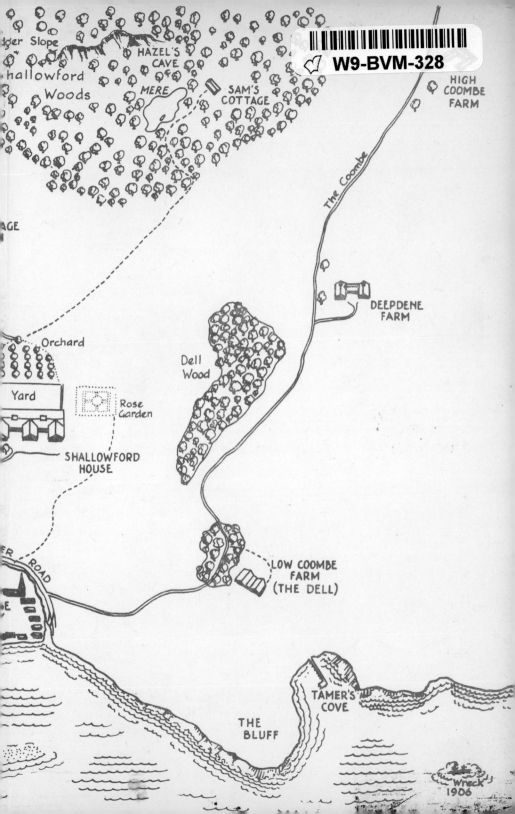

...dger Slope

HAZEL'S CAVE

...hallowford Woods

MERE

SAM'S COTTAGE

HIGH COOMBE FARM

The Coombe

DEEPDENE FARM

...AGE

Orchard

Dell Wood

Yard

Rose Garden

SHALLOWFORD HOUSE

LOW COOMBE FARM (THE DELL)

...ER ROAD

...E

TAMER'S COVE

THE BLUFF

Wreck 1906

A Horseman Riding By

by

R. F. DELDERFIELD

SIMON AND SCHUSTER
NEW YORK

For Deirdre Gibbens

and

Sir Geoffrey Harmsworth,

both old friends, with a genuine

love for the Westcountry.

In all corners of the West there are Craddocks and Potters, Codsalls and Pitts, Tozers and Stokes, Timberlakes and Willoughbys; no person in this book is intended to represent a living character but rather a race of people in a corner of the country as old as time. Similarly there are hundreds of Shallowfords, scores of Sorrell Valleys. If any reader is looking for identification let him seek it in the national spirit that, even in this day and age, still quickens the people of provincial England.

At Shallowford House   Paul Craddock = (1) Grace Lovell (m. 1903)

Simon (1904)

(2) Claire Derwent (m. 1907)

Stephen and Andrew	Mary	Karen	Claire	John
(The Pair, 1908)	(1910)	("Whiz")	(1918)	(1934)
		(1913)		

Ikey Palfrey (adopted 1902)

At Four Winds   Martin Codsall = Arabella (until 1904)

Will   Sydney

Norman Eveleigh = Marian (until 1932)

Gilbert   Deborah   Rachel   Harold   Robbie   Esther   Mavis   Susan

Harold Eveleigh = Connie (after 1932)

At Hermitage Farm   Arthur Pitts = Martha

Henry = Gloria

David   Prudence

At Perewinkle Farm   Will Codsall = Elinor Willoughby (until 1931)

Mark   Queenie   Floss   Richard

Rumble Patrick Palfrey = Mary Craddock (1934 onwards)

Jerry

At High Coombe   Edward Derwent = Liz (second wife)

Hugh   Rose   Claire   (all by first wife)

At Deepdene Farm   Edwin Willoughby

Francis   Elinor

At Low Coombe   Tamar = Meg

Sam = Joanie Smut = Marie   Hazel = Ikey

Cissie = Brissot   Violet = Jumbo
Bellchamber

Pansy =(1) Walt Pascoe
(2) Dandy Timberlake.
(3) Reg Willis

At Home Farm   Old Honeyman

Nelson = Prudence Pitts

Estate Workers (1902–40)   John Rudd, agent = Maureen O'Keefe, lady-doctor
Horace Handcock, gardener = Ada Handcock
(housekeeper)
Thirza Tremlett, parlourmaid and nurse
Chivers, groom
Matt and Luke, shepherds
The Timberlake family, sawyers
Gappy Saunders, gardener's boy

At Coombe Bay   Parson Bull
Parson Horsey
Keith Horsey = Rachel Eveleigh
Abe Tozer, smith
Ephraim Morgan, builder
Tom Williams, fisherman
James Grenfell, M.P.
Walt Pascoe, labourer
Professor Scholtzer
Bruce and Cecia Lovell
Aaron Stokes, reed-cutter
Willis, wheelwright

Book One

CHAPTER ONE

I

HE left the carriage, ascended the short flight of steps and walked briskly past the dozing porter sitting in the deep shade of the portico; a small, neat man, in dark, well-cut city clothes and glossy topper. He did not look incongruous out here in the open country under a blistering sun, but like a confident rook, or perhaps a raven, with years of combative experience well behind him; a sleek, utterly self-possessed and, in a subdued sense, deadly raven, with a bill best avoided.

The porter did not see him until he was inside the cool hall and in the act of turning the polished handle of the door, marked "MATRON: PRIVATE". The man rubbed sleep from his eyes and shouted "Hi there! You can't . . ." but the dapper man with the jutting Van Dyke beard was already inside with the door closed behind him, and the porter, baffled and dismayed, hesitated, bemused by the visitor's arrogance.

The matron, fourteen stone of starched linen, was almost equally disconcerted, at least for the moment. She was accustomed to deference, advertised by timid knocks, downcast eyes, abject mumbles and not merely because, as matron, she was Queen Empress of the Hospital for Convalescent Officers, but because, as a Countess who had given her country seat to the nation in its hour of need, she had been basking in a golden glow of patriotism ever since Black Week, in December 1899, when every capital in Europe was whooping at the spectacle of a few thousand Boer farmers trouncing the British Empire. Here she had sat ever since, flirting decorously with the Harley Street men, patronising the nameless doctors, cosseting heroes, and resolutely bullying her volunteer nurses. She had never realised a war could be so richly rewarding.

She looked up from her tea-pouring and saw the little man with the beard standing in front of her desk and his leisured removal of his hat was no more than a token courtesy. She was so astonished that she forgot to be outraged and could only suppose the insolent intruder had lost his way and blundered in here by mistake. But while she

13

was waiting for the porter to arrive and remove him he actually sat down. Actually seated himself, in the leather swivel chair, used by Sir Brian Wilmott, and all the other famous physicians who paid calls on her, and before she could exclaim he said, in a hoarse voice she could only describe as singularly common, "Lieutenant Craddock: Lieutenant P. Craddock, of the Yeomanry. He arrived here a day or so ago. I should like the latest report on him!", and he pushed a visiting card across the table.

She made a slight gobbling sound, handling the card as though it was a live cockroach. It read, "Franz Zorndorff, Zorndorff & Craddock, Ltd." and underneath, in neat script, "Canal Place, E.4 and Belsize Mansions, N.W.3." She found her voice at last, just as the porter, after a perfunctory knock, sidled into the room and looked at her for inspiration.

"How dare you? You had no appointment . . . ?"

"No," Zorndorff said, blandly, "none!", and then smiled in the most insolent and embarrassing way possible.

The porter arrived, passing a hand over his jowls. "He walked past!" he began, "he walked right past . . ." and then the little man looked at him and suddenly the Countess did not seem nearly as formidable and he retreated, muttering, so that the matron was abandoned to make what head she could against the visitor's armoury of invincible insolence.

She said, weakly, "Craddock, you said?", and made a miserable pretence of shuffling among the papers on her desk, whereupon the little man smiled, this time a charming although by no means ingratiating smile, and said, "Perhaps I should be more explicit, Countess; I am at present serving on the Board of Voluntary Hospitals in the London area. I have been a generous subscriber but in view of Lieutenant Craddock's presence here, I have decided to particularise. I have here a banker's draft for five hundred guineas, earmarked for this institution, together with a guarantee of another five hundred to be paid over the day my late partner's son is removed from the dangerously ill list!", and he took from his pocket a stiff, foolscap envelope, laying it beside the visiting card.

All the tension went out of the atmosphere and although the Matron began to gobble again it was not with supressed indignation but the effusiveness she hitherto reserved for Harley Street visitors, men like Sir Brian, known to have been consulted on royal births at Windsor Lodge and York House. Her blunt fingers shook as she withdrew the cheque from the envelope and all the time Franz Zorndorff watched her; with relish.

She began to bustle then, so that suddenly the room was full of the whisper of starched linen. Bells rang in far off corners of the mansion and a sister appeared, and then a hollow-eyed young man in a white coat, and finally the Chief Medical Officer, inclined to be irritable and impatient until the matron waved the cheque under his nose, after which he became almost cordial and produced a gold cigarette case from under his white coat, offering the visitor an Egyptian cigarette which was declined. He thought, "A Jew, almost certainly! And a Continental Jew at that! But who the devil am I to quibble? If we can nail that other five hundred we can expand and beat Marylebone's intake by fifty patients, what might that mean? A C.B.E. at the very least; and with the war virtually over and private practice in the offing, that will be one up on quacks like Sir Brian!" His mind began to juggle with the new cases in "H" Ward, whence all the recent arrivals had been sent but he found it difficult to isolate a Lieutenant Craddock, and held the visitor at bay with vague rumbles of "Craddock! Ah yes, Craddock. Leg wound, I believe. Smashed knee-cap. One of the stretcher cases that came in from the *Mondego Castle* on Monday . . . Monday was it, or Tuesday? . . . We've been inundated, Mr. Zorndorff, inundated . . ." and then, mercifully, the Matron (who at last seemed to have grasped the urgency of the occasion) placed the file in front of him, and he could stop floundering and seriously address himself to manœuvring this big fish to the bank. "Craddock!" he exclaimed, "Lieutenant Craddock, P. Why, of course, Mr. Zorndorff! Give Mr. Zorndorff some tea, Countess!", and he relaxed in his chair, like an ageing athlete who, against all probability, has breasted the tape an inch ahead of odds-on competitors.

Zorndorff watched the interplay with quiet enjoyment, looking more than ever like a raven, with deep-set, hooded eyes and supercilious beak. These people, he thought, were such tyros at the game. They gave themselves away so easily and they had no reserves of subtlety, no real knowledge of the blasting power of money. As if he would be here, scattering them all like a fox in a hen-run, if he had not made it his business to reconnoitre in advance, and satisfy himself that the rivalry between the various members of the minor aristocracy and their medical cliques had not already reached a point where, one and all, they were ready to bankrupt themselves, and submerge their entire professional lives in outbidding one another in patriotic endeavour, just so long as whispers of their efforts appeared in *The Bystander* and *Illustrated London News*. Patriotism, he reflected, was a kind of illness itself, and one that would respond to no other drug but public acclaim, public adulation. Before the war it had been who gave the largest house parties, and whose equipage attracted most notice at Ascot, but now only the slow-witted, clinging to Victorian traditions, raised these faded banners. Ever since Black Week, ever since national prestige had been spat upon by Kruger and his Bible-thumping peasants, these people had been at work on a new banner that was no more than a Union Jack; a man like himself, who knew that even Union Jacks had to be paid for, would be a fool not to take every possible advantage of their gavottes. He said, very civilly, "What are his chances? That's what I must know before I leave." and waited.

The Medical Officer was now in command of the situation. Lieutenant Craddock was on the touch-and-go list; Lieutenant Craddock's wound originated from a Mauser bullet entering on an upward course, half-an-inch below the right knee-cap and received whilst patrolling the blockhouses along the Pretoria–Bloemfontein railway. Two operations had already been performed, one in South Africa, one during the voyage home. Both were badly botched. The patient's condition had deteriorated during the voyage but he was now reported to be "holding his own". If gangrene was confirmed then the leg would certainly have to be amputated. So far his youth and health had served him well but he would appear to have rather less than a fifty-fifty chance. Everything that could be done for the boy was being done. The M.O. closed the file and searched the visitor's face for reactions. Seeing none he said, without malice, "His next of kin is given as 'father', Mr. Zorndorff."

"I buried his father yesterday," Zorndorff said without looking at doctor or matron for he appeared to be thinking so deeply that the process was almost visible.

The Countess said, in a voice entirely free from disappointment, "Poor laddie! You are a relative, Mr. Zorndorff?"

Zorndorff must have arrived at his decision for he looked up, brightly, and said, "No relative at all. I am his executor. His father was my oldest friend and business partner. He left his son the sum of twenty-eight thousand pounds, plus a third share in our joint undertaking."

He did not seem in the least interested in the effect of this statement and the ensuing silence in the room was embarrassing for the subdued. They waited, each conscious of the loudly ticking clock; there was nothing else they could do. When Zorndorff rose, asking, or rather demanding, to be led to the patient, they stood up as one and the Countess would have demurred if her half-hearted protest had not been cut short by the M.O.'s gesture. The gesture did not escape Zorndorff, who smiled grimly, standing aside for the surgeon to lead the way through a maze of corridors to a small ward, on the south side of the house.

There were ten or twelve patients lying there and it was insufferably hot, the strong May sunshine beating in at tall, half-curtained windows. One or two voluntary nurses stood about listlessly but straightened themselves as the surgeon strode in, with Zorndorff mincing behind. They went along the beds until they came to one containing a man with his right leg suspended in a cradle that looked like a miniature gallows. The patient was asleep, but fitfully so, for as Zorndorff looked down at him he moved his head left and right half-a-dozen times and his breathing was irregular. Zorndorff studied the face without emotion and the surgeon, watching him, thought, "He's a damned coldblooded customer! I wonder if the money reverts to him if the boy dies?" and then he flushed slightly, being half-persuaded that the Jew could read his thoughts.

Zorndorff stood by the bed looking down for more than a minute. He saw a narrow face, with a long jaw-line and slightly hollowed cheekbones sprouting a half-inch of blue-black stubble. It was a strong, obstinate face, still boyish under the flush of fever and a man's beard. The dark hair was thick and plentiful, the forehead high, the mouth rather thin and somehow fastidious, like the shapely fingers drumming feebly on the turned-back sheet. It had, he thought, very little in common with the squarish, stolid features of old Josh Craddock, whom he had first met when he was about this boy's age but there was, Zorndorff suddenly realised, a strong resemblance to the dark, silent woman, who had married Josh the Plumber and had watched him moulded, clinging desperately to his artisan background, into Josh the Merchant. It was the first time he had thought of Josh Craddock's wife in years and he did so now with reluctance and the merest flicker of guilt. He had forgotten even her name, for she had never been linked in his mind to the man who came forward out of nowhere to stand resolutely and illogically between him and deportation to Austria, at the time of his bankruptcy. Yet he recalled her face now and one other thing about her; she had been a countrywoman who had wandered into the city and never found her way out again. He remembered this clearly, and also that she had loathed the city and the claims it made upon her and that her loathing had broken her heart at the age of twenty-eight.

He said, without looking up, "You have private wards here?"

The M.O. said they had indeed, a few, but they were occupied.

"Be so good as to move someone out," Zorndorff said, "someone with a better chance of recovery." Then, before the surgeon could either agree or disagree, "Can you recommend a specialist a good one, who will make himself available for a second opinion?"

The surgeon hesitated, clutching the rags of his pride, but the prospect of the honours list jogged his elbow just in time and he said, sourly, "I was at Barts under Sir Jocelyn Ferrars but he would be extremely expensive!"

"His fee would not, I think, amount to more than twenty-eight thousand pounds," Zorndorff said, and the surgeon's resentment was swamped by a grudging tide of admiration for such preposterous insolence.

They were out in the cool hall again, where the smell of disinfectant followed them but the temperature was twenty degrees lower and suddenly Zorndorff was being very civil again, thanking him gravely for his courtesy, and begging him to convey his respects to the Countess. Then, in a twinkling, he was gone, and the porter lumbered forward to open the door and run down the steps to the visitor's carriage. The M.O. waited just long enough to see the fellow get a tip for his pains, and from the man's expression it was at least a florin, possibly as much as a crown.

He thought, as he plunged his hands into his cluttered overall pockets, "Damn him! I ought to have torn out a handful of beard and thrown it in his face!" but the mood of bitterness did not last as far as the Matron's door for by then his attention was fully occupied with other matters. Who could be ejected from a private ward with the least fuss? And how much should he offer Sir Jocelyn on that arrogant little bastard's behalf?

II

For a man lying flat on his back, with one leg suspended from a

18

pulley, the ceiling looked incredibly far off, yet not so far as to prevent Craddock conjuring fantasies from stains etched into the plaster by leaks that were stopped a century ago; during the long, hot afternoons, when pain and drugs were doing battle with one another inside him, the ragged edges of the damp areas resolved themselves into charging lines of infantry and squadrons of cavalry, with here the burst of a bombshell, there an angled standard.

The battle overhead distressed him far more than pain or weakness resulting from his wound, for in the months between the present, and the day he had pitched headlong into the dry watercourse beside the railway line, he had come to terms with pain. There never seemed to have been a time when small, darting flames were not searing the nerves between shin and groin. The battle overhead was something different. It would never resolve itself. The opposing armies were always on the point of advancing but when he looked again they were still ranged in lines, with bayonets advanced, officers' swords upraised, drums beating, bugles braying, and the smoke from the batteries billowing between the two hosts. It was a set-piece, but there was about it an immediacy that compelled him to cock an ear for the sob of breathless men and the screams of wounded. It exhausted him but unless he closed his eyes he found it difficult to look elsewhere, for the pulley, and the narrowness of the cot, exacted a penalty in terms of pain. Yet often enough he paid the fee, pressing his left cheek to the pillow to bring his right eye in line with the french windows opposite and staring out at the prospect beyond the terrace, where convalescents played their interminable games of pontoon.

Beyond them he could see the park sloping down a field or two, then up to a line of woods on the horizon. Nothing much happened out there. Sometimes a cow browsed into view, and occasionally a farm waggon crawled along the hillside track, moving so slowly that it seemed to take a very long time to cross his restricted line of vision. He could see clouds drifting above the elms, and patches of blue through the rents and somehow, as though to counter the poised strife overhead, the view brought peace and sanity, for he was aware that the stillness outside was real, whereas the battle on the ceiling was not.

Gradually he began to relate the two vistas, the one fraught with anxiety and stress, the other bringing him joy and tranquillity, so that, as the days passed, and the hillside view slowly began to assume mastery over the armies above, he knew that he would live, drawing more reassurance from the contrast than from anything the surgeon said or the soothing remarks made by the plump nurse who brought him drinks. And with this growing belief in his survival the battle on the ceiling lost its horrid significance, and the vision of serenity framed in woods resolved itself into a kind of Promised Land where he, Lieutenant Paul Craddock, whom they had given up for dead, roamed in the splendour of his youth.

That was after they had moved him to a private ward upstairs, a small room where his view was greatly enlarged and he could lie hour upon hour looking across at the great bow of the woods, and the brown, green, drowsing patchwork, between woods and park. By then the tide of pain had receded a very long way, but had been displaced by boredom and acute discomfort, arising from the angle of his leg, slung to the damned gallows at the foot of the bed. Dressings brought pain but also relief from the tedium of lying there alone. If it had not been for the magnificent view he would, he thought, have died of boredom. Yet there were adequate compensations. The leg, they told him, had been saved after all, and although the surgeon warned him that he would almost certainly suffer a permanent disability resulting from partial atrophy of the joint, it would not be much more than stiffness and he would walk with a slight limp, and could certainly ride; in fact, the more exercise he took the better. He had, they said, been extraordinarily lucky, not solely to have escaped amputation above the knee but to be alive at all. His cure, they explained, was due to a third operation performed by one of the most brilliant surgeons in the country, brought here at enormous cost at the instance of a Mr. Franz Zorndorff, some five days after his arrival from South Africa. He noticed that they all spoke of Mr. Zorndorff with awe and this puzzled him, for all he recalled was a secretive and rather flashy little Austrian Jew who, during his boyhood and youth, had been in close partnership with his father.

They let him ponder this for a day or so and then, with every manifestation of sympathy, they broke the news that his father had died the day he had landed in England. He was shocked by the news but not overwhelmed. He had not seen his father in almost three years and, on the last occasion they had met before he embarked for South Africa, their mutual antipathy, so long banked down by mutual distrust, had flared into a shouting match, with Joshua Craddock calling his son every kind of a fool to stick his nose into the Imperial quarrel, and Paul talking a good deal of vainglorious nonsense about his patriotic duty to assist in the chastening of Kruger and Kruger's

Bible-thumping farmers. Since then there had been a letter or two, and an occasional draft of money after his commissioning, but no exchange of affection, no show of warmth on the part of either one of them.

After they had left him with what they imagined to be his grief Paul found that, for the first time in his life, he could think of his father impersonally, a big, broad-shouldered, taciturn man, with a squarish face, deliberate hands, a large, walrus moustache, a deep voice that disguised his Bermondsey accent, and above all, a baffling inaccessibility due, as Paul now realised, to his obsession with business affairs that never seemed to bring him any real satisfaction for all the time he lavished on them. He had never, for instance, told Paul anything of his mother, who had died when the child was five, or how it came that he, Joshua, had fought his way from the top strata of the artisan class, a plumber with two or three men in his employ, to that of city merchant, or a kind of city merchant, for Paul had no knowledge of how his father earned a living, apart from some connection with scrap metals near the centre of his original endeavours as a plumber. It seemed to him, lying trussed up under this infernal gallows, a very strange thing that he should know so little about his family, particularly as Joshua had been insistent that he should come into the business on leaving the undistinguished little private school, where he had been sent as a boarder when he was eight years old. He had resisted this pressure solely because he had a strong disinclination to work in an office under artificial light, and had dismayed his father by announcing his intention of entering the artillery. He had already made application for entry to Woolwich when the War offered all young men a chance of immediate service overseas. One of the few accomplishments he had learned at the pretentious little school he attended (Joshua, in his ignorance, had always referred to it as "a public school") was how to sit a horse, so that it had been easy, under the impetus of Black Week and its humiliating defeats, to join the Yeomanry. Later, because of the gaps torn in the ranks by the enteric fever epidemic, it had been almost as easy to get a temporary commission, but for all that he had not seen much active service. By the time his training period had expired the war had degenerated into ding-dong encounters between patrols and Boer Commandos and it was in one of these scuffles that he had received his wound. Before that, however, he had changed his mind about a military career. He was unable, he discovered, to take pleasure in harassing the wretched

Veldt farmers and their families, and it was not long before doubts obscured his vision of Imperial infallibility. He wondered sometimes, what he would do with his life now that a gammy leg barred him from most outdoor occupations, yet his prospects did not dominate his thoughts during the earliest stage of his convalescence, when he was learning to walk again on sticks and a network of lines rigged along the terrace. What occupied his mind more often was the curious deference shown him, not only by the volunteer nurses but the Countess, the Chief Medical Officer, and the junior physicians. It puzzled him, for instance, that he alone, apart from one or two high-ranking casualties, had a room to himself, and also that any request he made—for a book, a magazine, or a variation of hospital diet—was granted, when in the crowded general wards below other junior officers, especially the non-professionals like himself, were treated like tiresome children and reacted accordingly, cursing the impulse that had involved them in a war for which many serving soldiers now felt a slight disgust, causing them to ask themselves if, after all, the pro-Boer Lloyd George and his following had not been justified in condemning the adventure from the outset.

He found the key to all this within a few minutes of receiving his first visit from Franz Zorndorff.

The little man strode on to the terrace unannounced about a week after Paul had been allowed downstairs. He was not wearing his city clothes today but had got himself up in what he imagined to be correct country-house attire, a pepper-and-salt Norfolk suit, a wide grey cravat with a diamond pin, and a billycock hat sporting a pheasant's feather. The staff made way for him as though he had been the Emperor of Japan or, at the very least, a racegoing friend of the new king, Edward. He seated himself in a creaking basket chair and opened his pigskin attaché case, producing a sheaf of papers tied with pink tape.

"Delighted to see you're making such excellent progress, my boy!" he began, gaily. "We've a little signing to do first of all. I trust you read all the letters the solicitors sent on?"

"No," Paul admitted, a little irritated by Zorndorff's brashness and the fact that he made no mention at all of his partner's death. "I began to read them but I found it difficult to concentrate. You wrote promising you would come over soon, so I decided I'd ask you to summarise them. They looked damned dull to a man who has read nothing heavier than the *Strand Magazine* for three years."

He saw to his amusement that he had succeeded in disconcerting the Jew, who now looked somewhat startled and then, recovering himself, uttered a short, neighing laugh.

"Then you won't know? Unless, of course, the whisper has gone round, as I rather thought it might!"

Paul asked him to explain, adding that visitors were only allowed a bare half-hour before the bell rang and the terrace had to be cleared.

"Oh, don't concern yourself over that!" Zorndorff said, contemptuously, "I've tamed everybody in this charnel-house, including that fraud of a matron! They won't shoo me out, I can assure you!" And then, placing his shapely hands on his knees and looking directly at Paul, he added, "You'll probably be surprised at the extent of your patrimony. I was myself, somewhat, although I realised of course that Josh spent very little over the years. That was his trouble, I think; he could never cease to think in sixpences, or free himself from the notion that he was still waiting on a plumber's harvest—a hard frost that is!"

"You haven't told me how my father died," Paul said, not altogether liking the half-veiled patronage of the man yet understanding now why he had been treated as a favoured patient.

The Jew lost a little of his ebullience. He said, seriously, "I suppose I owe it to you to admit that Josh Craddock died fulfilling what he imagined an obligation to me. As to the facts, he killed himself heaving a two hundredweight water-cistern from a cart!" He hissed through his teeth, one of the few Continental habits he had retained after forty years in England. "Imagine that! Josh Craddock, with cash and assets totalling something like forty-five thousand pounds killing himself to help a lazy oaf of a carter empty a cart!"

The figure stunned him and Zorndorff, enjoying the confusion his casual announcement caused, smiled as he waited for Craddock to recover a little. The Jew had a well-stocked wardrobe of smiles; this was an occasion for his thin one. He said, finally, "Well, and how much did you think he was worth?"

Never having given any thought to the matter Paul guessed, reckoning the ugly house in Croydon, at £750 and his father's share of the business at about £3,000. "Certainly not more than five," he said, "and hardly any of it in cash! You wouldn't be having a little quiet fun at my expense, Mr. Zorndorff?"

"I don't joke about money!" the Austrian said, sharply. "As to the estate, I based Joshua's share of the business on half our last offer to sell, a little over fifteen thousand; the rest is in hard cash, or readily saleable assets, and you are the sole beneficiary. That was something I insisted on when I witnessed the will."

He began to forage in his case but Craddock checked him, saying, "Never mind the documents, Mr. Zorndorff! I should much prefer you to explain, and as simply as you can! Am I to understand that the whole of this sum, including a half-share in the business, comes to me and that I can do as I wish with it?"

"By no means," Zorndorff said. "Your father remained an artisan all his life but he was no fool. We talked it over and agreed that you should inherit a third share of the business and the whole of the capital sum, but you won't receive more than five thousand until you are twenty-eight. That last provision was no suggestion of mine!"

Because Paul still appeared bemused the Jew became a little impatient. "Come now," he said, "even you must realise that the coarse metal trade prospers in wartime. We were doing well enough on sub-contracts before the war, but three years ago, when army contracts were put about, we forged ahead in relation to the blunders the generals made over there! I was optimistic from the start but I must confess that even I hardly expected a three-year war. The point is, we seem to be set fair indefinitely for the Kaiser has obliged the trade by entering the naval race. If you applied yourself I daresay you could soon convert your thirty thousand working capital into two hundred thousand."

Paul, who had heard nothing but the last few words, said slowly, "What the devil do I know of the scrap metal business? Or any business?"

"I would be prepared to teach you," the Jew said, earnestly now, and without a trace of patronage. "Joshua was the only friend I ever had and I have every intention of paying my debt to him, whether you like it or not, my friend!"

"Then you must find some other way of paying it," Paul said, "I may be half a cripple but I'm damned if I intend to devote my life to scrap metal, Mr. Zorndorff!"

The Jew did not seem surprised or disappointed. He looked thoughtful for a moment, drawing his brows together and contemplating his beautifully manicured hands. "With that capital you could do almost anything you liked," he said, at length. "Have you any preferences? Or is it something you would prefer to think about during the time you remain here?"

Paul said, briefly, "First I intend to learn to walk, Mr. Zorndorff;

24

properly, without sticks; like any other person, you understand? I think they have exaggerated my disability. In the meantime, would you care to buy me out at any figure you considered fair?"

The naïveté of the offer stirred Zorndorff. His head shot up and his eyes sparkled as he said, crisply, "Be satisfied with your loose change, and oblige me by allowing me to fulfil my obligations any way I choose!" and he stood up so suddenly that Paul made sure he was deeply offended but he was not, for his smile betrayed him and somehow, because of it, Paul was convinced of the man's fundamental honesty, and of the genuineness of the obligation he felt for the son of the man who had once stood between him and ruin. He said, half apologetically, "I know you have my interests at heart, Mr. Zorndorff, you have proved that already. I daresay I should have croaked in the general ward without first-class attention but the truth is I never expected this kind of opportunity and it alters everything. I had some idea of farming, in a small way, in one of the Dominions perhaps, but it's something I need to think about very deeply. I don't imagine I shall be out of here for a month or more. May I come to you then? Or write, if I form any decision?"

"By all means, by all means," Zorndorff said, expansive and avuncular again, and without any gesture of farewell except a vague pat on the shoulder he picked up his case, strolled along the terrace and went down the steps to the carriage park behind the forecourt.

Paul watched him go, thinking "Whatever he does is part of a charade. What could he and a dull dog like my father have had in common? Were they the complement of one another? And was my mother somehow involved in the improbable association?" His involvement with the dapper, enigmatic Austrian was to endure for another forty years but this was something he never discovered.

III

As the weeks passed and the sun continued to beat on the baking façade of the great house, there were many things he discovered about himself and not the least important of them was the durability of the bright crystals of thought left in the recesses of his brain by the long, exhausting fever duel between the static army on the ceiling and the serenity of the view of the park and downland, seen through the windows of the two wards he had occupied. Somehow the latter came to represent his future, and all that was pleasant and rewarding in life, and he saw it not simply as a pleasing vista of fields, woods and browsing cattle, but as a vision of the England he had remembered and yearned for out there on the scorching veldt. And this, in itself, was strange, for he was city born and bred, and although he had never shared the Cockney's pride in the capital neither had he been conscious, as a boy, of a closer affinity with the woods and hedgerows of the farmland on the Kent–Surrey border, where he had spent his childhood and boyhood. Yet the pull existed now, and it was a very strong pull, as though he owed his life to nectar sucked from the flowers growing wild out there across the dreaming fields near the rim of the woods, and with this half-certainty came another—that it was in a setting like this that he must let the years rescued for him unwind, yielding some kind of fulfilment or purpose. He had never had thoughts like this before and it occurred to him that pain, and a prolonged flirtation with death, had matured him in a way that had been leap-frogged by the other convalescents, many of whom had had more shattering experiences in the field. Some the war had left cynical and a few, among them the permanently maimed, bitter but all the regular officers seemed to have emerged from the war with their prejudices intact and talked of little else but sport, women, and the military lessons learned from the campaigns. They continued, Paul thought, to regard England as a jumping-off ground for an eternal summer holiday in the sun among lesser breeds, looking to them and the Empire for protection and economic stability, but had little or no sense of kinship with the sun-drenched fields beyond the terrace, or the chawbacons seen toiling there, taking advantage of the Coronation weather to cut and stack the long grass. He began to keep very much to himself, reading and browsing through the long afternoons on the terrace, and it was here, about a fortnight after Zorndorff's visit, that he came across the two-page advertisement in the *Illustrated London News* that gave him at least a glimmering of an idea concerning his future.

It was a detailed announcement of the forthcoming sale by auction of a thirteen hundred acre Westcountry estate, owned by a family called Lovell, that seemed to have been very hard-hit by Boer marksmanship, for the heir, Hubert Lovell, had been killed at Modder River after winning a Victoria Cross, and his brother, Ralph, in a skirmish outside Pretoria. Their father, Sir George Lovell, had been a considerable landowner, with other and larger estates in Cumberland and Scotland, and the Devon manor-house, the home farm and five tenant farms, together with areas of surrounding woodland and common, were destined to come under the hammer at the end of the month unless disposed of, either as a whole or in parcels, by private treaties.

It was an impressive and, he would judge, an expensive advertisement, for there were pictures of the house and the three dead Lovells, and a potted history of the family. The house looked impressive but neglected, a sprawling, porticoed building, built on the shallow ledge of a long slope crowned by woods, and seemed to Paul to be mainly Tudor, with Carolean or Georgian extensions east and west. It was approached by a sharply curving tree-lined drive and had clusters of spiralling chimneys that he associated with Elizabethan buildings. It looked squat, comfortable, weatherbeaten and commodious but it was not, in the first instance, the house that attracted his attention, so much as descriptions of the outlying farms, each of between four hundred and two hundred acres. The agents handling the sale announced that they would be open to separate sales of these properties, each of which had its own farmhouse and farm-buildings, and their names read like an Arcadian rent-roll—Four Winds, The Hermitage, Deepdene, High Coombe and Low Coombe.

The oval portraits of the three Lovells interested him. The old man, Sir George, was a bearded, heavy-featured man, with bulging eyes and, Paul would judge, a sensual, bullying mouth. He looked more like an evangelist than a country squire. His elder son, Hubert, was handsome in an unremarkable and slightly effeminate way, with a smooth face and rather vacuous expression, whereas Ralph, the younger boy, was an almost comic caricature of a Regency rake, with his sulky mouth, mop of dark, unruly hair, and an expression that suggested wilfulness and a certain amount of dash.

He mulled over the advertisement all the afternoon, wondering how much one of the larger farms would cost, and whether, in fact, a serious bid could be made in advance. Four hundred acres, he felt, was a large enough bite to begin with, and at length, almost on impulse, he tore the two pages from the magazine and enclosed them in a brief, tentative letter to Zorndorff. He would be discharged, they said, in time to accept Zorndorff's invitation to watch the Coronation procession from a private stand rented by the Austrian, and in his note he suggested that they might discuss the matter on that occasion if, in the meantime, his father's solicitors could extract some relevant

27

information from the agents of the sale. He was still only half-serious and wondered, as he sealed the letter, if Zorndorff would pour scorn on the notion, and employ arguments to launch him as a more genteel farmer in Malay or Africa, but after the letter had gone he felt curiously elated, as though at last he had done something positive to convert his fever dreams into reality. He watched the post eagerly during the week but all that arrived from Zorndorff was a telegram bearing the cryptic message, "Letter received; will discuss later; expecting you midday, Club, 24th instant," proving that Zorndorff, for all his apparent neglect, knew rather more regarding his immediate future than he knew himself. The Austrian's club was an establishment in St. James' and the address was on one of the cards he had left with the sheaf of documents that Paul had read with wandering attention. He thought, laying the telegram aside, 'Damn the man, why does he have to go out of his way to dominate everybody?" and then he thought he knew the answer in his case. He had, after all, been baulked by the flat rejection of the offer to launch his old friend's son on a money-making career in the metal trade and was still, in his insufferable arrogance, determined to have his way in the matter. "And I daresay the little devil will in the end!" Paul thought, glumly, "for he seems to have acquired the knack of making everyone bow the knee to him!" He had, at that stage, a great deal to learn about Franz Zorndorff's way of doing business.

IV

The newsvendor's cry reached the cab as a continuous high-pitched whine, at the junction of the Strand and Waterloo Bridge Road, and Paul leaned out to wave so that the man dived into the traffic and seemed almost to come at the cab from under the bellies of two enormous horses dragging a brewer's dray. The headline, in the heaviest black type, confirmed the rumour he had heard in the train; the new King was seriously ill, and the Coronation had been postponed indefinitely.

Craddock read the news unemotionally. The King was well over sixty and at that age any exalted man who took his pleasures as strenuously as Teddy might well be taken ill, might even die and be buried in Westminster Abbey. The cab swung into Trafalgar Square, merging into the solid stream of traffic debouching from the Mall, Whitehall and Northumberland Avenue, and here, over the Admiralty

Arch, hung two huge portraits, framed in gilt ovals, of Edward and Alexandra, gazing out over chestfuls of decorations and diamonds at the traffic below. Craddock glanced up at them, remembering the barrack-room jokes he had heard about the King's philanderings. He was, they said, the most persistent royal woman chaser since Charles II, but she was a woman whose regality made jokes about them seem in bad taste. He had waited, Paul reflected, forty years to mount the throne and now, at the very last minute, he was lying in bed awaiting a chancy operation. All the stands and scaffolding, the tinsel and bunting, were ready but now there would be no procession, no cheering crowds and no military bands but in their stead an orgy of impersonal grief for a bearded, corpulent man, fighting for his life and a chance to justify himself as man and monarch. Paul studied the faces of the people on the pavements but found there little indication of a national catastrophe, only the stress of scurrying through a whipped-up sea of horse traffic, pounding along to the accompaniment of a low-pitched roar. The sun continued to blaze overhead and the stink of fresh manure, blending with clouds of thick white dust, made Craddock's nostrils twitch. They shook free of the mêlée about half-way down Pall Mall and turned into St. James' Street, where Zorndorff awaited him at his Club.

"I suppose you've heard the news," Paul said, as he paid off the cabby, and the man grinned. "Couldn't 'elp it, could I, Sir? Been screaming their 'eads orf since first light! D'you reckon he'll make it, Sir?"

"Why not?" Craddock heard himself say, "he's Vicky's son; that ought to help!"

The cabby nodded eagerly and Paul noticed that he was no longer grinning. As he pocketed Craddock's tip he said, "Funny thing, can't seem to get used to the idea of a king. Kind o' permanent she was, like the Palace over there, or Nelson back in the square! You keep forgettin', gov'nor—you know, when they play 'God Save the Queen—King'!" and he saluted, flicked his whip and bowled away towards Piccadilly.

Craddock stood on the Club steps pondering for a moment. The man was right of course. Post-Victorian London was not the city he remembered of less than three years ago but he would have found it difficult to put the changes into words. The streets had always been jam-packed with slow-moving traffic, and reeking with odours of horse-sweat and dust, but the changes seemed to lie in the mood of

29

passers-by, more brash and brittle than he remembered, with a little of the class rigidity gone, more audacity among the vendors, porters and draymen, less assurance in the stride of those two cigar-smoking, top-hatted gentlemen, as they walked down the hill towards St. James' Palace. He went on into the plush-lined lobby and when he mentioned Mr. Franz Zorndorff the doorman at once became obsequious, and directed him to the dining-room, a vast, crowded rectangle, where the clatter of cutlery and the roar of conversation was as oppressive as the uproar outside. Zorndorff appeared through a cloud of waiters, calling, "Ah, my boy! Not in here, not in this babel! I've booked lunch in the members' dining-room upstairs," and he seized Craddock by the arm and steered him up a broad staircase and along a corridor to a smaller room, with the words "Members Only" painted in gilt letters on the swing-doors.

"You'll have heard the news, Paul? It must be a big disappointment for you," Franz said as the waiter, without waiting for the order, brought them two very dry sherries.

"It might have been this morning," Craddock told him, "but after crossing London from King's Cross I don't mind admitting it's a relief. Maybe I should have done it by stages, like a diver coming up from a great depth, but the noise and stink terrified me! I'm sorry for the Cockneys, though, they deserve a bit of glitter after putting up with this day and night."

"Come, you're a Cockney yourself, Paul. You were born in Stepney and that's within earshot of Bow, isn't it?"

"I'm not proud of it," Craddock said. "How the devil can you make decisions in such a hellish uproar?"

"Far more expertly than I could make them beside the old rustic mill," Franz told him jovially, "for in London wits are whetted every time one crosses the street and as for this," he waved his hand in the general direction of Piccadilly, "this is nothing, my friend, to the midday congestion beyond Temple Bar, or south of the river on a weekday. We shall wait until evening before going there and drive back to my house in Sloane Street at sunset. You can stay there as arranged. I shall be busy except for today, but I imagine you have things to attend to."

He went on to talk of general matters, the food, the King's chances of a recovery, the effect of his illness on the political scene, Paul's wound and the post-hospital treatment prescribed for it, anything, Paul soon realised, to steer away from the subject of purchasing a

Westcountry farm, but by now Paul had, to some extent, the measure of the man and felt reasonably secure in his affections, so that when the coffee and brandy had been served, and the waiter had ceased to make his swift, discreet dashes upon the table, he said, grinning, "Look here, Mr. Zorndorff, if you think I'm an ass to have written that letter you can say so! You don't have to avoid the subject, like a cat walking through puddles!" Zorndorff twinkled, put on his avuncular look and replied, amiably, "There is a side to you that indicates a latent business acumen, my boy! You possess a quiet obstinacy wedded to a somewhat shattering directness of manner, a formidable combination under certain circumstances!" He sipped and savoured his brandy, as Paul waited and then, carefully setting down the glass, he said seriously, "I hadn't forgotten the letter and enclosures but before I even discuss it you must do something for me. A very small thing, but also an obligation of a kind, I think."

"Well?"

"You must come down to the scrapyard. This evening, after my siesta. If you have really made up your mind to stick your nose in the dirt then you should give yourself the chance of deciding on the spot whether it is the three-per-cent-barring-acts-of-God dirt of a provincial farm, or the gilt-edged dirt of a bone yard! Afterwards? Afterwards we might get around to discussing your absurd proposition. Is that agreed?"

"Certainly I'll come to the yard with you. As a matter of fact I should like to, out of curiosity. I've never once been there, at least, not to my recollection."

"That," Zorndorff said, affably, "I already know, for your father fell into the error common to all artisans who have risen in the world. He was determined to ensure that his son wore a clean collar to work. This is very excellent brandy, but the flavour is a little elusive I think."

"Certainly no more so than you, Mr. Zorndorff," Paul said, smiling, to which Zorndorff replied, "From now on, my boy, it would flatter me if you would address me as 'Uncle Franz'. I have cohorts of indigent nephews but none, alas, with a float of five thousand and expectations."

The curious thing about this pronouncement, Paul noticed, was that, although larded with Zorndorff's brand of laboured irony it was uttered in all sincerity.

They paid off the cabby at Tower Bridge, walking south-east into the maze of streets running between the Old Kent Road and the

31

canal, and as they went along Paul was aware of a stronger and more tangible security than he had ever known. He did not understand why this should be so, only that, in some way, it emanated from the dapper little man tripping along beside him, an utterly incongruous figure here in his tweeds and billycock hat, twirling his cane to emphasise points in his flow of conversation. Zorndorff was obviously very much at home in this part of London, turning left or right without hesitation when, to Craddock, every seedy little street seemed the same and even their names ran in sets, the battles of the Crimea, the battles of the Indian Mutiny, the seacoast towns of the Cornish peninsula and a variety of flowering shrubs that had not been seen hereabouts for generations. The complexity of the brick labyrinth astonished him, for it went on and on until it melted into the bronze sky, under which the stale summer air was battened down by a pall of indigo smoke, rising from ten thousand kitchen-ranges behind the yellow brick terraces. The houses all looked exactly alike, narrow, two-storeyed little dwellings, bunched in squat, yellowish blocks, like rows of defeated coolies awaiting their evening rice issue. Here and there the occupiers (none were owners Franz told him) stood at the doors, obese, shirtsleeved men with broad, pallid faces, wrinkled old crones with furtive eyes and nutcracker jaws, shapeless, blowsy women in aprons, their moon faces curtained by great hanks of hair, and sometimes a very old man, like a Chelsea pensioner stripped of his uniform. The evening heat hung level with the chimney pots and although the litter cars were at work in the streets most of the rubbish escaped their revolving brooms and was whirled into the gutter. The curious thing was that Craddock did not shrink from the scene, as he had from the comparatively clean streets of the West End, for although, on this side of the river, there was airlessness, and evidence of an appalling poverty, there was also a sparkle and vitality that intrigued and interested him, as though he was exploring the seamier section of a foreign city. Watching the West End crowds that morning he had seen individuals hurrying past in isolation but down here, where the yards spilled into one another, and the house numbers ran up to two hundred in stretches of less than a hundred yards, the Londoners were obviously a community and, as far as he could judge, a more or less contented community. It was the urchins in the street that interested him the most, bedraggled little ragamuffins, with the zest and impudence of city gamins all over the world. He watched them spill out of their narrow houses, calling to one another in their

32

strong nasal accents, to torment the carter in charge of the water-sprinkler who was doing a very little towards laying the dust. Every time the cart-jets sprayed the urchins dashed within range of the nipples, accepting the flick of the carter's whip as part of the sport. Franz said, "It astonishes you? The richest city in the richest country in the world? Perhaps you find it difficult to believe but it is far more salubrious than it was. When I came here in the 'sixties no man dressed like us would have dared to walk these streets, not even in daylight. You have read your Dickens, I imagine?" and when Craddock told him that he had, he added, "There is still squalor to spare but not nearly so much vice, I think. That is largely because there is plenty of work within easy walking distance of these hovels. It is only down nearer the Docks that a man can get knocked on the head nowadays, and then only at night."

As they went along, moving further south of the river, Franz pointed out various local landmarks. There was Peek Frean's biscuit factory, employing over a thousand, and nearby the "Grenadier" match factory, where there had been a national scandal over a number of operatives who had contracted the dreaded "phossy-jaw", from contact with phosphorus. He did not need to point out the Tannery for the stench assailed them as they rounded the corner of the high boundary wall and then, within a quarter-mile of this enormous building, they passed through the double-gates of the scrapyard and Craddock looked with amazement at his inheritance.

It was about two to three acres of wasteland, enclosed on three sides by the backs of terraced houses, and on the fourth by an eight-foot wall, surmounted with broken glass. Debris lay on all sides, strewn in what at first seemed utter confusion but when he looked more closely was seen to be stacked according to some kind of plan. The junk rose in a series of twenty-foot pyramids, built row upon row, like a terrible parody of a cornfield full of stooks, and round the base of each pyramid was a patch of cinders rutted by cart wheels. Every imaginable article of hardware was represented. Craddock saw brass bedsteads, buckled bicycles, tin baths, skeins of twisted, rusting pipes, holed and handleless pails, cracked lavatory pans, stoves, both whole and in fragments, stripped perambulator frames and at one point, between two mounds of rubbish, the better part of a tanker engine, looking like a dying dinosaur in a swamp.

"Great God!" he exclaimed, "you say my father actually *liked* working here?"

33

"Most of the men and boys on piecework like it, at all events, they much prefer it to a steady job in a factory. We had a Salvation Army Unit here last summer, and about a dozen of them were talked into attending a free camp on the Downs. Most of them were back here before the week was out, and even those who stayed spent their time looking for scrap."

"How much do you pay casual labour for this kind of rubbish?"

"That depends on what they bring in. Certain metals, like copper, carry a bonus, but an average barrowload earns them about a shilling. If it comes by the cartload we weigh it on the weighbridge there by the office."

Craddock glanced in the direction indicated and saw that one half of the yard was dotted by a dozen, slow-burning fires. In the still evening air the smoke ascended vertically and all the time smuts floated across his vision, drifting by like cockroaches in a trance. The wooden hut that did service as an office was built on a steep concrete ramp and under the ramp were several carts, awaiting their turn to move on to the weighbridge. Franz led the way over, mincing along the narrow tracks between the rubble stacks, lifting his cane to acknowledge the checker's respectful greeting. Craddock followed him up the ramp and stood on the platform looking out over the vast desolation. It was like, he thought, an illustration of Dante's *Inferno*, that he had seen among sale catalogues that his father had kept in the glass-fronted bookcase at home, and the orange glow of the setting sun, lighting up acres of slate roofs to the west, shed an unlikely radiance on the squalor. Franz had gone into consultation with a beefy man in the office and Craddock stood quite still, looking across the yards to the vast huddle that surrounded St. Paul's, in the far distance. He thought, "Twenty-eight thousand pounds out of this! It's an ugly joke but the laugh is on poor devils who comb through refuse heaps at a shilling a barrowload!" and as he thought this his ear caught the pleasant warble of a mouth-organ, playing "Lily of Laguna" and he looked down beyond the weighbridge to see a boy aged about ten or eleven sitting on the nearside shaft of one of the carts, his bare legs swinging free, his hands cupped to his mouth so that Craddock could only see the upper part of a face, crowned by a mop of black hair. The child's face and air of rapt concentration arrested him, so that for a moment he forgot his disgust for the place and concentrated on the musician, noting the boy's breadth of fore-head, large, thoughtful eyes, and above all, the statuesque set of head

34

cocked sideways, as though listening intently to the wail of his own music.

Then something happened that made him shout a warning, for a carter ducked between the tailboard of the foremost cart and the head of the horse harnessed to the cart in charge of the boy, so that the animal, startled, threw up its head and the overloaded cart tilted, sending its load of scrap metal cascading over the tailboard and producing a clatter that set the terrified horse rearing, its hooves flailing within inches of the carter now boxed between the wall of the ramp and the rear of his own cart.

The boy must have moved at fantastic speed, for when Craddock turned his head he was missing from his seat on the shaft and Craddock could only suppose him to have been thrown down between the footboard and the hind-quarters of the frantic horse. He turned to run down the steps but at that moment he saw the boy bob up on the far side and spring on the animal's back, where he hung on with his knees as he tore off his jacket, leaned far over the neck and flung it over the animal's head, holding it there as his body was flung backwards and forwards by the violent heaves. Gradually the animal quietened, straining outward away from the ramp and then, after what seemed to Craddock a long interval, the checker came running round to the far side of the queue and grabbed the bridle, throwing his weight on the horse's head and then wheeling the cart out of line away from the ramp, so that the carter could rise shakily to his knees and stagger past his own vehicle to the weighbridge. The boy with the mouth-organ then swung his legs and slid to the ground and Craddock, to his amazement, saw that he was not only grinning, but still had his harmonica clutched in his right hand.

"Serve yer bloody well ri'!" he jeered at the man, "doncher know better'n to come on 'er from the blind side?" whereupon he perched himself on a bollard beside the scales and at once proceeded to suck at his mouth-organ, until such time as the foremost cart moved off the weighbridge and it was his turn to follow it across the grating.

Craddock, spellbound by the incident, now saw that Franz was standing beside him.

"That boy!" he said, "I've never seen anyone react as quickly and intelligently! Who is he? I . . . I'd like to give him something."

Franz glanced into the yard.

"I heard a lot of shouting," he said, "what happened?" and when Craddock described the incident he said, carelessly, "Oh, they're

35

always getting and giving hard knocks down there. You don't have to come here distributing your largesse!" and plunging a hand into his pocket, he called over the guard rail—"Here boy! That's one of Sophie's horses isn't it?" and the boy grinned up at them and said, "Yerse, Mr. Zorndorff, it's ole Betty, an' she's blind in one eye! Foster come up on 'er blind side so she turned nasty! She's orlri' now tho', Mr. Zorndorff!" but when Zorndorff continued to frown he lost a little of his perkiness, pocketed his harmonica and ran over to help the men clearing away the litter that had spilled on to the carriageway.

"Never mind that, come up here at once you rascal!" Zorndorff called and the boy, looking like a pupil answering a headmaster's summons, came slowly up the steps to the platform and stood before them, now looking furtive and dejected.

"You're one of Sophie Palfrey's boys yourself, aren't you?" asked Franz sharply and the boy nodded, throwing back his mop of hair and converting the gesture into a surreptitious wipe of his nose. "I'm the oldest. Me Dad's laid orf fer a bit, so Ma said to load up an' bring what was waiting out back from las' week!"

"All right," said Zorndorff, gruffly, "I'm not blaming you for what happened but that horse of your mother's is past working and we'll have trouble with the inspector if you don't send her to the knacker's and get another. You'd best tell your mother that, you understand? Here . . ." and he tossed the boy a coin, which the child caught expertly and thrust into his pocket.

"Cor, thanks Mr. Zorndorff," he said, carefree again, and skipped down the steps to help reload his cart.

"What did you give him?" asked Craddock, a little annoyed by Zorndorff's cavalier handling of the situation, and when Franz told him sixpence he said it wasn't enough, whereupon Franz turned on him fiercely and said, "It's more than enough! You don't know these people! Show them kindness and they'd be on top of you, with their tricks and excuses in two minutes! I know that family well. As a matter of fact that boy is a relation of a sort."

"A relation?"

"He's one of Sophie Carrilovic's brood. She came over here and married a tanner called Palfrey, a thorough-going scoundrel who drinks all he earns and beats her regularly every Saturday night. She's a Croat, one of the many who got word of me and migrated for pickings! It happens with every expatriate, the moment he gets his head above water! I've had them clamouring for work and somewhere

36

to live for years, and at first I did what I could, remembering my own troubles, but there comes a time when a man has to harden his heart or go under."

"But the boy's speed and courage saved that carter's life," Paul protested.

"I don't doubt it," Franz grunted, "but something of that kind happens here every day of the week. They have a saying, south of the river; there are only two kinds of folk—the quick and the dead! Damn it man, the mortality rate among children of his kind is forty per cent up to the age of five and it doesn't depreciate much in the next ten years."

Craddock was silent and they moved into the office, an airless little building, littered with spiked invoices, price-lists and grimy box files. Here, and among all that debris below, thought Craddock, his father had lived out his life, accumulating thousands of pounds but ultimately bursting his heart lifting a piece of rubbish from a cart. It seemed a pitiful waste of energy and initiative and his wife, the woman Craddock had never known, must have loathed it, and perhaps taken refuge in dreams of open country until the day she died. Down here, he reflected, the children of the poor fought for coppers, risking their lives handling half-blind horses and counting the acquisition of an extra sixpence a triumph. He thought again of all the men who had died in South Africa to maintain the momentum of the machine that opportunists like Franz Zorndorff thought of as a modern, highly-industrialised state. Well, at least the volunteers in South Africa had spent their final moments breathing fresh air, and under a sun that was not blotted out by sulphurous smoke and floating smuts but surely—surely to God there was a compromise between the England of yesterday, with its fat farms and thriving local industries, and the grinding, impersonal money-machine that England had become in the last few decades? Surely somewhere, somehow, the industrial skills of the Watts and Stephensons and Faradays could be applied to a land that could still grow good corn and breed the best cattle in Europe? He said, deliberately:

"Well, coming here has resolved any doubts I had, Uncle Franz. I'll sell all my interests in this graveyard at once! I'll accept whatever terms you propose, purchase over a period, or money down for a bargain price outright! And I won't have second thoughts on this! You can get the lawyers to make out the papers tomorrow."

He expected immediate protests, arguments, scorn, for down here, safe on his home ground, there was an edge to the Croat that was blunted in the West End, but Zorndorff only sighed and, lifting his case, spilled its contents on to the littered trestle table, poking among the papers until he found a slim clip of letters, with a buff telegram form on top. He said, with a shrug, "I had no real hope you would recant but at least I've done my duty by your father; it was always his wish you would take over this place and perhaps mould it into something as profitable but somewhat more conventional. However, I suppose I have a duty to your mother as well. You never knew her, did you?"

"No," Paul said, "and very little about her, except that she was a countrywoman."

"She came, I believe, from somewhere in the Severn Valley but I am not familiar with the English provinces. That would be a hundred miles or so due east of this Shallowford place you wrote about? Well," he smiled his thin smile, "what is a hundred miles to a plough-boy, eh? You'll see that I have secured an option on the place. You can go and look over it tomorrow, now that the Coronation is cancelled!" and he handed Paul the papers which included the original advertisement from the *Illustrated London News*. Paul glanced at the telegram. All it said was, "*Will meet Lieutenant Craddock Sorrel Halt 3.30 p.m. 24th instant. Latest information is thirteen thousand acceptable. Will confirm later. John Rudd, Agent.*"

"What the devil does it mean, Uncle Franz? It doesn't make sense! I asked for a price on one of the farms, not the entire damned acreage and house!"

"My boy," Franz said, "I told you your father found it impossible to stop thinking in sixpences. If you must farm then farm big! Don't nibble! Take the biggest bite offered you! And when you get there don't let this joker of an agent bluff you. They'll take thirteen thousand gladly, if only to save the extra delay in selling off by lots. It's clearly the best offer they've had. I should have stuck fast at twelve!"

"But hang it," Paul exclaimed, exasperation with the Croat's patronage overcoming his nervousness, "I haven't got more than five thousand, have I? And I don't know a damned thing about running an estate of this size! My idea was to learn farming, not set up as a squire over thirteen hundred acres!"

"Oh, you'll learn," Zorndorff said, with maddening unconcern. "This agent seems to know his business and doubtless he'll stay on

38

for a year or two. As to the money, you can leave that side of it to me. I'll waive a point and release another eight thousand, plus a working capital of a thousand or two to tide you over until the rents come in. As to disposing of your share in this bone-yard, you'll find me far less co-operative! You'll keep your interest as long as I think fit, and remember you can't sell to anyone but me until your twenty-eighth birthday and I daresay you'll be very glad of the income during the intervening period! It looks to me as if the place is badly run down."

Paul sat on one of the office stools, trying to grapple with the magnitude of the new situation and finding it difficult not to succumb to panic.

"How far am I committed?" he demanded and the Jew, looking at him kindly, said, "You aren't committed at all. This is an option, not a contract, boy. Go down and look at it. Ride about, ask questions, listen at keyholes if necessary. With this amount of money involved any safety device is permissible! But I'll tell you one thing! Don't come back here and admit that your nerve isn't equal to it, and start hedging your bets by becoming a pennypiece freeholder among a crowd of tenant-farmers, all of whom, I daresay, would buy their land if they had the guts and capital! If you do that you'll soon be squeezed out and make a mess of it. In other words, stay there as boss or not at all! There's only one way to farm in this country—on a big scale, with lesser men doing all the donkey work. That talk of starting at the bottom is put about by people at the top; those at the bottom stay there!"

"You didn't!" Paul argued, chuckling in spite of himself, "my father told me the pair of you started with a working capital of less than a hundred!"

"Ah," Zorndorff said, "that was before this country sold its soul to the devil! It's very different nowadays. The day of the small man is over, I'm afraid!" He pointed through the begrimed window to the weighbridge, where the line of carters was still awaiting their turn. "Do you imagine any of those ruffians will ever sip brandy in St. James', as we did today? Only if there is another war, on a far vaster scale than the South African affair, and then only the gamblers among them!"

"Why are you so eager to push me into this?" Paul asked, suddenly, "you know it can never make money, not as you understand money?"

Franz said, shrugging, "That's so, but apart from propitiating one's involuntary sleeping partner and one's sole, solvent nephew, I like a

39

young man to follow his destiny even if it leads to the Official Receiver!"

It was some kind of answer but it was very far from being a complete or even an honest answer. Franz Zorndorff's contempt for sentiment was genuine enough, but as he looked sidelong at Paul Craddock's strong, narrow face and obstinate mouth it was not of his old friend that he thought but of the stately, aloof woman, who had been Josh Craddock's country-bred wife. He fancied that, for the first time in all the years that had passed since he and Josh had thrown down their challenge to the world, she was regarding him with tolerance, or at least without disdain.

CHAPTER TWO

I

JOHN RUDD recognised him the moment the little train emerged from the cutting, a lean young man with a rather sallow face, head and shoulders thrust enquiringly through the window of a first-class compartment. Recognition did nothing to reassure the chunky, ruddy-faced man sitting the piebald cob and holding the grey gelding by a leading rein. Rudd thought, as the face disappeared, and the train ran alongside the platform, "That's him all right, an ex-Yeomanry show-off, still wearing uniform a month after peace has been signed! A kid too, by the look of him, with plenty of somebody else's money to burn, and all the answers in his narrow little head!", and he kicked the flanks of the cob and moved forward, deciding that he would be damned before he dismounted and went into the booking-office to help The Prospect with his luggage. He couldn't carry it anyway, since the idiot had told the Jewboy to wire asking for horses, and why should he have done that? Probably in order to cut a dash in his uniform so that now the luggage would have to come over on the carrier's cart, a service that would cost him a florin. Rudd waited, glumly, more than ever convinced that he would be paid off and turned loose within the next month or so. After all, an ex-Yeomanry poop would not be likely to need an agent to run a six-farm estate. He would be sure to imagine he could do the job better himself.

Craddock had seen Rudd and been intimidated by the man's moody stare, and the squareness of his seat on the piebald. He looked like a man who knew his business but also a person unlikely to give unprejudiced advice on matters involving his personal future. Craddock slipped on his rucksack, all the luggage he had brought with him, and left the train, noting that nobody else got out at the halt but that his arrival caused a ripple among stationmaster, porter and two or three idlers sunning themselves on platform seats. They looked at him incuriously but steadily, so that he had to walk the gauntlet of their stares, surrendering his ticket and stalking through the booking-hall and into the station-yard, which was more like a garden with its

41

tall hollyhocks, sunflowers and neat beds of geranium growing under the stationmaster's windows. Rudd touched his low crowned hat.

"Lieutenant Craddock?"

"Only 'lieutenant' until the first week of July," Craddock said, making a determined effort to smile as he shook the agent's hand. "I'm in uniform because I was discharged from hospital yesterday and didn't stop to buy civilian togs."

Rudd surveyed him coolly, a little disconcerted by his youth and cordiality. "Maybe I'm wrong," he reflected, "maybe he's a poop that can be handled with a little care," and he nodded briefly, swinging his leg over the cob and dismounting to slip the gelding's stirrup-irons down the leathers.

"She's fat but you'll find her comfortable, Mr. Craddock. Been out to grass since early spring. Nobody to hunt her back end of the season," and he stood holding the crupper, while Craddock hoisted his stiff leg across the grey's back. He managed it but not without a grimace and Rudd said, casually, "You got it in the leg then?"

"Knee joint," Craddock told him, "it doesn't look much but its given everybody a hell of a lot of trouble."

This seemed all there was to say so they set off down the curving white road side by side. It was not until they had crossed the main highway, and pushed on down a stony track leading across a wide stretch of gorse moor, that Rudd spoke again. To Craddock, who still found him intimidating, he seemed to do so with reluctance.

"Maybe it was a good idea riding back. At least I can show you some of the country before you look at maps. Our boundary begins down there in the hollow, a mile or so on. We shall go pretty well the entire length of our western border and pass two of the farms, Hermitage and Four Winds, both around three-fifty acres."

"How far is it?" Craddock asked for something to say, and Rudd told him that the distance from Shallowford to Sorrel Halt, their nearest rail point, was a little over six miles. "It would have been much shorter," he added, "if the family hadn't opposed the Great Western Railway crossing their land. As it is the branch line was kept to the far side of that main road that we crossed just now. That's one reason that has kept us in the Middle Ages."

He said this with a sneer and Craddock looked at him again, noting the firm flesh of his jaw which had the strength of a steel trap and the bleakness of hard, light blue eyes, now gazing straight ahead. He looked and rode, thought Craddock, as though he had seen service in a cavalry regiment and he might have been a year or so short of fifty. He said, without curiosity, "Have you been in the Army, Mr. Rudd?"

The agent's reaction was immediate. He swung round so sharply that the cob threw up its head and pranced a step or two as Craddock's grey, evidently accustomed to its tantrums, neatly sidestepped giving Craddock's leg a sharp twinge. They stopped, half-facing one another.

"So they haven't lost much time telling you!" snapped Rudd and Craddock saw that his cheeks were a network of tiny blue veins and that a pulse beat in his temples. He decided that he disliked the man on sight and replied, crisply, "Nobody's told me anything, Mr. Rudd. I explained that I was in hospital until forty-eight hours ago. All the arrangements were made by my father's executor, Mr. Franz Zorndorff, and neither he nor I have met or corresponded with anyone down here, save yourself."

The anger went out of the agent's face and he looked confused and shamefaced. He gave the reins a twitch and they moved on.

"Then I beg your pardon," he said after a pause, "I had no cause to say anything like that, no cause at all! Damned bad manners on my part! I apologise, Mr. Craddock."

"Very well," said Paul, his resentment ebbing, for the man now looked both depressed and uneasy, "we'll forget I asked, except to say that it was a perfectly innocent remark on my part. While we are at it, however, am I right in imagining you resent me coming here? If so, it might help us both if you explained why?"

Rudd reined in again and sat quite still, staring over the hillside to a great sprawl of woods on the far edge of the moor and it seemed to Craddock that he was almost willing the nearest clump of oaks to topple and crash. Suddenly he looked directly at Craddock and his full lips twitched in an unexpectedly frank smile.

"I don't blame you thinking me a rum 'un," he said, "but the fact is I'm pretty much on edge these days and there's reason enough for that right enough! I've been waiting here ever since Sir George died up north, and even before that I had no kind of instructions from him or his solicitors. They even let me read about Mr. Hubert's death in the newspapers. I suppose Shallowford means little enough to them but they might have had the decency to reassure me about my own future. After all, I've served them well for close on twenty years, and if they had any complaints I've yet to hear of them!"

43

"You mean your position as agent has neither been confirmed nor terminated since the estate was put up for sale?"

"I've not had a word, one way or the other, nothing except a telegram about the furniture sale from the solicitors."

"It all seems a bit casual," Craddock said, "and I can understand you feeling touchy about it. Did you intend leaving when Shallowford is sold?"

"I've nothing else in the offing at the moment," Rudd said grimly, "but it would be unreasonable to discuss that with you at this stage. In any case," he paused a moment, looking down at the cob's bristles, "to be honest it wasn't my position here that made me fly off the handle just now. I jumped to the wrong conclusion, that's all."

"That the Lovell family had written to me about you?"

"Yes, and rather more than that."

"You can't expect me to follow you there, Mr. Rudd. Either tell me what's in your mind or let's ride on and we can discuss your position as agent when I've had a chance to make up my mind. It isn't made up in advance, you know."

Rudd said, breathing heavily, "No . . . wait, Mr. Craddock! You've served overseas, so it isn't like talking to a complete stranger. I'd rather tell you at once why that 'innocent question' of yours encouraged me to make an ass of myself! The fact is, I *have* served in the Army. Until I was twenty-eight I held a commission in the Light Cavalry and I too served in Africa but another part of Africa." He paused a moment and then said, flatly, "I was cashiered, more or less."

"How can an officer be cashiered 'more or less'?" Craddock asked.

"What I mean is it wasn't official but it was a drumming-out just the same," Rudd said, "and it wasn't for debt either but something a damned sight worse! It was that that gave the Lovells, father and sons, the edge on me all these years, and they still have it, even though all three of them are dead now, damn them! And on top of it all Hubert had to win a V.C.! Well, thank God I wasn't called upon to congratulate him on that!"

"Then the Lovells were bad people to work for?"

"They were but I don't hate them for that," Rudd said, "any more than do the rest of the people around here, folk dependent upon them for one reason or another." He seemed to rise slightly in his stirrups and survey the whole sweep of the moor as far as the sea. "This has been a bad place to be," he said quietly, "rotten bad for three

44

generations if you had no means to escape from it! It need not have been but it was, for they made it so, one and all! It took me years to make up my mind about that, that it was them and not the place itself. However, that doesn't explain my touchiness does it?", and unexpectedly he smiled again and kicked his heels, so that the cob began to walk on down the slope and the well-mannered grey followed.

"I don't see that you are under the slightest obligation to explain things to me at this stage," Paul said.

"Oh come, Mr. Craddock," said Rudd, good-humouredly now, "suppose I left it there? You would only get to wondering and wondering and be driven to find out one way or another. Anyone would, especially a lad your age, who could never imagine it happening to him."

"A good deal has happened to me already," Paul said. "I only pulled through by a miracle. They gave me up time and again and I got in the habit of hearing my chances chewed over by doctors and nurses. That can teach you a thing or two if you'll let it."

Rudd looked frankly at him and for the first time there was tolerance in his eyes.

"Exactly what did it teach you that was new, Mr. Craddock?"

"Patience, I suppose, and gratitude for being alive. Also respect for people who seemed to go to a great deal of trouble to improve one's chances—those kind of things."

"I was a pupil at a different kind of school," Rudd said. "Did you ever hear of the Prince Eugène Napoleon? The 'Painted Emperor's' son, the one killed in the Zulu War?"

"Certainly. He was killed on June 1st, 1879, whilst on reconnaissance during the advance on the Zulu capital."

"Now how the devil do you come to know that?" exclaimed Rudd and Craddock chuckled. "Because it happens to have been the day I was born, so naturally I made a mental note of it when I'd read an account in one of the *Strand Magazines* we had at home."

"Now that's very odd," said Rudd, musing, "that's damned odd! If I was a superstitious man I'd say that was some kind of omen but good or bad I wouldn't know. Do you recall the circumstances?"

"No, I'm afraid I don't," said Craddock, "but I imagine you liked the Prince Imperial as much as you seem to have liked your late employers."

"About even I should say," retorted Rudd easily, "for both had a peculiar propensity for winning notoriety at other people's expense!

45

That young man had nobody but himself to blame for what happened. He off-saddled in shoulder-high grass out of range of the camp, with one wretched lieutenant and six troopers as escort. The Zulus jumped the troop and they had to bolt for it. Everyone got away but the Prince. He was riding a nervous horse and couldn't get a leg over when the firing started. He had about a dozen assegai wounds when they found him. All in front. Very proper."

"How were you involved?"

"I was sent after the patrol by an officer who should never have sent it out in the first place, and when I met them coming back hell for leather I turned and rode in with them. Was that so odd? What is a man supposed to do when he sees a reconnaissance patrol riding for their lives? Stop them and ask for a written report?"

It was strange, Craddock thought, how time had done nothing to dull the man's memory of that single moment of panic, now twenty-three years behind him. It was as though, up to that moment, nothing of importance had occurred to him, and after it he had lived a kind of half-life in which the most sensational event came a poor second to a wild gallop across the veldt, with troopers gasping out news that the Prince Imperial was back there, speared through by assegais.

"Why are you telling me all this, Mr. Rudd?" he asked and Rudd said, "God knows! I haven't mentioned it to anyone else in twenty years! Not that everyone here doesn't know about it, Sir George and Hubert saw to that."

"But they continued to employ you as their agent."

"That's *why* they employed me and also why I stayed. What kind of future was open to a man who had turned tail and abandoned a Prince Imperial to a few savages?"

They rode silently for a moment and then Craddock said, "Very well, now you've told me, but as far as I'm concerned I don't give a damn what bad luck you ran into all that time ago. I've done my share of dodging tricky situations and so has every other soldier, unless he's a fool, or a bit slow off the mark! I was hoping to rely on you for straightforward advice on my chances of making some kind of success with this place; if I decided to buy that is, but you ought to know right away that it wasn't my idea at all but Zorndorff's. I can't even legally buy it for another five years."

Rudd looked surprised. "You mean your money is tied up until then?"

"That's so but it needn't necessarily stop a purchase. Mr. Zorndorff

46

seems anxious that I should take the plunge, although administration of an estate this size was only a vague notion at the back of my mind, something I used to think about when I knew I would be invalided out. I've had no previous experience and wanted a single farm. The only qualifications I have are that I should be interested and I can ride. I'm not a crock either. When this stiffness eases I'll be as fit as the next man. I wanted an open-air life and Mr. Zorndorff seemed to think this was as good an opportunity as any."

Rudd was smiling again. The man had almost as wide a range of expression as Zorndorff. No trace remained of his previous sullenness and he looked, Craddock now felt, like a man one could trust.

"Well, I suppose you might do worse, things being what they are and I mean your circumstances, not those of the estate. It's badly run down and peopled with backward, lazy rascals but they ought to welcome you; if they have any sense that is! The Lovells took their rents every quarter day for a century or more and cursed them if they asked for a new tile on the roof. You'll need to put money into it for a spell but the land on this side is as good as any in Devon and there's good timber behind the house. The Home Farm is in shape, for I've seen to that, and Honeyman is a good farmer. It's in the Coombe area that you've got layabouts and they're mostly confined to one family, the Potters, of Low Coombe. However, there's no point at all in my influencing you one way or the other at this stage, you'll have to make up your own mind after you've gone the rounds." He chuckled and glanced sidelong at Craddock through half-closed eyes. "Well, this is a rum do I must say! I expected all kinds of developments when I got the enquiry but nothing quite like this, I can assure you." And then he seemed to brace himself in the saddle, assuming a paternal, businesslike air. "We're about half-way down," he said, "so I'll do what I should have done at first instead of crying on your shoulder, Mr. Craddock!" He pointed left towards the steep wood that bounded the moor. "That's Hermitage Wood, close-set oak and beech mostly but with a big fir plantation higher up. This moor is called Blackberry Down and it's common land, used by us and also by the Gilroy Estate, our nearest neighbour across the Teazel. That's the smaller of the two streams, this one on your right is the Sorrel that flows through our land as far as the sea at Coombe Bay, four miles from here. Coombe Bay isn't much more than a small village but we own some property there, held on long leases. The road runs beside the river here for a mile or more and the park wall is over there on your left, beyond Hermitage Farm. Martin Codsall's farm, Four Winds, is down there across the river, the biggest we've got, and fairly well run. Above you, hidden by that clump, is Hermitage, farmed by Pitts and his son, sound enough chaps but very unenterprising. Beyond the park wall . . ."

He broke off as Paul, lifting his head, trotted forward and reined in on the very brow of the hill where he could look across the long, rolling slope to the sea.

"One minute, Mr. Rudd," he called, "I've never seen anything quite like this before!" and he swept the prospect from west to east, from the thin sliver of the Teazel marking Gilroy's boundary on the right, to the high, wooded bluff above the outfall of the River Sorrel, that ran below in a wide curve to the left. He could sniff the sea breasting the scent of heather and gorse, a smell of summer released from the bracken by the grey's hooves, and hear the light breeze shaking Martin Codsall's corn on the slope where Four Winds' meadows met the great sweep of the woods and the Sorrel, ten yards wide, and spanned by a wooden bridge, began its final curve to the sea. He could even see the sun glinting on a roof in the distant village and as his eyes followed the course of the shallow stream a kingfisher flashed and then disappeared into the brake.

Rudd said, "Ah, it looks tame enough now, Mr. Craddock, but some of its moods are damned ugly! You should see it when the sou'westers come roaring in from over the Whin, and sleet drives at you from every point of the compass!", and he led the way down on to the track that followed the bend of the river, a broad path thick with spurting white dust that swept up in clouds and then settled to bow the stalks of cowparsley in the hedgerow on their side of the river.

It was this tall bank that held Paul's attention until they passed the angle of the grey stone wall, bordering the park, for its colour defied the dust every yard of the way. Tall ranks of foxgloves grew there, and at their roots a thick carpet of stitchwort, ragwort, dandelion, honeysuckle, dog rose and campion. The air throbbed with the hum of insects and huge bumble bees droned from petal to petal, like fat, lazy policemen checking the doors of silent premises. As they trotted past the wooden bridge Rudd told him that it was the only one spanning the Sorrel between the railway and the sea, and rightly belonged to Codsall of Four Winds but was used by everyone when the ford from which the estate derived its name was impassable. As the little grey lodge came in view beyond the Home Farm buildings, he added, "I took the liberty of getting Mrs. Handcock, the house-keeper, to make you up a bed in my lodge. There used to be a lodge-keeper of course, and I lived up at the house, but when he left I moved in and have been too lazy to shift. I'm a widower, and can look after myself although one of Tamer Potter's sluts looks in to clean up every once in a while. I live a solitary life down there and get sick of my own company, so you'll be welcome to stay with me as long as you are here. The guest rooms up at the big house are in poor shape. If we get a wet spell after this long drought the ceilings will leak."

"The lodge will suit me very well," Paul said but absently for he was still a prey to pleasurable excitement and nagging anxiety, sparring one with the other just below his belt. The whole place, he thought, was so immense, and not only vast and awesome but over-powering. By acquiring suzerainty of such a domain, he would be shouldering the cares of a small kingdom and that without a notion of how to rule unless he placed himself under the thumb of this square-faced, unpredictable agent, a man who rode with a chip on his shoulder, a chip the size of a French Prince. He must, he told himself, take plenty of time to think this out, and do his thinking in solitude.

The park gates looked as if they had remained open for years and hung by rusting hinges to a pair of fifteen-foot stone pillars, crowned by stone eagles. A stone's throw from the entrance was the ford, paved with flat stones and no more than six inches deep where the river ballooned into a pond. Geese honked among buttercups and anemones growing on the margin and the lodge, a snug little house with a pantiled roof and trim muslin curtains stood only a few yards inside the drive. All that Paul could see of the house itself was a cluster of chimney pots soaring above the last few chestnuts of the drive which curved sharply at the top of the steep ascent, where grew huge clumps of rhododendron, now in flower.

Mrs. Handcock, the housekeeper, came waddling to the lodge door as they clattered up and Rudd, dismounting, introduced Paul, giving the horses to a boy about twelve who somehow contrived to hoist himself on to the cob and rode away across the paddock to the Home Farm. The housekeeper was a large, pink-faced woman about fifty, with greying hair and a rich Westcountry brogue, the first purely Devon accent Paul had ever heard. She was respectful in her approach but by no means humble, as she shepherded him into the parlour where the table was laid for tea, a traditionally Devonshire tea of scones that Mrs. Handcock called "chudleys", and huge bowls of homemade strawberry jam, served with thick, yellow cream. Paul was too elated to do justice to her hospitality but he did his best and was afterwards shown to his room which was very small but scrupulously clean, with a copper can of hot water set ready for his use. He listened a moment to the rumble of Rudd's voice below, guessing that the agent was giving Mrs. Handcock his first impressions of The Prospect but then he thought that this was taking mean advantage of them and having washed, came downstairs again, to find Rudd very much at ease in his big armchair, with jacket off, feet up and a Meerschaum pipe between his teeth. Paul lit his own pipe and tried to pretend that he too was at ease but Rudd was not fooled. He said, "I didn't tell you the conditions of the furniture sale, Mr. Craddock. The curtains and carpets, together with various fittings labelled 'R', go with the property; all the other stuff is up for sale the day after tomorrow. Coombes and Drayton are doing it from Whinmouth, that's our nearest town, some three miles west of Gilroy's place, across the Teazel. If you have made your decision before the auction you can bid for anything you want, or I'll get someone to bid for you. Would you like to go up there now, or will you wait until morning?"

"I should like to go now," Paul said, "and if it's all the same to you, Mr. Rudd, I'd prefer to poke around on my own. I can make notes of anything I might want to ask and I expect you've got plenty to do."

"I've got an inventory to make out," Rudd told him. "The lawyers have been pestering me for it ever since the sale notices went up. The place is locked so you'll need the front-door key," and he handed Craddock a key that looked as if it would have opened a county gaol. "I usually have a toddy before bed," he added, "would you care to join me, after dusk?"

"Very much," Craddock said, "and convey my thanks to Mrs. Handcock for the tea." He left then, more than ever anxious to be alone, yet conscious of a growing liking for the agent and climbed the steep drive, discovering that the brazen heat had gone from the day and that long, evening shadows were now falling across the smaller paddock, beyond which he could just see what looked like a formal garden enclosed by ragged box hedges. It was so quiet that he could hear the rustle of birds in the rhododendron thickets and then, as he rounded the curve, there was the house twenty yards distant, looking like a great grey rock, with the last rays of red-gold sunlight lighting up its westerly windows but its eastern wing blank, as though such life as remained in the pile had gone to watch the sunset.

50

It was easier to assess its age and character than had been possible by studying the picture in the *Illustrated London News*; Craddock saw at once that it was really two houses, of widely separated periods. The centre block, notwithstanding its portico and Doric columns, was a stone Tudor farmhouse, with two squarish windows set low in the wall. The massive front door was the kind of entrance suggested by the key and although at first sight the two styles represented in the frontage seemed incongruous yet they seemed to have learned to tolerate one another over the years, the marriage having been accomplished by a mantle of creeper running wild along the whole front of the building. The main windows, opening on to the terrace, looked as if they gave upon spacious rooms and the terrace itself was unpretentious, divided in half by the semi-circular approach fronting the pillars, and bounded by a low stone wall spaced with stone cranes or herons.

Craddock stood looking up at it for several minutes, watching the west windows turn ruby in the sun and as he stared, eyes half closed against the sun, the silent building began to stir with life, so that he saw it as an ageing and once beautiful woman, awaiting the return of sons who had marched away centuries since and been swallowed up in a forgotten war. There was patience here, patience and a kind of desperate dignity, as though all hope of their return had never been abandoned, and that one day all the windows would glow with candles. Craddock tried to relate this dignity and repose with the little that Rudd had told him of the family who had lived here for a century or more but he found this very difficult, for somehow the house did not strike him as morose, merely forsaken and resigned. Yet about the middle section of it, the oldest, Elizabethan block, vitality lingered, the older tenants still seeming to exert more influence than the Lovells and this conviction was so real that Craddock would not have been surprised if, as he watched, lights had flickered in that part of the house leaving each wing dark and lifeless.

He climbed the stone steps and wrestled with the giant key, the lock turning more easily than he had anticipated, and the great door swung back with a sound like an old man's cough. He left the door open, for it was dim in the slate-slabbed hall and here he saw that the early-Victorian architect's work on the interior had been more bold than outside, for beyond the great empty fireplace a stair ran up in a well-contrived curve and each step was so broad and shallow that it promised an easy ascent to those short of wind. There was not much

51

furniture in the hall and what there was was shrouded in green dust-sheets. Some of the portraits had lot numbers attached to them and Craddock, recalling the hard faces of Sir George and younger son, guessed they were portraits of Lovells from 1806 onwards; they had the same bleakness of eye and stiff formality of dress that he had noted in the photographs in the magazine.

He glanced in two reception-rooms, one on each side of the hall, finding them half-full of shrouded furniture, most of which was lotted, but here and there was a piece labelled with an "R". The reserved pieces, he noticed, were mostly heavy oak or draperies, like the big refectory table and the faded curtains looped with silk ropes as thick as cables. He went back into the hall and down the stone passage leading to the kitchens but the light here was bad so he returned and ascended the stairs, hesitating at the top where there was a kind of minstrel gallery, trying to decide whether to take the left- or the right-hand corridor.

He was standing here when he heard the sound of a footfall on a wooden floor, and hearing it repeated identified the sound of someone walking in one of the rooms in the west wing. He was on the point of retracing his steps, and locking the door behind him, when he remembered that he was as authorised to be here as anyone else, so he walked quietly in the direction of the sounds until he came to the door at the very end of the corridor. It was slightly ajar but when he stopped and listened again the sounds had ceased, so after a preliminary cough he walked into what had obviously been a nursery, for there were toys strewn about, including a large dappled rocking-horse and over in the corner a vast three-fold children's scrap screen of the kind that every upper-class nursery possessed. Then, over by the tall window, where the square panes had turned to stained glass in the setting sun, he saw the girl.

Astonishment made him the trespasser. He stood just inside the door gaping, and she stared back, an instinctive defiance stemming from anger rather than alarm. She was, Craddock decided on the spot, the most exciting woman he had ever seen. Not in illustrated books, nor in the course of his visits to picture galleries or in his dreams, did he recall having seen anyone who made such an immediate impact upon his senses. She was wearing a light blue riding habit, hitched at one side, a white silk blouse frilled at the throat to give the impression of a stock and was bareheaded, her dark hair gathered in a broad grey ribbon. Her eyes matched her costume

52

exactly, her nose was short and straight and her small but very resolute chin had a large dimple an inch below a small, red mouth. But what impressed him more than her good features or bearing, was the texture of her skin, which was pale and waxlike, very firm and entirely without blemish. Her hair, removed from the strong rays of ruby light that flooded the window, would have seemed jet black, giving the taut skin of her cheeks and forehead an almost phosphorescent glow. She was not much above five feet in height but the cut of her habit, enclosing a small waist and emphasising the upward sweep of her breasts and downsweep of her sturdy thighs, added a fictitious inch or so to her figure.

He stood staring at her and she stared back, one hand gripping the curtain, the other holding a riding switch, and perhaps thirty seconds passed before she said, sharply: "Who are you? What are you doing here?" The voice betrayed no trace of fear, or even surprise, only a leashed and rather daunting anger.

He said, uncertainly, "My name is Craddock, Paul Craddock. I'm looking over the house. Mr. Rudd, the agent, gave me the key," and he held it up as though it had been his ticket of admission and she was the janitor. She considered him and the key for a moment but her expression did not relent. She still glowered at him, as though he had been a strange male who had blundered into her bedroom, so he tried again, this time a little hoarsely, for his throat was dry and his heart was pounding.

"I arrived this afternoon, Rudd and I rode over from the station."

"Why?"

She spat the word at him so sharply that it converted his uncertainty into indignation.

"Why not? My father's trustee has an option on the estate!"

Her expression softened and there was curiosity in the eyes.

"Does he intend buying the place? Buying the estate as a whole?"

"He might," Paul said, "and on my behalf but it's far from settled yet." Then, tentatively, "Do you live here? Rudd said the house had been empty some time."

Her eyes left him for the first time since he had entered the room. She glanced first at the bare floor, then out of the window.

"No," she said, less aggressively, "I don't live here. I used to come here a great deal; some time ago, before . . . before the war!"

"Her reluctance to speak the word gave him a clue. He said, lightly, "Ah, you knew the Lovells then?"

"Of course!", and that seemed to be all the information she was

53

prepared to give for suddenly she seemed to slump a little, as though bored with the conversation. After a pause, however, she went on, "I must go now, it'll be dusk before I'm home. I've got a horse in the yard and four miles to ride. I'm sorry I startled you, I should have asked Rudd for the key. I only came here to look at some furniture." Then, in a few long strides, she was past him and before he could think of an excuse to detain her she was half-way along the passage, her high-heeled riding boots clacking on the bare boards. A door banged somewhere behind the kitchens and after that there was silence, a slightly eerie silence he thought, as though she had been a ghost and he had imagined the encounter.

He crossed to the window asking himself impatiently why a chance meeting with a pretty girl in an empty house should disturb him, both emotionally and physically. She was obviously here without authority and had probably decided to bluff. He wondered briefly how she had managed to unlock the back door and why she should have seemed so resentful of him. She had, he decided, been musing and had made her way to this particular room for that purpose. Her pose over there by the window had betrayed as much and his sudden appearance, breaking into her reflections, had startled her so that, in a sense, her anger had been counterfeit. He remained standing where she had stood, wondering if she would circle the west wing and appear at the crest of the drive, but when he heard or saw nothing of her he fell to thinking about women in general and his relations with them in the past.

His experience with women had been limited but although technically still a virgin he was not altogether innocent. There had been a very forward fourteen-year-old called Cherry, who had lived in an adjoining house in Croydon, when he came home for school holidays and Cherry had succeeded in bewitching but ultimately terrifying him, for one day when they were larking about in the stable behind her house, she had hinted at the mysterious differences between the sexes and when, blushing, he had encouraged her to elaborate, she had promptly hoisted her skirt and pulled down her long cotton drawers, whereupon he had fled as though the Devil was after him and had never sought her company again, although he watched her closely in church on successive Sundays, expecting any moment to see forked lightning descend on her in the middle of "For all the Saints". Then there had been a little clumsy cuddling at Christmas parties, and after that a flaxen-haired girl called Daphne

54

whom he had mooned over as an adolescent and had thought of a good deal in the Transvaal but now he had almost forgotten what Daphne looked like and had not recalled her name until now. Finally there had been an abortive foray across the frontier in the company of a self-assured, toothy officer, called Prescott-Smythe, the two having ventured into a brothel at Capetown, where Paul spent a few embarrassing moments with a Hottentot whore. The experience was something he would have preferred to forget and indeed, almost had forgotten save for the girl's mousey smell and repellent gestures. After that the Veldt and the exclusive company of men until he was wounded, and in the hospital any attempts to establish extra-professional relationships with volunteer nurses had been nipped in the bud by the Countess who regarded every officer as her personal prerogative. So he stood thinking, glancing round the musty nursery and wondering what compulsive memories had directed the girl here when she had every reason to suppose that the house would be empty. The rocking horse, and the faded scrap screen offered no answer and apart from the few scraps of peeling wallpaper there was little else in the room. Then, unexpectedly, he saw her again, riding a neat bay round the south-western corner of the house below the window and as he watched she flicked the horse into a slow canter at the head of the drive and they passed out of sight under the avenue chestnuts. He saw a swift flash of blue as she passed the gate pillars and then nothing more, so that excitement ebbed from the day and he made his way down the shallow stairs, letting himself out and carefully re-locking the door.

Dusk was falling outside and a blue mist lay under the woods enclosing the house from the back. The front windows were blank and there was no life in the house, not even the original block beyond the pillars. He noticed also that paint and plaster were peeling from parts of the façade and that the old building now looked more like a near-ruin than a dignified woman awaiting the return of dead men. Yet the vivid memory of the girl's eyes and pale, waxlike skin remained as he made his way back to the lodge and as soon as he had settled over a toddy with Rudd he told the agent of his encounter, expecting surprise and possibly indignation at a trespass but Rudd only shrugged when he described the girl and her curiously aggressive reception.

"That'll be Grace Lovell," he said, carelessly, and when Paul asked if she was a granddaughter of the old Squire Rudd chuckled.

"By no means," he said, "simply a family hanger-on of a kind,

55

although perhaps that's a bit unfair on the girl. Her father, Captain Bruce Lovell, is the family ne'er-do-well and even he is only a cousin. He took one of the Lovell houses at Coombe Bay after his retirement from the Gunners and was quite a charge on them all until he remarried. His wife was a Voysey, very wealthy family from Derbyshire I understand. But in marrying her Bruce bit off more than he could chew, or so I'm told. The girl's been very troublesome too. She was to have married Ralph, the younger son of the old man, but Kruger put paid to that of course."

As always when he discussed the Lovells Rudd's manner hardened but somewhere at the back of Paul's mind a shutter opened and the girl's display of anger at being discovered in the empty house began to make sense.

"Was it a family match or were they fond of one another?" he asked but at that the agent's casualness left him and he looked at Paul with a kind of exasperation.

"Look here, if you've been smitten by Grace Lovell my advice is forget her. She's tarred with the same old brush, an indiscipline that can show itself in obstinacy, bloodymindedness, or a sort of madness. There's congenital rottenness in that family somewhere along the line. Sometimes I used to dismiss it as arrogance coming from always having had too much money, but other times . . . well, I'm not going to bore you with more confessions. They're all dead now, at least, the three I had to do with are, and I'm done with them, thank God, so take another glass before you go to bed and tell me what you thought of the house up yonder."

They talked for a spell of the fabric of the building and Rudd told him something of its growth from a manor farmhouse, older by far than any other farm on the estate, to its present unmanageable size. The main changes were made in the early eighteen-twenties, on the proceeds of prize-money won by the first Lovell's brother, who had been lucky during the long war with France. Paul listened with assumed interest but his mind was not much exercised by Rudd's estimates of how much it would cost to put Shallowford and surrounding property in order after two decades of neglect. It was engaged in following a flash of blue beyond the ford and across country to the sea. "Smitten" was the word the agent had used, and Paul was regretting now that he had betrayed interest in the girl. Rudd, however, interpreted his polite affirmatives as a desire for bed and presently arose, knocking out his pipe.

56

"We'll do the round tomorrow," he said. "I'll show you the worst part first, over in the Coombe, and then we'll look for something better at Hermitage and Four Winds in the west. Good night to you, Mr. Craddock. There's a candle on the hall tray."

He went up and Paul soon followed but it was a long time before he slept. His wound ached from the long ride and the owls in Hermitage Wood were hunting and making a great deal of noise about it. Soon the moon rose, flooding the tiny chamber with a silver light, and at last Craddock slept, most of his doubts unresolved.

II

Nobody could have said with certainty how the Potters of Low Coombe received warning of The Prospect's visit. They were usually the first to get news, even of insignificant events and Smut Potter, the poacher, who saw Craddock's arrival at the station probably passed the word around. The Potters lived with a communal ear to the ground and could hear and interpret every rustle of rumour between the sea and the far side of the moor beyond the railway line. The green basin they occupied under the wooded, sandstone bluff suggested a gypsy encampment but in place of caravans were ramshackle buildings centred on a ruinous cob farmhouse and life revolved around the pump which, at this time of year, was hidden by docks, chickweed and shoulder-high nettles. A long clothes-line stretched from pump to the nearest oak and along it, on any fine day, hung an astonishing array of threadbare garments, all the way down from Old Tamer's long woollen pants to the pinafore of Hazel, the youngest of the Potters, a half-witted nine-year-old, as wild as any animal in the woods.

Nobody, not even Tamer himself or his brown-faced, handsome wife Meg, could give the full strength of the clan at any given time. Potter boys and Potter girls were always coming or going and as often as not some of Meg's Romany kinfolk were encamped in the Coombe, although, under Sir George, this had been forbidden upon penalty of eviction, for it gave every local poacher an alibi. Tamer and his wife had been living at Low Coombe for as long as most Valley folk could remember, sometimes farming the ninety-odd acres between the sea and Edwin Willoughby's farm, higher up the Coombe, but subsisting in the main upon the driblets of money the children brought in, Sam, the eldest boy, from the sale of firewood, Smut, the second boy, from

57

poaching and the three elder girls from what they earned as part-time domestics and the occasional sale of their lusty, unwashed bodies. But for all their improvidence the Potters were a happy-go-lucky brood, each with their father's eye for a quick profit and their mother's resilience, nurtured by the systematic persecution of Romanies. They were ragged, dirty, thieving and irrepressible but they seldom went short of food and not one of them had ever been laid aside by a day's illness. Peasant cunning on the part of Tamer, allied to possession of the Evil Eye on the part of his wife, may have contributed to their survival, for although they were despised and avoided by respectable families like the Codsalls, the Pitts and the Derwents, and treated with tolerance by their immediate neighbours, the Willoughbys, few in the Sorrel Valley cared to incur the hostility of the men, or the witchcraft of Meg, who was credited with the power to distribute blessings or blights, according to her inclination.

The scene in Low Coombe that morning was akin to the scurry in a Highland glen after word had arrived that redcoats were arriving to search for arms and Jacobites. At first there was a wave of panic, showing itself in wildly disordered attempts to clear away litter, strip the clothes-line and shore up tottering walls but the Potters could never engage in sustained activity and after half-an-hour's running here and there Old Tamer called a conference round the pump, pointing out that perhaps, in the circumstances, it would be more profitable to advertise extreme poverty, rather than create an impression that the Potters were sober, industrious farmers. Rudd, the agent, would never be taken in by a last-minute spit-and-polish whereas the new young Squire (the Potters, one and all, already thought of Paul as such) should be given no excuse for thinking the family was self-sufficient and could survive without a reduction of rent and perhaps a loan of draught animals from the Home Farm.

"Us'll get nowt if us makes out us needs nowt!" Tamer reasoned, "zo us might as well let un zee us is down to our last varden!", and the family, standing in a semi-circle in the nettles, sanctioned this realistic approach with enthusiastic nods and grunts before dispersing to their various occupations, nine-year-old Hazel having been posted half-way up the cart-track to give immediate warning of the approach of the visitors.

She came flying down the path in less than ten minutes, shrieking the news that Rudd and New Squire were on their way and Cissie, the eldest girl, cuffed her for making such an outcry, whereupon

Hazel kicked her sister in the buttocks as she bent to replenish the fire and then fled to the safety of the oak which she climbed with the speed of a chimpanzee until she could look down on the dell from a height of some fifty feet. Meanwhile, all older Potters adopted expressions of deep humility, and the postures of absorbed artisans, Mother Meg at the huge washtub, Sam at the woodpile, the three elder girls at the osier frames and Tamer presiding over the tribe from the porch steps, his patriarchal belly clasped in his hands. Only Smut, the rebel of the tribe, continued what he was doing, skinning a rabbit taken from the Gilroy warrens across the Teazel in the small hours. Smut, twenty now, and as muscled as a professional wrestler, made no compromises with the enemy. His was a war without truce.

Half-a-mile or so higher up the Bluff, where the ascent flattened out to form a tiny valley east of the Coombe, Edwin Willoughby of Deepdene had also received warning of the inspection, for the Potters were on affectionate terms with Willoughby, a Christian who took the Sermon on the Mount literally. Willoughby was a Methodist lay-preacher, as well as a farmer, but his God tested him sorely. On the one hand he had, willy-nilly, to live with the Potters, and north of his border lived the dour Edward Derwent, who abominated the gypsy family. Thus Willoughby's land, a poor and stubborn two hundred acres, was a no-man's-land between two hostile clans and Edwin enjoyed little of the forbearance he preached each Sunday in one or other of the little tin chapels along the coast. He persisted, however, for he had experienced worse in the lifetime of his wife, Ada, now at rest in the Coombe Bay Methodist burial ground. There were many in and about the Sorrel Valley who declared that Edwin's devotion to the Almighty stemmed from His mercy in removing Ada in the fifteenth year of their marriage, for it was generally admitted that she had tormented her husband with tongue by day and loins by night and for good measure occasionally let fly at him with a saucepan or flat-iron. Since her death he had grown to look rather like a saint, with his long silky hair, white as hoar frost, high, pale forehead, and mild, deepset eyes that burned with love for all mankind, even such wayward sons as Tamer Potter and his crusty neighbour, Derwent. His sermons, although spiced with the traditional touch of brimstone, expressed his deep belief in an era when lions would lie down with lambs, and reformed Potters would hoe harmoniously alongside Derwents. He was fortified in his faith by the example of his sister

Mary, who had made her home with him after his wife's death and now divided her time between keeping Deepdene farmhouse spotless and presiding over a small school for Valley children too young to travel to the nearest elementary school, at Whinmouth, or the Church School, in Coombe Bay. All the children of the surrounding country had been Mary's pupils and among the present generation were Codsalls, of Four Winds, Derwents, of High Coombe, and Honeymans, from the Home Farm. Mary Willoughby was a sweet-faced woman, several years older than Edwin and had been mother to Edwin's children, Francis and Elinor, both of whom helped to run the little farm.

News of The Prospect's tour was leaked across the hedge to Edwin by Smut Potter but the Willoughbys had no need to prepare against the arrival of a new squire. Their land was poor but their buildings and outbuildings were in good trim and their livestock a credit to the hardworking Edwin and his prudent eighteen-year-old daughter, Elinor, who was responsible for the poultry. Edwin thought it wise, however, to tramp back to the farm where his sister was reading *Alice in Wonderland* to the children and inform her of the visit of a new master of Shallowford but all Mary exclaimed was, "There now, I do hope he'll zettle an' be happy yer," and went on reading of the Cheshire Cat, while Edwin crossed the Deepdene fields to see how his modest barley crop was coming along and pass the news to one of Farmer Derwent's labourers, hard at work diverting a small stream that ran along the Deepdene–High Coombe boundary into a shallow trench inside the Derwent holding. The man was rather outfaced to see Edwin's saintly face loom over the hedge but he need not have been. Edwin saw what he was about and offered him the loan of a larger spade.

Edward Derwent, his big son Hugh, and his two daughters, Rose and Claire, discussed the news over their breakfast after they had finished an early morning stint in fields east of the farm and in the stables, where the girls had their riding school. Neither husband nor children addressed a word to the second Mrs. Derwent, a nonentity at High Coombe who was not included in family councils. Hugh, broad and swarthy like his father, dismissed the news as a Potter-inspired rumour.

"No one with money to burn would buy this white elephant," he declared, "he could do better up country if he was looking for land.

Big House is leaking bad, I hear, and apart from us, the Codsalls and the Pitts, what of us got to offer but flint, dirt farmers and a tangle of woods? It's probably nowt but a swell from London after some o' they antiques upalong." Whereupon he wolfed his rashers and three eggs with the despatch of a man who has been forking hay since first light, and at once returned to the fields.

The two girls, Rose and Claire, were far more intrigued. "Gregory had it from Mr. Willoughby that Mr. Craddock is an army officer wounded in the war," Rose said. "I wonder if he's married, and if so what his wife can be thinking of to bury herself down here?"

Edward Derwent, always inclined to speak scornfully of the estate, was not prepared to extend the same privilege to his children. He was a powerful, dark-jowled man, with bushy black brows that met over a strong nose in a broad "V" and gave him an expression of permanent irritation.

"Why the devil does everyone here talk as if we lived in a desert?" he demanded aggressively, and his wife lowered her gaze penitently as though she too had erred in this respect. "We've done pretty well here, haven't we?" Claire, the pretty daughter, giggled. As her father's favourite this called for no reproof so he continued, rumblingly, "White elephant! Flint and woodland! A backwater! What kind of talk is that? There's nothing wrong with my land and if the riding stable books are to be believed we're showing a good profit on liveries, so why all this belittling of the place?"

Rose and Claire were well accustomed to their father's rhetorical questions and paid them no attention at all but continued to speculate on the possibilities of the new man's patronage.

"If he's a cavalry officer he'll be sure to hunt," Rose said, "and if he's wealthy enough to buy Shallowford he'll probably keep a second hunter, carriage horses and at least one hack!"

"He might even have a motor," suggested Claire but not seriously, for the lunatic improbability of this made Rose laugh aloud and even their stepmother gave a nervous little smile. Nobody in the Sorrel Valley had ever seen a motor, except in the illustrated magazines. The new King was said to own one but the Derwents thought it a clownish substitute for the royal coach.

The girls went on gossiping about a possible successor to the Lovells after they had returned to the yard to muck out and clean tack. Rose, big boned and freckled, confined herself to the more

61

practical aspects of the situation—whether the new man was likely to prove as reckless a rider to hounds as the late Ralph Lovell, who had ridden horses to death and broken limbs in the process, but her sister, fair-haired and soft mouthed, with dimples in place of her sister's rash of freckles, continued to harp on the possibility of the new squire being a bachelor. She had read and enjoyed *Jane Eyre*, and the prospect of a Mr. Rochester at large in the Valley offered all kinds of possibilities. They were still speculating when the hired man, Gregory, stumped into the yard and confirmed the presence of Agent Rudd and his "Lunnon gent, in Yeomanry togs".

" 'Er's down wi' the Potters now, Misses," he said, "an' they ole varmints'll be in a proper ole flummox, if I knaws aught about it!"

The embarrassment of the Potter clan was wishful thinking on Gregory's part. As a Derwent employee he naturally embraced Derwent politics, nurturing a dutiful hate for his master's principal enemies. The truth was, however, very different, for Old Tamer and his family had played fish like Paul Craddock far too long to lose the advantage of an hour's warning of the approach. Rudd and Craddock rode into the Coombe about nine o'clock and Paul was impressed by the scene of virtuous industry in the Dell. All the Potters except Smut genuflected and Tamer went so far as to reach for a forelock that was not there.

"Well, you damned rascals," Rudd said jovially, "you'll have to stir your lazy stumps round here! Mr. Craddock is considering buying Shallowford. *Considering*, mind you! Don't broadcast it up and down the Valley. God help me," he went on aloud, glancing round the Dell, "did you ever see people make such a tip of a place? Look at that yard, and those outbuildings?"

Tamer simpered and rubbed his hands, as though overjoyed to hear the agent enjoy a harmless jest at his family's expense, but inwardly Paul was obliged to agree, for what with the washing, the forest of nettles, empty tins and broken boxes, a smouldering ashtip, and the presence of a saddleback pig rooting under the trees, the natural beauty of the green basin was grotesquely camouflaged. As far as Paul could see the Potters were not farmers at all but down-at-heel vagrants, living on their wits. The two things that did impress him, however, was the heroic industry of Meg at the washtub, and the shining health of the three girls, weaving baskets beside the fire. He did not see Hazel Potter, perched forty feet above his head but she

62

saw him and tried, unsuccessfully, to hit him with an acorn. She was lying full length on a great limb of the oak, her mop of hair swinging free, her face pressed close to the bark, and as she looked down on the group she composed one of her secret prose poems about the newcomer, singing it softly under her breath and exulting in the fecundity of her imaginaton.

"He be tall and thin, like a birch in winter," she sang, "and the silvery bits on his soldier's clothes look like the birch bark I can peel in strips . . .", but then the new squire dismounted stiffly, and so did Mr. Rudd, and they all moved out of her range of vision so that she forgot them and turned her attention to the tiny brown stains oozed from the crown of the uncupped acorn in the palm of her hand. Hazel Potter was even less trammelled by the demands of duty and industry than her sisters. Some said she was short of wits, and this had kept her from attending school but others declared she had inherited her mother's powers of witchcraft and were careful to give her skimmed milk or a halfpenny when they heard her crooning to herself at their doors.

With Tamer as guide, and Sam bringing up the rear, Rudd and Paul were shown around the holding. Hens fled squawking at their approach, for a sudden turn of speed was a condition of survival to all birds and animals in the Potter farmyard. As they poked about among the sheds and litter Tamer maintained a running commentary of the difficulties of life at Low Coombe and Rudd, who cherished for him the amused tolerance law-abiding citizens show the picturesque burglar, let him whine to his heart's content.

"Us needs all manner o' things to maake a praper start yerabouts," Tamer explained, as they entered a stable half-full of rubbish and containing no beast of any kind. "You'll mind, Maister, that the military commandeered the ole mare us 'ad, and 'er 've never been replaaced, so as us must needs do our own haulin' from the shore."

"They use seaweed for manure on the Coombe farms," Rudd told Paul, "and most of our horses were bought up by the Army, in the first year of the war. I've made a note of this kind of thing so you needn't bother to memorise it all, I just want you to get a general impression."

"Be'ee reely going to taake Squire Lovell's place, Maister?" Sam Potter asked reverently, but Paul said, "I really don't know, it's too early to say but I'd prefer you didn't discuss it outside the estate."

He said this earnestly but he was already enjoying the sensation his presence had occasioned in the Valley. From the moment he had opened his eyes that morning, and looked over the ford to the long downslope to the sea, he had been uplifted by an elation that had eluded him since childhood and this was not caused by the novelty of the occasion or even by the beauty of Shallowford's southern vista but by a feeling akin to that of home-coming to a place and people who seemed, in some improbable way, to need and want him. He looked over the golden vista basking in slanting sunlight, noting the steep hedgerows and their riot of colour, and inhaling the scent of the baked, red earth, spiced with the whiff of the sea. He warmed to the soft burr of the Devon accent and the sharp hiss of indrawn breath that men like Tamer Potter used as an expression of assent, but buried deeper than this, glowing like a small, bright coal, was the memory of Grace Lovell and her pale, shining skin and he wondered if the tour would take them through the village of Coombe Bay, where he might see her again, although he was careful to say nothing of this to Rudd.

They left the Dell by the broken gate, taking the path across parched fields to the headland, east of the river. A few pigs rooted on the edge of Coombe Brake, and half a dozen lean cows browsed in the meadow. Rudd shook his head over the Potters' domain; "Lovell was always on the point of turning the rascals loose," he said, "but somehow he never did and I think I know why. People like the Potters have the power of survival and would endure under any system. They're a dirty, dishonest and thoroughly worthless bunch, but somehow one goes on tolerating them as a kind of counterpoise to stolid, law-abiding tenants, like the Pitts and the Willoughbys. Take those girls now—a trio of handsome, tawny animals; how do they manage to keep strong and healthy? It's probably on account of them that Old Tamer never got his marching orders, for young Ralph used to ride over this way rent-collecting and they probably took turns to pay him in a dry ditch every quarter day! We're crossing to the Willoughby boundary now —he's a harmless enough chap, notwithstanding a touch of religious mania, and his sister Mary is a credit to the Valley. If it wasn't for Mary Willoughby half the children round about wouldn't be able to read or write!"

"Aren't they compelled to attend school nowadays?" Paul asked but Rudd chuckled. "Common law doesn't operate in places like this as it does in cities, Mr. Craddock. We're four miles from the nearest main road, and six from the railway. Whinmouth, on the estuary

64

yonder, is a two-hour ride, and there is not even a village bobby between us and Paxtonbury, twelve miles inland. No, the folk about here are pretty well as self-contained as they were in the eighteenth century, and have their own ways of doing things. Mary Willoughby started that little school of hers twenty years ago and dispensed all the schooling Valley children have ever had or wanted. Listen!", and he reined in on the northern slope of the cliff field, pointing to a white cluster of buildings about half a mile below them. "That's Deepdene, the farm that keeps the Potters at Low Coombe and the Derwents at High Coombe from tearing at one another's throats! You can hear the children singing. I always like to listen when I ride out this way in the forenoon. It cheers me up after calling on the Potters."

Paul listened but at first could hear nothing but the slow suck of the sea on the pebbles below. Then, very faintly, the sound of children's voices reached him across Willoughby's barley field, and after a moment or so he could identify the strains of "John Peel". It had, as Rudd implied, a refreshing innocence and as they came to the road nearer the farm Willoughby's daughter Elinor came out of the hen-roost to greet them. She was a shy, slim girl and on being introduced to Craddock, lowered her glance and said she would warn Auntie Mary of the visitors' approach, using this as an excuse to escape. Paul saw her dart into the schoolroom, a long, half-timbered barn adjoining the house and was struck by the speed with which her bare feet covered the ground.

"How old is that girl?" he asked and Rudd said she was eighteen, and being courted by Will Codsall, the elder of the Codsall boys at Four Winds, just across the river.

"The Codsalls are against the match," he added, "for Arabella is a snob and thinks her Will could do better. I daresay she's right, but Elinor Willoughby will make a good farmer's wife for somebody. I've never seen her idling or flirting, and she's damned clever with her poultry strains. There's nothing much wrong with this farm, although it's too small to be profitable. Derwent, beyond the crest up there, has all the best acreage this side of the river."

The singing stopped in the middle of a bar and they dismounted, giving their horses to Francis Willoughby and going into the barn. Paul felt far less at ease here than he had in the Potters' Dell for the children, about a dozen of them, stared at him in curiosity, sitting on forms with their arms folded and expressions blank. When he was introduced to them as "a soldier gentleman friend of Mr. Rudd's"

65

they rose like so many clockwork figures and piped "Good morning, sir!", after which they subsided, again in concert.

Rudd brought a flustered Mary Willoughby over to shake hands but instead of doing so she dropped a swift curtsy, so that Paul was struck by the tug of feudalism among the Lovell tenantry.

"I heard the children singing," he said, for something to say and Mary Willoughby replied, eagerly, "Will you have them sing for you here, Sir? I'm sure they'd like to, wouldn't you, my dears?" and the children chanted "Yes, Miss Willoughby," opening and closing their mouths like two rows of puppets, then fixing their eyes on their teacher who picked up a tuning fork, tapped it on the desk and said, "Softly then! Watch the baton! One chorus of 'The British Grenadiers', because Mr. Rudd tells me Mr. Craddock is just home from the wars!"

The children, one and all, received this news with respect, their eyes leaving the tuning fork and returning to Paul. They sang in shrill, clear voices, the boys grinning, the girls repressing giggles, and when they had finished Paul said, hoarsely, "Thank you, that was splendid! Er—how many are there here, Miss Willoughby?" and Mary said there were fourteen today because two of the older boys were out helping with the harvest and little Hazel Potter was playing truant again.

Paul, on impulse, pulled out a handful of loose change, saying that everyone present was to have a reward for singing so well but before the squeal of delight had died away a bullet-headed little boy in the rear row shot up his hand and demanded, "Sir, sir! Did you kill ole Kruger?", a question that made even the demure Mary Willoughby laugh.

"No," said Paul, "nobody killed Kruger, because he got away before anyone could catch him!", but his questioner was not satisfied with this and saw Paul's presence as a means of beguiling a tedious hour's instruction. He followed up with, "Did all the Boers run away, please sir?", and Paul glanced at Rudd, hoping for some inspiration but getting none said, deliberately, "The Boers didn't run away at all. They were very brave. After all, they were farmers fighting for their country, just as we would!" This simple statement was received with a shocked "Cooo!", and Paul again glanced at Rudd who was now studying a knothole on the schoolroom floor. Feeling miserably embarrassed he got up and tried to smile. "I'm sure Miss Willoughby won't want me to stay and interrupt your lessons any longer," he said,

66

"so Mr. Rudd and I will have to say good-bye, because we have to ride over and see all the other farms."

When they were clear of the farm, and riding along the ridge parallel with the woods Paul said, "Did I do wrong to tell them the truth?"

"If you're only a visitor passing through it doesn't matter a damn what you say," Rudd told him, "whereas if you become 'New Squire', as the Potters rather hope, you can say anything you like! After all, they'll be tenants, and if a Tory doesn't mince his words with them why should a Radical?"

"I'm not sure that I am a Radical," Paul told him. "I never gave a thought to politics until I began to convalesce, and had nothing better to do than read the Parliamentary debates in the newspapers."

"Well," pursued Rudd, with one of his quizzical sidelong glances, "and what conclusions did you arrive at?"

"I don't know, one can't help admiring that chap Lloyd George's nerve defying the whole weight of public opinion about the war, and there were fellows out there who came around to agreeing with him, after they took part in chivvying the Boers from Hell to Hackney. It seemed to me, however, that once we were in it we had to choose going through with it or becoming the laughing stock of the world. Apart from that it now looks as if they'll get a better deal from us than they would have got from anyone else. What would have happened to them if the Germans or French had been in our situation?"

"Ah," said Rudd evasively, "that would be telling!" and Paul thought: "Damn him, he gave so much away yesterday that he'll be a clam from now on! However, I'd lay six to four that he's pro-Lloyd George, if only because the Lovell family were Tories!" and then he forgot politics, surrendering himself to the beauty of a long, easterly slope stretching from Willoughby's boundary, across the Derwent holding to the cloudless sky over the county border.

They met Willoughby on the ridge and introductions were exchanged. Rudd, glancing over the hedge, saw the evidence of Gregory's excavations alongside the stream and at once remarked on it.

"Derwent had no right to siphon off your water," he told the saint-like farmer. "You may need it badly later on, even if you don't now."

"Why, God bless you, Mr. Rudd," Willoughby said, "who am I to begrudge a neighbour water for his cattle in weather like this?"

Rudd said, "Well, it's your concern I suppose, but I doubt if he'd

67

do the same for you!", and they rode on down the slope and through the fir copse that shaded the freshly whitewashed buildings of the Derwent farm, Rudd saying that Paul was not to expect forelock-pulling from Derwent, who was anxious to become a freeholder and probably had the means to purchase his land if a new owner was willing to sell it.

"He's a cagey fellow, with a poor wisp of a second wife," he told Craddock. "Frankly, I've never liked him much but both he and his son Hugh are first-class farmers, and the two daughters are the leading lights of the local hunt. One's a very fetching girl but the other looks like a horse. They'll all be civil to you when I tell him why you're here, but don't be fooled by the Derwents. They're like the Codsalls; money and land are the only things they care about and after that, Independence Day!"

Paul's reception at High Coombe was much as Rudd had predicted, both father and children making a show of hospitality and the faded Mrs. Derwent bringing out glasses of sherry and some appetising little pikelets on a large, silver tray.

The house was well furnished, the stock in good condition and the farm buildings in repair. Paul was particularly impressed by the spotlessly clean stables where Rose, the daughter with a face like a horse, showed him a magnificent four-year-old gelding she intended hunting next season. Rose cared for nothing but horses but her sister Claire showed great solicitude when Rudd told her that Paul had been wounded in action. She was extraordinarily pretty, Craddock decided, with golden hair piled high on a small head, dark blue eyes and an undeniably kissable mouth. She pretended to scold Rudd for encouraging a convalescent man with a leg wound to undertake such a long ride on a hot day, and when she took Paul's glass to refill it her long fingers caressed his but in the nicest possible way. Craddock, somewhat to his surprise, found he was able to relax at High Coombe, notwithstanding Derwent's dourness. The yard and enclosures were pleasant places in which to linger after the seediness of the Potter farm, and there were no children to embarrass him with leading questions about Kruger and the war. They resisted an invitation to stay for lunch, however, and pressed on under a blazing midday sun, breasting the northern spur of the ridge and entering the blessed coolness of Shallowford Woods.

Craddock at once decided that this was the most enchanting part of the estate, a great belt of old timber rising from a jungle of under-

68

growth that covered the entire south-eastern section of the estate, two miles across and about a mile deep, with a dip in the middle filled by a shallow mere. He had not noticed the lake on the map Rudd had shown him before they set out and thus came upon it by surprise, an oval of reed-fringed water enclosed by oaks and beeches, some of which must have been centuries old. Waterlilies floated here and a tiny islet, half-way across, was the haunt of wild duck and moorhen, who took to the reeds as soon as the horses emerged from the trees. Paul saw that there was a building of mock oriental design on the islet and Rudd told him it was known as "The Pagoda" and had been built, half a century ago, by Amyas Lovell, father of the late baronet. Amyas, Rudd said, had been wounded in the head campaigning in Lower Burma and had been very eccentric towards the end of his life. The pagoda was supposed to be a miniature replica of a temple in Mandalay, and the old soldier had been in the habit of punting himself across the lake and painting atrocious water-colours from the pagoda steps.

They rode on through the murmurous woods, Rudd making estimates of the value of the timber, Paul telling himself that if ever he owned Shallowford he would prefer to sell Derwent his farm rather than fell any of the trees. Some of the beeches rose to a height of over a hundred feet and on the western edge of the wood, where they towered above younger trees, they had been planted according to plan for they were evenly spaced along the rides.

They emerged into glaring sunshine again east of the steeper and far less dense Hermitage Wood that rose behind the house. Paul could now see the back view of the manor lying in the little valley as they crossed rough ground heading for Hermitage Farm, which lay in open country between the curve of the Sorrel and the main road they had crossed the previous afternoon.

"You'll like Arthur and young Henry Pitts," Rudd told Paul, "they're a genial, hardworking pair and I don't ever recall having had a dispute with them all the twenty years I've been here. Although Arthur is no more than my age his father and grandfather farmed here before him and his father, Old Gaffer Pitts, is still living, although he's got Parkinson's disease, poor old chap, and now sits mumbling in the chimney corner. He can remember the harvest failures of the 'forties, and riots over the Corn Laws away in Whinmouth and Paxtonbury. He was in the militia at the time and broke heads on behalf of the Lovells, but his son and grandson are very easy-going and we'll stop off there for a bite of lunch, if you've room for it after all those pikelets Claire Derwent pressed on you. That girl is about desperate for a husband, Mr. Craddock! I daresay you noticed she made a dead set at you. What did you think of her? More fetching than the little dark ghost you disturbed in the nursery last night?"

Paul smiled but said nothing, determined to give the agent no opening in this particular field but as they urged their horses into a trot at the top of Hermitage he reflected that the Sorrel Valley seemed very well endowed with pretty girls, for he had encountered six in a single morning's ride and any one of them would have stood out in a crowd among the overdressed young women he had noticed in London. Musing on them as they jogged down the track he made comparisons, measuring the aloof appeal of Grace Lovell with the pink and white prettiness of Claire Derwent and the shy charms of the Willoughby girl, now courted by young Will Codsall. He recalled also the frankly sensual appeal of the three Potter girls and it came into his mind that they had the generous proportions of the Hottentot prostitute from whom he had fled in Capetown but looked infinitely more wholesome. Then he was required to face yet another series of introductions, this time to Arthur Pitts and his wife Martha, their son Henry, and Pitts' old father, The Gaffer. He took to this family at once, for there was a lack of ceremony about Hermitage that had been absent elsewhere, or perhaps it only appeared so, because Rudd was on more friendly terms with the Pitts than with the other tenants and he and Arthur began talking of the drought, and the harvest while Paul was faced with vast helpings of ham and tongue and mountains of green salad, served with a stone jug of potent, home-brewed cider.

Henry, Arthur's son, a thick-set young man with a pallor at odds with a farmer who had been out in a heatwave for a month was exceptionally welcoming and solemnly wished Paul well if he did in fact buy, reinforcing Rudd's hints that "the plaace would require a praper ole shower o' money" if it was to be put on a profitable basis. Martha, Arthur's busy little wife, had a brogue as broad or broader than Tamer Potter's and Paul had some difficulty in catching the drift of her conversation, spiced as it was with so many strange words, like "thicky" and "giddon" which he interpreted as "that" and "go along with you", whereas all animals, male and female, were referred to as " 'Er". She expressed her deep thankfulness that "they ole Boers were now parcelled up an' vinished with", and that no more young men would be required to "get theirselves shot to tatters", pointing out that if a man had a mind to die from gunshot wounds he might, with more profit, "stand the blind side of thicky hedge, when us iz rabbiting!" Her husband, Arthur, who happened to overhear this remark, said, "Dornee talk so daft, mother! You get a blamed sight more pay chasin' they Boers than us gets for the rabbits us knocks over hereabouts!" One way and another Paul delighted in their cheerful company and was sorry when Rudd said they must press on to Four Winds to meet the Codsalls; his failure to do so that same day would surely stir up jealousy in the Valley.

"Well youm right there," confirmed Martha, "but dornee let that Arabella Codsall give herself airs and you can depend on it she'll try, seeing as she can't never forget her father left her the best-dowered daughter in the Valley."

Rudd, laughing, said he would mind her advice and off they went again, Paul making light of the growing stiffness in his knee, which pained him somewhat when he swung his leg over the grey.

"I think they're delightful people," he told Rudd, when they were trotting down to the river road and Rudd said he had planned the tour this way because it had a natural rhythm, all the way from sleazy rascality in the Potters' Dell, to the farcical pretentiousness of Arabella Codsall, "the best-dowered woman in the Valley".

"Four Winds is the largest farm in the area," he told Paul as they went along, explaining that it had been stocked on Arabella's money, nearly two thousand left by her father, a Paxtonbury draper. "Mind you," he added, "Martin paid dearly for his stake, for Arabella never lets him forget that she married beneath her and considers herself a cut above any other farmer's wife in the Valley. Martin is a harmless sort of chap but of less account at Four Winds than Derwent's wife is at High Coombe. At least Mrs. Derwent can handle a knife and fork how she likes and that's more than Martin can when there's company. She's a tiresome, garrulous, over-weening bitch is Arabella, for she not only nags her husband from morning to night but discriminates between the boys. Will, the elder, is an amiable blockhead, who would make a good enough farmer if he was left to himself, but he isn't, and his mother makes a pet of Sydney, her younger son, who she is determined to make into a gentleman. How the hell she'll do that with Codsall blood and bone I can't imagine, for the Codsalls have been farming there for a century and Codsall's father, old Jeremiah, died in the infirmary after falling in the Sorrel dead drunk on New Year's night. However, we'd best call and round off the day by taking a quick look at the village itself. You can see the Home Farm any time, tomorrow if you like, if you don't want to hang about the sale."

Paul, elated at the prospect of riding down to the sea before the heat went out of the day, now addressed himself to the impossible task of sorting out the various families he had met so far but his memory boggled at so many Potters and Willoughbys and Derwents and Pitts, with here a husband who bullied his wife, and there a wife who nagged her husband, of the rivalries and jealousies and a bevy of pretty, chirrupy girls and their lumping great brothers, so that he gave it up as they clattered over the wooden bridge into Codsall territory and saw the sprawling cluster of buildings round the long, low farmhouse close to the western boundary.

It was obvious that word of his presence had reached the fifth farm, for the four Codsalls awaited them in the yard, dressed in their Sunday broadcloth and Rudd, spotting Martin Codsall's silk waistcoat from afar, let out a guffaw and shouted, "Codsall! You never tog yourself up for me when I come for the rent!", a jest that Arabella Codsall, towering half-a-head above her husband, and holding little Sydney by the hand, ignored but bobbed an abbreviated curtsy in Paul's direction, exclaiming, "Look now, Sydney! The gentleman's in uniform, and an officer's uniform, I declare! Welcome to Four Winds, Mr. Craddock!" Then, in a higher key that carried as far as the river—"Will! Don't stand gawping! Take the gentleman's horse! Martin! What are you about? Show the visitors into the parlour this minute!", and the Codsalls moved into action like a sullen detail surprised by a visiting staff-officer and watched by a zealous sergeant-major.

III

Arabella Codsall, notwithstanding her comparative affluence, was almost certainly the most unhappy woman in the Valley and her discontent stemmed from her disgust of the poor material with which she was obliged to work. Under no circumstances could she have proved a success as a farmer's wife. She had been born over a linen-draper's shop and brought up within the tight circle of a cathedral city's tradesmen's community, so that she thought of farmers as hobbledehoys in a social bracket equivalent to that of roadsweepers, lamplighters and Irish navvies. For all that she had been glad to marry Martin Codsall some twenty years before when she was then twenty-

72

eight and towered nearly six inches above most of the eligible tradesmen's sons, in her native Paxtonbury. She had the additional handicap
of looking rather like an indignant goose, with a large, curving nose,
small startled eyes, sharply receding chin and a mouth that was
always half-open, as though honking with fury. She had arrived at
Four Winds with a supply of linen and one hair trunk but any chance
she had of making the most of her situation was shattered by her
father's death and surprise legacy of nearly two thousand pounds.
She had not expected anything like this amount for Alderman
Blackett had been notoriously secretive concerning his savings.
Moreover, there had originally been two other children and the
Alderman, having made his will early, had not altered it when these
two died in a scarlet-fever epidemic in the early 'nineties, so that the
words "or surviving progeny thereof" trebled Arabella's patrimony.
She at once set about the task of hoisting the cumbersome Codsalls
into a niche above that occupied by their neighbours, and only a peg
or two below that of the Lovells, but it had been a wearisome, thank-
less task, for neither Martin nor her elder son Will seemed able or
willing to exploit their opportunities. Arabella mistook the symbols
and rituals of her linen-draper's background for reliable handholds
along the haul towards gentility, instituting at Four Winds such
incongruous items as four o'clock tea sipped from thin china, linen
napkins, a maid with a cap, and even a tablecloth at breakfast,
novelties that bewildered Martin Codsall and ultimately converted
both him and his son Will into farmyard fugitives, who stayed out
of doors whenever possible. Yet she persisted; year after year she
prodded and planned, and words of advice and admonition gushed
from her goosey little mouth like a cataract, so that in order to survive
her menfolk were driven to raise all kinds of defences against her
nagging. Martin took refuge in a weak man's obstinacy and a warren
of bolt holes. Will adopted the characteristics of a deaf mute, so that
at last Arabella was driven to direct most of her energy upon Sydney,
the younger boy. Sydney was more pliant—or so it seemed—and his
pliancy soon won for him the adoration of his mother. The moment
Arabella had word of Craddock's visit, and the possibility of his
succeeding as Squire, Four Winds erupted. She dressed Sydney in
his best, set the hired hands to scour the yard, instituted a spring-
clean inside the house (where most of the work was done by a be-
frilled half-witted child, called Minnie), flushed Martin and Will from
their hiding-places and ordered them to don their Sunday serge.

73

Martin, mumbling that he had work to do, took his revenge by somewhat overdoing the transformation and appeared downstairs in a starched dickey when it was too late to go back and changed his shirt. Son Will, his mind still searching for a permanent escape route from this hell upon earth, said nothing at all but eyed Craddock with interest when he rode into the yard, perhaps seeing in him some glimmer of hope for the future; for Will Codsall, madly in love with Elinor Willoughby and reduced to the status of an automaton, any change at Shallowford would be for the better.

Within two minutes of being seated in the Codsalls' airless parlour, listening to Arabella's uninterrupted flow of domestic clichés, Paul realised that Rudd had not exaggerated in his description of Arabella as an insufferable woman. Her approach to him was at once overweening and apologetic, overbearing yet grotesquely cringing, vain to the point of idiocy, yet voluble in her demands as a long-suffering tenant, so that Rudd, after listening to her gobbling for ten minutes, cut in with a terse, "It's not the slightest use burdening Mr. Craddock with all this, Mrs. Codsall! He hasn't even made up his mind to buy Shallowford and if you make everything sound run down I don't suppose he will!"

This remark had some effect upon her, inasmuch as she converted her flood of complaints into a detailed description of Sydney's astonishing progress under a private tutor, at Whinmouth, whereupon Craddock, taking his cue from the agent, said, "I really came over to look at the farm, Mrs. Codsall," and on that Martin bobbed up like a hare and led the way out into the sunshine with Will breathing down his neck and Mrs. Codsall, still gobbling, bringing up the rear. Sydney did not follow his parents into the yard. He was a well-schooled little boy and his Sunday suit anchored him to the parlour.

They inspected Codsall's excellent Friesian herd, then his pigs and finally his sheep down by the river. Here Martin disappeared, seemingly into a haystack, but Arabella and Will followed every step of the way, so that Paul had the impression he was being dogged by a goose and a soft-footed St. Bernard dog. Soon both he and Rudd ceased to comment, for the most innocuous remark increased the clack of Arabella's tongue and finally they made their escape, the honking of Arabella following them as far as the swing gate that led to the bridge. It seemed then that they had spent a long afternoon at Four Winds but on glancing at his watch Paul saw that their visit had occupied no more than forty-five minutes.

Neither of them spoke for a while and the silence in the river meadows was like a balm but at length Rudd said, "One understands under what terrible provocation some murders are committed! I've often thought how willingly I would give evidence on Martin's behalf, if he appeared at Paxtonbury Assizes one fine day charged with drowning that wife of his in a duckpond. Justifiable homicide! That's what the verdict would be." Paul asked if he knew the cause of Arabella Codsall's terrible volubility and he replied with a wry smile, "Well, I suppose I might quote our friend Donne about a woman's mouth only being full of words when she is empty elsewhere, but it doesn't apply in Arabella's case. I think it has something to do with the dismal nineteenth-century cult of 'self-improvement', foisted upon us by all those crackpot writers and philosophers, like Ruskin, Bentham, and all the rest of them! Buried down here for the past two decades I've seen less changes than most men but what I have seen could have taught those city sociologists something! It's a great mistake to teach everybody to read and write, Craddock, maybe the greatest mistake western civilisation has ever made, for it'll do for us all in the end, mark my words!"

"Now how can you possibly justify that?" Paul demanded, recalling the squalor of the area beyond Tower Bridge, "surely some of a nation's wealth ought to be ploughed back into its population. From what I've seen since I came home precious little of our industrial profits are being invested in the welfare or the fabric of the country. Isn't a compulsory education the key to a nation's progress?"

"It's a key all right," Rudd said sadly, "but does it unlock? When I was a boy the social scale here and in the cities was not adjustable. In the main you stayed what you were born, artisan, tradesman, professional man, gentleman. Hardly anyone in a district like this *could* read or write, or wanted to, but they were contented enough, they didn't resent the patronage of people like the Lovells. They got all they needed by hard work and peasant cunning, by making themselves indispensable to their so-called betters, and they didn't quarrel with the pattern either. People like Arabella Codsall wouldn't have been tolerated for a moment, but that isn't so any more. Arabella is laughed at by old-timers like Martha Pitts, but only behind her back! I've seen Arabella at village socials, queening it over all the other wives but impressing them, in spite of themselves. Nobody challenges her, not even me or you. And if her husband took an ashplant to her backside as he ought he'd be up before the magistrates If

75

Arabella hadn't been taught to read and write would she have had the impudence to complain to us about her damned rights-of-way or her roof tiles?"

"What do you think will happen in backwaters like this eventually then?"

"I can tell you that, now that we have universal male suffrage. The whole edifice will come crumbling down in a single life's span and the land, as we know it today, will go to pot, with nobody left to tend it. All the children you saw with their noses in books at Mary Willoughby's school will drift away to the cities and become an army of frustrated little clerks and busybodies. They'll all be Arabella Codsalls, wringing their hands over their neighbours' possessions, living in little brick boxes with a few square feet of garden. You might regard the talkative Mrs. Codsall as a local pioneer."

"Altogether too pessimistic," Paul argued. "Damn it all, we're all subject to evolution. Things never stay the same for long, either nationally or locally."

"That's so," pursued Rudd, "but my point is things are changing far too quickly. People can't absorb the social and economic changes of the last century. When technology leaves the mass of population far enough behind there's going to be a God-Almighty explosion."

"What kind of explosion?"

"How do I know? Go back to your history books. A revolution of some kind, or a war."

"We've just finished a war," Paul argued, "and it hasn't turned civilisation inside out."

"I'm not talking about colonial wars," Rudd said, "I'm talking about Armageddon."

They rode on in silence for a spell, the flashing stream on their left and the church spire of Coombe Bay rising clear of Codsall's cornstalks. It occurred to Paul that there was an affinity of a kind between Rudd and Zorndorff, both of an age, both addicted to sensational generalisations. He wondered what each man expected of him, and whether Rudd would be interested in Zorndorff's advocacy of the purchase of the estate but before he could continue the discussion they entered the steep village street of Coombe Bay and he found himself looking about him for any signs of Grace Lovell riding her neat bay mare.

There were none. Coombe Bay was deep in its afternoon siesta and the broad, single street was quite deserted. It was not much of a

76

village, a double row of thatched cottages curving away from the river and, lower down, a straggle of tiny shops, and a few Georgian terrace houses, with window boxes and polished knockers.

Rudd told him that the estate owned some of these houses let at fifty pounds a year, and that a larger house on the headland was occupied by Grace Lovell's father, the family parasite. They ambled down to the beach where the Sorrel, no more than thirty feet across, gushed into the sea under a rounded, sandstone bluff. There was a boat shelter, one or two blue jerseyed fishermen pottering about their nets, and further west, where the sand swept in a wide curve as far as a landslip, some children paddling and shrimping under the breakwater. It was all very quiet and still under the hot afternoon sun, so quiet that Paul could hear the plash of tiny wavelets falling on the white sand. They sat there resting the horses and Paul would have liked to have dismounted and bathed his stiff leg in the sea but was too lazy to dismount and pull off his boots. Presently a yellow gig, driven at a spanking pace swept out of the High Street and turned west along the waterfront, disappearing up a side-street beyond the inn, which had a double-headed bird on its signboard and the name "The Raven" in Gothic lettering.

"That's Doctor O'Keefe," Rudd said, "he never drives that poor beast at anything under a canter. He does it to spread the impression that he's conscientious when, in fact, he's usually half-pickled. He's a likeable old rascal though, and I daresay you'll meet him if you stay long enough. Came here years ago, after some kind of scandal in his native Dublin but he's a good doctor, drunk or sober. I've seen him do some remarkable patchwork in my time here," and then, as though he had suddenly made up his mind to be done with small talk and come to the point, "How do you feel about the place as a whole, Mr. Craddock? Is it anything like you imagined? Are you still serious about taking up your option?"

"Which question do you want answered first?" Paul asked, smiling, but Rudd said, rather peevishly, "It makes small enough odds to me one way or the other. You won't need an overseer like me if you intend living here and not leaving us to our own devices for years on end like the Lovells."

"Well," said Paul, "as to making up my mind I'd rather leave it until tomorrow if you've no objections. I'd like to think over what I've seen so far and I owe it to Mr. Zorndorff to discuss it with him. Is there a telephone on the estate?"

"Good God, no!" said Rudd, "what would anybody here want with a telephone? The nearest one is in Whinmouth Post Office, nine miles to the west."

"Very well," said Paul, "I'll decide before the sale opens tomorrow. As to what I feel about the place, I admit it intrigues me. It's so utterly unlike anything I imagined after reading that article in the *Illustrated London News*."

"Can't you be a bit more specific?" asked Rudd, and because he seemed genuinely concerned Paul added, "I think it's a private world, populated by a few hundred castaways from a wreck about a century ago! On your own admission its commercial prospects are very thin but frankly I'm not much concerned about that. I should expect to put money into any property I took and it boils down to this in the end; what kind of person are these farmers and their families looking for as a landlord, or 'squire' if you like? What would be his responsibilities to them? Or theirs to him? Wouldn't they prefer to buy their farms cash down or over a period? Do they really want a city stranger breathing down their necks?"

Rudd's spurt of irritation had spent itself, as it usually did in a matter of seconds.

"How can I answer that?" he said smiling. "They haven't confided in me all the time I've been here. I was little more than a rent-collector for the Lovells."

"That isn't quite true," Paul told him, "because it's obvious that you've formed an opinion about every one of them. Is Derwent the only one keen to become a freeholder? Wouldn't Mrs. Codsall jump at the chance of being her own squireen?"

"I doubt it," said Rudd, "she likes the link with Quality, you being Quality if you follow me. Derwent is an exception, and I daresay he'd quibble at the price you asked him. Neither Potter nor Willoughby would care to stand on their own feet, and Arthur Pitts is happy with things as they are. No, they'd jog along if they got a man prepared to put the estate in order. They'd all rather leech on somebody like you, so I'm afraid you would have the monopoly of obligations, Mr. Craddock."

"Well, that's honest enough," Paul said, "and I'll bear it in mind when I give you my answer tomorrow. Have you got a hip bath up at the lodge? I've overdone it a bit I think, and I'd like to soak this leg and take it easy for the rest of the day."

Rudd was instantly solicitous and swung his cob around.

"I'm an idiot!" he exclaimed, "I ought to have thought of that but the truth is I've enjoyed myself today in an odd sort of way. It's long enough since I saw Shallowford tenants hang out flags. We'll go home and Mrs. Handcock will fix you up with some soda."

An hour later Paul was enjoying a soda soak in the wash-house behind the lodge and after a high tea, and a smoke in the parlour, the ache of his wound left him and he surrendered to a pleasant drowsiness as the shadows moved across the paddocks. Rudd, sharing the silence with him, avoided reopening discussion on the sale but when Paul, on the point of going to bed, asked if the grey would be available early in the morning he promised to have Honeyman's lad see to it and tether the horse in the yard behind the wash-house by six-thirty. Paul thanked him and after a moment's hesitation, said, "I should like to own that horse in any case, Mr. Rudd. He isn't included in the sale, is he?" and Rudd said no, although the stable tack was, adding that Ralph Lovell had bought the gelding for fifty pounds shortly before he left for South Africa.

"I'd gladly give that for him," Paul said, "he's quiet and very well-mannered for a young horse, and I don't intend to take any chances until my leg is right."

"Then consider it sold," Rudd said, "you might go further and fare a great deal worse!", and with that Paul left him sitting in his big armchair, looking out of the open window across the paddock. "It's odd," he thought, as he mounted the little stair to his room, "but the prospect of leaving here is making him miserable notwithstanding all his grousing about the Lovells."

CHAPTER THREE

I

THE cock at the Home Farm awakened him soon after first light and on going to the window he saw that it promised to be another scorcher. A curtain of pale, blue mist veiled the downslope to the sea and wisps of cloud, coral pink over the sandstone cliff of the Coombe, were translucent and very still. Over in the rhododendron thickets the bird chorus was beginning and as Paul dressed the steady rhythm of its twitter built into a continuous murmur, like the patter of rain on glass. He stood at the window sniffing the morning and thinking that this might be a day he would remember all his life, yet he was free of qualms and felt as fit as he ever remembered, with little stiffness resulting from his twenty-mile ride the previous day.

The grey was tethered to the rail of the big paddock, stirrups high on the leathers, reins tucked under the crupper, and as he climbed into the saddle he thought that Honeyman's boy must be a very early riser, for it was still only six-forty and the boy was already a figure on the skyline, plodding the mile or so back to the farm.

He crossed the ford, now barely two inches deep and followed the track they had taken to Coombe Bay the previous afternoon, and it was only when the spire of the parish church showed above the corn that he realised why he was riding this way. His memory of the Lovell girl was no more than a vague impression of dark curls growing close to a small, neat head, and the swell of a sturdy figure under the blue riding habit, yet this was enough to persuade him, now that he was alone, that the girl was linked to his ultimate decision and somehow the conclusion did not seem illogical or facetious. By the time he was half-way down the village street, and passing the gardens of the Georgian houses, he had ceased to make excuses for himself and looked eagerly across to the wooded slope that enclosed the village on the east, searching for the house where Rudd had said she and her father lived, overlooking the harbour. He could see a couple of detached houses, each half-hidden in trees and facing due south but there was no sign that anyone else was astir, although from some-

80

where in the yards behind the cottages he could hear the scrape of boots on cobbles and the metallic clank of a pail.

There was more activity down by the waterfront. Fishermen were at work hauling a boat down to the water's edge and far out across the bay he could see two or three other small craft, pulling into the sun. Gulls flew squawking from the harbour wall when he edged his horse down the slipway, and along the beach to the hillocks beyond high-water mark, but the long, curving shore was deserted. As he climbed the hummocks to a sandy plateau above the tideline he made another effort to concentrate his thoughts on what he would say to Rudd at breakfast, or what he should write to Zorndorff that evening. He had a sensitive man's horror of appearing ridiculous in public and an awareness of his unfitness for responsibilities of this kind. Rudd had warned him that he would have a monopoly of responsibility in this small, tight community, made up of such unpredictable people as the sly Tamer Potter, uncompromising Derwent, and the voluble Arabella Codsall, their families and their hired hands. How many were there for heaven's sake—thirty, fifty, a hundred? And who knew what currents of jealousy and rancour lay in wait for him under their smiles of welcome and deferential greetings? Of the families he had met only one, the Pitts of Hermitage, seemed uncomplicated, whereas the Potters and Codsalls might present all manner of problems to an inexperienced young man savouring his first taste of authority. He sat astride the patient grey, his eyes squinting into the sun so that it was not until the horse threw up his head and whinnied that he was aware of movement below and to his right, where the white sand stretched as far as the distant landslip.

She came out of the west at full gallop, pounding along the flat within yards of the sea, the bay's hoof-thrusts sending up little spurts of sand, the rider pitched forward in the jockey's huddle that Yeomanry riding-masters had been at pains to eliminate from the seats of recruits. She was wearing a white blouse and a grey riding skirt and she was hatless, thus breaking another riding-school rule in her madcap gallop along the water's edge. As he saw her she set the horse at a drift-log and sailed over it and then, without checking her stride she swung left, heading directly for the hummocks on which he stood, whirling in a flurry of sand and breasting the incline at such a pace that it seemed to Craddock she would sweep past him on to the sandhills beyond. He tightened his rein, thinking that the grey might bolt in pursuit, but suddenly she brought the horse up short, rearing it

81

back like an Arab executing a mounted salute and he saw then, from his position twenty feet above, that she was smiling and had recognised him before he had seen her approach along the beach.

She called, in a loud, clear voice, "Mr. Paul Craddock, I believe!" and he raised his hat as the grey sidled forward and descended to the beach.

"I saw you half-a-mile away," she said, with her tight, slightly ironic smile. "That's a good horse you have! When you get his fat down and corn him up he'll carry twice your weight all day! Where's Rudd?"

"Still asleep in bed," Paul said, "or he was when I left him."

Was it his fancy that a change of expression registered a little of her suspicion when she realised he was alone? He felt unsure of everything about this hard, compact parcel of energy but she continued to look straight at him, as though his presence here on a public beach early in the morning required an explanation. He knew then that this was the sign he had been awaiting, that, notwithstanding his uncertainty and fear of ridicule he would this very day be master of Shallowford, and Grace Lovell's landlord to boot. He said, gravely, "I'm buying the estate. I'm taking over Shallowford," and was surprised by the firmness of his voice. "Will you be attending the sale?"

She stared at him, not resentfully as in the nursery, or ironically, as when she had whirled to the foot of the hillock but with a frank curiosity, as though he had been a curious object left on the beach by the tide.

"You've been a farmer?" she asked at length, dropping her glance to his breeches and military boots.

"No," he admitted, "I don't know a thing about farming. I've been overseas nearly three years and after that I was in hospital but from what I hear the Lovells weren't farmers either!"

She laughed at this, throwing back her head and squaring her shoulders. He said, "I'm sorry, I shouldn't have said that. You were a relation I believe?"

"No," she said, "not really and anyway it's true. Neither Sir George, nor Hubert, nor my Ralph cared a row of beans about what went on here, so long as rents were paid, but I suppose you'll be buying it for the hunting?"

"By no means," Paul said, "though I shall hunt, providing I have time."

She looked genuinely surprised at this. "Why shouldn't you have the time? If you can afford to buy Shallowford you must have all the time in the world."

82

He said, convincing himself rather than her, "I'm partially disabled, but at twenty-three I don't care to look forward to a lifetime of idleness. I suppose that sounds pompous but I don't apologise. Months on your back gives a man a chance to think and there should be a better use for capital than to make more money, and dissipate the interest cutting a fashionable dash. I believe I might be using mine on a place as old and potentially fruitful as this valley and I think I'd enjoy doing it."

It was strange, he thought, that he could speak so freely to her, whereas he had been unable to clarify his thoughts to experienced men of the world, like Zorndorff and Rudd, both people who wished him well. It occurred to him that this might be because she was of his generation and then his mind fastened on her words "my Ralph" and this, he thought, might be the key to her brooding presence in the nursery, implying as it did that she too was confused and, to an extent, dissatisfied with her life. She interrupted his conjecturing with, "How badly are you disabled, Mr. Craddock?"

"Enough to deny me the chance of doing what I wanted to do, take a permanent commission. I had a bullet through the knee joint. It's healed now, and in time I shall be ninety-five per cent fit, but it was enough to get me thrown aside as a crock!"

"You're bitter about that?"

"No," he admitted, truthfully, "I'm not bitter, or not any longer." He returned her steady gaze and asked, "Are *you* bitter? About Ralph Lovell getting killed?"

The question disconcerted her. He saw that at once, for she looked past him and seemed to be considering whether to protest at his curiosity.

"I don't know what Rudd's told you about Ralph," she said, "but whatever it was it was prejudiced. Rudd hated the Lovells and I imagine he had good reasons for hating them."

"Yes he did," Paul told her, "and I happen to know those reasons, Miss Lovell, for he made a clean breast of them as soon as I arrived." She seemed surprised at this, so he went on, before she could comment, "They never let him forget an incident that led to his resigning his commission, but I've been under fire myself, and if Ralph Lovell had survived I daresay he would have found it easy to understand Rudd when he came home. I like Mr. Rudd and I mean to keep him on as agent."

"I see; and have you got any plans for your tenants?" she asked,

83

slyly. "I'm one, you know, at least my father and stepmother are; we live up there," and she pointed with her crop.

"Well I won't put up the rent, if that's what you're hinting at," Paul said and she laughed so that Paul thought it was a long time since he had heard a more musical note. Her laughter had resonance, and sounded as free as the birdsong he had heard at the window an hour before.

"Look here, Mr. Craddock," she said, "I'd like you to know that I honestly wish you luck, and also that I'm sorry I was very rude back at the house the other night. I ought to be grateful to you really, I'd gone there to eat another helping of nostalgic pie. Your appearance gave me something else to think about."

"You were unhappy over Ralph Lovell's being killed? That's nothing to apologise for, is it?"

"Ralph was killed a long time ago," she said, "and I haven't had your chance to come to terms with the future. I've been feeling altogether too sorry for myself and it really doesn't do to start living in the past at my age. You'll be attending the sale, of course?"

"Yes," he said eagerly, "I shall bid for some of the things I might need up there. Furniture, fittings and tack especially. I daresay Rudd will advise me now that I've finally made up my mind."

"You mean he doesn't know?"

"That's right," Paul said, "I really came here this morning to decide. You just happen to be the first to hear, Miss Lovell," and he smiled.

The hand holding her crop shot up to her mouth and her lip touched the ivory handle, so that she suddenly looked like a child, puzzled by an unexpected turn of events. Then he saw the two bright spots appear on her cheeks once again and before he could say another word she clapped her heels to the flanks of the bay and dashed past him to the top of the sandhill. The grey whipped around, almost unseating Paul so that he was obliged to concentrate on the horse for a moment; then, looking up, he saw her again, sitting her horse in the precise spot where he had been when he had watched her gallop along the water's edge. She was smiling down at him like a child who had confounded her elders by a piece of showing-off and as he pulled the grey around she lifted her hand in a salute and swinging round galloped over the crest of the hill and out of sight in a few seconds.

84

Rudd received the news calmly enough until Paul added that he would like him to remain as agent on a three-year contract at a starting salary of three hundred a year. Then the agent's phlegm deserted him and he got up, standing by the open window with his face turned away and his hands clasped behind his back.

"You don't have to do that," he said gruffly, "you could manage very well on your own after a year."

"I should be an idiot not to take advantage of your experience," Paul told him. "You would be doing me a favour by staying."

At that Rudd swung round and said earnestly, "Well then, I accept, and I must say it's damned generous of you, Mr. Craddock! I won't pretend that I should find it a big wrench to leave here. As I said, I haven't been all that happy but I've always loved the place. There's been indifference here, and plenty of sloth too, but I still think the place could respond to a little care and imagination. You know what they say about a woman who is loved? She takes on self-confidence and beauty, and I've always thought this could happen here. Anyway, I'll promise you two things. I'll give you honest advice, and my heart will be in the job!"

"Well that should do for a start," said Paul and they shook hands on the bargain, spending the morning touring the Home Farm, which seemed to Paul well administered by Tom Honeyman, a plodding, bald-headed man, whose enthusiasm was reserved for Southdown sheep, for he was descended (or claimed to be) from the Newbury farmer who once won a thousand guineas from the local squire by making a hunting coat from wool sheared from a pair of Southdowns that same day. Honeyman was a widower, with grown children, all farming outside the estate boundaries, and managed the farm with a cowman, three or four boys, and two biblical looking shepherds, known as Matt and Luke, who were twins and, so Rudd informed Paul, unable to read or write. Later they went up to the house to select items of furniture that might be bought in at ten per cent above the reserve price. This seemed to Paul a very arbitrary way of doing business, for the sale had been advertised for the following day, and it occurred to him that bidders might be coming some distance to buy lots that they would now find withdrawn, but Rudd pooh-poohed his doubts. "It was laid down in the conditions of sale that anything the purchaser of the estate wanted he was to have," he told Paul. "The

85

executors are more interested in selling the estate than disposing of the bits and pieces, and anyway, a lot of the stuff here is either worn out or second rate." Paul discovered, on closer inspection, that this was so. Most of the furniture was heavy mid-Victorian pieces whereas the carpets were badly worn, except in the main bedrooms which did not appear to have been used much. He had an opportunity, on going round with Rudd, to get better bearings on the house and found it longer and narrower than he had imagined, with a spacious drawing-room, and a dining-room respectively east and west of the entrance hall, a smaller and very cheerful library, stocked with over a thousand books leading out of the drawing-room, a billiard-room adjoining the dining-room, and a warren of passages and pantries about the huge, Elizabethan kitchen that still had its great hearth, and antediluvian cooking implements. Kitchen and domestic quarters lay behind the east wing and opened upon a wide, cobbled yard, enclosed by stables and coach house. The woods here began at the end of the kitchen garden, which rose steeply, making the back of the house rather sunless, except in the late afternoon. Behind the garden, which was in good order and enclosed by a mellow brick wall, was an orchard and Rudd said that in springtime this was full of daffodils and narcissi, and that later bluebells grew there so thickly that the ground was a blue mist. Paul asked him if he was fond of gardening and he said no but had an interest in wild flowers, which he was usually reluctant to admit. "For a countryman to confess to a liking for wild flowers is tantamount to him saying he opposes blood sports," he said with a chuckle.

They went up the backstairs and along the rearward passage to the staff sleeping quarters. Evidence of neglect and decay were every-where, plaster and paper peeling from walls and at one place, on the east wall, a wide crack in the ceiling and a hole in the roof of the attic through which they could see the sky. Here the tiny bedrooms, some half-dozen of them, were airless boxes containing little besides an iron cot or two, a truckle bed and a few stools. Rudd told him that when Sir George had been in residence he kept a full staff of servants, sometimes as many as a dozen variously employed as kitchen hands, parlourmaids and grooms, apart from the resident housekeeper and three gardeners, but that when the house was empty all but the gardeners and Mrs. Handcock, the housekeeper, were paid off, "like a crew engaged for a single voyage". When Paul asked if this had not caused distress in the area Rudd said that it had, particularly in winter, but that regular work in the Sorrel Valley had never been plentiful and the family had not had difficulty in recruiting casual labour whenever they came down for a hunting season, or the period preceding or following the London season. "They wasted money they begrudged putting into the estate," he said. "I've known young Hubert pay out two hundred guineas for a hunt supper here but they paid atrocious wages, spending what they saved on any number of fads, like the old man's passion for photography. He had a dark-room off the library and his paraphernalia is still there, together with hundreds of photographs he took and developed. You can see what needs spending on the house before you start on the farms but I can find you a good local builder and if we get his estimate right away I daresay he'll move in and live here until the job's done. He can sub-contract for the painting and plumbing and we shall need Vicary, the Coombe Bay stonemason. After the sale we can make a plan as to what's necessary and what, if anything, you would like knocked down or built on."

There was no bathroom—the Lovells seemed to have washed in wooden tubs—but the three main bedrooms at the front of the house were in better repair than the reception-rooms on the ground floor. Two of these bedrooms looked over the paddocks and ford, and a string of smaller guest-rooms, ending in the nursery, faced west. Paul noticed that the scrap screen and the rocking horse were labelled Lots 250 and 251, and he wondered if Grace Lovell would bid for them. In the largest bedroom was a huge four-poster and two or three pieces of late eighteenth-century furniture, including a serpentine chest of drawers, a military chest converted into a wardrobe, and two or three rosewood wig-stands which he said he would buy, together with about twenty lots in the guest-rooms and the rooms downstairs. He also marked down the library furniture and books, promising himself some pleasant winter evenings in what seemed to him the cosiest room in the house. The windows here looked over Shallowford Woods and Coombe Bluff and there was a deep leather armchair promising solid comfort in front of a wide stone hearth. When the list was complete they made their way back to the lodge and Rudd totted up the cost of the items Paul had bought in, making a total of under four hundred pounds. This excluded the grey, the trap and the tack in the harness room, which came to another hundred and fifty, so that Paul told himself he had done a good day's business, particularly when Rudd explained that all the gardening tools were included in the overall purchase price. That night Paul told the agent the source of his legacy and something of Zorndorff's part in the

87

adventure. He was frank about his means, thinking it unfair to both of them if Rudd, who would be responsible for the initial outlay, remained in the dark and was tempted to either cheesepare or overspend.

"Well," said Rudd, bracing himself as though to speak an unpleasant truth, "I promised you good advice and I'll give you some right away. Don't tell anyone else what you've just told me—the source of the money, that is, or your association with trade of any kind. You are simply a fortunate young man who has come into a legacy and if you're wise you'll leave it at that! There's nobody in the world so snobbish as the peasant with a straw in his mouth!" As he spoke they heard the hooves on the gravel of the drive and through the open window saw Rose and Claire Derwent trot past on their way up to the house. Rudd said, with a chuckle, "One thing more, Mr. Craddock!" and pointed with his pipe at the disappearing horsewomen—"Are you the marrying type? Or committed elsewhere?" and when Paul admitted that he had never seriously thought of marriage the agent added, "Then I'd best warn you of something else while I'm at it! Every filly hereabouts will be anticipating the hunting season by a couple of months or more! There go two who have already started cubbing, so to speak, so sit tight until they move on to draw the next covert!"

It seemed that every man, woman and child as far afield as Whinmouth, and the villages north of the railway line, had taken time off to attend Shallowford House sale. By ten o'clock, an hour before bidding was due to commence, paddocks and forecourt were the scene of a vast picnic, with everyone in their summer best and ranks of gigs, traps, waggonettes and saddle-horses tethered to palings behind the avenue chestnuts. Paul and Rudd made their way to the house through groups of respectful strangers, some of them people Paul remembered having met on his tour. He saw Tamer Potter already refreshing himself out of an enormous flagon of cider, with his three girls gossiping with young men in corduroys under the trees, and their brothers Sam and Smut talking to a man in velveteens, who looked as if he was lecturing them, for he kept making emphatic gestures as Sam looked sheepish and Smut listened with a broad grin on his sunburned face. "That's Melrose, Lord Gilroy's head keeper," Rudd told Paul, as they walked up the drive, "giving Smut Potter another of his final warnings! There's Arabella, with Martin in tow. I daresay she'll make him bid for one or two of the fancy lots. And there's Dr.

88

O'Keefe," and Rudd pointed to a rather handsome old man, in a black frock coat leaning negligently against a tree, surveying the gathering with contempt. "And there's Lord Gilroy himself, out for an airing after his last spell of gout. He's a supercilious old rascal but I daresay he'll be civil enough and suspend judgment on you until somebody gets wind of your connection with a scrapyard! After that he'll cut you, but you can get along without Gilroy patronage—the Lovells did!"

"I'm a bit astonished by the grip the eighteenth century still has on the area," Paul said when they had been admitted by the back door and had moved into one of the rooms facing the terrace where they could overlook the crowd in the paddocks and drive.

"What else did you expect?" Rudd said. "We only got our railway link four years ago, and I can remember *The Times* being read aloud in the bar of The Raven once a week! You've caught us at an intermediary stage—say about 1860, and I think this might be the source of some of your biggest headaches! You saw one or two reach for their forelocks at the farms but when they realised they were doing it instinctively they felt shamefaced, and that's a bad thing. Either a man freely acknowledges power of wealth and class, or he doesn't think of himself as anything but a free man, with a free man's privilege of telling the squire to treat him as one or go fishing! Take that mob out there, flirting, guzzling and skylarking around the waggons. Not one in fifty has any intention of bidding for anything here. With one or two exceptions they couldn't afford to pay for it if it was knocked down to them, but does that stop them making a fête out of the sale? Why bless you, Sir George Lovell in his heyday would have had his keeper herd them the far side of the ford but today there they are and not a blush between them, except when Parson Bull buttonholes sermon-dodgers and threatens to name slackers publicly from the pulpit! There he is now, giving Arthur Pitts the edge of his tongue," and Paul saw a massively built clergyman, with a great mop of white hair, hectoring a downcast-looking Arthur, who stood with his wife Martha in the forecourt awaiting the auctioneer's signal to unlock the front door.

"What kind of man is Bull?" Paul enquired. "I daresay I shall have to attend church as soon as I settle in," and Rudd chuckled and said that even Sir George Lovell had been circumspect in his dealings with Bull, who was probably the last buttress of the eighteenth century in the Valley, for he hunted three times a week, swore freely in public and usually called for a tot of brandy before dispensing communion wine to his flock. "Willoughby, the Nonconformist, once challenged him outside The Raven, accusing him of setting a bad example to his parishioners," he said, "but Bull only shouted 'If you meet a man carrying a lantern on a dark night don't question his character, you dissenting knave! Just be grateful for the light he's shedding, in the hope that it will keep your erring feet clear of hell!' He's a hard man is Bull, but he's respected. He's a real man, you see, and they prefer that to someone who hands out the Gentle Jesus brand of Christianity!"

The auctioneer asked Rudd if it was time to open the doors and when Rudd said it was Paul withdrew and watched the bidding, almost all the lots on the ground floor being knocked down to a dealer from Whinmouth, rumoured to be bidding on Lord Gilroy's behalf, or to one of the auctioneer's staff acting for absent clients. He recognised Claire Derwent's blonde head under the rostrum and she saw him and smiled, nudging her sister Rose and then looking quickly away. Arabella Codsall bought a mirror and one or two figurines, and in addition to greeting the Pitts and Tamer Potter, Paul acknowledged the polite greetings of Willoughby, his shy daughter Elinor, and the grim-faced Edward Derwent, who never once took his eyes off the auctioneer but offered no bids, either by word or gesture. After a time Paul's leg began to ache so he drifted into the library and thence into the adjoining room that Sir George had used as a photographer's studio. The window was still draped with black cloth and when he had ripped it down, and opened the window, he saw a jumble of faded photographs, hypo baths and fixing frames left on the benches by the late owner. The pictures gave him a closer insight into the family than he had obtained from reading the *Illustrated London News*. He decided that George Lovell was no ordinary amateur but a technician with imagination and finesse, for there were some cleverly posed groups under the chestnuts, and several excellent pictures of horses and of meets in the forecourt outside. There were also souvenir pictures of fancy-dress balls of more than twenty years ago, dated and signed on the back in Sir George's spidery hand-writing—*Shallowford Christmas Rout, 1882*, and *Harvest Ball, 1883*, large photographs showing groups of Robin Hoods, Dick Turpins and fairy-tale characters. It all seemed to belong to an age as far away as Waterloo, or before then, when choleric squires dispensed lavish hospitality and drunk themselves insensible after gruelling days in the hunting field. Looking at them Paul thought of what Rudd had said regarding the transitional stage at Shallowford, and its time lag, reflecting that he would be the person responsible for quickening the tempo but he also wondered if good intentions and an injection of capital would be enough to drag this self-contained little community into the twentieth century? Did the people of the Sorrel Valley acknowledge the Age of Progress, that everybody in London talked about? Had they ever devoted a moment's thought to airships, and electric lighting, to motors, phonographs, and higher education? And even if they had, would any of these things add anything important to their lives?

He was returning yellowing photographs to the shelf where he had found them when he saw the brass-bound Bible, a ponderous volume on the one shelf free of litter. He pulled it out, wondering why its clasp was secured by a small brass padlock, and it occurred to him that a Bible of this size and weight might contain a family tree, or perhaps a record of Lovell births and deaths over the century. The little padlock presented no difficulties and he prised it open with his penknife, turning to a flyleaf which was disappointingly blank. Then, opening the book at random, he almost dropped it with astonishment, for it was not a bible at all but an album of near-pornographic photographs, most of them obviously the work of Sir George, for they were identical in tone, mounting and finish to the groups he had just laid aside.

He turned the pages curiously, glancing at twenty or more portraits of show-girls in various stages of undress and a variety of obscene poses. Some of them wore tights, others were draped in what looked like clusters of spangled tassels. The subjects were all plump, rather overblown girls, with great sturdy thighs, mountainous breasts and very ample behinds. Most of them were smirking into the camera, so that Paul found their poses grotesquely comic, as though the photographer, by housing them between the covers of a Bible, was playing a secret practical joke on society. There was nothing particularly shocking about the first half of the album. The girls were clearly the type who habitually posed for these kind of pictures, and their self-satisfied smiles and negligent poses, indicated that they were not in the least ashamed of earning an honest half-guinea catering for their patron's eccentric tastes. But then the nature of the gallery changed abruptly and Paul recognised, with a sense of shock, one of the older Potter girls, photographed against a background of artificial foliage and looking, he thought, a little frightened and incredulous, as well she might for she was stark naked, her disordered hair masking part of her face as she stood with shoulders slightly hunched, as though poised to run. There were several other pictures of this girl but in subsequent photographs she seemed to have gained confidence, for in two she was grinning and standing with feet astride and her hands on her hips. There were also photographs of a younger girl whom Paul did not recognise, a dark, wild-looking creature, who could not have been more than fifteen and had been permitted to retain an unlikely pair of drawers, frilled at the knee and very much beribboned, as though to heighten her forlorn appeal. She had been photographed standing in front of a full-length mirror and the result of the double reflection was somehow pathetic, as the camera had caught a pile of shabby discarded clothing in the bottom right-hand corner.

Paul stared at the pictures unbelievingly, wondering if chance had revealed to him a well-kept secret, or whether the whole Valley acknowledged George Lovell as a lustful old goat, whose secret pleasure was to coax young girls into this airless little room and bribe or frighten them into stripping and posing for his camera. The local pictures made him feel slightly sick and he pushed the window further open, wondering where he could hide the book until he had a chance to destroy it but as he moved a loose photograph fell to the floor and bending to retrieve it he saw that it was a study of another un-identifiable girl. This one, although naked, seemed to have clung to modesty of a sort, for she had turned her face away from the camera and used her hand as a screen. She was, thought Paul, an un-willing subject, but then he wondered, for a deliberate attempt had been made to pose her against the sylvan background and parody the pose of a surprised nymph. She was, he would judge, about the same age as the girl in the frilled drawers but better nourished, and pos-sessing a more mature figure and a healthy skin. He was slipping the picture between the Bible covers when he heard a step in the library and for a moment he panicked, glaring round for somewhere to dispose of the wretched album. He had just thrust it alongside the festive groups when the door opened and Claire Derwent's blonde head appeared. She did not seem surprised to find him there alone and smiled, showing beautiful teeth.

"Why *there* you are, Mr. Craddock! Mr. Rudd said you were in the library. I wanted to ask you if my sister and I can help about horses. He told me the news and everyone is delighted! Mr. Rudd also told us you had bought the grey and we're pleased about that too, because Rose bred him from Misty, one of the best mares we ever had in the Valley."

Paul, thanking God that Claire Derwent had not been numbered among Sir George's local models, made a determined attempt to compose himself, feeling almost that she had surprised him enjoying the old satyr's picture gallery.

"It doesn't matter a bit if it isn't convenient now," Claire went on, mercifully oblivious of his confusion, "we could easily discuss it some other time, but if you need a good groom we happen to know of one who was a soldier like you, and has just come back seeking a post. We should also like you to know that we could come over and look after any horses if you had to go away again before you settled in. What I mean is, if we can help in any way you have only to ask, and father told me to say he'll do anything he can to help because he's just as pleased as we are that you're going to be Squire!"

He had recovered sufficiently to pay some attention to her now and it struck him again that she was an extraordinarily pretty woman, with her small, neat head, tidy corn-coloured hair dressed in coiled plaits, Dutch fashion, clear blue eyes and soft, red mouth. Her figure was good too, not straight and lithe like her sister's, but rather full, with small hands and feet, so that everything about her suggested neatness and vigorous health.

"It's very civil of you, Miss Derwent," he heard himself saying, "and I daresay I shall take advantage of your kindness. I'm very much taken with the grey and I expect, soon enough, I shall want a good cob for the trap, and maybe a second hunter. However, my first job is to try and get some kind of order into this chaos. The house needs a great deal of renovation, don't you think?"

She looked round the room with a woman's appraising eye for defects.

"Eph Morgan will sort it out in no time," she said, "he's the local builder Mr. Rudd will recommend and what he can't manage himself he'll find somebody to do. It's going to be wonderful to have Shallowford come alive again after all this time. This could be a wonderful home, Mr. Craddock, it only wants somebody like yourself to . . . well, to love it, and care for it! The Lovells were always coming and going, taking on people and getting rid of them, and really keen farmers like Daddy felt rather wretched about it all, you understand?"

"It's going to be different from now on," Paul promised and was surprised at his enthusiasm. "I'm going to like it here and I've no interest in town life. We could pull the place together in no time, providing every family is as co-operative as yours!" And then, because he noticed a gleam of triumph in her eyes, he felt he had said too much, and added, lamely, "I'd like to see how things are getting on

93

out there if you'll excuse me, Miss Derwent, I only came in because it was so stuffy among the crowd in the big room."

"Oh, they're all upstairs now," she said gaily, "selling the stuff in the guest-rooms. We've come over in the waggonette and brought a picnic lunch. Would you care to join us when they break for luncheon? We're at the top of the drive and Daddy's got some rather good claret."

"That's kind of you," he said, "but I must ask Rudd if Mrs. Handcock is expecting us for lunch."

"Oh no she isn't," said Claire, "I've already asked Rudd and he said I was to ask you."

"Very well then, I should be delighted," said Paul, a little taken aback by her persistence, and they moved out of the library to join the crowd on the landing, at the point where the passages branched.

He could hear the auctioneer's voice droning away at the far end of the corridor and the crowd made way for him in a way that suggested the news had already spread far and wide. He shed Claire on the way and here, looking over people's heads, he saw that the room was packed with spectators and that some of the lots from the bedrooms had been carried in to provide more selling space. Then, in her familiar corner by the window, he saw Grace Lovell, and beside her, looking as if association with the crowd distressed them, was a slim erect man about fifty, and a handsome, hard-faced woman, in her mid-thirties, who held a lilac parasol and whose features were rigid with concentration. He identified them at once as Grace Lovell's father and stepmother.

The auctioneer was selling Lot 250, the nursery screen, and before he was done with his patter Grace called "Ten shillings!", speaking so quickly that her mouth was closed again before Paul had realised she was bidding.

"Ten shillings!" repeated the auctioneer, as one of his assistants lifted the screen, "Any advance on ten shillings? A lot of painstaking work has gone into this! How about some of you young ladies and gentlemen thinking of getting married . . . ?", and there was a dutiful titter, in which the Lovells did not join.

"Fifteen!" said a woman standing in front of Paul and he recognised Arabella Codsall.

"One pound!" Grace called, before the auctioneer could invite an advance and Arabella, with a tut-tut of irritation, said, crossly, "One guinea, then!" and Paul caught a glimpse of Martin Codsall's peaked face at his wife's elbow.

The auctioneer glanced across to the silent trio by the window. "Come now, Miss Lovell, you'll not let it go for that. Shall I say twenty-two and six?"

Grace shook her head and Paul, seeing her glance drop, said, "Thirty shillings, Mr. Auctioneer!", and everyone in the room turned to stare. There was a pause and then, swiftly, the auctioneer brought down his gavel. "Sold to Mr. Craddock, and I'm delighted something else is staying where it belongs, sir! Well, ladies and gentlemen, that's all in here and we'll break for luncheon. The remaining lots, including all those outside, will be sold commencing two p.m. sharp!", and the crowd began to surge out into the corridor, pressing Paul back to the landing and downstairs to the hall where they streamed into the open.

Paul waited beside the big fireplace, watching Bruce Lovell and his wife descend the stairs, and pass into the forecourt. They did not see him and were engaged in a low and earnest conversation. When Grace did not follow he went up again and along the corridor to the nursery. She was still there, standing with her back to the door examining the screen with care. He said, "I didn't really want it, Miss Lovell, but I could see that you did and it didn't seem right to lose it to Arabella Codsall. It's yours if you want it and I can see that you do."

She turned slowly, regarding him with disconcerting gravity.

"Very well," she said, almost inaudibly, "I'll send the money for it tonight. I daresay my father can get someone to collect it tomorrow."

"I don't want paying for it," Paul said, "I'd like you to have it for old times' sake. You said you used to come here as a child and I daresay this room has happy memories for you. I'd be very glad if you would let me make you a present of it, Miss Lovell."

She continued to gaze fixedly at him and he decided that he wished she would sometimes make an effort to put him at ease. As if she could read his thoughts she suddenly dropped her glance and said, still very quietly, "Happy memories? I don't know why I wanted the screen, I probably wouldn't have looked at it when I got it home, but I helped to make it from scraps, cut up in the schoolroom. I was about seven or eight then, but it seems longer ago than that!" She seemed almost as though she was talking to herself but suddenly her head came up and she smiled, "It was a kind thought anyhow, Mr. Craddock, and I don't intend to be churlish again! I'll accept it as a gift—a going-away gift!", and she walked past him into the corridor and down the stairs, leaving him as baffled as he had been by her two previous dismissals.

CHAPTER FOUR

I

ZORNDORFF, enthroned on his high stool overlooking the yard, adjusted his half-moon spectacles and re-read Paul's eight-page letter with the undivided attention he gave to every document addressed to him, even trade brochures and invoices. He had read it before that morning but hurriedly, to assess its factual worth. Now, with time on his hands, he dissected it, phrase by phrase.

It told of Paul's meeting with Rudd and the understanding they had arrived at during their ride over the moor; it described the scenery, house, farms, tenants, sale and the terms of his contract with Rudd. It even reported on the progress of his wound but it said nothing of Grace Lovell, or of the episode concerning the nursery screen. Zorndorff, however, had been prising undisclosed information from letters too long to miss the inference that there was a pretty girl somewhere between the lines and her presence intrigued him for he was aware of aspects of Craddock's character of which Paul himself was unaware and among them was a certain loss of confidence engendered by the shock of his wound, his long illness and the certainty that he now faced life with a permanent disability. It was because he was aware of these factors that Zorndorff had not been impressed by the young man's summary rejection of the scrap-iron business. To Craddock, as to any young man emerging from hospital with one leg shorter than the other, the world had a slightly sour taste and he would be ready to quarrel with everything until the period of adjustment had passed. The fact that a few days in the west had enabled him to mention his wound in passing satisfied the Croat that Paul had somehow succeeded in making that adjustment in a matter of days. Fresh air, soft scenery, and a visit to a few run-down farms, Zorndorff reasoned, would hardly have inspired a letter as jubilant as this; he wrote like a man in love and Zorndorff, who, despite preoccupation with business, had lived a full life, could appreciate the difference between the stimulus of a pretty landscape and that of a pretty woman. The only aspect of the letter that puzzled him was its postscript, obviously an afterthought. Paul had written: *"One other thing—I need a stable lad and remembered*

96

that urchin, the one who was so smart with that cart-horse. Would he care to exchange smoke for fresh air? Anyway, ask him and advance his fare if he'll come. He'll get full board and half-a-crown a week, together with expert training as a groom."

Zorndorff had to think hard before he recalled the incident and when he did he smiled wryly, judging that a street-urchin of Ikey Palfrey's temperament would not willingly exchange the freedom of the streets for Gray's Elegy in a Country Churchyard. He blew down the speaking tube to Scotcher, the yard foreman, and instructed him to send Ikey Palfrey, Sophie Carrilovic's boy, to the office as soon as he came in with a load.

The boy appeared within half-an-hour and Zorndorff guessed correctly that he had been playing truant again, for the schools, closed in anticipation of the coronation ceremony, had reopened as soon as it was known that the King would not be crowned until August. The boy stood before Zorndorff in his rags, eyeing him furtively, as though sure of a command to return to school at once which would mean a thrashing. Ikey Palfrey cared very little for a routine thrashing but he resented very much enforced separation from his barrow, for that meant loss of income. He said, with mock humility, "Gaffer said you 'ad special collection for me, sir," and Zorndorff chuckled.

"Gaffer said nothing of the kind, boy. He told you I wanted a word with you, and it isn't for skipping school either. Why should I care a damn if you remain illiterate?"

The boy relaxed a little, although he still looked ready to dart out of the door.

"Wot was it then?"

"It's this," Zorndorff said, and read the postscript aloud, watchin the boy's bewildered expression. "You don't recall Mr. Craddock then?"

"Yerse I do," Ike said at once, " 'Ee got me a tanner, didn't he? I ain't likely to fergit that—earning a tanner, just fer savin' that bleedin' carter's head from being kicked in!"

The boy's nasal accent jarred Zorndorff's nerves and he found it difficult to believe that Sophie Carrilovic, a woman born and reared in Zagreb, could have produced a child who could so outrage a foreign tongue. He would wager that the boy could not speak one word of Croat but then, why should he? He was probably nine-tenths the son of that layabout Palfrey, whom Sophie had been obliged to marry in order to acquire British nationality.

"Very well, you remember him," Zorndorff said shortly, "but you

97

don't know that he was Mr. Craddock's son, or that he was badly wounded in the war."

"No, I never knew that," Ike admitted, "but wot's the odds, Mister Zorndorff? What's that ter me?"

"Mr. Craddock seems to think you can be taught to handle horses," said Franz, now rather enjoying the interview.

"I c'n 'andle 'em nah, I don't need to be taught nothin' about 'orses," said Ike sharply but Zorndorff saw that he was impressed by the offer. " 'Arf-a-crahn an' all fahnd," he murmured. "Well, it don't sahnd bad, do it? Pervidin' you could pick up the odd bit o' scrap and flog it. Could you do that dahn there, Mr. Zorndorff?"

"I feel confident that you could do it anywhere," said Franz, "but I wouldn't like you to miss the main point. Mr. Craddock probably intends that you should learn a trade. You aren't likely to get that opportunity here if I know your parents, and as a stable lad on a big estate I daresay you would have a chance to ride real horses, not cart-horses. You might even become a jockey before you're finished!"

The boy's face shone. "Cor!" he said. "You ain't kiddin', Mr. Zorndorff? You wouldn't kid abaht a thing like that? I alwus reckoned I could be a jockey, ser long as I don't grow no more. I'll take it, Mr. Zorndorff, if you'll 'ave a word wi' Mum, but don't let the ol' girl talk you aht of it, will yer?"

It was all arranged with the maximum despatch and Franz Zorndorff, pondering the caprices of mankind, went along to Sophie Carrilovic's two-roomed dwelling that same afternoon, depriving her of her eldest son and partial support, comforting her with promises of a substitute, and despatching Ikey to buy himself a suit of corduroys and two flannel shirts in the Bermondsey Market.

The boy presented himself fully kitted and with undeclared small change in his pocket the following morning and Franz, after inspecting him, gave him a Gladstone bag to hold his scanty possessions, plus a sovereign for his travelling expenses. It was the sight of the coin that destroyed Ikey Palfrey's composure. As he stood looking down at it in the palm of his hand Zorndorff saw him for what he was, a grimy, raggletailed, undernourished little boy of ten or eleven, with the fear and cunning of the jungle lurking behind his eyes. He had seen thousands of such children during his lifetime both here and in Austria, but for some reason the sight of Ikey Palfrey touched him and he said gently, "You don't know what might come of this, Ike. Work hard and don't steal. Even if you're not caught you'll be likely to cause

Mr. Craddock trouble. It was very strange that he should remember you, so make the most of it for I have a feeling that you won't regret what you're doing. There now, make yourself scarce, tell him I'll write and might even come and see you both one fine day."

The boy, thrown off guard by Zorndorff's tone, stuck a knuckle in his eye and then, with a long sniff, jerked himself erect and bestowed upon his employer a Cockney wink. Zorndorff, shamed by his emotions, frowned but he watched him march down the ramp and through the debris to the double gates of the yard and the boy must have realised that the Croat was watching for, when he reached the road, he suddenly turned and lifted his hand, a gesture that surprised Franz very much. "Now why the devil did he do that?" he asked himself aloud. "Was he simply acknowledging my part in the business, or was he saying good-bye to the only place in the world that ever gave him anything but hard knocks?" Then he put the boy out of mind and addressed himself to totting up a list of fractions with the speed of an adding machine.

Ikey Palfrey was not entirely unfamiliar with the country. Twice in the last few years he had been hop-picking in Kent, and on two occasions he had travelled as far as Leith Hill in Surrey, on Sunday School treats, but always, when he had passed outside the rings of brick and stone that enclosed his entire world he had done so in the raucous company of two score of his neighbours, so that the terrible emptiness of a landscape had gone more or less unnoticed, had seemed, indeed, less real than the green patches on railway posters.

Now, for the first time in his life he was alone in it, and long before the train stopped to change engines at Salisbury the defensive crust of his urban cockiness had cracked and fallen away, leaving him as vulnerable as a country-bred child turned loose in a populous city. He was, however, very far from being a weakling. He in no way resented the cruelty of the society into which he had been born but fought back, more or less successfully, with fists, hobnailed boots, artfulness and lies. These weapons, however, were no defence against the loneliness that enfolded him as he sat looking out of the window at miles and miles of fields, coppices and picture-book farms, all as alien to him as the upper reaches of the Amazon. How, he wondered, did one find one's way about in a place bereft of landmarks, where every field and hedge were identical and every patch of woodland cover for nameless enemies? What did people do with themselves by day in

99

such a wilderness? And when night fell, and darkness pressed down like a thick wet sack, how could one sleep with a certainty of waking again? He was by no means an introspective child, and was incapable of rationalising his fears, but they were there just the same, multiplying with every clack of the wheels, and in the terrifying isolation of the frowsy third-class carriage they began to undermine his courage, so that he would have burst into tears had it not been for the coins in his trouser pocket. Zorndorff had given him a sovereign and the fare demanded of him at Waterloo had been half-a-sovereign; never having possessed this sum before he regarded it as a special talisman against evil, and when he was not looking at it he was holding it in his moist palms, together with the small change left over from the sum given him to buy clothes. Ever since he could remember money had been a guarantee against oppression and the everyday hazards of cold and hunger. He had enormous respect for coins, all kinds of coins. With a halfpenny one could buy a roasted potato on a frosty night; with a penny for a juicy meat pie one could not only avoid going to bed supperless but could exchange half the pie for a seat beside a night-watchman's brazier. These things were fundamentals and coins were the keys to them, so that even the nameless dread conjured up by the endless fields and woods must, he reasoned, be subordinate to so much wealth for today, by the mercy of God and his own prudence, he was worth thirteen shillings and sevenpence; in view of that there could not be much to worry about.

They had told him at Waterloo that the journey would take about six hours but as he had no means of knowing the time it seemed to pass very slowly. He had eaten his pies and sandwiches long ago, and had begged a mug of water from a porter at one of the stops, but now he was both hungry and thirsty, and also much agitated by the prospect of overshooting his stop and missing the junction where he had been told to change trains. His stomach cart-wheeled with relief when the guard looked in and told him to get out at the next stop and there was only one other train at the branch siding so that he was able, to some degree, to compose himself during the brief journey to Sorrel Halt. But when he arrived there, and there was no one to meet him, he gave himself up for lost.

He sat down on a platform seat, staring out over the empty moor like the sole survivor of a shipwreck gazing over a waste of water. The great moor, yellow with drought, stretched away in the distance, and across it ran the single white ribbon of a road. The sun, blood-red and ominous, was setting over the woodlands on his left, but the minutes ticked by and still no one appeared. What, Ike asked himself, did one do in such circumstances? What could one do but pray?

He had no real faith in the power of prayer. Every morning, at Alexis Street Council School, there had been a brief religious service that included a gabbled prayer and on the rare occasions when he attended Sunday School (in order to qualify for the annual treat) the bearded Superintendent prefaced and concluded his address with interminable appeals for Divine guidance and mercy. Ike had remained unimpressed by his appeals. They seemed to him to have even less meaning than the words of the hymns they chanted, yet who could say with certainty whether or not there existed above the bright blue sky an Omnipotent Sunday School Superintendent in a long white nightshirt who might be disposed to extricate a petitioner, providing he made his plea with eyes tightly closed and palms pressed together? He arranged himself in the conventional pose and murmured, swiftly, "Lord, get me aht of 'ere quick! *Make* Mr. Craddock show up! Amen," and when he opened his eyes, and saw a trap speeding down the ribbon of road, he was ripe for wholesale conversion, so much so that, in the act of grabbing his Gladstone bag and leaping on the seat to wave, he did not forget to comment on the despatch of Divine service, saying, breathlessly, "Lumme! It *worked*!"

Paul came driving out of the sunset in a fast trot and saw the small figure capering on the platform seat. He had misjudged the time it took to climb the long, winding hill from the Sorrel Valley and seeing relief shining in the child's pale face he was contrite, saying, "I'm sorry, kid, I took too long getting over the moor. It's six miles and rough going. Have you been waiting long?"

"No, sir," Ikey said politely, for his spirits had been uplifted by the remarkably swift answer to prayer which boded well for an easy solution to future problems, "No, Mister, I knew you'd show up sooner or later, I'd have hoofed it on me daisy-roots if I'd known which way ter go!", and he climbed up and settled himself, gazing round at the countryside with disdain and assurance. The trap, he thought, was a very smart rig, and the bay cob pulling it seemed exceptionally fat, for plump horses were not within his experience. "I think you're going to like it down here," Paul said. "I do myself, so much that I don't think I shall ever go back to London! The big house is the other side of the woods, and as you'll have to find your way about sooner or later I'll tell you the names of the places we pass on the way. But I expect you're hungry after that journey. Could you eat a pasty? A home-made one?"

"Could a duck swim, Mr. Craddock!" said Ikey, and for the next five minutes was silent whilst accounting for the largest and tastiest pasty he had ever seen or heard described and one, he would judge, that would set anybody back twopence in Berstein's pieshop, in the Old Kent Road.

As they jogged on over the moor Paul outlined what he had in mind for the boy, an apprenticeship in caring for horses and harness under Chivers, the middle-aged groom the Derwents had sent him. He had arranged, he said, for Chivers to teach him the rudiments of horsemanship and tack-room work, and added, "You may find the speech of the people down here difficult to understand at first, but don't forget that they won't understand you either! Very few of them have ever been within a hundred miles of London, do you understand?"

"Yes, sir," said Ikey dutifully but privately considered the warning unnecessary, for although he seemed to have travelled a thousand miles since eight o'clock that morning he had not crossed a sea and was therefore still within the confines of the British Isles, where everyone spoke English. As they breasted the slope of the moor, crossed the main highway and dropped down on to the river road, the boy stole a cautious look at his companion, seeing a lean, thoughtful face, with a flicker of kindness in the grey eyes and determination in the small, jutting chin. Ike was well versed in the art of gauging character by a study of adult faces and voices, and concluded at once that here was a soft touch, provided he didn't overstep the mark. His hunger temporarily satisfied by Mrs. Handcock's enormous pasty he said, with infinite humility:

"I done a bit o' trap-driving, Mr. Craddock, sir. Would you like me to take the ribbons fer a bit? Just ter make a change for yer?"

"If you like," Paul said, "but take her gently, I only bought her yesterday and she might have one or two tricks I don't know about," and they exchanged seats, Ikey clicking his tongue in the fashion of all the best London cabbies. The cob seemed to understand for it broke into a steady trot and Paul, his shyness making way for a kind of conspiratorial affection for the urchin, said, "I know your surname is Palfrey. What is your Christian name?"

The boy grinned, shamefacedly. "Me proper name's 'Percy'," he said, "but I 'ates it! I mean, anyone would, wouldn't they? Everyone back 'ome called me Ikey."

"Why?"

"I dunno why, Mr. Craddock, sir."

"Very well," Paul said, "it's 'Ikey' from now on," and he wondered if the name had been suggested by the boy's long, slightly curved nose, unusual in a boy from the South Bank where, Paul recalled, every other urchin's nose was snub.

II

Paul Craddock was to remember the long, blazing summer of 1902 as one of the happiest and busiest of his life. From early July, until the leaves of the avenue chestnuts began to fall, he was called upon to face an endless variety of problems, and to suffer not a few frustrations, but his spirits remained as unclouded as the weather. It was a joy to watch his home growing up around him under the ceaseless sawing and hammering of Eph Morgan's shock brigade, and to feel the pulse of a domain that seemed to him, admittedly a prejudiced witness, to be stirring after years of hibernation. He was fortunate during all this time, to have two such sponsors as Rudd and Mrs. Handcock, the resident housekeeper, for both made no secret of their liking for him, were ready to go to any lengths to help him adjust himself to the rhythm of country life, and also to mediate between a rank amateur and the people of the Valley. He was thus able to meet all the tenantry and their employees during this period, as well as most of the professional craftsmen and the few private residents in and about Coombe Bay, but he soon realised that conquest of the community as a whole was not something he could take for granted, simply because he had acquired Shallowford by a banker's draft. By August, when he had been living at the lodge for seven weeks, the Shallowford folk had sorted themselves into three groups. There were those like Rose and Claire Derwent, and Farmer Willoughby who openly proclaimed their relief that the estate was in the hands of an earnest if inexperienced young man; those like Arabella Codsall and Tamer Potter, who were somewhat fussed by his enthusiasm, and grumbled in private about city gentlemen who were prone to run before they could walk; and a third group of neutrals, like the Irish Doctor O'Keefe, Parson Bull, the head gardener, Horace Handcock, and some of the small tradesmen in Coombe Bay with whom Paul found it difficult to establish a close personal contact.

Some goodwill had to be purchased, as when Paul took Rudd's advice and gave Sam Potter the post of estate forester with a cottage at the far end of Shallowford Mere. Sam was grateful for both accommodation and post. He had lately married, and his wife Joannie was pregnant, and with winter coming on life promised to be bleak in the crowded family dell. Rudd reasoned that, with brother Sam drawing regular pay from the enemy's purse, brother Smut's poaching might be confined to robbing other people's coverts, east and west of Shallowford. Paul also won over the dour Edward Derwent, by buying in a small cliff pasture on the extreme eastern border and incorporating it into the High Coombe domain without an increase of rent, but in any case his relations with the Derwent clan, as with the amiable Pitts family, at Hermitage, were fairly cordial from the very beginning. Rose Derwent found him a good groom and a sturdy cob for his trap and her pretty sister Claire gave him plenty of frank advice regarding his approaches to the women of the Valley. "You have to pay each and every one of them the compliment of pretending they are equals of the men," she told him, when he came to her grumbling of Arabella Codsall's importunities one day. "It's a pure fiction, of course, except in Arabella's case, but it's Heads-I-Win-Tails-You-Lose for you because the women are flattered and their menfolk regard your approach as proof that they have married wives with good sense!" There and then Paul decided that Claire Derwent herself had more sense in her head than one could reasonably expect to find in a pretty girl of nineteen, but he was very careful not to discriminate between her and her sister Rose, for he soon discovered that Rose had a very warm heart, would go out of her way to help anyone and nursed no jealousy whatever in respect of her handsome sister.

In the immediate area of the big house Mrs. Handcock was his major-domo. Her immense weight did very little to reduce her mobility and she bustled breathlessly to and from her quarters in the domestic wing ministering to him and Rudd and engaging a troop of local girls to take service at Shallowford as soon as the renovations were finished. At first Paul had the greatest difficulty in understanding Mrs. Handcock's brogue, the broadest in the Valley not excluding Tamer Potter's, and would shake his head when she pounded into the parlour to ask if he would be available "to-zee-thicky-Lowry-maid-us-was-thinking-o'-taakin'-on-till-us-zees-'ow-'er-shaaapes!"

In the meantime the house was nearing the step of habitability, for Eph Morgan, the Welsh expatriate from Coombe Bay, had moved in the day after the sale and had since recruited a horde of local craftsmen on a sub-contract basis, setting them re-roofing, re-plastering, and papering according to the demands of Rudd's survey. The agent acted as architect but paid Paul the compliment of consulting him on important details. A bathroom was added, a passage cut through from kitchen to dining-room to ensure that meals were no longer served cold, joists in several floors were ripped out and replaced, every room upstairs was repapered with a cheerful floral pattern, new storage water tanks were installed in the loft, and Sir George Lovell's darkroom was fitted up as an estate office. Paul spent a great deal of his time watching the builders at work and Ephraim Morgan, their sponsor, intrigued him. He was a very small man, hardly more than five feet in height, but with a huge, round head that gave him the appearance of an intelligent gnome. He had first come into the district as a railway engineer and had decided, when the line was built, that he could earn a better living in Devon than in his native Wales. Yet, like all Welshmen, he cherished a fiery patriotism for the Principality and was a great admirer of Lloyd George, concerning whom he would deliver long, rhapsodic speeches in his sing-song voice while his men stood around grinning and sometimes throwing in a sly comment as fuel to the Welshman's fire. Eph Morgan had two principal hates, The Brummagers (represented by his arch-enemy Joe Chamberlain) and The Brewers, whom he declared the mainstay of the Tory Party and he saw his hero Lloyd George as a dauntless St. George ambushing both from morning to night. Paul gathered, however, that Morgan was an exception as regards his interest in radical politics, for all the farmers, and most of their hired men, were tepid Conservatives, who had followed the Lovell lead at the polling booth for generations without devoting a thought to topical issues like Irish Home Rule, Welsh Disestablishment, or the legacies of the South African War like the concentration camp scandal and the importation of Chinese labour into the mines. They were content to plod peacefully along the well-beaten paths of rural forefathers, looking to the gentry to govern and to the owner of the big house to keep their premises in repair, promote country sports and occasional social activities like the annual harvest supper and Empire Day celebrations. Notwithstanding the activities of prominent local dissenters like Farmer Willoughby, of Deepdene, and Eph Morgan, the established church had the local community well in hand. Parson Bull was not only feared but genuinely respected in the district. Rudd introduced them after Matins one Sunday morning, and Bull struck Paul as a man at least a century behind the times. He treated all his parishioners, rich and poor, with impatience and showed little traditional deference to his patron, the Squire. Rudd said that Bull's consuming interest was hunting and that he was an ecclesiastical parody of Surtees' Jorrocks, inasmuch as he hibernated in the summer and came alive again when cubbing began, in the last week of September. Then, Rudd promised, Paul would see the real Parson Bull astride an enormous seventeen-hand skewbald, roaring his way across country and threatening whiplash and hellfire to anyone who blocked his approach to a jumpable fence. "He's a frightful old tyrant, and makes nonsense of the Sermon on the Mount," he said, "but he's so Old English that one can't help paying him grudging respect. You've got half the gift of his living but that won't mellow his approach to you, as you probably noticed. They say that even the Bishop goes in fear of him and he's scared so many curates into resigning that now he doesn't have one but simply goes through the motions of taking a monthly service in outlying churches over the river."

Doctor O'Keefe, on whom Paul called for a routine check of his wound, was equally offhand, and the reek of whisky in his surgery went some way towards explaining the speed with which the doctor drove his gig around the district. He asked Paul one or two questions about the war, glared at his knee, then warned him that "he would have his hands full with a damned shambles like Shallowford", but they struck no sparks, and Paul left feeling the doctor lacked the saving grace of Parson Bull, who was at any rate a rumbustious character. Rudd said that O'Keefe had not always been surly and uncommunicative but had become misanthropic after his wife's death from tuberculosis some years ago. He had always been very fond of Irish whiskey ("the landlord of The Raven kept a special stock for him") and had turned to the bottle for solace. His wife had been a beautiful woman and the story was that they had been very attached to one another. "They've got a daughter somewhere," Rudd added, "a bonny girl she was, who ran off soon after her mother's death and is nursing or teaching up the country. If she had stayed she might have pulled the doctor through but it isn't a job I should have relished, and I daresay she'll keep clear of him until he floats into the grave."

When the morning temperatures cooled, and the period of drought was followed by a spell of soft rain and south-westerly winds, Paul rode far afield every day, sometimes alone but more often in the company of Claire Derwent, who showed him the maze of leafy rides between Coombe Bluff and the northern edge of Shallowford Woods and all the short cuts to the Dell, Hermitage, Four Winds and bracken slopes of Blackberry Moor. Together they rode over to visit Lord

Gilroy, in his elegant home, Heronslea, beyond the smaller, parallel River Teazel. Gilroy, stiffly polite, gave them tea in thin Rockingham china and threatened to send the local agent over to Shallowford in order to gather Paul into the local Conservative fold. He did not deign to ask Paul his politics, assuming, no doubt, that he was eager to ". . . stop the damned tide of Radicalism set in motion by that unspeakable bounder, Lloyd George", a politician, his Lordship declared, who should have been strung up on the occasion of his pro-Boer rally, in Birmingham during the war! Paul judged it tactful to make no comment upon this and after an hour or so they left, riding south to the sea, then east along the curving beach to Coombe Bay.

Paul had made one or two expeditions in this direction already but always unaccompanied, for although his thoughts constantly returned to Grace Lovell, and to their three improbable meetings, there was no one in whom he could confide regarding his infatuation. Rudd, he knew, would go out of his way to dissuade him from anything but a formal association with the family and on the one or two occasions he had mentioned her name the agent had abruptly changed the subject. It was clear that he carried his dislike of the family as far as the cadet branch still living on Shallowford property, for he once referred to Bruce Lovell as "a man who could borrow from a Hebrew pawn-broker and later have the man charged as a receiver of stolen goods!" Neither did Paul care to raise the subject of Grace Lovell to Claire Derwent, although their association had been completely circum-spect. He decided that he would like to keep it that way, for she was a merry and informative companion, who seemed to enjoy showing him off to scattered local families, and although she looked undeniably attractive with her corn-coloured curls peeping beneath a hard hat and her pink cheeks glowing with health, she did not stir him in the way that Grace Lovell had when they had met on that first occasion in the nursery, or when she had accepted his gift of the screen at the sale. The screen had been collected the following day and since then he had not even glimpsed her although, on two occasions, he rode slowly past her house in the early morning, and at various times had ridden the grey, now named Snowdrop, along the tideline of the Bay.

The grey's name derived from a remark of Mrs. Handcock's, greet-ing him as he rode down from Priory Wood with, "I zeed 'ee cummin', you an' that gurt beast o' yours! Just like a man zitting atop a gurt bunch o' snowdrops!" and thereafter Paul discarded the grey's Irish name, which was unpronounceable, and settled for "Snowdrop".

So the summer days slipped by, until Eph Morgan announced that renovations were finished, and Mr. Craddock might write to the upholsterers in Paxtonbury for soft furnishings he and Rudd had ordered on their one expedition to the city. The day before they were due to arrive Claire turned up at the house on foot dressed, for once, in blouse, skirt and white, straw hat, announcing that her horse had gone lame and asking if she could help arrange the furniture that was coming.

Paul told her the vans were not due until late that afternoon. It did not occur to him at the time to wonder how she had managed to walk the four miles from High Coombe to Shallowford, on a sultry day and arrive looking as fresh as a spring daffodil. She seemed so disappointed that Paul, telling her that she was welcome to ride Snowdrop home and return him the following day, suggested they took a picnic lunch to Shallowford Woods, returning before tea to receive the vans. Claire brightened up at this and said it was a wonderful idea, providing Paul's leg was strong enough to carry him that far over rough ground.

"Hang it, Claire, I'm not a cripple," he said indignantly. "The hospital surgeon told me to walk as much as I could and since I've been down here I've never been further than the lodge on foot. I'll get Mrs. Handcock to pack up some pasties and tea and sugar. We can make a fire and boil tea if we take my army canteen with us."

They set out in high spirits, following the narrow path along the left bank of the river and skirting the shoulder of the Coombe to the edge of the woods, seeing no one except Hazel, youngest of the Potter children, said to be queer in the head and much given to talking to herself. She was doing it now, staring up at an isolated oak in the meadow and watching something half-way up the trunk. She did not notice their approach and they were thus privileged to overhear one of her impromptu poems.

"I-zee-you-bobtail, a-patterin'-along thicky-bark," she sang. "Youm grey, and a varmint they zay! But I loves 'ee! I loves 'ee bettern'n the red, 'cause youm like me, chaased be everyone, baint 'ee?" but at this point Hazel must have heard their approach over the turf, for she swung round and took to her heels, speeding across the field towards the Coombe and covering the ground as fast as Matabele children Paul had watched in the kraals.

"She's an odd little thing," Paul said. "I don't remember seeing her before. Does she live about here?"

Claire told him that she was Hazel Potter, an afterthought on the

108

part of Tamer and Meg, and was reckoned half-witted on account of her tendency to spend her days roaming the fields and woods, sometimes holding conversations with trees, birds and animals.

"Well, I don't consider that convincing evidence of lunacy," he said. "She's a rather beautiful child and moves as fast as a greyhound. Doesn't she go to school?"

Claire said that she was enrolled at Mary Willoughby's little school but was absent more often than not, for the Potters could not be induced to make her attend regularly but she was clearly not interested in the subject and seemed preoccupied with thoughts of her own, so after watching the grey squirrel dart along the branch of the big oak and disappear into shadows cast by the leaves, he followed into the woods, wading through waist-high bracken to a ride that led down to the shore of the mere opposite the pagoda.

Despite his boast he found his leg tiring and was glad to sit and let Claire gather sticks for the fire. She had thrown aside her wide straw hat while he sat under a willow by the shore, admiring the grace with which she moved to and fro in the scrub, every now and again bending swiftly to add to her armful of sticks. She was, he thought, a very supple creature, with a figure shaped by healthy ancestors, years of hard exercise, and, he suspected, very little farm drudgery. Everything about her was neat, cool and somehow deliberate. She walked with a slight sway, like a tall flower in the wind, so that again he thought of a daffodil growing by a lake and he was glad now that chance had given him an opportunity of seeing her in feminine clothes. On all their previous expeditions she had appeared at the house in a brown riding habit and dull colours, he decided, did not flatter her as much as the cotton blouse and well-cut grey skirt she was wearing today. The water of the mere was very still and he could see the white ruin of the Burmese pagoda hiding in pines on the islet. The air was full of the hum of insects and far across the little lake the reeds stirred, affording him a fleeting glimpse of waterfowl — wild duck, teal or widgeon he supposed, making a mental note to ask Rudd if they ever shot down here.

She came back to him still looking pensive and not much inclined to gossip, so they lit a fire and made tea in his battered canteen, afterwards disposing of Mrs. Handcock's pasties and talking lazily of one thing and another. He admitted then that his leg ached badly and she asked him about his wound. To satisfy her morbid curiosity he rolled up his trouser leg and showed her the bluish depression, where the

Mauser bullet had entered, and the hollow where, after chipping the bone, it had emerged in the bulge of the calf. She studied it with concern, saying that until now she had been unable to relate all the papers had written of the war with actual physical suffering. Down here, she said, it had all seemed like something out of a history book happening to people in another age. Then she became embarrassingly silent again, sitting back, her weight resting on her hands and looking out over the water, so that after watching her slyly for a few moments he surrendered to an impulse that had returned to him since he had watched her gathering sticks. Leaning forward he kissed her on the mouth, not as any young man might claim a kiss from a pretty girl but more as a jocular attempt to re-establish contact between them. To his embarrassment she offered neither protest nor encouragement but continued to smile, saying, with the utmost self-possession "Well, what now, Wicked Squire?" and incongruously he thought of George Lovell's album and the question he had asked himself on the day of the sale when she had surprised him with the mock Bible under his arm.

"You wouldn't know a wicked squire if you met one," he said but at this she laughed and said, lightly, "Don't believe it, Paul! We had one here for years!"

He looked at her curiously then for her remark implied that Sir George's weaknesses were general knowledge in the Valley. "How much do you really know of him, Claire?"

"Oh, that he couldn't be trusted a yard with a girl over fourteen and his son Ralph wasn't much better! Everybody round here accepted that—after all, they had to, for people with that kind of money can behave pretty much as they like, can't they?"

It struck him then and for the first time, that there must be a great difference between country-bred girls like Claire Derwent and their social counterparts in the suburbs, for she, it appeared, could discuss this kind of thing with a man without embarrassment or coyness. More than that; Lovell's eccentricities seemed hardly to interest her.

"You mean you know about his . . . well . . . his photography, a rather unusual kind of photography?"

She looked at him frankly. "Why of course! Everybody did. But who told you about it? Was it John Rudd?"

He told her how he had found the album by chance, admitting shamefacedly that he had been looking through it on the day of the sale, when she had come into the library with her invitation to lunch and at this she gave a little yelp of laughter.

"Oh dear! How awful for you! What did you do with his famous collection?"

"I burned it," he growled, "what the devil else could I do with it?" but she still seemed determined to treat the thing as a great joke.

"I imagine most young men would have kept it for their own amusement and do stop looking so shocked, Paul! Do you think a girl can grow up in a place like this without knowing about things like that?"

"Did he ever ask you to pose for him?"

"No he didn't but he certainly would have if I'd given him half a chance! He did start pawing me in our barn one day and I dodged into the open and fled. But I didn't see anything very unusual in it at the time. Rose was a bit shocked, and thought I ought to tell father; I didn't though, because I thought it was—well—just silly. What I mean is, the Valley girls who did go into that messy little room of his and let him take pictures of them with their clothes off weren't enticed there. They did it with their eyes wide open and for what they could get out of it! I daresay the elder Potter girls' pictures were in that album, weren't they?"

Then, half-consciously, he noticed something else about her, that she was no longer smiling her slightly superior smile but was looking at him boldly as though assessing his mental confusion and perhaps weighing her advantage and his vulnerability; her eyes, watchful as a cat's, never wavered, so that he felt more than ever confused and began to bluster.

"Oh, I daresay you think me a greenhorn!" he began, but that was all he said for suddenly she was lying full-length beside him with his face held between her hands and was kissing him not as he had kissed her a moment since, but in a fashion no one had kissed him before. He was not, however, really aware that the initiative had been hers alone for it had all happened in a matter of seconds. One moment they had been sparring with words, the next embracing with a recklessness that swept away all traces of the restraint that had governed every moment of their relationship up to that time. He thought, fleetingly, of all that possession of her here in the summer woods might entail, a complete surrender of dignity for her and for him God alone knew how many obligations but the check was momentary. The softness of her mouth and the scent of her hair banished the last of his scruples and almost at once he began to assert his mastery, bearing down on her with his full weight, and fumbling at the fastenings of her blouse in

III

his eagerness to use her as she so clearly intended to be used. There was no flicker of tenderness in his handling of her. She might have been the half-caste girl he had purchased for a few sweaty moments in the Cape Town brothel, for when the blouse buttons resisted him he dragged at her skirt and continued to press brutally on her mouth. It was as he sought to extend his grip on her clothes that she somehow extricated herself, taking advantage of the bank and throwing herself sideways so that suddenly she was clear of him altogether and standing between the willow and the water's edge, with her face turned away and her hands busy with her blouse that had broken free of the waistband of the skirt. Watching her from the crest of the bank he suddenly felt very foolish and very deflated, and his shame was not less intense because it was fused with exasperation. He rose slowly to his feet and when she had finished tucking in her blouse, and was lifting her hands to her disordered hair, he began to mumble excuses. They emerged as half-finished sentences, without conviction and without much sense but almost as swiftly as she had left him she was beside him again, and her voice had an almost pitiful earnestness as she said, shaking her head so that pins fell in a shower, "*Don't*, Paul! Don't apologise! Just listen to me, so that we have a chance of starting again, of starting differently!" and when he stared at her uncomprehendingly, "Don't you see? I meant it to happen! Don't you *see*, you idiot?"

He said, slowly, "What the devil do you mean, *you* meant it to happen? I know you didn't mind my kissing you but . . ." She made a gesture and looked so distracted that he stopped, giving them both a moment to compose themselves. It was she who benefited from the pause, for suddenly she was calm again, and said, turning away, "It's just that I lied about the horse. Flash isn't lame. I dressed for the part and then got a lift as far as the lodge in Willoughby's trap. I knew very well that stuff wouldn't be coming until evening and that you would suggest coming here, or somewhere like here. *Now* do you understand?"

"Getting me out here was one thing," he mumbled, still greedy for a major share of the blame, "but don't try and tell me you hoped . . ."

She turned, interrupting him again, and this time she looked angry and exasperated, as though she was prepared to pound the truth into his head.

"Paul Craddock!" she said. "You've got to realise you had no part in it, do you understand? None that you could help that is, so do stop trying to be gallant, and face up to what I'm saying, because if you don't it'll come to you sooner or later, and then it'll seem far worse than it is! Will you listen? Will you stop pretending?"

"Well?"

She came a little closer to him, shaking her hair free and sitting on a stump a yard or so away. "Any man would have acted as you did given the opportunity, any man who was a man, that is! *That's* what I'm trying to make clear to you, and if you think back a little and put two and two together you'll see me for what I am, or what I almost was! I'll tell you again since I have to — I meant something like this to happen, it's what usually happens, it's how most marriages about here begin! The girl baits a trap in the grass and the man walks into it."

He baulked at this, moving swiftly across to her and saying, explosively, "For God's sake stop talking like that, Claire! You'll be damned sorry for it tomorrow!"

"I'm sorry for it now," she said, "about as sorry as I can be. The one thing I'm glad about is that I had enough honesty left in me somewhere to bring me up short at the last moment! Even that I can't take much credit for; if you had been just a little less clumsy I'd have gone through with it all right, and what would either of us gained by frankness afterwards? You would have resented me for the rest of your life I daresay, whereas now—well, at least we can go on being civil to one another!" She got up, brushing the shreds of bracken from her skirt. "Let's get the things and go home."

They gathered up dixie and basket and began the climb up the ride to the edge of the wood but it was not until they were clear of the trees that he spoke again. "Look here, Claire, we could pretend it never happened, couldn't we? Nobody else knows about it! Just the two of us!", and she stopped, looking at him intently, her head slightly on one side.

"Don't deceive yourself over that," she said. "Every busybody in the Valley knows about it! Oh, not that I hatched a silly schoolgirl plot, got you out here and encouraged you to seduce me, but the fact that I had it very much in mind! I could almost hear them as we rode around the estate together—'Claire Derwent is quick off the mark, isn't she? Claire isn't a girl to let grass grow under her feet!'" She gazed around, looking back at the woods, then forward across to Coombe Bluff and the sea. "Sometimes I hate this place and everybody in it! Including myself!", and she walked on so quickly that the effort of catching her up brought a sharp twinge to his wound.

113

CHAPTER FIVE

I

THE yellow-eyed herring-gull who, in mild weather is the scavenger of Coombe Bay fishermen, will fly inland as soon as the autumn gales blow from the south-west and the route he uses whilst awaiting better weather never varies.

He flies inland over the Bluff, crossing in two minutes a cliff that an active man cannot scale in under an hour and heads for Deepdene Farm to see if there are any pickings to be had from the Willoughbys. Then he flies low over High Coombe, veering north-west along the edge of the wind, croaking his way over Shallowford Woods and the mere, and on across the orchard of the big house to Priory Wood and the outbuildings of Hermitage, where he sometimes swoops to steal pig food from the troughs of Arthur Pitts and his son, Henry. Henry usually sees gulls and takes pot shots at them with his rifle, so this heads them into the wind, or almost so, for they fly on south-west by west across the Sorrel to Four Winds and if there is nothing to be had there on again over the moor to the Teazel, and so out of the Shallowford domain altogether.

The herring-gulls are greedy, cunning, inquisitive birds, with little sense of family but they are matchless aeronauts, cresting the strongest gusts and sometimes making pinpoint landings on chimneys and stable roofs to see and hear what is going on in the estate. If they could write diaries and read thoughts it would be possible to know everything that was happening hereabouts for they miss nothing, are witnesses to every trivial incident, and are so common that nobody notices them until they swoop to steal.

It was such a gull that saw Sam Potter and his pregnant wife Joannie loading their few things on to the family cart and setting out for their new home in Shallowford Woods, on the last day of September 1902. The first of the autumn gales had arrived ahead of time and the elms in the Potter Dell were creaking under strong, Channel gusts, with leaves that were still only half yellow floating down on the smoking camp fire over which the rest of the Potters sat trying to look as if Sam's departure caused them more than the minimum concern.

Tamer, as usual, sat removed from his family, on the steps of the ramshackle farmhouse and Meg was off somewhere along the coast selling mats and baskets that the girls had made when the Potters decided that it would be courting sunstroke to work in the fields, but the girls were all there—Pansy, Cissie, Violet and Hazel—talking and giggling among themselves and so was Smut, the poacher, helping brother Sam to stack the waggon with furniture that most families in the Valley would have discarded long ago.

Sam, his big, vacuous face wreathed in smiles and his stiff, carroty hair standing up like a forest of rusty pikes, was glad to be off, but no more so than his wife, for although her time was still two months away she was already enormous and there was little cheer in waddling about a leaking, draughty house where there was nowhere to sit and her gnawing hunger remained largely unsatisfied. She had inspected the little cottage in the woods and was very grateful for this chance to make a home of her own, with Sam drawing regular money at last. Climbing on to the box seat of the waggon she heard her husband warn Smut to confine his expeditions to the west of the estate, well beyond the limits of Shallowford Woods. He sounded apologetic but firm.

"Dornee come my way, Smut," he said gently, for Sam was a gentle man, "dorneé come out-a-long! Just you stay down-a-long or up-a-long, zee?"

To the Potters, indeed to everyone in the Coombe, "out-a-long" meant east, "down-a-long" meant south, and "up-a-long" indicated Priory Wood and Codsall land over the river to the west. Sam reasoned, no doubt, that as a woodsman living on the eastern border of the estate he could not be held responsible for the loss of game, chickens or geese beyond a three-mile radius of his cottage.

"Dornee fret," Smut reassured him, "I'll leave that zide to you, Sam! Anyways, I'll be across the Teazel mos' nights in and about ole Gilroy's coverts. Good luck to 'ee, an' you too, Joannie! If that li'l tacker o' yours be a boy you c'n call 'un Fred after me, for no one yerabouts uses me real bliddy naame, do 'em?"

That was the extent of the Potters' farewells to the eldest of the family and soon after, as the lurking gull rose and flapped inland, the waggon moved off up the steep track and across the meadow where Hazel watched squirrels in the big, isolated oak.

The gull, who should have known better than to waste time looking for scraps in the Dell, rode a gust over the elms and crossed the neglected stubble fields into Deepdene land where the children were in school chanting out spellings like two rows of besmocked choristers and Elinor Willoughby was talking to her hens in the neatly-fenced yard, north of the schoolhouse.

The gull hovered, hoping she would leave so that he could beat in with flapping wings, frighten the strutting cockerel, and grab a beakful of meal, but Elinor did not go away for this morning she had a great deal on her mind and there was no one but the hens in whom she could confide. Her father, the solemn Edwin, who thought of all love as the love of God, had never given a thought to the yearnings of his daughter or her lover, Will Codsall, over the river, whereas Elinor was far too shy to consult her spinster Aunt Mary on such matters as courtship and marriage, so she told her story to the hens who were obliged to listen if they wanted their morning corn.

" 'Tiz cruel," Elinor told the complacent Rhode Island Reds under her feet, " 'tiz cruel, and there baint a particle o' sense to it! I'd make Will a good wife, for I loves 'un as much as he loves me, so why shouldnen us go to Parson Bull an' put up banns, same as anybody else? I wish that mother o' Will's dead, that I do!" and she flung a handful of grain at the nearest bird as though she had been a feathered Arabella Codsall.

The gull heard nothing of all this. He was far too busy watching the scattering grain and had been far out on the sandbanks fishing all last evening, when Will Codsall and Elinor Willoughby had walked hand in hand along the rutted lane east of the woods discussing their dismal situation.

Will had confessed that his mother's nagging was driving him out of his mind, and that she returned to the subject of Elinor Willoughby every mealtime and often in between meals.

"Mazed about us, she be," he muttered, "fair mazed! To hear her prattle you might think you, your father and your Aunt Mary were wasters, like they Potters, yonder! Says I should vind a maid who could bring a dowry to the farm, same as she did, just as if money grew on trees like flamin' plums, and could be gathered all seasons of the year! I said to her, 'Listen here, Mother, *listen*, will 'ee, an' stop yammerin' for a minute, for the love o' Christ! They Willoughbys is decent folk, as good as any family about here, so doan talk about my Elinor as though 'er was hard up for a man, because 'er baint, bein' the prettiest maid in the Valley'."

The indirect compliment pleased Elinor so much that she made

116

light of her future mother-in-law's opposition. Now that dusk had fallen she lost her shyness in his presence and slyly plucked his sleeve as they passed the five-barred gate dividing Deepdene lane from the common pasture that separated the Coombe and the woods.

"Dornee fret about it, Will dear," she said, "it'll come right in the end," and she put up her face to be kissed which was thoughtless of her, for the discussion of his mother, followed by the gentle pressure of Elinor's body, fired Will with impatience to be separated from the one and have the other beside him all night. So he kissed her in a way that startled her, indicating that he might not brook further delays.

He said, gloweringly, "There's talk of a new farm Young Squire's trying to buy, a plaace up behind Hermitage on the edge o' the moor. It's rough land, and not much of it but there's no knowing what us might make of it. For two pins I'd call and ask if us could lease it and they could get along at Four Winds as best they could! The farmhouse is half a ruin, and the outbuildings are cob, with the water running down the walls but it'd be better than nothing mebbe! What do 'ee zay, Elinor? Would 'ee live in a plaace like that, providin' I fixed it up for 'ee?"

"Ay, I would that," Elinor told him fervently, and thought fleetingly of the new Mr. Craddock and all his money and of his junketings about the estate since last June, but before she could speculate on their chances Will, making the most of his time, kissed her again in a way that made her knees buckle and she said, although not very convincingly, "No, Will! Not now, Will, please!" as his big hand slid over her shoulder, across her tight bodice and then below the waist to fondle her little buttocks.

The gull, caring nothing at all for lovers' problems, decided that Elinor would stay in the yard all the morning so he flew off across the slopes of Deepdene to two small fields adjoining the cliff path, where Edward Derwent was leaning on a stile considering what use could be made of his new land and also what had prompted that unpredictable young fellow Craddock to incorporate it into High Coombe without raising the rent. There must, he reasoned, be a hidden motive for such an unrewarding act on the new Squire's part, for Derwent himself had never done anything without a profit motive. He pondered the possibility of Craddock's intention to sell High Coombe, and ask a higher price for a slightly enlarged farm but decided that this was unlikely for two small fields would not merit the addition of twenty-five pounds to the purchase price. It then occurred to him that Craddock might have made him the free gift of the fields at the suggestion of his daughter Claire, and this led to serious contemplation of Claire's involvement with the young fellow and whether it was within the bounds of credibility that he might have a real live squire for a son-in-law. The possibility, remote as it was, warmed his heart. The fellow obviously had a great deal of money (made in scrap iron it was rumoured) and was, on the whole, a likeable chap, as far as a city-bred man could be likeable. Perhaps it was not so improbable; perhaps Claire would steer the Derwents into a lawyer's office where the new Squire, enslaved by his bride's beauty, would hand over the entire acreage of High Coombe for a nominal sum! As he thought of this, and of Claire's golden hair and blue eyes, his stern face relaxed until it was about half-way towards smiling and he reflected that Claire was growing more like her dead mother every day and that between them, they must have been very clever to breed a young chit pretty enough to monopolise the attention of a rich scrap-merchant turned landowner. Then his pessimism caught up with him and he thought of the recent change in Claire, and her solemn face at the breakfast table that morning, and also of her silent withdrawal into herself of late which was very uncharacteristic of his younger daughter. If she was in love, he decided, then so much the better, for that meant that his hopes had at least some foundation and if she was not, and there was no more in this association than a bit of flirting on Craddock's part, then she was probably sickening for something and would doubtless get over it as quickly as she had recovered from chickenpox and measles in her childhood. At this point his practical mind reverted to the use of the new fields. Barley, oats or wheat? He wasn't sure yet, he would have to sleep on it.

The gull decided that there was no profit in hovering over Derwent's unploughed fields and whirled into the wind, coasting along its warm, wet currents to the window-sill of the Derwent parlour, beyond which, through small panes of glass, he could see the fair head of Claire Derwent bent over a letter she was writing. The envelope beside her was already addressed to "Paul Craddock, Esquire, Shallowford House", and the letter was by way of being a distress rocket, fired from a trim vessel adrift on a sea of uncertainty.

Four weeks had now passed since the picnic in the woods and she had not so much as glimpsed him as he rode up and down the Valley,

118

but gossip kept her abreast of his affairs and she knew that the big house was finished and occupied, and that all manner of other changes were in the planning stage. Many times during the month she had called herself a reckless, impulsive idiot, not so much for rushing her fences as for reining back at the last moment, for although, in the early days of their friendship, she had been attracted to him as Squire Craddock, of Shallowford, a wealthy and amiable young man (who would, she supposed, have to marry someone sooner or later) the few moments in his arms beside the mere had wrought a dramatic change in her daydreams. She would now, she told herself, welcome his re-appearance at High Coombe in any role, and his prophecy that she would live to regret her frankness had been miserably accurate, for it surely was this alone that condemned her to sit here inactive for as long as he cared to keep her waiting. Going back over the events of the momentous afternoon by the mere, Claire concluded that she had made three tactical mistakes in as many minutes. She had been far too forward, far too backward and ultimately, far too honest.

At the end of the fourth week she came to realise that her only hope lay in an entirely new approach, and although by no means so devious a young woman as she imagined herself to be, the plan she finally adopted had the hall-mark of first-class strategy in any kind of war-fare; it was simple, direct and preserved an avenue of dignified retreat. She decided to write advising him to give a combined coronation supper-dance and house-warming for the estate tenantry and their dependants, reasoning that even a young man who had held her in his arms would have some difficulty in interpreting this as anything more than a piece of friendly, patriotic advice. If he liked the idea then he could hardly fail to ask for further advice; if he rejected it good manners alone would compel a reply.

The composition of the letter cost her a good deal of thought and effort. Four drafts went into the waste-paper basket (each was torn into fifty pieces and scrambled) and she finally settled for a simply-worded note, pointing out the obvious advantages of such a gesture at this stage of his settling-in period. She addressed him as "Dear Mr. Craddock" and signed herself, "Your sincere well-wisher, Claire Derwent". Then she gave the letter to one of her father's farmboys who passed Shallowford House on his way home every evening, telling him that if Mr. Craddock should make him late when he called for a reply in the morning she would present his excuses to her father, a stickler for good timekeeping. The boy went off tipless, for Claire had no money in her reticule. Edward Derwent did not believe in women having money. It made them uppity and inclined to answer back.

The gull ignored the offal in the private trough of Sarah, the Derwent's prize sow. It looked tempting and accessible from twenty feet above the sty but Sarah had a savage nature and was notoriously averse to sharing rations with uninvited callers. The gull's new line of flight took it north-west across Shallowford Woods and there was nothing to be had in or about the mere, so it passed on, skirting the chimney pots of the big house, sailing into the cobbled yard and cocking an eye at Ikey Palfrey, polishing harness outside the tack-room and whistling the appropriate song from *H.M.S. Pinafore*.

Ikey always whistled at his work nowadays. He liked catchy tunes and he liked his new situation. He had a warm place to sleep, more than enough to eat, a chance to ride real horses at least twice a week and he had formed a deep but unspoken attachment for the "ex-Yeomanry gent" who, for some reason that was still a mystery to Ikey, had winkled him from the scrapyard and set him down in a great country house with, as Ikey might have expressed it, "all the trimmings".

Ikey had long since lost his fear of the countryside and soon replaced his familiar Thames-side landmarks with local ones, like the red, sandstone peak of Coombe Bluff, the steep green incline of Priory Wood, the lanes with broken gates and isolated trees, and the spire of Coombe Bay parish church in the distance. He got along very well with "the local swedes" although, as Paul had prophesied, he had initial difficulty with their dialect. By now, however, he could not only understand the Devon brogue but could speak it like a native. Some-times, to amuse the motherly Mrs. Handcock, he would exchange nasal Cockney for the broadest Westcountry burr, interchanging words and phrases and reducing her to a quivering mass of flesh by his expert drollery. He took a careful note of everything and forgot nothing. Chivers, the rather old-maidish groom whom Paul had taken on, spoke very well of him, and said he had a natural seat and good hands, but most of Ikey's thoughts when he was alone were concerned, in one way or another, with his hero, Paul Craddock. To the boy it still seemed incredible that a man in Paul's exalted position, virtually a king ruling a subject race, should treat him almost as an equal and sometimes, when he rode into the yard to hand over the grey, stay and chat with him about London. As a Cockney Ikey cherished his independence and this easy condescension on the Squire's part was the mark of true greatness.

Gulls do not have the weaknesses of magpies and the glitter of Ikey's polished harness made no appeal to the bird. Soon it flapped over the steep roof and into the forecourt, where the Squire himself was sitting on the balustrade of the terrace munching a pasty as he studied a map that fluttered in the strong gusts blowing from the sea. Rudd, the agent, was beside him but neither man seemed aware of the fact that this was not the best place to study a map measuring three feet by two but they persisted, talking to one another in earnest tones, as the gull edged warily along the balustrade towards the plate on which lay the Squire's half-eaten pasty. Here were pickings to be snatched from men who deserved to lose them and as soon as it was confident the snatch could be carried out with safety the gull swooped and was gone, Rudd shouting an oath and Paul throwing back his head to laugh at the bird's impudence. Then he forgot about the gull and returned to the map, which was one of the reasons why Claire had been left without word of him.

There were other reasons, the chief being that Paul felt that the next approach should come from her. As the memory of the frolic in Shallowford Woods receded it became no more than an embarrassing moment that he preferred to forget, along with all the self-righteous nonsense she had talked trying to explain it away. If she said she had set out to compromise him in order that he would marry her he was prepared to believe her but he was not, at the moment, in the mood to consider marrying anyone, being far too deeply engrossed in his work and in Shallowford. He had discovered that he loved the house now that it was warm, habitable and purged of its gloomy Lovell associations. He liked his big, sunny bedroom and the high-ceilinged reception-rooms, where his few pieces of furniture looked very much at home but best of all he liked his snug, red-curtained library, with its shelves of leather-bound books smelling of comfort, leisure and repose and here he spent his evenings with John Rudd for company, learning about crops and soil and livestock and exchanging stories of African wars separated by half a generation. He liked his staff, who were polite without being servile, and well-trained without being officious. His wound troubled him hardly at all and there was so much to do and so much to learn in this new world that there was always an overspill of jobs awaiting his attention. He thought about Claire now and again but by no means as often as she thought about him. He also pondered, at a somewhat deeper level, Grace Lovell, who had disappeared as completely as if she had emigrated to Australia. Sometimes he thought of them together, comparing their dissimilar natures, the one buoyant and frank, the other withdrawn and secretive. Then, about three weeks ago, Rudd had come in with news of the death of old Hardcastle, the moorside freeholder whose widow was prepared to sell the smallholding, so they went over and measured out the sixty-odd acres, and inspected the ruinous premises and the resultant negotiations had occupied nearly a week, during which time he had not thought of Grace or Claire at all.

"How does it compare with our calculations, John?" Paul asked and Rudd replied "It's an acre or two out in the east and north. These old estate maps are mostly guesswork. When we get time we ought to resurvey the entire Valley and bring the property in line with the national ordnance maps. I could do it myself, with a bit of help from you."

"You see now why I talked you into a three-year contract," said Paul grinning. "Very well, but it's a job for spring or summer, I wouldn't care to footslog over the fields from now on. Let's go into the office and trace the adjustments."

They tramped inside out of the wind and Mrs. Handcock brought them their morning beer. Sir George Lovell would have had difficulty in recognising his former dark-room for it was freshly painted in green, fitted with a small fireplace, a drawing board and had two walls of new shelves and cupboards, together with a large safe for estate documents. The two men settled down over the parchment absorbed and content.

Half a pasty had by no means satisfied the gull's hunger and after disposing of the titbit at the summit of one of the avenue gateposts it took off again, heading due north on the edge of the wind. Its flight led over Priory Wood and on to the plateau of Hermitage Farm, where the Pitts family were discussing new Squire's recent acquisition of the Hardcastle smallholding just north of their boundary. The gull saw nothing of them, for they were all inside the house but as it was not interested in unploughed land it flew on over the Hermitage fields seeking a worm, or an antagonist less formidable than the Derwents' prize sow. A small piece of luck came its way. Earlier that day young Henry Pitts, carrying two swill buckets to his sties, had staggered in a strong gust of wind and spilled a pool of swill on the path. A few other

122

gulls were already there and the lone bird joined them, ignoring their clamour.

Inside the big kitchen old Arthur Pitts was discussing his son's proposal to apply to new Squire for permission to absorb the Hardcastle smallholding into their acreage, offering an increase of thirty pounds a year in rent, but the older man would have none of it. His main interest had always been in market gardening and he had but a poor opinion of old Hardcastle's skill as a farmer.

"Us have got as much as us can handle now," he told his son, "and any money I lay out is going to be for a hot-house over by the hives. You can make a dam' sight more on early veg than on grazing sheep or fattening beef on that bit o' rough land!"

Young Henry had respect for his father's professional opinions, having seen Hermitage grow from a parcel of land not much larger than the Hardcastle holding into the second-best farm in the Valley.

"Arr," he said, gulping a pint of Martha's steaming cocoa, "it was on'y a notion I had, but what'll young Squire do with the plaace, now 'er's got his claws into it?"

"He'll make it pay," said Arthur, sagely, "that's what he'll do with it! For dornt none of you yerabouts underestimate that young feller-me-lad! 'Er knows nowt about farming as yet, but he's not like most lads with money at the back of him! He's willin' to listen an' willin' to learn, and John Rudd'll be better'n a father to him! What did you think of him, Mother?"

"A praper young man, when he's worked through his fancy ideas," said Martha, and young Henry, finishing his cocoa, winked at his father over the rim of his mug. They were a happy, well-adjusted trio and the keynote of life in the Hermitage kitchen had always been tolerance.

"There's one change he'll have to make soon if he really zettles isself in the gurt, empty house," Martha went on, gathering plates and crashing them into the vast tub she used for washing-up.

"Ar, an' what's that, Mother?" Arthur demanded, well knowing the answer.

"A wife, an' one who knows her bizness," said Martha, and she sighed for it was always a matter of regret to her that Henry, now twenty-four, was still a bachelor and seemed likely to remain one. She would have welcomed a buxom daughter to share her enormous kitchen and she sometimes hungered for grandchildren.

Henry might have taken her point and advanced a time-honoured

123

defence based on a preference for his mother's cooking but at that moment the gulls outside began a furious quarrel over the shrinking remains of the swill and shouting "They dratted gulls again!" he grabbed his rook-rifle and, loading as he ran, charged into the yard and fired into the squabbling group but he aimed to scare, not to kill. He was not only a warm-hearted young man but a superstitious one and he knew that every time a seagull died a sailor was drowned, their souls being interchangeable.

The gulls rose in a screaming cloud, circled and flew south in convoy. They read the weather signs and knew that within an hour the wind would abate and they could resume fishing on the beach, where food was plentiful. As they beat into the wind they flew over the Codsall homestead, their quarrel forgotten but as they passed it was taken up in the kitchen of Four Winds, where the smouldering resentment of Will Codsall had finally flared up, and he and his mother faced one another over the long oak table, with poor Martin caught between the hammer of his son's frustration and the anvil of his wife's furious obstinacy.

"You c'n take it or leave it, Mother," Will was shouting, "and that's the last you'll yer from me on the subject! Either me and my Elinor put up the banns on Sunday, an' fix a day this side o' Michaelmas, or I march out o' here and won't wait until Michaelmas to do it, neither!"

"*Neither! Neither!*" sang Arabella, in her high whining voice, "you're already beginning to talk like her! Would anyone ever know you were something a bit better than the yokels who swarm in this Valley? It's a wonderful catch for her I daresay, but what'll she bring with her apart from bad blood? It isn't as if you were kept from the girls, as all the young men were in my day! There was that nice, refined Miss Agate as I asked here to tea in the summer, daughter of a solicitor if you please, who spoke up like a lady, and had a decent education!"

"Aye," said Will, grimly, "and a face like one of our bliddy Friesian cows and she wouldn't ha' taaken a second look at us Valley folk if her mother coulder found her a man back in Whinmouth!"

"You're coarse-minded too," Arabella shrieked, "and it makes me shudder to think what kind of children you and that Willoughby girl would raise between you!"

"Couldn't we have Willoughby over and talk to him?" suggested Martin—courageously for him, for he knew very well the remark would direct the tide of his wife's scorn from son to father.

124

"No, we couldn't!" snapped Arabella, "for I won't give house-room to one o' them Nonconformist Radicals! What are you thinking of, both of you? During the war that man Willoughby prayed in public for the Boers didn't he, and was pelted for doing it! Have him up here for a talk? What about might I ask? Our eldest boy and his chit of a daughter getting wed before Christmas and from then on we should be related! *Related!* To a Coombe family if you please! What have I ever done to deserve this? Haven't I been a good wife and mother to you all? Hasn't this farm been stocked on my father's money? Don't anyone realise how I should feel to see everything I've worked for pass to the daughter of a psalm-singing smallholder, scratching a living out of his chapel collection plate and a few moulting hens?"

Martin Codsall considered this, wondering how far it was from the truth for the Willoughbys, although poor, had never been regarded as anything other than harmless, respectable people and the bitterness of his wife's prejudice against them puzzled him. It might, he reflected, be a pleasant change to hear another woman's voice raised in the kitchen, and personally he had nothing whatever against his son marrying into a Coombe family, so long as it wasn't to a Potter. He would have preferred it to be a pretty girl like Claire Derwent, who had made his mouth water when he watched her waltzing at the Victory Ball in the Whinmouth Assembly Rooms last May, but Will would be of age in a month and could marry whom he pleased, so where was the sense in making such an issue of it? He said, again in a low voice, "I don't want to lose our Will, Mother, I couldn't get along without him. It would mean taking on another man and another boy, and veeding 'em both, six days a week!" He thought this appeal to her pocket might make her think twice but he was wrong, for Will's revolt plucked at the taproots of her authority and in a way she was enjoying the dispute that must end in Will's unconditional surrender. She glanced at the white-faced Sydney, listening to every word and snapped, "Eat up your pie, and sit up straight, Sydney!" Then, like a boxer flexing his muscles before advancing to the centre of the ring, "If Will was so inconsiderate as to run contrary to my wishes I wouldn't receive him into the house again, or his wife either! 'Either' you'll notice, not *'neither'!*" and as though this was her final word on the subject she dabbed her lips with the napkin and cut into another portion of shepherd's pie.

There was a silence, Martin and Sydney looking down at their plates, Arabella looking past them at a brass warming pan over the fireplace. Then two sharp sounds were heard simultaneously, the scrape of Will's chair and the warning rattle of Arabella's cuckoo clock, which always made this sound a second before its doors flew open and the bird bobbed out to cry the hour.

"That's all I wanted to be sure of, Mother," Will said, "I'll be goin' along now, and don't *neither* of you come making a scene over at Deepdene when I'm zettled in! If you do I'll come back and do mischief!"

Arabella dropped her knife and fork and half rose to her feet as Martin stretched out his hand, as though to detain Will by force. Sydney remained quite still, masticating his mouthful of pie the requisite thirty-two times before swallowing.

"You go and I'll harness the trap and come straight over to fetch you back!" shouted Arabella. "I'll make such a fool of you you'll be the laughing stock of the Valley. You an' that girl too!"

Will stood facing her and Martin, looking up, noticed that the muscles of his son's jaw were twitching, and that his big hands, resting on the back of his chair, were trembling. Some instinct warned him that this was a real and final crisis and he jumped to his feet just as the cuckoo appeared at the double doors of the clock. Simultaneously Will's hands left the chair and reached across the table, grasping the heavy crock in which stood the remains of the shepherd's pie. It flew across the room and struck the doors of the clock in the act of closing, splintering them with a crash that sent the Codsalls' spaniel Nell scurrying for the back door. The crock itself, together with all that remained of the pie, ricochetted from the wall, fell on the table and then disintegrated, spattering Sydney with china, mashed potato and gravy, and shattering half the dishes. Sydney screamed and Arabella, after a single outraged yell, burst into a noisy flood of tears. Martin said nothing. He had been Arabella's husband for twenty-one years and therefore considered himself married to her cuckoo clock, a wedding present from the staff of her father's shop. There were no words to express the dreadful finality of such an act. But Will said one more thing as he turned at the door to the hall on his way out. "That's to show I baint bluffing, Mother!" he said. "I'll come back here, and do the same for every stick o' furniture in this house if you show your face at Deepdene arter I'm gone!"

They heard him stump upstairs and drag open a chest of drawers but after that there was silence except for Arabella's sobs and Sydney's intermittent sniffs but the horror of being abandoned by even such a silent ally as his son gave Martin a last spurt of courage.

"Well," he said, "I hope you're satisfied, Mother! I do 'ope you're satisfied!", and he left them to their mourning.

On their flight down to the beaches the gulls passed low over the two chalet-style houses standing in an acre apiece on the ridge above the harbour. The western one, "Channel View", was the home of Captain Bruce Lovell, his wife Celia (neé Winterbourne, of Winterbourne Chase, Derbyshire) and Bruce's daughter, Grace, by his first wife. No vulgar quarrel was in progress here but there was enough tension under the roof to charge a searchlight battery.

Bruce Lovell's second marriage had not been as disastrous as his first, which had ended in his wife's suicide in a Madras reservoir. Celia was a well-bred, handsome woman, who seldom raised her voice, preferring to correct her husband's many failings by more indirect means, such as sentencing him, every now and again, to terms of banishment in the country, or keeping him short of money at the height of the flat season. Bruce was undergoing punishment now and had been, ever since his disastrous losses at Ascot, and an involvement with a little milliner in Camden Town, but his sentence was almost up and he was now watching the calendar like a new boy approaching the end of his first term at a particularly dull boarding school.

Celia had promised him that they would return to town on the tenth of October and he knew her well enough to accept the fact that no social obligations, or pleas on his part would induce her to forward the date by twenty-four hours. They had now been at "Channel View" since the end of June, "a three-months' stretch" as he would tell his cronies at the Club, and it seemed to him a heavy penalty for backing an also-ran in the Royal Hunt Cup, and then seeking mild consolation in a rough and tumble with an amateur tart in Camden Town. He was, however, philosophical, so long as his philosophy could be practised in comfort, and life had taught him that a spree was usually followed by a flick of the whip by those controlling the purse strings. This was the pattern of life for a gentleman without private means of his own and he had followed it uncomplainingly as a cavalry subaltern, a tea-merchant, a stage-door Johnny, a remittance man, a tout, and finally as the husband of the elegant Celia Winterbourne. She paid up but she made him suffer and he was suffering now, by God, from the agonising pangs of country life by the sea. He hated

127

the country. Ennui engulfed him as soon as he saw a ploughed field or a wood and prolonged residence in the country reared inside him a kind of octopus whose tentacles explored his vitals, his greying temples and finally every cell of his brain, so that instead of screaming he yawned until his jaws ached and even the sporting page of *The Times* could arouse in him no more than a candle glimmer of professional interest. Celia knew he was nearing breaking-point and wished now that she had fixed the date for their return a week earlier but the Winterbournes had not made a fortune in pots of boot blacking without showing firmness at factory bench and fireside, so she set her face against a surrender that revision of the departure date would imply, hanging on and watching his long, yammering yawns with a certain satisfaction. It was some consolation for having been obliged to ask her father for an advance in order to pay his bookmaker and for having to listen to an unspeakably coarse private detective's report on what had transpired in a basement flat in Camden Town.

Celia had not minded Bruce's infidelity as much as the smell of the detective's beery breath, or the fact that he wore heavy brown boots with a navy blue suit. She was that kind of woman; little things pleased or irritated her. Bruce's sun-tan, when they first met in Madeira, had been a little thing and so had his discovery that freesia was her favourite flower. Little things both, but enough to encourage her to share life with a man whose sole qualification for a husband was that he looked a gentleman and could even behave like one in public.

What occupied Celia's thoughts just now, however, was not Bruce's breaking-strain, which she could assess out of the corner of her eye but the circumstances surrounding the new Squire's interest in her unpredictable stepdaughter Grace, Bruce's daughter by his unfortunate first wife. When Celia became the second Mrs. Lovell Grace had been seventeen and had spent the greater part of the year at a convent in the Lake District. At that time Celia had nothing against the girl and had set out to do her best on Grace's behalf, arranging a season for her and casting about for suitable escorts, one of whom might ultimately relieve her of the responsibility of a half-grown stepdaughter, but Grace had been unresponsive. There had been a succession of sulks and tantrums, leading, now that Grace was of age, to a wary truce between them. Bruce played no part in this, giving his daughter less thought than a promising colt entered for next year's Derby.

In some ways Celia respected the girl, for at least she had a natural

128

dress sense, caused her very little concern by cultivating unsuitable friendships and was an accomplished horsewoman who could have made herself a national reputation in this field. But Grace's disposition as a whole was baffling, for she was very difficult to type and this made it impossible to plan her future. The Winterbournes had been a very sociable family and Celia, in her youth, had met every conceivable type of young socialite at Winterbourne Chase. She experienced gawky girls, sulky girls, listless girls, dutifully innocuous girls and girls whose homesickness for the gutter led them to consort with grooms and bootboys. Among her friends were women who could be classified as Spartans, blue-stockings, religious maniacs, women who dieted themselves into a decline, and those who over-ate and acquired a matron's figure before they lost their virginity. She supposed that she understood the frustrations of every woman of her own class between the age of thirteen and forty but she had yet to make real contact with Grace, whose personality seemed to Celia a wild tangle of contradictions. That the girl had a good brain she had no doubt. She had heard her converse on equal terms with elderly men, and on subjects well outside the range of a convent-educated girl—Darwinism, the Oxford Movement and Universal Suffrage to name only three, but at Celia's "At Homes" she sat as mute as a mummy, and everyone left thinking her insufferably dull. Some days she looked pretty and on other days she was almost plain, her strange pallor without its lustre, her hair bundled any old how and always short of pins. Usually she had good manners but there were occasions when she behaved like an adolescent bore, anxious to attract attention to herself. She interested men, all kinds of men, but she never showed the least sign of wanting to exploit her conquests and often she seemed to Celia frigid and, what was far worse, aggressively so. In fact, regarding her stepdaughter, Celia was certain of only one thing. The girl hated her father and took no pains to hide it. Perhaps it was this, which, in a sense, was something shared between stepmother and stepdaughter, that encouraged Celia to persist in her efforts to help the child but so far her efforts had gone unrewarded. Grace Lovell continued to walk and ride in a strange world of her own; it seemed to Celia, a friendly, cheerful extrovert, to be a very arid, profitless world.

The incident of the screen intrigued her. She had heard a good deal of gossip about the young man who had appeared from nowhere and swallowed the Shallowford white elephant at a gulp. It was rumoured

129

that his money derived from guns or scrap metal, and Celia, who, to do her justice, was still unconvinced that her own income stemmed entirely from boot polish, fervently hoped that it was the former, for whilst there was a certain dignity in shot and shell there was surely none in old iron. She had been very curious to see the young man for herself and that was why she had nagged Bruce into taking them to the sale but once there, gaped at by every hobbledehoy in the Valley, and inhaling their body odours at close quarters, Celia would have left at once had not Grace insisted on staying to bid for two items of furniture in the nursery. Celia had humoured her because she thought the girl might feel nostalgic regarding her past association with Ralph Lovell, the rackety son of that old rascal Sir George, and when Bruce wanted to go home and asked what purpose there could be in lumbering the house with Ralph Lovell's playthings, Celia told him sharply to hold his tongue and squeezed Grace's unresponsive hand, standing beside her whilst a vulgar farm wife had bid more than the things were worth. Then the curious thing had happened. The lean-faced young man who had bought the estate had topped the bidding and presented the nursery screen to Grace, when, as far as Celia was aware, he and Grace had not even met.

Discreet questioning on Celia's part provided half the answer. Grace said, off-handedly, that she had encountered Craddock whilst riding on the sandhills one morning, but this was enough to set Celia's thoughts in motion along strictly circumscribed lines. Ever since her own nursery days she had been accustomed to think and talk about suitable marriages for this relative or that playmate. She said nothing to Bruce at first, allowing the possibility of bringing these two young people together to mature, but day by day she held the possibility up to the light, searching for possible flaws and blemishes. She discovered none, or none that mattered nearly so much as getting Grace off her hands, in order that she could devote all her time to moulding Bruce into someone for whom it was not necessary to apologise to one's friends.

Only when she was quite ready did she fire her first range-finding shot, aiming it at the neat crease of Bruce's *Times*, behind which he was taking cover after dinner one evening. Grace was not in the house at the time, having gone on a short duty visit to Celia's sister in Derbyshire, so they had an opportunity to explore the possibility at leisure.

"When," said Celia, suddenly, "would it be convenient to call upon

Mr. Craddock?", and Bruce, half-lowering his paper, replied, "Why in God's name should we want to call upon the fellow?"

"Well, for one thing he *is* our landlord," said Celia pleasantly, and Bruce, lowering the paper with a sigh, replied, "My dear; in the course of a life of movement, I must have had a hundred landlords, exclusive of one-night stays. I do not recall visiting any of them socially. Besides, they say the fellow's money comes from a boneyard."

"From munitions," Celia corrected, as Bruce raised his paper.

"A mere matter of processing," he said. "From what little I saw of him he struck me as a common little tyke."

"Perhaps," Celia conceded, "but the fact remains that he is very comfortably off, and has also been showing interest in Grace."

She knew her man. The paper came down again and this time it stayed down. Bruce Lovell was a snob but he never let his prejudices make a fool of him. All the same, he was not yet ready to surrender unconditionally. He said, thoughtfully, "Is that so? Well, I must say it surprises me, but notwithstanding his money I wouldn't care to make a friend of the fellow."

"No," said Celia, with smiling malice, "I don't suppose you would, Bruce. You've never put yourself out to make a friend of your daughter, but even you must see that, things being what they are, it might prove a good opportunity to ensure the girl's future. You recall the terms of my settlement no doubt."

How could he forget them? In the event of her death Celia's money passed directly to her younger sister, and although Celia was the least likely person in his world to reduce him to penury by drowning herself in a reservoir like his first wife, there remained the routine hazards of sickness and accident. He reflected glumly how securely his fortunes would have been buttressed against disaster by Grace's marriage to young Ralph Lovell, for although Ralph had been a younger son the Lovells had never been known to leave money to female relatives.

"Ah," he murmured, "that was a frightful thing, young Ralph getting himself killed in South Africa. He would have made Grace an excellent husband."

"Rubbish," said Celia, emphatically. "Ralph was a young blackguard and would have made her miserable but I daresay she had made up her mind his money was worth it. However, we are talking of the future, not the past. As I said, the new Squire has already met Grace, and there was that little matter of the screen upstairs. It may have

131

been no more than a polite gesture. On the other hand it may have some meaning, for I have a feeling she didn't tell me the complete truth about it. They have probably met not once, casually, but several times, and for my part I think it ought to be encouraged."

"My dear," said Bruce, suddenly feeling cheerful, "I have never quarrelled with your judgment regarding really important matters. I'll have a word with Grace when she returns home tomorrow."

"The day after tomorrow," said Celia, and without another word left him to go up to Grace's room and examine the screen in detail, moving round it much as a conscientious detective might inspect the luggage of a suspect in the hope of finding an overlooked clue.

II

The naïve formality of Claire's note suggesting a combined coronation supper and house-warming amused Paul but it was not until he and Rudd were having their night-cap before the study fire that he read into it anything more than a mild rebuke for his neglect of her.

"Claire Derwent seems to have a good idea here, John," he said. They had recently taken to addressing one another by Christian names and although Rudd had demurred a little, thinking it might encourage familiarity among tenants and staff, it had lessened the age gap between them and generally oiled their relationship. He read the note aloud, glad now that Claire had been discreet in her phraseology, for he knew that Rudd would strongly disapprove of what had occurred in Shallowford Woods.

"It's a better idea than she realises," he said, "but the object behind it is clear, of course. That girl is out to get you and I knew it the day I introduced you to her, but I don't see why we should hold that against her. Nothing wrong in aiming high, if you come into the field as well equipped as she is."

"You think a tenants' supper-dance would be a success? After all, I hardly know most of them. Mightn't it seem a bit pompous and patriarchal on my part?"

"It might in some circumstances but you have a cast-iron excuse in the coronation. There have already been countless local junketings, so why shouldn't we have one at Shallowford?"

He got up, sucking his pipe and stood with his back to the fire. "It's a damned good idea," he said finally, "for it can set the tone for what you want to do down here! They'll love it, every man jack of 'em and it's a pity I can't be here to see you through. However, I've a notion Claire Derwent will take over very efficiently."

"Why can't you be here?" asked Paul, surprised, and Rudd said, "Because I've given my word to attend the Spithead Review. It's my boy, Roderick. He's gunnery officer on the *Crecy* and I promised a long time ago. I haven't seen him in more than three years, he's been on the China station."

"I never even knew you had a son," exclaimed Paul, and Rudd replied with a shrug, "Oh, I told you more than enough of my life-story the day you arrived here! I was married soon after I got my first lieutenancy but Jean died, giving birth to the boy. I was overseas at the time and he was brought up by my sister and her husband and is closer to them than to me. But he's done well, or so I'm told. He doesn't write much, and I suppose his aunt persuaded him to insist on my attending the Review."

Something of the man's acute loneliness and the prickliness it had fostered over the years revealed itself to Paul, helping him to gauge the satisfaction John Rudd had derived from their comradeship, dating from that first conversation on Blackberry Moor. He said eagerly, "Couldn't we have our soirée later in the year when you're home again?" but Rudd said, "No, it wouldn't be the same. All the sparkle would go out of a 'do' like that if it was held after the national uproar had died down. Take my advice, and drop a line tonight to Claire Derwent telling her the idea has my blessing. Then ask her over and rough out some kind of plan. You'll need all kinds of things in the way of decorations, souvenir programmes and suchlike, and that girl obviously has the interests of you and the estate very much at heart. Leave all the catering arrangements to Mrs. Handcock, she'll be beside herself with bustle, and Claire can put you in touch with the local musicians. Mary Willoughby plays the piano well and the shepherd twins at the Home Farm are first-rate fiddlers."

"I'll do that," Paul said, his enthusiasm growing, "but I wish you could be here."

"So do I," Rudd said with a smile, "if only to see the girls scramble for you. By the way, *can* you dance with that leg?"

"I'll have a damned good try, if only in honour of King Teddy," Paul said, and after Rudd had gone home he sat at the library table and composed two letters to Claire Derwent, each covering a single page and respectively numbered "one" and "two".

133

The first was couched in terms that parodied her letter. "Dear Miss Derwent." it ran, "Your note arrived by runner this a.m. Have consulted my estate agent and he approves suggestion in principle. Perhaps, at your convenience, you would call, in order that we might discuss preliminary arrangements for staging some local festivities of a patriotic nature. Sincerely, P. Craddock."

The second letter was an attempt to revive their comfortable relationship: "My dear Claire, What a marvellous idea tucked away in a stuffy little letter! Rudd thinks your notion is just what is needed to play me in and is tremendously enthusiastic, as I am myself. Come on over, you silly girl, and we'll discuss what needs doing. I've missed you very much, but honestly I've been inundated with work and John Rudd keeps me at it day and night! Affectionately, Paul."

He gave both letters to the Derwent farmboy when he called next morning and instructed him to present them in rotation. Then he went whistling about his work, riding over to the Home Farm to discuss the introduction of a new strain of Southdown sheep, afterwards crossing Priory Wood to consult one of Henry Pitts' hired men regarding the construction of a new boundary fence between Hermitage Farm and the new sixty-acre smallholding, acquired from Mrs. Hardcastle. He was back at the house shortly before the lunch hour and was delighted to see Ikey Palfrey watering Claire's bay in the yard.

"Miss Derwent rode in about 'alf an 'our ago, sir," Ikey told him. "She's in the kitchen with Mrs. Handcock."

"Good," said Paul, handing Snowdrop's reins to the boy and watching him lead the horse into the stable, "Do you dance, Ikey? I don't mean 'Knees Up Mother Brown' but real dancing, waltzing and suchlike."

"Lumme, *no*, sir, Mr. Craddock! Why would I want to do a thing like that?"

"Oh, you never know, Ikey," said Paul and left him, with his mouth agape, and went chuckling up the yard steps to the kitchen.

CHAPTER SIX

I

THE soirée organisers soon resolved themselves into a committee of five, with Claire Derwent as an enthusiastic chairwoman. Rudd stood back and gave advice, and Mrs. Handcock made herself responsible for a buffet-supper that promised to give everyone who attended indigestion. Ikey Palfrey ran all the errands and Paul, enjoying every moment of the upheaval, spent most of his time seconding Claire, who added fresh touches every hour they spent together.

It was a happy time for Claire Derwent and her inspiration flowered under Paul's patronage. It was she who discovered how to enlarge the dancing space, recalling that the dining-room and adjoining billiard-room were still connected by a sliding door that had been sealed and papered over. Paul sent for Eph Morgan, the builder, and had him re-open the rooms and build a dais for the musicians at the western end. The billiard-table and heavy furniture were carried away and there seemed to be ample space for The Lancers. Claire also made out an invitation list, the cards displaying pictures of the King and Queen and sat for hours at the library table listing names, checking and rechecking to make sure that nobody in the Valley was overlooked. "Those with young children will just have to draw lots and set up a baby farm for the night," she said. "That way most of the mothers will be able to attend. I make the total of certainties one hundred and fourteen, allowing for child-minders and sickness. Altogether you'll need to write out a hundred and twenty-five invitations."

"Can't they be printed?" he asked, and Claire said they certainly could not because the whole idea of this party was to establish personal contact between the new Squire and everyone between sea and railway line, and therefore letters in his own handwriting were essential. "I'll get Ikey to take a note to the Whinmouth stationers," she said, "and while we're at it we might as well start the decorations. We've only got ten days and we need every moment of them."

In fact it occupied the pair of them exclusively, for two or three days later Rudd left for Portsmouth, and Mrs. Handcock grew very

135

testy under the strain of ordering and preparing huge quantities of food and drink, so that Claire and Paul were left to decorate the huge room unaided by anyone except Ikey. Two huge cardboard ovals, together with the gilded legend "*God bless our King and Queen*", were brought in to dress the walls, so that the two rooms were soon transformed into a vast green cave, lit by strings of Japanese lanterns and hung about with Christmas-tree decorations. The hall beyond became a kind of antechamber, for here Claire (who seemed to have ready access to the most improbable stage properties) hung pictures of Canadian forests, Australian deserts and Indian temples, together with the flags of all the nations, including some who would have disclaimed the suzerainty of Edward VII and Queen Alexandra.

The whole house was turned upside down and soon presented a more disorderly appearance than during its renovation period. Guest-rooms were prepared for those staying overnight, two cloakrooms contrived out of butler's pantry and estate office, washing facilities provided at key points off the main corridor and a dozen trestle tables hired for the kitchen staff, who were promised a Christmas party of their own to compensate them for their labours the night of the ball. For Paul had now begun to look upon it not as a supper-dance but a ball, hardly less important than the recent county event in Paxton-bury. Under Claire's driving force he saw the event mushroom from a local soirée, with a tinkling piano and a couple of amateur fiddlers, into the most important social event in the history of the Valley, and it pleased him to think that it might prove an evening that people like the Potters, the Willoughbys and the Pitts would remember all their lives.

As his excitement increased so he came to take more and more pleasure in Claire's company but although they were often alone after Rudd had left, and Ikey was usually out on one of Claire's missions, there was never a repetition of their mutual recklessness in Shallow-ford Woods and this not because Claire was always in a brisk, businesslike mood, but because of his shyness in her presence, that increased alongside admiration for her ingenuity and her skill in getting the last ounce out of over-worked maids and outside staff, like the head gardener, Horace Handcock, the old-maidish groom, Chivers, and particularly the stable lad, Ikey.

Only on one occasion, when he was helping her down a ladder, did their relationship enlarge itself slightly beyond that of a brother and

136

sister, organising a family party and that was when, in the act of steadying her, he held her by the waist rather longer than was necessary and kissed her lightly on the cheek. She did not acknowledge the salute but neither did she say, as he half expected her to, "Now then, we've no time for that kind of thing!" or some such evasive remark. She merely stood still at the foot of the ladder and said, carelessly, "Thank you, sir!" and then, to his annoyance, Horace Handcock came stamping in with another great bunch of evergreens and they sidled apart.

It was after twilight when she arrived home that night and Rose was anxiously awaiting her at the top of the lane with a lantern. She had driven the trap at a slow walk, for she wanted an opportunity to summarise the events of the last few days, before being obliged to gossip with her father, sister and stepmother, all of whom were showing the liveliest interest in the event.

She had entered upon the task of organising the soirée with enthusiasm but caution. It was obvious from Paul's second note that he had dismissed or forgotten all that silly talk in the wood, although she rather hoped he remembered the moment that preceded it. That he enjoyed her company she now had no doubt but he seemed, in some mysterious way, to have retreated into a kind of boisterous adolescence during their separation. It surprised her the more because, in matters that did not concern her such as the daily issue of orders to Home Farm and estate workers, he seemed at the same time to have enlarged himself and she could see that, even without Rudd's presence to guide him, he had grasped the essentials of administration. He gave his orders in a confident voice and she could have wished that, on occasions, he would employ this tone and manner with her, but he did not, and his deference was the one small cloud on Claire Derwent's horizon during this season and one to which she gave considerable thought during her journey home to High Coombe that evening. "Maybe I'm being too bossy," she told herself, as the trap wheels slipped on the loose surface of the Coombe ascent. "Maybe I should get him to make suggestions and applaud them, no matter how impractical they are!" and then the memory of his hands about her waist and his light-hearted kiss returned to her and she thought again of the hectic moment beside the mere, so that it was fortunate for both of them that the cob knew its way home for it got little or no guidance from the rein.

Paul Craddock too was reflecting on the trivial incident that same

137

evening, as he sat studying the invitation list whilst Mrs. Handcock prepared his supper. Under the incentive of her presence, he decided, the incident in Shallowford Woods had, to some extent, resurrected itself, and with it the distant tinkling of an alarm bell. He would need very little encouragement, he admitted, to whisk her off somewhere on a prefabricated excuse and begin the same kind of thing all over again but there was a very obvious disadvantage in this. The girl had already frankly admitted that she had marriage in mind and at the moment, enjoying the unexpected delights of the past few months, he had no desire to "settle" as they said; furthermore he was by no means certain that he was in love with the girl. He wished then that he had had more experience with women. What use was the ludicrous incident with the saucy Cherry in the barn, or his calf-love for the girl Daphne, or, indeed, the few minutes in the Cape Town brothel, in teaching him how to proceed with a purposeful and bewitching creature like Claire Derwent? He thought hard about the matter most of the evening when he should have been addressing invitations but the only certainties that emerged were that she was a very pretty girl and that he had no intention at all of being rushed into marriage by anyone. Later that night he found some comfort browsing through one of the big leather-bound books taken from a lower shelf. It was a rather windy account of Queen Victoria's youth, and he was a little amused by the admission she had made to Lord Melbourne when she declared that she was very satisfied with her situation and had no wish to marry for two or three years. That, he thought, was precisely how he felt himself. He would marry, almost certainly, when Shallowford was under his hand but not before. The challenge was there and he wanted to meet it, so that a wife and family could wait on events. It was fortunate for Paul's peace of mind, perhaps that he put the book aside and drove himself back to his homework, and thus did not read the pages concerning Victoria's ultimate surrender to dear Albert.

Claire was over again early next day, the last but one before the ball and, as it happened, Paul came forward with a splendid suggestion, without any prompting on her part. When the ballroom had received the last of its finishing touches, and they stood back to review their work, he said, suddenly, "What we need now, Claire, is something to cap it all! Something spectacular, like fireworks!" and then, catching her hand, "That's exactly it! Where could we get ten pounds' worth of fireworks? And why the devil didn't we think of it before?"

"They've been selling them for weeks in Whinmouth," she told him, "but if we want as many as that we should have to go to Paxtonbury, right away. Suppose we both go now, in the trap? We can be back by teatime if we take your cob, for my old Nobby would drag his feet all the way home!"

He was tempted; he had only paid one visit to Paxtonbury and the prospect of the long ride there and back, with Claire on the box beside him, appealed to him but he remembered then that he had not answered a business letter in ten days, and baulked at the prospect of Rudd returning to find the office tray full of headaches.

"I can't go, Claire," he told her, "there's a desk spilling over in the office, and some of the matters have to be attended to before the ball unless I'm to look a helpless, undecisive ass when Rudd comes home. You and Ikey drive into Paxtonbury and I'll wait tea for you. Then Chivers can take you home after dark. We ought to have fireworks, with a set-piece of the King and Queen if you can get one."

She promised to do her best and drove off at once, taking the delighted Ikey for company. Paul watched them leave, spending the next three hours in the office, wrestling with correspondence from seedsmen, county agricultural advisers, dairy contractors, insurance rates and ideas spawned by their observations during rides about the estate during the last three months. He had a bite of lunch and pushed on in the afternoon, so absorbed that he did not notice the sky darkening over the avenue chestnuts or the first slash of rain on the window. It was not until he saw old Handcock run along the rose-garden hedge in search of shelter that he realised that it was now pelting down, and that Claire and Ikey would have a very uncomfortable journey home, charged as they were with the responsibility of keeping the fireworks dry. He went across the hall to warn Mrs. Handcock to have a hot meal ready for them but as he turned for the kitchen archway the front door bell jangled so he retraced his steps, opening the heavy door and peering into the grey murk of the porch. A small bedraggled figure was standing there, holding the handlebars of a bicycle but for a moment he failed to recognise her. Then, as she raised her hand to her dark curls to push them aside he saw that it was Grace Lovell and he hurried out to relieve her of the machine, propping it against the wall. She said, breathlessly, "I'm sorry, I only wanted shelter until it slacks off a little. I was on my way home but the ford is deeper than it looked. The water will go down directly the rain stops, it always does this time of year."

"Well, for heaven's sake come in and dry yourself first," he said,

139

surprised at his delight in her unexpected appearance. "Leave the bike there and I'll get Mrs. Handcock to give you tea. You'll catch your death of cold for it isn't like getting wet on a horse. A horse keeps your blood circulating."

"I've never caught a cold in my life, Mr. Craddock," she said, but she stepped into the hall and he saw to his astonishment that she was wearing one of the new bicycling outfits, a costume that was a shapeless mass of pleats and pockets. He left her spreading her hands before the library fire and told a maid to bring tea and muffins at once. Then he put bellows to the coals and lit the table lamp, aware that she was watching him with the disconcerting concentration he now expected of her. Today, however, there was a difference for her scrutiny did not make him feel inadequate but rather the opposite, as though she was a child who had come in out of the rain expecting a scolding. She looked rather childish, he thought, in that absurd costume, and he decided that he heartily agreed with the people who were currently writing letters to *The Times* complaining that the bicycling craze had robbed young women of feminine appeal.

"I didn't know you were a bicyclist," he said, as the girl came in with the tray and left again, averting her glance from the steaming figure by the fire.

"Oh, it makes a change," she said, listlessly, and then, chafing her hands and looking at the pyramid of sealed envelopes on the table, "Are all those letters invitations for the supper-dance?"

He was surprised by her directness and stopped in the act of pouring. "Why yes," he said, "as a matter of fact they are and there's one there for you, and for Mr. and Mrs. Lovell. You can take it now if you like."

"Who will be coming?"

"Just about everybody," he said, laughing, "at least I hope so. Do you think your father and Mrs. Lovell will accept?"

"Yes, they will," she said.

"You've been discussing it then?"

"Everybody's been discussing it,"

He was pleased without knowing why and she went on, "My father can't actually attend. He's going to London tomorrow, but Celia, my stepmother, will, you can be sure of that!"

She said this almost as a threat and it occurred to him again what an odd young woman she was, for she seemed always to carry on a discussion from out of range, to be standing just inside the boundary of

140

good manners so that it was like talking to a precocious child, in the presence of strangers.

He said, handing her tea muffins, "I trust you'll be coming too, Miss Lovell."

She looked round the room carefully, inspecting the evergreen decorations before saying, this time with a tired smile, "Yes, I will, Mr. Craddock, for Celia, my stepmother, would be annoyed if I didn't. Anyway, I'd like to come now that I've seen all the trouble you've taken. Everybody ought to back you up, for nobody did anything like this for the Valley people in the old days."

"Don't give me the credit," he said. "All the organising has been the work of Miss Derwent, of High Coombe. She's been working on it a fortnight."

"Rose Derwent?"

"No, Claire Derwent, her sister. She'll be here in a moment I hope. The poor girl has driven into Paxtonbury for fireworks."

She nodded, sipping her tea and nibbling her muffin. She ate and drank, he thought, like a fastidious kitten and as he watched her, trying to think of something affable to say, the mystery that had surrounded her from the occasion of their first meeting returned to him, so that suddenly a breakthrough of some kind became a matter of importance to him.

"You keep coming back here, Miss Lovell," he said, "and always under improbable circumstances. Yet it seems to me as if being here makes you unhappy, and talking to me makes you angry—not with me exactly but—well, with yourself! Isn't there anything I can do to make you take me for granted? Almost everyone else is beginning to."

She listened with little change of expression but her pallor intensified a little, and her jawline moved as the small chin hardened. Her inflexibility made him uncomfortable so that he reached for her teacup, saying, "I'm sorry, it's bad manners on my part to say that when we hardly know one another. It's just that—well—we don't seem to make much progress, do we? Let me give you another cup of tea."

When he had refilled the cup and handed it to her he was surprised to see that she looked far more at ease than he felt.

"I don't blame you a bit, Mr. Craddock. The fact is, all the Lovells are odd, and I'm odder than most! Don't apologise for your breach of manners, I should do that, not you. You're wrong about something, however, I don't resent you being here. I did before I met you but I don't now. You'll make a better job of Shallowford than they did,

141

anyone can see that with half an eye, if only because you're an optimist. Coming here doesn't make me unhappy either. I expected it to but it didn't, or not after that second time, when you bought the screen. I suppose I'm curious and that's understandable. I once thought I should be running the house."

"Were you in love with Ralph Lovell?"

"No, never."

"But he was with you?"

"I'm afraid not, and he didn't ever pretend to be, but don't ask me to explain the mystique of dynastic marriages, or 'arrangements'. It has to do with money I suppose, but there's more to it than that. Ralph and I grew up with the thing more or less settled."

"But didn't you even like the man?" he persisted, but before she could reply they both heard the rattle of wheels on the gravel outside and then the heavy creak of the door and a ring of laughter followed by Ikey's explosive "Cor! What a carry-on!"

Her expression changed at once and she said, pulling on her gloves, "I must go now, the rain's stopped," and when he protested, saying it was only Claire Derwent and the stable lad returning with the fireworks she brushed aside his courtesies and hurried into the hall.

"I can get Chivers to drive you back, and take the bicycle in the trap," he argued, but she shook her head and opened the door.

"No, I've got a lamp and it's all downhill. Thank you for everything, Mr. Craddock, and I'll see you on the night. Post the invitation and I'll warn Celia it's coming. Good-bye, and thank you!" and in a swirl of skirts she was gone, yanking the machine round, hoisting herself on to the pedal and thence into the saddle without even stopping to light the lamp on the handlebars.

He called good-bye when she was half-way across the forecourt, noting that she seemed equally at home on a bicycle as riding side-saddle on a horse and then Claire, her skirt splashed with red mud, came through the kitchen arch and he saw that despite her wetting she was in high spirits and grabbing his hands said, "We got soaked, both of us! Just look! But we got the most wonderful fireworks you've ever seen and I wrapped them in an oilskin as soon as the rain came down. Ikey's unpacking them now and putting them in the still-room. Is there any of your tea left, while Mrs. Handcock makes fresh?"

He felt a little bewildered; the contrast between them was so great. "I've had a visitor," he said, taking her into the study and removing the fireguard so that she could enjoy the full benefit of the heat.

"Someone else came in out of the storm, and had to be warmed inside and dried off outside."

"Oh, who was that?"

"Grace Lovell, the girl who was to have married Ralph."

"Her? What on earth did she want?"

He was too preoccupied to notice that the laughter left her eyes, or that her voice now had an edge.

"I told you, she came in out of the storm, she was riding a bicycle and wearing one of those awful cycling costumes. I gave her tea and muffins, it was the least I could do, wasn't it?"

"Yes, I suppose it was," she admitted doubtfully, and then, "Didn't you bid for something for her at the sale?"

"A nursery screen she seemed to want. She was mooning over it the night I first arrived here. Do you know her? She seems to know you and Rose."

"I know her father is a bad hat, and she gets on better with her stepmother than with her father. What did you talk about besides me?"

He did not miss the reproof this time but met it good-humouredly.

"She implied that you were the Belle of Sorrel Valley, and I said I had heard as much but thought it rather undignified for the Squire to compete with all the other chawbacons in the Valley! I said you were employed here as an apprentice parlourmaid, but had agreed to help out as an interior decorator for the party. She said—" but by now she was mollified and flaring her skirts to the blaze, said, laughing, "I don't believe either of you mentioned me! She was probably too busy telling you you'd never make a go of this place. That was what everyone of them except me believed when you came." Then, changing the subject very pointedly, "That cob Rose sold you is a corker! He didn't drop below a trot all the way from Teazel Bridge, and I didn't have to flick the whip once!"

Over her shoulder he saw her reflection in the fireplace mirror. In the bright lamplight her cheeks glowed and her eyes shone with health. He put his hands on her shoulders and pulled so that her weight rested on him lightly and he could kiss the damp coil of hair above her ear.

"You look prettier than ever when you're soaked through," he said. "I was an ass to send Ikey. If I'd have driven we could have stopped somewhere, until the rain eased off," and he would have turned her and kissed her lips if, at that moment, they had not heard the rattle of

143

crockery outside as Mrs. Handcock bustled in, barging the door open with her enormous hips and exclaiming, "Mazed you be! Sixteen mile there, sixteen mile back, an' all ter vetch a bundle o' Roman candles! You too, Mr. Craddock, surely youm old enough to know better! That Palfrey varmint coming into my kitchen drippin' wet, an' Miss Claire here like to catch her death!" She swept the corner of the table clear and set down the tray with a crash. "There, get a hot drink inside 'ee and then strip they wet things off an' give 'em to me to dry!" And so the moment passed, and Claire began to chatter gaily about the fireworks, the storm and the wonderful paces of the new cob but he was not really listening finding that his mind, unaccountably, was elsewhere, following a small figure in a bicycling costume down the long hill into Coombe Bay, up the harbour slope to an ugly Victorian villa and into a room where the screen might remind her of him. And Claire, although she continued to chatter of fireworks, was half aware of the fact.

II

At ten minutes to midnight, on a clear September night, the Shallowford House Coronation Supper-Dance and Soirée had run about half its course. Dancing had been promised until dawn to those who intended to stay, but already, four hours after the opening Paul Jones, the party had lost the brittle civilities that had bedevilled its first hour or so.

The sluggish start had been no fault of the musicians. Mary Willoughby at the piano, and the two biblical shepherds, Matt and Luke, as fiddlers, had played with gusto from the moment Paul made a formal round of the ballroom, hall and terrace and coaxed self-conscious couples on to the floor. Now, after a noisy set of Lancers, the Boston Two-Step, two waltzes and a break for ices, the atmosphere had thawed a great deal and Claire had made up her mind that the event was building into a spectacular success. A second Paul Jones was a riot, even Mrs. Codsall joining the ring to be caught by a grinning and half-tipsy Tamer Potter, who swung her round the floor at such a speed that she had no chance to escape nor breath to protest.

From the forecourt the din rose like a waterspout, soaring into the night sky and making every roosting bird in the Home Farm coverts fidget. Standing half-way down the drive the tinkle of piano and the scrape of violins were puny, intermittent sounds all but submerged in the roar of voices and crash of feet, in sudden shrieks of laughter and the long rolling clatter of crockery, as Mrs. Handcock and her sweating team plunged mugs and ice-cream plates into vats of near-boiling water.

Almost everybody in the Valley was now inside the house or, in extreme cases (like that of seventeen-year-old Violet Potter), in the shrubberies surrounding the house, but Claire had badly underestimated the final tally of guests, for labourers' wives from the Gilroy Estate had been recruited as Sorrel Valley baby-minders. The only family so far unrepresented was the Bruce Lovells, of Coombe Bay, who had sent a message to say they would be late. Paul was too busy and far too elated to miss them, and Claire privately hoped they would not appear after all, for she had not quite forgotten Paul's vacant look after Grace Lovell had cycled home the night she had returned with the fireworks. It was not a serious worry, however. She too had her hands full, supervising the staff, the refreshments and even the run on the cloakrooms, and re-introducing Paul to late arrivals, whispering their names to him when they were still out of earshot.

The Potters had arrived *en masse* in a farm cart, every single one of them, including the pregnant Joannie (who spared the company's blushes by staying to help in the kitchen) and Hazel, the youngest Potter girl, who found herself a seat high up on a pedestal shorn of its bust and moved well back against the billiard racks. From here she could look down on the throng with her large, wonder-struck eyes, unnoticed by anyone except Ikey Palfrey, who, in his uncomfortably stiff collar prescribed by Chivers, the groom, had spotted her perch and staring up at her, shouted, "You look like a statcher up there, kid!" a remark, which, although made with friendly intent, caused Hazel to shoot out her tongue and put her thumb to her nose, a gesture that made Ikey slightly homesick for Bermondsey.

All the Derwents, together with their staff, were present, as were the four Willoughbys and the four Codsalls, with their hired hands. Three waggonettes had driven over from Coombe Bay, bringing many of the tradesmen and all the artisans, including Eph Morgan, who was already engaged in disputation with Derwent's foreman, Gregory, concerning the advantages of free trade over tariff reform. They could hardly hear one another but were enjoying themselves, for Gregory was the honorary treasurer of the Whinmouth Conservatives and Unionist Association and considered it his duty to engage the Radical, even at a coronation ball.

Parson Bull looked in for an hour or so but left early, despite

145

generous brandies. The vicar was a little confused by an event that, so far as he could recall, had no precedent in Valley history. He supposed there was nothing basically wrong with farmers and their hired hands making brief holiday once in a while, and there was, of course, a loyal excuse to be found in the coronation but at the back of his mind he found new Squire's common touch disconcerting and he was not easily disconcerted. Anyone else, he thought, as he drove off, could have been scolded in public for encouraging so much dangerous familiarity inside the walls of the manor but it was difficult to challenge a man who held the gift of part of his own living in his hand, and that in coronation year, so all he said to Paul on leaving was, "Well, don't let 'em drink too much, Craddock! If you do you'll regret it for there's no holding one of 'em once they're well liquored!" The admonition annoyed Claire who said, tartly, "That's rich, coming from him, a sponge in a dog-collar!", and she flounced off to confer with Mrs. Handcock on the supper relays.

Paul, primed in advance, chose a fresh partner every time and steadily worked his way through a rota of Mrs. Codsall, who was in rare good humour, Rose Derwent, who found it difficult to allow herself to be led after breaking so many horses, Meg Potter, the stern-faced gypsy, who marched round the room like a Hanoverian Grenadier, and the shy, eager Elinor Willoughby, who blushed scarlet when he took her hand, and mumbled replies to all his polite remarks. After that he joined Eph Morgan's set for the Lancers, and when it was over, perspiring from his enormous exertions, he sought out Claire and dragged her on to the floor for the Military One-Step. "I've earned more than this tame dance," he said, swinging her round in a final flourish and she replied, breathlessly. "We're not going home yet, are we?" and he left her to announce that, after the statue dance (which carried a prize), there would be first supper for those who were not remaining until morning and after that fireworks in the paddock, and finally a second supper for the bitter-enders. There was a good deal of ooing and aahing at this, and when the orchestra climbed down about forty of the middle-aged guests pushed their way into the hall, where a buffet supper was laid for them on trestle tables reaching from the hall door to the porch. After a hasty swig of lemonade the tireless trio returned to play supper music but the piano and fiddles were soon swamped in the roar of conversation and the rattle and clash of plates, cups, spoons and forks.

Mrs. Arabella Codsall was holding court below the big fireplace. Words flowed from her with her usual spontaneity but her tone was comparatively honeyed for her subject was the new Squire, and she wanted it known that, so far, she wholly approved of him and all his works. There were some present, she qualified, that Mr. Craddock might well have overlooked when compiling the invitation list. Nobody, for instance, would have missed that scoundrel Potter and his draggle-tailed brood but she supposed that dear King Edward, God bless him, had been called to rule over even such as these and she was ready to forgive a new man's difficulty in assessing the Potters and the Willoughbys for what they were. Martin Codsall, much embarrassed, whispered, "Shush, Mother!" but as Arabella's audience consisted of Martha Pitts, and the din was so great that even she heard less than half the words uttered, the warning was unnecessary.

Arabella Codsall's good humour was due, in the main, to the absence of her errant son Will but had she been privileged to see round corners it is doubtful whether any amount of cider cup would have prevented a shift in the wind. At that moment Will Codsall and Elinor Willoughby were face to face in the shadow of a stone buttress on the east wing, as far as they could get from the ballroom without breaking cover, and Elinor was having some difficulty in preventing a scene that would have anticipated the promised fireworks display.

"Dornee, think I'd *like* 'ee to cum inzide, an' 'ave 'ee swing me round, Will?" she said earnestly, "but where's the zense in it? Your mother'll up an' leave an' new Squire will want to know why, and where will us be then?"

"Dammit woman, she knows I'm livin' over your plaace, don't 'er?" demanded Will. "Us 'ave made sure us can't get married 'til January, when I'm twenty-one, unless us goes to court and if us does that the whole Valley'll know anyways!"

"I daresay," Elinor said shrewdly, "but let 'em get to know in dribs and drabs, not all at once with us bang in the middle of it! No, Will, us've talked it over with father, and he's promised to marry us in chapel on your birthday, so do 'ee let well alone an' go along home to baid, like you promised me!"

The distant music, and the softness of her body under the little gingham dress she wore, tested his resolution but he abandoned his protests and kissed her almost reverently on both eyes and the tip of her nose. Then, with a desolate, "Oh, Will . . . !", she left him but

147

he did not return home, as he had promised. Instead he continued to skulk within earshot of the party, scowling at the rustlings and gigglings that emerged from the rhododendron walk where Pansy Potter was sporting with a young fisherman from Coombe Bay — "Having her turn" — as she put it, for the Potter girls, although enjoying far more personal freedom than any of their contemporaries, realised that Tamer would disapprove of a family exodus from the ballroom and had agreed to take the air one at a time. Violet and Cissie were now back in the house and Pansy would be returning shortly in order to let Cissie take another stroll, perhaps with the same young man. The Potter girls were practical Communists. They shared men much as they shared rabbit pie, helping themselves to wedges whenever they felt like it.

As it happened Tamer had not missed them. He was in the yard with Sam, enjoying real beer from his own cask that he had brought along in the cart and offloaded into an outhouse. Tamer distrusted other people's liquor and on occasions such as this liked to top off every now and again with a brew on which he could rely. He was also glad of the opportunity to have a chat with Sam, always his favourite, and father and son were discoursing on the local changes that had been wrought since the end of the summer drought.

"Be'm proper mazed do 'ee think, Sam?" Tamer asked, nodding towards the house. "Is 'er goin' to keep this up, or will us vind us all have to pay for it, bimeby?" He found it difficult to believe that benevolence, on the scale practised by new Squire, could endure unless it was buttressed by an increase of rents all round but Sam reassured him. "Dornee worry about Mr. Craddock, Father! He's got religion, I reckon, on'y it don't show like it do in looneys like ol' Willoughby, who won't part with a bushel of maize unless youm prepared to pay in prayers an' hymns! No, he's different, for he don't want nothin' back for it, if you get my meaning! Think on this now — he rides up to my cottage a week ago and asks after Joannie, saying our tacker will be the first born to a tenant zince he took over. Brought along a bag o' seed for the patch and told her she was to have all the milk an' eggs she liked from the Home Farm, until we was zettled in, and had goats an' vowls set up at the back! Now could a man zay fairer than that? And him a gentleman, already paying for the roof over our heads?"

"No," said Tamer, impressed but not wholly convinced, "I don't reckon he could, but to be on the zafe zide you'd best ask him to stand

148

in as godfather when Joannie's nipper shows up! That way mebbe you'll get free milk an' eggs for the rest of your life!"

Sam nodded, admiring his father's far-sightedness. "Reckon I'll do that, Father," he said, "and now me an' Joannie had best get back along. Us can't bump along over they ol' tracks, with her zo near her time," and he carried Tamer's cask back to the outhouse and camouflaged it with straw.

Meg Potter sat with her back against the cue-rack, under the spot where Hazel squatted on her pedestal. Her expression was inscrutable, so that it was difficult to tell whether or not she was enjoying the spectacle of the dancers or despising their enthusiasm for the polka. The tactics of her elder daughters to mask their constant comings and goings had not fooled her for a moment but she was not concerned with their reputations or whether their repeated disappearances into the shrubberies resulted, nine months hence, in the appearance of yet another mouth to feed in the Dell. She took an extraordinarily broad view of life, all life, not simply that part of it prescribed by changing codes of social behaviour, for although she had left her tribe at sixteen to settle as the wife of a squatter, she was still very much a gypsy, with a gypsy's contempt for settled living. As long as the girls provided enough pence for necessities it was all she asked of them, or of her husband and sons. She was loyal to their clan but she did not love or respect them as individuals. All her respect was reserved for her second son Smut, who alone had inherited the spirit of her ancestors and was ready to challenge authority in every form and remain wholly free, not partially so, like her husband and the others. Smut had always been the exception. He looked like a gypsy, with his crow-black hair, swarthy complexion, and his curious, bouncy walk, as though wherever he trod he anticipated the snap of a mantrap. Mantraps were against the law now or so they said but Meg didn't believe it. A man like Lord Gilroy probably sowed them in his coverts, just as he was known to have issued orders to his keepers to shoot poachers on sight, but these hazards did not keep Meg awake at night, when Smut was out across the Teazel. She had faith in his skill and speed, in his ability to hear and interpret any movement in any patch of undergrowth and judge the thickness of shadows, and the distance of sounds. Smut could smell a Gilroy keeper at seventy yards, and move over the ground at night faster than any fox and almost as silently. So she sat erect, watching her favourite child casting his spell over Margy

Voysey, the Coombe Bay butcher's daughter, reflecting that he was a rare boy for his work, for even on a gala night such as this his mind was on his markets. She wondered if Smut would ever marry and decided that if he did he might do worse than pick someone like Margy, who could at least provide a legitimate outlet for his game. She watched him take the dumpy butcher's daughter by the hand and lead her gallantly on to the floor, and then she fell to a contemplation of ballroom dancing in general. It was not really dancing at all, she decided, just a sweaty clasping and a prancing about, like a lot of fox cubs at play. She could remember real dancing, in the light of pine torches and great, blazing fires, on the occasion of gypsy weddings long ago and for a moment she regretted the passage of the years. Then Smut and his partner swept by and her eyes glowed with pride; Smut was worth all the hard work and loss of freedom of the last two decades.

Claire Derwent carried her glass of lemonade to a corner of the backstairs where she could remain detached from the throng but stay within reach of it. She wanted a few moments alone in order to savour her triumph, for it was clear by now that the party—*her* party as she thought of it—was a triumph. She had been worried by its sluggish start, assured that an anticlimax would dowse her in ignominy, and undo all the good work that had been achieved since the moment of her inspiration three weeks ago. But there was nothing to worry about now; Paul was launched as Lord of the Valley and it was she who had, so to speak, broken the champagne bottle. Every day since he had answered her letter she had been growing more indispensable to him and now it was obviously a pleasure to him to seek her advice. She was equally sure that she was deeply in love with him, there could be no doubt as regards that, either. Of all people in the Sorrel Valley she alone understood his potential, and luck, encouraged by her initiative, had chosen her as his impresario, so she sat on, enjoying her moment of solitude and wondering if he would come seeking her during the supper interval. Fireworks were due in twenty minutes so perhaps he could then spare a few minutes from his obligations as host to stand close to her in the dark, watching the first rockets soar over the avenue chestnuts.

Paul did not appear but her sister Rose found her, elbows on knees and glass in hand, and because there was a deep affection between them Rose recognised the satisfaction in Claire's eyes, saying generously, "It really *is* a success, Claire! Everybody says so, even Father!" and then, cautiously, "I *do* hope Mr. Craddock appreciates all you've done! I don't suppose you've had time to talk to one another tonight."

"We had one dance," Claire said, so dreamily that Rose laughed, "I expect he'll stand with me to watch the fireworks. Do you think you can get Father and Liz to leave soon? After all, you'll be staying, so he oughtn't to mind, with so many people about the house,"

"Oh, he's on your side all right," Rose said, and then, fearful of probing too deeply, "Has . . . has he *said* anything, Claire? After all, you've been over here a great deal lately."

This time it was Claire who laughed. "Oh, there's always been somebody else around for a party this size doesn't organise itself! No, he hasn't actually said anything but does he have to? I mean, at this stage?"

"I'm afraid I wouldn't know," said Rose and Claire, because she was feeling more elated and secure than she ever remembered, threw her arms round her sister's neck and kissed her, exclaiming, "Dear Rose! I'm so lucky to have you! And someone will show up for you, just see if he doesn't! I'll tell you what, if—when—anything does happen, I'll persuade Paul to fill the house with chunky, hard-riding, sporty men, the kind who always have taken more notice of you than me. We'll select our victim and stalk him and he won't stand an earthly against three of us!"

"Oh rubbish!" said Rose, sincerely, "I'm quite content to stay single but you wouldn't be! I only hope Paul Craddock has the sense to appreciate you before somebody else grabs you! Come on, he'll be looking everywhere for you, and the fireworks are due to start any minute."

They went downstairs hand in hand and met Paul coming up. Claire shouted, "Paul, dear!" but Rose, perhaps because she had ridden so many half-broken colts was immediately struck by the exuberance of his stride, so that a prick of uncertainty punctured her serenity. His expression was odd too; the tolerant might have called it radiant, the more sophisticated fatuous. He said, without any attempt to conceal his excitement, "They've arrived! They're *here*!", and when Rose asked who had arrived he caught Claire by the hand and said, "The Lovells! Grace and her stepmother! They're downstairs, drinking hot cocoa! They drove over in an open gig!", but by now Claire's serene expression had clouded and the shock was considerable as she read

151

into his voice and manner a great deal more than Rose. She withdrew her hand from his and said quietly, "I'm sorry! We've run out of glasses, Paul!" and scuttled away, running back upstairs and down the corridor, as though making for the room they had converted into an extra cloakroom. He looked after her so blankly that Rose, in a sudden rage, wanted to strike him across the face. His insensitivity maddened her and she could have cheerfully flung him down the stairs. Instead she excused herself and hurried after Claire, so that he thought, briefly, "They've had a tiff over something," and went downstairs again, joining the group standing round the open fire, listening respectfully to Celia Lovell's praise of the decorations.

III

He never discovered how close Grace and Celia came to not making an appearance at all. Two of his tenants could have told him as much but neither of these was actually present when the Lovell gig stopped in the forecourt and Paul, warned by Mrs. Codsall, came running to help them down, direct the driver round to the yard and ask Mrs. Handcock for hot drinks for the late arrivals.

The first person to see the Lovell gig *en route* was Edward Willoughby, who was walking along the river road on his way from Deepdene. Willoughby had politely declined his invitation, for he disapproved of strong drink and also, although to a somewhat lesser degree, of dancing and non-sacred music. But there was nothing in the Bible against fireworks so he let his daughter Elinor persuade him to walk over in time to see the display. It was a fine clear night and he enjoyed his walk, seeing no one until he emerged from the Coombe track and joined the river road, where it ran towards the ford. It was here, under a mile from Shallowford, that the Lovells overtook him and then, to his surprise the gig pulled up a hundred yards further on and made as if to turn.

Will Codsall saw it about the same time from the far side of the ford, where he was enjoying his sulk while awaiting the fireworks and the seeming indecision of the driver puzzled him. He stood in the shadow of the gate, watching, and the murmur of women's voices raised in argument reached him.

The gig had stopped because Grace Lovell had called over the rail to the hired driver and then Celia had countermanded the order, and Grace had repeated hers, so that the man swore softly under his breath and halted while they made up their minds which way they wanted to go. Both women found it embarrassing to state their case in the presence of a part-time coachman but there was no alternative, short of getting out and continuing the dispute on foot.

"Grace, please don't be so tiresome!" Celia hissed, "we're almost there, and we've simply got to go! We told Mr. Craddock we should attend and it would be extremely rude of us not to at this stage, do you hear?"

Grace said nothing, being more inhibited by the coachman's presence than was Celia, so that after a moment, with a cautionary nudge of the kind administered to a wilful child, Celia told the driver to get started again, and the gig rattled over the ford and began to breast the slope of the drive. Neither passenger spoke another word until Paul greeted them at the forecourt and then Celia, an expert social liar, said sweetly, "We do apologise for arriving so late, Mr. Craddock! We had the *greatest* difficulty hiring transport," and Paul said, handing her down, "I'm delighted you got here in time for the fireworks but you must be cold! Let Mrs. Handcock get you hot drinks!"

They went into the hall, where their appearance caused a little stir among the supper guests, for apart from Parson Bull quality had been noticeably absent from the ball. Mrs. Codsall bridled, and dropped half a curtsy, while all the younger women stared enviously at Grace Lovell's gown, a many flounced affair of scarlet silk that whispered as she walked across to the fire and spread her hands to the blaze.

"Oh, but she's beautiful!" Elinor Willoughby said to Pansy Potter, who was gaping at the late arrivals and Pansy, her big red hands smoothing the serge of her stained, grey frock, murmured, "Ah, 'er is an' all! Like a princess, an' Mrs. Lovell along of 'er," which expressed, fairly adequately, the opinion of every other woman present who watched their entry.

The Shallowford House firework display began with a single rocket that soared over the chestnuts and fell, a far-off ember, on the Home Farm stubble three parts of a mile away. It ended with a large and rather smudgy set-piece of Queen Alexandra, Claire having been told by the dealer in Paxtonbury that all the set-pieces of the royal pair had been sold out long ago.

Between the rocket and the set-piece some thirty-five minutes elapsed, a split second in eternity and only about a sixteenth of the time spent by most guests at Shallowford that night, yet this was

153

enough to mould the destinies of fourteen men and women who stood among the hundred and twenty spectators.

Out here in the open, with the undersides of the chestnut leaves exposed in the lurid glow of Roman candles and the dark mass of Shallowford Woods rising behind the rose garden, the company seemed small and subdued. In the house there had been barely room enough to hold them and they had drawn courage from one another, performing prodigies of chaff and buffoonery, but out here they were awed and hushed, because the harsh glare of an exploding firework is not natural light, like that of sun, moon, or even lamp oil but has a talismanic quality that can betray the future to those who follow its path across the sky and watch it die. There were some who neglected to do this on the night of the Shallowford soirée, in late September, 1902, and each of them paid forfeit. It was not, after all, a very spectacular firework display, so perhaps its yield in heart's-ease or heart-break was out of proportion to the ten pounds Claire had paid for the rockets, Roman candles and rip-raps, but fireworks are unpredictable. They did their work and burned themselves out; what happened as a direct result to those on the ground was no concern of the men who made and sold them.

Perhaps the golden rain had the most to answer for in emotional by-products. Horace Handcock, cannoneer extraordinary, had planted a row of six to follow the initial discharge of his battery of sixpenny rockets and cries of delight greeted the first shower of green and crimson balls, erupting over the chestnuts and hanging suspended for a moment before drifting down and out of sight behind the trees. In the light of the shower of green balls Smut Potter made up his mind to remain a bachelor, while Walt Pascoe, a Coombe Bay bricklayer whose body and brain had been thrown in a ferment by the Potter sisters, made his choice, but these were only the results of the first discharge. As the second shower burst Edward Derwent came close to breaking his wife's heart, whereas Paul Craddock had a clear thirty seconds to study Grace Lovell's profile, not long but long enough to fall so madly in love with it that there was no hope of disguising the fact from anyone, certainly not Derwent or his daughter Claire, both of whom were watching Paul intently. At the third discharge, when both crimson and balls shot up and floated down, Mrs. Codsall saw the spare figure of Preacher Willoughby on the far side of the little square, and beside him, arms linked, her son Will and Willoughby's daughter, Elinor. She waited until the fourth discharge to make quite sure and then, with a squeal of rage, thumped Martin Codsall between the shoulders and roared, "So he's here after all! Look over *there*!" and Martin, following in the direction of her stabbing finger, caught a glimpse of Will and Elinor as the last laggard ball drifted behind the trees.

Of these few only Smut acknowledged his debt to the fireworks at the time. He had emerged from the steamy ballroom half-disposed to invest in the future and supply himself at one stroke with a dullish wife and a helpful father-in-law. For some time now he had been improving his relationship with Tom Voysey, Margy's father, possibly the one father in the Valley who would welcome such a wastrel into his family. The Potters, notwithstanding hearty appetites, had rarely been able to eat all Smut brought home from the Gilroy and Shallowford coverts. Sometimes there was a glut in the Dell, so that Smut had sought an outlet for his spoils in Coombe Bay and Tom, of late, had been buying his poached game at about half its market value. Smut, however, did not really poach for money but mainly to keep the family fed, and also for the hell of it, so he was happy to dump hare, pheasant, trout, conies and even venison in Tom Voysey's scullery behind the shop and go home with a half-sovereign in his pocket, knowing full well that Voysey's profit at Whinmouth weekly market would approach four hundred per cent. It had occurred to him lately, however, that if he became Voysey's son-in-law, as well as Voysey's main source of supply, he might in time become rich enough to buy his mother the painted caravan she had always coveted and give his sisters shop dresses, and himself green velveteens, a moleskin waistcoat and perhaps a good gun into the bargain. He was not ambitious but he had a strong sense of family loyalty, and to demonstrate it was almost prepared to marry a girl with two heads. Margy Voysey had one head but it was large, seemingly almost round and crowned by a topknot of mouse-coloured hair. More hair sprouted from a large mole on her receding chin but, as if to compensate for this, she had no eyebrows and lack of them gave her a permanently surprised look, so that sometimes Smut thought that her decapitated head, set alongside those displayed in her father's window, would have fooled all but the keen-sighted. He had remarked on this several times but it had not impressed him, one way or the other. Margy was Tom Voysey's only child and what she looked like had not seemed to matter at all until those revealing green balls in the sky exposed her face at close quarters. He made up his mind on the spot; Meg must continue to inhabit the leaking farmhouse, and the girls continue to wear rags, until he could hit on an alternative solution to comfort them. The gun he possessed was good enough for another season, and he would remain content with Voysey's half-sovereign. There were premiums that were too stiff for an insured future and marriage to a greenish-tinted pig's head was one of them. Mumbling, "Just thought o' something I got to do, Margy," he relinquished her hand, dodged out of the crowd and vanished into the starry night.

Edward Derwent had been his crusty, pessimistic self when he arrived at Shallowford that evening. Rose, his daughter, and Liz, his twittering second wife, had done their best to persuade him that something momentous was happening—that Claire's capture of a real live Squire was imminent but he refused to believe that anything so fortuitous could happen to him, a man who had seen the wife he worshipped lifted from a ditch with a broken neck. Even as a young man he had never been sanguine about life and it had taken him years to accept the fact that Molly Rodgers had married him, a penniless smallholder, and borne him children. When Molly was killed, early in the first run of the 1890 season, he had been overwhelmed but not surprised. Something of this nature had surely been lying in wait for him for years, and the only aspect of the tragedy that did surprise him was that it had taken some ten years to catch up with him.

He got over it in time and his doubting nature had helped, as had his capacity for long days of monotonous toil in the fields but when the shadow of his wife's death had passed another took its place. Buried down here, with no more than two hundred acres, he decided that it was hopeless to try and build a really prosperous farm to dower his two daughters and it worried him to contemplate what would become of them when he died. Rose, he imagined, could make some sort of a living out of her liveries but Claire, although a fair horsewoman, had no real flair for farming or the rearing of livestock and unless she married well who would provide for her? It was useless to tell him, as Rose often did, that Claire was even prettier than her mother, and that the odds against her becoming an old maid were about ten thousand to one. Derwent only countered by saying that, in this depopulated little backwater, there was no man Claire was likely to want to marry and who, so far, had come courting either one of them? So, in the main, he ignored their silly tittle-tattle claiming that Claire's constant attendance at the manor was a sure sign the new Squire was taken up with her; he did not believe it, it was far too good to be true.

Then, with his own eyes and ears, he had seen and heard acknowledgements of his daughter's influence at the big house, for as tenants arrived to pay their respects to the young man, Derwent noticed that he redirected their compliments to Claire and even received guests with his arm resting on her shoulder, and this evidence was reinforced by Craddock's cheerful, "Well, Mr. Derwent, my thanks for the loan of your daughter! Everything you see is her work, all I've done is carry out her orders, isn't that a fact, Rose?" And Rose had loyally agreed that the whole idea had been Claire's, after which Claire bustled away to introduce Squire to latecomers, for all the world as though she was already mistress of Shallowford.

Derwent was a slow-thinking man and continued thinking to some purpose, until past midnight, when everyone trooped into the paddock to watch the fireworks, and his thoughts, for once, were heartwarming, so that he sensed the spread of a satisfied glow deep in his belly that was not wholly due to rum punch and at length his rare feeling of well-being demanded physical expression. Hesitantly, as a man unpractised in familiarities, his arm stole round the waist of his wife Liz and he pressed her to him so that she almost cried out with astonishment and delight for it was the first public acknowledgement he had made of her in five years of marriage, the first acknowledgement at all discounting his lusty embraces in bed. She thought, for a moment, that he must be far gone in drink, and then she was ashamed of the thought, reasoning that perhaps she had misjudged him after all and perhaps the glorious conviviality of the occasion had wrought a miracle in him. She revelled in this illusion for two minutes and then Handcock discharged another shower of green and crimson balls, and the glare lit up the paddock like a searchlight, so that everyone there might have been standing under strong lamplight, and this was the biggest betrayal of all, for it showed both Claire and her father the face of Paul Craddock, who was looking down on Grace Lovell, standing close beside him. In that moment father and daughter conceded complete and utter defeat.

IV

Claire had been coaxed from the cloakroom by Rose and they had gone out into the paddock as the first rocket soared; she saw Paul

157

standing in the angle of the box hedge, talking to Mrs. Lovell, and at once made up her mind to edge round towards them during an interval of darkness, but unluckily, before the rocket dipped, her father saw her and called, "Well, Claire, this is a rare night for Shallowford! The Lovells never came up with anything of this kind at either of the Jubilees!" and his voice was so jovial that she hesitated in spite of herself, puzzled by his rare amiability and pondering its source. Then, as the golden rain went up, she noticed that he had his arm round Liz's waist, and in the light of the rockets they both looked so spoony that Claire's spirits lifted and she wanted to laugh but did not for it pleased her to see them standing like lovers, with faces turned to the sky. She kept her mind on Paul, however, and when the volley of golden rain erupted she looked quickly in his direction and then wished very much that she hadn't, for he was still there, no more than ten yards away but was no longer talking to Mrs. Lovell. He was looking directly down at Grace Lovell and his expression was even more fatuously captive than that of poor Liz, and as Claire stared, almost choking with humiliation and dismay, Grace Lovell's chin tilted so that she seemed to be returning his rapturous gaze and for several seconds, as the glare in the sky faded, they continued to look into one another's eyes at a range of no more than twenty inches. As soon as it was dark again she fled, pulling back from the enclosure so quickly that Rose called, "What is it, Claire?", but she could not talk, even to Rose, hurrying back to her seat on the backstairs with tears of disappointment streaming down her cheeks and a throat so dry and constricted that she could hardly get her breath. She sat here alone for the remainder of the display, oblivious of the winking flashes of reflected light, and the thunder and crackle of explosions over the paddock.

Derwent had not missed the exchange of looks between Paul and Grace, and it brought him up with a severe jolt. He knew then, and instantly, that his original estimate of this affair had been more accurate than the family's and that Paul Craddock, for all their prattle, was not the least bit interested in his daughter, except perhaps in the way a lazy curate courts an earnest spinster who rushes to arrange flowers in the church, and polish the brasswork of the altar rails. It was all a lot of damned nonsense, he decided, dreamed up by silly womenfolk in their idle moments, and as the certainty of this laid hold on him he suddenly felt enraged with himself for being so gullible. He loosed hold of his wife, Liz, so abruptly that she staggered, and thrust both hands into his breeches pockets, as though to make sure he would never again surrender to a sentimental impulse. Fireworks continued to explode all around but he paid no attention to them. He was too busy assuring himself that he must take immediate steps to prevent his daughter being further exploited. "Damn the fellow!" he muttered, "Who the devil does he think he is, keeping a girl of mine dancing attendance on him for the better part of a month, when she ought to have been at work in the dairy?" He wondered, briefly, if the association had progressed beyond the mutual hanging up of a few paper chains and evergreen sprigs but decided this was unlikely. Surely a daughter of his would have more pride than to let a callow townee make a real fool of her. He looked round as though to assure himself of the fact but Claire was not to be seen, so he switched his thoughts to the only source of comfort that presented itself—the prospect of persuading Craddock by any means, fair or outrageously foul, to sell High Coombe and thus make the Derwents independent of young men with too much money who came prancing down here to play at being farmers.

The flash that had sent Claire back to the house, revived her father's habitual pessimism and put a term to his wife's illusions, went flickering down the years to the end of time. Claire had gone, having seen enough, and Smut Potter had gone, having seen more than enough; Arabella Codsall was to leave as soon as she could tear herself from the engaging spectacle of a smouldering Queen Alexandra, and Paul Craddock, adrift on a sea of romantic speculation, was not thinking of fireworks any more. One golden rain beneficiary remained until the final discharge and this was Walt Pascoe, the bricklayer who had, that same night, spent fifteen minutes in the rhododendrons with Violet Potter, and about the same time with her sister, Pansy. He had not had an opportunity to sample Cissie, the third Potter girl, for Cissie was being squired by Bert Tidmarsh, a close friend of Walt's who was known to be very handy with his fists. This, as it turned out, was fortunate, for if Cissie had been added to Walt's immediate worries his problem might have proved insoluble.

The trouble was all three were as alike as peas in a pod and not only in appearance but in speech, gait and even courting technique. They both giggled and wriggled when he passed his hands over them and they both said "Dornee, Walt!" when he was quite certain they would have been very indignant if he had heeded their protests, for this was by no means his first brush with them. On several previous occasions he had skylarked with the Potter girls in coppice and hayfield, but that, he reflected sadly, was before his mother died, when he had every intention of remaining single. Tonight things had changed and he looked into a cheerless future, one of preparing his own meals before he went to work, and again when he returned, of making his own bed and keeping the cottage clean, of doing his own mending and fire-lighting and hearth-sweeping and generally leading the devil of a life as a bachelor. He had buried his mother in June and the loneliness of the cottage was getting on his nerves, especially at night. He had made up his mind that, sooner or later, he would have to share his life with someone, for he was a very amiable young man with a lively sense of humour but although, at first sight, it seemed that Violet would make him just as comfortable as Pansy, or vice versa, he was reluctant to make a hasty decision on a matter as final as marriage. Every time a rocket exploded he compared their upturned faces, noting their cheerful snub noses, their freckles, their thick chestnut hair and their strong, white teeth, and as he wrestled with his problem he did a sort of double-entry balance sheet of their merits and demerits, in so far as he was able on the strength of samples taken that evening. Violet, he noted, had drenched herself in some kind of rosewater scent, certainly home-made scent, and whilst it was pleasant and provocative it suggested that she might have something to hide. On the other hand Pansy used no scent, or none he could detect, but she had been slightly less accommodating than her sister in the rhododendrons whereas her sister Violet had surrendered to his embrace with apparent eagerness. On the other hand perhaps this was unfair, for he had sampled Violet first and now that he thought about it Pansy had proved harder to win, which surely implied superior virtue on her part. He was still undecided when the last Roman candle burned itself out and the darkness was only moderated by the glow of the set-piece. Then, with one sister on either side of him, Pansy made up his mind for him, almost as if she was guiding him towards the best prize in a lucky dip. Her hand moved up until it lay on his shoulder and then, as though caressing a cat, it moved slowly across his chest and down to his loins, a gesture that indicated two certainties. She had found him pleasing and had the kind of need for him that a man who worked hard all day and brought home regular money on Saturdays ought to look for when choosing a wife.

The caress was casual and probably absent-minded yet it made him

160

tingle from head to foot for it was as though she regarded him as a prize bull that had just been awarded the county accolade and he was ready to burst with manly pride. He said, hoarsely, "Come over yer, Panse! I got zummat to zay to 'ee, midear!", and they withdrew from the enclosure just as Queen Alexandra's right eye went out in a spiral of smoke and a long, satisfied, "Ahhh!" rose from the spectators.

It would be untrue to say that Paul Craddock's mind did not return to Claire Derwent this night, or that he spent every moment of the next few hours in a cloud. He continued to go through the motions of host to a shrinking company but he would have found it hard to say with any accuracy who had left and who had remained for the dawn stirrup cup. He danced with Grace twice, one waltz and one polka, but they exchanged little conversation, a few conventional remarks from him about the way people of the Sorrel Valley had received him, a comment from her praising his initiative and the prodigality of his hospitality but even then he did not think directly of Claire. It was much later, about three o'clock in the morning, that he wondered vaguely whether it was time to serve more ices, and learning that Mrs. Handcock had gone to bed, excused himself, went in search of Claire and was rather puzzled at not finding her or any member of her family.

There were then about thirty of the younger guests on the floor, the girls still full of zest but the men a little unsteady with all the refreshment they had taken between dances. The heroic orchestra was flagging but it continued to play, the twins, Matt and Luke, standing one on each side of Mary Willoughby, who had been relieved from time to time by Crisp, the Coombe Bay organist. Unable to find any of the Derwents, Paul went into the yard to see if their waggonette had gone and here he ran into Gregory, the High Coombe foreman, supping the dregs of Tamer Potter's cask in the outhouse. Gregory was drunk and Paul had to shake him before he could get any sense out of the fellow.

"Where is Mr. Derwent and his family?" he shouted in Gregory's ear, "When did they leave?" The man, recognising the Squire, made a supreme effort to collect his wits.

"They'm gone off 'ome, Mr. Craddock, long zince!" he mumbled, shaking his head violently in an effort to stop the roaring in his ears.

Paul thought it odd that they had left without saying good-bye, for he had understood both Rose and Claire were staying the night to help clear up in the morning but it occurred to him that Derwent might have objected to them staying so he returned to the ballroom and whilst Grace was dancing with Crisp, the organist, he sat out with Celia, eating an ice-cream. Mrs. Lovell was very gracious, saying that she and Grace much appreciated being invited and adding that dear Edward would certainly make a splendid King and keep the Kaiser in his place. She went on to say that she hoped he would be very happy at Shallowford and that she, for her part, was gratified that the estate had been bought by someone young, for under the Lovells it had been the resort of dull, middle-aged gentlemen, and had never had much to offer the young people in the district. "I have often thought," she said, laying an elegant gloved hand on his arm, "that this could be a happy house, full of noise and laughter and people who really cared for the land, and the families living on it," to which Paul, much encouraged, replied that he agreed whole-heartedly but was already finding his lack of experience a handicap. "There's John Rudd, of course," he admitted, "but a man ought not to put himself entirely in the hands of an agent, should he?"

"I should think not, indeed," Celia replied with an expert flutter of her fan, as though to shoo John Rudd from the place where important decisions were made, "but I should be flattered if you felt free to ask my advice about anything—well, anything social, you understand? After all, I grew up on a country estate—a much larger one of course but administered along the same lines and I believe I could be of service to you from time to time. We rejoin my husband in London the day after tomorrow, but we shall be back again shortly."

"I'm very obliged for the offer, Mrs. Lovell," Paul said, sincerely, "and I shall certainly take advantage of it."

"Well then, that's settled," she said, with a maternal smile and Paul thought how very gracious she was and what a pity it was she was the wife of a rake like Bruce Lovell, rumoured throughout the Valley "to have led 'er a praper ole dance".

Grace returned to them then, her smooth, pale cheeks flushed with the heat and exercise and Mr. Crisp, the organist, bowed himself out, after she had declined his offer to bring her an ice.

"I've been telling Mr. Craddock that he is very welcome to seek our advice about Shallowford, my dear," Celia said and Grace murmured, "He seems to be managing very well on his own, Mother!" after which she remained silent but although Paul observed that her foot tapped to the rhythm of the music and asked her if she would care to dance again, she said, "No thank you, Mr. Craddock," without looking at him but then, to his delight she added, "It's very stuffy in here! Could we take a breath of air, do you think?", and Paul leaped to his feet, expecting Celia to reach for her shawl for he could not believe that so formal a person would countenance an unchaperoned walk on the terrace at three in the morning. She made no movement, however, but smiled, saying "I haven't thawed out after watching the fireworks. Please take her on the terrace Mr. Craddock, but see that you have your cape, Grace dear!", and they passed through the hall to the terrace, turning left along the walk under the library windows.

It was a mild night for late September and a very still one now that the roar from the house had been greatly reduced in volume. The starlight was brilliant and they could make out the blur of Shallowford Woods but the glimpse stirred in him no memory of Claire. As she stopped where the terrace ended at the steps he said, "I'm very glad you were able to come, Miss Lovell. I was talking to your stepmother and she seems very pleased I've taken over here."

The girl turned, so quickly and so unexpectedly that she seemed almost to spin round and he saw, in the light shed by the library lamps, that her face had the same look of exasperation as on the occasion they first met.

"Of course she's pleased," she said sharply, "and why not? She sees you as a quite unexpected means of getting me off her hands. Surely you must have realised that by now?"

Her candour made him gasp but for all that he was no longer intimidated by her for it occurred to him that her attitude offered a short cut to a courtship that had promised to be tedious.

He said, "Very well, Miss Lovell, I'll accept that, but if you can say precisely what's on your mind whenever we meet I ought to have the same freedom. If you aren't prepared to grant it we'll go inside at once!" and he waited, watching her consider the challenge. She met it with the same disconcerting frankness.

"I really don't know why I have to behave this way with you," she said. "Manners aren't my strongest point but they really aren't as bad as they must appear to you. I suppose it's because, while I can't help admiring your enterprise and honesty, it makes me very angry to see people like Celia exploiting it. So here comes one more apology! You get one every time we meet."

"I'm not looking for your apologies," he said, "I'd far sooner say what's in *my* mind for a change. It might upset you, but it would save both of us a good deal of sparring and the rest of the Valley a great deal of speculation!"

163

Her rather bothered expression gave place to curiosity so that she looked at him sharply from under her brows, like a sleek little spaniel uncertain of whether a pat or a cuff was coming her way.

"All right, Mr. Craddock," she said, at length, "you can be as blunt as you like, and afterwards I'll tell Celia I'm tired and we'll all go home to bed!"

He did not feel much like laughing but he almost laughed at this. It was an aspect of her he had not suspected and somehow made her seem about fourteen.

"Then to be absolutely honest I'm rather flattered by what you say was in Mrs. Lovell's mind and also by her going out of her way to let me know she approves of me! I've only got your word for it, mind you, but I hope it is so all the same."

"That's odd," she said. "If I were a man in your place I should find it very degrading!"

"Well I don't," he said, "and I think I've got a good enough reason. After all, you came close to being the wife of the Squire so why should canvassing his successor seem so outrageous?"

She was smiling now and obviously had herself well in hand.

"You're a very extraordinary person, Mr. Craddock! You appear straightforward, sometimes almost naïve, but you aren't really! In fact, you're a far more complicated person than you pretend to be!"

"Well," he replied, "that being so or not I'm still sufficiently broad-minded not to resent local people like your stepmother trying their damnedest to marry me off! I suppose she regards it as her duty, like any other mamma, but I wouldn't like her to fall into the error of imagining I'm a substitute for a person like Ralph Lovell. I know absolutely nothing about the life or the needs of the people about here. I took this place on impulse so, without beating about the bush, I'll ask you on impulse to think seriously of your stepmother's intentions! I don't find them presumptuous or even embarrassing. As a matter of fact I find them very exhilarating!"

He heard her catch her breath and the fact that she did not whip round on him, as he half-expected her to, gave him a moment to control the tension building inside him. Seeing that she made no kind of reply he went on, "I can say this not only because you obviously prefer candour but because I think I know rather more about you than you imagine, and I didn't learn it all from Valley gossip!"

She was standing with her back to him, her hands resting on the balustrade, seemingly neither astonished nor embarrassed by what he

164

had said but considering it in a mood that was at once defensive and offensive.

"Whatever you know can't be much more than guesswork," she replied, at length. "People usually make guesses about me—it's all they can do. I'm an exceptionally private person!"

"Yes," he said, "you are but you can't hide everything. You can't hide the fact that you find your present life pointless and the future very uncertain. I have a special qualification for recognising that much about you!"

"And what qualification would that be?"

He hesitated. He was now so deeply committed that prudence, politeness even, seemed a worthless currency between them. "All my life I've been a very lonely person. I suppose I should have remained one if I hadn't taken the plunge last June and staked everything I had on this place. Well, it was a gamble but it seems to me to have an even chance of coming off. Ever since my first evening here I've wanted very badly to talk to you like this but it didn't seem possible without going through the rigmarole of calling and leaving cards. The point is, we've been lucky and found a short cut, so why don't we use it? It isn't reasonable to expect you to back your instinct as heavily as I'm prepared to back mine but you could tell me now if you are prepared to consider marriage."

Suddenly he ran out of words, or words that did not sound fatuous. She faced him then, and he would not have been surprised if she had laughed in his face but she was not even smiling but looking at him with a kind of wonder.

"My father lives by and for gambling," she said, "but he would never gamble on odds of this kind. What makes you want to take such a chance with your life?"

What indeed, he thought, regarding the loveliness of her skin and then, as though it was transparent, he could see her vulnerability and it stirred in him the same kind of compassion as that roused by the sight of the urchin Ikey in the boneyard but far deeper, and far more compelling. Yet all he said was, "You have a special kind of beauty for me but it's not simply that. I honestly think I could make you happy. After all, you would have married Ralph Lovell without love, on his side or yours!"

"Neither one of us had anything to lose. Why should you risk your happiness, or whatever you think you might achieve, for someone who is—well, bad luck to everyone?"

"That's nonsense," he said calmly, "a person's luck is usually regulated by the amount of confidence they have in themselves."

"I doubt it," she said, "but even if it is so I've never had a very high opinion of myself, Paul. That doesn't mean, however, that I haven't been flattered by your proposal — if it *is* a proposal!", and suddenly she smiled her small, secret smile.

"It's a proposal," he said stubbornly. "All I'm asking is that you should think about it whilst you're away in London."

"I shall certainly do that," she said, emphatically, and then again, "Yes, I shall certainly do that! There'll be very little else to think about."

"When will you be back?"

"Some time before Christmas. Celia likes my father to hunt in December. He'd sooner back horses than ride them but Celia calls the tune in our ménage."

There seemed very little more to be said so he took her arm and led her back to the pool of light outside the main entrance.

"Then we'd best go in now," he said, "or Mrs. Lovell will be wondering what I've done with you."

"She could compose herself, whatever it was," Grace said lightly, and stopping at the porch, asked, "You said — 'a special kind of beauty'?"

"Yes; for me."

She considered this gravely as though conceding that he might have a point. "And you never proposed to anyone before?"

"No," he said, laughing, "never, I'm afraid."

"Well," she said, "it was all very nicely managed," and as though rewarding an industrious little boy she placed her hands on his shoulders, stood on her toes and kissed his cheek, softly and swiftly. It was more of a salute than a kiss, something about half-way between mistletoe mischief and a benediction.

White light from beyond Coombe Bluff came stealing across the stubble field moving steadily west and north, as though unsure of what it might find in the paddocks separated by the line of chestnuts in the drive. It touched the charred stubs of Roman candles and the rocket sticks, still sagging beside the bamboos alongside the box hedge and then moved along the façade of the house. Everyone had gone. The ruts in the forecourt gravel were the only evidence that, an hour or so earlier, the diehards had wheeled and stamped here and shouted their hoarse good-byes. Only one guest remained, Gregory, the Derwent

166

foreman, who was sound asleep in the outhouse, beside Tamer Potter's empty beer cask. Ikey, and the gardener's boy Gappy Saunders, were snoring in their loft over the stable and even Walt Pascoe, now officially affianced to Pansy Potter, was walking home along the river road, congratulating himself on the final solution of his dilemma, for Pansy's final words to him, as they parted at the foot of the Dell ascent, had been, "I'll make 'ee comfortable, Walt! You can depend on it, midear!", which seemed to him as honest a pledge as had ever been made in the Valley.

The Derwents were asleep, all four of them, even Claire, worn out with weeping, and so were all the Willoughbys, with Elinor satisfied with Will's declaration, "Us'll see Squire about that freehold zoon us have slept on it!" Arabella Codsall had grumbled herself and Martin to sleep and Martha Pitts, who had returned home to the Hermitage after the fireworks, was already stirring in her sleep, as her fierce Plymouth Rock cockerel greeted dawn from the sty wall. Only one person was wide awake in the Valley and the wooded slopes enclosing it and he stood in the recessed window of the big Shallowford bedroom, in his shirt and dress trousers, looking south over the winding road that led across the ford to the Codsall fields, and the slender spire of Coombe Bay parish church. He was not thinking of the soirée as a whole but of its penultimate moment, when the Lovell gig had swept round the curve of the drive and Grace Lovell had looked back, lifting her hand as the fussy little equipage passed behind the line of chestnuts. There had been finality in the gesture, as though she had closed the first chapter of their association the moment of parting, but he was not uneasy, just tremulous and expectant. There would be other chapters, many of them, and all, he reasoned, would have more conclusive endings.

The white light became whiter and stronger over the Coombe, until the grey line of Shallowford Woods turned to green and russet where autumn was already thinning the oaks beyond Hazel Potter's squirrel tree. Somewhere out there a single blackbird piped up and the Channel breeze, an unfailing escort for dawn in the Valley, came soughing over the stubble and shook down a dozen leaves from the red creeper underneath the window. Their soft undersides, Paul thought, were like the texture of her skin where it was taut under her small, pointed chin. It was a pleasant thought on which to draw the curtain. Before the breeze had lifted the last of the leaves from verge to terrace he too was asleep.

CHAPTER SEVEN

I

LOOKING back on the half year between his arrival at Sorrel Halt and his first Christmas at Shallowford, Paul came to view it as his probationary period, a first term at prep school. It had the same doubts and uncertainties, the same discoveries and testing strain on patience, fortitude and nerve. The coronation supper-dance was the climax but until then, until the moment of Grace Lovell's wave from the disappearing gig, he had been tutored every step of the way. Throughout the early weeks Rudd had been there to hold his hand and when Rudd went away there had been Claire Derwent making light of his cares of office. It was when the tumult of the soirée was done and rhythm was restored to the big house that he was aware of the loneliness of power, for Rudd wrote saying he had slipped down a companion ladder attending a sherry party aboard a frigate and had cracked two ribs, an injury likely to immobilise him for another month, and Claire Derwent had disappeared from his life abruptly and completely. He sent Ikey over to High Coombe with a second message (the first having gone unanswered) and learned that she had left home a day or so after the ball and was likely to be away some time. The note returned by Rose was noncommittal. It did not say where she had gone, or why, and its vagueness sent Paul grumbling to Mrs. Handcock, complaining that the hunting season was upon them and that he had looked forward to some good sport with Gilroy's Teazel and Sorrel Vale pack of hounds but everybody seemed to have decamped, Rudd to Portsmouth, Grace Lovell to London and Claire Derwent, who should have known better, to heaven knew where. Mrs. Handcock was sympathetic. "Ah, theym a rare trapsey ole lot, Mr. Craddock," she told him. "It warn't zo in my young days. Us never stirred from the Vale, except mebbe to go once a year to Paxtonbury Market Fair or on a Sunday School treat, to Whinmouth. Now everyone rushes upalong and downalong to no purpose and if you ask me it all started wi' they pedally machines." Mrs. Handcock abominated the bicycle, refusing even to call it by its proper name for to her it signified the new era of restlessness in the Valley, promising an outcrop of reprehensible habits among the workshy, whom she said were multiplying with every local marriage. "No good'll come of 'em, mark my words, sir!" she would say, standing before him with hands on her enormous hips and sweat glistening on her forehead (for she was cook, as well as housekeeper at Shallowford). "No good'll be gleaned from they whizzing gurt things! A man's got two legs, baint 'ee, an' when theym too tired to carry un he's got four, waiting for un in the stable! Zo where be the reason fer a blight o' pedally machines about the plaace? Theym bad enough fer the men but the maids have taaken to riding 'em, showin' all they've got? I'd zee my daughter dade bevore I allowed her to zit 'er rump on one!"

This was a safe threat for, although Mrs. Handcock had been married for many years to the squat, bow-legged gardener, Horace, they were childless and she found consolation in a grotesquely exaggerated respect for her spouse, to whom she ascribed mysterious oracular powers. Most of her opinions stemmed from Horace, who rarely declaimed in public but hoarded his gems until he could bestow them upon Mrs. Handcock, in the privacy of the housekeeper's two rooms in the east wing. Paul alleviated his loneliness during the autumn days encouraging Mrs. Handcock to recount some of her husband's gloomier prophecies and was thus regaled with all manner of terrifying forecasts upon subjects as diverse as Kaiser Wilhelm's navy, submarine warfare, the future of the House of Lords, Irish Home Rule, women's suffrage and, of course, the main threat to the social system, the pedally machine. He grew very fond of the stout, talkative old body and she spoiled him outrageously, the more so as Rudd, whom she revered almost as much as her husband, had been obliged to abandon him after such a brief apprenticeship.

During these days Paul began to take a more personal interest in his protegé, Ikey Palfrey, for he was impressed by the boy's willingness and also by his considerable powers of mimicry, and cockney sense of humour. Sometimes, when he was waiting for Snowdrop in the yard, he would encourage Ikey to vary his Devon and London dockside repertoire, with caricatures of Lord Gilroy, or Parson Bull, and even the solemn Chivers, who condemned ribaldry at the expense of the gentry. It struck him that Ikey Palfrey possessed unsuspected gifts of observation, and Paul wondered if the boy was not wasted in a provincial squire's stable, and would benefit from such education as the Vale could provide. Accordingly, a week or so after the ball, he sent him to Mary Willoughby's school and the result was a permanent alteration in Ikey's routine. In the mornings he rode the house cob over to Deepdene, and in the afternoons and evenings resumed his work in the tack-room. Paul thought that Chivers, the groom, would disapprove but Ikey's charm had already enlisted the goodwill of his superior and when, as upon hunting days, there was much to do, Chivers would rise an hour earlier and go to bed an hour later, in order to make sure that Ikey did not miss his schooling.

Ikey himself accepted the change reluctantly, considering himself finished with droning schoolmasters, free with the cane and the casual cuff, and now regarded himself a wage-earning adult but after a day or so under the mild Mary Willoughby he reversed this opinion and thereafter he went willingly, enjoying the morning canter over Coombe Bluff, and along the edge of Shallowford Woods. Mary instilled into him an interest in lyrical poetry, in geography and in military history and loaned him books to take home and read in the light of a lantern in his hayloft. At first they were adventure books by authors like Ballantyne, Marryat and Henty but after she had loaned him *The Count of Monte Cristo* he became a very earnest reader and went on to tackle Dickens, Defoe and Scott, so that he could often be seen, to the astonishment of his loft-mate, Gappy Saunders, oiling saddles and polishing bits, with a book propped up in front of him on the tack-room table.

Until the third week in November, when hunting was in full swing, life was uneventful on the estate but towards the end of the month there was a flare-up in the smouldering Codsall-Willoughby feud, which erupted with unpleasant suddenness one dismal morning when the Valley was draped in mist, and the ford ran high with the rush of streams draining into it from Blackberry Moor, Coombe Bluff and Priory Wood.

Paul was at work on his draft plan for the rebuilding of the Priory homestead, hoping to have the work in hand by the time Rudd came home, when Mrs. Handcock ushered a shuffling Will Codsall into the office, introducing him with a sense of outrage for she had told him Squire was busy but he had demanded his rights as a tenant. The young man was dripping wet, having walked over from Deepdene Farm without a coat and his heavy hobnailed boots left a trail of mud on the way through the kitchen and hall to the office. Paul saw that he was agitated and told Mrs. Handcock to bring in a towel, a dry jacket and a mug of cocoa, and the housekeeper retired, muttering "Youm var too zoft with 'em!" but towel, jacket and cocoa soon arrived and

170

when Will had drunk his cocoa and changed his coat he told Paul the reason for his urgency.

"Me'n Elinor Willoughby are getting wed come Saturday, but tiz like there'll be a rare ole bust-up at chapel," he said. "I reckon Mother'll show up, shouting her objections, and Mr. Willoughby, who'll be marryin' us, is in two minds whether to go through with it! Elinor, she's back at Deepdene, crying her eyes out, and me, well I reckon I bin druv too far and that's a fact, Squire!"

He then recounted the story of his mother's implacable opposition to the marriage, leading up to his dramatic exit from Four Winds, after smashing Arabella's cuckoo clock. To Paul, who had managed to steer clear of Arabella Codsall except for his first visit to Four Winds, it seemed no more than a storm in a teacup and after pointing out that until Will was twenty-one his mother had a legal right to oppose the marriage, he asked if the couple could postpone the wedding until he was of age.

"Ah, that's what I reckoned on doing," Will said glumly, " 'til I had more'n I could stomach an' run out on her! But now us is in a right fix, for Deepdene won't keep another mouth through winter and I reckon on havin' to go abroad to find work. I can't take my Elinor along, unless us is man an' wife, an' 'er won't hear of me going backalong until I got me foot in a door somewhere!"

Paul had lived long enough in the Valley to differentiate between literal and local meanings of the word "abroad". To Will Codsall "abroad" meant anywhere outside a thirty-mile radius of Shallowford and to Elinor "backalong" was as final and desperate a removal as emigration overseas. Paul glanced at the plan of the Priory freehold lying on his desk and a solution at once suggested itself.

"Suppose I put you in the Priory freehold, Will?" he said. "Do you think you could make a go of it? It's no more than sixty acres, hardly enough to support a mixed farm like your father's, or even the Willoughby's but it would give you independence and I daresay you and Elinor could improve it."

The young man's eyes shone. "Well, sir, I had it in mind to come asking for that," he said joyfully, "but us heard you meant to lump it in with the Pitts' holding, at Hermitage."

"So I did," Paul admitted, "but the Pitts aren't greedy people, and yours is a special case. I'm planning to get Eph Morgan over there to rebuild the farmhouse and byres."

"Good God, Maister, you don't want to squander money like that!"

Will told him. "Me an' my Elinor could do it ourselves, if us had the use of the Home Farm sawmill and a trifle for nails, cement and suchlike."

Paul was touched; it seemed to him a wonderful thing that, in this mechanical age, there were still young couples eager to build homesteads with their own hands and Will's offer clinched the matter in his mind.

"Go there as soon as you've told Elinor," he said, "and then come back and tell me what you think you could do with the place. I'll write to the solicitors and get them to draw up a lease. The land is half derelict so I won't take a rent for the first four quarters. After that we'll fix a rental you can afford to pay."

Paul thought Will Codsall would have fallen on his knees and kissed his hand. His big, ruddy face glowed and he seemed unable to decide what to do with his enormous hands, first clasping them, then chafing them, and finally stuffing them in his breeches pockets, as though to keep them from shaming him. Nothing would deter him from going out into the rain then and there, in order to hasten back to Deepdene to tell Elinor the good news so Paul let him borrow the cob, telling him to ride over to Priory and leave it in the yard on his way back. He also promised to see Honeyman at the Home Farm about timber and the use of the sawmill and then watched a jubilant Will take the short cut to the river across the small paddock, and disappear in a flurry of rain in the direction of the Coombe.

"Well, there's something achieved at all events," he said to Mrs. Handcock, when she served his lunch, reminding her of Elinor's reputation in the Valley for breeding a good strain of poultry but the housekeeper had reservations. "I doan't doubt but they'll maake a go of it," she said, "providing they'm left be that is, but that Arabella Codsall, 'er won't let it go at that, you can depend on it! Us'll have a proper spuddle bevore us is done, you see if I baint right, sir!"

Her suspicions were soon justified. After breakfast the next day she announced the arrival of Arabella and Martin Codsall, showing them in, Paul thought, with a grim satisfaction, as proof of her powers of prophecy.

Arabella opened on a disconcertingly mild note, whining that spiteful rumours were abroad in the Valley alleging Squire's championship of her son but that she, as one sensible to the Squire's good heart, had refused to believe that he was a man to drive a wedge between mother and son.

172

Paul listened to this with impatience, feeling sorry for old Martin Codsall, whose embarrassment was obvious and at last Martin interrupted with "Squire don't want to listen to all that rigmarole, Mother! Stick to the point, and ask 'un if there's any question of our Will takin' that bit o' freehold upalong."

Paul said, "Will's been here, Mrs. Codsall, and I've granted him a lease on Priory," whereupon Arabella, turning red in the face, burst out, "Then he's more underhanded than I could have believed, Mr. Craddock! Everyone in the Valley knows that land rightfully belongs to the Hermitage holding, and that when Hardcastle died it would go back to the Pitts!"

"That was the intention, Mrs. Codsall," Paul said, patiently, "but after hearing Will's intention to marry I thought it fair to give him a place of his own. Honeyman says he'll make a first-class farmer if we give him encouragement."

The word "encouragement" lit a fuse in Arabella's brain.

"Encouragement!" she blustered, "you think that wicked boy *needs* encouragement? Or her either, that chit who's bewitched him, along of her ranting father? Do you know what Will did the day he walked out on me an' his dad at Four Winds?"

"Yes," said Paul, trying hard not to smile, "he threw a shepherd's pie at your cuckoo clock!"

"Is that any way to carry on in front of his own mother and father?" demanded Arabella. "You give him that tenancy, Mr. Craddock, and you'll rue the day! A boy that wilful won't make a success of anything —farm, marriage or what all!"

"Suppose I didn't," argued Paul, somewhat ruffled by her attempt to browbeat him, "how would he earn his living? Deepdene can't support two families and he'd have to leave the Valley and work as a hired hand."

Martin made his first real contribution to the discussion, and it seemed to Paul that for once he spoke without reference to his wife's prejudice.

"He's no call to go hiring himself to anyone outside the Valley," he growled. "He's our firstborn, an' Four Winds'll come to him in the course o' time. He can come home any time he's a mind to."

"With Elinor?" Paul asked and there was a pause, during which both of them looked at Arabella.

"Yes," she said finally, "with her, if he won't come alone. They can set up in one of the cottages, and we'll make the best of it, so long as they're married in church that is! I won't have a son of mine bedding his woman on the strength of a chapel wedding!"

For a moment Paul considered. It was obvious that Martin, irrespective of his wife, longed to have Will restored to him and as the elder of the Codsall boys his inheritance of the lease was protocol in the Valley but Paul doubted the wisdom of settling a truculent boy like Will, and a spirited girl like Elinor, on Codsall land, within close range of Arabella's tongue. He wished then that Rudd, or Claire were at hand to advise him, for instinct warned him that an incident like this could poison his relationship with the tenantry. Then he recalled Will Codsall's shining eyes and his heartfelt gratitude on the previous day and it occurred to him that Sydney Codsall, his younger brother, was his mother's favourite, so that Will might not inherit Four Winds after all. He said, bluntly, "It wouldn't work, Mrs. Codsall. Will's almost of age, and from what I've seen of him he'll be happier left to himself. He can still have Priory if he wants it but I'll see that he knows about your offer to return home."

"You'll advise him to?" This was from Martin, whose face, in contrast to that of his wife, had paled under the stress of the interview. "I'll tell him," Paul promised, "but he and Elinor must make their own decision."

"Well, I wouldn't have believed it!" said Arabella. "I just wouldn't have believed it!", and she marched towards the library door as Paul rose, saying "The boy's got his own way to make in the world, Mrs. Codsall. There's no sense in alienating him by making such a silly to-do over whom he marries. There are worse families hereabouts than the Willoughbys."

"Yes," she said, turning at the door and looking more venomous than he could have believed possible, "there *are* worse, Mr. Craddock, but I can only name one—the Potters! Maybe you would have helped him to drag us down to *their* level, if he'd taken a fancy to one of they harlots in the Dell!"

Her implacability was like a wall of ice and to overcome her monstrous prejudice, to touch her in any way, one would have to chip away at frozen blocks of pride, ignorance and pretension, accumulated over the years since she had been a child over her father's shop. He saw that he was unequal to the task but his failure saddened him, for he recognised her now as an enemy and he doubted if he could afford an enemy as formidable as the wife of the best farmer in the Valley. He tried once again.

"Don't you see I must do what I think is right, Mrs. Codsall—right for Will, and for the Willoughbys, as well as for you? Will doesn't really want to go his own way but your way wouldn't lead to anything but more trouble."

She gave him a final bleak look and was gone but Martin remained a moment, lifting his shoulders and spreading his hands in a gesture of despair.

"Can't you do anything with her at all?" Paul asked, and Martin, looking at him unblinkingly, said, "No, Squire, I can't an' never could! Nor can't anyone hereabouts! I've always been one for peace, for turning the other cheek as the Good Book says, but after twenty years of it I've come to realise that baint right way to go about it! Holy Writ can make mistakes, like the rest of us! You might spend your life sowing Christian seed but the harvest on my land'll be tares just the same!"

He went out after his wife and the chill in the room was not solely the result of the steady drip of rain from the verandah. Paul stood looking after them, trying to persuade himself that what had happened was a trivial incident, and would seem even more trivial in retrospect but he knew, deep in his heart, that this was not so and that Martin's tares would be much in evidence before a year was past. The certainty of this made him more angry with himself than with Arabella. Old Squire Lovell, he thought, would have managed it so much better.

II

He remained despondent all day, although Will Codsall's high spirits when he called to say he would have the Priory farmhouse habitable in a matter of weeks, confirmed Paul in the rightness of his decision. Then, for a time, he forgot the Codsalls, for Ikey came in with news that the carrier serving the triangle between Whinmouth, Coombe Bay and Sorrel Halt, had left a sealed wicker basket addressed to *P. Craddock, Shallowford House*, and that it contained some kind of animal, advertising its discomfort by scratching and whimpering. He followed Ikey into the yard and helped Chivers cut the fastenings. At the bottom of the crate, crouched and abject, was a half-grown puppy, with a label attached to its collar. On the label, in a neat feminine hand, was written, "*She has a defect in one eye and was condemned. No good for gun but rather appealing, don't you think?*" and then the angular initials, "G.L.".

175

He examined the dog carefully, finding it a well-bred golden Labrador bitch, and Chivers, inspecting the eyes, confirmed that there was indeed a slight defect but that otherwise the animal was very healthy although he doubted if it could be trained for the gun. Paul carried the puppy back into the house, setting it down before the library fire. He was touched not only by Grace's kindness towards the little reject but also by this proof that he had remained in her mind although it puzzled him somewhat to reflect that she should go to the trouble of sending a puppy all the way from London when she had not bothered to write a postcard. He sat on for a spell toying with names. "Grace" suggested itself but donor and dog had little in common. The pup was a shrinking little creature, already absorbing the warmth of the fire, and was clearly without a trace of Grace Lovell's prickly self-containment.

There was a meet the following day at Heronslea, Gilroy's place beyond the Teazel and because it was the first of the season within easy travelling distance the Valley contributed more than half the field. On his way down the river road Paul overtook a local cavalcade, consisting of Tamer Potter on a sturdy cob, Edward Derwent and Rose, riding two of the most mettlesome horses in the Valley and several farmers from further along the coast, some of whom Paul knew by sight. Rose was polite but distant but Derwent confined his greeting to a nod and a touch of his hat. Claire, Rose told him, was still away in Kent, but when Paul pressed her for details she seemed disinclined to gossip and he put this down to the fact that she was riding an untried gelding and had her hands full for, on reaching the crossing where Arthur and Henry Pitts came cantering down from Hermitage, the big horse threw up its head and screamed, sidling towards the river and only returning to the road in response to Rose's urgent whispers and firm, gentle pressures. Paul admired both her skill and nerve but secretly relished the fact that he was riding a horse as docile and well-mannered as Snowdrop, whom he could ride on a loose rein. Arthur Pitts was in his customary good humour and gave his blessing on Will Codsall's tenancy of the adjoining freehold.

"He's a good lad, and I'm all for seeing him start on his own," he said. "Me and Henry have as much as us can manage, Mr. Craddock, so dornee give another thought to what you had in mind about tacking they acres on to our boundary! That boy of Arabella's needs to be out of range of his mother's tongue and Willoughby's li'l maid will make un a praper wife, mark my words! There baint a girl between Sorrel and the county border as can rear better chicken, nor make better clotted crame!"

Paul thanked him and wished heartily that all his tenants had the amiability of the Pitts family. Skirting the Codsall farmstead they headed west over the shallow Teazel to Heronslea Woods, picking their way through the extensive larch coverts to the big white house, where old Gilroy and his son were standing on the broad steps under the portico watching the butler serve stirrup cup but otherwise remaining aloof. Gilroy had given up hunting some years before and his son confined himself to attending one or two lawn meets and the big Boxing Day event. Gilroy's chief whip, the virtual master of the pack, took charge of field operations, and at eleven o'clock they moved off to draw Folly Wood, behind the house, where they found at once and dashed off on a north-easterly line, across Blackberry Moor and over the railway.

There were several checks and Paul had leisure to enjoy the unfamiliar stretch of country and watch the antics of such of the field as he knew personally. Parson Bull lived up to his reputation as a thruster, pounding along on a barrel-chested piebald and cursing everyone who got in his way. He represented, thought Paul, a Christianity that was as dead as the Plantagenets and watching him plunge through a gap on the heels of the chief whip, it struck him that Bull had no business to be drawing an annual stipend for preaching the Sermon on the Mount, for anyone less meek would be difficult to find in the shire. Then a joyful shout from Henry Pitts made him qualify his verdict, for Henry, drawing level with Paul on an upslope, shouted, "Keep Passon in view, Mr. Craddock! If us loses un us'll never be in at the kill!", and Paul thought that whatever Bull's demerits he had at least won the respect of his parishioners to a man. Rose Derwent, giving the gelding his head, was away up in front and Derwent, who rode just as fearlessly, was not far behind. Tamer Potter panted along in the rear, and was soon left behind but Paul managed to keep up with the middle section of the field, a group that included the two Pitts, young Gilroy (who rode as though he was indifferent as to the outcome of the day) and several of the farmers along the coast.

They killed about a mile beyond the railway and found again an hour later but this time the field moved off so quickly, and became so scattered in the broken country north of Shallowford Woods, that Paul soon found himself alone and decided to call it a day. He took a bearing on the red knob of Coombe Bluff and following a stream that flowed south, pushed on through the woods until he saw the gleam of the mere below. He was skirting the eastern arm of the pool, within sight of Sam Potter's cottage, when Sam ran out and hailed him, waving his arms in a way that implied a certain amount of urgency, so Paul put Snowdrop at the ditch separating them and cantered into the clearing, where Sam came running, his brown face glowing with excitement, his huge boots crashing through the dead bracken stalks.

" 'Er's arrived, Mr. Craddock!" he bellowed, when he was still fifty yards distant, " 'er come sudden, two or dree hours since, and 'er's the prettiest li'l maid in the Valley!"

Paul looked for the doctor's gig and not seeing it said, "Well, I'm delighted, Sam! Is Doctor O'Keefe with your wife now?"

"Lord bless us no, he baint showed up yet!" Sam said, striding along with one hand on Snowdrop's leathers, "Joannie told me her time was come first light so I had the choice o' leavin' her, or waitin' until Aaron Stokes come up to the mere for his withies. Zoon as I zeed him I sent him off for doctor, but that warn't till noon! It don't signify tho', fer I managed well enough, and Joannie seems comfortable. Will 'ee . . . will 'ee go up, an' taake a look at 'er, Squire? I tell 'ee, 'er's the prettiest maid in the Valley!"

"You mean you delivered the child yourself?" Paul asked, incredulously and Sam shrugged his shoulders, grinning. "Well, there warn't no choice, was there? I fetched calves an' foals often enough, and there baint all that difference, Maister!"

Paul climbed the stairs with some misgivings and peeped into the bedroom, the one upstairs room of the cottage. Joan Potter, wan but triumphant, was sitting up in bed feeding the child and when she saw him she blushed, saying softly, "Why ever didn 'e call up first, Sam? Squire's a bachelor, and whatever will 'ee think of us?"

Paul said, "Well—er—congratulations, both of you! I didn't realise babies could arrive without a doctor but you seem to have managed all right. What are you going to call it—her?"

"Well," said Sam, "I was thinking us ought to leave that to you, Squire, seein' you'm the first bar us to zet eyes on the tacker! Baint her a pretty li'l maid? *Baint* her, tho'?", and he plucked aside the shawl to reveal a brick-red face crowned by a clownish patch of black hair. " 'Er's the spit of her Gran! Dark as a Gyppo, and likely as full o' mischief! Now *you* have the naming of her, Mr. Craddock, for us was goin' to call her after you, saving your presence, if 'er'd been a boy, warn't us, Joannie?"

178

His wife confirmed this, admitting that she had been disappointed at first but was now reconciled to the child's sex, "because Sam be as plaised as a mongrel wi' two tails and us can have a bushel o' boys laater on!"

Admiring their comforting directness and cordiality Paul thought how wise John Rudd had been to advise him that Sam, the pick of the Potter litter, was a man who would respond to trust.

"Very well," he said, "since 'Paul' is out how about 'Pauline'?" and Sam, scratching his head said, "*Be* there such a name for a maid, Squire? Then, so be it, 'Pauline Potter'! Damme they zeems to run together, dorn 'em? Arr, Pauline it is, and now you must wet the baby's head, Squire, and praise to God you was the first along to do it, for I reckoned it'd be old Aaron Stokes and he be one o' they bliddy Temperance loonies!"

Paul said good-bye to Joannie and followed Sam down to the kitchen, where Sam filled two pewter tankards with rough cider from a barrel under the sink. The brew was in the Potter tradition, about twice as potent as the cider Paul had drunk at The Raven and when he had emptied his mug he took from his pocket a five-shilling piece that he had carried as a good luck charm through the last year of his service in the Transvaal.

"Here, Sam," he said, "keep it for Pauline or buy her something with it if you'd rather. It was given to me in Pretoria, and although it didn't bring me much luck in the field I was too superstitious to spend it before I was wounded," and he pressed the coin into Sam's hand. Sam was overwhelmed. "Damn it," he said, "I'll bore un through, an' the maid can have it for a necklace. From Pretoria, you said, sir? Would 'er be Kruger coinage, with the old Queen's head on it?"

"No," said Paul, laughing, "it's English money. They paid us in crown pieces over there; they weren't so easily lost as smaller coins. If you want a real souvenir I'll give you a Boer testament, printed in Afrikaans, with a bullet-hole through it. I'll be off now, before the doctor comes. If you need anything for the baby, blankets or a cot, let me know, and we'll see what Mrs. Handcock can find in the attics."

"You done more'n enough getting me an' Joannie out o' the Dell," Sam said, solemnly, "and I'll maake it up to 'ee one way or another, sir. Things are good hereabouts an' like to get better, downalong and upalong and it's all your doin' I reckon, you an' Mr. Rudd's."

"Is that what most of them say, Sam?" Paul asked, feeling very encouraged.

179

"Arr, it be," Sam confirmed, "leastways, them as matters. Good-bye, and God bless 'ee, Mr. Craddock!" and he held the stirrup as Paul swung himself into the saddle.

It was dusk in the wood as he put Snowdrop at the long slope to the meadow, where he and Claire had surprised Hazel Potter talking to the squirrel, and as he went along he began to do a sum in his head, balancing the credit and debit of his account to date as Squire of Shallowford. On the credit side was an obviously happy and well-housed Sam Potter, and a liberated Will Codsall, to which could be added, perhaps, the coronation supper-ball, but on the debit side the Derwents had clearly taken the huff over something and there was also Arabella Codsall, who would not easily forgive his championship of Will and Elinor. At the foot of this balance-sheet, however, was Sam's heart-warming pronouncement, "Things are good hereabouts an' like to get better . . ." Well, he hoped they would get better as time went along and he could translate all he felt for the woods and fields and farms of the Valley into action but from this point his thoughts enlarged themselves into a more general contemplation of the future.

At the top of the slope he reined in to give Snowdrop a breather, sitting with his legs free of the stirrups and looking down through the straggle of woods to the mere. The basin was full of violet dusk and the great clump of oaks, immediately below, still showed traces of summer, like dowagers clinging to the rags of finery. All the other trees, except the evergreens, had surrendered to autumn and away to the west, where the woods ran down to Home Farm pastures, the beeches stood like huge, bronze mushrooms, marching through a shallow sea of green. Most of the hedgerow flowers were gone but here and there, as a pledge of spring, was a stray campion and on the very edge of the wood a few foxgloves, still standing sentinel with bells ready to ring. As always, unless the wind was in the north, he could smell the sea here, and its tang reminded him of ventures past so that he could isolate his purpose as never before.

What was his true purpose in the Valley? What was he trying to do with and for the scattered families, enclosed by the sea, the railway line, and Gilroy's boundary in the west? Had he elected himself judge, jury and custodian of their lives over the next half-century? Or was his role rather that of referee? Or, again, was he simply a landlord, with the power to pull on the rein or bestow occasional bonuses?

Did ownership of the soil that sustained these people give him the right to plot their destinies? And if not, then who would? Perhaps his true responsibility was confined to his pocket and even to Zorndorff's, so long as he kept the scrapyard revenue in reserve; or perhaps, by coddling them too much, he would sap their initiative. Was his a conception of Imperialism in miniature? Did the investors in Britain's overseas possessions think along these lines, when they poured in their capital, hogged all the lucrative posts, and talked of the white man's burden over their whiskies and sodas in jungle clearings and delta warehouses? How much imperial outlay and effort was inspired by benevolence and how much by the profit motive, or the sweets of personal power? Surely there was a parallel here, for had he not enjoyed the power he wielded within the Shallowford boundaries? And might it not, as he grew older and more cynical, corrupt him? The Lovells, presumably, had been corrupted by it, for what had any one of them been prepared to contribute to the Valley? A harvest supper once a year and an undertaking to do outside repairs on half-derelict property but only so long as local forelocks were stretched.

His mind explored the margins of his suzerainty but soon, under the spell of the creeping dusk, it lost its way in irrelevances so that he shelved the answers to these questions, promising himself that he would seek them again in the long winter evenings ahead. In the event, he did not wait as long. Riding into the yard, and giving Snowdrop's bridle to young Ikey, he was told that he had had a visitor, a Mr. James Grenfell, from Paxtonbury, who had left a card saying he would be visiting Coombe Bay this day week, and would call again to pay his respects to the new master of Shallowford.

Paul was intrigued by the tacit irony of the note and after a tradi-tional hunting tea of boiled eggs and toast, he took the trouble to sort through a pile of back numbers of the county press, certain in his mind that James Grenfell was someone of local consequence. He ran him down in the caption of a picture, illustrating the opening of a church bazaar, a slight, rather delicately built man in his late thirties or early forties, with a very earnest expression that gave his face a slightly fanatical look as he stood on the edge of a garlanded platform, present-ing prizes. He found the report on another page and learned that James (Jimmy) Grenfell was the Liberal candidate for the Paxtonbury constituency (a division that included the Sorrel Valley, as well as the Gilroy estate adjoining) that was at present represented by Lieutenant-Colonel Hilton-Price, an amiable nominee of the Conservative and Unionist Party, and this caused Paul to wonder if his chance remark at Mary Willoughby's school, advertising sympathy with the defeated

181

Boers, might have led Grenfell to anticipate support for the Liberals. He was glad then that he had been out when Grenfell called, for he was far too undecided as yet to commit himself but, in another way, the candidate's call flattered him so that he questioned Mrs. Handcock on local politics when she came in to clear away the tea things.

"What happens here when there is a general election, Mrs. Handcock?"

"Well," she admitted, "nothing much, as I knows of! Blue goes in, and Yellow maakes a praper ol' song an' dance about it! Us 'ave never been aught but Blue yerabouts, Mr. Craddock. My father voted for Lieutenant-Colonel Hilton-Price's father all his life but I never troubled myself with 'em one way or the other."

"How about your husband? Does he vote for the Conservatives?"

"Lord no," she said, "whatever would people like us want with either one of 'em? We both got more'n enough to do without draping they ole rosettes about us an' marchin' up an' down chanting they silly ole ditties."

"What ditties?"

"Oh, giddon, you must have heard 'em! They as begin '*Vote, vote, vote for Colonel Hilton, kick old Grenfell out the door . . .*', and suchlike ole rubbage!"

"But Mr. Grenfell has never managed to get his foot inside the door, has he?"

"Well no," she said, "and a good thing too when a body comes to think of it, for us could 'ardly do with a nobody like 'ee standing for Parlyment, tho' they zay his father did, only up-country tho', among the chimbleys! My Horace says he ought to be locked up, along o' that rascal Lloyd George, for encouraging they Irish the way he does! Paxtonbury be church folk you see, on account o' the cathedral!"

"Now what the devil has church got to do with Grenfell's politics?" he demanded, smiling, but she looked at him severely, replying, "Now what call has an educated gentleman like you to be askin' that of an ignorant old body like me? You must know that Blue be church an' Yellow be chapel, zame as it be all over the country! If you baint teasing me, as I think you be, Mr. Craddock, you'd best go to Parson Bull for the answer! He'd lose no time putting 'ee right!" and she waddled out, to the whisper of starch and the rattle of outraged crockery.

About a week later, on returning home early one bitter afternoon,

182

Paul was met by a flustered Mrs. Handcock on the steps of the kitchen. He had taken to using the back door and Mrs. Handcock, a stickler for the domestic proprieties, had complained of this more than once but today she greeted him with "You'll just have to go in by the front, Mr. Craddock! *He's* there in the library, waitin' for 'ee! And a fine to-do this be, I mus' say, marchin' up to the front door, ringing the bell, and zaying as he'll wait when I tell him youm about your business!"

"Who?" asked Paul, forgetting Grenfell's promise to call again, and she said, "*Him!* That little wisp of a body, 'Jimmy Gren' Something-or-other but he might have been Colonel Hilton-Price himself for the airs about him! You'd best show him the door, Mr. Craddock, before there's a praper upset yerabouts!"

"Good Lord," protested Paul, "why should there be? Can't a Liberal candidate call on me as openly as a Unionist? Don't be so damned prejudiced! He might talk your husband into using his vote before he's done!" but Mrs. Handcock was so horrified by this possibility that she shut the door in his face and left him no alternative but to walk round to the forecourt and come in by the main door.

He found James Grenfell examining books in the library and although he was polite and affable Paul thought his greeting was spiced with a certain irony. The newspaper picture had not done him justice, for although he was of insignificant build, and looked far from robust, his brown, deepset eyes held in them a kindness and humour that could be seen as soon as he smiled.

"Ah, Mr. Craddock, at last!" he said. "I shan't keep you long, but I thought I must call again, on my way over to Coombe Bay. Tuesday is my Coombe Bay day, you see, when I call on Ephraim Morgan, my chairman in the Valley. He did some work for you I believe, so I have the advantage of knowing rather more about you than you know about me!" Paul murmured something polite and Grenfell went on, "Morgan is a bit of a hothead but I really don't know how I should fare in this political desert without him! When I first came here I couldn't count on a single vote south of the railway line. Now I'm certain of at least fifty! But I believe you are numbered among The Great Uncommitted, Mr. Craddock?"

"Yes, I am," said Paul, a little breathlessly, for the man's assurance was formidable. "I've never had a chance to vote; I was overseas on my twenty-first birthday and in hospital during the last election."

"Very well, Mr. Craddock, then let's put you at ease straight away.

I'm not here to solicit, I came because I was curious! My intelligence service is the strongest part of my organisation (the weakest being finances) so I've already heard them speak of you."

"To my credit or otherwise?" Paul asked, smiling, for he found the little man engagingly original.

"Both," Grenfell said, "but somewhat loaded in your favour!"

"Look here," said Paul on impulse, "why don't you stay for lunch? What time are you due in Coombe Bay?"

Grenfell said, with genuine humility, "You'd really like me to stay?"

"I would indeed," Paul said. "I'm getting tired of my own company. Rudd, my agent, is laid up with an injury in Portsmouth, and the two other friends I've made since I settled in are also away. I haven't talked anything but pigs, crops, poultry and sheep in weeks."

Somewhat to his surprise Grenfell hesitated. "I don't know," he said, slowly, "maybe I oughtn't to take advantage of you. They said you were a friendly chap but I didn't expect this civility."

"It seems to me an ordinary enough civility," Paul said rather huffily but the little man lifted a protesting hand and said, smiling, "Look here, Mr. Craddock, don't take offence I beg of you. The fact is, entertaining me might easily damage your relationships with certain influential people round here. Ordinarily I wouldn't give a damn, but as you've admitted, you're uncommitted."

"And I daresay I shall remain so," Paul said, "but what the devil has that to do with inviting a casual visitor to have a bite to eat and a glass of sherry?"

"Nothing whatever," said Grenfell, chuckling, "I'd be delighted to stay and if I begin riding one of my hobby horses, just cut in and cap it with experiences in the Transvaal."

Paul told the girl Thirza to inform Mrs. Handcock that the visitor was staying for luncheon and then, as they drank sherry, they fell to discussing the recent peace-treaty terms which Paul knew in outline but Grenfell, he soon realised, knew in great detail. When lunch arrived, served by a blank-faced Mrs. Handcock, Paul told his visitor something of the reaction among rank and file volunteers concerning the herding of Boer families into camps that had been sited without regard to water supplies or sanitary facilities. He found Grenfell a good listener and went on to tell him of the change in the attitude of most of the civilian-soldiers after actual contact with the Boers, speaking without regard to the hovering Mrs. Handcock, whom he guessed was saving every titbit of the conversation for the oracular

Horace. When she left them to their cheese and coffee Grenfell said, with a laugh, "I presume the excellent Mrs. Handcock is an enemy camp-follower?", and Paul recounted his housekeeper's simplification of politics, adding that her husband Horace had never yet used his vote.

"Ah, that's a real trouble in places like this," Grenfell said. "Most of them are so out of touch that nobody can make them accept their responsibilities as democrats. Even when the Tories bundle them into carriages, and haul 'em off to the poll, they haven't the least idea what earns them the free ride, although most of 'em put a cross for the man who pays the fare out of a sense of fair play. I wonder what the Chartists would think about it all, or going further back, men like Hampden, and old John Ball? Sometimes I'd like to call a party truce for five years—the life of a Parliament, say—so that both parties ·could drive home the fact that the most important single gain of the British people over the centuries was the Reform Bill, and the Redistribution Act that followed it."

"How would you personally go about it?" Paul asked, and Grenfell's eyes blazed as he said, "Why, by real blood-and-thunder methods! By the use of magic lantern slides, showing how much blood was shed by Englishmen from the fifteenth century onwards! By lectures on incidents like Peterloo and the Tolpuddle Martyrs! By borrowing the techniques of the halfpenny press, to drive the lesson home in all kinds of ways—plays, pageants, debates and the use of every mechanical gadget on the market! Then, when everybody had been pricked in one spot or another, we'd have an election and the result would astonish us all! Maybe they wouldn't have one or other of us, or the Fabians either, because people would see the main issues more clearly and not let themselves be fobbed off with party propaganda."

"What are the main issues?" Paul asked and Grenfell suddenly stopped crumbling his bread and placing both hands on the table looked across at his host: "There are only two that concern me," he said. "One is tolerance and the other has been written into the first paragraph of every political tract of the last four hundred years—that men are born equal, and should enjoy equality of opportunity! Everything worth a farthing in politics are rooted in those principles."

The sparkle left his eyes and he smiled his winning smile as he stood up and extended his hand. "You failed to keep your promise, Mr. Craddock! You agreed to stop me if I began preaching. However, it has been delightful meeting you, delightful and . . . yes, I must say it, extremely encouraging!"

"I don't promise to vote for you," Paul said and Grenfell replied, "I told you—I didn't come here to solicit!"

Paul ordered Grenfell's trap to be brought to the front and when it was bowling away down the drive, with the little man crouched on the high seat flourishing his whip in farewell, he thought it was a long time since he had enjoyed such pleasant company at his table.

III

Will Codsall and Elinor Willoughby were married very quietly at the Congregationist Meeting House, in Coombe Bay, on the first day of December, when the seasons were still delicately poised between autumn and winter and the Sorrel Valley was awaiting the north-east wind to strip the last leaf from the Priory thickets and for the blue water between beach and sandbars to turn its wind-whipped winter grey. It was a day of strong gusts and the threat of sleet, no day for a wedding, or for anything more than the fitting of draught boards to cottage doors and a cursing of finches who had weakened the thatch in nesting forays throughout spring.

Paul and Mrs. Handcock drove over to Coombe Bay and took their places in the back pew of the whitewashed chapel, Mrs. Handcock gathering her coat about her, as though close contact with so many dissenters was a physical hazard. She was here at the insistence of Squire, reinforced by her dislike of the groom's mother who, or so Squire had warned her, had advertised her intention of causing a riot. Paul himself would have preferred John Rudd as a buffer between himself and Arabella but Rudd's ribs were slow to mend and he had now postponed his return until New Year.

Word must have gone round that there was likely to be free entertainment at the meeting house, for during the interval between the arrival of Will (buttoned into tight blue serge and wearing a three-inch collar that kept his chin at a sharp angle) and that of the bride, every pew filled with Valley folk, each of whom entered quietly and cautiously, as though expecting the roof to collapse at any moment. The Potter girls were there and with them Walt Pascoe, who would be a bridegroom himself in the New Year. Rose Derwent tiptoed in and bowed her head, just as if this was a real church, and Farmer Willoughby's minister from Whinmouth a real priest. Paul smiled

186

across at Rose but she did not return his smile and he wondered briefly about Claire, and her interminable stay in Kent but not for long, for he was far too apprehensive and his fears were not entirely allayed by having posted Ikey Palfrey at the head of the village street to warn him of the approach of the enemy. Arthur and Martha Pitts arrived late, causing everyone to look fearfully over their shoulders, and then came Willoughby's hired hand, who had obviously been detached as scout by the bridegroom, for he sidled up to the waiting groom and shook his head, indicating that so far there was no sign of Arabella. At this Will's chin shot up another point or two, and he ran his forefinger round the inside of his collar, sighing so loudly that some of the girls began to giggle. His embarrassment, however, did something to relieve the tension in the chapel, so Paul leaned towards the housekeeper and whispered, "Maybe she's thought better of it!" but Mrs. Handcock said nothing. She was wishing herself anywhere but here, abetting a young man whose kindheartedness was likely to be exploited to the prejudice of good order and discipline in the Valley.

She forgot her misgivings, however, when a stir at the rear of the church heralded the arrival of the bride and Elinor entered on her father's arm, a little wisp of a thing, in a white muslin gown, with a Honiton lace veil embroidered with true lover's knots held in place by an evergreen wreath. Edwin Willoughby looked very solemn as the two walked the length of the aisle and Will, nudged by his groomsman, jumped up with a clatter of boots and looked around helplessly, as though expecting to be told what to do next. Help was at hand for Elinor, half lifting her veil, smiled at him reassuringly and it was her smile that touched Mrs. Handcock as it did every other woman in the church. She looked so fragile, so pretty and yet so confident of her destiny.

After that the ceremony went off very smoothly, responses being uttered in voices that contained an element of defiance, and when the couple walked down the aisle to the chapel door, where they were showered with clammy handfuls of confetti by the Coombe Bay folk waiting outside, there was a general sense of anti-climax. Paul kissed Elinor on the cheek and shook hands with a beaming Will, who seemed almost dazed with relief that nothing had occurred to shame him or spoil the occasion for Elinor. There was no reception; the couple simply drove back to Deepdene in a hired Coombe Bay gig and the bride's father followed in his trap and everybody stood about in the wind until Paul, sensing that something was expected of him, issued

187

a general invitation to everyone to join him at The Raven and drink the young couple's health in beer or cider. Mrs. Handcock whispered urgently, "Now, dornee indulge 'em, Mr. Craddock!" but she came along nevertheless and drank tea with Minnie Flowers, the landlord's wife, in the kitchen, whilst Paul entertained the groomsman, Walt Pascoe and a dozen others in the bar. It was Walt, feeling himself half initiated in the mysteries of bridal rites, who expressed general disappointment with the ceremony when he said, cheerfully, "Well, here's your health, Squire, but 'twas all a bit of damp squib, wasn't 'er? I would ha' wagered half-a-sovereign to sixpence old Arabella would ha' sailed in and set about poor old Will with her umbrella, but 'er must have been tied to a chair last minute by Martin!" This was received as a great joke, Martin Codsall being recognised as the most hagridden husband in the Valley, yet there was a grain of truth in Walt's guess after all. Arabella had certainly intended making good her threat and it was Martin who had, in fact, prevented her.

Word had reached Arabella that the wedding was timed for 2 p.m. and at one o'clock she came into the kitchen dressed in her high-buttoned best with elastic-sided boots and a huge fruit hat, a kind of horned cornucopia made of hard, black straw and glutted with plums and grapes and cherries, that swung like so many coloured bells when she turned her head. Martin, also in his Sunday clothes, awaited her, having spent the entire morning in earnest attempts to dissuade her from disgracing the family. Arabella knew Martin well but not so well as she imagined, or she might have noted his unnaturally high colour, as though the wretchedness of providing a public spectacle and destroying the last bridge between him and his firstborn was already bringing blushes to his cheeks. He was unusually neat and tidy too, even for churchgoing, his greying hair damped down and his gold pin and boots twinkling in the firelight. He remained silent when Arabella consulted her bodice watch, saying that it was time to go if they were to arrive at the chapel in good time, but as they seated themselves in the high-slung trap he made a final appeal to her dignity, saying, "Then youm still bent on every layabout in the Valley laughing their silly heads off over us, Mother?", but all she replied was, "The sooner we get there the sooner it'll be over an' done with!"

"But damme," he protested, "it won't do a particle a good to any one of us! Do 'ee think this kind o' caper will fetch our Will back?"

"No, I don't," she said calmly, "but it'll make a fool of 'im an' shame her and that's all I care about at this stage!"

It was all he cared about too, and it tilted him into mutiny. She had not noticed that Flick, their sedate and ageing pony, was not harnessed to the trap or that Cobber, a recently acquired cob of doubtful sobriety, had taken Flick's place between the shafts. He was surprised that she had not commented upon this when they came out and even had an excuse on the tip of his tongue but he put her poor observation down to the cloud of spite that had settled on her brain. Saying no more he cracked the whip as the trap moved off down the track to the bridge at a spanking pace, the measured gavotte of Arabella's cherries and plums changing to a brisk polka and then a reckless can-can, as the cob lengthened its stride and bumped over the ruts at twelve miles per hour. "At this rate," thought Martin, grimly, "us'll be in Coombe Bay in under the half-hour, providin' we'm *going* to Coombe Bay this afternoon!"

The first indication that Arabella had of his treachery was when the trap shot across the plank bridge and swung left instead of right, taking the river road that ran under the slope of Priory Wood. She was so astonished that for a few moments she could find no words to comment and this, for Arabella Codsall, implied a very great degree of astonishment indeed. Then it occurred to her that Martin must be so emotionally disturbed that he had forgotten his way to the coast, so she shrieked, "Fool! Pull him up, and turn him round!", but instead of obeying Martin lifted his whip and brought it slashing down across the cob's haunches, and the cob, already going at a rolling canter, threw up its head and moved from canter to gallop, almost pitching Arabella over the seat rail and causing her to let out a sustained scream that startled every bird in the Valley. She realised then that he had gone mad, for only madness could explain open revolt and she realised too, with a coolness that did her credit in the circumstances, that if they continued in this direction at this pace they would soon pass a point where it would be impossible to retrace their steps in time for the wedding. The thought submerged her fears so that she made a wild grab at the reins, but madness upon madness, Martin switched them to his right hand and fended her off with the butt end of the whip, so that she suddenly abandoned all thought of the wedding in the certainty that he was bent on oversetting the trap and killing her and himself. She began to plead, holding tight to the rail with one hand and keeping her fruit hat from flying away with the other. The hat, in fact, was beginning to disintegrate, and cherries were already cascading into her lap. A plum, or a large grape, also worked itself loose but this went unnoticed, striking her shoulder and shooting into the back of the trap among some sacks.

The cob was now at stretched gallop, and on the uneven surface of the road the trap was bumping from side to side like a hay trailer, coupled to a recklessly driven waggon. Martin concentrated on preventing the hubs of the wheels touching the bank on one side or the flood posts on the other but Arabella had nothing to do but hang on and scream and this she did, shriek upon shriek issuing from her mouth in an almost continuous sound that sent every river bird wheeling from the reeds and caused a curious buzzard watching from an elevation of three hundred feet, to back up against the wind currents until it could decide what was happening on the ribbon of road below.

Then, as the cob saw the freedom of the moor before him, he shot off along the upland track that was not even as well surfaced as the river road and suddenly, to cap all, a shower of sleet came down, driving into their faces and tearing Arabella's hat from her grasp, so that she stopped screaming and began to plead but all Martin did was to lay on with his whip and the cob, that had been enjoying the outcry until now, panicked and swerved, shooting off into heather and then back again but without varying its frightful pace across the moor.

It was when they came to a gradient where neither whip, shouts, nor rattle could induce the blown cob to maintain its pace that the trap slowed to an uncertain walk but Arabella hardly noticed the change. She was sobbing and breathless, her unpinned hair obscuring her vision, her lovely fruit hat a sodden bundle half-a-mile back along the road, her mind tormented by the prospect of living out the remainder of her days with a lunatic husband. The sleet still came at them like a shower of spears but he paid no heed to it, sitting hunched over the footboard, reins and whip in hand, eyes fixed on the crest of the moor ahead.

"Well, Mother," he said at length, "I reckon that does it! Us couldn't get to chapel in time now if us went there behind racehorses so put up your hair and make the best of it! Us'll take it easy going backalong!"

She stopped wheezing then and glared at him through a matted screen of hair, for clearly he was not mad after all. Incredibly he had done this terrible thing deliberately, a crafty, premeditated manœuvre, aimed at cheating her of her revenge. She said, softly and murderously,

"I'll make you pay for this, Martin Codsall! As God is me judge, I'll make you pay!" but her threat did not disturb him unduly for he reflected, whilst turning the trap and heading back to the river road, that he had already paid all he had or was likely to have and what profit was there in plaguing a bankrupt?

Barely a mile from the spot on the edge of the moor, where Martin Codsall had turned the trap earlier in the day, his son and daughter-in-law were using the fading light to make the Priory farmhouse habitable. It was not really a farmhouse at all but a largish cottage, still half a ruin. Will and Elinor, helped by the biblical twins, Matt and Luke, had retimbered and rethatched the roof, and had also given the whole place a thorough scouring but their main efforts had been directed to the outhouses, for, as Will had put it on the day he had first taken Elinor there, "Us can only live in one room at a time and us must have somewhere for the livestock when the weather zets in." Now, on their owners' wedding night, a fat sow and her litter were snug in the small sty and two dozen saddlebacks were snoring in the big sty, while Gertie, the Alderney, old Willoughby's wedding gift, occupied a byre that was rather more comfortable than the farm kitchen where some of the broken windows were plugged with cardboard. Bride and groom made light of discomfort, however, for it seemed to them a very wonderful thing to be alone in a house of their own and as soon as they had changed they borrowed Willoughby's trap and drove over the moor in the teeth of the storm, stabling the horse in the ramshackle stable and lighting a roaring fire from sawn timber left over from the repairs. By the time it was dark and the lamp was lit, the kitchen began to look like a home although there was nothing on the stone floor but a rush mat and only a single wooden chair beside the open hearth, where Elinor had set a rickety table and the milking stool left behind by the Hardcastles. Fortunately Hardcastle's widow had also bequeathed them other pieces that had not been considered worth the trouble of hauling away after the funeral. Upstairs, in the now rainproof main bedroom, was a rusty iron bedstead, already neatly made with Elinor's hoarded linen, a chest of drawers warped by damp and a cracked sheet of backed glass for use as a mirror. In the scullery was a built-in dresser, with a few chipped cups and plates which would do for the time being for all their savings, including the Squire's sovereign wedding gift, had been laid out on pigs and winter feed.

About six o'clock Elinor called Will from the stairs, where he was replacing rotted boards and she might have been married years rather than hours judged by the casual way she summoned him to his meal and sat him on the only chair whilst she took the stool and began to ladle generous helpings of thick vegetable stew into which he dipped bread she had baked that same morning. They ate in silence and while they were occupied in everyday habits—eating, firemending, washing up under the scullery pump—they were neither shy nor withdrawn. It was only later, when Elinor carried the stone hot-water bottle upstairs to air the lavender-scented linen she had brought as her portion, that the fearful wonder of the situation touched her and she took the opportunity, whilst he was finishing off his carpentry, of slipping out of her clothes and pausing for a moment in front of the cracked mirror to study herself in the light of the candle. She was not sure that she liked what she saw, a small, girlish body, with honey-coloured plaits almost as thick as her wrists screening her small, hard breasts. "Well," she mused, "I wonder if he'll like me now he's got me?" and then, doubtfully but not altogether apprehensively, "and I wonder if he'll use me roughly, as he tried to often enough in the old days?" She already thought of their courtship as "the old days", belonging to the distant past but she no longer feared Mrs. Codsall's sourness or persecution. She was done with Four Winds and so, praise God, was Will! The few words, spoken by the red-haired preacher from Whinmouth, had banished Mrs. Codsall and all her works so that nobody, not even King Edward himself, could separate them now and the certainty of this warmed her belly and thighs, reaching to the tips of her little toes on the bare boards at the foot of the bed. She pushed the stone water bottle to "his side" and stood holding her long flannel nightdress against herself, fearful and expec-tant, yet somehow safe and rooted. Then she put the candle down on the box beside the bed and unlatched the door, calling to him as he knelt, hammering in the light of a storm-lamp hooked to the banister.

"Will," she said, "I'm going to bade now, unless you'll be wanting anything more."

"No, midear," he called back, "I'll damp the vire and come on up. Tiz a botchy ole job in this kind o' light!"

The mildness of his voice reassured her, banishing the last of her fears and she went back into the bedroom, folded her nightgown and placed it under his pillow, for he had told her some time ago that he liked to "sleep high" and the only pillows they had were two ratty old

192

cushions, loaned by Aunt Mary. Then she got into bed and inhaled the lavender scent, reaching out and touching the space where he would lie and finding it well-warmed by the bottle. He came in holding the storm lantern high and looked down on her with a great, broad smile, the first she had seen on his face that day.

"Ah, youm lovely, Elinor," he said, "and I dorn know what I done to deserve 'ee!"

"Youm a lovely gurt thing yourself, Will," she told him, "and never let no one tell you different! Make haste man and blow thicky candle out!"

IV

Winter entered the Valley like a white nun, austerely beautiful but pitiless, glorifying in mortification of the flesh and calling upon men to face realities.

Young Henry Pitts, of Hermitage, saw winter not as a nun, however, but as a malevolent clown who got under his feet and threw him headlong on the steep path to the sties, who clothed his Guernseys in their breath and sent them mincing over iced ruts to frozen pools, who sealed the very gate latches with ice and threatened his winter corn, sown with so much effort in early autumn. For the snow reached Hermitage first, moving in from the north-east and the heavy flakes floated rather than fell, each being set down gently and individually by a wind that had carried them all the way from the Russian steppes. Then, having frozen the imperishable grin on Henry's rubbery face, winter moved south-west, scattering diamonds across the Codsall stubble, slowing the Sorrel current, sealing its oxbow and stiffening its rushes, until it plucked at Martin Codsall's long nose as he stood cursing the clumsiness of his new cowman and declaring that Will had emptied udders in half the time taken by his replacement. Then the frost doubled to strike the Home Farm, silencing the sawmill and reminding the shepherd twins, Matt and Luke, that the lambing season was not far off and if snow fell now it might go hard with them in February. Down at the foot of the Coombe the snow lay lightly but the wind was just as keen and Meg and her thinly clad daughters shivered in their leaking kitchen and wash-house. Only Tamer, with over sixteen stone of blubber to protect him, could sneer at the sky and waddle across his turnip fields wondering who would do his spring sowing now that Squire had deprived him of Sam.

Higher up the Dell, where soon nobody could distinguish between

193

Potter's broken fences and the tiny hedgerows of Farmer Willoughby, drifts began to pile where the timber was sparse and Willoughby's hired man, plodding about Elinor's business in the henhouses, wondered glumly why the birds resented Elinor's abdication so much that they had gone into a mass moult. Mary still kept her school, for the Valley children were a hardy lot and as long as the river road was open continued to ride or walk to their morning lessons. There was a warm stove in the schoolroom and a long row of hooks over it to dry mittens and gaiters, and always, sharp at ten-thirty, cocoa for every scholar, even those banished to corners and wearing dunces' caps.

On the bleak upland of Derwent's holding tempers were sharper than the frost, for Edward Derwent sorely missed Claire and Rose was worried about her horses, realising there could be no hunting this side of New Year. Even at exercise the snow balled under shoes and brought animals down, so that they spent most of their time in loose boxes, eating the season's profits.

Perhaps the only two souls in the entire Valley to welcome the snow were Ikey Palfrey and Hazel Potter, the one because here in the country it was a novel experience, the other because it gave her an excuse to play truant every day.

Ikey had seen snow before, of course, but never snow like this, pure, unsullied and dazzling white, crisp, powdery and untrodden by man or beast. When snow fell on Bermondsey it never lay more than an hour but was soon slush under the pressure of boots, hooves and cartwheels. Under a mantle of snow every Thames-side factory looked like a prison and every dwelling was seen as the squat, defeated hovel it really was but down here, especially when the sun shone, the long slope between the big house and Shallowford Woods turned coral and rose-pink and every branch of every tree became a crystal chandelier. The birds grew tame, not merely sparrows and thrushes that always haunted the scrapyard but all kinds of birds, some of which he had never seen at close quarters, great tits and blue tits, crested wrens, greenfinches, bullfinches and dozens of perky robins, who perched on the harness pegs and ate crumbs from his hand. Then there were gloriously long slides in the drive and snowball fights with Gappy, the gardener's boy, when Chivers was safely out of the way but Ikey liked best his lonely tramps along the edge of the woods and up the west face of the Coombe to school, for here, in a silent, winter world, he could indulge his extravagant fancies and there was no one in sight to break the spell.

He saw himself in many disguises and by no means always against a background of snow and ice but sometimes crossing waterless deserts and mountain ranges and sometimes rafting across the Pacific or shifting for himself (and possibly Squire Craddock) on a coral island, like Jack, Ralph and Peterkin, in Ballantyne's book. During those tramps to and from Deepdene he was everyone he had ever met in Mary Willoughby's library—Robinson Crusoe, Monte Cristo, D'Artagnan, Sherlock Holmes, Jim Hawkins and David Balfour on the run from redcoats. Anyone watching him making his way across the meadow to Hazel Potter's squirrel tree, or along the southern edge of Shallowford Woods, might have thought him pursued by Furies. Every now and then he looked fearfully over his shoulder and darted for cover to emerge, bent double, to dash across the snow firing as he ran until he reached a bank where, it seemed, yet another ambush awaited him which he evaded by changing direction and disappearing into a ditch.

He was so engaged one overcast morning on his way home from Deepdene after Mary Willoughby had dismissed school an hour before time because Derwent had told her there would be another fall by mid-afternoon. Ikey usually went part way home with Sydney Codsall and children of a Codsall labourer, but they were an unadventurous group and preferred to take the track down the Dell and through the Potter holding to the river road, whereas Ikey liked the steep slopes of the Bluff, where he could toboggan down to the thick gorse that grew along the edge of the Coombe and then, by a frozen brook and two stiles, enter the meadows bordering Shallowford Woods.

It was very cold but he moved swiftly and kept his blood circulating, so that when he reached the woods he felt pleasantly warm and was tempted by a faint gleam of sunshine to use his extra hour's freedom by pushing through brittle briars to the top of the escarpment, overlooking the mere. He had not thought of the mere as being a solid oval of ice, with its mysterious, pagoda-crowned island as the sole break in its surface but now it occurred to him that he might be able to cross over and inspect the ruin, which was something he had been wanting to do for some time. He went on down to the margin and tested the ice but it was not strong enough to bear his weight so he moved round the lake to its far side to explore a part of the woods that was new to him. A tangle of evergreens grew here, close-set larch and dwarf pine, stockaded about with overgrown laurels and rhododendrons and it was here that he flushed a hare, who bounded from under his feet and dashed into the wood with Ikey in hot pursuit. He soon lost sight of the hare but found instead some deer tracks and followed them for about a mile along a narrow twisting path that split and split again, until he lost the tracks at a spot where a pine had fallen across the path barring further progress.

He had been so intent upon the chase that he had not noticed snow had begun to fall but when he turned back, seeking the mere, it drove into his face so harshly that he could hardly see his way and although he reasoned that it could not be more than two o'clock the wood seemed terrifyingly dark and gloomy. His outward tracks were now obliterated and soon he realised that he must have taken a wrong turning, for he blundered on and on in growing desperation without being able to break free of the tangled undergrowth or come within sight of the lake. Snow whirled down on him more and more thickly and in spite of his exertions he began to feel numb, particularly in the foot that got wet testing the ice. He tried to console himself with the thought that this was a real adventure but it was little comfort. His courage ebbed with every step and soon he realised he was wholly lost and likely to stay lost unless he could find help or shelter. He held on as long as he could, and perhaps a little longer, setting his teeth and slashing with numbed hands at the clawing briars and laurel branches but at last, as he entered a tiny clearing, the storm, the thicket and the paralysing cold defeated him and he uttered a wild shout of despair that issued from him involuntarily like a soul quitting a body.

The sound of his own voice encouraged him a little and he shouted again but when there was no answer he suddenly burst into tears and sat down on a log, thrusting his knuckles into his eyes and howling with terror and misery. He was still in this unheroic posture when he heard the crunch of feet and looking up, wildly hopeful, saw Hazel Potter standing gazing down at him in silent wonder, one hand pulling at her lip, the other swinging a small tin attached to her wrist by a string.

He recognised her at once as the child who had sat crosslegged on the pedestal at the coronation supper-ball and the horrid embarrassment of being caught by a girl in the act of blubbering made him glare as though she had been a predatory animal on the prowl.

"What are you doing here?" he blustered, but she did not seem to resent his aggressive manner and continued to pluck her lip and swing her tin, which Ikey now identified as a home-made handwarmer of the kind he had often used in winter in the scrapyard.

"Youm lost, baint 'ee?" Hazel said at last, and the corners of her mouth puckered as though she could easily have laughed at his dilemma.

It was useless to deny the fact so he said, loftily, "Yerse, I am, I never bin this side o' the woods and was caught in the storm. Tracking deer!" he added, impressively.

This interested her. "You was gonner kill 'em?"

"No," he said modestly, "I ain't got a gun an' Squire won't have 'em killed. I was tracking 'em, to see where they went."

"Ah, they went downalong," she said authoritatively, "they always do in the snow. Henry Pitts puts feed out for 'em but they don't stay, they come back, soon as they've eaten an' move over to the spruce where there's plenty o' bark to bite on! Most everything lives this side o' the mere—foxes, hares, an' badgers too, tho' there's a set 'longside my squirrel tree, upalong."

She talked as an expert, as someone privy to all the secrets of the wood and he had a strong impression that she thought of foxes and badgers not as creatures but as family units, inhabiting farms and living within prescribed borders, just like the Potters, the Codsalls and the Willoughbys. He had never heard the word "set" before in this sense and would have liked to ask about it but not wishing to display his ignorance he said, "Can you show me the way aht? I'm late 'ome, and I got work waiting in the tack-room."

She smiled then, and he noticed that her rather vacant face underwent a remarkable change when her mouth widened, exposing strong, white teeth. It was as though the smile was something she used for switching identities—from a dull-witted waif to a woodsprite in a homespun skirt of undyed sheep's wool and long gaiters of rabbit skin, tucked into patched, lace-up boots. One of the boots gaped like the mouth of a fish and exposed pink toes. He was enormously impressed by her yet was careful not to show it for although she clearly knew her way, which he did not, she was still only a girl and also a Potter and therefore of no account. She looked, he thought, only half human in her outlandish clothes, with a mop of matted red-gold hair and green eyes but as she continued to smile at him and her pink tongue emerged to moisten her lips, he had the impression that here in the woods she was a kind of queen and that all the creatures would come running to her whistle, that she could have told you everything in the wood that was good to eat and every berry that was poisonous, that there would be nothing that went on here that she did not know about

197

and this gave her a purely local omnipotence exceeding even the Squire's. She said, carelessly, "You'd ha' died o' the cauld, Boy, if I hadn't 'eard 'ee squawk! You shoulder kept walking 'til you dropped an' even then you should ha' crawled! Youm praaper mazed to zit yourself down in the snow. Coom, I'll tak' 'ee backalong!", and without giving him an opportunity to justify himself in any way she took him by the hand and led him into what looked like a low tunnel cut through the thickest part of the laurels.

What astonished him more than her anticipation of every twist and turn in this maze of undergrowth was her body temperature. The hand that clutched his was as warm as if it had just been withdrawn from a fur glove, and he reasoned that her feet must be just as warm for how else could she endure to walk through thick snow with a gaping hole in her boot? She not only knew exactly which rabbit run to follow and which to reject but also the strength and thickness of every obstruction. Without leaving hold of his hand for a moment she twisted this way and that, pushing through a tangle of branches without a second's hesitation, so that presently they came out on the side of the lake that ran directly past the island with the pagoda. He said gruffly, when he had recovered from his astonishment, "Orlright, I know me way from here," but she did not relinquish his hand but began hauling him up the slope to the crest of the escarpment where, in the gathering dusk, he saw the welcome yellow glow of the Big House lights.

"I'll leave 'ee here, Boy," she said, "but dornee stray that zide again 'til the snow's gone." She looked up at the sky and sniffed. " 'Er won't be long now; us've zeen the worst of it."

His respect for her grew and grew, whittling away at his male arrogance and making it seem mean and ungracious, so that he admitted, hesitantly, "I was lost orlright, an' I dunno what I'd have done if you hadn't bobbed up. What's your name? Mine's Ikey, I'm stable boy down there."

"Yes, I know. I've overlooked 'ee often enough," she said lightly. "I'm Hazel, and they zay I'm mazed. I'm not tho', but I let 'em think it's so, for that way I go where I plaises," and with this astonishing confession she turned away and seemed on the point of vanishing into the dusk but he called urgently, "Where can I find yer if I want to go that side of the mere again?", and she replied, pausing in her stride, "Come down by the Niggerman's Church and whistle. Whistle loud and I'll come to 'ee," and she put her fingers in her mouth and blew, producing a long, low and very piercing sound like the summons of a London cabby. Then, before he could ask her to teach him this engaging trick, or identify the "Niggerman's Church" as the old pagoda, she had disappeared, moving so silently that he could not have sworn whether she went back down the slope or east along the path towards the Coombe.

He stood there looking into the darkness where she had vanished and he thought how far from mazed she was but how completely she fooled everyone in the Valley. Then he wondered if he should tell Chivers or Mrs. Handcock of his adventure, of how, without Hazel Potter, he might have died down there in the wood but he decided not for this would be an admission of personal inadequacy and might also mean future prohibitions. At least, this was what he told himself but the truth was he was reluctant to share with others the knowledge that Hazel Potter was really a princess, masquerading as a half-witted waif, or that God who had once before come to his aid in a moment of despair obviously had a special interest in his welfare. Why else should He have directed her to him, barely fifteen minutes before daylight faded?

He brushed the dead leaves from his coat and went on down the slope towards the pool of orange light.

CHAPTER EIGHT

I

HAZEL POTTER knew her weather signs. The wind veered round to the south-west before Christmas and the snow was washed from the banked lanes by driving rain, so that after a spell there was hardly a trace of it save for pockets of slush under the trees.

Paul went about his business cheerfully enough, making his rounds two or three times a week, discussing spring sowing with unhurried men like Arthur Pitts and Honeyman, and pigs with Will Codsall, whose ramshackle holding was now gradually assuming a patterned neatness like Four Winds and High Coombe. Paul did not think of Grace Lovell much during the day but at night, when he was sitting before the library fire, loneliness sometimes stole upon him and the technical books on soil, shorthorns and land drainage, prescribed as evening reading by John Rudd lay undigested on his knees as he pictured the dark, compact figure of Grace in the leather armchair opposite, her eyes bent over some sewing or gazing abstractedly into the red glow of the Home Farm apple logs blazing in the hearth.

It was, he admitted to himself, a very improbable picture but his thoughts of her were always in this pleasant frame for after an interval of seven weeks, with no word from her except the scribbled message on the label of the puppy's collar, his memories of her arranged themselves in thicknesses, laid one upon the other like dockets in his office tray.

First there was the overall impression of mystery that her presence brought to him, with the certainty that somehow she belonged here in this house and by this fireside and this conviction was as strong and unreasoning as that which had possessed him concerning the estate as a whole on the day he had first ridden down from the moor alongside John Rudd. He could not say why this should be so; she had done little or nothing to confirm it but it persisted just the same, matching his possessive pleasure in the meadows, woods and leafy lanes between the Sorrel and the Bluff, the railway line and the silver sands of Coombe Bay. Then, adding a pinch of spice to her sense of belonging here, was the physical impact she made upon him—her neatness, her

200

containment, her cool, ivory skin seen against blue-black side curls and straight fringe, her dark, contracting brows arching over eyes the colour of dog violets in Priory Wood, her long cheekbones and firm little chin with the large dimple but above all, her presence as a whole, that seemed to him to promise so much to a man who could break through the defences she had erected against an invasion of her intense privacy and self-isolation. Was he such a man? He doubted it but doubts did not deny him reveries and flights of fancy, so that sometimes the sudden fall of the heavy book from his knees would drag him from an exotic dream in which he was mastering her in silent places about the house, while she, for her part, was submitting to his domination. The absurdity of these imaginings was sometimes brought home to him when he recollected that a proposal of marriage on his part had yielded no more than a vague promise to "think about it", but then, for comfort, he would look down at her dog and reflect that she must have thought of him as a man of compassion, gauche and unsophisticated perhaps, yet more eligible than the roystering Ralph Lovell, or any of the men she met in her father's rootless set, and this would launch him into fresh fields of speculation regarding the life she led in London, and what kept her there all this time, and if there was a lover in the background. He wondered too how much she knew about the source of his money and whether, indeed, such knowledge would disqualify him in her eyes, or those of her step-mother. It was then that the absurdity of his spontaneous proposal came down upon him with a rush, so that he told himself that he really had no wish to be taken seriously and that, for both their sakes, it would be better if they could look upon his impulsive advances as a flirtation, approximately in the same category as that he and Claire Derwent had shared before it went sour and she ran away to hide in Kent.

As the days passed it was this aspect of their relationship that began to gain ground at the expense of all the other daydreams. After all, he told himself, what did he know of the girl, and how much could one listen to instinct in matters as final as this? He had met her five times during a period of six months and on two of those occasions their conversation was such as might have passed between people in the street. He was sure, for instance, that a man like Franz Zorndorff would regard his infatuation as hopelessly immature, a park band-stand romance between adolescents, whereas John Rudd would have even stronger feelings about it, for he made no bones about including her family in his blanket of detestation of all the Lovells. And yet, behind all these misgivings was a curious inevitability of Grace Lovell as Mistress of Shallowford that could not be separated from his own identification with the estate and assumption of personal responsibility for all the people of the Valley. He had no clear idea of what he would tell either Rudd or Zorndorff about her, or what indeed he would say to Grace or Celia Lovell if either one of them took him at his word. He only knew that somewhere and somehow their paths would converge and that until they did real ownership of the Valley would elude him.

His thoughts were in this confused state when, a day or so before Christmas, a batch of letters arrived by a single post. He extracted all the seed catalogues, trade agricultural leaflets, bills and conveyances and carried the rest into his office, locking the door against interruptions.

The first was his fortnightly letter from Uncle Franz, to whom he had written in detail regarding his efforts to enlarge the estate to the north and east by the acquisition of the Priory freehold, now renamed Periwinkle Farm by Elinor and Codsall, and the cliff fields incorporated in High Coombe. Zorndorff had taken to addressing him as "My Dear Squire", using the form of address with restrained irony but he approved Paul's ready acceptance of a money draft from scrapyard profits, despite Paul's disclaimer which Zorndorff, it seemed, refused to take seriously. The Croat's letter was concise, businesslike and affectionate but there remained the hint of mockery in outwardly innocent phrases, as though, now that he had launched his "nephew", he could pretend that he was indulging the whim of an enthusiastic boy who would soon realise that the estate was all a bit of a joke between them, and could be wound up in the course of time. There was a footnote to the letter which seemed to Paul to underline this, for Zorndorff wrote: "If, by spring, you are persuaded that you have bitten off more than you can chew, don't despair, my dear boy! By pure chance you are batting on a safe wicket! Land values have jumped twenty per cent since the peace and we might even net a profit on your improvements!"

Paul smiled at this, made some notes in the margin and put the letter aside, opening a breezier one from John Rudd, who said he was up and about again and had been advised by his doctor to get as much exercise as possible in order that the cracked ribs could mend themselves. He added that he would be home again on New Year's Day, after seeing his boy Roderick off at Chatham.

The two letters in feminine handwriting Paul left until last and now opened a stiff envelope containing a very large Christmas card, with slapdash scrawl on the back. It was, he was relieved to discover, from Claire Derwent who had obviously emerged from her interminable sulk, for she wrote:

My dear Paul,
*   You must think me a presumptuous little fool! Perhaps Rose has told you why I went off without even saying good-bye, but the truth is, on the day after our party, I was so bored, restless and miserable, and everything seemed such a dreadful anticlimax that I just had to do something desperately different! The chance of a visit to cousins here (which I had previously declined) seemed one way out but I didn't know then, of course, that it would become permanent. Well, it has! I'm opening a tea shop in partnership with my Cousin Marion at a place called Penshurst that you may or may not have heard of because it's a famous Elizabethan house owned by the De Lisle family (Sir Philip Sydney and all that!) and lots of London visitors come here in the summer so it ought to be fun as well as profitable! I shall miss the Valley, of course, but not so much as you'd imagine, for the countryside here is just as pretty and Kent, remember, is the Garden of England! I do know (and how could I fail to know) what a little fool I made of myself as regards you. I was to blame from the beginning and hope you won't hold it against me for the rest of my life. I can only put it down to the dullness of life at High Coombe until you arrived to brighten things up a bit but now I've had lots of time to think it over and, like I say, it makes me blush to think of the way I behaved to someone who was such a good friend and had plenty of worries of his own! I do most sincerely wish you all the luck in the world, Paul, and I know you'll do well down there, "bringing all they ole 'puddenades' bang up-to-date, midear!" and heaven knows they need it! Keep at it, and bless you,*
*   Yours affectionately,*
*   Claire Derwent.*

The friendliness of her letter touched him deeply for he began to see how he had encouraged her more than she cared to admit and also that she had almost certainly been taken to task by her father and packed off home from the party with a flea in her ear. Her letter mellowed him so that he could think of her now with warmth and laughter and he reflected that a letter as frank and cheerful as this might do something to sweeten his relationship with Rose, whom he admired, and Edward Derwent, whom he respected. Ever since Claire had taken the huff relations between Shallowford House and High Coombe had been very cool and Paul realised that he could not afford to incur the enmity of both the Codsalls and the Derwents within six months of moving in. So, before answering Claire's letter, he wrote a note to Rose telling her that he had heard from Claire and was writing to wish her luck with her tea-shop venture.

He then opened his fourth letter, to find that it was a brief note from Celia Lovell, stating that they would be returning to Coombe Bay shortly and inviting him to call for tea, at 4 p.m. on December 31st. That was all. No hint that Grace had confided in her, no enquiries concerning their conversation regarding the estate, just that they were coming home and he was invited for tea on the last day of the old year. Re-reading the letter in an effort to learn something of Celia Lovell's character he thought of her as someone who never put pen to paper without recognising the possibility that she might be called upon to justify it in a court of common pleas.

After lunch the rain stopped and a watery sun came out, so he told Ikey to prepare the dog-cart and put a loose halter on Snowdrop, so that he might drive into Coombe Bay for shoeing the grey and the cob. As an afterthought he took Grace's retriever pup, perched on the box beside him. She was a gawky, lovable little bitch, with a pathetic eagerness to make friends with everybody and Paul lavished upon her a special affection of which she took shameless advantage, calling her "Goneaway" because of her ever-hopeful but always unsuccessful pursuit of game flushed from the thickets during her walks. She lolloped at his heels as he rode about the estate, sometimes following him so closely that her face was masked by a film of liquid mud thrown up by Snowdrop's hooves. Paul had come to agree with Chivers, the groom, that she was untrainable as a gun dog but he went on trying, calling her to heel when she was half-way down a rabbit hole, or scrabbling at a molehill, and thus a curious rhythm was established between man and dog that varied according to the time of day. Whenever Paul thought anyone else was present he used a stern voice but when he and Goneaway were alone in the study, all pretence of trainer and trainee was abandoned and the bitch leapt on to chairs, dragged bones under rugs and invariably positioned herself where she could monopolise the heat of the fire.

The Coombe Bay smith, a squat, mild-mannered man called Abe Tozer, promised to shoe the horses within the hour, so Paul, taking

Goneaway, walked up the east side of the slope overlooking the harbour, where stood Lovell's rented house, shuttered and silent. He was a little disappointed at this, and almost decided to call at the lodge and ask if the family was expected before Christmas, but thought better of it and walked on to the sandhills above the beach.

A high sea was running but the tide was out and beyond the empty beach he could see rollers throwing up a fine spray that travelled on the wind as far as the ridge. Beyond the bar, a mile out to sea, was a grey tumult of water and the horizon beyond Nun's Island and Whinmouth Head was empty and desolate, with the threat of more rain to come. He had walked perhaps a half-mile along the little plateau when the dog, barking furiously, dashed down the slope to the beach and began to worry the legs of a solitary figure who was so close to the water that Paul realised he was drenched by every wave. He called Goneaway to heel but the dog, as usual, took no notice of him, so he ran down the sandy slope to offer an apology. When he was half-way across the beach he stopped, recognising that the stationary figure was in fact Martin Codsall. The man was impervious to the dog or, indeed, to anything but the breakers crashing on the bar far out to sea.

He called, "Give the dog a cuff, Codsall!" but Martin seemed not to hear and made no movement of any sort but continued to stand in the overspill staring fixedly out to sea, as though fascinated by something happening beyond the bar. When he came up with him Paul was startled to see that his expression was blank and that his weather-beaten face was as unresponsive as the rest of his body. He noticed also that Codsall seemed very inadequately dressed for a wet day in late December, having nothing on his back but an old jacket, a collarless shirt with a pair of tattered trousers stuffed into topboots. Goneaway soon lost interest in him and scampered off to tease a stranded crab but Paul, taking Martin by the arm, shook him, asking, "What is it, Codsall? What do you see out there?", but still Codsall gave no sign that he was being addressed and Paul noticed that he was trembling, either from the cold or the rigidity of his posture. Just then a ninth wave drenched them both and Paul swore, jerking the man higher up the beach and here Codsall gave a long shudder, seeming to emerge from a trance. Paul saw then that the fellow was suffering from some kind of self-hypnosis and his mind returned to some of the cases of epilepsy he had seen in hospital. He said, leading Codsall away from the water, "Come on, old man, let's get back and dry off," and

205

they walked arm in arm back along the beach, Codsall stumbling sometimes and leaning more than half his weight on Paul.

It was only when they were ascending the slipway near the boat-shelter that he seemed to be aware of what was happening, for suddenly he withdrew his arm, stared at Paul for a moment, and said, hoarsely, "I thought I seed something out there! Out beyond the bar! A ship it was, but 'er's sunk now, I reckon," and he looked distractedly over his shoulder at the empty bay and stumbled slightly, throwing himself sideways, so that Paul had to brace himself to prevent his falling flat on his face. As this happened, however, he caught a strong whiff of Codsall's breath and was at once reassured for it reeked of cider and he came to the conclusion that Martin was blind drunk. It was strange, he thought, that he had never heard Martin Codsall described as a heavy drinker or, indeed, given to excess of any kind but as he watched him on their way up the street it was clear that Martin had been drinking very heavily indeed for his gait was dangerously uncertain and his speech so slurred that Paul abandoned all attempts to reason with him, hoisting him into the back of the dog-cart whilst he paid the smith and saw the cob harnessed to the shafts and Snow-drop tethered behind. The smith did not seem surprised at the piece of flotsam Paul had brought in from the beach. "Ah, Marty Codsall has been swilling like a good 'un lately," he said, grinning. "In the bar of The Raven most days he is and when he's had all Minnie Flowers will draw for him he wanders off along the beach, babbling about ships and suchlike! Catch his death o' cold he will, if he don't wrap up more and get the horrors too if he don't ease off a point or two, sir! Be you zeein' to him, or shall I?"

"I'll take him home myself," Paul told him, and then, "Does Arabella know that he's soaking it up like this?"

Tozer chuckled, saying, "Well, beggin' your pardon, Squire, if 'er don't it'd be the first bit o' tittle-tattles her's missed in a lifetime!", and Paul, reasoning this must be so, said no more, lifting Goneaway into the trap and driving off along the four-mile river track to the ford.

Once or twice during the journey he glanced over his shoulder at Codsall, who now sat slumped with his back to him, staring down the way they were travelling. Apart from heaving a long, gasping sigh now and again he remained silent. He seems drunk, Paul thought, but he doesn't look drunk, just completely bemused, and then it occurred to him that perhaps Martin was ill and wondered whether he should call at Doctor O'Keefe's before taking him home. He decided against,

206

however, for it was now getting dark and Codsall was obviously suffering from the cold, so Paul drove him as far as the yard of Four Winds, resolving to leave him there for he had no wish to tangle with Arabella again and began to feel rather sorry for the farmer when he thought of the reception he was likely to get from his wife. They crossed the plank bridge and went up the rutted lane to where a square of light glowed beyond the yard rick and here Paul dumped his passenger on one of the Codsall labourers, who emerged from the long row of byres housing the Codsall Friesians.

"Master's had a drop too much," he told the man. "Sober him up in the barn!" Then, as he began to turn the dog-cart, a strange thing happened. Martin Codsall seemed to shed his helplessness in a flash and suddenly hoisted himself to full height, his features losing their vacuity as they contracted into a kind of mask that suggested scheming servility or deep cunning.

"Obliged to 'ee for the lift, Squire," he said, clearly and distinctly, as though his slurred speech had been part of a practical joke. "I'll go along in to me supper, and thank 'ee, zir, thank 'ee kindly." Then, spinning round on the man, he shouted angrily, "Dornee waste no time on me, Ben! Get to tending the cattle, you bliddy layabout! Go on, before I kicks your arse through the barn door!", and having succeeded in astonishing Paul beyond measure, and effectively cowed the grinning farmhand, Codsall touched his forelock and marched steadily across the yard and in through the kitchen door.

Paul would have liked to question Ben on his master but the man had disappeared so he drove off down the lane, wondering if Codsall's heavy drinking had any connection with the recent abdication of his son Will, or with his wife's persistent nagging about the marriage. If it had, he decided, there was very little that he or anyone else could do about it. So long as the Four Winds rent was paid on quarter-day, and the farm continued to yield more than all the Coombe farms put together, it was none of his business yet he continued to think about the incident all the evening and went so far as to discuss it with Mrs. Handcock, who opposed his suggestion to call in O'Keefe on such a pretext. "The Codsalls 'ave all got a mazed streak in 'em," she declared, "but mostly it dorn amount to more than silliness. Marty's father, old Amyas Codsall, was a praper ole miser most of his life and then he got religion an' give three-parts of his money to missionaries in Zululand, or some such plaace. And *his* father, Sam, was mazed too! He once stood a whole night in Paxtonbury market-plaace in mid-winter, just to watch somebody hanged outside the gaol! No, zir, like I'm always atelling of 'ee, dornee bother with all their upsets! They won't thank 'ee for it! Like as not Arabella'll traapse about the Valley zaying youm persecutin' 'em!" That clinched it as far as Paul was concerned and soon he forgot the incident altogether, to recall it a year later, when he had reason to blame both himself and his housekeeper for not taking a more sustained interest in the current trials of Martin Codsall.

II

The Reverend Bull sent a message over on Christmas Eve saying he "confidently expected Squire to attend Seven Carol Service that evening" and had "marked him down" to read one of the lessons. This was Bull's way with parishioners. He never suggested or invited he "confidently expected". He never made requests, he simply "marked people down". Paul had already succumbed to the rector's tactics and sometimes even defended him against the attacks of his new friend, James Grenfell. The Liberal candidate admitted that he could not stomach the man and regarded him as a self-indulgent reactionary, using his cloth to patch a dying feudalism in the Valley, but Paul was growing tolerant of Sorrel Valley eccentricities and argued that a man of Bull's disposition at least projected the Church as something positive, a creed that men and women who lived with their noses in soil could understand and that Bull was an improvement on some of the professional hearties he had encountered in South Africa. He told the parson's messenger that he would attend the service and that he would bring along a contingent of Home Farm and indoor staff for the occasion. In the event Honeyman harnessed a couple of horses to the waggonette and they all rattled off to church with Mrs. Handcock, two of the maids, Ikey Palfrey, Chivers and the biblical shepherds, Matt and Luke, who seemed to Paul reincarnations of the originals in the popular carol. He himself rode over in the wake of the waggon for it was a clear, crisp night, lit by stars, and Snowdrop was familiar with the well-beaten track across the stubble fields and down the long slope to the village.

The little parish church was practically full and when he took his place at the lectern, sandwiching a passage from St. Matthew between "Once in Royal David's City" and "The Holly and the Ivy", Paul had some difficulty in restraining a smile on noting the incongruous assembly in the pews. The Potter clan was represented by Pansy and her swain, Walt Pascoe. She had persuaded him that attendance now might divert Parson Bull's wrath when they were married here in the New Year, for Parson Bull castigated loving couples at a marriage ceremony if they were known to have restricted church attendance to weddings, funerals and christenings. Arabella Codsall and her younger son Sydney, were there, but neither Martin nor Will, the latter having defected to his wife's denomination since marriage. Edward Derwent and his wife were present, with their daughter Rose, and so were all the three Pitts. The remainder of the congregation was made up of Valley farm labourers and their womenfolk and a majority of Coombe Bay villagers, exclusive of the little fishing fraternity, who were chapelgoers to a man.

They sang lustily and prayed devoutly and when it was all over and they dispersed in the churchyard, there was a babel of gossip, a noisy exchange of Christmas greetings and a good deal of kissing and giggling among canting tombstones. Paul had left Snowdrop at the smithy's and was leading him out, preparatory to mounting, when Ikey came up with a message that someone was waiting to speak to Squire by the rear lych-gate and that he was asked to go round by the church wall on foot. Somewhat mystified by this cryptic message Paul asked Ikey who it was but Ikey could not say. The message, he said, had been relayed to him by one of the choirboys.

"Very well," Paul told him resignedly, for he was cold and hungry, "put the grey in the forge and tell Honeyman to drive on home," and he went down the steep lane beside the church wall to the rear part of the churchyard, now cut off from the light of the church lamps by a belt of yews.

As he approached the gate there was a movement beside the buttress and Grace Lovell's voice came out of the darkness. "Well, Paul," she said, "this rendezvous should appeal to an incurable romantic!", and she gave him her small, gloved hand.

He was more astonished and delighted than he could say. It had never occurred to him that the message had come from her and he had assumed it was from one of the dissenting members of the parish who were invariably treated as trespassers by Bull.

He said, excitedly, "I had no idea you were home! I thought if you were you would be sure to attend the service!" but she told him they had driven over from Whinmouth only that day and that Bruce, her father, was now in Biarritz and likely to remain there until spring. Then she said, more urgently, "Let's not waste time, Paul! I've only a few minutes and Celia would explode if she knew I was here alone. I wanted to see you before you called. You got Celia's letter?"

"Yes," he said, "and I replied to it saying I should be very happy to come."

"She didn't have the decency to tell me that," Grace said, "but it doesn't matter now."

He could not see her in the deep shadow but he could smell her perfume and it came to him like the scent of summer hedgerows. He still held her gloved hand and she let him hold it, so that they stood there, levelled by the lych-gate step and her nearness stirred him even more deeply than when they last stood together on the terrace at Shallowford.

"What is it, Grace?" he asked. "Would you prefer that I didn't accept Celia's invitation next week?"

"No," she said but doubtfully, as though by no means certain about this, "you'll have to come, I suppose, because she won't let go of you now if she can help it! But there is something you can do before you see her; you can tell me the truth. As far as you know it yourself, that is!"

"The truth about what?" he asked.

"About how serious you were on the night of the ball. Oh, you needn't protest, and you don't have to sound a gallant fanfare for my daring to doubt your sincerity! I daresay you thought yourself in earnest at the time but it was a heady occasion. You were probably full of cider-cup and feeling very sure of yourself that evening!"

She stopped suddenly and he could hear her rapid breathing. "Do you want me to go on, Paul? Can we talk to one another honestly and openly?"

"Yes," he said, feeling deflated, "you had best say what's on your mind, Grace."

"Well," she went on, "things came to a head while we were in London. My father brought home a fat prize one night, and they both expected me to agree to marry it almost at once! You needn't know anything about him, except that he was going bald, was well over forty, likely to become a Member of Parliament, and very comfortably off! Naturally I wasn't forthcoming and there was a great deal of unpleasantness, not only about Basil Holbeach, but . . . well . . . about many other things! It was then that I told Celia about you. I didn't want to but I needed her support, and I got it. Celia is mad to get me off her hands but she is neither as cynical nor as money-grubbing as

my father, and neither is she more than an average snob. Besides,"—
there was laughter in her voice now—"you made a very good impression on her! She thinks you're going to succeed down here and
because her money originates from blacking she doesn't care about
your scrapyard!"

It was the first time she had referred to the scrapyard although he
had long since decided that she must be aware of it, as were most
people in the Valley by now.

"Tell me where these developments lead us," he said, "and how you
could be stupid enough to persuade yourself I was in liquor when I
asked you to marry me! That seems to me to be the only thing that
matters."

"Yes, it is, Paul," she said, choosing her words carefully now, "and
that's why I wanted to talk to you before you faced Celia's batteries.
I know what she'll say and how she'll approach the matter. She'll say
'Grace is a little wild and a little wilful' but that that she's still very young,
and will steady down the moment she has a husband and babies!"

"She's probably right at that," Paul said good-humouredly but in
the darkness he sensed her impatient gesture, as she withdrew her
hand from his. "She doesn't mean it that way," Grace insisted. "She
means I should enjoy being the lady of the manor down here, organising soirées like the one Claire Derwent arranged for you, doling out
blankets and logs to the poor at Christmas time, visiting the sick and
trotting dutifully about the country behind Gilroy's pack of hounds!
Because she's Celia she's convinced that this is the only destiny for the
provincial girl of good family!"

"Well I'm not so sure that it isn't," he protested, "or could be if
you didn't make it sound so damned dull!" and was surprised when
she laid her hand on his arm and said emphatically, "Perhaps it is,
Paul! For some provincial girls, but I've always known it wasn't my
destiny, even when I was engaged to Ralph Lovell! A woman brought
up to do that sort of thing, as I was, might achieve it without much
trouble, providing she was in love with the man she married."

"Very well," he said, gruffly, "you aren't obliged to say any more,
Grace, and in spite of everything I'd like you to know that I honestly
appreciate your frankness and when I meet Celia I hope I can be
equally candid."

"Oh stop being so *young*, Paul," she burst out impatiently. "How
many marriages of this kind, between people with money, are love
matches? Not one in fifty and only then between a cow-like couple

who do what they're told because it's so much less trouble! Of course I don't love you! How could I? Or you me, if you're really honest with yourself! I daresay you could learn to, and it's possible that I might learn to, but at the moment you're attracted to me by two factors; you imagine marriage to me would give you social security and you probably think it might be nice to have me in bed! Well, that isn't so original—a lot of men have been that much in love with me, but it doesn't mean we know each other, or could distil a particle of mutual happiness or usefulness from a permanent association!"

"Good God!" he said, "you make everything sound like a political tract! I think of you as the most exciting girl I've ever met, and I'm more attracted to you every time I see you, or hear you speak, or touch your hand! I can't reduce love to a kind of formula, like you seem to want to! I'm prepared to take something on trust and leave something to chance, the same as I did when I spent everything I had on this place! Everyone who falls in love and gets married takes risks. What about young Will Codsall and Elinor Willoughby? He turned his back on the best farm in the Valley to marry Elinor and she faced up to a mother-in-law with a disposition as sour as Kruger's! Can't you ever give your instincts a chance?"

She was not, it seemed, impressed by his arguments, or by the emphasis with which he presented them but she paid him the compliment of taking them more seriously than she had taken his proposal.

"I obeyed my instincts coming here and giving you the opportunity of unsaying what you said the last time we met," she said calmly. "I've got far more respect for you than for most men I've met so far, and there are things about you that I admire, Paul. But I don't love you, and I don't even know you sufficiently well to know whether I could love you. I've always had a contempt for the traditional responses of women on these occasions, particularly when faced with the chance to make what they call a good match! I'm not really interested in being the Lady of Shallowford. I think I might have bigger fish to fry, if Englishwomen as a whole ever break out of the seraglio! Good-bye, Paul!"

"But in heaven's name we haven't begun to decide . . ." he protested.

"There's time enough," she said, "and I daren't stay longer. If I'm missed, or seen here it will make things ten times more complicated for me than they are! Good night and a Merry Christmas!", and before he could stop her she had bobbed forward and kissed him lightly on the cheek and vanished. He called "Grace!" softly but there was no answer, only the scuffle of her shoes on the gravel of the path that emerged lower down the High Street, opposite the hill leading to her home.

III

Celia received him in her boudoir, a small room off the draughty landing that overlooked the bay. It was, he had decided by then, a gloomy, badly-planned house, overstuffed with heavy mahogany furniture that contrasted with Celia's fashionable clothes and hard good looks demanding an altogether lighter setting. She must have noticed his appraisal for she said, deprecatingly, "It's your furniture, Mr. Craddock! We rent it just as it is—antimacassars, stuffed elks-heads, and all! If I made you an offer for the place I should throw everything out but I wouldn't buy the house anyway, the only thing I like about it is its site," and she pointed to the view of the harbour framed in the sash window.

"I hope you won't be too disappointed at having tea with me instead of Grace," she went on. "When I dropped a hint that she paid a call in Whinmouth I expected tantrums but there weren't any. You never can be quite sure of Grace and she seemed to prefer you and I to meet alone at . . . er . . . at this stage! Does that surprise you?"

"No," he said, "I don't think she could surprise me, Mrs. Lovell."

Celia laughed, pleasantly and genuinely he thought, telling himself that there was something individual and very engaging about Celia Lovell as she sat pouring tea from a silver pot after boiling the kettle on a little silver spirit stove. There were muffins in a silver dish and cakes on a silver cakestand. Everything she used was expensive and delicately made, and all her movements were precise, as though she assessed in advance the exact amount of effort needed to lift a plate or pinch a knob of sugar with tongs. Then, when he was comfortably settled, she came straight to the point.

"Grace told me that you proposed marriage to her last October," she said, in a reasonable but businesslike tone. "I must admit to being surprised, as no doubt she was herself, but I was also delighted. I'm like her in one respect. I dislike fiddle-faddle and I'm glad to see that you don't seem to have much use for it, Mr. Craddock! I take it that she asked time to consider but has not written to you since?"

"That is so, Mrs. Lovell," replied Paul, feeling like a friendly witness being cross-examined by a sharp-witted barrister.

213

"Well now," she went on, kindly but expansively, "I should like you to know at once that I consider it very suitable! Very suitable *indeed*! In fact I think she would be a very silly girl not to accept!" She gave him a sidelong look, adding, "Upon my word, *I* should accept, Mr. Craddock!" leaving him in no doubt but that she spoke in earnest.

Paul said nothing for there seemed so little to say. After a pause, during which they both sipped tea, she continued, "In the circumstances, Mr. Craddock, I cannot but feel that you should know the full facts. The truth is, in some ways Grace has been causing both her father and myself a great deal of anxiety, but perhaps she told you something of this?"

It was a trap but he saw it in time. Celia obviously suspected that they had met since the family's return and he said, smiling, "No, Mrs. Lovell, although I have gathered she is rather uncertain about her future."

"She has no need to be, I assure you," Celia replied, quite sharply, "for Grace isn't a gel who lacks admiration. Her father would have encouraged her to accept another proposal, from a gentleman in possession of considerable means but he was a good deal older than Grace and I'm not at all in favour of marriages between people of different generations, notwithstanding settlements. It was then that she came to me for advice."

It was all, he thought, like something from an early nineteenth-century novel, with mamma using a set formula for the occasion, and in the light of what he already knew it was difficult for him to feel that Celia Lovell was free from hypocrisy. He said, slowly, "You said you don't like fiddle-faddle, Mrs. Lovell, so I gather from that you would prefer us to be frank with one another. Would you mind telling me *how* Grace has caused you and Mr. Lovell anxiety? Was it a love affair?"

"Oh no, certainly not," she said, seeming alarmed. "No, Mr. Craddock, it wasn't that! As a matter of fact Grace never has been attracted by younger men and, to be perfectly honest, I don't think she was as upset by Ralph Lovell's death as she ought to have been! Or if she was then she didn't show it! No, no, it was something quite different and it began when we were last in town and still remains a source of well . . . a rather strained atmosphere between Grace and her father. I imagine you must have heard about these dreadful suffragists?"

"The National Union of Women's Suffrage? Why yes, hasn't everyone? Is Grace a member?"

"I really couldn't say," Celia replied, obviously shocked by his implied tolerance, "all I know is that she has been associating with them, has even attended their public meetings! That we found distressing enough but the original group, although faddist and, to my mind, quite ridiculous, was at least constitutional! Recently there has been a breakaway movement led by a very provocative woman called Pankhurst and her two daughters, but perhaps you have read of them in the newspapers?"

Paul had but had not paid particular note of the cleavage. There had been brief reports in copies of the *Westminster Gazette*, that arrived in the Valley a day or two late and described lively scenes at political meetings and demonstrations. He recalled an instance of a woman climbing on to a roof at a Unionist meeting and being removed by firemen and policemen but even in his conversations with Grenfell, the subject of votes for women had never come under discussion and he was surprised to find that Celia Lovell took it seriously.

"It sounds quite harmless," he said evasively and was relieved to see Celia smile.

"I'm sure it is, so far as Grace is concerned," she admitted, "but her father took a very serious view of her involvement in this kind of thing and I must say I don't blame him! After all, a girl who makes an exhibition of herself is hardly likely to make a good marriage and that is what I want for Grace more than anything else. Being a stepmother carries exceptional responsibilities, Mr. Craddock."

"Yes," said Paul, "I can understand that, but it seems to me . . ."

"*Do* let me give you some more tea, Mr. Craddock!" she said, and he had the impression that this was to give her time to think as a barrister might drop papers when his witness was facing an awkward question. She poured tea and handed him the cakestand. When they were settled again she said, mildly, "*Do* go on, Mr. Craddock, and I hope you feel that you can confide in me. I most earnestly want to help in any way I can."

"I'm sure you do, Mrs. Lovell," he said, sensing that he had now got the measure of her, "but in the case of a girl like Grace I can't help feeling that the best way to help is to do nothing. I believe myself to be in love with her, and I'm sure that, in time, I could make her very happy here. However, I haven't any fatuous illusions about her being in love with me at this moment, and in this day and age surely a girl as intelligent as Grace should be allowed to make her own decisions."

215

She was now regarding him with admiration and he almost blushed for her, so artless were her tactics in contrast to those employed over the first cup of tea. He noticed something else too and it disturbed him a little, a glaze of ruthlessness in the alert, brown eyes and also the frank sensuality of the mouth. "By God," he thought, "I'll wager she can be worse than Arabella Codsall when she's roused! No wonder Bruce is keeping out of the way in Biarritz!" But again he was confident of handling her and the knowledge pleased and excited him, for he found his natural diffidence slipping away and he felt more assured than he recalled feeling in the presence of a woman. "Where is Grace now, Mrs. Lovell?" he asked and she replied, "I'm expecting her any moment, I thought we could have our little talk and then . . . well . . . I can find something to do and you could talk to her before you left. For that matter you could stay for dinner if you liked and . . ."

"No!" he said and stood up so abruptly that for a moment she looked at a loss. "I don't think that would be a good idea, Mrs. Lovell. It seems to me that it might . . . well . . . stampede Grace one way or the other! I think it would be wiser if I left before she returned, although I don't mind if you tell her about this discussion. There's no hurry, however, I'm not likely to fall in love again at short notice."

He said this as a joke but it was only after a moment's deliberation with herself that she could accept it as such. Then she was her assured self again, laying a long, elegant hand on his arm. "Do you know, I think I underestimated you, Mr. Craddock! I always thought of you as a kind, mildly ambitious young man but I also thought you had a great deal to learn about women."

"I have, indeed," said Paul, smiling, "and I daresay it will take me a lifetime."

"Nonsense!" she said, now almost caressing his hand, "you already understand Grace better than the rest of us. I don't suppose she is half as complex as we imagine and I'm sure that the time will come when she will look back on this votes for women nonsense and laugh about it! There now, let me show you downstairs, and when Grace comes I'll tell her I've been flirting with you, and that you would like her to ride over to Shallowford tomorrow."

"On a horse, not on a bicycle," said Paul, and Celia, again looking at him with approval, said, "We really do think alike, Mr. Craddock! And it's been a pleasure to talk to you! I can only repeat what I said,

216

I think she's a very lucky girl!", and she swept out in front of Paul and along the passage to the head of the staircase.

Paul was admiring the skill with which she handled her voluminous. lilac skirt, and the effect of a wan shaft of sunlight on her light brown hair, when the front door opened and Grace walked into the hall. She was wearing the bicycling costume she had worn when she called at the house to shelter and looked, Paul thought, even more windblown than on that occasion. Her defeated expression touched him so that he cursed Celia Lovell for not whisking him out of the house before she returned. They stood in embarrassed silence for a moment and it would have been hard to say which of them was the more dismayed. Then Celia flashed one of her brittle smiles, saying, "Mr. Craddock was just leaving, Grace dear. I tried to get him to stay to dinner but he can't, he's very busy it seems. You are sure you won't change your mind, Mr. Craddock?"

"No, if you'll forgive me," he lied, "I've got a great deal to do before Mr. Rudd comes back tomorrow," and he saw Grace's chin come up sharply, as though Rudd's return was an added cause for depression but she said nothing, continuing to stare at the tiles on the floor and fidget with her shapeless hat. Mrs. Lovell said, with a brightness that Paul now found irritating, "Would you like to ride over to Shallowford tomorrow? May Mr. Craddock expect you?"

It was like listening to an unimaginative mother encouraging a stupidly bashful child and suddenly he felt desperately sorry for the small, dejected figure, standing so irresolutely in her hideous costume.

"Come if you want to, Grace, and come on your bicycle if you like," he said. "You'll always be welcome and I'll tell Mrs. Handcock to make you comfortable in the library if I'm out. I'm usually there until about eleven and always after tea. I could drive you home in the trap," and he was rewarded by a look of gratitude and an almost inaudible "Thank you, Paul" as Grace sidestepped Celia and walked quickly through a curtained aperture at the rear of the hall. As he opened the front door to let himself out Mrs. Lovell seemed about to say something more but he cut her short, this time almost brutally.

"I don't want Grace harried, Mrs. Lovell! Please remember that, and tell Mr. Lovell the same!"

She made no reply to this but her lips parted and once again he had a strong impression that beneath her good breeding and natural amiability, she was as hard and ruthless as a professional whore. He went out into the gathering dusk and along to the yard of The Raven

217

where he had left the trap. Looking back over his shoulder he saw a light in the upstairs room and he thought, "That must be her bedroom, and I'll wager she's up there crying, and even if I marry the girl I doubt if I shall ever discover why."

IV

Paul Craddock would have won his wager. Grace was weeping but not, as he had half-imagined, face downwards on her bed, shoulders shaking with sobs for she had never wept in this fashion, not even when the Ayah told her that the Memsahib was dead and she was facing the eternity of childhood with the man whose pale, protuberant eyes had never looked on her without impatience or contempt. When Grace Lovell wept, which was seldom, the tears flowed sparingly and never for more than a moment so that presently she studied herself in the dressing-table mirror impatient with what she saw and wondering how an uncomplicated man like Paul Craddock could hoodwink himself into imagining that she would make a good wife for a young man who was already close on a century out of date. Yet she conceded his kindness, his rather craggy good looks and a streak of obstinacy that put him outside her experience. Her father was obstinate but only as regards matters related to his own comfort. Ralph Lovell had been obstinate in a different way, setting his face against the acceptance of any responsibility, even that of keeping sober in mixed company. Ralph's father, old Sir George, had been very obstinate indeed in persuading young females to take off their clothes and stand in front of his camera but neither could match the quiet obstinacy of this limping Cockney, with his nasal accent and dedication to a pastoral way of life that belonged in the reign of George IV.

Her tears ceased to flow and her features composed themselves into their habitual, vaguely mutinous expression, an expression that had defeated all but the most determined assaults upon her privacy. Up here, temporarily out of range of Celia's flashing smile and merciless solicitude, Grace did her thinking for when she was in the open her mind had a habit of shooting off at a tangent every few minutes. Sooner or later, probably sooner she thought, Celia would corner Paul Craddock, and persuade him to press his advantage. It had been touch and go whether Celia had declared in favour of the egregious Basil Holbeach and now that she had quarrelled with Bruce on his account her need to secure the substitute was imperative. Perhaps the impor-

218

tant thing to consider was, did Paul Craddock possess any "advantage"? He was well off—not nearly so rich as Holbeach but surely comfortable if he could find thousands of pounds for a run-down estate and then pour more money into its rehabilitation. Not that his means concerned Grace. Money was important to Celia and absolutely essential to her father, but meant little to her for she had never possessed any and had not even had indirect access to small change until her father's second marriage. She found that she was able to think about Paul Craddock with detachment in a way that she had never been able to review any of the men her father or Celia had introduced into her life, after news of Ralph's death in the Transvaal had reached them. He was healthy and whole, except for that damage to his leg, which did not seem to trouble him much and he was obviously very kindhearted. He thought her beautiful and had even confessed to excitement every time he approached her and the boyishness of this admission made her smile into the mirror, for the poor man was obviously besotted if he introduced considerations of this sort into a marriage of the kind Celia had in mind for him. He was probably the most genuinely disinterested suitor to present himself but did this make him worth the sacrifice of individuality? For all his kindness, and boyish enthusiasm, marriage to him would surely entail such a sacrifice, for clearly his idealism would never expand into wider, more adult fields and she could expect little from him but a humdrum life bounded by the sea, the main railway line, and the estate boundaries east and west, with possibly a monthly visit to Paxtonbury, which he would consider a rare treat. The prospect dismayed her almost as much as marriage to Basil Holbeach, soon to join the nameless ranks of Conservative and Unionist backbenchers at Westminster, a man who would lock his wife in her bedroom if he caught her reading a pamphlet of Mrs. Pankhurst's endeavours. Yet, unlike Basil or any of his predecessors, there was something appealing about Paul Craddock and what that something was she found it hard to decide. In a way it was a kind of sound, that seemed to reach him from a dead century, when Merrie England was an actuality and she fell to wondering about his background, and the strange impulses that had encouraged him to turn his back on opportunities that usually presented themselves to young men with fortunes. Even Ralph Lovell, lout as he was, with no other thought in his head beyond horses, wenching and whisky, had adventured further afield than Paul, whereas Ralph's father, the old satyr who pinched little girls' bottoms

219

and photographed them in the nude, had had interests that sometimes brought him in touch with men of modern ideas.

She tried to imagine how a man with such an archaic dream would acquit himself as a lover. He would probably be courteous, considerate or accommodating according to her moods. If she held her face stiff when he kissed her good night he would go to sleep and awake next morning without resentment. He could be roused, no doubt, whenever she felt inclined and the inevitable result would be several nicely-spaced children, growing up like a row of cabbages and receiving formal educations according to their sex. It was not a pleasing prospect but what was the alternative? A regular shuttle to and from this hideous house to Cadogan Square, and back again; wrangles with her father over her activities in London and tiresome importuning on Celia's part to capture the inevitable husband or, if not, to tread the social mill of her At Homes and the musical soirées, where young men prattled endlessly of pictures and tepid novels, and bombazined old hags chattered scandal, deferring to smug-faced husbands on every issue that really mattered. There must in the name of God be a compromise between these two fates and for the hundredth time in the last few months she thought of flight. But flight to where or to whom? With sixpence in her reticule? The prospect was even more absurd than marriage.

And then, as her mind shied at the years ahead, her strong sense of fair play reminded her that it would be a shabby trick to use a man as vulnerable as Paul Craddock as a harbour where she could never anchor herself for long. He might be a fool, might even be addressing himself to the task of putting the clock back, but at least he was honest, warmhearted and relatively harmless and deserved a wife who would expect no more of him than he had to offer. It was thinking along these lines that she made her decision and having made it felt carefree again. Tomorrow morning, she promised herself, she would ride over to Shallowford House and tell Paul Craddock, frankly and kindly, exactly why she could not marry him and afterwards acquaint Celia with her decision and direct her attentions elsewhere.

Downstairs the gong sounded for dinner and she changed into a green dinner frock without bothering to do more than wash her hands and tie a ribbon under her curls. She felt more than equal to Celia tonight, reflecting that she might even enjoy leading her partway up the garden path.

By ten o'clock on New Year's Day Grace Lovell was approaching the ford and as she walked her mare Roxy across the path-fields she was satisfied that her speech was word perfect. About half-a-mile from the crossing, however, a yellow dog-cart flashed past, going in the opposite direction and driven hard by a round-shouldered little man in an ulster and a billycock hat. She recognised him as Grenfell, the local Radical candidate, who had entered the field against Hilton-Price, Paxtonbury's Unionist M.P., and although she had almost as great a contempt for Liberals as for their political rivals, she wished him well if only for having the courage to plant a Radical standard on such Philistine soil. She soon dismissed him, however, readdressing herself to the business in hand, and it was only when she was crossing the river that she remembered him for ahead of her, on the point of turning into Shallowford drive, was another gig with two men on the box, and she recognised them as well. The driver was Lord Gilroy and his passenger, a thickset man about fifty, was Cribb, the local Unionist agent, a man whose job, so they said, was a sinecure, for how could anyone but a Conservative win Paxtonbury, one of the safest seats in the British Isles? There was nothing odd about Gilroy and his agent paying a call upon the Squire of Shallowford on New Year's Day but the circumstances began to seem unusual when she realised that their visit followed Grenfell's by less than ten minutes and suddenly Grace forgot about her speech in an attempt to draw conclusions from this coincidence. Had Grenfell just come from Shallowford? He must have done, for this track led nowhere else, except to the railway halt and no train stopped at Sorrel Halt until after midday. There was clearly significance in Gilroy's visit too, or why should he be accompanied by Cribb? Were both parties competing for Paul Craddock's support? And if so, could there be the least possibility of the brash young man challenging local mandarins as powerful as Gilroy and the Hilton-Prices?

She gave the gig time to increase its lead and dawdled in the area of the ford for a minutes. Paul could not receive her until they had gone and if they remained indefinitely she decided to postpone her call and keep Celia on tenterhooks for another twenty-four hours. The prospect of this did not displease her, and she rode round the paddock and entered the yard from the east, leaving Roxy with a perky little boy, who ran forward to take the reins. Gilroy's gig was in the fore-court, the horse tethered to a ring on a lamp socket and she could hear the murmur of voices coming through the library window. The garden door of what used to be old Sir George's studio was unlocked and by

221

opening it, and standing in the angle made by the terrace, she could hear very clearly what was being said in the next room. If she hesitated a moment from taking her stand here it was because she was debating whether anything Gilroy and Cribb might have to say merited her attention, for Grace Lovell had no misgivings about eavesdropping. In her guerilla war with her father and stepmother it had proved an indispensable means of survival. So she stood there, listening intently and so changed the course of her life.

V

Paul was map-tracing in the office when Thirza Tremlett, the parlourmaid, came in with the news that Lord Gilroy and Mr. Raymond Cribb were in the drawing-room on the other side of the hall. Thirza, the nearest approach Shallowford House possessed to a butler, was in what Mrs. Handcock would have described as "a rare ole tizzy", for the arrival of two such visitors in the forenoon frightened her and she came in flushed and out of breath. Paul himself was surprised, particularly as James Grenfell had only just left, and it occurred to him that the visitors might even have passed one another at the ford, so he was not entirely unprepared for the bleak look on his Lordship's face when Thirza ushered them into the library and fled. Cribb, however, was affable and quickly introduced himself, grasping Paul's hand with excessive firmness and apologising for having allowed six months to elapse before paying his call.

"Stopped by here a good deal in old Sir George's time," he said breezily, "but then, he was our local president before his Lordship stepped into the breach!" He went on talking about nothing in particular and Paul gained the impression that he was awaiting a cue from Gilroy but the dry old stick said nothing at all, seemingly less interested in Paul than in the room, for his eyes roved from book shelves to fireplace, then through the garden door to the office table where the estate maps were spread.

"Made a good many changes here," he remarked, gruffly, as though he resented not having been consulted. "Place didn't change at all in Lovell's time. Or his father's time either come to that!"

Paul murmured that the house and grounds had badly needed attention when he arrived in June and offered to show them round but when Cribb looked to Gilroy for a lead the old man waved a thin hand and said, rather impatiently, "No time today! Some other time!

Might as well come straight to the point, Cribb. Nothing gained by beating about the damned bush!", and he moved over to the fire and spread his hands to the blaze.

"His Lordship refers, I think, to some idle gossip that has reached him regarding your political sympathies," said Cribb, and Paul was surprised at his directness as though he was an employer rebuking an assistant who had just bungled a sale. He went on in a slightly more genial tone. "No more than rumour, of course, but it doesn't do to let these things go unchallenged, Craddock. After all, we've got to stick together, particularly now that the Government is making such heavy weather. Wouldn't you say so?", and he flexed his massive blue jowls, so that it seemed to Paul that he was looking at two purple puddings divided by the broad peninsula of Cribb's nose.

Paul's first reaction to this challenge was astonishment. It seemed to him impossible that two men of their years could be so sure of themselves on another's hearthrug. Then, in the wake of his astonishment, resentment rose in his throat and irritation changed to anger when Gilroy, without even looking at him, said in his thin, rustling voice, "They tell me that little rat of a Radical has been courting you, Craddock! Won't do, you know! Best show the rascal the door straight away! Don't stand on politeness with scum of that kind! Give 'em an inch and they take an ell!"

Amazement at the man's insufferable arrogance held Paul's anger in check for a moment and he said, vaguely, "Rascal? Ruffian? . . . I can only suppose you must be referring to Mr. James Grenfell. He's just been here. He looks in almost every week when he's over this way," and Gilroy said, with a glare, "The devil he does! Then it's true then?" but without the least indication that he was aware of Paul's resentment.

"Yes he does," Paul said, sullenly, "and I'm bound to say that I find him not only extremely civil but exceptionally good company! Moreover, I can't help feeling that he wouldn't speak of either of you gentlemen as you have spoken of him!"

He felt much better after he had said this and regained control of himself, a process made easier by the startled look that crossed Cribb's face and the blankness of Gilroy's expression. Cribb said, in a much more conciliatory tone, "Oh come now, Craddock, you aren't going to tell his Lordship that you vote for those damned Radicals?"

"I haven't had an opportunity to vote at all yet," Paul said cheerfully, "but after this extraordinary interview I shall think about doing so at the next election!" whereupon Gilroy made a move for the door saying, in a voice scarcely above a whisper, "Come, Cribb!", but the agent was less impulsive and stood his ground, saying firmly, "No, your Lordship! Wait a moment, I beg of you! Our job is to win votes, not throw them at Grenfell's feet!", and he turned back to Paul with a smile that came close to a grimace and said, "I take it you are un-committed, Craddock? Well, and why not? You're still a youngster and you've been out of the country throughout the war. There's no cause for a quarrel, my Lord, I daresay Mr. Craddock will learn as he goes along, and we ought, as neighbours, to give him the chance before we jump to conclusions."

Gilroy paused, seemingly undecided and Cribb readdressed himself to Paul with a great show of frankness. "Listen here, young man, I admit to being – well – a little shocked when I heard that Grenfell was a regular visitor here, and I daresay it seems presumptuous to have us pounce on you like this but you're a stranger in the district so you can't be expected to see through a wily bird like Grenfell. He's a good talker and I don't underestimate him in the way some of the party do but surely you must see that it can't be in your true interests as a landowner to get mixed up with that kind of rag, tag and bobtail! After all, if Grenfell and his kind had their way there wouldn't be any landowners!"

"Good God, man!" said Paul, "Grenfell isn't a Barcelona anarchist, or a Russian nihilist! He represents a respectable democratic party and what right have you or Lord Gilroy to call here and virtually order me to show him the door?"

"We're wasting our time," Gilroy said, quietly, "the fellow is obviously a damned Radical! I suspected it from the first, when I saw what a drubbing he had given the old place!", and he would have walked into the hall had not Cribb, very flustered now, seized his arm and protested, "That isn't the way to canvass, my Lord! Believe me, I'm an old hand and there's never anything gained by turning your back on a constituent! Craddock must see for himself the harm done by adopting this we're-all-Englishmen-together attitude!", and he turned back to Paul and said, "You're open to reason, I take it? You haven't actually promised Grenfell political support in the con-stituency?"

Paul said, deliberately, "No, Mr. Cribb, I haven't. As a matter of fact he's never asked for it."

"He wouldn't," said Cribb savagely, "that's his way! Now listen to me, young man . . .", but Paul, plunging both hands in his breeches pockets, said, "No, Mr. Cribb, *you* listen to *me*! Before I came down here I never gave a thought to politics, except to wonder sometimes, when I saw what was happening to the Boers, how our treatment of them could be justified but I've learned a good deal about politics this morning, and I don't like what I've learned! You say this isn't the way to convass votes and by God, you're right! I can't imagine a more hamfisted way of going about it! Grenfell, as I said, hasn't canvassed me in several visits here but neither has he treated me like a stupid child or a recently liberated serf! I'm not clear in my own mind what the Conservative Unionist Party stand for, or even what the Liberal Party stand for but you've made me eager to find out! I can see that your party lacks two things — tact and good manners, neither of which have been in evidence since you walked in that door!"

He moved above the fireplace to pull the bellrope but Gilroy cheated him by stamping out of the room before he could ring. Cribb remained, however, and seemed to be bouncing with rage, so that Paul, again seizing the advantage, said, "I'm sorry it had to happen like this, Cribb. I don't think you or I would have lost our tempers if you had come alone. But what else would you expect a man to do when complete strangers walk into his house and quarrel with his choice of friends?"

Cribb was clearly a man of mettle and apparently possessed a very keen sense of duty, for he somehow mastered his rage and said, in a high-pitched voice, "You're committing social suicide here, Craddock! Good God, man, why won't you let someone experienced in these matters help you?" and Paul, scarcely knowing why, felt rather sorry for him as he said, "I don't want to seem ungracious but this is supposed to be a democratic country and we're supposed to have outgrown political pressures on the individual! Why didn't you come here like Grenfell, and make some attempt to get to know me before blackmailing me into joining a party?"

"Because it never occurred to me that you needed anyone to teach you common sense!" snapped Cribb. "A man doesn't buy an estate of thirteen hundred acres without being prepared to defend it! You should have learned that much fighting Kruger!"

He must have decided at this point that any further argument would involve him in loss of face for he picked up his hat and crossed the room but because Gilroy had slammed the door he had to fumble with the handle and while he was thus engaged, with Paul watching

225

him, they heard a step on the stone floor of the office, and both turned as Grace Lovell walked into the room.

They saw that she was smiling a little sourly, as she said, with studied casualness, "I'm sorry to interrupt, but I just couldn't let you go without knowing I approve of every word my fiancé said, Mr. Cribb! You Unionists really are insufferable bullies, and I do hope we can make it hot for you down here! Shall I show Mr. Cribb out, Paul dear?"

Paul dear remained rooted, his back to the fire, but Cribb, now in a fighting mood, snarled, "I only hope your father feels the same way about it, Miss Lovell! And Mrs. Lovell also, both very good friends of mine, as you no doubt know!", and to Paul, "Good-day, Craddock! If it's war you want you won't find us as easy to beat as Boers! We have their kind of staying power and a great deal more money!"

"Oh, but they weren't all that easy to beat," Grace said, "as you would have found out if you had been in the field like Mr. Craddock!", but it is doubtful whether Cribb heard her for he was already outside the room and a moment later they heard the front door slam and then the crunch of the gig's wheels on the gravel.

They remained silent for a moment, Grace standing leaning against the door, her head cocked slightly to one side and her little crooked smile giving her the look of a clever, impudent child, who has just scored a point over grown-ups. Finally Paul said, breathlessly, "That was very sporting of you, Grace, but you didn't have to burn your boats in order to rub salt into the smart! You realise Cribb will spread the news up and down the Valley in a matter of hours, and you'll look pretty foolish if you have to back down on it!"

"Well," she said, cheerfully, walking across to the fire and giving the sullen log a kick with her boot, "I don't know how you feel about it but I haven't any intention of 'backing down' as you say! As for you, you had your chance in the churchyard on Christmas Eve and didn't take it!"

"You meant what you said? It wasn't said simply to confound that bully?"

"I meant it," she said coolly, "but it was a rather different tale from the one I rode here to tell you."

"You mean that you were listening all the time, and it helped you to change your mind about us?"

"I haven't been very clever, have I?" she said, "I'm giving away too much and too quickly!" Then, facing him, "It's the first time I've

226

ever *seen* you, Paul, can't you understand that? I thought of you as someone pleasant, kind, and well-meaning but I didn't know you were a rebel and I certainly didn't give you credit for that much nerve! I loathe people like Gilroy and Cribb, and everything they stand for, but until ten minutes ago I assumed you were only a watered-down version of them! Well, you aren't, quite obviously you aren't, and it makes a big difference! I'm not in love with you and it wouldn't be honest of me to pretend I was but we've got more in common than either of us imagined and that's a better basis for marriage than story-book slush!"

He crossed to the fireplace and lifted her hand, looking at it thoughtfully and noting the regularity of the long tapering fingers that somehow gave the hand strength as well as delicacy. "I don't know," he said, "without 'story-book slush' marriage must be a very dull institution, too dull to have lasted as long as it has. Maybe it emerges if the marriage is any good but I suppose it's much the same as any other endeavour—its success depends on what people are prepared to put into it. All I know for certain is that I'm willing to trust my instincts but I don't think you are, not really, and that's why it might be wiser to see a lot more of each other and be damned to what Cribb and Gilroy broadcast up and down the Valley!"

She looked at him steadily, without withdrawing her hand. "That's not how you were talking to them," she said, "it's more how I should have imagined you talked if someone had told me about what happened."

"The two things aren't the same," he said.

"Oh, but they are, because both are a calculated risk! You took one without a second thought but now you buck at taking another! You asked me to marry you and I said I'd think about it. Well, I have thought about it, and I'd be very happy to, so to the devil with hanging fire until all the fun's gone out of it! If we are going to marry let's do it without orange blossom and stale jokes!"

"You would be prepared to marry soon?"

"Today, Paul."

"We can't cheat Celia and the gossips out of everything. Half the Valley would regard marriage at Easter as indecent!"

"It's no concern of Celia's," she said seriously, "or of anyone else's in the Valley and that's important to me, Paul. This is one thing I'm not obliged to share with anyone but you." It did not seem preposterous that she should carry her passion for privacy into marriage

227

and he found that he was beginning, at last, to be able to anticipate her approximate line of thought.

"Very well, Grace," he said, "and you would probably like to be married away from here, in front of a couple of impersonal witnesses?"

"Yes," she said, "I should like that very much if it could be managed."

"It shall be managed," he said, grimly, "for all I want is a chance to prove how right it could be for both of us. We could get a special licence but that would require your father's permission and Celia would have to be won over. Could that be done, do you suppose?"

"All Celia wants is to get me off her hands. I can leave father to her. I don't imagine he'll be bothered to attend."

He began to understand something of the source of her bitterness, although he could not quite rid himself of a suspicion that she enjoyed over-dramatising a situation.

"All right then, that's how it will be! I'll ride back with you this afternoon and talk to Celia and if you'll stay for lunch I'll take her up on that dinner invitation I declined yesterday." Then, because her expression remained serious, he tried laughing at her. "I must say you don't look much like a girl who has just accepted a gentleman's proposal!" he said, taking her face between his hands and kissing her gently on the mouth. Her lips were no more than submissive, so that he thought of Claire Derwent's lips as he said, "You really *are* sure, Grace? We aren't under any obligation at all to rush things. I told Celia yesterday that I wouldn't have you hustled!"

She took her time answering this, looking at him steadily, so that he saw her in sharper focus, wondering a little at her composure but as baffled as ever by her remoteness. He marked other, equally familiar things about her, the clipped fringe, blue-black against her pale forehead, the ivory lustre of the skin stretching along the jawline to the deep cleft of her chin and one other feature that he had forgotten, dimples, starved of laughter, on either side of her wide mouth. She said, at length, "You have been good to me, Paul, and I know you mean always to be good. Well, you won't find one aspect of me wanting, and I'll prove it!" and suddenly she threw her arms about his neck and returned his kiss in a way that drove all doubts from his mind, so that nothing existed for him beyond her lips or the strong pressure of her body that seemed almost to clamour for him. When she drew back he was filled with a yearning for her that demanded immediate release and catching up her hand he pressed it to his lips and said, breathlessly, "I'll tell them, Grace! I'll tell them you're staying, dearest!" and rushed from the room as though he intended proclaiming his triumph from the housetops but when he bore down on Thirza Tremlett, dusting an engraving in the hall, he checked himself and said, gruffly, "Tell Mrs. Handcock Miss Lovell is staying to luncheon and ask Chivers to saddle Snowdrop and bring both horses round to the front door at two o'clock sharp!"

Through the open door Grace saw that the girl was startled by his eruption and wondered idly if she too had been engaged in eaves-dropping but the possibility did not concern her overmuch. Half the Valley would know about it by now and she wondered, smiling one of her small, crooked smiles, what they would make of it, and whether they would credit her with a technique superior to Claire Derwent, the hot favourite in the Shallowford matrimonial stakes throughout the summer.

VI

No one could say how the news spread to every corner of the Valley in such a short space of time. Things usually did, of course, but not quite so rapidly as on this occasion. Perhaps the news was blown back on the Sorrel by the indoor staff at Heronslea, who heard Lord Gilroy and Cribb discussing it over luncheon, or perhaps Thirza Tremlett, the housemaid, had been keyhole peeping after all; or maybe Ikey Palfrey, an exceptionally observant lad, noticed the way Paul looked at Grace when he helped her mount in the forecourt, and told Gappy, the gardener's boy, "It's 'er, like I said!", for Gappy, living on the Coombe side of the estate, had offered to wager on Claire Derwent. At all events, it soon got about and was common in the kitchens and barns.

Elinor Codsall heard it from Matt the shepherd that same after-noon and Matt must have got it from the wind gossip of Priory Wood pines for he had been outalong since first light and nowhere near the Big House. Elinor told Will as soon as he came into the kitchen and kicked off his boots and Will, for once, showed an interest in Valley tittle-tattle, exclaiming, "Well, I'm bliddy glad to hear it, midear! It'll ha' been lonesome for un in that gurt ole place, especially o' nights, eh?" and he winked, half-expecting her to blush, but twenty-eight successive nights beside Will had used up Elinor's blushes and all she said was, "Oh, giddon with 'ee! Come and zit down, man, I've made treacle pudding for 'ee!"

Martha Pitts heard it from the Bagman, who got it from one of the gardeners, Horace Handcock perhaps, who heard most things long before everybody else and Martha too was delighted. She had a great regard for the young city man who seemed so anxious to be a good landlord and had been hoping that the Big House would soon have a mistress to take some of the work off his hands. She told Arthur and Henry as soon as they came in at dusk and Henry said, "Well, damme, who'd ha' thowt it? The Lovell girl, you zay, who was to have been wed to that waster, Ralph Lovell?" His mother thought this a good opportunity to drive home a lesson on the subject of his bachelorhood and said, crossly, "Aye, and tiz time you thought about getting wed, boy! Baint the maids round here good enough for 'ee?" to which Henry replied, with a wink at his father, "The maids is well enough as maids, Mother! Tiz when they cease to be maids they shows their true colours!" and went on to talk about more serious matters, like the overflowing brook on the north slope of the wood.

Arabella Codsall learned it from one of the dairy-maids and it says something for the impression it made on her that she received the news in silence. There were times, these days, when Arabella retreated into silence, a change in her that disconcerted everyone at Four Winds. This is not to say she was mute. She still spoke approximately three times as many words each day as most people on the farm, but seemed to have ceased to expect replies to trigger off renewed outbursts and resorted to the long, muttered monologue, which family and staff could safely ignore. She had two repetitive themes nowadays, one directed at Martin, and the other at her younger son, Sydney. Martin's began, "Well on the road to ruin we are, you, me, the boy, the farm, everything about us and I'm sure I don't know what I've done to merit it . . . !", whereas the monologue addressed to Sydney was more cautionary than abusive, beginning, "You see the fruits of the lusts of the flesh, Sydney! Take heed of a man like your brother Will, who can turn his back on bottom land like this and banish himself to hill country, bringing shame on us and a pauper's grave on himself," and so on, a lamentation to which Sydney, ever a thoughtful, silent boy, would listen with rapidly blinking eyes, as his mother heaved herself about the big kitchen, going about her work with the joyless movements of a bond slave. But although Arabella made no comment on the new Squire's intention to marry she thought with sour satisfaction of his choice, for Bruce Lovell's reputation in the Valley was a scandalous one and it followed that his blood would bring tribulation to the deceitful young man at the Big House who had played his part in reducing her domestic audience to two.

News of the engagement reached the Potter Dell at dusk and Tamer Potter, lifting his nose, scented deprivation and strictures in the rumour. He had been relieved when the estate had been taken over by a bachelor, whom he sensed would regard him and his brood as characters and had done nothing since Paul's arrival to check the march of dock and nettle across Lower Coombe fields. Now, perhaps, changes might be on the way, for it was not improbable that a man with a wife to support would see him for what he was, a cunning and indolent old loafer, and urge him on pain of eviction to plough fields that had long lain fallow, or engage in the back-breaking labour of hedging and ditching. For his part he wished the young fool up at the Big House would remain single and count his blessings.

Farmer Willoughby, of Deepdene, heard the news with satisfaction. His gospel was love and Mr. Craddock's championship of Elinor had established him in Willoughby's heart as a patron of love. He knew nothing of the Lovell girl, whom the Squire was now said to be marrying but was sure that such an upstanding young man would choose wisely and he wished both of them well, even in the matter of procreation which, strictly speaking, did not feature in Farmer Willoughby's conception of love.

Edward Derwent was told the news at supper that night. His wife Liz should have known better than to broach the subject just as her husband was sitting down to a large helping of cold duck. She succeeded in demolishing his appetite with a single sentence for his eyebrows came together like the prongs of a badger trap and growling that here was another piece of women's tittle-tattle, he turned to Rose for corroboration. Rose confirmed the news. Alone among the Valley folk she was not much surprised by it for Claire had told her where the Squire's interests lay on the night of the fireworks. Now she wondered, a little wretchedly, whether she should relay the news to Claire, in Kent, but Derwent, satisfied that there must be something in it after all, left his food untouched and stumped off to the yard, lighting his pipe and leaning against the oak pillars of the byre to contemplate his cow stalls with masochistic gloom. He found himself wishing that he had never set eyes on the young fool up at the Big House. It was a tiresome and troublesome business to be levered out of one's comfortable pessimism only to discover that he had been right after all

231

and would live and die as a tenant, without graduating to the status of freeholder for surely this was certain now. Marriage implied continuity and a married squire meant a squire with heirs to consider. In addition to that it was now painfully apparent that any heirs Craddock produced would not have Derwent blood in their veins, as he had once been led to believe possible. It would have been better, he reflected bitterly, if the estate had jogged along in its old pre-war muddle for all that recent changes brought to High Coombe was two cliff fields and the loss of his favourite daughter, currently wasting her time in a tea shop on the other side of England. Ordinarily he would not have cared two straws whom Craddock married but it was hard to have glimpsed such a bright prospect and then see it vanish, together with his eligible daughter. Standing there in the January fog, puffing clouds of strong tobacco smoke at his blameless cows, Edward Derwent silently cursed Paul Craddock, his bride-to-be, and all his works.

Sam Potter heard the news from Aaron Stokes gathering reeds for thatching and Sam threw down his axe and ran at once to his cottage to tell Joannie. Sam was delighted. Ever since he had become a father himself he wished all men to be blessed with children, and neither had he forgotten young Squire's generosity and lack of condescension when he had called at the cottage on the day little Pauline was born. He got out the crown piece Paul had given him on that occasion and swung it from the string to which it had been attached through a hole, drilled in Queen Victoria's diadem. Joannie, a practical soul, said it was fortunate Pauline's arrival had preceded the Squire's marriage for had it not the christening gift might have been bestowed on one of his own children but Sam laughed at this, pointing out that young Squire possessed more crown pieces than he could spend in a lifetime, and that when an heir did make its appearance there would be junketings on an unprecedented scale and free beer for everyone in the Valley. He then replaced the medallion in its box on the mantelshelf, gave a gleeful imitation of his child's gurgle and returned to work in the wood.

Mrs. Handcock, who surely should have been one of the first to hear, was, in fact, one of the last, learning it from the lips of her own husband, Horace, when he was lying flat on his back in their double bed and she was struggling to free herself of her vast, whalebone corset. The act of undressing always occupied Mrs. Handcock upwards of half-an-hour and during this period it was Horace's custom to comment on life and the British Empire, with occasional

232

snippets of local gossip gleaned from heaven knew where. His awareness of all that happened, or was about to happen in the Valley, was a source of reverent astonishment to his wife, and contributed in no small measure to her respect for him. He looked small and insignificant when he was in bed, with nothing but his bald head and sidewhiskers showing above the coverlet but it was at these times that he was inclined to be more than usually oracular, staring up at the ceiling and giving her full benefit of his wisdom and logic. She still had nine hooks to free when he said, as casually as if he had been discussing compost, "You'll have heard, no doubt, that Squire'll be marrying Bruce Lovell's girl before the daffodils be out?" and she gave two yelps, one of surprise, and the other as her fingers slipped and she nipped a fold of flesh. He turned his mild gaze on her; "You mean you *haven't* heard? You've been on top of un and baint put two and two together?"

"I've heard no such thing," she said indignantly, "but I should ha' said if 'er was marrying anyone it would ha' been the Derwent maid!"

"Then youm behindhand, considerably so," he told her. "Squire'll wed the Lovell maid before you've time to bake a cake, and that's a fact, so you may as well make up your mind to it!" He did not need to look at her to know that his news had shocked her or that already, as she stood half-undressed, wrestling with her corset, she was boiling with uncertainty and resentment. This was understandable, he thought, for she was only a woman and therefore a fool, quite incapable of reasoning. Moreover, it pleased him that he had been the first to bring her the news for he was probably the only man in the world who could stem her panic.

"Now dornee get in one of your ole tizzies, midear," he said, mildly, "for there baint a need! Taken all round tiz well for us tiz the Lovell maid an' not the Derwent maid, because the Lovell maid, being a lady born, will be less likely to chase 'ee round than a varmer's daughter brought up to work with her hands! Let your mind dwell on that for a spell and mebbe you'll zee the zense in it!"

"But it won't be the same, Horace," she wailed, tearing at the last obstinate hook, "I've done for 'un ever zince he set foot in the Valley, and he's no more'n a baby to be taking a wife and unsetting things like this!" and she hurled the corset from her and burst into tears.

"Babies grow up, and gets interested in young wimmin," said Horace, unmoved, "so thank your lucky stars he's found someone who knows the plaace and not cottoned on one o' them townees who would

233

have brought her own housekeeper, along with her trousseau! Now put on your nightgown before you gets your death o' cold woman, and take it from me we'm lucky it's turned out as it has. The Lovell maid won't be one to count the linen, nor look too closely at the tradesmen's bills, I can tell 'ee that! You've had the ordering of the plaace all this time and you'll have it yet, zo blow the bliddy candle out and go to sleep!"

As always she was able to retreat under the mantle of his profundity and before she slept the worst of her alarms were stilled. She had been very happy mothering Paul, and before Paul, the widower Rudd, and before Rudd the tetchy Sir George on the rare occasions he was in residence but Horace was right, of course. A mistress had to appear sooner or later, and it might, as he said, have been worse, for at least Grace Lovell, a lady born, would be likely to leave the ordering of the house to servants. Then another, happier thought comforted her. There would soon be children about the house and she would like that very much and she smiled to herself in the darkness, listening to Horace's heavy breathing as she recalled the width of the Lovell maid's hips, in an attempt to estimate her child-bearing capacity.

The news reached Meg Potter when she was gathering herbs for her winter rheumatism cure. The Bagman, who had informed Martha Pitts, told her and passed on his way, leaving her to look for further enlightenment in the cards. Meg carried her cards everywhere, using them as a sailor uses a compass, or a stranger a signpost at crossroads. She now spread them on a beech stump, cutting, shuffling and re-cutting and three times out of five the face card that turned up was the Queen of Spades, Lady of Sorrow. This puzzled her, for she had gone to her cards on the day Paul Craddock first rode into the Dell and what they had told her had been very encouraging but today the turn up alternated between the Lady of Sorrow and the Knave of Diamonds, whom she recognised as her son Smut and no matter how often she reshuffled the result was the same. At last she gave it up, accepting the inevitable with the stoicism she brought to every turning-point in her life. There would be trouble in the Valley and soon and it would involve the Lovell maid and Smut, in the proportion of about five to two. She went back to her herb collecting, wishing it could have been otherwise.

Meg Potter had her cards and everyone else in the Valley had self-interest to guide them but John Rudd, the only one among them to hear the news direct from Paul, had no guide beyond a persistent

234

niggle under his strapped-up ribs and the niggle told him approximately the same story as the cards told Meg. He could not have said why this should be so. He was a man who usually rationalised his prejudices and he reminded himself that, whereas everybody knew Bruce Lovell was a bad hat, nobody knew much about his daughter, except that her mother had drowned herself in a reservoir in India, years ago. He listened, sucking on his pipe, to Paul's account of all that had taken place in the Valley during his absence, and could find it in him to admire the boy for his stand against Arabella Codsall and Lord Gilroy, but when Paul asked him outright what, if anything, he had against Grace Lovell he had had to choose between his niggle and his affection. He could not admit to a young man in love that he suspected a streak of madness in his darling's veins or that for a woman to drown herself on account of a Lovell implied a fatal lack of balance on the female side. He had nothing but rumour and conjecture to reinforce his arguments, nothing more than a vague impression that Grace Lovell was bad luck. And now, as he stood leaning on the fence rails of the paddock watching the moon rise over the Bluff, he knew that he had deceived himself when he had assumed that Craddock's arrival here, and the enthusiasm he brought with him, meant a permanent anchorage for himself. There could never be a safe anchorage with a Lovell in the Big House. As the soft, white light touched the shallows at the ford, John Rudd said to himself, impatiently, "Now who the hell am I to pour cold water on the boy? What gives me the right to advise him on a matter like this? He's in love with a pretty face and a pretty figure and if he brings the same enthusiasm to his marriage as he's brought to the Valley I daresay he'll prove me a superstitious old fool!" And hoisting himself from the rail he knocked out his pipe and went across to the lodge to bed.

CHAPTER NINE

I

A MARRIAGE between strangers is an uncharted journey; Will Codsall knew his Elinor and Walt Pascoe his Pansy, before marrying them. Within certain limits, they knew what they could expect of them as cooks, housekeepers and bedfellows, and their brides were equally well primed, so that such surprises as they encountered had no power to astound them as Paul Craddock was astounded and delighted by Grace Lovell.

The 8 a.m. ceremony at Paxtonbury Parish church was so short and simple that Paul had some difficulty in realising that he was indeed married when they said good-bye to Celia and John Rudd after breakfast at The Mitre. There was no one else present to shake by the hand or kiss; no rice, no confetti, no jokes, no old shoes tied under the carriage that took them to the junction and thence, by the Cornish express, to London, where they stayed one night before travelling to Dover and catching the cross-Channel packet for Boulogne.

Paul had asked her where she would like to spend the honeymoon and she had told him Paris, a city she had never visited although she was a seasoned Continental traveller and had stayed in several Belgian spas, sailed down the Rhine on a paddle steamer and spent several weeks beside the Swiss lakes. That was the first of his surprises but there were many more and they continued to explode at irregular intervals, like the green and crimson rockets on the night of the soirée.

He discovered, for instance, that she could speak fluent French, whereas he was obliged to grope for half-forgotten phrases from school text-books, and perhaps, if he had not been so much in love, her accomplishment would have dismayed him a little. As it was he listened with awe as she exchanged banter with porters, ticket collectors and the concierge at the sedate hotel which she had found for him off the Avenue des Capucines. Another source of amazement was her apparent familiarity with Parisian history. She took him to all kinds of out-of-the-way places connected with characters he had met in fiction or in encyclopaedias, and talked freely of people like Madame Roland, Catherine de Medici and Marguerite of Navarre.

236

She hustled him off to an obscure little museum to show him the proclamation Robespierre had been signing when the Thermidorians burst in and put a term to the Terror. She told him whimsical ghost stories as they walked the gravelled paths of the Petit Trianon and was even able to identify many of Napoleon's marshals from busts that seemed to him identical as they looked down from niches in the old Palais Royale. She seemed to enjoy guiding him as though he had been an adolescent son instead of her husband, so that, during their sightseeing tours he trailed dutifully behind her feeling no shame on this account but rather a surge of pride that sometimes made him almost drunk with exhilaration. To give expression to his pride he spent freely, buying her a present every day. Sometimes it was a confection that caught his eye in a milliner's window, sometimes a dress that she declared, laughing, she could never wear within fifty miles of the Sorrel Valley and sometimes a mere trifle like a book, trinket or even a posy of spring flowers. So it happened that by day the initiative was hers but when they were alone in their first-storey room above the rattle of the traffic she deliberately abdicated and became a bride again who, while not in any way shy or withdrawn, allowed the initiative to pass back to him. Yet here again she had the power to surprise him, for he had not yet forgotten her kiss and the promise that accompanied it on the day she had helped to rout Cribb and although he meant to implement his pledge never to hustle her this soon proved beyond his power. He had, on embarking on this adventure, been only too aware of his inexperience but in some indefinable way she gave him a measure of confidence so that, to some extent, neither one of them suffered the disenchantment that might have attended the essays of two people who had grown to maturity in an age when discussion of sex was taboo. It did cross his mind during that first week, however, that her intellectual curiosity might have led her to seek and find some printed source of enlightenment, for she seemed to know very well how best to accommodate him and it was only in retrospect that he wondered whether she had acquired this awareness in the arms of the roystering Ralph Lovell, reputedly an expert wencher. When he falteringly touched on the subject, however, she answered him with her usual frankness, saying that Ralph had certainly done his best to anticipate marriage but that she had had no difficulty in thwarting him for, like all the Lovells, he was an arch snob and drew a nice distinction between women of her class and village girls like the Potters. On this he let the matter drop, not liking to contemplate just how many

237

liberties had been extended to Ralph or to any other man. He was far too grateful for the patience and generosity she was prepared to extend to him and came to accept her accessibility as a physical manifestation of her exceptional candour. This was impressed upon him one afternoon about a week after their marriage when he had occasion to go into the bathroom of the little suite for his razor. The door was ajar and he called, "Can I come in?" and she said, laughing, "Why not? You're my husband aren't you?" and he went in to find her naked, with her tumble of blue-black hair reaching to her shapely buttocks as she stood before a mirror using her brush with long, sweeping strokes. She did not seem in any way embarrassed and went on brushing while he stared at her in wonder. He had never seen her more than half undressed and had thought of her as a rather sturdy little person, with muscles moulded by plenty of exercise but now he could marvel at the classic proportions of her limbs which, against all probability, contrived to give an impression of strength as well as infinite grace and softness. Nor, until this moment, had he appreciated the luxuriance of her hair that trapped the afternoon light in its bluish depths, or of the slenderness of her waist and the neatness of her feet. He said, gently, "But you're quite perfect, Grace! As perfect as a woman could be!" and she replied, in the assured tone of a wife of years rather than days, "It's nice to be told so!" and went on with her brushing.

Her manner of answering reminded him poignantly that, for all her recent submissiveness, she had never admitted to loving him but had only contracted to try and it seemed to him very strange that a beautiful young woman could stand before him stark naked and yet continue to hold on to her spiritual independence. He said, "I'll make you happy, Grace. That means more to me than anything."

She was rather too quick, he thought, with her reply, for suddenly she stopped her brushing and said, "More than the estate? More than that Valley of yours?"

"Whatever we do in the Valley we'll do together," he said, without finding her question irrelevant and forgetting his razor he swept her off her feet and carried her back to the bedroom.

So the days and nights passed, with the leadership shared equally but one day she gave him a brief inkling of what seemed to him her contempt for the dominion of men.

She had taken him, guide-book in hand, to a little lodging house on the Left Bank, telling him that it was here that the girl assassin, Charlotte Corday, had stayed on the night she came to Paris to kill

238

Marat. She seemed to have a very high regard for Charlotte Corday and to know facts concerning her that were not printed in the guide-book. She told him of the girl's indignation at the way the revolution had degenerated into an orgy of cruelty and bloodshed, and of Charlotte's determination to kill the man whom she identified as the chief author of the Terror, describing, with a certain relish, how she had bought the butcher's knife that she used on her victim. Paul said, jokingly, "She must have been a cold-blooded little devil!" but Grace snapped, "Cold-blooded? No, she wasn't that! Fearless and resolute, if you like, but not cold-blooded! The cold-blooded stayed home and talked of achieving something. She went out and did it, while all the men of her party were content to posture on the rostrum!" and as she said this he thought for a moment of Celia's warning concerning Grace's flirtation with the suffragists and wondered if she identified Charlotte Corday with the Pankhursts. She had never discussed modern politics with him and once or twice when he had mentioned Grenfell and his Liberals, she steered the conversation back to less controversial subjects but that same evening she opened the door on another unfamiliar world, conjuring two tickets for the ballet from a fellow guest at the hotel, and taking him, protesting complete ignorance, to the Opera, where *Giselle* was being presented by the Imperial Russian Ballet.

Until then he had always thought of ballet as no more than an eccentric form of dancing, but he tried to look as though he was pre-pared to enjoy it for her sake. It was not until he had stolen several glances at her during the performance that the magic began to work upon his prejudice and make his ignorance seem boorish. When the interval arrived he readily admitted this and was rewarded by a flash of enthusiasm in her eyes and an impulsive grasp of her hand as she said, "I was afraid you'd be bored and make nothing of it! This is an essential part of life, Paul! It makes up for so much ugliness, cruelty and stupidity! Will you promise me something? If the Ballet comes to London in the autumn may we travel up and stay for it? Will we get a chance to see something outside the Sorrel Valley every so often? Often enough to stop us growing cabbages for heads?"

He would have promised her the moon at that moment and replied, "Why certainly, darling, you can go to London any time you wish!" and then, recalling her enigmatic remark in the bathroom, "Is *that* what frightens you about Shallowford? The thought of being buried alive, and growing dull, like one of the farmer's daughters?"

"No," she said, "not really, but you must have hated the city very much to have gone there in the first place. They say you only visited Paxtonbury once, until we were married there!"

"Well, I suppose I do hate cities," he admitted, "particularly London, but my real reason for buying Shallowford wasn't as simple as that. I couldn't stand the thought of an office career and with my knee the field was very limited. Then, after I was committed, I soon grew to love every blade of grass in the place but I suppose it really began with the dream."

She showed interest at once. "What dream?"

"Oh, I can't tell you here and anyway it's time to go back."

"Will you tell me tonight?"

"Yes, but it will probably bore you. Other people's dreams always bore me."

She held him to his promise and when they were in bed he told her as much as he could recall of the conflict between the static hosts on the hospital ceiling and the compensating view of the country beyond the ward window that had seemed, at the time, to play such a vital part in his recovery. He could not tell whether she was impressed or dismissed the story as an unremarkable symptom of fever and drugs and would have been very surprised to know that she lay awake long after he slept, or that his story helped to convince her that he was by no means the amiable simpleton she had first supposed him to be. She lay there wondering if, even now, he understood that she had married him as cold-bloodedly as any fortune hunter and in retracing her steps over their various encounters she realised that already her conscience troubled her somewhat for surely his apparent need of her could no longer be dismissed as the self-delusion all men used to disguise their clamour for access to a woman's body and the incidental acquisition of a woman servitor. His approach, she thought, already indicated something more substantial than that and it would be folly not to admit it, for although his physical enjoyment of her was uncomplicated he already respected her as a person and not as a bedmate or a brood mare for children to perpetuate his name. For this, in the main, was how she had thought of him in the brief interval between her unconditional surrender and marriage but it was not, unfortunately for her peace of mind, how she thought of him now. He was, she admitted, far more imaginative than she had supposed, possessing also a certain originality and infinitely more patience than most young men, and even if his eyes were still fixed on contemptibly small

240

horizons his vision might, she thought, expand if she could teach him to look beyond Coombe Bluff. She made a half-playful attempt to separate the Paul Craddock of Shallowford from the Paul Craddock now sleeping beside her. The one she had thought of as little more than a gawky, earnest, ignorant boy who had served and suffered in a war but learned little or nothing about people and their overriding greed and self-interest. He could still suffer fools gladly, so much so that he accepted rascals like Tamer Potter and cranks like Edwin Willoughby as personal responsibilities. He liked to think of himself as a benevolent patron, administering a tiny kingdom of rustics when, in fact, he was no more than a lucky young ass, aping the country gentleman and lagging a century behind the times. He had probably never heard of people like Keir Hardie and his forlorn little working-man's party, or the vanguard of women prepared to sacrifice everything in an attempt to have a voice in their own destinies. Yet, and she was obliged to admit it, there existed, deep in this long, lump of a man, a spark of idealism that was never completely submerged by douches of sentimental claptrap or obscured by muddled thinking, and now and then she had glimpsed it. There was something even more rare—a male gentleness that she had never experienced in any other man. Intrigued by now, she lit the night light, turning carefully on her elbow and looking down on him as he slept. He was not, she decided, particularly good looking, with his long, craggy face, strong features and stiff, unruly hair almost as dark as her own. If they did have children they would probably have faces as long as a horse and complexions as swarthy as Spaniards. She rested on her elbow a long time, studying him calmly and objectively, noting his look of inno-cence that was offset by the unexpected firmness of the jaw and the fastidiousness of the long, thin nose. It was a face, she thought, that could have belonged to a ruthless or even a cruel person who would want his way with men and women yet she knew by now that there was no spark of cruelty in him and very little ruthlessness as far as she was concerned. She was aware too that she could, if she wished, manipulate him easily enough, either by appealing to his old-fashioned sense of chivalry or by the more direct method of throwing her arms and legs about him, and yet, was she capable of making him turn his back on his dream, so that they could advance as man and wife into the twentieth century? She looked at his jawline again. Perhaps, in time, when he grew a little but not yet, possibly not until she had borne him a child or two. A month ago this conclusion would have depressed her but tonight it only made her smile. She said, half aloud, as she playfully drew a lock of her hair across his cheek, "Well, Squire, we shall see! And anyway, I've been luckier than I deserve!" and she kissed his forehead, blew out the light, turned over and chuckled. It was a long time since Grace Lovell had indulged in a chuckle.

II

It was after their return to London, when they were being lunched by an attentive Uncle Franz, at Romano's, that she surprised him again, this time by demanding to be taken to the scrapyard to see the actual source of all the war profits that had been diverted to Shallowford. Paul, once he had recovered from his surprise, said, "Now what the devil can interest you down there? I promised myself I'd never go near the stinking place again!", but she replied, watching Zorndorff, "That's a very arrogant promise, Paul, and could only have validity if you had renounced your interest in what it yields! As long as you use its income you've got as much responsibility for it as you have for the farms in the Valley!" and Uncle Franz said the lady certainly had a point and soon twinkled Paul out of his sulks, ordering a four-wheeler to take them along the route Paul had taken on his first day out of hospital.

As they went along, weaving through the traffic, Paul noticed that Grace had made a singular impression on the old Croat and because he had a groom's intense pride in his bride her conquest warmed him, for although old Franz was a Continental, and could therefore be expected to pay court to any pretty, young woman, he knew his man sufficiently well to appreciate the difference between a genuine interest and conventional gallantry. They were talking now of motor-cars, one or two of which could be seen dodging about between the cabs and drays that flowed along the congested highway.

"I should have thought, Uncle Franz," Grace was saying, "that a merchant prince like you would have acquired a motor long ago! After the initial outlay upkeep must be far less than a carriage."

Paul, who privately thought of this as nonsense, winked at Uncle Franz but the old boy obviously took her seriously, for he said, "Oh, they'll have all the horses off the road eventually. Only a stick-in-the-mud like your husband will insist on keeping horses, but you're in error, my dear young lady, as regards the economics of the contraption. They cost more in oil than a horse eats in corn and you can't engage a trained chauffeur at the wage you pay a coachman. I daresay I shall experiment with one in a year or so, when they have got over their teething troubles, for it never does to rush in and buy mechanical devices until they have settled down. They tell me new developments are being made every week and a great deal of money has been sunk in promotion!"

They went on to talk of other topics, land development this side of the Thames, the prospect of a general election, and of Paris, which Zorndorff had not visited since he passed through it as a refugee. Paul noticed too that the Croat had also made a deep impression upon Grace, for she coaxed him to tell her something of his impressions of England, and how he had managed to make such a success of life in a land where he had arrived without knowing a word of the language. Paul could see that Zorndorff was flattered but he was only half listening, for the familiar reek of the streets made him homesick for the Valley and as they traversed the Old Kent Road, and passed the tanyard and Peek Frean's factory, he found himself comparing the dinginess and squalor around him to the charm of the French capital and wondered how Londoners could be so chauvinistic about their sprawl. Then, as they turned in at the gates of the yard and looked again on the jumble of desolation that filled the rectangle between the street and the backs of houses, he thought of the smell of the wind over Blackberry Moor and was impatient to be gone.

"I still feel damned ashamed of drawing money from the place!" he said, but his protest seemed to amuse her and she said, glancing at Franz, "How strange! Uncle Franz wallows in it, don't you, Uncle?"

"No, but I haven't a conscience about it," said the Croat, "and I imagine I tolerate it because it is alive."

"Would you say the Sorrel Valley is dead then?" demanded Paul but Grace was far too interested in the scene around her to take him up on this and began to bombard Zorndorff with questions regarding the collection, assortment and disposal of scrap, the prices it fetched and the use to which it was put when melted down. It baffled Paul that she could be so absorbed in such a dull subject when she had never so much as asked a single question about crops or cattle, so he left them to it, stepping out on to the platform above the weighbridge and gazing down at the yard, hating it all the more for the debt he owed it and would always owe it.

The last time he had been here it was in summer drought, when the debris had festered in the humid air but now, under a March sky, the vast array of odds and ends seemed to huddle together in the wind and the whole area had a pinched, dejected look. The scavengers looked pinched too as they pottered among the garbage and the rattle of their hobnailed boots came up to him like the chink of fetters. He was still there, glowering at his benefactor, when he felt her arm slip through his and her hand squeeze his wrist and at her touch his ill-humour left him. "I'm sorry to be so damned sour about it, Grace. I know I owe it money, and probably always will but I can't help it. The damned place disgusts me. Uncle Franz says my mother was a countrywoman and maybe that explains a good deal."

"Uncle Franz has just been telling me that," she said, "and it *is* a depressing spectacle, but don't you ever feel you could do something to improve it and with it the conditions these people work under? I think that's what would have recommended itself to me before I took on fresh responsibilities," and then she laughed, adding, "I'm sorry, Paul! That sounds mealymouthed!"

"No, it doesn't," he said, "but it shows a lack of understanding of the Cockney temperament! They don't recoil from the squalor, they feel safe in it and wouldn't give you a thank you for more than an hour or so in the country, or by the sea. If you don't believe me ask Ikey Palfrey when we get home."

"Who is Ikey Palfrey?" she wanted to know and he told her he was the stable-boy who had taken care of her horse on the occasions she had ridden over to Shallowford, and because she was interested he went on to describe the incident of the frightened cart-horse, and how he had felt impelled to give the boy a chance of growing up in clean air. "Ikey is the exception that proves the rule," he added, "but then, his mother was a peasant too, a relative of Franz's."

"How does Ikey like it down there?" she asked and he told her the boy was doing well and attending Mary Willoughby's little school in the mornings. "He's a very sharp kid and everybody's fond of him," he added and might have gone on to describe Ikey's cheekiness and powers of mimicry had she not stood back regarding him with a puzzled smile, saying "But don't you *see*? That's exactly what I meant! I just talked about it but you've already done something practical! You know, you're a very unpredictable person, and some-times bewilderingly human! I think I'm rather fond of you, really!" and she stood on tiptoe and kissed him on the cheek just as Franz, rubbing his hands, emerged from the office and said, "Get the man

244

back to his mangolds and let me attend to the business of supporting him!"

III

For some time now Paul had been playing a private joke on himself but had kept it a close secret, even from Grace and John Rudd, for he would have half-agreed with them that his estate diary was evidence of gross sentimentality on his part. When he was alone in his office, usually after breakfast, he unlocked a drawer and took out the Bible-covers that old George Lovell had used to camouflage his collection of photographs. Paul had long since disposed of the pictures but the covers he had laid aside and now it amused him to use the same bindings for his diary. He could hardly have been more secretive about it had the old goat's harem still smirked from between the leather-backed boards.

In the diary he wrote down the daily trivia of estate happenings and the first entry read: "*June 26th, 1902. Met at Sorrel Halt by John Rudd, and rode to Shallowford,*" and the second, dated two days later, "*Bought Shallowford Estate and the grey, Snowdrop,*" and so on, brief and often unrelated entries, recording such minor items as the birth of Sam Potter's daughter, the purchase of the Priory freehold, the marriage of Will Codsall and Elinor Willoughby, his first meeting with James Grenfell and a page devoted to his coronation supper-ball. So far there was nothing written there concerning his wife but the day after his return home he wrote: "*March 7th, 1903. Married Grace Lovell, my very dear wife!*" and when he re-read this entry a week or so later, he was somewhat embarrassed by it, as though he now saw himself as a patriarchal squire taking care that posterity would take heed of him and his chattels. He did not erase it, however but made no further entries until the last week of April, when he wrote, "*Grace began work on the lily pond in the rose garden: Horace Handcock thinks it practical.*"

The entry set him thinking and his thoughts ran through pleasant country. It was remarkable, he reflected how quickly she had settled, winning the friendship of indoor and outdoor staff and sometimes, as in the case of Handcock, the head gardener, enlisting a personal champion. She had dropped enough hints during the honeymoon to give him cause to worry, leaving him in little doubt but that she would only live permanently in the Valley on sufferance and would have much preferred to travel and winter in London. Yet, within hours of

245

their return she had found a small field of creative energy in the house and grounds and had at once set about banishing the bachelor atmosphere of the place so that within a month Shallowford was a home rather than a headquarters. She made no sweeping changes but made her impact everywhere and without fuss. She was careful not to antagonise Mrs. Handcock or the maids, particularly the parlourmaid, Thirza Tremlett, known to be prickly. She had a trick of persuading Mrs. Handcock and even Thirza that various improvements had originated with them and thus it was that a gay, patterned wallpaper found its way on the featureless walls of guest-rooms, along the length of the corridor at the rear of the house and, to Horace Handcock's amazement, on the walls of the housekeeper's rooms in the east wing. By a partial replacement of furniture, carpets and curtains, the main bedroom lost its austerity and the bleak dining-room, which Paul had abandoned to its original browns and greys, began to borrow something from the solid comfort of the library. This room she left alone, declaring it was his but she took a very active interest in the garden, persuading Horace to dispose of most of the overgrown shrubs that cluttered the lawns. Daffodils and narcissi that this time of year spread a yellow and white carpet from the stable-yard to the edge of Priory Wood, now reappeared all over the house, standing in earthenware crocks Grace had found abandoned in a disused stable.

It was this old stable that gave her the idea for the lily pond in what had once been a well-stocked rose garden, between the corner of the paddock and the river. Horace had declared that "they ole arbours need a good ole zet-to", by which he meant the rotting arches and trellis work should be replaced but Grace pointed out that the natural dip in the ground lent itself to the making of a sunken ornamental pond and water could be piped from the river if a culvert was deepened. The rose garden could then be laid out with flags taken from the old stable, and the pond, when complete, stocked with goldfish and bordered by great clumps of iris. Horace and his boy Gappy (occasionally assisted by Ikey to whom Grace had taken a liking) set to work at once and the pond was now ready for water. Grace did her stint arranging flags and Honeyman, of the Home Farm, sent over the Timberlake boys from the sawmill with a supply of freshly cut poles, so that soon this section of the garden was transformed.

She was equally successful as a hostess and they gave one or two little dinners, entertaining James Grenfell, Celia, and finally Parson Bull and his desiccated wife, Kate. Grace seemed to like Grenfell, although she crossed swords with him on several issues, including the political integrity of right-wing Liberals. Celia, for her part, was impressed by her stepdaughter's relaxed command of the house, easy relationship with such entrenched characters as the housekeeper and parlourmaid but, above all, by her seeming contentment. The dinner with Parson Bull and his wife went off far more successfuly than Paul could have hoped, for neither he nor Grace had much time for the rector, and Mrs. Bull was a nonentity, with even less to say for herself than the second Mrs. Derwent. Bull, however, was more genial than usual, partly because he had an eye for a pretty woman and when the ladies had retired congratulated Paul on his stand against Lord Gilroy, whom Bull dismissed as "a bloodless old stick", going on to describe Gilroy's heir as a "sack of potatoes strapped to a saddle". Bull, certainly no Radical, nonetheless declared it was high time somebody put a spoke in the wheel of the agent Cribb, who was for ever trying to hog the proceeds of local social events and divert money that belonged to the church into the local Conservative coffers. Paul asked Bull if he thought Grenfell had any chance of winning the seat and was surprised when the parson said he would probably triumph in the election after next, for the present member, Colonel Hilton-Price, was rarely seen in the area and the Liberals would soon sweep the country. Before they rejoined the ladies Bull made a direct reference to Grace, congratulating Paul on marrying "such a decorative and mettlesome gel", and one who could "sit a horse better than any filly between New Cover and Barnaby Clump"! Bull had his own names for Valley landmarks and seldom used those printed on an ordnance map, referring to uplands, bottoms and coverts according to how they presented themselves to a field in full cry. Thus the western part of Shallowford Woods was "that damned hairy place, where you poke about all day!" and the plateau of Blackberry Moor "that stretch where a fox covers the ground with its neck in splints!" One way and another it was a reassuring evening, although Paul felt very sorry for Grace, left to make heavy weather with Kate.

It was a day or so after this that Paul, working in the office with the garden door open, heard sounds of activity coming from the rose garden, so presently, when Ikey had brought Snowdrop round for him to ride over and see the Potters about the loan of a cart-horse, he led the horse along the terrace and looked over the box hedge at the group working in the excavation beyond. Grace was there with Handcock, old Timberlake the sawyer, the boy Gappy and the dog Goneaway,

247

the latter behaving as though the operation had been put in hand to entertain her. Grace looked up cheerfully when he called, wiping her forehead with the back of her hand. Her cheeks, he noted, had lost a good deal of their pallor and in the strong sunlight seemed to him almost as pink as the gardener's. She called "Gappy! Get that dog out of here! As fast as we dig out the idiot fills it in! If you're going out, Paul, take her along with you, please!" and Paul, laughing, whistled Goneaway over as Horace said, with quiet pride, "Us is gettin' along vamously, Squire! Us'll 'ave the watter in 'er be the weekend!" Paul left them to it but as he was climbing into the saddle Timberlake, who knew all about the cart-horse, said, "Dornee let that ole blackguard Tamer Potter talk 'ee into making 'er permanent, Squire! 'E'll try, mak' no mistake!" and Paul wondered at the changes Grace had subtly introduced into the place for before his marriage he had not been able to extract two words from the sawyer, who had stood about fidgeting and tongue-tied whenever he had called at the Home Farm and watched him at work.

He went on down to the ford and along the river road, pondering Parson Bull's comment that he was lucky to have found such a wife so quickly and he thought, as he turned up the steep lane to the Dell, "I'm lucky all right, but so are the staff and I believe they know it!" and because he was in such a good humour he listened with amusement to Tamer's catalogue of woes and his doubts as to whether the loan of a single horse would enable him to keep the wheels turning. "Tiz all on account o' me being zo shorthanded, Squire," he explained, "an' beggin' your pardon, zir, 'twas you who tempted away my Sam! Now my maid has gone an' wed that young Pascoe zo I'm obliged to attend to everything myself!" Paul reminded him that he still had two daughters to look after livestock and another son to help him work under two hundred acres, whereas Willoughby, higher up, managed with a part-time man and a boy.

"Ah," said Tamer, who had been ready for this, "but Willoughby's lad be a boy broken to varming, baint 'ee, whereas my Smut'll never do a handsturn about the plaace, an' my ole woman aids an' abets'n!"

The sun was shining for the first time in a month so Paul, reluctant to waste time arguing with the old rascal, said, "Well, you've got the horse and I'll ask Honeyman to lend you a man one day a week, providing you pay him. We all want to see you make something of this holding, Tamer, it's been a liability for too long," but Tamer was proof against this sort of talk and all he replied was, "Mebbe you'll be proud of us bevore us 'ave vinished hereabouts," but privately cursed the day when the new owner of Shallowford had taken a wife to hustle him into persecuting tenants. "Meg!" he bellowed, "come on out an' pay your respects to the Squire, will 'ee, you lazy slut?", and he turned his back on Paul to flush the survivors of his brood from the farmhouse. Meg Potter came out slowly and behind her the two girls, Cissie and Violet but Smut was nowhere to be found. "Do 'ee know where that Smut be to?" roared Tamer, who always enjoyed exercising his largely fictitious authority over his family but Meg said no, she did not know, although she was well aware that Smut Potter, at that precise moment, was overlooking the Heronslea partridge coverts, five miles to the east and that his presence there was a reconnaissance pending a descent upon a fat buck that had been using the covert lately. She gave a bob to the Squire, however, as he rode up the track towards Deepdene. He was entitled to that, she thought, seeing how much tiresomeness lay in wait for him but she said nothing of this to Tamer or the girls, returning at once to her ruinous kitchen to finish brewing her winter rheumatism cure. The sweet-smelling concoction seethed in a huge iron pot, and a long row of medicine bottles, taken by stealth from Doctor O'Keefe's dispensary over the years, stood waiting to receive it but as it was not yet on the boil there was time for a quick look into the future. She took out her cards and fell to shuffling and cutting them and out came not the Lady of Sorrow, as she had expected, but the Knave of Diamonds. Its appearance disconcerted her for it indicated that Smut's future was even more uncertain than the Squire's. It occurred to her then that she should warn Smut to leave the buck until it crossed into the safer territory of Shallowford Woods. Sam Potter, her firstborn, might have abandoned the tribe, but she knew he would never come between Smut and his livelihood.

IV

Spring, so Arthur Pitts told him, had been cruising offshore for long enough, but within days of Paul's return home it made up its mind, dropped anchor south of the sandbars and fired its green barrage over the Valley. The effect was salutary. The river went down overnight and all the Sorrel creeks and oxbows dried out. The banners of May appeared in all the hedgerows between Timberlake's sawmill and Codsall bridge. April showers still fell but were shot through with sunshine, so that the Teazel watershed was seen through a silver gauze and up and down the Valley there was bustle and expectancy. Henry Pitts sang as he herded his cows down to the water meadows and even Sydney Codsall, with a mind full of syntax and relativity, stopped his bicycle on the way to school one morning just to watch a ladybird on a sprig of cowparsley. A week or so later all the dwarf elms and beech hedges along the western edge of Hermitage Wood were full of nesting thrushes, blackbirds, tits and finches, and the vixens on the landslips further south were out all night hunting up food for their cubs.

There were plenty of other signs that the long, wet winter was done and that everything in the valley was bent on renewing itself. Over at Periwinkle Elinor Codsall, last year just a wisp of a girl, now dragged a thickening body across the uneven flags of the kitchen and in the woods north of the mere Joannie Potter, also pregnant, was wondering how, come the autumn, she would squeeze another crib into the cottage bedroom. Down in Coombe Bay were others with like problems, among them Pansy Pascoe. Pansy, once a carefree Potter, looked with distaste at her swollen body, envying her husbandless sisters who were not tied to a kitchen and one hungry male but the sudden warmth of the sun drove her out into the garden where, as she raised her snub nose to the sky, her spirits lifted and she set about peeling a mound of potatoes for Walt's supper.

Only Smut Potter, lying full-length in the bracken overlooking Heronslea, cursed the sun, for its sparkle complicated his scrutiny of the ground below where he suspected the fat buck he had earlier marked down was punishing the bark of the Norwegian pines Gilroy's forester had planted there. Smut had a customer for that buck and he meant to kill while the moon was up. He lay quite still, his eyes fixed unwinkingly on a patch of shadow under the trees, but it was not until the sun clouded over that he identified the movements down there as the chaffering of deer and gave a short grunt of satisfaction. "There 'er be!" he said aloud, "and I'll 'ave un tonight, sure as fate!" and he made a final eyesweep of the approach, memorising contours, gorse patches and places where the heaviest shadows would lie after moonrise. Then, crawling backwards on all fours, he worked his way down to a cleft where a stream ran down through a small coombe to the Sorrel. In less than five minutes he was hidden by the trees that grew on the steep sides of the goyle.

He had moved quickly and cautiously but somebody had observed him from the opposite ridge, a man not as well versed in exploiting cover as Smut but one who had the advantage of binoculars, borrowed for the purpose of keeping Potter in view. Nick Buller, Gilroy's head gamekeeper, had suffered a great deal on Smut's account and once or twice had come close to being sacked for failing to catch him. Recently, however, his luck had turned. A Paxtonbury butcher, who sometimes bought surplus venison from Heronslea when the herds were whittled down, had been heard to boast in The Mitre at Paxtonbury, that he could buy cheaper than Gilroy was prepared to sell and the outlay of a few shillings on Buller's part had traced his source of supply to the Dell. Buller was not such a fool as to hope that he could catch a poacher as wily as Potter in the actual act of taking deer but he thought he stood a good chance of being close on hand when the buck was killed, after which he could follow Smut to the Dell and confront him with a policeman while in the act of conveying the kill to Paxtonbury. He had made his plans accordingly but it was essential to know precisely where Smut would strike, and this explained Buller's presence on the hillside with binoculars. He returned to Heronslea in a happy frame of mind. If Smut Potter was out tonight he was as good as nailed.

If Buller had been allowed to follow this plan things might well have turned out as he had hoped. Smut would have been trailed at a safe distance and stopped by the police *en route* to the butchers but Gilroy's agent, Harry Kitchens, had more ambitious ideas. He argued that if Buller had marked the spot so accurately it would be a very simple matter to take Smut in the act and pay something off the score before he was brought before the Bench at Whinmouth Petty Sessions. Now Kitchens had been waiting for a chance to smash his fist into Potter's face as repayment for all the nagging he had endured on his account and he said, on receiving Buller's report, "Right! Get Scratton and Bostock and lay up both sides of the goyle before sunset. He'll come in by the goyle for there's cover all the way from the boundary. Meantime I'll take young Glover and we'll wait on the west side. We can close in from all sides as soon as we hear a shot! You can have five minutes with Potter yourself, Buller, but leave something for me. Then we'll lock what's left in the stable and hand it over to the magistrates in a sack in the morning!"

Meg Potter passed her warning to Smut but he only laughed at her. He was fond of his mother but took small account of her fortune-telling. All his life he had put his trust in his fieldcraft, his highly developed powers of sight and hearing and, in the last instance, his expert marksmanship, so why should he worry about the prattle of a greasy pack of cards? He cleaned his gun, smeared his face and hands with half-burned embers from the fire and left the Dell soon after dusk. It was a long haul in the trap to Paxtonbury and he wanted to be there by dawn, so that he could enter the butcher's yard before Beefy Bickley's staff arrived. He would then top off a good night's work with bacon and eggs at The Mitre, pay a brief social call on a lonely woman whose sailor husband had been so inconsiderate as to sign on for an Australian run, and be back in the Dell by mid-afternoon. Smut never wasted much time in bed. A siesta would follow and he would be out again as soon as it was dark, this time moving east instead of west. But it all turned out very differently and neither as Smut, Kitchens or Buller planned. Perhaps Meg, in the interests of the Valley, should have passed her warning to all concerned.

He killed the buck with a single shot, stalking upwind at a speed of about a yard a minute. The last sound the buck heard, the first to warn it of danger, was the soft snick of Smut's hammer. Then it was twitching at the foot of the tree and Smut, moving expertly and rapidly, bound forepaws and hindpaws, twisted a stick under the cords and braced himself to hoist it on to his shoulders. It was at that moment, when he was still bent double, that the first of the ambush party moved in.

Smut had passed within yards of Buller on his way out of the goyle but Buller did not possess the patience to play longstop for the agent. The moment he heard the gun he came plunging down the slope and would have fallen on Smut had he not misjudged his distance and overshot him as the poacher crouched above the buck. The butt of his slung gun struck Smut a glancing blow on the elbow, jarring it so sharply that he cried out in pain. Then, as he heard a confused shouting he realised that men were closing in from all sides and Buller had him fast by the ankle, bellowing for assistance at the top of his voice. For a split second, as he heard the others crashing through the undergrowth at the head of the goyle, Smut lost his head and swung his gun in an arc, the butt striking Buller's jaw with shattering force and causing him to utter a single agonised howl as he rolled sideways in the scrub. By then Agent Kitchens and young Glover were almost upon them and two more of Gilroy's men were crashing through briars between Smut and the goyle, so that instinct told him he must run due north towards the moor, unless he was to be caught and half killed on the spot.

He dropped his gun and broke out of the circle with only a yard to spare, Bostock colliding with Glover as the latter dashed up from the west and the pair of them, rolling on top of Buller as Kitchens, nearer the edge of the covert, bellowed, "Head him off to the right! Up to the moor!", and went blundering over the tangled ground in close pursuit. Glover followed but the others remained bent over the unconscious Buller and Bostock cried, "Strike a light, Tom, for Chrissake! He's killed un, I reckon!", and in the flare of a match they looked down on the keeper, his face a mask of blood, his feet across the body of the trussed buck and his gun snapped off at the stock where it had struck the roots of a pine.

It took Smut less than two minutes to lose his two pursuers. He was calmer now and ran with his head rather than his legs, doubling northeast, then north-west and once, for twenty or more strides, backtracking towards the cursing agent, now breasting the slope like an elephant pursuing a hare. After a hundred yards or so he gave it up and found his way back to the plantation where his raging temper was cooled by the shock of seeing Nick Buller, his head on Bostock's knees, as the other man, Scratton, kept repeating, dolorously, "He's done for un! He's done for un!" But Buller, although badly injured about his face, was far from dead and after they had lit the lantern he was able to sit up and gesture feebly, although he could not swallow the brandy Kitchens offered him from his flask. Working clumsily they bound his bloody chaps with strips of flannel shirt so that he sat with his back to the tree like a corpse ready for burial. Glover was sent on ahead to rouse the Big House and despatch a messenger to Whinmouth for the doctor and somehow, between them, they managed to carry Buller down to Long Covert and then across the paddock to his cottage. It was a tedious, troublesome journey and every step of the way Kitchens swore that somebody would pay a heavy price for their pains, as well as Buller's.

As soon as Smut was sure he had lost his pursuers he walked southeast, in a wide sweep that led him to the northern tip of Priory Wood and here, in a little glade, he sat down to ponder his situation. He was not at all sure that he had not killed that idiot Buller and now that he had won clear for a spell he had great difficulty in controlling a tide of panic and keeping his mind clear for his next moves for now it seemed his life might depend on them. He cursed himself for not throwing his gun aside the moment he felt his ankle grabbed and using his fists to persuade Buller to release his hold. That might have earned him six months for assault but nothing more, not the gallows, or penal servitude, and when these two alternatives presented themselves Smut's body, already bathed in sweat, began to shake from head to foot so that he had to hold himself rigid like a man clinging to a cliff. Presently, however, he began to regain self-control and the habit of logical thought that had extricated him from so many scrapes in the past. His first impulse was to put as many miles as possible between himself and Heronslea before daylight but he soon realised that he could not travel much beyond the county border before dawn and had neither food nor money to lie up, and move on the following night until he was clear of the district. He realised also that he could not go back to the Dell, for Kitchens would be sure to go there before reporting. He could take temporary refuge with Sam, in Shallowford Woods, but after calling at Low Coombe the police would probably make straight for the cottage and yet, a temporary hideout was essential if he was to get word to Meg and through her means to win clear. Smut knew every hideout between the Whin estuary and the county border and considered each, discarding one or another for different reasons and finally deciding on one that had the advantage of being within range of Meg but affording the most security. It was a cave formed by a fallen beech on the western shore of the mere and its main advantage lay in the fact that he could approach it wading along the shallows and through the running water of a rivulet, which meant that he would be safe from tracker dogs as well as men. It was an insignificant looking place and he felt sure he could remain here indefinitely, providing he could contact a member of the clan and get a supply of food floated downstream. He had found it some months ago whilst otter hunting and had occasionally slept there, warm and dry on a bed of bracken. To reach it before daylight he had to risk breaking into the open fields but he kept clear of paths and entered the western edge of Shallowford Woods with time in hand, passing within a few hundred yards of Sam's cottage on his way round the shore. He hesitated here, wondering whether it would be worth the risk to rouse Sam, beg some food and tell him where he was hiding but he decided against it, for rousing Sam meant rousing Joannie and Joannie was not, strictly speaking, a member of the clan. So he moved on, wading across the shallows and striking the stream a quarter-mile above its outfall. He followed it down to the great sprawling mass of the beech and then through the network of roots without leaving a single footmark in the silt. Once inside he felt secure and relaxed, his come-day-go-day philosophy

254

returning to still the tumult of fear in his heart but under this protective belt self-righteousness began to assert itself, so that soon, although sorry for Buller and sorrier still for himself, he began to see himself not as a man wanted for violent assault or perhaps murder but as a persecuted minority who had cleverly evaded an ambush prepared by those who denied him the right to live by his wits. A little comforted by these reflections he smoked a cautious pipe and curled himself up in the dry bracken to sleep. Ten thousand men could walk shoulder to shoulder from Heronslea to the county border and back again, but they would not find him here, snug, warm and within hailing distance of the first Potter to use the path to Sam's cottage. He would be hungry, perhaps, but that was no hardship; he and all his kin had been hungry often enough in the past.

V

They came down the road like a plantation posse, four mounted, with slung shotguns, two on foot leading dogs, as though flushing a dangerous beast into the open. Rudd, meeting them on his way up to help Honeyman plant a windbreak in the water meadows, stared at them in amazement. They looked so theatrical that he could not imagine for one instant what they sought, or why they looked so grim about it, so he called to Kitchens, the agent, "What's going on, Harry?" and the agent flung back, "You know what's going on, John!" Rudd, irritated by his tone, caught his horse by the bridle and said, "Now, why in hell should I ask you what's going on if I knew what's going on?" and then Kitchens looked slightly confused as the party surrounded Rudd. "Well, maybe you don't, John," he said, "maybe nobody has told you yet but we mean business, I can tell you that. Last night we almost caught Smut Potter, after he had killed a buck. He showed fight and Nick Buller is badly hurt. He had his face smashed in with a gun butt and they've taken him to hospital. We're looking for Smut now, so if you know where he is you'd best say, and save everyone a lot of trouble. My chaps aren't in the mood to fool around!"

John Rudd's jaw dropped. "Great God!" he said, "isn't this a matter for the police?"

"Yes, it is," Kitchens told him, "but you know how that lazy devil Price goes about his business. The Whinmouth police were told early this morning but by the time they get over here Smut will be miles

255

away. We thought we'd flush him out and we're on our way up to the Coombe right now. Come on, lads," and he kicked his horse.

"Wait a minute!" Rudd cried, running alongside, "you don't imagine Smut will be waiting for you in the Dell, do you?"

"We've got to start somewhere and we can begin with that gypsy mother of his. She'll know something and she'll either tell us or face a charge of compounding a felony."

Rudd said, "Listen here, Harry, Low Coombe is one of our farms and if you're going up there to raise hell I'm going with you!", and he ran back into the farm buildings and threw a saddle over Honeyman's pony, Squirrel. By the time he had the bridle on and was mounted, however, Gilroy's men were half-a-mile down the road and he had to gallop to catch them up. He had meant to send a message up to the house to inform Paul but there was no time and when he followed them into the Dell Kitchens was already hectoring Old Tamer and one of the girls. Presently Meg, the other girl and the Potters' simple child, Hazel, came out and they all stood in a tight circle, like partridges roosting in the open, with Gilroy men posted round them like sentinels. Rudd pushed his way through to them.

"Smut's in real trouble this time," he told Tamer, shortly, "so if you do know where he is you had best tell me. I'll undertake to hand him over to Police Sergeant Price. They won't dare maul him in my presence!"

Meg said, sullenly, "We dorn know where he be, Mr. Rudd, but if us did, do you think us'd tell'ee?"

"If you hide him you'll be in gaol yourself before you know it, the whole tribe of you!" Kitchens growled, but Meg only spat on the ground and said, "Aw, the devil take you all!", and walked calmly back to her farm followed by the two elder girls.

Rudd saw the veins swell in Kitchen's temples and heard the men muttering behind him. He said, ignoring Tamer, "You'd better follow me to Sam Potter's cottage in the woods. He might know something!" and Kitchens said, "All right, John, but don't try any tricks. These chaps are after blood and so would you be if you'd seen Buller's face last night!", and they rode out of the Dell with John Rudd leading, crossing the side of the hill and the big meadow and descending the long wooded slope to the mere.

"Listen here, Harry," John said, as they went along, "this is a ridiculous business and you know it! What'll happen if we run into Smut? They'll manhandle him and I shall be a witness, so you'll soon

be joining Smut in the dock! You'd far better leave it to the police and Mr. Craddock."

"Craddock?" said Kitchens, with a short laugh, "Craddock's a Radical isn't he? I wouldn't put it past him to be thinking Smut Potter had every right to that buck!"

"Then you don't know Craddock!" John said, shortly. "I'll answer for him. There's no harm in calling on Sam Potter but after that I'll see you all off our land and for your own sakes as much as Potter's! This isn't Czarist Russia and we aren't living in the Middle Ages!"

Kitchens seemed worried at this and dropped back to hold a brief consultation with his men, while Rudd dismounted and entered the cottage to find Sam and his wife at breakfast. He told them what had happened and asked if they could tell him where Smut might have gone.

"Lord bless you, no, I can't," Sam said, looking startled and unhappy, "he might be in any one o' a hundred plaaces, Mr. Rudd, and they'll have the works o' the world ter catch un, now he's won clear! Mashed in Nick Buller's face, you say? And with a gun? Well, an' what was they up to for such a thing to happen? Maybe Smut was on'y standin' up fer hisself, like anybody would?"

"He was poaching deer," Rudd said, "and they had every right to take him."

"Aye," Sam said, slowly, "but it depends on how they went about it, dorn it?"

"Perhaps, but if you find out where he is tell me or the Squire before you tell them, understand?"

"Aye," Sam said, readily, "I'll do that, Mr. Rudd. Smut? Well, he's wild all right, but he baint vi'lent, and you can tell 'em zo from me!"

Kitchens seemed in a somewhat more reasonable frame of mind when he rejoined them. Perhaps the hopelessness of flushing Smut Potter into the open had occurred to him, or perhaps he felt unequal to controlling the Gilroy keepers in their present mood. At all events he agreed to return to Shallowford and make a formal report to the Squire and sent the men home with a warning to be careful how they handled Smut if they were lucky enough to find him. They rode off still muttering and growling and Rudd had the impression that this business, coming on top of Paul's personal quarrel with Lord Gilroy, would be likely to widen the rift to a feud and that it was all very childish and unnecessary. He had always got along very well with Kitchens.

257

"I'll give you a piece of advice, Harry," he said, as they approached the house, "don't try and browbeat that young man. He isn't nearly as green as he looks and he's still very new to our kind of problems. It was Gilroy's manner that drove him into the Liberal camp." Kitchens said, sourly, "I'm sick of the whole business, John! Smut Potter is a waster, of course, but every landowner has poaching problems, and it needn't have come to this. But Gilroy means to make an issue of it and when Potter is laid by the heels he'll be for it! It won't make for peace and quiet hereabouts, I'm thinking!"

When they handed over their horses to Ikey in the yard they saw that Paul was already aware of what had happened, for the police sergeant's trap was there and Chivers, the groom, said he was in the office with the Squire now. "Has anything serious happened, sir?" he wanted to know but Rudd grunted, "Serious enough!" and left it at that.

They found Paul and the police sergeant in the library with Grace, whose presence disconcerted Kitchens, and when Rudd explained that they had been to the Dell and Sam Potter's but had drawn a blank the sergeant said, "Buller has a fractured jaw and two teeth through his tongue but there's no question of him not making a recovery. I saw his Lordship before I came over, and he seems to think it should be a charge of attempted murder. It's not for me to decide, of course, but my inspector will want to know the full facts, even if we do take our time catching him. He has a record, you know."

Grace said, unexpectedly, "Yes he has. Two spells of fourteen days for trespassing in pursuit of conies!" and everyone looked at her.

"That's so, ma'am," said Kitchens, "but this is surely a far more serious matter."

"I don't see that it has to be," Grace said, ignoring Paul's glance. "As far as I can see there were five or six of you on the spot and we have yet to hear Potter's version."

"No doubt we shall, when we catch him!" said the sergeant pacifically but Grace shrugged and said, "Will we? I doubt it! If I was facing half-a-dozen Gilroy witnesses ready to swear my life away, I think I should stay out of reach as long as possible!"

Kitchens said, "I was present when it happened, Mrs. Craddock. Buller jumped on him just as he was lifting the buck and when we came up our man was unconscious on the ground."

"Then you weren't actually present, were you?" she said, "and I also hear Buller's gun was snapped off at the stock."

258

Paul said, crisply, "Leave this to me, Grace! John and myself will sort it out."

"Oh, you'll sort it out I don't doubt," said Grace, thrusting both hands into the pockets of her overall, "but neither you, nor John Rudd, nor the sergeant here will be able to ensure that Potter gets a fair trial, with Lord Gilroy pressing the charges. Why don't we all admit it?"

The policeman looked miserably embarrassed and Paul said, "Listen, Grace . . ." but she turned and walked out of the room and Rudd noticed that her manner of exit had the effect of hardening Kitchens' mouth. Paul said, half-apologetically, "My wife and I crossed swords with Lord Gilroy on another matter, Sergeant, but that need have no bearing on this. If I get word of Potter I'll do my utmost to bring him in without further trouble, you can rely on that!"

"I'm sure I can, sir," Price said, in a tone that made Rudd doubt it.

There seemed nothing else to say so, after both the sergeant and Kitchens had refused a drink, they all left. Rudd said, slowly, "That wasn't very wise of her, Paul. Maybe you'd best tell me what you feel about it, personally."

"She has a point, John. It might be difficult to get an unprejudiced hearing in the circumstances, but we could get Smut a good lawyer to take care of that, couldn't we?"

"You'd want to do that?"

"Why yes, of course I would, and so would Grace. He's one of our people, poacher or not, isn't he?" And then, ruefully, "I don't seem to be able to put a foot right in Gilroy's direction, do I?"

"What has it to do with you? Smut Potter is jumped by Gilroy's keepers in the act of taking game. He hits out and lands himself in this kind of mess. Damn it, man, you can't be responsible for the behaviour of every Tom Fool in the Valley, can you?"

"No," said Paul, "I don't suppose I can, John, but I have an uneasy suspicion I'm partly responsible for the viciousness with which Gilroy is pressing charges. Battery and assault is one thing, attempted murder quite another. A man can go to prison for ten years or more for that, can't he?"

"Not in these circumstances," John said, "so stop worrying about it. If Smut keeps hidden for a while and Buller picks up, I daresay everybody's temper will soon cool."

"You really think that, John?" and he sounded, Rudd thought, pathetically eager to be reassured. "Yes, I do!" Rudd went on. "After

259

all, it sounds bad to begin with, a man surprised in the act of committing a felony using a gun to resist arrest but what does it amount to really? A scuffle in the bushes after dark. If Smut had fired a shot it might be different but he didn't and all I can say is it's a great pity he didn't use his fists. A good solicitor ought to be able to get him off with six months. Poaching is a national sport about here and has been since the time of William Rufus."

"Well, I hope you're right," said Paul, "I'd better find Grace and tell her. She's very worried about it."

"You do that," said John, but to himself, as Paul went on to the terrace, he murmured, "You'll get little comfort there, my lad! She's raised Kitchens' hackles just as I'd managed to lower them and every word she said will be stable gossip at Heronslea in an hour!" Grumpily he stumped out across the water meadows, reflecting that he could cheerfully wring Smut Potter's neck himself for landing them all in such a desperately embarrassing situation.

It was not until Paul was alone with Grace after supper that he was able to pursue the matter. He said, "It would have been better for everybody if you hadn't said that in front of Kitchens, Grace, and if he or Gilroy come here again I'd feel a lot happier if you kept out of it!"

She did not resent this rebuke, seeming to have expected it. "I'm not likely to seek either of them out," she said, and then, looking steadily at him, "but that doesn't mean I'm sorry for what I said! Somebody had to say it."

He flushed, saying sharply, "Why? Why couldn't you let things take their course? Or at least leave this kind of thing to me?"

"That's what you're upset about, isn't it?"

It was the closest they had yet come to an open quarrel and Paul wanted, above all, to be as honest as she always was. He said, flatly, "Yes, I suppose it is, Grace. No man likes his wife to do his talking for him and I think you made me look a fool."

"Well," she said, "I'm sincerely sorry about that but it had to be said all the same. You still don't know what you're up against down here and sometimes I don't think you ever will! If the Gilroys could lay hands on Potter now he would appear in court on a stretcher but that isn't what's so important. They'd pull every string within reach to get him gaoled for half a lifetime and partly to teach you your place! If I did speak out of turn this morning it was in your interests as well as Potter's."

"I think you're exaggerating," he argued but he felt uneasy all the

260

same. "Anyway, if I locate him I'll make sure the police get to him first."

"I don't doubt that you would," she replied, still speaking very calmly, "but that wouldn't stop him getting a savage sentence!"

"Damn it, Grace, don't let's overlook his liability," he said, feeling cornered. "He bashed a man's face in and the chap is still in hospital."

"What do you imagine they would have done to Smut if they had laid hands on him? When I was a little girl here a Whinmouth poacher was peppered with a shotgun and left to bleed to death in Gilroy coverts. The verdict at the inquest was 'Accidental Death' but everybody knew who was responsible."

"I've still got to do what I think is right," he said. "I happen to believe in civilised conduct."

"Yes, I know," she said in the same tone, "and that's why you should have stayed in a city," and she left him to his own gloomy company.

They did not refer to it again until they were going to bed. The implication that he was unqualified for his responsibilities rankled with him but he was too unsure of himself to make an issue of it.

"We don't have to quarrel over this, Grace," he said, when he blew out the lamp and was getting into bed beside her.

"No we don't, Paul," she said, "because, luckily for all of us, the issue has resolved itself already. Smut Potter is clear away by now and they'll have to take it out of the next poor devil they catch contravening the Ten Commandments and the landed gentry's Enclosure Acts! Good night, Paul," and she turned away. He lay awake a long time listening to the night sounds of Priory Wood and the muted hunting clamour of the river banks, dismayed by this unforeseeable rift that had opened between them but wondering, with the detached part of his mind, how much of his land and Gilroy's across the Teazel had once been common pasture, available to everyone in the Valley.

Grace was wrong in her estimate of Smut's margin of safety. At the moment, and every night until Midsummer's Eve, he was no more than two miles away, and far less as the heron flew from the river to the edge of Shallowford Mere. When the Valley worked he slept and when the Valley slept he was at one with the foxes in the glades further east and the otters fishing under the logs near his hideout.

He could have been gone by now, up the country, over to Ireland, to America even, for Meg had begun scraping money together the

261

moment Hazel brought news of his whereabouts, and by now she had somehow accumulated enough to spirit him out of reach of everybody, providing he travelled by night. But to her dismay he was still there, lying all day in his holt under the fallen beech and drifting about the woods all night, living on what he trapped and the food that Hazel floated down to him according to instructions given the day after he had gone into hiding. None of them had actually seen him, for even when he first made contact with Hazel he remained out of sight in the foliage that grew down to the water's edge and told her how to keep in touch with him by using the stream that flowed past the mouth of his lair. She had obeyed his instructions to the letter so that now he had most things a man could need, a blanket, a stewpot, tobacco and trap wires, with bread, salt and a stub of blacklead on which he could scrawl messages.

Yet it was not comfort that kept him here or fear of the Gilroy keepers and police, nor even the news that Nick Buller was now out of hospital, with a lopsided jaw and a slight impediment in his speech, caused by the passage of two teeth through his tongue. He was still there because he could not bring himself to turn his back on the fields and woods that had enclosed him all his life or separate himself from his kin in the Dell. He knew every bush and tree in the thirty-odd square miles about the Coombe but never once, not even for a day, had he travelled further afield, or wanted to and now that he was faced with the prospect of leaving it all and perhaps never coming back his resolution faltered and he hung on, waiting for some miraculous turn of fortune that would make everything the same as it had been before that unlucky incident in Heronslea plantation. He had never been called upon to make a decision as final as this, that would shatter the rhythm of his life and throw him among strangers, an act that would, in a sense, not only deprive him of his means of livelihood but compel him to come to terms with people who worked from dawn to dusk, lived in brick houses, raised families and paid rates and taxes. And so it was, in the end, that the decision had to be made for him by others, after news of his whereabouts leaked outside the clan.

Discovery of his hideout came through Ikey Palfrey, whose wits, always keen, had been whetted to a very sharp edge by his association with Hazel Potter, after she had found him lost in the snow. He had seen her several times a week since then and she had revealed to him most of her secrets of the wood but although he was an apt pupil, and learned all she had to teach him at remarkable speed for a boy reared

262

in a city, he remained in awe of her, regarding her as someone paying a brief visit from another planet. He marvelled at her strength and agility, at her ability to imitate bird calls and animal noises, from a moorhen skimming across the mere to draw an intruder from her nest, to the steady scrunch of a badger's claws enlarging a set. There was nothing, it seemed that she did not know about the woods and the countryside, about the weather and the whereabouts of plants and insect colonies. She showed him, at one time or another, each species in the wood at work and at play and about these things she could invent orations that seemed to him (familiar now with all Mary Willoughby's favourite ballads) an almost miraculous deluge of sounds, part monologue, and part chant, and delivered in a mixture of broad Devon and gypsy argot that contained words he had never heard uttered before. Her appearance bewitched him too, for it had little in common with that of any of the children who sat at lessons in Deepdene schoolroom. She was invariably dirty and unkempt but somehow strikingly beautiful, with eyes that seemed to change colour according to the strength of sunlight, with long, supple limbs, half-naked now that it was summer, and a great mop of tangled hair sometimes chestnut and other times bleached the colour of ripe barley. Her teeth intrigued him, so white that they shone like the underside of a cloud when she laughed at him, as she did when he stumbled or lagged behind her long, skipping strides. But the association was not quite so one-sided as it might have been, for slowly, as their friendship ripened, she began to show more interest in his background and ask him to tell her about "thicky gurt, smelly plaace", from which he had, by a miracle, escaped. And because this was all he had to offer at that time he was glad to tell her, painting heroic pictures of his struggles in the metropolis, where he had often seen carriages bowling along without horses, and had once cheered Queen Vicky in a carriage surrounded by her lifeguards.

All that spring, whenever he could escape from school or his work, he sought her out at their meeting place opposite the old pagoda which she continued to call "The Niggerman's Church", and together they ranged the woods and slopes as far as the railway line (but never over it) and the long curving shore of Coombe Bay. For him she was a kind of priestess and he told no one of his association with her; for her it was a taste of dominion over another soul, in whom she sensed a kind of worship that warmed her like June sunshine, so that it piqued her to sacrifice his company in the interests of clan loyalty, and to observe

263

him waiting for her by the mere when she was on her way to or from her brother's hideout.

One still evening, when she was descending the long wooded slope carrying a sack containing a supply of tobacco and fresh vegetables, she weakened and called to him, saying that she was on her way to "a beastie in a caave, yonder", and dumb with curiosity he had followed her, not knowing in the least what kind of pet she had hidden in the wood but guessing it was this that had kept her from him all these long sunny days. It was only when she emptied the sack and poked among the bushes beside the swift-flowing stream that flowed into the western margin of the mere, that he realised her beastie was a man and could be none other than her fugitive brother, Smut, and at once his heart sank, for he now saw himself faced with a choice of loyalties, to her, who trusted him, and to his other idol, Squire Craddock, who was rumoured to have quarrelled with his wife and with Lord Gilroy on Smut Potter's account. For the moment, however, he was too interested to worry over what he should do with the information but watched her fasten a carefully-wrapped parcel to a small, raised plank, attached to a long coil of parcel string and set this little raft adrift on the current, paying out the string until it was taut. The plank sailed out of sight through a clump of harts tongue ferns and when, after an interval she began to wind in, it reappeared without its parcel. He said, goggling, "*It's Smut, ain't it? He's holed up down there?*", and she smiled and laid a finger to her lips, saying, "Arr, that's zo! Us dorn mind *you* knowin' for youm different. Come on, us'll go an' zee they badgers, shall us?" But he was not interested in badgers now, or anything else she could show him, and as soon as he could he escaped pleading extra chores at the stable and here entered upon a terrible battle with his conscience for it seemed to him that he was obliged to betray one of them, the girl who had shared her terrible secret with him, or the man who had given him the keys to this new world.

He lay tossing and turning in his hayloft all that night and in the morning, red-eyed and yawning, he made his decision. It would have been different, he told himself, if Smut had been hiding in neutral territory but his presence here, inside the estate boundaries, involved the Squire in the poacher's crime, and the police had not yet ceased to search for him east of the river. Ikey was not unfamiliar with the police, regarding them with an inherited distrust. Police always meant trouble for someone and police here meant bad trouble for the Squire; it was therefore in his master's interests that he get rid of them and

264

once Smut's whereabouts were known Squire would manage that one way or the other.

He went through the kitchen and taking advantage of Mrs. Handcock's back slipped into the hall and thence to the library. Paul was at work in his office and Ikey braced himself to cross the room and tap on the closed glass door but as he did so he heard a step behind him and swung round to face Mrs. Craddock and for a moment he faltered, looking furtive and guilty. Then his expression cleared, for he knew Grace Craddock shared the Squire's interest in him and it occurred to him that the Squire would be certain in any case to pass information regarding Smut's whereabouts to his wife. He said, before she could ask him what he was doing, "I know where Smut Potter is, Ma'am! I was comin' to tell Squire."

He was startled by the expression of alarm that crossed her face and by the nervous manner in which she slammed the library door, leaning against it, with her hands behind her.

"You've seen him?"

"No, I ain't seen him, Ma'am, but I know where he is orlright. He's 'iding aht, the far side of the mere." He decided to skirt Hazel's involvement and the fact that his knowledge was shared by the Potter tribe as a whole. They could find that out for themselves if they wished. His responsibility ended with passing on the fact that the fugitive was still here, on the estate.

"You're quite sure of this, Ikey?"

"Yes, Ma'am."

"You could take us there?"

"I wouldn't need to, Ma'am, it's opposite the little island, in a kind of cave under a fallen tree."

She stood thinking for a moment and then, it seemed to him with an effort, said, "Very well, wait a minute will you?" and went into the office, closing the door.

He heard the rise and fall of their voices and presently both came out, Paul looking bewildered. "Go and fetch Mr. Rudd, Ikey," Grace said, "but don't mention this to a soul, you understand?"

"No, Ma'am."

He went out, shutting the door softly. Without exactly understanding why he realised that his news had shocked them and he had a sense of becoming involved in events that could bring trouble and discord and was already regretting having told them. He found Rudd at the lodge eating breakfast and the agent received the news phlegmatically.

"I always had a notion he hadn't run far," was all he said and told Ikey to go back to his work and keep his counsel, even from the groom.

When Rudd entered the library a few minutes later he was at once aware of the tension in the room but for all that he went straight to the point. "The best thing we can do is to urge Potter to surrender to us tonight," he said, "then we might be able to persuade him to give himself up to Sergeant Price first thing tomorrow."

"That's what I've been saying, John, but Grace is very much against it."

"What does she suggest?" he asked, as though Grace was not present, and she snapped, "That we send Ikey to tell him to clear out and take his chance as soon as it's dark! Are we to play thieftakers for the Gilroys?"

"To send Ikey would involve the boy," Rudd said, quietly. "If it came out, as it well might, he could be taken in charge himself and I'm not sure it wouldn't lay your husband open to being an accessory."

She did not seem impressed by this but smiled her tight little smile. "Why should it come out?"

"Don't forget, there's a warrant out for Potter, Mrs. Craddock."

"For attempted murder?"

"For malicious wounding and that carries a severe penalty."

She was silent for a moment and Rudd felt desperately sorry for Paul, who opened his mouth to say something but closed it again. Presently she looked up, first at Rudd, then at Paul, and when she spoke her voice sounded flat and defeated.

"No matter what I say you're both determined to give him up, aren't you? It's the law, isn't it? It's safe, for everyone but Smut Potter!"

"Damn it, you're twisting the facts, Grace," Paul burst out. "I wouldn't 'give him up' as you say, and neither would John. We want him to give himself up, in his own interests!"

"His own interests? Three to five years in a stinking gaol!"

"He won't get three to five years," Paul said, "he'll more likely get six months and less if the case is dealt with summarily, as one of poaching and common assault."

"Can you guarantee he'll be so charged?" she asked, and Rudd said no, they couldn't, but if he came in voluntarily his chances were far better than if he was arrested out of the district and committed for trial at the Assizes.

"I said in his own interests and that's precisely what I meant!" Paul argued. "Any other way, what are his prospects? He goes in fear of arrest every day of his life and can never show his face here again! I don't think he'd want that, not when he understands all it means and the fact that he's stayed so near home all this time proves as much, doesn't it?"

"I might prove he hasn't any money," she said.

"And you'd have me send him money?" Paul said.

"Yes," she said deliberately, "I would and if you wouldn't I would."

"Well I'm damned if I'll let you and that's final," he said, and Rudd thought, "Maybe he's beginning to learn how to handle her! Well, good luck to him, but this is no place for me," and he made as if to go but she called sharply, "Don't leave, John! That wouldn't be very brave of you!", and he stopped, his neck reddening, and said, "Surely this is something you have to settle between yourselves, Mrs. Craddock?"

"Fundamentally, yes," she said, "but not simply as regards Potter's fate. There will be other issues like this and Paul needs your advice as much as mine. You'd better say exactly what's in your mind."

"Very well," he said, turning back, "what's in my mind is clear. I think Paul is complicating the issue and you're sentimentalising it! Potter caused a man a serious injury while that man was doing a job he was paid to do. It doesn't matter to me who that man was, or who was paying him. The law is there to protect every one of us and Potter, who derides the law, got himself into this mess and must now take his chance with the magistrates! We'll do all we can to get him off lightly and I think Paul is right to want to provide him with a lawyer but beyond that I wouldn't go an inch, not for my own sake, or the sake of good relations hereabouts."

She said, looking at Paul now, "Well, there's your answer! You'd best do as John says, Paul."

He looked at her appealingly. "But you still don't agree with us, do you? You still think it a shabby trick on our part to deny him a sporting chance?"

"He's had one sporting chance and if it were left to me I'd give him another, that's all!", and left the room.

Rudd said, as her steps had ceased to sound in the hall, "It's a pity you told her, Paul."

"I didn't," he said, "but I'm glad she knows. Better this way than have her thinking we said nothing until it was all over."

"Does she know where he's hiding?"

267

"Yes, Ikey told her. Are you suggesting I should lock her up?"

"You might do worse," Rudd said, trying but failing to make it a joke. "I'll take a stroll there right away and tell Potter to come here after dark, shall I?"

"Yes, and tell him I'll leave the garden door of the office open." He paused and the agent saw that he was still not wholly convinced and that Grace's attitude had shaken him badly.

"You're doing right, Paul," he said, "and I believe you know that in your heart."

"Yes," he said, "I know it, John, but it's hard on both of us to have to face this situation so soon. It was working out, John, in spite of your misgivings and you did have them, didn't you?"

"Yes," Rudd said, "I did and it is a pity because I was beginning to lose them, Paul. I should like you to believe that," and because he felt his presence only increased the man's unhappiness he went out, turning east along the terrace in the direction of the woods.

VI

Smut's case came before Mr. Justice Scratton-Forbes, at the Devon Quarter Sessions in mid-July after he had appeared before the Petty Sessional Court at Whinmouth, where a procession of witnesses went into the box to testify against him. Kitchens had promised Rudd he would do his best to limit the charge to one of assault whilst trespassing in pursuit of game, but either Kitchens was a broken reed, or the authorities were otherwise inclined, for in the end Smut was charged with wounding so as to cause actual bodily harm and only the original charge of attempted murder was withdrawn. Yet Paul did not give up hope that something might be done to improve the situation when the trial opened. It was only when he saw the judge, a dry, withered nut of a man, that he realised that Grace had been right after all and Smut's chances of leniency were slim. There was so much to be said on one side and hardly anything on the other and the same procession of Gilroy witnesses, five in all, swore to Potter's murderous assault upon a man seeking to restrain him from carrying away the buck. The inevitable distortion of facts made Paul feel slightly sick, for it was soon clear the Gilroy team had been carefully rehearsed, and although the barrister he hired for the defence did his best to present another aspect of the case, arguing that Smut acted in panic when about to be assaulted by armed men, the story sounded lame in the dock, where

Smut cut a pathetic figure, far removed from the spry young rebel Valley folk recalled. A month of soul-searching in his cave, followed by another month's confinement awaiting trial, had cut him down to a bewildered young man with frightened eyes and the tan fading from his cheeks, clearly at a loss to know what was going on around him. Under his barrister's probing he told the truth in so far as he knew it and the testy little prosecutor did little to shake him, so that for Paul at least a true picture of the incident began to emerge at last—that of a man gripped by fear and fighting back with the first weapon that came to hand before taking refuge in flight. The picture was confirmed when Rudd leaned towards Paul and whispered, "He's right, Paul! They're after his blood! If things had turned out otherwise it would be Kitchens and his mob in that dock!"

The case excited a great deal of local interest and during the period the jury were out Paul saw Meg Potter and went across to her, against Rudd's advice.

"I should like to say how sorry I am about this business," he said, "and that I won't hold it against Smut if he comes back to the Valley," and she replied, to his astonishment, "It was in the cards and the only way he could have run contrary to 'em was to run faster! He couldn't bring himself to do that, Squire. There's less gypsy in him than I reckoned on. A real gypsy would ha' run and kept on running, but the Potters baint gypsies, except mebbe my youngest girl, Hazel. They others, they're their father's seed, although time was when I thought differently o' Smut!", and she walked away with her slow, stately gait, without waiting for the verdict. It was as though, by allowing himself to be netted, Smut had sacrificed her sympathy.

The verdict, as foreseen by everyone, was guilty and Mr. Justice Scratton-Forbes settled down to indulge himself in a little homily before pronouncing sentence. Dry and crisply righteous phrases issued from his lips like a shower of darts . . . "malice in your heart" . . . "despoiling property with the heedlessness of a savage" . . . "must be taught a severe and lasting lesson . . ."; the sentence was five years' penal servitude so that the limit of Grace's prophecy had been achieved.

Paul, and Rudd too, were appalled. Paul had resigned himself to eighteen calendar months and the agent would have been relieved to have seen the poacher go down for two years, but five seemed to them a savage and unwarranted penalty and others presumably shared their view for there was a murmur of indignation in the court that was instantly repressed by the ushers. Paul said, as they sought the castle yard, "Until now I never really believed there was one law for the rich and another for the poor, John!" and Rudd replied, "Well, perhaps we ought not to be shocked. Scratton-Forbes is a big landowner himself and we ought to have pressed for a trial outside the county. At the worst he would have got away with three years."

He glanced at Paul shrewdly, knowing that the young man's mind was not entirely monopolised by the memory of Smut Potter's blanched face, as he had stumbled from the dock with a policeman at each elbow but was trying to adjust itself to the prospect of facing his wife waiting at home. He said, slowly, "I still think you did right persuading him to come in, Paul, and this doesn't really change things, you know. The law is far from perfect, but it's the only law we've got and without it where would any one of us be? You've got to make your wife understand that, for if you don't then what you're trying to achieve back there won't amount to much. Would you care to see Smut before he's sent off? I expect it could be arranged."

"Yes," Paul told him, gruffly, "I owe the poor devil that," and Rudd went back into court, leaving Paul to look down on the city basking in the afternoon sunshine. John's reassurance regarding the rightness of his decision brought him no comfort. There was, he realised, a direct link here between his decision to coax Potter out of hiding and his own tenuous relationship with Grace, who seemed only to respect him as long as he was waving a rebel banner under the noses of authority. She would, he felt sure, back him every inch of the way if he resolved himself into a kind of Sorrel Valley Robin Hood, contemptuous of even such social reforms as those advocated by progressives like Grenfell. She was really, he reflected, a kind of anarchist who welcomed turmoil but he had no wish to live like that. He favoured steady, ordered, constitutional progress, where tolerance and education for the underprivileged promised hope of justice and stability but she had no faith at all in this dream. Her sympathies were with people like the Pankhursts, still raising hell up and down the country and it was on this cleavage that their relationship, so fragile from the beginning, seemed likely to founder, for what was that she had said when he told her Smut Potter had agreed to give himself up? "I was badly wrong about you, Paul. You aren't a rebel at all and could never be! That scene with Gilroy and Cribb was just a flash in the pan. Perhaps you knew I was listening and hoped to make an impression!" He thought it a bitter thing to have said and realised now that she

270

regretted it but they had been strangers to one another ever since, with Grace resisting all his attempts to put this stupid business into its correct perspective and stop her using it as a looking-glass held in front of his character.

John came back and said they could spend a few minutes with Potter. He looked around for Meg but she was not to be seen, so they followed the police sergeant down a long, gas-lit corridor under the court and were shown into a waiting-room where Smut sat with his hands on his knees, wearing the same dazed expression as he had worn throughout the trial. His pale, blue eyes kindled when he saw Rudd, whose approach to him had always been that of a jocular schoolmaster, dealing with a wilful but not unlikable scholar. "Well, it was a lot more'n I reckoned, Mr. Rudd," he said. "It was like I tried to explain, they'd ha' done fer me if I hadn't got one in first! *You* believe that, dornee, Mr. Rudd?"

"Yes, I believe it but it's too late to think about that now, Smut! Mr. Craddock is here to say you can come back to the Valley when it's all over."

The eagerness of the young man's expression as Rudd said this touched Paul more deeply than anything he had witnessed in court. He said quickly, "That's true, Smut, and I've told your mother the same. I'll find a place for you somewhere and perhaps give you a job like Sam's, where you could use your skill with the gun and all you know of the Valley."

A flicker of humour crossed Potter's face. "Me, a gamekeeper? That'll zet the boys laughing all right, Squire, but I'd like to come back some time. I'd like that, Mr. Craddock, Squire, and it's good o' you to tell me. It'll give me something to think on where I'm going."

"You'll get time off if you watch your step, Smut," Rudd said and Paul envied the ease of the agent's approach.

"Yessir, they told me that," Smut said, and then, hesitantly, "Do you reckon one o' you gentlemen could spare the time to look in an' give me news once in a while? I'd like to know what's goin' on back there and letters baint no gude. I never could read much more'n me own name!"

"I'll come and see you," said Paul, and felt better for saying it. "Good-bye and good luck for now, Smut, and don't worry about the family. I'll see they're left alone in the Coombe."

They shook hands and went out, walking into the hot sunshine of the castle yard and down the hill to the livery stable where they had left the trap. As it was being brought out, and Rudd was already on the seat, Paul felt his arm jogged and turning looked into the face of James Grenfell. "I heard about it," he said, "and it was a damned shame in the circumstances! It won't do Gilroy any good about here, if that's any comfort."

"It's no comfort," Paul told him, "but I tell you one thing, Grenfell. From now on, I'm your man! I'd like to help to break the crust around here and I think I can promise Rudd and my wife, too, will back me up."

"Well, we can certainly do with your help," Grenfell said, and then, with a smile, "But it won't always be this way, you know! It's going to change sooner than you think!", and he nodded and went on down the steep street, a small, insignificant figure among the lumbering farmers and draymen discussing the trial outside The Mitre.

It was in her heart to be sorry for him in the days that followed the eclipse of Smut Potter but she found it difficult to forgive pedantry on his part, and on John Rudd's, that had resulted in a man being shut behind bars for five years, and yet, she realised how humiliated he was in being proved so wrong so quickly.

The shadow of Smut Potter seemed to linger in the Valley and harvest prospects, which had looked so good, were cut back by heavy summer storms that left wheat and barley in disarray and put everyone's temper on edge. The semi-estrangement between them persisted because he seemed almost to nurse his defeat like a sulky boy but in the end it was his sulkiness that encouraged her to find a way of breaking the tension in the house. It was odd and a little pitiful, to see him fling himself into a frenzy of work alongside Honeyman's Home Farm team, to come home tired and skulk in the library, trying to lose himself in pamphlets James Grenfell had sent him, as though he sought there a means of reversing Smut Potter's sentence by social upheaval. Then a way out of the ridiculous impasse presented itself, for the certainty that she was now carrying his child persuaded her that two adults could not, after all, spend an entire summer brooding about a man in gaol.

Her own feelings about her pregnancy surprised her. She would have thought that it would compensate her for the life she had chosen to lead here in this wilderness, where every man, woman and child was a slave to the march of the seasons and men half-killed one another over the ownership of a buck, but this was not the case. A child, she reasoned, would be one more anchor, final proof of submission to men and their chattels and the only satisfaction she derived from the prospect was a conviction that, all things being equal, it was likely to inherit a world that was changing at speed and where ideas were likely to blow up under the noses of people like Gilroy.

About a fortnight after the trial she got up from the breakfast table and followed him into the office, where he looked up from a heavy leather book in which he was writing. She recognised the book with a start and for a moment was so astonished that she could only stare at it and her anxiety increased when he closed it hurriedly and seemed to wish it out of the way. She said, forgetting why she had come, "That was Lovell's Bible! But it wasn't a Bible! He kept pictures of girls in it!"

He looked, she thought, very embarrassed at this, so that the thought of him sitting here, seeking compensation for her withdrawal in contemplation of old Sir George's picture gallery made her want to laugh. He looked so shocked, however, that she bit her lip as he said, "You know about that? You saw them?"

"Yes, I saw them," she told him. "I imagine most people who were allowed in here were shown them. He wasn't ashamed of having them."

"He must have been a disgusting old reprobate!" he growled and then, rather pompously she thought, "Did you ever tell your father the kind of man he really was?"

"No," she said, "because he was quite harmless. He never molested his models, he was quite content to gloat over them, as you seemed to be doing!"

He flushed at this but then, perhaps because she was now smiling, he laughed and opening the book showed her that there was nothing between the covers but manuscript pages of cartridge paper, the first of them covered with his neat entries.

"It's my estate diary," he told her, "a kind of record of what happens. I destroyed the pictures the day I found them but I didn't do it as a puritanical gesture. It seemed to me the wrong people might have got hold of them and I recognised two of the Potter girls."

"Oh? Anyone else?"

"No, not even Arabella Codsall!"

He laughed, less at his little joke than with relief at being once again on joking terms with her and she joined in gratefully enough, reflecting that it would have shocked him into speechlessness to hear all she could tell of this little room, once so dim and stuffy, now so functional. It seemed a lifetime ago when she had stood over there where his map-

273

rack stood, posed against an improbable background of stage woods and ferns, with that old rascal Lovell, headless under his black cloth, his sibilant voice muffled and his elbows jutting as he crouched over his tripod. That was the first time, when he had persuaded her to be photographed as a faun and had loaned her a costume from a trunk of props he kept. At thirteen she had been flattered and, a year or so later, amused when he posed her as The Boy David, for a photographic competition, or so he told her, and then again as Juliet on a rustic balcony. She had not much minded his pattings and pawings, or even his sudden appearance round the end of the screen when she was half-dressed. It was some time after that, when she found out how her mother came to die, that she posed for him from entirely different motives, a thrust at the world of men, expecially her father, a sneer at all their shoddiness and cruelty. She wondered what had happened to those particular pictures. Obviously they had not gone in the book and neither, it would seem, had any of the more innocent ones, or Paul would surely have remembered them. Perhaps George had kept the nudes for his pocket book and sniggered over them among cronies at his club. She recalled then that she had hoped her father might see one of them and realise how whole-heartedly she despised him, and what venomous ways women had of proclaiming contempt.

He broke into her reverie. "You came here to tell me something, Grace. Or was it to hear me admit how right you were about Potter?"

She forced her mind back to him, saying, "No, it wasn't that at all. Something quite different and rather more cheerful! To the devil with Smut Potter and Gilroy. I came to tell you I'm going to have a child in the New Year!" and she waited for him to exclaim, or to do whatever expectant fathers did when they heard this kind of news. He did not whoop or coo or do any of the things she thought conventional. He simply took her hand, looked down at it for a moment and said, quietly, "I was wondering when you would tell me. I thought—'If she holds out much longer I daresay I shall hear it from one of the maids'!"

"But I really did believe you hadn't the least idea, Paul! I don't know why, but I did!"

"Well, I may be a bit slow on the uptake but I happen to look at you quite often," he said, smiling, and she was glad then that she had used this means of restoring the atmosphere of the early weeks of their marriage.

She said, suddenly, "It's a lovely day, Paul. Why don't we call a
274

truce and take a walk up through Priory and on to Shallowford Woods? It's surely time we did!"

He seemed pleased with the suggestion but said, "That's all of six miles. Do you think you should walk that far?" and she laughed, heartily this time. "Good heavens, Paul, the baby isn't due until January! It'll do us both good and when we get back we shall be too tired to argue the pros and cons of poor old Smut and his troubles."

He picked up the book, selecting a key from his ring. "Very well then," he said, "there's nothing here that can't wait!", but as he was putting the diary in his desk she said, "What exactly *do* you write in The Book From Which There's No Rubbing Out? Is it very private?"

He opened it at random and pointed to an entry, dated March 7th, "*Married Grace Lovell, my very dear wife*," and she thought, "Dear God! He doesn't belong to this century at all! Yet maybe a lot of us could do with his directness and simplicity!", and she kissed him impulsively and went upstairs to get a sun bonnet and a pair of walking shoes.

They passed one of the biblical shepherds (Grace could never tell one from the other) preparing a sheep dip in the hollow near the saw-mill and climbed the slope of Priory Wood to the spur where they could look down on Hermitage and away, on the very crest of the moor, the white smudge that was Will Codsall's little place, Periwinkle Farm. Up here, backs to the firs, stood great ranks of foxgloves, some of them as tall as grenadiers and each with its cluster of mottled bells at a regulation angle to the sturdy, green stems. The Sorrel below looked as lazy and heat-drowsed as everything else in the Valley and only one or two of Henry Pitts' big red Devons ambled along the shade of the hedge searching sanctuary from the flies. The sky was cloudless but what little breeze there was still carried the faintest tang of the sea and sounds travelled easily too, for over a distance of three miles they could hear the clank of the Four Winds' pump and the dry rattle of a trap on the moor road. He told her this was his favourite spot on the estate for up here there was a sense of permanence and in clear weather like today the Valley had the promise of eternal fruitful-ness so that one could discount days of sleet and snow when nothing thrived about here or could keep warm or find food. She did not say what lay deep in her mind, that it was fair enough but empty for all but those wanting refuge from new ideas and new thoughts.

They crossed the extremity of the Hermitage holding to the deep rutted lane that led down to the north-westerly tongue of Shallowford

275

Woods and then by a stile into the cool depths of the big beech grove and finally to the edge of the mere where the Lovells' ruinous boat-house still stood, with its half-rotted pier and punt. They used to fish here as children, she told him, Hubert, the elder boy, Ralph and herself and on summer days had sometimes bathed from the old punt, with the boys' tutor, then a much persecuted undergraduate, now a canon. He asked her what kind of man was Hubert, the heir and she said very stuffy and dominated by his livelier brother. "It seems curious that all those years of growing up here should have ended in a couple of skirmishes in Africa," she said, "and then you should come running from the same battlefields to step into their shoes. Why don't we punt over to the islet and take a look at the pagoda? That old tub can still float and I don't suppose you have ever been there, have you?"

He admitted that he had not, so they freed the punt and poled it through the reedy shallows, approaching the islet from the bank directly opposite Smut Potter's hideout. The island was no more than thirty yards broad and perhaps twice as long and the pagoda, a tiered structure roofed with shingles, stood in the centre, its lower half screened by firs and clumps of evergreen. She told him she had not been here for more than five years but did not add that the act of set-ting foot here gave her an extraordinary sensation of recapturing her adolescence, yet her mood must have communicated itself to him for when they sat side by side on a fern-grown terrace he suddenly turned her face to his and kissed her on the mouth and when she returned his kiss with an eagerness that surprised them both, she said, as his hand sought her breast, "You want me? Well, why not?" and although gratified by the invitation he was mildly shocked when she carelessly unhooked her skirt, slipped out of her single undergarment and motioned him nearer the pagoda where the ferns grew shoulder-high.

There had never been an occasion like this. From the outset she had been dutiful, complaisant even, but she had never once matched his excitement or, indeed, appeared to have more in mind than a wish to accommodate him. She matched it now but what surprised him as much was the deliberate and almost ritualistic manner in which she went about it, restraining him until she had removed the last of her clothes which she then used to make a bed among the ferns before embracing him with a kind of zestful gaiety. Only when the fire had gone from him, and she was lying still and contemplative in his arms, did he reflect upon the distance they had travelled since she had walked into his office that morning with her flag of truce and then the

276

humour of it struck him and he laughed, saying, "Well, I can't think of a better way of signing a peace treaty!" and set about helping her to dress. At the same time he glanced, a little apprehensively, at the mereside track opposite, remembering that it was often used at this time of day by Sam Potter and Aaron Stokes, the reed-cutter. Nothing stirred over there and when he met her eyes again he realised that she too was enjoying the comic element of the reconciliation and the pleasant absurdity of man and wife making love in such improbable circumstances.

"Was anyone over there?" she asked, and when he told her no, "It's just as well! Otherwise it would soon be all over the Valley that history was repeating itself and new Squire had got a love nest in the woods!"

"Squire could easily build one," he said, grinning, "it would certainly seem to recommend itself!" and steadied her as she stepped into her clothes. She laughed at this, the first wholly natural laugh he had ever won from her. It struck him as even more rewarding than her embraces.

Book Two

Book Two

CHAPTER ONE

I

ON the night of January 3rd, 1904, when the hands of the grandfather clock were ticking their unsteady way to midnight, Paul sat before the dying fire in the library listening for renewed sounds from the room above but hearing none or none that he could identify, as he had identified them in the late afternoon. Only the brusque voice of Daladier, the peppery little French obstetrician Celia had introduced as a reinforcement for the baffled O'Keefe, kept him from yet another restless prowl into the hall and up the stairs, to listen outside the room where Grace's labour had now entered its fourteenth hour. An hour or so ago the specialist had caught him there for the second time and sharply ordered him downstairs and Paul had gone, growling a protest to soothe his raw nerves and had taken refuge in whisky, half emptying the decanter with as little effect upon him as though it had contained barley water.

The silence upstairs, together with the steady, harsh movement of the clock and awareness of his own helplessness, made him sweat and fidget, and every moment that passed seemed to him to increase the chances of news arriving that the child had been born dead and that the mother was not expected to recover from her ordeal.

He tried, desperately, to think of other things, to occupy himself in office work, or a book, or more drinking, anything that would cocoon his imagination from what was happening up there, but every alternative thought seemed ridiculously trivial and the only escape route to his fears lay in contemplation of the specialist's blunt appraisal of the situation, delivered about four o'clock that afternoon, soon after his arrival.

He had made no bones about it being touch and go, for Grace, the child, or possibly both. It depended, he said, on a number of imponderables, some of which he tried to reduce to layman's language but Paul's mind was so blanketed by fright that he had not even tried to absorb the watered-down medical terms. All he did understand was that the labour was indefinitely prolonged and that it was something to do with the baby's position in the womb and the suspense of

281

waiting, after O'Keefe had come down about seven o'clock to help himself to a drink, was unbearable and had now continued, almost unbroken, for five hours. Listening intently Paul heard a few indistinct bumps, as of furniture being moved, then the rumble of conversation and once a long, low-pitched cry that made his blood freeze but after that hardly any sounds at all, except the maddening, metallic tick of the big clock, a far-off cough or two and the steady whoosh of the wind and the slash of rain against the windows.

The storm outside made it worse, for not only did its uproar drown sounds that he might have interpreted as progressive but brought with it a sense of onrushing doom that dispersed everything but fear. It also obliged him to endure his vigil alone, for Celia had promised to be here after tea and was not likely to appear now for the ford would be shoulder-deep after such a downpour. The staff had been sent to bed two hours ago, Mrs. Handcock having to be practically pushed from the room. He was very fond of the old soul but she had no stomach for this kind of crisis and the sight of her sitting there, puffing out her red cheeks and beginning sentences she could not finish, had maddened him. Rudd's presence would have been a comfort but Rudd was miles away, having driven off before luncheon to attend a farm sale in a village beyond Paxtonbury, with a promise to bring back an almost new threshing machine for a tenth its real price and although the subject had interested Paul a good deal the previous evening, he now thought of a threshing machine as of less significance than a feather in his wife's pillow.

Earlier in the evening he had, by degrees, succeeded in getting himself under control by looking round the room, itemising the changes Grace had wrought in it in less than a year's custodianship. He noted the glittering Sheffield plate candelabra, the warm red and gold wallpaper, the heavy velvet curtains with their tall pelmet, the rearrangement of the books, formerly shelved any-old-how, now neatly organised into sections. He was able to think of, and to appreciate, each of these things objectively and from them assess her value as a wife and a friend but this encouraged him to make a deeper survey of their marriage, remembering some of the other things she had brought to him and these too he began to itemise, like a man making an inventory of salvaged possessions after finding himself alone on a desert island. He could appreciate now, after ten months as her husband, his previous callowness and ignorance. She had opened so many doors that he could not even count them. She had

282

shown him, by example, how to strike a workable balance between familiarity and authority with staff, how to distinguish between good and indifferent wine, how to nurse a sick horse, how to make a garden grow, how to buy clothes and even how to conduct a public meeting, although she cared nothing at all for his wholehearted conversion to the Liberal creed and had refused to accompany him to a fund-raising ball in Paxtonbury. In one field alone, the management of the estate, she had left him alone. The submission of advice regarding Smut Potter's fate had been her single excursion in this sphere and she had learned her lesson, and so, perhaps, had he and there now existed between them an unspoken pact that such advice as he needed must be sought from John Rudd. There remained between them, however, the personal honesty that had characterised their association from the beginning. She accepted his possession of her as a woman if not as an individual, for her preoccupation with privacy did not extend to her body. She had once said something to him in this respect that he was never to forget, for it made a deep impression on him at the time. It was when he had expressed his appreciation of her generosity and she had replied, calmly, "When I begin to be dutiful you can turn me out. You know the convention in the West — men have orgasms, women have babies! Well, it was never intended to be that way between man and woman and if I had believed as much I would have gone out of my way to remain a virgin. The only way a marriage can hope to succeed is by yielding mutual satisfaction. Even then it can founder but without a physical basis it doesn't stand a chance. If it is there, or it develops quickly, then even incompatible people like us can get along."

Now, he reflected, as a direct result of her affection, she was in agony and perhaps at the point of death but he could do nothing whatever to help her and the awareness of helplessness made him grind his teeth and kick the dying fire with the toe of his riding boot that he had forgotten to draw off when he returned from High Coombe and Mrs. Handcock had told him, in her quaint, old-fashioned way, "Mrs. Craddock, poor dear, 'as been brought to baid!" adding that O'Keefe had been sent for, his mother-in-law notified and that he had best "zit down an eat a gude meal fer the three of 'em!"

That had been nearly twelve hours ago and since then there had been nothing but the arrival, wet through, of Celia's French specialist, indeterminate thumps on the floor, the rumble of voices and that one, low-pitched moan. He had just made up his mind to risk the doctor's wrath by a return upstairs when he heard a sharp rapping on the glass of the French doors opening on to the terrace. He thought at first that part of the trellis had come down in the gale but then the rapping was repeated and he pulled aside the curtains, fumbling with the stiff catch. When he got the window open the force of the storm almost wrenched it from his hand and a very bedraggled Ikey staggered into the room, holding a storm lantern tied to a short length of ash. Paul closed the doors and redrew the curtains and turning saw the boy crouching over the fire, rain streaming from his peaked cap and a look on his face that Paul remembered seeing on the faces of troopers awaiting the order to advance across open country in the face of Boer marksmen. He said, gruffly, "Well, what is it, Ikey? Why didn't you come in the proper way?" and Ikey replied, his voice shaking with excitement, "I couldn't make nobody hear, sir, I on'y just got back and tried Mr. Rudd's lodge first, but it was the same there, the wind's making such a racket!"

Paul remembered then that Ikey had taken the cob to the Coombe Bay forge for shoeing and had been told to summon Celia while he was in the village, but Celia would not come now as it was already after midnight. Where had he been all this time? The boy said, in the same shaking voice, "Something funny's bin happening over at Four Winds, sir! I follered Farmer Codsall along the beach, then back over the dunes. He saw me and tried to do for me with his shotgun!", and he held out the tails of his coat and Paul saw that they were shredded, as with buckshot. He said, urgently, "Go on, Ikey, tell me exactly what happened!"

"Well, I first see him when I was mounting the cob to get on 'ome, sir. He was drunk as usual, an' weaving about, so seein' he had his gun with him I thought—well, I thought I'd better keep him in view 'till I made sure he was clear o' the village."

"That was the sensible thing to do; then what?"

"Well, it was getting dimpsy by then so I follered him along the beach. He went right into the water once an' didn't seem to notice me, for I kep' back beyond the tideline but then he come out an' went over the dunes and I still follered, thinking he hadn't got a proper butcher's—proper *look* at me, but he must 'ave! When I crossed into the first field he let fly with both barrels and on'y just missed me!"

"Good God!" said Paul, forgetting everything else for the moment, "why didn't you get help in the village?"

284

"Well, I reckoned I ought to 'ave, sir, but I didn't want to let him out o' view, not knowing what he might get up to, once he'd reloaded. I skipped back out o' range pretty smart but he seemed to forget about me an' went off across the fields. It was pitch dark be then but I chanced he'd gone on home an' follered, tying the cob to the farm gate when I got to his yard. Then . . . well, then . . ." and suddenly the boy's face crumpled and he began to sob, so that Paul, acting instinctively, poured a measure of whisky into his glass and said, "Drink this, Ikey! Then tell me what happened at Four Winds."

The boy gulped down the spirit and it set him coughing but it steadied him for he was able to continue in a level tone. "I couldn't see nothing at first, it was so dark, but after a bit I heard a lot o' thumping and screaming from upstairs an' then, all of a sudden, the winder o' the end room crashed open an' all the glass blew out, an' out come the boy on to the sill an' made a jump for it, not into the yard but right across to the roof o' the barn opposite! I could see him jump in the light coming from 'is winder an' he landed orlright but was stuck twenty feet up 'till I found a ladder an' fetched him down. He was in 'is nightshirt an' awful scared. I tried to get 'im to show me the way to the foreman's cottage but 'e couldn't, he just started carrying on something awful, an' I couldn't make no sense of it, except that old Codsall had come for 'im an' 'is mum like a madman an' that's what made 'im jump for it!"

"Where is young Codsall now? What did you do with him?"

"I brought him back here" Ikey said, "and when I got to the loft I woke Gappy, an' we give 'im a good rub down an' put 'im in Gappy's bed, which was warmlike. I told Gappy to make cocoa for 'im, fer 'e was perished when he got here, 'im in his nightshirt an' all! But you don't want to worry about 'im, sir. Gappy'll take care of 'im. It's just that — well — I reckon someone ought to go over to Four Winds right away, sir!"

Paul began to think logically for the courage of the boy steadied him. He said quickly, "Throw some chips on that fire, Ikey, and warm yourself. Mrs. Craddock is having her baby and nothing is going right for her but I'll have to go to Four Winds at once. I daresay we shall need the police and help from elsewhere!" He thought of waking Horace Handcock but Handcock couldn't sit a horse and wouldn't even go close to one and apart from him there were only the doctors and the girls. He swallowed another tot and went into the hall, up the

285

stairs and along the corridor to the bedroom, rapping gently on the door.

O'Keefe's flushed face appeared instantly and from inside came a whiff of stale air and ether. He got a glimpse of the room, with the lamp beside the four-poster throwing its light on Grace's tumbled hair but saw nothing more, except the fire roaring up the chimney and an array of instruments on the table near the window. He said, urgently, "How are things going?" and reading impatience and irritation in the Irishman's face, added, "It's not nerves on my part, Doctor! Something bad has happened at Four Winds. Codsall seems to have gone off his head and he tried to kill my stable-boy! I shall have to go, no matter what happens here. Are you making progress?"

"Yes we are," O'Keefe said, and Paul felt a tremor of relief, "but it'll be about half an hour. It was a breech birth, if you know what that is but the worst is over and they'll both do well enough with luck! What's this about Codsall? You say he's gone crazy?"

"It seems so," Paul said, "can you be spared?"

"No," said O'Keefe, "not unless you want to run a very grave risk, Craddock!"

Paul made his decision. Whatever had happened at Four Winds wasn't worth the risk of mounting the old man behind Snowdrop and racing through a storm. If the boy Sydney had been left behind it would be different but Ikey, gallant kid, had whisked him out of harm's way and Arabella and the staff must look to themselves. He said briefly, "Well, I shall have to go, I can do nothing here and I may be useful over there. If my wife asks for me tell her I've had to see to storm damage at the Home Farm."

"Yes, of course," O'Keefe said soberly, "you get off right away and I'll come over as soon as it's light. Good luck, Craddock!"

"There's one other thing," Paul said hurriedly, "wake Mrs. Handcock, the housekeeper, and tell her to have a good fire and hot drinks ready. As soon as its light, or before if possible, send Handcock to rouse Honeyman and send the two shepherds to Four Winds right away!"

"I'll do that!" said the Irishman. "Mother of God, the trials we're called upon to face!" and at once withdrew, closing the door.

Paul returned to the library where Ikey now had a bright fire blazing. The boy's cheeks were flushed but he seemed to have himself well under control. He said, "Saddle up Snowdrop, Ikey, I'm going there right away."

286

"Who'll be going with you, sir?"

"Nobody for there's nobody to go! I can't waste time making a detour to Home Farm, I'll have to cut across the corner of the wood and head straight for the bridge. How was the water level when you came over?"

"About up to the planks, sir!" Ikey told him, and then, obstinately, "If you're on your own, sir, I'm coming with you! Young Codsall's orlright an' that drink you give me put noo life in me, sir!" and he grinned.

"Do you think you can stick another trip over there, Ikey?"

"With you along o' me I can," the boy said and Paul put his arm across the child's shoulder.

'I won't forget this, Ikey, you've done splendidly! None of the men could have managed any better. Have you got a dry coat and boots?"

"I c'n take Gappy's, sir. The cob's fresh enough and I'll 'ave Snowdrop ready in a trice!" and he shot out of the room giving Paul the impression that he welcomed the adventure now that he could share it with someone. Ten minutes later, with Paul riding ahead and carrying the lantern, they were picking their way along the edge of Priory Wood and round its western boundary, probing for the track that led down to the river road. The rain had slackened somewhat but the force of the gale tried to tear them from their saddles and twice Snowdrop stumbled, almost pitching his rider to the ground. Above the roar of the wind Paul heard a pine crash in the wood behind and again his thoughts returned to the steadfastness of the boy, splashing along in his wake. There was no chance to call to him. All he could do was to hold the swinging lantern high and trust Ikey to follow the light. If it went out they were finished. At last, after what seemed to Paul about an hour, they struck the park wall, groping their way along it to the gate that breached it opposite Codsall bridge. The boy was still in his wake and came alongside to take Snowdrop's bridle while he dismounted to wrestle with the stiff gate. It came open at last and they were out on the road, where it was less dark but they had now lost the protection of the wall and the wind made the horses restless. There were, he recalled, some white flood posts at the bridgehead and as soon as he saw them he dismounted again and led the grey forward, shouting at the top of his voice for the boy to follow. The roar of the current vied with the shriek of the wind and the river level was dangerously high, lapping the planks to a depth of nearly a foot.

Paul slopped across, however, remounted and followed the path that led down to the farm, trusting in the grey's sight more than his own and in this way they soon reached the first of the Four Winds' outbuildings, a great bulk of a barn, in total darkness. Here, in the angle of the building, they could talk again. Paul said, breathlessly, "Well, we made it, Ikey! We'll put the horses inside and go round the back, the front door is sure to be locked," and he groped along the face of the barn until he found the fastening, bracing his shoulder against the door to prevent it crashing back on the horses.

The barn faced east so the wind here lost some of its force and together they managed to lead Snowdrop and the cob inside. The first thing they saw, in the dim light of the lantern, was a shotgun resting against a small bale of hay and then, as Paul broke it to see if it was loaded, he heard the boy utter a cry and turning, holding the lantern high, he saw a pair of rubber boots swinging four feet clear of the ground.

"It's 'im!" Ikey cried, his teeth chattering, "it's Farmer Codsall!" and Paul dropped the gun and crossed the barn to where Martin Codsall swung in the strong draught from the door, suspended from a cross-beam on a length of baling cord.

They could see little more than his outline for the barn was large and its recesses beyond the range of the lantern's rays. Paul thought, fighting the shock, "Well, its best I suppose but its terrible that the boy had to see it!" and he took him by the arm and said, "Don't look, Ikey, let's go outside!"

He heard the boy retch and felt him shudder violently, so that his first thought, that of climbing the ladder and cutting Codsall down, was forgotten in concern for the child. He hustled him into the open, shutting the door in the teeth of the wind. "There's nothing to be feared from him," he told the boy, "but we'd best go in and see if Mrs. Codsall's safe and then rouse Eveleigh, the foreman and send someone for the police," and he took the boy's hand, groping his way across the yard to the Dutch barn and, moving between barn and farmhouse, to the gate that opened on the kitchen garden. He remembered the geography of the place with great clarity and found the back door at once. It was open and they went in, setting the lantern on the table and lighting a table lamp with a faggot from the fire still glowing red in the fierce chimney draught. Paul said, "Wait here, boy! I'll take a look upstairs!" and feeling Ikey would be better with something to occupy his mind, "Blow up the fire and boil a kettle. There's sure to be cocoa somewhere about and we could both do with a hot drink. Go on, get busy!" and he lit one of the candles on the mantelshelf and went through the kitchen to the wide staircase.

Winter gales both tormented and stimulated Martin Codsall. As soon as the winds freshened in the south-west, and the Channel spray whipped across the dunes, he would sniff the air like a retriever and presently, as the elms began to creak, he would wander off, telling no one where he was going and make his way to the shore to watch the breakers crash and cream along the flat sand. The power of them fascinated him and the inevitability of their spill gave him confidence in the sureness and certainty of nature, as though here was the one thing upon which he could rely utterly, the rush and swirl of green-grey water, foaming round his feet and tossing its flotsam high up on the beach. Sometimes, but not always, he would fortify himself against the thrill of the spectacle by drinking a few pints of rough cider and a dash of rum at The Raven but lately the landlord had been reluctant to serve him and when he entered the bar other customers drew together, so that he knew very well they were telling each other he was off his head. He would strain his ears to catch the drift of their conversation but they were not always talking about him, it seemed, for on the third day of the New Year, when he was sitting in the saw-dust bar settle, he heard them reopen the topic of Smut Potter's assault on Keeper Buller back in the summer. The Potter-Buller incident interested Martin almost as much as the curl of the breakers in the bay. He had kept all the newspaper accounts of the trial and paid particular attention to Buller's injuries for to him they were the highlight of the whole incident. They said that when they carried Buller back to Heronslea his face was a mask of blood and Martin wished very much that he had been there to see it, for it was not often that a man got a chance to witness such a sight. He fell to wondering sometimes how much blood a man had inside him. Some more than others, he would think. Arabella, with her high colour and over-weight, would have a great deal, but young Sydney, pale and slight, not very much, hardly worth the shedding. It was on this particular day, when he heard them talking of Buller, that his obsession with blood and with the breakers fused so that he had a sudden revelation. After leaving the pub he wandered far along the shore, noticing that the waves had changed colour. They were no longer grey-green but bright crimson, the colour of blood and he took even more pleasure in them than usual, standing with water washing about his knees and the spray beating in his face, watching and watching the curl and crash of the great crimson waves, oblivious of discomfort and the growing force of the gale.

It was only when he glanced over his shoulder to follow the rush of a particularly big wave that he saw the boy on the brown cob, standing back against the dunes and watching him intently. Codsall was aware, however, that it was not really a boy on a cob but the Devil, masquerading as a boy, and mounted on a horse that could move in any direction without its feet touching the ground. Fortunately he had brought along shotgun and cartridges, hoping to get a shot at a partridge or two if there were any in the stubble fields and standing there in the water Martin felt more than equal to a mounted devil disguised as a boy. He pretended to take no notice but turned his back on the water and climbed the dunes as far as his first field, where there was a stile set in a gap between clumps of elderberry. Here he loaded his gun and waited and sure enough the little devil came on at a walk, presenting a fine target against the skyline of the dunes. When he was twenty yards off Martin fired both barrels and saw the devil's skirts fly out, saw him reel in the saddle and slump forward, the cob wheeling and tearing back the way he had come. That disposed of the boy and he could now carry on with his main task which was to discover just how much blood Arabella had, and whether it was enough to make a really big wave like one of those he had just seen break on the sand.

He did not go straight home but wandered slowly along the river bank, making sure that he really had scared the devil out of range, for he was not such a fool as to suppose that a devil could be laid low with buckshot. One needed a silver bullet for work of that kind, and sooner or later the boy would get over his fright and follow on, perhaps in some other guise, as a labourer, or a buzzard, or even a harmless little creature like a vole. He saw nothing, however, and when it grew dark he was in the vicinity of the farm but even then he did not go in but continued to skulk in the spinney near the river, sheltering as best he could from the slashing rain and terrible wind that came out of the west. One thing worried him a little. His coat was so wet that his spare cartridges were damp and probably useless, so he threw them away, promising himself to get more as soon as the kitchen lights went out and he could enter the house without being seen. He saw his hired men trudge off across the fields and later, his foreman

Eveleigh go down the lane to his cottage but even then he waited and it must have been close on nine before he crossed the yard and tried the front door. It was locked but he knew he could get in through the buttery window which had a broken catch and on his way round he looked into the big barn and lit one of the storm lanterns. It was here that he had another inspiration for immediately under the lantern, wedged in a bale of hay, was a hay knife more than two feet in length and freshly whetted, as he could tell after running his thumb along the edge. He gave up all thought of finding fresh cartridges and laying the gun aside picked up the knife. He was wet to the skin but hot and sweating rather than cold. He felt stronger and happier than he had felt for months and he stayed snug in the barn until he was sure that Arabella, Sydney and the two maids were in bed and asleep. The force of the gale shook the wooden building to its foundations but he enjoyed the uproar for to be alone in it made him feel superior to everyone. At last he got up and went out into the storm, not forgetting to latch the barn door. He tried the back door and was surprised to find it open and the kitchen fire still bright. He stood there listening and heard Arabella, or someone else, moving about upstairs and that made him glance at the clock, noting that it was still only half-past nine. Suddenly he could wait no longer. He opened the kitchen door very quietly and went upstairs.

Arabella was half-undressed when he entered the bedroom. She was standing beside the bed, great folds of flesh straining at her corsets and her hair screwed into a cluster of ringlets, as though she had been a girl of fifteen instead of a fat woman of fifty. He had never realised just how fat she was, with breasts like huge pink cushions and thighs that were like saplings stripped of bark. She turned when she heard him enter and when she saw him standing there, wet through, and with the hay knife in his right hand, she began to gobble like a turkey, perhaps, he thought, to scare him off but he made no move, for a man who had disposed of the devil was unlikely to be intimidated by Arabella Codsall. So they faced one another for what seemed to him a long time, he regarding her with mild pleasure and Arabella with her pale blue eyes almost popping from her head and her turkeycock cheeks getting more turkey-like every second. He had never seen her look at him like this before, without contempt or exasperation but without fear too, for her expression was one of the blankest astonishment, as though he was not a man at all but a freak of nature like a midnight sun. She seemed to be trying to say something, for her lips moved but no sound issued from her and it seemed to him that both of them had been turned to pillars of salt like Lot's wife fleeing from the cities of the damned. Then, with a single, well-aimed kick, she upended the little table on which the candle stood and plunged them into total darkness and at the same time she began to scream so that her voice rose above the continuous roar of the storm. She began to run, too, although in which direction he could not have said except that it could not have been towards the door for he had his back to it. Then a little of his calm left him and he advanced into the room, groping with his free hand and after a few moments of blind man's buff they collided and he took hold of her by the hair, striking outward and downward, twice and then, standing back a pace, a dozen times but without being sure that he was hitting anything except the bedpost, or the pile of her discarded clothes on the armchair. Then she seemed to melt away and her screaming ceased and he despaired of finding the candle among the wreckage of the room but it did not matter for he realised at once that he had failed in his essential purpose. He had not seen a wave of blood after all and disappointment choked him so that he flung down the knife, turned and began to grope for the door.

It opened before he got there and he saw Sydney was standing just outside in his long, white nightshirt, with a candlestick raised above his head. Martin rushed upon the boy with relief meaning him no harm at all but Sydney, uttering a single shriek, flung down his candle and fled. A moment later there was a loud crash of glass and Martin forgot about Sydney in his efforts to find the second candle and light it from matches he kept in his waistcoat pocket. He had some difficulty in lighting it for the matches were damp and his hands trembled violently. He managed it at last, however, and turned across the doorway to survey his work. There was blood enough in all conscience but it was not curling over in a wave, as he had imagined it would, whereas the untidy bundle that had been Arabella, although it looked rather like a large piece of flotsam, was not floating as surely it should have been. His sense of failure began to drag at him, like a cart being drawn up a steep hill and presently he understood the truth. Now, having made such a muddle of things, the devil would get him after all so he had best use what time there was to make away with himself in his own fashion. He clumped down to the kitchen, across the small yard to the barn and then up the ladder to the loft where he knew that baling cord was kept in a barrel. He found a length and in less than five minutes was out of reach of the devil in any guise. He hanged himself expertly, without even bothering to relight the storm lantern and see where to anchor the rope.

II

Paul came slowly downstairs and found Ikey had already made the cocoa for the kettle had been on the boil and the cocoa was on the long table, together with sugar and a can of milk. For a few seconds, pausing outside the bedroom door, Paul had been sure that he was going to faint, but the sight of the boy pottering about in the kitchen was like looking through a window on a sane, workaday world, where folk went about everyday tasks and children of thirteen were sometimes capable of tremendous exertions and matchless courage. He said, hoarsely, "We'll go for the foreman, Ikey. Don't bother with the drinks!" and he grabbed the boy and almost pushed him out of the house and into the blessed open air, stumbling over the slippery cobbles and down the muddy lane that led to the foreman's cottage a hundred yards away. All the time he held Ikey's hand tightly but for his own comfort more than Ikey's and together they staggered through the slush until the lantern, which he had picked up instinctively in his flight, revealed the outline of the squat, thatched dwelling under the bank. Paul hammered on the door, shouting into the wind and when no one answered he fell to kicking the door with all his strength until a voice above called, "What's to do? Who is it?" and Paul shouted, "It's Craddock, the Squire! Open up! There's been bad trouble at the farm!" and a moment later the door was unlocked to reveal Eveleigh, the foreman, his flannel nightgown stuffed into his corduroys and a bemused expression on his narrow, intelligent face. They went into the kitchen and Mrs. Eveleigh called down from the top of the stairs, "What is it, Norman?" and Eveleigh told her to come down and blow up the fire and make sure that the children stayed in bed.

Inside the little kitchen Paul's senses again began to swim and it required a stiff tot of Eveleigh's rum to steady him. Mrs. Eveleigh, a pleasant-voiced, ginger-haired woman, bustled about getting hot drinks and it was not until she put a mug in his hand that Paul said, "Martin Codsall is dead, Eveleigh! He's just made away with himself!" but he made no mention of the bundle upstairs, waiting until Ikey's eyes were lowered over his cocoa before jerking his head to

293

indicate that they should get the boy out of the room. Evcleigh seemed an exceptionally quick-witted man. He said, briefly, "Pop the boy in with young Gil, Marian. He's chilled through and we can send him back in the morning, when he's got a good breakfast inside him!" and Ikey went off without another word. Eveleigh said, sombrely, "Did the lad see it?"

"He saw Martin hanging from a beam in the barn," Paul told him, "but thank God he saw nothing worse!"

"Arabella? And their boy, Sydney?"

"Only Arabella. Ikey was there earlier and got Sydney away. Arabella is lying in the bedroom."

Eveleigh looked thoughtful and Paul, who had always respected the man, could not help admiring his remarkable self-control and complete lack of blather. The foreman said, finally, "Well, I can't say I'm surprised but I never thought it would run to murder. How did he go about it?"

"With a hay knife," Paul said, "it's still up there and nothing will induce me to go back, Eveleigh. In any case, everything had better be left as it is until the police get here. It's a miracle the boy escaped," and he told briefly of Codsall's attempt on Ikey's life with the gun and how Sydney had jumped from the window.

"It might easily have been my missus and my kids," Eveleigh said, soberly. "Doctor O'Keefe should have put the old fool away months ago!" Then, glancing at Paul under his dark brows, "Do you think you could help me take The Gaffer down, sir?"

"Yes," Paul said, "I think I could manage that after another glass of rum!" and Eveleigh poured him a measure and went into the scullery to get his rubber boots and mackintosh. He called upstairs, "I'm going up there now, Marian! Better dress and start breakfast," and Paul marvelled at his matter-of-fact tone and phlegm. "How many children have you?" he asked and Eveleigh told him six, four girls and two boys, the eldest of them eleven. "Gaffer was a hard man to work for," he said, as they trudged up the lane, "but his son Will would have made things all right. She was the main trouble, of course; she never could get to grips with a farm. A man oughtn't to go looking for a wife outside the place where he was born and raised!"

It was only then that Paul remembered Grace and the child she was struggling to bring into the world. It seemed to him incredible that he could have completely forgotten her during the last two hours but it was so. All his nervous energy had been expended getting here

294

through the storm and after that the sight of Codsall, and the shambles in the bedroom, had wiped everything from his mind. He said, "Mrs. Craddock is having her first child tonight, Eveleigh. There were serious complications and I had to leave before it was born," and he thought the man glanced at him sympathetically although he could not be sure. The storm was subsiding rapidly now and the comparative silence, after the uproar, was uncanny, as though everything in the Valley had been smashed down and beaten flat like Arabella. Eveleigh flung the barn door wide and there was just light enough to see the two horses, munching hay beyond the partition and, over to the left alongside the loft ladder, the thick-set figure of Martin Codsall gyrating in the draught.

"God's mercy!" Eveleigh said, softly, "how did he manage it? Did he leave a lantern burning?"

"No," Paul told him, "it was pitch dark when we came in. He must have gone about the whole business in the dark!" and he thought, "That's curious! Eveleigh's first thought was the danger of fire! He's a good farmer and deserves something better than this," and he found himself drawing strength from the man's stillness as he respectfully directed Paul to climb the ladder and cut the cord, while he enfolded Martin's body in his strong, wiry arms and gently lowered it to the floor. Codsall did not look much like a man who had hanged himself. His eyes were closed and his mouth tight shut. He looked almost as calm as someone who had died in their sleep. "He must have done it soon after the boy left here," Eveleigh said, "for he's stone cold, poor old devil!" Paul noticed that the soles of Codsall's boots were caked with blood and turned away, so that Eveleigh said gently, "You go on home, sir, and see to your wife. I can manage here, me an' the missus will take care of your stable-lad. He must be a spunky kid to ha' done all he did."

Paul, ashamed of his weakness, said, "What about informing the police?" and Eveleigh told him that Ben and Gerry would be here in an hour and he would send one of them to Whinmouth and meantime keep everyone out of the house. "You might send one of Honeyman's men over, sir," he suggested, "we shall need help one way and another," and Paul recalled then that Honeyman would have been informed by now and would probably arrive before the labourers. "Now you'd best get off, sir!" Eveleigh said, impatiently, as though he would prefer to handle things alone. "I'm mortal sorry about it, Mr. Craddock, and somehow I feel it's partly my fault not keeping an eye on him. Still, a man has so much to do, things being what they have been about here lately."

Paul thanked him and led Snowdrop out of the barn, leaving the cob for Ikey. It was almost light now and the temperature was surprisingly mild for January. He rode out of the farm gate half resolving never to enter it again but as he forded the river, and rode along the road under the wood he thought more anxiously of Grace than of Four Winds. Half-way up the drive he overtook the forlorn figure of Horace Handcock, the gardener, swathed in an immense overcoat and splashed to the waist with the red mud of the paddock. Paul reined in at once and asked him if Honeyman had been alerted.

Handcock's red face emerged reluctantly from the folds of his coat but he brightened when he recognised the horseman.

"Aye, I've done that! He's on his way now, along with Matt but there's good news for 'ee, zir! It's a boy, and Doctor O'Keefe told Mrs. Handcock they're both doing well! May I be the first to wish 'ee good luck, zir?"

"Yes, you may indeed," Paul said, thankfully, "and I'm sorry we had to get you out in the middle of the night! Mrs. Craddock is bearing up?"

"The missus has been in to her and 'er's taken broth," Handcock told him, gleefully. "It all happened minutes bevore I zet out. Seven pound odd he be, zo they zay an' bawling like a young calf when I left, zir!"

A great wave of gratitude engulfed Paul and he began to feel lightheaded, as though all the whisky he had swallowed earlier in the evening and the rum poured him by Eveleigh, were mounting to his brain. He thought, "There's good and bad here and its all mixed up! Martin Codsall runs amok with a hay knife, children leap from windows in their nightshirts, a man hangs himself in a barn but then, as counterweights, I've come up against Ikey's guts, Eveleigh's steadiness and this little character's goodwill!" And suddenly he felt braced and optimistic, riding into the yard where everyone was astir, and there was an air of bustle about the house. Mrs. Handcock beamed at him from the top of the kitchen steps and Chivers, the groom, took Snowdrop's bridle with an air of deference, as though the arrival of an heir improved the status of the father. He found O'Keefe supping tea in the kitchen and was at once reminded of Four Winds but he did not have the heart to wipe the smile from the housekeeper's face by telling what had occurred. Instead he said, "May I go up and see her now?" and the doctor said he could and that the specialist had agreed to accompany him to Four Winds as soon as he had washed and packed his bag. "Well, there's little enough you can do over there, except certify!" Paul told him as soon as Mrs. Handcock was out of earshot and the doctor shrugged and lit his pipe. As a practitioner of nearly fifty years' experience he was proof against the shock of violent death.

Paul went up the stairs hesitantly, a little shy at the prospect of seeing her. Thirza, the parlourmaid, wearing the mantle of nurse as though she had been created a baroness, slipped out of the room as he entered and said smugly, "'E's a praaper li'l tacker, Mr. Craddock, but 'er's had a turrible bad time, I can tell 'ee!"

He saw that Grace, although propped up, was asleep and stole across the big room to the window where the cot stood in the angle of the wall made by the bay. The baby's eyes were open and he looked back at Paul with a kind of shrewd interest. Newborn babies, Paul recalled, were usually brick-red, as bald as coots, and generally regarded as ugly by all but their mothers, but this child was neither red nor bald. His skin was as pale as his mother's and his hair as dark as Grace's but the tufts looked as though they had been stuck on his pate by a practical joker. Paul lowered his finger gently, letting it slide along the baby's cheek and the child opened his mouth like a day-old thrush.

He was still standing there, back to the bed, when he heard a movement from the bed and turning saw that she was not asleep after all but looking directly at him. He tiptoed over, aware of the filth on his boots and the clamminess of his clothes, noting that she looked exhausted but very composed. Her skin glowed and her two large dimples played hide and seek in the lamplight. He said, quickly, "I can't kiss you, Grace. I'm filthy. I never stopped to wash but came straight up thinking you were asleep!" He tried to say something conventional, to ask how she felt or whether she was pleased the child was a boy, but the sharp memory of Arabella's bedroom confused him and he dropped his gaze, waiting for her to speak. She said, calmly, "You had to go out somewhere?" and he told her something had happened during the storm at Four Winds but that it was attended to now.

"It must have been important," she said but without irony and he answered that it had been important and that was why he had no choice but to go. "The baby is a lovely child," he said, trying to steer

297

her away from Four Winds, "but it was terrible to have to go through all that, Grace! I was downstairs most of yesterday and felt absolutely useless."

She smiled faintly, "Well, I imagine you were, Paul, but that's a husband's prerogative. You're pleased it's a boy, I suppose?"

"I didn't care what it was," he said truthfully. "All day yesterday I don't think I gave the baby a thought as anything except a source of your pain and my fear. I'm glad now, though, and happier still that it's behind you. You'd best sleep, dear. I'll get a bath and change and if you're awake I'll come up after luncheon." He wished that he could bend over her and kiss her but he checked the impulse, moving towards the door. He had his hand on the knob when she called, "Paul!" and he turned, looking at her anxiously.

"What is it, dear?"

"What did happen at Four Winds?"

"I'll tell you about it later."

"But I want to know, Paul. I want to know why you're in such a mess, and why you're so upset. I don't like people treating me as if I was a sick child and you should know that by now!"

He knew it well enough and cursed himself for not stopping to wash and change and compose himself a little before blundering in here. He said, "Martin Codsall went off his head and took a shot at Ikey on the Dunes."

"Ikey was hurt?"

"No, but Martin — well . . . he killed himself and we've sent for the police."

She nodded, slowly. "Thank you for telling me, Paul. I knew it must be something grim. So you've had a bad time, as well?"

"It wasn't very pleasant," he mumbled, "but go to sleep and don't worry about it!"

"Tell Thirza I'm hungry," she said suddenly, "and do impress upon everybody not to creep about the house as if I was in a decline! I'm not, you know, Daladier said I managed it pretty well, considering it was a breech birth."

"I'm sure you did," he said and suddenly vertigo assailed him again so that he gripped the door-knob with all his force and glanced over his shoulder to see if she had noticed. Luckily she was looking towards the window and it relieved him to see that her expression, seen in profile, was serene and even a little smug. He thought, savagely, "I suppose Codsall never meant much to her and why

298

should he? But this Arabella business will have to be kept from her for a day or so and I'll punch anyone's head who blabs about it!" The moment of faintness passed and he was able to go out, closing the door softly. He went along to the guest room they had prepared for him and peeled off his wet clothes, throwing them in a heap. He gave himself a vigorous towelling but he was too spent to bother with a bath and climbed into bed not expecting to sleep but soon he was snoring and they let him lie until late afternoon.

His first thought, on waking, was not of Grace or Arabella but of Will Codsall, whom he supposed must have been told by now. He wondered how he would take it and whether he would blame himself for his desertion of a year ago, thinking, "If he does, then that wife of his will soon drag it out of him," and it occurred to him that Will might want to return to Four Winds and this would mean finding another tenant for Periwinkle. At once he remembered Eveleigh and his six children, surely the safest bet in the Valley. He lay there wondering at himself for worrying about estate routine when, a few yards away, was his wife and son, and thought, "If the child was born soon after I left last night he entered the world just as Martin left," and the notion of a simultaneous birth and death remained with him as he took his bath and went along to the big bedroom, opening the door an inch to see if she was asleep. She was awake and was combing out her hair and it seemed to him a very striking thing that she could be so engaged when, only twenty-four hours ago, she had been battling for her life and the child's, or so it had seemed to him waiting below. He took the brush from her, imitating the long, sweeping strokes that he had first observed her make in their bedroom in Paris.

"I've been thinking about names," she said. "Have you any particular preference?"

"None at all," he said, "as a matter of fact I expected a girl."

"I didn't," she told him, "not for a moment. I always knew it was a boy all right. An athlete too I wouldn't wonder, judging by the way he kicked out! It was probably his restlessness that caused the trouble."

She sounded calm and relaxed and he remembered reading somewhere that this was a common reaction after an aggravating labour. "I quite like your name," she went on, "but it's a nuisance to have two Pauls about one house. What was your father called?"

"Saul," he told her, grinning, "so that's out of the question!"

"There are too many biblical names around here already," she said.

299

"Joshuas, Samuels, Jacobs and Micahs, and most of the popular ones get shortened, all the Bills and Bobs and Walts and Dicks! No, I want him to have a two-syllable name that nobody lops. Who is your favourite historical character?"

"Oliver Cromwell," he said, "and I don't see him as 'Oliver', do you? There's another man who always intrigued me, however—Simon de Montfort!"

"That's it!" she exclaimed, " 'Simon'! It's clean and uncompromising like a . . . like a blade!"

"All right then, 'Simon' it is and I don't know whether we can take that noise for his approval."

The baby had begun to whimper but before Paul could pick him up Thirza had rushed in, all rustling skirts and galvanised efficiency and looking sternly at Paul said, "It's time for his feed, sir!" but when Grace held out her arms and Paul seemed in no hurry to go the girl looked so embarrassed that Grace laughed and said, "Oh, don't be so stuffy, Thirza! How do you think I got the baby anyway?" and without more ado slipped her nightdress from her shoulder and gave the child her breast. Thirza left the room in three strides, Grace's laughter following her down the corridor as Paul said, "Every convention in the book is a kind of hurdle you have to jump, isn't it?" and she replied, "Most of them, so you can tell me the truth about Codsall!"

He was unprepared for this and growled, "What idiot has been telling you things while I was asleep?"

"No one mentioned it," she said, "but I should be witless if I didn't know something was being kept from me! What really happened over there?"

He sighed, reflecting that it was never any use trying to cushion her against facts for every time he attempted it she made a fool of him.

"It was a ghastly business; Codsall killed his wife with a hay knife but if you want all the gory details you can read them in the newspaper after the inquest." He added, however, the story of Ikey's part in the tragedy and said how well the boy had acquitted himself, and this seemed to interest her as much as the murder. "We shall have to do something for that boy," she said, "and we ought to do it at once!" and when Paul pointed out that Ikey was perfectly happy as a stable-lad she said, impatiently, "I daresay, but he won't be later on! The time to start on him is now, while he's young enough to do as he's told."

"What can we do for him we aren't already doing?"

"We can send him to a proper school where he'll get a real education," she said, emphatically, and it was useless to suggest that Ikey might be unhappy at a school where his outlook and Cockney accent would put him at a disadvantage for her agile mind was already grooming the boy for a career and at last Paul had to admit that her plan had possibilities, for she reasoned that if Ikey could mimic anyone on the estate he could also learn to speak and behave conventionally, particularly if Paul made demands on him. He grumbled, "Why saddle me with the responsibility? It was your idea, not mine!"

"He worships the ground you walk on," she said, "he always has and always will. Why do you suppose he tracked Codsall like that and then insisted on going back to the farm? Everyone has to have a hero and you happen to be Ikey's, whether you like it or not, so talk it over with him and if he backs down because going away to school would mean parting from you then I'll have a talk with him!"

"You're always in such a damned hurry," he said, laughing, but she replied, seriously, "Yes, I am, Paul, and I always will be while things like that business at Four Winds and others like the Potter case occur so needlessly!"

He could see very little connection between the poaching incident, Codsall's craziness and his stable-boy's education but reflecting that this was no time to argue with her promised to speak to Ikey after the inquest at Whinmouth, the next day. She seemed satisfied with this and handed him Simon to return to his cot. He cradled the child for a moment and she watched him, her eyes alight with secret amusement. It was curious, she thought, that women produced children but never sentimentalised over them in the manner of men. She was glad about the child but more for his sake than her own. She felt no sense of achievement, as Celia and all the other sentimental old bodies had promised, no more than relief that it now had an existence of its own and that she could retreat into her own privacy. Then, away at the back of her mind and hardly as a conscious thought at all, she wondered if it was this kind of prejudice that set her apart from other women and whether, indeed, she had any real right to a man's protection and love.

III

The inquest produced no surprises. It was a survey of known facts, volunteered by a short procession of witnesses, beginning with

301

Doctor O'Keefe, who said he had treated Martin Codsall over the last year for headaches and had cautioned him on the probable results of his excessive drinking. He also mentioned the strain of eccentricity in previous Codsalls he had known, notably Martin's father, and when he was talking of this Paul glanced at Will Codsall, who was sitting on the witnesses' bench between his wife Elinor and the stolid Eveleigh but Will did not seem to resent this implication but merely blinked and absentmindedly scratched his chin so that Paul thought, "Nobody ever asks the important questions or digs for the real facts, like Arabella's eternal nagging or Martin's terrible sense of inferiority, engendered by years and years of denigration." He gave his own evidence briefly, as did Eveleigh, and was glad when the Coroner complimented Ikey on his dogged pursuit of the deceased and his prompt rescue of the hysterical Sydney. It was over and done with inside an hour and outside the little court Will Codsall told Paul that the funeral would be at Coombe Bay parish church the next day, murderer and victim being buried in the same family grave, despite a rumour that Parson Bull would prohibit it. His family, he said, had been churchwardens at Coombe Bay for more than a century and having regard to Martin's mental illness Parson Bull agreed to stretch a point. Elinor stood by tight-lipped while they talked, only joining in when Paul asked Will if he would like to return to Four Winds as master.

"No," she snapped, "'er woulden, an' you can taake that as vinal, Squire! Thankee all the zame but tiz 'No'! Four Winds be a bad plaace an' us is better off where us be, at Periwinkle!"

Paul agreed but noticing that Will looked shifty thought it right to press the point somewhat.

"There's no comparison between Four Winds and Periwinkle as farms, Elinor," he said. "One is well established and close on 350 acres, the other a mere sixty, enclosed by Pitts' land and the moor."

"It's no odds," she said stubbornly, "us want none of it, do us Will?"

"No, I reckon not," Will said slowly, "we'm zettled enough, Mr. Craddock," and Paul pondered the tendency of Codsall males to let their women speak on their behalf as Elinor added, "As to what that old vool in there said about the family being mazed, I don't reckon nothing to that! Will baint mazed, nor my little Mark neither! A man's what he maakes of himself to my mind, or what his woman maakes of 'un!"

302

"I daresay you're right about that, Elinor," said Paul, and thought how much luckier Will had been in his wife than Martin. "Stay on at Periwinkle and good luck to you both! Will you be taking young Sydney to live with you now?"

Elinor glanced at Will. It was plain that she did not relish the prospect but she said slowly, "I reckon that'd be our duty, Squire, providing he wants to come, but he'll never maake a varmer, he's too zet on book-larnin'. Maybe whoever moved into Four Winds would board him. He don't eat much and he's at school most o' the time."

"Then leave Sydney to me," Paul said and went across to the black-browed foreman, Eveleigh, who was adjusting the harness of his pony and deliberately avoiding involvement in the conference.

"Suppose I transferred the tenancy of Four Winds to you, Eveleigh?" he asked and the man's head came up so sharply that the pony shied. To cover his agitation Eveleigh shouted, "Quiet, damn you! Stand still, boy!" and glanced across at Will and Elinor, now on the point of moving off.

"That wouldn't be right, would it, sir?" he asked, "not with Will 'avin' to make do on sixty acres o' rough land?"

"Will doesn't want the farm," Paul told him, "I've just offered it to him. He'll have the contents, of course and some of the stock no doubt, for Martin probably left a will but he's only got sixty acres and I daresay you could come to some arrangement with him and buy stock over a period? Or perhaps you could split the Friesian herd between you. The point is, how would you feel about running Four Winds?"

Eveleigh considered, making the decision of a lifetime. Finally he said, "I could make it the best farm for miles around but I've got nothing put by. How could I, wi' six kids and the pittance Codsall paid me? I couldn't run it alone, and I couldn't pay the hired men a week's wages. It isn't Will I'd have to come to terms with, but you, Squire. It'd be five years before you saw money come back but by then my boys an' girls would be old enough to lend a hand so I wouldn't need hired help. I'd say it was you who had to make the decision, Mr. Craddock!"

Paul remembered the man's steadfastness and the gentleness he had displayed lowering Martin's body. He recalled too, the relationship between Eveleigh and his wife, and the way she had hustled Ikey into bed with one of her own boys. He said, "I'd take a chance on you both Eveleigh! The place is yours if you want it and I'll get Rudd to draw up a new agreement. You can have it rent free for three years and I'll undertake to pay the two men until you see something back from your harvest. Did Martin sell all his milk locally?"

"We do right now," Eveleigh said eagerly, "but my missus is a wonderful hand with the churn. I've always thought we could send butter an' cheese up the railway line to the cities if we got things on a proper footing. There's money in that if you can cut out the middlemen." And then, his dark eyes glowing, "You'll not regret it, Squire! You give me this chance and I'll make something of it, you can rely on that!"

"I'm sure I can," Paul said, and wondered briefly what Rudd would say when he heard he had struck the best farm in the Valley from the rent roll for three years. Then he thought, "To hell with John! Grace would agree and it's time I made some of my own decisions!" To Eveleigh he said, "You'd best go back now and get things moving. Come over and see me on Sunday morning."

Eveleigh nodded, too moved to say more. He climbed into his trap and drove off after Will Codsall just as Rudd came out of the courthouse looking more than usually gloomy. "I always seem to be missing when anything serious happens around here," he said glumly, "but it looks as if you and that stable-boy managed as well as anyone could have done. However, I can take over from here so get back to your wife and baby and take it easy for a day or two." He did not give expression to the thought that crossed his mind as he mentioned Grace, or how events seemed to be justifying his nagging suspicion that, in some way, Grace had revived the bad luck of the Valley simply by being who she was, a hangover of the Lovell tradition. There had been the quarrel with Gilroy, then the Smut Potter affair, and now this, a murder and a suicide, all within a matter of a year. And there was more to come he wouldn't wonder!

He went back to confer with the Coroner and the Police Inspector, while Paul mounted the trap Ikey had brought round and the two set off along the coastal cart road towards Coombe Bay. Ikey, to his delight, was allowed to drive and they were soon clear of the town and breasting the long hump of the red cliff that enclosed Whinmouth on the east. They were walking the horse down the next hill into Teazel Coombe when Paul said, "Mrs. Craddock and I have been discussing your future, Ikey. She thinks you should go to school, a real school, you understand?"

The boy looked startled. "You mean, away to school, sir?" and

304

when Paul told him this was so he burst out, "But I like it fine where I am, an' what I'm doing, sir! I don't want no more upsets. This aint because o' what 'appened at Four Winds, is it, sir? I did right the Coroner said, and so did you when we was doing of it!"

"Of course you did right," Paul said, "but both Mrs. Craddock and I feel that the way you've shaped since you've been here and the progress you've made at Miss Willoughby's school, entitles you to a real education. You can't get higher than Chivers if you stay a stable-lad, and you can never earn more than a pound or two a week. How old are you?"

"I couldn't say for sure," the boy said, "but I reckon I'm thirteen, or near enough. My Mum told me I was eleven when I first come 'ere but what would it mean, sir, going away and being put to a big school? Would it mean . . . well . . . that I grew into a gent, like you, sir?"

Paul chuckled. "By no means," he said, "for I'm only half a gentleman, Ikey. I bought my place here with money made from the scrapyard, and I didn't even make that myself, it was all earned by my father and Mr. Zorndorff. No, that isn't the point, at least Mrs. Craddock wouldn't think it was. She says that you've got a naturally quick brain and if you put your mind to it you could learn to speak properly and stand a far better chance of getting on in the world. Apart from that a good education is a fine thing in itself. I didn't have one and I've missed it, I can tell you! You can never really catch up, you only think you can."

The boy glanced at him curiously. "There's nothing you can't do, sir," he said, "so I don't see what . . . well . . . I don't see what the way a bloke talks has to do with it!"

"It has, believe me," said Paul feelingly, "in England it's the most important thing of all. I don't know why it should be but it is. Your accent, and mine, for that matter, would hold us back all our lives so long as we stayed at home. It wouldn't hinder us in America or the Colonies but here it's a kind of password. But I'm not the person to give you the best advice about this, go and have a word with Mrs. Craddock when you get home?" and when Ikey still hesitated, "You like Mrs. Craddock, don't you? You'd trust her, the same as you would me?"

Ikey said reverently, "I think she's the most beautiful person I ever see, sir. She's like . . . like a picksher in a book. I'd talk to her

305

about it, sir, but I'd tell her same as I told you, that I'm 'appy enough as I am!"

They left it at that and Ikey saw Grace but the result was as Paul had expected. She converted him to her point of view in half-an-hour. He at once sought Paul in the stables and said, grinning shame-facedly, "Mrs. Craddock reckons I could board out a bit with a schoolmaster she knows in Paxtonbury, sir, so I'm orf tomorrer! Then I got to try fer one o' them nobs' school, I dunno where exactly, but I 'ope it's 'andy!" That was all; the guardianship of Ikey Palfrey had passed from man to wife.

Paul learned the details later, when Grace was up and about again. The staff, he noticed, now treated her with increased respect, as though, by producing a male heir, she had accomplished a very singular feat indeed and although he was amused by this he was dismayed by her curious lack of interest in Simon, whom she cheer-fully abandoned to Thirza, now promoted from parlourmaid to Nannie. Grace breast-fed the baby, O'Keefe telling Paul that she had made an excellent recovery, far more rapid than he had anticipated, for the difficulties of the breech birth had evidently rattled the old man. Daladier, the specialist, came over once or twice to re-examine her and Celia accompanied him. Grace was convinced that the French surgeon was Celia's lover, for Bruce, her father, remained abroad. The notion of her forty-five-year-old stepmother enjoying a Continental lover amused Grace but in a strange way it seemed to bring them closer together so that Paul thought, "I suppose it's because she finds this one more example of flying in the face of convention, or is it just another score off her father?"

Rudd, to Paul's surprise, unequivocally endorsed the new tenancy of Four Winds, declaring that Eveleigh was far more likely to make a success of the farm than Will Codsall. After Eveleigh had settled in Paul rode over once or twice and was impressed with the transforma-tion of the place. Its air of explosive gloom had gone and the ghosts of Martin and Arabella seemed to have been laid by the teeming, tumbling Eveleigh brood, four flaxen-haired little girls, all lively and pretty and two stolid boys. Marian Eveleigh more than fulfilled her husband's promise in the buttery and the results of her industry was soon going up the line to London markets, where her butter and tinned yellow cream was reputed to appear on the tables of famous res-taurants. The two elder girls were initiated into the art and might have increased the dairy output if Eveleigh had not been a stickler for their regular attendance at Mary Willoughby's school. He had, Paul noticed, a great respect for the value of education and later on, when he would have been glad of his eldest boy's help about the farm, he preferred to see him canter off on the Four Winds' lively pony and ride the eight-mile round trip between Deepdene and Four Winds every weekday.

The weather that spring was mild and crops were forward. Up at Periwinkle, on the edge of the moor, Elinor Codsall was busy building up a strong strain of poultry that promised to improve on the hens she had left behind at her father's farm. She favoured a sturdy crossbreed, Rhode Island Red and Light Sussex and she too availed herself of city markets made available by the railway. Paul sometimes met her at Sorrel Halt unloading crates of eggs in the siding and noticed that she was pregnant again. He thought, "That was one of the best things I ever did, promote that marriage! How Will would cope without her I can't imagine," and he looked upon Periwinkle as one of his successes. Elinor made no secret of her relief that Four Winds, with its fine Friesian herd, had passed into other hands. "If Will had gone backalong," she told Paul, "I'd ha' lost him! 'Tiz as well for us things happened as they did and young Sydney is better along of all they Eveleigh children. Mebbe it'll taake him out of himself for he's got too much of his mother about him, whereas my Will has no particle of 'er, Glory be!"

Henry Pitts, at Hermitage, was courting at last, to his mother's satisfaction and his jolly father's amusement. He had been taken in hand, with little impetus on his part, by a grenadier of a girl, full-bosomed and red-haired, who was employed as dairymaid at one of the Gilroy farms and occasionally, when Paul was riding along the lanes of an evening, he would pass them walking slowly and in step, with Henry's arm tucked firmly under the girl's, so that he looked like an amiable prisoner being exercised by an affectionate wardress. As he passed them and Henry gave him a good evening Paul reflected that the women of the Valley were more vital and purposeful than its men and seemed also to have a clearer conception of what was important and what was not and that in most cases it was they who made the decisions. There was Elinor Codsall and her Will, Henry and his tall red-head, Martha and the easy-going Arthur Pitts, Mary Willoughby and her preacher brother, and, to some extent, Eveleigh's wife Marian, now keeping the pot boiling through the difficult period of the take-over. He wondered briefly if Valley folk thought the same of him and regarded Grace as the originator of policy at the big house but thought this unlikely, for Grace's interest in the estate was purely personal, like her patronage of Ikey Palfrey. He wished sometimes that she would show a more active interest in the estate and not continue to regard it, as he was sure she did, as a tiresome hobby on the part of a boyish husband. Their relationship as man and wife remained tranquil enough but he failed utterly to interest her in his political activities and so did James Grenfell, for all his persuasive charm. Paul had been a witness to their last skirmish, when Grenfell, arriving at Shallowford with news that a bye-election was a probability in the constituency in the summer, admitted that, whilst favouring the principle of the woman's vote, he thought it should await the settlement of more important issues, such as tariff reform, the bridling of the House of Lords, the Irish question, and a mass of badly-needed social legislation on subjects as divergent as shop-assistants' hours and pensions for the aged. He could not regard women's suffrage as a major issue; for Grace it dwarfed every other.

"You Liberals will never get your major reforms through without enlisting the support of every intelligent woman in the country," she declared. "You prattle about social reform until your platforms disappear behind a cloud of gas but you don't really believe in it, not you, not Lloyd George, not that cold fish Asquith, or Oh-So-Courteous Mr. Grey! The right of women to have a say in the kind of society in which they live ought to be self-evident! We produce the children you need to play 'Snap' with the German Kaiser but you still relegate us to the kitchen and nursery! Well, it won't do, James, and I'm hanged if you'll get my support until you stand up in Paxtonbury Drill Hall and admit that a woman is no longer a second-class citizen! If a male cretin can vote, why deny the same right to a qualified woman doctor?" It seemed to Paul that she had a point, but James only laughed and replied, "When a modern political party aims at rebuilding the entire fabric of that nation, my dear, it has to select priorities and deal with reforms one at a time. It dare not risk hard-won gains on a highly controversial domestic issue. You'll get your vote all right but you'll have to wait until you're thirty-odd instead of twenty-odd!" and Grace had snapped, "It's too long to wait, James!" and had retired to her rose garden in one of her withdrawn moods, not mentioning the subject again until Paul was getting into bed when she said, astounding him with her guile, "Why don't you work on the local committee to persuade Grenfell to stand down and

308

put you up instead? I'd work hard for you, providing, of course, you stood for women's suffrage. After a trial run or two we'd get to Westminster!"

"But I haven't the slightest desire to get to Westminster!" he protested and she replied, with a sigh that troubled him, "No, Paul, I'd forgotten that!" and dropped the subject.

After that they had kept off the subject of politics and the spring days passed pleasantly enough. One day, to his genuine pleasure, Claire Derwent appeared at the last hunt of the season and contrary to expectations he found that he could talk and joke with her without embarrassment. They seemed, in fact, to slip into the easy, unexacting relationship of the earliest days of their friendship, when she had ridden beside him all over the Valley and introduced him to people he now addressed by nickname. She was a little less plump, he thought, but her figure, if anything, was the better for it and she looked very fit for a girl who, according to her own account, spent most of her time indoors and had not sat a horse since leaving the Valley. She made no reference to the abruptness with which she had decamped after the Coronation soirée, or to the fact, now clearly established in Paul's mind, that she had felt certain he would propose to her but she still seemed interested in everything that was happening in the Valley and congratulated him warmly on the birth of his son, Simon.

"Why don't you come over and see the place again, Claire?" he said. "You ought to meet Grace and I'm sure you'll like one another. She's a great gardener and has made all kind of changes outside, although she won't even give advice on the administrative side. Come over to tea and bring Rose?" and Claire said that she would be happy to visit them the day before she went back to her teashop in Penshurst to prepare for the summer influx of visitors.

"I can't imagine you pottering about a teashop, Claire," he said, as they rode part-way home together, "you're an open-air girl and that's a city job," and she had glanced at him, a little sharply he thought, and said, "I'd sooner do that than spend my life as an unpaid servant for father!"

"Well, I don't suppose it will be for long," he said lightly, "you'll be married very soon for sure."

"Maybe," she said, and left it at that, but she redeemed her promise and she and Rose arrived in the Derwent's yellow dog-cart the following Saturday, both dressed in their best and Claire looking very smart in a diagonally-striped blue and white silk dress, with a huge picture hat of matching straw, openwork mittens instead of gloves and a long-handled parasol of saxe-blue silk.

Handing her down from the box Paul thought it was going to be a rather trying occasion but it proved exactly the opposite. As he had predicted she and Grace seemed to find a good deal to talk about and abandoned him to Rose, who lured him into the yard on the pretext of talking shop with Chivers the groom and then set to work to sell him a cob and exchange the old Lovell trap for a smarter equipage. He was easy game for this, having already made up his mind to buy a more modern drag before Grace, with her modern notions, persuaded him to get a motor, still foreign to the Valley but sometimes seen in the steep streets of Paxtonbury. When they had more or less clinched the deal he asked Rose outright if she thought Claire was happy away from home and Rose said she was as happy as most girls who could never settle for anything short of a husband and babies. Paul half expected her to make some reference to the general belief that he had jilted her but she did not and he was grateful. She praised Grace, saying that she thought her "quite lovely", and adding that she was popular among the tenants and then they returned to find Grace and Claire in the drawing-room after her inspection of the baby. Claire paid him the usual compliments and they left, declaring that they had enjoyed the visit enormously, and that Paul and Grace must come to High Coombe and not wait until Claire came home again, for that might not be until Christmas-time.

As the yellow trap passed out of view behind the curve of the chestnuts Grace said, "She's still madly in love with you, Paul, but perhaps you don't need telling that."

He was shocked and angry, not so much by the statement but by the blandness with which it was uttered, as though this had been a subject of debate between them and that it was now time to concede her the winner and pay the bet. He growled back, "That's a damned silly thing to say! And not a very kind thing, either!" and stumped off into the library, leaving her smiling on the porch steps. A moment later, however, she opened the door softly and came in and he saw that she was quite unruffled by his touchiness.

"It wasn't such a silly remark," she said, after a pause, "and I didn't mean it maliciously! There are all kinds of things wrong with me, Paul, but I'm not catty about other women."

"All right then," he said, resignedly, "let's regard it as bad guess-

310

work. I don't think she ever was in love with me, in fact, I know she wasn't! She may have been a bit infatuated when she was nineteen but it was never more than a flirtation on my part or on hers, no matter what you might have heard to the contrary!"

"I've heard nothing about it," she said, in the same reasonable tone, "I was just using my eyes. Her sister knows it's true and I daresay old Edward Derwent was disappointed too; that would account for his grumpiness! You didn't see her as I did, holding your Simon just now. She's not only in love with you but unselfishly so, and that's rare!"

He said, sullenly, "All women look that way holding babies! And he isn't just 'my Simon', Grace, he's yours as well!" but then, sensing that this might lead to a discussion that provoked one of her dismal withdrawals, added, "As a matter of fact she behaved rather badly at the time. Rose knows that and is still ashamed for her. She made the running and when it was obvious to her that I was in love with you she flounced out of the Valley and has never returned until now! It was more pique than anything else, as she frankly admitted in a letter to me!"

"Have you still got the letter?"

"I don't keep Claire Derwent's letters tied up with chocolate-box ribbon," he said. "Why should I?"

"Oh, I don't know—as a scalp, perhaps. Do you keep mine?"

"You've never written me one," he told her and she laughed, in a way that encouraged him to treat the whole thing more lightly than he was disposed to do.

"No, that's right, I never have! But there really wasn't time, was there and we've never been parted since then!" She came across and perched herself on the edge of the table close to his chair, her skirts rustling pleasantly. "Come on Paul, admit it! Don't you find me a little cloying? Like David Copperfield's Dora?"

"No," he said, "you're much more like Agnes, the practical one!" but she had coaxed him out of his sulk so that they were able to discuss the Derwents objectively, Grace saying that Claire had done herself a good turn without knowing it by fleeing the Valley. She was now living less than an hour's journey from London and could therefore enjoy the best of both worlds. Suddenly she added, "As soon as she sat down, holding her knees close together and sitting half sideways as I handed her tea, she reminded me very vividly of someone and I couldn't think who but now I think I've got it! Wait a minute . . ."

and she went over to the lowest shelf of the bookcase where there were several bulky volumes of coloured reproductions of famous masters, returning to him with a book called *Famous Paintings of the Western World* that Paul had never opened.

"Here it is," she said triumphantly, "and I was right! There's your Claire, three centuries ago!" and she laid the book open at an illustration of Rubens' "Bathsheba receiving King David's letter", a picture described as "one of the master's most enchanting later works, a fiery love song and a poem in praise of sensual beauty". Paul looked at the reproduction with interest, seeing a handsome, full-breasted girl sitting with bare knees pressed together and her body turned half-left as she received the letter from a Negro page. Grace's memory had been remarkably accurate, for the girl, listed as Helène Fourment, whom the painter had married when she was sixteen, was Claire Derwent in almost every particular. She had the same rounded face, the same air of mild provocation and the identical attentive pose, for it seemed to Paul that this Bathsheba might have been checking her shopping list rather than receiving the advances of a royal seducer. He studied the picture with interest, struck by its superb composition, by the way the painter had directed light on the carelessly bent arm, the soft, drooping fingers and the chubby knees. Grace, watching him closely, said, "Well? And what has she got for you, Paul?"

"Detachment more than anything else," he said, but Grace shook her head violently and said, "Oh no! It isn't that! It's a kind of *fruitfulness*, a ripeness that he's captured. A man could enjoy that girl very much but without ever getting emotionally involved. She would have children very easily, I'd swear to that!"

"Well," he said, closing the book, "I daresay you're right but there's something missing for my taste."

"What is it?"

"There's no 'secret' about her and I suppose that's what initially attracted me to you! Besides," he went on, more jocularly, "I'm partial to brunettes and always have been," and he told her something about the girl whose surname he had forgotten and the fourteen-year-old hoyden who had scared him so badly in the stables as a boy, reflecting that both had been dark, rather sallow girls. It was good to be able to talk to one's wife like this and he thought, "If I had married Claire Derwent I daresay we should have made a go of it, but it would have lacked adventure!" He said aloud, "Let's go and

312

look at your garden, Grace. Horace tells me it's almost finished," and they went out through the french doors and along the terrace to the corner of Little Paddock.

Great clumps of daffodils and narcissi were growing on the grassy bank dividing field and the path that led to the rose garden. There had been none about here last spring and he remembered now that she had planted more than a thousand bulbs hereabouts and more on both sides of the drive. It struck him as odd that a woman as self-contained as her, someone who worried about imponderables like women's suffrage, should expend so much energy on a garden, for surely the Pankhursts and their supporters would deride anything not brought to their notice by a pamphlet. As always when they were alone out here, with the great house silhouetted against an evening sky and blackbirds piping in the thickets, a glow of possession and satisfied memories stole over him, embracing not only the scene, and the long vista of woods and fields to the south and east, but her also and when they stopped at the stone wall she and Horace Handcock had built he slipped his arm round her waist and said, "I shall never want anything more than this and a man ought to think himself lucky to have found all he needed at twenty-five! Does that saddle me with a sluggish imagination?"

"No," she said, "not necessarily but it's a fortunate state of mind, Paul, and uncommon enough to be valued I think."

"Well then, I appreciate it to the full," he admitted and he bent to kiss the lobe of her ear.

CHAPTER TWO

I

IT came stuttering down from the moor like a lean, lamed hen, moving in short, uncertain flutters, pursued by a rolling cloud of white dust and because of its erratic progress the cloud occasionally overtook it and loitered just ahead until it emerged into clean air with an undertone of *bub-bub-bub* and an overtone like the bleat of a deprived ewe.

Henry Pitts was the first man in the Valley to see it, abandoning his plough to run wide-eyed across two acres of downslope where he could stand on the crest of the moor and look down on the road it travelled. It was the first horseless carriage he had ever seen for he rarely travelled as far as Paxtonbury and had never really believed the stories his drinking companions told them in the bar of The Raven. Yet here it was, careering along the track that led from the moor to the river road, a real and unmistakable horseless carriage, propelled by noisy magic and steered by a stranger in heavy goggles, a peaked cap and a long white coat, like the cloak of a French horseman in "The Squares at Waterloo", the only picture on the walls of Hermitage Farm.

Henry stood on the bank with mouth agape, telling himself that seeing was believing yet not fully acknowledging what he saw as fact, for the thing was now moving at the speed of a galloping horse and the dust streaked behind it like the wake of a ship. Its wheels, Henry reasoned, must be made of iron, for they struck the uneven surfaces with murderous force and several times the driver would have been thrown out had he not clung to a wheel perched on the end of a long vertical rod rising from between his knees. Henry thought it a very clumsy device for this purpose, reasoning that something fixed and square would have afforded a better grip but while he was still standing there the squat vehicle reached the junction of track and cart-road and suddenly stopped, its trailing cloud of dust again rolling down on it until Henry thought it had been an illusion and feared for his reason. It was still there, however, for when he ran down from the bank and advanced along the track the dust cloud had settled and the thing could be seen clearly for what it was, a kind of foreshortened brougham, with spoked wheels like exceptionally heavy bicycle wheels and rims swathed in thick bands of rubber. He saw now that the wheel to which the man had been clinging was obviously used for guiding because, just as Henry approached, the goggled man began to haul at it so that the front wheels moved around in a half-circle. There were, in addition, all manner of levers and appurtenances attached to the rigid brass frame, a pair of fishy-eyed lamps, another thick iron rod fitted with a handgrip and a bulb that looked to Henry like a hunting horn with a cricket ball attached to it. The young man smiled encouragingly when he saw Henry make his cautious approach and shouted above the *bub-bub-bub* of the little monster's voice, waving his arms as if urging Henry to come nearer but Henry stopped a good ten yards away and continued to stare, knuckling the dust from his eyes and trying to make up his mind which way to run should the thing explode in his face. So must his ancestors have approached a local pit in this same Valley when word came that a strange and ferocious beast had been trapped therein.

"*Hi!*" the young man continued to shout, "*Hi*, there! Am I right for Shallowford? Do I turn right or left?" and then, gauging the extent of Henry's uncertainty, he made some adjustment so that the shattering *bub-bub-bubbing* stopped and the thing stood as silent and unoffending as a dog-cart.

Henry said slowly, "Gordamme, maister, I never zeed such a thing! Never in my bliddy life!" and advanced a step or two as the young man climbed down, stripped off his goggles and turned on him a pair of laughing blue eyes under sandy, upsweeping brows. He was, thought Henry, a very cheerful-looking fellow and Henry's trepidation put a twinkle in the eyes as he said, "You mean that I'm a pioneer? The very first?" and he was clearly delighted for he went on, "Now that's one up for Diana because she's nearly seven now! It'll be something for her to remember in her old age, won't it, Di?" and he patted the casing at the front of the contraption just as though it was a horse. Henry was now half persuaded that he was dealing with an amiable lunatic but, remembering Martin Codsall, reflected that even amiable madmen were subject to violence so he continued to keep his distance and said, "Youm almost at Shallowford, zir! Baint no more'n a mile along the river 'till you strike the lodge!" Then, but still moving with caution, he sidled nearer, reaching out to touch the casing, finding it very hot and withdrawing his hand as though it had been bitten.

315

" 'Er's *seven*, you said ?"

"Yes," replied the young man, "she's a Benz, you see, a German model, copied from one of the early Rileys. I only bought her yesterday. She's not half bad on a good road but this stretch almost did for her."

"Where . . . where've 'ee come from, maister?" Henry asked and he would not have been much surprised had the young man told him from the moon.

"Plymouth," he said, "I started about noon. Not bad, is it?"

"Not bad!" Henry echoed, "forty-five mile in dree hours? It's a bliddy miracle, maister! Dornee mind risking your neck?"

"Good God, there's no danger!" the man said laughing. "Not half as much as riding a young mare across country!"

"Jasus!" said Henry, fervently, "you gimme the mare, maister! Be 'ee callin' on Squire Craddock?"

"On my father," said the sailor, "John Rudd, the agent. Do you know him?"

"Arr, that I do," Henry said, losing a little of his awe. "So you be Maister Rudd's on'y son? The Naval gent?"

"That's me!" said the motorist cheerfully. "I've just finished a short cruise and I've got a long leave, so I'm off all round England. If Diana lets me down I'll sell her and buy a Wolseley. Mind you, there's a lot to be said for this model. They have a mechanically-operated inlet valve and you don't get so much trouble with fuel intake. She's ten horse, you know, and can do thirty-five on the straight and flat!"

He might have been talking High Dutch as far as Henry was concerned and must have realised as much, for suddenly he hopped on to the seat, fiddled with levers, hopped out again holding a crooked piece of iron and ran round to the front where he seemed to tease the contraption's secret parts with his uncouth weapon. Suddenly there was a series of shot-gun explosions causing Henry to leap for the cover of the ditch but when he peeped out again the staccato *bub-bub-bubbing* had recommenced and a cloud of bluish smoke was pouring from Diana's hindquarters. With a wave the young man was off again down the river road, the noise of his progress stampeding Eveleigh's Friesians half-way across the water meadow.

"Gordamme!" Henry said softly, "to think I should live to zee a bliddy dog-cart driven be smoke!" and as he returned to his plough, realising that he would now have to treat his drinking companions' stories with more respect, for Willis, the wheelwright, had told him only a week ago that he had seen one of these same carriages climb Cathedral Hill in Paxtonbury at a speed twice as fast as a man could run.

One or two of the Home Farm workers saw the Benz turn into the main gates of the big house and pull up at the lodge, but either they were more sophisticated than Henry Pitts or they lacked his curiosity for they merely stopped work to see what would happen when the driver turned his back on the contraption. Then, calling encouragement to one another they edged nearer, watching the young man in the white coat hammer on the lodge door. Nobody answered, for nobody was there, but when he returned to the drive he saw what his wardroom companions would describe as "a fetching little filly" bending double over the controls in such a way as to expose a pair of exceptionally neat calves. He coughed twice, expecting her to bob up blushing, but she remained absorbed, her head half under the steering rod so that, in her light summer dress, he had an unlooked-for opportunity of appreciating what he would have described as "her upholstery", all the way from ankles to shapely little bottom. At length he had to admit to himself that he was taking a mean advantage and said, "Excuse me, Miss! I'm looking for my father, John Rudd. Do you know if he's around?"

The girl straightened up slowly and he noticed, with surprise, that she had oil on her fingers. He noticed also that her front view was even more attractive than her back view, that she had dark, close-growing curls, a pretty, heart-shaped face, deep blue eyes, a short, regular nose, and something he always looked for in a girl, two large dimples, not counting one in the cleft of her chin. He thought, "My God! What a little peach!" but he had good manners and instantly whipped off cap and goggles, giving her a quarterdeck bow, of the kind he used when the captain brought ladies aboard and he was under orders to make himself sociable.

She smiled, a slow, friendly smile and said, "Mr. Rudd is up at the house I believe. Are you Roddy, John's son?" and he stood to attention, looking rather ridiculous in his long, shapeless coat and said, "Yes, Miss! I'm on leave and I thought I'd look him up before setting off on a motor tour. I seem to have caused a bit of a sensation in the Valley. A chap back there told me they'd never seen a motor here before but that can't be true, can it?"

"Yes, it's true," she said and he noted her low, almost masculine voice and thought, "By George, I wish the skipper had invited somebody like this aboard during one of his blasted chit-chat parties!" But she was to surprise him further for she said, pointing to the motor, "It's a Benz, isn't it? The model the Germans copied? I've never seen one before but I've ridden in a Panhard and a Daimler. One of the original Daimlers it was, assembled in Wolverhampton. Does she boil on hills? Do you have to wait for her to cool off every now and again?"

"Why no," he said, eagerly, "she's not a bad little crock at all! I tackled a one-in-five on my way across Dartmoor this morning. Had to take it quietly, of course, and nurse her, but she only stalled once. The main thing is to find even ground. She's apt to move in jerks on rough surfaces, like the moor road back there. I say, would you like a lift up to the house?"

"Indeed I would," Grace said, laughing at his enthusiasm, "but perhaps I'd better introduce myself. I'm not a 'Miss' I'm a 'Mrs.' — Mrs. Craddock, the Squire's wife. I expect your father has told you about me."

"No, he hasn't," he said, disappointment clouding his good-looking face, "but I do beg your pardon and I'm delighted to meet you, Mrs. Craddock! You don't often encounter a lady who doesn't think of a motor as an infernal machine, liable to blow the curious to smithereens! Where did you ride in a Panhard? They're the best, so far, but the whole industry is in a state of flux and Panhard won't lead for long. Wolseley has something very lively coming up, I hear, and now that His Majesty has taken to motoring I wouldn't wonder if they aren't all the rage in a year or so!"

"I'm sure they will be," she said, as he handed her into the passenger seat, "and I wish I could persuade my husband to buy one but he's just bought a brougham, so I'm afraid it's unlikely."

She watched him start up and the Benz coughed its way up the steep drive. Conversation was impossible while they were in motion but they arrived in the forecourt without incident, just as Rudd came out on to the terrace and saw his son handing Grace Craddock down from her perch.

"Good God!" he exclaimed, "what the devil are you doing here in that thing?" and Grace explained, noting that for all Rudd's scorn he was nonetheless pleased to see Roddy.

They all three took tea in the library, Rudd explaining that Paul would not be back until late that night, for the long-awaited bye-

318

election had just been announced and he had driven to Paxtonbury to sponsor James Grenfell, in the Drill Hall. "I daresay he'll try and talk you into campaigning for him," John said. "Grenfell might like a modern approach and display a poster on a motor 'Keep abreast with the Liberals' or something like that."

"Good Lord, I couldn't allow that!" Roddy said, with genuine alarm, "we chaps aren't allowed to side with either party, although we're naturally expected to vote Tory! Will you be helping your husband in the campaign, Mrs. Craddock?"

"No, I'm afraid I won't," declared Grace, "I'm every bit as opposed to the Establishment as he is but I don't think the Liberals offer anything better. I'm a Suffragist, you see."

He was surprised more than shocked, although a trace of shock showed on his face. He said, "You surely don't mean you're one of Mrs. Pankhurst's women?"

"Well, not yet," Grace told him, laughing, "but I certainly would be if I lived in town. I attended a few meetings in London, before I was married and I still get all the literature through the post, I even subscribe five guineas a year to the cause."

Roddy said, gaily, "Well, jolly good luck to you, Mrs. Craddock! Those politicians need a shake-up! I think you'll get the vote, if you keep tormenting them!" But John Rudd, who knew his son rather better than the latter was aware, was thinking, "Now why did he say that? He doesn't believe in women's votes any more than I do," and he smiled, thinking it amusing that a boy who had never had a serious thought in his head should be so obviously smitten by Grace Lovell, for he was still unable to think of her as Grace Craddock, any more than he could adjust himself to other changes of names in the Valley. He said, rising, "Well, I've work to do. We shan't see much of your husband for the next month! He can hardly wait to take a crack at Gilroy's nominee and I can't help feeling that Grenfell chap stands a chance this time," but when he proposed that Roddy should ask Mrs. Handcock to make him up a bed at the lodge Grace said, "Why does he have to do that? The spare bedroom there is like a cupboard and our guest rooms are hardly ever used!" and without waiting for his assent she went to find the housekeeper.

"Were you surprised to find Paul Craddock was married, Roddy?" Rudd asked and when his son admitted that he was, he added, "Well, the truth is I've never liked our Mrs. Craddock until lately and I suppose that was simply because she was a Lovell. I'm ready to admit, however, that I was prejudiced. It's been a much better match than I hoped."

"She was interested in the motor," Roddy said. "Imagine that! A woman like her, getting oil all over her hands!"

"Oh, she's very much in favour of the new century," John said, "but the Squire isn't and never will be! However, he's a good chap, and you'll like him. He's made a big difference to my life, I can tell you. It's the first time I've ever felt needed and I'm beginning to like it!"

Roddy looked at him with affection. They had seen very little of one another but the boy was not unaware of the source of his father's surliness, or the difference in him since Shallowford had changed hands. He said, as proof of their new relationship, "Look here, Gov'nor, I hope you've put that silly business about the Prince Imperial behind you! It's ancient history now and nobody my age has ever heard of the damned Frog! There was no future in the Army anyway and you were lucky to get clear of it. The Navy is the only thing that counts, the Army is just a glorified polo club."

John said, slowly, "Yes Roddy, I have put that drumming-out business behind me but I only succeeded in doing it since the change-over here. As I say, I feel I've found a purpose in life after more than twenty years and it was Craddock who helped me find it. He's become a kind of son to me, you understand, and not only because of what I owe him but because I believe in what he's trying to do down here."

"What exactly is he trying to do?" Roddy asked, innocently. "I hear he has plenty of money and can't imagine why he doesn't want to cut a dash with it! Most fellows of his age would."

"I daresay," Rudd said defensively, "but Craddock isn't that kind of man. He's an anachronism maybe, but he's a sincere one and the country has to be nursed into the twentieth century, as well as the cities. Will you stop a day or two?"

"I'd like to," Roddy said but without adding that it was the prospect of driving the fetching Mrs. Craddock about the district and not an interest in a rural renaissance that attracted him.

II

Paul was enjoying the campaign more than he anticipated and this not solely because he was much encouraged by the local support

Grenfell was getting. In spite of the Candidate's careful priming Paul mounted his first public platform with a shrinking sensation in his stomach but he soon realised that he was not expected to juggle with political issues but to act as a buffer between the Candidate and Tory hecklers, who followed them everywhere and did their utmost to prevent Grenfell getting a hearing. Soon he found himself looking forward to engagements, for James proved himself adroit at handling the opposition and, as Jorrocks might have put it, the campaign had all the excitement of war and only half the danger. The adoption meeting was an unqualified success. Several small landowners from the area north of Paxtonbury came forward with support and subscriptions and as they drove about the constituency Paul realised that they could count on the Nonconformist vote to a man, as well as on a proportion of the smaller tradesmen and professional men. Gradually, and with a wonderful display of patience, Grenfell mustered his array and by the first week of the campaign candidates were running neck-and-neck and local excitement was mounting. Lloyd George himself wired his promise to travel down for the eve-of-poll meeting, and after hearing the new Gilroy nominee speak, Paul's confidence in turning the tide grew with every meeting, so that he was caught up in the whirl of the battle, devoting every moment of his time and every ounce of his nervous energy, to presenting James Grenfell as the only fit and proper man to represent the constituency at Westminster.

The big farms provided their toughest opposition for the more successful farmers feared the entry of cheap food into the country and were thus fiercely Protectionist but among their labourers the Radicals made progress, although they had to work very carefully, for many of the men feared for their jobs if it became known that they would vote contrary to their employers' interests and this was especially so within Gilroy boundaries, where Grenfell was received like a poacher.

Paul's singlemindedness, and the enthusiasm that he could bring to the cause on account of his sincere admiration for Grenfell, kept him absent from home for the greater part of the month, so that he saw little of Grace and observed their unspoken pact not to involve her in a cause for which she lacked conviction. Sometimes, a little forlornly, he wished that James would openly espouse the cause of Women's Suffrage and bring Grace in but he did not, holding to his theory that, while universal franchise was bound to come, it was an issue that would cost precious votes and to some extent Paul agreed with him for whenever Women's Suffrage was raised at a meeting the issue was invariably greeted with derision. In the main they stuck doggedly to the major issues, Free Trade, Chinese labour in South Africa (where Paul's local knowledge was useful) and social legislation, including workmen's compensation in factories, better housing, public health and education. Now and then they touched on broader topics, like the Irish Question and the Kaiser's new fleet but these subjects had small appeal for countrymen who regarded the Irish as noisy clowns, the Germans as bandsmen and the Kaiser as a sausage-eating buffoon in an eagle-crested helmet. Germany's attempts to rival the British Navy was an even better joke than votes for women, for down here, within rumour reach of Devonport, most voters took a personal pride in Britain's ironclads and dressed their children in sailor suits with the names of dreadnoughts braided into the ribbon bands of their hats.

Paul had been introduced to young Rudd and privately considered him a rather shallow young man, preoccupied with explosive mechanical toys and moulded to a type by the traditions of the Senior Service. He lacked, he thought, John's steadiness and confused prejudices with judgments. The campaign had made Paul edgy and even Rudd, who had promised to vote for Grenfell, smiled at the Squire's lurch towards demagogery, but whereas Rudd was old enough to enjoy watching a young man get drunk on politics Grace was not, and Paul's obsession began to irritate her a little as the campaign moved to its climax.

"You really should try and keep a sense of proportion," she said to him one night, after he and Young Rudd had exchanged acrimonious views on the causes of the South African war. "After all, a Devon bye-election isn't the end of the world and Roddy is not only a guest but hardly more than a boy!"

"He's only a year younger than me, so it's high time somebody put him right on his facts!"

"He's had a Service upbringing," Grace argued, "and in my opinion he's weathered it very well! He isn't nearly as stuffy as most naval officers and at least he makes an effort to keep abreast of the times, which is more than I can say of you!"

He was outraged, if only momentarily, by her criticism. "Good God!" he said, "Roddy Rudd's political thought is lagging behind Palmerston's! He believes in sending gunboats to discipline natives! How can you say a thing like that?"

322

She said, with the moderation she always used when they disagreed, "He knows about motors and he's interested in flying, that's all I meant. There's nothing personal about it! I find him intelligent and he's been good company all the time you've been barnstorming. However, if you really dislike him, and want him to go, all you have to do is to drop a hint to John!"

As usual when they approached an impasse Paul pulled back. Her championship of Roddy had pricked his self-esteem but he was hampered by the realisation that he had neglected her shamefully since the campaign had opened. "I don't dislike him," he said, "and I'm glad he's been fun for you but you must understand I've got to do all I can to help Jimmy Grenfell. He's got a terrific fight on his hands and every vote counts!"

"I don't quarrel with that in the least, Paul," she said, in the same quiet tone, "but please don't pretend that you are making domestic sacrifices! I've never seen you enjoy anything so much!"

"Why does a thing have to become a drudgery before it qualifies as a virtue?" he demanded, asking the rhetorical question that millions of husbands had asked before him. "Damn it, that's the trouble with women . . ." but he stopped for she was now regarding him over her shoulder as she sat at her dressing-table mirror and he recognised her look at once. It recalled the Smut Potter issue and warned him that there was a boundary to their truce over which it might be unprofitable to stray. He said, grumpily, "You have to admit that it would be easier if man and wife could pull together on this kind of issue. After all, it is fundamental, isn't it?"

"No," she said, laying down her brush, "not in the least fundamental, Paul. If you haven't learned that after nearly eighteen months with me you can't have learned anything! *Your* kind of politics, Grenfell's and Gilroy's politics, aren't fundamental! That's what's wrong with them!"

"But yours are?" he countered. "The only fundamental issue in politics today is women's suffrage?"

"Now you're being very tiresome, Paul," she replied, wearily, but he was so nettled that he did not take her hint.

"Isn't that what you meant?"

"No," she said, very sharply now, "it isn't what I meant! Women's suffrage is very important to me but I concede that it isn't to you, or to your precious James Grenfell. There are plenty of fundamental issues but political parties dependent on a flow of wealth from one

323

class or the other, aren't deeply concerned with them! Their impetus doesn't depend on a cause but on personal ambitions. That isn't true of you and it isn't true of Grenfell but it is true of all the other rabble rousers!" Then, with the edge of her voice blunted, "Do we have to prolong this stupid quarrel, Paul? It began over Roddy Rudd."

He had forgotten that and now that he thought about Rudd again, he realised that he had been rather boorish, and ought, perhaps, to be grateful to the young man for entertaining Grace while he devoted his attention to the campaign.

"I'm sorry, dear," he said, stooping and kissing her shoulder, "the fact is I'm overtired, and liable to fly off the handle. We're having to fight every step of the way and today was a bad day. We couldn't even get a hearing in Whinmouth."

She turned slowly on her stool and regarded him gravely.

"When is election day?" she asked and he told her on July 20th, about a fortnight from now.

"Do you remember a promise you made to me on our honeymoon, Paul? A promise you made the night we attended the ballet? You said that when the Company came to London we would go up to town for a few days."

He did not recall such a promise, although he did remember how much she had enjoyed the occasion. "Are they in London now?" he asked, knowing that he would have to refuse her and wondering how it could be gracefully achieved.

"No," she replied, to his relief, but I hear they are to pay a two-night visit to Bristol soon. If they do, will you take me? No matter what?"

"Darling, of course I will," he said, happy to be out of it so cheaply and she replied, quietly, "Thank you, Paul, I should like that very much."

"As to Roddy," he said, "I admit I was a bit short with him, and as you say, he is a guest. I'll apologise to him in the morning!"

In the morning, however, one of Grenfell's runners arrived with sensational news. There had been a major split over policy in the local Tory Party and Sir Keith Cresswell, a wealthy manufacturer of agricultural machinery on the northern edge of the constituency, had declared for Free Trade, so that the balance was now tipped slightly in favour of the Radicals. In the excitement he forgot all about Roddy and all about the ballet, galloping off on Snowdrop to the Liberal headquarters, to be seen no more for three days for he was canvassing fifteen hours a day. To save journeys he slept at Grenfell's rooms in Cathedral Close each night.

III

That same day Roddy had an idea. It was fine and warm and he suggested that they should drive to a village near the Somerset border where a former shipmate of his, a young man who had recently come into money and left the Service, had just bought one of the latest models assembled by Charles Rolls, the man who had converted King Edward to motors.

"It should take us about three hours each way," he said, "and Branwell will give us lunch. He keeps a big place near Dulverton!"

Grace agreed to go and Roddy asked his father if he would accompany them but Rudd, with too much work on his hands, declined but promised to wait dinner for them. He watched them chug down the drive with Grace at the wheel, her wide straw hat tied on with a chiffon scarf and her body shrouded in a long white dustcoat, borrowed from Roddy. He thought, "I suppose I understand their enthusiasm for the honking, snorting little abortion! It's their world, one of machines and gadgets of one kind or another and Paul might as well invest in a motor, if only to keep her happy, for she seems to get plenty of fun out of Roddy's!" He made a mental note to suggest as much and this led him to a morose contemplation of Paul's entry into politics and the change it had wrought in him. It was only temporary, he hoped, for ordinarily the youngster was a tolerant, easy-going soul but the campaign had shattered the rhythm of the estate and this displeased him, for things had been progressing very well lately, particularly over at Four Winds, where the Eveleigh family were proving their worth. Life was quiet in the Coombe, too, now that Smut was out of the way and even Tamer seemed resigned to using hired labour and the equipment the estate had loaned him. It was years, John reflected, since Low Coombe fields had been properly ploughed and now the old rascal was said to be going in for sugar beet, as had Derwent, on his new cliff fields. Willoughby's lad was proving his mettle too, and so were Will and Elinor over at Periwinkle, whereas he had never seen the Home Farm so fruitful after its record lambing season and the introduction of a small Guernsey herd during the winter. It was a pity, he reflected, that Paul had to be absent now, when the promise of the Valley was so rich. Political issues were

325

ephemeral but the land was always there, waiting to be loved, coaxed and cared for and he would have thought that Paul was old enough to get his values right. It did not occur to him, however, to give more than a casual thought to Roddy, driving off with an unchaperoned Grace, for he had never been able to take Roddy or his enthusiasms seriously. He was like his mother, who had romped through her short life without a thought beyond how pretty she looked and he wondered what she would have thought of her son and his obsession with mechanical toys. Then, remembering he was due at a sale across the county border, he forgot about Paul and the motorists and did not remember them again until a message reached him from Paul saying he would be away for the night and he was to tell Grace what had happened and how they now had a more than even chance of "giving old Gilroy a thrashing at the polls". He thought, "Much she'll care!" and ordered dinner for seven-thirty, returning to the lodge and sitting at his open window smoking as he watched the ford over which the Benz would come. Soon the heat went out of the day and the shadows of the chestnuts fell across the paddock but there was no sign of the motor. Grumpily, because he was both hungry and lonely, he trudged up to the house and ate a solitary meal. By nine o'clock he was irritated; by the time darkness had fallen he was worried and considering saddling up and riding along the river road down which they must come.

It would have availed him little. At that moment the Benz was stationary in a deep, leafy lane, fifteen miles north-west of Paxtonbury and about the same distance from the house where Roddy and Grace had lunched.

The outward journey had been made in record time, forty miles in one hour forty-five minutes, and after lunch Roddy's host had taken them for a drive in his Panhard, allowing Grace a turn at the wheel and encouraging her to coast over a flat stretch of moor at a speed just under forty miles per hour. They had returned about tea-time and Roddy had persuaded Grace to stay for dinner, pointing out that the drive home would provide them with appetites for another at Shallowford. Branwell, his friend, had been so kind and hospitable that Grace did not like to refuse, so they made a latish start, taking a cross-country route aimed at the main road north of Paxtonbury. It was growing dusk when they stopped in the lane to light the big brass lamps and then, to Roddy's astonishment, the Benz refused to start.

He swung her until he was wet with perspiration and had Grace hold one of the unscrewed lamps while he opened the bonnet and probed in the engine. It was no use. The Benz remained silent and Roddy said they would have to accept a humiliating tow from a cart-horse.

They set off together for the nearest farm but this proved all of three miles and when they got there the farmer, an unobliging fellow, declared that he had a market-day ahead of him and needed a fresh team for the twenty-mile journey to and from the city. He sent them on to another farm but they could get no response to their knocking and as it was now past eleven o'clock Grace said they had better return to the car and try in the opposite direction at dawn. She made very light of their dilemma, although Roddy was depressed by it and a little anxious about her reputation. When he mentioned this, however, she laughed and told him not to be stuffy, adding that both Paul and John would rejoice in the triumph of horse over motor.

Fortunately it was a fine night, with stars blazing and no breeze but under the trees, where they had left the Benz, it was pitch dark and they had to grope their way down the long lane towards the owlish glimmer of the lamps. All the way Roddy stammered apologies; he was an idiot, he ought to have set out before; he ought to have been capable of restarting the blasted car; she would think him a fine kind of escort to get her stranded in this ridiculous fashion, until at last she said, "Oh stop accusing yourself, Roddy! It's my fault as much as yours and anyway, I don't care that much! It's a long time since I had any kind of adventure and if you want the truth I'm rather enjoying it!"

He was very thoughtful at this, interpreting it as meaning she found little joy in her life at Shallowford, or in marriage to that hectoring fellow Craddock who was such a crashing bore about politics. His experience with women, although fairly wide, did not include anyone like Grace who was calm, competent and beautiful but also so much wiser than any of the girls he had met voyaging round the Empire. She was essentially English but without the helplessness or the coyness of the average English country girl. She treated him as an equal but she did not try and flirt with him, as so many married women had done in the past and she was, moreover, genuinely interested in the really important things of life, such as petrol-driven engines and heavier-than-air machines. Looking back on the past two weeks it seemed to Roddy that they had known one another for years, that she was a kind of heaven-sent sister, but a

327

sister who was able to disturb him in a way he had not yet been disturbed by a pretty woman. She had a stillness that he had not found in another human being, man or woman, and also a self-sufficiency that, in most girls, would have intimidated him but in her could be dissolved by a single light-hearted remark so that she was both attainable and unattainable. He could even marry a woman like that and decided that Craddock, who did not seem to appreciate her uniqueness, did not deserve his luck. He supposed she had married him for his money and he did not blame her for that, for he too intended to marry for money and yet, as he continued to reflect on their relationship as man and wife, he could not help wondering whether Craddock would be capable of rousing her as he felt himself capable of doing, given the opportunity.

His musings had made him very thoughtful during their progress back to the car and it was only when they arrived there, and had made one more unsuccessful attempt to start the engine, that he realised the open Benz would afford inadequate shelter for the night and suggested sitting under the bank and lighting a fire to ward off the night chill. She said this was a good idea but that it had better be at a safe distance from the car. A hundred yards back they had passed a shelter of the kind used by sportsmen on a winter shoot and she suggested they should return there and seek help at first light. He was just the slightest bit shocked by this suggestion but accepted it eagerly enough so they took the unscrewed lamp and retraced their steps to a three-sided shelter built on the edge of a wood above the level of the road. Here, in the glow of the lamp, they got a small fire going and in its light saw that the hide was carpeted with dry bracken. They went inside, sitting with their backs to the log wall and watching the fire flicker in the opening. She refused the loan of his coat, declaring that she was quite warm and when he suggested that she should try and sleep she said that she did not feel sleepy and would rather talk. As she said this she came a little closer to him, leaning some of her weight on his shoulder, so that he began to think benignly of the obstinate ignition of the Benz.

She had taken off her hat, tying her scarf about her neck and the scent of her hair mingled with the pleasant tang of resin and burning twigs, so that he found it very easy to convince himself that all she awaited was his seizure of the initiative. Yet the courage to take it eluded him and he wondered if he was losing his touch, as they talked of one thing and another and the scent of her hair stole upon him

328

like inecnse, so that he found himself growing vague and leaving her questions unanswered. At last, when the fire had burned low, he made a rather clumsy essay to get things going. Turning, he tilted her chin and kissed her lips. He kissed them expertly, or so he thought, but the kiss did not seem to give him the license he needed, so he kissed her again, this time extending his arm round her shoulder and slipping his hand under her breast. Gently she disengaged herself, saying, with laughter in her voice, "You can have my lips, Roddy, but no more! I'm very comfortable here and not inclined to spend the remainder of the night wrestling with you!"

He was very piqued at this, muttering, "I don't know what to make of you, Grace! You put a fellow in an intolerable situation!" and she laughed again, saying, "Come, be fair, Roddy! *I* didn't get us in this situation, I'm just making the best of it, so why don't you?"

"Because you obviously don't intend to let me," he said, his sense of humour reasserting itself.

"No, I don't, Roddy, but not for my sake, or even Paul's."

"Whose then?"

"For yours and your father's."

"Now where the devil does the Guv enter into it?"

"Because he's proud of you and very fond of Paul! In addition, he doesn't wholly approve of me although I believe he is beginning to!"

"Then he must be senile," Roddy said, "because any man between twenty and sixty ought to approve of you! I did, the moment I set eyes on you and now . . . well, now I'm very much in love with you, Grace!" He felt her shrink a little at this so he went on, hurriedly, "I know I don't stand any sort of chance and that you aren't in the least in love with me but you can't blame a chap wanting to make something of an opportunity like this! I've never met anyone the least bit like you before, Grace."

He waited, feeling that he had said enough and she was silent for some time. Finally she said, "You aren't in the least in love with me, Roddy! Paul is, but you aren't and I don't think you'll be capable of loving anyone until you're about thirty-five! *Then* you might, when you've had your fill of gadding about. You might even make someone a very charming husband!"

"How can you know that?" he demanded, irritably.

"How? I imagine because I've never been in love myself and that gives me a rather special kind of detachment. I made a misjudgment, Roddy, and my only excuse is that I didn't, as you probably imagine,

329

marry Paul for money. I really did think myself capable of making a success of it and in a way I suppose I have, or still could! What I won't do, however, is to make a fool of him the conventional way, or console myself by imagining that I can still try elsewhere and involve somebody I like, such as you. You don't understand love, Roddy. You could make love to me here, and persuade yourself it was extra-physical, and as for me, well—I'm sensual enough to enjoy it more than you but what could it lead to but self-deception on your part and cheapness on mine? No, Roddy, my dear, we shall have to behave I'm afraid, whether we like it or not!" and she settled herself comfortably against his shoulder and half-closed her eyes, looking out at the dull glow of the fire and the blue blackness of the trees on the opposite bank.

Her bland summarisation had a finality that divorced this from any parallel situation in his past. He had never thought deeply about anything but her honesty appealed so strongly to his commonsense that he remained silent, and presently (incredibly when he looked back on the occasion) he dozed but she remained awake, half-aware of the night scuffles of hunters in the wood behind them and the blaze of stars in the gap of sky between the belts of trees. She thought, "He's just another Paul but he'll never suffer like Paul! All the men I met when I was capable of being hurt were so-called men of the world, who enjoyed putting the screw on women, but now that I have learned to give as good as I get all I meet are boys with men's bodies! There ought to be some kind of half-way house between these extremes but there isn't. One has to settle for one or the other. If Paul could see me now he would never believe how innocent Roddy was and would still be if I did let him take me in his arms but thank God he's kind enough not to exploit the situation." She found that she could think of Roddy Rudd objectively, as she had often thought of Paul in the last few months, and of how he would have behaved had she given him the chance. The speculation amused her a little, for Roddy, thinking himself such a ladies' man, would surely pride himself on a fancied technique but his love-making would probably lack Paul's masculine approach, which was something she had deliberately fostered knowing that Paul Craddock would always need an injection of confidence in everything he attempted. She half wished it was possible for a woman like herself to experiment with men. It would be interesting, she thought, to really know men, all kinds of men, and acquire knowledge in such a simple way. All they needed to persuade

330

them that they were godlike was a little physical flattery and one could practise in gratifying them in this respect. The fire was a heap of red ash now and disengaging herself from the sleeping Roddy she moved to the entrance of the hut to replenish it, sitting there watching the sky pale and wondering what she should tell Paul and John Rudd of this escapade. Perhaps it would be better to lie and pretend they had spent the night with Roddy's friend, Branwell. He was an ex-sailor and could easily be persuaded to back the story, and thinking this she was relieved that she would not have to comfort Paul with real lies.

It was almost light when she heard the far-off jingle of harness and returned to the motor to see a startled carter whose horse had shied at the Benz blocking its path. The man was delighted to accept a half-sovereign for a tow to the main road and she left him attaching a drag rope to the motor. After washing herself in a brook and brushing the bracken fronds from her coat she woke the snoring Roddy.

"It's all arranged," she said, "a man is giving us a tow and you can probably get her started when we can get to a slope."

He sat up, rubbing his eyes, looking so bemused that she laughed.

IV

Paul, although reluctant to admit it, was beginning to be disenchanted with politics. He believed what he preached, and desired most earnestly to send Grenfell to Westminster, but his common-sense bucked at the racket and claptrap of the campaign and the ranting of half-intoxicated supporters of both candidates who swaggered about shouting their silly catch-phrases at one another. The business of government, he told himself, ought not to depend upon this kind of thing, upon the moods and impulses of leather-lunged yokels marching up and down with their banners and chanting doggerel like:

"Vote, vote, vote for Jimmy Gren-fellllll!
Kick Verne-Jonesy out the door . . . !"

but obviously it did so depend, and scenes like this were repeated all over the country at a General Election. Later, he supposed, all the Jimmy Grenfells and Verne-Joneses who had out-shouted and out-postured each other at the hustings forgot their rivalry in the genteel atmosphere of the House of Commons, where real policies were

331

formulated in cold blood. The more strident the campaign became the less he could identify himself with it, and at last he was obliged to carry his misgivings to Grenfell who, as it happened, had a rational explanation on the tip of his tongue.

"It's simply the price one has to pay for the use of democratic machinery, Paul," he said. "Under an autocracy you could dispense with it. A man would become one of the legislators by reason of wealth or position in a particular locality but now that all adult males have the vote this farcical nonsense is inevitable! It's really quite harmless, you know, and it does jolt some of the more thoughtful into making an honest and deliberate choice. I've heard people like you ask why we need parties at all or why a man like me can't judge every issue on its merits but whenever you get more than a score of men together they tend to divide into groups thinking roughly along the same lines. Then, hey presto, you have a political party and all the trimmings!"

Half satisfied with this Paul went back to his canvassing and stumping, drawing comfort from his belief in James Grenfell's integrity, for Grenfell did indeed practise restraint, rarely resorting to platform tricks and it now looked as if his careful nursing of the constituency was bearing fruit, for he was said to be leading the Tory Bernard Verne-Jones by a short head and the odds were five to four in favour of a Liberal victory. Once or twice, in his movements about the country, Paul's path crossed that of Gilroy and on one occasion, on a Paxtonbury market-day, he saw the crusty old patrician drive his brougham through a milling crowd about Martyr's Cross, on the Cathedral Green. He could not help admiring the old man's bearing, as contemptuous as that of a French aristocrat in a tumbril. The crowd surrounding the carriage was part hostile and there was a good deal of catcalling and booing but the expression on Gilroy's face remained impassive. He might, thought Paul, be taking a drive across Blackberry Moor, or paying an afternoon call on a duchess. He sat erect, enclosed in his aloof, glacial cage that was proof against plaudits and insults. Grenfell, standing beside Paul, said admiringly, "Well Paul, there goes the last of eighteenth-century England! You want to take off your hat to it, don't you?"

It was that same day that Paul had his brief and rather mystifying conversation with Farmer Venn, pot-bellied supporter from a farm a mile or so north of the city, whom he had met in the early stages of the campaign. He was eating a sandwich lunch at The Mitre when

332

Venn waddled in, his broad chest half-covered by a huge yellow rosette and he greeted Paul heartily as he ordered ale and pasties.

"A rare ole fix your good lady was in t'other mornin'," said Venn jovially. "'Er an' that young shover o' yourn an' their ole motor! Crawling along behind Ned Parsons' cart they was, an' at two mile an hour all the way to Norton Edge bevore they managed to get 'er goin'! 'Twas news to me you'd got yourself one o' they ole stink-pots, Squire!"

"I hadn't heard of their breakdown," Paul said, so far only slightly puzzled, "but I haven't been home much lately. And it isn't my car, Venn, it belongs to my agent's son, a naval lieutenant. Where did you see them?"

"Coming up the hill, towards Norton Edge backalong," Venn told him. "Early on, it was, as I was comin' in to market, an' both lookin' pretty sorry for 'emselves! Tiz a rare come-down to be towed home by a grey mare when they'm all so pleased to talk about 'horse-power', baint it?"

Having heard nothing about the incident Paul's impulse was to question Venn further but then it seemed to him that this would make him look ridiculous in Venn's eyes and perhaps start a rumour about Grace's relationship with that young idiot, Roddy, so he drank his beer and hurried away but found it difficult to give his mind to the chairmanship of meetings during the afternoon and excused himself at teatime, telling Grenfell that he had an accumulation of work at home and wanted to clear it before preparing for the eve-of-poll meeting.

He learned, on arrival at the lodge, that Roddy had left for London earlier in the day but Rudd was evasive when he asked about the breakdown, saying, off-handedly, "Oh, I believe they had several about the country, Paul. Motors aren't all that reliable, you know, but I daresay we shall have to have one in the end!"

"Over Snowdrop's dead body!" Paul told him and sought out Grace, less disturbed by the realisation that she must have spent a night away from home without telling him than by Rudd's implied championship of the motor. He found her alone in the rose garden, absorbed in her work and when he walked round the lily pond she looked up saying, "Hullo! I didn't expect you until after midnight!"

"I decided to take an evening off," he said and wondered how a husband began asking the kind of questions he wanted to ask whilst leaving room to manœuvre. He said carefully, "A farmer came to me today with a silly story about you and Roddy having to be towed home

333

one day last week," and found himself watching her eyes for signs of guilt. She gave a shrug and dusted earth from her gardening gloves.

"It wasn't a silly story, Paul, it was quite true. We were stranded overnight and a cart towed the Benz half-way to Paxtonbury."

He was startled and showed it. "When was this?" and she told him last Friday, the night he sent a message saying that he would be staying with Grenfell.

"Why on earth didn't you tell me about it?"

"Why? I suppose partly because I didn't have a real opportunity, and partly because I thought you might put a wrong construction on it, as you seem to be doing now."

"Is that unreasonable?"

"I think it is."

It was clear that she considered him ridiculous in the role of the outraged husband and was determined not to rise to the bait but he read in her impassivity an evasiveness that was not there. He said, shortly, "You can imagine what a fool I felt, having to stand in a public bar and hear about my own wife coming home with the milk! Doesn't that mean anything to you? Don't you care if I'm made to look as if I enjoy my wife gallivanting all over the county with a young idiot in a motor?"

She looked at him compassionately now but he was too angry and humiliated to notice it.

"Yes, I care, Paul," she said, quietly, "I care very much, but in this case my share of the blame is confined to not telling you about it and for that I apologise. Now I think we'd better go in."

He followed her along the flagstones and across the corner of the paddock to the terrace. When they were inside the library he said, petulantly, "Well, what *did* happen? Were you stranded at that friend of Roddy's? John told me you had paid a call there."

The white lie she had intended telling him changed colour with his attitude and now she felt under an obligation to tell him the insignificant truth.

"As a matter of fact we were stranded half-way between there and home," she said, "and spent the night in the open."

"Roddy and you?"

For a moment he was too outraged to speak. When he did the violence of his tone surprised her. "What do you mean, *'in the open'*? How could he let such a thing happen? And how could you be a partner to it?"

334

"It wasn't Roddy's fault," she said wearily, "it was just bad luck. The car broke down miles from anywhere and we couldn't get help . . . We tried but there was no alternative."

"You were together in that damned motor all night?"

For the first time since he had challenged her, she could smile.

"No, not in the motor, Paul. We found somewhere a little more comfortable."

She had not said this with the intention of goading him but he reacted as if she had, taking her by the arm so that at once the smile left her eyes. "Please don't act like that, Paul!" and she wrenched herself free yet still contrived to give the impression that she was in control of herself. She said, more patiently, "Do we really have to go on with this, Paul? Are you interested in chapter and verse?"

"Yes I am," he shouted, "what husband wouldn't be?"

"Very well then. There was a pheasant hide close by that offered some kind of shelter. We lit a fire and stayed there until it was light. Then a cart came along and pulled us on to the main road and on a hill Roddy managed to start the motor so we got home about breakfast time. It wasn't as romantic as it sounds, just the kind of thing that might happen to any pair of travellers. At least, I thought so at the time."

"And that's all?"

For the first time she seemed to resent his questions and her jaw hardened. "What am I supposed to read into that? That Roddy is my lover? Is that what you're trying to make me say?" He was so taken aback by this that it was plain to her he had no clear idea what he believed and again she felt compassion for him, although it astonished her to discover that a man could share her life for more than a year but learn so little that was important about her.

"Roddy wasn't my lover, then or at any time, but if you can't bring yourself to believe that there's nothing I can do about it, Paul. I'm sorry, but there it is," and she walked past him and out of the room.

He stood there cursing himself and her; himself for his ham-fisted approach, her for allowing herself to be squired by a man whose incompetence involved women in compromising situations. For it was a compromising situation, as even she had tacitly admitted by withholding the facts from him, although he did not doubt her innocence for a moment. There was no reason, however, why anyone else should believe in it; Farmer Venn, for instance, or the carter who

335

found them, or even John Rudd, whose evasiveness regarding the incident he now recalled. The thought of another man spending the night in a pheasant hide with his wife annoyed him but it did not frighten him, as it might have scared a man married to an unpredictable woman. For Grace was predictable, at least as regards fundamentals. She had always been candid with him, even when he would have secretly preferred her not to be and it was this that baffled him, the fact that, but for Venn's chance remark in the pub, he might never have discovered that she had spent a night in the woods with the type of man likely to boast about the experience. It was the thought of Roddy, and the ease with which he had captured and held her interest from the moment he came honking up the drive, that crystallised his resentment and it was not resentment against her for a single indiscretion but for their failure, after more than a year, to achieve harmony as individuals. She was his wife in bed and about the house and garden but beyond these narrow limits they shared nothing and while, for some men, this was enough to make a marriage work, for him it was not. Here he was, striving to make a way of life for both of them, while she continued, in her secret way, to deride him and the Roddy incident, so trivial in itself, emphasised the cleavage. He thought, wretchedly, "If this divergence continues there can be no real happiness for either of us! God knows, I've been patient but where has patience led me? To within a few inches of being cuckolded by a lady-killer who uses a blasted motor instead of a bouquet. I'll be damned if I give way again, the way I did over the Potter affair, the election, and everything else that gives purpose to my being here!" and he flung himself into the office and tried to cool his temper assaulting the accumulation of work in the desk-trays.

Yet, as a measure of calmness returned to him, he did not relent towards her or not in the real sense. When he went upstairs about eleven o'clock she was reading in bed and he was still inclined to deliver an unrehearsed ultimatum and would probably have done so had she not forestalled him by laying the book aside, looking across at him mildly, and saying, "It was very wrong of me not to have made a point of telling you, Paul. Will you believe me if I say I'm genuinely sorry about that?" and again he felt he had lost the initiative. He said, "Yes, of course I believe you. I realise you have far more dignity than to let a man like Rudd take advantage of you but that isn't the real issue, Grace!" He was standing at the foot of the bed, feet astride

336

and hands behind his back, and for a moment it was all she could do to stop herself laughing at his unconscious caricature of an outraged husband as depicted by Mrs. Braddon or Mrs. Henry Wood. The moment passed, however, for he went on, "It's your whole attitude to our life down here, to what I'm bent on doing and what I've set my heart on. I don't just mean the political aspect but everything, the estate, the attempt to . . . well . . . to *create* something lasting and rewarding."

"I've never concealed the truth from you about that," she said. "You know very well I could never see it through your eyes, Paul."

"You could try!"

"I have tried, far harder than you imagine."

"You haven't tried hard enough, Grace! Take this election; you aren't committed to the Party but I am and as your husband I'm entitled to at least a pretence of support from you."

"I've never been the least good at pretending, Paul. That's something you should have learned by now."

"But damn it, lots of wives aren't deeply interested in what their husbands are doing but they make some kind of show. They stand beside them once in a while!"

She said, slowly, "I don't think it's much use prolonging this argument, Paul, at least, not in your present mood. Perhaps it won't seem so vital in the morning!" and she reached out an arm with the object of turning her bedside lamp out.

"Leave that light alone!" he snapped. "I tell you this *is* vital, Grace, and it won't seem less so in the morning! Are you prepared to discuss it or aren't you?"

He had never addressed her in this tone and she was more astonished than hurt, probing among the probable reasons for the loss of his sense of humour and the male tenderness that had been his most endearing characteristic. She was angry because hectoring always angered her yet she retained a very real regard for his sincerity and it was this that kept her temper in check. They faced one another in silence for a moment and it was as though each hesitated to push the quarrel further but then it seemed to her that so they might stand for ever, unless she made a gesture, something that, however inappropriate, would restore the delicate balance of their relationship. She said, "That ballet company, Paul, they are due in Bristol on Thursday for two nights so I wrote off for tickets. I think you badly need a change and I'm sure it would help us put this nonsense

337

behind us before we start saying unforgivable things to one another. Will you take me, as you promised?"

It was probable that, had the approach been made earlier, he would have surrendered but he was under no illusions as to what surrender would mean. It would be the final acceptance of a measure of spiritual isolation down the years ahead and they were still young, and there were many years, too many to renounce all hopes of the full partnership on which he had set his heart. He said, miserably, "Thursday is eve-of-poll and Friday is polling day. I couldn't be away from here until Saturday but that doesn't mean you can't go, if you have to. It seems to me, however, that we could make a better start by you joining me on the platform at the rally on Thursday. You do what you think best, Grace," and he picked up his robe and walked out of the room, making his way along the corridor to the guestroom beyond the nursery. Simon's cot was visible through the half-open door with a night-light burning under a pink glass between cot and door. He hesitated outside but he did no more than glance inside. At that moment the child did not seem to belong to either of them.

v

The eve-of-poll rally was scheduled to open with a small-fry warm-up at seven-thirty. Paul, and several other local speakers, had undertaken to keep the audience occupied until nine o'clock, the earliest hour the candidate could be expected to arrive with the Great Man, for Lloyd George had wired that he would cover the last five miles of the journey by four-horse brake and act as chairman for Grenfell on the last stage of his eve-of-poll tour. The Tory Party had not succeeded in getting anyone of comparable weight into the West and Grenfell's foresight had baulked them of the opportunity to hold an equally big rally for he had booked the only large hall months ago and the opposition was reduced to an open-air gathering in the cattle market. Liberal luck was in flow during those last few days for the weather turned dull and showery, to the delight of the nine hundred ticket-holders queueing outside the Drill Hall hours before the doors were opened.

Paul, as chairman, welcomed the responsibility thrust upon him, for at least it kept thoughts of Grace at bay and when the meeting commenced and he faced the difficult task of controlling a restive audience (in addition to a few hecklers who had slipped in with forged tickets),

338

his nervous energy was fully deployed. He had never addressed a meeting of this size or importance, certainly not without Grenfell's professional support. He was no more than adequate as public speaker but tonight he was better than he imagined for all that was needed was a summary of the candidate's achievements in local government, his fitness for wider horizons and the unique treat in store for everyone present—that of seeing and hearing the most celebrated firebrand in the country.

Paul himself had been looking forward to the occasion, for Lloyd George's brazen attacks upon the Boer War had made him a byword among the troops overseas and since then hardly a day had passed without examples of his wit, impudence and debating skill providing headlines for the newspapers. It was known, for instance, that he had attacked privilege in a hundred dynamic speeches, that he had hounded Joe Chamberlain up hill and down dale, had trounced the brewers financing the Tories, had even challenged the Lords and cocked a snook at Royalty, generally keeping the country in an uproar. Grenfell's success in getting such a lion to the remote provinces was the best card he could have played and as soon as news of the visit was made public the betting on a Liberal victory shortened from five-to-four to two-to-one.

The stewards, to Paul's relief, soon disposed of the scattered hecklers and the stop-gap speakers, inveighing against the sins of the Government and howling for Free Trade and Irish Home Rule, gave him a chance to scan faces in the hope of recognising Grace among the converted. It was just possible, he told himself, that she had taken advantage of his order to Chivers to bring the carriage and pair into town by the time the meeting began and, being Grace, she might have entered the hall by the speakers' door and taken her place among the anonymous at the back. They had not reopened the quarrel during the last few days but had said very little to one another during the brief intervals that he had been at home. He thought it possible that she might have gone to Bristol by herself but more likely remained at home, nursing her imagined grievances. At last he saw Chivers sidle in by the platform door and take his stand behind one of the side benches and then there was a stir at the back of the hall and a great shout went up as Grenfell marched down the centre aisle and behind him, hardly able to progress because of the hysterical surge on either side, came the Great Man himself, short, thick-set, smiling and apparently well satisfied with his reception. As he mounted the

339

platform the audience threw off all restraint, rising to their feet and roaring a welcome so that Paul, after a formal handshake, indicated by gesture that it was useless to begin a speech of introduction and that Grenfell must take over from here on. Grenfell was given an almost equally enthusiastic reception but wisely limited his speech to a simple statement of his intentions if returned the following day. Then, to the accompaniment of another prolonged roar, he ushered Lloyd George forward and the famous Welshman began to weave his spell about the hall, his first words compelling a hush that seemed frightening after such a din.

He began very quietly, his soft, persuasive voice seeming to reach out and caress the rows of upturned faces, as he spoke of the certain dawn of the Celtic revival, of the kinship of Welshmen and West-countrymen, of the rising clamour for justice and security in a world of plenty that, for centuries past, had been reserved for the wealthy, the privileged and their nominees at Westminster. It was not a political address so much as an inspired fairy-tale, related by a man who not only knew every trick in the book but could use subtle inflexions and wide, graceful gestures to highlight the pathos of the story and point the way to the infinite possibilities that lay ahead for a race already the envy of every community in the world. His theme was The People, a majority poised to enter the ark of the covenant of Democracy. He extolled their patience, their courage and their determination to transform the social pattern of Britain but without —and here his voice gained volume—without resort to pike and tumbril and without endangering gains won since the ancestors of all those present had sweated as villeins on acres stolen from The People! He said that there had been an awakening among some who had been their masters for so long and that a few of the unselfish landowners (such as their young chairman tonight) had already espoused the cause and were marching with them, and at this direct reference Paul found himself hoping very much that Grace was present, so that he missed a searing comment on the enclosures of common land that must have had local relevance for a growl of anger rose up and was instantly checked by one of the speaker's swift, heaven-pointing gestures. And then Lloyd George began to speak of the candidate, turning to smile paternally upon Grenfell, asserting that he and Grenfell had much in common for both, he understood, had known what it was to hoard their pennies to buy an education and that Grenfell was the type of man so badly needed in Westminster, a man of The People, with The People's interests at heart! By this time tomorrow, he went on, "as sure as the sun will set over these beautiful Westcountry uplands", they would have a champion in Westminster whom they could trust to work selflessly and unstintingly in their interests, in their children's interests, and, above all, a man in step with the march of the twentieth century!

It was difficult to determine whether the speaker had intended to finish on this flourish for at these words the tension broke and suddenly everyone in the hall was on his feet, surging and swaying towards the platform, so that stewards, poised for such an emergency, had to rush in from all sides to head off a dangerous stampede. Paul slipped down to floor level to help and almost at once was buffeted against Chivers, who clutched at him as if he was a lifebelt and the two of them were swept involuntarily on through the exit that had been flung open to ease the pressure inside the building. Chivers said breathlessly, "God Almighty, sir, I never saw aught like this bevore! Nor my old dad neither, notwithstanding his tales o' bygone elections! I brought the trap, not the carriage, sir. The new cob would have dragged her feet all the way back after two outings, I reckon!"

"You mean the carriage has been out today?" said Paul, breathless and rather irritated by the change. "How far did Mrs. Craddock drive?"

"Why to the station, upalong," the man said, "with her heavy luggage. I would have taken her in the trap but there wasn't room to stow the baggage, sir!"

The din from the hall beat across Paul's brain like breakers and in the wild confusion about him only a word or two registered so that he took Chivers by the arm and dragged him round to the rear of the hall, where the uproar was partially subdued. Bewilderment made him sound furious. "What happened, Chivers? Never mind about what's going on in there, just explain why you brought the trap instead of the brougham, as I ordered!"

Chivers peaked face stared up at him in the glow of the gas lamp above the platform entrance. The man's wits seemed lost in the noise and excitement.

"It's like I said, sir, I had to use both cobs for the brougham and I didn't reckon they could stand the fifteen-mile trip here and back tonight, not after taking Mrs. Craddock up over the moor to the station! I know you give orders for the brougham, sir, but there wasn't room in the trap for Madam's luggage."

The gist of the groom's stuttered explanation filtered through to him. Grace had needed the brougham to convey luggage to Sorrel Halt and she would not have taken heavy luggage for a two-day trip to Bristol. The transport of her and her trunks in the brougham, instead of the trap, could only mean one thing. She had left home for a prolonged period.

The effort needed to absorb the shock was the more difficult inasmuch as he was prevented from advertising astonishment or alarm to Chivers, who seemed no more than puzzled by his master's failure to excuse his switch of vehicles. Paul said, quickly, "Mrs. Craddock must have changed her plans, she intended going on Saturday. She probably left a message with Mrs. Handcock." And then, sharply, "Bring the trap round here now. We shall be going home in a few minutes," and he climbed the steps into the band-room behind the platform, shouldering his way through a crowd of party workers until he saw Grenfell standing talking to the treasurer. He said, briefly, "I must have a word with you at once, James!" and they edged into the scullery where the Women's League were brewing tea in huge urns and here they could hardly see one another for steam.

"I shall have to go home at once, James," Paul said. "I'm sorry but I can't avoid it. You can manage without me now, can't you?"

Grenfell, struck by his expression, said, "It's nothing serious I hope, Paul?" and Paul replied, "Serious to me, Jimmy! Grace has left home. We had a quarrel, partly over this business, but I never dreamed . . . well, I can't burden you with my domestic troubles at a moment like this, I just wanted you to know I couldn't stay and may not be able to get over tomorrow."

He was grateful for the man's serenity. Most people, he thought, would have plagued him with questions and offered a choice of fatuous possibilities but all Grenfell said was, "Of course, and please don't worry about me. It's decided now one way or the other and we've got all the transport we need for tomorrow. I'll get in touch with you the moment I can and I'm sorry, Paul, truly sorry."

He had no opportunity to say more for one of the local secretaries spotted him through the steam and shouted, "Hi, there, Jimmy! There's to be a torchlight procession! They're getting drag-ropes on the wain now!" and Paul thought, "What the devil am I doing here anyway? How childish it all seems, and how vulgar and noisy!" and he thrust his way into the cool night air, half-running down to the Close and standing at the junction of Angel and Resurrection

342

Streets, until Chivers should appear with the trap. He was sweating and trembling and the dull roar coming from the Drill Hall was like the clash of gongs inside his head. He thought, savagely, "I must get hold of myself! I mustn't let Chivers see what's really happened! It would be all over the estate by morning and suppose there was nothing in it? Suppose she had just decided to take a trip to town and give this idiotic quarrel a chance to blow over or teach me a lesson?" Yet he knew that this was not so, that there was a measure of finality in what she had done and that it would take all his tact and persuasion and pleading to induce her to return on even the old terms. The certainty of this made him grind his teeth for he now saw himself humiliated as never before in the face of every man, woman and child in the Valley; a squire who had stepped into the shoes of the Lovells and had been deserted by his own wife, herself a Lovell.

The steady clip of the cob's shoes on the cobbles made him aware of Chivers' approach and he climbed on to the box, saying gruffly, "I'll drive and for God's sake let's get away from this pandemonium!" and Chivers glanced at him curiously. He was not a sensitive man but was puzzled to find the Squire in such an ill-humour after such a personal triumph. He said, respectfully, as they descended the hill outside the town, "They say Grenfell will win, sure enough, sir. If 'ee does it'll be your doing as much as his!"

"He'll win right enough," Paul grunted, "but tonight I've had enough of it, Chivers! Let's get on home, let's get clear of it!" and he whipped the cob into a trot as they breasted the level stretch that led on to the first fold of the moor.

CHAPTER THREE

I

ALL that autumn and the winter that followed there was a conspiracy of sympathy in the Valley. Nobody could have said how it communicated itself to Paul, or how and where it originated but it was there, perhaps the first bittersweet fruits of his stay among them. It was this, more than anything, that encouraged him to hold on.

He owed little enough to time or to the counsel of the more articulate of his friends, men like John Rudd, James Grenfell or even Uncle Franz, who wrote several sympathetic letters before the one that brought Paul post-haste to London. It was as well, perhaps, that this letter did not arrive until spring, for by then the link between himself and the people of the Valley had helped him to climb to his feet again and take stock of the future. Without it he might have continued to brood until his thoughts festered and destroyed him.

It was strange, in view of his active role in the election, that he should have been one of the last to learn of James Grenfell's resounding victory at the polls. It was Mrs. Handcock who enlightened him long after he had arrived home to find no note and no message, nothing but half-empty wardrobes and a dressing-table swept clean of feminine clutter. She had gone, and that was all that could be said. Gone, God alone knew where, and although reason told him that this was monstrous and ridiculous, that it was the gesture of a hysterical woman and that she was not given to theatrical gestures, he was certain in his own mind that she would never come back and that threats and promises would leave her unmoved. For this was the sum total of the little she had taught him of herself.

It was pathetically plain that Mrs. Handcock had no idea of the finality of what had happened, was unaware that there had been more than a lovers' tiff between them. She bustled in with his breakfast the day after the election announcing, "Well, you won so I yer!" and when he replied with a noncommital grunt she decided that he was disappointed with the statistics of the victory and waddled out again, seeking out Horace for further enlightenment. Horace, with his

344

sensitive nose for scandal, guessed the source of Squire's ill-humour at once.

"Tiz about her running off, Ada," he confirmed, rubbing the nose that made him the Shallowford oracle, "tiz her doin' an' tiz taaken the 'eart out o' the boy! Mark my words, Ada, tiz a bigger up-and-a-downer than you give me to understand! They've had but a rare ole bust-up, and us baint heard the last of it!"

She soon realised that he was right. Day after day, as Paul lounged about the house, she noticed that he had been at the decanter during office hours, that the swing had gone from his step, and that when he addressed any member of the staff there was a hesitancy in voice and manner that belonged to his first uncertain days among them.

Then, after John Rudd had rushed off and reappeared a day or so later with his motor-mad son in tow, the alarming truth spread through kitchen, stable-yard and gardens, whence it crossed the paddocks to the Home Farm and into the Valley beyond, rumours that crept along belly to ground and the first of these was also the most obvious, involvement with the agent's son. Soon, however, there were fresh rumours, the most persistent being the refusal of Squire's wife to have another child and, when Horace Handcock pooh-poohed this, came whispers of a lover or lovers in London. Finally the Valley found itself discussing the most bizarre explanation of all—a bitter cleavage of political thought, brought to the surface by the triumph of the Valley Liberals.

It was natural that Paul should think of Roddy first and just as understandable that John Rudd should deny it and set about proving his point. Nothing would stop him hurrying off to Portsmouth and bringing his son back like a fugitive under escort. Roddy was scared, not by the threat of scandal but by his father's attitude for he had never seen him so truculent and vindictive but he had no trouble persuading him that he was innocent of any part in Grace Craddock's abdication, saying that during their drives she had never spoken disloyally of Paul and Rudd realised the boy himself was astonished by what had happened. For all that he insisted on Roddy confronting Paul and they met, the three of them, in the library, an hour after father and son had returned. By this time however Roddy was exasperated and said, indignantly, "I give you my word of honour, Mr. Craddock, I haven't set eyes on your wife since I left here! She hasn't written or communicated with me in any way and she doesn't even know my address." Then, seeing Paul and his father exchange

345

glances, he added, sulkily, "Mrs. Craddock isn't the slightest bit interested in me if that is any consolation to you!"

It was not for Paul, feeling that he had been made to look even more ridiculous by his agent's confrontation, had to apologise on Rudd's behalf and thank Roddy for coming right across country on such a fool's errand. He realised then that he had been a fool to suspect the boy. He was not the kind of man to hold Grace's interest for more than a day or so, and her temporary absorption with him had its origin more in the motor than its owner.

After Roddy had gone Rudd spoke very frankly. "I did what I could to warn you when this began," he declared, "and I say this even though I realise that to come between a man and his wife is unforgivable! She never did belong here, Paul, any more than the Lovells belonged! It was no more to her than a pleasant place to spend a summer's day and as to loyalty, as people like you understand it, no member of that family ever possessed any! It's not their fault, I suppose. At fifty I've come to realise people can't help their temperaments but if I was in your shoes, hard as it sounds, I should wipe the slate, boy! I wouldn't waste an hour looking for her!"

Paul took this harsh advice more impassively than Rudd had anticipated, saying, "That's easy enough to say, John, for you never trusted her, did you? As for me, I happen to be in love with her, although I fully appreciate all you say about the streak in the family. It's a kind of congenital amorality, an opting out of the ordinary rules that most of us take for granted. Old Sir George, that boy Ralph of his, Bruce Lovell, and now Grace prove as much. But there were times, many times, when I thought she was fond of me, or at all events respected me."

"Well, I'll tell you something else," Rudd said, unhappily. "I never trusted her or her me but I was beginning to think I was prejudiced and although you may not believe it this gave me a good deal of satisfaction, if only for your sake! And she did respect you but in a way you might find it difficult to understand. I believe she could stand outside and see what you were trying to do down here and although nothing could convince her it was worth doing she could still admire the helping hand you gave people like Will Codsall and Elinor, Eveleigh and his family, and even Smut Potter, in spite of the friction he caused between you. However, people can admire an effort without wanting to take part in it. I've cleared Roddy and that's a personal relief to me!" and he left, feeling he had presumed enough.

346

John Rudd's logic yielded Paul small satisfaction, for his main purpose now seemed as sterile as Grace had always regarded it and his work no more than a dullish method of passing time and tiring himself physically. Grenfell's counsel brought him even less comfort than Rudd's. He drove over the night after the rally, when his place was at the polling booths, and was frank enough to confirm Paul's growing belief that this was an irrevocable decision on Grace's part.

"I don't think it has much to do with you personally, Paul," he said. "I believe there were far more complex reasons for her disassociating herself from what you're trying to achieve down here!"

"You're not going to tell me that women's votes are that important to her," Paul growled. "Damn it, a wife doesn't turn her back on home, husband and baby in order to march about with a banner and make a fool of herself at public meetings! Frankly, I'd prefer to hear she had left me for a lover and so would any man!"

"That's your trouble, Paul," Grenfell said seriously, "you try and rationalise every issue that presents itself. You can't do it with most political issues and you certainly can't with personal ones! Her preoccupation with the Women's Suffrage movement is a manifestation of what she feels about everything important to her, and I believe that goes for a good many of those gallant but misguided women! They want a *purpose*, Paul, like yours or mine and we have been denying them one ever since they lived in caves."

"But surely a home like this and a family is a purpose in itself?"

"It was and still is for most women but not for women like your wife! That's the price we are beginning to pay for universal education and men might find it a heavy one in the near future. It isn't *you* she is rejecting, Paul, but your whole way of life."

"You mean you suspected this might happen?"

"Not precisely this, but something less drastic perhaps."

"You said nothing!"

"Who the devil am I to criticise a man's wife to his face, Paul?"

"Yet you're now telling me, as kindly as you can, there's absolutely nothing I can do about it?"

Grenfell considered. Far more clearly than Paul he saw the wider issues confronting him and could view them free of bias. "Not at present but after an interval there may be; it would depend on all manner of things."

"What kind of things?"

"On what happens to her and to you. On how quickly the pair of you mature and on the changes in the world we live in, perhaps. She may not have the moral strength to struggle on alone. If she tried and failed, would you take her back on her own terms—freedom of action to go where she wished and to do what she liked? To make her own friends so long as she was loyal to you in the conventional sense?"

"No," he said, after a moment's hesitation, "I don't think I would, Jimmy. That isn't enough to stop a marriage like ours going sour. At least, not the kind of marriage I need so long as I stay here."

"I daresay you're right at that," said Grenfell, sighing. "God knows, your outlook as a landowner who puts human beings first and profit second is rare enough and a man needs peace in his own house to project it in this day and age! I'm desperately sorry about this, Paul, but not as sorry as I would have been if she had gone off with another man. All I can add to that is to tell you that I owe this seat to your loyalty and single-mindedness and I won't ever forget that! If ever you need me I should be more hurt than I can say if you didn't call on me!" and he shook hands warmly and left.

Good enough advice but it did little to help. To Paul, through the rest of the summer, the Valley seemed stale and profitless, and this in itself was strange because she had been such a quiet, unobtrusive person. Thirza, in her new role of Nannie, now took undisputed charge of Simon and was fiercely jealous even of Mrs. Handcock's interference. Rudd saw to it that he had plenty of work and at length he taught himself to stop anticipating the post. It was now, he soon realised, known throughout the Valley why she had left him and that she was unlikely to return but at least, as time wore on, he could stop speculating on what they said to one another when he rode by, or passed on having spoken to one or other of them on a routine matter. It was during these daily excursions that he became conscious of their mute concern, although it was months before he was able to distinguish between sympathy and a conspiracy of embarrassed silence. Throughout the autumn and a cheerless Christmastide he wasted few words on them, saying what he had to say then riding off with a nod. Yet his sullenness and bitterness was contained and perhaps it was this that won their respect. Slowly, and imperceptibly, he was able to translate their curiosity into warmth, so that he became aware of a kinship with them that had not existed in his most sanguine days before his marriage, when he had thought of himself as a well-meaning, bungling amateur and hoped that they would make generous

348

allowances for his inexperience. Something was reaching out to him from all of them and he noted and welcomed it in all parts of the Valley. It was there in the twinkle of Martha Pitts' brown eyes, when she insisted he stayed to a meal and ate a little of "Henry's gurt duck". It was recognisable in Eveleigh's stolid respect as he submitted his harvest figures and marshalled his little regiment of children to present home-made Christmas cards to "Young Squire". He found it in Elinor Codsall's voice, when she thanked him (as she did almost every time she saw him) for helping her rescue Will from Four Winds, and it was present in Sam Potter's determination to name his second daughter Grace, notwithstanding, as he explained to Joannie, that "Young Squire's missis 'as up an' left 'un, the poor, mazed crittur, not knowing a gude man when one be lyin' bezide 'er!" These subtle communications of their friendship would have gone unnoticed by anyone who had grown up among them but to Paul they were the first evidence that he was accepted, that his good intentions were recognised and that he was already regarded by them not as a brash young man with a bushel of fancy ideas but as the natural leader of the community. It was this realisation that encouraged him to look back and reconsider Grenfell's advice, and it was the same current of unspoken sympathy that enabled him to read Celia Lovell's startling letter objectively.

II

Celia's second letter arrived towards the end of January, more than six months after Grace had left. Her first, replying to his angry demands for news of his wife's whereabouts had merely annoyed him for he concluded from it that Celia was not much surprised by what had occurred and that it was not, in her view, an astonishing thing for her stepdaughter to have abandoned home, husband and a six-months-old child after an apparently trivial disagreement. The letter, moreover, expressed a neutrality that he would not have expected from her in view of her eagerness to arrange the marriage and he thought, bitterly, "Damn the woman! She might at least have said something sympathetic, even if she does make it very plain she won't accept the job of umpire!" He had not written again and was therefore surprised by a message from Coombe Bay one grey morning, informing him that she had returned to the Valley and would be glad if he would call as soon as convenient. He rode over that same afternoon but as he stood outside the door awaiting an answer to the bell his mind returned to the first occasion he had stood here, also in response to Celia's urgent invitation; it seemed to him more like fifty than two years ago. She received him graciously when the trim maid showed him up the narrow stair to her little boudoir, looking out across the restless winter sea but he was in no mood for polite preliminaries and said, bluntly, "I could make no sense at all of your first letter and can only suppose that you now regard the marriage as a mistake on everybody's part!"

She looked at him with her head on one side and then, laughing heartily, took his hand in both of hers and kissed him on the cheek.

"Paul," she said, "you might have frightened Grace with that baronial approach but it doesn't impress me in the least! Sit down, unbutton your coat and tell me exactly what led up to it. More important still, tell me how you got along *before* it happened."

He was nonplussed by her heartiness but her charm began to re-assert itself after a few moments so that he found himself thinking not so much of Grace or his own situation, but how she managed to look so young and attractive. He discovered too that he envied her assurance, reflecting that it was no wonder she had taken his news so lightly for there was so much experience behind her friendly brown eyes. He told her, without embroidery, of the passive period of their marriage and the sense of security it had given him, and then of their two quarrels, one over Smut Potter and the other over Roddy Rudd, and their exchange of ultimatums in respect of the rally and the visit to the ballet. She was a good listener and he saw that she did not miss a point but when he had finished, describing how Grace had packed her trunks and disappeared, she said, with a smile, "I daresay that's all very relevant, Paul, but if I'm to bring you together again I shall have to know a great deal more than that! How did Grace behave as a bride, before and after Simon was born?"

It crossed his mind then that she was using the occasion to satisfy a prurient curiosity and he recalled her more than maternal approaches to him when he had called upon her the first time, and again when they had parted after the wedding and she had drawn him aside and whispered, "Don't stand any nonsense from her, Paul! Remember the old proverb—'Thou goest to a woman? Do not forget the whip!'"

Then, without understanding why, he knew that she was drawing him out for a purpose of her own, that she could tell him a great deal more if she chose but had not yet made up her mind to tell what she knew.

350

The thought put him on his guard and he said off-handedly, "Grace was a perfect wife in the way most young men look for one, although maybe 'wife' isn't the word you had in mind!"

She nodded, eagerly. "Now that's odd, but very interesting! It knocks the bottom out of a theory I had about her before you were married."

He said, impatiently, "Look here, Mrs. Lovell, I'm only interested in getting her to behave like a reasonable human being. I know she's bored down here and I'm willing to make allowances. The estate is running itself now and we could go to London occasionally and maybe visit the Continent. Damn it, I'd even buy one of those blasted motors she seems so keen on and have a telephone and electric dynamo installed, if those things are that important to her! The one thing I won't do is change my way of life and I don't think she has the right to demand that. If you know where she is—and I believe you do—you can tell her that! She made a bargain and I intend to hold her to that part of it!"

"I should have no patience with you if you didn't," Celia said, eyeing him carefully, "and the fact is, you happen to be right—I do know where she is, I saw her less than a week ago."

"She's abroad?"

"No, in London."

He got up with an air of exasperation but she motioned him to sit again, adding, "Don't rush me, Paul! I have to consider very carefully what to do, for I'm genuinely fond of you and would like nothing better than to restore her to you on your own terms. Her kind of nonsense would have been thrashed out of a young wife when I was a girl but times change and she happens to have a little money of her own, for which you can blame me. Then again, I suppose there is some kind of excuse for this silly revolt against men. She did watch her father drive her mother to suicide but perhaps you never heard about that?"

"I knew her mother drowned herself in India," Paul admitted, "but naturally I never discussed it with her."

"Perhaps you should have done, for it goes some way towards explaining her oddity. Bruce Lovell drove that poor woman to her death with his debts and women and rather special brand of cruelty. I ought to know, although I didn't hear of it until it was too late."

"You mean that Grace, seeing that happen, conceived a contempt for men? That this suffrage nonsense is a kind of revenge?"

351

"What other reason could there be for an intelligent girl like her trading security and comfort for a fad?"

He knew that he could never convince a woman of Celia's background that some people might consider themselves more deeply committed to a political principle than a trend in fashion, so all he said was, "I made a point never to quarrel with her political views. After all, she has as much right to hers as I have to mine."

"Quite," said Celia, "but yours haven't led to the police court!"

He sat up, alarmed and astounded. "Police court? When?"

"She would be in gaol right now if I hadn't read of her case in the papers and paid her fine, very much against her will. These women hate to be deprived of their martyrdom."

"Grace was actually charged in court? What the devil for?"

"Throwing a bag of flour at a Cabinet Minister or so I understand. It's all so futile! What would they do with the vote if they got it? March around in hideous clothes campaigning for one nincompoop or the other I imagine. But perhaps you, as a Radical, sympathise with them?"

"I've never been convinced," he said, "but I'm damned if I think that issue is worth my marriage! Besides, Grace's desertion hasn't all that much to do with votes for women. I realise now that it's more of a repudiation of our way of life down here, a kind of compulsion to see everything new as miraculous and everything old as fuel for a bonfire. In that respect we should never see eye to eye but it need not prevent us from leading a normal married life? Do you see any prospect of convincing her of that."

"Well, I suppose we could try," she said, sighing. "Would you be prepared to travel up to town and talk to her if I could arrange it?"

"Yes I would," he said eagerly, "I should be glad of the opportunity. I don't think I would have been but now—well, I've always regarded dignity as a rather negative virtue Mrs. Lovell and I threw mine away when I bought myself a leading position among people who had been farming land since the Conquest."

She gave him a long, affectionate glance and once again he was conscious of something frankly sensual in her contemplation. "You know, Paul," she said at length, "the thing I admire most about you is your lack of complacency! I think Grace is an absolute fool. You're a real man, and you'll be a big one hereabouts one of these days! Will you stay to supper?" and when he declined she looked very disappointed and said, with a lift of her elegant shoulders, "Oh very well, hurry home and stick your nose in your beloved dirt! I'll write the moment I can arrange something!"

She kissed him then, warmly on both cheeks, inclining her body towards him with rather more pressure than necessary and he recognised the perfume that Grace used. For a moment he was half-inclined to accept her invitation, and perhaps demonstrate his contempt for personal pride and she would have welcomed him, he was sure of that. The vague prospect of a reconciliation, however, caused him to recollect himself and he thanked her, turning for the door. Little, he reflected, had been achieved, but enough to make him feel more cheerful than he had felt for months.

III

January passed with a spell of mild, muggy weather and white, drenching mists came in from the sea, shrouding those parts of the estate free of timber. All along the Valley, except for brief periods about noon, the clouds remained dense and almost motionless. The mist muffled the continuous whine of the Home Farm saw and moon-faced cattle loomed out of the fog along the river road, their hooves making sounds like soggy corks being withdrawn from bottles as they squelched across the half-seen landscape. Paul had resumed the rhythm of his work by then and was drawing up plans for a communal marketing scheme that he had been pondering a year or more but with the arrival of hard frosts in late February, and flurries of snow and sleet beating in from the north-east, it was difficult for busy men like Arthur Pitts, Eveleigh and the Derwents to assemble and exchange views on prospects of pooling resources instead of competing for the Whinmouth and Paxtonbury markets. Travel along icebound roads was irksome and hunting, where they might have conferred in the field, was at a standstill. Celia kept in touch, writing once from the village and twice from London but apparently it was not proving easy to locate Grace, and although Paul thought of her frequently some of the ache had gone from his heart and he was able, for long periods during the day, to put her out of mind altogether. John Rudd took to spending his evenings in the library again and once James Grenfell, down from London, dined with them, talking of events that might have been happening on the moon for all they affected life in the Valley. He said that the Tsar's régime in Russia was tottering under the stresses of revolution at home and a disastrous dispute with the Japanese in the Far East. Grenfell, to

Paul's amazement, backed the Japs to win the war that was on the point of breaking out but said he had scant sympathy with Russia, a nation that was the social equivalent of England about the time of the Wars of the Roses. The M.P. also discussed home affairs and prophesied an early general election, with a landslide victory for the Liberals but when Paul asked him if the cause of women's suffrage was likely to make progress under a radical government Grenfell said it would not, for no government could allow itself to be blackmailed and blackmail was the strategy of the militant group dominating the movement.

They sat talking until the small hours and Paul was grimly amused to note the subtle changes wrought by a few months in what Grenfell now called (rather self-consciously) "My Workshop". He was already a little thinner and a little greyer, Paul thought, but some of his tolerance had departed and Paul now thought it unlikely that he would suffer fools gladly. There was also a slight formalism in his manner and in his ways of pronouncing judgments, as though his opinions were unchallengeable statements of fact that no one in his senses could dispute. It was all barely noticeable but it went some way towards confirming Paul's distrust of professional politicians, who, once translated from candidate to Member, seemed to take on the pedagoguery of schoolmasters unable to distinguish between children and adults. Perhaps Grenfell himself was conscious of this for, on saying good-bye, he suddenly seemed less sure of himself as he said, hesitantly, "You've heard no more of Grace I suppose?" and when Paul told him there was still a possibility of a reconciliation he perked up at once exclaiming, "That's splendid! As for me, to be honest I'm sometimes very homesick for the Valley and I wonder she isn't! It can be disappointing up there at times. One begins hopefully enough but inside the House one sometimes has a curious sensation of having joined an all-party conspiracy against the people we're supposed to represent! However, I hope I'll outgrow this when we are a government and not an opposition," and he climbed into his trap and rattled away down the drive, leaving Paul with a conviction that Grenfell had found travelling more rewarding than arrival.

A day or so later, when the weather had mended somewhat, Meg Potter arrived sitting sidesaddle on the cart-horse they had loaned Tamer, fording the swollen stream as unconcernedly as if it had been a brook. She told him that Tamer was laid up with sciatica, that she and the girls were busy with spring-sowing, and that she had heard

354

Smut had been transferred to Paxtonbury gaol. "He's mentioned you in every scribble us've had," she said, "so he'd take it kindly if you could bring yourself to go up to that bad place, Squire." Paul said he would be glad to, for such visits as Smut had been allowed during the first two years of his sentence had been made by Meg herself. Twice Paul had loaned her the trap and she had driven right across Dartmoor and over the Tamar to Bodmin gaol, to spend a bare thirty minutes with her son, and Paul realised that she was relieved he was now back in Devon, for at least this was an earnest of his ultimate return to the Valley.

In a day or so Ikey Palfrey was due to start his first term at High Wood, a small public school in the north of the county, so Paul let him accompany him to Paxtonbury and wait with the trap whilst he approached the red-brick prison and presented his visitor's ticket. The vast bulk and silence of the ugly building oppressed him, and he wondered what on earth he could say to a man who had been locked up in such a place for more than a hundred weeks but when the wicket gate was opened and he was escorted to the waiting-room, curiosity conquered his distaste and he looked around with interest, watching a group of convicts at work in the courtyard with besoms and drain rods, and noting the blank faces of the other visitors who lined the bench like patients in a dentist's surgery. Eventually he was conducted to a low-ceilinged room furnished with a long table and divided down the middle by a wire mesh and after another delay a warder jangling keys at his belt entered, escorting a small, shrunken man in a mountebank's jacket and breeches of coarse canvas. For a moment Paul failed to recognise this clownish creature as the spry, suntanned poacher, with the insolent glance and soft, springy step, for Smut looked as if he had been confined in a small, sunless cupboard for weeks and hardly a trace of his natural ebullience survived. There were still irregular areas of brown on his cheeks but they were mere blotches, emphasising the moist pallor of his skin, and only the light blue eyes that lit up on seeing Paul recalled the Smut Potter he had met his first day in the Valley.

Smut said, in an odd, jerky voice, "It was rare gude of 'ee to coom, Squire! Mother zed you would, tho' I didn' taake it as zo 'till I zeed 'ee zittin' there!"

"Well, at least you're back in the county and only a few miles from the Valley," Paul said, feeling uncertain of his own voice. "What kind of work do they give you, Smut?"

355

Potter winked and his mouth pretended to grin. "Well, tiz better'n downalong in Bodmin, Squire," he said, "where us is sewing they ole bags most o' the time. I'm a trusty now, you zee, an' I work in the gardin, zo tiz altogether diff'rent. A man can turn his faace to the sky every so often an' smell the sea when wind's in the west! Oh, tiz well enough now, Squire, and they zay if I minds me P's and Q's I'll be gettin' more'n twelmonth off an' be backalong in just over the year. How be things in the Vale, Squire? Mother, 'er can't write, an' tiz six months zince I zeed her, that time she come over the moor to Bodmin."

"Things are going along very well," Paul told him, "especially in the Dell. Tamer and the two older girls have been raising sugar-beet and I'm going to have Eph Morgan mend the roof before you come home!"

"Arr," said Smut, absently, "youm gude to us varmints, Squire! Mebbe, if someone like you had been backalong when I was a tacker I wouldn't have taaken the wrong turn I did! Do 'ee ever zee that Gilroy keeper I drubbed?"

"Yes, I've seen him," Paul said, "and he's not even showing a scar. Gilroy's made him head keeper so you'd best stay our side of the Teazel when you do come out!"

"I'll do that right enough," Smut said earnestly, "for I woulden chance more time in a plaace like this, Squire! Tiz never worth it, an' they'll all tell 'ee the zame but mind you, most o' the ole rascals will be back in again zoon enough for they've no other means of earnin' a livin'!"

It was curious, Paul thought, how carefully Smut disassociated himself from the ordinary convict and he wondered if he thought of himself as a felon, or rather as an honest poacher who had fallen on hard times.

"You really do intend to finish with poaching, Smut?" he asked and Smut made a throat-crossing gesture and swore that he did indeed, and that if the Squire had meant what he said about having him back in the Valley, he would prove that the Potters could be as industrious and law-abiding as anyone in the county. "Us'll maake the Dell show a profit, even if us has to harness ole Tamer to the plough!" he added.

"Very well," Paul said, smiling, "I'll remember that! As soon as you come home we'll go to work on the Dell. I'll talk to your brother Sam and maybe we can clear part of the thicket north of the Bluff and add twenty acres to the holding. By the way, I suppose you know Sam now has a girl and a boy, and that your sister Pansy has one girl and a baby boy?"

"No, I never heard tell o' that," Smut said, with awe in his voice. "Lor bless us, to think on that! Four little tackers, in just over the two years! But then, we Potters is a rare tribe for breedin'. I dessay I've got a few around somewheres, tho' none o' the maids ever took me to court for 'em!"

It was this remark, uttered as the warder rose and brought the session to an end, that made the visit worthwhile, for in the final moment it seemed to Paul that the original Smut triumphed over the ingratiating penitent. He was hustled away and Paul went down the steps and through the wicket gate to the embankment, where Ikey trotted up and asked, in his ironed-out Paxtonbury accent, if Smut had had chains on his feet. "Good God, of course not!" Paul replied, but as he said this he thought, "But they still treat convicts like half-tamed beasts and dress them as buffoons. It's a pity they can't be spared a few shreds of human dignity," and was silent half the way home.

When the trap began to descend to the river, however, he cheered up, reflecting that he had left Smut something to think about and to hope for and then he glanced curiously at the boy sitting on the box beside him thinking, "Well, Grace and the *avant-garde* can sneer as much as they like but there is some point in my being here! Would the Lovells have given Smut Potter a second thought? And would this boy Ikey be getting a sporting chance? She might have originated the idea but she didn't stay and see it through!" and he went on to ponder the Eveleighs at Four Winds and Will and Elinor's success at Peri-winkle and then smiled at himself for seeking personal reassurance in a balance-sheet of good works. "Are you scared of going to a real school?" he asked, suddenly, and to his surprise and slight embarrass-ment the boy gathered up the reins and brought the colt to a sudden halt. He turned and met Paul's enquiring gaze steadily and Paul realised, for the first time, how greatly he had matured in the last two or three years. His skin, once fish-belly pale, was brown and healthy, his eyes were clear and his hair neatly cut, so that there was about him an air of confidence altogether different from the perkiness of the scrapyard urchin.

"Yes, Mr. Craddock, sir," he said, "I'm scared all right but you don't have to worry, I won't let you down, sir! The tutor told me all

357

the new boys got ragged and that I'm not to mind because it's an old English custom!"

He had lost, Paul noted, all traces of his thin Cockney accent and it came as rather a shock to realise that he had almost forgotten the poor little devil during his own troubles. The boy, he thought, could hold his own anywhere, for the toughness and resilience of the street Arab was still there under the looks and manners of a conventional lad on the point of exchanging prep. school for public school. He said, as though to excuse his recent neglect, "Well, I've had troubles of my own lately as you've probably heard and that's the reason why I appeared to lose interest in what you were doing over at the crammer's. You remember it was Mrs. Craddock's idea that you went in the first place?"

"Yes," the boy said, "I'm not likely to forget that, sir," and then more hesitantly, "Will she ever be coming back, sir?"

"I don't know, Ikey, probably not," he said gruffly, and Ikey taking the hint, shook out the reins and they moved down from the moor to the swollen Sorrel in a rather embarrassed silence.

Wild daffodils and yellow iris showed on the margins of the half-flooded meadows and the blackbirds were noisy in the Hermitage thickets. The sun, which seemed to have been away visiting another solar system since autumn, had returned to play a spring game with the darting current and a bay hunter, out to grass on the Four Winds side of the stream, whinnied a casual greeting to the cob, before throwing up her heels and galloping madly across the levels. Paul said, "Tell me, Ikey, are you ever homesick for London now?" and the boy replied, "No, sir, never! I don't think I should ever want to go there again. This is my home now, sir."

"Me too," Paul said and the kinship that had been born during their first ride down this road during the coronation summer, suddenly reasserted itself as he thought, "I must write to Uncle Franz and find out more about the boy. If there's a likelihood of Grace coming back, I'm damned if I won't think about adopting him officially for he is the only soul about here who shares my feeling for the Valley and that makes him a kind of heir!" They said no more until they were passing under the long park wall for each was absorbed in the familiarity of the scene, the swift river and wide stretch of meadows to the right, the sweep of Priory Wood to the left. Then Paul said, "There's something else, Ikey, I don't know whether your tutor mentioned it but at a school like High Wood they will expect you to have some

358

kind of domestic background. Did he ever talk to you about that?"

"He did mention it, sir, but said it was a matter for you and Mrs. Craddock."

Paul considered. He was confident that Ikey would pass muster in all outward respects but he recalled his own limitations as an officer in the Yeomanry, reflecting that there was no accounting for the graduations of the English caste system and the snobberies it spawned but there it was and one either accepted it or withdrew from the game altogether.

"Do you ever write to your own parents, Ikey? Do you keep in touch with them?"

"No, sir, I don't," said the boy, unsentimentally.

"All right," said Paul, "then we shall have to do a bit of bluffing. Sooner or later the subject of your family is bound to crop up. Did you have any story in mind?"

The boy grinned, suddenly an urchin again, and said, "Well yes, sir! I was going to say my guv'nor was dead, and my mother was still living abroad. Could I say that you were . . . well . . . a kind of cousin, looking after me over here?"

"You can do better than that," Paul said, laughing, "you can tell them I'm your stepbrother and official British guardian. The word 'guardian' always seems to impress the snobs somehow. Would you like to do that?"

"I would, and thank you, sir."

"Well, then that's settled. When you leave on Tuesday do you want me to take you to school, and see you settled in?"

"If it's all the same to you, no sir," Ikey said unexpectedly. "I'd sooner take the plunge on my own, sir."

Paul glanced at him, noting the set of the jaw and his mind returned to the child's gallantry and initiative on the night Codsall had hanged himself. "By God," he thought, "that snob school is lucky to get him, even though he might be the product of a drunken docker and a Hungarian emigrant!"

"Very well," he said, "that's something for you to decide but I'll drive you as far as Paxtonbury in the brougham. We must have the brougham for an occasion like that!"

"Thank you, sir," Ikey said, "I should like that, in case any of the High Wood chaps are going by the same train."

"Any of the High Wood chaps," thought Paul, grinning. "Damn it,

359

he's half-way home already!" and they turned in at the gates and set the cob at the steep drive.

IV

As it turned out it was Chivers, the groom, who drove Ikey to Paxtonbury in the brougham that warm spring day for Paul was already on his way to London. Celia's telegram arrived the night before, delivered by a perspiring telegraph boy who had cycled all the way from Whinmouth but it told Paul very little. "Essential you are in London early morning of the third," it said. "Will meet 10.40 a.m. from Paxtonbury, Love Celia." That was all and Paul had to make what he could of it, reshuffling his programme, saying good-bye to Ikey and catching the main-line train at Sorrel Halt. Celia had a carriage waiting for him at Waterloo and he was at her town house in Devonshire Square by late afternoon finding that he was expected to stay the night, for Celia had arranged his meeting with Grace at seven-fifteen the following morning.

"Where and why so early?" he demanded but the Frenchman Daladier was present and he did not press the enquiry after Celia's warning glance. They ate dinner together, making polite conversation and afterwards the Frenchman, who seemed to live on the premises, wandered off into the billiard-room. As soon as they were alone she said, urgently, "Pierre knows nothing about the real reason for your coming and I don't want him involved, you understand? He's practising here now, and any kind of scandal would injure him. I won't have that happen, Paul!"

It was not, he reflected, the Celia who had received him at Coombe Bay in January, but a taut, nervous woman, manifestly irritated by the situation. He said, seeking to reassure her, "There's no reason why either of you should be involved. Just tell me what kind of arrangement you've made with Grace."

"I haven't made any arrangement with her," she said, sharply. "I haven't set eyes on the little fool since I paid her fine at the police court, a day or so before I saw you in Devon! The fact is . . . she's in Holloway Prison at this moment!"

"Holloway Prison? For suffragist offences? Good God, Celia, what the devil has she been up to now?"

Celia looked as if she was about to cry. "I've had the greatest trouble keeping it from him," she wailed, "he's a very perceptive man and I daresay he's guessed the truth but he's very tactful and hasn't

360

brought it into the open." She looked at Paul defiantly and he noticed that she was vulnerable and beginning to look her age. There were wrinkles under her eyes that he had never noticed before and the skin of her neck was slack. Suddenly he felt sorry for her, sorry but at the same time grateful, for it was obvious that a decision to get him to London had involved her in risks she did not care to take and that her fear of involving her lover by public scandal was real. He said, "Look here, Mrs. Lovell, don't think I'm unappreciative of what you've done. Just give me the facts and then let me go to a hotel. I'll see you aren't involved in any way. After all, this is my responsibility, not yours. How long has Grace been in gaol? And what did she go there for this time?"

She said, only slightly reassured, "There is a very militant section of this suffragist movement led by that dreadful woman Pankhurst and her daughters. It seems that Grace is one of the most irresponsible of them, she and a woman from the North, called Kenny. You must have read about them in the papers?"

Paul said, shortly, "The last I read about them they were organising a petition to the Opposition leaders, to Campbell-Bannerman, I believe but Grenfell tells me they'll get even less change from him than from Balfour!"

"That's so," she said, "but they have begun to picket the big Liberal meetings in the provinces. Up in Manchester, a month or so ago, Grace and some others climbed into a loft over the platform of a hall when Churchill was speaking. They had banners that they let down when the meeting started and were thrown out neck and crop, as you would expect them to be."

"Well?"

"Most of them went meekly enough but Grace didn't. She hit a policeman with an umbrella and was later charged with resisting arrest. She was put on probation but would you believe it she did the same thing two days later down here and this time they sentenced her to a month without the option! She comes out early tomorrow. That's why I sent for you."

"Why didn't you send for me straight away?"

"What good would that have done? She had legal representation in court and he couldn't stop her going to prison!"

"I can't understand how I didn't hear about it," he said, "it must have been in all the papers."

"She was charged under a different name. She didn't use yours or

361

her father's. She used her mother's name, 'Philimore' and I don't know what her grandfather, the canon, would have said about it if he had been living!"

"You've written to her?"

"Yes I have but she didn't even answer. I told her that I'd seen you and that you were anxious to talk things over, and asked if I should get in touch with you. Listen Paul . . . " she spoke with a kind of desperation, "if you like, you . . . you can bring her back here! I'll get Pierre to take me to the races and if you could keep her out of the way until midday, you are welcome to do that! All I ask is for time to get Pierre away before she arrives. The French can be even more censorious about this kind of thing than the English, and I just won't face the risk of losing him, you understand? I've got a right to my happiness. God knows, I earned it, with Bruce Lovell!"

"Yes you did," he said, thinking of John Rudd's comment about the Lovell streak and the misery it introduced into the lives of everyone associated with them, "but I won't risk bringing her here. I'll take her straight home. It was very good of you to go to so much trouble and I'm not sure that either of us deserve it!"

"She doesn't," Celia said, "but I don't know why you should blame yourself! Millions of women would consider themselves lucky to have had her chance and I can't forgive myself for bullying you into marrying her."

He smiled at that. "Nobody had to bully me into marrying Grace Lovell," he said, "I made up my mind to marry her the first time I saw her. As to blame, I must have gone wrong somewhere or other or perhaps there wasn't a chance from the beginning. I've got Simon, and he's part of her, and in spite of what you think I've got some pleasant memories."

He kissed her for the first time as a friend and not a relative and it amused him to see the effect, for at once she shrugged off her despondency and said, "Let's join Pierre in a drink. If he asks after Grace say something pleasantly noncommittal," and they went into the billiard-room where the big Frenchman was potting with what appeared to Paul to be the expertise of a professional. He was a heavy-jowled, phlegmatic man, more like a middle-class Englishman than a Frenchman and it was difficult to see what an elegant, fastidious woman like Celia found so engaging about him. Then it was obvious, for the surgeon put up his cue, took her hand and raised it deliberately to his lips and Celia smiled over his head and for a moment looked

362

almost girlish. She said, "My son-in-law has to be away very early. Would you like a drink before he goes up, Pierre?" The surgeon looked at him very carefully, as though assessing his chances of surviving a tricky operation and Paul thought, "He knows quite well why I'm here but he's probably got hundreds of more important secrets in his head!" They drank brandy and soda together and Paul left them listening to a scratchy Mendelssohn recording on Celia's latest extravagance, an Edison Bell phonograph. The tinny (and to Paul, wholly unmusical) sounds penetrated as far as the first landing. It was not solely his instinctive recoil from mechanical contrivances that made him aware of the mockery of the song.

She came out of a little wicket-door that might have been the twin of the one by which Paul had entered Paxtonbury Gaol and it was of Smut Potter's shrunken frame and mountebank garb that he thought as he saw her stand uncertainly under the great stone gate, a pitiful little figure against a blank and grotesque background. Then, with a sob, he dodged between carts and cabs and ran across the shining wet surface of the road towards her, expecting to see her stiffen with surprise but she did not seem in any way agog at his presence but merely smiled, politely rather than joyfully, and said, with her customary containment, "I thought it would be you, Paul. Celia isn't very good at concealing things, is she? Have you got a cab?"

He told her a cab was waiting across the road and asked if she had had breakfast.

"A sort of breakfast," she said, casually. "Smut Potter might have kept it down but I couldn't!" and a sensation of pity and desolation engulfed him, so that for a moment he felt sick and dizzy and must have showed it, for she took his hand and piloted him across the road to the side-street where the cab waited. It was an old victoria and the interior smelt like a neglected tack-room. He called to the cabby, "Anywhere! Back to the West End," and they moved off at a trot, sitting isolated from one another, like a young couple having a tiff and waiting for each other to capitulate. After a few moments he had mastered himself sufficiently to look at her, deciding with relief that she did not seem to have changed much in the months that had passed since they had parted. If twenty-eight days in Holloway had marked her in any way there was no outward sign of it. Her skin had the same wax-like transparency, her hair was neatly if plainly

363

dressed, and her eyes, reflecting the glint of morning sun after the dawn showers, were still hard and clear and blue.

He said at length, "I only heard you were there last night. I came up here expecting Celia to give me an address," and when she made no reply, "She promised to arrange a meeting between us as long ago as last January; I've been waiting to hear ever since."

She turned suddenly, swinging her small, compact body at right angles to him and looking at him with a kind of desperate resignation.

"I'm not coming back, Paul! You might as well know that at once! It was good of you to come, and I'm glad to see you, but I'm not coming back, for your sake as much as mine!"

It came as no real surprise but it had plenty of power to wound. "We can at least discuss it, can't we?" he muttered, fighting to keep the note of pleading from his voice.

"We can talk like civilised human beings, I suppose, but only until ten. After that I've got to report to H.Q."

"Report?" he said savagely. "What the devil do you mean, 'report'? Are you a private in some kind of army? Whoever you have to 'report' to can wait! We're still husband and wife and I've neither seen you nor heard of you in almost a year."

"Well, I'm sorry, Paul," she said quietly, "but I still have to report. And we *are* an army, fighting impossible odds. That's why every individual counts."

He could not trust himself to reply at once and they bowled along in silence for three or four minutes. Then he said, sourly, "I don't begin to understand you, Grace! Anyone can be absorbed in an abstract idea but not to the extent of throwing everything life has to offer on to the rubbish heap! You've got a home and a child, even if I count for nothing, and you'll never persuade me that you weren't happy down there most of the time! I'll concede the right of women to vote, I've never seriously challenged it but it can't be this important! Nothing can!"

"What about your own 'abstract idea', Paul?"

"Shallowford? That's entirely different! It doesn't hurt anyone and it doesn't make nonsense of other people's lives!"

"No, perhaps not," she said, as though debating the substance of a breakfast-table remark, "but it obsesses you just as much as mine obsesses me."

"You knew about Shallowford when you married me, Grace. It's true that I also knew you were interested in women's suffrage but

364

whereas I made it perfectly clear what I had in mind you didn't! You didn't see fit to warn me that you wanted to spend your life between committee rooms and Holloway!"

It seemed that he had scored a point for she considered some time before replying. "That's true enough, Paul, that's quite true and I suppose it puts me in the wrong. But it doesn't make any real difference who is right and who is wrong, not now that I've had a chance to look back over the past and forward into the future!" and to the cabby she called, "Take us to the Embankment and stop by Cleopatra's Needle!" and addressing Paul again, "I wonder if it's possible to make you understand? It was very wrong of me to marry you, I realise that of course, but I think it would be far more wrong to go on pretending to make the best of it, and prevent you from leading a useful life as well as me. No, Paul," as he opened his mouth to protest, "let me say what I have to. We haven't very long and we might never have another opportunity."

"But that's monstrous!" he burst out. "It makes me wonder if you understand what you're doing!"

She looked at him sharply. "You mean that I'm slightly insane? Like my mother?"

"No, I don't mean that, and don't keep twisting my words! You're as sane as anyone in London but you're allowing yourself to become the victim of a kind of mania. We could agree to differ, couldn't we? Millions of husbands and wives do, without tearing their lives up by the roots! You say you didn't love me but you gave a good imitation of love sometimes!"

"Yes," she said, "I did and in that way I still could, Paul. But it doesn't stop me from despising your whole way of life."

"You never shared my way of life and I never insisted that you did!"

She said, with a final attempt at reasoning, "Suppose I came back with you now? I should have a choice of playing nursemaid to a community with a medieval outlook, or accepting the role of a toy shut in a cupboard all day and taken out to be played with after dark! I know what would happen well enough, and so do you if you face up to it! You wouldn't be content to let me develop wider interests of my own, and anyway, even if you were, I couldn't do it down there, cut off from every new idea and everyone with a spark of intellectual curiosity. In the end you would retreat into a permanent sulk while I bore a child a year and pottered about in the rose garden

365

between pregnancies! You think there is worthwhile work to be done in a place like Shallowford and maybe there is, for a man. But there's nothing there for me and could never be and that's why I decided to leave before we began to destroy one another, before it was too late for you to make a fresh start!"

The cab had stopped opposite the incongruous monument and they got out, Paul paying the man and following her to a seat facing the sluggish river. The sun shone brightly now and the Thames traffic was in full swing. Behind them trams sang back and forth along the Embankment and in front of them fussy little tugs towed strings of barges downstream, like ducks teaching ducklings to swim. Paul said, when a group of pedestrians had passed by, "How can you talk about a fresh start? We're man and wife, aren't we? We could only make a fresh start with each other but you won't even discuss it!"

"It isn't easy to discuss it, Paul," she said earnestly. "When I was back there, alone in that horrible little cell, I could separate everything in my mind and I did think of you a great deal and could see very clearly the differences in our points of view but now, seeing you so hurt and desolate . . ."

"Our points of view can't be all that different, Grace," he interrupted. "I remember you saying that if we were able to bring physical joy to one another everything else could fall into place."

"I said there was a *chance* of that happening, Paul. It took me eighteen months to appreciate the real sacrifices demanded of marriage! Don't you see, you're concerned with the particular, and I'm concerned with the whole! Your outlook is honourable and useful enough but you're content with a tiny field — a few dull-witted villagers, a little bad housing, involving maybe a dozen families. I want to work for an entire change in the system and I can't even begin until women are admitted into the counsels of men! It isn't a fad, Paul, it's my reason for being alive!"

"Nobody can move mountains alone, Grace. You've got to begin somewhere and in a modest way."

"That's well enough for you, Paul and I've always understood that, but can you imagine a Raphael happy to paint miniatures? That's what's been wrong with us from the beginning. When I married you I thought I could change you, that perhaps I could use your idealism and money to create something worthwhile and enduring! But I can't, and I never will! I see now that in trying to enlarge you, you will diminish me, until I go dry and sour inside. Neither one of us is to

366

blame for this. You are new to patronage and see nothing contemptible in it but I grew up hating it, and determined to do battle with it! How could I do that if I was still part of it?"

She put her hand on his and looked at him with great earnestness. "You can get married again, Paul! You're the kind of man who desperately needs a wife but the right kind of wife. I'd make it easy for you!"

He looked at her with an expression of such incredulity that she made a hopeless gesture with her free hand, as though to reduce the width of the gulf opening between them. "I owe you that much, Paul! It was a selfish, stupid act on my part to marry you but to hold on to you, as a kind of long-term insurance, would be unforgivable! Can't you see that this isn't really a personal issue? I'll never cease to think of you as kind and generous and honest but we don't make a pair. We never have, in spite of all the self-deception you've indulged in about me!"

It was a spiritual annulment of their marriage and the final dissolution of his hopes. He knew then, and with certainty, that he would never hold her again, that there would be no more embraces, no more companionship by the fireside and certainly no more children of the marriage, nothing but a dry interchange of ideas that he only half understood and her insistence on reducing everything to words and phrases that belonged in pamphlets rather than hearts enraged him.

He stood up, brushing away her hand as though even her touch was repugnant and then he saw tears in her eyes and rejoiced that he had found a means to hurt her. He was surprised at the intensity of his feelings and his sudden move away from her, across to the embankment wall, was a recoil against the violence of feeling that urged him to strike her across the face, to beat her senseless, to fling her down on the pavement and jump on her. He understood then how Martin Codsall must have felt as he struck Arabella, and recalled Rudd's observation concerning the provocation under which some murders occur but the moment passed. By the time she was beside him again he was almost drained of emotion and conscious only of a sensation of inertia and drabness, that drained all the colour from life and set him apart from the passage of people and vehicles on the pavement and roadway behind. He stood there silently for a moment but at length managed to say, "Simon? I suppose you took Simon into account when you did your thinking back there in the cell?" She made no reply so he remained looking fixedly at the river until he realised that the touch on his elbow was heavier than hers and turning looked directly into the face of a middle-aged policeman, a man with a heavy walrus moustache and a look of professional concern in his eyes. "Are you all right, sir?" the man said and when Paul stared as though he had materialised from the base of the monument, added, half-apologetically, "I thought you looked a bit queer, sir."

With a tremendous effort Paul pulled himself together. His sense of humour was too far off to help but his sense of irony remained. He said, "I'm all right, officer. It hadn't occurred to me to jump in!" and then, "Did you . . . did you see which way the young lady went?"

"Yes, I did," said the man, looking relieved, "she boarded a tram, heading for the tunnel! Bit of a tiff, sir?" and he grinned and waited.

"You could call it that," Paul said, "but she's more accustomed to them than me it seems. She's a suffragette—and my wife!"

The policeman looked surprised and then amused. "You don't say, sir? Then do you mind my giving you a piece of advice? Don't go after her, just take it out in beer. Then, when you're braced up, take a dog-whip to her! If all you chaps did that we chaps would have a quieter time on the beat, sir!" and as though feeling that he had shown too much levity he suddenly straightened his face, nodded and continued slowly on his walk towards the Boadicea statue.

The encounter had the effect of steadying Paul somewhat, so that, for the first time since he had seen Grace leave the prison he was able to make some shift at viewing the situation objectively, putting aside thoughts of pursuit, compromise or following her to the head-quarters of the suffragists and perhaps dragging her home by the hair. Yet he did not abandon all thoughts of violence, for his mind conjured for a moment with male license of the past, when, as the policeman had hinted, a husband in his situation could have legally thrashed his wife in public and been applauded by the magistrates for setting a good example. But as he considered this, the ultimate sacrifice of dignity, the sheer hopelessness of the situation over-whelmed him and again he almost succumbed to a physical nausea and thought he might do worse than follow the policeman's advice as regards a drink, or several drinks. He crossed the road and passed under Charing Cross arches, turning in at the first public house in Villiers Street and ordering a double brandy. It was only after he had swallowed his second dram, and had nibbled at a beef sandwich, that the forces of resentment began to reassemble inside him, swelling until they embraced not only Grace and the suffragettes but all womenkind and yet, as he continued to drink, his thoughts began to sort themselves into a less extravagant pattern. He knew that his immediate need was for companionship and thought first of Celia, then of Uncle Franz across the river, and finally of Grenfell, over at the House, but after a moment's thought he rejected all three. Celia would not be available, Zorndorff was too cynical and Grenfell might even sympathise with Grace, for he too was preoccupied with pamphlets, white papers and codifications compiled from the raw material of human emotions. "God help me, I have to talk to someone," he said aloud and a cheerful voice beside him said, "Well, I've bin hoping you would, dearie! You wanter buy me a stout?"

He did not recall ever having seen a more obvious harlot plying in public. She was a study in bright mauve, mauve summer dress, with old-fashioned leg-o'-mutton sleeves, mauve straw hat, openwork mauve mittens and it struck him at once that she was approximately Grace's age, with Grace's sturdy hips and shoulders and narrow waist. Her cheeks were heavily rouged and her lips gleamed with salve. She had on a pair of ear-rings made of some dull metal and a cheap coral necklace. Her hair, dark at the roots was dyed straw-blond and her eyebrows had been so mercilessly plucked that they had almost ceased to exist. He noticed all these things, misery sharpening his perceptions to an unusual degree and decided that her brittle smile was the saddest welcome he had ever been offered. He said, politely, "I'll buy you a stout; you can have as much stout as you can drink."

She laughed uncertainly, as though a little wary of him, but said, in her grating, Cockney voice, "Christ dearie, you wanner be careful wi' your invitations!" and to the impassive barman, "Fill 'er up, Fred!" as she coiled herself on the high stool next to him, throwing one leg over the other and exposing a few inches of booted calf.

"Whatever it is you don' wanner do mor'n damp it down, dearie," she said, gaily. "Too much too quick an' where are yer? Back where you was in no time at all with an 'angover as a bonus! You wanner take it nice an' steady like me," and she downed half her stout in a gulp and he asked the barman for another brandy. As he raised it to his lips he saw that the girl was now looking at him closely and that her brittle smile was gone. She said, "Well, just that one if you're really interested, dearie!" and finishing her stout stood up and adjusted her hat in the gilded mirror. He followed her out into the sunshine, she slipped her arm through his and they went slowly up the hill towards Charing Cross Station. Seven brandies on an empty stomach left his mind free to conjure with irrelevancies, the warm colour of a pyramid of oranges on a coster's barrow, the gap-toothed grin of the vendor, the words "Latest on Far East War" on a billboard beside a newsvendor. The girl said, "My place is behind the Turkish Baths. Lot o' my gentlemen friends like to pop in after. Do you good it would, dearie, in your mood—quick game o' Mums and Dads then sweat it aht an' sleep it orf!"

She steered him into a narrow alley between two vast, slabsided buildings, then through a door and up two flights of uncarpeted stairs. At the top of the first flight an obese, bald-headed man was deeply absorbed in a newspaper, flaunting a heavy-type headline, "Japs Rout Tsar's Army at Mukden!" and Paul thought, "Now there's idiocy for you! What real interest could a bald-headed old whoremaster have in Mukden?" but the man did not look up as the girl ushered him into a small, sunless room that seemed full of stale steam. The bed was unmade, the single wickerwork chair piled with litter and there was unwashed crockery on the bedside table. The impact of unrelieved squalor sobered him within seconds but the girl seemed disinclined to waste time. She reached behind her, unhooked her dress and let it fall, lifting her feet from the folds and stooping swiftly to unlace her boots. He watched her stupidly as she kicked them off, then picked up her dress and tossed it over the back of the chair, before making a half-hearted attempt to straighten the sheets. She wore no petticoat, only a punishingly tight corset and a pair of white, beribboned drawers the legs of which fell short of the top of her black stockings. He saw now that he had been misled by her padded shoulders and that although she had broad, fleshy hips that strained at the grubby rim of the corset the upper part of her body was very slender and her shoulders narrow and stooping. She said briskly, as she slipped off her drawers, "Are you one o' the altogether boys or will near-enough do?"

"How long have you been on the streets?" he asked suddenly, not because he was interested but because it was the first conversational gambit that occurred to him but she looked at him now with amused exasperation. "Oh Gawd!" she said, with mock despair, "you ain't one o' them nosey parkers are you?" and then, as though deciding for herself that he was not, she said, "Let's say long enough to send you on yer way rejoicing, dearie! Well, is it the lot or not? Or would you

370

like a cup o' cawfee first to clear yer pore head? No extra; all on the 'ouse!"

"No coffee but thank you, thank you very much," he said foolishly, and for some reason this pleased her and she said, "I like you! You're diff'rent! I dunno why, but you don' go with the girls neither, do you, or not all that much! You c'n alwus tell, mos'ly be the way they stand gawping, like you! Either that or they're in such a perishin' hurry! Tell you what," she put a finger in her mouth so that suddenly she no longer looked like a tart but like a lewd parody of a little girl teasing an adult, "we'll 'ave our cawfee after an' jus' for you we'll 'ave the altogether, so as you c'n swank to yer pals after!" She swung round, putting her back to him. "You'll 'ave to un'ook me, tho'!"

He stared at her narrow back, noting the contrast between the slack hooks at the top of the corset and the terrible tautness of those sheathing her buttocks. The stench of stale steam filled his nostrils so that he found it difficult to breathe and his head seemed hardly to belong to him at all, yet it continued to record details with the accuracy of a man making an inventory. He noted that the closed window was half covered with peeling paper, that the paper had a fussy pattern and that the girl favoured mauve above every other colour, for even the ribbons on her discarded drawers matched her outdoor clothes. Then, as though these facts revealed to him the absurdity of his presence here, he said quickly, "I'm sorry, I'm going now! Here . . . !" and fumbling in his pocket he found a sovereign, slammed it down on the bedside table and hurried from the room.

The girl was so astonished that he was half-way across the landing before she realised he had gone and then, darting as far as the threshold, she shouted, "Come on back, Soppy! I'm *clean* I tell yer, I'm *clean*!" but he went blundering down the stairs two at a time, rushing past the old man and down the second flight to the passage-way.

The clean air of the streets seemed as heady as the rush of a gale over Coombe Bluff and he gulped at it as if it was liquid. He went up Northumberland Avenue and into the Square, hurrying through the slow-moving traffic, across to St. Martin-in-the-Fields, then up Charing Cross Road as far as Leicester Square, where at last he slackened speed, crossing under Shakespeare's statue to a seat opposite the Empire. He sat down with a vast sense of relief, as though he had just escaped suffocation in a sulphurous tunnel.

Traffic flowed round the Square and people passed to and fro in front of him but he seemed to have lost the knack of recording inconsequential detail and the only thing that impinged upon him, apart from relief, was a hoarding, advertising "Pearson's Preserved Peas" fronting a building in the process of demolition. It struck him as being a very eye-catching advertisement, calculated to inspire almost anyone to have the utmost confidence in Pearson's Preserved Peas. It was a great splash of colour, a compound of greens, yellows and blues, depicting a sea and country landscape not altogether unlike that of the Vale south of the final bend in the Sorrel. He thought, "By God, I believe it *is* the Valley!" and then he realised that no corn was ever as golden as that and no sea as blue, not even on windless days in high summer. The illusion braced him and in a persistent way worked upon his fuddled brain, so that presently, when he had recovered his breath, his head began to clear and he was able to review the events of the day, from the moment he had issued from Celia's and hired the four-wheeler to his irrational flight from the sordid little room behind the Turkish Baths. He thought, "It can't all be due to too much brandy on an empty stomach. I must have had a kind of brainstorm!" and he wondered idly where Grace had gone after boarding the tram and then, by degrees, what he should do about her or himself, now, or later, or at any time in the future. He thought of hailing a cab and calling on Uncle Franz, or walking down to Westminster and sending in his card to Grenfell but a growing self-disgust prompted him to put both courses aside. What could either of them do beyond tendering advice? And what use was advice against an obstinacy like hers? Then he looked up at the hoarding again and this time it seemed to have a message for him, reminding him not solely of home but of all the people of the Valley, women and children whom, he supposed, had come to rely upon him to some extent. He thought, "As long as I'm here I can't even think! I can always think down there so why don't I just go home, out of all this fume and clatter to people I need, even if hardly one among them really needs me?" Then, as he stood up, he thought of Ikey Palfrey, now launched upon his first full day at school and buttressed by his bogus kinship with the Squire of Shallowford, a boy with a manu-factured background and a superimposed accent but with the courage of a hunted fox. The inevitable comparison between himself and Ikey made him shudder, so that self-pity ebbed from him. "Crad-dock," he said to himself, "that boy would make a baker's dozen of you at this moment! For God's sake pull yourself together and get out of here!" and he got up and began to walk swiftly down the hill towards the Strand, remembering that there was a train from Waterloo at midday and if he could get a cab at Charing Cross and promise the cabby double fare he might conceivably catch it.

V

It did not take Ikey long to realise that he was an exceptionally privileged new boy at High Wood for whereas all the other first-termers possessed but one background he had three. He had arrived at the school adequately supplied with academic qualifications, for the crammer had brought him up to prep school level with little trouble to either of them. High Wood, however, was not an establishment that set great store upon common factors, French verbs, and Latin declensions. It was a comparatively new foundation and was thus hard at work fashioning an image of itself calculated to persuade middle-class parents that they were getting Harrow and Winchester polish at half the cost and yet it was by no means a sham institution. The headmaster was a northerner and a realist who naturally made the most of the fact that his predecessor, High Wood's first headmaster, had actually sat at the feet of the great Arnold of Rugby. Outwardly the school had a good start over most of the smaller public schools that had sprung up all over the country in the last half-century with the object of catering for sons of a newly-prosperous industrial class, together with those of private gentlemen with limited means. It was a vast, isolated group of buildings on the edge of the Exmoor plateau, six miles from the nearest market town and endowed with more playing fields than its two hundred and fifty boys could use. A youngish staff was qualified to equip these boys with what was advertised as "a comprehensive modern education" and encouraged pupils to set their sights about half-way between city counting houses and the outposts of the Empire, boys in short, whose fathers were prone to quote Kipling without taking him too seriously. Unwittingly, in his original conversation with the crammer as to where Ikey would be most likely to succeed, Paul had made an ideal choice. Had he aimed any higher even Ikey's wits might have been severely taxed to maintain the charade but here, among prosperous farmers' sons, and the sons of merchants, doctors, dentists and clergymen who had married a little money, he was given time to adjust himself. He was to take unique advantage of the opportunity.

He was made aware of his head start by his habit of careful observation underlined by a personal experience arising out of the mild system of bullying new boys, something High Wood had adopted as a matter of course in the same way as it encouraged senior boys to wear fancy waistcoats and walk arm in arm to chapel, or called its Annual Speech Day "Speccher" and its nightly call-over "Bill".

During his first term Ikey was assigned as fag to Juxton, vice-captain of cricket and a notable "blood", with the faintest shadow of a blonde moustache. Juxton was an amiable oaf whose study was usually crowded with other bloods and whilst going about his chores, whitening cricket boots and making tea and toast, Ikey learned from their conversation precisely what was done and what was not done, what could be worn and what would brand a man as an "Oick", a "Yob", or a "Swedebasher". There was, in fact, a very great deal to learn in this field and a single bad mistake on the part of a new boy might have taken a good deal of living down but Ikey's acute observation, together with his unerring ear for accent stood him in good stead, so that he was soon Admirable Crichton to all the other first-year boys in the Lower School. He could tell you, for instance, at what angle one's cap should be worn at any stage up the school; how much familiarity it was safe to show certain masters and certain boys, and even such minutiae as exactly how long one should hold on to the second syllable of the Dervishlike howl of "High *Woooode*", whilst applauding the inter-school cricket matches. He found it absurdly easy to absorb these essentials so that his quick eye and ear kept him clear of trouble with the seniors, who came to accept him as a deft hand with the toasting fork, a notable polisher of sporting equipment and a quiet but respectful scrag-end of humanity. With the Middle School, however (where dwelt the Flashmans, the Scaifes and the Beaumont-Greens), other tactics were required and it was here that Ikey's triple background gave him an enormous advantage over all the other little toads who arrived at the school from moderately prosperous homes and cheap prep schools. This was made clear to him at the first New Kids' Concert, half-way through his first term.

At stipulated intervals every newcomer to High Wood was required to mount the fifth form rostrum and divert his betters with songs or recitations and whereas most of the new boys, giving of their poor best, received nothing from the audience but a shower of books and inkwells, Ikey's imitation of a Cockney coster rendering "Knocked 'em in the Old Kent Road" won genuine applause. The audience was,

374

in fact, stunned by what they naturally assumed to be a superb mastery of the Cockney dialect and when he obliged with an encore, giving them "Widdicombe Fair", as it might have been sung by Tamer Potter or Horace Handcock, he was at once acclaimed "A Turn" and thereafter treated with a degree of geniality by boys whose Sundays (Sunday was dedicated to the persecution of new boys) were long vistas of unutterable boredom.

It would have been fatal, of course, had he let it be known that the coster idiom was his native tongue, or that he had learned broad Devon whilst employed as a stable-boy on an estate only fifty miles away but he was far too astute to allow this secret to fall into enemy hands and preserved it jealously from all, including his cronies in the Upper Third. In fact he did the reverse, using his mastery of the two accents to imply that he was a man of the world, familiar not only with the music-halls, but the idiom of grooms and house-servants in the provinces. It was this, more than anything, that gave him not only stature among his peers but also a chance to bring his wider, overall strategy into play for in one way he was handicapped, the crammer not having had the time to teach him the important things about life at a minor public school. He was completely ignorant, for instance, of Rugby football, he could not swim, and his experience of cricket was limited to standing before chalked stumps on the scrap-yard wall and hitting an underhand ball with a piece of plank. His prospects in the athletic field were no more promising. He discovered, for instance, that he had short, rather clumsy legs and was usually the last to arrive at the tape in a 100 or 220 yards junior house sprint. He knew that, somehow or other, he must make this deficiency good by the end of his second term, and perhaps he was fortunate in beginning his school life in the summer term, when cricket occupied the seniors and nobody took the junior events seriously.

He thought about his handicap a great deal, and at length arrived at a possible solution. If he could never expect to run fast then he might train himself to run a long way, for he was told that in the term ahead cross-country running took precedence over every other sport except Rugby football. Rugby, he felt, he might learn from a book and as a new boy he was unlikely to be called upon to play in even a Junior House match. He thought it best, therefore, to concentrate on long-distance running and during his first holidays, when his new status as gentleman freed him from chores in tack-room and stable-yard, he went into strict training, refusing all Mrs. Handcock's heavy

375

pastry and going out over the stubble fields as far as Coombe Bay morning and evening in sandshoes (known at High Wood as "stinkers"), running shorts and vest. He had seven weeks in which to translate himself into a potential winner of marathons and here again he was lucky, for he soon made another discovery that he could never have found in a book. Early in his training, he discovered that a run across firm, springy turf was far less demanding than a run along the tideline of Coombe Bay and that to cover a mile on the beach was far more punishing than the same distance on the hard-packed track beside the Sorrel. It occurred to him then that if he trained on sand his calf muscles and wind would develop very rapidly so that he would have the edge on boys who did not have the luck to live beside the sea. Thereafter he merely jog-trotted to the beach, or sometimes rode the cob across the dunes and tethered him to a tide-post after which he ran as far as Nun's Head and back, using the landslip boulders as the equivalent of High Wood's hedges and ditches. By the time the autumn term arrived he was confident of giving a good account of himself in the first series of runs and so it proved, for at the first cross-country event he was the first junior boy into the quad and this feat set him apart in a way that might have gone to the head of a less wary athlete. Thereafter, in five successive runs, he scored a total of seventy-nine points, a record for a first-year boy. Nobody seemed to remember his dropped catches and gasping sprints of the previous term.

His efforts to master the mystique of Rugby football were not so successful, for he found the game complicated by rules against forward passing, by dropped kicks and the off-side prohibitions but his stamina, developed by his concentrated training, soon won him a place as a forward in the Junior Grenville pack and here he put into practise a trick of falling on the ball and letting the field storm over him, something he had marked down as worth remembering in *Tom Brown's Schooldays.*

Juxton, his fagmaster, developed an interest in him and the fact that Ikey privately considered Juxton a pompous fool did not prevent him taking full advantage of the great man's patronage, even to the extent of obliging study guests with song and dance, so that seniors came to refer to him as "That Palfrey kid, Jumbo Juxton's fag, an amusin' little devil, who can run like a hare but doesn't put on side".

And so, after a couple of terms, the metamorphosis was almost complete and a boy who began earning his bread as a collector of old

376

iron at the age of nine, and had subsequently shared a loft with the gardener's boy over a stable, was absorbed into the narrow, formalised life of boarding school without one of his contemporaries suspecting for a single moment that he was the victim of a bizarre practical joke. Yet there was a curious element in the transformation and this was Ikey's own appreciation of it, for not once did he cease to regard it as a social experiment practised upon a community not so much by himself but by Squire Craddock and there grew in Ikey a terribly urgent sense of obligation to Paul, a longing, so far unappeased, for the means to repay a little interest on the investment represented by himself. As the weeks passed, however, he could see less and less hope of achieving this for he was all too aware that the Squire had changed a very great deal during the last year and Ikey connected the change, as did everyone else in the Valley, with the inexplicable disappearance of the Squire's wife, said by some to have run off with a man in a motor, and by others to have gone raving mad so that she turned her back on hearth and home in order to chain herself to railings and throw soot at politicians. Ikey considered these theories separately but could make no sense of either, being reluctant to accept the view of Mrs. Handcock, who declared, "Missus 'as gone mazed, same as all they other suffragettes, an' Squire's well shut of 'er, the daaft baggage!" He was, in fact, persuaded to the contrary, it being clear that Squire was quite unable to put his wife out of mind and Ikey, having an affection for Grace Craddock, refused to believe that she could have lost her wits in the manner of Farmer Codsall. He was ready to admit, however, that her behaviour was eccentric and altogether outside his experience. He had been witness to many quarrels between man and wife in his childhood and remembered that they had all ended in a cuddle and a quart of beer and was therefore convinced—provided the means could be found of bringing the principals together—that all could be settled in minutes. In the meantime, concern over the Squire's despondency grew as the months passed and on the whole he was inclined to blame Mrs. Craddock the less, for a careful study of the Squire's demeanour during the Christmas holidays left him with the impression that Paul was almost enjoying his sulks and this made him wonder if, in some mysterious way, that man with the motor was at the back of it all. When, therefore, he learned that the agent's son was now cruising the China seas it struck him that something should be done before he came home again to charm Mrs. Craddock into committing further indiscretions

377

in his motor and Ikey gave the matter the same careful consideration as he had given to the process of consolidating himself at High Wood. It was some time, however, before he hit on a plan to improve the situation.

Part of his duties in Juxton's study was to light the fire and Juxton, who read the sporting page of the *Daily Mail* every day, saved the political pages for this purpose. It was in this way that Ikey came to read a lengthy report dealing with suffragette activities in London and he put it aside to study in the latrines, the only place at High Wood where new boys could expect privacy. The article interested him far more than he thought it would. He had never dreamed that suffragettes had so much fun, or were regarded so seriously by the police. He read an account of various outrages committed by these extraordinary women and became excited when he found the name "Mrs. P. Craddock" bracketed alongside the name of "Grace Philimore". It worried him a little, this name "Philimore", for it might mean that Squire and his wife were already divorced and that she was now married to someone else but he soon discarded this possibility, reasoning that such a dreadful scandal would certainly have reached the Valley and become common gossip in the kitchens. It must mean, therefore, that Mrs. Craddock had two names, one as the Squire's wife and another as a suffragette. He read on to learn with some dismay that she had actually been to prison, just like old Smut Potter and was not wholly reassured when he gathered (lower down the column) that suffragettes were always going to prison, and were, in fact, more often to be found there than not. The value of the report, however, lay in the address of the movement's headquarters which he ringed in pencil before putting the clipping in his pocket book. It came to him then precisely what he must do to restore happiness to the Squire. Somehow or other he must travel up to London, find her, and bring her back with him, and although he realised that this might prove a very difficult undertaking he had faith in his lucky star, and more in his ability to tell such a harrowing story that she would have little choice but to accompany him home at once.

He spent the last week of term perfecting this story, toying with a variety of illnesses but finally settling upon a fiction that could not be verified by a call upon the doctor, or indeed exploded by Grace returning home to find Paul in excellent health. He would tell her bluntly that he had proof that Squire was considering suicide but he was too good an artist to draw directly upon the well-known circum-

378

stances of the Four Winds tragedy. He would simply tell her that, on one occasion, Paul had been dragged half dead from the Mere (and his rescuers sworn to secrecy) and that on a second occasion he himself had caught Paul's bridle just as he was putting Snowdrop at an impossible fence. He thought it almost certain that she would check these reports but he could probably delay this somewhat by warning her that Paul had also sworn him to secrecy, and that he alone was cognisant of the cloud that had settled on Squire's brain. The important thing was to bring them face to face and shock the Squire out of his unforgiving sulk. After that he was sure that God would wade in and help. After all, he would have done the spadework and how many times had it been proclaimed from pulpits that God helped those who helped themselves?

Having settled his approach he went to work on practicalities, realising that he would have to explain absence from home during the first two days of the holidays. He would also have to pay his own railway fare to London and as it was near the end of term, and his wealth amounted to tenpence, at least ten shillings would have to be raised for journey money. First, however, at the final Sunday letter-writing session, he wrote to Mrs. Handcock telling her that he had accepted an invitation to spend a couple of days with Rawlinson, his particular friend, who lived near Plymouth, adding that Rawlinson's father owned a car and had promised to drive him back to Shallowford. He did not post this letter but held it back until the final evening, in order to guard against a cross-check with the headmaster. Then he buttonholed Davis Minor and offered his tuck-box at the knockdown price of ten shillings. He selected Davis not simply because he was the Lower School miser but because he was also the only boy in the Third who did not possess a tuck-box, his father being a faddist who disapproved of the tradition. He knew that Davis was secretly ashamed of this and when the boy, having inspected the tuck-box, offered seven-and-sixpence, Ikey closed his locker and said he would accept Martin's offer of nine-and-sixpence. Money changed hands at once, and Davis carried away the tuck-box in triumph, having decided to torment hungry companions throughout the following term by praising the fictitious delights of the contents.

All was now ready for a descent upon the suffragette headquarters, and when, during prep, on the last night of term, he was summoned to his housemaster's study Ikey obeyed the order promptly, anticipating that Mr. Ralston would issue him with his ticket to Paxtonbury and probably half-a-crown journey money, a sum that would bring expeditionary funds to thirteen shillings and fourpence halfpenny. There was, of course, the return fare to be considered, but he assumed that the erring (and by then penitent) Mrs. Craddock would pay for both tickets.

He knew that something was seriously wrong as soon as he saw Ralston's expression. He looked, Ikey thought, sympathetic and began, with a brave but false smile, "I'm afraid I've a bit of a disappointment for you, old chap!" At this form of address Ikey's stomach contracted but Ralston went on hurriedly. "You will have to stay over a week or two, Palfrey. I've just had a . . . well, a rather sensational message from your guardian's agent, a Mr. John Rudd . . ." and Ikey, suddenly feeling sick, said, "What's happened, sir? Is the Squire dead?" so that Ralston went on reassuringly, "Oh, it's not that bad, old man, it's well . . . something rather unusual, something I think you may well be proud to hear when you get over the shock! There was a shipwreck a few miles from your home and your guardian, along with a number of his tenants, was instrumental in saving several lives. The place has been turned into a hospital and everything is at sixes and sevens. Mr. Rudd telephoned to ask if we could keep you here for a day or so."

His bright smile did not deceive Ikey for an instant. This was only Ralston's second term as a housemaster and his first attempt at breaking bad news to a boy, so that he would have done well to have rehearsed his speech. Ikey said, quietly, "Is the Sq . . . is my guardian all right, sir?" and Ralston, unable to meet the boy's eye, replied with tell-tale hesitancy, that "Mr. Craddock had been knocked about a bit during rescue operations. He's getting the best attention and there's absolutely no need to worry," he added, "but for a week or so he needs rest and quiet, so I agreed that you could either stay on with us or, if we can arrange it, stay with a chum. Who is your particular chum? Is it Rawlinson or Hooper Two?"

"Rawlinson, sir," Ikey said but before Ralston had finished speaking he had made up his mind. The conclusion was obvious; if the Squire had been injured in such an improbable event as a shipwreck, it was obvious that God was already taking a hand in his plan, for now there was no need to cod Mrs. Craddock with stories of attempted suicide. All he had to do (and surely the need to act was more urgent than ever) was to go through with the main part of his scheme, that is, get to London, find her, and tell her Paul needed her

380

desperately. If that did not bring her back by the first train then nothing would but, as he decided this, he was aware that certain difficulties had arisen to cancel out such unlooked-for advantages and that the Almighty was rather overdoing it. As things were it now looked as though he would remain a prisoner at school until Squire was in a fair way to making a recovery and this milked the urgency from his mission. He looked carefully at Ralston and decided that the housemaster was telling the truth, or most of the truth, and that Squire was neither dead nor dying. He said, quietly, "Thank you, sir, I'd sooner stay at school until I can go home. Will that be all, sir?" and Ralston beamed at him and said heartily, "Why of course old man, and I'm bound to say I admire your pluck! Would you like to spend the rest of the evening with Mrs. Ralston and take supper with us? Or would you rather go back to prep and keep this to ourselves until tomorrow?"

"I'll go back to prep, sir, I should like to write a letter home straight away!"

"Naturally, naturally," said Ralston, patting his shoulder. "I'll look in after dormitory bell tonight, just to cheer you up," and Ikey, muttering "Thank you, sir!" slipped from the room.

He knew that he must act at once. He must go to the bursar's office, find his ticket to Paxtonbury among the tickets drawn in advance and get clear of the school before the morning papers made him the centre of attraction and flight was impossible.

The bursar's office was unlocked and the tickets were in their marked envelopes on the desk. He soon found his own, pocketed ticket and half-crown, and hurried back to Big School, where reading prep was still in progress. He took out his letter, read it over, scribbled a brief postscript and then readdressed it. When supper bell rang he posted it on the way to the dining hall. It would be collected early in the morning and arrive at Shallowford the following afternoon. By then he would have been missed, and Ralston would be trying to get in touch with his home, but this would be difficult since there was still no telephone at Shallowford (Rudd must have telephoned from The Raven) and it would increase his already excellent start. For a moment or so Ikey felt almost sorry for Ralston but the moment passed after the housemaster came softly into the dormitory to whisper something to Geary, the dormitory prefect. Ikey saw Geary glance across at him and then say something back, so that when the housemaster came down the aisle between the beds he pretended

381

to be asleep. He did not want to risk discovery of the fact that he was wearing his nightgown over shirt and rolled-up trousers. He would give them a couple of hours to settle down before slipping out and walking the six miles to Barrow Market. He would have to walk fast if he was to reach there in time to stow away on the late goods train that crossed Barrow viaduct in the small hours every week-night. Ikey knew all about that goods train, even to the time of its arrival in Paxtonbury, having made it his business to find out from Gobber Christow, the school lamp-trimmer. Gobber's son was an engine-driver and drove it three times a week.

He lay still listening to the excited chatter and end-of-term laughter until silence bell and to the scrunch of Geary's feet as the prefect came up, undressed and got into bed. He waited for Geary's contented sigh, for his neighbour's high-pitched snore and finally the far-off clank of the earlier goods train crossing the viaduct, the rattle telling him it was now almost midnight. Ten minutes later he was out of bed and he had jacket and boots on before he remembered the prayer. He did not need reassurance of the kind he had sought long ago, when he had prayed for Squire Craddock's appearance at the railway station the day of his arrival in the Valley, but thought it might be just as well to buy some insurance on the Squire's health. He knelt by the bed and muttered, "Keep Squire in bed and everyone busy until I get back with Mrs. Craddock, Oh Lord!" In his unseemly haste to get started he forgot the obligatory Amen!

CHAPTER FOUR

I

On the afternoon of March 14th, 1906, Tamer Potter was also in communion with God, having decided that it was high time he made a survey of his private beach, in order to see what the Almighty had sent him in the way of a bonus to his conventional activities. He went through the cliff-top rabbit-run and down the dry gully to the tiny bay that he thought of as Flotsam Cove (although it was unnamed on the Ordnance maps) and there began a meticulous examination of the boulder-strewn margin between high- and low-water mark, commencing at the knob of sandstone in the east and working westwards as far as Coombe Bluff, where the overhang of the cliff had kept this tiny section of coastline out of reach of less knowledgeable beachcombers.

The Cove was not more than eighty yards across but the points enclosing it were never uncovered, not even at extreme ebb tide, so that nobody could walk here from Coombe Bay or from the area further along the coast. High tides surged almost to the foot of the cliff, all of two hundred feet high at this part, and the sole approach, save by boat, was by the Potter tunnel, discovered forty years ago by an inquisitive lurcher called Kitty that Tamer had owned as a boy. The tunnel was really a long, steep rabbit run, beginning below the cliff path and weaving a path through thick gorse to the head of an old water-course, dried up since the stream had dug itself a new channel. It was a tricky descent but safe enough for anyone knowing it as well as Tamer, who usually went down there about twice a year, once after the autumn gales and again in early spring, for these were the times of the year when he could expect a harvest from the gales and the cross-tides sweeping up Channel to meet the outfall of the Whin further west.

Flotsam Cove had brought Tamer several slices of luck in the past. Once he had salvaged a watertight box of Virginia tobacco, which had kept his pipe filled throughout three winters. Another time he had found a strongly-built dinghy which he had repaired and still used for inshore fishing. Then there had been an almost new buoy and an anchor, which he sold for a sovereign to Tom Williams, a Coombe

Bay fisherman, and later still, after a week of gales, he had salvaged a thing that had been a man, still wearing sea-boots and a few rags of clothing. Tamer was not squeamish. He searched the corpse and found a leather bag containing a gold crucifix and two sovereigns. He pocketed them and reported the presence of the body to the proper authorities.

On this particular day the weather was wet and wild, with an unseasonal south-westerly gale blowing itself out and a particularly dense sea fog creeping in from the west when the wind lost some of its force. It was warm, however, almost muggy, and Potter, who was a cold mortal, never minded rain so long as the temperature stayed round about fifty degrees. He buttoned his reefer and dragged his sixteen-stone-ten through the narrow tunnel to the gully where, with surprising agility for one so gross, he lowered himself to the beach and began his square search.

About five o'clock, when the weather was setting in really thick, he came across a park bench. It was an odd thing to find wedged between two knife-edge slabs of rock but a close inspection showed it to be in good condition, with its iron rails and back supports intact, the latter stamped with the letters "U.D.C." indicating that it had been washed out to sea when a storm lashed some esplanade. Tamer assessed its worth at about thirty shillings, providing he could prise it loose and get the girls or Sam to drag it up the cliff. In all cases of salvage it was Tamer who prospected and the family who supplied the muscle work. The Potters never called in auxiliaries, no matter how heavy the task, for this would have meant revealing the secret of the approach to the cove.

He worked away doggedly for half-an-hour and all the time the wind was dying and the sea fog getting thicker and thicker along the coast. After an hour or so he could not even see the long tongue of rock that split the cove into two parts, a kind of natural causeway that ran south for perhaps a hundred yards ending in a solitary bastion of sandstone that had resisted thousands of years of erosion and formed a tiny island shaped like a broad-bladed dagger embedded on a shelf of rock. At last he worked the bench free and stood upright, grunting with satisfaction and it was just then that he heard some confused and subdued shouting that seemed to come at him from all points of the compass. He located it, however, as soon as he had made allowances for the echo in that enclosed place, realising that its centre was the sandstone pinnacle about a cable's length from the beach. It was an eerie sound, a combination of human and metallic noises, a steady grinding and crashing, with overtones of voices raised in fear and punctuated by hoarse shouts and just once a long and piercing scream, almost certainly the scream of a woman.

Tamer was a very stolid man and not easily frightened by noises. Some people might have interpreted the shouts as the wails of long-drowned creatures revisiting the scene of a tragedy long ago, but Potter understood at once that, whoever was making them, was in danger of being drowned at that particular moment. He forgot all about the seat and climbed over the rocks to the causeway, thinking that he might edge along it in the face of the rising tide and get some notion of what was happening behind the thick, wet blanket of mist, but when he was less than ten yards from the beach he realised that to go further would be suicidal, for the sea was running high and there was nothing to grasp for support on that narrow, weed-covered rock. So he put his hands to his mouth and bellowed "Ahoy, there!" and at once a man's voice answered "Ahoy!" after which there was more confused shouting and several isolated shouts for help.

Even at that distance, and with the voices distorted by fog, Tamer knew that the poor devils stranded there were foreigners, for in the answering voices an accent was clearly noticeable. The presence of foreigners on the reef did not surprise him. He was familiar with the Whinmouth coastal trade, a coming and going of Dutch and German brigs, some of them operating under sail with a single auxiliary engine, that carried cargoes of apples, timber, cattle food, coal and coke. He thought, gloomily, "They'm in a rare ole fix, an' there's no 'ope for 'em in this sea while the tide goes on risin'! They'm stuck on that ole point for sure and although the sea's goin' down it won't zettle 'till it ebbs and by then there'll be thirty voot o' water on that slab!" He hesitated a moment, his instinct to help at war with his strong reluctance to reveal a close family secret to coastguards, police and even local foreigners west of the Whin, but then he realised that he could not let a personal consideration prevent him from doing what he could for the poor wretches out there in the fog, so he shouted, "I'm a-goin' for 'elp! I'm a-goin' fer the lifeboat! 'Ang on, will 'ee, now?" and without waiting for an answer he hurried back to the beach and began the steep ascent of the gully.

By the time he was half-way up he was sobbing for breath and his heart was pounding at the cage of his ribs. He paused to strip off the reefer jacket and then continued climbing, moving from foothold to

385

foothold until at last he struck the mouth of the rabbit run and went on up to the cliff-top on all fours.

When he reached the top he was convinced that he was dying. His eyes misted over and he fell on his knees, bowing his head to the grass but after a few minutes his vision cleared and although he could not see five yards through the fog and still knew precisely where he was, he was uncertain where to go for immediate help. He was kneeling there, wheezing and gasping, when he heard the chink of iron shoes and to his relief a mounted figure loomed out of the east, looking gigantic in the dense trailers of mist. Tamer at once recognised the horseman as Farmer Willoughby, his neighbour, returning no doubt from one of his evangelistic missions at one or other of the chapels along the coast, and well mounted on his strong, barrel-chested cob. Willoughby stared at the thick-set figure in mild surprise.

"Why Potter," he said reproachfully, "you shouldn't be out in this weather without a coat, man! Jump up behind and I'll take you across to the Dell," but Tamer, still very breathless, grabbed his stirrup leather and gasped, "Tiz a wreck! Down on the reef below! They'm out on that ole rock ledge an' if us dorn get 'em orf before high tide they'll drown, every man jack of 'em!"

Willoughby's gentle face crumpled with dismay and he said, "Dear Lord, are you sure?" and Tamer, who had some regard for the man but privately thought him quite daft, shouted, "Gordamme, o' course I'm sure! I bin talking to 'em, baint I?" and at once made a decision, based on the potentialities of himself and his neighbour. "Lookee," he said, "stay yer to mark the spot and I'll take the cob and rouse Meg an' the girls! One of 'em can ride on into Coombe Bay and talk into that ole telephone at The Raven and another can roust out Squire an' Mr. Rudd. Us can't wait for the Whinmouth lifeboat nor the coastguard! Time they get 'ere the tide'll be full, and there's a big sea running! They'll be drowned, the whole bliddy lot of 'em! Stay right where you be an' when us hollers holler back, an' keep on hollering, do 'ee mind?"

In a situation like this Willoughby was ready to concede leadership to an erring brother. He had lived for so long in celestial regions that he felt helpless in the face of an urgent, earthly problem, so he dismounted and helped Tamer into the saddle and a moment later the latter's bulky figure had disappeared in the mist, leaving Willoughby to seek the counsel of God. No one in the Sorrel Valley could have done this as well as Edwin Willoughby, noted for his long, improvised

386

prayers, which invariably contained a plea for distressed mariners. He stood there like a biblical prophet on the edge of the cliff and one might have thought, by the urgency of his voice and posture, that he was asking Providence to aid him in staying the flow of the tide immediately below.

II

Tamer reached the Dell less than ten minutes after leaving Willoughby and minutes after that the Potter household had dispersed, Violet mounting the cob and riding for Coombe Bay, Hazel running through Coombe Wood and across the meadow to warn the people at the Big House and Cissie (alone among the Potters without the gift of moving across country by instinct) along the track that led to Sam's cottage in the woods. Sam was a good man in an emergency and Tamer, sweating and wheezing in his stable as he searched for ropes, cursed the authorities for depriving him of the services of Smut, who would have known just what to do and how to go about it. His wife Meg, however, was a good substitute. Once she understood the basic facts she wasted no time bothering him with questions but slung baskets each side of the cart-horse and helped him load them with coils of one-inch rope. She also had the forethought to drag out a hurdle that could be used for a stretcher, fastening it to Bessie's saddle by a length of cord. Once or twice, as they were getting ready to return to the cliffs, Tamer spared a thought to worry about himself, for the speed he had climbed the gully and the mad ride through the mist to the Dell, had left him dizzy and his heart continued to pump with the savage beat of a piston. He thought, savagely, "Damme, I'll 'ave another o' my ole turns if I doan't taake it easy but how can a man bide, when the water will be under the cliff in two hours and us 'aven't got down to 'em yet?" Meg noticed his distress and ran into the house, returning with a leather bottle on her girdle. "Here man," she said briefly, "take a swallow or two o' that," and he swallowed gratefully, feeling the potion warm his belly and put new vigour into his calves. A moment later they were off, Tamer riding the horse, and Meg following the sound of the dragging hurdle; only Potter could have found the still-praying Willoughby in under half-an-hour.

The Potter girls also accomplished their journeys in record time. Cissie reached Sam's cottage in forty minutes flat and was on her way back in another five, Sam accompanying her with more ropes.

387

Violet entered Coombe Bay village like another Paul Revere, shouting the news right and left as she cantered down to The Raven, to tell her story to Abe Tozer, the shoeing smith, who then made his first ever telephone calls to the Whinmouth coastguard and local police. He told them as much as he knew and what was being done in the way of rescue, then ran down to the quayside cottages in the hope of getting Williams to launch his boat and go round by the Bluff to the Cove but Williams was appalled at the news. "That'll be the German boat," he said, "I seed her beating out o' Whinmouth about noon and if 'er's gone ashore no one'll get her off! As for going round under the Bluff, well, us c'n try, but tiz risky. The tide is beatin' inshore now an' not due to turn 'till near midnight. I'll talk to Ned Hockings an' us'll see what us can do! Meantime, get the landsmen together and go over the headland to see if you vind some way down to the beach."

"You can't never get to that beach from the top," Tozer protested. "There baint no way down and with the tide running how can any of us get into the bliddy Cove, save by boat?"

Williams said soberly, "Tamer Potter got there Abe! Tell him to show 'ee the way while I get a boat party together. Has anyone told Squire?"

"Aye," Tozer said, "Hazel Potter is there now. Well, good luck to 'ee, I'll do the best I can!" and he ran back to The Raven, where a party led by Eph Morgan, the builder, had already assembled. They set off across the headland at once and on the way somebody thought to call in and leave a message with Doctor O'Keefe, telling the old man to prepare for casualties. They were leaving the street for the path to the headland when Abe Tozer's boy, a notable hunter of gull's eggs, had another thought and doubled back, rejoining them later with his thirty-foot rope-ladder.

III

Paul at once recognised the shipwreck as yet another of these sudden crises he had been called upon to face at intervals during the last four years and yet, for the first time, there was a difference, for here was a challenge that involved not only him but every able-bodied man and woman in the Valley and it was because of this that he could meet it with more cool-headedness than when caught up in the Smut Potter scandal, or the fatal madness of Martin Codsall, or even the quarrel that caused the split of the Four Winds family. For here, at last, was something that demanded swift planning and

388

resolute action, something akin to a junior officer's work in the field and whilst with one half of his mind he was issuing orders and making the decisions necessary to rally the manpower of the estate, at a deeper level of consciousness he was uplifted as he had not been for close on two years.

He was standing talking to Rudd in the stable-yard when Hazel Potter came panting out of the mist with news of shipwreck off Coombe Bluff, and at once Paul acted entirely on his own initiative, without consulting his agent. His first impulse was to ride for the village but when Hazel said her sister was already on her way there he gave the child a moment to catch her breath and then questioned her patiently, whilst John called for Chivers and together they saddled Snowdrop, the agent's bay, the youngest of the cobs and the trap pony. Hazel, who soon recovered from her cross-country run from the Dell to Shallowford, could not tell them much, for Tamer had been badly blown when he came in with the news and had despatched his daughters in all directions without telling them more than the barest facts. In addition, Hazel Potter's brogue was the thickest in the Valley and sometimes almost unintelligible. Paul gathered, however, that Coombe Bay had been alerted, the coastguard and police almost certainly informed by telephone, that Sam Potter would soon be on the spot, and that under the Bluff were an unknown number of persons in imminent danger of drowning. He made his dispositions accordingly, despatching Chivers to summon all the available men and two carts to the Dell, instructing him to call at the Home Farm, Hermitage, and Four Winds, in that order, before riding to the edge of the moor to fetch Will Codsall. Chivers rode off at once on Rudd's bay and before setting out for the Dell, where he hoped Potter or his wife would have more detailed information, Paul told Mrs. Handcock to prepare guest rooms and make a cauldron of pea soup against the probability of visitors. He would have taken rope from the stables but the girl said, breathlessly, "Dornee bother, Squire! Pa will ha' taaken rorpe, Pa's got bushels o' rorpe!" so they cantered off unencumbered, Hazel leading the way through the mist as far as the junction of the Dell cart-track where Rudd pulled up and said, "I'd better check on the village, Paul. They'll send out a boat party no doubt!" but Paul replied, "Not until ebb tide, John! There's no power-driven boat in Coombe Bay and no one could pull round under Coombe Bluff against a flowing tide!" and as he said this he was surprised by his instinctive knowledge of local conditions. Later that night Rudd was to remember this and say to himself "By God! And he has talked to me about throwing his hand in! He's been here less than four years but he knows the ebb and flow of the tides as well as Potter!" He said, "Lead on then, and we'll hope to God they had the sense to make straight for the headland and bring along tackle. All I hope is that she's struck well to the east, where we can climb down to the beach!"

They found the Potter farmhouse deserted, although the doors were open and the lamp was still burning in the kitchen and for a moment Paul was baffled. The mist was shredding a little here but visibility was still reduced to yards. The girl said, in a matter-of-fact voice, "They'm gone upalong! And they've taaken rorpe, like I told 'ee!"

It was this second reference to ropes that gave Paul a clue she was holding something back. In general with the rest of the Valley he had always regarded Hazel Potter as a halfwit, and partly because of this and partly because he was worried by the time factor, he seized her by the arm, shaking her impatiently.

"Do you *know* where the wreck is, Hazel?" he demanded. "Can't you tell us exactly where your father and mother have gone?" and the girl said sullenly, "Arr, us knaws! But he'll flay the hide offen me if I taakes 'ee there!"

"But you've got to take us, Hazel," he said. "People are out there, drowning at this moment.!"

"Wait a minute, Paul," John said as he edged his cob alongside the pony. "Listen, Hazel, your father told you to take Squire to wherever he's gone, didn't he?"

"Arr," said the girl, hesitantly, "he did that, but tiz funny for he zed he'd flay the hide offen any one of us who chattered!"

"What the devil is she talking about?" Paul demanded irritably, but John readdressed himself earnestly to the girl. "I *know* about that, Hazel! Tamer knows a way to the Cove and you know a way to the Cove but the Squire will give your father the Cove if you take us there now, do you understand?"

"Will 'ee zo?" said Hazel, looking wonderingly at Paul, and Paul, only half comprehending, hastily endorsed the promise and at this Hazel seemed satisfied and said, "Well, get along then and I'll show 'ee the tunnel, an iffen 'er belts me for showing 'ee I'll run off to the woods 'till 'er's safe an' drunk again!", and she clapped her heels into the pony and trotted off up the steepest side of the Dell and over several Potter hedgerows to the level ground of the cliff-top.

Up here the visibility was better and they could hear the roar of the breakers under the Bluff. John said, "We're damned near the edge, Paul, take it easy and let the girl lead. I've always had my suspicions about Tamer's unwillingness to cultivate these fields and it takes a shipwreck to prove them justified!", but before Paul could answer Willoughby's bewhiskered face loomed out of the fog and he called in a high-pitched voice, "Praise God you've come, Squire! Potter and his wife went down nearly an hour since, leaving me to show others the way! It's yonder, through the gorse to the head of that dry gully and after that the Lord go with you, for it's more than a hundred feet and close on sheer!"

"Great God, that's suicide in this mist," Rudd exclaimed. "They've gone to their deaths!" but Willoughby said, civilly, "No, Mr. Rudd, sir, they took ropes and Meg Potter came back to tell me she would wait by the steepest part to help others down! She's there now, I believe, at the head of the gully!"

Paul peered over the belt of gorse but it was impossible to judge the angle of the cliff. Rudd said, "If you go, I'm coming with you, Paul!" but Paul, turning back to him, replied, "You damned well won't, John! You're over fifty and that's a young man's climb in the mist or in the clear! Wait here with Willoughby and send some of the young men down if they've got the stomach for it! As for the girl . . ." and he turned back to the thicket just in time to see Hazel's heels disappearing through a hole in the gorse and went after her, crawling on hands and knees along a tunnel less than two feet high until he could hear the voice of Meg Potter chiding her daughter from a perch about half-way down the cliff. A moment later he was beside them on a small platform of sandstone over which two ropes had been flung, the ends running back into the bushes.

Meg said, in a matter-of-fact tone, "Oh, tiz you, Squire! Well, my man needs help below but if so you'd sooner bide here me and the maid'll go down. Thicky tide has about an hour to flow!"

"Have you made contact with the poor devils?" he asked and Meg said she believed not, apart from the initial exchange of shouts when Tamer first located them.

"I'll go down at once," Paul told her. "You and the girl stay here and guide the others," and he seized the ropes and lowered himself over the ledge, hanging by his hands until his feet found partial holds in the clefts each side of the gully.

It was, as Willoughby had said, almost sheer but the surface was rough and the descent was not as fearful as he had anticipated, although how anyone had ever managed it without the ropes he could not begin to think. Then, when he was part way down, a soft orange glow showed through the mist, and then another and a third, and he realised Tamer must be lighting fires along the beach and using fuel more inflammable than driftwood. As soon as his feet touched shingle he saw Potter's thick-set figure silhouetted between the cliff and the most easterly of his fires and smelled the sharp tang of burning pitch. Tamer called, "Who is it?" and he called back, "It's me, Tamer, Squire!" and Tamer came crunching over the loose shingle looking, Paul thought, preoccupied but by no means excited.

"Rudd's on top and others are coming down as soon as they get here," he told him. "Are they still alive out there?"

"Aye, they'm there," Tamer said, "but whether there's two or dree or a dozen I can't say in this bliddy ole fog! They'll do 'till the tide's full but if us don't get 'em off the ebb will taake 'em as far as Conger Rocks. I reckon they was comin' ashore from there in a boat when they capsized on the rocks yonder!" and he cupped his hands to his mouth and bellowed, "Ahoy there! Dornee move! Us is comin' for 'ee!" There was a faint answering hail and Tamer turned back to Paul. "It baint a particle o' gude waitin' for the lifeboat," he said. "Us'll have to taake a chance on it an' use my boat paid out on cable from the western zide o' the cove."

"You've got a boat down here?"

"Aye," said Tamer reluctantly, "but us can't use un 'till others get here. Then, wi one other along o' me, and a shore party holding us, I could let her drift downalong 'till us touches the rocks an' maybe bring off dree or fower of 'em."

They stood facing the sea for a moment, seeing nothing but the dense wreaths of mist and occasionally the cream-flecked crest of a wave as it crashed on to the shingle and beach debris. Paul said, finally, "Show me the boat," and Tamer led the way along the beach just as a rattle of stones higher up announced the arrival of the first newcomer at the foot of the descent.

IV

The alerting of the Valley beginning with Violet Potter's arrival in Coombe Bay, and carried inland by Paul's despatch of Chivers to rouse the farms, was not really a haphazard operation. It had about

392

it a speed and precision absent from the war games of professional generals working with trained soldiers and this was because, basically, it was a tribal exercise, performed by men who had been dependent upon one another's goodwill all their lives. The impulse to unite in a common cause was in their blood and bone and although, in fact, twentieth-century apparatus had been employed to summon Whinmouth lifeboat and coastguard, these factors played no part in the attempt to rescue eight men and one woman, marooned on a shelf of rock eighty yards seaward of Tamer's Cove and invisible behind the veils of mist. The feat was achieved by the people of the Valley and was due not so much to the courage and ingenuity of a sixty-year-old gypsy farmer and his twenty-six-year-old landlord, or even to the men who controlled the boat from the beach, but to the tribal instinct that had assembled them on an inaccessible stretch of shore in a little over one hour from the moment Tamer had galloped into the Dell with news that men were needed and time was short.

The Whinmouth lifeboat crew spent the whole of that wild night circling the hulk of the *Sulzbach* that was straddled on Conger Rocks, three miles south-east of the Cove but rescued nobody, for there was no one alive on the wreck. It was only when dawn came that they were able to recover two or three bodies from the sandbank inside the bar and cruise off-shore, watching Tom Williams' boats move in and pick up the stranded survivors, and such of their rescuers who preferred to return to Coombe Bay by sea rather than tackle the ascent of the gully after such a strenuous night. Then the lifeboat rounded the Bluff to put into the little harbour and its crew learned what had happened but by that time the story was known as far away as Paxtonbury.

The alarm had travelled the Valley in a wide circle, using the reverse route of gulls flying inshore when gales cut them off from their offshore feeding-grounds. The gulls always flew in on the wind, north-east from Coombe Bay to the Coombe farms, then west from Derwent's yard across the woods to the big house before passing Priory Wood to the Hermitage, and finally over the Sorrel to Four Winds and south to the coast. The cry for manpower took the opposite course, beginning at the Dell and moving via the big house across the river to Four Winds, then back again to Hermitage and Periwinkle Farms and finally over the woods to Derwent's farm at High Coombe. This clockwise circuit had an unlooked-for advantage. It meant that men like Hugh Derwent, and the younger Willoughby,

393

were the last to learn of the shipwreck but they had less than half the distance to travel to the shelf below the rabbit run, where Meg Potter remained all night lowering gear and showing the more awkward among them how to descend the gully. This was why widely scattered units arrived more or less together just as dusk was setting in and the wind was getting up, dissolving some of the sea-fog but driving the full tide hard among the boulders of the cove.

The Coombe Bay party, seven or eight in all, were the first to cross the headland and grope their way down the cliff path to the spot where Rudd and Willoughby awaited them. They had between them more than a hundred yards of good rope and a small inflatable canvas raft of doubtful age. They also had Davy Tozer's rope ladder, which proved invaluable in replacing the last two lengths of Tamer's rope and thus adding forty feet of cable to the coil on the beach. Rudd took charge of the cliff-top team and nobody questioned his authority when he told them Squire Craddock was already on the beach. The younger men, like Davy Tozer and Walt Pascoe thought little enough of the descent but some of the others, Eph Morgan, the builder, and Rudd himself, could not have attempted it had not Tamer pioneered the climb. In the red glow of the flaming canisters those at the top could just make out Squire and Tamer working at something wedged in a cleft under the shoulder of the headland and at first supposed them to be trying artificial respiration on somebody washed ashore. Then, after Davy and Walt Pascoe had gone down and secured the ladder to the shelf, Hugh Derwent appeared out of the mist and after him young Willoughby and then, in ones and twos, Will Codsall, who had had the longest ride, Sam Potter, Arthur Pitts and Henry, and Old Honeyman, with the shepherd twins, Matt and Luke. Last of all came Eveleigh with his eldest boy Gil and his two hired men, Ben and Gerry. Rudd, now using Hazel Potter to maintain contact between cliff-top and Meg's shelf, sent the most active of them down to the beach as soon as they appeared and when he saw they had arrived safely he said to Willoughby, "You take over here, Edwin, and send a message when you get news of the boats. I'm going down myself." Willoughby did not try and dissuade him and would have followed had not Rudd forbidden it. A responsible man was needed at the top, for hope that the lifeboat would arrive offshore before high tide had now faded and Davy Tozer, who made nothing of the climb, had come up again with news that Potter had a skiff in the cove and they were about to attempt a direct rescue with a paid-out cable.

394

"When the coastguard arrives explain what's going on down there," Rudd told Willoughby, and sent Hazel back to the village with a written message for Tom Williams or his deputy. He scrawled it on an envelope in the light of a lantern, making no attempt to explain details. All he wrote was, "*Shore party and possible survivors in cove just east of headland. Try and pick up at first light or soon as ebb begins. Rudd.*" Then, after a moment's hesitation, he added, "Per pro Squire Craddock," without thinking that Tom Williams would be most unlikely to know the meaning of 'per pro'.

There had been one spluttering rocket from the end of the reef, so that it was clear that someone there was still alive but the drenching spray had already doused two of the tar canisters and only the most westerly still burned brightly. In the light of this the men worked methodically, knotting the assorted ropes until they had a cable about a hundred and thirty yards in length. Abe Tozer tested every knot and Tamer showed them where to anchor the shore end, looping it over and through a twisted snarl of iron buried in the shingle, itself a relic of a wreck on the Conger Rocks a generation ago. Then, with the skiff stern firmly lashed to the long rope they carried the boat over the boulders to a point where sand had piled up in a broad crevice and there was a chance of launching between breakers, for here the beach was partially protected by the isolated rock and the causeway connecting it to the shingle. The causeway itself was already under four feet of water.

Paul took no part in these operations. Tamer obviously knew the tides and rock formations like the back of his hand, and Abe Tozer made himself responsible for briefing the shore party, emphasising the doubtful quality of the cable.

"She'll hold so long as youm careful to pay out an inch at a time," he warned them. "Dornee be in no bliddy hurry or they'm all gonners, an' Squire too!" He said nothing about Tamer's prospects but the old fellow was not slow to remind him.

"Aye, and me along of 'im," he growled, and because this was the nearest thing to a joke uttered on the beach that night everyone laughed and Eph Morgan, in his sing-song Welsh accent, said, "There's a brave thing you're doing, Tamerboy! The Lord go with both of you!"

It was now close on high tide and waves were breaking within twenty yards of the cliff wall. Glancing round the circle of faces Paul realised that there could hardly have been a more representative

395

gathering of the Valley families. Not since his Coronation soirée had he seen so many of them in one place at one time. The Coombe Bay folk were represented by the two Tozers, Walt Pascoe and Eph Morgan, the Dell by Tamer and his son Sam. Young Willoughby was there from Deepdene, and so were the Derwents, father and son, from High Coombe. Will Codsall and Eveleigh's team represented Periwinkle and Four Winds and although old Arthur Pitts had remained at the top with Willoughby and the Home Farm men, Henry Pitts was there to represent Hermitage and had, in fact, already quarrelled with Paul in an attempt to take his place in the boat. Paul counted them, without knowing that he did so and numbered fifteen and only when they were ranged each side of the skiff, waiting for the lull after a ninth wave, did he realise that his own presence brought the total to sixteen.

For a moment, on launching, the sea under the headland seemed almost calm and they made it in a single rush, Tamer at the oars, Paul sitting astern with his weight, in accordance with Tamer's instructions, pressed on the rudder bar, causing the skiff to swing south-east as the bows struck the first breaker and brought a drenching shower of spray into the boat. The rope went taut, then slack, then taut again, so that at first Paul thought they would be dragged back into the eddy and thrown at the feet of the shore party but the scour, sweeping round the extreme tip of the Bluff, caught them within seconds and glancing over his shoulder he could still see the beach in the glow of the tar beacon. Then the buffeting of the waves drove every thought but self-preservation from his head and they seemed to be spinning in wide circles, with Tamer grunting and wheezing in the bows and every now and again lifting his starboard oar clear of the water as he lashed away with his port blade to increase his sea room and hold a course for the rock.

Without the cable they would have been helpless, for the scour here had the force of a cataract and they seemed to be rushed towards the causeway at fantastic speed. The wink of the beach fire had been blotted out yet they could see no sign of the big rock or of the men clinging to it. Paul saw that Tamer was back-paddling with all his might, doing what he could to check the onrush of the boat for each time the cable went slack they feared that the next jerk would rip the stern from the boat or tumble them both in a heap in the bows. The shore party, however, seemed to know their business. Soon the sickening jerks ceased as the cable remained taut and Tamer,

396

glancing over his left shoulder, drew in his starboard oar and set to work solely with his port, so that in smoother water west of the break-water the sheer weight of the wet cable steadied them somewhat and when Tamer shouted "Hard up, Squire!" Paul found the boat answered to the rudder perfectly and they drove right in under the rock, Tamer breaking the force of the collision with the oar. Then a minor miracle occurred. At the very moment of arrival the mist parted and they must have been visible for a few seconds from the beach for Paul heard a faint cheer and was astonished by it. It seemed to him that they were now miles out to sea.

It was to this momentary break in the mist that the survivors on the rock owed their lives, for although the shore party might have been able to drag the boat within reach of the beach, they would have had to guess the moment to do so whereas now they could see enough to show them when to let the cable slacken and give Tamer an opportunity to make his own last-minute approach. He achieved it with a skill Paul would not have expected of an expert seaman, standing upright in the tossing boat and somehow steadying it between a platform of rock on one side and the unbroken wall of the pinnacle on the other. The first man fell on them as from the skies and it was only when there was a concerted movement on the plat-form that Paul saw where the survivors were huddled, wedged in a compact group under a concave slab of sandstone and covered, every few seconds, by vast sheets of water spouting through gaps in the pyramid of fallen rocks about there. It was astounding, he thought, that anyone could still remain on the shelf, for each big wave flushed it from end to end and even more astonishing that, in the tiny runnel where Tamer was holding the boat steady, the overspill cascading from the shelf did not capsize them. The second man reached the boat between two smaller waves and then came a young woman, with a great mop of dark hair, who managed it more skilfully, judging her moment and crawling crablike across the level surface before somer-saulting into the bows. The survivors obviously had fight left in them for at once they set about baling with sea boots and it was time some-body did for the skiff, with five adults aboard, was shipping water in alarming quantities. Tamer, however, remained erect, arms widely spread and looking like an old prophet pronouncing a blessing as a half-naked boy with an injured leg was handed down. Then the mist closed in again and the men on shore began to haul, so that there was no chance of plucking anyone else from the shelf as they were bounced away, the keel scraping on the submerged causeway in its rush for the beach. They shipped so much that it was a miracle the boat bobbed up again as the next wave crested past and then, in a bound it seemed, they had grounded on shingle and the shore party were then hauling them in, dragging woman, boy and the two men from the boat and carrying them up the beach to the fire. Tamer, chest deep in the swell, still held on to the waterlogged boat, bellowing "Dornee mind 'em! Drag the boat clear, you bliddy vools, bevore 'er's smashed to tatters!", and enough of them heeded him to lift it clear and carry it along the tideline to the point where it had been launched fifteen minutes before. Eveleigh said, hoarsely, "How many more be there for God's sake?" and Paul told him four or five, as far as he could judge and they would have to return for them at once.

It was odd how every man seemed to find himself a task and needed little direction, either from Paul or Tamer. The little cove now seemed crowded with figures, all moving cumbersomely among the scattered boulders and crossing the dull glow of the fire. Paul noticed that the shepherd twins and Meg Potter had now made the descent and came forward to carry the injured lad out of reach of the spray. The woman with the wild mop of hair walked alone, seemingly little the worse for her experience, and Paul left them to help Eveleigh and the others gather up the cable and follow the party with the boat back along the tideline to the western edge of the cove.

They had, perhaps, another fifteen minutes in hand, for the sandy runnel from which they had made the launching was now knee deep in water and although the mist was dispersing, the sea, even at this protected point, still ran high. They had upended the skiff and drained it before moving off but although it was no great weight it was very difficult to manœuvre over broken ground in semi-darkness, with yards of heavy rope trailing behind as they slipped and slithered on the bladder wrack and weed-covered limpet shells. When they regained the launching point Paul saw that Tamer was near the end of his strength and said, as the men positioned the boat and began coiling the cable, "Can you make another trip, Tamer?", to which Tamer replied, bluntly, "I got no choice, 'ave I? There baint one o' these lubbers knows the cove like me, nor that skiff neither! Suit yourself whether you come along, I reckon I could manage alone if I shipped the rudder and trusted to the skulls!" Paul said, briefly, "There's no time to argue. Line up each side and push us clear again!"

398

It was by no means so straightforward an operation as before. The fire had burned low and with water splashing all round them they got in one another's way, so that twice the keel fouled ledges of rock and hurled the boat back on the shingle. At the third attempt they won clear and the improved visibility helped Paul steer a more direct course for the rock while Tamer, shipping his starboard oar, used the other to prevent them swinging broadside on to the breakers. Almost at once, or so it seemed to Paul, they were running straight for the niche where the survivors crouched and immediately Tamer rose to brace his oar against the rock two men scrambled aboard, one using the spare oar to offset Tamer's pressure in an attempt to keep the boat comparatively steady. A second later a middle-aged seaman, whom Paul judged to be the captain, left the rock but rolled over the stern into the water shouting to the last castaway, a young man naked but for a pair of canvas trousers, to join him on the tow rope. Paul and the rescued men at once began to bale but the moment Tamer withdrew his oar the shore party must have begun to haul for the boat shot stern first from its tiny haven, ploughing straight into the backwash of a spent breaker recoiling from the big rock. It was not a large wave compared to those breaking beyond the causeway, or even those falling on the beach eighty yards distant, but it was more than sufficient to capsize them into the trough. Paul, losing hold of the rudder bar, was pitched head over heels into the bows and for a moment he, Tamer and the two men amidships, tangled as the stern lifted under the suck of another backwash. Then he was flung clear and an oar, shooting past like a javelin, struck him a shattering blow on the temple. He felt the sharp sting of salt in the wound as the next wave crested over him but after that nothing but a confused buffeting as a tumult of water rolled him six feet under towards the breaker line.

They dragged them from the surf more dead than alive, Paul first, then the captain who kept his hold on the rope and made a lucky landing on sand at the launching point, and finally another man, who made a successful bid for his life by striking seaward, judging his moment to dive and finally landing in the arms of the shepherd twins as they stood waist deep in water to catch him. Minutes later a big wave tossed Tamer on to the ruins of the most easterly of his tar beacons. The other two sailors did not come ashore in the Cove. One was washed up a fortnight later on the Whinmouth bar, twelve miles to the West; the body of the other was never recovered.

They carried them beyond the shingle barrier and nobody had any comment to make at that time. After a few mouthfuls of spirit from Meg's leather bottle the captain recovered enough to tell them in precise English that there were no more survivors out on the rock and certainly no one alive on the wreck three miles out to sea but in any case further efforts were out of the question for the cable had parted, the boat was in splinters and both oars had been lost.

Rudd, as soon as he heard the news, came down the gully again and in the light of lanterns rigged on driftwood spars watched them at work on the survivors, himself kneeling to bandage the deep gash in Paul's temple. It was still bleeding freely and the rush of blood gave him hope. One of the sailors, who had been unconscious when brought ashore, responded to artificial respiration but Paul, although they worked on him for thirty minutes, yielded no more than a dribble of water. His pulse still registered and he muttered a few incoherent words when they lifted him and laid him between the replenished fires, wrapped in dry blankets brought down by the tireless Davy Tozer, making his fourth ascent of the gully that night. Tamer Potter would never be revived and everyone realised that as they dragged him ashore. His jaw had been smashed to a pulp but no blood flowed from the wound and his body was so bloated that it was all they could do to lift him clear of the boulders and carry him up the beach. By then it was after eleven o'clock and they could expect help any time now, for the sea was going down rapidly and the tide was on the ebb. Tom Williams, who had made two unsuccessful attempts to round the Bluff, sent word by Hazel Potter that he would come in and land before it was light and that they were to keep big fires burning and mark the sand runnel with two rows of lanterns. Meg Potter made no outcry when Eveleigh told her that Tamer was dead but accompanied him along the shingle to the spot where he lay slightly apart from the others. Rudd went with her, the others standing back in a silent huddle. She looked down on the disfigured face for a moment and said, camly and quietly, "Well, Mr. Rudd, 'er was a rare ole waster but 'er died a man's death come to last." She then took off the short, braided jacket she was wearing and covered his face, afterwards busying herself among the others and administering carefully regulated sips of her cordial.

Just before the boats arrived a group of them, wet, shivering and little realising what they had achieved, gathered round the body of Tamer, muttering among themselves, shamed by the corpse of a

400

man whom all had regarded with varying degrees of contempt. Presently Ephraim Morgan, the only man among them born outside the Valley, said, "There's a name you give the poor chap—'Tamer'. Was he christened so?" and Honeyman growled, "How would a man get a given name like 'Tamer', you old fool? When he was a boy living hereabouts a circus come to Whinmouth and he won a gold sovereign for staying five minutes in among they mangey ole lions! Seed him do it I did and his father gave him a belting for it, but he was Tamer Potter from then on. Anyone in the Valley could have told you that, I reckon."

They drifted away, moving among the survivors, who were sitting round the fire huddled in blankets. Pride was beginning to steal upon them and with it impatience for Williams and his boats to take them off this accursed stretch of beach. They stopped at the still figure of the Squire, watched over by a grim-faced Eveleigh and the silent Rudd. The bandages about his head showed white in the grey murk and once, as they watched, he groaned and moved his hands in a futile little gesture. Perhaps Edward Derwent voiced the general opinion when he said, "There's more to him than I supposed and it's a blessing, maybe, he came among us! Pray God he's not mortally injured," and he moved on to warm himself at one of the fires, remembering the time when he thought to have this man as son-in-law. It seemed a lifetime ago.

V

Grace, from her seat on the platform, first noticed the boy during the chairman's preamble and wondered at his presence. He was too far back for her to recognise him as the stable-boy whom Paul had rescued from a scrapyard but she could assess his age at about fourteen and supposed him to be the son of someone in the audience. Then she forgot him until spotting him again, marching along the kerb in pace with the procession. This time she recognised him at once and wondered what on earth he could be doing there and whether Paul was somewhere in the crowd and using the boy as his emissary.

As she had predicted in Committee the park rally was proving a dismal failure. She belonged to the élite of the movement, who understood that the time had passed when processions, banners and appeals to the public conscience produced any effect. With two prison sentences behind her she was stripped of democratic prejudices and contemptuous of rearward troops who still believed in persuasion by leaflet and argument. She was no longer a campaigner but a revolutionary, one of two or three hundred, whose bruises taught that a revolution demanded sacrifices of a kind that few spinsters, and even fewer wives, were prepared to make. She thought of the great majority of women marching behind her as emotional adolescents, ready enough to carry a banner, or perhaps bait a harassed bobby but untested by the ordeal of pain that the hard core of the movement now expected its initiates to seek out and suffer.

She had changed a great deal in the last year, changed physically, having lost close on two stone on Holloway diet but also psychologically, for she believed that she had at last won the battle against herself and had renounced all men, from Prime Minister Campbell Bannerman down to that chubby-faced boy trotting along beside the vanguard and apparently searching for her in the ranks. It had been an uphill struggle this complete and utter renunciation and throughout it, every step of the way, she had envied the spinsters of the movement their virginity and their apparent physical repugnance of men as men, reflecting that it must be a very simple matter to renounce something one had never sought or enjoyed. She found the renunciation of the claims of motherhood (a subject some of the newcomers debated with the ecstasy of young nuns) a relatively simple matter for although she sometimes felt curious about her son she did not yearn for him, as she did for a man who could solace her and to whom she could bring solace. There were sleepless nights in Holloway when she read more into the occasional howls of women in the cell block than a desperate loneliness, or deprivation. They were keening perhaps, for their men, for some stupid, patronising, pompous overlord, who was probably sharing the bed of some other hapless slut but they keened nonetheless and their outcry set Grace Craddock's teeth on edge. Yet it was her prison spells that had won her the battle in the end, for there were men on the staff of Holloway, as well as wardresses, a few of whom singled out suffragettes for special persecution. There were chaplains, doctors and visiting magistrates, men with bland, rubbery faces and well-nourished paunches; doctors who threatened forcible feeding, chaplains who talked about duty to God, which meant, of course, duty to men, and magistrates, who would cheerfully have reintroduced the horsewhip and the ducking stool had those methods of persuasion remained on the Statute Book. These occasional reminders of the sex had done more to stiffen her resolution than the bullying of the wardresses, with their harsh, morning cries of "Slops outside!" and their habit of standing by whirling a bunch of keys on a short chain whilst prisoners crammed spoonfuls of revolting grey porridge in their mouths. She could sometimes sympathise with the wardresses, some of whom were disconcerted by having to deal with educated women, but the men were like all men outside, ready with a smile, a pat or a pinch but only if wives, daughters and serving wenches were prepared to jump through hoops like a string of performing bitches. They were just as ready with their fists and their heavy-booted policemen to prevent any enlargement of a woman's role, or any claim by women to reshape society.

When the procession had been broken up, as she knew it would be the moment she saw the decoys march in with their Union Jack, she slipped away from the scrimmage and made across the park towards the Serpentine and it was here, away from the cheering, hysterical buffoons around the rostrum that she saw that the boy had followed her but was keeping his distance, like a cautious private detective. She sat down on the first available seat, watching him stop, edge forward uncertainly and finally touch his cap and grin in a rather rueful way, as though by no means sure of a welcome. She called, "All right, Ikey! What do you want?"

He came up quietly and sat down beside her. He was looking, she thought, travelworn and dishevelled, as though he had slept in his clothes. His wide Eton collar was a limp rag and his dark hair tousled. She noticed too that his boots were coated with dust and that under the dust was a stiff layer of red, Devon clay. He said, with a more cheerful grin, "I had a job keeping track of you, Mrs. Craddock. I found the place easily enough but when you started marching there were so many ladies and they were all dressed the same."

His accent struck her as unfamiliar. The nasal Cockney twang had been extracted from it and yet, somehow, it was not yet a normal speaking voice. She said, briefly, "Is Mr. Craddock with you?", and he looked very surprised and said, "Good Lord, no, Mrs. Craddock! How could he be? Haven't you heard?"

"Heard what?"

"Why about the wreck, about this!", and he took a crumpled copy of the *Daily News* from his pocket and opened it. On the front page was a banner headline, the second feature of the edition. It said: *"Westcountry Wreck Drama; Villagers Save Seven Lives,"* and underneath, in smaller type, *"Gallant Rescues by Squire and Farmer; Five*

403

Believed Dead." He let her read the story through without comment. It was a garbled, inaccurate version but its outline was factual. In the stop press, under the heading "*Wreck Drama*", was a three-line paragraph reporting that Squire Craddock had been critically injured getting the last of the German sailors ashore under the cliffs. She said, sharply, "How bad is he? Is he likely to die?", and Ikey admitted that he did not know for he had not come to her from Shallowford but from school, having run away early the previous morning. She looked at the newspaper again and saw that it was a day old. It did not surprise her that she should have missed the story. She seldom read anything but political news.

"Ikey, when did this happen? And why did you run away?"

"Three nights ago," he said. "My housemaster told me I was to stay on at school but I was coming to find you anyway—in the holidays that is! I knew the address of your headquarters, so I rode a goods train to Paxtonbury and then caught the main line train."

There were so many other questions she wanted to ask but she noticed now that his grin was forced and that behind it his features were drawn. She said, "Where did you sleep last night?"

"I found somewhere," he said defensively and she remembered then that he had once been a wharfside boy. "Have you eaten anything?"

"I had a meat pie, early on."

She got up and took his hand. "Well, let's get something inside you and then you can talk. After that you can sleep at my lodgings while I tell them where you are. They'll be frantic and I expect the police are looking for you!"

They walked along to the Achilles statue and hailed a cab and in a Kensington teashop she watched him eat ravenously yet with punctilious attention to his table manners. When they were going up Sloane Street to her bed-sitting-room she said, "How do you feel now, Ikey?" and he grinned again, this time without effort and said, "I feel fine, Mrs. Craddock! Are we going back home now?"

"No," she said, "that is, you are, but not until you've had a good sleep. I've got to let them know you're safe and well, Ikey. If the Squire is as ill as they say they won't want a thing like this worrying him, will they?"

"No," said Ikey, mildly, "I hadn't thought of that. How will you do it?"

"I'll telephone the Whinmouth police," she said, "and ask them to take a message to Mr. Rudd. Then he can let the school know and after that you can take your time going back." He was about to protest at this but a yawn caught him unawares and while he was stifling it she said, "We can talk later, after I've done what I have to do." They climbed the stairs to her room overlooking the Square. It was simply but pleasantly furnished for her austerity did not extend to the deliberate sacrifice of comfort. Enough sacrifices of that kind were required in gaol. She made tea while he went behind the draw curtain to undress and when she took him a cup of tea he was sitting up in bed and blushed when she looked at his neatly folded clothes. She thought to herself, "Somebody is working hard on Ikey and I don't believe it's just Paul—he's changed a very great deal but the little ragamuffin is still there, under the straitjacket they're knitting for him!" She sat on the end of the bed watching him and liking what she saw, and presently said, "Did you really run away with the idea of finding me and taking me back with you?"

"Yes, I did," he said, with another yawn, "it was the only way I could think of to help Squire," and he handed her the empty tea cup and snuggled down under the sheets. Before she had passed beyond the curtain he was asleep.

She chose a police station where she was not known and gave her real name. She took Ikey's paper along and showed it to a serious-looking sergeant, explaining who Ikey was and saying that she would like to get a message sent through to Whinmouth police station. She would have preferred to pass the information by telegram but this would have taken longer. As it was the sergeant, gravely interested, allowed her to speak to the Whinmouth sergeant and she asked him to telephone the landlord of The Raven and tell someone to ride over to Shallowford and report to Mr. Rudd that Ikey Palfrey was safe and would be coming home on the first train tomorrow. Then she asked for news of Paul and was told he was on the mend, although likely to be laid up for some weeks. The head wound, she learned, had caused severe concussion but more serious injuries included two broken ribs and a fractured arm. The serious-looking police sergeant at her elbow listened to every word, and when she had concluded the call he said, trying hard to sound nonchalant, "The er . . . gentleman concerned in the rescue is your husband, ma'am?" and she said that was so and thanked him for his assistance but left without satisfying his curiosity. It was a long time since she had scored over a member of the Metropolitan police.

It was growing dusk when she climbed the stairs to her room again to find him still asleep. She made some vegetable soup and a ham salad, and set two places at her little table. Then she woke him, showing him where he could wash, and while he was splashing in the cubicle she told him what she had done and gave him the reassuring news from Shallowford. When they were sitting at table she said, "Very well, Ikey, now I'll listen," but suddenly he was tongue-tied. It had seemed so clear-cut when he had set out but now the purpose of his mission was getting blurred, and his presence here, drinking her soup and eating her ham salad after sleeping in her bed was farcical, like an elaborate practical joke that had misfired. She said, trying to reassure him, "Whatever you say, Ikey, will remain between the two of us! After all, you must have had very strong reasons for doing such a silly thing, particularly when you already knew the Squire had been injured and the whole Valley would be in an uproar without you adding to it!"

"I don't properly understand it any more, ma'am," he admitted. "I thought I did but I don't. I suppose I just wanted to . . . well to *help* him! He's been jolly decent to me, and it seemed right to pay back somehow. You see, he was so different when you were there and even before you came but now, well, it isn't like it was, not for me and not for any of us! I reckoned that if you came back it would be all right again but I daresay it's none of my business, ma'am."

Suddenly she felt great compassion for him. If she could have been sure that it would not have embarrassed him horribly she would have flung her arms round him and kissed him for his confusion. The honesty that prompted it seemed to her one of the most genuinely touching things she had ever witnessed and for the first time in a very long period she could have wept without shame. She said, mastering herself, "I can't ever come back, Ikey, and I don't think the Squire wants me back, not unless I changed my whole life and I can't do that. Far too much has happened but I don't blame you for trying. I think it was a rather wonderful thing to do and you're quite right to look up to the Squire the way you do because he is a very good man and not simply because of what he did for you or what happened in Coombe Bay the other night. It's just that he and I have different work to do and neither of us could do it if we went on living together in Shallowford or anywhere like Shallowford." She paused, adding, "Do you understand anything of what I'm trying to tell you, Ikey?"

"No," he said, stubbornly, "I don't reckon I do, ma'am. Married people live together for always, don't they?"

She tried another approach. "What do you believe in most, Ikey? I mean . . . what *idea*? What's terribly important to you, apart from Squire Craddock? Would it be your new school?"

He considered the question carefully, as though resolved to give as truthful an answer as his understanding of it permitted. "I suppose, England," he said finally, and then, doubtfully, "is that what you meant, Mrs. Craddock?"

"Yes," she said, "that's exactly what I mean and now see if you can follow me a little further. England is your country and it's very important to you. So it is to me and to the Squire, only we don't all have the same ideas of how to work for it, or make it a better place for everyone to live in."

His eyes never left hers as he said, "I can't see what that's got to do with you and Squire, ma'am."

"Oh yes you can, if you think, Ikey. You're very sharp! If you weren't you wouldn't have got the idea of coming to find me in the first place and even if you had you could never have found your way here alone. What I'm trying to say is this — the Squire and I don't live separate lives because we've quarrelled in the way that lots of married people quarrel. It's just that he wants the *old* kind of England and I want a very different one. When married people think as opposite as that they cease to get any pleasure out of one another's company."

"You mean you ran away just to join the suffragettes?" he asked, incredulously.

"Not exactly," she said, smiling, "but that was what decided me. I really left because there was no real place for me in the Valley and I believe Squire understands that now. If you give him time I don't think he'll continue to hold it against me!"

"Then why is he so miserable?" demanded Ikey and she said, quickly, "Because he's very lonely! You're away at school most of the time and Shallowford is a big empty house for a man to live in alone. Besides, I don't believe he is miserable all the time or not when he's out in the open. Maybe he'll marry again!"

"How could he do that when he's married to you?"

"People can get unmarried — divorced, and I've already gone into that, although he doesn't know about it yet. I suppose it must sound terribly complicated to you, Ikey, so you'll just have to take my word for it until you're older! It wouldn't be the slightest good my coming home simply because he was injured. You see, I believe in what I'm doing here, with all my heart and soul, just as much as Squire believes in what *he's* doing, and besides, I wouldn't want to live in the country again." She paused. "Have I made any kind of sense to you?"

"Yes, I reckon you have," he said, slowly, "but it doesn't help much, does it?"

"I believe *you* might help straighten things out," she said, "but you would have to give me your word of honour never to tell a soul, not even the Squire, that I had a hand in it!" and she paused, looking at him speculatively, scrutinising and ultimately sanctioning an idea that had occurred to her with disconcerting suddenness. "Do you remember Farmer Derwent's daughter? Claire, the pretty one?"

"Yes, of course," he said, "she used to ride a lot with Squire. She was always over the big house before . . ." He was going to say "before you came" but checked himself, feeling this might annoy her and said instead, "before I started taking lessons in Paxtonbury."

"That's right," she said, "and since we seem to have so many secrets now, Ikey, I'll let you into another. If the Squire hadn't married me he would have almost certainly married Claire Derwent! It was me who stopped him marrying her but she's still very much in love with him."

"How do you know that?" he demanded, unequivocally.

"Well, I do know," she said, "and what's more I know where she is at the moment. She's running a tea-shop quite near here. She owns it but she also trains as a nurse. I met her by accident some time ago and we . . . well, we talked! It was before the news got around that I had run away and she thought I was up here on a visit. She's the one you ought to spirit back to Shallowford, not me."

A small bubble of mischief popped through the crust of his bewilderment and he said, with an engaging grin, "You mean, he might fall in love with her again and marry her?"

"Why did you say 'again'?" she said sharply and he said, half-apologetically, "Well, they were laying odds on it when I was a stable-boy!"

"Who were?"

"All of them, Handcock the gardener, Chivers the groom, and the rest! Mrs. Handcock was sure Squire would marry Claire Derwent and I remember her and Thirza grumbling about it in the kitchen." He grinned again. "She clouted me for telling Chivers what they said!"

She noticed something new about him as he said this, that his loyalty was wholly Paul's. Her patience and cosseting had made no impression upon him, for he did not see her as an individual, or even as Paul's legal wife, but merely as a possible means of improving the humour of his hero, Squire Craddock. She realised something else — that she had grossly underestimated his intelligence and had been wrong to deal with him as one might deal with a child. He was not a child — in many ways he was far more mature than Paul and seemed almost to be mocking her as he said, "And how would I go about that, Mrs. Craddock?" His cold-bloodedness, his apparent readiness to regard her as something expendable was chastening.

"You came to me out of the blue so you'd better do the same to her, Ikey," she said and got up, with the intention of checking on Claire Derwent's address in the directory she used for canvassing. The initiative, however, had now passed to him. He seemed to be considering the matter with clinical detachment.

"That wouldn't do at all," he said finally, "not now you've told them where I am. If Miss Derwent got to know I'd been here first she wouldn't believe a word I said! No, that wouldn't work, or not with a lady!"

He seemed to imply that her sex was not so much tiresome as impossibly devious, and while this might have enraged her had he been a grown man she found herself admiring his easy familiarity with human weaknesses, so much so that she felt she had done her part by reminding him of Claire Derwent's existence and could safely leave the mechanics of intrigue to him. When she spoke again she was the pupil, he the instructor.

"What new mischief are you planning now, Ikey?"

"It would have to be done by a letter," he said slowly, "and the letter would have to be posted in Shallowford. I could write it here tho', and you could read it. Then I could post it as soon as I get home and it would have a local postmark on it and she wouldn't suspect." He had clearly made up his mind on the essentials. "Could you lend me a sheet of paper and pen and ink, ma'am?"

She gave him some plain writing paper, a pen and a bottle of ink, and left him to himself while she cleared the supper things. All the time she was washing up and drying he was bent over his task, his pen scratching away, his tongue peeping from between his teeth in the effort of concentration. When she had finished she lit the gas fire and sat beside it, pretending to read but actually giving him her whole attention. At last he straightened up and handed her the paper, now covered with his half-formed schoolboy scrawl and signed "*Ikey Palfrey*" and in brackets, below the signature, "*the one you may remember as stableboy.*" The naïveté of this afterthought made her smile but the letter itself was by no means naïve but a little masterpiece of special pleading. If she knew Claire Derwent as well as she thought she did the girl would find it irresistible. Ikey had written:

"*Dear Miss Derwent, I got your address from the Xmas Card you sent Squire. You may think it rood of me to write like this but I take the chance because I love Squire and can't think of any other way to help. You will have hird all about how he and Tamer Potter rescued the German sailors, and how he got badly hurt and is still laid up, also how Mrs. Craddock run off a year ago and hasn't been seen since. Well Miss Derwent, now I come to the mane thing. I was in and out of his room before he began to come round from the whack on the head and he kept asking for you, not nowing it of course but calling out your name as if you was in the room. I asked Mrs. Handcock about it and she said maybe he was remembering all the good times you had when I used to saddle up for him and you rode in the woods I thought you might like to know about this so as you could call in and cheer him him up a bit if you were down this way to see Miss Rose or Farmer Derwent soon. I know he would like that because he's been very low lately, nothing like he was in the old days so again appollergising for writing and hoping you are well as I am since Squire sent me to school Respectfully, Ikey Palfrey.*"

She read the letter through twice and handed it back to him, together with Claire Derwent's latest address in Bayswater.

"Ikey," she said, "either you'll end up in gaol like Smut Potter, or you'll be Prime Minister! I couldn't improve on that in a thousand years. Now tell me about yourself, and how you're getting on at that big school in North Devon."

CHAPTER FIVE

I

IT was not until she was alone in the room that Claire Derwent knew with certainty she had come home for good, that never again would she willingly exchange this view and these scents, for the asphalt of Bayswater or the genteel atmosphere of Tunbridge Wells. It was mid-April now and in the afternoons the sunlight over the paddock was the colour of buttermilk, with wide belts of river sedge lying like strips of green velvet on either side of the stream, and flocks of starched clouds moving slowly down from the Bluff casting patches of creeping shadow over the stubble fields of Four Winds and the long slope dividing the two rivers.

She stood by the big window a long time, occasionally glancing at the man on the bed, unworried by his restlessness, for they had warned her that he would be feverish for a day or so and the doctor had promised to look in on the way back to the village to "make him a little more comfortable". Claire had attended enough V.A.D. lectures at St. Thomas's to accept this phrase as a cliché that not even a lady doctor like O'Keefe's down-to-earth daughter could avoid using.

He looked, she thought, supremely uncomfortable, with his left arm awkwardly angled in its shiny metal splint, his body slumped in a position half-way between sitting and lying and his head turbaned in bandages, like the heads of wounded soldiers in illustrated magazines. He needed a shave too, and perhaps tomorrow they would allow her to shave him. That was something she had learned in the first series of lectures—"How to remove hair from the helpless"—and the memory of the sub-title made her smile, so that she had to chide herself for feeling so cheerful in a sick-room and turn again to look at the view, taking a brief mindseye ramble over the horizon where the Shallowford beeches formed the eastern frame for the landscape.

She had not realised how little thought she had given this place in the last few years. Once the first wave of homesickness had receded, and she had become absorbed in the teashop adventure, she had felt rather patronising about the Sorrel Valley and Sorrel Valley folk,

411

thinking of them as a collection of raggle-tailed rustics without benefit of the urban delights of a fashionable spa and out of reach of the great city, where she had spent the final year of her exile. But now, only three weeks since she had been lured home by that fantastic letter (penned by what was surely the Squire's most devoted tenant!) it was the people of the Spa and of the faceless houses along the Bayswater Road whom she thought of as underprivileged. What had any one of them to compare with this except a formal park or two, or a village already cluttered with honking, dust-trailing motors and enclosed by clusters of red-brick houses, where prosperous merchants were caricatures of men like Craddock? Yet, she had only made the journey on impulse, and with no intention of doing more than pay a hasty call on her father and Rose, and perhaps, in response to that devoted stable-boy's plea, to congratulate the hero of the Valley on having put the Sorrel Valley on the front pages of the newspapers for the first and probably the last time in history.

She had made her call and had returned to High Coombe shocked by his appearance and afterwards, with no real object in mind, she had hung on, waiting for the crisis of his attack of pneumonia, a not unexpected result of his incredible exertions on the night of the wreck. She found the rhythm of the big house shattered. People came and went, and the place seemed half full of foreigners, not foreigners who lived within half-a-day's ride of the Valley but real foreigners, who spoke a foreign tongue. Poor old John Rudd went about with an undertaker's face and Mrs. Handcock wept freely into her pastry. The only lively person about the place was two-and-a-half-year-old Simon, who soon made friends with her and clamoured to be taken for rides on the pommel of her saddle.

Then, like the false dawn of a new era, Doctor Maureen O'Keefe, the Coombe Bay physician's fully-qualified daughter, swept into the Valley, the first lady-doctor that any of them had heard of much less attended, with her mixture of sardonic humour, brisk efficiency and shrewd Irish charm that had succeeded in routing prejudice in less than a week. She had brought with her a sense of rapid change, fresh air and wide open windows, so that soon news began to spread that Squire Craddock was on the mend, and "thicky lady-doctor" had miraculously repaired his damaged ribs and set one of his fractures, using the big kitchen as an operating theatre. Even John Rudd was seen to perk up a little and Mrs. Handcock ceased her eternal snivelling. The boy Ikey lost his look of tragedy and optimism returned to the Valley in the wake of spring. Yet, although Doctor Maureen showed a certain interest in Claire's claim regarding a V.A.D. training at St. Thomas' it was not until after the second operation on Paul's arm that she accepted her offer as sick-room nurse, whilst she drove her gig about the Valley, bullying blushing labourers into peeling off their shirts and answering her questions about diet and cottage hygiene.

At any other time the invasion of a woman doctor in the Valley would have provided a pub topic for a month but so many things had been happening here of late that Doctor O'Keefe's daughter was able to play herself in in a matter of days. Rumours rushed up and down the Valley like flights of starlings. The Squire was dying. The Squire was recovering. Old Tamer Potter was being buried in a common grave with seven German sailors. Old Tamer Potter was having a granite memorial tombstone all to himself paid for by the Kaiser. And then rumours that grew out of these rumours; young Palfrey, the stable-boy Squire was trying to turn into a gentleman, had run away, been caught and sent back by the police; Claire Derwent, who was once said to be marrying Squire, had been rushed down from London to nurse him as soon as it was known that Squire's wife, that mad Lovell girl, had been locked up yet again; Smut Potter, languishing in Paxtonbury gaol, was said to be due for early release, an official reward for his father's heroism, and finally, perhaps the most disquieting rumour of all, old John Rudd, a widower with a son old enough to drive motors and seduce wives, was said to be madly in love with the lady doctor and courting her, while her father was taking a cure in an alcoholic ward of Paxtonbury asylum! It was too much, too quickly served and the Valley was unable to digest it, so that soon it gave up trying, the weather being warm, spring well advanced and work waiting upon idle hands in field and byre.

Slowly the great springtide of speculation receded but the Valley families were never to forget their moment of high drama. In farms and cottages newspapers containing stories of the wreck, and the funerals that followed it, were carefully folded and laid away in chests of drawers, so that future generations could appreciate the national importance of the Sorrel Valley in years to come.

II

He saw her sitting sideways to the bed, an open book on her lap

413

and the afternoon sun, flooding through the tall, mullioned windows, playing games with tendrils that had escaped from her golden "bun" and hung like tiny tongues of autumn bracken over her ears.

It took him a moment or two to realise who she was for when he saw her sitting there, with her knees pressed together and her head bent low over the page, he at once associated her with a picture he had seen somewhere and the effort of establishing the link tired him, so that he closed his eyes again and went about disentangling the fabric of dreams from reality. Then, when he opened his eyes again, he remembered. The woman sitting beside the bed, knees pressed together, smooth, rounded face half-turned to the window and a book on her lap, was Bathsheba, reading the message from King David, yet also—and this was puzzling—she was Claire Derwent, late of High Coombe farm. He studied her very carefully, or as carefully as his damnably awkward posture would permit, trying to remember whether she had been there during his few lucid intervals when he had exchanged a word or two with John Rudd before being pulled this way and that by a strange woman said to be a doctor and the daughter of that drunken old Irishman, O'Keefe. He could not recall seeing Claire in the room then and this disturbed him, for it suggested that he was still dreaming and that Claire Derwent, or Bathsheba, belonged to the world of fantasy. Then she looked up and saw that he was awake, and her eyes lit up as she smiled in a way that somehow reassured him. She said softly, "Hullo, Paul! More yourself?", and reached out to take his pulse. This again struck him as odd, for it seemed extremely improbable that there should be two lady doctors in the Valley.

"What are you doing here?" he asked, "and why the devil am I still trussed up like this?" but this time her smile was professional as she said calmly, "Which question would you like answered first, Paul?" and because her voice and touch soothed him he smiled back, saying, carefully, "They were going to reset this damned arm. That's the last thing I remember. Is it done now? Is this why I'm still in a straitjacket?", and she told him that this was so, that "the lady doctor" would be in to look at him again soon and that meantime she had volunteered her services as nurse. "Semi-professionally," she added, with a touch of pride, "for I did V.A.D. training in London but I don't think you should talk much now. Suppose I get you a cup of tea?"

"I don't want a thing to eat," he said, "but I could do with some tea! I've got a mouth just like the bottom of old Honeyman's saw-pit! Chloroform I imagine. Get tea Claire, but don't go away, because I want to know what's happened. I'm still very hazy."

"Of course you are," she said, "you've just come round from an anaesthetic but you'll be all right in the morning. I'll get tea now," and she rustled out of the room and hurried down the backstairs to the kitchen.

Without understanding why she felt elated, perhaps because his recognition of her, and his inclination to chat, gave substance to Maureen O'Keefe's assurances of a swift recovery. Mrs. Handcock read good news in her face and in the demand for a pot of strong tea. "Is 'er comin' round, then? Is 'er really on the mend, do 'ee think?" she asked and Claire told her that he was very definitely on the mend, and that she could pop in and have a word with him after the doctor had been. The bulletin transformed the housekeeper. She puffed out her cheeks with relief and waddled to and fro laying the tea-tray, saying, "Tiz been a turrible carry-on about yer, Miss Claire! A *turrible* carry-on! Right plaized to zee *you* back I be for mebbe you c'n maake 'un smile again! What with one thing and another us didden know 'ow 'twould end sometimes. My Horace has been in a rare ole tizzy about 'un, I can tell 'ee!"

"I can believe it, Mrs. Handcock," said Claire, and took the tray up the backstairs to the bedroom, cooling the first cup with plenty of milk in case he spilled it, then putting her arm round his shoulders to steady him as he lifted it to his mouth with his free hand.

He drank it gratefully and asked for another and hotter cup but while she was pouring he passed his hand over his chin and exclaimed, "Good God, I've got half-an-inch of stubble! Why the devil didn't somebody shave me before they brought you here?" and she laughed and said she would shave him herself if the doctor gave permission and then let him drink his second cup without help, remembering the stress laid upon such niceties in the lecture entitled "Convalescence!"

"All right," he said, when she had relieved him of the cup, "now you can tell me how you happen to be here and something of what's going on. That woman doctor can't because she's a stranger here and as for John Rudd, he fusses like an old hen every time I ask him a straightforward question! All I get from him is 'Don't fret, Boy! Leave everything to me!' as if that helps a man to clear his head!"

"Well, he's right," she said, "for you have been rather ill, you

415

know. Apart from being badly knocked about you had pneumonia and pneumonia plus broken ribs can be very dangerous."

He grinned and she realised he was laughing at her readiness to dispense medical knowledge.

"So you sold that wretched tea-shop and took up nursing?"

"No," she said, "but I might. I was always interested in nursing and would have gone in for it years ago if Father hadn't sat on the idea. I enrolled for a V.A.D. course at St. Thomas's when I left Penshurst and opened a shop in London."

He remembered vaguely that she had taken new premises in Bayswater about a year ago and that news of this had reached him through Rose after the arrival of a Christmas card showing a sketch of her shop. It gratified him that he could remember such things and that his brain seemed to be working normally, and after being prompted to tell him more she explained that she had read of the wreck in the London newspapers and decided to come home and hear about it first-hand. She said nothing of Ikey's letter, deciding that it was not for her to tell him that her presence here was in fact due to the boy's statement that he had called out for her in a delirium. Then he asked her the date and seemed surprised when she told him that it was April 8th, nearly a month since the night of the wreck yet with this reminder she witnessed a mild puff of pride when he said, being careful to speak collectively, "We did a good job down there, didn't we? Seven out of the nine on that rock but it was more by luck than judgment! Poor Old Tamer was the real hero and I wish to God he'd lived to realise what he'd done, and have people respect him for once! Will you remind John Rudd to see that Meg and the girls don't want for anything until I can get about again?"

"You really can't start fretting over things until you're really well," she told him severely. "For heaven's sake let the Valley look after itself, Paul! It's been doing it for centuries, you know!", and then she regretted having said this for it implied that his leadership was a non-essential, so she added, quickly, "That doesn't mean that everybody round here doesn't think a very great deal of you, Paul! I realised that the moment I talked with Father and you know how difficult he is to impress! He said the Valley people would never have achieved anything like that under a Lovell and that you've done a wonderful job here and this proves it."

He pondered this for a moment and she took the oportunity to draw the curtains. When she returned to the bed he was asleep and

416

as she stood looking down at him it crossed her mind that he had the face of an Elizabethan, with a jaw-line and high cheekbones that were uncommon today, especially about here, where almost everyone had the squarish Anglo-Saxon cast of features or, where the Celtic strain predominated, a smoother, chubbier face. There were plenty of dark-skinned men in the Valley but their beards had a bluish gloss that his lacked. All in all, she reflected, he was a strange, alien man to want to make his life here where he had no roots yet his doggedness was making itself felt, even upon men as conservative as her father. He was like a wedge that had first attached itself to the soil of the Valley by its own weight and every blow strengthened its bite. There had been that awful Codsall business, then the dismal Smut Potter affair and the quarrel with Gilroy and finally the strange abdication of Grace Lovell but nothing seemed capable of dislodging him, not even the recurring scandals of his wife's gaol sentences. He absorbed all these setbacks, still clutching at his rather old-fashioned conception of duty. His outlook would have amazed his predecessors and was said to have exasperated his wife but this ought not to have surprised him — anyone could have told him that a well-bred woman like Grace Lovell would be incapable of seconding his arch ideas.

She stood there a long time and the memory of their association returned to her like a windsong, pleasant but unsubstantial, without a clearly recollected beginning and with no promise of renewal. She had once thought of herself as madly in love with him but now she understood that her self-deception had grown out of the prospect of co-owning the acres on which she had been born and where she had spent such a happy childhood. She had forgiven herself all those clumsy schemes to capture him, supposing that any girl of her age and limited experience would have done her best to catch a husband who was rich, young and very amiable. Perhaps he was the real loser, for surely no one else in the Valley understood him as she did and had done from the moment when she had been able to evaluate his terrible earnestness. The thought interested her. Had Grace Lovell really been obsessed with the campaign to win votes for women or had she run off simply because she was bored to death by his obsession with chawbacons and their affairs? And wouldn't any intelligent, educated woman be bored with them if she had access, through his money, to a richer and fuller life? It was, she decided, unfair to ask herself this question, for she had never regarded herself as an educated woman and had been brought up to accept the authority

417

and the wilfulness of males as uncomplainingly as one faced up to a wet haymaking season, or a false spring half-way through January. A Valley wife did not necessarily have to embrace her man's enthusiasms; she either absorbed them or shrugged them off and went about the business of making a home and rearing children. Yet would it be as simple as this with Paul Craddock? Whoever married him would marry the estate and personal happiness with a man as obstinate as him could only be achieved by a fusion of interests that went beyond those of hearth and nursery. It was not simply a matter of acreage either, of cob, thatch and husbandry. Whoever shared his life would be required to know the Christian names of every soul dwelling inside the magic circle, together with their needs, hopes, fears and capacity for skilled and unskilled work. It was something to which she had not given a thought when she made such a goose of herself beside the mere and in the days immediately before the Coronation soirée.

There was a scrunch on the gravel outside and she looked down from the window to see the doctor's gig cresting the drive. As she watched Doctor Maureen handed down by John Rudd, she thought, "Well, O'Keefe's clever daughter may know what's wrong with his body but I could do a better job on the real man, so I'm hanged if I give that teashop another thought until I've made him laugh again!"

III

No poet lived in the Valley so there was no one to idle along the banks of the Sorrel, or sit musing beside the mere that season and make some shift at capturing the magic of spring in the fields and bottoms, or the effect it had upon the men and women who lived there. Hazel Potter sensed what was happening because she communed with each successive season but Hazel had great difficulty in writing her name and her poetry either stayed in her head or was expressed through gibberish or the flash of her nut-brown arms and bare legs, as she ranged the woods, or crossed the moor as far as the railway line. Hazel saw the drifts of bluebells under the beeches west of the mere and the trailing clusters of primroses nestling in the steep banks of the back lanes between Hermitage plateau and the thickets of the Bluff. She heard the oratorios of the thrushes, blackbirds and finches in the birch woods and laurel clumps, and saw the voles slipping along the Sorrel flats between the straight, green stems of wild iris. She knew some of the otters by name and the badgers too,

418

where they had their holts in the broken hillside north of the mere, and she often stood for an hour talking to darting squirrels in the oak on the meadow above the big house.

Tamer's death brought her no sorrow. She had never been afraid of him, as were the older girls, and her appraisal of death differed very materially from that of almost everyone else in the Valley. When the Valley folk heard Parson Bull intone at the graveside of the German sailors, using phrases like "man springeth up and is cut down like a flower", or "in the midst of life we are in death", they did not understand these warnings as Hazel understood them, regarding them as no more than extracts from the Prayer Book. Hazel, so accurately in tune with the rhythm of the Valley and with the cycle of life and death that involved every living thing in the Valley, accepted the phrases as plain statements of fact. Every creature, every leaf and every flower in the Valley lived its hour and died its death, sinking back into the earth again and reappearing in changed form next spring, or the spring after that. There was no profit in deploring this, or in wearing mourning and uprooting flowers to pile on pits at places where men and animals and even windfalls and the husks of horse chestnuts were recommitted to the earth. There they had been and there they went and that was that; there was no dividing line to be drawn between a pot-bellied old drunkard like Tamer Potter and, say, a hedgehog struck down by a hawk. It was the pattern of things and to question it or even think about it was futile. Yet this did not mean that Hazel Potter was deaf to the muted trumpet of spring, or that the throb of renewed life in the Valley aroused no response in her heart. Her step was lighter and her eye and ear sharper than when she trod these same paths in autumn or winter and her heart beat faster as she silently dogged the movements of Ikey Palfrey (whom she still thought of as "The Boy") in his lonely tramps through the coppices and bramble brakes behind the big house.

She had been surprised to see him again for they said that Squire had sent him away to a big school, and it must have been so for he had stopped coming down to the mere opposite the Niggerman's Church to wait for her. She did not resent this severance of their association, supposing him to have passed out of her orbit after being condemned to sit all day scratching among papers like a squirrel making a dray but sometimes she was curious to learn what had induced him to abandon the jolly life of a stable-boy for a wearisome life like the Squire's and whether, in fact, the change had been imposed upon him as a punishment, perhaps for stealing away and meeting her in the woods. Her curiosity encouraged her to keep a close watch on him and one morning she followed him across the bluebell orchard behind the house and through Priory Wood to the high-banked lane linking Hermitage land to the northern boundary of the Home Farm. When he turned east, as though making for Shallowford Woods, she stepped from behind a big ash and called so that he stopped in his tracks looking surprised and undecided. Then, when he saw her slide down the bank, he blushed and seemed on the point of running back the way he had come.

"Where've 'ee been, Boy?" she demanded, "an' why didden 'ee come upalong, like 'ee used to?"

His embarrassment left him as soon as he heard her voice but was replaced by a kind of wariness. He said, "I thought maybe you wouldn't be there, on account of your father being drowned," and at this she looked surprised, not so much by the remark but by the dramatic change in his voice, as though it had been dug out of him, put through a mangle and replaced, a lisping relic of the original.

"You spake diff'rent," she proclaimed, gleefully. "How cum you do that, Boy?"

He said, with dignity, "My voice has broken. All men's voices change when they are fourteen."

This seemed to interest her, as though it was one of the few processes of nature that had somehow escaped her notice.

"Is it zo?" she said, "I never heard tell of it bevore," and then, forgetting his voice, "Do 'ee want to zee the badgers, Boy?", and he conceded gravely that he would like to see them and they went up the lane, across the wood and round the edge of the mere to the hill near where she had found him in the snow.

They did not see any badgers but they saw many other things that interested him, a bullfinch's nest with three eggs, an otter diving near the island, a lame vixen at the entrance of an earth close to Smut's hideout, and soon a little of their effortless relationship returned so that he found himself slipping back into her brogue and wondering about her again. He asked her if her father's death had made her as miserable as the Squire's illness was making him and was shocked by her seeming indifference.

"Giddon, no," she said, contemptuously. " 'Er's dade idden her? And 'er diden know a dandelion from a daisy!"

420

Unable to follow this logic he said, "Well, he was a hero down in the cove, Hazel!" and she replied, glumly, "Ar but 'er smashed our boat to tatters bringin' they foreigners off the rock!" The discovery that she valued the boat far above her father gave him another clue to her character. She had always intrigued him, with her astonishing knowledge of woodlore and her free communion with wild creatures, but now he saw her as the one person of his world who had achieved complete independence and it seemed to him a very wonderful thing, this ability to remove oneself at will from the ties of authority and wander over the Valley, impervious to social obligations and the weather. In a way he thought, she was a kind of queen with privileges denied men and women tied to chores and caught up in the rhythm of the seasons. She was beautiful too, with her great brown eyes, healthy, freckled skin and wild mass of chestnut hair that fell, free of all pins and ribbons, to her shoulders. Contemplating her, as they sat side by side on an old log beside the mere, he said, enviously, "You have a marvellous time, Hazel, doing exactly what you please! Why can't everyone do as they please, just the way you do?"

She gave him a shrewd, sidelong glance, her strong teeth flashing in a merry smile. "Mebbe tiz along o' they ole books, Boy," she told him, "they'm all mazed about books. I dunno why. What can 'ee vind in 'em that baint starin' 'ee in the faace about here?" and she reached out and plucked a celandine growing in the bank behind them, holding it between a grubby finger and thumb and twirling it, so that the moist gleam of its petals changed it from a flower to a golden ring. "Idden 'er pretty, now? Dorn 'ee think on that when youm in skuel, along o' they ole books?" It was a salutary object lesson and impressed him tremendously for somehow it revealed to him his own duality, part waif like her, part gentleman-in-the-making and for the moment the latter role seemed very sterile. He reached out, tentatively and touched her hair, finding it unexpectedly soft and glossy. She did not move or smile but sat quite still as the tangled tresses slipped through his fingers but when the impulse to touch her was spent, and he shyly withdrew his hand, she said, "Tiz soft, baint it?" and shook her head so that hair tumbled about her shoulders and then, with her head on one side, "Do 'ee think I'm beautiful, Boy?" He said, sadly, "Yes, you are beautiful, Hazel, and the best times I ever had have been out here with you but I'm going back to school tomorrow, so I shan't see you again until the summer holidays. Suppose . . . suppose I write you a letter from school?"

"No dornee," she said, laughing, "I coulden read un," but then a thought struck her and she added, "I could get Pansy to spell un out mebbe. 'Er's the best scollard of us."

"No," he said, hastily, "I wouldn't like that!" and suddenly feeling deflated he got up and began skimming pebbles into the mere, watching them break the surface all the way to the islet.

She sat on the log watching him, plagued by emotions that she did not understand and moved by impulses that were the first she had been unable to obey as soon as they were felt. The recollected touch of his hand as it passed over her hair made her shiver and this puzzled her greatly, for the sun was very warm on her bare neck and legs. She got up, puzzled and angry with herself, and went quietly up the slope through the close-set timber. When he tired of throwing stones and returned to the log she had disappeared behind the trees.

IV

The fingers of spring were probing everywhere in the Valley now and their license was not restricted to the young and untrammelled. High on the long slope of Blackberry Moor, Elinor Codsall was aware of them that same morning, when the persistent twitter of birds awoke both her and Will at first light, and in yielding to him she casually conceived a third child, despite their plan to limit the family until they had enough capital to buy some portable hovers Will had coveted at the experimental poultry farm, north of Paxtonbury. He had thought at first that he could make hovers as good as these but the days were far too short and they could not afford hired help like the other farms in the Valley. As soon as he had done with her Will began to snore again, a gross indulgence on his part in view of the fact that it was time to rise and start work, so she prodded him, calling "Will! Will! Dornee drop off again! I'll brew tea an' us'll make an early start today!" He grunted and sat up, knuckling his eyes and then, in the soft light of dawn, grinned down at her fondly and possessively. "By God, Elinor," he declared, "youm prettier'n ever, midear! I reckon I could taake 'ee again if us had time," and although she said, "Giddon with your ole nonsense!" and slipped hurriedly out of bed in case he was tempted to waste more time, she was pleased with the compliment, reflecting that most men of Will's type, having been so recently indulged, would have grumbled at being dragged from sleep.

The sun almost shouted at Sam Potter, striding over the dyke-banks at the eastern end of the mere on his way to fell timber for a pheasant compound. He walked as though all his joints were fitted with small, steel springs, covering just over a yard at each stride, and as he loped along he sucked in great mouthfuls of sharp April air, sparing a thought for poor old Smut, now ending his third year behind bars and due, so they heard, for release on licence in the new year. He did not think of his father, Tamer, lying in Coombe Bay churchyard surrounded by such unlikely names as Ledermann, Schmitt and Kohlhoff, for it was not a morning to contemplate death and shipwreck. Instead he watched, with an admiring grin, a great dog-fox leap clear of the bracken and bound across the soft ground towards the badger sets. "Show a leg, you ole thief!" he shouted, "us'll be arter 'ee when the nights draw in!" Then, having selected a sapling, he swung his axe in a wide, slashing arc and the sound of the stroke rang through the woods, flushing out three moor-hens and sending them skimming across the lake for their sanctuary on the islet.

The Codsalls and the Potters were habitual early risers but Arthur Pitts and his son Henry over at the Hermitage worked to a more leisurely schedule and ate enormous breakfasts before issuing out of doors. They were munching away now with their womenfolk moving to and fro from the stove, Martha and her great tawny daughter-in-law from over the Teazel, absorbed into the cheerful atmosphere of Hermitage kitchen and privately thanking her lucky stars that she had chosen the genial Henry for husband, instead of the buck-toothed kennelman at Heronslea. The Hermitage, she often reflected, was a home in the very best sense of the word and she now thought of her-self as settled for life, although it sometimes puzzled her that Henry, with so much to offer in the way of good temper and security, had remained a bachelor for so long. She was not entirely convinced by Martha Pitts' explanation that "Henry was waitin' on Mrs. Right an' you be 'er, m'dear!"

Four Winds usually erupted about the time Will Codsall, at Periwinkle, was making his first rounds of the hen-roosts, and filling the hoppers while Elinor followed in his wake collecting the eggs. It was strange that a cautious and sober man like Norman Eveleigh and his practical wife, Marian, should have produced between them such

423

a noisy, rollicking brood, or that they should suffer them to make so much noise as they trooped down the uncarpeted stairs to breakfast, spilling over one another in their eagerness to get to the table and squealing with laughter when Sydney Codsall (now regarded as one of the family) used one of his long, unintelligible words when making a simple request, like "Pass the marmalade!" Their father and mother had impressed upon them that they must show great kindness to Sydney, who had lost both father and mother and thus qualified as an orphan but they found it difficult to avoid teasing him, for he was so unlike any other boy in the Valley, so solemn, studious and unblinking behind his steel-rimmed spectacles that he sometimes seemed more like a little old man than a schoolboy.

Sydney ate sparingly, paying more attention to a book propped against the cruet than to the home-made bread and jam piled on the wooden platters. Marian had given him permission to read at meals for he was already recognised as an exceptionally clever boy, who would go far, although in what direction nobody had yet decided. The headmaster of the Whinmouth Secondary School was said to take a keen interest in him and had told Eveleigh that he was a boy to be encouraged. He was therefore absolved from any work on the farm and spent hours in a room upstairs that was not much bigger than a closet. Up here, although he worked methodically, he did not spend every moment of his isolation preparing lessons. Sometimes he gazed out of the little window at the sons and daughters of the new tenant of Four Winds as they moved to and fro about their regulated tasks in the yard and deep in his heart he despised them all as a gaggle of geese, boys and girls who would never amount to anything but hewers of wood and drawers of water. He had inherited his mother's hunger for gentility but even at fourteen he could see quite clearly where his mother had made her first and fatal mistake. She should never have married a clodhopper like his father, for the road to gentility lay not through labour but through attentive study and the accurate memorisation of cohorts of declensions and tables. The headmaster had told him that knowledge was power and power, sometime and in some undefined sphere, he was determined to possess. Then all those giggling, skylarking Eveleighs would work not for their father, a jumped-up farm foreman, but for him, Sydney Codsall, the real master of Four Winds and all the acres beyond. After breakfast he set out on his bicycle to pedal the nine miles to school. The sun was hot by then and the birds sang in chorus all the way to the bridge over the Teazel but spring had no message for Sydney. He did not even notice it, being fully occupied repeating to himself a list of irregular French verbs.

The warm spring weather and the tumult it provoked in the thickets and hedgerows of the Valley did have a very dramatic effect upon someone old enough and experienced enough to know better. This was John Rudd, rising fifty-three, and a widower for more than twenty years but age and experience had not prevented him from falling hopelessly in love with Maureen O'Keefe, M.D., and that at first sight, when she drove her gig over to the lodge a day or two after the shipwreck and told him, in her pleasant Irish accent, that she was "after taking Father's place for a spell".

From the moment she consented to take tea with him in his little parlour, and they had discovered in the city of Cork a topic of mutual nostalgia, he found her the most engaging young woman he had ever met and he continued to think of her as young after she had admitted to thirty-seven. It was her humour and frankness that engaged him during that first meeting, but later, after she had paid several visits to Paul, she rapidly enlarged her hold upon him so that he began to think of her small, puckish features as beautiful, and her sturdy, thick-set figure as statuesque. Yet he was not such an old fool as to imagine that she was in the least attracted to him and would have been more than satisfied with her friendship, for she was the only "liberated" woman in his experience who did not make a tiresome fetish of emancipation. He was as astonished at the arrival of a qualified doctor in petticoats as every one else in the Valley for it was a phenomenon that he had neither encountered nor imagined but after watching her at work on Paul and other equally embarrassed males in the Valley, he had conceived an enormous admiration for her skill and her easy approach to cottagers that overcame their prejudices and won their confidence in the course of a single visit. She was obliged to rely on him a good deal that first month, for she was a complete stranger to the Valley and her close relationship with O'Keefe did not help, for the old man had been losing his grip lately and even patients who had suffered him half a lifetime were beginning to distrust his diagnoses and his rough and ready surgery. She was very frank, however, about her father's shortcomings, admitting that the old man was no longer fit to attend a sick cat and this, she said, was the real reason she was here, to save him making a mistake that would

425

"blot his copy-book and mine, on account of our names being one below the other in the Medical Register"!

She soon packed him off to take his cure and had the practice to herself. "Playing herself in", she called it, while she continued to search for a firm of practitioners who had not taken the pledge to stop the infiltration of women into the profession. One of the things that John Rudd most admired about her was her cheerful acceptance of male prejudice in the medical field, for in spite of it she preferred male doctors. "Women in authority," she told him once, "are usually hell-cats, like the matrons and nursing sisters I trained under before going on to take a degree in Dublin!" She was like her father in one respect. She drove everywhere and did everything at high speed and with enormous gusto but she enjoyed her work enormously and was very proud of having wrested her M.D. from the English. Although born in Ireland she had spent part of her childhood and some of her training period in Scotland, so that her accent was of a Celtic hybrid, half County Kerry, half Lowland Scot. Her outlook and sense of humour, however, was all Irish and her long struggle to qualify had done nothing to moderate a natural ebullience. During her five years in Dublin she had lived, she told Rudd, on about fifteenpence a day, "doled out in threepenny bits" by the Scots uncle who took her in when Himself (Doctor O'Keefe) had made his one-way crossing to England thirty years before. John Rudd would have liked to have satisfied his curiosity as to why O'Keefe had come here in the first place but reserved the question until he could be sure it would not give offence.

Like so many Irish patriots Maureen O'Keefe could laugh at her enthusiasm for Home Rule and even sympathise with the English for having to contend with such an indigestible morsel as Ireland. Perhaps John Rudd's intimate knowledge of Ireland, and the fact that he had enjoyed many a day's hunting in the West, did something to draw them closer together at a time when the agent was depressed regarding the Squire's slow crawl back to health. She was a good talker but an even better listener and within a few days he had unburdened himself regarding his own situation and his relationship with Paul. This was touched off by a direct question she addressed to him after he had watched her encase Paul's ribs in plaster. Before he could congratulate her on what seemed to him a very dexterous display she said, as they drove off down the drive, "You love the man, do you not, John? Now would you be after wantin' to tell me why?" and he

426

had replied, impressed by her discernment, "Yes, I love him and I'd be glad to tell you why if you have the patience to listen!"

"I have that," she said, whipping up the cob, "for it's no more than a trotting road here," and as they bowled along to Four Winds on their way to dress the septic hand of a labourer, he told her of his years under the Lovells and of Paul Craddock's sudden appearance in the Valley and how, over the last few years, they had made the estate their life. He told her too of the manner in which he had left the Army and settled in this remote corner admitting that until Craddock had come his entire existence had seemed profitless. Then, in response to her frank questions, he described the recurring crises they had shared culminating in Grace Craddock's flight and the night, just before her arrival, when they had seen the spirit of the Valley at work in the cove and Paul had twice risked his life to save seven lives. It was this incident that he saw as the first fruits of their partnership and it seemed to him a bitter thing that Paul was too ill to evaluate it. "If I could only get that across to him I swear he'd begin to mend," he declared but at that she laughed, saying she knew a better tonic for the boy and that luckily it was at hand in unlimited supply. She said merrily that she had only drawn him out on the subject in order to confirm her diagnosis. "You'll not be put out by what I say, John? You'll not think me presumptuous for interfering?"

"You're the doctor," he said, "and any judgment you made would be based on good sense and a kind heart."

She stopped the trap, sucked in her cheeks in a way she had and let her body slump back on her hands. "Paul Craddock is as strong as an ox!" she said, "and there's no reason in the world why he shouldn't be up and about again in a fortnight, providing he looks ahead instead of brooding on what lies behind! Sure, he did a man's job of work there in the cove, but his physical hurts aren't important! There's more to it than that, John, the boy's pride is in ruins!"

"How could you know that?"

"I guessed it the moment I heard tell of the little baggage he married. It's a special balm the boy needs and you can't buy it by the pot at the pharmacy!"

"Baggage or not," said John glumly, "he's still in love with that madcap and neither you nor I can do a thing about it."

"You think not?" she said. "Then you've a thicker head than I suspected, John! I was five and a half years working for my degree and there was nothing in the lectures about broken hearts. Maybe there will be when there are more women in the field but there isn't yet! We still leave it all to the ladies of the circulating libraries, who make a very good living out of it I'm told. Do you pay no account to this other girl—the one who rushed down from London the moment she heard of his plight?"

"Claire Derwent? Don't be misled by her they're old friends and I daresay after reading the papers she . . ."

"If you think she came simply because he was laid up with broken ribs and pneumonia, John, you must have your nose so deep in the soil that you'll end up down a rabbit hole!"

"Oh, he was fond of her but mildly I'd say and before he married Grace. It never amounted to anything serious."

"It's taking a serious turn right now," she said, "and I mean to give it a push! Why do you suppose I engaged Miss Derwent, in preference to a real nurse from Paxtonbury? Did you think I was impressed by her having played nursing games at a V.A.D. lecture course?"

"Well, to tell the truth I was a bit sceptical," he admitted, chuckling, "for I made sure you would get a professional in for night work. After all, he can afford it and you can't be on the spot all the time."

"John," she said, with Irish mock solemnity, "I'll tell you something else about the patient and I'll risk shocking you! It's a little night work the boy needs, bless him, and given time and patience on both sides I think he'll get it!"

He laughed outright at this, one of the few honest guffaws since his garrison days in Ireland twenty-five years ago. "Maureen O'Keefe," he said, in a very fair imitation of her brogue, "as Almighty God's me witness it's a brazen, scheming hussy you are and I have it in mind to pass your prescription to a medical council and plaised they'd be to get shut of ye!"

"You do that, m'boy," she replied, "and I'll argue the diagnosis before any number of them! Now will you not admit it's high time the country had more of us petticoat quacks? And what's so different about my prescription either? Sure, it's no more than the mixture as before!" and she cracked the whip and pulled the cob back on to the river road. It was a week before he learned how to look impassive when listening to Maureen's solemn and detailed instructions to "Nurse" Derwent, when she reported for night duty after the evening visits.

The situation in the sick-room linked agent and doctor in con-

428

spiracy for as Paul's wounds began to heal and he could move around a little John found himself studying the relationship between patient and nurse with an attention that sometimes made him nervous. It seemed to him that both Paul and Claire were very much on their guard, as though determined to keep their distance but when he mentioned this to Maureen she scolded him, saying that he would do well to keep away from the sick-room when Claire was on duty. If the girl got so much as an inkling what was expected of her she would be over the hills and far away in a flash. He took her advice and thereafter confined his visits to daylight hours but he went on worrying all the same and presently it occurred to him that the boy Ikey might be able to supply a clue regarding the latest situation between Paul and Grace. In the turmoil surrounding Ikey's return he had not exchanged more than a few gruff words with him, whereas Ikey had kept out of his way, probably anticipating a rebuke. John waylaid him one morning in the orchard and called, sharply, "Hi there! I want a word with you young feller-me-lad," and when the boy put on a virtuous expression, added, "You don't fool me! I haven't forgotten all that extra trouble you caused us skipping to London like that and I hope you get a hiding for it when you go back to school tomorrow!"

"I daresay I will, sir," the boy said, but so cheerfully that John at once suspected the boy was laughing at him.

"What in the name of God possessed you to do such a thing?" he demanded. "You must have known we had enough trouble on our hands and that having you home only made work for everybody!"

"I know that," said the boy, enigmatically, "but it was something I had to do!" Then, more doggedly, "I can't tell you, sir! I'd like to but I can't! I promised, you see."

John said, coldly, "Will you tell me why you went to Mrs. Craddock? Did she send for you?"

"No, sir," he said, "it was all my idea. She was surprised to see me and sent me back the next day."

"How the devil did you know where to find her?"

"I read it in the newspaper, Mr. Rudd."

"You found her address in a paper?"

"No sir, just where those suffragettes met. I guessed she'd be there and — well, she was, sir."

Curiosity tormented him but his army training stopped him bullying the truth from the boy. He had heard cornered troopers use this stalling technique in the orderly room and had, in fact, used it

429

himself when he was Ikey's age. The boy, he was sure, was not being evasive out of cussedness but from motives which he regarded as honourable, loyalty to a comrade perhaps, or maybe loyalty to Grace. He said, with a pretence of bad grace, "Very well, Ikey, I daresay the Squire will want to know all about it when he is better. After all, you're his responsibility, not mine!" and he walked back to the stable-yard. When he looked over his shoulder, however, the boy was still standing where he had left him and his expression suggested a certain amount of distress and uncertainty. For no reason that he could think of the interview both puzzled and disturbed Rudd but when he saw Maureen's trap enter the yard he shrugged off his doubts muttering, "I daresay it's all trivial enough but how the devil is a boy to know that at his age?"

V

John Rudd was correct in surmising that his questions had upset Ikey. In fact, one way and another these holidays had been a disconsolate period apart from the hours spent in Hazel Potter's company. The rush to London, the tracking down of Mrs. Craddock, the dramatic switch to Claire Derwent and the luring of her to Devon, had seemed achievements at the time and when Claire actually arrived he had enjoyed a moment of triumph. But since then events had slipped and slithered beyond his comprehension and the more he contemplated the adult world the more baffling and illogical it became, lacking the fixed loyalties that regulated the world of school and stable-yard. He suffered badly from lack of a confidant and, as the days passed, with Squire in the sick-room and Claire Derwent spending her nights at the big house, Ikey's elation began to moderate so that he passed from bewilderment to a permanent state of anxiety, seeing himself as the author of a plot that had gone awry and might ultimately touch off a domestic explosion involving everybody concerned and himself most of all. He could make nothing of the situation. The Squire, presumably, was still married to his wife, who had not only refused to visit him when he lay critically ill but had actually connived at the introduction of another woman into the house. It was this that ran counter to all Ikey's conceptions of the married state, indeed, to his conception of human nature. He was familiar with sporadic domestic eruptions in the backstreets but wives south of the Thames, however resentful and vituperative they felt towards their husbands, stopped far short of encouraging rivals. They would, he reflected, be more likely to tear the clothes from their backs and claw out handfuls of hair, at which stage, in Ikey's experience, husbands usually intervened and tempers were cooled in the nearest four-ale bar. And there was another aspect of the affair that bewildered him. He would have thought that Claire Derwent, once installed, would have been sure to seek him out and question him very closely about that letter but not only had she failed to do this, she had gone out of her way to avoid him and had, in fact, not addressed a word to him since her arrival. He could get little reassurance from Mrs. Handcock or Thirza Trimlett regarding Squire's health and yet they were forever whispering together and he guessed that their furtive confidences concerned Claire Derwent's more or less permanent presence in the house. He would have talked it over with Gappy, the gardener's boy and former room-mate over the stable, but since going away to school his relationship with Gappy had changed and Gappy now regarded him as one of the gentry, hardly less exalted than the Squire and had even taken to addressing him as "Young Sir", a form of address that made Ikey blush. After John Rudd's crusty interrogation he wandered away along the river bank towards Codsall Bridge, having considered but rejected the idea of seeking Hazel Potter's advice. With the best will in the world, he decided, Hazel could be of no assistance here and having decided this he again envied her her freedom and from this it was a short step to gloomy contemplation of his own changed status in the Valley and a conviction that it might be better for his peace of mind if, the moment the Squire was approachable, he applied for reinstatement as stable-boy. He drifted along the path beside the river, hands deep in pockets, forehead creased with melancholy, reflecting that here was a rotten end to a thoroughly rotten holiday.

He had always preferred the Sorrel banks to any other corner of the estate, except perhaps the green depths of the woods near the islet. Last term the English master had introduced him to a poem called "A Boy's Song", and the lea, described therein, seemed to Ikey to refer to this particular reach of the river. Recollection of the verses, however, only served to deepen his gloom for he had no Billy with whom to share his enthusiasm for the darting trout and the tremble of tree shadows over the pike pool. He stood leaning on the rail of the bridge staring down into the clear water like a man contemplating suicide and was so drenched in self-pity that he did not hear the whirr of the trap wheels or turn aside when hooves beat on the planking. The first indication he had of the presence of the lady-doctor was her hail of,

431

"Hi, boy! *You*, boy!" and then he turned and flattened himself against the rail, supposing himself an obstruction to her passage. She did not advance, however, but stared down at him, her eyes glinting with amusement.

"You're from the big house, aren't you?" she asked, and when he admitted that he was, "Aren't you a relative of Squire Craddock's?"

Now this was not a simple question to answer. At school the Squire was his stepbrother but he had never made such an impudent claim on home ground, so he said, evasively, "I'm Ikey Palfrey and I used to work yonder but now Squire sends me to school!"

"That's it," she said, triumphantly, "I knew you belonged! I don't forget faces that easily. Squire adopted you, didn't he?"

"He sends me to school," Ikey repeated obstinately, privately thinking her a very nosy woman and wishing she would stop pestering him.

"All right, have it your own way," she said cheerfully and then, to his dismay, she hoisted herself from the box, looped the reins round a post and joined him in contemplation of the water.

"Any fish down there?" she said casually.

"Trout," he told her, "and sometimes grayling but Squire won't let it off. Anyone can fish free so long as they work on the estate."

"Ah," she said, with an air of satisfaction, "the Squire's a sensible man! And a good one to work for I'm told."

"Yes, he is," said Ikey, somewhat mollified, "the best! Anyone will tell you that, Doctor."

They remained side by side squinting down at the stream and presently he saw, or thought he saw, a chance to relieve at least one of his private anxieties. He said, bluntly, "Is he going to get better? *Really* better?"

"Why, of course he is! He'll be out and about as soon as we get the plaster off his ribs and his arm out of splints. He's through the worst of it."

He felt himself warming towards her, so much so that he was tempted to break the first seal of his confessional and said, "You . . . you heard about me running away to London when it happened? They all said it was a bad thing to do but I didn't mean to cause Mr. Rudd or anyone any trouble. I . . . I had an idea, that's all."

She said, with elaborate unconcern, "You did? Well then you must have a clear conscience so don't bother!" And then, even more casually, "What kind of idea?"

432

"A daft one it turned out," he said, beginning to suspect that he had already said too much.

They fell silent again and perhaps two minutes passed before she said, suddenly, "Look here, Ikey, if you want to get anything off your chest get it off and it won't go any further! If you don't then I'm not in the least worried. It's a fine spring day and a boy of your age ought to enjoy it! No dam' sense in taking troubles seriously at your age!"

The advice, and the fashion in which it was offered, levelled them in a way that astonished him for he might have been leaning on the rail alongside one of his Third Form cronies. This woman, whom everybody for miles around regarded as a freak, seemed far more approachable than, say, one of the prefects at school. He put a finger in his mouth and pulled at his lower lip, screwing up his face in an effort to assess her trustworthiness and then, as he recalled his miserable confusion of mind, he made a decision in her favour. "I can't explain how it all happened," he said, "but it was me that began it! Now I don't know whether I did right or wrong and that's a fact, Doctor!"

"All right," she said, equably, "suppose you explain and leave me to sort it out for you? Why *did* you run off to London, instead of staying at school until you were sent for?"

"I went to find Mrs. Craddock and tell her she ought to come home," he said.

He must have succeeded in astonishing her for she gasped and then chuckled, a rich chuckle, beginning deep in her throat so that he was prepared to share the joke to some extent.

"He was very low," he explained, grinning, "not like he was before she ran off. I got to thinking about it and then, before he got hurt rescuing those sailors, I thought I'd . . . well . . . get her back if I could. I would have managed it without anyone missing me if it hadn't been for Mr. Rudd ringing up and telling them to keep me at school for a week!"

She was regarding him now with admiration. "Glory to God!" she said, "but you're a deep one and no mistake! How old are you, Ikey?"

"Fourteen," he said, wondering what his age had to do with it and she added, "So you put it to her, just like that? What on earth did she say?"

"She said she wasn't ever coming back."

"And then?"

He licked his lips having now arrived at the most improbable part of the business. "Well," he went on, reluctantly, "she was nice to me and we had a talk about things. She said the person who could really cheer him up wasn't her at all but Miss Derwent, the one who was daft about him when he first came here."

"I see," she said, "so all you did was to hop round the corner and enlist Miss Derwent as Comforter-in-Chief?"

"No," he said, "I wrote her a letter saying the Squire was calling out for her in his deliriousness!"

"In his deliriousness? But was he?"

"How should I know, I wasn't here then."

She annoyed him then by exploding with laughter and he added as though in extenuation, "Well, it worked! It worked a lot quicker than I thought it would! She was down here almost at once."

"I'll wager she was," said Maureen O'Keefe, standing with feet astride and hands on hips as she regarded him with the closest attention. "Well then, since it worked what are you so bothered about?"

"It doesn't seem right when he's not married to her but to Mrs. Craddock," he said and the genuine note of piety in his voice told her that it would be boorish to laugh at him again; instead she laid a hand on his shoulder, pulling him round facing her. "Look here, Ikey," she said, "I think you're marvellous, do you understand? You went right to the root of things, and didn't let the prospect of trouble for yourself stop you! Did they give you a hiding when they got you back?"

"No," he said gloomily, "but I daresay they will when I get back to school tomorrow. Not that that bothers me, for a walloping doesn't amount to much. What really worries me is . . . well . . . not knowing whether I did right and whether . . . the Squire really *wants* Miss Derwent around all the time."

"You can set your mind at rest on that," she said. "You did Squire the best turn anyone could have done him and he does like having her around, take it from me! As to getting a thrashing from your housemaster for running away you can forget that too. I'll give you a note to take back and you'll hear no more about it."

"Look here, Doctor," he said, wriggling out of her grasp, "that won't do at all! I don't want anyone at school to know what I ran off for and I don't want anyone here to know, especially Squire! I wouldn't have told you if . . ."

"Don't be so stupid," she said, "do you think I'd split on a pal?

434

Me? The person responsible for getting him well again? I won't breathe a word to anyone upon my honour!"

"Not even to Mr. Rudd?"

"Least of all to him," she said. "It'll be between you and me and for always!"

"Well, thanks," he said gratefully and then, "I don't reckon it would do for Miss Derwent to know Mrs. Craddock read the letter first!"

"*She* read it? Mrs. Craddock did?"

"Yes. I wrote it while she was there and took it back to Devon to post so as it would have the right postmark."

"Ikey," she said, "there's a word you wouldn't have heard yet that just about describes you so remember it and you can recognise yourself later on! You're Machiavellian! Remember that— *Mack-i-ah-vellian!*"

"What does it mean?" he asked and she said, gesticulating, "It's having an instinctive understanding of people and how their minds work and it's a priceless quality to possess, particularly if you ever think of going into business!"

"I'll not do that," he said, scornfully, "I'm going to join the cavalry!"

"Ah," she said, "then I'm afraid it won't be much use to you. Still, it's nice to have and I daresay it'll help you get along with the ladies!"

"I shan't ever marry either," he said, firmly, "it muddles things up so!"

"Well, it needn't," she said, "but while we're on the subject I'll let you into my secret. I think it very likely that Squire will marry Miss Derwent in the end. You see if I'm not right."

He stared at her in amazement. "How could he do that?" he said and then remembered what Grace Craddock had said about "getting unmarried", a remark he had not taken seriously at the time.

"Well," she said, "we won't go into it right now but it'll happen about this time next year, maybe. The thing is, if it does, what would you think about it?"

"I don't know," he said, slowly, "Miss Derwent and me always got along. She's a sport and I like her all right but I liked Mrs. Craddock. One time everyone up at the big house thought Squire and Miss Derwent would marry so I suppose it would work out all right!"

He began to wonder if, after all, there might be some kind of pattern

435

to the strange behaviour of adults, even if it was so complex that it could not be related to everyday life. He said, "She'd *fit in* better I mean, she *belongs* and somehow Mrs. Craddock never did, did she? She was well . . . a *town* person!"

"You've hit the nail on the head again," she said and unlooping the cob's reins hoisted herself on to the box. "Would you like to finish the round with me, Ikey?"

"No," he told her, suddenly feeling a glorious sense of release, "I think I'll cross Hermitage and cut through the woods to the mere. We've got woods round the school but they're not like our woods, mostly just pine where nothing much grows."

She lifted her whip in respectful salute and rolled across the bridge towards Four Winds. He looked after her a moment and then ran across the road, scrambled up the bank and disappeared into the ash thickets on the river side of Hermitage Wood as she drove to Four Winds at a spanking speed. "Well," she said to herself as she clipped through the gate, "I came here thinking a country practice might be dull but I'm learning otherwise and that's for sure!"

VI

He was aware of her less as a nurse and a personable young woman with a glowing complexion and corn-coloured hair, than as an agent whose presence completed a cycle of years, beginning with the long weeks of drought when he had first ridden about the Valley in her company, and ending in another spell of unbroken sunshine that followed the mild spring and promised a record crop providing sufficient rain fell by the first week of July. Thus, in a sense, she was impersonal, not a woman at all but a spirit of the Valley unexpectedly restored to him and bringing the promise of better times.

He did not remember her as a tranquil person. Spirited and joyous perhaps, and always eager for laughter but certainly not a woman who could communicate repose. Yet she was so now and sometimes he wondered what experience outside the Valley had changed her, calming her without making her moody and withdrawn. Her stillness was now an essential part of her, like her watchful blue eyes and a head of hair that was sometimes gold, sometimes almost auburn and sometimes the bronze shade of the sea an hour or so before sunset. He would watch her for long minutes as she stood by the tall window, supposing him to be taking his afternoon nap although in fact he

436

seldom did take it, but maintained the pretence of doing so for a fortnight or more in order that he could study her through half-closed eyes when she thought herself unobserved. He would lie still and wonder about her, comparing her in a thousand ways to Grace and pondering questions that never suggested themselves during their brief conversations in the evenings. Privately he thought it odd that she should sit here at all through the short nights, for once he became accustomed to the awkwardness of his posture caused by the splint and the plaster that itched so mercilessly, he felt he no longer needed a night nurse and wondered why the woman doctor John Rudd had introduced into the house insisted someone should watch him until splint and plaster were removed. He did not quarrel with the decision, however, because Claire's presence gave him something to think about and he much preferred her to a stranger.

After a time her tranquillity communicated itself to him so that he found he was able to think of Grace, and Martin Codsall, and Smut, and poor old Tamer objectively, and was even able to regard the misgivings they aroused as a by-product of illness and high temperature, like the fantasies of his long spell in hospital. He got accustomed to her neat ways and patient method of hoisting him this way and that, and even to her shaving him each morning. Soon, in a sense, he began to enjoy his comparative helplessness for it was very pleasant to lie here with nothing to do but read and think abstract thoughts. The doctor told him that the plaster would have to remain at least a month and at first this had exasperated him for he had sharp memories of the boredom of sickbed life, but soon he was more than resigned to it and Claire Derwent's presence reconciled him to inaction. It was Claire who encouraged him to pick up the threads of everyday life about the house and here she had the power to surprise him, first in the matter of her piano playing, then as the only person at Shallowford capable of overcoming young Simon's distaste of the sick-room.

He knew nothing of music and had been curious to learn who was playing the old upright piano in the drawing-room one evening, just before she came on duty. The piano had stood there since Lovell's day and nobody had played it since the Coronation soirée. When she admitted it was her and told him the instrument needed tuning, he was astonished. Nobody had ever told him that she could play.

"Who taught you?" he wanted to know and she said that her mother had given her elementary lessons but after her death she had taught herself to play by ear. Now she was able, in her own phrase, to tinkle up and down and pick out a tune providing the basic chords had stuck!

"It sounded pleasant enough from up here," he said. "Go down and play again and leave both doors open."

She seemed mildly embarrassed by the request but she went and the muted melodies of Strauss waltzes and popular student songs reached him from the stair-well. He said, when she returned, "That was delightful! I'll persuade Doctor O'Keefe to prescribe it night and morning!" and she said, laughing, "It wasn't really playing at all! You must have a dreadful ear, as bad as Simon's!"

"Have you played for Simon?"

Yes, she said, now and again when he was particularly tiresome but he was only interested in discords and the squeak of the pedals.

"How is the poor kid?" he asked and for a moment her tranquillity deserted her and she said, sharply, "He's playing Thirza Tremlett up. You ought to have him in here and talk to him, so that he knows you mean it."

"Oh come, he's only two and a half," Paul protested, "and besides, he won't come in here while I'm trussed up like this. We've tried it and he nearly screamed the place down!"

"That depends on the approach," she said. "He wouldn't make a fuss if I was here!"

"Very well," Paul said, "go and get him and I'll wager he kicks up the devil of a row!"

She went out at once and returned a few minutes later leading the child by the hand. He looked uneasy but subdued, staring at Paul with Grace's expression and a finger in his mouth. Paul thought, not for the first time, "He's all hers, there's hardly a trace of me about him. He's got her looks and her obstinacy but Claire seems to know how to manage him." Claire said, addressing the boy, "Well, there he is, Simon, and he isn't so frightening after all is he? He got hurt saving people from drowning and it isn't very kind to leave him on his own all day! He'd come and see you if you were hurt and had to stay in bed!"

The boy considered this, regarding the patient thoughtfully and presently he put out his hand and scratched the plaster where it showed under Paul's open nightshirt. Then, to Paul's surprise, he chuckled and said, "You could write on it! You could, couldn't you, Auntie Claire?"

"Yes, you could indeed," Claire said, picking up a pencil from the

438

bedside table. "Draw something. It'll give Daddy something to look at when he's bored."

The boy took the pencil, sucked it a moment and then, with neat, careful strokes, drew a crude sketch of a sailing boat. Paul laughed so heartily that his sore ribs gave a twinge and the laugh ended in a gasp, whereupon Claire lifted Simon down and said, "All right, run along now but don't forget to come in and say hello in the morning and good night when you go to bed! Go on, off with you!" and she patted his rump and shooed him out.

"Well I'll be damned," Paul said, "I've never seen him behave like that before! You must have a flair for children, Claire. I've hardly been able to approach the boy since Grace went."

"That's not wholly your fault," she said, "it's the fault of the women about the place. Thirza spoils him, so does Mrs. Handcock and so do all the maids and Chivers, the groom. A child getting that much attention is naturally going to bellow every time something doesn't please him. You'll have to look into the Simon situation when you're up and about again."

He knew that what she said was true, that the staff did spoil the child outrageously, particularly since Grace had left and also that Thirza, his nanny, had come to regard Simon as a personal possession but it was obvious that the child had respect for "Auntie" Claire.

"You've changed a great deal since you went away," he said.

"You've changed yourself," she told him cheerfully, "and not altogether for the better!"

"Well, at least you don't over indulge me in goo-goo invalid talk," he said, smiling. "*What* changes, particularly?"

She looked down at him coolly, perhaps considering whether or not he was prepared to digest home truths and apparently decided that he was, for she said, "What I liked about you when you first came here was your enthusiasm for people rather than ideas. You didn't settle here simply because you like unspoiled country but because you were lonely and found a couple of hundred ready-made friends. It was your warm approach to people like Rose, the Codsalls, the Pitts, and the Potters that gave you a flying start but if you don't watch out you'll lose all the headway you made! Then you'll stay here not because you want to but from force of habit and from lack of an alternative and I think that would be a shame."

"You really think I made headway then?"

"Good heavens, of course you did, tremendous headway!" she

snapped, "and that remark only illustrates what I'm trying to say! You see setbacks of the kind anyone attempting anything new is bound to encounter as . . . well . . . as personal failures but what's so disappointing is that you are beginning to hug them to yourself like a hypochondriac! Why don't you try balancing them against your successes? There isn't a person about here who doesn't wish you well and that's very different from feeling sorry for you!" She stopped and he noticed to his surprise that she was blushing. "I'm sorry," she added, "it's really no concern of mine, is it? What would you like for supper tonight?"

"A straight talk," he said, writhing himself into a more upright position, "finish what you were going to say! I'm still cock of the roost round here but nobody talks to me any more, not even old John."

She sat down beside him, saying, "You're a natural optimist, Paul, but lately you've been hard at work converting yourself into a pessimist, just like my father! There isn't so much enthusiasm about that we can spare it, least of all in a place like this, while everyone in the big world outside is making money and mistaking it for progress! All right, you took a toss over Martin Codsall, and another over Smut Potter. Then your wife walked out on you and from what I hear you've been sulking ever since, or at least until the wreck. But things like that happen to everyone who lives anything but a fenced-in life. They shouldn't stop a man with your kind of enterprise, at least, not at your age! Perhaps you don't realise it but you've already made a name for yourself round here and not only because you fished seven people off that rock! Folk round here believe in you and believe in what you're trying to do, although some of them don't really understand it yet. My advice, for what it's worth, is that you should go right on doing it, not gloomily and doggedly, the way you have since Grace left but the way you began, with a sense of fun and adventure, do you understand?"

"Yes," he said slowly, "that's easy to understand Claire but by God I badly needed someone to spell it out for me!" He was going on to defend himself by citing the loneliness of authority but before he could phrase it the sentiment seemed pretentious in the face of her outspokenness so he held his tongue and said: "I'll have supper now, Claire, and when Mrs. Handcock brings it up stay down there and play some more. I haven't much musical taste but your playing stimulates thought and maybe it's time I did some real thinking!"

She left him and went down to the kitchen and a few moments later he heard the tinkle of the untuned piano. She had, he thought, a very light touch, as though youth came out of the tops of her fingers coaxing melody from a battered old instrument that he would have thrown out long since if it had come to his notice. He thought, "She's a damned good sort to bother with me after all that's happened and I hope she doesn't take it into her head to fly off again as soon as I'm out of this blasted straitjacket!" The flesh under the plaster itched and in twisting to seek relief he noticed Simon's drawing. "She's right about the kid too," he mused, "and I won't wait until I'm up before doing something to sort that out. I'll get Mary Willoughby over and talk her into occupying the boy's mind with the alphabet or something and after that I'll draw up some kind of programme for him, for as long as they treat him like a baby he'll stay one!"

He was still reassuring himself along these lines when Mrs. Handcock waddled in with her rich bedside manner and said, referring to the music, "Tiz real pretty, baint it? 'Er's a rare maid an' no mistake!" and Paul smiled, knowing precisely what was in her mind, and what she and Thirza, and possibly everyone else about the house were speculating. Tonight the thought amused him and he said, in excellent imitation of her brogue, "Oh, giddon with 'ee Mrs. 'Ancock, I dorn reckon 'er be a maid no more! I yeard tell 'er got 'erself married to someone in London but ab'm got around to braaking the news to us yet!" and the look of pained astonishment on the housekeeper's face was ample reward for the twinges produced by his struggles to sit upright and balance the supper tray on his knees.

441

CHAPTER SIX

I

THE estate record book, enclosed between the Bible covers of Sir George's photograph album, had grown into an estate encyclopaedia. Personal data, births, deaths and marriages, were still entered in Paul's tall, sloping handwriting on the left-hand pages but on the right was a summary compiled from hundreds of jottings of how each farm was stocked and what was grown on its acreage. It could tell you, for instance, how much fallow land Eveleigh had at any one time, how many acres supported his Friesians and how many were devoted to wheat, barley, oats or root crops. It could correct Henry Pitts when the latter stated that his twelve-acre field had been given over to kale the year before last when, in fact, it had produced mangolds, or rye for green fodder. Paul set everything down there in black and white, season by season, year by year and daily access to this book had formed certain patterns in his mind, so that he thought of Periwinkle as a chicken farm, of Four Winds as the mainstay of the estate's dairy output, of Deepdene as the principal source of market-garden produce. Similarly, everyone on the estate had a mental tag. Sam Potter was the tree-feller, Edward Derwent was the best stockman in the Valley, and his daughter Rose, Shallowford's most accomplished horsewoman and breaker of horses. Yet, for all his passion for detail, Paul was an easy-going landlord. He had let old Honeyman have his way about sheep and suffered the Potters to farm any way they liked, for away at the back of his mind, too remote to find expression even in casual shop-talk with John Rudd, was the outline of a collective scheme in which every tenant farmer, and many of their employees, became specialists operating within self-chosen and clearly-defined limits, a communal plan that would one day—perhaps a generation hence—establish the Valley as the most productive in the West. This was his dream but he was not yet fully aware of it; it was also the spring-board of his patriotism, for England beyond the Sorrel and railway line had little meaning for him, save as a kind of impersonal audience.

In four years he had still to show a credit balance and had not

442

ceased to feed money into the estate but the amounts ploughed back grew smaller each year and by Lady Day, 1906, he was close to breaking even. He thus had cause to thank Franz Zorndorff for his insistence that he paid into Paul's account his share in scrapyard profits, for in the first two years, when so many implements had had to be replaced and several tied cottages rebuilt in addition to routine renovations on some of the farmhouses, he had drawn heavily upon his capital whereas the original income of the estate had shrunk, partly owing to his arrangement with Eveleigh at Four Winds but also by default on the part of the Potters. Now, however, John told him that they could anticipate a steady climb towards solvency, for Will Codsall was reclaiming land north-west of his borders, Derwent paid slightly more rent for additional acreage on the cliff, Eveleigh was making a spectacular success of Four Winds and two houses and several rebuilt cottages in Coombe Bay had been let on long leases at increased rentals.

The stock on every farm in the Valley had improved, even the Potters coming up with several fine litters of saddlebacks, that thrived under the oaks on the edge of the woods. Eveleigh boasted one of the best herds in the district and Will and Elinor Codsall had recently produced a sturdy cross between Light Sussex and White Leghorn and were said to be despatching forty dozen eggs a day. Honeyman's last lambing season had been a success owing a good deal to the exceptionally mild winter and over at Hermitage, where the Pitts clung to the mixed economy of their ancestors, the rent was never a day overdue. Old Willoughby kept few animals at Deepdene but because of improved transport his fruit and vegetables were finding a ready market in Paxtonbury and he was also sending cut blooms to Covent Garden during part of the year. All in all, Paul decided (once he was chipped out of his plaster and could move about more comfortably), prospects seemed very fair, especially if the fine weather lasted into July and there was occasional rain at night, as there had been throughout the summer.

During the long days of June he would stand in his office, propped against the drawing-board (a position he found more comfortable than sitting) and thumb through his own and John Rudd's notes, occasionally turning aside to write a letter, or make a ledger entry but often filling the big white pages of his bible, for this was something that gave him a sense of achievement, his personal index to the circulation of the estate in terms of stock, crops, income and human

443

beings. He noted, for instance, that his "population" had risen sharply during the last few years. When he took over there had been six farms supporting a hundred and two men, women and children, a tally that included some forty craftsmen and casual labourers, some of them part-time workers and almost a score of them women, wives or daughters of Coombe Valley men who were not employed on the estate. Mary Willoughby at that time had seventeen children on her roll call. Now there were seven farms, supporting one hundred and nine people and Mary had twenty-five children in her farmhouse schoolroom, for the fecundity of the Valley seemed to extend to the women living in it. Elinor Codsall had produced a girl and a boy and was now expecting a third child. Joannie Potter had two girls and a boy. Pansy Tozer had a girl and a boy and Henry Pitts' rawboned red-head had recently presented him with a great lumping boy, weighing ten-and-a-half pounds at birth. Over at Four Winds Marian Eveleigh dutifully produced an annual addition to the long family and there was also his own child, Simon, born in January, 1904. It was almost certain that Cissie and Violet Potter, still officially unclaimed, had done their share out of wedlock but their efforts were not entered in the record.

There were, of course, more sombre entries in the book, one relating to the Four Winds tragedy, another to the death of old Tamer Potter, but deaths were lagging far behind births, for people seemed to live to incredible ages on this side of the Sorrel. There was one entry, dated March 20th, 1905, marking the hundredth birthday of old Floss Timberlake, the estate sawyer's grandmother, who had been born the year of Trafalgar. Paul sometimes called in on the old lady, who lived in a cottage close to the Home Farm and found her enjoying a clay-pipe and berating her long-suffering daughter, aged eighty, whom she continued to treat as a child in a pinafore. In Coombe Bay there were three nonagenarians and Arthur Pitts' father, who still lived at Hermitage but never left his room now, claimed to be as old as young Floss Timberlake. Arthur said this was nonsense for it made him out to be eighty, whereas records at the parish church showed that he was only sixty-nine.

Paul did not spend all his time in the office during the latter part of his convalescence for Maureen O'Keefe was no coddler of invalids and told him that by far the best way to heal his cracked ribs was to keep them at work, no matter how painful it proved and that, providing he was careful, he could ride Snowdrop at a walk. His arm was

444

fully healed and apart from stiffness gave him no trouble at all but despite his eagerness to get about and take advantage of the long spell of fine weather he found that he tired very quickly after more than five weeks in bed and at first was subject to occasional spells of dizziness, so that on the doctor's instructions Claire Derwent acted as escort when he went afield on horseback or on foot. Her orders in this respect were so peremptory that John Rudd, that most cautious of suitors, went so far as to warn her one day when they watched Paul and Claire walk their horses down the drive and cross the ford to the river road, with the intention of going as far as the landslip at Nun's Head and taking a swim.

"Look here, old girl," he said (having progressed this far in the last few weeks), "I'm not at all sure you ought to encourage that in the circumstances!"

"What? Forbid them a health-giving bathe on a day like this?" she said, innocently, but he replied, "You know damned well I'm not referring to the curative properties of salt water! You are determined to throw those two together willy-nilly and one ought to remember that he's still a married man and she has a reputation to protect!"

"Oh, stuff and nonsense," she burst out, "you talk just like one of those circulating library queens! Who gives a damn about reputations around here? She's good for him, any fool can see that, and as for his wife, is she likely to object?"

"She might. She might even have them spied on for grounds for divorce!" he argued but this was too much for Maureen, who exploded with laughter and was tempted to break faith with Ikey by explaining Grace's part in luring Claire back to the Valley. She checked herself in time, however, and said, "Well, you should be the last to come forward with that kind of pious notion, John Rudd! Everyone in the Valley is gossiping about you and I and heaven knows we give them all the amunition they need!"

"Ah, that's different," he said, secretly delighted by her admission, "for I'm a widower and you're old enough to look to yourself in that respect! All the same," he added, as an afterthought, "we could easily put a stop to their gossip, Maureen!"

He had not meant to make such an informal proposal, not here, on a bright June morning, as they walked down the drive to where her cob was tethered. It had slipped past his tongue before he could stop it but now it was done he was relieved when she neither laughed at him nor so much as checked her stride but only said, calmly, "So you'd be after making an honest woman of me, John? You'd like us to be married, providing, of course, I decided to stay down here and give up all idea of joining a city practice?"

"I should like that very much, my dear," he said, "but you don't have to commit yourself to a country practice. My contract with Paul Craddock has run out and we haven't got round to renewing it yet. I've got a little money, never having spent much down here and I daresay I could find part-time work wherever you went. I could do your accounts, too, and make sure you didn't work sixteen hours a day for nothing."

She stopped as they reached the gate of his lodge. "You would be prepared to leave here? To let Young Lochinvar manage by himself?"

"Why not? He's quite capable of doing so! For a town-bred man he's learned more of estate management in four years than the Lovells acquired in two generations. The point is he's genuinely interested and doesn't really need me now, or won't by this time next year."

"But John," she said, and he had never heard her speak so softly, "I'm well on the way to being an old maid and I'm also a freak, with far more dangerous ideas about women's rights than the laddie's wife! I'm not much to look at either and you know well enough my job would always come first."

"You're the most intelligent woman I've ever had the luck to meet," he said, "and as for being an old maid, you've no qualifications for the role! You're thirty-four—you told me that the first day we met—whereas I'm fifty-two but we're both fit and in our right minds. Incidentally, you're as handsome a woman as Claire Derwent in your way, so don't get to thinking otherwise!"

It was the first time he had ever seen her blush and it gave him confidence. He went on, lifting her hand from the iron knob of the gate, "Did I know anything of your character or qualifications that first day you took tea with me here, when I was desperate with worry about all that had happened down in the cove? I didn't care a straw what you were—an actuary, a governess or an Irish seamstress! You put me on an even keel in ten minutes and I said to myself, 'Now there's what they mean when they talk about Irish charm!' I could have proposed on the spot and that's the truth of the matter!"

The blush faded as she said, in a businesslike tone, "Come inside a minute, John!" and pulled him into the porch and then, without closing the door, into his untidy parlour, with its bachelor jumble

446

littering table, armchair and sofa. The impetus of his declaration had spent itself and he seemed bewildered. She said, bluntly, "Now what is it you're looking for, John? You've been twenty years a widower so how do you expect a dedicated woman like me to give you back two decades? Tell me true, John Rudd, wouldn't you be scared out of your wits if I took you up on this, put the city out of mind and agreed to marry you next week or the week after?"

"No," he said, deliberately, "that I wouldn't! A man doesn't have emotional impulses at my age and neither does a woman of your experience respond to them! I was deeply in love with my wife, but I don't expect to recapture that kind of feeling at my age. This is something quite different and I'm not going to dress it up in fancy language. I was lonely and crotchety during my time here with the Lovells, and I owe my fresh start to Paul Craddock. But when he married I was lonely again, and after his wife left him I was lonely and miserable into the bargain. Your coming here was a kind of miracle, a third start in middle age, which is something no man has a right to expect. I'd make you a good husband and I think we should suit one another. I'm interested in your work and I envy your self-confidence and high spirits, two things I've always lacked. However, if you think the idea is ridiculous, say so. You won't give offence to me and we can remain good friends and leave it at that!"

Her laugh seemed to fill the stuffy little room and momentarily he was disconcerted but then he saw that there was no derision in her merriment and that she looked younger and prettier than he would have thought possible.

"John," she said, taking his hands, "I like it so much better when you speak off the cuff and forget to rationalise! Sure I'll marry you, the moment you give the word but I'm not so long in the tooth as to seek nothing better in marriage than twilight companionship! You make it sound damned dull, so you do, and this is to prove there's a chance it might have its livelier moments!" and she gave him a resounding kiss on each cheek, after which she skipped over to the corner cupboard where he kept his drinks and poured a couple of stiff whiskies, bringing them back to him and raising her glass with the toast, "Here's to us, John, and bless you for everything but your modesty!"

II

The bay was as smooth and as flat as a silver platter and looked

447

just like one from the top of the drowsy village street but when they had gone down the slipway and walked the horses along the tideline, the water lost its silver gloss and turned forget-me-not-blue inshore, with great belts of emerald-green under the sandbanks of the bar. Everything on the beach was lazy in the hot, morning sun. Gulls idled about the pools pecking listlessly at their catches and two of Tom Williams' boats, a mile out to sea, were stationary specks and seemingly unmanned, which told Paul that Tom and his crews had dropped anchor, set their lines and gone to sleep until the sun should pass beyond the headland that marked the outfall of the Teazel.

There was not a soul about on the beach and when the horses reached the shade of the giant boulders, scattered like giant's marbles for more than a quarter-mile below the largest landslip, they were reluctant to leave it, so Paul found a tiny bay backed by steep rocks where there was a rock pool half-way up the beach. It was a pleasant place to linger so they unsaddled and let the horses potter about in the shallows, while Paul peeled off jacket and shirt and stretched beside the pool, luxuriating in the sun and saying this was something he had longed to do throughout his weeks of confinement.

She stood on the far side of the pool smiling at him and presently she called, "Are you a swimmer, Paul?" and he told her he was not but could thresh about in a calm sea and enjoy it, providing the water was lukewarm. "This pool has a Table Bay temperature," he told her, "so I'm having my dip right here. Do you swim?"

"Yes," she said, pensively, "Rose and I used to come here often when we were children. My mother could swim like a fish, and taught us when we were still toddlers. I often wonder where she learned to swim as well as she did, for she wasn't a local girl. Father was always vain about her horsemanship but he thought sea-bathing unladylike and often told her so but she never let his old-fashioned notions worry her. She was an extraordinary woman in her way, Paul. All the older people in the Valley still remember her, some of them more vividly than Rose and I."

He recalled then the little Rudd had told him about the dashing first Mrs. Derwent and for the first time realised that Claire and her sister Rose must have been old enough to recall the day their mother had fallen to her death at a jump over the Heronslea border. He would have asked her more about it but it was neither a time nor place to probe disagreeable memories so he said, "Well, here goes! I'll paddle about as Doctor Maureen advised and then sunbathe,"

448

and she took the hint and wandered further down the beach towards the horses while he slipped out of the rest of his clothes and lowered himself gently into the pool.

It was deliciously warm and the water soothed the sore belt of flesh where the plaster had been. Presently he struck out and crossed the pool, using a clumsy sidestroke and telling himself that he had been a fool to let four summers pass without once coming down here to swim. He had been splashing about for half-an-hour before she returned carrying a parcel wrapped in oilskin.

"What's that?" he called, "you didn't say we'd picnic. I was going to suggest lunch at The Raven on the way back."

"It isn't food, greedy," she told him, "it's only my bathing costume. It's a hideous thing and one might as well try and swim in a crinoline! You men don't know how lucky you are being able to bathe in a single costume. Just look at it!" and she held it up, a voluminous garment in heavy serge, with sleeves and wide ornamental frills ending in bloomers tied with ribbon just above the knee.

"Good God!" he exclaimed, laughing, "I've seen pictures of them in the newspapers but I didn't think people actually swam in them! Won't it drag you down?"

"I'll chance it. Will you be a perfect gentleman and watch the horses for a few minutes?"

"Not me," he said, "I'll wait and watch you go in and I wish I had old Sir George's camera! You'll look ravishing in that outfit!"

She made a face at him and went off behind the shoulder of the rock, emerging after an interval in the costume, with her hair crammed under a mob cap of the kind that Lovell's housemaids had worn but Paul had long since banished. It was odd, he thought, that she could enhance a costume as sexless as that, investing it with an element of comedy. The only parts of her exposed were face, shins, feet and hands, five pink and white patches relieving yards of navy-blue worsted. He said, regretfully, "They don't leave much to chance, do they? Do all the girls dress like that when they bathe from the machines at Folkestone and Margate?"

"More or less," she said, "but the men don't see them because usually they're shooed to the far end of the beach. Only the really go-ahead resorts allow mixed bathing and as for what I'm doing right now, I'd be drummed out of society altogether in any self-respecting Spa if it got about that I'd actually shared a rock pool with a man and him married into the bargain! Well, as you said, here goes!" and she

449

poised herself on a rock three feet above the water and plunged, very expertly he thought considering her handicap but the dive did not astonish him so much as the pace at which she raced the length of the pool, turned, disappeared under water and swam back to him with a powerful over-arm stroke.

"By George, you make my efforts look silly!" he said admiringly as she went up and down again with a back stroke, climbed out and plopped herself breathlessly beside him.

"I was always a lot better than Rose," she said. "Mother made up her mind to produce the best horsewoman and the best swimmer in the county. She was only interested in bests and as far as Rose is concerned she succeeded but I don't think I could have learned to swim in this outfit. She used to let us swim in the nude. Nobody ever comes here except an occasional beachcomber from Coombe Bay but of course we had to keep it from father."

"She sounds a great deal of fun," Paul said and then, throwing his towel over his shoulders, "Look here, if I promise not to play Peeping Tom would you like to take it off and have a real swim? I can see you're longing to!"

"All right," she said, doubtfully, "if I can trust you not to cheat. Go along the beach to where the landslip begins and stand guard. No one can come from the west because low tide doesn't clear the point and Tom Williams is way out of range."

"Perhaps he has a telescope," Paul said and she replied, "If he has good luck to him!"

He picked his way over the boulders to an empty stretch of sand and was still standing there, presenting a chivalrous back, when she called and he rejoined her to find her dressed with her great mass of golden hair tousled and loose about her shoulders. She said, "It was wonderful! I felt a little girl again and I could almost hear mother laughing at us! Lend me your towel and I'll try and do something with my hair. It'll have to dry before I can show my face in Coombe Bay or the truth will have run as far as the railway line by sunset!"

He said, handing her the towel, "Do we have to bother that much about gossip, Claire?" and she replied, without looking at him, "Yes Paul, I'm afraid we do! If we stopped caring there's an end to the fun we're having and the prospect of more in the future."

"You mean your father?" he said, remembering Edward Derwent's coolness towards him that had been maintained until the night of the wreck but she said, calmly, "No Paul, nothing whatever to do with

Father! And nothing to do with anyone else in the Valley, except you and I, but me especially! I wouldn't care to go through that experience again and if I thought I was likely to I should go back to London tomorrow."

It was the first real indication he had had that she had suffered on his account, having always regarded her flight from the Valley as an exhibition of pique.

"I didn't mean to act shabbily, Claire," he said. "It honestly didn't occur to me that you were really hurt."

"If I was I had no one but myself to blame," she said, "and it didn't take me long to realise that! In any case, I imagine you've since been hurt a great deal more, so let's forget about it and get lunch at The Raven."

She got up and went down the beach to collect the horses, leading them back to him where he stood beside the pool. The sun still shone but for him at least the sparkle had gone from the day. As she was saddling up, he said, "You only met Grace that once—the time you came over to tea. Didn't Rose write to you and fill in the blanks?"

"No," said Claire, sharply, "Rose did not! She isn't given to tittle-tattle! All I heard was that . . ." She stopped and addressed herself to tightening the girths so that he said, impatiently, "Well? What did you hear?"

"That you weren't getting along," she said, briefly, "but do let's stop discussing it, Paul."

"No," he said, suddenly exasperated with the conspiracy of silence regarding Grace and irritated that it should run all his personal relationships into cul-de-sacs where the mere mention of her was regarded as unmannerly. "I'm over it now and I haven't forgotten what you said about making a fresh start. How can I do that if everyone shies away from the subject the way John Rudd and Mrs. Handcock always do, the way you are doing right now? Grace isn't ever coming back so we can all stop pretending it didn't happen!"

"I'm not so sure we can," she said, regarding him steadily across her saddle. "Everyone here says you're still very much in love with her and that you'll never give her up!"

He was not much astonished by this, reasoning that he must have given this impression by his churlishness over the last two years but it struck him now that it was no longer true, that in the last few weeks most of the resentment and humiliation had been purged from him, although just how this had happened he did not understand. It was something to do with a shift in the centre of gravity, removing Grace as the dominant factor in his life and filling the vacuum with the Valley, and the people of the Valley and he supposed that this shift had been brought about by the wreck but it was clear that Claire's return had a share in it. "I was very much in love with her," he admitted, "but it seems to me that love can only stand up to a certain amount of battering, Claire. Grace walked out on her duties as wife and mother and I'm reconciled to the fact that I never will understand why. It's one thing to lose out to another man but quite another to be made a fool of by a political fad! I suppose the heart of the trouble is that Grace didn't simply turn her back on me and Simon but on our whole way of life down here. That being so there comes a time when a man has to accept what can't be altered!"

She had finished adjusting the girths now and was holding both horses by the bridles. She looked, he thought, very young with her damp hair tumbling about her shoulders but for the first time since her return she also looked resentful.

"I don't see why you have to involve me in it," she argued. "I won't have people thinking I'm waiting in the wings, waiting . . . well, for things to happen! I've already made a fool of myself twice over you, Paul Craddock, and there isn't going to be a third time, I promise you!" and with that she dropped Snowdrop's bridle, swung herself up and set off at a smart trot down the beach. He did not follow her at once but remained standing by the pool, smiling to himself. Perversely her flash of temper had overthrown the barrier their mutual wariness had raised and unaccountably he felt more light-hearted than at any time since that ridiculous quarrel with Grace over young Rudd and his motor. And this was not because he was flattered by her demonstration but because he was able, for the first time in years, to get his dilemma into perspective and view it objectively without self-pity or indignation. It was this glimpse of himself that opened up an entirely new vista on his marriage. He could see it now for what it was, no more than a compromise from the very beginning, an arrangement entered into with reservations on the part of a woman with her back to the wall. Surely there could be no such thing as a marriage conditioned by such strictures and anyone but an infatuated fool would have realised as much from the beginning. He had been too obsessed with her to weigh the cost against the probability of failure. He had temporised and gone on temporising, buying time with intermittent flashes of hope, like her interest in the garden and her ability to hypnotise credulous peasants, like Horace Handcock. There had never been a real marriage between them, no real fusion of interests and responsibilities, only the mutual appeasement of physical appetites, together with resignation on her part and hope deferred on his. Standing there on the rock, with the sun warming his body and Claire a solitary figure on the tideline, he saw this so clearly and unmistakably that he felt like proclaiming it at the top of his voice, for self-knowledge brought with it a sense of release that was immensely reassuring and uplifting. "Damn it," he said aloud, as he retrieved his clothes, flung them on, and swung himself on to Snowdrop, "a man ought to be guided by his head when he goes looking for a wife! If I'd had a ha'porth of sense I'd have finished what she started in Shallowford Woods years ago!" and forgetting Maureen O'Keefe's caution he clapped his heels into Snowdrop's flanks and pushed him into a canter, so that Claire, looking over her shoulder, stopped and swung her cob round as he came up with her.

"Get down," he said, curtly, "for I can't say what I've got to say to you jog-jogging along the beach!" and when she only stared at him, he jumped down, threw both sets of reins over his arm and half yanked her from the saddle, although the effort gave his ribs a twinge that made him grunt with pain.

"Listen to me . . ." she began and he guessed that she was on the point of reassuming her role of nurse.

"No I won't," he said, "I've been 'listening' long enough and always to women of one sort or another! I don't give a damn what your father or the Valley think about it and I'm not interested in what happened four years ago, or two years ago, or two minutes ago! If I get a divorce will you marry me? And if you do will you guarantee to stay put and not run off and open a teashop at our first difference of opinion?"

"You're insufferable!" she said, trying to dodge between the horses but he caught her round the waist, dropped the reins and kissed her on the lips. It was a claim advanced with such determination that it threw her weight against the bay, who shied seawards and made off at a smart trot with reins trailing over the sand.

"Well?" he said, without relaxing his hold, "what else do I have to do to convince you?"

"You might ride after Rusty and take me somewhere a little more private!" she suggested, "for if anyone sees us from the cliff path I

453

shall be packed off to Tunbridge Wells again within an hour of getting home!"

"I'll catch him but wait here!" he said, and dashed off after the bay. She stood watching him circle and head the horse off, hands pressed to her tousled hair, a slow, half-rueful smile puckering the corners of her mouth. How was she to know that her thoughts were identical to his when she said to herself, "Well, if we had pushed that first encounter in the woods to its logical conclusion we should have saved everybody a great deal of time, trouble and expense!"

III

Paul saw Zorndorff's motor standing in the yard when he rode in shortly before sunset, a shining, snub-nosed monster considerably more impressive than the first motor to descend the Valley under the inexpert guidance of young Rudd two years before. He was surprised, for he had not expected Franz to respond in person to his letter and had in fact resigned himself to making another journey to London.

He found the Croat already established in the library, with Mrs. Handcock fussing round him, impressed by his air of polite patronage and treating him as though he was a distinguished relative of the family, paying a duty call on Squire and his chawbacons. He was as neat and dapper as ever, in what he imagined to be "country clothes", a pair of salt-and-pepper knickerbockers, a pleated Norfolk jacket, heavy brogues and brown worsted stockings; there was also a carnation in his buttonhole. He embraced Paul warmly, at once issuing orders for supper, as though this was one of his shooting lodges and Paul was a welcome but unexpected guest. Paul said, "I didn't expect you to come down here, Uncle Franz. I intended coming up to see you as soon as you had news from the solicitors," but Franz replied, patting his shoulder, "Nonsense, my boy! I know you loathe London and I've been promising myself to pay you a visit for I don't know how long."

"For four years," Paul told him, smiling, "and it took a situation like this to get you here! How long do you intend staying?"

"Oh, I'm afraid I shall have to be off bright and early in the morning," the old man said and the regret in his voice was so counterfeit that Paul laughed but made no protest, realising that the country had the same effect upon Franz as urban sprawl had upon himself. It occurred to him also that this distaste of open spaces might have

454

helped to establish the contact between Franz and Grace and that had led to the casual postscript of Uncle Franz's last letter, for he had written, *"Grace called at the yard and I took the unfortunate little pigeon out to dinner."* The use of the word "unfortunate" had irritated Paul at the time, implying as it did that Grace was the injured party but after reflection he had made allowances for Franz's kind heart and had obeyed an impulse to write him a frank letter expressing his wish to marry again and asking Franz to sound their London firm of solicitors on the prospect of a divorce. And now here he was in person, barely forty-eight hours after receiving the letter, yet for all his despatch he did not seem over-anxious to discuss the situation. It was not until after supper, when the glow of sunset filled the room and Franz had examined Paul's current bank statements, that he pushed the papers aside, removed his half-moon spectacles, and said, "Well, my boy, you've shown me your figures so I'll show you mine!" and had unlatched his briefcase giving Paul the impression that he was due for yet another lecture on the amount of money he had poured into the estate over the last few years. Instead Uncle Franz opened a buff folder and took from it the receipted bill of a hotel called The Golden Angel, at Windsor, handing it to Paul without comment. The bill related to a two-day stay at the hotel by a "Mr. and Mrs. James Monteith", and for a moment it meant nothing at all to him. Then he turned it over and found a piece of notepaper attached to it with a paper-clip. On the note, in Grace's handwriting, was written, *"Will this do? If not let me know at once—Grace."*

He stared at the note curiously, conscious of the old man's eyes on him and said, without any attempt to hide his distaste, "Is this how one goes about it? Is this the legal way?" and Franz chuckled, replying, "Not strictly legal, Paul, but it serves. More than half the divorces granted nowadays are arrived at by similar means and you might consider yourself fortunate that Grace is willing to accommodate you without being paid for it! Most wives would value that evidence, at, say, a thousand guineas or a settlement but then, she's an eccentric girl, wouldn't you agree?"

The receipt, the note and its obvious implications moderated Paul's pleasure at seeing the old man again after so long an interval. He said, briefly, "I don't know much about this kind of thing but I was under the impression a divorce could be obtained on grounds of desertion."

"So it could," Franz said, "providing you and the lady you hope to marry are prepared to wait about five years, plus the time the suit will take to get heard. This is by far the quickest and cheapest way of going about it."

"And the most unsavoury," Paul said.

"That's for her to judge, isn't it?"

He said this with such a ferocious lift of his eyebrows, that Paul's sense of injustice was roused.

"Damn it Franz, am I to understand from that that you sympathise with her?"

"To some extent," the old man replied frankly, "but also with you, my boy, for now that I know her better it seems to me to have been an extraordinarily ill-considered affair on both sides! To my mind you are entirely incompatible and you aren't such a fool as not to have recognised that by now!"

A few months ago Paul might have argued the case with some heat but now he had enough philosophy to appreciate the old man's difficulties as go-between and also his obvious willingness to help in any way he could.

"There's no point in raking over the past, Uncle Franz," he said, "and I daresay it's sporting of you to involve yourself. If we did proceed along these lines would Grace and I have to meet again?"

"No," he said, "not necessarily. The fact that she sent me that bill means she wouldn't defend the case. You would have to attend, of course, but it isn't the ordeal most people imagine, it's becoming rather fashionable I'm told."

"Fashionable or not it's something I don't relish," said Paul. "Did you see her more than that one occasion when you took her to dinner?"

The old man twinkled. "Yes," he admitted, "I've seen her several times. As a matter of fact she came to me to discuss the possibilities of letting you go free before you wrote but I didn't take any action because I couldn't be sure you weren't anxious to have her back on any terms. As soon as you wrote I got in touch with her and that bill arrived by return of post."

Paul studied the bill again and asked, "Who is James Monteith?" and Franz, sighing, said, "You really do live in another age down here, Paul! He's no one in particular."

"He isn't someone Grace has taken up with?"

"Knowing her I should think it extremely unlikely. He's almost

456

certainly a professional, someone to whom she paid money for the purpose of getting evidence."

"Good God!" Paul exclaimed, "I've heard of women employed in that respect but never men!"

"I still don't think you really understand the situation," Franz said, patiently. "In almost all these cases it's accepted that the man takes the initiative, on the assumption that he has less to lose than the woman, but as the law stands you would have to provide evidence of adultery and cruelty and refuse to have her back. Well, for your information, Grace won't hear of anything like that but not simply because she recognises you the injured party. She won't be under an obligation to a man, so as far as I can see it will have to be that evidence or a long wait. You would have to write inviting her back and she would have to reject the offer. It could drag on for years and she considers this would be most unfair on you. If I was in your shoes I should give me instructions to go right ahead on what you have there."

"Tell me honestly, Franz, does it make any kind of sense to you? I don't mean simply her approach to divorce but her entire attitude to life?"

"No," said Zorndorff, "not sense but there's a kind of glory in it."

"Glory?"

"Yes, glory. These women see themselves as a vanguard carving out a new social structure. There have always been minorities set on martyrdom. The early Christians were one and some people might even include the Lollards and Lutherans in the parade. The world usually begins by mocking them, then slams them behind bars and ends by canonising them! Today the fabric of society is changing at frightful speed and although the process has now been going for quite some time it's only recently that people are sitting up and taking notice."

"Then I suppose you class me with the minority who won't face up to change and takes refuge in a bolt-hole like this?"

"No," said Franz, "not altogether and neither, I think, does Grace. A man ought to follow his destiny and yours is clearly here doing what you believe yourself capable of doing. Take my advice my boy and let her have her own way about this and I tell you that not because I agree or disagree with her but because I happen to know it will ease her conscience. Believe me, she has one, and it's troubling her a good deal!"

He seemed to prefer to leave the matter there and went on to talk of more general matters, of the stimulating effect the dreadnought race

457

with Germany was having upon the price of scrap iron, the increasing pressure building up under the new Liberal Government for an avalanche of social legislation, of matters that were common currency to him but to Paul were little more than London newspaper topics. They talked on into the small hours and when Paul had shown him to his room, and they stood together at the open window looking out over a paddock bathed in moonlight, Franz said, "Well, it doesn't look as if much has changed around here since the Tudors but it will, although I daresay it will last you out, or maybe you'll be so set in your ways you won't even notice the differences."

Paul said stubbornly, "I'm not afraid of differences, Uncle Franz. My policy here involves change. What I am opposed to is dissolution."

"Ah, I daresay," he said, cheerfully, "and who isn't? Sometimes I think we're all heading for perdition but so long as we get a choice of route I'm satisfied. You stick to yours, Paul, and let Grace stick to hers! That's my advice, for what it's worth."

Paul said good night and went along to his own room, where Mrs. Handcock had lit the small lamp and shadows were playing hide-and-seek in the window draught. He sat on the bed and pulled off his tall boots that he wore almost exclusively in these days, for he was on horseback most working days. The strong Maxwell boots gave support to a leg still inclined to trouble him where the tendons surrounding his Transvaal wound had been strained during his buffeting in the cove. Tonight there was an ache in his heart as he thought, with a touch of nostalgia, "This room was her creation and whenever we were alone in it we were at peace. If I marry again I suppose Claire will make changes but a man doesn't slough off a woman as easily as all that, not when he's held her in his arms through long winter nights." He got up restlessly and padded over to the window, flinging it wide and sniffing the night air, heavy with the scent of the woods. "Franz talks of changes," he thought, "but I feel their presence myself tonight. So many things have changed since I spent my first night here; Martin Codsall and Arabella were alive then, and Tamer Potter, and poor old Smut was ranging the woods, poaching deer; Lord Gilroy's tame M.P. represented us at Westminster and now Grenfell's up there at my instance, making what he can of this clamour for change. Simon was born in this room and Grace spent her last night at Shallowford here, with me beside her, never dreaming what was in her mind. All this, in four years! I wonder what the next four will bring?

458

Over in the chestnuts an owl hooted and from the rhododendrons nearer the house, came the sounds of a stealthy scuffle. He yawned, feeling detached from the past yet near enough to look back and savour its bitterness and sweetness. Then he thought of Claire, of her smooth oval face, pink and white freshness and the repose she seemed to have acquired during her exile and suddenly he felt more cheerful, flung off his clothes and climbed into bed. "Maybe I'll stop shaping things and let 'em happen in future," he told himself and on this compromise he slept.

IV

Paul's moment of self-revelation, and what came of it down by the landslip, released a spate of letter-writing up and down the Valley. The Sorrel people were shy of pen and ink. Some of them had never written a letter in their lives and a majority were content to scrawl greetings on Christmas cards once a year but events in the cove during the early spring, and their appearance on the front pages of newspapers, made the Valley folk aware of themselves as a clan. Some, with relatives in other parts of the West, followed up with news of events that grew out of the wreck, notably the Squire's intention to divorce his wife and marry Claire Derwent as soon as he was free.

Claire herself was not guiltless of rumour-spreading. Having written to her cousin and partner, arranging to sell her share of the business and stating that she was unlikely to return to London, she added an enigmatic postscript: "*Have been seeing a good deal of 'P'. There is talk of him divorcing his wife, who left him some time ago and has since been mixed up with the suffragettes.*" What her cousin made of this is not certain but if she recalled Claire's four-year-old confidences on the subject of "P" she probably put two and two together.

Maureen O'Keefe wrote two letters in illegible scrawl (deliberately cultivated for writing prescriptions) to the only woman who had shared her medical course in Dublin, a glum, Hebridean girl, now junior partner in a Belfast practice where women doctors were just tolerated, providing they were good Protestants. Maureen succeeded in astonishing her friend by adding, after saying she was taking over her father's Westcountry practice, "*. . . and I expect you will be even more surprised to learn I am to marry in September! I still can't believe it, especially when I (a) look in the mirror, and (b) check up on my birth certificate! I think you would like John—John Rudd that is, for in some ways he reminds me of you being dour, very solemn and wonderfully kind.*"

459

He is fifty-two, a widower with a son in the Navy, and has been agent on this estate for years . . ." She rattled on about Paul, Grace and even Claire Derwent, but mention of Claire reminded her of another letter she intended to write, so she cut short the Irish mail and began a slightly more legible letter to Ikey Palfrey.

"*My dear Ikey,*" she wrote, chuckling again as she recalled the encounter by Codsall bridge, "*I think the time has come to keep you up to date but burn this as soon as you have read it, or we shall find ourselves on the carpet again! I took care not to breathe a word about your MACHIAVELLISM but I felt you should know that it worked out better than any of us could have hoped, for Squire, so I hear, is taking steps to get a divorce and there isn't the slightest doubt that if and when he does he will marry Miss Derwent, and jolly good luck to them! By the way, he's quite his old self again now. Today, when I was visiting in Coombe Bay, I watched him go past without him seeing me and he was whistling loud enough to loosen his front teeth. He's very fit and putting on weight and Mr. Rudd tells me he's just not the same man at all, so we can both take credit for that! Good luck to you, Ikey, and I do hope you're happy at school and are looking forward to the holidays. Affectionately, Maureen O'Keefe.*"

Ikey read this letter in the Fives court, having first extracted the five-shilling postal order enclosed with it and fortified himself with two cream horns at the tuckshop. He was gratified by the news, although it seemed to him that the slightly crazy woman doctor must be pulling the longbow somewhat, for he still found it difficult to believe that people could change wives like horses. The information regarding Squire, however, was cheering and having obeyed her instructions, and carefully burned the letter, he occupied his Sunday letter-writing period composing a suitable reply. "*Dear Doctor O'Keefe,*" it ran, "*Many thanks for P.O. which is now spent and also for news. There are lots of things I should like to know more about but better not write them as you never know with letters do you. I am looking forward to coming home for summer half hols and entered in the under-fifteen mile sports day which is soon and I hope you and Squire will come up for it because I might win Cooper our running capt. thinks so. Good-bye and thanks again for the P.O. Respectfully, I. Palfrey.*"

Maureen O'Keefe did not burn this letter. It amused her so much that she put it away in her souvenir box, alongside her degree and collection of trainee photographs.

Sam Potter, at the instance of his wife Joannie, wrote one of his very rare letters to Smut, who had completed his third year and was expected to be released on licence by autumn. Sam had accompanied his mother on a visit to the gaol immediately after Tamer's death and had decided that nothing would induce him to go there again but his wife thought he should tell Smut about the special headstone the German Mercantile Marine had erected over Tamer's grave. After a great deal of laborious pen-chewing and chair-squeaking as he writhed in the agonies of composition, he produced the following: *"Dear Smut, this is to let you no they Germans paid for a stone over Father and chipped out a lot of wot hapened on it — must have cost I dont no how much but you can read it when you get here — I cant rite it even if I could think on it. They say Squire is puttin aside his missus and there is tork he will take Ted Derwents dorter to church the pretty one I mene see you soon Sam."*

Smut was intrigued by this letter, although both items of news puzzled him for, although there were a number of Potters laid in Coombe Churchyard, none had attained the dignity of a headstone which, as he recalled, were luxuries reserved for freeholders and prosperous tradesmen. He was even more mystified by Sam's reference to the Squire's possibility of taking a second wife, supposing that this privilege extended only to heathens and was against the law in England, even for a man as exalted as a Squire. His memories of Claire, however, were vivid for she had always been reckoned the most fetching girl in the Valley and he had suspected that she might one day make a good match, although not quite as good as this.

Something of Smut's natural exuberance had returned to him of late for they had recently put a card on the door of his cell, explaining that the legend thereon, *"E.D.R.15.10.06"* meant *"Earliest date of release, Oct. 15th, 1906"*. If things continued to go smoothly he would be back in the Valley in less than three months but the nearness of his release date was not the sole reason for his cheerfulness. Since his shift back across the border into Devon, where he could smell the sea and, if the wind was in the right quarter, the scent of gorse blowing down from Blackberry Moor, some of the sting had departed from confinement behind stone walls and iron doors and under the encouragement of the officer in charge of trusties working in the prison grounds, he had found a new interest in growing flowers. Smut, although he had lived his life in the open, had always taken flowers for granted but he did so no longer for in here a small splash of colour

461

riveted the eye and sometimes made a man catch his breath. All summer he laboured away tending geraniums, lobelia, calceolaria and marguerites and bit by bit, as he watched the results of his work, the occupation became the focal point of his existence so that he sometimes thought a little fearfully of the time when he would be separated from them and some other clumsy lout would have charge of them. He pondered this a good deal and wondered if it would be possible to make some kind of livelihood out of potting plants in the Coombe. If so, then he would prefer to devote himself to a job like this rather than share the casual husbandry of Meg and the girls, for here a man could see something in return for energy expended whereas nothing ever prospered under his hands in the Dell. He made up his mind to broach the subject to Chief Officer Phillips as soon as the opportunity presented itself.

In the meantime, however, unknown to Smut, a place was being prepared for him in the Valley, for the manner in which Tamer had died forged a personal bond between Paul and the shiftless tenants in Low Coombe. At harvest-time Paul rode across to the Dell and had a talk with Meg on the family's future, after which he crossed the corner of the Bluff and descended the wooded slope to Sam Potter's cottage beside the mere.

He found Sam at his midday meal and Joannie, always flustered by a visitor, wiped a damp cloth across the jam-smeared face of his goddaughter Pauline, who held the distinction of being the first child born on the estate under the new régime. Paul always felt very much at home in Sam's cottage and accepted a brew of tea whilst Snowdrop was given a feed in the lean-to stable.

"I've been discussing with Meg what we can do about Smut," Paul told him. "He's due out in the autumn and I'm officially responsible for him until his full sentence expires. Do you think he'll go back on poaching?"

Sam said that he thought not but he was clearly worried by the possibility. Despite their temperamental differences the brothers had always been close and Sam's visit to the gaol had strengthened the link, for he found it difficult to imagine a worse fate than that of being locked inside a grey fortress for years on end. He said, reflectively, "Ah, tiz a real problem an' no mistake, Maister! Smut were never a varmer, no more'n any one of us, an' like as not he'll be praper rusty after being cooped up in that gurt ole plaace! God knows, Mother needs help over there, and I bin in two minds to ask 'ee to give

Smut this job o' mine and let me move downalong, wi'Mother an'the girls. I'm no great shakes at varmin meself but I could best Tamer's efforts and maybe end up a credit to 'ee, Squire."

"It's more or less what I had in mind, Sam," Paul told him, "but you and Joannie have been happy here. How will you really feel about moving out and letting Smut take over as keeper and woodsman?"

Sam looked glum and said, with a glance at his wife, "I'll be honest with 'ee, Squire, us won't like it at all, will us Joannie? Us've maade a praper nest for ourselves here an' us don't fancy going downalong, an' bedding down in that old muddle! Still, us'd maake a better job of it than Smut and I zee no help for it if us is to give the varmint a fresh start!"

The same thought had already occurred to Paul. Sam had more than justified his faith when he had set him up here and it was asking much of Joannie to leave her clean, tidy home and share a kitchen with Meg and her sluttish daughters. He said, "I don't like the idea of uprooting you at all and maybe there's another way round it. Perhaps I could get your mother a permanent hired man and settle Smut somewhere on a patch of his own."

"Beggin' your pardon," Sam said, regretfully, "he'd never prosper on a patch of his own, Squire. 'Er's a good sort at heart but 'er's more shiftless than ever Tamer was. But if us dorn settle 'im somewheres you can be certain sure us is in trouble again, and neither me nor Joannie would like that, seein' how good you been to us! No, us'll get packed up, I reckon, and Smut can move in here. Mebbe he'll marry an' zettle down an' if 'er does, then it will have been worth it. What do 'ee zay, Joannie?"

Joannie said, without looking up, "Aye, us have got to stand by the family and there's an end to it!"

As he rode back through the woods it occurred to Paul that there must be some good blood in the Potters somewhere for how else could they produce courage like Tamer's and loyalty like Sam's? He wished, however, that he could buy a few acres west of Four Winds or north of Priory, in order to give Smut a fresh start without disrupting the lives of his brother and sister-in-law.

v

The announcement that John Rudd and Maureen O'Keefe were to marry in September intrigued and amused the Valley but it surprised no one. John, although much respected, had never captured the affection of the Valley people and when it was known that he was openly courting the lady-doctor (who, although acknowledged a far more skilful healer than her father, was judged even more eccentric) people like old Honeyman and the shepherd twins told one another that here was someone who might succeed in shaking old John out of himself and maybe encourage him to take himself less seriously. For in some ways Rudd remained a symbol of the Lovell régime and this despite the fact that he was known to be held in high regard by Squire Craddock.

Paul himself was not surprised by the news. It had been obvious from the first days of her sojourn among them that Maureen O'Keefe had bewitched the agent, who had trotted up and down the Valley behind her like a big collie, blind to the smirks and deaf to the innuendos of his beloved's patients. The doctor made a great joke out of his subjection, sniping at her fiancé's dignity without mercy but in some mysterious way warming a place for him in the hearts of tenants and their dependents. As soon as John had proposed she drove up and down the Valley broadcasting the news like a town-crier and very soon, on a sunny September morning, the marriage was solemnised in the parish church. Every pew was crammed and the entire population of Coombe Bay, including freeholders who had no dealings with the groom, assembled in the churchyard to witness the event. The bride arrived in the Squire's waggonette, attended by a male cousin and the two Derwent girls as bridesmaids, for Maureen O'Keefe, declaring that she had never expected to be a bride, had announced that she intended making the most of the occasion and doing the Valley full justice.

Paul was already inside with the groom and much relieved to get him there, for John's natural phlegm had basely deserted him when Paul called at the lodge an hour before the ceremony. In the act of fastening his high collar the agent had dropped both hands and exclaimed, "Damn it, this is bloody ridiculous at my age! Why did I let her talk me into making a spectacle of myself? Why can't we slip out of the Valley and marry in the Paxtonbury Registry Office?" Paul had replied, laughing in spite of himself, "Look here, John, it's her day and you damned well do as you're told! As soon as you're properly dressed I'll get you a stiff drink and the moment Parson smells it he'll gabble through the service at top speed in order to get across to the house and drink his quota!"

After his favourite toddy John calmed down somewhat and as there was time to spare he sat on the edge of a chair puffing away at his pipe and ruminating on the present situation in terms of mild astonishment.

"Now who the devil would have thought of anything like this that day I waited for you to get off that London train, Paul? Did you know that I hated you before I set eyes on you? And I made sure the first thing you would do was send me packing! Damn it, it's like a crazy fairy-tale and this is a fitting climax I must say! Me, sitting here in a frock coat and a Come-to-Jesus collar, waiting for you to steer me down the aisle and be sniggered at by every yokel for miles around!"

"Well, it's improbable, I'll grant you that," Paul admitted, "but as for getting married in a registry office you thank your stars you didn't! I have no choice in the matter, for the Church won't marry a divorced man and that's a big disappointment for Claire, I can tell you. I daresay she'll be thinking of it today and I wouldn't wonder if she doesn't plague me to have a go at Parson Bull about it if we ever get around to marrying."

"Oh, you'll marry the girl all right," said John, "and if you ask me . . ." but Paul decided this was not the time to involve the nervous groom in his own problems and said quickly, "Will you have one more before we leave?"

"Yes I will," said John, "for God knows I need it," and then, glancing at his watch, called to Chivers who was waiting with the trap in the drive and asked if he thought the cob would make it comfortably in under the half-hour. Paul said, "Were you as jumpy as this on your first wedding-day, John?" and the remark must have steadied the older man for he smiled, relit his pipe and replied, "Do you know, I'm hanged if I can remember? I've been trying to ever since I woke up this morning but I can't, it's all too long ago—three years before you were born!"

"And that's strange too," Paul said, "for I seem to have known you all my life, John," and he poured himself another small drink to make up for the groom's excessively large one.

"There is one thing I would like to say," John said, suddenly, "and since we've still got five minutes I'll say it before we get caught up in the clamour awaiting us yonder. You aren't under any obligation to renew my contract. I told Maureen only the other day that you don't really need me any longer and you could save yourself three hundred a year and plough it back into the estate. I'd manage well enough, I've

465

saved you know—and my first wife left me a little money. I wouldn't be idle either. I can always drive Maureen around and do her accounts."

"You'd prefer that?" Paul said, looking at him sharply, and John said, "Well no, I don't say I'd prefer it but . . ."

"Then don't make a fool of yourself on your wedding-day! I can afford three hundred a year and anyway you earn it and always have! I've got plans for next year, John, and you're included in them. It wouldn't be the same without you. You're the best friend I ever had and certainly the most honest!"

"Thank you, my boy," John said sincerely, "you couldn't have said anything more calculated to steady me!" and raising his glass, added, "I daresay there'll be a lot of gaff talked before the day is out, Paul, but this is my toast—to you and what you stand for in the Valley!" and as though fearful of seeming over-sentimental he tossed down the drink, cleared his throat, picked up his hat and gloves and marched out into the drive where Chivers helped him on to the box as though he had been a chronic invalid.

The gathering in the big marquee erected in the paddock was the most representative since the Coronation soirée four years before and many of those present recalled as much. There were over sixty official guests and about a hundred unofficial ones but after the first glass of champagne, and the cutting of a spectacular cake baked by Mrs. Handcock, the two categories intermingled for this was as much a Shallowford event as the wreck and the funeral of Tamer Potter that had followed it.

All the farmers, their families and employees were present and most of the estate and Coombe Bay craftsmen and fishermen, and when the honeymoon drag arrived from Whinmouth to convey the couple to Sorrel Halt everybody surged into the forecourt for the send-off. By this time, however, several casks of beer had been broached and many of the unofficial guests, together with several of the official ones like Henry Pitts, were in fine fettle. The bride's appearance on the porch steps was the signal for so much scuffling and shouting that the be-ribboned greys harnessed to the drag would have bolted had it not been for Sam Potter and young Willoughby, who hung on the reins and shouted for Paul and others to clear the drive. When this was done John stood up on the box and made a little speech, pointing out that the age of those gathered to wish them well covered a span of over a century and it was a point well taken. Among those on the

466

verges were Marian Eveleigh's six-months-old baby and old Floss Timberlake, who disgraced her chapel-going daughter-in-law by reciting a traditional wedding toast that had not been heard in the Valley for three generations. As John concluded his speech of thanks she bellowed, for all to hear:

"Yer's to the hen who never refuses,
An' lets un tread whenever 'ee chooses!"

a couplet that produced a frenzied "shhh!" from her family but laughter so immoderate from Henry Pitts that he came close to choking. Then the drag was off, trailing its strings of tin cans and old boots but the professional greys expected nothing less and were well in hand by the time John reined in at the lodge where Paul, Rose and Claire waited to remove the garbage. As Chivers (charged with bringing the vehicle back from the station) took his seat Paul said, "Well John, this isn't a day we'll forget in a hurry! Good luck, and all the happiness in the world!" but this did not satisfy Maureen, who thrust aside his proferred hand, threw her arms round his neck, and kissed him half-a-dozen times, after which she climbed back in the box and threw her bouquet at Claire who caught it so expertly that Paul was half-persuaded the gesture had been rehearsed. Then Chivers cracked the whip and the drag moved off at a bowling trot along the river road, best man and bridesmaids returning to preside over the meat tea provided for the invited guests. Rose was excited and talkative but Paul noticed that Claire seemed thoughtful and when, on reaching the house, she excused herself and went upstairs, he said, looking after her, "You don't think she's having second thoughts, Rose?"

"She's enjoying every moment of it," Rose replied, equably, "and she's perfectly reconciled to having a very quiet wedding if and when things are sorted out. However, there is one thing you could do and today seems a very good opportunity, for I've seen to it that father had plenty to drink. Could you ... well ... could you try and explain the situation to him? He's terribly old-fashioned, and neither Claire nor I have had the nerve to do it, although I daresay he's heard all kinds of rumours up and down the Valley."

"I don't mind telling him" Paul said, although by no means relishing the task, "but wouldn't it be better to wait until I'm actually free to remarry?"

"No," said Rose, "it would not! He'd far sooner hear it from you

467

than from outsiders, so if I were in your place I'd get it over and done with right now. I know Claire would be very relieved if you did!"

He said, squeezing her hand, "Very well, I'll be guided by you, Rose. He's talking to Arthur Pitts now. Get Arthur out of the way and I'll bring him in here."

They went out on to the terrace and Arthur was skilfully detached with news of a new snaffle Rose was using on the half-broken trap pony. Paul said, approaching Edward Derwent with a glass of champagne in his hand, "Do you think we might have a private word in the study, Mr. Derwent?" and was relieved to note that the farmer's stolid features assumed a slightly startled look as he followed Paul along the terrace and into the house, standing with his feet planted well apart and looking as if he envied Paul his full glass.

"It's about Claire," Paul began. "Rose thought it proper that I should tell you precisely how things stand between us, if only to anticipate the gossips. You will have heard that I'm suing for a divorce?"

He was glad then that he had not waited to replenish Derwent's glass for he had him at a slight disadvantage, but then he suddenly felt sorry for him, reasoning that he must find it damnably embarrassing to be bearded by his landlord on the latter's home ground and added apologetically, "I'm assuming you had heard Claire and I hope to marry when I'm free?"

"Aye," Derwent said, or rather growled, "I heard that right enough and who hasn't? Well, she's twenty-three now and has usually gone her own way no matter what but there's limits, Squire, as to what a father is prepared to put up with! Notwithstanding you owning the land I farm I'd see you in hell before I let you drag my Claire's name through the Courts!"

His truculence, Paul thought, did him credit but it was plain that Rose's suspicions were well founded and that some of the more extravagant rumours must have reached him. He said, quietly, "There's absolutely no question of that, Derwent! I'm divorcing my wife, my wife isn't divorcing me. The lawyers are dealing with it now but it will take time, these things always do. What I should like you to know is that, if and when I'm free, Claire and I want to marry at once. Would you have any objections?"

Derwent frowned, biting his dark moustache and looking, Paul thought, less embarrassed than exasperated. Finally, however, and with what appeared to be considerable effort, he said, gruffly, "No,

468

Squire, I wouldn't stand in your way and I don't mind saying why. Time was when I would have set my face against any girl of mine taking up with a man in your position, and him with a wife living into the bargain but most people about here realise Mrs. Craddock's capers were no fault o' yours, and most of us were right sorry about it at the time! I never held with divorce. If you make a mistake you bide by it, or you did in my time but times are changing and, as I said, she's not a girl and can earn her living independently! If she's set her heart on you I'll neither say nor do anything to turn her aside."

It was not, Paul thought, a particularly gracious answer but it was a more conciliatory one than he had anticipated and it amused him slightly to hear the unsmiling master of High Coombe dismiss Grace's desertion as "a caper". The man's unexpected tolerance, however, tempted him to press the subject further and he said, "Well, that satisfies me, Derwent, but I'm not sure it will satisfy Claire! She's always had respect and affection for you and she'll want your blessing! Would you give it to her?"

Since the day, more than four years past, when Rudd had first taken him over the bluff to High Coombe he had seen Edward Derwent in a variety of moods, all the way from brusque civility to downright truculence but he had never, until now, seen him humbled. Derwent's face, dark under its suntan, flushed as he stood looking down at his large, well-polished boots.

"Yes," he said at length, "I reckon I could do that for her mother would have given it soon enough," and then, meeting Paul's eyes defiantly, "The fact is, Squire, I was badly wrong about you and a man of principle oughtn't to mind admitting a bad judgment when it's come back on him, as mine did the night o' the wreck! They others about here, they'm flippety-gibbets for the most part—anyway for a pint o' cider as they say, but me—I'm not easily taken in and I don't mind admitting it always seemed to me you were a young man wi' too much money playing the fool at farming! Well, I was dam' well wrong, as I saw wi' my own eyes when you and Potter took that cockleshell to sea in the cove! If I don't admit a fault I'm under an obligation and that's something I don't care to be to any man, not excepting my landlord!" Paul murmured acknowledgement of this apology but Derwent went on, relentlessly, "Wait now, there's more to it than that! Before you came, and many times since, I wanted badly to be a freeholder but now I'm not so set on it, particularly as you want to marry my girl soon as you can! Maybe I'm too old and

469

too set in my ways or maybe I'm content for my boy Hugh to take it up with you later, but seeing what you're bent on doing in the Valley I'm well content to let things remain as they be. From now on, whether or not you take my girl, I'm your man, Mr. Craddock!"

There had been many occasions since he had come to Shallowford when Paul had been heartened by individual recognition of his intentions. Arthur Pitts and Henry Pitts had always encouraged him, and so, in a more roundabout way, had John Rudd and old Honeyman. Eveleigh, and his wife Marian, had never ceased to show their appreciation of his faith in them whereas Sam Potter and Will Codsall had been his partisans from the beginning. But this blunt statement from the tight-lipped Edward Derwent was something different. It was the conversion of a man whom Paul had always recognised as the hard core of opposition to his policy and because of this it touched him far more deeply than the loyalty of men like Henry Pitts, or even a farmer like Eveleigh, who had plenty for which to thank him in the material sense. He reached out and clasped Derwent's hand and for the first time he felt he had gained a powerful ally, not as a prospective father-in-law but as a friend whose weight counted for something in the Valley.

They went back into the hall just as Claire came downstairs and called, as though it had been she who had been kept waiting, "Oh, *there* you are, Paul! Really, we ought to be getting them seated. Some of them have a long way to go before dark!" and Edward Derwent looked at Paul with an expression that could not, under any circumstances, have been called mischievous or even sardonic, but somehow suggested an alliance between men who, from time to time, would be called upon to suffer jointly the maddening illogicality of wives and daughters.

Book Three

CHAPTER ONE

I

LESS than an hour after sunrise, on the last morning of April, 1908, Claire slipped out of bed without waking Paul and went downstairs, through the big kitchen and across the stable-yard to climb the path that led through the orchard to the cart-track dividing kitchen garden from the first trees of Priory Wood.

She walked barefoot as she usually did on these early morning expeditions, enjoying the sensation of the dew passing between her toes and savouring the smell of the long grass, and the great clumps of late primroses and early bluebells that grew all the way up the slope. Up here, looking down on the great sprawling house, was a favourite viewpoint, for here she could take out her life and prospects and examine them, as a craftsman might examine a half-finished piece of work; here, in the past twelve months, she had spent her most complacent moments.

Today, her wedding anniversary, was especially propitious and she was glad that Paul had been late to bed the previous night, having ridden across the Whin to look at a pair of cart-horses. He would sleep on, she decided, until about seven-thirty and the next ninety minutes were her own, for even Mrs. Handcock and Thirza would not stir for another half-hour and Chivers, the groom, rarely appeared until eight.

The scent of wild flowers and pine sap came out of the woods on a westerly breeze and she sniffed it like a pointer, deciding that it was among the most evocative scents in the world, along with the smell of the sea and the whiff of autumn bonfires. It had stillness in it and promise, and so far most of its promises had been kept for she had wandered up here to listen to them in the very earliest days of her marriage and could look back on no more than a single disappointment, an early miscarriage more than six months ago but now forgotten in the certainty of a second pregnancy. For the last two months, ever since Maureen O'Keefe had confirmed that she would have another child at the end of August, she had been able to view her disappointment with detachment, reflecting that Maureen must have

473

been talking sense when she had said that Claire had no one to blame for the miscarriage but herself. She had been too exuberant and too active, continuing to ride and swim, stay up late, overtire herself entertaining, and join Paul in all his political jaunts and market researches. She would not make the same mistakes this time, although she knew quite well why she had made them last summer. She had been so eager to be the kind of wife he wanted and needed, resolving to share all his enthusiasms and achievements and had laughed at Maureen's warnings until it was too late, but youth and natural vitality had limited her depression to a matter of weeks and ever since Christmas, by which time she suspected that she was pregnant again, she had been serene and cheerful, although this time she had been careful to follow Maureen's advice in every particular.

Apart from this one setback the year had passed happily and eventfully, with his plans slowly taking shape and the Valley expanding under his thrust and initiative. His touch was surer now and she gave herself a little credit for this, for he was always relaxed and seemed to find in her someone who could match his enthusiasm for the Valley. Yet there was far more to it than that. After the barest minimum period of adjustment she had become wholly his, as much his as this wide, wooded valley and everything growing on it, as much a part of him as his secret dreams. She could laugh now at old wives' whispers of the indignities demanded of a woman given in marriage, and had, indeed, never taken their warnings very seriously, for she had been born and raised on a farm and a witness from earliest childhood of the farm cycle.

For all that marriage presented her with a variety of surprises and not the least of them had been his unexpected gentleness during their first few weeks together. Although far less inhibited than the average city girl of her generation Claire had experienced a certain amount of anxiety as regards the purely physical aspects of marriage and her doubts were centred on his previous marriage to a woman of a different *milieu* from her own. Grace Lovell had been accepted in the Valley as a "modern" woman, possessed, no doubt, of all kinds of mysterious "modern" ideas, some of which she may well have communicated to her husband and it was this that caused Claire to magnify her own ignorance. Her mother had died when she was nine and no one had taken her place, for Rose, and later Edward Derwent's second wife, Liz, were even less experienced than she was herself. She had read very little apart from the romantic lady novelists of the period and such information as they could supply on the subject of marriage stopped short at the altar. This was why, once the modest tumult of the wedding was over, Claire Derwent found her confidence at low ebb, particularly after they had arrived in Anglesey where she had elected to spend the honeymoon.

They took a suite in a hotel and it was here, in a matter of hours, that she was blessedly reassured, for she found him not merely tolerant and patient where tolerance and patience were not to be expected of a groom but able, in a way that was peculiarly his own, to spice his ardour with a humour that soon demolished such reservations as had survived her upbringing on a farm under the eye of a man of her father's temperament. With this shedding of false modesty on her part came other discoveries, chief among them a secret delight in his frank worship of her body. She had never thought of herself as more than pretty and even that in a somewhat countrified way, but he obviously thought of her as beautiful and under the stimulus of his glorification she learned to respond to him in a way that not only brought him gratification as a lover but stature and authority as a man, and to a degree that had eluded him since he first came to live among them. It pleased her enormously that she should have been able to achieve this so rapidly and so effectively that, on their return, even people like John Rudd noticed it, but for all the accord and delight they found in each other's arms laughter was never quite banished by urgency. These lighter notes were struck, in the first instance, by his appetite for love which had mildly surprised her until she remembered that he was only four years her senior (which was something she had half-forgotten during his long illness) and also that he had been deprived of a woman for almost two years and had not, it seemed, consoled himself elsewhere after Grace's desertion. Sometimes, when he was asleep beside her and his arm lay across her breast, she would feel herself blushing at the memory of an encounter, of words that had escaped her and extravagances she had actively encouraged and sometimes half initiated but then her sense of humour would reassert itself and she would smile in the realisation that there was surely health and resilience in the sharing of so much ecstasy compounded with so much silent laughter.

She stood by the stile at the north end of the orchard watching the coral pink sky shedding its veils of light over the Bluff as the sun topped the eastern slope of the cliffs. The bluebells were already half out, spreading handfuls of pale blue dust between the older apple

475

trees, and in hedges crowded by clusters of primroses, solitary campions, violets and periwinkles peeped, like shy neighbours in a street of extroverts. She thought, "God knows how scared I was, scared of comparisons, of him accepting me as a second-best, a good-intentioned hobbledehoy but there was nothing to be frightened of after all! All my instincts about him were accurate, for where there is kindness and courage anything is possible given goodwill on my part and that he always had in abundance!" And suddenly life and prospects seemed as smooth and round as her belly and the future as predictable as the seasons. With a song on her lips she went on down through the wet grass, stepping in her own footsteps and then round to the forecourt and in at the big door that they never locked since the night of the Codsall tragedy.

There was still no one astir and she went through the library and into the office to get the Bible-camouflaged estate record. His gesture in giving her this book to maintain had been one of the most rewarding in her life and she took great pains to justify it although, under her pen, it had become less of a record and more of a great, gossipy diary. She carried the book back to the library and sat facing the empty grate, and as her eye fell upon the bearskin hearthrug she laughed for this morning the rug had a special significance for her and for the child in her womb, conceived here on the blustery night they had both taken too much of Martin Pitts' punch at Hallowe'en and had rattled home by moonlight to find a great fire burning and the room more inviting than the bedroom overhead. She paused, after opening the book, to reflect on the moment, half in wonder and half in amusement, recalling his boisterousness and her own halfhearted protests about the possibility of prowling servants. A single kiss had driven all thought of them from her mind and there they had lain for an hour or more, with the room lit by the flicker of pungent-smelling apple logs and the familiar tide of gratified accomplishment sweeping over her, for although he was soon asleep, and the punch or the makeshift couch made him snore, she would never forget what he had replied when she had said, "We're behaving more like a pair of precocious adolescents than a respectably married couple!" He had said, running his hand through her disordered hair, "Having you restores my adolescence, Claire! Every time I touch you, look at you even, I feel about seventeen, and surely it must be good for a man to have that kind of wife within reach!"

She remembered this now and it produced the satisfied glow she

476

had experienced at the time, so that she no longer had patience with the book and put off writing an entry about his purchase of the cart-horses, flicking through the later pages and scanning items like *"Smut Potter's second hothouse erected"*, and *"Stream End block of four cottages, in Coombe Bay, bought and rethatched"*, until she arrived at blank pages and wondered what events would be recorded on them after the final one which read, *"April 22nd, 1908. Jem Pollock signed on as foreman, Low Coombe. Dell problem solved but in what a curious way! Squire's approval still conditional."* Then she closed the book, replaced it in the safe and went out to brew some tea, filling two china mugs and carrying them trayless to the main bedroom.

He was still asleep when she drew the curtains and she woke him by holding a braid of her hair and drawing it slowly across his face. He opened his eyes and looked bewildered for a moment and then, with a laugh she said, "I've been out! It's wonderful! Just like the early morning of the world up there in the orchard! Take it, it's freshly made"—and she gave him his tea, but as he sat up to drink it he noticed her bare feet.

"You ought to wear shoes out there, Claire! Maureen warned you to be more careful this time!"

"Not about getting dew on my feet," she said, and lifting her foot invited him to feel it, which he did, finding it unexpectedly warm.

"Well, I don't know," he grumbled, only half seriously, "if old Chivers saw you walking barefoot in the orchard at crack of dawn he'd probably tell old Horace Handcock you do it to elude my early morning demands on you!"

"He's only got to look at me to discover I didn't succeed!" she said and faced the full-length mirror on the clothes closet door, adding ruefully, "I'm enormous, Paul! About twice as big as I was last time. Is that a good sign, do you think?"

"It's probably a sign that you've badly miscalculated," he said grinning.

"Oh no it isn't. I'm not likely to make a mistake about that. As a matter of fact I've just been in the library remembering. You and your Hallowe'en parties! A fine climax to nibbling apples in a bowl and wearing turnip lanterns I must say!"

He put down his mug and clasped his hands behind his neck, regarding her humorously. "Come over here!" he ordered, and when she came a little closer but remained out of reach, "What were you

477

doing when I opened my eyes just now? Were you pulling the bed-clothes from me?"

"Nothing so heartless," she said, kneeling on the bed so that her hair covered over his face. "Just this! Surely the most enchanting awakening a man can expect, even from such a doting wife as me!"

"Yes, it is," he said, seriously, gathering a double handful of tresses and kissing them, "but I'm hanged if I don't believe you've forgotten what day it is," and before she could indignantly deny the fact he threw aside his pillows and produced a small leather box, pressing the spring and showing her a beautifully wrought brooch, with a heavy gold circlet and a central star composed of one large and a score of much smaller diamonds, the whole being suspended on a thin gold chain. She showed the wild excitement of a child opening a Christmas stocking.

"Paul, it's lovely! I didn't expect anything, honestly I didn't! I didn't dream . . .", and then, as her hand reached for it, "Did you really buy those cart-horses yesterday? Is that really why you went all the way to Torhaven?" and he told her, chuckling, that it was indeed and that the purchase had been an afterthought that occurred to him minutes before the quay curiosity shop had closed, that he had walked inside without an idea in his head and had seen the brooch on a blue velvet cushion, surrounded by a lot of trumpery jewellery.

She crossed to the mirror and fastened it to her blouse, jerking her head this way and that and cooing like a pigeon.

"Well, it's wonderful and I wouldn't have given you credit for such marvellous taste!" she said. "Look! Isn't it right? Isn't it *different*?"

He said, smiling, "No, it's you who are different, Claire! And you don't need jewellery to convince me!"

II

The Dell problem had indeed been solved and it was not flippancy on Claire's part that had prompted her to write "in a curious way—Squire's approval conditional" in the record book. The Dell had always been a nursery of Valley scandal but never more so than in the spring of 1908, some time after Smut came out of gaol on licence, having served three years, eight months of his five-year sentence. He at once astonished his welcome committee by declaring that he intended to become a horticulturist, specialising in hothouse and bedding-out plants for sale in the city.

478

This ambition baffled everyone who had known him but in many other ways he was a parody of the Smut Potter they recalled as the terror of Shallowford and Heronslea coverts with his gun and traps. His impudent smile had gone and in its place was a sleepy, ingratiating grin; his stubby hair had streaks of grey and his loping, poacher's walk had shrunk to a careful shuffle. Instead of balancing himself on his toes, as of old when he had always seemed on the point of leaping for cover, he now stood with joints relaxed, as though awaiting the bark of command before he moved in any one direction. Yet one thing about him had not changed. He was still extremely obstinate and nothing could induce him to have a hand in uprooting Sam and his family from their cottage and taking Sam's place as woodsman and keeper. Yet, to their dismay, neither would he consent to having Tamer's lease transferred to him and settling himself on the derelict farm. He was done with poaching, he said, but also with pig-farming and crow-starving. All he wanted to do was to grow flowers in a greenhouse and if Squire Craddock, bless his warm heart, could see his way to dismantle and re-erect the dilapidated glasshouse now standing empty behind the Shallowford rose garden, then he would raise pot plants that had never been seen in the Valley and sell them as far afield as Paxtonbury. He knew he could do it if only he had a single quarter-acre under glass, and if Squire would not part with his greenhouse he would set to work, collect discarded panes from all over the Valley and build one on the long, sunny slope where the Potter land ran down to the river east of Coombe Bay.

The Potters went into conference with Paul and the upshot of their deliberations was that the project was just possible, although Meg expressed private doubts as to Smut's staying power, saying he would be more likely to keep out of trouble if he went to work in the woods. It was Claire who finally won them over. She came out as an enthusiastic ally of the ex-poacher, reporting that Smut had obviously acquired an extraordinary amount of expertise in the prison gardens and not only knew the names of a wide variety of fashionable conservatory plants but could designate them in Latin! This piece of information convinced everybody that Smut was in earnest and for three days after Paul had given assent to his plan the Potter haywain trundled to and fro along the river road with its load of glass panes and metal frames to be reassembled on the southern slope known as Seafield, and subsequently repaired and repainted by a team of volunteers, including one of the Eveleigh boys who enlisted as an apprentice.

Old Willoughby, of Deepdene, himself interested in horticulture, gave Smut a good deal of useful advice and a supply of seeds and most of the other farmers chipped in with second-hand tools and supplies of manure, so that Smut was soon established and working sixteen hours a day, sleeping in a poacher's shelter built against the greenhouse boiler that had been hauled over the bluff on Timberlake's tree waggon, along with its complement of cast-iron pipes.

It was encouraging, Paul thought, to see the Valley folk rally round the rascal, giving their labour free and taking collective pride in the ungainly structure on the downslope of the Low Coombe boundary. When all was as ready as could be Claire presided at a half-humorous official opening, launching the enterprise with a bottle of Meg's hedgerow wine smashed against the boiler at the southern end of the house. Everyone, it seemed, was pleased to see Smut home again and all wished him well in his unlikely venture. His initiative, however, did nothing to solve the vexed future of the Potter farm as a whole. Meg had little interest in steady farming or animal husbandry and spent most of her time collecting ingredients for her elixirs, or making the mats and baskets she sold across the Teazel, whereas the girls, who could make a shift at looking after pigs and occasionally ploughed a few acres, were unsuitable as long-term tenants for they were now in their mid-twenties and unlikely to remain single indefinitely.

It was through their agency that the matter was settled, and although the manner in which this took place caused scandalised comment in the Valley, the arrangement drifted on until it was hallowed by time, and Big Jem Pollock was generally accepted as the master of the Dell, and in some ways proved a worthy successor to old Tamer.

Jem was not a farmhand, although he had worked on farms during his semi-vagabond life before appearing in the Valley with a travelling fair licensed to set up on Blackberry Moor each Whitweek. The fair billed him as *"Jem Pollock, the Goliath of Bideford"* and his act consisted of tying knots in iron bars, hauling struggling teams of yokels across the ring and driving six-inch nails into billets of wood with his bare fists. The fair was a seedy little attraction, with the usual collection of swings, roundabouts, giant-slides and catchpenny booths but it attracted a public from as far away as Paxtonbury in the north and Whinmouth in the west whereas the Valley folk always attended *en masse*. The Potter family, very much at home in this kind of atmosphere, invariably downed tools and attended every evening, the two girls, Cissie and Violet, acquiring trinkets and entertainment by means of their personal cunning. It was here that they encountered and passed under the spell of Jem Pollock, the Bideford Goliath, or it might be more accurate to say that it was they, a pair of slingless Davids, who brought Goliath low, for having arrived in the Valley with no intention other than making sport of panting locals at the end of a rope Jem remained there until attracted to the colours by Kitchener's arresting finger.

It happened on the final night of the fair. Jem had a barker and a tent to himself, and during the previous visits the Potter girls had watched spellbound as he bent over knotted bars, buried nails in tree-trunks with blows of his enormous fist and won frenzied cheers by marching round his patch of sawdust trailing six of the lustiest Heronslea estate workers on a tow rope. The Potter girls had always appreciated a man and were connoisseurs in this field, having, between them, sampled most of the available men living within walking distance of the Dell, but never before had they looked upon a man like Jem, whose calves were like half-grown pine trunks and whose biceps and magnificent torso reminded them of illustrations of the famous Sandow. But it was not his display of muscles that drew giggles from them so much as his working costume, consisting of a leopard-skin toga augmented by pink and excessively tight-fitting hose that left very little to the imagination and had spectators comparing him to Eveleigh's prize bull. Another unusual thing about the Bideford Goliath was his geniality and the vacant mildness of his expression as he performed in the ring. He had the innocent gaze of a timid girl and features that were delicate for one so huge and muscular. On his splendid limbs grew forests of short, golden hairs that glistened with sweat as he stood flexing his muscles between each act. He also lacked the vainglory of the professional giant and seemed to find nothing very remarkable in his extraordinary feats of strength, which was strange considering the effect they produced upon his audiences, particularly upon the ladies, who flocked to his tent in large numbers for every performance.

Meg Potter was on familiar terms with several of the showmen and it was over a bread-and-cheese supper in the acrobats' tent one night that the girls were introduced to Jem as a man rather than a performer. They found him so shy that they made little progress with him on that occasion, beyond extracting from him an admission that he was not forsworn to circus life and was, in fact, "looking about for a likely place to zettle" and perhaps set up as a smith or forester. On hearing this the girls sounded their mother on the possibility of engaging him as a permanent replacement for the hired hand, loaned to Low Coombe by Four Winds after Tamer's death. The prospect of having so magnificent a specimen of manhood within call day and night, was inviting from a variety of aspects, for the Potter girls hated their farm chores and Meg, looking on Goliath with an unprejudiced eye, agreed that he would more than earn his keep at Low Coombe and promptly offered him fifteen shillings a week, plus board and lodging. He promised to think it over and the girls saw that he did, following him about the fair every night and stupefying him with affection. On the last night of the fair he made up his mind and it was years before they learned what had tipped the balance. In a rare moment of expansion he told them saying, in his broad North Devon burr, "I zeed the pair of 'ee cum sliding down thicky giant slide showin' all 'ee had which was considerable!"

The Potter girls, although promiscuous, were not harlots within the meaning of the word. It was simply that they delighted in the company and admiration of men and always had, ever since they were fourteen-year-olds but they did not consort with them from motives of personal gain alone and regarded anything material that emerged from encounters as a bonus to the simple pleasures derived from jolly companionship. They wandered among the world of men like children gathering wild flowers, each subject to furious, short-lived enthusiasms over one bloom or another and although, in the view of the Puritan, they possessed no moral sense whatever, they exercised discrimination and had learned something from their sister Pansy's dolorous experience of life pledged to one particular man. For poor Pansy, who had been so elated when she had secured Walt Pascoe as a husband, was now anchored to a cottage teeming with squalling children and seemed not to have any fun at all whereas Cissie and Violet were still gloriously free and valued their freedom far too much to form a permanent attachment. The establishment of Jem Pollock in the Dell would not, as Violet had pointed out, commit either of them in any way. As a hired hand, they reasoned, they could take him or leave him at will at the same time relieving Meg and themselves of the irksome responsibilities of work on the land. They found nothing distasteful in the prospect of sharing him, turn and turn about. They had shared all their lovers and sometimes extracted a good deal of amusement comparing notes. They had made their mistakes and there were

482

two toddlers in the Dell to prove as much, but a child or two under their feet did not bother a Potter, for the Dell seemed always to have been teeming with children. So the fair moved on, leaving the Goliath of Bideford behind as man-of-all-work at Low Coombe, and soon the whisper ran along the Valley that the Potter girls had at last found a male capable of accommodating them and had established a cosy *ménage à trois* in the Dell. That, however, was before the story broke new ground and an unexpected sequel forced the true state of affairs into the open. This might never have happened if the girls had been able to adjust themselves to their new way of life, and their antics had not awakened a fierce possessiveness in the heart of their willing captive.

It happened about a month after Jem had moved in. He soon proved himself a sound investment from Meg's viewpoint for his willingness and strength, expertly applied to the rundown acres, transformed the farm almost overnight. He was more tireless than any cart-horse and under Meg's direction cleared all the brushwood and weeds from the southern-facing slopes, later ploughing three of the largest fields for winter wheat and planting kale in the more enclosed part of the Bluff. When this was done he cut timber and built several new sties, sinking a small well on the edge of the wood and also repairing the ten-year-old leaks in the farmhouse thatch. His stamina was amazing, for although he worked hard all day he seemed to need very little sleep, so long as his huge frame was nourished by cauldrons of Meg's savoury stew, enormous helpings of fresh vegetables and an average of three loaves of home-baked bread between sunrise and dusk. He ate about ten times as much as a normal labourer but even so he more than earned his board, and everyone in the Dell was delighted with him, blessing the day he had been detached from the Philistines. Then, one mild summer evening, he suddenly presented his bill and it was seen to be a formidable one for it included, in addition to about a basketful of food each day and fifteen shillings a week for beer and baccy, the personal freedom of the girls who were dismayed to find themselves more married than their sister Pansy in Coombe Bay.

He was returning to the Dell at dusk when he heard a ripple of laughter in the long grass on the eastern edge of the wood, close to the spot where he had dug his well. He recognised the sound as Violet's laugh and stolidly changed direction to plod to the top of the slope, where he almost fell over the girls and the two Timberlake boys. Jem was neither a talkative nor an explosive man, his tongue being the one

483

organ of his body that wanted for exercise. After blinking down at the recumbent couples, who were unabashed by his presence, he gave a short grunt that some might have mistaken for the sigh of a man who finds a small task overlooked as he is about to climb into bed. He bent down, gathered a Timberlake under each arm and ambled on as far as the well where he paused for a moment, as though uncertain how to dispose of his double burden. The Timberlake boys, Dandy and Jerry, were not weaklings. Each of them measured around six foot and weighed around thirteen stone but when Jerry heaved himself round and struck the Bideford Goliath a heavy blow on the back of his head, he minded it no more than the impact of a descending beech nut. All it did, it seemed, was to remind him that he had yet to dispose of his rivals and lumbering a few strides further up the hill he dropped both young men into the new well.

Cissie and Violet, screaming their protests and scrambling in pursuit, now made a concerted rush at him, their shrieks carrying far across the meadows and startling gulls on the rock ledges over the cove but the outcry was largely a reflex for the well was only nine feet deep and after floundering for a moment in thick, red mud the boys scrambled out and ran for the woods, without so much as a glance over their shoulder. The ease with which they had been transported from near heaven to the pit convinced them that counter-attack would invite further humiliation and possibly grave personal injury, so they did not pause in their stride until they had circled the Bluff, crossed Shallowford meadow and reached the sanctuary of their father's saw-pit.

Bereft of their champions the two girls looked at Jem a little apprehensively, never having seen him in such a ponderously active mood but for a moment they were cruelly deceived by his apparent amiability as he poked about in the hedge and seemed disposed to begin some new task. When he took out his clasp knife, however, they looked anxiously at one another and Cissie said, sharply, "Put up that knife, you gurt fool! They're half-way home be now and us don't want real trouble!"

He made no reply but as he came back to them they saw what he had been doing. He had cut himself three or four pliant ash shoots and was binding them together with a piece of bast. Violet said, "What be at now for God's sake?" and he replied, mildly, "I'll show 'ee in a minute or so, midear," and swished his birch through the air in such a manner as to dispose of their doubts in the instant. Hitching their long skirts they turned and fled towards home almost as precipitately as the Timberlake boys but it was not until they reached the head of the winding path leading down to the Dell that they realised they were barefoot, having shed their brogues in the long grass before Jem arrived to spoil a pleasant evening with a display of uncharacteristic vindictiveness. Jem was close behind them and apparently in no hurry so that they could easily have out-distanced him had it not been for the tangle of briars and roots that grew over the path here. Cissie said, "We got to get our shoes, Jem . . ." but the remark ended in an agonised yelp as the birch landed its first blow and after that there was no more talk of shoes or anything else but a clamour that startled everything in the thicket as the girls made a rush down the steep path. Jem managed to keep just within range and every now and again landed a casual swipe on the nearest posterior, so that the sisters jostled with one another for the honour of leading the procession. Violet, who had been in the rear, overtook her sister about a third of the way down but here, where the trees grew thickly, it was difficult to see in the gathering dusk and she stumbled, Cissie falling over her, so that Jem, still administering leisurely swipes, stood over them as they rolled together in the nettles. Smut, who happened to be visiting the Dell, heard the uproar from the campfire and ran to see the cause. He was just in time to witness the climax and the spectacle, once he had recovered from his surprise, made him double up with laughter for the two girls came down the incline at a stumbling run and behind them came a fast-striding Jem, herding them along like a drover escorting a couple of frisky heifers to market. Thirty yards from the glade Violet made a grave tactical error. Thinking to increase her speed she whisked up her skirts waist high and Cissie at once followed suit but it was a sad mistake on their part, for as long as he could keep them moving Jem was not specially vindictive and seemed in no particular hurry. With two such tempting targets, however, he settled to his task and scored a bull's-eye on one or the other about every three yards. With renewed shrieks the girls dropped their skirts and settled for a good steady pace so they soon arrived, leaping this way and that like a pair of Chinese crackers, while Jem, his humour restored, came up with a broad, gap-toothed grin, as though proud of the brisk manner in which he had headed his cows for home.

The girls disappeared into the house and Meg, glancing after them, absorbed the situation at once. She did not join in Smut's uproarious laughter but her stern features relaxed sufficiently to register approval of the way in which affairs at the Dell had been set in order. She said, incuriously, "Was it they Timberlake boys?" and when he nodded, "Ah, then us'll see no more o' they, Jem! You did right, boy, and they'll be the better for it! 'Ave 'ee vinished with 'em now or be gonner give 'em a real tannin'?"

"Leave 'em be, Mother," he said, carelessly, "I skinned the arse off 'em all the way 'ome," and then, sniffing, "What's for supper?"

"Rabbit stew," she told him, "and I should eat yours, midear, an' tak' theirs into 'em later. They'll be busy now putting lard on one another's backsides I reckon."

This was, in fact, precisely what they were doing in the light of the kitchen lamp and after they had quietened a little Violet, the sharper of the two, grumbled "Well I doan 'ave to tell 'ee what this means do I?" and Cissie said no, she supposed not, and that it meant they were now Jem's exclusive property and that the sooner everyone in the Valley got to know it the fewer broken heads and whole skins there would be hereabouts. Silently, as they inspected one another's welts, they reviewed the prospect of lifelong bondage to the Bideford Goliath. It was, they felt, a sorry ending to a life of freedom but it had certain advantages that were expressed, perhaps, in Violet's summing up after they had peeped fearfully out-of-doors and watched their tormentor stolidly supping his stew by the fire. "Well," she said resignedly, "it could be worser I reckon! After all, there's only two of us but Jem makes six of any other man in the Valley!" And Cissie agreed, adding wistfully, "I can smell that stew from here, Vi! I wish I dare nip out an' get some but I darn't, dare you?"

"No," said Violet grimly, "I dasn't, fer I shan't zit comfortable for a week as it is! Us'll bide yer and be real nice when 'er brings some in, and if 'er comes in among us tonight dornee start that ole nonsense about you bein' a year older than me! Us'll cut cards for it now – ace high same as Mother decides!"

They cut the cards and Violet drew a queen to Cissie's eight and from that night on there was peace and modest prosperity in the Dell. It took a world war to upset the equilibrium established there by the Bideford Goliath.

III

On the day that Claire's twins were born old Parson Bull breathed his last and the double quota of news ran up the Valley like a heath fire.

Claire had not really believed Maureen O'Keefe when she had told

486

her to prepare for two babies but Maureen had done some investigating into parish registers and discovered that, unknown to Claire, and even to Edward Derwent, there were twins on both sides of her family and that there might well be on Paul's for all she was aware. When she was half-convinced Claire began to worry but Maureen said, impatiently, "You can forget about last year's mishap for you know well enough what brought that about! You're a strong, healthy girl and the theory that twins are more difficult to bring into the world than one child is old wives' prattle! I'll undertake to deliver them if you do your part by taking things easily instead of gadding about after your husband as if you're afraid to let him out of sight!"

The event occurred on the second day of September with the minimum of alarms, although John Rudd had to be summoned as nursemaid to Paul, who spent the day walking about the house like a man awaiting a last-minute reprieve from the gallows. He had just descended from seeing her, and peering dutifully at the pink, bawling scraps in the cot, when Chivers asked for him and said word had, arrived from the Rectory that Parson Bull had died after a long illness dating from a fall he had received in the hunting field more than a year ago. Paul was so relieved that Claire was safely through her ordeal, and so intrigued at becoming the father of twin boys (weighing, they told him, respectively a shade over six pounds apiece) that he could find little regret for the passing of the choleric old parson, although he had always half-admired the man as a genuine left-over from the eighteenth century; in any case, Bull had reached the age of seventy-eight, had been hunting at seventy-seven and was usually well ahead of the field. Paul wondered, as he sipped his brandy in the library, who would succeed him as rector and it was not until John reminded him that he was a patron of the living that he realised that this, in large measure, would depend on himself.

"However, there's no hurry," John said, "a locum will come over from Whinmouth until we've had a chance to look around. You don't know any parson who would be likely to fit in here with your policy, I suppose?"

Paul said he did not but supposed that he would get guidance on the subject from the Dean and Chapter at Paxtonbury.

"Oh, they'll have someone in mind, you can be sure of that," John said, "but if we have a candidate they'll have to consider him seriously. Bull was appointed by Sir George Lovell and must have been rector here all of forty years and it's odd that the old battleaxe should have passed on today. Why don't you occupy your mind entering it in the record book while I go down and make sure that Maureen has a hot meal ready when she's finished upstairs? She'll have to go out again afterwards, she has three evening visits to make yet."

Paul was glad of the excuse to be alone, for his nerves were calmer now and after John had gone, and he sat listening to the indeterminate thumps from upstairs, his mind went back to the wild evening he had spent alone here the night Simon was born, when Ikey, dripping wet, had burst in with news of the Codsall tragedy. It occurred to him that the contrast between the occasions was symbolic of his two marriages for that night the world outside had gone mad, with volleying rain slashing at the window and trees threshing in a full south-westerly gale, whereas tonight the evening sun filled the landscape with soft, golden light and the curving rows of chestnuts were as still as trees painted on canvas. He took out the estate book and read the last few entries, noting how proudly and self-consciously Claire had written of his trial scheme to set up a shuttle service of carts moving on a planned route through the Valley to dispose of produce from points as far apart as Smut's greenhouse in the east and Eveleigh's dairy in the west. He saw that she had referred to the innovation by the name used for it, in the Valley—"Squire's Waggon Train", an offshoot, he supposed, of the recent visit of the Buffalo Bill's Wild West Show to Paxtonbury, but although they made jokes about it it seemed to work satisfactorily and eliminate a great deal of duplicated labour. In the past each farmer had used his own transport to take his milk, eggs, vegetables and plants to the railway halt, or to collection points established by the Paxtonbury and Whinmouth wholesalers but now, with three light carts and their teams in constant commission, they were relieved of this chore and their individual output had soared as the latest figures proved. He took his pen and wrote, at the head of a new page, "*September 2nd, 1908. The Rev. Horace Bull, Rector of Shallowford-cum-Coombe for forty years, died today, aged seventy-eight,*" and underneath, in his neatest writing, "*My dear wife, Claire, gave birth to twin boys, as yet unnamed. They were born at two in the afternoon and safely delivered by Doctor Maureen O'Keefe, M.D. All three reported to be doing well.*" He smiled at the entry and was tempted to add to it a light-hearted comment, expressing his delight or astonishment but he decided against this, reflecting that as soon as she came downstairs Claire would rush to the book and fill in her own comments. If she took pleasure in writing of his waggon train how much more would she extract from describing the arrival of the twins? He put the record away and listened for fresh sounds but all seemed silent now, so he lit a cigar and went out on the terrace, turning to look up at the window which was wide open, Maureen being a stickler for well-aired sick-rooms. The doctor found him there and said, gently for her, "She's asleep now and there's not a thing to worry over, Paul. Congratulations if I haven't said it before. They're a couple of sturdy brats and should do well. By the way, she can nurse them—no reason at all why she shouldn't and she was happy to learn as much!" Paul said, "Did she have a bad time, Maureen? It seemed so quiet most of the time," and she answered, "It was just as straightforward as I expected, thank God, but you've got her to thank for it, not me! I always have thought the mental approach to birth is as important as the physical—given no complications of course and Claire wanted to bear you children more than anything else in the world. And why not? After all, she has everything now, bless her! She's a wonderful wife, Paul, but I don't have to tell you, do I, boy?", and she kissed him impulsively and went down the terrace steps to the lodge, now half a dwelling and half a surgery. He looked after her gratefully, not knowing how close she had just come to explaining how Claire Derwent had been reintroduced into his life as the direct result of an alliance between her predecessor and *That Boy*. She supposed she would tell him one day but right now he had enough to think about and all of it reassuring.

IV

There seemed no reason why the vacant living of Shallowford-cum-Coombe should concern Ikey Palfrey, yet it did and in more ways than one. Indirectly it was to teach him to box; years later it helped to change his entire cast of thought.

Ikey returned to school soon after the birth of the twins (by that time, and after interminable discussions, christened Andrew and Stephen) and found himself saddled with the melancholy task of chaperoning a new boy, Keith Horsey, fifteen-year-old son of the Reverend Edward Horsey, who had replaced Bull as Rector of Shallowford-cum-Coombe.

The Reverend Horsey's appointment came about through a combination of chances but the most important factor, unknown to Squire Craddock until much later, had been the bishop's anxiety to hide a troublesome shepherd in a remote pasture, where his embarrassing

489

social and political views would be likely to cause the minimum number of ripples in the diocese.

The newcomer was recommended to Paul as a Radical, and at the initial interview Paul found him a pleasant, scholarly little man, although somewhat too innocuous for his taste. After consultation with Rudd, however, it was decided to offer him the living on the theory that Bull's overbearing ways had isolated the substantial nonconformist minority in the Valley whereas it seemed likely that a man of Horsey's temperament would contribute to the spirit of teamwork Paul had worked hard to foster.

The new rector was short and slightly built, with myopic brown eyes and a few wisps of grey hair that made him look years older than in fact he was but he had a soft, persuasive voice and, as Paul was quick to realise, a very lively appreciation of the problems of the poor. He had been engaged in missionary work in China but his health failed under the strain and he had taken a curate's post in London's dockland. Here again, however, his physique proved unequal to the strain and he was given a curacy in a residential stronghold of the newly rich, in a Birmingham suburb where he soon alienated parishioners by pulpit attacks on conditions in local factories. From here he drifted south-west but it was apparent to his superiors that no Tory parish would keep him long and when Bull died, and the bishop recalled that the area south-east of Paxtonbury had just sent a Liberal M.P. to Westminster, he made a gift of Horsey to Paul. Horsey was quick to settle in, passing as harmless and establishing contact with dissenters like Farmer Willoughby and the Methodist fishermen of Coombe Bay and this he achieved without any noticeable falling-off of his official flock who had become accustomed to regarding the local pulpit as a source of entertainment.

A month after his arrival the Reverend Horsey made a request of the Squire, informing him that his only child, Keith, had gone to High Wood much later than most new boys. His education had been interrupted by illness and he would not have gone away to school at all had not the doctor prescribed upland air as the best medicine for the child. Horsey, however, was anxious about his son, fearing that his stammer and poor physique might invite persecution, and when he heard that the Squire had a relative established in the Upper School he asked Paul to write to Ikey and request him to keep an eye on the boy.

Paul complied without a second thought but Ikey received his letter with misgivings. The ragging of new boys, particularly well-grown

490

ones, was traditional at High Wood and Ikey was now removed from the hurly-burly of Lower and Middle Schools, for he was almost seventeen and his progress up the school had been spectacular in the last year or so. He was not yet a "Blood" but was in a fair way to becoming one after being awarded his running colours and a place in the pack of the House fifteen.

Ikey had never varied the original technique of his entry into public-school life via scrapyard and stable-yard. He never made the mistake of trusting to luck and was therefore never wholly offguard. From the moment of arrival he had but one object in mind—to do Squire Craddock credit and justify the faith reposed in him. His entire stock of nervous energy, plus his not inconsiderable powers of mimicry and assimilation, had been directed towards this end so that, four years later, he still had everyone at High Wood thoroughly hoodwinked. They thought of him, from the headmaster down to second-form urchin, as an accomplished eccentric and within certain limits eccentrics were encouraged. As a scholar he was reckoned capable of achieving far better results than he did in fact achieve, but in general deportment he was accepted as a gentleman and the son of a gentleman. He made friends easily, dressed casually but not too casually, employed the careless drawling, "g"-dropping speech that was *de rigueur* in the Upper School, was earmarked for a prefecture and a house-captaincy, and was permitted to despise all forms of sport except running in which field he was supreme, holding the under-fifteen and under-sixteen school records for the mile. Everybody at High Wood believed that Ikey Palfrey (rumoured to be the son of a Hungarian countess) could have excelled at cricket, football, shooting, swimming and even fives had he been so inclined but he continued to devote himself exclusively to cross-country and track events, never hurrying, or never appearing to hurry, but making light of all opposition. It was even said to his credit that he could have lapped most of his competitors had he chosen but checked his stride in order to encourage them and this was, in fact, partially true, although Ikey himself never admitted it; it would have seemed to him putting on side and he set great store on modesty, at least outwardly.

Yet Ikey's performance as a Highwodian was not entirely a charade. As the terms passed he began to develop an almost mystic affection for the place, for its dove-grey stones, for the music of distant shouts rising from the playing fields, for the bells, the fads, the newish traditions but more particularly for the country beyond the ridge of beeches from which the school derived its name. Imperceptibly it grew on him like another skin, covering his two other personalities— the Ikey Palfrey of Bermondsey, and of the Shallowford stable-yard, so that his pretences were subconscious and there were times when he almost came to believe in the fiction of his relationship to the Squire. Paul's marriage to Claire, and the secret understanding this had developed between himself and the lady doctor, removed the source of anxiety that had clouded his first school year and as he increased in importance and felt more a part of the place, his life became serene and untroubled by anything more urgent than a house-match or an end-of-term examination.

And now, when he was poised for the final leap into the top echelon, when he looked like getting into the first fifteen and perhaps succeeding Henley-Jones as Captain of the House, the Squire was asking him to play nursemaid to a new kid, the son of the Shallowford parson and whereas Ikey's loyalty to Paul was absolute, and therefore any request amounted to a command, it was also an insufferable bore and Ikey hoped fervently that the wretched kid would not place too much reliance on a chap to steer him through his first, troublesome year. He was soon disillusioned. When, after some slumming in the Lower School Keith Horsey was unearthed and interrogated it did not take Ikey long to assess the new boy's vulnerability or the risks one would invite attempting to pilot such a drip through the Lower School rapids. To begin with he was as thin as a beanpole, with a tin-whistle voice and, to crown all, old-fashioned steel-rimmed spectacles and as if these were not sufficient handicaps, the whey-faced toad also possessed large, nobbly knees and was clearly outgrowing his strength, for although very thin he was also tall and his height made him noticeable among the bullet-headed scruff who had joined the school as newcomers that year.

Yet it was not merely Keith Horsey's physical oddities that singled him out as a target for the second-year boys, all resolved to exact payment for their own sufferings in the past. He was also, it seemed, a brilliant scholar and proved as much by beginning his school life in the Upper Fourth, which was rather like an enlisted civilian starting an army career as a first lieutenant. Ikey found the new boy hiding in the latrines (where he himself had sought refuge a thousand years ago) and after ordering him out led him behind the sanatorium where they were unlikely to be overlooked.

"Squire told me to look you up," he mumbled, "your pater being the new rector at our place. The fact is, you're likely to get hell this term but if you don't let it bother you it'll soon ease off, the same as it does for all new kids." He stopped and ran his eye over the shambling figure. Having just finished *Nicholas Nickleby*, the set book for half-term exams, it occurred to him that the new boy was curiously like the wretched Smike and he added with a sigh, "Is there anything you are likely to shine at? Anything at all? Just to start working on?"

"Lllatin," said Keith hopefully, "I'm gggood at Latin!"

Ikey winced, not so much at the discovery of yet another handicap, but at the idiocy of the reply. The toad did not even know enough to understand that familiarity with Latin verbs was as good as a leper's bell among the Middle and Lower School riffraff. Just in time, however, he recalled his duty to the Squire and said, patiently, "No, kid! Cramming don't count! I mean *sport*—games, football, *anything!*"

"I haven't played any games," admitted Keith blandly. "I was too anaemic they said. I didn't go to a Prep School you see but had a private tutor. Pater taught me too, he's a first-class classical scholar, you know."

"Well," said Ikey heavily, "you can keep that under your thatch to begin with! If I was in your shoes I should muff your first term exams and aim for somewhere near the bottom. If you got moved up at the end of your first term God help you, because I couldn't!"

They walked in silence for a moment, Keith relaxing in the patronage of this tremendous being, whom he knew to be one of the most popular boys in the school. He had had a wretched time so far but now, it seemed, the worst part was over, for surely nobody would dare to put him through the Sunday new kids' ritual when Palfrey was his champion. He said, pleasantly, "Do *you* lllike it here, PPPalfrey?"

"Yes, of course I like it," Ikey said irritably, and then, defensively, "why shouldn't I? It's the best school in the West, isn't it?"

"Pater said it was," admitted Keith doubtfully, "but I'm not so sure now. The classical standard isn't all that good, you know, and that Latin master made a shocking mistake on the board this morning."

Ikey's small stock of patience burned itself out and he stopped, swung round, took Keith by the shoulders and shook him so hard that the new boy's glasses slipped down his long nose.

"Listen here," he said savagely, "I told Squire I'd keep an eye on you and I will, but you've got to help! You've got to stop . . . *asking* for it! If Henley-Jones had heard you say what you've just said about the

493

school he would have tanned your hide so hard that your arse would have looked like a ploughed field! You've got to . . . got to . . .", and he broke off, for the boy's chapfallen expression proclaimed the magnitude of his task. "You've just got to keep out of sight, that's all! Hide in the bog when the chaps aren't playing rugger and are milling about in the quad and passages! Keep out of *sight*, you understand? And don't try too hard at half-term tests—get things wrong on purpose . . . and well, play the fool in class, just to make some kind of a name for yourself!"

He could think of nothing else calculated to help the boy, deciding that he would have to give the matter more thought. He walked swiftly away, leaving Horsey standing under the beeches, with tears in his eyes and a sense of having somehow mislaid the key to the citadel.

Ikey did give the matter thought, indeed, he thought of little else during the next few days, during which time he took care to keep clear of his new responsibility. Then he had an inspiration; he would solve Keith's problem, and incidentally his own, by providing The Beanpole with a foolproof alibi, something that would not only explain why he was the kind of person he really was but also blunt and disarm his tormentors into the bargain. He buttonholed the new boy during morning break, pushed him into the band-room and carefully closed the door.

"Now look here, Horsey," he said, "I've thought of something! All you have to do is back me up when anyone asks you. You got that stammer, and you had to wear those glasses, after being shipwrecked on the way from New Zealand! You were thirty days adrift in an open boat and were the sole survivor! When they picked you up your eyeballs were scorched and you couldn't remember who you were but now it's coming back, very slowly, get me? They'll all swallow that, providing I vouch for it as coming from Squire via your pater and because it's dramatic, it'll make everybody . . . well . . . decent you know, at least for a term or so!"

"But it isn't true," Horsey said, blinking his owlish eyes, "it isn't a bit true, not a word of it, Palfrey! I've never been to New Zealand and I've never been on a boat, except round the Isle of Wight on a paddle steamer."

Ikey stared at him, half in amazement and half in anger so desperate that he too began to stammer.

"Ttrue?" he said, "well dammit, man, of course it's not true! I made it up, didn't I! I made it up to keep you out of trouble, as Squire

494

asked me. I daresay it sounds mad to you but I know this place and I know how these chaps think! I've been through it all myself and I *know*! You do what I say and spin any yarn you like, so long as we both stick to the same outline."

The boy's face was now almost as white as the pipe-clayed O.T.C. belts hanging on the racks behind him. He said, falteringly, "But I . . . I couldn't, Palfrey! It's jolly decent of you, and I'm grateful, really I am, but it's a lie just the same and I couldn't say that to stop boys like Williams and Vesey Minor kicking me and pouring ink down my neck! It wouldn't be right, don't you see?"

Ikey saw far more than Horsey suspected and more than he would have preferred to see. The boy's rejection of the carefully-thought-out alibi was, in a sense, a revelation to him. He saw, for instance, that one could not always judge by appearances, that heroes sometimes appeared under strange disguises, and that this weed's regard for the truth was likely to prove unassailable. He realised too that it did not spring from self-righteousness but from deeply ingrained lessons learned at home and because, from earliest childhood, Ikey had had the ability to gauge the potentiality of human beings he re-assessed Keith Horsey at once, docketing him as a fool and a physical weakling unlikely to collect anything but bruises on his way up the school but also as an individual possessing something quite rare among people – moral courage untarnished by piety. He knew also that he was beaten, that he could never hope to protect Keith Horsey from the Williamses and Vesey Minors of this world and that the best he could do would be to stand by and see fair play within the limits of the code. He said, glumly, "Very well, Horsey, forget what I said! I'll keep an eye on you if I can but it wouldn't help if I interfered too much, you'd only get it worse!", and he opened the door of the band-room and mooched, hands in pockets, across the quad.

He was faced with the challenge again the following Sunday, the ominous Last Sunday But Four, when new boys, according to pre-scribed ritual, were required to Scrub-The-Floor with their tooth-brushes and tins of tooth powder. The ritual began with the rising bell and ordinarily Ikey would have paid no attention to it, for he now regarded these practices as the prerogative of The Scruff, that is to say, boys in the Lower Middle School. His disdain, however, was by no means general among other seniors. Some of the more loutish among the Fifth clung to their toys and one of them, a hulking seventeen-year-old, whose idleness accounted for his presence in the Fifth for the fourth term, had elected himself Inquisitor-in-Chief. It was soon clear to Ikey that Piggy Boxall had selected Horsey as his sacrificial lamb, for although Keith, in common with the other new boys, scrubbed his bedspace until it was coated with froth, dust and blanket fluff, Piggy directed him to the bedspace of a boy who had the misfortune to sleep alongside Piggy. This boy protested, not out of sympathy for Horsey but because he did not relish having to stand in the mess of toothpaste but Piggy overruled his objection, standing over the kneeling Horsey and encouraging him with occasional toe-flips.

Ikey watched for a moment in silence. Boxall was a head taller and probably two stone heavier, but he did not intimidate Ikey. His reluctance to intervene stemmed from distaste in becoming involved in such a kindergarten sport and it was only with difficulty that he forced his responsibility to the front of his mind, saying at length, "That's enough, Horsey! Get on and dress now," and when Piggy Boxall demanded of Ikey who was senior Ikey cheerfully admitted that Piggy was but that Horsey had already done his quota and had no business messing up someone else's bedspace. Horsey scuttled off into the wash-room but Boxall seemed disposed to press the point. "You're getting damned bucky for someone who only moved into the Fifth this term!" he said, "I've a good mind to wallop you here and now!"

"You're welcome to try," Ikey said, quietly, as half-dressed boys gathered round, relishing the promise of a fight to relieve the fearful tedium of an autumn Sabbath. "The fact is, Piggy, I'm tired of watching a weed like you take it out on Scruff and as far as Horsey is concerned you'll have to stop picking on him because he happens to be the son of my guardian's new rector and I've been asked to keep an eye on him. Sorry and all that, old man!"

The murmur of conversation in the big room had ceased. Everyone there regarded Ikey Palfrey as an eccentric, given to elaborate jokes of this kind but championship of a first-termer, and a first-termer of Beanpole Horsey's type, was carrying a jest too far, particularly if it entailed challenging the only boy in the dormitory who shaved. They moved closer, interested and expectant but Henley-Jones, senior boy in the House, said, "Well, you can't leave it there, either of you. You'll have to fight and you can't do it today. Sunday fights are taboo."

"I'd be happy to oblige tomorrow," said Ikey, "but only on conditions. If I beat Boxall he doesn't touch Horsey again, not until he's played in."

496

The nicety of the challenge intrigued them. Henley-Jones said after a moment, "That's reasonable. I'll get the gloves during dinner-break. We haven't had a proper House fight for a year or more but you'll get a hiding, Palfrey."

Boxall said, angrily, "Look here, why do we have to wait until tomorrow? I'll give him his rations now since he's so damned hungry for 'em! It's time someone took Palfrey down a peg or two!" but Henley-Jones replied, as the five-minute bell rang, "Please yourself about that, Piggy, but if you're caught fighting in the dorm a House perk has to dab whoever he catches and Toothy Gilbert is on duty today. He's about half your size and you'd look damned silly bending over the radiator for him! If I were you I should go about it according to rules."

There was a murmur of agreement. A properly organised fight was infinitely preferable as a spectacle to a dormitory scuffle ending in the contestants getting caned by the duty prefect, which was something they could see any old day. Ikey said, "There's sense in what he says, we'd best make it tomorrow, Piggy!", and he walked back to his own bed.

He had been grateful for Henley-Jones' intervention for it was no part of his plan to leave things to chance and there was something that had to be done if he was to face Boxall in the Fives Court with any chance of beating him. He dressed quickly and went down in the boiler-room to consult Gobber Christow, the school lamp-trimmer. Ikey had a relationship with the school servants that his intimates found difficult to understand. Without hint of patronage he could talk their language and for two years now any favours demanded of them— the purchase of cigarettes, the backing of horses and other infractions of the rules where their services were in demand, Ikey had been chosen to bribe them. It was his familiarity with the world of sculleries, boot-holes and furnace basements that had won from Gobber Christow a reluctant admission that he had once been a professional bruiser.

"Gobber," he said, without preamble, "I've got to fight Piggy Boxall tomorrow afternoon. He's a good deal heavier than me and his reach is longer. How would I go about beating him?"

Gobber had been boilerman at High Wood for twenty-five years and thought he knew boys. He screwed up his bloodshot eyes and summoned to mind the image of Piggy Boxall, mentally staking out the distance from solar plexus to chin and equating it with the weight, reach and spunk of Palfrey, a young gentleman who never forgot to tip

497

him at the end of term. Ikey, making a guess at the reason for his deliberation, said, "It's late in term, Gobber, but I could raise a bob or so."

"I don't want no bob," Gobber said, "not 'till Christmas that is but you can lick that long streak easy enough, if you mind what I say. You'll 'ave to dance about out o' reach of 'im for a round or two and wind him. Then you lets fly a right to the head and his guard goes up. Before it comes down again you land a left on 'is belly-button, hard as you c'n drive and down comes 'is guard agin. With any luck he doubles within reach and you c'n weight in left and right, many as you c'n land. Mind all I say and I'll bet on you."

"Would you go over it with me again, Gobber?"

Gobber stirred his tea, swallowed a mouthful and got up from his box.

"I will that," he said, "a dozen times jus' so as you don't forget. Now I'm Boxall, pretty well a head taller . . ." and the lesson continued, the pair dancing a gavotte round the confined space and the ponderous Gobber, blessed with strong stomach muscles, taking punishment without the satisfaction of being able to exploit Ikey's rushes. Afterwards, as they drank more boiler-brewed tea together, Ikey said, "You don't have half a bad time down here, Gobber, with nothing expected of you but to keep the lamps trimmed and the boilers stoked up! I suppose you'd think I was stretching it if I told you I envy you sometimes. The fact is," he went on, forgetting his usual caution, "I'm a bit of a misfit and sometimes I think I don't belong out there at all." But Gobber, with the keen perception of the lowly and middle-aged, replied, "I don't reckon you do neither an' I made dam' certain of it long since but I wouldn't let on if I was you, not even to me! It wouldn't do, you see, for come to think on it you're a bloody sight luckier'n the rest of us! You got the best o' both worlds, so make the most of 'em and don't forget—keep out o' range 'till he's blown! Meanwhile I'll see if I can get long odds on you, four to one mebbe."

The fight after second school the next day followed the predicted pattern so closely that, looking back on it, Ikey wondered if the boiler-man was clairvoyant.

Henley-Jones refereed and Ikey endured the storm of jeers from the gallery throughout the first three rounds when the enthusiasm of spectators spent itself in derisive shouts of "*Mix it*" and "Oh, *stand up* to him, Palfrey!" but Ikey was never seriously rattled, bringing to the fight the same patience as he brought to all his complex personal problems. In any case he was in far better training than Boxall and came out of his corner at round four comparatively fresh, whereas the older boy was breathing heavily and resolved to make a speedy finish of it. Driven into a corner Ikey rode out a heavy punch on his shoulder then swung wildly at his opponent's head. Just as Gobber had predicted Boxall's guard shot up, leaving his solar plexus open to attack and the straight left that followed folded him like a penknife, so that several spectators cried "Foul!" but Henley-Jones, revelling in his official role, shouted, "Balls! It was above the belt! Go in and win, Palfrey!" and Ikey stood back to deliver the only telling blows of the match, two lefts and a right to Boxall's head that brought him to his knees.

It was the first technical knock-out ever witnessed at High Wood and they would have made much of him but Ikey slipped away on the excuse of changing and, again making sure he was unobserved, sought out Horsey and led him into the cover of the beech plantation. There was a seat overlooking the cricket pavilion and they sat there in the dusk, Horsey tight-lipped and blinking nervously, Ikey without a mark on his face and triumph in his heart. He said, at length, "Well, you won't have any more trouble from Boxall but you'll still have to take it from the others. I can't fight everybody and I wouldn't if I could. It's accepted that new kids should go through the mill!"

"Why is it?" Horsey asked, unexpectedly, and Ikey, mildly outraged, replied, "If they didn't they'd get bucky and start putting on side."

"It's funny," the boy said, slowly, "we have Chapel twice a day and lessons read from the New Testament, but nobody really listens, do they? I mean, the Head might be reading the call-over list because nobody here actually believes in Jesus Christ!"

Ikey had the same disinclination to discuss Jesus Christ as any other sixteen-year-old but he could not help wondering at the new boy's detachment, as though he was a kind of a missionary plumped down among a swarm of heathens, appalled by the hopelessness of his situation and the improbability of witnessing justice or mercy. He said, uncomfortably, "It's nothing to do with the Bible. You just got to learn to look after yourself! It's not so hard as it seems at first and it gets easier every term," and then, recklessly, "You'll be spending the hols on the estate and I daresay I'll see something of you. Maybe I

499

can give you a tip or two. You don't have to play everything their way but you have to pretend to, like me."

The boy looked at him curiously. "You mean you don't believe in it either? In all this fighting and bullying? Because if you don't, then why did you fight Piggy Boxall? I didn't ask you to and I wish you hadn't. I think fighting is uncivilised and stupid," and for some reason Ikey was humbled, the mantle of patronage falling from him so that suddenly he felt naked. He said, irritably, "It's no use talking to you, Horsey! Your pater ought not to have sent you to a place like this!" and he got up and stalked through the dusk towards the pool of light shed by the lamps of the quad arch. "Blast the kid" he said to himself, "he'll make a lily of me if I don't bloody well watch out!"

v

At the extreme north-west corner of the mere, beyond the maze of rhododendrons in which Ikey had lost himself in the snow, the ground rose steeply to a great outcrop of sandstone where the older woods fell away, oak, beech, sycamore and thorn giving place to a straggle of dwarf pines and Scots firs that had crept down from the evergreen belt of the Hermitage plateau. It was here that the Shallowford badgers had their sets and from her eyrie at the top of the slope Hazel Potter could watch them lumbering to and fro, like paunched merchants in the streets of a sleepy country town. This was the spot she preferred beyond all others, for nobody ever came here now that Smut had turned horticulturist and it was here, under the overhang of a great, slapsided rock, that she had made her home.

It was unlike any other house in the Valley. Its hearth was a triangle of flat stones and its south side was open to sun and wind but inside it was always dry and warm, with a floor of crushed bracken, a wicker screen that kept out the slanting rain and cavities to store her modest utensils, a pitcher, a few tins, a stock of kindling, a roasting spit and some flour sacks that she used for bedding when the fancy took her to stay here overnight.

In the spring, when the woods below were opening their vast green umbrellas and the birds were busy all day in and about the shrubbery, she spent most of her time up here, composing her prose poems about the creatures she overlooked, cooking a mash of vegetables and rabbit meat in her iron pot and sometimes braiding wild flowers into her hair so that she looked like one of the allegorical goddesses for whom

500

Edwardians blushed at the Royal Academy, the type of floral-crowned beauty painted by popular artists, like Henrietta Rae. When the sun was warm, however, she advanced even further into the world of the painters, throwing off her rags of clothing and sprawling naked on the jutting slab that was her roof. The sun warmed her through and the vantage point gave her a temporary affinity with starlings rushing down from the plateau into the puffs of pot-bellied cloud drifting down the Valley. Cataracts of sounds that were more expressive than words would slip from her tongue to lose themselves in the woods below, heard but unheeded by the stoat, the field mouse and a swarm of tits, wrens and robins in the thickets. She had as much company as she needed, for almost all things living between the red outcrop and the rhododendron forest below had come to accept her long ago. The badgers never gave her a second glance and neither did the lame vixen, nursing cubs in a shallow earth under the wreck of an eighty-year-old pine that had crashed into the Valley. The hedgehog passed her with his belly clear of the ground and the field voles, who frolicked on the stumps of charred firs sometimes scuttled into the cave to look for dry leaves for their nests. During her long watching spells she took careful note of everything that went on around her and because she had the power of remaining utterly still she added a little to her store of secrets every day. She had her favourites, among them the otter, who occasionally left the mere and sunned himself on a rock half-way up the slope; and the old, mad cat, who grinned at her over the remains of a chicken dragged all the way down the escarpment from the most easterly of the Periwinkle runs. She had often heard Will Codsall curse that cat and run for his gun when he caught a glimpse of yellow-white fur in the long grass but she never told Will where it might be trapped at the expense of an old hen. It had to live, she supposed, the same as the white-waistcoated stoat and the brindled water vole and the vixen who also raided Periwinkle runs. Here, where the bracken grew shoulder high, there was always movement and changing colours. Kingcups, willowherb, ragged robin and dwarf red rattle covered the ground near the overspill of the stream at the foot of the slope but nearer the summit grew cowslips, battalions of fox-gloves, sea-pinks and wild thyme and in and out of this riot darted a hundred varieties of birds, some as familiar as the golden plover and as impudent as the magpie, others shy summer visitors who came back year after year, like the sand-martin and the monotonous cuckoo, one of the few birds Hazel did not welcome. She was not always absorbed by the panorama or the creatures going about their business between the haze that was the summit of Blackberry Moor and the more definite blur to the south, that was the sandstone cliffs of the Bluff. Sometimes, if the mood came on her, she could forget all else in a long, self-satisfying appraisal of herself, contemplating her golden-brown legs, her flat belly and her high breasts that were a source of special wonder to her for she could not recall anything more regularly formed, unless it was the spread of the lower branches of her favourite oak in the meadow a mile south of her eyrie. She would sit cross-legged and study herself minutely, beginning with her flower-decked hair that reached to her waist and ending with a dedicated scrutiny of her supple toes, usually coated with the fine red dust of the rocks. Then she would leap down from the slab and fetch the burnished lid of one of her tins to use as a mirror, holding it up at an angle and glancing sideways at her shoulders, then moving it in a slow, tilted sweep, until she could catch a distorted glimpse of her rounded buttocks and the deep dimples above them. Usually she was pleased and would shake out her hair, raise her arms and wriggle like a savage beginning a ritual dance, exclaiming with the deepest satisfaction, "Youm bootiful, Hazel! Bootiful, do 'ee yer, now? Youm the most bootiful of all, for youm smooth an' white an' goldy and you baint much fur about 'ee, neither!" If anyone living in the Valley below could have seen and heard her their suspicions that she was mad would have been confirmed and perhaps someone would have set out to capture her and put her away for her own safety, but they would have been making a terrible blunder, for Hazel Potter was not in the least mad but simply primitive and her method of self-appraisal differed little from that of her sisters' or any other woman in the Valley, twisting and cheek-sucking before a bedroom mirror. She was, moreover, probably the happiest woman in the Valley, or any other valley in the West, for her isolated way of life was accepted by her mother Meg and her brother Sam in his cottage below. She never harmed anyone or anything, if one excepted the rabbits she trapped and roasted or the gulls' eggs she gathered and swallowed and even when they did not see her for days at a time no search-parties went to look for her and bring her back to the Dell. They had long since given up sending her to Mary Willoughby's school and she had completely forgotten what little she had learned there, so that at seventeen she could neither read nor write but seemed little the worse for it for she gave Meg far less trouble than had either of her three sisters when they were growing up

502

and quarrelling with one another over men and ribbons. She would appear and disappear like a half-tamed bird and she made no demands upon anyone. Every now and again, usually during spells of bad weather, she would reappear in the Dell and eat sparingly from the family stewpot, or steal one of her sister's discarded garments, but apart from this she fended for herself and even a conventionally minded soul like Edward Derwent did not remark on her when he caught a glimpse of her flitting across a glade or standing silhouetted against the skyline.

And yet, although exquisitely self-contained, there were moments in the spring of the year when Hazel was vaguely conscious of her isolation, when it made itself known to her by a curious sensation, a faint and remote pricking, located somewhere between her breasts, as though, without leaving a puncture, a sliver of gorse had got under the skin and was trying to work its way out.

At first she paid little attention to it but as the warm April days succeeded one another, and the murmur of the woods swelled so that it reached her rock like the wash of the sea, the pricking became more insistent and sometimes converted itself into a choking feeling in the base of the throat that made her eyes smart, so that she could no longer lay inactive staring down at the green umbrellas and would spring up, pull on her dress and plunge down the pine-studded slope to the rhododendrons and through the green tunnels to the mere and here, if she was lucky, she would see Sam, or Joannie, or old Aaron the osier cutter, and would forget what had brought her here in such a hurry.

It was during one of these brief melancholy spells, on a warm April day, that she saw something break the calm surface of the mere on her side of the islet. She was lying naked on her rock, screened from above and below by gorse and bracken and the landscape, usually so alive, was listless under the noonday sun. At first she thought the wide ripple was caused by the pike that Sam said had lived there since Old Tamer was a boy but soon she saw a swimmer moving slowly across the mere to the western shore. As she watched, surprised and a little alarmed, she saw the figure make a landing near the spot where Smut had hidden from the Heronslea keepers. She recognised him at once, even at this distance, and her heart gave a great leap of pleasure, as a tear, after hovering for half a minute, splashed down her cheek and beaded a hart's tongue fern growing on the edge of the rock. She jumped down into her cave, pulled on her ragged dress and without knowing

503

why held up the shining lid to study her reflection, noting that she had a string of bird's foot trefoil braided into her hair and also that she was smiling and that her eyes were moist. She stood still for a moment, pulling faces at herself and tossing her hair this way and that and said with deliberation, "I'll bring un yer! I'll show un the house, an' mebbe he'd stay on a bit to watch things!"

It was not a light-hearted decision. No one, not even her brother Sam who tramped the rabbit run below three or four times a week, knew of the existence of her house for her instinct had always been to guard the secret against the time when they would come looking for her to put her to work or send her back to that stuffy schoolroom at Deepdene. But The Boy could be trusted, for The Boy was different, half-way to being wild like herself, for if not why should he swim naked across the mere as if the old pike, the underwater bogies and the clutching weeds were not lying in wait to drag him where he would never be seen again? She went swiftly down the slope and through the rhododendron tunnels to a rift in the lakeside foliage, moving cautiously until she could see him towelling himself under a Douglas fir, and as he rubbed he whistled softly through his teeth, flapping his arms as though he was cold. She would have called out to him but at that moment, still flapping, he turned away and reached up to take his shirt and trousers from the lowest branch and she had to smother her giggles for he looked so funny standing there with the filtered sun playing on his long, pale back, lean legs and small, chubby behind. She remembered then that men were ashamed of their bodies and with good reason it seemed, so she waited until he had struggled into his trousers, shirt and sweater before crackling twigs underfoot and calling, "Boy! Boy! Dornee know the ole pike'll get 'ee swimmin' in there?"

He looked startled for the moment but when she stepped down to the shore to meet him he smiled and flicked back his dark hair, saying that he had crossed to the islet twice without landing. He seemed to her much broader and taller in his clothes, no longer a boy but a man nearly as broad-shouldered as her brother Sam.

"It's years since I set eyes on you," he said, "where have you been? They said you were still about but I never saw you, not once!"

"I've seen 'ee many times," she said gravely and he remembered then that she sometimes took it into her head to watch the yard from the meadow behind the house.

"But you're never at the Dell," he said and the truculence in his voice pleased her so that she shook out her hair and twirled her body,

504

saying, "I've got a house o' me orn and I'll tak' 'ee there if you mind to! No one knows it, not even Sam, nor Smut! Tiz mine, fer 'twas I as found un and vurnished un and there I bides as long as I likes?"

It was evident that he did not take her very seriously for he said, carelessly, "Oh, you mean one of those gun hides? Well, there's a dozen of them in the woods. Which is yours?"

She said, pouting, "You follow along, like you did time you was lost, an' I'll show 'ee but I'll kill 'ee if 'ee tells, mind!"

He followed her up through the green tunnels and the long, pine-studded slope to the outcrop of rock where she disappeared as completely as if the ground had opened under her feet. A moment later he heard her mocking laughter and looked all round but still could not see her until she climbed half-way out of the cave and showed him where he should enter the wicker screen and scramble over the loose rocks to the overhang. She had her small reward for once inside he looked round in astonishment, noting everything, the fire-blackened stones, the utensils and the flour sacks neatly folded in the corner.

"You actually live here? Sleep here?" he said, unbelievingly.

"On'y when tiz warm," she said carelessly, "other times I go down-along. Do 'ee like my li'l home, Boy?"

He scratched his head looking very puzzled but finally smiled, sat down with his back against her wicker screen and said, "Don't keep calling me 'Boy', Hazel. I've got a name and anyway I'm not a boy any longer, I'm seventeen and I shall be shaving next term!"

"Will 'ee now?" It was information that interested her, so that she tilted her head and searched his chin for evidence. Presumably she found some for she went on, eagerly, "Will 'ee grow a beard then? Like ole Varmer Willoughby's. A bushy one?"

"No," he said laughing, "just a moustache. I'll see how it looks anyway and if I don't fancy it I'll shave it off!"

Suddenly he dismissed the subject of problematic whiskers. "What do you do up here? I mean, aren't you ever lonely? Don't you get sick of your own company?"

"Yiss," she admitted slowly, "but if I'm lonesome I go and have a talk with Sam or the girls; other times, when the wires baint hooked me a coney, I go to the varms and they gives me skimmed milk and home-baked bread!"

"Are they all kind to you?"

"Mrs. Pitts dorn let me go hungry," she said, and then, tiring of so dull a subject, "Do 'ee like it up yer, Boy?"

505

"Yes," he said, "I think it's a wonderful place to be in summer but my name is Ikey. Call me Ikey, 'Boy' sounds soppy!"

" 'Ikey'!" she repeated slowly, "that's a daft name for gentry, baint it?"

"I'm not gentry," said Ikey firmly but she said, "Oh but you be! Youm Squire's boy and you lives along o' Squire, dornee?"

"I live with him when I'm home from school," Ikey said, patiently, "but I'm not related to him. In fact, I'm no more 'gentry' than you are. Squire Craddock gave me a job years ago and then sent me to school. But surely you knew that, didn't you?"

"Yess," she said carelessly, "but I forgot. I most always forget. Truth is I forgot about you 'till I zeed 'ee tempting the old pike in the mere!"

He knew then that she must have watched him dry and dress but it did not bother him for in most ways she seemed no older than little Simon or the twins. He was piqued, however, that she had forgotten him so readily for he had never forgotten her or the pleasant days he had spent in her company. Now that he looked more closely at her he saw that she had changed a great deal in the last two years. He had continued to think of her as a child, the rural equivalent of urchins with whom he had run and fought in his scrapyard days but he could now see that she was a woman, moreover the kind of woman his town-bred study partner, Tovey Major, would jest about, might even boast that he had kissed and cuddled and perhaps, in Tovey's own phrase, "run up and down the scales, don't you know?" The thought set his heart pounding, for surely a Blood like Tovey would never miss an opportunity like this, and because of this sudden awareness of her sex he found it difficult to continue to talk to her as though she was a cottager's child and he was duty-visiting. He made the effort, however, saying kindly, "You're quite grown up, Hazel. Is anyone courting you?"

She smiled and by no means innocently. She was familiar with the routine of courting, having watched the antics of her sisters over the years and knew that "courting" implied squeaks, protests, gusts of laughter and stealthy movements in the long grass. She had even had an encounter of her own when the youngest Timberlake boy had cornered her in the barn and run his hands over her before she kicked him in the shins and fled. She said, mildly, "No, I baint courtin'. I keeps to meself mostly", which did not help him very much, for the answer at once relieved and disappointed him. He had gathered from

506

the books and magazines Tovey had introduced into the study that a girl as pretty as Hazel Potter might have a great deal to offer a man of the world, although he did not understand precisely what, or how to begin seeking it. At the same time, he felt under a moral restraint, reflecting that she was, after all, the daughter of Squire's lowliest tenant and perhaps even Tovey would classify a flirtation with Hazel as "infradig-old-man". Then, noticing that she was still watching him intently, he blushed and had a mind to get up at once and leave her absurd "little house" but he found that he lacked the resolution to do anything so final and not solely because he seemed to hear the sound of Tovey's derisive laughter echo in the Valley below. The wonder she had always stirred in him was working its magic again but this time it was not based on an objective admiration of her independence or envy of her way of life. Her mouth, he thought, looked like a rosebud in the early morning and her thick chestnut hair, starred with tiny blue flowers, reminded him of the hair of a goddess in a painting. He said, in a low voice, "You're beautiful, Hazel! You're the prettiest girl in the Valley!"

"Yiss," she said, blandly, "more beautiful than Cis an' Vi an' Pansy." She had watched and absorbed the courting techniques of animals and birds from the rock above. Pride, caprice and ferocity she had seen but never humility on the part of the female. "Woulden 'ee like to kiss me?" she added with shattering directness and at once he was immensely grateful to her for it seemed, by taking the initiative so fearlessly, she had resolved his doubts and also, to some extent, accepted the responsibility. He put his arm round her and turned her warm cheek, kissing her gently but with an air of decision and then, to his dismay, the situation complicated itself again, for the bravado of the act evaporated the moment their lipst met and his heart pounded so insistently that he thought he must be ill. For all that, contact with her mouth was the most delightful sensation he had ever experienced, making nonsense of all his triumphs on the playing field. He put up his hand and let it run smoothly down over her hair so that it crackled, as though protesting against the liberty. As he stroked her hair she gave a tiny shudder that somehow increased his delight and there seemed absolutely nothing to say or nothing that would make the least sense. When he had turned her head to begin this extraordinary adventure he had been very conscious of marching forward in step with Tovey Major but now Tovey and all his kind were left behind along the road that led back to his childhood. He was acutely aware of the awful solemnity of the moment and notwithstanding its sweetness and poignancy, he recognised its implications. There would never be another moment quite like this, never another mouth and cheek as soft and sweet as these, and it was this, and not his characteristic caution, that caused his hand to stop half-way in its instinctive move towards her breast and to fall to the bracken floor, for he knew very well what would happen if he touched and caressed that soft roundness; within minutes this beautiful, half-wild creature would be reduced to the status of one of the simpering, broad-hipped blondes in Tovey Major's magazines and that would be to convert a symphony into a discordant jangle. Instead he sought and took her hand and their fingers interlocked, and as the kiss ended his lips brushed her cheek and found her hair wherein was the scent of everything growing in the Valley.

They sat quite still for a long time, only half aware of the sunplay on the floor of the cave and the restless twitter of birds outside. It crossed his mind that they should make some kind of pledge, a promise that would ensure repetition of this unspoken declaration but he had no idea how to convert his feelings into words and in the end, after kissing her softly once more, he gently removed his arm, saying, "I'll have to be going now, Hazel. I told them at the house I was trying to swim the mere and Chivers will worry if I don't show up."

She said, unemotionally, "You'll come yer agaain? Zoon, mebbe?", and he said he would, at about the same time tomorrow and went out through the tall bracken screen and down the long slope hardly aware of his direction, for every thought that entered his head disappeared at once into a maelstrom of guilt and joy.

She gave him time to pass the rhododendrons before she climbed out of the cave and on to her flat rock, where she could catch occasional glimpses of him as he moved along the northern margin of the lake. In her mind there was no confusion, only the satisfied relish of his lips and the light touch of his hand on her hair. The pricking sensation under her breast had gone and it was some time before it returned to gall her but in its place was a glow that demanded release in words, so that seeing the old, mad cat on a stump partway down the slope, she called, "Did 'ee zee un, Tibb? Did 'ee zee my man, then?" but the cat only turned his head and gave her a long, supercilious glance. He had just disposed of a shrew and the sun was very warm. He had seen Ikey pass but he was not interested in a man without a gun.

CHAPTER TWO

I

IT WAS with a sense of shock that Paul heard the name of Lord Gilroy announced as he sat working in the library one sunny July morning but before the man had been shown in he realised that his visitor must be the successor to the man who had once bearded him in this room and played an unconscious part in Grace's decision to marry.

The old man, the "dry, bloodless old stick" as John Rudd described him, had died a year since and Paul had only a vague recollection of his son, whom he had met once or twice in the hunting field. He found him a great contrast to his desiccated-looking father, a tall, broad-shouldered, chubby-cheeked individual, who looked and dressed more like a prosperous city business man than a landowner. He wore expensively cut country clothes, the kind of clothes city men always don when travelling ten miles outside London and his approach was well-bred, genial and confident, so that Paul got the impression that his visit was friendly and possibly directed at improving relations between the estates. Paul had no quarrel with him and had indeed written him a formal letter when he read of his father's death on the Continent. He offered him whisky which Gilroy promptly accepted.

"I do apologise for interrupting you at work, Craddock," he said glancing at the littered table, "but I'm away up north tomorrow and I gave Owen-Hixon my word I would call, although"—and he smiled, pleasantly—"I must confess it was at his insistence rather than mine! You won't have met Captain Owen-Hixon yet? He'll be opposing your man at the next election, and the local party were lucky to get him! He'll give Jimmy Grenfell a good run for his money, I'm told."

As Paul waited for Gilroy to come to the point it struck him that father and son were about as unlike one another as was possible in an inbred family like the Gilroys. Whereas the original Lord Gilroy had stood on this same hearthrug, looking and behaving as if he was paying a call on a recalcitrant cottager, his son had the cheerful expansiveness of a company director trying to interest a prospective shareholder in a doubtful bill of goods.

Paul said, hoping to shed light on Gilroy's presence, "The Unionist

509

candidate asked you to call? Didn't he know I was deeply committed to the Liberals?" and Gilroy said laughing, that he did indeed but the candidate had described Squire Craddock as "a lost sheep who might be happy to return to the fold in view of Lloyd George's 'People's Budget', a frontal attack on every landowner in the British Isles."

"Did you agree with him?" Paul asked and Gilroy said that he did not, for he flattered himself that he knew his enemy better. "However," he said cheerfully, "since I'm here I might as well say what I came to say, providing you'll pay me the compliment of listening! Frankly, some of the local committee feel that recent events might have caused you to have second thoughts about Liberal policy. They wanted to descend on you with a deputation, the fools, and I give you my word that it was me who stopped them! I remembered the drubbing you gave my father when he called soon after you took over the estate!" and he chuckled, appreciatively. "You were the only person about here who ever sent my father packing with a flea in his ear!"

"It wasn't really me," Paul admitted ruefully, "it was my first wife and I daresay she could do better now. From what I read in the newspapers, however, she seems to expend all her ammunition on the Government!"

Gilroy looked uncomfortable for a moment, as though he had expected Paul to gloss over his oblique reference to Grace but he said, "You are still in touch with her?", and Paul said he was not but that the antics of suffragettes were breakfast-table talk all over the country.

"Ah, yes," Gilroy said thoughtfully, "but I can't help feeling that militancy won't get them far, although our people ought not to complain. They have intervened in several important bye-elections already and very much to our advantage. Asquith, I hear, can't speak in public for five minutes without being expertly heckled! However, it wasn't suffragettes that I came to talk about, Craddock."

"Go ahead by all means," Paul said, deciding that the son was infinitely more likable than his crusty old father.

"Well," said Gilroy, "there are people on our committee here who find it difficult to believe that a man owning your acreage can stay in step with firebrands like Lloyd George and that pirate Churchill! After all, social progress in an industrial state is one thing but highway robbery is quite another! I imagine you keep in touch with national issues or is your interest in politics purely local?" He paused but when Paul said nothing, he went on, "You don't have to answer my questions, of course, not even out of politeness. You can send me packing as promptly as you sent my father and I'm damned if I'd hold it against you! After all, we may be at war but wars can be fought by gentlemen."

"I don't mind answering your questions in the least," Paul said slowly, "but there's no prospect of me crossing the floor if that's what your committee hopes. I'm not deeply concerned with what happens in Westminster, it's true, for I've always thought of an M.P. as a man who ought to concern himself with his own constituents. After all, that was the original intention, wasn't it?"

"A long time ago," Gilroy replied, "but I'm entirely with you. Have you studied these latest proposals, the way the Chancellor proposes to get the money for this insurance scheme of his? It'll come largely from us, you know. Don't you feel any resentment at all?"

Paul had asked himself this several times during the last few weeks, after the London papers had carried reports of Lloyd George's sensational proposals to raise income tax to 1s. 2d. in the pound, increase death duties by a third on estates of more than £5,000, and slap heavy taxes on land of enhanced value, even if it remained undeveloped but the proposals had not weakened his loyalty to the party as a whole, or to James Grenfell in particular. It would sound, he thought, rather smug to admit this to a far wealthier landowner like Gilroy but the fact was he had never really thought of himself as a wealthy person, and had never been able to interest himself in money as money. He regarded it still as a means of feeding and improving the estate and he could not see how Lloyd George's proposals, that had set most landowners about the ears, could make much difference to the future of the Valley. In any case some kind of insurance scheme was surely due to poor devils cooped up in shops, offices and factories all the year round. He did not say this, however, for it seemed to him a holier-than-thou attitude. Instead, he said, guardedly, "I imagine the Chancellor has to get money from somewhere. You people have been insisting for years that we play snap with the Kaiser as regards naval strength and dreadnoughts can't be built for nothing, Lord Gilroy."

"Indeed they can't," Gilroy replied affably, " 'We want EIGHT And We Won't Wait!' but although I'm not surprised by your attitude — your personal attitude that is — I must admit that I am by its broader implications. After all, it's plain to me looking across the Sorrel that you're as deeply traditionalist as was my father and you're far more attached to the old way of life than I am, who was born to it!

511

How do you marry your cricket-on-the-green notions to the clamour for a New Order, led by men primarily concerned with industrialisation?"

"I've never set my face against change," Paul said, defensively, "and I should have thought that was known in this area. I admit I want to preserve, and even people like Grenfell regard me as a bit old-fashioned but if the old system isn't prepared to bend it will break and I wouldn't like that to happen. I suppose that's why I'm a Liberal."

"Curious," Gilroy said thoughtfully, "for I believe the exact opposite and that's why I vote Unionist. I don't think our system was built to bend but if it's tampered with too much it will break, and then we'll all be in trouble! Still . . .", and he stood up extending his hand, "I'm bound to say I respect your views, Craddock. I'll fight you when the election comes up and I'll fight damned hard but I hope you'll never regard me as a personal enemy, or associate with me all the party mudslinging that is inevitable!"

"I'm delighted you called," Paul said and meant it, for the feud had always seemed to him very childish. "I take it you will inform the new candidate and the committee that the lost sheep prefers to remain lost!"

"I will indeed," Gilroy said, chuckling, "as a matter of fact I shall rather enjoy doing that, Craddock!" and Paul walked him to the fore-court where his shiny French motor awaited him, a straight-faced chauffeur sitting erect behind the enormous brass steering wheel. The big car moved off smoothly, trailing a cloud of blue exhaust and Paul thought, "Damn it, one can't help liking the chap, but if he's so keen on preservation why the devil does he have to poison the Valley with that stinking contraption?"

Claire came to him, calling "Who was it?" as she crossed the paddock and he said, helping her over the rail and slipping his arm round her waist, "That was only young Gilroy kite-flying. He wanted to know whether I would jettison Grenfell on account of Lloyd George's land piracy!" and her laughter comforted him, for he could not help reflecting how differently Grace would have reacted. "It's odd," he said, "the last time a Gilroy called here he succeeded in getting me married! Did you ever hear about that?"

"No," she said, "but before I forget to tell you the twins are talking!"

"That's Simon's idea of talking, to me they only gurgle."

"No," she protested, "Andy can say a word or two—he's already about three months ahead of Steve and he'll be walking in a matter of weeks. Simon has him in the nursery now. He's very good for them, you know, and they worship him," and he forgot all about Gilroy as she talked of the relationship between the three children so that he thought, as soon as she had gone, "She's so different from Grace and I suppose some husbands might be bored with her but I'm jiggered if I am!" and went whistling into the yard calling to Chivers to harness the trap for a seed-buying trip to Paxtonbury.

As though Valley drums had relayed news of Gilroy's visit to Westminster, Grenfell wired that he was coming down that same week and Paul, meeting him at Sorrel Halt, drove him across Blackberry Moor and listened to lobby gossip that never found its way into the West-country editions of the London newspapers.

He found the Member depressed and glad of a few days' rest in the country, as well as an opportunity to confide in Paul his fears of the outcome of the next election.

"In spite of our majority we're having to fight every inch of the way," he admitted. "We've had to compromise on the new dread-noughts to get the support we need for social legislation and Irish Home Rule but the P.M. has his hands full with that Cabinet and finds them a difficult team to drive! Some would call the Kaiser's bluff and let him build as many blasted battleships as he likes but at the other end of the scale we have the well-britched, who think L.G. is biting off far more than he can chew! The Lords will throw the budget out, of course, but that only means we shall have to go to the country. I promise you, it's been a devil of a sitting! I can't tell you how glad I am to turn my back on it for a day or so."

He talked, with his customary lucidity, on a wide variety of topics but Paul noticed that he avoided mentioning women's suffrage and the havoc the militants were causing at the public meetings, doing this, he felt, out of motives of delicacy. In the meantime, however, Paul was content to listen, receiving an account of Grenfell's stewardship up to the end of the third year of the Government's span and asking for details of the Chancellor of the Exchequer's proposed new land taxes. Grenfell, he thought, hedged a little on this, as though he shared the local Unionists' suspicions that a man owning fourteen hundred acres might jib at facing a stiff increase of taxes including a levy on incre-ment value and the exploitation of mineral rights, so that when Paul told him of Gilroy's visit he made no attempt to hide his relief. "By George," he said, "I'm delighted to hear that, Paul! I couldn't help

513

wondering if you'd be tempted to ditch us and I suppose one could hardly blame you if you did! Was it loyalty to me that made you spit in his face?"

"No," Paul admitted, "not entirely. If I was that interested in money I wouldn't be down here pouring it into the Valley. I'm all for giving the working chap a larger slice of cake but not, if I'm honest, for philanthropic reasons. Universal suffrage means they'll get the slice one way or another and if it's denied them indefinitely they'll just up and take it! Gilroy and his people don't appear to realise that. They think that they can keep all the advantages of feudalism and still use the short cuts of a highly industrialised society. I notice he's running around in a damned great motor and it wasn't even British made! Maybe you could score a point there in one of your election speeches, James."

Grenfell did not respond to this quip but continued to look preoccupied, so that when they reached the river road Paul reined in, saying, with a smile, "Well, what is it, James? Has it anything to do with the suffragettes?"

The Member looked confused for a moment but then his brow cleared. "You're getting very sharp in your old age, Paul! I always did say you'd make a politician. Yes, it *has* to do with the suffragettes! The fact is, I intend to back them at the recall in the autumn," and when Paul exclaimed in amazement, he went on, hurriedly, "No, wait! I haven't told anyone this because I felt you should be the first to judge my motives. I suppose, knowing your first wife so well, I got in on the ground floor of the controversy but for a long time I wasn't convinced. There was so much else to be done and all of it uphill work. Then it became clear that the Cabinet was very divided on the subject and that many Liberal Members, as convinced as I am that women's suffrage is inevitable, are hoping to hold it at bay as long as possible and maybe pass it to the Tories as a hot potato! Well, some of the colours have faded for me since I graduated from soap-box to the House and discovered how fiendishly difficult the art of government really is but not so much as I can't distinguish black from white! What our people are doing to those women at the moment is a damned outrage! If the Tories did it we should make all the capital we could of their manhandling women in the streets and forcibly feeding them in gaol!"

"I've only unpleasant memories and newspaper talk to help me form an opinion," said Paul dryly, "but it does seem to me that some of them enjoy martyrdom! Besides, can we really afford to let a noisy minority blackmail Parliament?"

"One thing at a time, Paul," Grenfell said. "First, are you capable of viewing this issue without prejudice?"

"No," Paul admitted, "I don't suppose I am, for 'The Cause', as they call it, made a bad joke out of my first marriage. For all that I don't still bear a grudge against Grace. Why should I? I'm happier now than ever I was in my life and by every conceivable yardstick Claire is a far better wife and, for that matter, a better mother to Grace's own child. However, no man cares to remember he was once the laughing-stock of everyone about here!"

"That's prejudice for a start," Grenfell said, "for you were never that, Paul! I've always had my finger on the pulse of the Valley and everyone who mattered was deeply sorry for you at the time."

"All right, they were sorry for me but either way I'm not pre-disposed to suffragettes!"

Grenfell picked up his briefcase, unstrapped it, and took out a buff folder. "Take a look at this," he said, "it's one of several and not the worst by any means! It isn't a fake either, although it was suppressed by the editor whose photographer took it. He thought it might enlist too much public sympathy."

Paul looked at a picture, an eight by six photograph, reproduced on coarse newsprint. It was a close-up of a mêlée outside the Houses of Parliament. In the foreground two bearded policemen were frog-marching a young woman through a mob of bystanders, most of whom appeared to be shouting abuse. The woman had been well dressed but her clothes were in terrible disarray, blouse torn, one shoe gone and hat lying on the ground under the horse of a mounted policeman in the background. The woman was screaming. He said, handing it back, "Well, I must say it doesn't do the London police much credit," and James, dipping into his folder again, handed him another picture, this time printed on glossy paper. It showed a similar scrimmage but in this case a policeman was looking on, whilst three young men in straw hats bundled a middle-aged woman down a flight of stone steps outside a hall. The policeman was grinning and so were several male bystanders standing under a banner reading, "*Liberal Rally, Men Only*". The most unpleasant aspect of the incident, Paul thought, was not the violence used, although this was shocking but the obvious source of male merriment. The lower part of the woman's body was exposed showing her underclothes as far as her waist and her skirt was ripped almost in half.

"I could show you a lot more," James said grimly, "I've made a collection of them. I think I'll call the dossier '*England, 1909— Under a Liberal Government Pledged to Reform.*' "

Paul said bitterly, "Is there one of Grace?" and James, touching his arm, said "No, but I have an accurate cartoon from the paper she edits. It shows forcible feeding in Holloway. Will you look at it?"

He handed him a small magazine and on the front page was a drawing of a woman held by four wardresses in a tilted chair. A man bending over her was inserting feeding tubes into the prisoner's nostrils. There was a dark smudge where the woman's mouth should have been, arrowed with the words "*Metal Gag*".

"Great God," Paul muttered, "is that what the papers call 'hospital treatment'?"

"I haven't seen forcible feeding," said Grenfell, "but I've seen practically everything else! The police aren't so bad—they're often in a difficult position—it's the public who make me vomit! I've seen young men drag women along the ground holding them round their breasts and some of these poor devils, whose only desire is to want a share in making the country's laws, are half dead when they come out of gaol! I'll tell you something else too! When a man takes his seat in Parliament he soon learns to vote with his head rather than his heart, for it is never much use judging an issue emotionally. However, a line has to be drawn somewhere, unless one is to become a mere voting machine. I've been pushed over that line after witnessing W.S.P.U. lobbying of Members of Parliament. Apart from that I've attended all-male political meetings they managed to penetrate and seen them manhandled by dirty-minded stewards. When I make my next public speech down here I'm pulling no punches! I'm not simply paying lip-service to women votes, I'm going to attack what's happening inside gaol and out of it!"

"How will that affect your poll?"

"Very adversely, I should say."

"This new man of theirs, Owen-Hixon, is supposed to be a man-eater," Paul said. "Do you know anything about him?"

"Yes," said Grenfell, "I know all about him and it'll be touch and go whether I hold the seat! He's fought two strongly held Liberal boroughs and came near to pitching our man out on both occasions. It's odd that Gilroy should have approached you like that but I hope you believe me when I say I would have warned you of my decision in any case. Would you like to think it over for a day or so?"

"Yes, perhaps I would, James," Paul said, "but for a personal reason that isn't affected by my own views. Will you lend me those pictures until tomorrow?"

Grenfell gave him the file and they drove on in silence. Presently Grenfell said, "You were wise, I think, to stay here and accept limitations, Paul. If more of us did that, we wouldn't need a London talking-shop at all!"

Paul noticed at dinner that James paid Claire the same grave courtesy he had shown towards Grace, although Claire's complete ignorance of political issues, which she was not ashamed to admit, meant that she was unable to spark him off, as Grace had done so effortlessly. The conversation was therefore confined to Valley topics and when she had retired to take a final look at the children, James said, puffing at his cigar: "There's not much doubt about your luck having changed, Paul, and you need not have proclaimed your personal happiness back at Codsall Bridge—it shouts at me from all parts of the house!" Afterwards, in the dusk, they walked together through the orchard and across the meadow as far as Hazel Potter's squirrel oak and Grenfell stood for a moment looking down the Valley to the Bluff: "Keep it like this, Paul!" he said suddenly, "don't ever let them change it, so long as you've breath in your body!", and Paul replied, "I made up my mind to that the first day I stood here, James!" and they went slowly back to the house, now lying half invisible in a bowl of violet dusk.

It was after midnight when Paul went up to find Claire still reading in the glow of her bedside lamp. She kept a bedside book called *Rural Anecdotes* and often read a page or two before she slept. Paul knew the book well, a selection of passages from Goldsmith, Cobden, and Borrow, interspersed with lighter passages from Surtees and verses from Wordsworth, Raleigh and Kit Marlowe. He said, throwing Grenfell's buff file on the bed, "Here's a different sort of reading, Claire! It isn't likely to induce sleep but it's important to me that you see it! I'll tell you why in a moment."

She took the file and looked at the pictures one by one. He saw her mouth tighten once or twice but she made no comment until he had slipped in beside her and, without extinguishing the lamp, settled her head on his shoulder. This, for him, was always the most rewarding

517

moment of the day and they would sometimes lie so for half-an-hour before going to sleep, talking of this and that, of the children and domestic problems, of topics like Will Codsall's intention to reclaim more heath land and the comic situation in the Dell, where the Goliath of Bideford was still maintaining his brace of submissive wives, of anything and everything in their tiny world bounded by sea, the Sorrel and railway line. He told her then of Grenfell's decision and of his own dilemma. If women's suffrage was made a platform issue at the coming election how would he stand as Grenfell's chairman at the meetings? Would not people find it curious that he, once cuckolded by The Cause, was publicly advocating it? Then he touched on the real issue. Might not his backing of James in this field imply that he still hankered after his first wife? For this, he admitted, was something of which he must be sure before James returned to London.

She said, after hearing him out, "I think you're being morbid, Paul! It's plain from these pictures that James has made the right decision. I don't know what you think of votes for women but I know how I feel right now! If I was a man, committed to politics, I think I should know precisely what to do."

"And what's that?" he said, shifting slightly so that he could look down at her.

"I should back him for all I was worth!" she said, "and to the devil with what people think or don't think! I'm sure of you now and that's all I care!"

"Turn out the lamp," he said, "and don't reintroduce politics again tonight on pain of getting your bottom smacked!"

She reached out and turned the screw and it was only then that he remembered that the moon was almost full, for the big room was flooded with a light as hard and bright as silver. Yet she disobeyed him after all for just before she slept, she said, as though addressing not so much him but herself, "I suppose I must be as far behind the times as any woman alive! I'll use the vote if we get it but I can't work up much enthusiasm on the subject. Is that why they have to fight so hard do you suppose? Because so many women like me are satisfied to trot between nursery, kitchen and double bed?" He made no reply and his regular breathing told her he was already asleep.

II

The campaign of January 1910 saw the most bitter electioneering in the history of the constituency. Neither candidates nor leading supporters emerged unscathed from the contest.

Captain Owen-Hixon, the new Unionist contender, fought a merciless campaign, appearing, however, in the role of a puff-adder rather than the lion they had been promised. He not only employed conventional ammunition to attack the Government but the brickbats supplied by Grenfell himself after he had openly proclaimed his belief in women's suffrage.

The main issue in the fight was the proposed land taxes and the Unionist, an exceptionally accomplished speaker with a knack of cutting hecklers down to size, hammered out his thesis day after day and night after night, warning the electorate, most of whom looked to agriculture for a living, that the budget would mean all round contraction on the part of landowners and therefore unemployment among farm labourers in the area. Paul, as the only landowner supporting the Liberals, came in for persistent sniping for Owen-Hixon lampooned him as an amateur farmer, protected from the full effects of the new taxes by a steady flow of capital from a London scrapyard. He implied, and came close to stating openly, that the Shallowford estate was bolstered by profits from the South African War and the jibe was the more lethal because Grenfell had never ceased to denounce the war as a capitalist adventure. Owen-Hixon also made play of an alleged attempt on the part of the Government to sacrifice national safety to a vote-catching policy built on the new insurance scheme, painting lurid pictures of what would happen to Britain when the Kaiser's growing naval strength enabled Germany to challenge the Empire on the high seas. As to Grenfell's sudden infatuation with "the livelier ladies"—the Unionist turned Grenfell's criticism of forcible feeding back upon him by saying that he was puzzled to know why, since his friend felt so strongly on this matter, he was still aligned with Lloyd George, Asquith and Winston Churchill, the principal persecutors of the suffragettes.

In only one exchange did the Liberals come off with the honours and that was at Owen-Hixon's eve-of-poll rally, in the Paxtonbury Corn Exchange, where the heroes were a pair of determined Liberal hecklers. On this occasion Owen-Hixon, carried away by his own eloquence, made a jeering comparison between Lord Gilroy, a landowner with three centuries of tradition behind him and his neighbour Craddock, who, no doubt, would lose interest in farming as soon as the new tax was imposed and seek some other diversion, perhaps milling flour for the suffragettes to throw at Liberal Cabinet Ministers! In the laughter touched off by this sally Henry Pitts, of Hermitage Farm, rose from a gangway seat about a third of the way down the hall and demanded to know of Lord Gilroy, in the Chair, how much he paid his workers on the Heronslea home farm? The question was ruled out of order but Henry remained on his feet, buttressed by the immovable Sam Potter and read out a short list of weekly payments made to Heronslea and Shallowford farm-labourers. The wages showed a difference of around seven shillings a week in favour of Squire Craddock and in the momentary hush that followed this announcement Henry added, genially, "So mebbe tiz as well us didden get an answer from the Chair! Saved ole Gilroy tellin' a string o' bliddy lies, didden it?"

At this the Unionist stewards made a concerted rush for Henry, now standing one seat in from the centre aisle. In their eagerness to eject him, however, they overlooked Sam Potter who threw his chair under the feet of the foremost and floored two others with his fists. Before reinforcements could be rushed round from the sides of the hall the two Shallowford men had escaped via an exit, Henry felling another steward *en route*. They left the meeting in an uproar and made their way to Liberal headquarters, congratulating one another on the success of their sally. Neither man, out of his cups, was a talkative individual. All Henry said was, "Well, us *told* un, didden us, Sam?" and Sam replied, "Arr, an' us *showed* 'un, didden us, Henry?"

Claire stood beside Paul and Grenfell on the day following the ballot and watched the votes pile up on each table as the boxes were opened by the tellers. By midday the result was announced from the balcony of the Town Hall. James Grenfell had lost his seat by the narrow margin of eighty-seven votes. Captain Owen-Hixon was the new Member for Paxtonbury Vale.

Grenfell, Paul thought, took his defeat stoically. On the way back to Shallowford, as their trap breasted the northern swell of the moor, James said, with a sigh, "Well, Paul, nobody could call it a clean fight but at least it was a lively one! Without you I could never have saved my face, let alone my seat and I'd like you to know I'm grateful for that! Maybe a year or so on the home beat won't do me any harm, for it's my guess we shall be at it again before long. Today's result all over the country is something and nothing, the main issues can never be resolved without a clear-cut majority."

Paul said nothing, feeling far too raw to take pleasure in an inquest but he reflected glumly that Grenfell's championship of suffragettes had cost him far more than eighty-seven votes. It was left to Claire to comment further on the issue and as they turned on to the river road she said, cheerfully, "Well, I wouldn't worry if I were you, James! To my way of thinking you didn't lose out on your policy but on your chivalry and it was about the only spark I saw struck in that mud-fight!", and to emphasise her point she squeezed his hand so that Paul, seeing the movement out of the corner of his eye, thought, "By God, if James was lucky enough to find a wife like Claire she'd put him back all right and with a thumping majority!"

As they passed Codsall bridge they saw Eveleigh and his family standing in a forlorn cluster to give the loser a cheer and Grenfell, waving acknowledgement, looked across the winter fields towards the Teazel watershed and said, "The grass roots are right here, Paul, We ought never to forget that, lad!"

III

News of the sudden death of King Edward came to the Valley in the full flush of Maytime; to Paul, who had settled here the summer Edward was crowned, it seemed as if the brief reign completed a personal as well as a national cycle.

The first rumour reached the Valley by one or other of the two tele-phones in Coombe Bay, and was later confirmed by the heavy black border round the front-page advertisements of the *County Advertiser* but Paul, knowing that some of the tenants living off the main road would be unlikely to see the weekly newspaper for another day, decided to go his rounds, at least, this was the excuse he offered Claire at breakfast. She was not taken in, remembering the long drought of the coronation summer when he had first arrived among them and well knowing his trick of separating the phases of his life into little packages of seasons and years. He would see the death of Edward, she thought, as the end of a Valley era and for an hour or so would want to ride alone, savouring his modest achievements here. She said, kissing him, "Go along then Paul Revere, and proclaim the news among the Potterites and the Codsallites in the Wilderness," and he rode off, taking the river road along the park wall in the direction of Codsall bridge.

He noticed, on passing the Timberlake cottage, that someone had hung a bunch of crepe on the knocker and drawn the parlour blinds,

521

as though the royal corpse lay inside. Old Mrs. Timberlake, allegedly one hundred and four, had died the previous summer, and perhaps it was her late mother-in-law's incredible age linking her with George III, that had prompted Mrs. Timberlake junior to show this special mark of respect to royalty. Yet Paul found himself unable to share in a sense of loss that morning, for the sun was bright, kingfishers flashed along the Sorrel stream, the hedgerows were a riot of flowers and he had never seen King Edward in the flesh. He could think of him with mild affection, however, recalling the headshakes of the wiseacres when the portly, sixty-year-old rake succeeded his mother. Everybody had said he would introduce sweeping changes in the Court and they had been right but some of their other prophecies remained unfulfilled. He had proved an unexpectedly popular monarch and even his weaknesses, the chain-smoking of cigars and his obsession with pretty women, the Turf and rackety characters associated with racing, had endeared him to the mass of English people. He was also said to be the only man alive who could browbeat the German Kaiser, his sabre-rattling nephew across the Channel, and if this was true, it was a pity that he had not ascended his throne earlier and saved everybody a great deal of money by discouraging Wilhelm from building a navy. He thought, as he rode down the Four Winds track, "I suppose we shall have to do something to mark the occasion. Perhaps Parson Horsey will want to hold a special service and if he does I shall have to appear with Claire and the children," and then he saw the oldest Eveleigh boy forking dung and called, "Hullo, there! Is your father about?", and at that moment Marian Eveleigh emerged from the dairy with her daughter, Rachel, a rosy sixteen-year-old, carrying a pail of skimmed milk for the pigs. Marian said, "Good morning, Squire! You've heard the news I suppose?", and Paul said he had and was sorry but all Marian replied was, "Well, to tell 'ee the truth, Squire, I'm surprised 'ee lasted so long! He was very weak in the chest you know!"

She talked, Paul thought, as though the King had lived in one of the tall, red-brick houses in Coombe Bay where the royal bronchitis was a parish topic. It occurred to him that modern communications were already having their effect upon people cut off from the cities, for how would a Tudor peasant have been able to comment on, say, the bronchial tubes of Henry VIII?

Eveleigh himself came out of the byre while they were talking and declared that Edward had proved a better man as King than as Prince

522

of Wales. Paul suspected that Eveleigh, an austere man dedicated to hard work and simple living, was a republican at heart and the farmer seemed to confirm this by adding, "Well, it won't make much difference to me, I reckon! His son'll succeed him and they say he's a quiet sort of chap, don't they, Squire?"

"I believe they do," Paul said, smiling and deciding that Eveleigh was anxious to get on with his work he said good-bye and went on down the gangway between house and barn towards the higher ford. As he passed under the gable of the farmhouse he glanced up at the window of the room where he had looked on the bloody remains of Arabella Codsall but the memory had no power to dull the sparkle of the morning. Eveleigh, and his family of romping, rosy children, had exorcised the ghosts of Four Winds long ago.

He forded the shallow river a mile above the bridge and climbed the edge of the moor to Periwinkle, where Will and Elinor Codsall had heard nothing of the news from London and seemed more deeply impressed by it than the Eveleighs. Elinor's oldest child was now five, and already earning his keep egg-collecting. The farm was nearly double its original acreage, Will having reclaimed a wide strip of moorland and his poultry arks were dotted about the fields like a shanty town. Paul thought, as he gossiped with man and wife, "That was the first real decision I ever made about here—to get Will and Elinor married off and settled on their own and it was a good move, despite what happened afterwards." He remembered his first glimpse of the little woman now standing by Snowdrop's head, a slim, shy, slip of a thing, with hardly a word to say for herself and here she was, the mother of three children, the real master of the farm and the acknowledged poultry expert of the Valley. He wondered if the lumbering Will Codsall resented taking second place to her but decided not, for even now, as they stood in the yard talking, he was looking at her as though he would like to whisk her off into the clover. Codsall said, "Will us be havin' some kind o' funeral service, Squire? Us did for the Ol' Vic, I remember, Parson Bull preached a sermon on her, didden he, midear?" but Elinor said this was a matter between Squire and parson and that he had best get about his work upalong, while she brewed Squire a dish of tea.

He drank her tea and rode down across the great swathe of heather to Hermitage, wondering if any of them were ever put out by his casual visits. After all, they were tenants holding long leases, and were not answerable to him so long as they paid their rent each quarter-day, but as soon as he saw the broad, beaming face of Henry Pitts he knew that he was wrong and that most of them were flattered by his interest in their stock and day-to-day improvements and also that what little remained of their prejudice had disappeared since his re-marriage. Henry called, "Top o' the marnin', Squire! Mr. Grenfell was passin' by yesterday an' I told un, us'll 'ave him back in no time! Us will too, you can depend on it!"

Paul recalled then that Henry's triumphant foray in the Corn Exchange had made him an enthusiastic supporter of Grenfell and that he was now honorary treasurer of the Valley Liberals. Leaving him to his beloved saddlebacks Paul rode into the yard and entered the big kitchen where Martha Pitts and Henry's great tawny wife, Gloria, were apparently enjoying a private joke for they stopped laughing and looked shamefaced when they saw Paul on the threshold. There was always laughter here, he reflected, and enquired after Henry's eldest boy, who had recently broken an arm climbing an elm to get at a rook's nest.

"Oh, er's well enough, Squire," Gloria said casually. " 'Twoulden surprise me if 'er didden come in with t'other one broke tomorrow! Bones mend zoon enough at his age, dorn 'em now?" He told them that rumours of the King's death had been confirmed by the newspapers and at this they both put on straight faces, holding the expressions until Gloria said, nudging her mother-in-law, "Well, if all I yer about 'un be true, he had a wonderful run for 'is money, didden 'er?" and Martha said, "Shhh! Dornee talk like that!" and pretended to be shocked, so that Paul left them hiding his own grin and rode to the top of Hermitage plateau where he could look down over the wide Valley, something he never failed to do when he was this way.

It was a day for remembering. He recalled coming here with Grace on a summer morning, a long time ago it seemed, the day they had punted across to the temple on the islet and made love like lovers meeting by stealth, and he wondered, briefly, where Grace was at this moment, and if she ever thought of him and remembered vistas like the one at his feet. Then a pair of coal-tits distracted him and he watched them flirting on the lower boughs of a chestnut, making a mental note to tell Horace Handcock, the local oracle on all matters ornithological, who had told him only last week, that, whereas the Valley was teeming with great-tits and blue-tits, he had not seen coal-tits hereabouts since he was a boy. The birds seemed almost tame, flitting about Snowdrop's head, darting in and out of the widely-spaced trees. He went down the main ride to the steep-banked lane leading to the mere, finding it alive with all kinds of water birds, moorhens, dabchicks, coots, a mallard and her family, and even a heron, standing like an old post in the shallows near the islet.

Sam's cottage seemed to be half-full of children, although Paul counted but four on the premises. The eldest, his godchild Pauline, was playing with her sister Georgina and the babies, making daisy chains for each of them as Paul called "Catch, Pauline!" and threw a penny which Pauline caught expertly, abandoning her charges to run in and fetch her mother, who Paul noticed was pregnant yet again, the fifth time in eight years. He thought, "Dammit, if they don't call a halt soon I shall have to build on to the cottage!"

"Sam's upalong, hauling timber," Joannie said, pointing towards the northern end of the woods, "did 'ee want un special, Squire?", and Paul said no, he had only looked in to tell them that the King was dead and Joannie said, "Cor! *Be* 'er now? Will Alix have to manage on 'er own then?", and Paul had to explain that Alexandra would not be Queen any more but would live in retirement, while her duties were taken over by the new Queen Mary, King George's wife. Joannie was interested but unconvinced. "Well, I daresay his missus will manage," she said, "but.I can't say I call 'er to mind. Sam don't read, you see, so us don't get a paper but he sets a store by Queen Alix because we got her in the parlour," and she led Paul into the tiny front room that seemed never to be used and there on the wall was a gigantic double portrait of the late King and Queen Alexandra, Edward looking half-asphyxiated in a tight, gold-laced gorget and red tunic. "I alwas thought of 'er as the beautifulest woman I ever set eyes on," Joannie said solemnly, as though she too had died. "I mus' say I'm sorry for *her*, that I am!" and moved by the same instinct as the Timberlakes she pulled down the blind so that the room was almost in darkness despite the brightness of the sun outside.

He left her and went through the wild wood behind the cottage and over the escarpment, to strike the Bluff about half-way up where a briar-tangled path led to the Dell. Only children were there so he put Snowdrop at the path down which the Bideford Goliath had whipped his mistresses, and there, in the level field adjoining the cliff top, he found the Potter girls drawing water from the new well and emptying it into a great wooden pig-trough under the oaks.

They were obviously glad of an excuse to stop work and came running, their broad, good-natured faces glistening with sweat. "Jem's

525

off across the Teazel to buy wire," they told him in chorus. "He's minded to fence the strip under the trees tomorrow," Violet added, "on account of the pigs fattening quicker if they don't stray. We had to fetch a sow back from Deepdene and it put Jem in a rare old tizzy, didn't it, Cis?" Cis said it had indeed and Paul got the impression that the Potter girls were far more effectively subdued by their hired hand than were the Valley wives by their lawful husbands. He had been discussing the Dell situation only yesterday with Claire, expressing himself in agreement with Parson Horsey that something should be done to regularise the position, particularly as, in the New Year, the Potter sisters had presented Jem with a child apiece to add to the two whose fathers were the subject of much speculation in the Valley. Claire, laughing at his misgivings, told him to let well alone, pointing out that the Dell was paying its way for the first time in living memory. "He seems to have tamed them and that's an achievement," she said, and he had told her she was shameless and that sooner or later Parson Horsey would insist Jem married one or the other.

"How does your mother get along with that fellow?" he asked and Cis said that Meg looked upon him as a son, Vi adding, resentfully, "An' no wonder, for since Jem come 'er's never done a stroke o' work about the varm, the lazy old slut!"

"Well," said Paul grudgingly, "I must say I've never seen the place looking tidier but Parson Horsey was very shocked indeed when he heard about those babies. It wouldn't surprise me if he doesn't pay you three a visit soon and insist on one of you getting married and living a respectable life, like your sister Pansy."

The girls' faces fell and Violet said, virtuously, "What bizness is it o' the Passon how us arranges things? Jem loves the pair of us equally, dornee, Cis? Besides, Jem won't take no account o' what Passon says, 'er was brought up strict Baptist!"

Paul could think of no reply at all to this so he left them, chuckling as he crossed the cliff fields to call in upon Smut, whose glasshouse was now a blaze of colour and who greeted him cheerily. When Paul told of the death of the King he stood to attention, as though on parade and said, " 'Er's dade is 'er? Then God bless him, Squire, us'll miss him, I reckon!", after which, having paid his respects to the House of Hanover, he drew Paul's attention to a well-stocked wire basket swinging from the cross bar of the greenhouse and said, "Do 'ee think Mrs. Craddock could vind a place fer that on the terrace o' the big house, Squire? I've a few left over and I'd like to maake her a present of un, seein' as she so admired the early ones us had when her was yer last."

"I'm sure she'd be delighted, Smut," Paul said, "but she would want to pay the proper price for it."

"No, 'er worn't, Squire!" said Smut, "for you stood by me like a brother backalong and I'm the last man in the Valley to forget it! Us'll put the basket aside and the boy can drop it off on the way back tonight!"

Smut was sufficiently unprejudiced, Paul decided to give advice on the situation in the Dell and after thanking him for the gift said: "Can't you persuade your mother to talk Jem into making a choice between Cissie and Violet? She must know that everyone from here to Paxtonbury is sniggering about what is going on down there!"

"Well," said Smut, with a grin that recalled the poacher for a moment, "tiz been goin' on ever since they was young maids, Squire, an' the only diff'rence is that now all us knows where they be whereas us never did in the old days! If you want my advice, Squire, leave things to zettle 'emselves, for not even old Tamer could keep the drawers hoisted on they two, nor their sister Pansy neither 'till her got 'erself married and was brought to bed once a year reg'lar! The fact is Jem's a match for the two of 'em and they lives in fear an' dread of 'im half the time, which do make for peace an' quiet over there as well as gettin' a yield out o' fields that was left lyin' fallow in Tamer's day!"

"You mean Jem is a brute to them?" said Paul, surprised that such a genial-looking man could terrorise two such experienced harlots as Cissie and Violet Potter, but Smut said he was not, not by any means, and would always defer to Meg, but was not above whopping the girls when they needed it, a privilege the law did not deny any husband in the land!

"But hang it man, Jem isn't married to either one of them," Paul argued. "He's only a hired man as far as I'm concerned."

"Arr, that may be, Squire," Smut conceded, "but they maids have never been partic'lar about churching, 'ave 'em? And since you ask me I woulden wish either one of 'em on any man in the Valley save Jem, who can look after himself! No, Squire, you let the tongues wag, same as they have ever since the girls growed big enough to start 'em waggin'! Us is doin' very well over this side an' tiz all on account o' Jem knowing when to give rein an' when to shorten it!"—and with that Paul had to be content, reflecting that it was precisely the same advice given him by his wife on the subject. He turned the grey on to the cliff path and rode over the shoulder of the Bluff to the head of Coombe Bay's single, broad street, lifting his hand in acknowledgement to almost everyone he met and recalling the first, scorching day he had ridden down to the tiny harbour in the company of John Rudd.

The village was a good deal changed now. Nearly a score of cottages had been gathered into the estate, rethatched and let on long leases. There had been social changes too, for the low-church Parson Horsey had reconciled the agricultural church folk and nonconformist fishermen. A sub-post office had opened next door to The Raven, so that it was now possible to send telegrams if despatchers did not mind their contents being broadcast all over the Valley within the hour. One of the ugly Victorian villas, where Grace's stepmother Celia had lived, was occupied by a retired army major who collected butterflies, and the other by an elderly German, called Scholtzer, said to have exiled himself as a protest against the Kaiser's militarism and to save his son from being conscripted into the Prussian army. Paul had spoken to the German once or twice and found him civil enough, a short, fat, moon-faced man, who looked as if he had strayed out of a German band but was, according to John Rudd, a former professor of history at Jena University. He stopped and had a word or two with Abe Tozer, the smith, and saw Mrs. Walter Pascoe, Pansy Potter that was, with her tribe of children on the strip of sand where the nets were drying. Then he turned west, through the back lanes, intending to cut across the dunes and rejoin the river road beyond the Four Winds southern boundary, but on the outskirts of the village he stopped at the ruined brickworks, recognising a slim, bespectacled youth engaged in some kind of survey of the derelict area. It was Sydney Codsall, now nineteen, and articled to Snow and Pritchard, solicitors of Whinmouth.

It was over a year since he had seen the boy, so he reined in and hailed him across the ruined wall. Sydney looked startled and fumbled with the reel of tape he was holding, so Paul called again, "What's going on, Sydney? Is somebody thinking of restarting Manson's kilns?"

The boy came towards him reluctantly and Paul realised that, although he had always felt sorry for him, he was a difficult boy to like. He was a misfit in the Valley and his year or so in an office since leaving school had encouraged him to slough off what little influence the jolly Eveleigh family had had upon him, when he lived at Four Winds. His face was long and narrow and his carroty hair was sleekly brushed and evidently oiled, for it gleamed wetly in the afternoon sun. He favoured neither his father nor mother, Paul thought, and walked

528

alone, exuding a faint odour of patronage, as though he had been glad to shed the stigma of sweat and stable straw and climb into the more genteel atmosphere of streets and offices. Seeing who it was Sydney touched his cap politely, composing his sharp features into an expression of cautious humility.

"I'm sorry, I didn't see who was calling," he said in a reedy voice that recalled Arabella nagging her husband across the kitchen table. "The fect is, I was busy! I was sent heah by Mr. Vicary himself!"

"Who is Mr. Vicary?" Paul asked and the boy's expression slipped a little, as though this was a question that only a fool would ask.

"Why, he's our Chief Clurk, Mr. Craddock, my immediate superior at Snow and Pritchard's. He's not articled, of course, but he had the responsibility of training me and this is the first assignment I've been given, measuring up so that the deeds can be proved you see." He went on to explain that Manson's heirs had disposed of the property and Paul did not conceal his surprise. He knew Manson had died back in the spring and that his odd bits of property, including the brick-yard, had been willed to a relative in London but it piqued him that the solicitors had not approached him to buy the plot, for it was known that he was always in the market for land or cottages adjoining the estate boundaries. He had bought what was now Periwinkle Farm through Snow and Pritchard, and also the cliff land added to the High Coombe holding, and it now struck him that the boy found his presence here embarrassing. He said shortly, "Who bought it, Sydney?" but Sydney's face went blank once more.

"Well I . . . er . . . I'm not at liberty to say, Mr. Craddock! I don't think Mr. Vicary would like me to discuss the firm's business with a third party!"

"Damn it, I'm not a third party, and both you and Vicary should know it! Half the houses hereabouts are on the Shallowford maps and I particularly asked Mr. Snow to tell me when any others came on the market. Do you suppose he forgot about it?"

"I reely couldn't say, Mr. Craddock," replied Sydney, slightly intimidated now, "but I'll certainly tell him you enquired. However," —and Paul was now reminded of Arabella in a malicious mood— "I do assure you it is sold and that the purchaser won't consider re-selling. Shall I make an appointment for you, sir?"

"No," Paul growled, looking across the brick-strewn yard and deciding that it was hardly worth his trouble and then, relenting somewhat, "How do you like working in an office, Sydney?"

"I'm very well suited, thank you," Sydney said primly. "I find the work very much to my taste."

Paul smiled, reflecting that this was the way Arabella might have replied. "Well, that's splendid," he said and rode on, finding his humour slightly soured by the encounter but forgetting Sydney the moment he caught sight of the sun dancing on the shallow river under the Bluff. Sydney, however, did not forget him and pondered the conversation all that day, wondering if Vicary would cover up for him when the Squire raised the matter and deciding that he probably would, for it had been Vicary who had suggested Sydney should lay out some of his savings on the Manson property. Having reassured himself as regards this he began to rejoice in his brush with the Squire, telling himself that he had got the best of it. Sydney Codsall had never heard of the Chinese proverb "Why do you hate me? I have never helped you!" but he would have appreciated its wisdom. It was some years since he had declared secret war on Shallowford and the purchase of the brickyard, and other bits of Manson property, were his opening shots in this war. Vicary, the ageing clerk of Snow and Pritchard, had taken a liking to his junior, seeing in him the makings of a first-class businessman and an astute legal mind. Childless, he had set himself the task of guiding and inspiring the boy for it was no secret that Sydney Codsall would share equally in Martin Codsall's estate when he was twenty-one and at sixty-plus, with small prospect of a pension, an unarticled clerk had to look out for himself. He found the boy quick to learn, very neat and tidy, but, above all, refreshingly lacking in sentiment. When the matter of the Manson property had come up he had counselled Sydney to buy, pointing out that, although the new land taxes made it something of a liability this would be more than compensated by an inevitable rise in the price of building land and that Coombe Bay, a trifling community today, would expand as time went on and seaside holidays came within reach of all. Sydney had thought this sound reasoning and learning that brickyard, cottage and derelict shop were to be had for a little over a hundred pounds, he put his money down straight away. What he would do with his purchases he did not know but whatever it was it must, he felt, yield a profit. In the meantime it added greatly to his status. Perhaps, as time passed, there would be other and better opportunities but in the meantime he could wait. He was only nineteen and there were many examinations ahead; after all, Lloyd George had started life in a solicitor's office and was now Chancellor of the Exchequer.

530

In mid-July that year, Paul, Claire, John Rudd and Maureen travelled to High Wood to attend the annual athletic sports, the last Ikey would take part in, for he was due to leave at the end of term. They took with them six-year-old Simon, who was much attached to Ikey and sick with excitement at the prospect of watching his hero win races and collect cups. "I shouldn't be too sure about it, Simon," Claire warned him, as they climbed out of the carriage and joined the gaily-dressed crowd lining the ropes. "We can't guarantee Ikey will win, he might only come second, or third."

"Really, Mamma, how can you be so stupid?" Simon replied. "Ikey can run further than anyone in the world without even puffing!" and it was Simon rather than Claire who was proved right for Ikey, eighteen now, a double colour and Captain of his House, almost literally walked away with the half-mile, the mile and the steeplechase, as well as winning second place in the long jump and throwing the cricket ball.

Paul listened to the cheers with quiet pride, noting that Ikey was idolised by the smaller boys who screamed their enthusiasm when Ikey's long nicely-judged stride carried him ahead of the field. He thought, as he watched the boy step up to receive five silver cups from the local countess, "By God, it's a miracle! The first time I saw him he was wearing trousers three times too large for him, had a running nose and was driving a cart in a Bermondsey scrapyard! Today nobody could distinguish him from the best dressed of these languid young devils!" Maureen Rudd had other thoughts, recalling her first meeting with Ikey on Codsall bridge when he had been bewildered by the outcome of his plot to help the Squire. She glanced sideways at Claire, cool and elegant in green and white striped silk and showing off a very trim figure indeed for a mother of two expecting a third around Christmas-time. The boy, she thought, must have had an instinct about her; how else could he have known that a mis-spelled letter written on the advice of another woman would restore serenity to the Valley? And again she wondered if anything would be served by bringing it all into the open and telling Claire and Paul exactly how much they owed the boy passing back and forth across the headmaster's lawn to collect his cups but as always she decided to leave well alone and she hoisted Simon level with spectators' shoulders, so he could get a clear view of his hero.

It was during the tea interval, when Ikey was changing, that she asked Paul what Ikey intended to do now that his schooldays were ending and Paul said that as far as he was aware Ikey intended to try for a commission in a cavalry regiment and sit for the Sandhurst exam in the autumn.

"Well, I daresay the life will suit him," she said, without enthusiasm, "he's a sociable type and has plenty of—what do they call it—'Leadership qualities'? Still, the boy's undoubtedly got brains and he'll spend money rather than make it in the Officers' Mess. Couldn't he do something more original?"

"I'll have a word with his headmaster before he leaves," Paul told her and her enquiry set him thinking for, until then, he had never considered Ikey a person with money-making propensities.

Claire was enjoying herself very much in her own way. The mothers and sisters seemed to her a very fashionable set and it wasn't often she got a chance to mix with smartly-dressed women. The setting, she thought, was as remote and rural as the Valley, but today seemed self-consciously so, as if everyone here was taking part in an elaborate pastoral masque. There was an endless flirting of gloves and twirling of parasols, and the women swayed as they walked, wearing bright, fixed smiles and using courtly inclinations of the head. She thought, "If anyone wanted to paint a scene representative of England in the first summer of the new reign they couldn't do better than plant their easel by the long-jump pit and turn out something like Frith's 'Railway Station' or 'At The Seaside'. If they were good enough they might even catch the smugness and the well-fed looks on the faces of that picnicking group over there, or the strained, newly-arrived expression on the face of that little boy's plain sister, sitting alone near the hurdles." Then it occurred to her how very out of touch with the social world she and Paul were becoming down in the Valley and how unrepentant she felt about it, although she wasn't so sure it was altogether right for them to live such an enclosed life. For the first time since she had left London she reminded herself that this voluntary withdrawal on his part had been the rock on which his first marriage foundered and this encouraged her to think that perhaps there was something to be said for Grace after all. Taking advantage of a moment when everyone was talking to somebody else she said, "I'd forgotten people still followed fashions, Paul! Will you promise me something, while I remember?"

"You look attractive enough to extract any number of rash promises

532

today, Claire," he told her but she said, "No, I'm serious! After the baby's born will you take me to London for the Coronation? I haven't been east of Paxtonbury since we married?"

"Well," he said, "I'll tell you what. Present me with a girl instead of another damned boy and it's a promise! And I don't give a row of beans if it's twins so long as it isn't one of each!"

"I'll see what can be arranged," she said and squeezed his hand as Ikey, looking self-consciously smart in his swallow-tailed coat and three-inch butterfly collar, joined them to say the Head could see Paul now and save him a special journey to school before end of term. So Paul followed him along stone corridors to a heavy, pseudo-Gothic door on which Ikey knocked and said, by way of introduction, "My guardian, sir!" and withdrew, leaving Paul confronted with the thick-set, scrubby-haired man about fifty, who shook his hand absent-mindedly and seated him in an obvious "parents" chair that engulfed him.

Paul had met the headmaster on several previous occasions and had found him rather remote, with a tendency to grant an interview with a parent as though it was unavoidable but a crashing bore just the same. Today, however, the man came alive and Paul concluded that his change of manner had some link with Ikey's athletic triumphs for he began by saying, "Delighted you could get over, Mr. Craddock! In view of the fact that Palfrey is leaving this half I should have written in any case, but I appreciate an opportunity to tell you how wrong I was about the lad and how pleased I am to be wrong!" When Paul looked rather nonplussed at this he continued, "The fact is he began rather badly—that time he ran off to London and I admit that I wrote him off as a lad anxious to advertise himself as an individualist!"

"Isn't that encouraged?" asked Paul, deciding that he did not like the man much but the Head disarmed him with a professional smile and said, "Well, to be frank we don't cater for individualists here—not yet, at all events. It was during the last year or so that we began to succeed so spectacularly with your lad."

Paul murmured that his ward (he remembered just in time that "Ikey" was never used at High Wood) had been very happy at the school and that he was relieved to hear him well spoken of by his headmaster.

"Oh, it's rather more than that," the headmaster went on, "the fact is Palfrey has always puzzled me somewhat. He was never any trouble apart from that one time. He pulled his weight and made friends easily

533

enough but frankly, I always had the impression he was . . . well . . .
laughing at us! Does that sound extravagant?"

Paul thought, privately, "No, I'm damned if it does for he almost
certainly was and jolly good luck to him! He got away with it, and
I wonder what the old bird would say if I told him Ikey came here
from a London junk yard via my stables?" He said, aloud, "I've been
wondering if we're doing the right thing encouraging him to take a
commission, Headmaster. Have you any thoughts on the matter?"

The headmaster put on his "careers" look and said, with slight
hesitation, "That . . . er . . . rather depends. Has he an army background?"

"I served through the South African War," Paul said, at last beginning to get the measure of the man, but all the Head said was, "Ah,
that's not quite the same thing! You were Yeomanry, I expect, and
you're his guardian, not his father."

"The old bird is fishing now," Paul thought, "but he'll catch
nothing from me!" "I'm a relative," he said, brazenly, "his sister was
my first wife. Perhaps I never told you he was born on the Continent,
or that his mother was an Austrian subject?"

The Head seemed vaguely impressed, remarking that the Austrians
produced a large number of first-class equestrians, whereupon Paul
said promptly that the boy could ride anything and had always had an
exceptional flair for horses.

"Then I don't really see how we could improve on the cavalry," the
headmaster went on. "After all, it's a pleasant life, particularly in
Ireland and India. If he does well enough in Army Entrance he might
get a good regiment although there's tremendous competition, I'm
told," and when Paul made no reply he added, "Did you have anything else in mind?"

"No," Paul admitted, "I didn't but I think I should prefer him to
take up a profession with more future in it."

"But surely there is a future in an Army career, Mr. Craddock?"

"Not in the cavalry," Paul said promptly, "at least, not in my
opinion!"

"I'm afraid your opinion isn't generally shared," the Head said
kindly, as though applying a gentle damper to a boy who had made
a bad gaffe but needed encouragement. "The Chairman of our
Governors, Lieutenant-General Manners-Smith, thinks the exact
opposite and he was on Buller's staff in the Transvaal."

"I wouldn't wonder," Paul thought, "and got a lot of good chaps killed playing at Waterloo outside Ladysmith!" and suddenly he tired of phrase-juggling and began to wonder if, after all, High Wood was the kind of place he wanted for Simon and the twins when they had passed through Prep School. It had performed a miracle on Ikey but did his own boys stand in need of miracles? He said briefly, "I'll have a talk with the lad during the holidays, Headmaster, and if I need further advice perhaps I could write. If he really wants the Army I won't stand in his way," and he got up, extending his hand. And then another, more important thought struck him and he said, "You spoke well enough of him as a product of the school. How did he show up as a scholar?"

"Oh, average, average," said the Head airily, "but scholarship isn't everything, Mr. Craddock," implying that it counted for rather less than the ability to convert a try into a goal.

The matter was carried a step further early in the holidays as Paul and Ikey rode into Paxtonbury to look at a hunter recommended by Rose Derwent as "being worth a guinea over the odds". They had often travelled this road in company and for each of them it was usually a sentimental journey. Paul recounted the gist of his interview with the Head and Ikey was amused by Paul's confession that he had found the man too pretentious for his taste. "Oh, Sandy Mac is stuffy all right," he said tolerantly, "but he's a trier, a bit like you and I in a way," and when Paul asked what this meant he added, "He's not public school, you see and has to walk pretty carefully. His father was a postman, I believe, and he won a scholarship to a grammar school up north and afterwards went on to win first-class honours at Cambridge. You have to hand it to him for that. It was really why I played along with him."

Paul was intrigued by the boy's eye for the chinks in adult armour and also by his ability to judge people's real worth but the comment reminded him of the Head's remark—"I believe he was laughing at us" and he quoted it, expecting to outface the lad. He evidently failed for Ikey laughed so heartily that he lost a stirrup.

"He said *that*? Old Sandy Mac admitted that to you? Geewhiz! He must have come close to twigging me after all!"

"The point is," said Paul seriously, "you've been playing charades ever since you went to school and I've been aiding and abetting you! Frankly I think it's been worth it but we don't have to go on playing them indefinitely! You're eighteen now and can make your own decisions!"

535

"Can I?" The boy was suddenly serious. "I can't you know, not really! Far too much has rubbed off on me. Oh, I'm not complaining, Governor, and I should hate you to think I was, I'm grateful for everything you've done for me but sometimes . . ."

He broke off and kicked his heels against the horse's flanks causing it to break into a trot. Snowdrop automatically increased his pace and when they drew level again Paul saw that the boy's eyes were troubled. "Look here, Ikey," he said, "you don't have to confide everything to me but I'll always listen if you want to and don't ever forget it! I started this conversation with the idea of finding out if you had made up your mind about taking Army Entrance in October and going to Sandhurst. The last time we talked about it you had no doubts. Have you had any since?"

Ikey reined in and both horses stopped near the brow of the hill; another fifty yards and they would top the crest and begin the long descent into the Paxtonbury bowl.

"The Army would cost you money, Governor; it could go on costing you money indefinitely."

"I can afford it and if you really want to take a commission I'll back you. The real issue is—would you prefer to train for something else, for one of the professions? Or would you care to go on to University and make your final decision there?"

The boy said, with a shrug, "It isn't that easy, Governor. At my reckoning I'm only about two-thirds a gent; maybe not as much as that, maybe only three-fifths! You couldn't anticipate that when you sent me to High Wood but that's how it happened, a good part of me was still . . ."

"In the scrapyard? That's damned nonsense, Ikey, and I believe you know it!"

"I wasn't going to say 'scrapyard'," Ikey said, gently, "I had that beaten *before* I went to school. But I was happy in the stable-yard and deep down I never wanted or expected anything better."

"I'm hanged if I follow you," Paul grumbled, now more than a little exasperated, "you made a success of High Wood and whether you like it or not you've moved up in the world. What is it you really want?"

"I suppose, more than anything, to justify your investment in me," Ikey said and Paul was instantly sorry for his impatience. "Where would I be now if you hadn't brought me down here?" And suddenly he looked less serious and added "I can guess—doing a stretch probably, for knocking off the railings of Buckingham Palace or the Monument!"

536

They rode on in silence for a spell, Paul puzzled and a little disturbed by the boy's view of himself as a partial misfit but the more he thought about it the less credible it seemed for his mind returned to his obvious popularity and the vision of the trim, swallow-tailed youth who had escorted him into the headmaster's study less than a month before. He said finally, "When you were at school were you homesick for the stable-yard, Ikey?"

"Not the stable-yard," Ikey said, "but the freedom that went along with it! A chap outside looking in on a place like High Wood is entitled to imagine it's all beer and skittles but it isn't, you know! Nobody's life is that simple—I mean, there were plenty of times when I was homesick for the days when I didn't have to live up to anything and that's what I mean when I say I'm still only two-thirds a gent. The other third was always back here, deep in the woods."

He was tempted, at this moment, to confess what lay behind this admission, to tell Paul of his long association with Hazel Potter and his identification of her with everything that grew and hunted in the coombes and coverts of Shallowford, but consideration for the man checked him. He had been living with snobs too long not to realise that their kind of snobbery had no place in Paul Craddock's nature but he knew also that there were limits to tolerance and that Hazel Potter, the half-wit of the Valley, was beyond those limits. To say that he had often wished he had stayed a stable-boy with free access to her and her irresponsibilities would be throwing dirt in his benefactor's face yet he was aware that, to some extent, she was the most rewarding person in his life, except for the man riding beside him. As he pondered this he felt a great yearning for her, for the sound of her soft, Devon burr and the broom-thicket scent of her hair, for the security and isolation of her little house over the badger sets and for the touch of her warm lips. He said, suddenly, "Look here, Governor, I don't have to confirm my Army Entrance application until September but I can tell you one thing—I've decided against the cavalry, if only on the grounds of your pocket! A chap I knew at school has an uncle in the Engineers and I met the old boy when he came over one day. The R.E.s are the only up-to-date branch of the Army and if we ever do have a showdown with the Germans or the Russians they'll make rings round the lancers and hussars! And that's not all, either! I don't think I could stick the mumbo-jumbo of what they call a 'good' regiment. If I am to be in the Army then I should certainly want to earn my keep—you know, *really* earn it—and at least I should have an outdoor job with a chance to travel at Government expense. I couldn't stick an office life so maybe we have got somewhere with this pow-wow!"

"You mean you want a week or two to think it over?" Paul said, laughing and Ikey said maybe only a day or two, so by common consent they dropped the subject and rode on into the city talking of horses.

V

Every day, wearing his old training sweater and a pair of soiled slacks, Ikey climbed the orchard to the high-banked lane, circled the mere and threaded the rhododendron maze that he now knew as expertly as Hazel. She was always waiting for him, high up on her rock, and would lift her hand when she saw him tackle the steep, pine-studded slope leading to the cave. And when he saw her a sense of urgency would rush down on him and he would set himself at the sandy slope as though he was on the home run of the most important cross-country event of the season for all summer there had been a clock ticking in his heart, setting a term to boyhood.

One day, soon after the conversation on careers, he did not come until evening, after the sun had passed Nun's Head in the west and the bowl below the escarpment was drowsy with summer, as though everything living there had been used up by the heat of the day. She shouted, from her platform, "Where've 'ee been? I've been lookin' out for 'ee zince noon!" and he told her he had been to a tea-party with some of Mrs. Craddock's friends in Coombe Bay and had only now managed to change and steal away. He went through the wicker screen to the little house and because everything there was familiar to him he noticed a stone jar, standing in one of the cavities she had scooped in the soft sandstone.

"What have you got there?" he asked and she told him it was a gallon jar of Meg Potter's hedgerow wine she had stolen from the washroom behind the Potter farmhouse. "Tidden *really* stealing," she added, "for backalong, when 'er was out after blossoms, I went along of her an' helped. Besides, there's nigh on a dozen jars stored there to cool off. 'Er sells it, you zee, over in Whinmouth, so when 'er wasn't lookin' I skipped off with some, thinkin' us'd taake a mug when us was dry!"

He sniffed it, finding that it smelled a little like damp corn. "What does she put in it, Hazel?"

"Oh, all sorts," the girl said carelessly, "zertain nettles 'er knows,

538

cowslips, elderberries, turnips, dandelion, sloes, quinces and I don't know what, fer 'er's proper stingy with 'er book o' charms an' never lets none of us peep, not even me, who coulden read what's writ there! Would 'ee like to sample it? Tiz rare stuff and good for rheumatics they say."

"I don't have rheumatism yet," he said laughing, "but I'll down a mug if you will," and she produced two earthenware cups, shook the jar and tipped a generous measure into each.

It was like drinking the Valley at harvest time. Clover was there, as a kind of base, but so was every other ingredient Hazel had mentioned and many others besides, including honey. It slipped over the palate like nectar.

"By George!" he exclaimed, "it's marvellous! Better than any drink I ever tasted! Pour me another."

"Tiz heady stuff," she warned him, "us dorn want to zend 'ee 'ome tipsy," but he boasted that he had a good head for liquor and could walk a straight line after half-a-bottle of the Squire's burgundy with brandy to follow so she poured another measure and sat sipping her own, her great brown eyes watching him over the rim of the cup.

When he had finished his second drink and smacked his lips with appreciation she put the stopper on the jar and returned it to the cavity.

"I dorn reckon you'd better have no more, Ikey," she said, "for even our Smut can't taake a pint of it and you've had two gills. 'Ow do it feel? Do it warm your belly and maake your ears sing?"

It would have baffled him to tell her exactly how he felt. There was, it was true, a great glow spreading under his navel and his ears were singing but not unpleasantly so, the murmur of the woods coming to him as a chorus chanted by angels and the evening light, filtering into the cave through the gorse, appearing as the radiance of a celestial sunset. He said, giggling, "Let's have another half cup, Hazel—go on, be a sport!", but she refused him and stood with her back to the cavity. He got up then crouching because the roof was low and made a playful grab at her but she pushed him and he staggered, grazing his head on a rock buttress, not heavily, but enough to make him yelp and sink to his knees. She was beside him at once, with her arms round his shoulders, pressing his head to her breast and uttering soothing noises, as she might over a puppy struck by a blundering foot.

" 'Ave I 'urt 'ee? Did 'ee knock yer poor ade on the rock? Tiz gone to your legs, like rough cider! Bide awhile an' I mak 'er some tay!", and she held him like a child, rocking him to and fro while a wave of sweetness passed over him and he forgot the smart of his head in the softness of her breasts and the scent of her hair tumbling about his face. Then the glow in his belly seemed to explode so that its warmth invaded every vein in his body and he broke from her embrace, bearing her backwards and crushing her into the bracken with his weight and covering her face with kisses. She seemed inclined to resist him for a moment for when, breathlessly, he turned his head aside and caught up a handful of her hair, which he pressed against his mouth, she twisted from beneath him and said, "Dornee, Ikey boy, tiz the drink in 'ee!", but he saw to his relief that she was only laughing at him and that her remark was more of a statement than a protest. He released her, however, rolling on his elbow and laughing at himself but also at her for she looked comical squatting back on her hams and looking down at him like an affectionate wife contemplating a husband far gone in drink who had returned home and fallen on the doorstep. She seemed to contemplate him a long time, as though not sure what to do with him and as she sat there, head on one side, hands on her knees, he thought her the most beautiful creature he had ever seen and blurted out, "I love you so much! I love you, Hazel!", and because, despite the choir and the golden haze, his inner consciousness was still sharp and clear his voice sounded false and stilted so that he slipped back into her vernacular, saying, "Youm mine, Hazel Potter, and I'll kill any man who touches 'ee, do 'ee hear, now?", and this must have sobered her for she stood up with a slow, graceful movement, and without taking her eyes off him, said, "O' course 'ee would! But I woulden let un, Ikey! *Never*, do 'ee hear? No man but you!"

The effect of the wine on his brain was two-fold, for while his body presented him as an amorous, half-helpless clodhopper his thoughts about her were diamond sharp and he saw her as he had always thought of her, the concentration in a woman's body, of all the colours and scents and fruitfulness of the Valley under the mantle of summer and desired her not as a woman but as a kind of key to her world and everything it offered. Yet the prospect of possessing her seemed to have nothing to do with his body but was an emphatic gesture of the mind. He stood up, unsteadily, and because he staggered a little she took his hands, saying, "You'd best bide a spell, Ikey, youm drunk as David's sow!" and she giggled as she propped him against the canting wall and spread her flour sacks on the bracken at the back of the cave.

"You'll bide tu?" he said and she told him she would but he was not to worry for he would soon be asleep and when he awoke he would be none the worse for the drink; " 'Er dorn carry no ade with 'er," she added. By now, however, the glow had spread to every part of his body, so that the atmosphere of the cave became insufferably hot and he began to struggle with his sweater in an effort to pull it over his head. She said, as though it was the most natural question in the world, "Be 'ee *that* hot then? Do 'ee want to strip to lie down?", and pulled his sweater free after which she removed his trousers by the simple process of unbuckling his belt and hoisting his legs clear. He suffered this indignity without protest, without even thinking of it as an indignity, and watched her make a pillow of his clothes. When the makeshift couch was ready he collapsed on to it and lay flat on his back as she knelt beside him, inspecting his body with a kind of amused tolerance and saying, with the utmost mildness, "Ah, youm a praper-looking man now, Ikey, a praper man to be sure!" He lay staring up at her with slightly glazed eyes and might have succumbed at once to the drowsiness that was already playing tricks with his consciousness, distorting his judgments of sound and distance but then, almost with resignation, she stood upright again and without taking her eyes off him for a moment slipped out of her odds and ends of garments, folded her ragged dress with great care and put it to one side, standing erect between where he lay and the fading light filtering through the gorse screen of the entrance. His drowsiness left him then but he did not move a muscle, remaining on his back looking up at her, marvelling at the tawny smoothness of her long, straight legs and the rim of browned skin where the tide of sunburn had been checked by the dress just above the shallow downsweep of her breasts and above her knees. Then, with a curiously remote expression, half abstracted and half deliberate, she knelt again and began passing her hands over his body, lightly yet with an air of purpose so that the touch of fingers induced in him a state that was a kind of suspension between elation and the richest daydream of his experience. He was aware that they were naked and that she was caressing him with deliberation but he felt no shame or, at that moment, desire. Her manipulation of his senses was without significance and thus made no direct impact on him and he did not move, neither did he reach out to return her caresses. It was only when she placed both hands on his shoulders, leaning over him to kiss his mouth that her presence beyond his reach became intolerable and he pulled her down beside him, kissing her face and breasts and shoulders and slipping his hands

541

down the full length of her back. She said, with a tinge of sadness in her voice but without urgency, "You gonner tak' me now, Ikey? Be 'ee clear-aded enough to know what youm at!" and he said, sharply, "Youm mine, Hazel Potter, I'll tak' 'ee whenever I wants!" and she sighed as he enfolded her and was done with her in a few painful seconds.

He slept then, almost on the instant and she slipped gently from him, aware of the evening chill rising out of the Valley and striking cold on her back. She paused a moment to look down on him, noting the tiny fronds of dead bracken adhering to his chest and hair so that suddenly he looked a boy again, younger by far than her and she hastened to cover him with another of her sacks. She did not regard what had happened as momentous and could contemplate it without fear or regret. She did not invest it with any special significance. He had always been her man and she was aware that men's desires and demands changed as they grew older. It was just that today, unexpectedly, a few draughts of hedgerow wine had hastened his growth and he had moved on, taking her with him as was the order of things. She did not look for a solution to their committal for she had never troubled herself about solutions and explanations of human or animal conduct, taking each new experience as it came and extracting from it what she needed and what life was disposed to give her. It had granted her him and for a long time now she had accepted the inevitability of this bounty and the limitations that accompanied it, for she supposed now that he would demand access to her every time they met and that she would grow accustomed to being seized by him and crushed under him, with dry bracken stalks scratching her back and her body a soft target for his explosive energy. She did not resent this in any way. All she knew of life in the woods and on the moors taught her that violent possession of the female was the unquestionable right of the male and if, beyond this acceptance, there was a single spark of sadness it was struck by his impatience that had involved pain, certainly to her but perhaps also to him. Yet she knew instinctively that this need not always be so, that it would not necessarily be a clumsily contrived act and that perhaps, when the wine was out of him, they could find ways to prolong preliminaries that had brought her infinitely more joy and satisfaction than the climax. She shook out her hair and pulled on the ruin of her dress thinking with yearning of his smooth, white body under her hands and of the way she had gentled every part of him while he lay still staring up at her as though she was an angel appearing

542

out of a cloud. And as she thought this she lifted and studied the hands that had touched him, extending her fingers and bringing them to her lips, smiling secretly as she performed this act of homage. Then, with a final glance at him, she made her way out into the open and through the gorse to the slope. She knew somehow what he would not want to find her there when he awoke.

He got back to his room without disturbing anyone, remembering little of his scramble through the rhododendrons, and round the edge of the mere in almost total darkness. Once or twice he fell and bruised himself and on the climb up the escarpment to the edge of the woods he was clawed by innumerable briars but he struggled on, careless of hurts so long as he could reach the privacy of his room and lock the door against intruders and thought.

She had been right about the comparative harmlessness of the devil's brew that had drawn him into this terrifying situation. There was no hangover; his head did not ache and although his mouth felt parched there was no sour taste on his palate as there had been when he, and Manners, and Hicks Minor, had drunk three pints of stout in the fourth form and gone reeling to bed. But the lack of a hangover was a trifling compensation when he was weighed down by so much guilt and shame and by so many desperate fears that rushed at him like gusts of wind from behind every tree. He did not know whether her absence, when he awoke to find himself naked under her sacks, had been a relief or not. He would have found the greatest difficulty, he thought, in meeting her reproachful eyes, but it was pitch dark by then and they could have talked, and she might, somehow, have been able to reassure him, although he doubted very much if she would have forgiven him his handling of her. He thought savagely of his worldly-wise cronies in the Sixth, who boasted so lightly of their conquests of shop-girls and street-walkers. Either they were liars, which he was disposed to believe, or they were made very differently from him, without consciences, and without any sense of moral responsibility towards other people. For a few minutes only after finding himself alone in the cave and the Valley below dark and silent, he had attempted to dismiss the incident as an initiation into the world of men. He had got drunk on Meg Potter's nectar. He had kissed and fondled a girl. And finally he had pushed the encounter to its logical conclusion. After all, she was only a Potter and everyone in the valley knew that the Potter girls were to be had for a shilling. But soon he recognised this as a deliberate distortion of the truth, knowing that what had happened after the wine had started a fire in his loins had not been a casual encounter with an accommodating girl but something approaching a rape, with her a virgin crying out as she was ravished, and, what was worse, ravished by someone whom she trusted. If his memory of all that had taken place had been at all clear he might have found ample self-justification in the fact that it had been she who had undressed him, she who had pushed him down on the floor and then virtually offered herself but the devil of it was he was by no means clear on the details, only upon the fact. That brew of Meg's seemed to have scoured his memory of all that had occurred between his swallowing of the second mugful, and her sharp, single cry as he took possession of her. He could hear that cry now and it tormented him all the way down the sunken lane and across the orchard to the stable-yard. Then, as he reached his room, guilt was driven out by fear and the most urgent of his fears was that she should find herself with a child, his child, whom he would have to acknowledge before Squire, the elegant Mrs. Craddock, Doctor Maureen, Hazel's family and, indeed, the Valley at large! What would follow if this dread possibility materialised he did not know. He would, he supposed, be thrown out of the house, for surely Squire Craddock would be outraged to discover that the protegé upon whom he had lavished so much affection and money had behaved in such a base fashion. Ignorance buttressed his fears for in spite of the long talks over the study fires in his last year at school he still did not know whether a baby was the inevitable sequel to what he had done. He hoped and prayed not, telling himself that if this was the case then the world would be overpopulated in a matter of years, and he clung to this straw of comfort while he pulled off his clothes and stealthily washed himself in cold water. Then, as he climbed into bed, it occurred to him that if the worst happened perhaps he might not be turned out of the house, but reviled and herded to the altar to be married to Hazel Potter out of hand. Possibly her mother and brothers (and almost certainly the Squire and Mrs. Craddock) would insist upon marriage and for a moment the pricks and stabs of gilt and fear ceased to assault him as he tried to picture their life together as man and wife. He supposed he loved her for how else could he have behaved with such criminal recklessness? And he was convinced that she still loved him, in spite of his brutality but he also knew that there was a good deal more to marriage than rolling about on a couple of sacks spread on dried

544

bracken. How and where would they live? How did one earn enough money to maintain a wife and the children resulting from every encounter such as the last?

He found sleep impossible and watched the dawn draw the curtains on his window. Away across the fields, in the yard of the Home Farm, a cock shrilled and birds began to rustle and sing in the creeper above the porch. He got up, sluiced his face and dressed, leaning his elbows on the sill and looking across Big Paddock to the river. It was still only five-thirty and he had an hour or so before people crowded back into his life and addressed him, expecting lucid, everyday replies. He knew that before then he must find some kind of solution to his problems and he thought, for a moment, of flight. Then he remembered that there was no immediate urgency, for a baby, so they said, was nine months in the making and with this thought came another, a recollection of something Tovey Major had said about virgins being unable to have children. He was unsure how much reliance could be placed upon this or in what measure it affected him, but he began to cheer up a little, a very little and returned to his bed, lying fully-dressed on the rumpled sheets with his hands clasped behind his head as he searched among his memories for significant details. He found none but some of his fears, and a little of his guilt, began to recede and as the room grew lighter he found to his astonishment that he could look back upon the incident with a certain amount of detachment. The more he succeeded in doing this the less urgent it seemed, and slowly his panic began to subside so that he could think of Hazel with tepid warmth and of his savage use of her with a certain amount of awe. He said, half-aloud, "I shall have to leave here at once for if I don't I know very well what will happen, I'll go to that damned cave again and it will happen as often as I go with or without that jar of hedgerow wine the little fool introduced into the place! After all, it was the liquor that began it all for without that stuff inside me I should have stopped short after kissing her, or maybe fondling her a little. Surely the best thing is to disappear and I can tell Squire first thing I've decided on the R.E.s, and that I need three months' cramming before sitting Army Entrance! I can give him the name of Manners' crammer, near Eastbourne, and go there at once." But then, as he rejoiced in this easy escape route, he remembered Hazel Potter's brown eyes looking across the rim of her mug when he was supping his second gill and he knew that he could not leave without explaining to her why and where he was going. He would have to see her once again, and tell her how sorry he was, and perhaps kiss her but very gently and impersonally on the cheek. He hoped she would understand and agree that things could not be left as they were. If she did not then he would go anyway, leaving her to make the best of it.

He knew where he could find her at this hour. If she had not slept at the cave then she must have gone to the Dell and after what had happened he guessed that she would not remain there long but would make her way back to the woods at first light. He would try the Dell first and if he drew blank he would go to the cave. He slipped out and down the backstairs, cutting round the house and crossing the sloping meadow to enter the scrub on the west side of the Bluff where the field path joined the Dell track. Having made a decision he felt almost lighthearted and it was difficult to remain gloomy in the early morning woods, where it seemed as if every bird in the Valley had congregated to swell the clamour. He waited here, watching a woodpecker at work, and presently he heard her coming along the track and moved behind a bush for his curiosity regarding her had increased rather than diminished and presently she came in view, dawdling along and actually crooning to herself, as though she found the world a particularly pleasant place that morning.

"Damn it," he said to himself, "here's me, worried half out of my wits about her and feeling the biggest cad on earth and here she comes strolling along singing! What the devil am I so bothered about?", and he called, "Hi there! Hazel!"

She stopped, turning her head slowly and her mouth curved in a warm, welcoming smile as he edged out of ambush and stood uncertainly in her path.

"Youm right early, Ikey!" she said, as though she had half-expected him, " 'Ave 'ee come from my little house?" and he said, sulkily that he had not, that he had awakened to find her gone and blundered home in the dark but had not slept a wink because he was worried about what had happened. "It was that awful stuff of your mother's," he excused himself, "and I . . . I'm sorry, Hazel, upon my honour I am! It was a cad's trick and that's a fact!"

She was puzzled by his troubled expression and far more so by his words, for there was nothing, as far as she could remember, to be sorry about. His manner, however, must have enlisted her sympathy for she took his hand as they moved along the path towards the squirrel oak, saying, "Lord, Ikey, what's 'ee long-faced about, boy? You on'y got tipsy, didden 'ee?"

"I . . . I don't mean about getting drunk on that stuff," he protested, indignantly, "I mean . . . well . . . you must *know* what I mean! I wasn't so drunk that I can't remember what happened and it was the first time ever, you understand?"

"Well," she said, mildly, " 'twas first time for me but what of it? It baint nothing to worry over, be it?"

For several minutes he could make no reply. The gulf between them, between her view of life and the tight, circumscribed code of people who lived in houses, sat at tables and made polite conversation with one another was unbridgeable and the realisation of this renewed his feelings of guilt and apprehension. He said at length, "Look, Hazel love, I . . . I've got to go away, I've got to study to be a soldier and I'll be gone some time! That's why I came to meet you—I thought, well, that maybe you'd think I was staying away from you because of what happened."

She was undismayed by the news. Ever since she had known him he had always been going and coming and the passage of time meant very little to her. He had been with her last evening, he was here now and would be gone tomorrow but he would come back, sooner or later, as he always did and today she felt particularly sure of him. They stopped on the edge of the wood where the heavy timber began its march down the slope to the mere.

"You'll come zoon as 'ee gets 'ome?"

"Yes, of course I will." Suddenly, and inexplicably he felt totally reassured and with reassurance came tenderness and concern. "Hazel," he said, urgently, "why don't you go home and live with Meg and the girls? And why don't you go back to school at Miss Willoughby's? You can't always live in the woods, you know, you're grown up now!"

She said wonderingly, "Go back home? Wi' all that ole racket? Go back to skuel? Now whyfore should I do that?"

"Because I should like you to," he said, "because I want you to . . . I want you to read and write like everyone else. Will you think about it while I'm away?"

"Ooahh," she said, lightly, "mebbe I will, tho' I doan zee much zense in it! Dornee like me as I be?"

"Yes," he said desperately, "of course I like you but . . . well . . . I'm thinking about what's to become of you if you go on living rough and wandering about the way you do."

She interpreted this as caution on his part against the possibility of

547

some other young man in the Valley waylaying her and demanding oi her what he had been granted and the thought made her smile.

"Giddon," she said scornfully, "I baint afraid o' no one an' a worn't let none of 'em come near me, same as I told 'ee last night! I c'n run faster an' any humping gurt man in the Valley and I keeps meself to meself, mostly! Will 'ee be goin' outalong now? Or shall us go to my li'l house?"

"I'm going now," he said, sighing, and she said, "Oo-ah," putting up her face to be kissed.

He kissed her gently. Not, as he had promised himself, on the cheek but on the mouth. Her breath was as sweet as the morning air and he held her for a moment until he began to tremble again and stood back, dropping his hands to his sides and looking at the ground, but she did not seem to notice his confusion and said, gaily, "Well, dornee forget then, zoon as 'ee comes back. I'll save what's left in the jar for 'ee. T'won't 'urt fer waitin'!" Then, as in their early days, she was gone, melting into the foliage and he was alone, as bewildered as when he set out but no longer weighed down by shame and fear. He thought, "There's nobody like her, nobody the least like her but I wouldn't have her any different so to hell with everything!" He went slowly down the field to the sunken lane and into the orchard by the stile.

CHAPTER THREE

I

CLAIRE must have set her heart on going to London for the Coronation. She had spent the long autumn afternoons of her pregnancy turning the pages of catalogues of children's emporiums, paying particular attention to little girls' frocks and bonnets and when her third child was born, towards the end of the old year, she was delighted, although not much surprised, when she heard Doctor Maureen exclaim, 'Glory to God, it's a girl!'

Paul was not in the district when the baby arrived, about 2 o'clock on an unseasonably mild afternoon. He had accepted Maureen's assurances that the event would not occur until the New Year and had embarked, with James Grenfell, on a whirlwind tour of the areas north of Paxtonbury to fight a second election within twelve months. He had been reluctant to go but both doctor and wife persuaded him, the one because, in her own words, "I hate having husbands under my feet at a time when they are less use than a wet clout!", the other because she knew that Grenfell would be fighting the battle of his life and had real need of Paul.

Local passions over the People's Budget had not cooled throughout the summer and Grenfell regained lost ground after the announcement that a Women's Suffrage Bill was to be placed before Parliament; so Paul rode off in the trap, promising to be home before New Year's Day.

The baby gave them very little trouble although she was a plump little thing, tipping the scales an ounce short of seven pounds, more than either of the twins had weighed at birth. She had, Claire noted, an abundance of dark hair, darker even than Paul's and her eyes, now cornflower blue, looked as if they intended to stay blue and not change to grey, as had the eyes of the boys within six months of birth.

"Well, Maureen," she said later that night, "you have to admit she's pretty and Paul will certainly spoil her. He'll be in a real tizzy when he comes home and finds we managed without him."

Maureen said that after breakfast next morning she would post Thirza to watch for Paul at the gates, so about 10 a.m. Thirza was

549

despatched to the ford to give warning of the Squire's approach. An hour or so later he came spanking along the river road at about twice the pony's normal pace and seeing Thirza hopping about between the great stone pillars, shouted, "Has anything happened? Is Mrs. Craddock all right?" and Thirza, gasped, "It's a girl, Squire! Prettiest li'l maid you ever did zee!" and without a word he dragged her into the trap and drove furiously up the drive to the forecourt where he left Thirza, now giggling hysterically, to lead pony and trap round to the yard while he went up the stairs three at a time and thumped on the bedroom door, as if alerting occupants of a burning building.

Maureen came out scolding him for his impatience, and telling him that, as the father of four, he ought to know better but then she relented and said, laughing, "As God's my witness she's an angel from heaven, the prettiest baby any of us ever saw, and there's no doubt who's the father! Wait a minute, lad, I'll tell Nurse and you can go in, for they're both doing marvellously."

A moment later he was looking down at the child with an awe that he had not experienced on either of the previous occasions. Thirza and Maureen had not exaggerated. There was nothing of the brick-red, puckered look about this child; she had perfectly formed features, a peach bloom complexion and exquisite little hands and feet. He stood gazing down at her so long that Claire said, "Well, don't I count any more?" and although aware that she was teasing him he blurted his apologies and kissed her a dozen times, saying, triumphantly, "By God, Claire, she's a treasure! She really is! I've always had to pretend to like newborn babies but this one. . . ! Damn it, I'd quite resigned myself to another lump of a boy! Did you have a bad time? Maureen swore she wouldn't arrive for days—I wouldn't have thought of going if I'd dreamed you were so near!"

"She came very quickly and it was about ten times as easy as the twins," Claire reassured him, "so much so that I can't still persuade myself that it's all over. Do you know, Paul, I've got the pleasantest feeling about her. Something tells me she'll never be any trouble to any of us! There's something . . . well . . . something reasonable about her and I'm glad she was born earlier than we reckoned because 1910 was a wonderful year for us and what happens in 1911 is anybody's guess."

He said, stroking her hair, and wondering at both her radiance and resilience, "Every year with you is a good year, Claire, and 1911 will be better than 1910, more sensational anyway, for James is getting us places on the House of Commons stand for the Coronation. Had you forgotten that bargain we made at Ikey's Sports Day?"

"Certainly not," she said, "in fact I've already picked out a dress! It's in the catalogue on the study table, with the corner of the page turned down, so look at it and tell me you approve. But how can James get us seats unless he's re-elected?"

"He'll be re-elected all right," Paul said grimly, "we've got them on the run again! A year on the local doorsteps has worked wonders and I'll wager he goes in with five hundred majority!"

The nurse came back then and shooed him out. Downstairs, before she dashed off to complete her rounds, Maureen told him over a stiff brandy that the birth had indeed proved one of the most casual in her experience and said, raising her glass, "Well, here's long life to the pair of you and that's no conventional toast either! She's a healthy, happy girl and she's made you a wonderful wife, so don't forget to count your blessings, lad!"

"I'm not likely to," he said seriously, "as John could tell you. You never did meet Grace so you can't imagine how different they are but the odd thing is I don't think I should have ever fully appreciated Claire if I hadn't been so much in love with Grace. There's a conundrum to work into one of your fancy theories."

"It's not much of a conundrum," Maureen said chuckling but refused to be drawn and hurried away, promising to send John up to "wet the baby's head" immediately after supper.

Paul sat by the log fire stroking the retriever's head and feeling his hand nuzzled for she loved having her ears fondled. The dog was his one permanent reminder of Grace and of the hours they had spent together in this room. Simon, her child, had never interested her much but the dog she had sent him had always remained hers and although she had long since attached herself to Paul she always behaved as if she half-expected Grace to walk through the door again.

It seemed strange to him, sitting here alone with Claire and her new baby overhead and the house quiet after the turmoil of the last two days, that his thoughts should centre not upon Claire but Grace, whose ghost had never been banished from this particular room, although it seemed to have vanished from all other parts of the house. He wondered vaguely what had happened to her, if she had tired of passing in and out of Holloway under the Government's Cat and Mouse act, or whether, by now, she had another husband, perhaps a fellow campaigner who could share her implacable hatred of the old society. He thought, "I wonder if Claire realises how much she owes Grace and how they would behave to one another if they ever came face to face? Claire probably thinks of her, if at all, as a crank, whereas Grace would certainly despise Claire for her domesticity and deference to men. For all that I'm glad Grenfell and his minority have forced the Cabinet to recognise the right of people as intelligent as Grace to vote," and he heaved himself up and fetched his beloved estate record to which he usually turned on these occasions. He wrote, on the last page of the 1910 Section, "*About 2 p.m. on December 29th my wife presented me with a daughter weighing six pounds 15 ounces; she has dark hair and blue eyes*" and then fell to pondering a name embodying the tranquil temperament Claire had prophesied for the child. A string of Biblical names presented themselves — Deborah, Judith, Naomi and Sarah, but none of them appealed and, finally he hit upon the most English of all names, Mary, and savoured it, murmuring, "Mary — Mary, Claire, Craddock", deciding that it had a roundness and simplicity that pleased him. He wrote, feeling sure Claire would confirm his choice, "*I am calling her 'Mary'*" and then, perhaps infected by the inconsequence of Claire's entries, "*Everyone about here describes her as a rare pretty li'l maid and so she be!*", signing his name under the frivolous entry.

The new year opened in triumph, for Paul's prophecy was fulfilled and Grenfell was returned with over a thousand majority. The sardonic Captain Owen-Hixon disappeared like the Devil in a pantomime but the new Lord Gilroy took his defeat very handsomely, congratulating Paul at the declaration of the poll and promising him "a return match" in the years ahead. "Sour grapes notwithstanding I don't envy your chap," he said, "or any Government taking office today! They have so many hot potatoes they can't help but drop some of them! They can't get a clear majority without leaning over backwards to bribe the Irish Home Rulers or the Labourites and what with Ulster, Home Rule, the reform of the Lords, the Navy League outcry, that ass of a Kaiser and the suffragettes, I wouldn't wonder if the more thoughtful among them isn't damned sorry they won!"

The prospects of stormy sessions ahead, however, did not seem to depress James when Paul drove him across the moor to catch the connection for the Cornish express, at Sorrel Halt. A whole year on home ground had revitalised him and his increased majority had boosted his morale, and yet, Paul told himself, he was a very different

James from the man who had gone blithely to London after the 1904 bye-election. The struggle to relate conscience and humanity with the cut-and-thrust of life in the House showed in his face, deeply lined at forty-two, and in patches of grey at his temples and he made a jocular reference to the wear and tear of his nerves as they paced the little platform awaiting the train. "I've always said you have the best of it, Paul, guarding the grass roots down here and I don't suppose you'd care to change places, would you?"

"I'd sooner change places with Smut Potter or Norman Eveleigh," Paul said. "I haven't been near London since I went there to try and bring Grace home; that was more than five years ago.'

"Well, you'll be combing the straw from your hair in June," James reminded him, "Claire is holding you to your promise to bring her up for the Coronation."

"Oh, I'll do that," Paul told him, "for I can't get out of it now but it'll be a three-day stay and no longer. A drive round to see the decorations, a day watching the toing and froing and another for Claire to show off her new clothes — then home, with the harvest just round the corner!"

"Well," James chuckled, "you were a born townsman but they always say converts are more catholic than the Pope! Here's the train, so good-bye and again, thank you for your loyalty!"

From his seat on the box of the trap Paul watched the train round the long curve and then walked the cob over the moor, congratulating himself on his luck.

II

They had booked a small hotel overlooking St. James' Park and on the day of their arrival, whilst Claire was busy unpacking, Paul sat on the balcony and looked down on the evening idlers moving slowly along the wide paths and across the acres of parched grass. There seemed to be hundreds of thousands of them and the bunting entwining the lamp-posts and the gilded arches catching the last rays of sun in the Mall, reminded him of the day he had crossed a city preparing for Edward's coronation nine years ago. He thought, "I was young and green in those days, with no more than instinct to guide me in leaving this stew and breaking new ground! I hadn't even made up my mind to buy Shallowford then, but now it seems as if I was born there and my father before me! Well, a devil of a lot of water has passed Codsall bridge since those days. People were still flaying poor old Kruger, and Lloyd George, now turning the country upside down with his precious budget, was no more than a comic turn with the Welsh gift of the gab! I wonder if Claire ever hankers after city life? She tried it for a spell but she soon came home and although she says we're developing into a pair of bumpkins I don't believe she really likes cities any more than I do!", and he heard her call from the dressing room and came in to ask if she wanted to go out before dinner.

"Go out? Why, of course I do!" she called, still invisible, "why else do you suppose I've dressed myself up?"

"I didn't know you had," he said. "Come out and let's have a look at you."

"Close your eyes then," she said and he closed them, hearing the pleasant swish of her skirts as she moved into the bedroom and giving a gasp of astonishment that ended in a shout of laughter which he hastily choked back when he saw her frown.

"What's so funny about me?" she demanded, tartly for her, but he moved round her once or twice and was no longer disposed to laugh but rather to wonder how a woman who so seldom got an opportunity of dressing for the town, should succeed so spectacularly when the chance offered itself.

"By George, you're absolutely sensational, Claire!" he told her, sincerely, "I only laughed out of shock! I've never seen you looking like that, not even on your wedding day!"

She was a summer's evening study of white and apple green, with a high-waisted skirt flowing away into a whipped-up torrent of sprigged lace that foamed out behind her like a small, neat wake. Over a tight bodice she wore a green velvet hussar jacket, with frogged lapels and a stiff, turned-up collar. She had on a huge Gainsborough hat, one of the largest hats he had ever seen, worn at a tilt and crowned with green organdie gathered in half-a-dozen loosely tied bows and she was wearing the pearl necklace he had given her after the birth of the twins. In her right hand, clothed in an elbow-length suède glove, she carried a long-handled parasol with a white sword-knot swinging from it. He had noticed, of late, that she had been putting on weight but she was obviously well corseted under her coronation regalia for her figure seemed to him quite perfect, the waist as neat as the day he had first seen her in the yard of High Coombe farm, although even the merciless corset could not conceal the roundness of the hips and the generous contours of the bust. She blushed a little under his scrutiny and said, regretfully, "I didn't realise how much I'd put on since Mary's arrival! I ordered this dress in advance and I suppose it ought to be let out a little."

"Rubbish," he comforted her, "you've only put a little on in the right places and you don't have to apologise to me. I like a woman to look like one, especially when she's my wife! My only complaint is that the hat hides your lovely hair!"

"I could hardly watch the Coronation bareheaded," she said. "After all, it's only once in a lifetime and I don't suppose we shall ever see another king crowned." Then she laughed, adding, "Do stop staring, darling, it can't be that sensational! I bought every stitch of it in Paxtonbury," but he told her that he enjoyed staring and so would everyone else when they went out but that he wished they hadn't got to go out, because she not only looked vice-regal but very provocative indeed.

"I daresay," she told him, "but I'm not available for more than a chaste kiss right now and anyway my breathing is restricted, so do please behave yourself!"

"Well, temporarily," he promised but drew her gently to him, complaining that the corset she was wearing converted her lovely rump into a rampart. She laughed at that and kissed him warmly saying, "Oh, we *are* lucky, Paul! I do love you so much! And this is for bringing me up, because I know you'd far sooner have stayed home!", and she kissed him again, this time on the mouth but skipped away at once sensing that another kiss or two would make him unmanageable.

They went out, walking sedately along the edge of the lake and thence into the Mall, now crammed with sightseers, and from here to the Palace, to stare at the railings and royal standard, and then back again along Constitution Hill to Piccadilly, unrecognisable under a thousand flags and pennants and huge, cardboard portraits of the King and Queen, printed in garish colours and wired against the tug of the breeze. She was so gay, and looked so desirable, that he felt they were well launched on a second honeymoon and Claire, when he told her this, admitted that she was, in fact, far more ready to enjoy herself than she had been on her real honeymoon in Anglesey, four years before.

"Now why should that be for you weren't a particularly nervous bride," he said. "As a matter of fact I was agreeably surprised now I come to think of it."

"Well, I started out terrified I can assure you," she admitted,

555

"because I couldn't hide the fact from myself that I was a country daisy succeeding an orchid! I suppose it didn't show because . . . well . . . you didn't rush me! You probably don't remember, Paul, but you were very patient with me.'

"Was I?" he said as they passed into the foyer of their hotel and the commissionaire saluted. "Well, I'm not likely to be so patient on my second honeymoon, my dear," and because it was obvious from the doorman's smirk that he had overheard, Claire whispered urgently, "Shhh, for heaven's sake! I shall blush scarlet when I see that man in the morning."

"It's my belief that you'll have good cause to!" he said, laughing, and in this mood they went in to dinner.

As usual, he was soon heavily asleep. She knew no one who could drop off to sleep so quickly and sleep so soundly, notwithstanding the unfamiliar symphony of rattling carriage wheels and honking motors that was such a contrast to the midnight stillness of Shallowford. She did not feel sleepy, in spite of all the wine they had drunk and the boisterous interlude that had followed. Always, at times like this, she liked to lie still in his arms, and smile at herself and at him and as the increasing flow of traffic rolled under the window she thought, "He really does behave as though he married me this morning! It can't be my new clothes, in spite of the impact they made on him, for he could hardly wait for me to take them off!", and she chuckled, wriggling from under his arms and sitting up, hugging her knees and feeling happier than she ever remembered. It was a very wonderful thing, she thought, to have attained the degree of balance and intimacy that was theirs and had been theirs since the very beginning, and her mind went back to the day soon after his arrival in the Valley, when she had set out to capture him without knowing or even caring what kind of man he really was, or what qualifications she had for marriage to someone with his unusual sense of purpose and singlemindedness. She was glad, looking back, that there had been that near-fatal rift in their association and for the first time in her married life she could contemplate his first wife without jealousy, reflecting that she probably owed her a good deal for seasoning him as man and lover. She must, Claire thought, have been a sensual little minx, for the man now asleep beside her had very little in common with the shy, rather gawky youth she had enticed down by the mere. All his boyishness and uncertainty had been ironed out of him during his first marriage

556

and the unhappy period that followed it yet it had left him with no kind of a grudge against women, as might have been expected. He was masterful but, to her mind, accomplished as a lover and what was more unusual unselfishly so. That, in itself, was a contradiction to all that young women of her generation had been taught to expect of a man once he had got a woman to bed, for how many husbands in the Valley regarded lovemaking as a mutual experience or took pains to ensure that it was so? Precious few, she would say, for the dice was heavily loaded against her sex in this respect, yet it was not so in their marriage and for this she would never cease to be grateful. She leaned over and kissed him lightly and wriggled back into his embrace and as she drifted over the edge of sleep she thought, 'If we go on like this I shall have a baby every year and lose my figure altogether but I don't care a row of beans! Not even if they arrive in pairs, like Andy and Steve!"

The next morning they toured the city from Aldgate Pump to Marble Arch and when they had had their fill of sightseeing he asked her if she would care to renew her acquaintance with Uncle Franz and see the scrapyard in all its squalid glory.

"It hardly qualifies as a Coronation attraction," he said, "but the Valley owes it a good deal. If I'd had my way I should have cut myself off from it altogether and it would have taken all of twenty years to put the estate in good heart."

She said she would enjoy meeting Franz and spending an hour among his old iron, so they crossed the river and drove through the sweltering streets to the yard, where Paul noticed that there had been some extensive changes.

The place was as forbidding as ever but there was a certain grandeur about its disorder and multiplicity of its pyramids of junk. Several more acres had been enclosed on the far side and the fires now burned in braziers, mounted on brick hearths. Uncle Franz's shack had given place to a red-brick building with waggon-sheds alongside and among the carts Paul noticed two or three cumbersome motor vehicles, shaped like barges on wheels and called, he was told, "lorries". There was an air of efficiency about the place that had not been there in the earlier, more casual era. Doors in the office building had wooden plaques with "*Foreman*", "*Weigh In*", "*Chief Sorter*" and "*Cash*" painted on them; he said to Franz:

"My word, things must be looking up! It used to be just a frowsy dump and now it's a slum empire!"

557

Franz was his usual chirrupy self, extending to Claire the same Continental courtliness as he had shown Grace and he amused her very much by gravely kissing her hand and telling her that, whilst he was grubbing among scrap in a brick jungle the luckier and more discerning Paul had found "A pearl beyond price in the provinces". Paul said, "Don't take the slightest notice of him, Claire! He talks like that to every woman he meets under sixty! It comes from a lifetime of coaxing housewives to empty their attics!" but to Franz he said, seriously, "You seem to have made a lot of changes round here and I must say the place looks a lot less sleazy than before. Have you taken in more land over there by the viaduct?"

"Another four acres," Franz said casually, "and business was never better, my boy! Thank God for Kaiser Wilhelm and his shining armour! He's the man who put new life into the scrap industry! I don't suppose you ever look at the balance sheets I send you?"

"No," Claire told him, "he doesn't, only the dividend slips and even those have to be brought to his attention by the bank manager."

"Well, you might be interested to know that our turnover last year was treble that of our best South African War year," said Franz. "If this naval race continues until either us or Germany goes bankrupt you'll die a rich man, Paul, providing, of course, you don't pour the whole of it into those Devon quicksands of yours!"

"At least I do something practical with it," retorted Paul, slightly nettled by the old man's irony, but Claire said, quickly, "Don't tease him about the Valley, Uncle Franz! Ordinarily his sense of humour is good but that's his sensitive spot!" and Paul, suddenly ashamed of his huffiness, was grateful to her for her intervention.

They took Franz back to the hotel for tea and afterwards to a theatre, a musical extravaganza that Paul privately thought ridiculous but which Claire obviously enjoyed. During the interval, as he and Franz smoked a cigar in the foyer, the old man said, affably, "Well, Paul, I must say you should be congratulated on your taste for wives! She's just as pretty as Grace and more tolerant of your eccentricities! You're obviously a happy man."

"Yes I am," Paul admitted readily, "and, in a way, I have to thank you for it, Franz, for I don't suppose I should have bestirred myself to try again if you hadn't jogged my elbow! Claire is a wonderful wife and mother and there's no fear of her disappearing into the blue to join the Militants! Have you seen anything of Grace?"

"Oh, once or twice, for an hour or so," Franz replied, rather too airily Paul thought, "she pops across the river to collect her subscription."

"What subscription? She gets her allowance regularly, doesn't she?"

"Oh, I'm not referring to the hundred a year you allow her," Franz said, laughing, "I mean the subscription I make to the Sacred Cause."

"You subscribe to suffragette funds?"

"Certainly I do, twenty guineas annually!"

"Good God!" exclaimed Paul, genuinely astonished, "I didn't think you cared two straws about votes for women."

"I don't," Franz said, "but I like to see politicians harried and anyway, I admire their spirit."

The thought crossed Paul's mind that the real reason for the wily old Croat's support of a movement that was embarrassing a Liberal Government lay much deeper than this, and had far more to do with his preference for a government inclined to spend even more upon armaments and thus, by inference, upon scrap, but he only said, "How is she, Franz? Still as fanatical?"

"More so I'd say," Franz replied but no longer joking, "their frontline fighters have been getting a very rough handling up here. They don't put everything in the papers."

Paul was going to tell him about Grenfell's championship of the movement and of the photographic evidence he had seen but at that moment the intermission bell sounded and they rejoined Claire in the stalls. The old man refused an invitation to accompany them on the morrow and see the procession from the M.P.s' stand, so they watched him drive off across Leicester Square to his Portman Street home, after he had promised to make another appointment by telephone before they returned home at the end of the week.

That night, when they were alone, Claire said, suddenly, "You can't help liking Uncle Franz, Paul, but . . ." and she hesitated, as though fearing to offend him.

"Under his charm he's rather frightening; is that what you were going to say?"

"Yes, it was, but maybe all people who make money are frightening."

"Well," Paul said, "I don't suppose we should be sanctimonious about it. We put the money he makes to good use in the Valley and have been damned glad of it. I daresay we could struggle along without it now but it seems to me that to reject it would be a rather pompous gesture; all the same, I would do it, if you had strong feelings about it."

She made no immediate reply, sitting on the dressing stool brushing her long hair, so he added, "Well? *Have* you?"

"No," she said, as though she wasn't altogether sure, "but the time could come when I might have. Do you suppose all this battleship building could lead to anything serious; to people actually killing one another, as they did in that war between Russia and Japan?"

"No," he said, "I don't, for in my opinion it's all a game of bluff played by men like Franz and by others, bigger and more ruthless than him! I don't think the Kaiser ever wants to use his dreadnoughts; he simply has them so that he can strut about the decks in fancy dress but our people take him seriously—or they pretend to. No major power could afford that kind of war for more than a week or so!"

"Well, I hope not," Claire said, "but the next time I see Franz I shall ask him that one!"

In the event they did not see Franz again. Within forty-eight hours of parting from him they were on the way home, bolting very much as Paul had bolted six years before. The Coronation procession proved even more spectacular than the newspapers had promised. Watching the cohorts of splendidly uniformed men march past, and hearing the deep-throated roar of the densely-packed spectators as the Royal coach and its escort of Household Cavalry came in view, Paul was gripped by a sense of climax about the spectacle, as though it symbolised the extreme high tide of the Victorian and Edwardian eras and had been deliberately staged to advertise the enormous thrust and weight of British Imperialism. It had seemed strident enough in the days of the Transvaal War but now, to him at all events, it was even more vociferous and glittering. He said, aloud, "My God! It's like a Roman triumph!" but his voice was lost in the wave of sound that seemed to rock the tall buildings and a moment later the coach and escort were gone, the roar moving forward like a boosted echo.

"Did you say something, dear?" Claire asked when the next military band was still a hundred yards off and Paul said nothing of any consequence but suddenly he felt homesick for the simplicity of a national celebration in the Valley, attended by no more than two hundred people and patronised by the beaming Henry Pitts and the biblical shepherd twins, who asked no more of a national holiday than a tug-of-war between "Outalong" and "Downalong".

The next afternoon they were given tea on the terrace at Westminster by a sprucely-dressed James Grenfell, who seemed optimistic about the prospects of getting ahead with the Liberal programme, provided nothing disturbed the existing arrangement with the Irish members and Labourites, whose support gave them their overall majority in the House. They were standing near the West door of the great hall on the point of saying good-bye when Paul saw a party of police dash by, coming from the direction of Westminster Bridge and disappear, whistles shrilling, in the direction of the railings fronting the House.

"Hullo, what's happening there?" he asked and James, looking anxious and uncomfortable, said, "Probably another raid by the Militants, their headquarters are just across the Square and this happens pretty frequently now that the Suffrage Bill looks like being talked out. I'll get a cab, Paul, you should get Claire away."

Although he did not say so it was obvious that he felt there was more than a likelihood of Grace being among the demonstrators and Paul, sharing this misgiving, said, "All right, James, let's get away!" but unexpectedly Claire spoke up, facing them and saying, "*Why?* Why do we have to turn our backs on it? We backed you in two elections on this issue, James, and I think we ought to see for ourselves!" Then, as neither made a reply, "It doesn't matter if Grace *is* there! We ought to judge the issue on more than photographs, James!"

James said, uneasily, "I suppose she's right, Paul, it might be important for you to see what I've seen often enough in the last year or so," so they moved towards the vortex of the disturbance under the statue of Richard I but were soon obliged to link arms to prevent being separated by the crowds now moving in from all directions.

"Sometimes it's no more than a scuffle," James said but they saw at once that it was more than a scuffle today, for the whole area in front of Parliament was boiling like the scene of a revolution, with mounted police laying about them with rolled-up capes and foot police fighting to seal the area in front of the statue where two prison vans were drawn up with doors open and police on the steps. Then a larger section of the crowd swept in from the far side of the Square and they were all three, together with a bearded police sergeant and two younger officers, washed back against the railings, the sergeant losing his temper and shouting to his men, "Get *through* to them, damn you! Use your fists if you have to!" and after a renewed heave Paul was parted from the others and carried closer to the vans as the police drove a passage through the mob enclosing him in the cordon.

Here, the ugliness of the struggle was revealed to him far more vividly than in James' photographs and scenes were being enacted

561

that he would never have associated with an English political demonstration. The cordon re-formed behind him and although he looked everywhere he could see no sign of James or Claire and forgot them as he was swept closer to the heart of the riot. He saw about a score of women, most of them well-dressed, grappling with as many police and plain-clothes men and there was no evidence of docility on the part of the suffragettes, or of chivalry on the part of their assailants. It might have been a police descent upon a thieves' kitchen, south of the river. Fists were flailing, hats and umbrellas flying, helmets skidding under the feet of horses and, here and there, police and women were rolling on the ground in a flurry of blue tunics and white petticoats. Paul stood aghast at the brutishness of the spectacle. He saw a middle-aged woman propelled up the steps of the Maria with a punch in the back aimed by a straw-hatted man whose face was distorted with fury and whose nose streamed blood; he saw that one van was already full to overflowing for suddenly a young woman, hair streaming over her shoulders and mouth open in a soundless scream, appeared for an instant at the door before being dragged back by someone inside; he saw an elderly man, whom he identified as a sympathiser by the rosette he wore, wave a banner on which the single word "Votes" was distinguishable and then a mounted policeman tore the banner from him and began using it as a stave to clear the struggling pedestrians from the area about his horse. Then, almost under his feet, he saw a young woman in grey, crouched on hands and knees, hatless and with a mass of dark hair masking her face as she contracted herself to avoid being trampled.

He recognised her as Grace even before a young, helmetless policeman seized her by the shoulders and half raised her and he grabbed the man just as someone laid hold of him from behind, so that all four of them, locked in a grotesque chain, lurched and cannoned into the group struggling around the remains of the banner. The din was hellish for by now the cordon had broken and the crowd, predominantly men, were pressing in from all sides so that the van lifted on two wheels and would have overturned but for the plinth of the statue. A certainty that, in a matter of moments, Grace would be crushed to death in the mêlée, gave him the impetus to shoulder the young policeman aside and break free of the restraining hand on his collar. His hat flew off and his collar burst loose but he steadied himself by shooting out his arms and bracing himself against the plinth so that, for a moment or two, he formed an arch over Grace who now lay flat on her face, the man who had been holding the banner crouching almost on top of her. At that moment mounted police moved forward three abreast, clearing a small space under the statue and an inspector, running round the plinth, shouted to Paul, "Get her on her feet, man!" and he shouted back, on impulse, "She's nothing to do with the damned riot! She's my wife, we've been in the House . . . !" and taking advantage of the momentary lull, tore out his wallet and flourished Grenfell's card under the inspector's nose. The man glanced at it and shouted, "Hold hard, there!" as if he had been in the hunting field and to Paul, "Work your way behind the statue! I'll get the van moving! If some of these fools are run over so much the worse for them!"

Paul lifted Grace as the van began to plough through the mob, moving diagonally across the Square so that soon there was space enough to edge round behind the statue where there was a measure of sanctuary after the crowd had streamed away in pursuit of the vehicle. The inspector had forced his way round in their wake and said, breathlessly, "You can vouch for her? She's your wife you say?" and Paul said, savagely, "Yes, and I'm damned if I ever thought I should be ashamed to be English! What the hell has happened to people? Has everyone gone raving mad?"

"It's those women, sir," the inspector said, "it happens day after day but we weren't prepared seeing it's Coronation week. We thought they would have given over until the celebrations were done. Is she hurt?"

His manner was friendly but by no means anxious until James appeared, also waving a card and announcing that he was an M.P. and intended raising the subject of the riot in the House at the first opportunity. As soon as the link between the unconscious woman and a Member of the House was established the policeman's attitude changed abruptly and he said, a little desperately, "I hope you don't hold me responsible, sir! She was right in the thick of it, and so was this gentleman! You can see for yourself the hopelessness of our job when they start trouble at peak hours! They've been warned often enough, God knows." James said, with a glance at Paul indicating that he was to stay out of the discussion, "Well, this one wasn't, Inspector! I was showing her where English laws are made when this happened!" and the man said, "I'm very sorry, sir, but how can we distinguish? Let's take a look at her; maybe it's only a faint!" And then, as all three of them peered at the limp figure in Paul's arms, Claire rejoined them and the crowd melted away, running towards the Abbey. A helmet-less policeman, who seemed to have sized up the situation, bustled up and said, "I've got a cab, sir! Over there by the Members' entrance!" and the inspector, giving him a look of approval, said, "Good work, Crutchley! Get her in first and look for your helmet afterwards!"

James remained for a moment with the inspector while Paul fol-lowed the constable across the littered paving stones to the Members' entrance and climbed into a four-wheeler. As they edged through the door he saw Grace open her eyes, then close them again, rather too swiftly. He thought, "Damn it, I don't believe she's hurt at all! She's just using us to make the most of the situation!" and instead of telling the cabby to drive to the nearest casualty ward he gave him the name of their hotel, saying, "All right, Officer, I realise you couldn't help it and I'm a witness to that!" The man saluted and looked very relieved, wiping the sweat and grime from his forehead as James rejoined them.

"Well," he said, as they moved slowly across to Whitehall, "I've given him something to think about but I did it with my tongue in my cheek! The poor devils are in a hopeless position. It's the politicians not the police who should be censured for this kind of thing! Is she hurt, do you think?"

Grace herself answered the question by opening her eyes and sub-jecting all three of them to an ironic scrutiny. There was, Paul re-flected, an element of glee in her expression but as soon as she saw Claire she wriggled out of Paul's grasp, tossed back her hair and said, carelessly, "Well, that's one up for us anyway! I'll wager that inspec-tor has a sleepless night or two! Thank you, James, it was clever of you, and you too, Paul!" and to their amazement she plunged her hands into a sachet fastened to her waistband, extracted a handful of hairpins and began to tidy her hair.

James said, with a note of mild reproof, "I guessed you were spoof-ing all the time, you little devil! But he didn't, did you, Paul?"

"No, I'm damned if I did!" Paul growled, feeling very foolish and avoiding Claire's glance. "She looked to me as if she was heading straight for martyrdom! The next time I'll do what I intended to do then—keep well clear of a mess like that!" and then he remembered the woman who had been punched in the back and the elderly man with the banner banged over the head with his staff and suddenly he felt neither foolish nor irritated, but almost proud of the way she had used them to save herself from arrest and another spell in gaol and also to hit back at her persecutors. He noticed too that she was much

564

thinner than the last time he had seen her, with her pleasing round-ness gone and a strained, white face that reminded him of an under-nourished adolescent. Her clothes, well-cut and once smart, were now wildly disordered. The shoulder of the blouse had been ripped across, exposing the strap of her petticoat and her skirt was stained with patches of manure and road dust. He said, with awe in his voice, "Is it worth all that? Isn't there some other way?" and James replied, quietly, "They've tried all the other ways, Paul," and a look of under-standing passed between Grace and James so that Paul felt shut out of their confidence.

Claire said, as the cab stopped at the hotel, "You'd best come in and tidy up, Grace. Then we can all have tea," and when Grace hesitated she added, laughing, "You really do need a wash and brush up! They'll probably arrest you if you go home in that condition," where-upon they all got out and whilst Paul was paying off the cab the two women went through the foyer, causing the commissionaire to open his eyes wide as they passed him on their way to the stairs.

The men remained below, James ordering two stiff whiskies, while Paul went into the cloakroom to make what repairs he could on his burst collar. When he returned James said with a grin, "Leave 'em to it, Paul, they understand one another well enough!" and Paul thought that perhaps he was right for during the cab ride he had been aware of a curious intimacy between the women. He said, "Very well, but afterwards, I'm going straight home, James! Every time I come here something damned unpleasant happens and from now on I'm avoid-ing this blasted city as if the Great Plague was still raging!" and James told him he was probably well advised to do just that but from now on he hoped Paul would support universal suffrage with more enthusiasm.

"Yes, I'll do that, James," Paul said, slowly, "but out of disgust, rather than conviction! I never thought to see Englishmen behave like that towards demonstrators. On the Continent, perhaps, but not here and not against women, however misguided! As a matter of fact I'm half-persuaded that people like Grace enjoy it in a way. Is that prejudice on my part, would you say?"

"No, not entirely," James said, sipping his drink, "but even if they do I don't see why they should apologise for it. There's self-satisfac-tion in fighting that hard for something you believe in deeply and sincerely and they'll win, quite soon I believe."

"It can't be soon enough for me," Paul grumbled, "for right now I feel like a bath and not simply to wash the dirt from my body!"

While Grace was in the dressing-room Claire sat in the bedroom sewing up the rent in her blouse and when this was done she set about beating the dust from the heavy folds of the skirt and sponging away the great yellow stain. She worked methodically, her mind contemplating the unlikely situation, that seemed to her as improbable as a story in a chain-library novel but it did not embarrass her, for instinct told her that Grace had long since renounced any claim on Paul. When she came out drying her hair with a bath robe, she studied her dispassionately, noting her boyish figure, and the prominence of her collar-bone as she slipped on her blouse and stood before the long mirror tidying her hair. There was hardly a trace, Claire thought, of the trim, self-assured young woman who had entertained her to tea at Shallowford in the first year of her marriage. All her curves had disappeared and with them her indifferent, half-vacant air that had seemed at that time close to boredom. Now the lines of the face were taut, the cheek-bones prominent and every movement she made whilst brushing and underpinning her hair was crisp and decisive, as though physical energy was something to be carefully husbanded. Only yesterday, Claire recalled, she had thought of this woman as sensual but she changed her mind now and wondered if dedication to a political cause, to the extent that this woman had dedicated herself, demanded the discipline of a nun entering an order. She thought, "There must be enormous strength of will there for I know myself well enough to realise that I couldn't exchange life with Paul, or the security of the Valley for an abstract idea. I might have done once but not now, not having enjoyed a man's vigour and protection, not having borne him children as she bore him a child. She has resilience, too, she isn't in the least put out by this turn of events and seems almost to take it for granted," and she began to comprehend some of the sources of the failure of the marriage, reasoning that, beside Grace, Paul was an adolescent, with an adolescent's dependence upon flattery. She said, as she handed Grace her skirt, "Would you think it impertinent of me if I asked you if you were happier now, Grace?" and Grace stopped in the act of stepping into her skirt, smiled and said, with the utmost candour, "Certainly not, providing you'll be equally frank with me!"

"I've always been grateful to you," Claire said slowly, "and I don't mind admitting that. There was a time when I was very jealous but that's done with, I'm not jealous now, any more than you are of me! I'm happy and I think Paul is; in fact, I know he is. Yet I know too that he wonders about you sometimes and that he'll be very upset by what happened today."

Grace hitched her skirt and tucked in her blouse so that Claire thought she put on clothes more like a soldier hurrying to parade than a young woman dressing in the presence of another. She had a trick of conducting an intimate conversation like this, on a flat, impersonal level, as though Claire was a recruit to the Cause and she was instructing her in tactics.

"I'm quite sure Paul is happy, Claire, far happier than I could have made him and believe me, I'm grateful to you too! You were the means of soothing my conscience about him. All the same, I still think you should have fought for him in the first place."

"But it wouldn't have worked that way," Claire retorted, although it secretly pleased her to have proof of the fact that she knew Paul so much better than this strange, eclectic creature, "and you haven't answered my question! I've got a reason for asking it."

"I don't want to know reasons," Grace told her, "I made a bad mistake and so did he but I made mine deliberately, so it wasn't fair that he should help pay for it! Am I happier? I don't know, I had never much expectation of happiness so it's difficult to judge. I'm doing what I want to do, I've found a purpose to justify myself so I suppose that's something. The only way I did that when I was a wife was over there," and she inclined her head towards the bed. Claire said nothing, so she went on, as though answering her own questions, "That's half a marriage but Paul isn't a man satisfied with half, is he? I soon found that out and that's what decided me to stop pretending. I imagine it's very different with you for you always belonged in his precious Valley. It's still the whole of his life, I imagine?"

"Yes," Claire told her, it was, that and the children.

"You have children? Yes of course you have, Uncle Franz told me—two girls, wasn't it?"

"Two boys, and now a girl."

"You haven't wasted much time!"

"The first two arrived together—twins—the girl last December."

Grace looked then as if she was trying to make up her mind to say something important but was not sure how it would be received and for a moment Claire suspected that she was going to flaunt her "liberation" by inquiring into the sex relationship of man and wife. Then, suddenly, Claire understood the reason for her hesitation; she was thinking, no doubt, of her own child Simon and said quickly,

567

"You were wondering about your boy?" but Grace shook her head vigorously and replied, "No, that wasn't it! It just occurred to me that a woman like yourself must regard a person like me as a masochist."

Claire had never heard the word "masochist" and frankly admitted as much whereupon Grace laughed and said, "By god, Claire! I was right about you! You were the only person in the world for Paul and I admire your honesty! Not one woman in a hundred would have admitted that in your situation!" and when Claire's expression showed she was unable to follow her reasoning, she went on, "It's just a fashionable word meaning someone who derives pleasure from pain. Some of our people fall over themselves to use all the new words, you know, and I suppose some of them really are masochists. Well, at least my affiliation is not that much of a fad! I'm the person I am simply because I watched my mother driven to suicide by the cruelty of a man and I suppose this is my way of hitting back but perhaps Paul never told you about that?"

"No," Claire said, "he never did."

"Well, if you're interested ask old John Rudd when you get home but I shall have to go now, I'm probably the only one who survived that raid and Headquarters will want a report," and she picked up a yellow straw hat of Claire's from the window seat and said, "Could I borrow this until tomorrow? I lost mine in the scrimmage."

"You can have it, a donation to the Cause," Claire said, "but before you go I would like you to know that both Paul and I campaigned for Women's Suffrage at the last two elections in the West."

"I do know it," Grace said, "for that comes within my terms of reference. However, this isn't the kind of war won on platforms, as you probably noticed outside Parliament this afternoon."

Claire said, "If you'd been arrested and taken to gaol would you have gone on another hunger strike and been forcibly fed?"

"Not necessarily," Grace replied carelessly, "they're so frightened of the prospect of one of us dying in gaol that they've introduced a new method now. They watch us starve for a few days, turn us loose, then arrest us again as soon as we're strong enough to totter along between two fat policemen!"

"It's outrageous," Claire burst out, "how many times have you been in Holloway?"

"I've lost count," Grace said, "but I can tell you how many times

568

I've had the steel gag and been fed through the nostrils. That's something you do remember."

Suddenly Claire felt sick and miserable. The thin, erect figure standing by the window was a rebuke, not only to her but to all of them and contemplation of her, and all that had happened to her over the last few years, made a mockery of the brilliant procession they had watched the previous day. She said, falteringly, "How . . . how long will it go on, Grace?" and Grace, shrugging, said perhaps another two or three years, depending upon all kinds of factors, the staying power of the Militants, the supply of funds, the state of public opinion and the obstinacy of male legislators of both parties. Then, as though bored with the subject, she crammed on the hat and said, "We'll go down now. Paul will be tormenting himself guessing what we're talking about up here!" and she moved for the door but Claire caught her arm and said, "Wait, there is one thing more! We haven't told Simon about you. It isn't easy to explain divorce to a seven-year-old. We shall, of course, but sometimes I wonder . . . well, wouldn't you like to see him? You could, at any time you wished."

Grace gave her another of her long, thoughtful stares before saying, "No, I don't think that would be very wise of me, would it? He's happy and fit, I imagine?"

"Yes, he is," Claire told her, "he gets on well with the twins but Ikey, the boy Paul more or less adopted, is his great favourite."

"Ah yes, Ikey," Grace said, as it struck her that Claire must be quite unaware of Ikey's role as the link between them. "How is Ikey shaping? I always had great hopes of that boy."

"He's doing very well," Claire told her, "he's in his first year at Woolwich. He was going to be an Engineer but he's changed to the Gunners. Having his own children hasn't made any difference how Paul feels about him."

"No," Grace said, slowly, "it wouldn't, not with people like you and Paul, but . . ." and she stopped, biting her lips so that Claire said, "Well?"

"In a place like the Valley," she said, with less than her former assurance, "Simon won't be in ignorance about me long. If I was in your place I should get Ikey to explain to him and not lose any time about it. It wouldn't help if he heard it from one of the farm hands. Will you do that for me, Claire?"

"Certainly, if Paul agrees," said Claire, although privately she thought the assignment eccentric.

"Paul will agree to anything you suggest," Grace said and suddenly, inexplicably, she bent forward and kissed Claire on the cheek, after which she pulled open the door and marched out into the corridor. "No wonder Paul could make very little of her," Claire thought, as she watched the yellow straw hat bob down the staircase, "for who on earth could? Certainly not me!" and she hurried to catch her up before Grace found the table where Paul and James sat smoking, each looking as sombre and ill-at-ease as an expectant father.

CHAPTER FOUR

I

THERE was no persuading him to remain in London another night and catch the 11 a.m. train from Waterloo, that all Valley travellers used, for it was the only main line train that stopped at Sorrel Halt. He fled the city like a fugitive, telling her that this was not the first time but would be the last. At first she was depressed that their holiday, which had begun so well, should have ended so abruptly and on such a dismal note but as the lights of the tenement houses fell away, and the train ran on into dark, open country she began to share his relief at going and was soon lulled to sleep by the clack of the wheels. When she opened her eyes again it was light and she could smell parched summer woods, a few miles short of the Devon border.

He had not asked her about her conversation with Grace and she had not told him, thinking that it would keep for when he felt less jaded but he remained moody and silent over breakfast at The Mitre, in Paxtonbury. It was not until they had hired a horse and trap at the livery stables, and were breasting the incline on the first stage of the fifteen-mile journey to the Valley that he began to perk up a little, for she saw him lift his head and sniff the air like a pointer, as though he was searching the rendezvous of the west wind and the whiff of Channel spindrift. He said, as though she had been privy to his thoughts all the way home, "That glitter and all those blaring bands! Pomp measured out by the chain mile and what is the point of it if the vast majority are just lookers-on? Can you answer me that now?"

She said mildly that she supposed the spectacle itself was there to be enjoyed by taxpayers, and this, in essence, was the object the authorities had in mind but he growled, "Yes, I daresay! Bread and circuses, to keep the mob yammering for more red on the map! But they'll bellow for local blood if given the chance, as you saw outside the House yesterday! Damn it, if we put on a show down here to mark a national occasion every man, woman and child in the Valley would be personally involved in it! But not in London, for London isn't England any more! Monarchs used to make progresses to places

571

like the Valley. Now they use London as a reflecting mirror and a bloody flyblown one at that!"

He seldom swore in her presence but she said nothing, knowing his mood would blow itself out in a few growls and gusts and that every turn of the trap's wheels would improve his humour and she was right. After a rumble or two he subsided, his features relaxed, and he began to look about him as they tackled the last lap of the interminable hill to the saddleback where the real moor began. A hundred yards or so below the crest he pulled on to the heather and let the reins drop between his knees. It was then about 8 a.m., and the morning river mist had long since been sucked up by the sun so that the open stretches of the Sorrel winked at the sky and the salt taste of the wind was unmistakable. She saw him grin and stretch himself, and in his sudden enthusiasm he thumped her knee so vigorously that she shouted, "Hi! That'll leave a bruise, you great bully!" but she smiled because she was so relieved the magic had worked again.

"Look at it!" he said. "Six miles wide and twelve deep!"

"And we don't own the half of it," she said, "so stop crowing!"

"It doesn't matter a damn who owns it," he said, "for even old Gilroy's patch is more English than Trafalgar Square! I'll tell you what I have in mind and you're the first to hear of it! We'll put on a coronation show of our own that will be talked about when George and Mary are nudging their jubilee! And I don't mean simply a Valley affair but a *real* show, with brass bands, a sports programme, fatstock competitions, rifle butts, a gymkhana, a cart-horse parade, the lot! We'll get entries from the Paxtonbury territorials, who start their annual camp in a fortnight and from the Yeomanry over in Heronslea Park and we'll get Gilroy to bring his hirelings across the Teazel to get a drubbing from our chaps in everything from pig-skittling to Cornish wrestling! How does that sound for a start?"

"Absurdly ambitious," she said, her lip trembling, "but I'm all in favour if it improves your temper!"

He kissed her then, a great, hearty kiss full on the mouth, like a farmer returning home after a successful day at the market. Back here he was so like a great, hulking boy that she could never think of him as a person born and raised in a city. He said, "By God, we'll show them how to go about things! Get up, Ned!" and he slapped the reins on the cob's back and began the steep descent to the river road.

His enthusiasm infected the entire Valley within a couple of days, as he lunged up and down the estate, dashing off letters to Honorary Secretaries as far afield as Whinmouth and—this astounded everyone who knew him—getting the house connected to the Paxtonbury Telephone Company, so that he could make direct contact with the Gilroy estate and the people and organisations to whom he looked for active co-operation. There had been all manner of free luncheons and sports meetings arranged in the district as part of the national coronation fiesta but most of these had been organised on a local basis. The promise of valuable prizes and free beer worked wonders upon the isolationist spirit of communities half-a-day's journey north, west and east of the Valley so that the event, given good weather, looked like proving the most spectacular since the Heronslea three-day fair at the time of Victoria's first jubilee, a celebration still spoken of by the middle-aged and elderly of the Valley as "the day us all got dead drunk at Gilroy's expense".

The local military organisations proved co-operative, Territorials and Yeomanry entering sports teams in most of the contests, and when it was clear that the number of contestants and spectators was likely to exceed two thousand Paul shifted the venue from Big Paddock to the Codsall stubble fields now lying fallow. Tents and enclosures began to mushroom there within days of his return home and the ringing of the new telephone bell in the hall drove Mrs. Handcock frantic, for she swore that she could never disassociate it in her mind from a fire-alarm. Only the sudden return of Ikey, on a month's furlough, saved her from resignation as Chef Extraordinary, and her husband Horace had to be taken on one side and told to persuade her that the Coronation Jamboree would make Shallowford history, so that her loyalty to the Squire was at stake. Apart from this Horace was a great help to Paul during these feverish days for he was a great authority on the many slumbering feuds that existed between Heronslea and the county border and showed the Squire how to exploit them in the interests of competitive events. Three silver and four brass bands entered in the band contests and there were over a hundred and forty gymkhana entries for a dozen major events. Two hunting packs promised support and rural athletes came in from as far away as Barnstaple, whereas the rifle and clay-pigeon events were so popular that they had to be shot off in heats days in advance. A fifty-yard stretch of the river was dredged for tub-racing and a wrestling ring was built west of the ford. There were all manner of agricultural contests, from fence-splitting to hedging-and-ditching and the inevitable

573

firework display advertised a magnificent set-piece of the Spithead Naval Review, with guns firing rocket salvoes over the avenue chestnuts.

John Rudd, although approving of the venture as a whole, shook his head over the probable cost, declaring that it would set the estate back five hundred pounds, but Paul said they could regard it as money spent on advertising and that the Valley as a whole would benefit from new contacts and the opening up of fresh markets in the area. Rudd thought this was eyewash but he did not say so for by then he had had a word with Claire, who described what had happened on their last day in London. Thinking it over he agreed with her that a diversion on this scale was what Paul needed. As for the others, the hard core of the Valley tenantry, they formed a kind of staff about Paul and, notwithstanding the fine weather, work on the farms was shamefully scamped throughout the first week of July. The stolid, conscientious Eveleigh took charge of the sports meeting, Sam Potter the agricultural competitions, and Henry Pitts, glad of such a good excuse to take a holiday, appointed himself Squire's adjutant, with Ikey Palfrey as an aide-de-camp tearing up and down the Valley on his chestnut hunter. And each of these officers had auxiliaries outside the Shallowford area, men like Eph Morgan, the builder, who, as a Welshman, declared himself the only man qualified to supervise the musical programmes, and Tom Williams, the fisherman, who provided tubs for the river-race and cartloads of hazards for the obstacle races. The women of the Valley rallied to Claire's sub-committee so that the smell of baking rose over the Sorrel like a benediction and so much food was prepared that Martha Pitts, carrying her quota into the refreshment marquee, declared that the twelve apostles would be needed to carry away the surplus by the basketful as they had when the five thousand were fed beside Galilee.

The sky began to cloud over on the last day of preparation and it looked as though the spell of fine weather was about to end so that the men worked on frantically after dusk and when it was too dark to swing a mallet assembled to broach the first of the fifteen-gallon casks that had been hauled into the Valley by Whinmouth drays and were now ranged in an imposing row in the refreshment tent. Said Henry Pitts, his cheerful face clouded with anxiety, "All us wants now is a bliddy downpour, an' us looks as if us'll get it!" but to Claire's relief Horace Handcock (whose oracular powers extended to the weather field) licked his thumb, looked wise, and announced majestically that

574

there would be a change of wind during the night and that the sun would shine all the following day. Then Sam Potter, raising his pewter tankard, declared that as the place would be full of foreigners tomorrow he proposed they all took this opportunity to drink the health of the Squire and everybody murmured agreement and downed their pints in one while Claire, glancing across the table at Paul, saw that he was touched by their loyalty and added her silent prayer for a cloudless day.

She was awake and at the window soon after five, watching the grey light creep over the Bluff and cross the river to the little town of tents, booths and enclosures west of the ford. It was childish, she thought, to be so concerned over a country fête of which there were probably a thousand arranged for that day in various parts of the British Isles but it seemed to her an issue of tremendous importance for so much work had gone into the event and not an inconsiderable amount of money. She continued to stand watching the sky while his snores reached her from the bed, and presently the shadows across the river retreated to the Teazel Valley and she saw cotton-wool mist steal in from the sea, which told her that calm weather could be expected for the surest sign of rain in the Valley was a clear view to the south-west. She went back to the bed and shook him and when he only muttered and rolled over on his back, she slid her hand along the dark stubble of his chin so that the short bristles crackled and he sat up suddenly wide awake and exclaimed, "What's it like?"

"Set fair," she said, "so get up and shave! You forgot to yesterday and your chin is like a quickset hedge!"

He passed his hand across his cheek and grinned, "So I did," he said, swinging his feet to the floor, "I was so damned busy! Have you been lying awake worrying about rain?"

"Yes I have," she said. "I invariably do your worrying for you! Now hurry up, Paul, there's a lot to do before breakfast!"

"Aye, there is that," he admitted, but despite her impatient protest he caught her round the waist as she crossed to the dressing-table and holding her for a moment said, "It wouldn't be any fun without you, Claire! I don't suppose I should lead a different life married or single but it wouldn't be any *fun*, you understand?" and he gave her a bristly kiss on the neck and went whistling along the passage to his tub.

She looked at herself in the mirror, wasting more precious time she told herself but there was time enough to smile at her reflection and say, "Claire Craddock, you're odiously smug and he's smug too!

575

Maybe we're all rather smug down here far away from it all and we'll stay so as long as we can!"

II

By extending the area of the Jamboree beyond the Valley and inviting entries from districts north of Paxtonbury, east to the county border, and west to Gilroy's estates, Paul had not intended to stress the competitive element but, as Horace Handcock warned him, an occasion like this would unleash local patriotism on a formidable scale and Horace must have known his west-countryman for the Jamboree soon lost its national flavour and entered the arena of local partisanship, with substantial bets being laid on the top score of the various competing units. These units were basically geographical and the intense rivalry between them was not finally resolved until a match had been applied to the set-piece of the new King and Queen. That, however, was very late in the day and in the meantime competition was intense, for superimposed upon geographical backgrounds was the rivalry between the civilians and the Territorials and the Yeomanry, so that sometimes there was a conflict of loyalties. By afternoon the general scheme of the contest had sorted itself out and the amateur bookmakers were at last able to introduce some kind of pattern into their wagers.

The Valley gained a headstart when Rose Derwent, on her steeplechaser Tawnyboy, won the principal event of the Gymkhana. One of Gilroy's stable-lads rode her to a close finish after a pile up at the water-jump and she streaked down the flat with little more than a nose to spare.

Then, to the Valley's surprise and disgust, the famed Goliath of Bideford, a hot favourite for the Cornish wrestling championship, was vanquished in the final by a Horse Artilleryman from Paxtonbury. It seemed that clearing Potter land and digging Potter wells had not provided the right training for this kind of contest, despite the fact that Jem Pollock still looked a magnificent specimen of manhood in his leopard-skin. The men of the Valley, however, seeing him thrown three times in succession in the heats, were not deceived and dispersed wondering if any man, no matter how thick of thigh and broad of chest, could be expected to keep two Potter girls quiescent and still triumph in the wrestling ring. Anyway, he was badly beaten, and several less well-regulated fights threatened to break out between territorials and agriculturalists as a result of the verdict. Jem took his

576

defeat well, declaring his opponent a master of the art but in the dressing tent Cissie and Violet Potter felt ashamed and blamed the issue on Meg's insistence that Jem should enter the contest with a full belly. They had cause to complain. In the interests of the Valley they had denied themselves his comforting presence for almost a week and had looked on glumly that morning when Meg had sent him out fortified by five fried eggs, three pounds of fried potatoes and a dozen rashers of green bacon.

Lord Gilroy's team won the hedging and ditching contest and a West Dorset silver band was judged the winner of the band contest but Sam Potter brought the Valley to the forefront again with his brilliant exhibition of rail-splitting. It was a joy to watch him straddling a great beech log, whirling his woodsman's axe as though it had been a conductor's baton. The sweat poured down his naked back as he worked his way towards the tapering end, occasionally exchanging his axe for wedges and a fourteen-pound sledge until, like a neatly divided apple, the log split down the middle.

A curious thing happened in the final of the clay-pigeon contest where Smut Potter, to everyone's amusement, came face to face with Dave Buller, the Heronslea keeper whose scars had cost Smut three years and eight months behind bars. Paul, when he saw the pair take up their stand, expressed anxiety but John Rudd laughed at him, declaring that Dave bore Smut no malice. And neither did he, it seemed, for when Smut won, he went up to him and wrung his hand saying, cheerfully, "Well, Smut, you baint lost your touch I zee!" and everybody within earshot applauded the keeper's sportsmanlike attitude.

Other highlights of the day were the tub race, won by the Yeomanry after all their competitors had capsized and the Ladies' Pancake Tossing sprint, won in fine style by Elinor Codsall, mother of three but still as fleet of foot as when she was a slip of a girl. Ikey increased the Valley's lead before tea by winning the mile, with half a lap in hand but the tug-of-war proved almost as big a disappointment as the wrestling for despite Jem Pollock as anchor, the Territorials dragged the Sorrel men over the mark in a series of expert heaves and pulled into overall second place by going on to win the open relay.

By six o'clock, when points had been totted up after the ankle competition and fancy-dress events (events sporting men discounted and excluded from their wagers) the Valley was only one point ahead and the atmosphere was charged with excitement as competitors lined up

577

for the most spectacular event of the day, a two-lap trap-race, with no pettifogging trotting conditions imposed on it and here, it seemed, the Terriers were favourites and a win would give them a clear five-point lead.

The day had been intensely hot, with distant thunder rumbling beyond the Bluff and when the stewards cleared the course word came that Eveleigh's eldest boy, Gilbert, who had been training the Codsall skewball Firefly for the event, had sprained his wrist getting ashore in the tub race and had been obliged to withdraw. In the few minutes left the Valley was canvassed for a substitute but none with any chance of holding off the strong challenge came forward, so that a howl of dismay rose from the ropes as Eveleigh, looking even more unsmiling than usual, began to lead Firefly out of the line-up. Paul, standing alongside the starter, said philosophically, "Well, that's that, John! The Terriers have it in the bag," but John said suddenly, "Look here, they needn't have! You can handle a trap smartly enough, get up there and show 'em," and to Paul's surprise Claire, overhearing the challenge, said, "Do it, Paul! Even if you don't really care who wins everyone else in the Valley does!" So Paul peeled off his coat, donned a steeplechaser's crash hat and climbed into the box to the accompaniment of the biggest cheer of the day but feeling far less confident of his ability to negotiate the bends than were his supporters.

There were five entries but only the Terrier looked dangerous and Paul was relieved to be drawn on the inside, a starting position that seemed likely to exploit Firefly's reputation as a flying starter. He thought, as he picked up the reins. "Good God, this is ridiculous! I feel more nervous than I did out on the Veldt, or fishing those Germans ashore in the cove and all over a footling chariot race in one of my own meadows!"

Then they were off, with Firefly gaining a clear yard in a couple of bounds and he held on to his inside place round the first bend as the ponies went into a stretched gallop on the slight downslope of the flat. The pace was terrifying. Never had he moved so fast behind a horse and he thought, as he dragged Firefly round the second bend and into the straight to complete the first lap, that he must have been an ass to let Henry Pitts and Will Codsall override him on the potential dangers of this event. On the third bend he heard a wild shout, and the splintering of wood behind him but it was not until he had started the final lap that he saw what had happened. Three of the traps had crashed in a wheel-lock on the second bend and were only dragged

578

clear as he pounded straight down on the mêlée with the Terrier drawing level and half-standing in his box as he lashed his pony to overtake at the second bend.

The spectators now seemed to go mad in a body, for as the two traps flashed by neck-and-neck they poured from behind the ropes and capered into the centre of the course, and then, as the two survivors entered the straight again, Paul realised he had the race in hand for the Terrier dropped back and Firefly crossed the finishing line with a length in hand and Paul had to use all his strength to avoid ploughing on into the crowd now scattered all over the track. He said, as an exultant Henry Pitts jumped for the pony's head and brought him to a halt, "The next time you insist on a chariot race you can damned well compete yourself, Henry!" but Henry only banged him on the back and bellowed, "Us 'ave shown 'em, Squire! Us 'ave shown 'em!" and every man, woman and child in the Valley agreed with him, even Claire, who had watched the race with her heart in her mouth feeling sick at the thought that, if Paul had been injured, she would have blamed herself for the rest of a guilty life.

Paul went over to inspect the damage to the others and found, to his great relief, that all three drivers had escaped with bruises, although their vehicles were shattered, two of them beyond repair. The Yeomanry competitor was undismayed for his entry had been official and the trap was on the inventory of the barracks, but Paul felt sorry for the Dorset man, a young farmer now dolefully inspecting the wreck of his gaily-painted rig. "What do you value it at?" he asked, and the man said it was his father's trap and the old man had paid four pounds ten shillings for it at Paxtonbury market only a month ago. "My agent, Mr. Rudd, will give you the money out of funds," he said and feeling magnanimous as winner of such a contest, added, "and here's an extra ten shillings for danger money!"

Over in the east thunder continued to mutter but the rain held off and it was decided to hold the dancing in the open air. Paul went into the refreshment hut for a badly needed drink and was served by a tall, thin, bespectacled young man, whom he did not recognise until Doctor Maureen, sipping a brandy close at hand, told him the volunteer barman was Keith Horsey, son of the rector, still known as New Parson, although he had now occupied Parson Bull's pulpit for more than three years. He went across and talked to the youth, finding him very shy and afflicted by a slight stammer.

"Does Ikey know you are here?" he asked, "you were at school together, weren't you?" and Keith said that this was true but that he had returned home from Oxford only that day and had so far not spoken to Ikey although he had watched him win the mile. Paul said, "There's dancing going on now and a chap your age would be better employed following his fancy. I'll find someone to take on here!" but the boy began to protest and his stammer increased, so that Paul would have left the matter there had not Ikey lounged into the tent at that moment, greeting Keith with genuine pleasure. Paul noticed that the parson's son lost his stammer at once and the way he looked at Ikey, with myopic brown eyes, reminded him of Grace's retriever anticipating an ear-rub in front of the library fire. He thought, smiling to himself, "He's got a way with him has Ikey! There isn't a soul here who doesn't perk up when Ikey walks in and this poor little toad obviously worships him!" and on the pretence of buying Maureen a drink he disposed of Keith for a moment and said, "Take that kid down to the dancing enclosure and make sure he gets a girl! He'll do no good standing here serving drinks for the rest of the night!"

"A girl! Beanpole Horsey with a girl?" said Ikey, laughing, "I know you've just bankrupted the bookies by winning the chariot race, Gov'nor, but don't ask for miracles! Beanpole wouldn't know what to do with a girl if he was locked up with one."

"What sort of chap was he at school?" Paul asked, and Ikey replied a first-class brain but that was about all. "He's a trier all right," he added, "and he's got guts but somehow they don't show. I like him and always have, I'll get working on him tomorrow, Gov.," but for some reason Paul persisted, saying, "No, Ikey, not tomorrow, now! All the girls will have gone tomorrow and some girls like the self-effacing type! They don't all fall for the cocky bounders like you!"

"Well," Ikey said, "always willing to oblige, especially after your performance!" and he ambled over to Keith and Paul watched them stand chatting for a few moments after which Keith took off his barman's apron, folded it neatly and left the tent like a poacher's lurcher trotting at its master's heels. It was a trivial incident, perhaps the most trivial of the day, but he was to remember it long after the excitement of the chariot race had faded from his memory.

III

Keith Horsey, now eighteen, would not have survived his first year at High Wood without the patronage of Ikey Palfrey. After fighting

580

for him, and giving him an essential breathing space, Ikey had found it difficult to shed partial responsibility for the ungainly youth and although Horsey was regarded as a useless weed by almost everyone in the school Ikey soon realised that this was by no means the whole truth about the Beanpole. He possessed, for instance, a great deal of moral courage and moral courage was in short supply at High Wood. As it was, buttressed in some measure by Ikey's friendship, Beanpole not only survived but made some kind of impact by his stand against the code of Bloods, notably, that part of it condoning smut and cribbing. In the course of this lonely crusade he collected innumerable beatings, both official and unofficial, but he never yielded ground and no one succeeded in extracting from him so much as a yelp. As Hillman, the Captain of Fortescue, once put it, "It's like walloping a deaf mute and a man can't do it and then sit down to tea and buns with an easy mind." So, in the end, they left him to himself and to Ikey, and the Beanpole shot rapidly up the school to the Sixth where he won the coveted open scholarship to Oxford at the unprecedented age of seventeen and left to read economics and philosophy. Although Ikey had lost touch with him since entering Woolwich the previous year he had by no means forgotten him and was genuinely pleased to see him at the Jamboree. For an hour or more they talked, watching the dancers moving over the clipped turf to the blare of the Yeomanry band and it was not until Ikey saw Rachel Eveleigh partnerless on the far side of the square that he recollected his instructions. Bidding Keith wait for him he lounged across and greeted her.

Rachel was the second daughter of the Four Winds string of children and the most like her placid mother, Marian. She had red-gold hair, a good-natured, slightly freckled face and blue eyes that tonight had something of a snap in them.

"I'm pairing up on Squire's instructions, Rachel," Ikey told her, "do you know Keith Horsey, the parson's son?" and when Rachel admitted that she knew him by sight, "I wonder if you would do Squire a favour and bring him on a bit? He's a nice chap but on the shy side so you'll have to make the running," and to Ikey's surprise Rachel replied in her soft Devon brogue, "I'd love to meet him, he's always seemed a very polite boy and there aren't so many around tonight!" and without waiting to be introduced she walked across the enclosure and stood smiling in front of him while Ikey, temporarily losing the initiative, said, "Er . . . Keith old man, this is Rachel Eveleigh from Four Winds . . . Rachel . . . you've er . . . you've seen him in church, maybe?" Keith said nothing but stood blinking at the girl who took him by the hand with a cheerful, "Come on, this is an easy one, the Military Two-Step. Follow me all the way round!" and Ikey was left standing with his mouth open having always thought of Rachel Eveleigh as hardly less shy than Keith. He did not notice another solitary figure, a boy about his own age wearing spectacles nearly as thick-lensed as Keith's, slightly apart from Rachel when he approached, and who remained to watch the couple merge into the long file of dancers circling the bandstand but Rachel was very much aware of Sydney Codsall, standing by with an expression of baffled irritation on his face for her ready acceptance of Ikey's appeal had been the direct result of a sharp exchange between them earlier that evening.

Sydney Codsall had not wanted to attend the Jamboree, regarding it as a mere chawbacon's carnival with little to offer a man who "worked clean"—that is to say, wore a starched collar and cuffs. He was only there because, of late, he had been cultivating Rachel for reasons that had nothing whatever to do with her amiability, her red-gold hair or her pleasing, freckled face. He had grown up with the Eveleigh family and had no great affection for any of them, having always regarded them as interlopers whom circumstances had contrived to make him a lodger in his own house. He had been glad to break out of the family circle when he became articled to Snow and Pritchard and took lodgings in Whinmouth but his recent foray into the property market had caused him to have second thoughts about abandoning the Eveleighs altogether. A month or two back he had learned by chance that the parcel of land adjoining the brickworks site was registered in the name of a Mrs. Amelia Page and he recalled that Marian Eveleigh had been a Miss Page before her marriage. A little cross-checking during the lunch interval when he was alone in the office had confirmed his guess regarding the ultimate owner of the land, no other than Mrs. Eveleigh, old Mother Page's only surviving child. He also discovered that old Mrs. Page was pushing ninety-three. The land comprised no more than a couple of acres but it had a common boundary with his holding in Coombe Bay and if it could be had cheaply was clearly worth a great deal more to him than to anyone else. Sydney gave matters like these very careful thought and it seemed to him that, whereas a direct approach would probably result in drawing the land-hungry Squire's attention to the parcel, an oblique approach through the most pliable of Marian Eveleigh's daughters

582

might lead to a bill of sale before anyone else was aware that there was another plot of land to be had on the outskirts of the village.

He set to work at once to court Rachel and made what he considered steady progress, for Rachel had never forgotten her father's instructions that they were to be kind to the orphaned Sydney. Soon, or so it seemed to her, kindness cracked the crust of Sydney's aloofness, for he seemed willing to sacrifice precious hours that should have been devoted to study walking her along summer lanes and telling her how much he appreciated the kindness her family had shown him and also — and this interested her rather more — how much more ladylike she was than any of her sisters. It was some time, however, before Rachel, a modest soul, could persuade herself that the rather prickly Sydney was actually courting her, for there were aspects of his attentions that were very puzzling. For one thing he never once tried to kiss her or even to hold her hand; for another all their walks, no matter in which direction, seemed to bring them to the fence surrounding Grannie Page's field, alongside the old brickworks. For some reason Sydney seemed more bemused by the field, which was quite an ordinary-looking field, than by her red-gold hair, her blue eyes, her dimples, or anything about her, including her "ladylike" conversation. It was not until the tea interval at the Jamboree, a month after the sombre courtship had begun, that Sydney confessed to a keen, personal interest in the field and asked her outright if Grannie Page was likely to live much longer and if Rachel thought her mother would be prepared to sell it for, say, ten guineas per acre?

Rachel Eveleigh was a very amiable girl but she was not stupid. Moreover she had the advantage, which Paul Craddock, in his dealing with Sydney, had not, of having lived cheek by jowl with him for years, so that it did not take her more than a moment to price Sydney's courtship at twenty guineas, less solicitor's costs. She had her mother's complaisance but her father's pride. After pondering a moment, in order to be quite certain that she was doing no one an injustice, she lifted her right hand and smacked Sydney's face so hard that he lost his balance on a tussock and fell backwards into the shallow river. By the time he got to his feet she had gone and before he could condemn his stupidity for rushing his fences so recklessly she was dancing with the parson's son, Keith Horsey, and looking very much as if she was making the running. He watched them sourly for half-an-hour but she did not even glance in his direction and before the first rocket soared over the paddock he was bicycling back to Whinmouth, having learned

583

a valuable lesson in tactics but lost a golden opportunity of enlarging his Coombe Bay holdings.

In the meantime Keith Horsey was blithely unaware to whom he owed his adoption by the prettiest of the Eveleigh girls, the titian-haired one, whom he identified as the second unit of a descending row of heads when the family took their places in church. Although shy and ill-at-ease with men he was more relaxed in the presence of women, for he had grown up among church workers who were pre-dominantly female and was thus familiar with feminine topics of con-versation. Rachel, who had only taken him in hand as a means of alleviating the smart caused by Sydney's baseness, soon found him agreeable company and was secretly flattered at having one of the gentry all to herself, although she could have wished for one with rather more experience in the art of dancing. By the time the fireworks were due to begin, and the band had disappeared into the refreshment tent, all her toes were bruised and on her right thigh was a tender patch of skin where Keith's knee struck a blow every time they turned. It was very pleasant, however, to find a man ready to admit his short-comings, especially after a month's courting with Sydney who had never confessed to one. Keith made no excuses for his clumsiness, saying that his cousins had long since given him over as a hopeless hobbledehoy but if he could not dance he at least treated her with an elaborate courtesy that she found very welcome after the fumblings and neighing laughter of partners at village hops she had attended since putting her hair up. Rachel had pride, as her reaction to Sydney's proposal had proved, but like all the sons and daughters of tenant farmers in the Valley she recognised her place in the graded society into which she had been born. On one side of the fence lived Squire, the freeholders, the doctor and the parson, and on the other the ten-ants, the tradesmen, the cottage craftsmen and the hired hands, in that order of progression. To be asked for a single dance by a young man from the other side of the fence was one thing, and might happen to any girl on an occasion like this, but to dance with a college boy who was also the parson's only son eight times in succession, and then to be escorted by him to the refreshment hut for ices and lemonade, was quite another. By the time the fireworks were started, and Keith still showed no desire to rejoin the gentry, Rachel had decided that the Squire's Coronation Jamboree promised to be a milestone in her life, the more memorable, perhaps, because there had been so few. Then the Valley gods took a hand in the affair. As the third volley of rockets soared forked lightning flickered over the Bluff and seconds later thunder rolled, so that she had every excuse to reduce the space between them; and because he was such a gentleman, and had such nice manners, his hand, cool if bony, took hers and she told the first deliberate lie of her life saying, in reply to his inquiry, "Yes, Mr. Horsey, I *am* frightened of thunder," hoping that he would ask her to address him less formally. He did not but she made progress in another direction for he at once enlarged his hold upon her plump hand and held it tightly for the remainder of the display.

For those in charge of the fireworks it was a race against time. With the fall of dusk the atmosphere over the field became oppressive and the rumbles of thunder beyond the Bluff ever more frequent. Presently, before the set-pieces had been touched off, a few heavy drops of rain splashed down but nobody minded them much for it was not often the Valley could watch a fireworks display and some of the spectators recalled the display here in honour of King Teddy, in October 1902. Among these was Pansy Pascoe, plain Pansy Potter when watching the last descent of green and crimson balls over the chestnuts. She was here again tonight, with her brood of four, three cooing and ahhing and the fourth, two-year-old Lizzie, asleep in the go-cart, which Pansy now realised she would have to push all the way home to Coombe Bay for Walt, her husband, had been last seen far gone in drink in the refreshment tent with certain other revellers. Pansy was not given to brooding but the link between the firework displays was too obvious to be ignored. In 1902 she recalled, she had been as one with her sisters living a semi-gypsy life in the Dell taking her fun wherever she found it; now she was a woman apart, with a house to keep clean, a husband to cook for and a steadily increasing tribe of children to make impossible demands on her time, so that fun passed her by and she was also losing her figure. She could not help wondering if she had chosen wisely in settling for Walt, simply because he owned a cottage and earned a pound a week, summer and winter. There were times, particularly of late, when she yearned for the cheerful muddle of the Dell as it had been in old Tamer's time, for up there an odd baby or two had never seemed to matter much and children did not get under one's feet as they did in a four-roomed cottage. At the firework display of 1902, she recalled, she had considered herself the sharpest of the Potter girls but tonight she was not so sure, in spite of the rumour that Big Jem, the hired hand, kept Cissie and Violet on

585

a very tight rein. Her thoughts, becoming more nostalgic with every new discharge, were interrupted by an impatient tugging at her arm and in the glare of golden rain she looked down into the face of her eldest boy, Timothy, now rising seven and said, without troubling to ask what he wanted, "Go over there, Timmy, an' dornee be tiresome! No one'll look at 'ee an' iffen they do then who gives a damn, boy?"

Then, as Timothy slipped away, she was aware of the gleam of a waxed moustache at her elbow and sensed the not unwelcome presence of Dandy Timberlake, eldest and by far the sprucest of the Timberlake boys. All the Timberlake boys had a roving eye but Dandy's roved to more purpose than his brothers' and with another pang Pansy recalled larking with him in the hay about a thousand years ago, when everybody in the Valley was free and young and spry. He said, sorrowfully, "I've come to tell 'ee, Panse, Walt's dead drunk and like to stay for the night! How be gonner get the family back home?"

"On shanks' pony," she said grimly, "how else do 'ee think, Dandy?" but she was pleased to see him nevertheless and not much surprised when he said, "If I walked so far with 'ee, would 'ee ask me in for a brew o' tea for old times' sake, Panse?"

She considered; Walt would probably lay up in the barn with all the other over-indulged loyalists and she had always liked Dandy, with his penchant for fancy waistcoats and fierce Kaiser moustaches, the effect of which was softened by a pair of twinkling brown eyes. There could be no harm in him walking her home, cumbered as she was by four children, for it would not be practicable to stop *en route*. If, at journey's end, he claimed a small reward for his services as escort and go-cart pusher was that so unreasonable?

"Mebbe I would at that, Dandy!" she said, "but tiz time us started backalong, for the kids is tired out, baint 'ee, my loves?"

The nature of the reward, she decided, could be left in abeyance and would depend upon how tired she was on arrival, but it might have been otherwise had she known that Dandy had set his sights elsewhere only a few moments before their encounter, having edged along the line of spectators until he stood very close to Violet, her sister, sandwiched between Cissie and Jem, all standing with their faces to the sky. Dandy had always had a slight preference for Vi and seeing that she and Jem were engaged with the fireworks he approached from behind, pinched her bottom, squeezed her hand and let it run lightly upward until it had sufficient purchase to incline her towards him. She turned then and flashed him a smile, for Jem's pitiful performance in the wrestling ring had blown upon embers of resentment in her heart. Like all the Potters she had been born free and tonight she chafed at the bonds of honourable captivity. Jem continued to stare upward and she was so deceived by his air of abstraction that she reached out and touched Dandy, her hand moving tentatively, like the hand of a penniless connoisseur fingering an exhibit in a museum while the curator's back is turned, yet she ought to have remembered that Jem had eyes in the back of his head. He said, quite amiably, and without turning, "I was worsted be that sodger but I could still maake mincemeat o' Dandy Timberlake!" whereupon Dandy moved on to seek Pansy Pascoe and Vi, much piqued, grumbled, "The trouble wi' you, Jem, is youm so bliddy greedy!"

"Ahhh," said Jem, still without taking his eyes off the suspended green balls in the sky, "I daresay I be but that's how it is, Vi midear! I've told 'ee bevore an' I'll tell 'ee again, dornee let me catch either of 'ee we' no man or I'll tan the hide off 'ee, do 'ee mind now?"

"So I should think!" said Cissie virtuously and Violet, reflecting bitterly that her sister had not been tempted, ground her teeth with rage but judged it wise to make no further comment.

Edward Derwent, standing at the foot of the avenue with his wife Liz, his son Hugh and his daughter Rose, watched the rockets soar with more satisfaction than any man in the valley. It was not that he set much store by fireworks, considering them pesky, noisy, unpredictable things but simply that they helped to reveal the fat of the years, particularly the last few years, that had done so much to mellow him. For in that brief span of time Claire had *shown* them. Not only had she married the Squire and presented him with heirs but, almost in passing, she had cured her father's land-hunger, for where was the sense in yearning to own High Coombe when, in a way, he already owned it, together with every other farm in the Valley? His mind returned to the occasion he had last stood here watching fireworks and he recalled his bitter disappointment at the apparent inaccuracy of their assurances that Young Squire was madly in love with his prettiest daughter, and likely to demand her hand at any moment. Well, Young Squire had taken his time but it had come to pass in the end and now he was the Squire's father-in-law, just as they had predicted. As the years passed his pride in his daughter had grown and grown, just like one of his neighbour Willoughby's vegetable marrows

587

earmarked for the harvest festival, and whereas everyone in the Valley had, in some degree, warmed their hands at the glow issuing from the Big House, Derwent had been warmed through and through by events up there. And some of this warmth had passed through him to his wife Liz, she who had tried so hard and so unsuccessfully to fill the shoes of her predecessor, for whereas, in the early days of her marriage, Edward had treated her like a scullery-maid, he now yielded her the respect due to a tolerably efficient housekeeper and with this she was more than content. Silently, as a set-piece of the Battle of Trafalgar began to sputter, Liz Derwent breathed a prayer of thankfulness that things had turned out so well for all of them.

A few yards removed from the families and lovers a thickset figure sat perched on a shooting stick, also contemplating the fireworks although not as a source of entertainment. Professor Hans Scholtzer, formerly of the University of Jena, liked firework displays because they reminded him that the early Chinese civilisations had shown so much more sense in their use of gunpowder than had their imperial successors in the West. Here, in this remote valley, however, the old German had found something of the peace he had sought all his life and at least once a day he relished it, as he was relishing it at this moment. He hoped with all his heart that the simple folk around him (who reminded him sometimes of peasants he had met in the forest clearings of Lower Saxony) would never be tempted to put gunpowder to other uses and involve themselves in the interminable bickerings of the Hohenzollerns, the Romanoffs and the Hapsburgs, to say nothing of the shifty politicians in Paris. For if they did not only would his peace be shattered but also the peace of the valley, possibly for generations, and the Kaiser's minions would reach out and pluck the Professor's fine son Gottfried from his studies and enrol him as a private soldier under the Kaiser's double-eagle. The Professor sat on his shooting stick like a carefully balanced toad but in the white glare of the rockets those about him did not see him as a toad but as a caricature of a fat German bandsman, such as they had often seen in the streets of Paxtonbury. His round head shone and his eyeglasses twinkled and every now and again he blew out his cheeks, as though he was flexing his facial muscles for an assault on the trombone.

Then, when everybody had quite forgotten the mutter of thunder over the Bluff, the storm that had been threatening all day burst and rain began to hiss down on upturned faces and lightning shamed the puny flashes over the chestnuts. The Battle of Trafalgar was left to fight its way through to an indecisive finish and everyone ran clear of the trees and made for tents or outbuildings, remaining there while the giant thunderclaps echoed all the way down the Valley and the rain drummed on taut canvas, telling one another what a good thing it was that the storm had held off all day and spared the Squire's Jamboree.

Claire was already in the house when the storm burst, happy to kick off her shoes and shoot her long legs towards the empty grate, reflecting that she had been very wise to insist that the helpers' dance was postponed until the debris was cleared from the paddock and stubble field for she did not think she could have kept awake after such a long day in the open. She did not light the lamp but sat sipping hot, sweet tea, watching the lightning play over the chestnuts and hoping Paul would be along soon and they could go to bed. It had been, she reflected, a stupendous success and had done everyone credit, particularly the man who was to foot the bill for all the beer consumed and all the gear hired. There could be little doubt but that everyone had enjoyed themselves immensely but then, it did not take very much to amuse the people of the Valley. The men, she reflected, invariably used these occasions to drink, wench, and air their collective rivalries, whereas the women concentrated on displaying their clothes and practised a different kind of rivalry, and Claire, valley-born, could view these activities without patronage. After all, were the so-called gentry very different? Their own life, hers and Paul's, trod an equally narrow circle; they ate, drank, made love, slept and planned the expansion of family and estate, which was only another form of rivalry.

The rain continued to pour down and she wondered how people would get home and how many would stay overnight in the barns and lofts. Well, they were welcome, every one of them, but their presence would mean another early start in the morning, and the thought made her yawn. At last Paul clumped in and greeted her just as she was slipping into a delicious doze.

"It's set in for the night!" he said, "thank God it held off until now! We got most of the fireworks off the ground before the fuses got wet. Is that tea? By thunder I could do with a cup! Is it long made?"

"No," she said, heaving herself out of the chair, "I fell asleep drinking mine—here you are." He stood, feet astride, looking her over with a smile and said, as she handed him his cup, "I couldn't have brought it off without you, Claire. And the food was first-class, everybody says so!" but she was far too sleepy to be flattered and replied, "Good! Well drink it up and let's get some sleep, dear!"

He was on the point of following her up when a thought struck him and he went to the bottom shelf of the big bookcase, taking out a heavy volume called *Famous Paintings of the Western World*. He turned the pages until he came to Rubens' "Bathsheba Receiving King David's Letter", the picture that Grace had shown him the first time she had met Claire. He had never looked at it since but now that he did he saw how accurate Grace's observation had been. Claire *did* look extraordinarily like the fair Bathsheba, with her habit of sitting with knees pressed together at an angle to the chair and a kind of overall ripeness —that had been Grace's word—in every line of her strong, plump, flowing figure. He thought as he closed and replaced the book, "Well, no one could blame David for trying, although I daresay Claire would think him a dirty dog for putting Uriah in the forefront of the battle! I'll ask her, if I remember."

He went on up the broad, creaking stairs as, peal on peal, thunder crashed over the Bluff and went rumbling up to Sorrel source beyond the railway.

CHAPTER FIVE

I

THEY were the vintage years, the brief, crowded period immediately after the fillip given to the Valley by the Coronation Jamboree; the second half of 1911, then 1912 and 1913, and into summer that, on looking back, seemed as remote as the Middle Ages.

Some guide as to what occurred in the Valley during those thirty-six months could be found in the Bible-bound estate record, kept up to date (although in fits and starts depending upon events) by Claire and also by Paul himself when he felt more than ordinarily complacent.

There was his entry dated *"February 12th, 1912"* reading *"Today Doctor Maureen Rudd, M.D., wife of John Rudd, agent of Shallowford, delighted and astonished Sorrel Valley by presenting her husband with a bouncing boy! It was her first and she is, I think, more surprised than any of us, for she declares her age to be 39 although, privately, we think she is 37."*

Whether or not Maureen Rudd was indulging in a little blarney about her age Claire was not exaggerating when she wrote that "Lady Doctor" (as her patients continued to call her) was quite astounded to discover that she was pregnant. She had dashed up and down the Valley inviting all and sundry to witness the miracle, and would say, when they hastened to congratulate her, "It's the air in this damned Valley, so it is! It's a forcing-house for women! Every woman, married or single, this side of the Teazel calls me out in the middle of the night sooner or later! And now who the Devil can attend to me?" They all laughed with her and reassured her, for she was one of the most popular figures in the Valley and the initial prejudice against her sex had long since disappeared, banished by her explosive laughter and her habit of cutting the cackle and coming straight to the point but John Rudd, who loved her dearly, and had never quite recovered from the shock of having his diffident proposal accepted, voiced his anxiety to Paul after Maureen had returned from seeing a specialist in Paxtonbury.

"She says Clifford Goreham has assured her everything will be all

591

right," he said, "but it's obviously a risk for a woman to have her first child at that age. If anything happened to her I'd never forgive myself."

"For God's sake don't say that to her," Paul told him, "or she'll throw something heavy at you, John! It's the kind of remark that would infuriate her if I know Maureen."

"Oh, it's well enough for you," John grumbled, "Claire is only twenty-nine and she's already had three children, but damn it, I just couldn't believe it when Maureen told me and strictly between ourselves I feel a bit of a fool! After all, my son Roddy is thirty and I'm not far off sixty!"

"Obviously a young sixty," Paul joked, having been warned by Claire to laugh John out of his anxieties. "As for Maureen, she's as fit as a fiddle, whether she's thirty-nine or, as I'm inclined to believe, thirty-seven for it's just like her to make the most of a situation like this! Believe me, John, everything is going to be all right, so let's wet the baby's head in advance."

And so it proved when Maureen's baby was born in a Paxtonbury nursing home "on the anniversary of Abraham Lincoln's birthday" as the almost incoherent father informed Paul and Claire by telephone. Maureen had had a stiffish time, he said, and was very tired, but Goreham who was attending her was pleased with her on the whole. The baby weighed seven pounds and they were going to christen him Paul, after his godfather!

"How many godchildren have I got around here?" Paul asked Claire, after he had passed the news to the anxious kitchen staff and Claire, after consulting the record, told him seven, four girls and three boys, and she would have to make a special entry in the back of the book so that he did not overlook anyone's birthday. She kept her promise the next day and read the list to him over the luncheon table. The first, Sam Potter's eldest daughter, was now nine and between Pauline Potter and Paul Rudd came one of Will Codsall's boys, Eveleigh's youngest daughter, a son of Henry Pitts, a child of Honeyman's foreman at the Home Farm, and the daughter of a cottager employed by Edward Derwent, whose wife had died in labour.

"Well, it's enough," he said, "we'll have to call a halt to this nonsense. How can I be responsible for seven children learning their catechism when I'm going bald and putting on weight? Maureen's right about this Valley. Every woman who sets foot in it finds herself in the family way sooner or later."

"If they didn't you'd be the first to complain about diminishing returns," Claire told him. "Who knows, I might have some interesting news for you myself in the spring."

He looked at her so sharply that she laughed and said, "It's all right, I'm only teasing but don't look as if I could go about it without your enthusiastic co-operation! Sometimes I'm surprised we haven't got as many as the Eveleighs! I do hope they've finished or we shall be saddled with the expense of extending Four Winds."

Maureen returned to the Valley in early April and Thirza, who had been Simon's nurse, was flattered to be taken on in like capacity at the Lodge, her place as parlourmaid-nanny being filled by a pert fourteen-year-old called Joy, the daughter of the eldest Timberlake girl.

Another entry in the record, dated "*March 1st, 1912*," told of Paul's acceptance of the mastership of the combined Teazel Vale and Downland Farmers' Hunt, on condition that he was not expected to hunt more than three days a fortnight and could hand over to Rose Derwent on alternate hunting days. The invitation originated from Lord Gilroy, who, despite their political rivalry, flatly refused to perpetuate his father's feud and took little or no interest in country activities.

The Teazel Vale pack was sadly run down but the Downland farmers, who hunted the country east of High Coombe where the Shallowford boundary ran inland from the sea, were only too anxious to halve their expenses by bringing in new hounds and combining the two hunts, renamed the Sorrel Vale Hunt and housed in kennels built on to some old outbuildings belonging to the Hermitage. Gilroy provided his own huntsmen and Eveleigh's eldest boy was engaged as whipper-in and kennelman, so that after a shaky start the new hunt settled down to a lively season in the autumn of 1912.

To see the motley field move off on a fine autumn morning and draw one of the Hermitage coverts, or cross the moor in a north-easterly direction to the rough country behind Shallowford Woods, was like watching a column of moss-troopers embark on a border foray. It was by no means a fashionable hunt for Paul was no stickler for etiquette and most of the followers wore corduroys, leggings and hard, low-crowned hats. Only Rose Derwent and one or two of the wealthier freeholders were well-mounted but there was an easy familiarity about a company where most of the field addressed one another by Christian name and once they were in full cry over open country there was often some hard riding and a good deal of rivalry to be in at the death. Paul, who considered himself no more than a

593

competent horseman, was outclassed by the small group of thrusters to whom a day in the saddle was the breath of life. Always up with the leaders, and usually in advance of them, was Rose Derwent, who would ride straight at the most formidable fence; not far behind whenever he was home on furlough, was Ikey, with young Gilbert Eveleigh, Gottfried Scholtzer, the son of the German historian, little Pauline Potter, Sam's eldest daughter (who was Rose Derwent's chief apprentice), and two or three others. Paul himself, Chivers his groom, Henry Pitts, Edward Derwent and Eveleigh when he could spare the time, usually followed in a pounding bunch, with stragglers sometimes as much as a quarter-mile in the rear, those who turned out for the exercise like John Rudd, old Arthur Pitts and even, on occasion, the German professor himself, who splashed along on a barrel-chested cob, his Teutonic passion for tidiness requiring him to see the last of the cavalcade out of a field and make sure every gate was shut and fastened. Rose Derwent had taught every child in the Valley to ride, accepting fees from no more than half of them but relying on their services as stable-hands during school holidays and week ends. Claire came out occasionally but, unlike Rose, who shocked some of the older members of the hunt, preferred to ride side-saddle. Whenever she appeared at a meet Paul noticed the sad, proud look in her father's eye and guessed that he was comparing her with her mother, who had died in a gully across the Teazel more than twenty years before. Although he did not take his mastership very seriously (it was difficult to think of the Sorrel Vale and Southdown Farmers' in terms of the Quorn or Pytchley) he always enjoyed himself and felt better for the day out. He liked best, however, the long treks home to Shallowford when the deep goyles intersecting the moor were bowls of blue dusk and the smell of wet leaves came out of the woods. Sometimes he would ride partway home with Eveleigh, or Henry Pitts, and they would discuss the day's run, chuckling over John Rudd parting from his cob at a jump or telling each other that young Gilbert Eveleigh and little Pauline Potter would make first-class steeplechasers in the years ahead. For there always seemed to be so many years ahead and whenever he was alone on the final stage along the river road or crossing the shoulder of the Bluff, Paul was aware of the timelessness of the Valley, and the rhythm of its seasons that seemed unrelated to the passage of time elsewhere. When Claire was with him they would sometimes talk of the future and speculate on the probable careers of Simon, the twins, Andy and Steve, and their daughter Mary, but secretly, and

594

sometimes a little guiltily, Paul preferred to make these homeward journeys in solitude, for then he could kick his legs free of the stirrups and let his thoughts range back across the years to the days when he first ambled over this familiar ground, surely the greenest and possibly the luckiest landowner in the Westcountry.

II

Old Willoughby died in the new year, the direct result according to his boy Francis, of travelling to Whinmouth in foul weather to conduct a service and riding home the same night. It was partially true, inasmuch as he died only a week later of pneumonia but Willoughby was nearly seventy and had never enjoyed the robust health of the other tenants although, for some years now — ever since his Road-to-Damascus conversion at a Methodist camp-meeting — he had driven himself hard, sometimes making a journey of forty miles to witness The Truth. At his funeral in the tiny Nonconformist burial ground adjoining the Methodist Chapel in Coombe Bay Paul noticed that the Valley was as well represented as it had been at old Tamer's funeral, when the whole countryside had turned out to pay tribute to such an unlikely hero. The centuries-old feud between church and chapel-goers was finally buried with Willoughby, for Parson Horsey attended, standing a little apart from the dry-eyed Elinor Codsall and her hulking husband Will, who looked clownish in his blue serge suit. Paul said to Francis Willoughby, as they walked back to the lych-gate, "He was a good man, Francis, and I shall never forget how well he behaved on the night of the wreck. He didn't have an enemy in the Valley, did he?", and Francis said no, not now that Parson Bull had gone but that the old man had been inclined to let Deepdene take second place to his preaching and the place was now in bad heart.

"You'll be carrying on, I hope," Paul said and Francis replied that it depended on how much money his father had left for there was very little profit in poultry now that Elinor had gone and for some time the farm had been badly understocked. "I always wanted him to go in for beef," he added, "but he never would, for he couldn't stomach the idea of fattening animals for the slaughter-house. He ought to have been a vet instead of a farmer, he was clever with a sick beast."

Paul said, "Look here, Frank, if you think you can make a success of beef go ahead and chance your luck! I'll ask Honeyman to see what he can do to give you a start and you know that I'm all for specialisation

595

It's certainly worked over at Four Winds, and at your sister's little place. You don't have to show a profit for a year or two for I shouldn't press you," and Francis, a young man of few words where his father had had so many, murmured his thanks but little else, so Paul sought out Elinor who agreed that it was a sound notion and told Francis so on the spot.

The upshot of the conversation was that Francis Willoughby sold his poultry to his sister, his pigs to Henry Pitts and thereafter concentrated on beef cattle and Paul noticed that he seemed to flower within weeks of his father's death, as though, for the first time in his life, he could farm instead of deputising for a man who preferred the pulpit to the strawyard. He had always been a very reserved young man, small and neat like Elinor but lacking the stamina she had shown from the day Will Codsall carried her as a bride to the half-ruined holding at Periwinkle. Paul first noticed the dramatic change in Francis while crossing a Deepdene meadow on his way home from the last meet of the season. He saw him driving a bunch of steers into a kale field and at first he thought the lad must be having trouble for he darted this way and that, waving his jacket and uttering sharp, staccato shouts but after watching a moment he realised that Francis was only amusing himself by pretending to be a matador so he rode on without advertising himself, realising that the new master of Deepdene would be very embarrassed if he thought his charade was overlooked. He thought, "Well, that's another little problem sorted out but it's a pity the old man had to die first! That's the way it seems to be, however; Martin Codsall goes crazy and Eveleigh steps in to make a go of Four Winds; Tamer Potter gets drowned and his two daughters take up with a tireless clodhopper who succeeds in revitalising the Dell; and now Frank Willoughby plays at bullfighting in his own meadow and that within a month of his father being laid in the earth!", and he rode on down to the Ford musing and feeling that, although the Valley seemed always to stand still, this was really a delusion and that its blood was circulating all the time as new approaches were made to old problems and new hands laid on old tools.

III

Ikey Palfrey passed out of Woolwich with creditable marks in the late summer of 1912 and came home on furlough for a month before joining his battery in India. Claire thought he had changed a good deal during the last two or three years and Paul admitted that he had, at least outwardly, for he was now a shade short of six feet and had also filled out, losing the lean, rakish build of his cross-country days. Yet to Paul he was still the Ikey Palfrey plucked from the scrapyard ten years ago, a waif with an impudent way of looking seniors in the eye as if, whilst prepared to be lectured now and again, he reserved the right to treat scoldings as so much pi-jaw without much significance.

Claire had never felt wholly at ease with Ikey and, without in the least knowing why, went out of her way to maintain the slightly impersonal relationship that grew up between them. In the early days of her marriage, when Ikey was only a boy and away at school most of the time, it had been easy to patronise him but later on, when he was about eighteen, she began to suspect that, more often than not, and in the kindest possible way, he was laughing at her and this led her to discard patronage in favour of propitiation, although she could think of no reason at all why she should adopt such an attitude. It might, she sometimes thought, have something to do with that curious letter he had written her all those years ago, the one urging her to visit the injured Squire after he had called out for her in a fever. She had never mentioned this letter to anyone, not even to Paul, yet here again she could find no adequate reason for keeping it a secret, for she had never once doubted its substance. Ikey was always very polite to her and she did not think it likely that he still regarded himself as the agent who brought man and wife together, reasoning that he had probably forgotten the letter by now and yet, every now and again when their eyes met over the table, or she found herself alone with him, his knowing air put her at a disadvantage. He still addressed her as "Ma'am", as though she was a queen to whom he owed an indirect allegiance, and this slightly uncomfortable relationship had not been eased by a recent exchange over Simon, occurring soon after her discussion with Grace concerning the boy.

Claire took her duties as stepmother very seriously and had gone out of her way to avoid discriminating between Simon and her own children, often to the latters' disadvantage. Simon was a difficult child to know and inclined to walk alone but she had persisted and was confident that he had a genuine affection for her. She had thought a good deal before taking Grace's advice, and discussing with Ikey the possibility of telling Simon some form of disguised truth about his mother. She would have preferred to leave things as they were and let him grow up thinking of himself as her child but she remembered that the

Valley relished scandal of every kind and with Simon approaching his eighth birthday it was likely that he would soon learn the truth from an outside source which it was surely her duty to anticipate. So, in the end, she told Ikey the gist of her conversation with Grace in the hotel bedroom after the suffragette scuffle and as always he listened gravely and politely to what she had to say. When, however, she told him that Grace had advised her to employ him as her agent, he smiled his rather irritating smile and said, "I'm afraid it's too late, Ma'am. Simon already knows all there is to know." She said, shocked by this news, "He does? Who told him?" and without a blush he admitted having told Simon himself more than a year ago, after the child had made an appeal to him for information on the subject.

At first she was furiously angry but then common sense warned her that she was being unjust and that Simon must have got an inkling from one of the tenants or estate workers before approaching Ikey in the first place. She said, crisply, "He *came* to you? After hearing gossip from somebody else?"

"I couldn't say," he replied calmly, "I didn't ask him."

"Why didn't you ask him?"

He lifted his shoulders, refusing to be rattled. "I don't know, perhaps because it seemed to me to be prying. He had probably been eavesdropping and heard something he wasn't meant to hear. He asked me about his mother so I told him."

"Wouldn't it have been wiser to have sent him to me or his father?"

"I don't think so, Ma'am. If he had wanted that he would have gone to you or Squire instead of me."

She bit her lip and at that moment she could cheerfully have boxed his ears but behind her resentment she could not help admiring his grasp of essentials. She said rather sharply, "Well, how did he take it? Was it a shock to him?"

"No," he said, "I don't think it was a shock. I cushioned it as well as I could, and I got the impression he had always known there was a difference between him and the twins and Mary. How can we be sure he didn't get a hint years ago, a chance remark made by any one of us when we thought him too young to notice?"

She considered this and the pause gave her a chance to master her temper and make an honest effort to put herself in Ikey's place. After all, he was quite possibly right, for adults often made this mistake and in any case it was done now and her relationship with Simon had improved rather than deteriorated in the last year. She said with a shrug,

598

"Well, I'm glad it's over and done with but I shall have to tell Squire what happened and I daresay he'll want to hear more details."

Ikey nodded, absently she thought and said, "I did what I thought best at the time, I'm sorry if I put my foot in it. It seemed to me that, by making an issue of it Simon might have been more confused than he was. That was why I made light of it, Mrs. Craddock."

Devil take the boy, she thought, he's infallible! It occurred to her then how odd it was that Grace should have singled out Ikey for a mission already accomplished and with this thought came another, more disquieting one for it seemed to her that Ikey's loyalty was to Grace rather than to her and it distressed her to think this for until then it had always seemed that all trace of Grace Lovell had been banished from the house whereas it was now evident that something of Grace lingered. The uncertainty caused by this reflection must have shown in her face for, with his strange faculty for reading thoughts, he said, gently, "I wouldn't worry about it any more, Ma'am. Simon looks on you as his mother and why shouldn't he? You haven't failed him in that respect and I'm sure you never will."

Suddenly, and shamefully, she wanted to cry and he must have seen this too, for he turned away and lounged off, hands deep in his pockets while she stood there feeling more unsure of herself than at any time since her return to the Valley. But she was Edward Derwent's daughter and had emotional reserves at her disposal, so presently she blew her nose, threw up her head and marched off along the terrace to the rose garden where she remained until she had regained control of herself.

She found a way of telling Paul without making an issue of it, throwing the information into a general conversation about her talk with Grace at the hotel and saying, with a casualness that deceived him, "Grace wondered if Simon knew I was his stepmother; I told her that Ikey had explained it to him long ago," and all Paul replied was, "Ikey did? Well, good for him! It was something I should have put off indefinitely."

And that, so far as Claire was concerned, would have been that had not a new development involving Ikey and Simon taken place during Ikey's embarkation leave, a year later. This time Claire found herself in uneasy alliance with Ikey, siding with him at the risk of engaging in her first serious quarrel with the man she adored.

It happened at lunchtime, on a day towards the end of October after Paul and Simon had come in from a morning's cubbing in the woods. Paul seemed very put out about something and Simon, after kicking

599

off his little boots and throwing down his hard hat and riding switch, disappeared upstairs, remaining there in spite of being called for lunch. The twins and Mary were in the nursery and the only other person at table was Ikey, who had seemed very preoccupied this leave, a circumstance Claire attributed to the imminence of his first tour overseas. Claire said, as Mrs. Handcock appeared with the vegetables, "I'll see to that! Go up and get Simon, I've already called him three times!" but Paul said, unexpectedly, "Leave him to work out his sulks!" and Mrs. Handcock departed, buttoning her lip as she always did when there was an atmosphere at table.

"Did anything happen this morning?" Claire asked and Paul grunted that sometimes he couldn't get to the bottom of "that boy", and that it was time Simon went to school to get sense knocked into him.

Ikey perked up at this, winking at Claire who at once demanded to know what had happened. It was something very trivial, he told her — Gilbert Eveleigh, as whipper-in, had posted Simon on his pony in the north run while most of the others stood back from the covert. The boy had been told to holler back as soon as the fox in the thick undergrowth crossed the ride towards a known earth north of the mere. The fox went in that direction — Gilbert and others would swear to that — but no holler came from Simon, and when they had all dashed round to his side of the wood he was seen walking his pony down a ride nearly a mile from the spot where he had been stationed. The fox got clean away and when Paul demanded to know whether Simon had seen it he admitted that he had but had turned away rather than holler.

"Why ever did he do that?" asked Claire much surprised, and Paul said that on the way home Simon had told him he did not want to go hunting again and that he thought hunting "wasn't really a gentleman's sport!"

This was too much for Ikey who let out a loud guffaw and even Claire smiled but Paul, whose sense of humour was unpredictable, said, "What's funny about it? I felt a damned ass I can tell you! And as for him feeling squeamish about hunting we don't want the boy to develop into a milksop, do we?"

"He'll not do that," Ikey said and with so much emphasis that Claire saw he no longer treated the incident as a joke. "If the kid really feels that way," he went on, "then jolly good luck to him! He's probably right anyway!"

"Now what the devil am I to make of that?" demanded Paul angrily and Claire said they were both making too much of the matter, and that if he took Simon at his word, and left him behind next time, the boy would probably be disappointed.

"I wouldn't bank on that," Ikey said, quietly, and when they both looked at him, added, "He's got a natural sympathy for the fox. He always has given me the impression he's signed on with the hunted!"

"Sometimes, Ikey," Paul said, gruffly, "I wish to God you would stop favouring us with undergraduate drivel when you're at home! It doesn't suit you and it damned well irritates me!"

It was the first time Claire had ever heard him address Ikey sharply and she suddenly was aware that the clash between them went beyond Simon's quixotic sympathy for a hunted fox. She said, hastily, "All right, all right! Don't let's quarrel about it, it isn't that important."

"It might be," Ikey said, ignoring her cautionary glance, "if the Gov'nor is determined to warp Simon into being the kind of person he isn't, and never will be!"

"Well he isn't likely to do that," snapped Claire, feeling annoyed with both of them but she could not help noticing that Paul winced at Ikey's remark as he said, sharply, "Look here, Ikey, I happen to think young Simon made an exhibition of himself turning his back on the field the way he did! I daresay the incident seems trivial to both of you but to my mind it was a blatant piece of showing off! If he really felt that way he could easily have made some kind of excuse."

"What kind of excuse?" Ikey asked, and Paul replied, irritably, "Any kind! He could have pretended he wasn't looking, or that he had just taken a toss!"

"Yes," said Ikey, still quietly, "he could have done that and revealed himself as a liar and a coward when he's neither."

"Oh do let's get Simon down and forget about it," said Claire but Paul said, "No, I'm damned if I will for I'll not have Ikey trying to teach me how to bring up my own son! I tell you the boy was showing off and nothing more!" whereupon Ikey growled, "That isn't true and you know it, Gov'nor! It's a damned pompous attitude and I'm hanged if I'll sit here and listen to it! The kid was perfectly justified in doing what he did and as his father you ought to sympathise with him instead of bullying him!" and he got up, nodded to Claire and strode towards the door.

He was stopped by Claire who shot out her arm as he passed and caught him by the wrist. She said, in a way that made them both feel slightly ashamed of themselves, "You can't walk out on this now,

601

Ikey! And neither can you, Paul! You've both said too much for my peace of mind and it's quite wrong to begin an argument like this and then turn your backs on it!"

"I wasn't turning my back on it," Paul said, although he had in fact half risen. "All the same I can't see any sense in prolonging it and upsetting everybody. You'd better go, Ikey, and I hope you mind your manners better than this in the mess!"

"Stop it, Paul," Claire almost shouted, "just stop it and let me say something!"

They both looked at her then, Paul settling back in his chair, Ikey standing irresolutely by the door.

"Now then," she said, trying hard to get her voice under control, "this is something we must have out here and now if only because I happen to be concerned. Very much concerned!"

"I don't see how," Paul grumbled but in a more reasonable tone. "What are you driving at, Claire?"

Claire looked at Ikey, realising that he was very well aware what she was driving at and went on, "Ikey is implying that Simon is . . . well, is his mother all over again! That's what you meant, isn't it?"

"Yes, it is, Ma'am," he said, "and I'm sorry."

"You needn't be sorry but for heaven's sake do stop calling me 'Ma'am', as if I was someone who had usurped Queen Victoria!" she snapped and a ghost of a grin plucked at the corners of his mouth and then vanished as he saw thunder in Paul's glance.

"I've never heard such damned nonsense in my life," Paul said but Claire, turning on him, said that it wasn't nonsense and if he would have the patience to think about it he would see that it wasn't. Paul said, helplessly, "But hang it, woman, Grace hunted twice a week! She was one of the best riders to hounds in the country."

"It isn't simply a matter of hounds and foxes, Gov'nor," Ikey said, patiently, "it's an attitude to life, an inherited attitude maybe. That's what you meant, wasn't it—Claire?"

Colour came back into her cheeks and through the fog of the issue that had them snapping at one another she saw that, for the first time since they had sat around this table together, they were of a single generation, no longer a man, his wife and a boy but three adults, each equally involved. She said, more calmly, "Yes, Ikey, that was exactly what I meant, and because of it I entirely agree with you! It would be quite wrong of Paul to bully Simon into hunting against his will, or looking on him as a ninny because he wouldn't! I don't like saying this,

Paul, but you can be very stupid about some things and you're being stupid now, because your pride as the local M.F.H. is involved."

Ikey looked at her admiringly and for a moment nobody spoke. Then, when Paul moved as though to get up, and they both made sure he was going to storm out of the room, the door opened and Simon came in, silently taking his place and helping himself to vegetables. Claire said, gently, "You really must come when I call, Simon, we've all been waiting for you," and the boy, looking slightly startled, said, "I'm sorry, Mother, I was changing," and began to eat with catlike deliberation.

It was the strangest meal they had ever sat through but any prospect of further discussion was averted by Ikey's tact for he talked to Simon about one thing and another and occasionally included both Paul and Claire in the conversation so that Claire, whose heart was still beating an uncertain rhythm, had cause to be grateful to him but wondered bleakly what Paul would say to her when they were alone.

After about twenty minutes Paul rose, saying, "Run along and give Chivers a hand rubbing down, Simon, he's on his own this afternoon," and the boy slipped off, glad to be out of it so cheaply.

"Well, I'm not exactly climbing down," Paul said, as soon as he had gone, "but there might be something in what you say. It's worth thinking over at all events because if it is so then it will need tackling one way or another! To have Simon go Grace's way wouldn't bring him much joy, would it? Or us either?" and with that he stumped out. Ikey said, "I'm sorry I let you in for that, Claire. If I had to open my big mouth I shouldn't have done it in your presence!"

"It's just as well you did," she told him, "for there's little enough you could have done on your own, Ikey. Paul is hard to drive but I do flatter myself I've learned how to lead him."

"Yes," he said, with a grin, "I'm quite sure you have!" and he thought, "Grace certainly knew her business when she urged me to write that letter, for Claire understands him better than any of us, yet he can manage her when he wouldn't have managed Grace in a thousand years!" He moved across to the window, looking across the paddock under its green and gold autumn mantle.

"Are you depressed by the prospect of exchanging this for India?" she asked him suddenly but he said no, on the contrary he was relieved but he did not add why. She said, after a pause, "Well, if ever you want to talk, Ikey, I'll listen and do anything I can to help. We've at least made that much progress today."

603

He came back to her then, holding his head slightly to one side as though considering. And then he did something he had never done in the ten years she had known him. He bent and brushed her cheek with his lips and was gone before she could decide what had prompted the gesture. When she thought of him afterwards, however, it was not as the brash, affable young man of whom she had once been so wary, but rather of a youth as confused and uncertain as any of them, despite a convincing show of self-containment.

IV

Claire was learning about him. The shifts of his life had taught him how to deceive most people, to cod them into believing that he had all the self-confidence necessary to make a place for himself wherever he went, but he had stopped deceiving himself long ago, soon after finding himself in a straitjacket tighter than any he had worn at High Wood or Shallowford. Yet he still might have worn it comfortably had it not been for Hazel Potter who stood squarely between past and future and was always there, clutching her rags and freedom no matter how many new friends he made, how many cadet sprees he embarked upon, how enthusiastically he threw himself into the business of learning to be a gunner. He would see her in his mind's eye at odd times of the day and night, when his thoughts should have been engaged elsewhere and it was not only his body that yearned for her. She had the power to make everything he did seem profitless, sometimes almost fatuous, as if she alone was the one substantial force in his world and everything else — the ritual of mess life, the airs and opinions of instructors and fellow cadets, the menace of the great tools he was learning to use, were toys in a nursery of men and women clinging to the fantasies of childhood. Yet he did not accept this duality without a bitter, inward struggle for he sensed, somehow, that it would bring him down in the end whichever way he turned and he was still tormented by the demands of loyalty to the Squire, the man who, from the kindest of motives, had turned him loose in this desert. But it was Hazel Potter who triumphed. Only a day or two after he had returned home for his first leave his good intentions were forgotten. Shedding his fashionable clothes with his army drawl he slipped off into the woods to find her and here, so long as they were alone, he was happy again, his tensions miraculously eased.

They did not become lovers again, or not on that first occasion, for

604

as long as their association remained innocent he could hold the door on the other world ajar but when he came home again in the spring the temptation to slam that door and go to Heaven or hell with a flower in his mouth was too strong for him; and having once recrossed into her world he had no regrets, although he sometimes wondered what would become of them both and how loud the crash would be when it came.

He no longer felt shame or fear when he parted from her but he took great pains to ensure, as far as possible, that the woods kept their secret, riding out on his chestnut mare, Bella, and unsaddling and haltering her below the hill where Hazel kept her little house. As long as he went out mounted Paul and everyone else would assume him to be riding for exercise and sometimes on his return he would describe the imaginary route he had taken. Chivers might have noticed that Bella always looked fresh when he stabled her but Chivers was an unimaginative soul and would have found it difficult to believe that horse and rider had gone no further than the north side of the mere, there to part company for an hour or longer.

Hazel received him gladly but without excitement. She was aware of the obligations he owed the world beyond the screen of the woods and had long grown accustomed to his erratic comings and goings at odd times of the year. Whenever she saw him emerge from the rhododendrons and begin to climb the hill she would slip down from her rock, mend the fire and, after propping the polished tin lid on a niche, shake out her hair, crooning softly to herself and admiring her reflection in the surface. Then she would fill her battered kettle at the spring and put it to boil, for he liked her strong bitter tea and the honey she gathered to spread on bread baked in her Dutch oven.

There was nothing urgent or impetuous about these occasions. Sometimes, after they had kissed in greeting, they would sit together and look out over the Valley and she would tell him of her trivial encounters since he was last here, of lumbering badgers visiting one another's sets on the slope, or another attempt of the stoats to rob the woodpecker's nest and the struggle that followed. There were always fresh flowers in a jam jar on her "table", not only the more homely flowers of the woods, bluebells, harebells, primroses, foxgloves and campion, but much shyer plants that she alone knew where to find and had gathered to give brief splendour to the cave. Then, when they had talked and sipped their tea, he would sometimes stroke her hair, caressing it with a gentle, unhurried touch and looking at her as if he

605

never ceased to wonder at the texture of her skin, the lights in her hair, or the suppleness of her limbs tanned nut-brown by sun and wind. Whenever he spoke to her he used her familiar burr but without self-consciousness, for it seemed to him an affront to talk to her as he talked to the cadets and the people up at the Big House. He would say, stroking her breasts, "Youm beautiful, Hazel! Youm the prettiest creature yerabouts, that you be! An' I loves touching 'ee, do'ee know that?" and she would smile a gratified, vacant smile and shiver under his hand or lift her own to trace a path down the side of his face with a forefinger, as though to assure herself that he was real. Then, without explanation, he would be gone again and she would busy herself renewing the bracken on the floor, or scouring her battered pots, or would resume her aimless movements about the Valley. She was always happiest in the hour when he had gone for then her memory of what had passed between them was fresh and she could compose one of her long, rambling prose poems in which they ranged the woods and river valley together but soon she would half forget him until some sixth sense told her he was home again and it was time to resume her vigil on the rock. They had tried to coax her back to the Dell or to take service with one of the farmers but she resisted their persuasions, disappearing completely for days at a stretch so that, short of locking her up, there was no way of stopping her wandering. Meg saw her and talked to her from time to time, but Meg did not join the crusade to tame her; she alone, with the single exception of Ikey, understood what freedom of movement meant to the only true gypsy in the family and would do nothing to threaten it.

Two or three days after the dispute about Simon Ikey set out across the woods on foot in the dusk of a dry autumn day. He did not hurry for he was depressed at not having had the courage to tell her that he would be gone in the morning, this time for at least three years. He knew that she took little heed of time and that even if he told her the truth she would not be much concerned but the finality of the occasion weighed on his mind nevertheless. It was almost dark when he threaded his way through the rhododendrons but she heard twigs crackle under his feet and lit a candle to guide him to the screen of the gorse at the mouth of the cave. He was a long time coming up and the kettle, which had been simmering, was boiling when he reached her little house.

"Will 'ee tak' tea now," she said, as though she had been a polite hostess welcoming a guest and he said he would and squatted on a truss of bracken, balancing himself on his heels. Sitting in that posture, with the candlelight flickering over his dark hair and strong features he looked a little like an Arab pondering a purchase and she said, handing him tea, "Youm sad, Ikey boy; be 'ee off outalong tomorrow?" He said this was so and that he would be outalong much longer than usual for they were sending him across the sea. This did not frighten her but it must have astonished her for she uttered the low hissing sound she used to express surprise.

"Across the sea?" she repeated. "Baint 'ee scared?"

"No," he said, "I baint scared but I'm mumpish, mumpish to be leavin' 'ee so long."

"Aw giddon," she said, carelessly, "you'll be back zoon enough, dornee mope along o' that!" and she sidled up to him and tweaked his ear. He seized her then with an urgency he had never used, not even when he was drunk on her mother's hedgerow wine, throwing her across his knees and covering her face with kisses so that she laughed and pretended to resist and they rolled sideways into the bracken, their shadows dancing a crazy pattern on the wall. Then, breathlessly, she freed herself and said, "Wait on, boy! Dornee rush zo! Tiz dark now, so why dornee stay the night zince youm going? Tiz mild too and us'll be snug if I mends the fire!"

He said, for once not using the brogue, "I can't stay, Hazel; it's my last night and they'll expect me to dinner," but he made no effort to go and she was puzzled by his sudden listlessness. "I don't like leaving you and that's a fact," he added and she smiled for he had never previously committed himself so deeply, "I don't like to think what might happen to you up here alone with me thousands of miles away. Dammit, you can't even read a letter I could write! Why the devil won't you go and live in the Dell, at least until I get back again?"

He had suggested this many times, just as he had urged her to return to Miss Willoughby's school and learn to read and write, but tonight she saw that he meant it and his sudden concern baffled her.

"Now whyfore should harm come to me up yer?" she demanded. " 'Er never has, has 'er?"

"No," he admitted, "it never has, and I suppose you can look after yourself for if you can't, who can?"

"I likes it yer," she said, doggedly, "so yer I stay 'till I dies!"

"*Why* do you like it so much, Hazel? Tell me, if you can."

"Because I can zee what goes on," she said, but then he saw that she was teasing him and that this was not the real reason, and said, "That isn't why! I don't mind about you being here by day, it's sleeping out that matters."

"Aye," she said, now looking at him slyly, "but mebbe I stay on because o' you!"

"Because of me? But I only get up here once in a blue moon!"

"Ah," she said, "that's zo but when I'm yer *youm* always along o' me in a manner o' speakin'. Do 'ee mind that, now?"

He minded it well enough and it filled him with a tenderness that no words, in or out of the brogue, could convey. He put his arm round her and drew her close so that they sat there with their backs to the shelving wall, her head on his breast as he stroked her tumbling mass of hair. They sat thus for so long that he thought she was asleep and presently the candle guttered and went out but as though to replace it a sliver of moonlight crept into the cave. Time passed and neither of them moved but when, shifting slightly to glance at his luminous watch, he saw that it was already long past dinner-time, she stirred and said, plaintively, "Youm turrible mumpish tonight, Ikey! Dornee want me no more?" and he took her face between his hands and said, "I'll always want you, Hazel, wherever I am and I'll always come back to you, don't ever forget that! I'll always come back!" It seemed to satisfy her for she brightened up at once, saying cheerfully, "Well then yer us be an' tomorrow you'll be outalong zo tiz no use frettin', be it? Us best maake the most of it, Ikey-boy!"

Her philosophy, thus expressed, boosted his spirits for he thought, "They all call her 'mazed' but she's more sense than any one of us! She doesn't live by the week or the day but by the hour, so that's how I'll think of her, always!" and he pulled her down and would have taken possession of her with the impatience he usually displayed when time was short, but tonight a subtle difference entered into their relationship; after the first moment or so it was she who led, as though she realised he was the one standing in need of comfort.

It was after ten o'clock when he kissed her for the last time and, taking his lantern, went out along the track to the north end of the mere and home by the long but less overgrown route, approaching Shallowford from the east. He slipped in by the yard door and up the backstairs to change his clothes and when he came down to the library he found Paul and Claire waiting up but they did not ask him where he had been, or why he was so late, remembering that he was almost twenty-one and might well have some private good-byes to say in the Valley. In fact they had laid a wager on the subject, over dinner, Paul betting that Ikey was mildly interested in the eldest Eveleigh girl, Claire wagering that Deborah Eveleigh was not Ikey's type and suggesting that his fancy had strayed over the county border during his summer furlough and fixed on the daughter of a retired cavalry major called Ella Stokes, who lived at Brandon Chase or the next village on.

"It's a damned long walk in the dark," Paul said, when ten o'clock struck, "so you've lost your money, old girl!"

"Not so long at his age, and with the prospect of three years pig-sticking and polo playing in the company of men," she said. "In any case, don't you dare question him unless he volunteers information!"

"Not me," he told her chuckling, "I know that much about Ikey!"

He apologised for missing dinner when he came at last but he did not explain where he had been, except to say, off-handedly, that he had lost track of time. Claire, kissing him good night, noticed that he still looked a little wan and decided that the bet would be null and void, for he had almost certainly been mooching around in his own company all evening and this did not surprise her. If she had been exchanging Shallowford for India it was what she might have done.

CHAPTER SIX

I

KEITH HORSEY'S wooing of Rachel Eveleigh was progressing but at such a pedestrian pace that sometimes Rachel would lie awake for an hour wondering how to bring him to the boil. It was almost two years since she had correctly assessed the worth of Sydney Codsall and, miraculously it seemed at the time, switched to Keith who had undoubted possibilities as a swain but whose technique was even more cumbersome than Sydney's, although for very different reasons. Sydney had held off because he had no intention of committing himself, whereas Keith was clearly enslaved but was so humble about it that it had taken him nearly twelve months (spaced by absences at Oxford) to reach the hand-holding stage. Now that the fine weather had arrived, and they could take long walks together in the cool of the evening, she had managed to apply the spur once or twice but the entries in the diary she kept recorded only three kisses and two of them were hardly more than pecks in the region of the right ear. It was depressing to compare her recent experience with those of her pre-Sydney period, when, in the company of Debbie, her sister, she had attended harvest suppers and an occasional hop in the Coombe Bay Village Institute. Here she had had the greatest difficulty in extricating herself from bucolic embraces without crossing the line that might have led to a thrashing from father, endless nagging from mother, a shotgun wedding and a life-sentence in a tied cottage behind one of the farms. Faced, however, with Keith's abject humility Rachel sometimes wished that the Devil his father was always preaching about would take fleeting residence in his son, just long enough to enable her to turn temptation to permanent advantage.

It was not to be, however. Keith must have imbibed so many warnings against the lusts of the flesh that he was more or less inoculated against the Devil's wiles, for even when their fingers touched he trembled and began to stutter, and once, when he was helping her over a stile and her dress had caught on a briar to expose about two inches of shin, he had blushed the colour of a ripe plum and they walked all the way home unlinked.

Reviewing the situation as it was when he came home for the summer vacation in June, 1913, Rachel concluded that she could only hope for an appreciable advance if something dramatic occurred during one of their silent evening rambles, something calculated to galvanise him into action and precipitate his suit by involuntary personal contact. She visualised a number of bizarre situations — Keith throwing his arms about her to shield her from a falling bough, Keith clasping her to him in defiance of Honeyman's prize bull, or, better still, Keith lifting her dripping wet from the Sorrel and attempting artificial respiration on the bank. In the event she was not required to set the stage for any of these occurrences.

It happened on a warm June evening as they were moving round the shoulder of the great escarpment north-west of the mere, using the overgrown path above the hill where the Shallowford badgers had their sets. Their walk had been even more uneventful than usual for the ground was rough over most of the route and for the last two miles they had been walking in Indian file, with Keith ahead, beating a passage through the brambles. Like most countrybred girls Rachel took the glories of nature for granted. Woods, ferns, wildflowers and brambles were to her little more than a growth on what might be converted into arable land and she was sorry now that she had agreed to turn off the sunken lane that ran a half-circle behind the Big House. Since he had returned home a few days earlier she had been growing desperate. Stile after stile had been negotiated and she had seen any number of available logs to sit upon but he had passed every spot where, on such an evening as this, and under a bronze and heliotrope sunset, lovers might have been tempted to linger. She finally made up her mind to try the simplest expedient of all, a stumble and a sprained ankle, that would encourage him to stop and perhaps try a little gentle massage, for by now Rachel was convinced that only close physical contact would give her a sporting chance of casting a net from which he, as a parson's son, could hardly escape with honour. She did not expect miracles but a miracle was unnecessary, a little patting and probing would do the trick and a proposal would almost certainly follow, particularly if she prescribed the areas where the patting was done. And then, just as she was looking out for a suitable briar to entrap her foot, the Valley mating gods took a hand and a low, choked cry issued from a gorse thicket within a few yards of the path. They both stopped, surprised, and a little alarmed to hear such a sound in such a place, and he said, seeking corroboration, "That was human!
611

Somebody is hurt in there!" and although the cry had sounded human common sense told her that it was far more likely to be the moan of an animal caught in a trap and she said as much. "Squire has forbidden the use of steel traps on the estate," he said. "I'll push through and see!" and he barged through the gorse that grew close against the summit of a large, flat-topped rock on the crest of the slope.

She did not follow for the gorse was dense and she was wearing her Sunday stockings. She sensed, however, that a crisis in their relationship had arrived, or was on the point of arriving and was therefore partially prepared for his re-emergence within a matter of seconds with an expression of terror on his face. She had never seen so much horror in a man's eyes, or a face more tense and blanched and cried, "What *is* it, Keith? What's in there?" and he gibbered. "It's . . . it's a *woman*, a gggirl! She's . . . she's . . . there's a bbbaby coming!" and for a moment she thought he was going to faint. Then a second cry came from the base of the rock and another and another, each louder and more pitiful than the other, so that Rachel rushed past him and dived through the gorse to find that it screened a small, shallow cave, evidently the hideout of a tramp or gypsy, for there was a burned-out fire and a few trumpery utensils scattered about. Beyond the fire, close against the wall was a girl, her knees drawn up and her single garment, a faded grey dress, rucked up level with her breasts. Her matted hair tumbled as she heaved and when her mouth was not open in a yell her teeth were clamped over her lip.

Rachel recognised her at once as Hazel Potter, the half-crazed postscript of the Potter tribe and a glance told her that Keith, unbelievably, was right and that the poor little wretch was indeed giving birth to a child, for the baby's head was already showing and it seemed to Rachel, who had witnessed the birth of innumerable foals and calves, that labour was about half-way through and progressing rapidly before her eyes. She had inherited courage from her father and any amount of common sense from her mother, so that even before the shock had receded she knew what she must do and also what Keith must do if he could keep his nerve. She dived back through the bushes and seizing him by the shoulders shook him as though he had been a troublesome child.

"Listen!" she shouted, "listen, and then do exactly what I say! Are you listening? *Are* you?" and when he nodded, his head wobbling on his long, thin neck, she went on, "It's Hazel Potter and she *is* having a baby! I'll have to stay and help but you must go for the lady doctor as fast as you can. Don't go the shortest way but across the stream to Sam Potter's cottage and send his wife here to help me—tell her to bring towels and a sheet and . . . and string and scissors, can you remember? Then take Sam's pony, ride on to the Lodge and guide the lady doctor back here."

She was agreeably surprised to see that he pulled himself together at once and repeated her instructions like a recitation. Then he set off at a long, loping run, disappearing round the bend in the track while she ran back through the bushes and flung herself on her knees beside the girl, looking wildly around for something approximate to a bed and rejecting the pile of sacks in favour of a great truss of freshly-cut bracken bundled against the wall. She saw the kettle beside the almost extinct fire and would have crawled across to revive it by blowing on the embers had not Hazel, at that moment, clutched her with both hands as her mouth opened in another fearful yell. Then she understood that everything else would have to wait, that her immediate presence as someone to cling to for as long as the ordeal lasted, was more important than water or bedding or linen, so she wriggled in a half-circle that brought her in a position where Hazel's head could rest on her lap and Hazel's hands could retain their grip on her wrists and in this way she rode out the girl's successive heaves, pouring out such words of comfort as she could invent while the climax mounted and mounted until there was no interval between the spasms that touched off the girl's cries.

She was never able to recall how long they were alone before Joannie Potter arrived. It might have been twenty minutes, or an hour, or even longer before Rachel saw the child lying there and Hazel's grip on her wrists relaxed, so that she was able to shift her position and spill the truss of lean bracken across the floor, dragging some of it under the girl's shoulders, then scrambling round to revive the fire. The water in the iron kettle was still warm and in one of the cave's recesses she found the deep earthenware bowl that Hazel used for baking. She cleaned it as best she could, using strips torn from her petticoat and half-resting the squirming little creature on her knee sponged it from head to foot with her best cotton blouse. She had no means of separating mother and child, for although there was a large wooden-handled knife among the utensils its blade was rusted and she remembered that Jamieson, the Valley vet, had impressed upon them the importance of using clean instruments. It did occur to her to hold the blade in the fire but she shrank from this and anyway it did not seem to matter for the terrible urgency had ceased with the girl's cries. She was still making sounds of distress, long, whistling gasps, like a cider-sodden harvester asleep in the hay but her big brown eyes followed Rachel's every movement and noting this Rachel said, softly, "It's a boy, Hazel! I think he's all right!" The girl twisted herself to look at the child but even this small effort exhausted her and she slumped back on the bracken while Rachel, now using the hem ribbon of her petticoat, tied the cord tightly in two places about twelve inches apart as she had seen Jamieson do in the byre at Four Winds. When the water had been changed and the baby sponged again it looked, Rachel thought, more like a baby and less like a slimy pink monkey. It let out a single yell and its tiny feet pressed feebly against Rachel's knee, so that she forgot her terrible anxiety in a surge of achievement, wondering again whether or not to use the knife to cut the cord but again rejecting the idea from motives of hygiene. Instead she cradled the baby against her soiled skirt and with her left hand tore off another strip of material from her petticoat, using it to wash Hazel's face and the lower parts of her body. The girl spoke, suddenly, her voice seeming hardly to belong to her after all those cries:

"Where's 'er tu?" she demanded. "Where's The Boy?" and Rachel, surprised that she should have remembered Keith's fleeting appearance in the cave, said that he had gone for Joannie Potter, who would be here any moment and also the lady doctor, who would come as soon as Keith Horsey guided her here. Hazel received this information thoughtfully, lying back with her eyes fixed on the roof of the cave and Rachel noticed that her breathing was slowly returning to normal and that she seemed, miraculously, little the worse for the ordeal. Then, as the light in the cave waned, they heard someone call from the path and Rachel shouted, "In here—through the bushes under the rock!" and Joannie Potter appeared clutching an armful of bedding and towelling and with barely a glance at the baby began to make a couch at the back of the cave, spreading the sacks as a base for heaped-up bracken. The little cave seemed very crowded now and Rachel realised that Joannie was very much out of breath, so much so that it was minutes before she could gasp, "You've washed the mite? 'Twas warmish, I 'ope?" and Rachel told her the kettle had contained lukewarm water and that the baby, a boy, had cried out within a moment or two of birth. Joanie paused in her work of doubling the blankets. " 'Er baint crying now an' her should be! Turn un over, an' give un a smack or two!" and Rachel, smiling now, began to turn the child face down and then remembered that the cord was uncut.

"I tied the cord but couldn't cut it, Mrs. Potter!" she said and Joannie, without a word, poked her head under Rachel's elbow and bit so that the cord parted and Rachel was able to administer a smack on the child's tiny behind. The baby opened his mouth as wide as it would go and roared its resentment, the volume of his yells astonishing Rachel almost as much as the mother's unaided scramble on to the bed. The baby continued to bawl so loudly that Joannie said, grimly, " 'Er'll do! Just 'ark to un! Still, 'twas lucky you was by, with nought but a few dirty sacks to hand!" and she sighed as though the birth of a child in these circumstances was a bit of a nuisance but otherwise unremarkable.

'Be 'ee gonner tell 'em whose tacker tiz?" she asked carelessly but Hazel replied, sharply, "Tiz mine! Dornee pester me, Joannie!" whereupon Joannie sighed again, grumbling that Sam would want to know and so, probably, would the lady doctor but implied by her tone that the identity of the father was not very important.

"Be 'ee strong enough to give un the breast, child?" she said and Hazel, in answer, reached out for the baby and Rachel, a little regretfully, placed him carefully in her arms while Joannie pulled the crumpled dress over the mother's shoulders and busied herself tucking the blankets around her. The baby's outcry ceased so suddenly that the silence inside the cave seemed uncanny. Joannie said, dispassionately, "You'd better go an' watch for 'em. That boy was so scared I woulden wonder if 'er dorn taake lady doctor to Hermitage! I'll bide 'till they come, for Sam's with the children, young Barby bein' sick abed!"

Rachel went out into the open, surprised to find that it was now almost dark. In the glimmer of light over the Bluff she saw the foliage stir down by the north corner of the mere and presently, where the trees fell away around the stream, she caught a glimpse of two figures on horseback moving at a trot and yelled at the top of her voice in case, as Joannie had suggested, Keith had difficulty in locating the spot. Somebody answered her and they came on at a canter, the ponies' hooves chinking on the stones of the ascent like bottles in a basket. Keith appeared first, rolling from the saddle of Sam Potter's chestnut pony and shouting the moment he saw her, "Are you all right, Rachel?" and Rachel said, "Of course I'm all right! It wasn't me who had the baby, stupid!" but then she understood why he had asked for she was blouseless and her hair was falling over her bare shoulders so that for once it was she who blushed and was glad to answer the bark of Doctor Maureen, who climbed out of the saddle holding her bag, demanding to be shown the way to the patient.

They left Keith with the horses and pushed through the gorse, guided by the gleam of a lantern Joannie had lit but Rachel, acutely conscious of her dishevelled appearance, and feeling suddenly helpless in the presence of a professional, was glad to wash her face, hands and neck in what remained of the water before despatching Keith to the stream for more. While he was gone she hitched up her skirt, tore away the trailing edge of her petticoat hem and tried to tidy her hair by rearranging pins but she could do nothing about her bare neck and shoulders until Joannie said, "Taake my jumper, child, and go along home! Us can manage now and you can ride Sam's pony backalong, and Passon's boy can return un in the mornin'." Gratefully Rachel slipped on the soiled jumper that hung about her like a cloak, tucking it into the waistband of her skirt and giving a final, fascinated glance at Hazel, as she sat propped against the rear wall of the cave, the child at her breast. Then she went out to find Keith and said, apologising for her appearance, "It's Joannie Potter's jumper! I . . . I had to use my blouse in there," but she didn't mention her petticoat thinking that the poor boy had had a surfeit of embarrassments that evening. It was when he helped her climb up behind him and she had clasped him round the waist, that she began to feel happier and more serene than she had felt in twelve months for somehow, after all that had happened back there in the cave, his angular body was a source of comfort and what had occurred seemed, perversely, to have given him more confidence, for he said as they crossed over Codsall Bridge, "You were wonderful, Rachel! I was proud of you, and some time . . . some time I'd like to . . . to speak to Mr. Eveleigh about you, Rachel."

It was not the proposal she had daydreamed about either before and since the entry of Keith Horsey into her life, but it was valid she supposed and she hugged him in silence. There was really nothing she could reply to such a delightfully old-fashioned statement of his intentions. When they reached the yard and got down, unbridling the pony and turning him loose in the duck field, Keith found an excuse to linger by the gate. She could have wished that he had sought an elbow-rest further from her own kitchen door for she could hear the clatter of dishes and the voices of the children, any one of whom might appear bawling, "It's Rachel, Mum!" for it was late enough to merit explanations. She said, therefore, "I must go in now, Keith dear. It's late and Dad's very strict about time," and then, without the slightest prompting on her part, he seized her by the shoulders and kissed her on the mouth, and she kissed him back and ran swiftly across the cobbles towards the oblong of light in the kitchen yard. As she ran she giggled, partly with excitement but also with relish at the thought that it had taken Hazel Potter's bastard child, born in a cave in Shallowford Woods, to convert him from a possible into a certainty.

II

There was less speculation in the Valley as to the identity of the man responsible for bringing Hazel Potter to bed than there was comment regarding her reply to every inquiry, a sullen, reiterated, "Tiz mine an' my man's, baint it?" to which she would sometimes add the admonition directed at Joannie Potter at the time—"Dornee pester me!" as though requests for enlightenment on the subject were not merely impertinent but frivolous. Her sisters, who were shocked by the event, came up with a list of probables that included a half-witted crowstarver employed on the Heronslea estate and all three of the Timberlake boys. Fathers were canvassed in Coombe Bay and among the labouring population on the western side of the estate, the Potter girls reasoning that if Hazel's lover had lived on the eastern side they would have been sure to have seen him coming and going about his shameful business. Meg, for her part, did not seek information, realising that one might as well ask a vixen to name the dog-fox that had crossed into Shallowford country when she was last in season. She was, moreover, resigned to the arrival of babies without fathers and in any case did not consider it her business. In her view any grown woman could renew herself if she felt so inclined and with whom she went about it was a personal matter. Doctor Maureen, however, had other views and after making no headway at all with Hazel consulted her husband, declaring that the father of the child should be sought out, encouraged to marry the girl or if he was disinclined, compelled to contribute towards its upkeep but John told her not to waste time and shoe leather. "That child has lived rough in the woods for years," he said, "and I'm surprised it hasn't happened before! It might be any one of a score of men and no one is likely to own to it."

"If that child is promiscuous I'm Boadicea!" Maureen declared. "It wouldn't surprise me to learn that she'd been raped and threatened

617

and that's why she's holding her tongue!" but John said, wearily, "Why do we have to put such a dramatic construction on a Potter producing a bastard? They were doing it when I came here!"

"The circumstances are different," his wife said, "*very* different and not on account of the child being born in a cave! That Hazel Potter is fey for how else did she conceal her pregnancy all the time?"

"With the help of the Great God Pan I wouldn't wonder," John said, grinning and resumed his attempt to teach his seventeen-month-old son to walk a straight line across the carpet.

So Maureen turned elsewhere, questioning patients up and down the Valley but adding nothing to her knowledge. Few recalled having seen Hazel Potter during the last few months and those who had declared she was always alone. She persisted, however, and it was while casting about for some means of providing for the child's future that she was approached by Keith Horsey, the son of the rector, whom she recalled as being a friend of the absent Ikey. Keith came to her with a practical suggestion. If Hazel would domicile herself within walking distance of Coombe Bay, he said, the rector was prepared to pay her a small weekly sum out of parish funds for cleaning the church and helping Marlowe, the sexton, keep the graveyard free of weeds. She thanked him and recalling that it was he who had summoned her the night the child was born asked if he or Ikey had any knowledge of the company Hazel kept. He was on the defensive at once.

"Certainly not," he said, stiffly, "why should I have? Or Ikey either for that matter!"

"Oh come, lad," she chaffed. "I'm not suggesting it was either one of you but you and that lass you're courting walk the woods of an evening whereas Ikey, whenever he was home, was through them on horseback often enough. He's sharp enough to have noticed and remembered if he did see her with anyone. Will you mention it when you write?"

The boy turned aside and it seemed to her that he found the subject distasteful. Then she realised why, recalling that he had burst into the cave and seen the girl in labour and it had probably been a considerable shock to a person as shy and withdrawn as Keith Horsey. He said, finally, "I'll write and ask Ikey but I don't think he'll know anything. Won't the girl say?"

"No," said Maureen "she won't but for your information that isn't at all unusual in these cases."

618

"Why?" he asked, genuinely surprised. "Why should that be so?"
"All manner of reasons—fear, a bribe perhaps, or even mistaken loyalty. Sometimes they break down when they are faced with angry parents but this won't happen in Hazel's case, for that gypsy mother of hers thinks no more of a bastard than a litter of kittens under the stairs."

He flushed and she was sorry she hadn't chosen her words more carefully but after repeating his father's offer he left abruptly and she tackled her husband again, this time on the subject of accommodation for Hazel.

"There's a half-ruined cottage near the old mill a mile or so along the river road," she said. "Do you think Paul would do it up and let the girl have it on a peppercorn rent?"

"I daresay he would," John said, "he's soft enough, but why can't she and the child move into that harlots' nest in the Dell?"

"Because, if she does, she'll be in the family way again within six months," she told him, shortly. "I wouldn't put it past that great lump of a Jem adding another to his harem!"

"Ah," said John, chuckling, "you've got something there, old girl! I'll have a word with Paul," and he did with the result that Hazel and her baby moved into Mill Cottage adjoining the long abandoned water-wheel, at the junction of the Sorrel and the stream that ran down from Deepdene goyle. Surprisingly she soon made herself at home, cultivating the vegetable patch and keeping a few goats in the water meadows and every weekday morning she carried her baby along the river road to the parish church where she scoured and polished for nine shillings a week, with a bonus of sixpence an hour for helping in the churchyard. Motherhood had sobered her somewhat, inasmuch as she did not wander so far afield but in other respects she was the same half-wild creature who had lived rough in the woods and Maureen, Irish enough to have faith in the Little People, thought of her as one and often passed to Hazel some of the payments in kind given her by cottagers for medical attention. She also took a keen interest in the baby, standing in as godmother when, at her suggestion, he was christened Patrick. As Maureen explained to her patients, saints had lived in caves all over Ireland when the English were still painting themselves blue, so why shouldn't a broth of a boy be born in one on the Shallowford estate?

As soon as Hazel had settled in the doctor ceased her random inquiries regarding the child's paternity, quite forgetting that she had

619

advised Keith to write to Ikey on the subject. She never did learn how close she came to discovering the truth then, for Keith had few doubts on the subject but remained silent for reasons so complex that, notwithstanding his familiarity with Greek, Latin and Hebrew, he would have found it difficult to set down. Alone in the valley Keith had strong suspicions regarding the paternity of Hazel Potter's child and they stemmed from a single word uttered by the mother at the moment he had burst through the screen of gorse to find her lying up in agony beside the half-dead fire. She had seen him through a haze of pain, standing agape with his back to the evening light, and in the moment before he had turned and rushed back to Rachel, she had confused him with the tall young man who had come here so often and had cried out, in desperation and perhaps relief, "Ikey-boy!", clearly and distinctly, thus telling Keith when he had time to reflect, all he needed to know. He was aware, of course, of his duty even if he found it very hard to believe that his one time champion had seduced this girl and left her to face the consequences alone. It was clearly obligatory on his part to write to Quetta, asking Ikey to confirm or deny but he did not write, regarding the child or anything else. The chain-reaction that would almost certainly follow Ikey's admission would be shattering and result in so much trouble for everyone that he did not possess enough resolution to light such a fuse. Whatever happened it was he, Keith, who would suffer most, for if Ikey admitted paternity there would be legal claims that would broadcast the facts up and down the Valley and surely Ikey would find it hard to forgive the Judas who had so invoked the wrath of the Squire and Mrs. Craddock and the contempt of rustics like Sam and Smut Potter and everyone else who sympathised with the girl. Yet if Ikey denied the fact, as he probably would, the accusation would destroy their relationship for life and it was a relationship that Keith prized almost as highly as his love for Rachel Eveleigh. The more he considered putting what he knew on paper the more profitless it looked and so, in the end, he kept his counsel, persuading himself that if the girl herself was determined to keep her secret then he was entitled to do likewise. It did not satisfy his conscience completely but it helped and because, at that time, his head was full of dreams involving Rachel, and the rosy future they would share when he had his degree, he was able to put the secret into cold-storage and even half-persuade himself that Hazel Potter's agonised cry qualified as a kind of audible hallucination on his part.

In September of that year, 1913, Squire Craddock, that resolute hater of motors, confounded his friends by buying one. He made the gesture on the occasion of his wife presenting him with another daughter and the Valley was never to forget the unlikely association of baby girl and horseless carriage, for it was perpetuated by a quip of that inveterate Valley joker Henry Pitts. On hearing of the simultaneous arrivals at the Big House, he exclaimed, "He give 'is missis a bliddy motor? For coming up with another maid? Well damme, I suppose he knows what he's at, but it sounds to me as daft as namin' the baby Whiz-bang!" This comment soon reached the Big House where Paul, having been told by Maureen that the child's arrival was the quickest on local record, said, "Well, maybe Henry's hit on something! Let's call her 'Whiz', since she obliged her mother and me to that extent!" and from then on his second daughter (officially named "Karen") embarked on life as "Whiz", or "Whizzo", just as the twins were known as "The Pair", and Simon as "Si"; only Mary, now almost three and as pretty as a Devon violet, enjoyed the dignity of having her Christian name put into general use.

Claire had been very relieved by the child's safe arrival, for the previous year she had had another miscarriage, her second in five years. Her tendency to miscarry worried her much more than it need have done. There were plenty of wives in the Valley (Marian Eveleigh for one) who welcomed an accident of this kind but Claire derived the deepest satisfaction from her ability to produce healthy, good-looking children and her joy in doing so was closely linked to her consciousness of intellectual inferiority to Grace. She always thought of herself as rather a "goose", with no pretentions towards intellectual tastes and pursuits. She could play the piano by ear but that was the nearest she ever came to the arts. She seldom read anything but the county newspaper or the lightest of romances and thought Holman Hunt's *Light of the World* as the last word in masterpieces. She could strum any number of ballads on the old upright piano but the thunder of Wagner, the phrasing of Mozart and Mendelssohn, meant far less to her than, say, a waltz by Johann Strauss, and although Paul was by no means artistic he had a very lively appreciation of current political issues and was a wide if undisciplined reader, particularly of the eighteenth-century classics and modern history. He had also cultivated a taste for period furniture, English porcelain and pictures and over the years had gradually transformed the reception rooms, getting rid of most of the pieces he bought when he first came to Shallowford and replacing them with furniture in the Chippendale and Sheraton periods and beginning a modest collection of Rockingham, Worcester and Swansea china. What he did not know about these things he was prepared to find out so that Claire now thought of him as an intellectual which he was not and never would be but because it was important to him to stand well in her eyes he encouraged the fiction, pretending to an erudition that he did not in fact possess. Grace would have rumbled him in an hour but Claire was not Grace and thanked her stars that she was not. She was a woman who knew her limitations and cherished them, her vanity resting in her children and her face and figure, which she regarded as her dowry as far as Paul was concerned.

She had ample excuse for this. Her placidity, that concealed a strong vein of obstinacy, occasionally irritated him but physically he was more in love with her than he had ever been. He still thought of her as an exceptionally beautiful woman and told her so, several times a week, which possibly helped to explain why, at the age of thirty, she still looked twenty. A pedant would have described her as fresh, and perhaps pretty rather than beautiful; she still had her pink and white complexion, unremarkable blue eyes, a very ripe mouth with its rather sensual underlip, and her small, determined chin. She worried about putting on weight but her fears were largely imaginary. Despite four children in six years she retained a surprisingly neat waist and a high, shapely bust but by far her most remarkable feature was her high piled corn-coloured hair, of which she was as vain as the late Empress of Austria. When it was unpinned it reached as far as her buttocks and under lamplight it glowed like a river of gold. He was always encouraging her to display it and no miser derived more satisfaction from a hoard of guineas than Paul Craddock on one of these semi-ceremonial occasions. He would gaze at it and stroke it with boyish wonder and she would sit smiling a little self-consciously but basking in his admiration, telling him that they were really too old for this kind of nonsense, yet he was always immensely gratified by her complaisance, telling her at the time, or in retrospect, that she made herself available to him so often in order to flatter his masculinity and although this was said as a joke between them it was really no more than the truth, for at moments like this neither of them forgot the scars left on his pride by his first marriage. She had, however, developed a sure instinct about him. If things were going well an act of love between them was a celebration; but if things went awry her generous body was an instrument of solace. She may not have been as clever as Grace but she was much wiser and far better versed in the art of giving; her mind was uncluttered with theories and the sores of humanity and concentrated, in the main, upon enlarging him as a person.

There was little or no rhythm about their love making. He would be stirred by any number of tiny, inconsequential things, a cluster of stray tendrils on her neck that caught a gleam of winter sunshine, the slow ripple of her breasts as she reached up to put something in place and what was singular about her in this respect was that she never used the excuse of a task or appointment to bridle or postpone his demands but would say, with a frankness that amused him, "Now? Well really . . . !" and would cease whatever she was doing and accommodate him, initially with an almost complaisant air but soon with a cordiality that began to manifest itself the moment he laid hands on her. In this respect, as in others, they remained lovers and were seldom conventional as regards time and place. If the impulse touched him after the children and servants had gone to bed and they were together in the library of a winter evening, they would sometimes repeat their impromptu encounter of Hermitage Hallowe'en night before the fire and whenever this happened the process assumed a kind of lighthearted, unselfconscious ritual, beginning with his leisurely undressing of her and praising of each part of her, as though to prolong the occasion as long as possible. There was a stage, however, beyond which she would show impatience and then, when they were still, she would pretend to a modesty and delicacy that she did not possess and never had possessed, and he would tease her unmercifully but secretly he was immensely vain of his ability to awake such unthinking response in her. Intimate moments such as these brought her a disproportionate satisfaction, for she too had her vanities and they concerned, as well as his delight in her body, his virility, a virility that seemed somehow to spring from the valley around him, as though he were able, by some acquired magic practised over the years to catch and distil the fecundity of the countryside, storing it in his loins to bestow upon her as proof of his achievement. This enormous gusto in him, this bonus bounty of the fields and woods he loved, was something she prized even above her children, for she was persuaded that it was something rare that neither Grace Lovell nor any woman in the Valley could have conjured from him. It was partly this naïve pride in his masculinity that invested her with the power to match and surpass his easily aroused passion. She sensed that he possessed her not only

623

as a woman but as the consuming instrument of his lust for life in the place he had made for himself in this gentle wilderness. She was a woman not much given to extravagant fancies but in this realm the wildness of her imagination had few limits. She saw herself then not as Claire Derwent, a farmer's daughter married to a man who had purchased his place among them with pounds, shillings and pence, but as consort to an almost godlike being who used her flesh as an altar to express his strange obsession with the fruitfulness and timelessness of the Valley, with every flower and cornstalk that grew in it, and every human or animal who lived and multiplied hereabouts, and it was acute awareness of this that made her reckless of giving, so that she felt at times that she could never absorb enough of him or demonstrate how dedicated she was to the gratification of his senses. Eagerness to convey this, communicating itself as it did to every nerve in her body as she enfolded and enclosed him sometimes half-stupefied him with delight.

And yet, in more mundane spheres, there were times when she called the tune, when an issue arose that encouraged her to make a stand and whenever this happened, when she once made it clear that she was determined to have her way, she could usually influence him without much trouble. This had been so in the case of Simon's renunciation of hunting and like matters but perhaps her most signal victory was in respect of the car he brought home on the occasion of the birth of "Whiz".

It was a 1911 Belsize, a great, square, brass-snouted monster, purchased second-hand from a Paxtonbury draper who had lost his nerve on the second outing and left it unused in his coachhouse for almost two years. Paul decided to buy it after hearing Claire say it was a pity the family could never travel far afield as a group and after getting Frisby, the Paxtonbury coach builder, to service it and give him a few lessons in driving he piloted it home across the moor in dashing if somewhat erratic style, deriving unexpected pleasure out of his mastery of the brute and causing Eveleigh's foreman, who saw him come bouncing down from the water-shed, to run up the hedge in alarm, scarcely able to believe his eyes when he recognised the driver.

About a fortnight after Claire had come downstairs he suggested a family expedition into Paxtonbury and after some hesitation Claire got the elder children ready, veiled herself in a beekeeper's bonnet and they set off, little Mary sitting between Paul and Simon in the front, Claire and the exuberant twins in the back. Simon, holding Mary's hand to give her confidence, looked very solemn but The Pair squealed in unison when Paul clashed the gears at the foot of the drive and wedged the lever into its tortuous gate, so that the Belsize (christened The Juggernaut by Claire) leaped forward like a steeplechaser and came to a shuddering halt between the stone pillars.

"Are you sure you can manage it, Paul?" Claire asked anxiously and he said huffily that he certainly could for how else could he have driven the fifteen miles from Paxtonbury? He got out and swung the heavy starting-handle and soon they were moving at a steady twenty miles an hour along the river road, past the Home Farm, where one of the biblical shepherds swung his hat and cheered, past Codsall Bridge, where Eveleigh's cows turned tail and stampeded across the water meadow, then hard right up the unsurfaced incline to the moor where, long ago, Martin Codsall had taken his wife Arabella on a John Gilpin's ride to prevent her intervening at her son's wedding. And here, almost at the top of the hill, the engine coughed and fell silent, so that they were poised on a gradient of one-in-six, with no room to turn and no hope of breasting the hill.

He climbed out again, assuring them of his confidence in himself as an engineer and swung the starting-handle until the sweat ran down his face but nothing happened and Mary's faith in her father's infallibility faltered so that she began to cry. Simon did his best to comfort her, declaring that Father would soon have them on the move again, while the twins shrieked offers of help from the back but Claire held them back, privately regretting her share in sponsoring the expedition and reflecting that, apart from the baby safe in her cot, all her eggs were now wedged in a single, unpredictable basket. Paul said there was nothing for it but a careful reverse back to the river road, where, if necessary, Simon could run and borrow ropes and a pair of Eveleigh's cart-horses.

He pretended to treat the matter as a great joke and had she been alone with him she might have humoured him but the safety of her brood was no laughing matter to Claire and she said, very sharply, "Wait then, while we all get out!" and when the twins clamoured to remain she gave each a smart box on the ear that sent them scrambling on to the road, after which she opened the nearside front door and ordered Simon to bring Mary out and wait with the twins on the safe side of the hill.

"Look here," Paul protested, "if I get her started I shan't be able to stop again without the engine dying. Why can't you stay put and wait for her to spark when I slam her in reverse?" but Claire said firmly that her duty was to look after the children, and what he did with The Juggernaut was his business, so after telling her she was making an unnecessary fuss he released the brake, missed his gear again and zigzagged all the way down the hill backwards, his steering made wildly erratic by the pressure he was obliged to apply to the handbrake.

He got safely down and they followed him in a cautious group, finding his temper had not improved for he was using language that made the twins and Simon giggle and Mary glance fearfully at her mother. Claire said then that she would walk the children home and send Honeyman out with two cart-horses and ropes but Paul, declaring that such mass desertion would make him the laughing stock of the Valley, ordered them to remain, saying that all he needed was a shove along the flat. An open quarrel was averted by the timely arrival of Tod Glover, an engaging nineteen-year-old who was Old Honeyman's nephew and had recently forsaken the land to work for a Whinmouth hackney-carriage proprietor owning an eighteen-seater charabanc. Tod, cycling back from the Whinmouth direction, at once offered his services, inspecting the Belsize with the respect his ancestors would have reserved for its owner. As the only man within artillery range with the rudiments of a mechanical training Tod was regarded as the Valley witchdoctor and Paul welcomed him as the one person capable of rescuing his dignity. The lad had the bonnet cover off in a trice and after tinkering for some moments, and giving the handle a swing or two, he said, with a grin, "All she needs is a drink, Squire! When did you last fill her up?"

"I haven't put any petrol in since I brought her home," Paul admitted ruefully and the insertion of a twig showed that the tank was bone dry.

"How about the can on the running board?" asked Tod, trying not to look superior when Paul admitted that he thought the can contained water and after a sniff to make sure Tod made a funnel of paper and within minutes the Belsize was climbing the hill again, Paul maintaining a discreet silence all the way to Paxtonbury.

"Well," said Claire, after an uneventful journey home, and insistence upon the entire family taking a bath to rid themselves of layers of white dust, "it was nice of you to buy a motor for us, but I can't help thinking we should be much cleaner and far safer without one! It would be promising, I think, if you had a mechanical bent like young

626

Tod but you haven't and never will have, so why not admit it, and stick to horse and trap?"

"That's a ridiculous stand to take simply because I ran out of petrol," he said. "It's high time we got used to motors and I'll master this if it's the last thing I do!"

It almost was; a day or so later, having refused to engage Tod as a chauffeur, he came bumbling down the steep drive, clashed his gears at the gate and shot across ten yards of soft ground straight into the Sorrel, carrying ten yards of paling with him. There had been some heavy rainfall and the water above the ford was five feet deep. The Belsize plunged in nose down, looking like a primeval monster maddened by thirst and only the fact that he had managed to unlatch the door whilst ploughing through the iris bed enabled Paul to free himself before the heavy vehicle sank into the soft mud of the river bed.

Help came from all directions. Matt, one of the shepherd twins, hauled him ashore and Honeyman and Henry Pitts, summoned from the lodge where they were conferring with John Rudd, managed to get a rope under the rear wheels just before they disappeared from view. When Claire was summoned she found the river bank seething with activity as Home Farm horses struggled with the hopeless task of hauling the Belsize clear. What astounded her was the fact that Paul did not seem cured of his obsession. Instead of going back to the house to change he remained on the bank to supervise salvage operations, snarling at everybody who advised him to get into dry clothes. He was there for an hour or more during which time no progress was made, apart from the motor being anchored by ropes to saplings and the following day, to nobody's surprise, he had a heavy cold which did not improve his temper.

Claire said, as she dosed him with whisky and water, "What do you intend to do with The Juggernaut if you ever do get it out?" and he said, grumpily, clean it up, get young Tod to service it and have another go.

She said, with unexpected firmness, "You'll leave it right where it is!" and when he exclaimed in protest, arguing that it was she who prompted him to buy, she went on, "That was before I realised you haven't the temperament essential to anyone setting out to master one of those things! I admire you for trying and I shouldn't have to remind you that I usually back you to the hilt when you set your mind on doing something, but this is different; the children are involved and I'm obliged to make a stand."

"Now how the devil are the children involved in my driving a motor?" he demanded. "I'm not likely to let them play with it, am I?"

"Sooner or later you'll expect them to ride in it," she said. "It's only by chance that Simon wasn't beside you yesterday and if he had been he would have been drowned! Did you think of that while you were prancing about on the bank in wet clothes, catching this cold and working off your bad temper on people who were trying to help you?"

He had not thought of it but he knew it was true. Up to the last minute Simon had intended to accompany him but Paul, impatient to be off, had made a trial run down the drive whilst Simon slipped inside for coat and scarf. He said, reflecting how specially protective Claire always felt about Grace's child, "You're right. If anything had happened to him you would have found it hard to forgive me, wouldn't you?"

"I should have found it impossible, Paul," she said, calmly, "even though, indirectly, it would have been my fault! As it is, we were lucky and I mean to profit by the lesson, even if you won't! I can't stop you amusing yourself with your new toy but I won't have you take any of the children out ever again and that's final!"

It was an edict and he accepted it as such but for all that her attitude still piqued him, perhaps because, for the first time since marriage he had failed to impress her.

"Suppose we retired old Chivers and signed on Tod as a chauffeur?" he suggested. "He could give me lessons and I can't be such a damned fool as to fail to get the hang of it in time."

"Paul," she said, more gently, "I know you better than anyone and a lot better than you know yourself! You'll never make a motor-driver because you haven't got that kind of patience. You're a bull-at-a-gate person and machines need a light touch. You are entitled to risk your own neck but you're not risking my children's! I don't often oppose you but in this I'm adamant and I'm not saying this because of what happened yesterday but because your prejudice against gadgets is so great that you ought never to be trusted with one as lethal as that motor!" She smiled, for the first time since the subject had been raised. "Shall I tell you what my advice is? Leave The Juggernaut as a local landmark and go back to horses!"

And this, after a good deal of grumbling about wasted money was what he did. All that winter, when the river was high, the Belsize was the plaything of otters and water voles but when the floods receded part of the wreck was revealed, a permanent testimony to the Squire's

628

short-lived attempt to adapt himself to the twentieth century. From then on the mechanisation of the Valley proceeded without him. Soon the German professor appeared in Coombe Bay High Street in his new Humber, driven by his son, Gottfried, and then Eveleigh hired a traction engine to haul away the trunks of elms felled on his western boundary. Now and again, in that final glow of the Edwardian afternoon, an occasional motor was seen on the river road and occasionally, very occasionally, power-driven engines were used to harrow stubborn ground that had long lain fallow. But for the most part the horse continued to flourish and Claire consolidated her victory and in the main the people of the Valley were at one with her. It was Henry Pitts, watching the hired traction-engine pull roots as easily as a dentist extracts teeth, who voiced the opinion of witnesses when he said, with one of his slow, rubbery grins, "Tiz quicker an' neater than us can do it wi' chains an' plough horses but somehow it baint real farmin', be it?"

Book Four

CHAPTER ONE

I

LOOKING back on the last summer of the old world Paul was always struck by two features of that time; the weather and the focus of attention on Irish affairs to the exclusion of everything else, including Germany.

The weather he remembered as being the most pleasant of any comparable season he had spent in the Valley, warm and consistently sunny by day, with gentle rain at night so that crops ripened early and even the habitual pessimist Eveleigh, spoke guardedly of excellent harvest prospects. In some ways it resembled his first summer at Shallowford when there seemed to have been blazing sunshine for weeks on end but there was no accompanying drought, as there had been in 1902, and under a temperate sky the Valley burgeoned with promise and fruitfulness so that people went gaily about their work and only a few local wiseacres like Eph Morgan expressed doubts about what was likely to happen when the Irish were given their precious Home Rule and began civil war.

James Grenfell was down in early June and Paul invited him to dine with Professor Scholtzer with whom he was now on cordial terms. James liked the old German on sight and it was over their port that night that Paul took part in his first discussion on the dangers inherent in the rivalry Germany, France, Russia and Great Britain had been practising for more than a decade. He was mildly surprised when the Professor put forward a theory that, without justifying the Kaiser's antics in the diplomatic field, at least shed a little light on them for he declared that, rightly or wrongly, fear of encirclement was very real to many Germans, even intelligent Germans. The Junkers, he told them in his expansive but guttural English, were anxious to come to some agreement with Great Britain and their fear of France and Russia was not merely a ruse to compel politicians into granting more and more money for military and naval purposes. They saw Russia as a steamroller driven by barbarians and France as an irresponsible nationalist mob determined to avenge the defeat of 1870. "I am not excusing them, my friends," he went on earnestly, when James Grenfell pointed out that sooner or later Germany would be obliged to restore the privinces of Alsace-Lorraine, "I try to make you look at Europe through German eyes. Only if you British do that can we stop this Gadarene rush to destruction." James said, with a smile, "Oh, I don't question your thesis, Professor, but surely it is generally accepted that war, even on the scale of 1870, is an impossibility? Threats and border incidents yes—we'll always have those, but cvilised nations, grinding one another to pieces? That's a very different matter, if only on account of cost!"

"Guns," said the Professor sadly, "have a vay of going off by themselves and vonce theÿ bang there are always plenty of people to profit from refilling cartridge pouches! That has been my reading of history; it remains my greatest fear! Not a vor started by the Emperors or by the politicians or even the Junkers but by those who profit by conflict!"

Neither Paul nor James took the Professor's warnings very seriously, James because he was too deeply imbued by Westminster's views that no power could afford to fight a modern war, Paul because he found it difficult to believe that anyone, even a crass idiot like the Kaiser, would, when it came to the touch, challenge the British Empire. He did not say this; it would have seemed to him a breach of good manners but he mentioned it to James after the Professor had gone home and they were smoking their last cigars in the library. James dismissed the Saxon's fears as the result of studying the past at the expense of the present. "Even if the guns did go off by themselves, you can take it from me, Paul, that we should stay clear of it and I have that on the best authority—Asquith's, Morley's and even Grey's! For your peace of mind we couldn't get in even if we wanted to. The pacifist group in the Cabinet would resign in a body and we should lose the backing of the Labour Party. That would mean an election and by the time we had gone to the country if would be all over bar the shouting! So in case we don't run our full term I advise you to concentrate on the Ulster question. That's real enough and they mean to fight if they have to! A good many Tory M.P.s are egging them on and you can imagine how I feel when I see suffragettes sent to prison for long terms on charges of conspiracy when idiots like Carson are openly advocating armed rebellion!"

When at length he went to bed it was not of German aggression and Russian steamrollers that Paul thought but of women like Grace, Annie Kenney and the girl Davison, who had died under the hooves of a Derby horse the previous summer. James' parting remarks robbed him of sleep for an hour or so, or it might have been the heavy meal and all the cigars they had smoked, for he lay awake beside Claire for a long time, wondering what had become of the woman who had entered and left his life so abruptly, so long ago it seemed that it might have happened in childhood. He thought, recalling the scenes they had witnessed outside the Houses of Parliament, "It's their staying power that astonishes—that and their sense of dedication! But they don't seem to be getting anywhere, poor devils, and now this Irish business has edged them out of the spotlight!" When at last he fell asleep he had one of his meaningless dreams about her, a prolonged waiting in all manner of improbable places for Grace to keep a muddled rendezvous. If ever he did dream of Grace it was always along these lines.

In the decade after the Great War historians made play of the general anxiety caused by the shooting of Franz Ferdinand by a tubercular youth in Sarajevo that June but Paul, knowing the Valley and its people so well, never subscribed to this fiction. News of the Archduke's death came and went but hardly anyone in the Sorrel district remembered the incident until it was thrust under their noses a month later and even then they looked on it as no more than a scuffle in a far-away country where the crack of the pistol and the roar of a home-made bomb were commonplace occurrences. Few in the Valley bought any newspaper but the *County Press* and although this publication carried a small section devoted to foreign news, its local readers did no more than glance at it before turning to the market section or columns dealing with county cricket.

There was one man, however, apart from the German professor, who was very much aware of the open door of the European powder magazine. Horace Handcock's hatred of Germans dated from the day their Kaiser decided to compete with the British Navy and build himself a clutch of dreadnoughts. From then on Horace had waged a one-man campaign in the Valley, aimed at alerting his neighbours to the menace of Potsdam, and his warnings were so stark, and so original, that he was always able to enlist an audience in the Shallowford kitchen or the sawdust bar of The Raven. Horace appeared as a Solomon Eagle, preaching of wrath to come, and the regulars in the bar, seeking diversion, would sometimes encourage him to pronounce upon the latest forms of frightfulness Potsdam had in pickle for their British cousins. Nobody had ever discovered the source of Horace

635

Handcock's information, which was so extensive and so detailed, that the simple-minded among his listeners might have been forgiven for supposing him to have had access to the Wilhelmstrasse wastepaper baskets. He would talk of bombs disguised as mangolds dropped over agricultural districts by Zeppelins, of bags of poisoned sweets for unwary children delivered by the same agency and of giant howitzers planted as far away as the Baltic coast and capable of destroying half London. He was obsessed by the presence of cohorts of spies, landed nightly by submarine, to rendezvous a night or so later at deserted coves like Tamer Potter's, east of the Bluff. To Horace every foreigner (Italian ice-cream vendors excepted) was in the pay of Von Moltke and quite aside from the personnel of German bands (spies to a man), he knew of at least two resident agents in the Valley, the mild-looking professor and his gentlemanly son, Gottfried. It was useless to point out to Horace that the professor himself was hostile to German militarists, or that he was on visiting terms with the Squire. Horace declared these instances typical examples of Teutonic guile and that they would not see the professor and his son in their true colours until the Kaiser's fleet out-numbered the British by two ships to one. Then, one awful morning, they would find the German's Coombe Bay house silent and shuttered, the occupants having been taken off by submarine the previous night in order to be spared the terrible naval bombardment that would follow and the sack of Paxtonbury and Whinmouth by field-grey hordes landed by fast torpedo boats, of which the Kaiser already had several thousand, with more building.

The only person agitated by these dire prophecies was Mrs. Handcock, who was obliged to listen to them after everybody else had gone home to bed, and because she had always entertained a great respect for her husband's erudition she had long since convinced herself that a German invasion of the coastal strip between Coombe Bay and Whinmouth was a virtual certainty. Fortunately for her, however, she was optimistic by nature and had made up her mind that the balance of naval power was unlikely to be tipped during her life-time, so there was really no point in worrying about it, especially as they were childless. And yet, in the end, Horace was caught on the hop just like everybody else for like a fool, he allowed the Mutiny at the Curragh to distract his attention during the critical months leading up to August, 1914. It was only when he learned of the Austrian ultimatum to Servia, in late July, that he saw that events had overtaken him and by then it was too late to rouse the countryside.

The task would have been beyond him in any case for during the last few days of July, with hot weather continuing and the harvest upon them, the men of the Valley did not even pause to read the *County Press*. While the telegraph systems of Europe quivered under a ceaseless exchange of threats, proposals, counter-proposals, accusations, denials and politely-phrased disclaimers, the respective masters of Four Winds and Hermitage were bargaining over a Jersey bull, and Smut Potter was working sixteen hours a day in his greenhouses. Nearby his two sisters, burned almost black by the sun, were digging an irrigation channel across the cliff field under the threat of the Bideford Goliath's hazel switch and all over the estate men and women were discussing such things as the fruit crop, water shortage, field pests and the likely price of cow fodder in the autumn. On the very day that the Tsar of All the Russias was posting his ukase to the remotest villages in his vast domains, Sam Potter was blazing the next belt of firs to be felled in the plantation behind his cottage and Sydney Codsall was taking a posy to old Mrs. Earnshaw, who was ninety-eight and making a new will at the expense of a niece in New South Wales. Sydney was one of the few who was half-aware of a crisis but it did not seem to him anything like so important as the transfer of Mrs. Earnshaw's ropewalk to a company known as Coombe Bay Enterprises, Ltd., who were offering hard cash for an enterprise that had failed even before Mr. Earnshaw was drowned at sea in the eighteen-eighties.

In only one kitchen in the Valley did the distant roll of kettledrum cause dismay and this was at Periwinkle, on the edge of the moor, where hostilities had already begun in a sharp engagement between Will Codsall and his wife, Elinor. Like the bigger conflict over the sea the dispute had its origin in a scrap of paper, not a treaty exactly but a printed summons ordering Will to present himself at the Devon Yeomanry barracks within forty-eight hours, on pain of arrest.

The arrival of the summons stupefied Elinor. Until then she had looked upon Will's territorial activities as a silly male game, for which, however (and she also considered this ridiculous), he had been paid a regular quarterly sum, ever since he had signed on the day of the Coronation Fête, in 1911. Will had been won over by the Yeomanry's smart turnout on that occasion and in the refreshment tent after the tug-of-war had got into conversation with a troop sergeant, who had pointed out the advantages of a Territorial engagement which required of a volunteer no more than one drill a week and a fortnight's camp each summer. Will signed on the spot and had never regretted his impulsive act. He had enjoyed the drills and found the money useful for new stock, whereas the period in camp had been a welcome change from farm chores. It had never occurred to him that he might, at some time, be required under the terms of his engagement to fire a rifle in anger, and if anybody had told him there was the remotest possibility of his being transported across the seas he would have paid his solicitor brother to extricate him from such a menacing situation. Elinor, once the meaning of the summons was made known to her, flew into a temper that gave Will a foretaste of the drum-fire and box barrages he was soon to encounter near Armentières. She stormed and raved for an hour, likening him to various vegetables of the coarser kind, and using phrases that would have stunned her lay-preaching father, mercifully at rest in the churchyard. Will reasoned and pleaded, pointing out that all Territorial units were earmarked for home service, for guarding viaducts and suchlike, and that even if there was a war it was unlikely to last more than a month and that he would be paid for his time with the colours, just as he had for his periods in camp, but Elinor's wrath continued to break over him in waves until at length he fled to the privvy in the garden and locked the door against her. When it was dark he stole out and foraged around for his kit. It took him back a few years to be moving about a house with stealth, as though, at any moment, he would hear the shrill voice of his mother, Arabella, but when Elinor found him packing in the kitchen he saw that her rage was spent, that her eyes were red and at once felt small, mean and wretched. He said, dismally, "You'll get the separation allowance, Ellen, and I daresay tiz all a lot of ole nonsense and us'll be 'ome be weekend," and he put his arms round her and kissed her as she wailed, "How be I goin' to manage with harvest almost on us? What's to become of everything we built up yerabouts if youm gone for months? Was 'ee mazed Will Codsall, to put us in this kind o' fix for a few shillings?" He admitted glumly that he must have been, as mazed as a March hare, adding that there was a possibility of him getting temporary exemption until the harvest was in, and after that he would see Squire and anyone else who could pull strings to prolong his deferment indefinitely. She cheered up a little at this and cooked his supper and afterwards, in the evening haze, they walked the boundaries of their eighty-acre holding and he issued his final instructions in case exemption took time to arrange. That night, while he slept, Elinor lay awake and her mind went back to the first night they had spent in this room after their wedding at the little chapel in Coombe Bay. They had, or so it seemed to her, achieved a great deal since then, enlarging what had been a ruined patch into a real farm, very small but prosperous. Then they had nothing but a few hens but now they had the biggest egg yield in the Valley, besides a cow, ducks, turkeys, pigs and several acres of former heathland under the plough. Was this to be sacrificed because Will, almost an illiterate, had signed a paper he didn't understand? It was a monstrous price to pay for a small mistake and what kind of soldier would he make anyway, despite a hulking frame and hardened muscles? He had never been able to bring himself to wring a fowl's neck and all the killing was done by her. Perhaps they would find this out and send him back; perhaps, but somehow she thought it unlikely.

II

Will Codsall's summons was the plucking of the first brick from the parochial wall. News that he had been hustled away overnight sobered the Valley and sent some of the more thoughtful to the foreign news sections of the *County Press*. Henry Pitts, of Hermitage, was not among this minority, giving it as his opinion that the German Kaiser, long recognised as mad, had now degenerated into a homicidal maniac and that Will was fortunate in finding himself among those charged with hunting the lunatic down and packing him off to St. Helena, which Henry regarded as the traditional lock-up of all unsuccessful challengers of British naval supremacy. It was an extravagant theory, and Henry's father Arthur said there was surely more to it than that, for the British Army must have been very hard-pressed indeed to need the services of an amiable chap like Will. He was more inclined to think that the Yeomanry was being called out to replace regulars who had refused to bear arms against Ulster. Eveleigh, at Four Winds, being a more serious-minded man than either of the Pitts, was one of those who sought an answer in back numbers of the *County Press*, there to make what he could of newsletters published under such headings as "Austria Threatens Servia!" "Tsar Pledges Aid to Slavs", and "Where Britain stands in Balkan Dispute", but he soon lost his way in a maze of despatches from St. Petersburg, Vienna, Berlin, Paris and Belgrade, suspending judgment until he could consult Horace Handcock, the Valley oracle on foreign affairs. Eveleigh was a practical man and found it very difficult to connect the sudden disappearance of one of his neighbours with revolver shots fired at a bulging-eyed foreigner in a town of which he had never heard.

When he entered the sawdust bar of The Raven about seven o'clock that evening he was amazed to find more than a score of the Valley men already assembled and all, it appeared, in search of the answer to the questions he had sought in vain in the newspapers. Rumours, some of them too absurd to be credited, converted the usually peaceful atmosphere of the bar into a Tower of Babel. Churchill, they said, was calling out the fleet; the King had written a strong letter to his crazy German cousin ordering him to back down at once; Kitchener had been recalled from Egypt and was standing by to land the Army on the Continent whereas Horace Handcock, his face the colour of a ripe cider apple, proved quite unequal to the task of sieving these rumours, having been so generously plied with brown ale that he could only babble incoherently of spies, Zeppelins and lethal mangolds. About eight o'clock Eveleigh left in disgust, none the wiser save for confirmation that Will Codsall had left the Valley in uniform.

He should have waited a little longer. About eight-thirty Smut Potter looked in on his way back from Sorrel Halt and in his pocket was a special edition of a London newspaper, thrown from the window of a through express. It told of troop movements all over Europe, of Germany's pledge to support Austria against Russia, and of France's pledge to back Russia and Servia against Germany and Austria. There was no mention of England's involvement and this was a source of disappointment to those present, so much so that, as the evening progressed, and after a labourer who could actually vouch for Will Codsall's departure arrived, Will's stock declined, for it was thought discreditable on his part to have slunk away without a word to anyone, as though resolved to fight the Kaiser single-handed. Then, to everybody's relief, word was circulated that Squire was in the bar parlour with John Rudd and Sam Potter asked the landlord if he would convey their respects to Mr. Craddock and ask for enlightenment. A moment or two later Paul appeared and damped everybody's spirits by announcing that Mr. Grenfell, who was surely in a position to know, had told him over the telephone earlier in the day that Great Britain was almost certain to remain neutral if war broke out but that he, personally, did not think it would because the latest news in London was that the President of the United States and the Pope had offered their services as mediators. This information fell upon the heated company like a cold douche and Smut pinpointed the only consolatory crumb by saying, "Well, that'll bring old Will home with his tail down, for it dorn zeem as if any of us'll get a crack at 'em!" a remark that indicated to those who had known Smut in the old days that the poacher was not exorcised after all. Soon the forum broke up and the Valley men, their belligerence mellowed by beer and cider, dispersed, all but Horace Handcock who had progressed beyond the jovial stage and had to be forcibly restrained from staggering up the hill to denounce the German professor as a spy.

Paul was silent during the ride home and it was not until they were approaching the ford that he said, "Do you suppose I'm right, John? Are those idiots really disappointed with the prospect of us keeping clear of it?" and John said that this was more than probable, for there wasn't a man in the Valley apart from themselves who had ever been involved in a war. Paul digested this in silence but when they reached the end of the tow-path, said, suddenly, "It doesn't make sense, John! What the devil would any of them get from war but death or wounds? And what would happen here if only the half of them rushed into uniform?"

"I can't answer that," John said philosophically, "but I can tell you this; there wasn't a man among them who wasn't damned envious of Will Codsall and that's ironic, if you like, for he's probably the only one in the Valley who would prefer to be ordered about by his wife than by a sergeant-major!"

"But they always seemed contented enough," Paul argued. "Why should they want to go off and get shot at?"

"You did it yourself once, didn't you?" John reminded him, "but this time it's more than high spirits and boredom, I fancy. For a century or more we've been telling everyone we're top nation and now we look like having to prove it."

Paul said, "Come, John, you heard what Grenfell said; there's no chance of us being involved, except as mediators. Do you honestly believe there's a likelihood of us siding with France and Russia?"

"Yes I do," John replied and Paul noticed that there was an edge to his voice. "Politicians like Jimmy Grenfell think they know better than most people but the fact is it must be difficult to see the wood for the trees in Westminster. I've been watching this damned naval race for a long time and I've thought about it too, more often than I cared to. If it doesn't come now it'll come next year or the year after, so maybe it's as well to get it over and done with while we still have the pretence of naval superiority. At all events that's what the Navy thinks!"

As John said this Paul had a vision of Roddy Rudd, the fresh-faced, motor-mad boy who had been dazzled by Grace and had once incurred his jealousy. "Where is Roddy now?" he asked, and John said somewhere in the South Atlantic, serving as gunnery officer on the cruiser *Good Hope*. "And damned well out of it, I hope, at least for the time being," he added, "for don't run away with the notion that the German Navy won't fight or that, ship for ship, it isn't a damned sight more up-to-date than ours!"

"Good God, you can't mean that, John," Paul said, for having grown up in the belief that one British-manned ship was worth ten of any other nation's he found his agent's disparagement unpalatable.

"I do mean it and I have it on excellent authority," John said, "although it isn't the kind of thing one should noise abroad. They've got better range-finders and thicker armour-plating and many of them can show a better turn of speed! And now, to more practical issues; will you do anything to give Elinor Codsall a harvest hand at Periwinkle?"

"Certainly I will, providing Will doesn't come back looking sheepish the day after tomorrow. I'll tell you what, John, I'll lay you two to one in half-crowns that he will!"

"You're on," said John, "for if we're to have everything turned upside down for the rest of our lives I don't see why I should miss a chance of making five shillings out of it!"

Paul knew that he had lost his bet some time before the crowds began to gather outside the *County Press* offices in Paxtonbury awaiting the appearance of the latest posters, and before packets of newspapers screaming "War!" were flung among excited newsagents' boys when the Cornish Riviera made its three-minute stop at the cathedral town. He knew it even before the sombre Foreign Secretary, Grey, had made his prolix but unequivocal speech to the House on that tense Monday afternoon, for his telephone, still one of three in the Valley, linked him with a man whose sources of information were just as good as those of Grenfell's and whose interpretation was more expert.

At about 2 a.m., on the night that Paul deflated the Valley jingoes in the bar of The Raven, he awoke to hear his telephone-bell shrilling in the hall, where it stood in an alcove under the stair well out of sight of Mrs. Handcock who still regarded the instrument as a direct link with the Devil. And in a way, on that close August night, it was.

When Paul went downstairs to answer it the voice at the end of the wire had the fruitiness of Satan who had just succeeded, against all probabilities, in winning over half Christendom.

Paul said, a little breathlessly, "Who is it? What's happened?" and through a soft chuckle Uncle Franz replied, "Now who would it be, my dear boy? Who else, among your bucolic friends, would be awake and abroad at this hour?"

"What the devil is the point of ringing me at this time of night?" Paul demanded, although he felt relieved. "Is it about Grace?"

"Not specially," the old man replied, enjoying his advantage, "although I do have news of Grace. The Glorious Cause has come to terms with their Tormentors. I understand Holloway is to be emptied of the dear ladies on condition they wave Union Jacks in a day or so!"

"Oh, get to the point, Uncle Franz," Paul growled, "I'm standing here practically naked and it's gone two o'clock! It's a miracle I heard the bell at all."

"Well," said Franz, slowly, "there isn't a point, not really, particularly as you are not a man of affairs looking for a profit motive. I just thought you might like to know that I've leased the scrapyard for almost exactly the sum that you inherited from your father back in 1902! *Leased* it mark you, not sold it! It reverts to us again after five years!"

"Good God!" Paul exclaimed, "who is the tenant? The Tsar of Russia?"

"Only indirectly," Franz said, "but I won't bother you with details now. I rang because papers will arrive for you to sign in a day or so, and you won't be under an obligation to read them! You have my word for it that they are . . . well . . . advantageous, shall we say?"

"Did you ring to tell me that or for some other reason?" Paul asked, suddenly seeing a chink of daylight through the old Croat's smokescreen and Franz replied, blandly, "I suppose I really rang to stop you ringing *me* when the documents arrive for I won't be available; I shall be on the move as soon as the balloon goes up!"

Paul said, breathlessly, "You really think it will?" and there was a pause before the old man replied, as though he was choosing his words very carefully. Finally he went on, in a slightly more serious voice: "I don't imagine it will affect you much one way but if you do have emergency measures in mind take them now! Don't even wait for the morning papers. Germany, France and Austria have mobilised and Austria is over the frontier into Servia. Germany will declare war on

France tomorrow, if she hasn't already done so. As for us, we shall be in by Tuesday at the latest!"

"How can you be so sure?" Paul demanded, "Grenfell rang two days ago and said it depended upon half-a-dozen unknown factors, any one of which might result in us standing aside."

Franz said, "My dear boy, the politicians are the clowns who provide the curtain-raiser, an entirely different cast act the play! If I thought you would follow my advice I could put you in the way of making another fortune between now and next Sunday but you have always had your nose too deep in the dirt to do that and, in a way, I admire you for it! At least you know yourself, don't have self-doubts about your destiny, and have hit on the secret of real success, which is living one's life the way one wants to live it! Judged that way you're a very spectacular success indeed! Good night my boy! Sleep well . . ." but Paul cried, "*Wait*, Uncle Franz! You've hauled me from bed to say this much so you can tell me a little more! What'll be the outcome of this madness on everybody's part?'

"A very long war," Franz said, "so don't be taken in by the Kaiser's promise of Home-before-the-Leaves-Fall! Most of the poor devils won't come home at all and those who do will never be the same again. Kitchener's view is three years, although everybody is laughing at him right now. Personally I think he's an optimist!"

"Three years!" Paul exclaimed, "but Great God, that would bankrupt everybody wouldn't it?"

"It will bankrupt a good many," Franz said, fruitiness re-entering his voice, "but I am reasonably confident that neither you nor I will be among that number. I'll give you one piece of advice that you may be inclined to take. Put every acre you've got under the plough while you have chawbacons to do it! Who knows? You may come out of it better than I!" and he rang off, leaving Paul holding the receiver and conscious, despite his half-nakedness, of sweat pouring from under his arms and striking cold in the draught from the big door. He reached beyond the telephone and slipped on an old hunting coat, too agitated to go back to bed and disinclined to wake Claire who had not heard the bell. He went through the library and out on to the terrace where the heat of the day still lingered and the cloying, old-world scent of wall-flowers hung on the air like the perfume of meandering ghosts. There was a waning moon low in the sky over the Home Farm meadows and the night was so still that the whisper of the avenue chestnuts reached him across the paddock. He thought, grimly, "All over Europe men

644

are shuffling along in the dark with their packs and weapons, and I daresay, by now, every main road in German is noisy with the rattle of waggons. Almost everyone here and there thinks of war as I thought of it, during the voyage to Table Bay fifteen years ago, but it didn't take me long to discover that war is a boring, bloody muddle, punctuated by moments of fear and disgust!" And suddenly his memory turned on a peepshow that he would have thought forgotten, of smoke rising from a burned-out Boer farm, of sun-bonneted women and snivelling children standing behind the wire of a waterless concentration camp, of a private of the King's Royal Rifles with a Mauser bullet in his belly calling on his mates to put another through his head. "It was bad enough then," he said half-aloud, "but that was a piffling affair by today's standards! I don't suppose a hundred thousand ever met on one field and now there are millions, and fighting will occur in densely-populated areas! Who the hell is to blame for misery on that scale? The Kaiser? The Tsar? Those tricky French politicians or the starchy British ones, like Asquith, Grey and that Jack-in-a-Box Lloyd George?" He moved along the terrace to Grace's sunken garden and when the perfume of roses she had planted reached him he thought of her again, and how pitiful The Glorious Cause looked measured against a European war. What, precisely, had that cynical old rascal Franz meant when he implied there were men behind the politicians and generals pulling the strings? Did he mean merchants like himself, who made a profit on war as his father had done years before? Or rabble-rousers, high and low, obsessed by the cult of nationalism who used their influence to convert happy-go-lucky chaps like Smut Potter and Horace Handcock into bloodthirsty patriots? And how did he himself view the prospect of war against the Kaiser's Germany? He had never considered it a serious possibility, not really, in spite of all the years of newspaper talk and even now found it difficult to whip up rage or resentment against the Germans. The only two personally known to him, the professor and his son Gottfried, were amiable, intelligent chaps. What he did feel, however, pressing like a girdle about his ribs, was a sadness at the finality of the occasion, and the sensation reminded him of the time he had lost Grace and fled from the sleazy lodging of the prostitute near the Turkish baths. It was a profound certainty that the way of life that was his he was about to lose and with it the promise the future had offered, for if Grenfell's predictions proved right it would be a savage, bloody business, no matter how long or short it proved, and if it did drag on, as Franz seemed to think, then nothing could ever be the same again for any of them. He wondered, objectively, if he would involve himself in it; if, before it was over, he would find himself alongside men like Will Codsall and some of the others who seemed eager to show their mettle but decided against, remembering that he was now thirty-five, with a wife and family to consider and that war was a young man's business.

The perfume of the roses from the sunken garden seemed to drench this end of the terrace so that when he heard a step on the flagstones and a voice calling him, he thought once more of Grace, whom he always associated with this garden. Then he saw a blurr of white in the doorway and called, "I'm out here, Claire!" and she came along the terrace towards him, her hair tumbling over the pink shawl he had given her last Christmas. She said, anxiously, "I wondered where on earth you were! What's happened? Is it anything serious?"

"Serious enough," he told her and repeated the gist of Franz's conversation over the telephone. He was amazed to note that she seemed relieved rather than startled, as though the clash of armies had nothing to do with themselves or the people of the Valley. She said, "Well, all I can say is I'm glad you're too old and the children are too young!" and he thought the remark very typical of her and envied her ability to view catastrophe in such a personal light. He said, however, "It will make nonsense of all we've been trying to do down here, Claire. You realise that I suppose?"

"I don't see why it should," she argued, "James told you it couldn't possibly last more than a month or so, didn't he?"

"I'd sooner take Uncle Franz's word than Grenfell's on an issue like this," he said. "If there are people around prepared to pay that much money for a five-year lease on a scrapyard they must have a good idea what's likely to happen! Those kind of people, Uncle Franz's kind, don't make mistakes that cost money, not their money!"

"Oh well," she said, cheerfully, "there's nothing we can do about it is there? I suppose they must fight it out and then go home and pick up where they left off!"

He smiled, putting his arm round her and kissing the top of her head. It would be a shame, he thought, to try and explain to her what a conflict on this scale could do even to a place as remote as this, or to a woman with a civilian husband and children in rompers. She would soon find out if Uncle Franz's gloomy prophecy came true. Then he thought how differently Grace would have reacted to the news and remembered that it was here, on this very spot, that he had proposed marriage on the night of the Coronation soirée. It was disturbing but also significant, he reflected, that Grace should seem so close tonight and the sharpness of his memories seem almost an affront to Claire standing with her head on his shoulder inhaling the sweetness of the night air so he said, shortly, "Come on, there's no sense standing here, let's go back to bed!" and they went in and up the broad, shallow stairs. She curled up and was asleep almost at once and again he envied her narrow world. "There's Ikey," he thought, "he'll have to go but she never bothered much with Ikey. He always seemed to belong to the era of Grace and anyway, he's a professional and might even welcome war as offering prospects of promotion." Then, as it began to grow light, he borrowed something of Claire's complacency, thinking, "Dammit, maybe she's right! There's no sense in losing sleep over something that can't be helped or altered! I'll do my worrying when I have to!" and was sorry then that she had gone to sleep for the scent of the roses seemed to linger about her, and it occurred to him that casual access to the woman beside him was a more exciting prospect than storming every citadel in Europe.

III

In the first week of November a persistent north-easterly, showering Channel spray and needles of sleet across the Valley, drove the yellow-eyed gulls from their fishing grounds on the sandbanks and launched them on one of their periodical circuits across the shoulder of the Bluff, west to the upper reaches of the Sorrel then back across the shorn fields of Four Winds.

The gulls knew the features of the Valley better than any earth-bound creature and as they hovered over the woods and streams, peering down for unconsidered trifles, they must have been aware of some of the changes that had taken place there in the last few weeks. They no longer had to contend with the wild cries of Eveleigh's crow-starver, or the ill-aimed pellets of Henry Pitts, because, at these two points of flight, they maintained height and swooped upon easier pickings behind the field kitchens of the vast tented camp that covered the moor between Periwinkle Farm and the Paxtonbury road. There was always food to be found here and nobody minded when they helped themselves from the bins ranged along the hedge that bordered the camp to the north. Thousands of men were living there but were either clumping about in cohorts, encouraged by bellowing

647

figures out on the flanks, or cowering in their sopping tents, sheltering from wind and rain. So the gulls dived on the offal and hunks of bread scattered all around and flew off gorged to Coombe Bay, where the more observant of them might have noted other changes in and about the village, the absence of Tom Williams and his fishing team for instance, or the stillness of the house and garden where the old German professor had lived above the dunes, a man who had always welcomed them and encouraged them to take bread and bacon rinds he saved for them. This house, a favourite port of call for storm-driven gulls, was unoccupied now, its windows open to the rain and there were slivers of shattered glass lying on the lawns back and front, reflecting the pale gleam of the sun on the rare occasions it penetrated the low cloud. This, perhaps, was the most significant change of all, for there had been Territorial camps on Blackberry Moor in years gone by but never a scene like the one enacted outside the old German's house one warm evening in late August.

It began with an advance up the hill of a knot of Coombe Bay men, including Eph Morgan, the Welsh builder, Walt Pascoe, Tom Williams shortly before he joined the Naval Reserve and others, women and children as well as men. If the local posse could have been said to have had leadership it was vested in Horace Handcock, the Shallowford gardener. He it was who had preached the crusade in the bar of The Raven but he was too old and too drunk to take his place at their head when they stormed up the hill to register their disapproval of the Kaiser's rape of Belgium.

The professor was at his desk when the clamour reached him and he got up to look out of his window. The first stone, flung by Walt Pascoe, smashed the glass and grazed his head, causing blood to flow. A moment later stones or clods had shattered every window at the front of the house. The professor remained downstairs long enough to bundle up his manuscripts but while he was doing this a fragment of glass struck his chin, inflicting another small wound. He went upstairs and locked himself in Gottfried's bedroom overlooking the garden but soon this window was shattered and he saw that people had made their way round the house and were cavorting about his flower beds, pulling up plants and shrubs and howling like dervishes. Then Eph Morgan remembered the German had a motor and at once linked it in his mind to the Squire's derelict Belsize, still embedded in Sorrel mud. It seemed to Morgan a good idea that there should be two derelict cars in the district so, with the help of many willing hands, he trundled it out of the coach-house and on to a rose bed where, with the tools taken from the shed, it was soon reduced to a wreck. More people continued to arrive from the village and as it was nearly dusk someone suggested a bonfire, so Pascoe punctured the petrol tank with a garden fork and soon there was a very good bonfire indeed, one that could be seen a great way off. Paul saw it as he crossed the ford and set off at a gallop for the village, making the journey in the record time of eleven minutes, for he was riding a mettlesome four-year-old that Rose had sold him just before the outbreak of war. He had been warned of the riot by Pansy Pascoe who had the forethought to use The Raven's telephone and she urged him to come quickly before murder was done. Pansy was probably the only person in the village who disapproved of the riot. She had been employed by the professor as a daily help and he had treated her with kindness and generosity. She realised, however, that it was useless to argue with her husband Walt in his present mood, for he was full of beer, having enlisted that very day at Whinmouth and was due to depart the following morning. She said, on the telephone, "Do 'ee come quick, Squire! They'm murderin' the poor ole toad!" and Paul had set off at once shouting to Chivers to send John Rudd after him and during his wild ride along the river bank he thought savagely of the strange madness that had seized people since newspapers had begun calling Germans "Huns" and printing stories of crucified Belgian babies that no man in his senses could believe.

They would not have gone as far as to lay hands on the German. He could see that as soon as he flung himself from his horse and rushed round behind the house, where it seemed as though the entire population of the village was dancing round the blazing wreck of the Humber. The house, with all its windows shattered, looked empty but someone said the old professor was inside, hiding under a bed probably. Paul's informant seemed to assume that the Squire had arrived to share in the fun and was astounded when Paul grabbed him by the lapels of his jacket and shouted, "What the hell do you think you're doing? Has everybody gone stark, staring mad? *Who* started this business? *Who* began it? Do you realise you could all go to prison for this?" and he punched his way into the centre of the ring.

His words had immediate effect. For a long time now they had been content to have him do most of their thinking. Tom Williams said, a little shamefacedly, "I told 'em they was goin' a bit far, Squire. Breaking the old devil's windows would ha' been enough to frighten the ole bastard out o' the Valley!" but he too had a shock when Paul spun round on him, shouting, "You bloody idiot, Tom! What harm has the old fellow ever done any of us, and how the hell can he be responsible for the Kaiser's doings? He's a fugitive from the Junkers himself! He only came here to get a bit of peace!" Then, having cleared a ring and seeing people beginning to slip away round to the front of the house, he shouted, "The next person to throw a stone or touch anything here will be reported by me to the Whinmouth police, do you hear?"

They heard, those who were not already gone, and within a few moments Paul had the garden to himself, except for some wide-eyed children who should have been in bed. He said, sharply, "Get on home. The policeman will be here in a moment!" and they fled so that he was left to wonder whether, when John Rudd arrived, they should round up the rioters and make them extinguish the blazing car with water taken from the rain butt. He decided not to bother for the motor was all but destroyed and there was no danger of flames spreading to the rear of the house. He stood in the centre of the lawn and called, "Herr Scholtzer! Professor! It's me, Squire Craddock! They've gone now, you've nothing to fear!"

There was no answer so he tried the back door and finding it open went in. On the first landing, holding a lamp above his head, he saw the old man looking down and seeing the blood on his face, Paul called, "I'll send one of those fools to telephone for the doctor!" but the German said, briefly, "No! Please! It is nothing, Mr. Craddock!" and came down to the hall where glass from the coloured panes in the front door crunched underfoot.

They went into the library, Scholtzer dabbing his head with a towel and in here was the same litter of broken glass and pages of manuscript blown to the floor. The room had always looked scrupulously tidy for the professor was a very methodical man and somehow, to Paul, the disorder emphasised the sheer idiocy of the assault. He said, grimly, "You must let me deal with this, Professor. I'll have every one of them in court for this night's work!" but the old man lifted his hand and said, "No, Mr. Craddock, it was goot of you to come quickly but please, you will not make the case of it! That would do no goot for you and I have plans to leave very soon. The police were here with my papers this morning," and he began gathering up manuscript from the floor and sorting it into little piles.

"You don't have to leave on this account," Paul said, "they'll not bother you again. Get a few things together and come back to the

650

house with me. We can clear up in the morning and I can guarantee you plenty of assistance!"

The old man made no immediate reply but having finished collecting his papers he poured two glasses of gin and handed one to Paul. He seemed, Paul thought, very calm and resigned, as though a frenzied assault upon his property and person by people he had regarded as friends brought sadness but neither rancour nor fear. He said, finally, "You must not blame them so much, Mr. Craddock! It will be happening all over Europe. It is kind that you should ask me to your house but it would not be wise, I think, to go. They would remember it against you as long as the fighting lasts. It would be different if my boy was here but there is nothing they can do to me. It is your glass that has been broken."

"And your motor that has been burned," growled Paul. "Where is Gottfried? I heard he had gone abroad earlier in the summer."

"He is in Germany," the old man said. "He went to Italy for a music examination in June. Then the foolish boy went tramping in the Dolomites and I have since heard that the authorities refused to allow him to leave. Perhaps, by now, he is in uniform. After all, he is German born, with German parents, and your Government would not consider him eligible for exchange. Perhaps his whereabouts are known and that is why your people come here to break windows."

"I'm sure that had nothing to do with it," Paul said but the fact that the shy young German was possibly serving in the Kaiser's Army astounded him almost as much as the demonstration on the lawn. Gottfried had grown up in the Valley and seemed to Paul almost as much a part of it as Eveleigh's children or Sam Potter's daughter, Pauline. He said, "Can they compel him to serve in the Army?" and the professor replied, with a shrug, "It will be a choice between the Army or prison. If I had foreseen such a thing I would have applied for his naturalisation papers when he was a child but one cannot blame oneself for not foreseeing what is happening in the world today."

"You say the police were here? Is it likely that you will be sent to an Aliens Camp?"

"No," said the old man, "I have been given permission to go to the United States. My publishers and certain Oxford gentlemen were kind enough to vouch for me. It is a pity that Gottfried cannot change places with me, for even the Junkers could not use me as a soldier."

There seemed nothing more to say and Paul felt trapped in a mesh

of circumstances almost as frustrating and bizzare as those encompass-
ing the German and his son. It was as though the entire structure of
the estate and its way of life was crumbling and all one could do was to
stand around wringing one's hands and making fatuous comments on
each new development. Will Codsall had disappeared, then Gottfried,
now the old professor, whom he had always thought of as popular in
the Valley, and others would be going soon, among them some of
those who had created this mess on the floor. He supposed that he
would get used to what was happening in time but the rhythm of the
Valley had been so smooth and settled, and the process of readjustment was not easy, for he was unable to subscribe to the strident
patriotism that had been surging down the Valley ever since Bank
Holiday; so much of it seemed as shrill and childish as the recent
behaviour of sober men like Tom Williams and Ephraim Morgan.

He said, as a valediction, "You were happy here, Professor, you
won't forget us easily?"

The old man smiled, drawing a mottled hand across his great
walrus moustache. "No, Mr. Craddock, I shall remember Shallowford
with gratitude. I found what I sought here, the chance to live and
work among kindly people and a single night's stone-throwing cannot
erase the memory of more than ten years' peace!"

They shook hands and Paul left him, letting himself out of the
shattered front door and crossing the road to the spot where his bay
was tethered. The street was empty, so empty that Paul wondered if
everyone had gone into hiding, but outside The Raven Pansy Pascoe
came out of the shadows, calling softly, "Is 'un all right? Did they
'arm the poor ole toad?" and Paul told her that the professor had
escaped with a few cuts but that the police would be making enquiries
in the morning.

"Well," she said, philosophically, "I daresay that'll put the fear o'
God into some o' the gurt fools but it won't bother Walt! He's off
first light an' dam' good riddance to 'un! Us 'aven't 'ad a word o'
zense out of 'un zince it started!"

He wondered how she would manage on the meagre separation
allowance and a house full of half-grown children but then he remembered that she was a Potter and that the Potters always managed somehow. He thanked her for telephoning and rode off up the empty
street. Glancing over his shoulder he could still see the orange glow
of the burning motor on the hillside; it looked, he thought, like a
beacon warning the coast of invasion from the sea.

There were changes that the sharp-eyed gulls did not see as they made their circuits waiting for the wind to change and enable them to return to their fishing grounds on the banks. By early November the Dell was beginning to assume its once familiar look of neglect and near-squalor, with tools and faggots scattered around, and rubbish accumulating behind the sheds and byres. Jem, the Bideford Goliath, who had reigned here ever since he quit his job at the fair and imposed his genial discipline upon the two Potter girls, had followed Will Codsall into the Army soon after the Miracle of the Marne, and although he was over thirty his giant frame had ensured acceptance by the fast-talking recruiting sergeant at the Paxtonbury Territorial centre. Jem had been followed, almost at once, by Smut, who had abandoned his greenhouses to the younger Eveleigh boy and gone gladly enough, as though, in soldiering, he saw an opportunity to recapture the excitement of a poacher's life. John Rudd warned him that his prison record might result in rejection but John was wrong for when Smut admitted that he had served a term of imprisonment for belting a gamekeeper over the head with a gun butt the recruiting sergeant was delighted, saying that this was precisely the type of recruit needed. Smut's musketry instructor was equally impressed. At the initial five-round shoot-off Smut scored four bulls and an inner and that with a type of rifle he had never before fired. On the strength of this, plus a pint or two of beer, the instructor withdrew him from the awkward squad and sent him on a sharpshooters' course. It was astonishing how rapidly Smut reverted to type, how quickly and completely he forgot his patiently acquired horticultural skills and became, in effect, a poacher again. He found that he could still move across country quickly and noiselessly at night and interpret and locate the sounds made by blundering adversaries opposed to him in training exercises and with the rediscovery of his skills he sloughed off the new personality he had acquired after his release from gaol, progressing rapidly in his new profession. After Will Codsall he was the first of the Valley men to cross to France and move into the soggy ditches that already reached from Switzerland to the sea, and here he adapted himself far more easily than did most of the men of his battalion. Alone among them, save for a tramp or two lured into the recruiting office by the promise of beer and the leonine glare of Kitchener, Smut could spend successive nights lying out in the open in all weathers and he did not find a five-day spell of front-line duty very different from life as a boy in the Dell in Tamer's time, or as a young man subsisting on what he could trap and kill between the Sorrel and the Whin. He had no personal quarrel with the Germans but he was more fatal to them than many of those who regarded all Germans as unspeakable swine. To Smut they were simply the equivalent of the hares, bucks and pheasants he had stalked in the past, and the techniques he employed against them were much the same. He would lie behind the parados for hours disguised as a roll of wet sacking on a pile of rubble, as still and patient as a famished cat at a mousehole. Whenever he caught a fleeting glimpse of a moving cap or a hunched shoulder in the trenches opposite, he would wheeze with satisfaction and gently squeeze the trigger of his specially-sighted rifle. Sometimes, if the weather was good, he would take a chance after making a kill and wait for a second victim but more often he would be inside his own trench within seconds of his quarry hitting the ground. Then, after carefully notching his rifle, he would meander along to another sector, pick a fresh vantage point and begin another vigil. He would fire at almost anything that stirred but the mark that excited him most was a sun-reflecting *pickelhaube*, for this meant the passage of an officer and therefore a slightly longer notch on his score-board. He was held in high esteem by his officers not because of his sniping but because he was now a fully-licensed poacher and an enormous asset to men short of almost everything that made life bearable under conditions of constant danger and appalling discomfort. He never hurried and never acted impulsively. Before making a swoop he would study the routes of ration parties, just as he had marked out the rabbit-runs in Heronslea coverts and sometimes, when his platoon was desperately short of firewood, duckboards, sandbags, wiring stakes, plum and apple jam, bully beef and even the almost unobtainable navy rum, Smut would be permitted to lay aside his rifle and drift back towards brigade headquarters on some spurious errand. Here he would make a careful reconnaissance, and after selecting three or four of the more robust of his mates, return after dark to the areas he had memorised. Sometimes one or two of his carriers would be caught and mercilessly punished but Smut was never among this minority, for he never carried anything himself and could always melt into the darkness and try again the following night. They soon made him a corporal and he could have risen higher but he was content with two stripes, explaining that a third would cramp his style. The night he appeared at the

654

entrance of his officers' dugout with a case of Scotch whisky his Company commander swore that he would recommend Potter for the D.C.M., declaring that men had been decorated for far less but Smut talked him out of it. One of the very earliest lessons he had learned as a poacher was to remain inconspicuous and after some discussion he settled for ten shillings which he sent home to Meg, telling her that more would be coming for he was now doing a brisk trade in the sale of souvenirs.

Smut was not the only member of the Potter clan to find release in war. All three of his elder sisters had their burdens appreciably lightened when their men marched out of the Valley whistling "Tipperary". Pansy let her cottage at an advantageous rent to a major at the camp on Blackberry Moor and moved herself and family into the farmhouse at the Dell and here, restored at last to the congenial company of the recently liberated Cissie and Violet, she began her war work.

The Potter girls were the first women in the Valley to make war show a credit balance. Although past their prime (Cissie and Pansy were on the wrong side of thirty and Violet was twenty-eight), they were still strong, vigorous, handsome, healthy women and the Lancashire Fusiliers, occupying the tented camp on the moor, were a jolly set of boys, all far from home and unfastidious. Often, of a winter evening, the Dell farmhouse erupted with song and laughter and even a man as formidable as the Bideford Goliath would have found it impossible to defend the fort as he had defended it against the raids of the Timberlake boys. The girls still thought of Jem affectionately and sometimes sent him parcels and money to eke out his rations and pay in the dismal Welsh camp, where he was learning to disembowel Germans with bayonet and Mills bomb but they did not wish him back, telling one another that war had opened their eyes to the pitiful state of servitude into which they had lapsed. Such work as was done on the farm was now performed by volunteers and paid for in kind, and whereas Jem laid the mark of his despotism on the fat posteriors of his handmaidens if they so much as winked at another man they now had a battalion of men at their disposal, with no question of any one man, or even two, claiming proprietorial rights over them. Meg, as usual, kept to herself and Hazel rarely appeared in the Dell. One way and another the Potter girls were set fair to enjoy the war, for when the Lancashire Fusiliers moved out the Shropshires moved in and the pleasant rhythm of life in the Dell hardly faltered.

In the last week of November there was a flare-up in the kitchen of Four Winds, where domestic scenes had once been commonplace but had been unknown since the Eveleighs had replaced the Codsalls. The cause of the only serious dispute that had ever broken out between the black-moustached Norman Eveleigh and his wife Marian was Gilbert, their eldest boy, who had been whipper-in to the Sorrel Vale Farmers' Hunt ever since Squire Craddock had reorganised it, in 1911. Gilbert was now nearly eighteen, a slim, serious-minded boy, whose appearance favoured his mother but whose character was more like his father's. He was withdrawn and sparing with words but known in the Valley as a conscientious boy and the best rider to hounds for miles around. Squire Craddock liked and trusted him and the hounds, each of whom he could identify at a glance, adored him. The demands of the Government Remount Department, however, cost Gilbert his job. By early October there was hardly a horse left in the Valley, apart from those reserved for the plough and all prospects of hunting ended. Without consulting anyone Gilbert walked into Paxtonbury, added a year to his age and joined up, and this folly on his part disrupted a very united family for Mrs. Eveleigh, who prized her eldest boy above all the rest of the brood, said she would disclose Gilbert's correct age and get him discharged at once. To her dismay Eveleigh told her to hold her silly tongue, saying that he, for his part, was proud of the boy. Periwinkle Farm had contributed a man to Kitchener's Army and the contemptible Dell had sent two; if Gilbert wanted to rescue the honour of Four Winds who were they to deny him?

All the children were present during this dispute and what astonished them more than their father's stand was their mother's obstinacy. Never, so far as any of them could remember, had Marian Eveleigh contradicted her husband but here she was actually screaming abuse at him, with the white-faced Gilbert trying to reason with both and although the matter seemed to end when Eveleigh also lost his temper and threatened to strike her, it was Marian who carried the day, for she flung herself out of the house, walked into Coombe Bay and telephoned the military depot at Paxtonbury so that Gilbert's enlistment was declared void.

After that, although tempers gradually cooled, things were never quite the same between man and wife. It was as though the ghost of Four Winds had not been banished after all but was still lurking in one of the attics awaiting an opportunity to sidle into the bedrooms and kitchen and foment trouble between man, wife and children. In the event all that Marian's defiance achieved was four months' deferment, for Gilbert re-enlisted on his eighteenth birthday and the controversy seemed likely to flare up again for there were two more boys, aged sixteen and twelve, and by the time Gilbert had gone nobody could say if the war would last three years, ten years, or the remainder of everybody's life.

It was not long before the Eveleighs, man and wife, were at one another's throats again and the dispute on this occasion centred round their second daughter, Rachel. Rachel Eveleigh had been going steady with Keith Horsey ever since the Coronation summer but it was only after they had been instrumental in bringing help to the crazy gypsy-child, Hazel Potter, that the Valley showed any interest in the association. Now it was generally understood that Keith would marry the farmer's daughter as soon as he passed his finals at Oxford and was assured a good teaching post and Eveleigh was thought to look upon the match with satisfaction, for a parson's son with a university degree was a rare catch for the daughter of a man who had begun as Codsall's hired hand.

Keith Horsey, luckier than most young men that catastrophic summer, sat for his finals in June and the result, a double first, gave him a choice of several careers. The couple had planned to marry in early spring but the war was rushing along at a speed that bewildered all but the very young and in mid-October Rachel informed the family that the wedding was being put forward to the last week in November.

The Valley was still apt to look suspiciously upon hurried weddings and none more so than the dour Eveleigh, whose unexpected opposition to the changed date was reinforced, it seemed, by sudden and inexplicable second thoughts regarding the groom. Challenged by Rachel and her mother to explain them he said that he had been told that Keith Horsey was associated with a group of students dedicated to the ideal of international brotherhood. Rachel looked blank at this but Marian laughed in her husband's face, something else she had never done in more than twenty years of married life.

"You can't be serious, Norman!" she protested, "what can it matter to us what Keith thinks about politics? He's a nice, well-mannered boy, capable of earning a good living independent of his father's money and in any case he's head over heels in love with our girl! I say the sooner they're wed the better!"

"Well I say different!" snapped Eveleigh, "and seeing she isn't

657

twenty-one until next summer she'll have to get my permission before she ties herself up to that snivelling little pro-German!"

At this Rachel burst into tears and rushed away but Marian stood her ground, for it occurred to her that this was her husband's way of punishing her for intervening in the matter of Gilbert's enlistment. Then another somewhat darker thought struck her and she came out with it at once. "Have you got it into your silly head that our girl has got to get married?" she demanded and Eveleigh, to her amazement, replied, "It wouldn't surprise me none, not with a boy of his type! Have ye not heard it said he's agin the war?"

"No, I haven't heard it," said his wife stubbornly, "but if I had it wouldn't cause me to think less of him! Anyone in their zenses is against the war I should think and the zooner more of them make it known the zooner this wicked slaughter among Christians'll stop!"

Now when Eveleigh had begun this conversation he had had no serious intention of withholding his permission but had merely sought to express disapproval of his future son-in-law's unpatriotic views. To a simple man like Norman Eveleigh lack of enthusiasm for the war amounted almost to treason. He had never given a thought to European politics before August 1914 but newspaper accounts of German atrocities in Belgium had stirred his anger so that he was among the most belligerent men in the Valley, growling that the world would never be safe until the Kaiser was put away, the German generals backed up against the wall and German towns given over to sack on the scale of Louvain. He was a man who had always driven himself remorselessly but he considered himself just and the German advance across France and Belgium surely called for retribution without mercy. The discovery that his own wife, the mother of his children, wanted the war stopped before justice had been done shocked him and hardened his resolve to make an issue of his daughter's marriage to a pacifist. He said, flatly, "Lookit here, Marian! If she marries that milksop she'll do it without my blessing! I'll have no part in it, you understand? I'll not show at the wedding, and if she won't abide until she's of age then she can run off for all I care!" and having delivered this ultimatum he stamped off and took it out on a frisky bullock who had unwisely chosen this moment to break out of the pen behind the barn and career up the lane towards Codsall bridge.

Rachel, watching him belabouring the animal, said, "He's mad! He must be! It's this place! This farm! Everybody who lives here ends up going off their heads, like old Martin Codsall and Arabella!" Then,

658

drying her tears, "Well, I'm not going to let *his* silly notions ruin *my* life, Mam, and you can tell him so for I shan't have another word to say to him! If he tries to stop us I'll go before the magistrates and get permission! They'll give it me and why shouldn't they? I'll be twenty-one in less than a year and Keith's father will stand by us!"

In the event this proved unnecessary, for although Eveleigh persisted in his opposition he was persuaded by Paul to sign the papers on the grounds that, if he did not, the couple would marry in any case, war-time courts having little patience with parental opposition to weddings. Every day girls younger than Rachel were marrying soldiers, often after courtships of less than a month. All the same, the new quarrel deepened the unpleasant atmosphere at Four Winds and the ghost of Arabella had reason to be pleased. After Rachel had married and settled in Leeds, where Keith took a university post, the Eveleigh family sat through a succession of silent meals and when Gilbert re-enlisted Marian Eveleigh fastened on her old grievance, going so far as to tell her husband that he had driven the boy to his death! So many things were happening so quickly in the Valley, however, that it was some time before Paul was aware that strife had returned to Four Winds after a lapse of ten years. He was usually alive to most happenings in the Valley but at that season he had other and more personal matters on his mind, notably an unexpectedly violent dispute with his own wife. The disagreement centred on another war-time marriage.

V

Late in November, less than a week before Keith Horsey and Rachel Eveleigh were married in Coombe Bay parish church, Ikey Palfrey reappeared in the Valley, home with his unit from India after an absence of more than two years and destined, in a matter of days, for France.

There was no time to warn anyone of his approach for he was granted but seventy-two hours' leave and travelled west on a night train that did not stop at Sorrel Halt. He arrived very early in the morning, driving a hired car of uncertain vintage and came into the kitchen just as Mrs. Handcock was brewing her ritual cup of tea. She let out a squawk of joy as he came bounding up the yard steps, pouncing on her, kissing her on both cheeks and declaring that she had put on ten stone since he had seen her last. He had always been her favourite and she bustled about frying him eggs, bacon and potatoes, bubbling that she would "share un wi' no one, not even Squire, 'till 'e 'ad summat hot in his belly and had thawed-out-like!" She told him that he was "as chock full of 'is praper ole nonsense as ever, the gurt varmint!" adding, with satisfaction, that he had "villed out summat" and "looked more like a nigger than a Christian!" He had indeed broadened so that his height was less noticeable and the Indian sun had burned his face and hands berry-brown, but already his tan was fading and looked, she told him, "more like grime than zunburn!" While he ate she gave him the news, or such of it as she could recall, for there had been so much in the last few months, although, prior to that, little enough save for the birth of the Squire's second daughter Whiz, "the prettiest li'l maid you ever did zee!" She told him Will Codsall had gone for a soldier as soon as war started and that his wife, Elinor, had been in a rare ole tizzy but had now got a good hand working for her, the son of Tom Williams (now mine-sweeping), who had a dread of the sea, having witnessed, as a child, the rescue of the German sailors in the cove. "And a praper zet o' bliddy vools us maade of ourselves that day!" she added, "for, like as not, they us dragged ashore are vighting for that varmint Little Willie!" She told him that Smut Potter had enlisted and was said to have already killed hundreds of Germans and that Jem, Dandy Timberlake and Walt Pascoe had gone after him, leaving Walt's slut of a wife to move in with her sisters at the Dell, there to earn more money on their backs, the hussies, than they were ever likely to earn standing upright! She also mentioned the rumour that Farmer Eveleigh was opposed to his daughter's marriage to Keith, scheduled for next Saturday, and this seemed to interest him most for he questioned her as to the reasons for Eveleigh's opposition but she could supply no satisfactory answer beyond saying, "Tiz rumoured about yer that Passon's son be one o' they preaching agin the war and that's enough to turn any man sour, baint it?"

He surprised her by saying that before long a great many people would be preaching against the war, for it now seemed certain that it would not be over by Christmas or the Christmas after that and that he expected to be in France himself within days which was a pity for he would have liked to have attended Keith's wedding on Saturday. Mrs. Handcock was dismayed that he would only be home for days after an absence of more than two years and at once recalled her duty to notify Squire and Mrs. Craddock of his arrival. Ikey made the brazen suggestion that he should carry in their early morning tea but Mrs. Handcock would have none of this for it would mean him seeing man and wife in bed together and this outraged her notions of propriety. She entered into a conspiracy, however, to tell Squire that someone had called on urgent business, bidding Ikey to wait at the top of the stairs so that she could watch the fun. Soon Paul came hurrying out, struggling into his dressing gown and his shout brought Claire on to the landing without a dressing gown for she interpreted Paul's bellow as an accident involving somebody's tumble downstairs.

They were delighted to see him and touched by the presents he had for them in his valise, a cashmere shawl for Claire, a pair of silver-mounted Mahratta pistols for the library wall and a cunningly-made Indian toy for each of the children. Mary, three and a half now, blushed with pleasure when he gave her a doll dressed in exquisitely worked embroidery closely sewn with amber and ruby-coloured beads.

News of his return ran down the Valley like a heath fire and all that morning tenants and Valley craftsmen made excuses to call and shake his hand, for he was the only professional soldier among them and Mons had raised the standing of a professional soldier in public esteem.

Among the last to arrive was Keith Horsey, who came into the yard as Ikey was saddling Paul's ageing Snowdrop for an amble round the estate before dusk. His greeting seemed so restrained that Ikey put it down to nervousness regarding his imminent marriage. It was when Keith curtly declined the loan of the stable's sole remaining hack and an invitation to accompany him that Ikey noticed there was a reticence about him reminiscent of the nervous, shambling youth who had been the butt of High Wood during his first school year. He told Chivers to exercise Snowdrop and walked Keith up the orchard as far as the sunken lane and here, exercising the privilege of an old friend, he said, "Are you scared about getting married, Keith?" but Keith looked at him defiantly and replied, quietly, "No, Ikey. I'm not a bit scared about Saturday. Rachel and I will be very happy once we get away from here."

"I heard that your prospective father-in-law was flag-flapping," said Ikey, "but I'm damned if I'd let that bother me."

"It isn't that either," Keith said, stubbornly, "in fact, it isn't anything much to do with me really. I suppose I should have written but it wasn't the kind of thing one could put to paper, at least, *I* couldn't!" and when Ikey raised his eyebrows, very puzzled by the other's embarrassment, he went on "It's . . . about you, Ikey, but before I make an idiot of myself will you tell me something?"

"Anything?"

"Well, before you left here, how . . . how well did you know Hazel Potter?"

Ikey, still bewildered, said, "What the devil are you driving at? If you've anything on your mind, Keith, for God's sake stop drivelling and come out with it."

"Very well, I will," said Keith primly. "I don't suppose anyone here wrote to tell you for there was no reason why they should but Hazel Potter—she had a child about eighteen months ago and I've always believed it was yours!"

It took Ikey thirty seconds to get a grip on himself while Keith, his eyes directed to the ground, stood with shoulders hunched and hands clenched like a man expecting a blow. At last Ikey said, quietly, "If Hazel had a child it would be mine, Keith. Whose child do they think it is?"

"They don't think anything about it now," Keith said, "she wouldn't say and nobody cared much so after a bit they gave up guessing."

"Where is she now?"

"She's living in the cottage beside the old mill on the river road. Doctor Rudd got her fixed up there and I found her a job, cleaning the church," and when Ikey made no reply he described how he and Rachel had found the girl in labour and how, when he had burst into the cave, she had shouted Ikey's name. "No one knows that," Keith added, "not even Rachel, for naturally I didn't say anything. I couldn't be sure anyway, not until the child began to grow but then, somehow, I knew! Well, it's off my conscience and I'm glad. I did what I could for her, Ikey, and she seems happy enough down there, happier than any of us I imagine."

Ikey lowered himself slowly to the step of the stile while Keith continued to hover, seemingly more embarrassed than ever. They remained like that for a moment, neither speaking nor moving, until finally Ikey said, "It was damned decent of you, Keith, decent to say nothing but even more so to take care of her. However, I'd sooner have known! Do you believe that?"

"Yes," Keith said, "I believe it now."

"You could have told Doctor Maureen. She would have written and maybe she would have understood too."

662

Keith said, wretchedly, "I almost did but I couldn't be sure, not absolutely sure and it seemed . . . well, so disloyal I suppose. How could I forget all I owed you? Oh, it wasn't just watching out for me at school but everything, including Rachel. I suppose you've forgotten it was you who brought us together?"

"Yes, I had forgotten," Ikey said but he remembered now, and a picture returned to him of a gawky, stammering youth shaking hands with the pert farmer's daughter against a background of swirling couples and the blare of a brass band.

He said, "You're sure nobody knows?" and when Keith reassured him, "It seems incredible that nobody saw us, not once. Maybe her mother Meg does know but she'd never say anything, she doesn't waste many words." He got up, passing a hand over his hair. "That old ruin beside the water-mill you say?"

"It isn't a ruin now, Squire had it done up for her."

"She stays in it all the year round?"

"Why yes," Keith said, "why shouldn't she?"

"Ah," said Ikey, "that's something you wouldn't know, Keith. Well, I'll go there right away."

"Would you like me to come?"

Ikey smiled. "No, we had no witnesses in the old days so there's no point in enlisting one now. You could do something, though; tell Mrs. Handcock to tell Squire I'll be in to dinner but that I would prefer it wasn't a celebration, I believe the Gov was planning one. There's something else you can do too, if you will. I've only got three clear days, and God knows if I'll ever be back. Would your father marry us if I got a special licence?"

Keith opened his mouth and closed it again, perhaps knowing his man better than anyone in the Valley. He said, "I expect Father will help, if he can," and hoisting himself over the stile walked down the orchard path towards the house.

The cottage stood on a low bank on the left of the road, a squat, three-roomed dwelling, built of cob with a pantile roof and around it a quarter-acre of vegetable garden hedged about with a criss-cross of angled beanpoles.

The setting sun over Nun's Head was a narrow sliver of orange, turning the small, deep-set windows to flame and when he climbed the winding path and looked inside he could see them both in the light of a log fire, Hazel squatting on the floor, with her back to him and the

663

child, facing the window, on the point of tottering across the floor into her outstretched arms. It was a set-piece, like a woodcut illustration of a sentimental magazine serial, yet curiously moving in its banality. He stood watching as the child staggered the distance on chubby, bowed legs and the mother caught him round the waist and tossed him the length of her arms. What awed him was not the child's likeness to himself, which seemed to him so striking that he was astonished she had kept her secret so well but the domesticity etched on her and the room, as though the single act of giving birth to a child had changed her as no other pressures had been able to change her, drawing out her wild blood like wine from a cask and replacing it with the blood of a cottager's wife, who slept in a bed under a roof, cooked regular meals and worked to a domestic timetable from sunrise to sunset. The evidence was all there before his eyes, not only in the playfulness between them but in the clean hearth, the shining pans suspended from the whitewashed walls, the patchwork rug neatly spread beside the scoured table where lay a pile of ironed linen and two bowls and spoons set before a high and a low chair. He thought, "It's like looking into the cottage of the Three Bears and I wouldn't wonder if she wasn't pretending to be a bear," and suddenly a rush of tenderness choked him and he felt his eyes pricking and for a moment was a child again himself but one shut out of the simple delights of childhood looking in upon security and certainty he had never enjoyed. He stood back from the window making a great effort to collect himself and in a little he succeeded, so that he was able to pass the window and reach for the gargoyle knocker; yet he was unable to rattle it, thinking desperately, "God help me, she has to know and there isn't much time! Maybe Dr. Maureen or the parson can sort it out somehow but it's for me to make the first move," and he thumped the knocker hard, hearing her steps scrape on the slate slabs and the slow creak of the heavy door being dragged open.

He had expected her to whoop, or scream, or make some kind of outcry but the only sound she uttered was a kind of prolonged hiss, expressing no more than a mild and pleasurable surprise and then she smiled, almost absently and stood back, waving him into the cosy room as though he had been a casual visitor calling with the parish magazine or a parcel of groceries. Then he remembered that she was endowed with the priceless gift of reckoning time by her own clock and calendar, and that her months had always been days and her days minutes or seconds. Yet erosion of this bastion must have started for she said, carelessly, "You been gone longer'n I recall; *zeems* longer any ways! Will 'ee mind the tacker while I maake broth?"

He could think of nothing adequate to reply to this and so compelling was her bland acceptance of his presence that there was no necessity to say anything, or to begin the grotesque task of convincing her that more than two years had passed since he had climbed the long slope to her little house and that within that period her womb had yielded up his child, the fat youngster now perched on his knee and gurgling with delight at this unlooked for variation in its routine. He said, as she bustled between hob and table, "He's a proper li'l tacker. What do 'ee call un, midear?"

"Well, 'er's christened Patrick along o' the lady doctor," she said, "but I dorn call un that, 'cept to plaise 'er when 'er's about! I calls un anything as comes to mind and 'ee answers to most. When us is yer alone tiz 'Rumble' on account o' the noise that comes out of un! He's lively enough, mind, and us never has to worry over 'un but he do zeem to have a man's share o' the wind! Give un a pat and judge for yourself!" and as if to support her claim the baby belched, a long, rumbling, almost dutiful belch so that Ikey shouted with laughter and Hazel smiled too as she poured soup into the two bowls and then, using a piece of muslin as a strainer, a third portion into another bowl she had taken from the dresser.

They sat and ate supper, slowly and ceremoniously, Hazel lifting the spoon to the baby's mouth and turning aside every now and again to help herself. It was as though they had sat there through eternity, a man, a woman, and a child, snug and smug between four thick walls, warmed by the fire and their own complacency and it was only when he had watched her put the baby to bed in a cot made from a lidless coffer of ecclesiastical design that he was able to escape from the cocoon of fantasy that she and the child had spun around him from the moment of entering the cottage. Then, as she coiled herself like a housecat on the rag mat and leaned her thin shoulders against his knee, he realised that, whether he willed it or not, he would have to coax her a few steps towards reality and said, still using her brogue, "I'm a real sojjer now, midear, and theym zending me to the war in a day or zo. Suppose us goes down to the church an' marries, same as Rachel Eveleigh an' Passon's son be doing this week? Would 'ee marry me, an' zet up house here for me so as to have a cosy plaace to come back tu?"

665

She turned and stared up at him and at first he thought the movement was one of protest but she looked no more than mildly surprised and said, chuckling, "Now why ever should 'ee live yer along o' me? Us all knows you bides wi' the Squire, at the Big House."

"Ah," he said, "that's zo but tiz a draughty ole barn of a plaace an' I've a mind to zet up with a plaace o' me own. Seein' as that tacker o' yours be mine tu I dorn need to look no further, do I?"

His logic appealed to her but she had reservations. "Well, 'twould suit me well enough," she said, "seein' youm comin' an' goin' most o' the time but will the Squire let 'ee? Worn 'er fly in a tizzy at you leavin' 'un?"

"Lookit yer," he said, "I'm a grown man, baint I? And I can live where I plaise, so hold your chatter woman and give us a kiss!" and after kissing her he went on, "I like the notion so well, I'll zet about it right away! I'll see Squire, then I'll have a word with Mother Meg for she'll have to give 'ee away, seein' Tamer's dead an' buried. You bide on yer an' I'll come to 'ee in the mornin', and us'll be married same as your sister Pansy, for that way us'll get the money from the Army for 'ee so long as I'm away."

It was as simple as that and after a peep at the sleeping child he went down the bank and along the river road into the dusk and it was here, by pure chance, that he met Meg returning from one of her autumn hedge sallies, with pannier baskets full of roots slung across her shoulders.

She stopped in her stately swaying walk and greeted him with customary civility and although she made no direct reference to Hazel he was aware that she knew where he had been. Meg knew everything that happened in the Valley and therefore showed no surprise at all when he told her that the child was his and he had only known of its existence that same afternoon. When he said he was determined to marry Hazel by special licence, however, a shade of doubt crossed her face and she said, clicking her teeth, "Ah, you've no call to do that! 'Er's well enough as she be, an' Squire won't favour it. You baint our sort and never could be, not now!"

"I'm not gentry either," Ikey told her, "and everyone about here knows that well enough. Hazel, she knows how to care for the child as well as any woman in the Valley and at least the baby has stopped her wandering."

"Aye," said Meg, thoughtfully, "it has that and I'm glad on that account, for the Valley baint safe for a maid to wander the way it once

666

was," and she jerked her head to the north where lay the camp beyond the hump of the moor. "Still," she went on reflectively, "they won't take kindly to a man from the Big House marrying a Potter and come to think on it that makes no sense either, for youm better blood stock than the Quality! One can look into the baby's hand for that!" and casually she reached out and peered attentively at his hand, drawing her dark brows together as though resigned to what she read there. She said, suddenly, "Will you be doing this to give the boy a name?" and he told her no; he was doing it because he should have done it long since, before he went away, before he finally crossed over into the gentry's world by taking the King's commission. It had been a bad mistake and he admitted it for now he belonged to neither world. Only with Hazel did he feel rooted and at peace. If he survived the war, he went on, he would resign his commission and live out his life in the Dell or on some other holding. By then people all over the world would have seen the folly of money-grubbing, flag-waving and airs and graces and many would go back to agriculture, the family unit and simple basic things.

She nodded, as though disposed to agree with him and promised that if he sent a message to the Dell she would attend the ceremony and afterwards she watched him wade the ford and pass between the great stone pillars of the gate; they had never exchanged more than a few moments' conversation, yet she felt closer to him than to any of her own kin for somehow she recognised him as a spirit attuned to the rhythm of the seasons and privy to some of the earth's secrets that were no longer secrets to her. Now, having read his palm, she knew something of his future too and was glad that he had spawned a son in whose veins ran the oldest blood in the Valley. What the Squire said or thought about legalising the union was not important. Marriages performed in the church down on the shore were no more than a ritual not much older than some of the oaks in the Shallowford woods. She supposed that the mumbling of a priest and the signing of papers had significance for some but not for such as her, whose ancestors had hunted about here before the first church was built. She hitched her baskets on to her shoulder and set off again down the river road, walking like a queen bringing gifts to gods older than the sad-faced Jew they called Jesus.

VI

News that the Squire's protégé was to marry the half-witted

667

postscript of old Tamer Potter and Gipsy Meg created a sensation in the Valley comparable to that of the Codsall murder or the wreck of the German merchantman in the cove. For a week or so, as a talking-point, it ousted the war but then news of the Valley's first casualty was broadcast and it was half-forgotten by the Eveleighs, the Pitts, the Derwents and the Willoughbys. The topic lingered, however, in the kitchen and sculleries of the Big House, for here it was recognised as a flashpoint of a tremendous family row, a long, rumbling affair leading to weeks of monosyllabic conversation at table, to sudden out-bursts of temper by the complacent Squire's wife and—this was the thing the servants noticed—a stricken look on the face of the Squire that reminded some of them of the dismal interval that had followed the flight of his first wife.

They were not far off the mark; in the days after Ikey had gone to France and Hazel Potter had become Hazel Palfrey, Paul was almost as miserable as in the months leading up to the wreck and his second marriage. He had enough to depress him in all conscience and without the added irritation of a semi-permanent quarrel with Claire. In four months he had watched the patient work of twelve years crash under the demands of war, with men leaving the Valley in ones and twos, impossible demands being made upon the Valley livestock and all the dislocations attendant upon the presence of the huge tented camp over the hill. Added to this were the constant appeals made to him for help from the bereft womenfolk, as well as personal embroilment in other people's brawls, like the sour quarrel at Four Winds. He could have managed and perhaps, at a pinch, extracted a measure of satisfaction from tackling these problems, had he been able to share in the general enthusiasm for the war and view the slaughter across the Channel in the unequivocal terms of newspaper leader articles but to a man of his essential tolerance and slow habits of thought this was not easy. He had always regarded Germans (the professor and his son ex-cepted) as noisy ridiculous people, with their posturing Kaiser and childish preoccupation with military display but he could not, at a bound, subscribe to the popular view that they were a race of sadistic monsters, hell-bent on rape and plunder with homicidal tendencies reaching down from the All-Highest to the humblest private soldier in the field. Nor could he, as an unrepentant provincial recognising his own limitations, convince himself that Britain's involvement had been inevitable. For these reasons, and for others he sensed but could not put into words, he was depressed, frustrated and dismayed, without
668

the compensating intoxication that the wine of patriotism seemed to produce in his neighbours.

Then Ikey arrived and Paul looked to him for reassurance and perhaps professional enlightenment but within hours of his return he calmly announced that he had fathered the Valley half-wit's bastard and was determined to advertise the fact by marrying her! This was depressing enough; what was far worse, from Paul's standpoint, was Claire's hysterical efforts to stop the marriage and, when she failed, her inclination to saddle him with the blame as a man who had side-stepped his responsibilities. Her attitude, he felt, was as illogical as Grace's had been all those years ago, for both instances proclaimed the maddening unpredictability of women and their brutish obstinacy in defending indefensible positions. He recognised at once that Ikey would have to make his own decision, no matter what any of them said or did and although he was hurt and baffled by the boy's gesture he understood, or thought he understood, the chivalrous impulse that prompted it. Moreover, as temporal leader of the Valley (a position he had always taken very seriously) he felt he had a duty to the child and questioned whether he had the right to dictate to a man of twenty-three, for although still in receipt of a modest allowance Ikey was no longer dependent on Paul's money and would not benefit by Paul's will. At his own instance, shortly before leaving for India, Ikey had insisted that his name was removed from the list of beneficiaries, de-claring that Paul had already done more than enough for him and that any money or property he left should go to the children. Only thus, he told him with a grin, could he hope to remain in Claire's good graces for the rest of his life.

For all his reservations, however, Paul found it hard to look upon the marriage as anything but a madcap decision, pointing out that all the Potter girls were promiscuous and that even if Hazel was of different clay she was unlikely to prove a suitable wife for an officer, even in the middle of a war fought on behalf of democracy.

Ikey's reply to this counsel had astounded him and yet, in a way, half-convinced him. Declaring that no man other than himself had ever had access to the girl he said it was his intention, at the earliest opportunity, to resign from the Army and take a small holding on the estate, perhaps the Dell if it was vacant. As for the generally-held opinion that Hazel was dotty he would not subscribe to this and neither would Paul if he spent an hour in the company of the girl.

Paul then tried another approach, pledging responsibility for mother and child and promising Hazel a life tenancy of Mill Cottage, rent free. Ikey listened to him politely and when he had talked himself out said, quietly, "I suppose you find it impossible to believe I want Hazel for herself? For what she has been and is in my life?"

"Yes, I do," Paul grunted, "I find that quite impossible to believe!"

"Well, it's true anyway," Ikey said, "and I realised it soon after I went overseas. Every woman I've met since is a bore or a harpy, especially the eligible ones! I suppose that's what comes from being a changeling, Gov'nor?"

"Damn it, you're not a changeling!" Paul yelled at him, "you've got a better brain than any of us and I've always been damned proud of you!"

"Yes, I know that Gov," Ikey said, "but the difference between you and me is that, although both of us started from the scrapyard you never worked there! Ever since I came down here as a kid I've had an affinity with Hazel Potter, a far closer one than I ever had with any of the jolly old Empire builders I met at school or since. In the ordinary course of events I don't suppose I should have had the guts to turn back and appear to throw everything you've done for me in your face, but now it's different! The whole damned lot of us are slithering down the slope and if I have the luck to come through, which seems to me pretty unlikely, then I'm done with pretence for good! All I shall want is a cottage, a bit of land, Hazel Potter and Hazel Potter's kids!"

After that Paul gave up and went grumbling to Claire and she listened with impatience as he recapitulated all that Ikey had said and when he told her that he supposed they would go ahead no matter what anyone advised she snapped, "Nonsense! You must stop it, Paul! I won't have Ikey marrying that trollop, I *won't*, do you hear?"

He said, despairingly, "But I've just explained, he'll marry her no matter what we say! He's twenty-three, independent, and he'll be in the trenches this time next week!"

"I don't care," she said, stubbornly, "you mustn't allow it! You must think of a way to stop it at once!"

"Maybe you can think of some way," he said grimly and she replied, "Yes, I can! You can tell him that if he goes ahead with this ridiculous marriage you'll turn the entire Potter family off their land and evict that girl from the cottage!"

"Good God!" he said, appalled, "you can't mean that! It would be damnably unfair on Tamer's widow and the girls, to say nothing of Jem, who's away fighting for us!"

She said, with calculated emphasis, "You've always been a sentimental idiot, Paul, and mostly I haven't minded because none of the issues were important enough to quarrel about. But this one is! I won't have you and I made a laughing stock from here to Paxtonbury!"

"Now how the devil are you involved?" he demanded and she said that they were both deeply involved for he had sponsored the boy when he was a waif of ten or eleven and she was his wife. Marriage to a half-witted slut would hold the estate up to ridicule.

"I don't agree with you for a moment," he said, "but even if I did I'm damned if I'd take it out on the girl or the girl's family! This isn't like you, Claire! You aren't a vindictive woman, but you're talking just like Arabella Codsall when she came bleating to me about Will marrying the Willoughby girl all those years ago!"

"I'm not apologising for that," Claire said, "for maybe Arabella Codsall had a point of view after all! You have always given everyone about here far too much rope and let them impose on you. Now it's time I stepped in and cracked the whip a little for if I don't I wouldn't like to think what might happen when our own children grow old enough to get themselves into this kind of situation, providing they are stupid enough that is! And that isn't all, either! The tenants are taking shameless advantage of you in all kinds of ways. They come down on us for everything nowadays and some of them are coining money out of that camp! As to this Ikey nonsense, I'll settle that in two minutes, if you'll back me up!"

"I certainly won't back you up to the extent of turning the Potters adrift!" he retorted. "You can talk to Ikey if you like but you might as well understand he's genuinely attached to the girl!"

She looked at him steadily, no longer pale and tight-lipped but with a bright pink flush on her smooth, oval face. "You actually believe that rubbish? Attached to a girl who won him in a ditch, a technique she probably learned from her sisters in the Dell?"

It occurred to him then that there had been a time, long years ago, when she herself had come very close to winning a man in a ditch but he knew that to remind her of the encounter beside the mere would only make a bad matter worse, so he shrugged and said:

"You argue with Ikey. I've had my say and as far as I'm concerned Hazel stays in Mill Cottage, married or single! I'm damned if I'll put her out to flatter your snobbery!" and he stalked off, leaving her trembling with rage.

He never discovered whether or not she made a direct appeal to

671

Ikey for no one from the Big House attended the ceremony in the parish church three days later. It was held at 8 a.m. and Ikey was gone from the Valley by afternoon. Paul heard that a number of the curious had gathered at the church, among them Henry Pitts' big, rawboned wife and the kindhearted Mary Willoughby, who had once tried so hard to teach the bride the alphabet. Others watched the couple leave by the lych gate and drive off somewhere in Ikey's hired motor and one of them, Rachel Eveleigh, herself due to marry in the same church the following day, told Mrs. Handcock that she had never realised how beautiful Hazel Potter was and how serene she had looked as she sat smiling down at them while the bridegroom cranked the car. Ikey came in to say good-bye to Paul before driving off across the moor to catch his train but neither made a direct reference to the wedding. Ikey said, shaking hands, "I don't suppose I'll be back for at least six months, Gov'nor; if at all, that is," and Paul growled, "I wish to God the women of this Valley would be less bloody-minded and the men a bit more optimistic!" but he wrung the boy's hand and wished him luck.

Outside, as Ikey humped his kit into the little motor, he added, "I'll keep an eye on her, Ikey!" and Ikey replied, "I didn't have to ask, Gov!" That was all and Paul watched him swing round the bend of the drive to reappear again for a moment between the leafless chestnuts as he shot the gate. He thought, "What the devil does it matter anyway seeing that he's heading for all that slush and slaughter? Somebody ought to remind Claire that she was young herself once, and a neighbour of the Potters but I'm damned if it's going to be me! In her present mood she'd probably sulk for an extra month!" and he went into the library and poured himself a stiff whisky.

He was standing there, his back to the fire, when Maureen came in from the terrace. She seemed very breathless, as though she had climbed the drive too quickly and she had a worried expression that looked odd on her broad, humorous face.

"Could you go down to John?" she said, quickly, "he'll need you for an hour or so. It's Roddy, his boy. He had a telegram about an hour ago," and as Paul exclaimed she said, "Oh, you don't need to worry to that extent, Paul, he's taken it on the chin, but Roddy was all he had left of his youth and a wife who died young. I think you could give him more than me. I was a late-comer in his life."

"Tell Claire," Paul said, savagely, "but don't have her come fussing! She's been damned difficult over this Ikey business," and slipping a bottle of his best Scotch in his pocket he hurried across the paddock to the lodge.

John was sitting in his old leather armchair beside an untended fire, the last light of the short winter's day excluded by the closely latticed panes of the little window. He did not look grief-stricken, only small and a little shrivelled, an unlit pipe in one hand and the buff telegram form in the other.

He said, as Paul came in, "It was that affair off the Falklands. Our squadron was outgunned, just as I said they would be. There'll be more naval shocks before it's all over, mark my words. You can't win a war by singing 'Rule Britannia', Paul!" and he handed over the telegram containing the flat, impersonal expression of royal regret on the snuffing out of a life in its prime. Paul was to see and handle many of these telegrams in the next two years but because this was the first he read it carefully twice before laying it down.

"I do wish you hadn't taken Roddy's bit of nonsense with Grace so much to heart, John," he said. "There was never anything in it, and I knew that, even at the time. We ought to have laughed him out of it and encouraged him to spend another leave here. Was he married?"

"No, and I've got my own theory on that. It doesn't matter a damn now, so I suppose I can tell you. The truth is he never really got Grace out of mind. Does that surprise you?"

"Yes, it does," Paul said, "for Grace never regarded him as anything more than an engaging boy. Did they meet after he left here that time?"

"Oh yes," John said, "after the divorce they met often but you're right, she never took him seriously. They used to dine and visit a theatre whenever he was in town or whenever he could catch her between spells in Holloway. Would you mind if I let her know about this?"

"Not in the least," Paul said, "why should I?" and he took glasses from the cupboard and half-filled them with his special brand of "Loch Leven". "Here," he said, "I need one badly myself," and with the object of giving John something else to think about he told him of his quarrel with Claire over Ikey's marriage.

"She's wrong and the boy's right," John said, when he had finished, "for here's another who never thought of Hazel Potter as dotty. Fey but not dotty. Anyway, who are any of us to talk about half-wittedness, when we've all got ourselves into this kind of mess? As

673

for Claire, wanting to take it out on the Potter clan, I suppose I can understand that in a way."

"I'm damned if I can," said Paul, "it came as a shock to me that she even suggested it."

"It's odd," John mused, sipping slowly, "the Valley always clung to its class distinctions, even in the Lovell days. There were the Derwents and the Codsalls on either border, the workaday Pitts and Willoughbys in the middle and finally the Potters. Claire was brought up to regard the Potters as scum and I suppose they are in a way, all except Meg, who comes closer to ancient royalty than any of us. Marrying into the Big House was a triumph for High Coombe and I don't think old Edward Derwent has ever stopped congratulating himself. The prospect of his grandsons inheriting High Coombe and every other farm in the Valley is a very unlooked for bonus and I daresay he'll side with his daughter on this issue. Still, I ought to have a fellow feeling for him today I suppose," and when Paul asked why John said Roddy's death had stirred in him memories of the boy's mother that he had thought forgotten and that Derwent too had lost a wife when she was about Myra's age. "They were a bit alike," he added, "both pretty, dashing and maybe a little showy like poor old Roddy. It's funny, but that kind usually burn themselves out before their time. It's the plodders like you and me who die a little every day."

Paul said, suddenly, "How do you see this war, John? As a crusade, the way most people seem to? Or more as I see it, an appalling, stupid waste, without a shred of glory about it? It hasn't anything in common with the wars you and I fought in, you against those poor devils of savages, me against a few thousand Boers. They were incidents but this is genocide or will be if fought to a finish. Dammit, the way things are going, we shan't have an able-bodied man left in the Valley by this time next year!"

John Rudd lit his pipe and puffed it stolidly and Paul thought he looked much as he had that summer evening he first sat there after their ride from Sorrel Halt. He took his time answering, it was not often that anyone extracted a snap judgment from John Rudd.

He said at length, "I happened to have professional tips from Roddy and some of his shipmates on which I based my opinion of the Navy's unpreparedness. That doesn't make me a wiseacre."

"But you were the only one who was sure they wouldn't capture Paris," Paul reminded him and John said: "I'll be sixty next year;

apart from the Zulu campaign I've lived all those sixty years in Britain. A man ought to learn something about his own people in more than half a century. He'd be a damned dull dog if he didn't!"

"What did you learn that makes you so cocksure, John? For you are cocksure, aren't you?"

"About the outcome? Yes, I am. We'll win all right though I don't know that it will do us much good in the end. I suppose I've seemed to you to take the war in my stride because I've been anticipating it so long and there isn't much point in arguing the rights and wrongs of an inevitability. The line-up started round about the time you settled here and if it hadn't been poor little Belgium this year, it would have been poor old Turkey next year, or hands off India the year after that! Now it's here the only thing left is to hold on and the British do that much better than most of them!"

"It looks to me as if it's all that's left to us," Paul said, "so what makes you confident about us getting anything better than a stale-mate or a compromised peace?"

"Ah no," John said quickly, "you can rule that out! A nation that achieves all this one has in a century has to have special qualities and I don't say that in the spirit of somebody paid to write for the popular press, it's just a feeling, down here," and he tapped his paunch with his pipe-stem.

"Then all I can say is I wish to God I had it," Paul said emphatically. "It seems to me we rushed into the business without a thought as to what was at stake and these people here, the Walt Pascoes and the Smut Potters, are amateurs. We all know what happens when an amateur takes on a professional!"

"They'll stay amateurs for a bit," John said, "but that's what I'm driving at. When they get desperate enough they'll knock hell out of everybody. Go up to that camp and watch those cotton-spinners at bayonet practice."

"Not me," Paul told him, "I've no stomach for the business and I still think we were damned stupid to get drawn into it."

"Well," John said, "I can understand that, knowing you. For too long now you've been giving your attention to what happens in your own backyard but when you realise that backyard is at stake you'll outdo the rest of them! That'll be when your Puritan streak shows. Puritans only show fight when they've convinced themselves their way of life is threatened. After that there isn't many who can stand up to them for long." He got up and knocked out his pipe. "Will you tell

675

Maureen not to wait supper? I think I'll take a turn along the river road."

"Do you want company?"

"No," John said, smiling, "but if I did I should prefer yours to anyone's. Thanks for coming down and thanks for getting my brain working on an abstract issue. I don't know whether it was intentional but it worked!" and he took his hat and stick and went out abruptly leaving Paul to contemplate two framed portraits on the mantelshelf, one of Roddy in his rakishly tilted naval cap, the other of the fat surprise packet Maureen had produced not so long ago, now asleep in the little room over the porch where Paul had spent his first night in the Valley. He thought, as he lit the lamp, "I wish those bloody fools who had poor old John Rudd drummed out of the Army on account of that Prince Imperial incident could have shared the half-hour I've just spent with him! Could I show that much dignity if I'd just had a telegram telling me Simon or one of the twins had been blown to bits in somebody else's quarrel thousands of miles away?" He sat finishing his whisky, having heard the girl whom Maureen employed as a maid clank off into the dusk on her bicycle. Presently Maureen came back and he gave her the message. "Well, that's John's way," she said, "he always is greedy with his troubles. Can't bear to share 'em with any one of us, but maybe you've noticed?"

"Yes," Paul told her, "it was something I learned about him very early on. Did you see Claire?"

"Yes and made a point of not telling her about Roddy, tho' I rather wish I had. She almost bit my head off and the twins came in for a slap apiece. Is she that much upset about Ikey marrying the Potter girl?"

"About as upset as I've ever seen her."

Maureen said, as though to herself, "I find that very odd!" and then, turning to face him, "Top up your drink, Paul, for you're going to need it!" and when he protested that he had already had too much whisky she took the decanter and half-filled his glass. "I'll tell you something I've never told anyone, not even John, and you can please yourself whether you make use of it or not! If it wasn't for Ikey, Claire Craddock would almost certainly still be Claire Derwent. At all events, she wouldn't be mistress of Shallowford tucking your children into bed!"

Paul said, "What the devil did Ikey have to do with me marrying Claire?" and Maureen, trying but not altogether succeeding to keep

676

the chuckle out of her voice, replied, "It was a letter written by him saying you were calling for her, that got her down here that time you were laid up after the wreck. And that's not all either, not by a long chalk! He wrote to Claire at the instance of Grace. The letter was written in her rooms that time he ran off to London."

Said like that, bluntly and factually, it did not make an immediate impact on him. After a pause, while she waited for it to sink in, he said, "How do you know that? How long have you known it?"

"I've known it ever since I came here."

"*He* told you? Ikey told you?"

"He did that, down by Codsall bridge a week or two after it happened."

"You believed him?"

"Of course I believed him. Would a boy of his age manufacture a story like that? Besides, Ikey was never a liar."

The implications of her story began to register. He said, wonderingly, "But he was only a kid! Claire came home on chance and finding me laid up volunteered as a nurse. If I remember rightly you engaged her."

"Claire never mentioned that letter to you? The one telling her you had been calling for her when you were running a high temperature?"

"Never! I didn't know there was a letter!"

"Well boyo, there was! You can depend upon it and there isn't much doubt that the girl took it at face value, believing what she wanted to believe. Knowing that, I'm sorry I blabbed. She probably had good reasons for forgetting. Still, I've told you now so it's up to you if you jog her memory or not. The fact is she owes Ikey Palfrey her happiness, but come to think of it, so do you, for this silly business will blow over soon enough and taken all round you and Claire are as well-matched a pair as I've ever doctored!"

He said nothing for a moment so that presently she picked up his glass and pushed it into his hand. "Get it down, lad," she said, "it's not Irish whiskey but it'll serve!" and after he had swallowed the measure and still remained silent, she cocked her head on one side and said, humouring him, "There now, it's not worth brooding on. What began as a hoax turned out well enough for all of us, didn't it?"

"In the light of what you've told me," he said, slowly, "her present attitude to Ikey is impossibly arrogant! Ought she to be reminded of what she owes him?" and it was Maureen's turn to consider.

"No," she said at length, "I don't suppose it would help in the

677

least, it would probably harden her against him. How many of us enjoy coming face to face with a generous creditor after a lapse of ten years?"

For the first time since he had heard of Ikey's intention to marry Hazel Potter Paul was able to smile. "You were in attendance as doctor at the time so will you tell me one thing more? *Did* I cry out for Claire?"

"If you did I didn't hear you," she said, "but you have to give that boy full marks for originality!"

He went out and up the drive feeling a good deal less despondent than when he had descended it. He found that his memories, jogged by Maureen's story, were sharp enough when he summoned them. He could recall waking up after they had set his bones on the kitchen table and seeing Claire over by the window, looking as if she had always been there and would always remain there, and he could also recall his sense of relief at her presence, as though the excitements and terrors of the wreck had, in half-battering the life out of him, filled a vacuum left by Grace and given a new twist to his life. He thought, a little smugly, "Let her sulk! Let her indulge her damned Derwent pride, for that's all it is now I can get a close look at it! I could puncture it by telling her what I know but Maureen's right—it would only drive a permanent wedge between her and the boy, for what woman likes to be reminded of the tricks she played to get what she wanted? And she must have wanted me pretty desperately and Shallowford too I daresay, although I don't blame her for that. She's been a good wife and mother and she cares for this place as much as I do, so what have I got to complain about?"

He took a long sniff at the damp evening air and went in to begin his penance. He might have dragged his step a little if he had suspected that it would see him through Christmas and well into the New Year.

678

CHAPTER TWO

I

By early spring, 1915, the people of the Valley were dispersed as they had not been for two-and-a-half centuries. The last exodus on this scale had occurred as long ago as July 1685, when the Duke of Monmouth came recruiting and some of the Sorrel men had been rash enough to volunteer for a shorter war that had ended, for most of them, on the field of Sedgmoor or in transportation to the sugar plantations of Barbados.

Will Codsall, Dandy Timberlake, Walt Pascoe, Jem Pollock, Smut Potter, Gilbert Eveleigh, Tremlett the huntsman and Tod Glover, the mechanic, were already in khaki, the first three overseas the others in training camps up and down the country. Others were on the point of going, including the sons of Eph Morgan, the Coombe Bay builder, and Abe Tozer, the Coombe Bay smith, and Willis, son of the Shallowford wheelwright. Tom Williams, who was a naval reservist, and his nephew Daniel had been at sea for months, minesweeping on the same vessel off Rosyth and by the time primroses were fading in the river road hedgerows one or two of the women had left, among them Rose Derwent, of High Coombe.

The war had given Rose's life a painful jolt but it happened that the enforced closing down of her riding school brought compensations. By May, 1915, she was married and mistress of an estate larger and more impressive in every way than that of her sister Claire, so that Edward Derwent, who had once dreamed of being freeholder of three hundred acres, now had prospects of seeing his grandchildren (providing thirty-four-year-old Rose bestirred herself) inherit two appreciable slices of the English countryside. It was an astonishing turn of fortune for the glum, taciturn man who, only a decade before, had resigned himself to dying a tenant farmer and sometimes he found it difficult to believe that both his daughters had, against all probability, made brilliant matches. Yet it was so, for Rose married Major Barclay-Jones, D.S.O., on the first of May, 1915, and whilst Edward Derwent could claim no credit for getting Claire off his hands he played a vital role in disposing of the amiable, horse-faced Rose,

679

whom everyone declared would die an old maid and that in spite of inheriting her mother's seat on a horse.

There had been little to occupy Rose after the Government had emptied her stables in the hectic days when the High Command still had visions of cavalry charges over open country. Almost every hunter in the Valley had been bought and carted away and Hugh, her brother, ran High Coombe very efficiently with the help of his father, a hired hand too old to enlist and a couple of boys. For a time she mooched about in the dairy and then, at her father's instance, volunteered to serve in the Y.M.C.A. canteen at the camp on the heath where she found herself the only woman among several thousand men. This would have been gratifying to most spinsters of thirty-four but it caused hardly a flutter in Rose's heart. She had always preferred horses to men and easily parried the passes made at her by homesick middle-aged men and even a few younger ones desperate for feminine society. She made friends with some of the senior officers, however, among them the stoutish, loud-voiced Major Barclay-Jones, who, as a former hussar, bitterly resented his enforced association with sweaty infantry-men and stinking motors. The Major, a rather explosive little man of five and fifty, had been blown out of retirement by the trumpet blast of August 4th and it was not long before the frequency of his visits to High Coombe put a thoughtful look on Edward Derwent's face. Un-like everyone else in the Valley he had never quite despaired of getting his elder daughter off his hands. He made a few discreet inquiries and was encouraged to learn that Major Barclay-Jones was a widower, owned a large estate in Gloucestershire, had two sons serving with the Army overseas and had been joint master of a famous hunt up to the time of rejoining the colours. It was this last piece of information that stimulated Derwent for he was a man who struck bargains with the minimum of sales talk, his method being to concentrate upon the most obvious selling point of the merchandise. Claire's selling points had been numerous, among them her pretty face and what Grace would have called her "ripeness", but Rose's selling point, if she could be said to possess one, was limited to her seat on a horse, a factor hardly likely to be overlooked by a man who had served thirty years in the 11th Hussars and had been master of a fashionable hunt.

In a matter as important as this Derwent could curb his pride. He approached his daughter, expressed a mild liking for the major and asked her bluntly "If the man had said anything as yet?" Rose, who could be obtuse, replied, "Said anything about what, Father?" where-

680

upon Edward, with a grunt of exasperation, took himself off to Shallowford and came riding home on Snowdrop, one of the two hunters left in the Valley, the other being Rose's mettlesome four-year-old, Prince, the horse she had once hoped to school into a national steeplechaser.

To give Rose any real chance at all, Edward decided, it would be necessary for the major to see her mounted on a good horse and also to watch her handle an animal that even the grasping Government Commissioners had left behind as too spirited for their requirements. By this time Derwent had taken Claire into his confidence and on her advice left nothing to chance. There being no hunting anywhere within hacking distance he arranged to borrow Snowdrop for a week and offer the major an hour's pleasant exercise in the saddle on the afternoons he was free. Once he saw Rose in the saddle, once they were alone in the woods Derwent decided, it seemed likely that Rose's selling-point would become apparent to him. If nothing resulted what had any of them got to lose?

It succeeded with a speed that astonished him. On his return from their third excursion Major Barclay-Jones was so full of admiration for Rose that he stayed on for supper, drinking nearly a bottle of Edward's sloe gin and pronouncing "The Gel", as he called her, "the possessor of a spanking seat and the neatest pair o' hands in the business!" Encouraged by Derwent and another noggin of gin, he went even further: "Watched a lot o' good nagsmen in my time," he added, after Derwent had murmured modestly that Rose was reckoned the best horsewoman west of Melton Mowbray, "but she tops 'em, Derwent! Tops 'em by inches! Dammit man, I watched her put that temperamental joker at a five-bar on the far side of the wood! Nothin' rotten, mind you — good solid timbah, by God! *Flew it!* Flew it with a foot in hand and at full gallop! Joy to watch! Lovely action! Dam' sorry I couldn't follow but the old grey is past it, like me, since I tied in with those blasted foot-sloggers!"

A day or so later, however, the major showed that he was not quite past it and put the seventeen-year-old Snowdrop at the bole of a fallen elm which he cleared with less than an inch in hand. He was so delighted with himself that he proposed on the spot and Rose, too astounded to accept or refuse, stuttered that he had "better talk to Father", providing, of course, "that he wasn't joking". He laughed all the way home at this but he was not joking. He was among the dwindling number of optimists who still believed that as soon as better weather set in the two-million-strong German Army dug in across north-eastern France would be herded back across the frontiers by a few regiments of British cavalry, waiting with drawn sabres to exploit a gap torn in the enemy's lines by Sir John French's Territorial drafts. It therefore followed that by midsummer he would be back at Lavington Court with all his commandeered horses restored to him and a new pack of hounds in the kennels. The mere prospect of sharing life with a gel of Rose Derwent's calibre persuaded him that he was good for another twenty years in the saddle.

So Rose travelled to Gloucester to meet his elderly half-sister (fortunately for everyone the possessor of yet another spanking seat) and because it was war-time, and everybody's movements were uncertain, the wedding took place almost at once, a colourful little ceremony in Coombe Bay church with the groom in full regimentals and an arch of swords provided by officers from the camp. It was the first military wedding that had taken place there since the days of the South African war and the Valley was delighted. There were no bridesmaids, Claire acting as Matron of Honour, but the little church and yard was crammed, boys scrambling on to the granite obelisk of Tamer Potter's grave in order to get a better view. Nobody in the Valley remembered Tamer that sunny May morning, but, by a macabre coincidence, Tamer was remembered vividly elsewhere that very same night.

All day on May 1st, 1915, the German U-boat that had been lurking off the Firth of Forth for a week or more stalked the minesweeper *Venturer*, butting north towards Scapa Flow and the *Venturer* had two Sorrel Valley men in her crew. One was Tom Williams, the leader of the fishing fraternity in Coombe Bay and the other was Tom's nephew Dan, who had been his uncle's crewman up to the time they left the Valley together. Dan was not a naval reservist like his uncle but had decided to share his active service because he was attached to him by ties stronger than blood. During a severe squall off Nun's Head in the winter of 1910, when Dan was an inexperienced lad of seventeen, Tom had put life and boat in jeopardy to rescue the boy swept overboard in a heavy sea and ever since they had been inseparables. The boy had a great respect for his uncle's seamanship whereas Tom was now linked to Dan by one of the strongest superstitions of the sea; having saved a soul from drowning he must abide by him for the rest of his natural life. At 2 a.m. sharp, on the morning of May 2nd, the U-boat fired two torpedoes, striking the *Venturer* aft and amidships and folding her like a hinge. She sank in six minutes and as there had been no chance to launch boats the nine survivors, including Tom and Dan, climbed aboard the only means of escape, a venerable life-raft that looked about as seaworthy as a soup-plate. Luckily the sea was no more than choppy but as they had but one paddle, and were all half choked with oil, their chances of making landfall seemed slim. Then, to their dismay, the U-boat surfaced, an officer addressing them by loud-hailer and speaking, to Tom's amazement, what he would have called "Gentry English".

"How many are you?" he asked and when Tom replied "Nine!" the sleek, grey shape manœuvred alongside and someone lowered a jar of rum and a bag of ship's biscuits. The officer then gave Tom his position but when Tom told him that they had no means of making way, and that their only chance was to be picked up by daylight, a tow-rope was thrown aboard. For more than two hours the strange convoy moved westward, travelling at a speed designed to prevent the men on the raft being washed clear. When the U-boat cast off as the first streaks of dawn showed in the sky Tom saw that the Scottish coast was not more than five or six miles distant. It was difficult, he felt, to thank the man who had just sent his ship and most of the crew to the bottom but clearly some kind of acknowledgement was required, so he climbed unsteadily to his feet and bowed and the U-boat captain, standing on the conning tower, waved his hand and shouted, "Witness, gentlemen, we are not barbarians! Good luck!" and went below. Within minutes the vessel had submerged and Dan Williams, drunk with excitement and several draughts of German naval rum, said, "Well, sod me? If that don't beat all!" but his uncle sternly admonished him for profanity and set about trimming the raft and distributing biscuits while the second mate, having fetched up what he hoped was the last of the oil in his stomach, set off the first distress flare.

It was not until they were being counted aboard a destroyer's launch three hours later that Tom remembered another shipwreck, one that had occurred more than five hundred miles south-west of their present position, an occasion when, so to speak, the boot was on the other foot and roughly the same number of Germans had been hauled ashore half dead in Tamer Potter's Cove and ferried to Coombe Bay as soon as the tide-race permitted. He did not see these two rescues as a coincidence but as an exercise in Divine book-keeping. They

683

were nine German survivors out on that rock and there was enormous significance in the number. He thought about it all the next day when they were being fed, cosseted and fitted out at the Sailors' Rest in Aberdeen and when, a day or so later, he and Daniel boarded the train for a nine-day survivors' leave, he said to the young man, "Daniel! There's zummat us'll do the minute us gets to the Valley, zummat as *calls* for doin', I reckon!" Daniel could think of several things that he would like to do but since they included petting Eph Morgan's daughter and sinking a quart of homebrew at The Raven, and since he was aware that his uncle would frown on both indulgences, he merely said, "Arr, an' what'll it be, Uncle Tom?"

"Us'll pay our respects to Tamer's grave, boy," said Williams, "and us'll lay some flowers there mebbe, for come to think on it Tamer shares that grave wi' the Germans us fished ashore dade time o' the wreck and I dorn reckon anyone's give a thought to any one of 'em zince!"

Daniel followed his uncle's reasoning although privately he thought him sentimental. Everybody knew there were a few good Germans and a lot of bad Germans and that they had been fortunate in encountering one of the few good Germans with a punctilious sense honour. He was ready to admit that they owed their lives to the tow and the rum but he did not see how laying flowers on the graves of Germans drowned when he was a boy had any bearing upon their recent experience. As usual, however, he was prepared to defer to Uncle Tom in all matters affecting the sea and said, "Arr, Uncle Tom, us'll do what you say! Come to think on it, I dorn reckon anyone has given old Tamer a thought for years never mind they Germans along of him!"

He was probably right although, at that precise moment, two men of the Valley were thinking of Tamer's kin in the person of his daughter Pansy, wife of Walt Pascoe.

Four months guarding the Sweetwater Canal, the victim of sandstorms, suffocating heat, sand-dusted bully beef, thirst, flies, scorpions, boils and the whining importunities of Egyptian hucksters had encouraged Walt Pascoe to regret the impulse that had led him to exchange corduroys for khaki and the Sorrel Valley for the Sinai Peninsula so that when his unit was hustled off to Alexandria to embark for Gallipoli he went with alacrity, happy to leave the riddle of the Sphinx unsolved. On the troopship he had the luck to encounter an old friend, one who helped to ameliorate the pangs of homesickness

684

that Walt had endured ever since he ate tinned Christmas dinner in a temperature of 105 degrees in the shade. He was trying to find bed-space on the overcrowded deck when he heard his name shouted from among a group of soldiers wedged in the bows and he recognised Dandy Timberlake at a glance, for Dandy still wore his four-inch waxed moustaches that had given him a quasi-military look even in peace-time. The two greeted one another boisterously and teamed up for the voyage, celebrating their reunion with several bottles of warm, weak beer.

All day and much of the night as the troopship ploughed its way across the eastern Mediterranean they beguiled the hours with nostalgic talk of the Valley and Valley personalities and had she been able to hear them exchanging confidences and Wild Woodbines Pansy Pascoe's sense of humour might have been tickled, for she would have recalled an occasion, shortly before her marriage when Walt had blacked Dandy's eye for slipping his hand down her neck in Codsall's stubble field, and another, years later, when Dandy had walked her home through the violent thunderstorm that concluded Squire Craddock's Coronation Fête. Neither occasion was referred to during the endless flow of reminiscence but Walt remembered the fight in the stubble field and Dandy remembered the night of the Coronation Fête and both felt guilty for behaving so churlishly towards a comrade-in-arms, now bound for the same battlefield. Walt hoped that Dandy had forgotten the cornfield squabble and Dandy derived some consolation from the fact that, even if the fourth of Pansy's children did look more of a Timberlake than a Pascoe he had been the means of contributing, albeit anonymously, to Pansy's separation allowance. They parted temporarily at Mudros but met again under even more cramped conditions in a gully under Achi Baba, about a month later. From then on they were inseparables until a Turkish sniper shot Dandy through the lung and Walt, his concern for the wounded man overcoming his caution, was cut down by a burst of machine-gun fire at less than two hundred yards range. Dandy was not mortally wounded, but his long convalescence, first at Mudros and later at Alexandria, was not made easier by reflecting how and why Walt had died. He thought about it a long time and it made him feel mean, small and treacherous. When he was well enough to sit up he composed a long letter to the widow which puzzled her a good deal for as well as recounting how Walt had died the letter hinted that he was prepared to wait in the wings indefinitely as a possible replacement

685

and she had never thought of Dandy Timberlake as the marrying kind. In her fashion Pansy had loved Walt, and in the lighthearted way of the Potters she regretted him, but she had plenty of reminders of him under her feet and life was very hectic in the Dell just then, so she did not read into Dandy's letter all she might have done. In any case it would have seemed to her ridiculous that Dandy's conscience should trouble him on Walt's account, or on account of Timothy, her youngest boy. After all, Walt had been blind drunk that particular night and one could not reasonably expect a bachelor to walk three miles in pouring rain pushing a pram-load of another man's children without receiving some kind of reward for his chivalry.

Spring, 1915, found Smut at the celebrated Bull Ring at Harfleur, not far, as the gull flies, from the scene of his triumphs in the Armentières sector but far enough to deprive him of prey whilst improving his stalking techniques. At Harfleur they taught him new but less precise methods of adjusting the imbalance between the Kaiser's hordes and the British Army, showing him, for instance, how to use a Mills bomb and a light machine-gun. He was an apt and attentive pupil, for although neither weapon demanded the degree of skill that had won him a reputation as a rifleman, he was the first to concede that they were likely to prove more lethal when he returned to the line. He was probably the happiest man in all the huge, dismal camp for, unlike most of his comrades, the ties that had bound him to his native heath had all but broken. The only thing awaiting Smut across the Channel was a couple of greenhouses and it seemed to him unlikely that people would worry overmuch about a shortage of petunias, lobelia and fuchsia so long as this gigantic spree endured. Meanwhile, for the new Smut, or rather the old one reborn, there were many compensations. The area was rich in merchandise of a kind that did not have to be watered or kept at an even temperature, all manner of things that careless people left lying around to be carted away and used, given away, or disposed of at a modest profit, loot as varied as sides of bacon, cases of spirits and French wines, items of harness, automatic pistols taken from dead German officers, high-grade German binoculars, boots, tins of jam, periscopes, torches, blankets and sometimes even a mule that had strayed within earshot of someone who knew how to persuade it to follow him without re-course to oaths and blows. To Smut Potter the untidy landscape about Harfleur was a kind of university wherein he was fed, clothed, housed

686

and even paid to perfect new skills and enlarge his mental horizon. For now he spoke a fluent patois that could engage and sometimes captivate the most grasping estaminet patronne. He could drive a Leyland lorry over bad roads at night without headlights or pilot a motor-cycle combination across a turnip field without clinking bottles stowed in the sidecar. He could strike an advantageous bargain with a Scotsman or a Yorkshireman who, in their home towns, had been the despair of professional salesmen and he could exact by way of toll almost any privilege from admiring company officers who often benefited directly from his highly developed sense of local loyalty. There was talk, now that spring had arrived, of an advance that would harry Fritz back over the Rhine in a matter of weeks but Smut hoped that the enemy would not be in too much of a hurry to depart. The prospect of resuming life as a reformed character had no attractions for him. He did not see how he could avoid becoming a poacher again once the Kaiser was accounted for and thought it likely that he would sign on for as long as they would have him and stalk other of the King's enemies, Arabs perhaps, or cannibals of the kind who had once engaged the attention of some of the time-serving men now instructing him. He liked everything about his present life, its constant movement, its boon comradeship, its glorious uncertainties and in this strange contentment he was not alone among enlisted Valley men.

Fifty miles south of the camp where Smut was perfecting new killing techniques the Bideford Goliath, sometime Lord of the Dell, had also had the seal of official approval placed upon dormant skills. As a private in a pioneer company Jem's weight-lifting techniques were invaluable. They had first advertised themselves when an ammunition limber slipped off the greasy pavé into a shell-hole and might have passed beyond recovery had not Jem, standing close by, grabbed a trailing rope, anchored it round a stump and held it there as nonchalantly as another man checks the flight of a frisky terrier. Others hurried to his assistance and the limber was hauled out but the story of his feat passed from mouth to mouth throughout the sector and soon assumed Homeric proportions, bringing to Jem the kind of notoriety that Samson must have enjoyed among the Israelites. After that he was watched every time he shouldered a load of iron staples to carry up to the line and it was remarked that, not only was he capable of shifting roughly twice as many as the strongest of his comrades could bear along a slippery communication trench, but also that he was, or seemed to be, impervious to shell-fire. When a whizz-bang or a five-nine came crashing out of the sky, and others flung down their loads and flattened themselves in the mud, Jem seemed only to contract a little, carefully shifting his load to interpose between flying shrapnel and the upper part of his hulking body. He never winced. He never cowered. And he never got hit. Soon he became a kind of talisman so that men were comforted by his presence and under their admiration his personality began to flower. Once again he could take pleasure in the popularity he had enjoyed as a youngster in the booths of the travelling fair and had savoured, briefly, as Master of the Dell. He had never demanded much of life, no more than a full belly, a little affection and public acknowledgement that he was the strongest man in the world. Here, in a Pioneer battalion a mile or so east of Béthune, these simple requirements were his and like Smut he thought it improbable that he would willingly return to the Dell and readdress himself to the hopeless task of guarding the virtue of his two wives. This was not to say that he had resolved, like Smut, to prolong his service with the colours. There were things he missed, among them the evening peace of the Valley, and the tang of the sea meeting and mingling with the scent of freshly turned soil, but he did not miss Cis or Vi as much as he had anticipated. The spasmodic chatter of machine-gun fire in and about the cluttered pitheads was a fair substitute for their clacking tongues and the occasional whoosh of a five-nine, a split second before impact, sometimes recalled their fierce, raucous laughter. On the whole, and on thinking it over carefully, he preferred the overtones of war, so long as projectiles fell on the extreme front line, or the back areas, whence came all these miles and miles of wire and all these millions of pit-props and iron pickets.

II

Smut was enjoying the war and Jem could bear it but less than two days' march to the south-west was the very first of the Valley volunteers, Will Codsall of Periwinkle, and Will shared neither Smut's enthusiasm nor Jem's tolerance for the situation in which he found himself alongside the Albert Canal, whence he and the few survivors of the dismounted Yeomanry had been sent after a hectic four months in sectors further north. The appalling reality of modern war had been brought home to Will before any of his neighbours had crossed the Channel. In October, 1914, the Paxtonbury bunch had been fed into the line to plug gaps torn in professional ranks by the First Battle of Ypres and were at once engaged in a string of ding-dong battles in shallow, flooded ditches running on and on through unpronounceable towns and villages. In those touch-and-go days Will had seen the Paxtonbury group shrink from three score to about a dozen exhausted, lice-infected scarecrows, who regarded themselves as a squad doomed to spend the fag-end of their lives performing the horrid cycle of five days in the line, five in support and five "resting" in areas that came in for nearly as much round-the-clock shelling as those within pistol range of the Germans.

For a man who had never been able to bring himself to drown a litter of kittens Will had acquitted himself well, performing, in those first mad weeks, miracles of enterprise, hardihood and even ferocity. He had seen at least a dozen men fall to his rifle and had used the bayonet, cosh, and crude bomb on many occasions but that was before the day during a trench raid near Rue de Bois when he stopped in the business of tidying up to look closely at a German Corporal he had killed with a spade about an hour earlier. The sight of the faceless thing lying on its back in six inches of churned-up clay opened the door of an attic in Will's mind that had been kept locked and chained for more than twelve years and soon after that he began to see himself not as Will Codsall, the soldier husband of the brisk and business-like Elinor but as Will Codsall, son of Martin Codsall, whose craving for blood had directed him to cut off his wife's head with a hay-knife. The dissolution of his self-control was not instantaneous. Even in his present pitiable condition, with nerves raw and brain and body numb after terrible physical exertions and lack of sleep Will was still game enough to coax the spectre back to the attic and slam the door but the odds against keeping him there were great. Soon the whole orchestra and landscape of the battlefield enlisted with Martin and Martin's obsession, so that Will began to see the churned-up fields not as violated French farmland but as the margin of Four Winds' duck-pond on a wet November afternoon, and hear the rumble of the guns as an echio of Arabella's assaults on his privacy as she flushed him out of hid ng places during the struggle that had ended in his flight and marriage. It was as though everything about him conspired to re-create and widen the tragedy of long ago and the sense of doom emerging from this vastly amplified projection of destruction caused him to ponder aspects of the murder and suicide that had not occurred to him during the twelve-year lull. He came to believe, for instance, that his

689

father had not been mad at all, or not in the clinical sense but a man who had yielded to intolerable pressures upon his self-control, pressures supplied by the steady lash of Arabella's tongue, and it was during a pitiless bombardment a day or so after contemplating the man he had killed with a spade that Will understood precisely how his father had felt when he reached breaking-strain. From here it was only a step to personal identification with Martin at that point in his life where he had fired his gun at the Squire's boy, murdered Arabella in the bedroom and hanged himself in the barn.

No one around Will suspected that he had passed the extreme limit of endurance for as-yet there was no such thing as "shell-shock" in the R.A.M.C. handbook. There were heroes and there were cowards and in between a majority who could endure a spell in the line and slough off the fear of death the moment they passed out of range of all but the heaviest artillery. It was this majority that Will Codsall envied but they were now cut off from him by the ghost of Martin, who seemed never to leave Will after they moved into a comparatively quiet sector, in April. Will came upon him in all kinds of improbable places, masquerading as the platoon sergeant in the bath-house, or sitting beside him on the companionable four-seater latrine, behind the billet, but it was not until Martin's ghost began to speak that the confusion became intolerable for then, largely out of cussedness, Will began to defy the old fool and curse him as he sat beside him at battalion sing-songs, or advised him to draw his bayonet and prod the belly of the corpulent reserve officer, who had replaced Captain Bagshaw, blown to bits at Rue de Bois.

Leave saved his sanity for a time. Once he was tidied up and embarked on the long, cross-country journey back to Base, Martin's ghost began to recede and by the time Will had reached Sorrel Halt, after a two-day journey of almost uninterrupted sleep in jolting trains, he felt reasonably assured that the old devil had been unable to escape from the lunar landscape about the Albert Canal and would stay there to be sniped, shelled, or bayoneted to death in the next local foray. And there, for all Will cared, Martin could suffer with all the other ghosts; he had never had much affection for his father when Martin was living and the recent persecution had put him on a par with Arabella.

III

Lieutenant Palfrey, the only man in the Valley to fight as a regular, spent the month of April, 1915, in the area of the dreaded Cuinchy brickstacks, where the Germans held one half of the rubble and the British held on to the lower, disadvantageous half. As a gunner and an officer he was spared a good deal of the terror, misery and discomfort that had driven Will Codsall to the edge of a mental breakdown but he saw more of front-line conditions than most heavy gunners for he was employed, sometimes for days at a stretch, as an artillery spotter and was either aloft in a captive balloon or, more often, checking map references with divisional infantry officers in and about the grotesque ruin where the two lines of trenches ran as close as fifty yards.

Ikey had now been in France for five months and the fact that he was a professional conditioned his outlook and moderated his prejudices. He was unable to view the sprawling, bloody muddle of Armageddon with the enthusiasm of Smut, the phlegm of Jem, or the frantic dismay of Will, for to most professionals the war was looked upon as a tiresome interruption in the fashionable art of soldiering mitigated, to some extent, by the chance of rapid promotion. Regimental protocol was still enforced and time-honoured mess customs were still sacrosanct, a frigid welcome being extended to youngsters drafted in to replace casualties. Ikey, who had always been inclined to look upon regimental ritual with tolerant contempt, was grateful for his keen vision and highly developed sense of observation, that offered an excuse to absent himself from the battery and regimental H.Q. He cheerfully accepted the risk of being shot down from his balloon or sniped on his way to and from the front-line if he could spend whole days out of reach of the sahibs further back. By the time spring had come round he had developed a theory about the war that, to a degree, blunted its impact upon his sensibilities. All his life, or so it seemed to him, he had stood exactly half-way between the possessors and the possessed, between people who jingled the bell when the fire burned low and those who came trotting up to replenish it. He had been acutely conscious of this personal neutrality during his schooldays and whilst engaging in his clandestine association with Hazel, and although it would seem that, by marrying Hazel Potter, he had crossed from one social sphere to the other this was not really so. As long as the war continued or as long as he was actively engaged in it he still retained a foot in each camp. It was this time-truce that helped to clarify and then buttress his sense of detachment so that he came to see the war as a kind of surgical operation that civilisation was performing upon itself, an agonising but extremely interesting attempt to demolish class-barriers that had been building in Western Europe since the early days of feudalism. Possibly at that particular time, he was the only man in France who saw the war as the last eruption of feudalism, a gigantic and masochistic combined assault by masters and men upon the bonds they had forged for each other over twelve centuries of pride, bigotry and licensed greed. Unlike the majority of his comrades-in-arms he could not view it as an exercise in nationa, rivalry or even, as the more sophisticated were beginning to regard it, as a cynical struggle for world markets that would last, perhaps another few months, or at worst another year. He saw it for what it was, the explosion of a magazine of myths and the trappings of myths such as flags and tribal cultures and although its barbarity horrified him, and he could pity the little people trapped in the cogs, he could also accept the slaughter as inevitable during a vast shift in the pattern of life on the planet. It was his sincere belief in this that enabled him to shorten the recoil of his emotional reaction to scenes that he would have thought himself incapable of witnessing without disgust and perhaps a protest that would have led, sooner or later, to direct conflict with brother officers.

His letters to Hazel encouraged the growth of his detachment. He enclosed one, at least once a week, in his cheerful, factual letters to Paul, who now paid Hazel a weekly visit for the express purpose of reading Ikey's letters to her. To Hazel herself Ikey said little about the war but confined himself to irrelevant minutiae, a patch of clover growing beside a trench; the fatness and multiplicity of rats and their dexterity in dodging revolver shots; the wandering flight of a chalk-hill blue butterfly braving shellfire over the brickstacks; and sometimes even a comic quote from the gunners' letters he censored. He did not know whether Paul, in reading his letters aloud, ever attempted to convert his words into the brogue that he himself had always used when talking to her but he deeply appreciated Paul's kindness in fulfilling his promise to keep an eye on wife and child and was touched when Paul enclosed a letter allegedly dictated by Hazel, describing his small son's attempt to wade the Sorrel that had ended in a drenching. He had no means of knowing that it was Paul's regular visits to Mill Cottage that precipitated a second crisis at the Big House, or how near Claire came on his account to allowing the wound inflicted by his marriage to fester.

Claire had done her share of flirting. In the days before Paul came to Shallowford when she was belle of the Valley she had enjoyed the stir created by her arrival at a Hunt Ball or at one of the charity dances in the Paxtonbury Assembly Rooms and because he was proud of her good looks and fine figure, Edward Derwent had given her far more freedom than her competitors received. Then, after her humiliation at the Coronation soirée, she had taken it out on the Tunbridge Wells beaux but without a serious thought for any one of them. Since her return to the Valley, however, and certainly since her marriage, she had never given anyone the slightest encouragement to flirt with her although a good many tried, particularly after the establishment of the camp on the heath where the permanent staff included a dozen regular officers in their early thirties, including one or two accomplished mashers.

She would certainly not have involved herself with Aubrey Lane-Phelps, the twenty-five-year-old musketry instructor, had her relationship with Paul resumed its tranquil pre-war course after the Hazel Potter incident but Lane-Phelps was not a man to wait upon encouragement. He possessed, besides hard and rather flashy good looks, an easy way with men and women, a small but adequate private income and, above all, a colossal but carefully camouflaged vanity. He met and marked down the Squire's wife on his first visit to Shallowford House and the suspicion that, in due course, he would be drafted to France applied a spur to his determination to make one more conquest before he was sucked into the Flanders mincing-machine, where the life of a junior officer was estimated at six to eight weeks.

He had sampled Claire, so to speak, at a Christmas party given by Paul for the permanent staff and had kissed her, very expertly, under the mistletoe in the hall, accomplishing this when everyone else's attention was engaged elsewhere. It was getting on for eight years since Claire had been kissed by any man other than her husband and she decided that it was a wholly pleasurable experience, particularly the way Aubrey Lane-Phelps went about it. All the same she broke from him rather indignantly and went out of her way to avoid him for the remainder of the evening. For several days afterwards her thoughts returned to him at odd moments when she was pondering how she could capitulate to Paul without losing too much face or when she was

sitting in front of her mirror combing her long golden hair and wondering if, after all, she wasn't beginning to spread a little in certain
directions.

Then he took to riding over to the house on one of the dejected
screws they kept at the camp and usually appeared towards the end of
the short winter afternoon, when Paul was out on his rounds, seeking
the means of putting more acres under the plough or selecting timber
to meet the demands of the Government's Forestry Commission.

At first she was rather distant with him but then, under the accurately sustained bombardment of his lively conversation, she began to
thaw and at length made no secret of welcoming his company. The
day he bent low over her hand and told her that he was in love with
her she was far more flattered than outraged but after a moment of
confusion, decided to treat his declaration as a joke, returning his
heart with the sweet firmness of a broad-minded matron redirecting
an infatuated youth. She misjudged him hopelessly. His experience
was far wider than hers, so that he moved in smartly to pick up the
next trick, projecting himself as a young man marked down for death,
whose emotions had been cruelly mocked. Had she been less kind-
hearted, or better grounded in the business, she would have told him
to mend his manners and not come again until he could resist the
temptation to play the fool but it so happened that he caught her at
a special disadvantage. Claire, at this time, was going through a very
disturbing phase in her relationship with Paul. The quarrel concerning Ikey's marriage had died down but it had left a sensitive spot and
whereas Claire had emerged from her long sulk, Paul unwittingly kept
the issue alive by avoiding mention of Ikey or Hazel and keeping
Ikey's letters to himself, so that a sense of strain crept into their relationship, showing itself in artificial silences and a marked slowing
down of the physical rhythm of their marriage. It was not that he ever
rejected her or she him but something of the gaiety and excitement of
pre-war exchanges was missing and when they did make love it
seemed to her that he roused himself with an effort, as though performing a duty expected of him. She had no way of knowing that this
apathy on his part was due far more to his brooding preoccupation
with the war, and his own uncertainties regarding it, than to their
quarrel over Ikey's marriage but she had too much of her father's
pride and obstinacy to broach the subject. It was because of this, and
really for no other reason, that Lane-Phelps' interest in her as a
woman and not merely as a convenient hostess excited and flattered

her and when he threw in his reserves of pathos she faltered so that he was able to gauge her state of mind with considerable accuracy. He said, humbly, "I know I haven't the slightest right to expect love in return, Claire. In any case, apart from you being married, I'm due to go overseas any day and my chances of coming back to you are not more than fifty to one. I've said what I feel for you because I had to but I can bow myself out with dignity I hope."

It was a virtuoso performance, particularly as he knew well enough that there was not the slightest chance of him going to France until the new Kitchener armies were fully trained and that he meant to do his damnedest to land a staff appointment, for which he was fortunately placed. She said, miserably, "Don't say that, Aubrey! Let's hope to God it'll be over before any of you men up there are killed!" but as he turned away she caught his hand and the kiss that followed was somewhat more adventurous than that exchanged under the mistletoe, for in the course of the embrace his hands performed a light but very expert reconnaissance over two areas of his field of operations. Then, her Derwent commonsense catching up with her, she broke from him violently but experience told him that it was from motives of panic rather than repugnance and he decided not to press his luck but await a more opportune occasion. He picked up his hat, cane and gloves saying, "If I should be posted suddenly, as usually happens, you'll see me again?" and she said she would, although he was not to call when Paul was out and she promised nothing.

She was in a very confused mood for the next day or so, a curious but not altogether unpleasant compound of guilt, fear, recklessness and elation. Paul seemed not to notice as much, being excessively engaged just then persuading the Government commissioners that, whilst they were welcome to all the soft timber on the estate, the war could be won without sacrificing Shallowford timber that had been maturing over two centuries. Suspense, and guilt also, made her amorous and at ordinary times he could not have failed to notice this, for she came very close to parading herself before him in the intervals between the time he came stumping up to bed and the turning down of the bedside lamps but although he was talkative it was not of love that he spoke but of Valley men overseas and the maddening perversity of officials pestering him for timber and agricultural returns, so that she was thrown back on her own thoughts and they were thoughts that might have dismayed him. She began to reflect that they must have reached a stage in their marriage where a spur was needed to remind him that she was something more than an audience for his rumbling complaints.

It was after the signal failure of her most brazen attempt to stimulate him that she made up her mind to adventure one step further with Aubrey. In the early days of their marriage Paul had always taken pleasure in brushing her hair and when they retired about eleven o'clock one night she made sure there was a bright fire in the grate, undressed, put on a beribboned summer nightgown, loosened her hair and invited him to brush it. His response would have made her laugh at any other time. He took the brush, performed a dozen, absent-minded strokes and said, vaguely, "Won't you be cold in this? Shouldn't you wear something thicker?", so that she snatched the brush away and climbed sulkily into bed, thinking, "If Aubrey does call I'll receive him whether Paul is here or not! At least he'll pay me a few compliments instead of deluging me with estate problems and other people's troubles!"

He did call and with regularity, seeming to have accurate information on Paul's movements, for he never once appeared when she was not alone and able to be coaxed out of the orbit of the servants. They walked in the rose-garden and they sat in the little conservatory, talking gaily of this and that and sometimes skirmishing a little. By this time her feelings of guilt had almost disappeared and she flattered herself that she could handle him as surely as her sister Rose handled a young horse. There were half-a-dozen light kisses and one or two pats on the bottom, or make-believe accidental contacts between his hand and her breasts, but his progress was disappointingly slow until the afternoon when, in teeming rain, he came to tell her that he was expecting to join a draft in less than a week. They took tea in the conservatory where he kissed her rather more ardently than usual and she discovered, to her surprise and dismay, that his good looks, expertise and quietly aggressive masculinity roused her more than she wanted to be roused. It was only when his hand slipped from her shoulder, passing casually over her buttocks and then, swiftly and accurately, moved lightly between her thighs that she recollected herself and fended him off with genuine indignation. He said, sulkily, "You can't blame me wanting all of you, Claire, not in the circumstances!" a protest that fell short of his usual high standard in the give and take of mashing. She replied as she turned for the door, "It's a good deal more than you'll get, Aubrey, circumstances notwithstanding!" which at least showed him that she was learning. He followed her abjectly,

696

mumbling apologies and blaming her magnetism for his unforgivable lapse, and although she parted from him coldly she remembered all he had said when she sat musing before the library fire that evening, waiting for Paul to come home from an overlong session of the local agricultural war committee in Paxtonbury.

Paul telephoned about nine saying he would not be in until midnight so she went yawning to bed, still unable to make up her mind whether or not she should forgive Aubrey's insolence sufficiently to say good-bye to him before he left for France. She decided, on drifting off to sleep, that she would; any man going out into that deserved the benefit of the doubt.

She was not much surprised when, soon after breakfast the next morning, a lance-corporal arrived with a message couched in impeccably polite terms. It told her that Lieutenant Lane-Phelps was due to leave camp within forty-eight hours and would appreciate an opportunity to thank her for her hospitality since he had been in the district. He added that he would telephone if she would tell the lance-corporal "when she was likely to be on hand" and she did not miss this hint, telling the messenger Lieutenant Lane-Phelps might telephone mid-morning, a time when Paul was certain to be out. Sharp at eleven a.m. on the following day he 'phoned, first asking if she was alone. She said, hesitantly, that she was, astonished that the note of pleading in his voice brought colour to her cheeks.

"I'm due out of camp late tonight," he told her, "but I'm free all this afternoon. Will you ride out and meet me at the battery on the Bluff?"

She hadn't bargained for this; a sad, semi-platonic farewell in the security of her own drawing-room with delicately balanced cups of tea and Mrs. Handcock within earshot was one thing. A meeting in the wooded country on the western slope of the Bluff involved risks she was reluctant to take but then she reminded herself that he was manageable and could hardly get out of hand if they were both on horseback—so she said she would do her best to meet him between three and four o'clock, providing he promised "not to be silly".

She was beginning to suspect that she had no talent for the role of erring wife and blew hot and cold all the morning, changing her mind half-a-dozen times. When, at lunch, Paul said he intended taking the trap to Whinmouth that afternoon—"to have another go at knocking sense into those damned timber pirates"—she had difficulty in not exclaiming with relief, for somehow his absence from the Valley

697

converted an act of gross disloyalty into a kind of schoolgirl romp and she thought, as he gave her a casual kiss and marched off, "It isn't as if I was the least bit in love with the boy! I'm damned sorry for him — sorry for anyone going to France but even that isn't the real reason I'll go and say good-bye! I'm really going because all the sparkle has gone out of life since last summer and this is the only bit likely to come my way until it's all over!", and she went into the yard and saddled Snowdrop, telling Chivers that she was riding over to High Coombe to see her brother Hugh.

It was a dull, windless afternoon when she emerged on to open ground from the high-banked lane that ran down to the woods. There was rain about but it fell on the Valley as mist, filling the hollows and blurring the landscape on the far side of the river. She rode at a slow walk, as though, by dallying, she still had leisure to change her mind but when the belt of mist had crossed the stream to idle at the base of the Bluff she was conscious of mounting excitement and almost admitted to herself that it was the prospect of being grossly flattered by a good-looking young man that made her feel so reckless. When she reached the outskirts of the Dell Wood, that clothed the western shoulder of the Bluff, she had renewed qualms of being spotted by one or other of the Potter tribe whose farm lay less than two hundred yards beyond the first trees, so she made a wide circuit to within fifty yards of the river road intending to skirt the garden of Mill Cottage and use a track that ran across the steepest part of the Bluff before trailing off into a gorse-grown section of the cliff, overlooking the battery. From here, she thought, she could look down into the copse without being seen and perhaps, even then, change her mind and ride on to High Coombe, as advertised.

She had reached a point where the cottage came within twenty yards of the road when she pulled hard on the bridle, seeing a figure suddenly emerge from the river mist and turn in at the wicket gate of the cottage. He was on foot and because the stiff latch of the gate engaged his attention he did not look over his shoulder and see her reined in between the high banks. There was no mistaking the long stride and short-peaked cap. The man entering Mill Cottage was her husband, who should, by now, have been more than half-way to Whinmouth to confront his enemies the timber pirates.

Her first reaction was extreme astonishment at seeing him there and she only just checked herself calling out. Then, like the crackle of Chinese rip-raps, came other responses, all painful and most of them outrageous, for the sight of him turning casually into the gate of Mill Cottage, as though he visited there alone and on foot every day of the week, set off a chain reaction in Claire's already over-stimulated imagination, exhuming factors that her memory had recorded subconsciously over the last three months. There was his recent habit of walking rather than riding about the estate; his extreme reluctance to mention Ikey, or the trollop Ikey had married; his obstinate championship of the girl at the time of the wedding and his evasiveness to engage in any kind of truce-talk after the initial flare-up between them on the subject. All this, she reasoned, as her brain skipped from signpost to signpost, might or might not have significance but there was something else that presented itself as a particularly glaring piece of circumstantial evidence. There never had been a time since their marriage when he had failed to enjoy her as his bedfellow, not, that is, until recent weeks. In other spheres she had, at one time or another, had self-doubts but never in this respect for here was the thread they used to spin the pattern of their marriage, a mutual and deeply-rooted satisfaction in access to one another of the kind that Grace, as he had once told her, had proclaimed the true basis of marriage but had, for so many other reasons, been unable to achieve with him. Time and again over the last eight years she had exulted in her power to engage him at the level of an accomplished mistress rather than that of a workaday wife and while she had no yardstick but him to assess the vigour of men it had always seemed to her that his was exceptional. What pleased her even more was his boyish frankness regarding her power to stimulate him. She could look back on a girlhood and early womanhood when the topic of sexual adjustment between man and wife was taboo, not even discussed between mother and daughter. To her his approach had seemed not only healthy but immensely flattering. He had never used her without complimenting her, often in such wildly extravagant terms that she blushed in the secrecy of his embrace and as a lover he contrived to combine enormous gusto with a gentle reverence of her body. Sometimes she had not hesitated to exploit this when eager to win him over to her point of view yet, even here, he had knowingly submitted to exploitation, so that they had achieved a harmony she believed to be rare between two people. She was so conscious of this, and of her power to rouse him at will, that she often smiled at her own smugness but she had never ceased to value his need of her, hugging it to herself as the most precious acquisition of her life. It was because of this that the mere suspicion

699

that her ascendancy was threatened frightened her as never before. To see him walk through that cottage gate, across the little garden and in at the back door without even knocking made her almost sick with rage and the alarm bell that buzzed most persistently in her head was not that he was clearly a regular visitor here but that he was prepared to lie about his visits.

She sat the horse without moving for five minutes or more while Snowdrop munched the long grass growing out of the bank. She went over the evidence piece by piece, balancing one fact against another without troubling herself to seek alternative explanations. There could not, she decided, be any other explanation, for everybody in the Valley knew what the Potter girls had for sale. Their availability to any man with a shilling or two in his pocket was a byword for miles around and had been, ever since she had been a girl growing up a mile or so above the Dell. It followed that this girl, the half-witted Hazel, who was by far the prettiest was also, on account of her lack of wits, the most accessible for she would be unlikely to blab of her conquests. It was all, Claire decided, very much of a piece—his moodiness, his deliberate attempts to turn the conversation whenever Ikey's name was mentioned, his obstinate advocacy of the idiotic alliance, and, above all, his currently tepid approach to her own person, for surely only a man who spent himself frequently with a strumpet could fail to respond to her invitations during the last week or so when she had, as she now realised, been seeking reassurance from him.

It was the thought of Lane-Phelps, waiting for her at this very moment in the copse under the Bluff, that changed her dismay to humiliation. The base inequality of the sexes stuck in her throat like a plum-stone, for here she was, feeling guilty and troubled about a mere kiss or two, while her husband was paying regular visits to a harlot whom he had married off to his own ward! The reflection braced her to gather up Snowdrop's reins and half-wheel in the lane with the object of riding openly to her rendezvous with Aubrey and avenging herself on the spot but she did not proceed with this intention. Deep down, under the welter of indignation that boiled in her, was a pin-point of Derwent commonsense and it told her that there was a chance, just a chance, that she might be wrong, or half-wrong, or misled in some way, so that she knew she would have to make certain before committing herself finally and absolutely.

She judged that almost ten minutes must have passed since she saw him enter the back door and he was not, as she knew better than anyone, a man likely to make a ritual of the business. By this time, no doubt, they were already upstairs and in bed. The prospect of actually confronting them was dramatic, providing she could go through with it, which she doubted, but perhaps this would not be necessary. All she had to do was to creep into the house and listen and after that events could take their course. She swung herself out of the saddle, knotted the bridle round a young ash, and taking advantage of the overgrown bank moved down the lane to the gate which, most fortunately, he had left ajar.

The mist proved a valuable ally. It had been thickening minute by minute and now the hollow in which the cottage stood was half-filled with the seeping cloud drifting in from the south-west. Looking over her shoulder she could no longer see Snowdrop, so, moving with great caution, she approached the door and laid a hand on the latch. As she did this she glanced through the tiny rear window of the building, her eye attracted by the flicker of the fire within and here she stopped, hearing the murmur of Paul's voice rising and falling in a continuous rumble, as though he was reciting. He sounded so unlike a man passing a casual half-hour with a harlot that she hesitated and then, hardly knowing what she did, edged back from the porch, flattening herself against the cob wall and inching forward until she could look directly into the big room, with its window facing the river and its hearth on her immediate right. What she saw made her gasp. All three of them were there, Paul, Hazel and the child, the latter on his mother's lap with his fat little legs dangling like great, pink sausages as Hazel listened attentively to Paul reading aloud from a letter. Claire watched in amazement. It was like looking in upon an animated scrapbook illustration, the tall, broad-shouldered man, still wearing his cap, his shoulder resting lightly on the mantelshelf and holding the letter in his hand, the young woman sitting in an old basket chair, an expression of rapt attention on her face, the child, disinterested but relaxed in the grip of his mother's forearm, his legs clear of the floor. Claire could even hear a snatch or two of the letter . . . *"thought of you when I saw the wind catch the poplar leaves and throw a handful of silver into the air"* . . . *"hoping to come on leave"* . . . *"heard your brother Smut had been promoted corporal"* . . . odd, inconsequential snippets that nonetheless made everything perfectly clear, so clear indeed that she could have smiled had she felt less ashamed at being here at all. She had been right about one thing, however. He obviously did come here regularly but for the purpose of reading Ikey's letters that were obviously enclosed in his own and Claire suddenly remembered that Hazel Potter had never learned to read or write, despite all Mary Willoughby's efforts to teach her the alphabet.

The long trailers of mist seemed to bore their way into Claire's bones and she shivered so convulsively that she could remain still no longer and began to retreat along the wall towards the door, and into the weed-filled garden, moving backward step by step, as though from something terrifying. On reaching the open gate, she turned and ran through the mist to the spot where the grey was tethered; seconds later she was in the saddle and using her heels vigorously so that the horse broke into a trot and then a slow canter, swinging left into the sloping field at the head of the path and finally, still at a canter, down the broad sweep of meadow to where the Shallowford track ran down to the orchard.

It was not until Snowdrop had been stabled and Claire was sitting hunched over a smouldering library fire that she spared a thought for Aubrey Lane-Phelps, still waiting for her in the mist below the battery but it was no more than a fleeting thought. "Damn Lane-Phelps!" she said, aloud, "he can go to France, Egypt or Timbuctoo for all I care! I shall squirm every time I think of him and maybe weep as well but not for the reasons he thinks!" and she snatched up the poker and attacked the fire as though the smouldering logs had been responsible for bringing her within a hairsbreadth of reducing her well-ordered life to chaos.

V

He did not come in to tea and when she nerved herself to make an inquiry from Chivers she learned that he had returned home about three-thirty, collected the trap and gone to Whinmouth as scheduled. She knew then that he would not be home again until supper and deciding that she could not face him across the table went up to the bedroom, telling Mrs. Handcock that she had a headache and was retiring early. She did not attempt to undress but sat in her favourite chair over the coal fire, curtains drawn against the world.

She tried to read and failed and tried to think and failed. In the end she just sat and looked at the shifting coals, awaiting his step in the library below.

About nine Mrs. Handcock tapped on the door and said a Mr. Lane-Phelps was asking for her on that there telephone. Claire said, shortly, "Tell him I'm not available! Tell him that if he wants he can ring later, after Squire returns!" and her contemplation of Aubrey's reaction to this message was the one cheerful spot in an interminable evening. Soon after Mrs. Handcock had gone she heard Paul come in and after a brief pause the chink of china, as his cold supper was set before him; she thought, "Do I go down or do I wait for him to come to bed? If Mrs. Handcock has told him I've got a headache he'll creep about for fear of disturbing me. Well, I could hardly be less disturbed and am likely to remain so unless I tell him everything now, before I weaken! I daresay it's inviting disaster but I'm sick to death of watching us drift the way we've been drifting since Ikey came home! He'll surely fly into a fearful rage and assume I'm going the same way as Grace but I can't help it if he does for anything's better than this. We had a good marriage, a wonderful marriage, and if we can't mend it and put it back on the rails it won't be for want of trying on my part!" She decided to wait for him to come up and undressed, putting on a winter nightgown, for this was no time for ribbons. It was whilst rummaging in the cupboard for her nightgown that she saw some of Simon's discarded riding kit, jodhpurs and jacket that he had outgrown put aside for the next jumble sale. There was a riding switch, a short, brown cane that she picked up, recalling the story she had heard of the Bideford Goliath's use of a stick on the Potter girls every time they tried to make a fool of him. She thought: "I wouldn't blame him if he treated me like Cis and Vi Potter for I'm really no better for all my airs and graces!" and the reflection made her more depressed than ever, for all her life she had regarded the Potter girls with a contempt not far removed from disgust.

He did not keep her waiting long. Soon she heard him call good night to Mrs. Handcock, who usually drowsed by the kitchen fire until nearly midnight and then he came in, looking mildly surprised to find her sitting there and the lamps still burning.

"I haven't got a headache, Paul," she said at once, "but I came up early. I've got something important to say."

He did not seem particularly surprised by this unusual greeting but for a moment looked almost amused and then straightened his face, kissed her lightly on the forehead, and said, "Well, you do look a bit off colour. Anything unpleasant happened?"

She said, with a deliberation that surprised her, "Yes, Paul, a great

703

deal has happened and it *is* unpleasant but not nearly so bad as it might have been, or would still be if I made light of it!"

He sat down on the hard chair across the fireplace and shot out his long legs. He was still wearing his tall boots and breeches and he looked, she thought, a good deal more cheerful and relaxed than he had looked for some time.

"All right," he said, "if it's that important my news can wait," and she experienced a wild flutter of alarm and cried out, "You haven't enlisted!" at which he laughed louder than she had heard him laugh since before the war.

"No," he said, "I haven't enlisted, I doubt if they'd have me! It's just that I've saved our timber, at least for the time being."

"I'm glad," she said, slowly, "and I expect you are!" and then, as though restarting a race after a false start, "I've let you down rather badly, Paul! In two ways, different ways! I've been very unhappy about what's been happening to us lately and I suppose that's my only excuse, although it's a very poor one."

He still did not seem much concerned although his expression hardened a little. He said, "What the devil are you driving at? Come right out with it, it's easier that way and I'm damned sure it isn't half as bad as you think it is! *How* have you let me down?"

She said, flushing, "I've been having a very heavy flirtation with Aubrey Lane-Phelps, up at the camp. *Only* a flirtation on my honour, but . . . well, it might easily have led to something more serious if I hadn't suddenly come to my senses this afternoon!"

"Why especially this afternoon?" he asked, so mildly that she was thrown off balance again and began to stammer, her cheeks flushing as bright as the core of the fire.

"I . . . well . . . I followed you to Hazel Potter's—Hazel Palfrey's cottage! I saw you go in. I was coming down the lane on the grey."

"Yes, I know," he said, grinning, "I saw you and I wondered what you had in mind. Why didn't you call?"

For a moment she was speechless and then, her colour receding somewhat, "You . . . you *saw* me? You *knew* I was there while you were reading Ikey's letter to her?"

"Well no," he admitted, looking surprised in his turn, "I didn't know that. I had it in mind you rode off in a huff as soon as you saw me. As a matter of fact that's why I've never told you I always call there and read his letters. She wouldn't make much of them herself. What induced you to peep in and then creep away?"

She had to plunge now for what had seemed too certain this afternoon now seemed not only grotesquely ridiculous but downright insulting. She went on: "Sitting here this evening I made up my mind to admit everything and here it is! I was certain you were calling there for . . . well, for the reason most men call on the Potter girls!"

If she wanted to astonish him she had succeeded at last. His jaw dropped and his heavy brows shot up more than an inch. Then, mercifully for both of them, his unpredictable sense of humour came storming up and he let out a bellow that might have been heard in the stable-yard on the far side of the house. "Great God!" he said, once he had composed himself, "you thought *that*! But you dear silly idiot, how often have I got to tell you that Hazel hasn't a thing in common with her sisters? Ikey's wife? And him in the trenches? Why, Great Scott, even if I was so inclined she'd kill anybody who tried to make a fool of Ikey!" Then, quite suddenly, he became serious again and went on, "What the devil *is* the matter with you, Claire? It can't be just this nonsense with a cocky young masher like Lane-Phelps. I knew all about that, knew you were very flattered by his attentions anyway, but it didn't worry me or not seriously! I suppose I was irritated to watch him buzzing round like a wasp over a jam-jar but since everybody is a little crazy these days I didn't grudge you a bit of fun, so long as it remained fun!"

"It did, Paul," she said, urgently and he ripped out, showing his first flash of impatience, "Good God woman, I *know* it did! Do you imagine I wouldn't have known after all this time?"

Suddenly she felt both relieved and deflated, as though she was a child with long plaits confessing a fault to an indulgent parent, expecting a slap and getting nothing but amused tolerance. The transition from one extreme to the other was so painful that tears welled in her eyes and she made a helpless gesture with her hands. He must have realised how she felt for amusement and impatience left him at once and he said, quietly, "All *right*, Claire. I'll listen, if you really want to unburden yourself and I don't mean that cynically! What exactly did happen between you and that ass? He kissed you once or twice, I suppose?"

"Yes he did, half-a-dozen times."

He still looked indulgent, even when he said, "And let his hands stray a little, I wouldn't wonder? Well, I hope his private technique is better than his public display for his tactics went out with the crinoline! Dammit woman, chaps like him are ten a penny in every mess or were until we got caught up in a real war! I suppose he told you he was being drafted to France and hadn't long to live?"

"Yes," she admitted, "he did, only this morning and I . . . I . . . was on my way to say good-bye when I saw you! He's going overseas tomorrow."

"He's going tomorrow but not overseas," Paul told her, shortly. "When I saw him preening himself on his progress I asked the adjutant about him. He's going on a course to Aldershot, then straight back here and after that he'll land a staff appointment that'll keep him out of the firing line! He'll work it all right, the Lane-Phelps of this world generally do but what was it that made you 'come to your senses' as you say?"

"When I looked in the window and realised why you were there."

He pondered a moment. "And suppose I had been upstairs with the girl? Would that have resulted in Lane-Phelps getting another scalp?"

"Yes, I think it would."

"Well, I dare say you would have been justified, for I suppose it did seem to you I was lying about going to Whinmouth. I met the postman in the drive and thought I'd pop over and read her letter before I crossed the river. It's all rather silly, isn't it? I mean, not just this but the situation we've allowed to develop between us, and I daresay it's partly my fault; I couldn't have been easy to live with during the last few months."

She was by no means disposed to grant him his share of the blame. "That's rubbish!" she said, "you've been grossly overworked and because you identify yourself with the Valley you suffer for everybody in it! You always did but now it's a hundred times more strain and I should have tried to help instead of fooling around with a man like Lane-Phelps. Most men in the Valley would have given their wives a damned good hiding for far less!"

"Well," he said, cheerfully, "I haven't the slightest desire to knock you down and black your eyes but I'll turn you over and smack your handsome bottom if you insist!"

His facetiousness confused her, so much so that, in a perverse way, she felt cheated.

"I'm sorry, I can't laugh it off, Paul. The truth is I've never felt so small and mean and wretched in my life!"

"I'm sorry too," he said, more seriously, "but I find it difficult to go berserk over a show-off like Lane-Phelps!"

706

"But it isn't Lane-Phelps," she argued, "I see now that he was just a kind of game I was playing with myself. This afternoon was different. How could I have been so wrong and stupid? And suppose I hadn't waited and had ridden off to the Battery?"

"Well you didn't!" he said and she replied, biting her lip, "I came within an inch of doing so and that makes me unfit to share a bed with a man as honest as you!"

Her contrition, carried to these extravagant lengths, exasperated him. He said, impatiently, "Oh, for God's sake! Let's forget the whole bloody thing!" expecting her to shrug and climb resignedly into bed. In all their previous clashes she had remained open to reason and tact on his part, had even managed to half-heal the one serious rupture in their relationship. Tonight, however, it was as if she enjoyed wallowing in guilt and she stood staring at him with a curiously wooden expression that he had never seen on her face all the years he had known her. She said, at length, "I don't seem to be able to convince you do I?" and he snapped, "No, you don't! I think you're just being stupid and enlarging a peccadillo into a crisis!" but because she still regarded him with that odd, woebegone expression he suddenly relented and made one more attempt to laugh her out of it, saying, "Look here, if it will soothe your conscience at the expense of your rump wait while I slip down and fetch my riding-crop!" and he reached out, intending to gather her up and throw her on the bed. To his dismay she stepped back sharply and backed against the cupboard. "Whatever happens this is going to take me a very long time to live down," she said. "Your come-come-now-now approach isn't likely to help, Paul!" She turned then, flung open the cupboard and picked up the brown switch, thrusting it at him and throwing up her head with what struck him as a gesture of almost hysterical defiance. Then his astonishment was doused by laughter and he said, taking the cane, "Very pretty, but if I took you at your word I daresay I'd never hear the last of it!"

Her head came down again and now, as defiance ebbed, she looked spent and defeated. She said, very quietly, "It wasn't such an empty gesture, Paul. What you can't understand is that a woman who has behaved as I have would prefer a week with a sore backside to a lifetime with a sick conscience. Very well, leave it at that, but for God's sake don't stand there making excuses for me!"

It was only then, as she made a step towards the bed, that he realised she was in earnest, that she was in desperate need of some kind of penance and would have been grateful for a blow across the face the moment she had confessed to Lane-Phelps' fumblings and her suspicions regarding Hazel. He understood too that her emotions were essentially primitive, far more so than his, a newcomer to an area where the emotional relationship between man and wife had nothing to do with statutes and codes of behaviour written into books. He felt pity for her and compassion made him wiser yet without altogether banishing humour from such a grotesque situation. He said, thoughtfully, "Has anyone ever beaten you?"

"My mother, when I deserved it."

"Never your father?"

"He left that kind of thing to her. Perhaps it's a pity."

"It's not too late. Bend over that chair and stay there until I tell you to get up!"

Even then she had power to shock him. Without a word or a change of expression she did as he bid, hoisting her nightgown and bending low so that her hair brushed the carpet. She was trembling but it was not from fear and no longer for shame. The very humiliation of her posture brought a sense of release as though, by calling his bluff, she was already atoning in some degree for the self-abasement of the day. She might have felt differently about this had she seen his expression as he stood contemplating her defenceless buttocks. It held no trace of irritation or astonishment now. He was grinning, broadly, and as the cane dropped to the floor, she felt in place of its bite, a tremendous slap that would have precipitated her over the back of the chair had he not saved her by grabbing the folds of her nightgown and robe. Then, before she had half-recovered her balance, he had spun her round and was holding her in a grip that drove the breath from her body.

"Don't be such a damned fool!" he shouted through his laughter. "I'm no wife-beater and you're no Potter girl! Take those damned things off before I tear them off and then get into bed and turn out the light! I know a way to teach you who is boss around here!" and he kissed her, swung her off her feet and tossed her bodily on the bed.

It was his tone more than the gesture that sobered her, that and his abrupt stalk round the end of the bed and into the dressing-room where he kept his riding clothes.

She got up and stood in the centre of the room massaging her tingling behind and then, catching sight of her reflection in the tall mirror, was amazed to discover herself smiling. They were over it, through it, and had the rhythm of their lives by the tail again and she could have shouted her relief and thankfulness at the top of her voice. She heard him grunting as he tugged at his long boots and called, after a moment, "Do you want a hand with those?" and he shouted back, "No! Get into bed for God's sake woman!" and a few moments later he was beside her handling her as impatiently as she ever recalled.

Yet it was she, exhausted by the emotional demands of the day, who slept first while he lay awake awhile, going about his familiar business of sorting out and docketing his impressions, his thoughts returning to her accurate diagnosis of his ill-humour over the last few months – his personal identification with the turmoil that had reigned in the Valley since Franz had 'phoned that August night telling him that war was inevitable and would be anything but the field-day-jubilee that everyone expected. She was right of course; she knew him better than anyone, better even than John Rudd who had shared the adventure from the very beginning. He saw the Valley people as a family, as dear to him as Grace's boy Simon and the twins, and his daughters Mary and Whiz, all sound asleep in their quarters along the corridor. He shared the mounting desperation of wives like Elinor Codsall and the misery of mothers like Marian Eveleigh, at war not only with the Germans but with her own husband. He worried, with Old Honeyman, over the shrinking manpower of the farms and dreaded the impossible tasks that would face them all at harvest time. He brooded, with Rose Derwent, on the probable fate of her horses, bought up and driven away by Government scavengers to drag great hunks of metal along foreign roads. He had saved the old timber of the estate for the time being but how long would it be before they presented him with fresh ultimatums? And if the deadlock in France showed no signs of breaking how would it be possible, in two years or three, to reharness the Valley to his dreams? It was a depressing role, this witnessing of twelve years' thought and toil being swept away like bubbles of silt on a Sorrel freshet but tonight, for the first time in months, he felt comparatively optimistic and this was not on account of his victory over the timber pirates. His cheerful mood stemmed directly from the woman asleep in his arms, a wife of eight years' standing and the mother of four of his children but also, at this moment, a living symbol of the Valley, of its fruitfulness and beauty season by season. Her breasts were its contours and in her thighs lived its abundancy. "And not so damned fanciful either!" he thought, "for there were Derwents hereabouts when the first Tudor arrived and probably before that if they could be traced! I didn't get my hands on this land simply by paying the Lovell family a cheque but by taking her into partnership and giving her children in this house. All I've done since I got here is to play stud-horse and caretaker, and I daresay I'll go on doing just that as long as I live for it won't become Craddock land in the real sense until her children, and her children's children, take on where I leave off!" The conclusion and the glow of possession engendered by it, was a balm and warmed his belly like a glass of Burgundy. He pulled her closer, his lips brushing her hair and as he drifted off to sleep the knowledge that whole armies were locked in conflict across the Channel seemed a trivial thing compared to the eternity of red soil and the race who cared for it.

CHAPTER THREE

I

JOHN RUDD, Eveleigh, Sam Potter, indeed anyone who claimed to know Paul Craddock at all well would have argued that he was anything but an impulsive man. He had a reputation for slow, cud-chewing thought, and carefully weighed decisions, for assembling every scrap of available evidence and carrying it away to study in privacy before taking action on any matter involving the administration or development of the estate. And yet, viewed in retrospect, all of the important decisions of his life had been arrived at impulsively, almost recklessly—the purchase of thirteen hundred acres after a twenty-four hour survey; his marriage to Grace Lovell and later to Claire Derwent; his adoption of Ikey Palfrey and, finally, in the summer of 1915, his final conclusions on the war which led, more or less directly, to his personal participation in it.

Until then he had qualified as a guarded neutral, an object of distrust by the Kaiser-hating fire-eaters, men like Horace Handcock who saw in the conflict vindication of the prophecies of a decade. Almost alone among the menfolk of the Valley Paul was not visited by the virus of war-fever, devoting his energies exclusively to buttressing the Valley against the pressures exerted upon it from the hour Paxtonbury's newsagents' boys had run shrieking along the down platform proclaiming Armageddon and summoning the more impressionable to the Bosphorus and the Sweetwater Canal. On that momentous occasion Paul did not even get his feet wet. He looked upon the involvement of Britain in the Franco-German quarrel as a grave misjudgment on the part of the Government, whom he had always regarded as pacific and conciliatory. When it was clear that there could be no withdrawal and that, for good or evil, there would be a few months' carnage, he moderated his attitude, saying that he supposed they would all come to their senses sooner or later and he made no secret of the fact that he intended to continue minding his own business, taking full advantage of the Government's reawakening of interest in the land. Fortunately for him (for patriotism could be menacing) he was qualified to stand aside. He was thirty-five when the war began and still suffered from the leg wound gained in the last epidemic of patriotic hysteria. He also had considerable responsibilities, including a wife, a young family, a seat on the local Bench and suzerainty over six prosperous farms each expected to do its share in stocking the national larder. At that stage, indeed, at any foreseeable stage in the war, he could have been said to be serving national interests more usefully at home than overseas and he continued to tell himself this until the war was about a year old. Then, brick by brick, the protective barricade he had raised against the outside world began to crumble so that he was obliged to take stock of it and ponder how long it could sustain mounting pressures from all sides and how much longer he could justify his neutrality. For thirteen years now his life had been the Valley, the people who lived there, the crops they raised and the cattle they reared, and for him no other obligations existed. Under the tremendous stresses of a war however, with half the world already involved and every participant bent on total victory, the entire social structure of the Valley began to change at a velocity that made his head spin. The slatternly camp arose on the moor and raucous north-countrymen flocked in like so many Viking invaders. Machines proliferated and their stench poisoned the air of the countryside but, what was worse, his own men drifted away in twos and threes leaving every farm short of labour and at a time when official demands on the yield of the land were assuming fantastic proportions. In one way he welcomed those demands. They gave him plenty to do and justified his faith in the land and in the improvements he had made over the years. With the expert knowledge of John Rudd, and his own not inconsiderable experience to help him, he grappled with manpower and equipment problems, solving them all one way or another but hard work and improvisation could not rescue him from personal involvement in domestic problems, or, as time passed, from involvement in the tragedies of the Valley. It was here that his detachment foundered.

In the last ten years Paul Craddock had developed a knack found in the best type of regimental officer. He had a remarkable memory for the kind of personal trivia that convinced tenants and estate workers that their interests were his and this was neither a pose nor an oblique way of keeping the estate machinery oiled. He really did think of the Eveleighs and the Codsalls as his friends and the Derwents and Rudds not as relatives or deputies but as allies and he went far beyond that, reaching right down to the level of the two- or three-score hired men and maids employed on the farms and in the workshops of the Valley, craftsmen who were all, in some degree, dependent upon the estate. He knew everybody in the vale by Christian name. He knew whether they were married or single, how much they earned and how many children they supported. He knew the age of most of them and, in some cases, how long they had occupied their cottages and what kind of home-makers they were. Thus, when the men began to drift away and face death or disablement he was concerned for every one of them and for their families. Each brick knocked from his wall had a name upon it and when a sufficient number had been removed, or knocked askew, he was as deeply committed to the war as the least of them and they all knew it and looked to him to solve some of their immediate problems.

The first of these to confront him was the loss of Will Codsall's labour at Periwinkle, smallest of the Valley farms and as time went on, he and John Rudd formed a pool of part-time, migratory labour to fill this and other vacancies so that soon Valley farming became almost a communal venture. This system broke down, however, after a mere eight months and with far more land under the plough than in peacetime, adjustments had to be made in the way of concentrating stock and merging machinery and even borders. Some local trades withered altogether. Thatching was the first of them and Nick Salter and his boys went to work at High Coombe and Four Winds. The fishing industry at Coombe Bay died after the recall to the Navy of Tom Williams and two of his crewmen and the local building industry was soon at a standstill, for Ephraim Morgan lost Walt Pascoe and three other specialists and although, in a sense, the failure of subsidiary trades was no immediate concern of the estate, Paul felt it incumbent upon him to do all he could to keep them alive against the return of the volunteers. Apart from using all available manpower on the denuded farms he also reduced nearly a score of his cottage rents and provided cart-horse transport for the pupils of Mary Willoughby's little school. He maintained good relations with the camp and indulgent officers sometimes turned a blind eye to his temporary enlistment of a craftsman or agriculturist from among the swarm of recruits.

Then the casualties began to occur, the first of them, Roddy, John Rudd's boy, who had written home in September, "*We are looking for Von Spee: when we find him we shall go to the bottom!*" thus fulfilling John's prophecy regarding the emptiness of boasts regarding the

713

Navy's invincibility. After that came news of Walt Pascoe's death in Gallipoli but although Paul regretted Walt, whom he had liked, he did not waste much sympathy on his widow, one of the few local women who seemed to be enjoying the war. After that, in May, 1915, came news that Tom Williams and his nephew had been torpedoed and of the near-riot that occurred in the churchyard when Tom was seen to put flowers on the grave of the German seamen buried there. Then a letter came from the old German Professor, who wrote from America to say that his only son, whisked into the Kaiser's Army whilst on holiday, had been killed in Champagne. It was foolish, perhaps, to mourn the death of an enemy yet Paul did regret a boy whom he had always regarded as a charming, friendly lad with a splendid physique and courtly manners. He did not and could not see Gottfried Scholtzer as a ravisher of Belgian women and bayoneter of infants notwithstanding the report that the Germans had just used poison gas at Ypres. For all that reports of the use of poison gas as a weapon of war between civilised nations helped to set Paul thinking along new lines, for it began to seem to him that unless the war was won, and that within a reasonable period, civilisation would go to the devil and, what was more to the point, all prospects of the Valley resuming its pre-war rhythm would disappear for his lifetime. In this context he said to Rudd, "You can count me in from now, John! It might be the craziest thing that's ever been allowed to happen but it has happened and as I see it we've no choice but to win," and old John, sucking his pipe, had replied, "The longer it goes on the less chance there is of a negotiated peace. For my part I don't think it's possible; everybody's blood is up and it won't cool until all European males between eighteen and forty are dead, or home with a limb missing! There's another thing too. Win or lose don't deceive yourself into thinking it can ever be the same again, here or anywhere else! All the wrong people are getting killed and all the flag-flappers are making money. Thank God I've had most of my life. Chaps your age will have to adjust themselves to something very different when the bloody thing does run itself into the ground!" In a year or so there were many who subscribed to this theory but in the early summer of 1915 John Rudd's views were regarded as eccentric and even his wife Maureen derided them.

And so the barricade began to tumble but there was no major collapse of Paul's defences until the Will Codsall episode. Once again it was a Codsall who supplied an unpleasant jolt to the Valley.

Will came home on leave in April and everyone was shocked at his appearance. He had left the previous August a thick-set, bumbling, broad-shouldered man, with a mild, friendly and slightly bucolic approach to all. He returned a shambling scarecrow, with a vague, shifty expression behind his eyes and a jumpiness that made his callers nervous when he handled his rifle and shot rats in the yard. Few could forget that Will's father had died raving mad and to those who remembered Martin there seemed a disturbing resemblance between Will and the man who had taken to staring out to sea and had one day gone home to murder his wife. Will mooched about, answering questions of "What was it like?" vaguely and unsatisfactorily, beginning sentences and leaving them unfinished but everybody made allowances for the fact that he had gone through a bad time after being rushed into the line in October and seeing most of his Paxtonbury cronies blown to pieces. They cheered up when Will, fortified by a few pints of ale, worked himself up into a ferocious mood at The Raven and described in detail, and with seeming relish, how he had brained Germans with spades and shot them down at close range when they advanced in close formation outside Ypres. Then, on the night before he was due to return, Paul was summoned from his office to find a tense Elinor Codsall awaiting him in the hall and Elinor, who seldom wasted words, went straight to the point regarding her fears for Will's sanity.

" 'Er's goin' just like 'is old man!" she declared, "and I've 'ad a rare ole do with him, I c'n tell 'ee, Squire! Tiz no good carrying on about 'ow 'ee got 'isself into this ole pickle be joinin' they Territorials backalong. The fact is he'll do someone a mischief if us don't tell they Army people there's alwus bin daftness in the Codsall family! He's talking about staying on yer and hiding hisself, same as Smut Potter did time he crowned Gilroy's keeper! Says he's done his bit 'an won't taake no more part in it and if I hadn't got un half-slewed with cider he'd ha' been gone by now an' us would have had the police over yer to march un off to prison!"

Paul accompanied her back to Periwinkle where he found a half-stupefied Will in the kitchen. Will had drained a gallon jar of home-brewed cider but he was not uplifted by it. Although he could hardly stand he was sour and intractable, declaring with idiotic persistence that he had no intention of returning to the colours but would "lie up somewheres 'till tiz all over!" Paul tried to reason with him but in the end he had to fetch Doctor Maureen, who suggested getting Will's leave extended. She made out a certificate to the effect that he was suffering from chest trouble and got it countersigned by the camp doctor, who was under an obligation to her for helping him free of charge during an epidemic during the winter. The Army doctor then examined Will and contacted his base at Paxtonbury with the result that Will was put to bed and remained there for a fortnight, after which he was, so the camp doctor assured them, regraded for duty at the base and was unlikely to be sent back to France for some months. The night before Will left home for the second time he called on Paul and at first seemed almost himself again but Paul was disturbed by his declaration, made on leaving, that he had seen his father on the battlefield. Under careful questioning he admitted that it was only Martin's ghost he had seen and Paul put this down to some form of hallucination brought on by shock and exhaustion and was relieved to learn that Will could now anticipate a few weeks' rest at base. Neither he, nor Will, nor the camp doctor were aware at that time of the tenuousness of the Ypres defences, after the counter-attack that had followed the German use of gas. Will reported to base on Saturday night; thirty-six hours later he was back at Le Havre and a month later the second of the dreaded buff telegrams arrived in the Valley. Will Codsall, the first man in the Valley to go to war, had been killed in action.

The Valley mourned him as a hero and Elinor mourned him as a grotesque sacrifice to local big-mouths like Horace Handcock, the Valley's unofficial recruiting agent; they were all wrong, for Will was neither Hero nor Sacrifice. He had been executed as an Example!

The trial occupied far less time than the Whinmouth inquest on Will's father and mother all those years ago. A row of granite-faced senior officers heard another officer and several witnesses describe how, during a local attack ten days previously, one of a party of bombers who captured a section of German trench threw aside his rifle, ran back across no-man's-land, scrambled into and out of the British trench and went on running until he was arrested by a couple of Red Caps well beyond the supports. On the way he felled two men who tried to stop him and one was now a casualty with a broken jaw.

The sentence was death. It could hardly be anything else for a man who had thrown away his arms in action, and Will, asked if he had any comment, uttered four short words. To his judges they amounted to a confession for he said, in a low voice, "They was right there!" The President of the Court, who had won a V.C. on the North-West

716

Frontier, winced at hearing such a craven admission, particularly as there had been no Germans in the trench when Will fled except, of course, any number of dead ones. How was Will to explain that it was the dead who had caused him to fly; not the German dead but two dead civilians, sitting side by side on the firestep of the captured trench and both shouting at him which was very odd for Martin, his father, had a rope round his neck and Arabella, his mother, was headless.

It is doubtful whether Will understood his sentence or the plea of mitigation made by his defending officer. He felt more secure inside the buttery, which did service as a condemned cell, than he had felt for a long time. The door was barred and there was a sentry outside so that neither Martin nor Arabella could approach him. When they marched him out, blindfolded him and stood him against the wall he may have thought they were playing some kind of game for in the few moments before the volley he discovered that he could see through the bandage and was not much surprised to see Elinor climb the broken farmhouse wall, swinging a pail full of eggs and calling in her shrill voice to laggard hens. It was early but the sun was warm and beat on his face and neck and he wondered, although not urgently, what she could be doing there in a foreign farmyard, and how she came to look so slim and young, not the least as she had looked when he parted from her a month or so ago, with a tense, pinched face and a thickening figure but as she had looked when he used to slip across to Deepdene to do his courting. Then the sun must have burst for pieces of it exploded all around him and he knew he was in the line again and under bombardment and called to Elinor to look what she was about for shells could kill civilians as well as soldiers.

The provost, biting hard his stringy moustache, looked down at the body and said, under his breath, "Poor sod! Any road you're out of it, chum!" and then barked at the firing-party who filed away, one of them reeling like a drunkard.

That same day in the House of Commons the Foreign Secretary was asked how many executions for cowardice there had been in France during the last ten months. He replied that, according to his information, none at all. His information must have been out-of-date. There had been four that month in Will's division alone and there were many divisions within a hundred miles of the place where Will was shot. Perhaps it was to keep the record straight that they sent a telegram saying Private Codsall had been killed in action.

717

A month or so later the Valley learned that Jem Pollock was dead but this time the telegram was followed by a letter giving circumstantial detail. The letter, written by Jem's company commander, was addressed to "next-of-kin" but as nobody in the Valley knew Jem's next-of-kin it found its way to Paul.

It told a graphic story. Apparently Jem had been attached to the Engineers for the purpose of tunnelling under the German line near Cuinchy, where the two systems of front-line trenches sometimes came within forty yards of one another. Rumours of his enormous strength had reached R.E.s responsible for the shaft and for more than a month Jem shovelled away in safety while, overhead, men were killed at the rate of about one every five minutes, for the Germans had gauged the mortar range to the nearest yard. Then it was discovered that the Germans were tunnelling directly opposite. When Jem laid aside his spade he could distinctly hear the chink of tools and sometimes a man coughing. The officer came along and listened with him and then left to telephone H.Q. for instructions but while he was gone the sounds from the German tunnel ceased and the sergeant left in charge ordered work to recommence. It was an unwise decision, for the German shaft must have progressed far beyond the British and they exploded their mine soon after dawn, a day before the British were scheduled to explode theirs and Jem, just going on shift, was about twenty yards down the tunnel when it went up. All the men in front of him were buried alive but the entrance of the British tunnel had been riveted with steel rails and held for a matter of about fifty seconds, before slowly subsiding like a gently squashed matchbox. It would not have remained open that long had not Jem instinctively reached up and braced himself against a key crossbar, an act that enabled the five men behind him to run back into the trench and crouch under the crumbling firestep. One of them reported what had happened and Jem's name was sent in for the Military Medal which he did not get because none of the witnesses had been officers. He was, however, toasted that night by the survivors, who thought of his death as almost biblical so that, in a sense, the Goliath of Bideford was transposed into Samson of Cuinchy, who died supporting the pillars of a crumbling temple. The men who drank to him that night knew little or nothing of Jem's past so that they could not be expected to appreciate the roundness of Jem's end. All his life he had both paraded and used his strength for the benefit of others. In the jobs he held before joining the travelling fair his

718

muscles had been at the disposal of North Devon craftsmen and in the fair ground he had drawn crowds and more than paid his way. Later, when he forsook the gypsy life and settled in the Dell, his strength had been at the disposal of the Potter girls and he had spent it freely, in the fields by day and in their beds by night, so that the Dell was rescued not only from weeds but from the threat of dwindling population. Then, when he went to France, he used his strength unsparingly on behalf of the Pioneers and there was still enough left over to save the lives of five of his comrades.

Paul, musing over the officer's letter, hoped Jem would get the medal and rode over to the Dell to pass the story on to Cissie and Violet whom he found pregnant and rather depressed. As Violet put it, "He were a gurt handful was Jem, and us'll never see the like of him again, Squire!" He took the letter away with him and it was pasted into the back of the estate diary by Claire. She must, Paul thought as he watched her, have travelled a long road since the day she had railed against Ikey's marriage to a Potter, for when he told her that Violet had borne Jem a strapping boy, now aged six, she said, "I'll fix the letter by the corners so that when he's old enough I'll be able to take it out and give it to him."

He was touched by the thought and kissed her neck as she busied herself pasting the letter into the record. "Claire Derwent," he said (for he could rarely think of her by any other name), "that flare-up we had over Ikey and Lane-Phelps did us a power of good! It cleared the air, like a heavy thunderstorm. I love you, woman, more than I ever did!"

"Prove it," she said without turning aside from her task but he laughed and said, "Not me, I've got to ride over to Hermitage. There's a problem blowing up over there, a very tiresome one!"

"Oh?" she said, "and what's that?"

"I'll tell you about it in bed tonight," he said and when she replied, laughing, that knowing him and seeing that spring was in the air she doubted this very much it struck him that since the crisis they had become lovers again and that she could cheer him up with a glance. He rode off reflecting, "I'll soon settle this nonsense of Henry Pitts! He must be older than me and Hermitage can't manage without him! Damn it, if it comes to the worst, I'll write to the Agricultural Committee and get him starred for the duration!"

Paul's attempts to nail Henry Pitts to his farm for the duration proved unavailing. By early September, when everyone in the Valley was working sixteen hours a day getting in the harvest, Henry was plodding up and down a dusty parade ground near Oswestry, with a dummy rifle over his shoulder. By the time the British Army in the field had made good its losses at Loos he was in France.

Henry's urge to enlist was the outcome of his mid-morning visits to his piggeries, on the north-east corner of his holding. From here, high up on the shoulder of Hermitage Wood, he could look directly down into the basin of the camp parade ground where columns marched and wheeled all day and the hoarse shouts of N.C.O.s reached him like the distant wail of gulls. Henry was fascinated by the patterned precision of their movements, which seemed to be animated by clockwork. He liked best to see a company respond to the command, "At the halt, by the left, form close company of pla-*toon*!" and see the long, snaking column waver, break up, unfold like a spreading fan, reform and come to a tidy halt in front of the saluting base. As a child he had always liked playing with lead soldiers, forming them into assault columns and giving the closest attention to their dressing but here, before his eyes, was a game of soldiers come to life and played on a huge scale. The crispness and precision of their movements was a kind of poetry to him and he revelled in it, day after day, week after week, until it seemed to him that he could never be happy until he identified himself with those khaki-clad automatons, responding smoothly and ecstatically to the bark of their drill-masters. The precise beauty of drill banished all other aspects of soldiering from his simple mind. He did not ponder the possibility of wounds, or death, or discomfort in the trenches, or even prolonged separation from his land and his great tawny wife and plump, tawny children. All he could think of was the synchronisation of arms and legs *en masse* and at last he knew that, no matter what it might cost him, he must absorb himself in it at once.

He expected opposition from his wife, Gloria, and from his father, Arthur, but although there was an awed hush when he announced his intention to join up no one attempted to dissuade him except Squire Craddock, who was furious. His wife Gloria, the red-haired grenadier of a woman who had forsaken the Heronslea estate to marry him, openly applauded his decision. After Horace Handcock, Gloria Pitts was the most indefatigable patriot in the Valley and thought of any male out of uniform, if he was neither child nor dotard, as a poltroon. Gloria was the first woman in the Valley to engage in the popular pastime of distributing white feathers to civilians and actually slashed one of Martha Pitts' best down cushions for ammunition. She said, delightedly, "Youm reely *goin'* Henry? Youm actually takin' a *smack* at that bliddy Kaiser? When then, good luck to 'ee boy! And when you comes back on leaf in kharki I'll show 'ee off all round the neighbourhood, you zee if I don't!"

Martha's reactions were more restrained. She pointed out that Henry was thirty-six and that they would probably keep him at home, guarding bridges and viaducts, but old Grandpa Pitts, who could recall watching redcoats embark at Plymouth for the Crimea, chose to regard this as an insult on the family and said that Henry would almost certainly return with a Victoria Cross pinned to his breast and a personal letter of thanks from Lord Roberts. They had told him several times that Bobs was dead but he chose not to believe it. Without both Bobs and Kitchener he could not believe in the inevitability of victory.

Paul argued that food-growing was just as important as killing Germans and that Henry, as a professional farmer, would almost certainly be rejected by the authorities. Henry countered by saying that his eldest boy was already big enough to take his place and Gloria, outraged by the Squire's attempt to snatch the halo of patriotism from the Hermitage, said she would never hold up her head if theirs was the only farm in the Valley that failed to contribute a man to the forces of the Crown. Seeing how determined they all were Paul withdrew his opposition and because of his personal regard for Henry did not write the threatened letter to the local committee with the result that Henry, fearing rejection in Paxtonbury, travelled to Bristol and enlisted in the Gloucestershire Regiment. Within a matter of hours, he was being taught the simplest of those great sweeping movements he had witnessed from his vantage point beside the piggeries.

His only grouse during his training period was that it was a long time before they issued him with a real rifle and until they did, until he could smack his huge, horny hand against a real gunstock, it seemed to him that he was only playing at soldiers. In due course, however, he got his arms and equipment and came home on embarkation leave about Christmas-time, when the Valley was under a light mantle of snow and everything looked lifeless and forlorn. Everything, that is, except his wife, Gloria, who shrieked with excitement when he marched into the yard, the living justification for an entire handful of white feathers for now she could say, as she distributed them, "Get on an' join, boy! My Henry's rising forty and he's out there, so what be doin' in corduroys?" Her delight in him was such that, had Henry been given more than a short leave it is doubtful whether he would have had the stamina to hump his fifty-six-pound pack into Paxtonbury on the morning of departure. Their relationship up to then had been cordial but humdrum, for man and wife habitually worked a thirteen-hour day and Gloria, with three children, had more than once declared that she had no intention of cluttering herself with more. Now, however, she had the immense privilege of actually sharing a bed with a real live soldier, a man trained and eager to slaughter Huns and she was determined to do her part by sending him off to war fortified against a period of celibacy. She had never heard of the Roman custom of introducing harlots into gladiators' quarters on the night before the Games in order to give them memories worth fighting for but it was in precisely this spirit that she refused to let Henry rise at the customary hour of six-thirty and perform his usual duties about the farm. She clasped him to her capacious bosom and enfolded him with her great, muscled limbs, so that it was sometimes past nine o'clock when they came down to breakfast and Henry began to wonder if life in the trenches could demand more of a man. He went off on Boxing Day with something like relief but all the way to Paxtonbury he chuckled reminiscently over his experiences of the last few days. "Gordamme," he said to himself, shifting the weight of his pack as he braced himself for the stiff climb to the crest of Blackberry Moor, "I never knowed 'er had it in 'er, for 'er was always inclined to ration a man after our first tacker showed up!" Then, as he swung into the rhythm of a step that was brisk and satisfying after the countryman's peace-time plod, he began to whistle, "Plum and Apple" and "Do Like a Nice Mince Pie", alien songs to a Valley man and learned during his training period. Probably no man ever went to war in better heart.

III

Pansy Pascoe, widowed nine months ago, expected Dandy Timberlake to pay a courtesy call when he was invalided home from Egypt that Christmas, but was surprised to see him climbing the steep, stony track to the Dell within an hour of his return to the Valley.

Pansy was as good-natured and affectionate as any other Potter but, like her sisters Cissie and Violet, she had always found difficulty in throwing down roots strong enough to bind her to any one male and although she was saddened by Walt's death she did not mourn him long. As the months passed she was able to bracket him in her mind with all the other men of the Valley, including Dandy and his brothers, and was therefore delighted to see the tall, stooping figure amble into the yard and pause, regarding the scene with distaste, for it was washing-day and the Potter farmyard looked more like a nomadic encampment than ever, an untidy crisscross of lines supporting innumerable flapping garments and an air of jerky, unplanned industry pervading the outbuildings and washtubs.

Pansy abandoned her tub and ran to greet him, a big, beaming, blowzy woman, radiating a vitality that, for a moment, affronted a man who had spent six months in a hospital cot. She said: "Why, Dandy, youm fair blown be the climb! Come inside an' us'll brew some tay!" but Dandy refused the invitation with a gesture, saying he preferred to sit in the open where they could talk privately, and then, glancing round the Dell once again, realised that he had forgotten the fecundity of the Potters and exclaimed, "Tiz like a bliddy fairground yer! How many tackers be there for God's sake?"

"Oh, I dunno," she said carelessly, "getting on fer a dozen I suppose but dornee mind 'em boy, nor the soldiers neither! I'll get my li'l Liz to carry on with the wash," and raising her voice she bellowed to her eldest daughter, a dark girl of about eleven, telling her to attend to the tub while mother took a breather.

The girl detached herself from a swarm of children round the waist-high nettles and Dandy, watching them, said tolerantly, "How many o' that lot be yours, midear?"

She told him four and pointed them out, a boy favouring his father, two girls favouring her, and a toddler with straw-coloured hair who was staggering up and down with a huge marmalade cat that seemed not to mind being hooked under its belly and dragged about with its paws clear of the ground. It was the toddler who interested Dandy and he scrutinised the child carefully, noting his slightly buck teeth and narrow head topping a thick neck and solid little body. "That little 'un," he said, thoughtfully, "what's un called, Panse?"

She knew, or thought she knew, why he asked and her generous

723

mouth split in a grin. "Albert," she said, "but I alwus thinks of 'un as 'Dandy'! What's eatin' 'ee? Be 'ee thinkin' I was comin' down on 'ee for a maintenance order?" and when he was silent she pressed him, adding, "Well? Do 'ee own to the boy? Do 'ee mind the night I come by him, you ole rascal?"

Her sophistry shocked him and he blushed under his tan. "Did Walt ever guess?"

"Giddon no!" she said impatiently, "for Albert were only a tot when you went off and bevore that, down at that cottage, us was treading on one another, so I don't reckon he ever got a close look at him! You baint *worryin'* about it, be you? Not after all this time?"

Dandy cleared his throat. It was embarrassing to confess to worrying over such a triviality to a Potter girl but he went on, desperately, "Yes I be! I got to thinkin' on it many a time when Walt and me was out there together and that's why I made up my mind to speak, zoon as I set foot in the Valley! Fact is, me and the Army have parted company, Panse, and I'll be back at me old trade soon as I'm fit to do a day's work. There's no help for that anyways, for Pa and Ma are moving out come New Year, on account o' Pa's arthritis and theym goin' to live in one o' they new jerry-builts, at Nun's Bay. With them gone, and the other boys away, Sawmill Cottage'll be empty and if I quit Squire will have to move a new sawyer in seein' house-room's mighty short about here." He paused and cleared his throat again, irritated by the bewilderment on her broad, freckled face. "Fact is," he went on, with a rush, "I got to thinkin' maybe you'd turn your back o' this knacker's yard and live decent again! There's room enough for all of us at Sawpits. The boys and the maids can share the two back bedrooms and we'll have the front! What do 'ee say, Panse? Dornee reckon Walt would sooner you took up with me than one o' these bliddy forriners? And baint there a good enough reason for it, seein' us've already made a start with a family of our own?"

She had been amazed and then amused by his stumbling earnestness when he began, astounded by his apparent willingness to accept responsibility for four children when only one of them was his but then, as he ploughed on, she was touched very deeply, not so much by his troubled conscience but by his eagerness to salvage something out of their past. It was as though he was offering her not marriage exactly, and certainly not what passed for respectability in the Valley, but something much more than that and of infinitely greater value, for here was a fruity slice of her half-forgotten youth being restored to her

724

by someone who had once contributed to its gaiety. Then she reminded herself of the more practical issues, a father for the children and regular money coming in from his work and part disability pension but these things did not seem important. What impressed her was the tremendous compliment he was paying her and for the first time since she was a twelve-year-old, smarting under one of Old Tamer's casual clouts, her eyes filled with tears and she was so disconcerted by them that for several moments she was incapable of speech.

He waited, having the kindness to avoid looking at her and presently, collecting herself, she gave expression to the warmth she felt for him by reaching out and letting her plump hand slide from his shoulder to his knee. It was the gesture that had won her Walt Pascoe all those years ago, when they stood together watching Coronation fireworks, and it must have communicated itself just as surely to Dandy for he suddenly grabbed her and kissed her so enthusiastically that she was transported back to the time when she was a neat-waisted girl of seventeen skylarking in the hayfields. She said, with a slight quaver, "You . . . you baint makin' game o' me, Dandy? You baint, be you?" and he denied hotly that he was, declaring that he would prove as much by making arrangements with the rector this very day but that in the meantime she was to restore Walt's wedding ring to her finger—"So as none o' they bliddy forriners get to trespassing zoon as me back's turned!"

He left her then and she watched, with compassion, his halting progress down the track before running to give Cissie and Violet the news. She was not much given to vanity but she could not help feeling elated by the thought that, whereas the three of them had shared many men, she alone had received not one proposal but two. It seemed to her, thirty-three and with four children, confirmation that she was the flower of the flock.

The big hearth at Sawpits Cottage had no time to cool. The older Timberlakes moved out on New Year's Day and Dandy and his bride, trailing their ready-made family, moved in that same afternoon so that for the first time in close on twenty years the whine of the Home Farm saw was challenged by the tumult of children. Pansy, reconciled by the solid comfort of the place to the loss of her regained independence, was in high spirits, having drunk a pint of her mother's hedgerow wine at the impromptu wedding breakfast in the Dell but Dandy, exhausted by the excitements of the day, admitted frankly that he felt unequal to the statutory exertions of a bridegroom. "Well," she said,

725

genially, "we'm neither of us chickens be us and there baint no particular hurry, seein' youm back for good midear! Why dornee go up along an' rest while I put the tackers to baid and make supper? I'll call 'ee when I'm ready and tidden as if you dorn know what youm gettin' be it?" He took her advice and climbed the stairs, thinking wryly on the days when he had bounded up them three at a time and was soon so heavily asleep that when she called there was no response so she went up to find him, sprawled fully-clothed on the bed in his new blue serge suit, its crumpled flower still pinned in the buttonhole. She thought, smiling, "He's aged, the poor toad! They must serve 'em cruel in that bliddy war! I'll let un bide and tak' supper alone!" and then she giggled, reflecting on the unlikeliness of her wedding night, with four of her children under the same roof and the groom sound asleep and still dressed in his Sunday suit. She went out quietly and ate her supper in front of the fire, thinking not only of Dandy, whose snores she could hear through the oak floor, but also of Walt and Smut, and Henry Pitts and poor old Will Codsall and young Gilbert Eveleigh, and all the other Valley boys dead or scattered or just tired out like Dandy upstairs and for the first time, not excluding the moment when the buff telegram had been delivered to her, she thought of the disruption of their lives as something sad and disturbing.

IV

Nun's Bay village was a small island of freehold land sandwiched between the coastal borders of the Heronslea and Shallowford estates, a tiny community that had been no more than a hamlet up to the time old Farmer Blair had died childless, a year or so before the war. The Blairs had freeholded here for generations but when the last of them died the farm went up for sale. Local landowners had made a bid for it but it eluded both Gilroy and Paul, passing into the hands of a local firm that practised under the enigmatic title of *The Whinmouth Development Company (Bricks and Tiles) Ltd.* whose boards had been mushrooming in the district ever since Coronation year. The chairman of this shadowy company was supposed to be old Widgery, of Whinmouth, but nobody believed this for Widgery was in his eighties and his neighbours thought it unlikely that he would launch out into land development after a lifetime as a dairyman. Whinmouth folk said that Widgery, who owned a few houses in the Whinmouth harbour area, was the front for a group of men that included two or three Urban

726

District Councillors who did not want their association with local building publicised but although these pundits were groping in the right direction they were wide of the mark. The secretary, and major shareholder in the Whinmouth Development Company, was a young man who was too knowing to waste time and money fighting local elections or concerning himself with other people's drains and water supply.

Sydney Codsall, as a qualified solicitor, had left Whinmouth two years before the war and was now junior partner in an older firm of country solicitors, with offices in Cathedral Yard, Paxtonbury. Sydney had enlarged himself a great deal since the days when he had courted Rachel Eveleigh in the hope of getting a slice of freehold land for a wedding present. At twenty-one he had come into the money left by his father and mother. Ordinarily he would have only inherited half but in the event every penny of it came his way, partly because of Will's careless nature but more on account of Elinor's independent spirit. Having abominated Arabella when she was living she had no wish to profit by her death. Sydney had an eye for a bargain and used the money wisely, chiefly in the purchase of odd parcels of land. His years at a solicitor's desk had taught him, among other things, that the only really permanent form of wealth was land, and after land, bricks and mortar, preferably unmellowed bricks and mortar. Having ready access to advance information, and also the cash to tempt impatient beneficiaries, he soon acquired an oddly assorted patchwork of strips and corners in and around Whinmouth and formed a loose kind of partnership with a local builder called Tapscott, whom he tamed by taking out mortgages when the builder's going was rough during spells of bad weather. By the spring of 1914 he was in a fair way of business and having temporarily exhausted the Whinmouth vein, where Tapscott had a bad reputation, the partners ranged further along the coast in search of promising sites. At Coombe Bay they were blocked by the Shallowford estate, whereas inland most of the property was in Gilroy's hands but the death of old Blair, who owned over a hundred acres at the mouth of Nun's Bay goyle, proved a god-send, for Blair's heir was farming in South Africa and wanted a quick sale. The farm was purchased and building began almost at once.

The war, however, caught Sydney off balance and after the completion of a mere half-dozen of the twenty-four bungalows planned, the scheme looked like petering out and might have done if Sydney had not taken out insurance by cultivating the Paxtonbury Borough

727

Surveyor who put him in touch with the Government department responsible for siting training camps in the west. The temporary camp on the moor had never been very satisfactory. It was badly exposed, south-westerly gales made havoc of the tents and its water supply was poor, so that Sydney was able to lease his Nun's Bay site for the duration and secure Tapscott a meaty contract for erecting a permanent hutted camp on farmland overlooking the sea. There were several rewarding by-products to this development, the most important being the securing of Sydney's enrolment as a permanent member of the Camp Siting Commission, and its offshoot, a committee concerned with the acquisition of local timber for Government needs. Sydney could scent an Act of Parliament as a fox scents the taint of man. He reasoned that, if the Army was so short of manpower as to rush a clodhopper like his brother Will into the front line, it would not be long before the supply of patriots was exhausted and Lord Kitchener began prodding the hesitant. Friends told him that England would never stand for conscription but he did not believe them and was soon proved right. Within weeks of his attachment to the camp-siting and timber commissions the newspapers announced the Derby Act, under which all single men below the age limit were ordered to attest pending enrolment in the forces and Sydney hastened to take out further insurance by getting himself a wife. He also bought the services of a co-operative doctor, who addressed himself to the task of discovering minor ailments afflicting Sydney's person, ailments that had been quiescent since childhood.

By this time Sydney had come to terms with the war. The establishment of Nun's Bay camp enabled him to exploit his somewhat panicky marriage to the only daughter of a Paxtonbury provision merchant and he persuaded his father-in-law to adventure into the field of confectionery and toys on premises adjoining the camp, where five thousand potential customers were wired in and ten miles from the nearest competitor. The village shop prospered under the personal supervision of Sydney's wife Dora, who was not as winsome as some girls Sydney had contemplated marrying during his apprenticeship days but had the advantage of a good head for business and a father with a cellar full of sugar bought at pre-war rates.

So much progress in such a short time would have turned the heads of some young men and would have mellowed others. Sydney not only kept his head but remained loyal to his original dream, a resolve to establish a new balance of power in the area surrounding the

728

twin valleys of Teazel and Sorrel. He could have told you most things about his ambitions as a whole but would have found it difficult to describe this secret driving force, which was really no more than a resolve to arrive at level pegs with Paul Craddock, of Shallowford House. He could not have said why he resented the man, or why everything he did in the way of increasing his substance was an attempt to wriggle beyond reach of Squire Craddock's patronage. It might have had something to do with Paul's championship of his brother Will's marriage to an ignorant farm girl, or the fact that Paul had been the first to look upon his butchered mother the night of the double tragedy, or something much more complex, a deeply buried resentment linking Paul in some way with all that had occurred at Four Winds that night, or a combination of all these factors that had made him a pensioner in the home of his father's foreman, Eveleigh, to suffer years of drenching pity from the uncouth children of Eveleigh and his wife. He had never explored his motives in depth, preferring to lump them together under the general title of *Getting On*, or *Getting Ahead*, or *Being Someone*! And now, as the war entered its second year, he was someone, as was evident when he paid a call on the Squire in his capacity as a Government forestry official and was sufficiently sure of himself to attempt reversing their roles.

Paul had already had one brush with the Commission when they had tried to make him include hard timber in the existing contract to supply pine-lengths for pitprops, so that it came as a mild surprise to him when he opened a letter bearing the official note-heading, informing him that a Mr. Sydney Codsall would be calling on him by appointment on behalf of the department. Paul had always felt rather sorry for Sydney, whose spirit, he felt, must have been scarred by his terrible experience in 1904, when he had so narrowly escaped sharing his mother's fate. He had seen him often enough while he was growing up in the Eveleigh household but had lost track of him until their encounter on the land adjoining the Coombe Bay brickfield but Paul had almost forgotten that by now and decided that it was rather fortunate that the new local agent was under some kind of obligation to him, and not a foreigner eager to despoil the countryside of trees that had been growing before the German Kaiser's grandfather had pulled on his first jackboot. He was slightly amused by Sydney's pomposity when the young man was shown into the office but remembered that young Codsall had always been a pompous boy, utterly unlike his amiable brother, Will. He shook hands, offered Sydney a whisky and remarked jocularly that he had put on weight and seemed to be having a tolerable war. Sydney was disconcerted by this breezy reception and a little irritated by Paul's inclination to treat him as though he was wearing his first pair of long trousers. He said, in the slightly lisping accent he had cultivated since taking his articles, "Time rettles on, Mr. Craddock! Perhaps you have forgotten that I'm older than you were when you bought Shallowford from the Lovells!"

He hoped that this would put Squire in his place but all it did was to make Paul chuckle. "By God, you're right, Sydney!" he exclaimed and then, looking at him carefully, "You seem to have made good use of the time. Is this Government job full-time or a voluntary effort?"

Sydney considered this question so naïve that he disdained to answer. He said, removing his rimless glasses with a deliberate air, "I think I can put you in the way of doing yourself a bit of good, Craddock."

Paul did not miss Sydney's self-conscious dropping of the word "Mr.". He said, sharply, "How do you mean, 'good'? In respect of what?"

"Timbah," Sydney said, smirking openly now, "Timbah and Pocket!"

Paul suddenly decided that he not only disliked but distrusted Sydney Codsall, that he had always disliked and distrusted him, from the day he had paid his first call at Four Winds and seen the boy standing beside his insufferable mother. His first instinct was to pull him up short, re-establishing the relationship that had existed between them since Ikey brought him back to the big house but his curiosity was aroused by the young man's fatuity. He said, "Why don't you say exactly what you have in mind?"

Sydney must have been completely deceived for he at once became conspiratorial. "You're selling your pitprops well below par," he said. "I could get you another fifty shillings a load! Providing, of course, we came to an arrangement."

"You mean other local suppliers are getting more?"

"There's no standard price, the Government have to have pitprops by the million so long as trench fighting lasts and a smart supplier can get what he asks, providing he stands firm and . . . er . . . providing he has contacts our side of the fence! It's the same with everything isn't it and after all, the Government don't have to make another profit do they?"

730

"No," Paul said slowly, "I suppose not but this . . . er . . . 'arrangement' you mention; do I assume it would be between you and I?"

"Naturally," Sydney said, not surprised by the Squire's ingenuousness, "I should be satisfied with twenty-five per cent of the increase. It would be worth that much to you, wouldn't it?"

Something in Paul's expression must have warned him, for suddenly he faltered and made a play of replacing his glasses. Paul stood up, looking directly down at him, and finding it very difficult indeed to check an impulse to knock him backwards over the chair. The desire to do just this sprang not so much from the amateurishness of Sydney's technique as from the recollection of Will Codsall's tormented eyes shortly before he returned to the Front to be killed and with this recollection came others, equally unpleasant, as though, instead of looking down on Sydney Codsall's neatly-parted hair he was staring into a pool where scum gathered in poisonous-looking bubbles which were bursting softly in his face. All kind of bubbles — the brutishness of the Coombe Bay mob howling under the Professor's window, the stricken look on Marian Eveleigh's face when he had called to console her on the death of her boy Gilbert and the satisfied smirk, not unlike Sydney's, on the face of Lieutenant Lane-Phelps who had done his best to seduce Claire. He said, breathing heavily, "There's only one thing that stops me telephoning Paxtonbury Town Hall and reporting every word of this conversation, Sydney! Do you know what that is?" but Sydney, flushing now, jumped up so quickly that he smashed his glass, making a gobbling sound as Paul went on, "The thing that holds me back is that everybody associates you with poor old Will and Elinor, so for Christ's sake get out before I kick you out and don't ever come back, not on any pretext whatever!" and he passed behind Sydney, flinging open the terrace door and glancing towards the porch where a sallow man sat waiting in a trap outside the main door. His movement gave Sydney a moment to recover a little of his bluster. He said, shrilly, "Look here, you can't play the God Almighty Squire with me any longer! Things have changed and they'll change a lot more before it's over! I could have been a good friend . . ." but Paul made a vicious sweep with his hand and Sydney dodged round him and leaped on to the terrace as Paul shouted, "If that's your trap get into it! I can't think why you didn't arrive on a snake!" and then, as the last of his self-control left him, "Get out, blast you! Get out before I kick your arse all the way back to Paxtonbury!" and at this Sydney ran along the terrace, shouted

731

something to the driver and scrambled on to the box. A moment later the vehicle had passed behind the screen of chestnuts, leaving Paul standing with fists clenched and head thrust forward and that was how Claire found him when she came on to the terrace saying, "I heard shouting! Who was it, Paul?"

He swung round aggressively, almost as though he expected to find Sydney had eluded him and returned to the attack and she saw at once that he was in one of his rare, white-hot tempers. "Who *was* it, Paul? Who were those men?"

"I don't know who one of them was," he growled, "but the one I was talking to was a bloody sewer rat, the kind that seem to be proliferating about here!" and he stalked past her into the room, pouring himself a whisky and tossing it back in a gulp.

She followed him not asking other questions but not leaving the room for she sensed he would need her in a moment or two. When the spirit had steadied him somewhat he told her what had happened, cursing the social infection that was poisoning the Valley and declaring that the only place for an honest man now was alongside chaps like Henry Pitts and Smut Potter. She heard him out. She was growing accustomed to these outbursts, although they were seldom so violent and usually tailed off into a rumbling monologue that had as its theme the avalanche of change that had swept over the Valley in a little over a year.

"There are more Henrys and Smuts than there are Sydneys," she reminded him. "It's important not to lose one's perspective."

"You're about the only one who hasn't, Claire," he said but smiled grudgingly, adding, "I was a damned fool to myself anyway! I don't want his filthy bribe but if I'd handled him more tactfully he might have saved our timber! Now he'll go out of his way to hit back any way he can."

"I doubt it," said Claire, "he'll be far too scared you'll inform on him."

"Not him! There weren't any witnesses. He'd deny it and say I was slandering him out of pique!"

"Oh, I wouldn't be too sure of that," she said lightly. "*I* was a witness, wasn't I? And in a cause like that I'd swear to it in Court if necessary! So would Horace Handcock because his patriotic principles would be outraged. One way and another we could sew Sydney into a sack and drop him into the river!"

Suddenly and irrationally he felt immensely grateful for her, for her

732

balance and strength and her great granary of commonsense that made his own impulsive protests sound like the bleat of a child. He crossed to her where she stood by the terrace door, pulled her towards him and kissed her on the mouth.

"Damn it, I don't believe you'd have the slightest compunction in perjuring yourself if the Valley was involved! I believe you would do it without a blush if you had to!"

"Certainly I would," she told him cheerfully, "and I should do it a great deal more convincingly than you! That's why I'm glad the children favour you more than me for there isn't an unblushing liar among them! Well, have you got Sydney's taste out of your mouth or shall I pour you another small one before lunch?"

"Go away," he told her, good-humouredly, "and attend to your business so that I can attend to mine! Whenever that perfume wafts about the room in the morning I get a dozen different answers to the same column of figures!" and he speeded her on her way with a slap on the bottom.

Her perfume remained, however, and it was not Sydney who hindered his concentration, so that presently he threw aside his work and began to browse through the pages of the estate diary, noting recent entries written in her neat, rounded hand. It was only then that he realised that he had not made an entry since the note recording the declaration of war but she had, more than four pages of them and he marvelled at her detachment for nobody could have guessed from the factual statements on subjects as commonplace as repairs to the tithe barn after a gale, that their lives had been mercilessly disrupted. Then he noticed, starred with an asterisk, an entry reading "*For enlistments, casualties, etc. see last page*", and turned to the end of the book where, in fact, there were two pages devoted to war-time entries, one headed "*Shallowford Estate Enlistments*", the other "*Casualties, Decorations, etc.*". It surprised him very much that she had kept such a meticulous record, one that included the antecedents, regiment and even dates of departure of recruits. He read the long list of names under the Enlistment column, then turned to the shorter list on the page opposite. Roddy Rudd's name led it with the information *Falkland Islands, November 1914* alongside and below were the names of Walt Pascoe, Jem Pollock, Will Codsall and Gilbert Eveleigh and he thought grimly, "And I wonder how many more names will be there before it's over?", resisting a strong impulse to score the page through and reflecting that, despite an occasional flippant note in some of the

733

day-to-day entries, Claire took the job of local Recording Angel very seriously.

Contemplation of the book led him to ponder the future of the Valley as a whole and the ultimate effect the war would have upon it. Right up to the last minute on August 4th, 1914, everything had been reasonably predictable but what could anyone be certain of now, save shrinking manpower, shortages of things one once took for granted, and the brooding fear of news that another familiar face had been blotted out? His own detachment, maintained into the New Year, now failed him altogether and he was fully committed, if only because the Valley itself was committed, but involvement had not yet convinced him of the justness of the war or enlisted him among the patriots who seemed able to regard it as a latter day crusade. And he was beginning to sense that he was not alone in his reservations, that the Horace Handcocks and the Gloria Pitts of the Valley were already outnumbered by the doubters. Will Codsall's terrible apathy had sobered some of the men in the bar of The Raven and the news that, notwithstanding his shattered nervous system, he had been thrown back into the whirlpool to vanish for good had shocked women whose sons and husbands were in training camps up and down the country. Only a few months ago people still hoped it would end any day with a glorious victory in the style of Waterloo or Agincourt, orchestrated by high-sounding sentiments of the kind written by the poet Brooke that had found their way into the *County Press* in 1914. Now the temperature had dropped, not alarmingly but noticeably, so that the odd cynic raised his voice, questioning the infallibility of news bulletins and even the qualifications of generals like the pot-bellied Joffre, who had once been everybody's favourite uncle. Perhaps, after all, the smell of Sydney Codsall's hair-oil had not been entirely vanquished by Claire's whiff of Parma violets, for suddenly Paul felt restless and uprooted and, despite access to Claire's granary of commonsense, lonely and desolate.

CHAPTER FOUR

I

WINTER in the Valley had been mild but generally wet, cheerless and without much promise. There had been no heavy snowfalls but ever since November the sun had been hiding behind seeping skies and by January the flurries of hail that came in horizontally, like a shower of assegais, had given way to a steady downpour that beat the dead bracken flat and changed the meandering Sorrel into a brown, froth-flecked torrent twenty yards wide carrying floating islands of drift-wood imprisoned in briars that snagged in the shallows, causing floodwater to lap half-a-mile across the flat fields of the west bank. The woods, were thinned, strewn with the victims of the autumn gales blocking the rides or leaning drunkenly against hardpressed neighbours and the river road below Hermitage Farm, robbed by Lord Kitchener of Henry Pitts' watchful eye, soon became pitted with pot-holes and obstructed by bank-slides. As winter groped its way towards spring the landscape withered under ceaseless rain and its inhabitants withdrew into themselves, almost forgetting to keep Christmas and New Year. The only really cheerful face to be met with in the Valley that season was that of Horace Handcock, for he alone, it seemed, held the secret of the year's promise in his heart and was willing enough to share it with anyone with patience to listen.

For Horace this was the year of decision; the year when Kitchener's trained hosts, instead of being fed piecemeal into the line, would charge forward *en masse*, an irresistible force that would scatter the cowardly German hordes like stubble wisps and surge over the Rhine to Potsdam, carrying ropes for the Kaiser, Little Willie and the Junkers who had planned to enslave the world but had forgotten that the British Lion had strong teeth. They would be dealt with, Horace assured everyone, as the Lion had dealt with everyone in the past who made the fatal error of twisting the tail of the passive but indomitable islanders and disposed of, once and for all, as had Napoleon, the Mahdi, and Kruger but with a slight difference. This time there would be no honourable banishment for the defeated but an eighty-foot gallows for the leaders and years of hard labour for the misled. Neither

735

were Horace's hopes pinned entirely upon the British field army. Poised to issue from Scapa and Rosyth were the ironclads that would steam down the east coast, corner the craven German Navy in or around the Heligoland Bight and blow it out of the water so that never again would the Hohenzollerns, or anyone else, presume to seek parity with the supranational dispenser of justice which was how Horace regarded the British Grand Fleet.

There were men of the Valley, however, who did not share Horace's optimism in the early spring of 1916, men who would have liked very much to look forward to a midsummer victory-march down the Unter den Linden to the music of "The British Grenadiers" but who were prevented, by evidence that they found difficult to discount, from believing in the likelihood of gaps being torn in the German line for the exploitation of Haig's cavalry.

Several of these dismal Jimmies lived within rifle range of Horace's cowardly grey hordes whom they sometimes met face to face in trench raids or on patrol in no-man's-land and who saw no shame in flattening themselves in deep slush when they heard the oncoming shriek of a five-nine, or watched the deceivingly slow roll of the dreaded Minnenwerfer coming out of the sky like a great wounded bird. Henry Pitts could be numbered among the doubters for in one way active service had disappointed him. He had arrived in France shortly after the lost Battle of Loos but so far no one had ever asked him to perform any of the evolutions he had perfected on the home drill-grounds during the previous summer. Instead they shuttled him to and fro along the greasy pavé, humping a Christmas tree of equipment that taxed even his patience and stamina when they left the road and entered narrow communication trenches where, every few yards, there was a shell-hole, a hangman's noose of barbed wire, telephone cables, a cave-in or a stretcher-party battling along from the opposite direction. He remained cheerful because, in place of precise, heel-clicking drill movements, they offered him comradeship. He had always preferred the company of men and here was good company in abundance, its society and steadfastness releasing the full force of his jovial, tolerant disposition, so that like Smut Potter and Jem Pollock before him, he soon became a great favourite in his company and could be relied upon to squeeze laughter from the most melancholy incidents, like the upsetting of the rum ration jar or a mortar explosion that smeared the section's breakfast rashers against the parapet. He had never had an eye for natural beauty so that the hideous disfigurement of the landscape did not distress him in the least and there was another aspect of active service that commended itself to him. When in the line nobody nagged him about his personal appearance, which was almost worth the sacrifice of home and family, for first Martha, his mother, and then Gloria, his wife, had never ceased to berate him for failing to care for his clothes or scrape the stubble from his chin. Over here, as long as he was out of range of the martinets, he could go days without removing mud that adhered to him and as to shaving regularly he often grew a tramp's stubble half-an-inch long. There was, in fact, a freedom that a man could not fail to appreciate after years of nagging at the Hermitage. For all this, however, he had no great hopes of seeing Germany's defeat by midsummer for what had impressed him most out here had been the apparent permanence of the war, with its miles and miles of deep ditches, its unending forests of wire, its deep, roomy dugouts (especially in captured sections of the German line) and the multiplicity of expensive-looking mechanical transport that swarmed everywhere between support lines and rest billets. To Henry's simple mind it seemed ridiculous to suppose that so much effort, and so much money, should have been poured into an enterprise due to end in a month or so. Frugal use of stock and plant had been practised by generations of Pitts at Hermitage, where a five-barred gate was expected to do service for twenty-five years, and sometimes the evidence of waste that he witnessed in France depressed him. He could not help thinking how useful some of these things would prove if he could have transported them to the farm.

A dozen or so sectors north of Henry's was another Valley man who would have challenged Horace had he heard him prophesying victory by June. This was Smut Potter, whose estimate of the duration of the war was based upon the strength of German counter-attacks during the Loos fighting last September. Smut had never shone at arithmetic. One of his drawbacks throughout life had been his inability to count beyond ten. At Mary Willoughby's little school he had used his fingers for counting but a fog descended on his brain when he had used up all his fingers and thumbs and was obliged to start again. Yet numbers impressed him and he made a point of counting the German dead when the company occupied one of the enemy's trenches. Until Loos this had been an easy thing to accomplish, for he was engaged in nothing but local sorties where the dead and prisoners seldom exceeded a dozen, but in the big push that autumn Smut's counting system broke down the first day, for he was in the second wave to cross no-man's-land and jump into a deep trench previously held by the Brandenburgers and here he found acres of Germans killed in the preliminary bombardment. It had seemed to him then, that the German Army must have been eliminated, that only a few dazed survivors would be left to scramble out of range of the British guns but he very soon discovered that this was not so for, by midday, he and his friends were counter-attacked, bundled out of the captured trench and were soon back at starting-point, where they were pinned down by fresh hordes appearing as from nowhere.

The seesaw went on for four days. Every time a few yards of rubble was won it was carpeted with German dead but the enemy soon reappeared with any number of fresh men until the offensive ground to a halt and the survivors of Smut's company were withdrawn for rest and refit.

During a spell in billets behind the line he pondered his experiences so deeply that he missed several chances of relieving his quartermaster's worries in respect of various shortages. At last, finding no answer to the mystery, he turned for enlightenment to his particular chum, a Stepney coster, called Harry. " 'Arry boy," he said, "where do 'ee reckon they all come from?" and Harryboy, whose familiarity for humanity *en masse* was the natural product of an East End upbringing, replied, unhelpfully, "All them mucking Fritzes? Blimey, doncher know? They collects all the dead uns after every show an' puts 'em through a bloody great mincer in the Kaiser's palace! Then they cart all the sausage meat to a bloody great bakery where they bake it, an' out they come good as noo ready fer the next show!" Smut, of course, did not accept this as a satisfactory explanation of the inexhaustibility of the Kaiser's manpower but secretly he felt that the real explanation came as close to necromancy.

Young Harold Eveleigh, seventeen-year-old brother of Gilbert, who had profited by Gilbert's false start and enlisted in a town a hundred miles from the Valley, would have taken issue with Horace on yet another count—that of the popular belief that all Germans were cowards, who ran away once they were bombed out of their deep shelters and called upon to "face cold steel". Harold had been in France since early September, despite his mother's frantic efforts to trace him and haul him out of the Army as she had once succeeded in doing as regards Gilbert. Harold looked at least twenty, having in-

738

herited his father's height and had joined up for devilment but whilst he was still in training, and serving under a false name, he learned that his elder brother had been killed in a bombing accident at a neighbouring camp. He and Gilbert, as the two elder boys in a long family of girls, had been very close and Harold had to take it out on somebody, so he managed to wangle his way into a draft on the point of leaving for France and soon became as enthusiastic a slayer of Germans as Smut Potter, although he never approached the latter's efficiency. There was already a belief among veterans that a newcomer was at his best during his first few weeks in the line and that thereafter he deteriorated as a fighting machine. Harold Eveleigh's recklessness during the Loos push justified this theory. He arrived in France only a fortnight before the battle opened and when his shattered unit was withdrawn he had accounted for at least five Germans and probably one or two more. He came through unwounded, one of four in his platoon, and the experience taught him, among other things, that war correspondents who described the Germans as a nation of cowards were either deliberate liars or very badly informed for he witnessed acts of heroism on the part of enemy personnel that would have surprised him had they been performed by some of the élite British regiments, like the Coldstreamers, or the Royal Welch. He saw three Germans killed in quick succession trying to rescue a wounded comrade from the wire and the next day came across a dead machine-gunner, lying beside his weapon with seventeen wounds in his body and a deep trench down which he could have withdrawn within yards of his emplacement. He saw German stretcher-parties walk through a box barrage carrying British wounded and he studied the impassive faces of some of the dead Saxons who had refused to surrender a surrounded sap when their nearest reinforcements were pinned down by an incessant rain of shells. After Loos, Harold was in and out of the line for another six months and was sent back with a slight wound, in February 1916. During this period he learned many basic facts about the war but perhaps the most important of them was that a man's courage under fire did not depend upon his nationality but upon such factors as how much sleep he had had in the last seventy-two hours, what kind of training he had received, how much rum had been available before an attack and even on the arrival or non-arrival of his mail. It also depended, just as the veterans argued, upon how long a man had been out and what kind of sectors he had served in, so that when, to his amazement, he was included in a group of survivors and

739

sent home to train for a commission he would have admitted to anyone, Hórace Handcock included, that the respite he had gained represented the difference between Harold Eveleigh the Hero, and Harold Eveleigh the Coward.

It is doubtful whether Ikey Palfrey, still serving with the artillery in or around the Cuinchy brickstacks, would have bothered to argue with Horace Handcock upon the subject of how long the war would last but if, for some reason, he had been drawn into a discussion at The Raven his rebuttal of Horace's prophecies might have led to him being branded as a defeatist. After nearly eighteen months at the front, broken by a single spell of leave in June, 1915, Ikey had formed certain theories about modern warfare and they were not of the kind likely to win preferment for a professional. He had artillery-spotted for several small-scale offensives and two major pushes, including the Loos débâcle and had come to the conclusion that at least two drastic changes would have to be made on the Western Front before the Allies could advance as far as Roulers and Lille, much less Cologne and Berlin. In the first place all British ex-cavalry generals bent over maps at H.Q. would have to be put out of harm's way, preferably by a bullet through the head, although, in this case, shots would have to be fired point-blank for it was a well-known fact that all cavalry generals had bullet-proof skulls. This having been done, and a new General Staff having been recruited from men who had ceased to think of war in terms of Balaclava, some new tactical method would have to be devised as a means of penetrating the German trench system and covering the advance of infantrymen across open ground traversed by enemy machine-guns. Ikey had watched, through powerful binoculars, the advance of successive waves at Loos and for four days had seen the clusters climb out of their assembly points, plod a few yards over churned-up ground and wither away before they had travelled half the distance to their first objective. They looked, he thought, like a swarm of clockwork dolls moving across a brown tablecloth and when, during the first two days, attack after attack failed, he was at first surprised, then furiously angry and finally filled with hatred for men who ordered their advance without regard for the vulnerability of flesh and bone to bullets and shrapnel. Then, as his duties required him to keep the surging attacks and counter-attacks under constant observation, he was able to eliminate the human element altogether and study the battle in a tactical sense, reasoning that before

740

the fortified ground on either side could be taken and held something far more imaginative than a preliminary bombardment was needed to fortify the attacker during the initial stage of a breakthrough. His mind began to toy with smokescreens, low-level aerial machine-gunning and even bullet-proof vests but he rejected all three as too clumsy, too revolutionary and too ineffectual. Then, on the third day, he had the germ of an idea and it excited him; what was surely needed out here, what would have to be found before substantial progress could be made, was some kind of war chariot mounted with quick-firing guns, something impervious to all but a direct hit from a mortar or long-range shell, a machine, moreover, that could crush wire and circumnavigate all but the smallest shell-holes, a moving fort behind which the hardy infantry could advance without being scythed down by traversing machine-guns and rifle fire. That night, back in his dug-out, he took pencil and paper and began to sketch but he was less than half-satisfied with the drawing he produced, thinking that it resembled a memory copy of one of the sketches of military engines made by Leonardo da Vinci that he remembered seeing in a magazine in the mess at Quetta. He persisted, however and at last evolved something that seemed to him to be at least partially practical, a kind of squat armoured car, with broad, steel-plated wheels looking a little like an armadillo. He was so absorbed that he got behind with his real work and it was not until the candle burned low that he put the sketch-pad in his valise, marked his maps and finally rolled on to his wire-netting bed to sleep. Outside the guns went on grumbling, not violently but persistently, somewhere to the south and before he slept Ikey thought the distant cannonade sounded exactly like autumn thunder in the Sorrel Valley.

There was a woman, formerly of the Valley, abroad that same night not forty miles from the sector where Ikey sat sketching war-chariots and although she had always prided herself on being a realist, she would have done her utmost to extract a crumb of comfort from Horace Handcock's optimistic prophecies. Having come to regard the war as the most hideous tragedy that had ever beset the world she would have welcomed any terms, including unconditional surrender, that brought the suffering she witnessed each night to an abrupt end.

As an ambulance driver shunting regularly between casualty-clearing station and hospital, Grace Lovell was more familiar with the extremes of pain and human desolation than even a front-line infantry-

741

man. A fighting man was primarily concerned with his own plight, and either stuck it out, like a terrified mole, or was caught up in a struggle for survival demanding a quality of exclusive concentration. Grace Lovell did most of her work outside the range of all but the howitzers and therefore found it very difficult to isolate herself from the load of misery in her vehicle and devote her entire attention to the task of driving over shell-pocked roads with quarter-power headlamps.

She had been in France for close on a year now, having volunteered for ambulance driving after a brief, unhappy spell in a London hospital when the 1914 amnesty freed all imprisoned suffragettes. She emerged from Holloway half-way through her sixth sentence and her experiences during the previous decade had not been such as to encourage her to embrace a patriotic crusade. Ever since 1904 she had been hounded, hunted, manhandled, forcibly fed, and hectored by men and to the hard core of the Movement, some of whom, like Grace, were reduced to skin and bone by hunger-strikes and nervous strain, the war was regarded as a fitting punishment for a world of men who had been callous, sadistic and mulish in responding to a demand for basic human rights.

This savage mood endured through the autumn and into the spring of 1915, while she was recuperating at a holiday home in Scotland run by a wealthy sympathiser but she began to relent a little as the casualties of the first winter's fighting appeared on public platforms at meetings loosely associated with women's suffrage, men who, for the most part, were no longer men at all but patched-up parodies of men lacking arms, legs or even half a face. As news of the death or mutilation of some of her personal friends reached her, the shift of sympathies kept pace with her improvement in health and although she still regarded the war as the climax of years of blundering inefficiency on the part of the male cabals of Europe, she could find it in her heart to feel desperately sorry for the millions of young men urged to lay down their lives at the toot of a bugle and the flutter of a Union Jack. Veterans of the movement, women like Annie Kenney and Christobel Pankhurst, assured her that this was the opportunity for which they had been working since 1904 and that after the war every woman in Britain would have the franchise. She did not know whether she believed them but after a spell as a V.A.D. in a London hospital it did not seem to matter much for the keen edge of her fanaticism was blunted by a factor removed from the purely physical suffering she witnessed in the wards. This was a creeping doubt as to whether

742

women in authority were any more reasonable, or even as efficient as men. She had the bad luck to come within the orbit of a fat-rumped martinet whose only qualification for her position as Commandant was newly-acquired wealth and Grace soon had good reason to despise this type of woman as wholeheartedly as she despised Cabinet Ministers. The titled Commandant administered the hospital like an eighteenth-century school, treating her volunteer nurses much as the more ignorant of the wardresses had treated prisoners in Holloway. Grace came to suspect that, again like some of the wardresses, the Commandant was not only a bully and a snob but also a Lesbian for she made favourites of all the doll-faced little nurses from aristocratic houses and was hostile to any member of her staff who had been a suffragette. After two or three months of back-breaking toil and humiliation Grace knew that she would have to choose between resigning or changing her hospital, and since almost every reception-centre for the wounded was in charge of middle-aged women enjoying the exercise of despotism she managed, by pulling various strings, to transfer to the transport section of the Department and was sent to France in time to evacuate some of the casualties of the battle of Neuve Chapelle, in April.

It was here, driving between clearing-station and base, that her re-orientation really began, for during her ten years in and out of gaol she had forgotten that men also possess the capacity to suffer. Back in the hospital wards at home, freshly washed, rid of their filthy uniforms and with their wounds covered by clean bandages, wounded men could be regarded with a certain amount of detachment but out here, where they were lifted into ambulances much as they had quitted the battlefield, compassion came near to prostrating her until she was able to convince herself that every stretcher case needed instant, practical help far more than tears. By the time the Loos fighting began she had become an extremely efficient driver and assistant orderly so that she was put on a regular run through devastated territory wrecked during the previous autumn's fighting.

Although the oldest woman in her section she withstood the demands of active service better than most. Her experiences had bred in her an iron self-discipline and once she was rested, and had recovered from successive hunger-strikes, she put on weight and regained her taut, resilient physique. She had need of strength. In addition to the strain of night-driving over bad roads, where every jolt produced screams of agony, and the sickening morning routine of scrubbing out the ambulance, her seniority made her a target for all the younger women seeking a confidante. There were those whose health proved unequal to the demands of the work but who wanted most desperately to acquit themselves well, and there were those who had rushed starry-eyed into the Service at the beginning of the war and were now driven to distraction by nagging superiors. There were others, perhaps the most pitiable, whose greatest fear was to succumb to fear, and there was, of course, a steady stream of pregnancies among girls from good-class homes in city suburbs, girls whose staggering ignorance of the basic facts of hygiene caused Grace to rage against the social taboos of the last few generations.

Some of the girls who came to her for help and advice were only half aware of how they had become pregnant and there were even more hopeless examples of girls who had been virgins when they stepped ashore at Le Havre and had contracted venereal disease in a matter of weeks. Grace did what she could, exploiting her many personal contacts at home, delivering impromptu lectures on sexual hygiene and contraception, using her campaigning and even her prison experiences to alleviate distress wherever possible, but sometimes it seemed to her she was distributing a handful of oats in a meadow full of donkeys. Whenever possible she conserved her nervous energies, making few close friends and spending her meagre spare time sitting alone in the sun and letting her mind go blank, a substitute for sleep that she had learned in the cells. But this was not always easy, particularly after an offensive, when, night after night, she had to handle men with wounds in the lungs, wounds in the stomach, wounds in the groin, legless and armless men, men with hideously disfigured faces and, worst of all, gas cases, so that she sometimes thought what a blessed relief it would be to look upon a young man who was whole and unblemished.

Perhaps it was this subconscious longing that urged her, in the early spring of 1916, to make a deliberate sacrifice of her privacy and involve herself, physically and emotionally, in what proved to be the most bizarre yet in some ways the most rewarding of her campaigns.

He returned to her for the third time in April, a gangling boy of no more than twenty who had been wounded in the shoulder at Neuve Chapelle and again, this time in the forearm, at Loos. She remembered him because of the terrible distress he showed after vomiting over her as they were helping him to board the ambulance and when they sent him back into the fight a third time in anticipation of the summer offensive on the Somme, he went to a great deal of trouble to seek her out explaining, naïvely, that he had never ceased to think of her all the time he was home and had written several times although his letters seemed to have gone astray.

She was oddly flattered by his attentions for it had seemed to her that never again would she earn the sidelong glance and smile of a young man. At thirty-four she still had an excellent figure but her dark curls were showing streaks of grey and her eyes seemed too big for her small, rather pinched face; in any case years had now passed since she had given more than a passing thought to a man who was not, automatically, a persecutor. Because of his insistence she let him take her out to dinner once or twice at a hotel that could still provide an excellent meal for officers attached to the transport centre, and she was touched when, on escorting her back to her quarters, he asked shyly if he might kiss her. For all his battle experience he was still no more than a timid boy and was also good-looking, she supposed, in the conventional English way, with his wavy, light-brown hair, a straight, short nose, clear eyes and fresh complexion. She let him kiss her, more as a joke against herself than from any desire to be kissed but the gentle pressure of his lips, and his reverential approach to her, renewed in her the yearning for a fresh, clean man, someone who was whole and whose clothes were not infested with lice and about whom there was no stale smell of sweat, blood and Flanders mud.

She must have responded to his kiss more eagerly than she intended for he began to pour out protestations of love, saying that the younger women at home meant nothing to him and that he had been unable to get her out of his mind during his convalescence after Loos. She tried teasing him, pointing out that, as an enterprising girl of fourteen, she could have been his mother but when he raised his hand and stroked her hair she succumbed to the crazy pressures of war and after one or two furtive embraces in the limited privacy of the base she promised to spend three days' leave with him after he had completed his gas course, at Montreuil.

She regretted it the moment he had gone, realising that she did not regard him as a person at all but as a symbol of all the millions of young men marched into this inferno by paunched, bewhiskered generals and ageing politicians on both sides of the line, boys who, like this one, would die virgins if they were too fastidious to visit the Blue or Red Lamp establishments during rest and training periods behind the front.

She kept her promise, however, and far from regretting it found in

745

his clumsy embraces a measure of solace for her years of deprivation and dedication before and during the war. They did not go to Paris, as he had urged, but to the village high up the Seine where, as a girl, she had boarded out for a time after her father had brought her back from India and where, among the friendly peasants, she might have found peace had she remained there to grow up as an exile instead of being fetched home after her father's remarriage.

They stayed at a little inn near the bridge. Before their window was the broad sweep of the river and its tidy fringe of poplars, limes and chestnuts and above them towered the walls of the castle, squatting like a white hen on a clutch of half-timbered, many-gabled houses. For Grace it was a recuperative interval, for here the war seemed to belong to another century. For David, "The Boy David" as she called him, it was an idyll. He could hardly have been as deeply in love with her as he professed himself to be, yet she represented for him a romanticised ideal of womanhood who somehow struck a precise balance between a mother and a mistress, offering comfort in the one role and the grossest flattery in the other. He asked her many questions about her past but she parried most of them, telling him good-humouredly to mind his own business and although he talked eagerly about marrying her during his next leave, he did not press for details of her first marriage or her involvement in politics. On the final morning, just after dawn, she left him to sit by the tall window looking down on the sliding river and when she returned to the bed the terrible poignancy of his sleeping face brought tears to her eyes. To her he was as dead as though he was lying out on the battlefield and the knowledge that she had been the means of bringing him a little ecstasy seemed to her the most positive achievement of her life.

David was the first and perhaps the most innocent of them, for as the war dragged on she took other lovers, all of them young and resigned to death in the immediate future. She derived small physical satisfaction from these encounters for some of the boys were greedy while others were excusably clumsy yet she derived satisfaction of another kind that had nothing to do with their bearlike embraces and fearful impatience. She saw herself, as the Somme petered out and the even more costly assaults of 1917 began, as a healer and again as a kind of janitor, opening the door to give these condemned men a glimpse of a world they would never inherit. It was an extravagant thought and perhaps a vain one but it seemed to her a more rewarding endeavour than any she had attempted in all the years of platform storming and

746

window smashing, or, for that matter, anything achieved during her short reign at Shallowford.

II

One morning in April, 1916, the Reverend Hubert Horsey, Rector of Shallowford, was shown into Paul's office in what Mrs. Handcock might have described as "zummat of a tizzy". Like his son Keith he was afflicted by a slight stutter and Paul, aware of this, gave him a moment or two to collect himself before offering him a sherry which he politely refused.

"It's about my boy, Keith," the rector said. "I'm here to ask you a favour, Mr. Craddock, or maybe find someone else on the estate who would do me the favour." He went on to say that his son had recently been summoned before a Leeds tribunal to explain why he had not enlisted under the Derby Act of the previous December, Keith having declared himself a conscientious objector. Paul was not surprised. Both father and son had always been regarded as eccentric among the Valley folk and the rector was as unlike his predecessor, the Reverend Bull, as it was possible to be for he neither hunted, hectored his flock, nor challenged members of his congregation to explain why they had missed matins. He had also succeeded in establishing cordial relationships with the Nonconformists in Coombe Bay and for this reason alone Paul had always liked the little man but Horsey had not been a success in the Valley. Having been bullied by Bull for a generation the local Anglicans regarded clerical tolerance as weakness and church attendances had fallen sharply until the war encouraged parishioners to seek Divine protection for absent menfolk. Paul said, "How convinced is he, Rector? What I mean is, there seem to be many varieties of conscientious objectors. Is Keith a religious boy?"

"I never thought of him as such," Horsey admitted. "We've had a good deal of argument on religious dogma since he went up to Oxford but he seems to have made a stand on this issue. I have a newspaper report here; perhaps you should read it."

It did not take Paul long to discover that Keith Horsey's objections were political rather than religious. He had recently resigned from the Paxtonbury tribunal himself and was familiar with all the stock questions and most of the stock answers. To the old chestnut, "What would you do if you saw a German soldier raping your mother or sister?" Keith had replied, rather fatuously Paul considered, "I have no mother or sister," and when pressed said he supposed he would

747

attack the rapist with his bare hands. There was nothing dramatic about the examination. It had the same tiresome note as the Paxtonbury hearings and the same futility that had prompted Paul to resign.

"Will he do farm work?" Paul asked and Horsey said that he probably would but that he, as Rector, had already made the rounds of the Valley farms and had been unable to place his son. At Hermitage Farm Gloria Pitts had abused him and at Four Winds Farmer Eveleigh had refused to discuss the proposition. There was no demand for unskilled labour at the Dell or High Coombe and neither Willoughby at Deepdene, nor Elinor Codsall at Periwinkle, could afford extra help.

Paul considered. He was aware that both the Pitts and the Eveleighs could use extra help; indeed, Four Winds, with the biggest acreage and a herd of seventy Friesians, was desperate for a cowman and Keith could surely be taught to milk in a week or so. He said, "Leave it to me, Rector. I'll get him taken on at Four Winds. Get the boy down here and as soon as he's fixed I'll write to the Leeds tribunal."

"It's very kind of you," Horsey said. "I couldn't bear to think of him going to prison, they say they treat them so badly, but I should be less than honest if I didn't say I understood how people feel who have a son or a husband out there." Then, pausing for a second, he said glumly, "This business makes me feel useless, Mr. Craddock. I'm not one of those parsons who can unblushingly bless a cannon, or claim that the Almighty is fighting for us! Sometimes I wish I were; it would make things a lot easier and I daresay I should make more impact here."

Paul, deciding that he had never liked the man so much as at this moment, said, "I'm not all that enthusiastic myself, Rector! However, there's little you or I can do about it."

The man's head came up and Paul noticed the baffled look in his brown eyes. "Is there no prospect at all of a compromised peace this year?" he asked, and Paul told him he had asked the same question of their M.P., Grenfell, only a few days ago and had received a negative answer. "Grenfell says the Government mean to fight to a finish," he added. "There are reasons for supposing the Germans have already approached both the Allies and the Americans and been turned down," and then, when he saw Horsey was prepared to unburden himself further, he made the excuse that he would try and catch Eveleigh before the farmer went off to weekly market. He was not in the mood to share the rector's troubles, having more than enough of his own just

748

then. As he was leaving however, Horsey said, "This war and everyone's approach to it—it makes absolute nonsense of my work, Squire."

"Mine too," Paul said grimly, "I put fourteen years into building this estate into a useful community and I thought I was progressing but here I am going cap in hand to one of my own tenants, to ask him to help prevent a brilliant brain like Keith's being scattered about France, or dulled by prison!" and he took his cap and went out, not in the best of tempers.

Eveleigh proved exceptionally stubborn. "Look here, Squire," he argued, "I've had one boy killed and I've another in uniform! Why the devil should I help a damned shirker?"

"Maybe because he's your son-in-law!" Paul reminded him, "and I'm sure your wife would be relieved."

"I daresay she would!" growled Eveleigh, "but the truth is I've never liked the boy! Rachel ought to have found herself a man, not a walking encyclopaedia who hasn't the guts to fight for his own kin! Besides, I've made arrangements to get a land-girl here."

"You could do with two extra hands and I'm asking this as a favour," Paul said.

Eveleigh hesitated. The war had changed him, more than any of them, Paul thought. He had always been dour and uncommunicative but in spite of this Four Winds had been a happy, prosperous farm since they had moved in, man, wife and children working in close accord and seeming to possess mutual respect for one another. Now the atmosphere of the farm was uncomfortably like Four Winds in Arabella's time, with Eveleigh snarling at his wife and younger daughters and the kitchen charged with explosive bad temper and suppressed resentment.

"Well," he said at length, "I'll do it on your account, Squire, for I don't need reminding it was you gave me my chance, backalong. If you hadn't I'd still be a hired hand living in the cottage, so get the boy here and Rachel too, and we'll see how they shape. If they pull their weight they can abide but I'll tell you straight, I won't have ought to say to 'em."

That was the best Paul could do and a week later Keith and Rachel arrived from the North and took up residence in the cottage the Eveleighs had occupied during the Codsall régime. The rector called in to thank Paul but Keith himself did not seem particularly grateful for the reprieve and Paul guessed that he regarded farm work as an uneasy compromise. Rachel also was estranged from her sisters, who were

749

inclined to share their father's view that Keith was a coward, a pitiful creature compared to their splendid brothers Gilbert and Harold but the arrangement served as a temporary measure and at least kept Keith out of gaol. Paul heard, however, that a month or two after their arrival, Eveleigh went ahead with his intention of employing a land-girl and soon after her arrival he saw her, a buxom, auburn-haired young hoyden, who looked as though she would be more at home in a munitions factory than a field of cows. Paul happened to pass her by Codsall bridge whilst she was driving the herd home from the river pastures and saw her take out a pocket mirror to apply a powder puff to her broad, freckled nose. He thought, "Well, I don't know what Eveleigh's thinking of but Keith can't be much more of an amateur than her and at least Rachel can make butter and care for hens!" but he did not think any more about it until a week or so later when, on returning late from a meeting of an agricultural committee at Paxton-bury, Claire met him on the doorstep and he saw at once that she was worried.

"Rachel Horsey is in the library," she told him, "but don't go in until I've told you what it's about. There's been more trouble over at Four Winds."

She took him into the little-used drawing room and shut the door.

"What do you know about that land-girl Eveleigh has over there?" Claire asked, and Paul told her nothing at all except that she did not look like a girl who could earn her wages on a farm."

"I daresay you're right at that," Claire said, "for it seems that Eveleigh isn't interested in her vertical activities!"

"Now what the devil do you mean by that?" Paul demanded, "Eveleigh's not that kind of chap? You've been listening to gossip started by the fact that she's the first land-girl who has shown up here!"

"Not in this case," Claire said, "she was Eveleigh's fancy piece when she worked behind the counter at Foster's, the drapers, and has been for a year or more. He got her drafted to him by delivering cream and butter on councillors' doorsteps. Ben Godbeer, the seedsman, is on the County Council and allocates land labour, doesn't he? And Ben is an old crony of Eveleigh's. It looks to me as if Rachel has hit the nail on the head."

"And what does she think I can do about it?" Paul demanded. "Eveleigh's a paid-up tenant running the best farm on the estate and I'm already under an obligation to him on account of placing Keith."

"Well," Claire said, hands on her hips, "you can't ask him to get

750

rid of the girl just like that but Rachel thinks you might make some kind of indirect approach. Since this afternoon everyone at Four Winds knows about it."

"What happened this afternoon?"

"A French farce," Claire told him, "Old Ned Fosdyke, the pigman, went into the loft over the barn to get meal and trod on the pair of them. Eveleigh had his breeches down and the girl was stark naked in the hay!"

"It's nothing to grin about, woman!" Paul growled, but Claire, still chuckling, said, "I'm sorry, Paul, but I can't help it. If it were anyone else but Eveleigh it wouldn't be funny but he's such a sententious, self-righteous kind of chap and so strict with his children! The idea of him taking both time and breeches off for an ex-shop girl is enough to make a cat laugh!"

"Damn it, he might have been more discreet at all events," Paul grumbled. "How did Rachel come to hear about it?"

"How could she help hearing? Eveleigh was so mad he knocked poor old Ned Fosdyke down the ladder and everyone came running, including Marian! The point is he's absolutely unrepentant and won't even hear of getting rid of the girl!"

"He damned well will if I've anything to say in the matter," grunted Paul and after a talk with Rachel, who was crying in the library, he would have accompanied her straight back to Four Winds had she not begged him to wait and hear something of her personal problems. "It was good of you to get Keith fixed up," she said, "but it isn't going to work, quite apart from this development! Father's so changed you wouldn't know him. I don't know whether it was the boys going, or the war, or what, but life is impossible for Keith and I over there and Keith is thinking of walking out and taking the consequences. He thinks the war is a crime against humanity and that the only way it can be stopped is for people like us to make a stand but what good will it do him going to prison? Besides, I'm expecting a baby in the autumn!"

He looked more closely at her and realised that this was a fact. Claire said, "Then his first duty is to you, Rachel, and not to a theory!" and once again Paul felt grateful for his wife's grasp of essentials. He said, "Leave me to deal with Keith and when Ikey comes home on leave I'll get him to talk to him. He's due in a day or so unless leave is stopped. Meantime Keith can work on the Home Farm. Can Rachel move in with us, Claire?"

"Certainly," Claire replied, "and the sooner the better. It'll suit a plan I've had in mind for some time now."

She did not tell them what her plan was and it was months before they found out but Rachel, very relieved, accompanied Paul to the Home Farm where he told Honeyman to make room on the staff for Keith. They moved in bag and baggage within twenty-four hours, making a home out of a ruinous cottage adjoining the tack-room where Lovell's coachman had once lived.

Feeling that the reins of the place were slipping out of his hands, and that the spirit of the Valley was being poisoned by the stresses of war, Paul rode over to Four Winds and had a frank talk with Eveleigh on the subject of the buxom land-girl. He found him truculent and unresponsive.

"You baint heard my side o' the business," the farmer growled. "Marian's not been a wife to me for close on a year now and I'll be honest, Squire! I'm a man as works hard, eats hearty and dam' well needs a woman night-times! Alwus 'ave and please God alwus will! I wouldn't have thought to get Jill yer if things had been as they were between me an' the missis but they baint an' won't be again. She holds me responsible for Gilbert being blown to tatters and Harold runnin' off an' enlisting, although you know same as I do that they'd ha' gone be now in any case! As for Rachel, and that four-eyed scholard she wed, I don't give a damn what happens to 'em, so long as they get from under my feet! Jill stays here as long as I've a mind to keep her and that's all I'm disposed to say about it!" and he stumped off to his work leaving Paul to find his own way out of the house. He saw one of the dairymaids in the hall and asked her if her mistress was available.

"No," said the girl, carelessly, " 'Er's table-rapping in Gil's room."

"She's *what*?"

"Table-rapping! 'Er's at it all the time now. 'Er says if 'er keeps at it long enough 'er'll get through to Gil and vind how he's going on beyond the veil! It's a real carry-on I can tell 'ee, Squire."

Paul began to understand why Eveleigh had sought solace in the barn and on the way out he passed the land-girl Jill forking hay in the yard. She gave him a smirk and the time of day but he did not acknowledge her greeting. It might have been fancy but, as he climbed on to Snowdrop and clattered out of the yard, the atmosphere of the place seemed so stale and sinister that he pushed the grey into a trot and had just reached the bridge when he saw a motor turn off the

752

moorland road and accelerate along the flat beside the river. As it drew level he saw that the driver was Ikey and without knowing why his heart gave a tremendous bound and he shouted as the car slowed and stopped.

"We weren't expecting you yet, Ikey," he said. "Claire will be delighted! You look very fit, far more yourself than most of the youngsters who come home from time to time."

Ikey grinned and Paul thought how much of the impudent gamin had survived the successive strait-jackets of public school, hill-station, and Armageddon.

"It's having had the sense to join the artillery, Gov," he joked, "the P.B.I. do all the slogging and we chaps just sit around and make things tough for 'em by tickling up Fritz every now and again. I'm back in Blighty for several weeks, special course at Aldershot. Very nice and very secret!" and he winked.

Paul laughed, feeling cheered already and cutting through the paddock cantered ahead to give Claire the good news. That night, however, after everyone had gone to bed and they were sitting over their brandy, Ikey was not so flippant, warning Paul that within a month or two there was going to be a push to end all pushes on the Western Front and that, in his opinion, it was likely to be far more costly than Neuve Chapelle and Loos.

"The point is, will it be successful?" Paul demanded, "will it break the deadlock and hasten things to a finish?"

" 'Ah, that I cannot say'," quoted Ikey, " 'but 'twas a famous victory'!" and then, seriously, "Let's say it stands a better chance than anything we've tried so far. We've got some surprises and we shall certainly rattle old Fritz, the poor old sod but I can't say more than that, not even to you, Gov. Now, to hell with the war. What's happening on the home front?"

Paul did not think he could be seriously interested but Ikey listened attentively when Paul recounted the Valley news and seemed particularly struck by the information concerning Keith Horsey.

"I ought to have written to him," he said. "He wrote several times to me. I wouldn't like Old Beanpole to imagine I thought less of him for telling those bloody hearthrug patriots to look elsewhere for cannon-fodder! I'll go over and see him first thing in the morning."

"What strikes me as odd," Paul said, "is that you chaps aren't anything like so emphatic about the war as the people at home. You don't foam at the mouth about the Germans and I get the impression

753

you half admire people like Keith Horsey. Is that cussedness on your part or is it general among men on active service?"

"General I'd say, at least below the rank of colonel but I don't see why it should surprise you. Fritz lives under the same hellish conditions as we do and you can't help admiring his guts. Most of the chaps feel more akin to him than to the people at home and I daresay he feels the same way. You can't live a week out there and go on believing all the bloody nonsense people write and talk back here, not unless you happen to be on the staff that is!"

"But if things are as bad as that," Paul said, "isn't there a chance of it petering out of its own accord?"

"Not a snowball in hell's chance, Gov," Ikey told him cheerfully, "but if you ask me why I couldn't give you a short answer. It has to do with self-respect, regimental pride, the habit of discipline and even the warrior cult thousands of years old but more than any of those things it's probably reluctance to let other chaps down. I suppose that sounds facetious but it isn't, it's just that we're all so closely involved with each other and, in a way, with Fritz. I don't think things are like that on the other fronts, or at sea, but out there, in that great sprawling mud-bath where, to show the top of your head is certain death, a man ceases to have anything in common with ordinary civilised people. They've stopped believing in the war, or in the way it is regarded in London or Berlin, but they'll go on sticking it until one side breaks. Do you find that impossible to understand?"

"Not entirely," Paul said thoughtfully and he did understand in a way, in fact he went to bed thinking he had learned more about the war from Ikey than from any other source over the last eighteen months.

Ikey crossed to the Home Farm the next morning and he and Keith went off together, high up to the source of the Sorrel, which had always been Ikey's favourite place on the estate. Here, where the river was no more than a shallow stream winding through thickets of brambles and shoulder-high ferns, he identified the locality with the first poem he had ever read, "A Boy's Song" in Mary Willoughby's *Poetical Reader*. Paul never heard what they talked about that day but whatever it was it had an immediate effect upon Keith's thinking, for on his return he announced that he intended to volunteer for a stretcher-bearing unit, formed from conscientious objectors who had refused to carry arms and soon after Ikey left to begin his course he said good-bye to a tearful Rachel, and to Paul and Claire, and returned

754

to the North. A month later Rachel received a letter from him from France. Two months after that she gave birth to a stillborn child and left the Valley for good.

III

The Somme offensive, following swiftly upon Jutland, fulfilled Paul's gloomiest forebodings regarding the blank page at the back of the estate diary. In a single week, the first week of July, a string of familiar names were entered under "Casualties" by the dogged Claire, who had made a vow to keep the record up-to-date even though the task depressed her almost as much as it would have depressed Paul.

The first two names written in were Jutland casualties, Tom Williams and his nephew Dan, both lost aboard the battle cruiser *Queen Mary*. Within a fortnight Smut Potter was posted as missing, believed killed, and after Smut came news of the death of Evan Morgan, son of Eph Morgan, the Coombe Bay builder, and then Tremlett, the hunt servant, both killed on July 1st. Later the same week Nick, second of the Timberlake boys, Jeff Marlowe, son of the sexton, Will Salter the thatcher's son, Jim Willis, the wheelwright's younger son and two others, were killed, bringing Valley casualties up to fourteen. Despite these appalling losses the general news was encouraging. London papers, arriving a day late, told of spectacular advances, enormous German casualties and the capture of innumerable prisoners but long before the first of these prisoners appeared in a small P.O.W. camp, sited a mile or so north of Shallowford Woods, the note of triumph had gone from the leading articles and Paul began to suspect that, as Ikey had prophesied, Fritz had been badly rattled but far from defeated. By harvest-time the familiar deadlock seemed to have been resumed, with no hope whatever of the war ending with a flourish of cavalry trumpets.

It was the establishment of a prisoner-of-war camp beyond the northern rim of the woods that led, indirectly, to the next outburst of Valley hysteria, an incident that pushed Paul that much nearer despair.

The camp was not a large one. It held no more than two hundred carefully-seeded Germans, mostly Saxons, selected from larger camps for timber-felling in the area. They worked in conditions amounting to freedom for none showed the slightest inclination to escape and Paul gathered, during a conversation with one of their reservist guards, that they considered themselves fortunate to be out of it and still sound in wind and limb.

They worked in gangs of six under the supervision of Sam Potter, the woodsman, and Sam, having free access to such splendid muscles, was not above allocating one or two of his charges to do urgent work on the estate, besides the felling and shaping of pitprops in the plantations between the border of Periwinkle in the west, and the boundary of High Coombe in the east. When Elinor Codsall complained to him that her patch of pasture under Hermitage Wood was reverting to moor and stood waist-high in brambles and nettles, he readily agreed to lend her a prisoner for a week or two to get it cleared. Soon the man arrived, a tall, broad-shouldered Württemberger, with a great moon face not unlike Will Codsall's and hands like raw hams that assaulted the briars and docks as if they had been collectively responsible for uprooting him from his farm near Ludwigsburg and setting him down on alien soil.

Nobody seemed to think it ironic that he should be clearing the land of a man at whom he might well have shot a year or so ago and that under the eye of his widow, who trudged to and fro among her shanty-town of hen houses on the opposite slope of the hill; nobody, that is, except Elinor herself, who was morbidly fascinated by the spectacle of the German's great broad back and the swift gleam of his scythe blade as it caught the sun in one of its wide, expert sweeps. Soon she found herself looking for him and sometimes wondered what Will would have said at having a German soldier working his way across the tussocks over which he had walked so often on his way to the fringe of the wood. His lumbering movements, Elinor thought, were strongly reminiscent of Will's, particularly when he stooped and gathered great armfuls of weeds to carry to the fire, and one day, impelled by nothing more than curiosity, she took him a stone jar of cider to refresh him at noon and thought, as he clicked his heels and bowed from the waist, that this was something Will would never have done, not even to a Lovell. He could speak a little English and she asked him his name. When he told her it was Willi, Willi Meyer, she walked swiftly away but after that, during the hot spell, she took him his cider each day and sometimes a hard-boiled egg and a crust of home-baked bread spread with butter from her churn. He seemed pathetically grateful for these modest gifts but whenever she approached he always dropped his scythe or billhook and stood stiffly to attention as though she had been an inspecting officer. Each time she saw him he seemed to have grown more like poor old Will and even the children must have thought so, for they often crossed the dip and climbed the hillside to talk with him and play about him as he worked and he was always careful to warn them to stand well clear of his scythe, although he beamed at them and sometimes made faces that produced squeals of laughter and excited jumpings up and down. There were four children, the elder, a boy, Mark, two girls, Queenie and Floss and the baby Richard. Elinor was glad to let Mark take them all out of her way as soon as he had finished his morning chores. He was a slim, serious-minded boy, with his mother's neat build and Grandfather Willoughby's beaky nose and grey eyes. When dinner was ready Elinor usually called to them from the farm wall on the opposite slope and she had summoned them one hot morning and seen them run down to the rivulet, when she heard a sudden outcry and saw the Württemberger throw down his scythe and dash down the hillside, moving at considerable speed for so clumsy a man. She ran down her slope to join them and was horrified to learn that Mark, in jumping the brook, had landed almost on top of a sleeping adder, curled on a slab of sandstone and had been bitten in the ball of the thumb. There had been one or two cases of snakebite in the Valley in the past year and one child, over at Coombe Bay, had died before she could be treated but it looked as though Willi Meyer had some experience in this field for he acted with commendable speed, sucking the puncture for a full minute, then whipping out his penknife, sterilising the blade in a match flame and scoring a deep double cut before sucking again. Then, still moving so quickly that he appeared almost to be turning somersaults, he threw the boy on his back, knelt on his forearm and made a tourniquet with his bootlace, twisting it until the leather bit into the flesh. Doctor Maureen said later that the German's first-aid had undoubtedly saved the boy's life for it was nearly an hour before she was located and could use the serum she had sent for after the fatal Coombe Bay case. Mark was out and about again in a week and boasting of his experience but Willi's skill and initiative made a deep impression on Elinor, who could not help thinking it strange that her son's life had been saved by one of the men who had helped to make her life and work meaningless. After this incident she made a habit of giving Willi a hot meal at the farm and gradually an undemonstrative friendship developed between them. He learned English rapidly, and seemed deeply interested in everything about the farm, particularly her methods of cross-breeding fowls to produce a good laying strain and soon they were on mildly convivial terms, discussing farm and family problems. He told her a good deal about his own farm in Württemberg, and how the South Germans always resented the domination of the Prussians and had only supported the war because Germany, as a nation, felt herself encircled by enemies. It was a point of view Elinor had never heard expressed and she thought, privately, that if most Germans were anything like the amiable Willi Meyer then the war was even more stupid and wasteful than she had supposed, and her husband's enlistment had been his first act of insanity.

The association never progressed beyond a neighbourly stage but it did not go unnoticed. Vicky Tarnshaw, a sullen, middle-aged woman who worked part-time for the Pitts family, at Hermitage close by, marked it and discussed it darkly with Martha Pitts and Gloria, the Valley Amazon. The good-natured Martha made allowances both for Elinor's loneliness and Vicky's addiction to gossip but Gloria was outraged. It seemed to her an act of the basest treachery to introduce a German, any German, into one's house at a time when half the Valley men were engaged in a life-and-death struggle with the baby-crucifiers and rapists overseas and having gone one noontime to the edge of Hermitage Wood, and watched Willi respond to Elinor's shrill call for dinner from the far hillside, Gloria convinced herself that there could be but one explanation to this act on the part of her neighbour, telling Vicky, in Martha's presence, that Elinor Codsall's lust for a man had driven her to form an association that shamed the Valley. Martha, a kindly soul, pooh-poohed the notion but Gloria argued, "For what other reason would 'er ask un inside? *Inside*, mind you! Gordamme mother, dornee lean over backwards maaking excuses for everyone! Us 'ave 'ad conshies an' our spies too 'till us bundled that Hun professor out o' the Valley! So why shoulden us 'ave a woman who dorn mind beddin' down with a Hun when there's nought but children about the plaace?"

Thereafter Gloria and Vicky, taking turn and turn about, kept a close watch on Periwinkle Farm but they did not, by common consent, broadcast the story in the Valley. They had a plan of their own and were reluctant to share the pleasure of its execution with anyone.

One October evening, soon after supper, Gloria left the house on the excuse of collecting mail from the box at the end of the long track that led down to Hermitage Farm from the river road but instead or going its full length she climbed through a gap in the hedge and crossed the shoulder of the hill to the wood. As she went she heard the clink of hobnailed boots approaching higher up the lane and wondered who might be calling on the farm at this hour but she did not wait to find

758

out for she had a rendezvous with Vicky and soon located her, standing on the fringe of the wood looking across at the single yellow blurr that marked the kitchen window of Periwinkle. "Us'd better go about it straight away," Vicky said, "bevore 'er locks up for the night! Did 'ee think to bring the big scissors?"

"Arr, I did that," Gloria said briefly. "Come on then and us'll make a quick job of it!" and they went down the slope and up the opposite hillside to the farm where a peep through the uncurtained window showed them that Elinor was inside alone, bottling plums at the long table. They lifted the latch and rushed in, startling Elinor so much that she jumped back, smashing a large glass jar of fruit on the slate hearth. It must have seemed to Elinor that her neighbour, together with the hired woman who accompanied her, were victims of the same homicidal urge that had destroyed Martin and Arabella, for they rushed at her shouting curses and before she knew what was happening they had her pinioned in the high-backed chair, her feet in a mush of spilled plums and broken glass that littered the hearth. Then she saw the big scissors and let out a wild shriek and young Mark upstairs tumbled out of bed and came pattering down the wooden stair but by then Vicky, who was a powerful woman, had the prisoner fast with her arms twisted behind the chair and Gloria, hearing Mark approach, wedged an oak form under the knob of the stairway door. After that the kitchen was in an uproar with all three women shouting and screaming and Elinor's wild struggles upsetting the table lined with bottling jars that crashed and rolled in every direction. It was not until Gloria had torn Elinor's hair loose and sliced more than half of it away that the victim had an inkling of what lay behind this assault, for Gloria screamed, "There now! No one'll look at 'ee twice now, not even that bloody Hun!" and went on snipping away until all Elinor's honey-coloured hair lay in the great pools of plum juice on the floor. It was the presence of so much sticky liquid underfoot that gave Vicky Tarnshaw another idea. She shouted, gibbering with glee, "Now us'll strip her naked an' roll her in it, Mrs. Pitts!" and without waiting for affirmation she ripped Elinor's cotton dress down the back and did the same with her petticoat, while Gloria wrestled with her drawers and stockings. It was this final indignity that gave Elinor a brief access of strength. She kicked Gloria in the stomach and lurched sideways so that the chair, entangling itself in Vicky's legs, brought the pair of them crashing to the floor within a foot or two of the fire. The struggle then became general, with the winded Gloria joining in and getting

759

half her own clothes ripped off and they were all threshing about in a whirl of garments and plum-syrup when the outer door crashed open and Henry Pitts rushed in to stand with mouth agape looking down at the extraordinary scene.

It had been his footfall, home on unexpected leave, that Gloria had heard in the lane and when Martha Pitts seemed evasive about his wife's whereabouts he lost no time in getting her to voice her suspicions and had at once hurried in pursuit. Now he stood stock still on the threshold hardly able to believe his eyes. He was still wearing his uniform and patches of dried Flanders mud still adhered to his breeches and puttees. For a terrible moment he mistook the pools of plum juice for blood and assumed that the women were in the process of attacking one another with knives. Then he saw the shorn tresses lying behind the chair and it must have given him a clue for he started forward, seized his wife by the hair and hauled her clear, after which he planted a hefty kick on Vicky's behind that caused her to roll sideways and expose the crushed, hysterical Elinor whose cropped head was only an inch or so from a smouldering log that had fallen on to the hearth. He lifted her to her feet and saw that she was almost naked and plastered from head to foot in bottling syrup, as indeed, were all three of them. He said, with a trench oath, "What in God's name be thinking of, all of 'ee?" and when Elinor, feeling her head, burst into hysterical weeping he turned to his wife whose dress hung down as far as the waist exposing her bare breasts and whose head and shoulders were dripping with plum juice so that she stared at him through a great mat of clotted red hair.

Vicky Tarnshaw was the first to recover. She scrambled to her feet and said, backing away, "Us was marking her, Mr. Pitts! 'Er's been lying wi' one o' they Hun prisoners up at the camp!" whereupon Elinor suddenly ceased her outcry, snatched up the scissors and would have plunged them into Vicky's face if Henry had not caught her by the shoulders and held her. Then Henry became conscious of a heavy thumping and wild cries from behind the stair door and asked Gloria who was there. She told him sulkily that it was the children trying to get in and the information seemed to steady him for he released Elinor, pocketed the scissors and went across to the door, opening it but blocking the boy's entry and saying, "Tiz all right, Markboy. Us 'ave had a bit of an accident wi' the bottling and us was quarrelling who was to blame! Go back upstairs and quiet your sisters!" and then, very deliberately, he closed the door and addressing Elinor said, "Now give over snivelling, Elinor, an' tell us the facts. Is it true you been larkin' wi' one o' they Fritzes? Not that I give a damn if you 'ave but to satisfy these varmints, be it true?"

"No, it baint," screamed Elinor, "it baint true! Willi Meyer saved my boy's life when he was bit by an adder an' ever zince I give 'un a bite to eat mealtimes! You c'n ask the children, any of 'em! Theym always yer when he comes inside the 'ouse!"

"Right," said Henry, "then go along upstairs and don't upset the tackers telling 'em what really happened!" and as she moved across the littered floor he picked up a besom from the corner so that Vicky, mistaking his intention, made a sudden rush to the door. He caught her a buffet on the ear that sent her sprawling, shut the door and threw the broom at his wife. "Clean this bliddy mess up," he said briefly, "every particle of it, do 'ee hear?" and when Vicky, dazed from the blow, struggled up on her hands and knees, he added, "You too! Get to work the pair of 'ee! Or I'll beat the daylights out of 'ee!"

He was very calm now, more deliberate and serious-looking than Gloria had ever seen him. He took a seat astride a chair near the door and watched their every movement and when the litter of squashed plums and broken glass was shovelled up he said, "There's a bucket yonder, under the sink. Fill it from the kettle and give the floor a swab over!"

"I'm not gonner scrub for the likes o' . . ." shouted Vicky but she changed her mind when he got up and moved towards her and scuttled into the scullery for bucket and floorcloths. He reseated himself, placidly smoking his pipe as they moved about straightening furniture and washing the stone floor. When it was done, and the litter had been thrown out, he said, "Right! Get on home now, Vic Tarnshaw, an' if you so much as shows your face at Hermitage again I'll drown 'ee in the bliddy duckpond, you zee if I dorn't! As for you," he continued, addressing his wife, "I reckon I'll serve you zame as you served Elinor!"

"Don't you lay hand on me!" shouted Gloria, jumping back towards the fireplace but he turned his back on her and flung open the door just as Vicky made a rush to pass him and escape into the yard. She arrived there even quicker than she had intended for, as she flitted by, he kicked her so accurately that she flew across the cobbles and landed face-down in the midden heap. He did not even wait to watch her scramble up and run shrieking into the darkness but shut the door, bolted it and crossed to the hearth, extracting Gloria's scissors from

761

his pocket on his way. When she realised that he meant to put his threat into execution she let out a wild squawk and tried to run round him and escape by the window, but he caught her easily enough, throwing his arm under her chin, dragging her across the window seat and making five quick snips with the blades. In a matter of seconds one side of her head was shorn even closer than Elinor's. Then she began to beg and plead—"Dornee boy! *Dornee do it, Henry!*" and half-escaping his grip clasped him round the knees but he snipped and snipped until all her sticky auburn locks lay in a heap on the floor and the despairing face that looked up at him was the face of a stranger and not Gloria's at all.

He released her then, kicking the shorn tresses into the hearth, after which, still quite impassive, he took a ten-shilling note from his breeches pocket and laid it on the table, calling, "Us iz goin' now Elinor! I've left 'ee zummat to pay for the damage and I'll be over to zee 'ee in the mornin'!"

There was no answer, no sound in the big kitchen but the loud ticking of the clock and the whimpering of the woman huddled under the window. He said, briefly, "Be these our scissors?" and when she nodded he flung them in the fire saying, "I woulden care to own 'em after this! Come on 'ome you gurt stoopid bitch, an' thank your stars I don't take a harness strap to your fat backside zoon as us gets there!"

She got up, still gulping and sniffing and went out into the yard. After a last look round he followed her, walking close behind as they crossed the shoulder of the hill, skirted the wood and went on down the far slope to the Hermitage track. It was a strange home-coming for a man who had been in and out of the trenches for the better part of a year.

The story of the assault upon Elinor Codsall was common knowledge in a day or so. The Pitts did not broadcast it, and Vicky Tarnshaw left the Valley to work in a munitions factory in the North, but two closely-cropped heads on adjoining farms could not be concealed and Paul heard about it from the postman and made direct enquiries from Henry. Henry said, grimly, "Arr, tiz tru enough, Squire, I come 'ome after nigh on a year overseas lookin' for peace an' quiet an' what do I find? A bliddy war on me own doorstep, started be me own missis! Still, 'er won't start another I reckon, and I've squared the damage they did upalong. What the hell have got into the folk back here? Be they all clean off their bliddy heads?"

Paul said he thought most civilians were and after paying a call on Elinor arranged, through Sam Potter, to get the Württemberger sent away from the camp in case he was victimised. The sight of Elinor's unevenly shorn head distressed him more than anything he had witnessed in the Valley lately and leaving her he rode on up to the highest point of the estate, on the edge of Hermitage Wood, looking down across the autumn landscape and trying to understand the hysteria and savage intolerance that changed simple, workaday folk like Gloria Pitts and Norman Eveleigh into the kind of bigots one might expect to find in the fifteenth-century lynch mob whipped up by fanatical priests. Was it fear, he wondered, sponsored by the shattering of their settled way of life, or had a vein of tribal brutality always existed below the surface to be laid bare by the shock of war? It was hard to determine, particularly as the fighting men, like Henry, Ikey and Dandy Timberlake, seemed to have become almost gentle and were certainly more tolerant for their terrible experiences whereas cruelty only showed in the people at home. He sat his horse up there a long time deciding that he no longer belonged to any of them in the way he had belonged before the war. There were the fanatics, like Gloria, Eveleigh and Horace Handcock, the Smart Allicks, like Sydney Codsall, and the passives, like Elinor Codsall and Claire; there were those in the thick of it all, like Ikey and Henry and the odd ones who saw the war as the negation of human dignity, people like Keith Horsey and poor, half-crazed Marian Eveleigh. He himself was a category of his own. By now he had learned to accept it as a kind of visitation, a plague that would one day die out and perhaps leave the land purified but today he felt utterly isolated, belonging neither to those under fire, to the patriots, or even to the honest doubters. He thought, grimly, "Damn it, I'll have to find my way back again somehow and surely the only way to do that is to come down on one side or the other. I couldn't honestly proclaim myself a C.O. but I'm damned if I'll let my judgment be warped about the Keith Horseys and the Elinor Codsalls! I suppose the only thing left is to jump in head-first, alongside Ikey, Henry and all the others around here who have been sucked in!" and at once he felt more clear-headed but because he was doubtful whether they could use a man of thirty-six with the scars of the last war on his body he said nothing of his decision to anybody, not even Claire, until he had written to his old Yeomanry Colonel who had a staff job in Whitehall and asked for advice on the quickest way of getting to France.

He had made insufficient allowance for the terrible attrition of the Somme battles. A reply came by return of post and he was offered,

763

subject to a routine medical check, a temporary commission in the Royal Army Service Corps, Transport Section. He sat staring at the letter hardly knowing whether to be astonished, elated or dismayed and then, remembering Will and Smut and Jem and all the others, and weighing their worth against that of Sydney Codsall and Gloria Pitts, he made his decision. Fearing that Claire would try and talk him out of it he filled in the application and posted it, asking for an interview at the earliest possible date.

IV

He confessed that same night, when he and Claire were sitting late in front of the library fire. Her temperate reception of the news confounded him, so obviously so that she laughed, telling him, in Mrs. Handcock's phrase, that "she could read 'un like an ha'penny book!" She could have said a great deal more on this subject, how she had watched him, anxiously and sympathetically, for months past as news reached the Valley in dribs and drabs of casualties, as fissures opened between combatant families and those who, by luck or design, had made money and managed to remain uncommitted. It was this, she felt, that was wearing him down for she had long ago accepted the fact that the social health of the estate concerned him very deeply, perhaps even more deeply than their domestic accord. This was the yardstick he used to measure his worth as a human being. She had watched him wince at the emergence of the Sydney Codsalls and their ilk, at rifts between men like Eph Morgan, whose only son had been killed, and men like Abe Tozer, the smith, whose son-in-law was said to be coining money in a Birmingham foundry. She too had been dismayed by the attack upon Elinor Codsall and by the traces of slime that survived Henry's earnest attempts to make amends and yet, in the main, she had been unable to help him much for although she was Valley born she still looked at the Valley through clear glass and not, as he so obstinately did, through a stained-glass window. It was because she knew him so well that she had known it would end like this, in him going off in the wake of the others and she said, in reply to his question as to how she could know something he had not finally decided himself, "Oh, I knew you would go, sooner or later, and if I were in your shoes I suppose I should do the same. I don't say I'd do it in the spirit of the slop one reads in the papers but, from a man's viewpoint, it must seem that all the best are being sucked in and the discards

764

spewed out! If you were ten years older you'd have to grin and bear it; as it is, thank God, you aren't likely to be sent into the line; if they accept you at all, that is!"

"They'll accept me," he said, so huffily that she laughed again. "Yes, I suppose they will, for you're a good deal lustier than some of the men they've taken. However, don't run away with the idea that leg of yours will stand up to unlimited demands. What kind of jobs do they do in the Service Corps?"

He was so relieved that she accepted his enlistment as inevitable and was not disposed to make a song and dance over it that he became expansive. "The R.A.S.C. take all the ammunition, stores and rations up the line. I shall try and wangle my way into a horse or mule section!" but she reminded him that Ikey had told them mechanical transport had now all but superseded the horse in France, and that if he was judged on his handling of the old Belsize he would prove an expensive addition to the forces of the Crown. He was not entirely fooled by her gaiety but caught himself admiring her performance.

"I don't know why you should be so ready to consign me to the awkward squad," he grumbled, "I was in uniform the first day you saw me and you fell over yourself to catch my eye if I remember rightly!"

"Yes I did," she agreed, "but you were young bones then! Besides you were the best catch in the county!"

"I've still got a shot or two in my locker," he told her. "Come over here and I'll prove it," but she declined the invitation and instead sat on the hearthrug looking into the coals as Paul watched the effect of firelight on her hair. As he mused he thought of something he had always been meaning to tell her but had somehow forgotten, not once but a dozen times, since their encounter with Grace at the time of the Coronation visit to London.

He reached out, heaved one of the heavy books from the shelf at his elbow and thumbed through the pages until he found the colour reproduction of Rubens' young wife, Hélène Fourment, as Bathsheba, receiving King David's letter.

"I don't know whether you'll be flattered or otherwise," he said, "but this was something I always meant to show you. The first time you and Grace met, that afternoon you came here with Rose soon after we were married, she produced this as soon as you had gone, and said you were Hélène Fourment reincarnated. It wasn't wholly a joke either, I think she half believed it."

765

She showed interest at once, taking the book and studying it carefully. "Grace said that? All those years ago? But I was slim then and this girl would turn the scale to eleven stone! It was probably an attempt to put you off, I expect she saw you looking me over too attentively!"

He laughed, saying that even then he was inclined to think that Grace had been considering abdication. He could say that now and half-believe it for somehow, in the last year or so, he had begun to share a little of Grace's impatience with parochialism. "You were never slim," he said, prodding her. "You had a neat waist and still have but you were always what the Edwardians called 'a fine woman', meaning that you had plenty to catch hold of! However, Hélene was reckoned a great beauty, so I always regarded the comparison as a compliment, tho', if I remember rightly, she did use the adjective 'ripe'."

"It's one that certainly suits me now," Claire said. "Are there any more of Hélene? Did he paint her often?"

"He was always painting her. Damn it, the man was over fifty and she was sixteen when they married so can you blame him? If I could paint I'd have you sitting for me nude, half-dressed or over-dressed, eight hours a day!" He took the book from her and looked closely at it again. "That's an idea, Claire," he said triumphantly. "Would you like to sit for someone really good? After all, we look like being here permanently, so it's time we laid down an ancestor or two!"

She was secretly delighted at the suggestion but made a protest nevertheless, saying that it would have been a pleasant notion ten years ago but today, at thirty-three, it was too late for that kind of nonsense.

"Rubbish," he said, "look at some of these old hags of the Lovell family! I'd a damned sight sooner sit looking at you and pack this lot off to a sale. If we could get a London artist down he could do the children as well. I'll write off to Uncle Franz, for I wager the old codger would know someone and keep his price down."

She said slowly, "All right then but don't be so eager to throw your money away. As a matter of fact I've a confession myself. I didn't mean to tell until the plan was a lot further advanced but if you really are likely to go soon you ought to know at once. Has it ever occurred to you that *I* might want to play a more positive part in the war?"

"No," he said, "frankly it hadn't! You always seemed far better at carrying-on-as-usual than me." And then he remembered that long

766

ago she had an ambition to nurse and had taken a course at St. Thomas's Hospital during her exile in London. He said bluntly, "Look here, I'm damned if I'll stand for you working yourself to death as a V.A.D.! I want you here when I come home and you have the children to think of."

"Oh, it wouldn't involve leaving here," she said, airily, "but if you do go I don't think I could hang around here passing the time, living for leave periods or the end of the war. I should have to have something to keep me occupied and as long as John Rudd is active he can care for the estate far better than I. I had . . . well, it occurred to me that we could turn this barn of a place into a hospital!"

"A hospital? For stretcher-cases!"

"No, that isn't practical, something more modest like a convalescent home for about fifty to sixty wounded men who wouldn't arrive until they were on the road to recovery. As a matter of fact I've already discussed it with Doctor Maureen."

"The devil you have!"

"She thinks it's a first-class idea. We've got at least ten rooms we now use for lumber. I could shift the children out of the east wing and clear the furniture from the big drawing-room that we hardly ever use. Then we could have a main ward on ground level and patients that could move about could sleep three to a room upstairs. If we needed more space we could get a couple of Nissen huts put up in the paddock. I got the idea watching Dandy Timberlake after he came home from Gallipoli. Men get patched up in big hospitals and then they go on leave, most of them to industrial cities and some, I suppose, to near-slums. Then, as soon as their scars heal, they get reboarded but they aren't really well at all, they're still suffering from shock and nervous exhaustion like Dandy and some of the others about here who have been out a long time. A month or so in a place like this, with organised exercises, fresh air and sea-bathing from May to October would work wonders. I should like to do it, providing you agree."

"Well," he said, greatly impressed in spite of himself, "I suppose it's possible but who would you get to run it?"

"I'd run it," she said. "I've kept up-to-date reading Maureen's journals and if we gave the house the Government couldn't very well turn us down, could they? As to staff, there are more than a dozen wives in the Valley who would be glad to do something useful. We could even organise a local crêche, with a roster of nannies and older children taking their meals at Mary Willoughby's so that their mothers could work part-time over here. The only drawback I can see is whether you really want the place knocked about by strangers and turned into a kind of barracks. After all, this is what you'll be fighting for, and in spite of anything you might think at the moment your dream isn't dead, Paul, only hibernating. Do you think I don't know why you divert every penny you receive from the scrapyard into a special account, earmarked for post-war development!"

"This is ridiculous!" he exclaimed, laughing, "I don't have a shred of privacy! How the devil did you know I had made up my mind not to make a personal profit out of munitions or other fiddles?"

"Oh, I keep an eye on your papers when you're on your rounds," she said carelessly, "and for all you know I go through your pockets from time to time. You ought to know that, seeing you're likely to be turned loose in France among the mademoiselles and the WAACs! But don't sidetrack me, I've got to know exactly how you feel about this plan. It's got to have your blessing before I go ahead with it."

He said, pulling her down on his knee, "I think it's a damned good idea and with Maureen to keep an eye on the venture you'll make a sensational success of it! Yes, it has my blessing, Claire. You're nearer the truth than you know about the home background of those poor devils. There isn't one in fifty who owns a square inch of the land he's fighting for and Grenfell says their physique compares very poorly with the men they're up against! Take a look at some of those strapping Fritzes in the camp and see for yourself, it's a point worth taking!" Then, teasing her, "I suppose when I do get leave and come back here pawing the ground I'll be met by a starchy matron who regards me as a patient rather than a warrior in search of solace?" and he ran his hands over her thinking what a fool he must be to sacrifice her society for the desolation Ikey had described to him in Flanders or even the cheerlessness of a base camp populated exclusively by men. She said, after a moment of this, "I'm always telling you we're too old to do our courting in an armchair! Let's go to bed," but the prospect of forsaking the warm fire and putting a term to one of these rare moments of intimacy was uninviting, so she remained where she was holding the future at bay and presently provoked him into enacting one of those boisterous scenes that always made her chuckle in retrospect, as though they were not man and wife, with a growing family and a longish partnership behind them but a couple of youngsters making the most of a lucky opportunity in the front parlour, when everybody was out of the way.

768

V

Paul's summons to report for initial training at a nearby Officers' Training Camp came in late November, 1916, but before he left Grenfell travelled down from London and spent a night or two at Shallowford. He was a very different James, Claire decided, from the buoyant, quietly confident professional they had often entertained in the days following his return to Parliament. The strain of long-night sittings and a share in decisions involving the slaughter of thousands of men showed in the lined face and patches of white hair above his ears. He had lost most of his jauntiness and now walked with a slight stoop. He was not, he told her, in the best of health, being sadly troubled with chronic indigestion and periods of sleeplessness, aggravated by his growing disgust for the jealousies and scramble for power among some of his senior colleagues and opposition members of the wartime Coalition. It was like, he told them, being aboard a crippled vessel among a lot of elderly passengers who had dismissed the crew and taken upon themselves the job of charting the ship's course. Paul soon realised that he was not only losing faith in his revered leader, Asquith, whom Grenfell said was too much of a gentleman to survive in such a scrimmage but had also come to dislike and distrust the firebrand, Lloyd George, who was openly flirting with Unionists, men like Bonar Law and the newspaper magnate, Alfred Harmsworth, in the hope of replacing Asquith as Premier. "I'm not so prejudiced as to think The Welsh Wizard wouldn't make a good pilot," Grenfell admitted, "but the way he's going about it could split the party down the middle and we are going to need men of Asquith's integrity when this business is over. Sometimes I find myself more in sympathy with the men who had the guts to stand up in August, 1914, and condemn the whole business as an international crime! I wasn't one of them butI supported the idea of a negotiated peace months ago and I've suffered for it since! Maybe Old Keir Hardie was right when he said, 'If I had my time over again I should steer clear of politics and preach the gospel!' "

He and Paul sat late over the study fire and Grenfell told him something of the overall strategic position of the Allies and spoke of hidden factors that influenced decisions and could not be made public in the newspapers. The Dardanelles campaign, James said, had almost succeeded, and might have done had it not been bedevilled by inter-Service rivalry. Now, in his opinion there was no real chance of either side achieving a breakthrough in the West. James admitted to being an

769

"Easterner", believing that a final decision could only be reached on some other front but the High Command, of whom he had an even poorer opinion than Ikey, were now committed to a war of attrition in which the victory was based on the Allies' superior manpower. "Almost as if they were playing with counters rather than people of flesh and blood!" he declared bitterly. He deprecated Paul's decision to join up, saying that he would contribute more doing his part in making good the terrible losses caused by the U-boat campaign. "Damn it man," he protested, when Paul told him he was due to leave in a few days, "hasn't the Valley contributed its quota already? What sense is there in you rushing out in search of a medal and a lump of shrapnel to balance the Boer bullet that's still travelling round inside you? I should have thought Claire would have had the sense to talk you out of it!"

Paul realised that it was useless to try and explain how he felt about staying home while men like Smut Potter and Henry Pitts wallowed in the mud. By now Grenfell was incapable of regarding the war in a personal light but was compelled, by reason of his familiarity with the overall picture, to look at it as a complicated exercise in checks and counter-balances involving not merely men but entire races and imponderable economic factors. One other thing he said did impress Paul and made him increasingly anxious for the future and that was his contemptuous dismissal of the Russian "steamroller" myth. He gave it as his opinion that Russia would be out of the war in a matter of months. "And can you wonder," he grumbled, "when the Tsarist system is rotten right through! Peasants are going into action unarmed while scoundrels in Petrograd are making fortunes, and all the time that ass of a Tsar and his neurotic wife behave as though they are playing chess instead of a game that will sweep them all under the carpet, along with all that's left of human values!" He went off to bed in a despondent mood and presumably found it difficult to rest for in the small hours Paul awoke to find Claire getting him a bismuth mixture. She told him she had heard James pacing his room, assailed by one of his stomach cramps and said, on climbing back into bed, "He's going to pieces, Paul! I don't think it's indigestion but something more serious, probably ulcers. I've insisted that Maureen gives him a good going-over in the morning and if necessary you'll have to persuade him to stay here and rest for a month or so."

"I'll try but I don't think I'll succeed," Paul said and he was right, for when, in the morning, Maureen diagnosed irritation of the duo-

770

denal cap he shrugged, pocketed her prescription, and said that while men who had voted for him were having their heads blown off in France, and dying of dysentery in the Balkans, he could hardly take a month's holiday on account of a bellyache. "And in the circumstances," he said to Paul, "who are you to argue with me? They'll probably invalid you out half-way through your initial training, and I hope to God they do! At least there will be one person hereabouts to preserve a small corner of England that I like to regard as a counterweight to all their damned factory chimneys and red-brick jungles!" Paul saw him as far as Sorrel Halt and as the train pulled out James leaned from the window and waved his billycock hat, revealing, for a brief instant, a flash of the jaunty campaigner who had once shocked the Valley by barnstorming his way into the heart of a Tory citadel. Paul was to remember his swift smile, and the wave of the billycock hat. It was a long time before he saw him again.

Two days later he stood on the same platform but this time it was he who was quitting the Valley and Claire, dressed in her fashionable best, who was putting a tolerably brave face on their first separation since she had come home in the spring of 1906. He said, jokingly, "Well, cheer up, I'm not off to France yet, just to camp over the county border!" but there was finality in the occasion and they both sensed it, possibly because, further along the train, khaki-clad figures leaned from the windows watching them. Paul said, as they awaited the guard's whistle, "Listen, Claire, get moving with that convalescent home the minute you get back, it'll give you something to think about! As for me, I daresay I shall be on the move but I'll write and if I don't get leave soon I daresay I'll put things in my letters aimed at taking some of the starch out of the matron's linen!" She smiled at that and said, "It'll be odd getting a letter from you. You haven't written me one for more than ten years. I daresay, when you get down to it, you'll find it downright embarrassing!"

"Not a chance," he said. "I could compose one between here and the junction and maybe I will!" and with that the train started and her hand flew to her mouth, and looking back he saw her standing against the open skyline of the grey landscape. It was confirmation, he thought, of the belief that had been gaining strength in him through all the years of their marriage. She and the Valley were one and could never be separated in his consciousness. There was comfort and a certain reassurance in the knowledge.

771

CHAPTER FIVE

I

THE first of them began to arrive early in the New Year, men wounded in the later stages of the Somme offensive, some having already spent up to four months in hospital and were now on the road to recovery, although about a third were permanently maimed in one way or another. These were the most cheerful. They had survived and could never be sent out again, whereas the more able-bodied lived in permanent fear of being reboarded fit for active service and were inclined to retard their own recovery, sometimes with Maureen's connivance.

At first there were only about a score of them but within weeks the Government sanctioned the erection of three Nissen wards in the small paddock on the right of the drive and thereafter the odd chronic case began to appear, including gas casualties, one or two who had lost limbs, and a few cases of shell-shock, men who sweated and trembled and dribbled and were sometimes sent off again to mental hospitals. By then a permanent Medical Officer had been allocated to Shallowford, together with three downgraded medical orderlies, themselves former casualties of 1914 fighting.

The weather that winter was cruel, with months of severe frost and several heavy falls of snow, so that, for the most part, the men remained indoors, some of them permanently in bed and it was this that compelled Claire to reorganise the staff almost as soon as it had been enrolled. She had not bargained for so many immobile casualties and the M.O. and his orderlies were fully occupied in the wards and could give no help in cooking, cleaning and organising recreational facilities. Doctor Maureen was equally busy, sometimes working an eighteen-hour day but she seemed to thrive on it and soon gained ascendancy over Captain Gleeson, the M.O., who had served with the Oxford and Bucks Light Infantry from Mons to the battle of Loos, and been invalided home with bronchitis in the autumn of 1915. Gleeson was a cheerful but irascible man who looked a little like a grizzled Father Christmas and could swear fluently in Hindustani. He was inclined, however, to take things easily, reckoning that at fifty-eight he had done his bit. He told Claire that only compassion kept him at his post for he had been on reserve when recalled in 1914. His three orderlies worked extremely hard for they were anxious to remain on home service but when, in early March, the number of patients rose to eighty-five the demands upon Claire, Mrs. Handcock, Thirza and the scratch team of dailies she had enlisted in the village became intolerable and she began a local recruiting drive that was met with immediate success.

Her first triumph was the enrolment of Marian Eveleigh, whom she managed to coax from communion with the spirits when everyone else, including Marian's exasperated husband, had given her up for lost.

The death of her eldest son and the fear of losing Harold, his brother, now commissioned and serving in the Near East, had brought Marian to the edge of a nervous breakdown and Eveleigh's uncharacteristic involvement with the land-girl Jill had coincided with her change in life so that the wretched woman's world had crumbled to pieces. She shut herself up for days on end in the boys' old bedroom where she was alleged to have established contact with a Red Indian spirit, who acted as intermediary between mother and son. Her daughters and the hired hands at Four Winds took it for granted that she was going the way of old Martin Codsall but Claire had known Marian all her life and remembered that she came from good, yeoman stock and was therefore not prepared to accept this verdict. In her initial approach she worked on the lines that, by taking service at the hospital, Marian could do something practical on behalf of her surviving son. She won her victory on the afternoon she persuaded Marian to call at Shallowford and meet some of the patients. One of them had served in Harold's battalion in France and from that day on the cloud that had been settling on Marian Eveleigh's mind began to disperse and she agreed to go to work in the kitchen. Doctor Maureen described her as a classic example of the value of occupational therapy, declaring that Claire had a natural gift for healing. She then urged her to try her luck on Elinor Codsall who, since the night of Gloria Pitts' assault, had stayed within the confines of Periwinkle and was said to be developing into a recluse. Elinor proved more stubborn. To Claire's first appeal to hand over the outdoor work to Old Matt, one of the biblical shepherds (who was the Valley stopgap these days) she advanced a flat refusal.

"They took my man Will an' then spread bliddy lies about me so they can vinish their war without my help!" she said. Claire was puzzled by her truculence, remembering her not so much as the wife of Will Codsall but as the shy daughter of old preacher Willoughby tending chickens at Deepdene and Elinor's casual use of the favourite male adjective in the Valley was an indication of the changes that had engulfed the Valley in the last two years. She persisted, however, pointing out that the wounded men at Shallowford were ex-comrades of Will and therefore entitled to her concern and when Elinor protested that she had young children to care for, in addition to thirteen-year-old Mark, Claire said that she might bring the toddlers to work with her each day and leave them in charge of Thirza, who had charge of the nursery for encumbered helpers. Elinor said she would think about it but when Claire artfully remarked that she looked years younger with short hair, and reminded her of when they were girls on neighbouring farms, the widow's surliness disappeared and she even shed a few reminiscent tears, brushing them away with the query, "What's to become of us all, Mrs. Craddock? That's what I'd like to know, what with the Squire gone too at his time o' life!", and Claire hiding a smile, made a mental note to write and tell Paul that at least one of his tenants had ceased to think of him as "Young Squire" and had already advanced him to his dotage.

Claire then enlisted the two Potter girls who grasped the opportunity to move within the orbit of eighty convalescent males, despite the fact that most of them were free with snapshots of wives and children. Time was pressing on the unmarried Potter sisters these days, for Cissie was thirty-three and Violet not much younger and although each could boast of a small spread of handsome, healthy children, neither could lay claim to a separation allowance or even a shared pension in respect of Jem, who had gone to his death unable to make up his mind which of them he would wed. As Violet put it to her sister, the night after Claire had offered them a pound a week each for a daily five-hour spell at the Big House, "Us'd better taake 'er up on it, Cis! Tiz reg'lar money and us dorn zeem to be gettin' far with the boys zince they shifted that dratted camp the t'other side o' the Valley!" to which Cissie replied, thoughtfully, "Aye, and us baint gettin' no younger neither, be us? They zay half the men downalong are short of a limb but they can't all be married, can 'em? Maybe tiz time us thought o' zettling down like Panse; after all, if theym took us'll get the pension, providin' us can get a pair of 'em to church, that is!"

774

And so they went and were soon in their element among the more cheerful and active of the patients and as more and more men arrived, and nearly half the women of the Valley were absorbed in shift work about the wards, kitchens and wash-house, they suggested to Claire that she signed on their sister Hazel, whose second child had been stillborn early in the New Year and whom they now described as "Uncommon low in sperrit on that account". It was a sharp reminder to Claire that she had not called on Hazel since she had lost her baby but before going along to Mill Cottage she consulted Maureen on the possible usefulness of Hazel on the staff. Maureen's response surprised her. She said, shortly, "Leave her be, she's not fit for any kind of work, although I daresay pottering about helping the sexton doesn't overtax her."

"Do you mean she's ill, that she hasn't recovered from losing her baby?" Claire asked but Maureen only sucked her lips, looked irritated and said grumpily, "Oh, she's well enough physically, and if I was asked for a professional opinion I should say her wits were sharper than they had ever been but having Ikey home for a long spell and then losing him again had a bad effect on the poor little wretch."

"Well, since you've told me that much you might as well tell me the rest," Claire said. "I should have thought working here might cheer her up. She'll be with other people all day."

"Not the kind of people we have here," Maureen said, "men lacking an arm or a leg and shell-shock cases! Hazel isn't a child any more. She was never really half-witted you know, just retarded and always, I thought, in a rather privileged way. For one thing time meant nothing to her. The months separating That Boy's visits were only days, perhaps even hours. She was never a prey to doubt, jealousy, or even fear of death in the way ordinary folk are bothered about these things. The fact is she's now beginning to grow up and could prove as much a shell-shock case as some of the lads yonder! Leave her be, Claire, I'll be responsible for her!" and with that Maureen rushed off on her rounds leaving Claire regretting that she had not found time to call at Mill Cottage the day Meg brought news that Ikey's daughter had been born dead shortly after his return to France. She resolved to go at the first opportunity but that night one batch of men left and another came in so that she was occupied every waking minute of the next two days. On the third day, as she was setting out, she met John Rudd trudging up the drive with news that put Hazel Palfrey out of mind. He reported, gloomily, that there had been a second rick fire during the night, this time at Deepdene, and that, following upon the first fire at High Coombe earlier in the week, it seemed probable that a pyromaniac was at large in the Valley.

II

John had had his suspicions after seeing the burned out ricks at High Coombe. He had a long experience of rick fires and this one, breaking out in the middle of the night after a week of drizzle, baffled him. Spontaneous combustion would have been preceded by smouldering and Hugh Derwent told him that he had passed the ricks only an hour before and would have certainly smelled smoke on such a windless evening. There were so many ways a stack could catch fire that John assumed that the outbreak was due to carelessness with cigarettes on the part of soldiers taking shelter there earlier in the day. When news came of a second fire, however, this time at Deepdene, he realised that it must be deliberate and made a report to the police, circulating all the farms in the Valley to keep a sharp lookout and report the presence of any stranger in the lanes and tracks after dark. No information came in but within forty-eight hours there had been two more outbreaks, one on the extreme boundary of Four Winds and another on the eastern edge of Hermitage. John recruited a patrol from the officer at the Nun's Bay camp and for a week or more no new outbreaks occurred. Then, in the first week of April, smoke was seen coming from a large stack of pitprops in the plantation beyond the badger slope north of the woods and this time evidence of kindling was discovered and there was a whiff of lamp oil about some of the half-burned billets. John was in the act of telephoning the police when Claire told him that Meg Potter was asking for him and had expressed a wish to say something of importance to "Squire's agent and the Lady Doctor".

"What the devil does she want with Maureen?" John demanded and then, a thought striking him, added, "I'll get her in any case, she's down at the lodge now."

They assembled, all four of them in the library, the old gypsy standing with her back to the door, arms folded, face impassive, like a queen receiving an embassy. She said, without preamble, "I can tell 'ee where to look for the rick-burner!" and when they exclaimed, went on, "I dorn say I *will* but I could! Providing us keeps it clear o' police an' foreigners!"

John said, sharply, "Look here, we can't promise anything of that kind! The matter has already been reported to police and the military. The whole damned place is up in uproar!" Then, when her expression did not change, "Is it one of the patients here? A shell-shock case?"

"No it baint!" Meg replied stubbornly, planting her sandalled feet widely apart as though to resist a combined onrush. "It's along o' my girl, Hazel!"

"Great God!" John exclaimed and Claire rose from her seat but Maureen sat still looking at the floor. "Are you certain of that? You've seen her at it?"

"Nay, I've not seen her," Meg said, "but tiz Hazel right enough. The point is, what'll become of her if the police learn of it? Will 'er be shut up, same as my boy Smut backalong?"

Maureen said: "Not in a prison, Meg, I could make certain of that!"

The gypsy turned, ignoring the others and said, "*Where* then? In one o' they asylums for mazed folk?"

"She'd have to be," John said, "you couldn't expect us to leave her free to do worse. Suppose she started setting fire to cottages with people asleep in them?"

"She'll not do that!" Meg replied grimly, "tiz just the ricks and handy kindling, like the props up yonder."

"How can you know that?" Claire asked and Meg said bluntly that she knew it well enough, implying that she had no intention of saying more than she could help.

"Listen Meg," Maureen said urgently, "suppose I could promise Hazel a course of expert treatment? I've got a friend in Bristol who runs a clinic. It isn't an asylum, or anything like an asylum. It's a place where they treat all kinds of people who have cracked under war-strain. I don't think this is a permanent derangement, it's linked to the girl's post-natal physical condition and maybe a sudden awareness of what's going on in the world. We'd get her well, given time."

"Damn it," protested John, "what proof have we anyway? To put the girl away we should have to catch her in the act, wouldn't we?"

"Has she admitted the facts to you, Meg?" Claire asked.

"No," said Meg, shrugging, "I've not spoken a word to her on the matter and neither will I, except maybe to warn her should you and Mr. Rudd set the police on her. I baint forgot what the police did to my boy backalong or the kind of place they kep' him shut up in for taking a deer and fightin' free o' Gilroy's men! Tiz like Mr. Rudd says, you've no proof and us'll zee you don't come by none!"

"Then why are you telling us?"

The gypsy shrugged. "Because you an' Squire always played straight with me an' mine!" she said and left it at that.

There was silence for a while. In a way, Claire thought, it was almost as if she was gloating over their impotence, yet if this had been so she would hardly have come here with information that her own daughter was a pyromaniac. She said at length, "The Doctor could go and talk to Hazel, then report back to the four of us. Would you do that, Maureen?"

"If it served any purpose," Maureen said, "but it wouldn't, I can tell you that."

"Why not?"

"Because, since her baby died, she doesn't trust me. I've tried talking to her, I've tried explaining about the war but it was easy enough to see she thought I was romancing. The only German she ever knew was the old Professor over at Coombe Bay. When I said Ikey was away fighting Germans she laughed in my face. She thinks of the Germans as a race of fat, wheezing professors, so it isn't surprising she finds it hard to believe Ikey and everyone else is fighting them. No, I could do something for her with Ikey's consent but she wouldn't admit anything to me."

"She might tell her mother," Claire said but the gypsy shook her head. "I've generally known what the girl is about but there's been no bond between us," she said. "In the old days I had to stand with Tamer, him being my man, and as for the others they stood together. But Hazel, she's different, she stood alone 'till The Boy took up with her and now tiz his concern I reckon."

"Could Ikey get special leave under these circumstances?" Claire asked John and John said he might, providing the facts were laid before the military authorities. Claire caught Meg's eye and said, "We won't break faith with you, Meg, not unless we have no alternative," and to Maureen: "Would it do any good if I tried to talk to her?"

"It might," Maureen said, "she always trusted the Squire, and you're Squire's deputy. Maybe, if you let her know that you know, fear of the consequences might stop the next rick going up. What do you say to that, John?"

John said, gloomily, "I'm hanged if I know. It would depend on whether Meg was prepared to back us, providing, that is, Claire extracted some kind of confession from the girl. If I'd known when I came in here that it wasn't a shell-shock patient I'm damned if I would have given half a promise to keep the police in ignorance for at least they could have kept a watch on the cottage. My duty has always been to the estate and it still is. I don't clutter myself with personal responsibility for everyone who lives on it!"

"No," Claire reminded him, "but Paul does so it seems to me I ought to try and put myself in his place. Would you agree as regards that?"

John blew out his cheeks and groped for his pipe. "Yes," he said reluctantly, "I suppose I'd have to agree to that. I've worked alongside the man fifteen years and flatter myself I know him that well. Go and see what you can do but if you run into trouble don't stay and handle it yourself, come straight back here for help!" He got up and went out, saying he would tell Chivers to bring the trap round to the front and Claire thought she had never seen him look so old and tired.

They had forgotten it was a Thursday, the day for the weekly war game over at the camp. Troops swarmed on the rising ground beyond the Four Winds' border, and the peace of the river road was shattered every now and again by a convoy of lorries, the ear-splitting rush of a despatch-rider's motor-cycle, or the passage of the big Crossley staff car that advertised its approach by a series of imperious honks. Claire cursed them one and all as she jogged along towards the cottage, for the noise and bustle put an additional strain on her nerves and the presence of transport here, where it had always been so quiet and changeless, underlined the fearful urgency of the war, as though a great bird of prey was beating its way up and down the Valley in search of fresh victims. She reined in beyond the ford to let the staff car rush by and did not answer the cheery wave of the officers in the back. The car disappeared in a cloud of exhaust towards Coombe Bay and she went on to the point where the lateral track joined the road beside the cottage, tethering the pony to the gatepost. In the garden she saw the child Patrick absorbed in the task of nailing pieces of wood together with a hammer that seemed almost as large as himself. She was struck not only by his neatness and cleanliness but also by his likeness to Ikey. There was little of the Potter stamp about his face or build for he was very slender, with a dark, slightly sallow complexion and sharp, intelligent eyes. He stood up when Claire asked him if his mother was in the cottage.

"Arr," he said, in the broad Valley burr. " 'Er's upstairs, ma'am.

779

Leastways, 'er was!" and then, with an unexpectedly engaging smile, "I'm making a nairyplane! I'm gonner fly in un when 'er's done!"

She had come without the least idea of how to approach the matter but now she saw that, with a little luck, she might use the child to win Hazel's confidence. She said, "If I sent my Simon over for you would you like to come up to the Big House and play with the twins? They're making aeroplanes too."

Patrick considered. He had, Claire thought, his father's charm as well as his polite but definite sense of privacy. "Arr," he said finally, "I'd like that! When will 'er come, then?"

"I don't know, I'll go and ask Mummy," Claire said and went into the cottage.

It was, she thought, very neat and clean. It seemed a lifetime since she had spied in at the window watching Paul read Ikey's letter aloud, her heart torn with jealousy, but today a different kind of confusion assailed her and she stood just inside the door, wondering where to begin. Everything in the room shone and twinkled in the afternoon sun and the hearth had been newly swept. It did not look like the home of a crazy woman who ran about the estate at night setting fire to ricks and the responsibility of her mission dragged at her so that, not for the first time since Paul had left, she was conscious of her own inadequacy to deal with problems of this kind, her uncertainty reminding her of his strange talent for administration. Every man, woman and child living in the Valley trusted him implicitly and he would have had such a headstart on an occasion such as this.

She went up the short stair and found Hazel sitting beside the window looking out across the stubble fields beyond the river. There was something birdlike about the way she sat perched on a milking stool, her knees and hands pressed tightly together, her expression not exactly tense but very alert. She said, as Claire entered, "Be'm still searching, then? I zee the soldiers go by just now," and Claire wondered if this remark was a defensive diversion, as though Hazel understood very well why she was here and was hoping to forestall interrogation. She said, gently, "I should like your boy to come over and play with my twins. If I send Simon over will you let him come? Tomorrow afternoon, say?"

"Arr," Hazel said, readily, "you could have un over to stay for a bit if youm minded, for I fret sometimes on account o' leavin' un alone o' nights. 'Er sleeps like a winter squirrel mind but if 'er did awake, to vind the plaace empty, I daresay he'd be lonesome!"

"You have to go out? Of a night?" Claire asked, and was dismayed to find herself trembling.

"Oh arr, sometimes," Hazel said cheerfully, "on account o' lighting they beacons. Tiz a praper ole nuisance but seein' theym all lost it has to be done, dorn it now?"

"Yes," Claire said, feeling her way step by step as one might descend an unfamiliar staircase in the dark, "I suppose it does, but does nobody ever help you light those beacons, Hazel?"

The girl looked sharply at her but then suspicion left her eyes and she smiled.

"Giddon no," she said, impatiently, "for there's no one can vind their way about in the dark like me! I'm accustomed to it, you zee. There baint no plaace yerabouts where you could lose *me*!"

It was her emphasis on the word "me" that gave Claire her first real clue and for a moment compassion choked her. She reached out and took the girl's hand. It was very soft, she thought, for a woman who had lived rough all her days and spent every morning in the church-yard helping the sexton dig graves and cut grass.

"How . . . how *long* have they been lost, Hazel?"

"Time enough," said Hazel briefly. "First one and then the other, and tiz puzzling, somehow. The Boy was lost first time I ever zeed him but he was a proper ole townee then, so there baint nothing sur-prising about *that*! Tiz the others losing theirselves that's queer — Henry Pitts, Will Codsall and young Gil Eveleigh, all reared in the Valley; and then Smut, that's queerest of all! Smut knew the plaace better'n any on account of the poaching he did from the time he was a tacker in the Dell! I should ha' thought Smut could have showed 'em the way home easy enough but 'er hasn't, zo it crossed my mind to zet light to they beacons. Tiz a rare pity there baint more ricks nearer the shore. If theym all across the water, like The Boy says, they won't zee the blaze unless theym looking for it!"

Suddenly it was very simple to understand, like a jigsaw puzzle when the centre pieces were assembled making a picture of what had been a jumble of torsos and severed heads. All the men of the Valley were lost and unable to find their way home again and the beacons were to guide them home. Claire said, releasing Hazel's hand, "Sup-pose I took the boy back to the Big House now? The twins would like someone to play with and my trap is just down the road. The lady doctor is coming too and I think she wants to talk to you. Could I take Patrick, if I promise I'll bring him back as soon as his Dad gets back?"

781

"Arr, you taake un," Hazel said, carelessly, and losing interest in the conversation resumed her scrutiny of the fields across the river.

Claire went downstairs, impatient with the tears blurring her vision and pausing for a moment in the living-room to absorb the terrible poignancy of the situation. Then, with relief, she was able to concentrate on the most urgent measure to be taken — the whisking away of the child outside, to a refuge where he would be secure in the company of her own children. She thought of other things too, what she would write to Ikey and Paul and how Maureen would find the words to persuade Hazel to abandon her vigil and quit the Valley for the first time in her life but she pushed these misgivings into the back of her mind and went swiftly out into the garden, telling the child that his mother wanted him to go to the Big House at once. He agreed eagerly enough and they went down the winding path to the river road hand in hand. As she closed the gate Claire looked up and saw the girl still sitting in the same crouched posture, looking out across the slope of the watershed between Sorrel and Teazel.

She was back within the hour with John and Maureen. The agent was more relieved than dismayed at her report and Maureen, having telephoned the Bristol hospital, suggested they should persuade Hazel to join her child in the Big House until arrangements could be made for her to be taken away. Neither seemed to think it would be difficult to coax the girl out of the Valley and, looking back on what happened with such appalling unpredictability Claire sometimes wondered if he exaggerated her own misgivings in this respect.

She went on alone, leaving John and Maureen in the lane but her return after such a short interval must have alerted Hazel, for when she suggested she should move out and join Patrick at the Big House the girl looked at her suspiciously and said, flatly, "For why? What would I do there, along o' they voreigners?"

"You could help me and your sisters," Claire reasoned, "we're nursing wounded soldiers now and some of them are friends of The Boy."

Hazel showed a flicker of interest. "Do they know where he be tu then?"

"We could ask them?"

Hazel considered a moment before rejecting the proposal. "If theym voreigners they'll be worser lost than the Valley men! I'll bide yer and look to the beacons!"

782

Claire hesitated whether to accept this for the time being and consult Maureen and then made what she later realised to be her fatal mistake. She said, trying to sound casual, "You mustn't light any more beacons, Hazel. It's better that you should stay up to the house, really it is!" and laid a hand on her shoulder. It might have been the touch, the strained expression in the eyes of the Squire's wife, or the sixth sense that had served Hazel throughout her wild life in the woods; whatever the cause she leaped back, throwing up her head like an animal scenting danger and gathering herself for flight. Before Claire could utter a word of reassurance she had dodged round her and dashed down the stairs and within seconds she reappeared on the flood barrier that served for a front garden on the river frontage. Claire's shout brought John Rudd running but Hazel spotted him before he had moved two strides and changing direction without checking her pace crossed the patch and leaped down on to the road, turning south for the edge of Dell Wood a hundred yards distant.

It had all happened so quickly and so inexplicably that Claire, although leaning far out of the bedroom window, did not even see the big Crossley staff car until it came swinging round the bend at full throttle. There was no time for the driver to brake or even to honk and car and running figure met head-on thirty yards from the gate. Claire saw the car swing right and then left in a long, twisting skid as Hazel, mounting the bonnet, was flung upwards and outwards, to pitch like a bundle of rags in the iris clump at the stream's edge.

Maureen and the driver were bending over her when she ran from the cottage and like the sound of a far-off bell submerged in the thunder of shock she heard herself crying, "Thank God the child wasn't here—thank God, thank God!", and after that images fused so that she had no more than a glimpse of men spilling out of the car and John Rudd, white and shaking, grasping her arm and saying, with a kind of pitiful emphasis, "You couldn't help it! It had to happen— something like this! Maybe it's better!", and although Claire understood quite well that he was only trying to mitigate her grief and horror she remembered his words in the days ahead and derived comfort from them.

There was nothing Maureen or anyone else could do beyond lifting the broken body into the car to be driven to the potting-shed behind the Nissen huts, a place that had already done duty as a temporary mortuary that year. Hazel must have been dead when she struck the ground for her neck was broken, as well as her right arm and several

783

ribs, but miraculously her face was almost unmarked and Maureen, sponging it clean and awaiting the arrival of the Camp Commandant and police, wondered at the curious serenity of expression reposing in the features of one who had died so suddenly and violently. She wept a little as she worked at straightening the clothes and tidying the hair, recalling her old affiliation with That Boy, who would have to be told by someone—not her, please God—that violent death was not the prerogative of young men in khaki. Perhaps Paul would come home and afterwards write, explaining as best he could that even this was preferable to shutting a wild creature like Hazel Potter behind walls and subjecting her, possibly for years, to the nameless indignities of the mentally deranged. There was the child to be thought of and mercifully he was young enough to be lied to until the memory of his mother grew dim. She supposed Claire would concern herself with Rumble Patrick and as she thought this she felt a terrible, choking pity for all of them—for Ikey, for Claire, for Paul, for the Valley wives and even for the miserable little Cockney driver of the car, who had whined in his thin nasal voice, "She come straight at me! Never giv' me a chance, not a chance!" Well, that was true enough and luckily for him there were witnesses to back him up, so that he, at any rate, was out of it. She would have trouble, she suspected, with John, who was sure to hold himself equally responsible with Claire but was any one of them to blame in the smallest degree? It was, at bedrock, simply a case of the world's present madness catching up with one of the few who had managed to keep ahead of it for so long. Looking down at the calm, blank face of the girl Maureen found her crumb of comfort in the reflection that, when all was said and done, Hazel Potter's life had been more fruitful, tranquil and rewarding than most.

III

It was ironic that, within days of Hazel Palfrey lighting her last beacon to bring the Valley wanderers home, two of the strays should make such dramatic reappearances, the one on Valley soil, the other two hundred miles to the east where the youth of Europe was entering upon its third successive summer in the trenches.

The camp despatch-rider carrying the findings of the court of inquiry and coroner's report on the accident actually crossed beneath the route of the first of these returning warriors, who came sailing in at a height of about eight hundred feet, pushing his S.E.5 biplane up

784

to its maximum of 120 m.p.h. as he swung into a following wind between the hills enclosing the two rivers. Then, to the delight and astonishment of every man, woman and child within running distance, the aircraft swooped down over the avenue chestnuts and went bump-bump-bump along the turf of the pig paddock to stop barely a hundred yards from the house.

They came scrambling from every direction, spilling out of the barns of the Home Farm, crowding from the stable-yard and tearing new gaps in half the hedges along Hermitage and Four Winds boundaries, all converging on the dapper, leather-jacketed young man who half-rolled from the cockpit and pushed up his goggles to shake hands with the first arrival. This happened to be old Horace Handcock who nearly choked with excitement when the S.E.5 (a machine that he alone in the Valley could identify) dipped over the rose garden and, according to his account told later in The Raven, "Dam' nearly knocked me bliddy 'at off!"

Few of those who crowded round the little machine, or reached to touch the smooth blades of its propeller, recognised the aviator. His snug helmet, heavy jacket and goggles gave him a Martian look and the nature of his arrival reinforced this notion. But Claire recognised him at once and told Thirza to take charge of the twins, who would have persuaded Simon to hoist them into the cockpit if they had not been held back. Claire remembered the young man's half-apologetic grin, and also a familiar smear of oil on his forehead, for Tod Glover, the Valley's first motor mechanic, had always worn a smear of grease on his face, carrying it like a trademark. When she pushed forward to greet him Claire recalled the occasion, years before, when Tod had rescued the family from the ignominy of being towed home in the Belsize. He was a fully-fledged pilot now, he told her, having completed his course at Montrose, in Scotland, and been transferred to a flying camp near Bristol. He had been there, he told his astonished audience, only an hour or so ago and would have to return at once but had decided to try a practise landing on home ground, having remembered that the paddock was the most level stretch this side of the river.

He stayed about half-an-hour, drinking tea (he refused alcohol) and munching a huge slice of Mrs. Handcock's plum cake and still they surrounded him like the figures in the engraving that hung in the bar of The Raven, entitled News of Waterloo. He had retained his Devon burr but few among them could recognise his slang and concluded

785

that, on taking to the air, these young men had been taught a new language. He apologised for his short stay but on taking off promised to loop-the-loop and the younger ones understood this well enough and hopped about with excitement, clutching one another and saying that Tod was going to perform the legendary feat right over big paddock and that if the war lasted long enough not one of them would enlist as a soldier but in the Royal Flying Corps, like Old Tod, where they could kill more Germans in two minutes than an infantryman killed in six months. As Tod shook them off, warning them to stand clear whilst he swung the propeller, Horace Handcock began a patriotic speech that might have lasted some time had it not been obliterated by the roar of the engine and a wind that carried his words away like dry beech leaves. Then, after a short, uncertain lurch across the turf, the S.E.5 was airborne and everybody stared at the sky as it gained speed and height, sweeping in a wide graceful circle round the fringe of Shallowford Woods and then shooting downwind as far as Codsall bridge. Tod kept his promise. Before heading off up the Valley he actually did loop-the-loop, not once but three times. The ecstatic sigh that arose from his audience was more prolonged than anything the Squire's rockets and set-pieces had produced at either of his Coronation displays. Then Tod and his trim little steed were a disappearing speck over Blackberry Moor and all that was left to remind the earthbound of his miraculous visitation were two streaks and a brown skid-mark on the turf. The twins looked at the scars reverently every day until they were obliterated by the boots of hospital patients passing to and from the Nissen huts. The patients, as a whole, did not share the Valley's enthusiasm for fliers. One private almost caused a riot in the bar of The Raven that same night by remarking, sourly, that "The bloody airmen had it cushy! They didn't have to face barrages and they slept under a roof every night!"

The return of the second Valley wanderer did not create such a sensation as the appearance of Tod Glover, for he was unable to make a personal appearance but news of his miraculous reappearance this side of Jordan was a nine-day wonder. Smut Potter—poacher, gaol-bird, horticulturist, and slayer of innumerable Germans, missing and believed killed during the early days of the Somme offensive, returned from the dead, seemingly none the worse for dying.

Smut had been given up for lost by everybody in the Valley except, possibly, by Meg who consulted the cards on the subject any number of times but had not turned up the ace or jack of spades, signifying death or mutilation. She was not much surprised, therefore, when an official letter arrived informing her that Smut had rejoined his unit and would be home on furlough in due course. This was followed, within a day or so, by a single sheet written in Smut's laborious scrawl, explaining that he had been taken prisoner in July last year but had escaped and holed up until he could rejoin the British field forces. Meg showed his letter to Horace and Horace showed it to John Rudd but neither of them could make very much of it for it sounded a very tame account from someone who had returned from the dead. It was, however, the simple truth and Smut himself was puzzled by the furore his reappearance caused in what remained of his battalion. He was interviewed by at least four intelligence officers, one of them a taciturn Red Cap whom Smut hated on sight. It was only when his own colonel interviewed him that the full story of Smut's survival emerged, and was copied into the regimental record, forming the basis of several newspaper articles, one of which Smut read but understandably failed to recognise himself as the hero.

His odyssey began ordinarily enough. On July 2nd, 1916, together with a wounded lieutenant and about a dozen other men, he was overrun in a shell-hole during a counter-attack. Smut, whose blood was up, was for fighting it out but luckily for the other men in the pocket the lieutenant decided to surrender when ammunition ran low. They were not murdered out of hand, as Smut rather thought they might be but were employed as stretcher-bearers until there was a lull and afterwards marched to a ruined farm behind Péronne. They were lightly guarded and Smut could have left the column without difficulty but he was tired, hungry and in no physical shape to attempt the feat of threading his way through the fluid German positions. An opportunity occurred, however, later in the day, when a large number of prisoners were packed into a large farmyard and dusk came down before they were recounted. On one side of the yard was a vast midden heap and near it Smut found a length of lead piping from a shattered pump. The pipe reminded him of an occasion, long ago, when he had given Gilroy's gamekeepers the slip by taking to a pond and breathing through a long reed while his pursuers beat a patch of marsh without flushing him out. His chum, "Dinty" Moore, to whom he confided his plan, was sceptical of burrowing into the midden and using the pipe in the way Smut had once used the reed.

"I'd as lief spend the rest o' me bloody life behind wire as lay up in that stinking mush!" Dinty said but Smut, who had spent three and a half years behind bars, valued freedom more highly and was soon deep in the midden, his pipe projecting a few inches above the wall.

He lay there until he was half suffocated but the plan worked. As soon as the men were marched away he had no difficulty in emerging and walking unchallenged into the eastern outskirts of Péronne. By the time he got there, however, he was near the end of his tether. Forty-eight hours had passed since he had eaten his iron rations in the shell-hole and although by no means a fastidious man the stench he carried with him was enough to overpower a man travelling on an empty stomach. There was a shaded light at the back of the first house he reached, a tumbledown building with a large, stone-built barn abutting on to the street. Smut hesitated outside the half-open door wondering whether he should risk foraging for something to eat and perhaps lie up during daylight hours after making shift to remove traces of his sojourn in the manure heap. He was incredibly lucky. As he stood there, trying to make up his mind, he was assailed by a delicious smell of freshly-baked bread so that he pushed open the door and walked in, coming face to face with the baker, a handsome, statuesque woman of about forty, who might have weighed around eighteen stone. She came out of the inner bakery, stared at him in the dim light issuing from the open door, gave one or two long sniffs and then recoiled, as from a fiend of the pit but the smell of baking bread had now overcome the last of Smut's reservations and he followed her up, closing the door and announcing himself as a British soldier on the run. Thus began an association that was to last a lifetime and form the starting point of his miraculous return from the dead.

The woman was a Fleming called Marie Viriot and had been widowed twice, once by a sack of flour that fell on her first husband and broke his neck, and later by the Germans, when Monsieur Viriot was killed in the Ardennes offensive. She was now struggling to run her business in territory that had been occupied by the enemy since the first weeks of the war and her unremitting hatred of the Boche stemmed more from their innumerable petty restrictions than from the fact that they had killed Sergeant Viriot in 1914. She was a vigorous, affable woman, with a loud, neighing laugh and her sense of humour, dormant for so long, was revived by the appearance of Smut standing in her bakery steaming in the heat of the oven and giving off the acrid stench of a neglected farmyard. In her youth she had been a waitress in an Ostend teashop that catered for tourists and her quick

788

mind had picked up a working knowledge of English. Smut's estaminet French was better than average so that they were able to converse freely almost from the start. They took to one another at once. Both Madame's husbands had been short, stocky men of Smut's build and after he had stripped and washed in her presence, and she had fed him on hot bread and thin vegetable soup she had made her decision.

"You stay vile I brebare the bapers of my sister's husband, Jules!" she announced, in her thick Flemish accent. "Then you vill work until the poilus return to cut the Boche into bieces!"

It was not until several days later, when she dragged him from hiding in the flour store and brandished a set of papers half-covered with official stamps that he understood his refuge was to be permanent. Madame Viriot's brother-in-law, it seemed, had decamped shortly after the Germans arrived in the district and had left his identity papers behind, together with wife and family, who afterwards obtained permission to go south to other relatives. In a strictly rationed area like Péronne Madame Viriot exercised considerable influence in official circles and it had been a simple matter to bribe civil authorities into converting Smut into the absent Jules Barnard. When Smut protested that his French was unequal to so great a strain Madame Viriot said, disdainfully, "Poof! Jules was half the idiot! I shall give out that he has returned from the war all the idiot!", and thereafter she coached her protégé to such good effect that Smut was able to move about quite freely, indulging a hopeless stammer, a distressing twitch and a mild, cherubic grin. He rather enjoyed the charade and in any case was glad of a rest after more than twenty months in and out of the line. His obligations in the bakery by day were not as exacting as those by night, in Madame's vast, canopied bed, for Marie Viriot, husbandless for two years, was a virile woman and used her stray Tommy with an energy and dexterity that Smut found astonishing in one so ponderously built. He did not mind, however. He was well-fed and well-housed and when he was not at work derived a good deal of pleasure from watching the enemy's second-line troops sweat and bustle in their efforts to withstand the interminable British pressure on the Somme. By the time the attacks had petered out he was accepted everywhere as a bonafide French idiot and could walk about the town without much risk, under cover of his distressing stammer and carefully cultivated twitch. He soon reverted to his wartime trade and brought home a variety of carelessly guarded trifles. He collected information too of a sort, the names and numerals of German drafts passing through to the front, the type of transport used to shift stores and ammunition and the approximate location of ammunition dumps and long-range howitzer batteries, more than enough to have got him shot had he shown more diligence as secret agent. He was happy enough, save for occasional bouts of homesickness. The monotonous, featureless landscape around Péronne, he decided, must have been depressing in peace-time but war had converted it into a half-rural, half-industrial slum, housing a sullen population harassed by German regulations and fear of death from air-raids and the long-range shelling. Once, early in the new year, he gave expression to his disgust for the French provinces, telling Marie that, après le guerre, she would do well to sell up and take refuge across the Channel where trees sometimes grew and occasionally the sun shone for a week at a time. He was startled by her reaction to this innocent remark. She bounced at him, held him firmly by the ears, planted kisses on both cheeks and exclaimed, rapturously, "It iss the brobosal of marriage you make! I accept! We will go to your native place and establish ourselves as pastry cooks! Did not the fortune-teller in Bruges tell me I should haf the three husbands but no little ones? Come now! Embrace Marie, Tommy!", and she crushed him to her buttressed bosom while outside the thin, slanted rain fell and fell, and limbers moving up to the front passed in endless procession.

Early in March rumours began to circulate of an imminent German withdrawal to a new line many miles to the east and soon afterwards all able-bodied civilians within the requisite age limit were faced with a choice of going into hiding or being forcibly evacuated. It was time, Marie announced, for Jules Barnard to disappear again so Smut was salted away in the flour store once more, remaining there while the town emptied He had, by now, a very high opinion of Marie's ingenuity and naturally expected her to evade the evacuation order. But at the last minute something must have gone wrong for she suddenly appeared in his hideout with news that she was being moved to Lille and that a demolition squad would blow up the bakery at six o'clock the following morning. She did not seem to resent the wanton destruction of her property so much as her enforced separation from Smut, declaring that the French Government would be obliged to pay her compensation after the war and that she had already made out the bill. She made him memorise her new address and gave him back his uniform, which had been boiled, mended, and pressed against the day of liberation. She then issued final instructions, telling him to convert

790

the flour store into a bomb-proof dugout, strong enough to resist the blowing up of the adjacent bakery and to be sure to write to her through the Red Cross as soon as he was free. If he failed in this respect, she said, she would hunt him down wherever he was, commencing the day the war ended.

The big bang came precisely at six a.m. and for a few minutes it seemed to Smut that Marie Viriot would be widowed a third time. The plaster ceiling of the store descended in an almost solid mass and only five layers of flour-sacks, reinforced by a girder, saved him from being buried alive. He poked a small hole through the debris but remained hidden all that day and the following night. Early on the second day he heard what he recognised as the sound of cheering and donning his uniform made his way across the ruins of the bakery to the street. By that time it took a great deal to excite Smut but he was more stirred by what he saw in Péronne that morning than by any experience that had come his way in the past. The advancing allied troops were Highlanders and they came swinging into the town to the bagpipe strains of "Scotland the Brave". Smut was still capering with excitement and cheering himself hoarse when he was arrested by two Red Caps as a deserter and clapped in the lock-up to await interrogation. After that it seemed to him that he told his story approximately five hundred times but in due course he was welcomed back to the rump of his unit. It was, he noted sadly, full of strangers. Only the adjutant, one former lieutenant now a captain and five men of his original company recognised him. All the others had been killed or wounded in the last ten months. The adjutant, however, was delighted to see him and promised to recommend him for a Military Medal on the strength of his experiences. He also re-enlisted Smut as his personal servant. He had had a string of servants since the previous July and had mourned Smut every time one of them returned from Battalion H.Q. with nothing but demands for returns on how many tins of plum jam had been consumed during the last ten days or what instructions were being given the men on keeping their feet dry. Smut had never bothered with this kind of thing but he had seldom returned without a bottle of whisky or a pound of candles.

IV

The day he received Franz's letter, telling him that he was now a sleeping partner in a firm producing grenades, pistol ammunition and

791

other familiar articles, Paul had just returned from a night haul up to the support lines, behind Messines. He read the letter carefully, partly because its unconscious irony fascinated him but also to make quite sure that Franz had no commercial links with heavy pumping equipment, for that, Paul decided, would have been too grotesque. He had now been hauling pumping equipment up to Messines on thirty-five consecutive nights and had been strafed every night but two, when they had to turn back owing to traffic jams.

Paul's section had been assigned to the group of Engineers responsible for the fabulous mine-galleries running directly under the ridge, mines that promised to provide the loudest bang since the beginning of time and blast away a whole section of the high ground from which the Germans dominated the area, pin-pointing every cross-road and trench junction, every artillery position and, or so it seemed to the Transport men, every yard of pavé over which they moved. He had been in this sector ever since he had arrived in France in January and he already knew it as well, or better, than he knew the Sorrel Valley. It was a landscape that fascinated him, perhaps because, for so long now, he had been preoccupied with landscapes. The starkness and emptiness of this one was so awful that it sometimes took on a kind of beauty, like engravings of Blake that he remembered having seen in one of the books left behind by the unknown Lovell who had a taste for art. It was not a merely tortured landscape where nothing grew and not a single building of any kind remained whole; neither was it a lifeless landscape for over it, at widely-spaced intervals, little figures crawled and motor and horse transport moved at funeral pace. But for all the unlikely symmetry of some of the ruins and the presence of half-a-million human beings, it had a kind of bloated emptiness, like the mottled remains of a half-eaten crab stranded above the Coombe Bay tide-line and everything that crossed it was contaminated by its foulness, its utter and stupid uselessness. At all events this seemed to be so, until one stumbled across groups of men in dugouts or billets. Then, hearing them laugh or cough, or noting their watchful eyes and cumbersome movements, Paul discovered by degrees that many of them seemed to have found fulfilment in their troglodyte lives here and in the terrible intensity of their personal experiences during their spells up the line or in one or other of the offensives. They had acquired, almost incidentally, the maturity he had been seeking so long in the Valley and their communal life presented the kind of perfection he had been striving to create in the community of the estate

but without getting anywhere near the ideal of comradeship and inter-
dependence of this array of clerks, labourers, factory workers and
schoolboy officers, in their faded, mud-stained tunics and clay-caked
boots and puttees. It was this sense of discovery and his absorption
into the fellowship that converted Paul's initial pessimism into a secret
optimism, an optimism that grew a little every day as he moved to and
fro across the lunar landscape for it seemed to him that, if this almost
holy relationship between Englishman and Englishman survived the
war, no obstacle likely to be met with in peace could defeat or discourage him. Had it not been for this Franz's letter would have made
him sick with shame.

The old man had not intended to sound so cynical. His letter, in
essence, was no more than a business bulletin informing a shareholder
that the firm was doing well under the current demand for scrap and
the end products of scrap. Paul remembered that even in a sideshow
like the Boer War, Franz and his father had made modest fortunes so
that it was surely inevitable that ten such fortunes could be wrung
from Armageddon. He was also sufficiently balanced to appreciate that
his instinctive disgust on hearing that he personally was profiting from
the war was frivolous and emotional. A British shell shortage would
spell defeat and defeat in the field would almost certainly entail the
loss of another half-million lives, even if its ultimate consequences
were not as terrifying as prophesied in Fleet Street. He looked at the
final page of the letter again and re-read the old rascal's tailpiece, this
time with a sour smile, Franz ended — "*So keep your head low, my dear
boy, and every time one comes over inviting a Teutonic response remember
it means another threehalfpence, to your credit, another droplet to pour
into that bottomless pit of yours in the West!*"

By the same mail there was a letter from James Grenfell explaining
at some length why he had sided with Asquith in the recent Lloyd
George coup that had ousted the great patrician and split the Liberal
Party from top to bottom. The seizure of power by the Welsh Wizard
had occurred when Paul was still in England and had seemed an event
of enormous significance but out here it was very small beer, and
although he sympathised with James, who was appalled by the ruin of
his beloved party, Paul found it difficult to concentrate on the closely
written pages of his old friend. James rambled on about loyalty and
integrity, of the importance of holding the Asquith group together
against the days of reconstruction and then covered a page railing
against the intrigues of public figures like Northcliffe but over here,

793

where men were being killed at the rate of about twelve thousand a day, the quarrels of politicians crossed the Channel as the echoes of kindergarten squabbles and if soldiers heard them at all they dismissed them as the prerogative of "The Frocks"!

He put James' letter aside half-read and opened Claire's, the one he had been saving, as he might have saved the icing on a rather soggy cake. It was, he soon saw, one of her cheerful, gossipy letters which disappointed him but he paid it the compliment of close attention and although its content was even more trivial than Grenfell's it held his interest. She pattered on for several pages; there were now one hundred and four patients at Shallowford; a new attempt on the part of the forestry pirates to throw Shallowford beeches had been frustrated; there had been an outbreak of fire at the camp at Nun's Bay; the twins, little traitors, had succumbed to German measles but so far Mary, Whiz and Ikey's boy had escaped; and so on, down to the bottom of the last page, where, in a postscript dated the following day, lay the promise of a real letter in the near future, for Claire had written: "*This is only a hotpotch dearest—jottings I might forget if I didn't set them down between times and even this has been two days in writing! I do miss you so. I'll explain how and why as soon as I get an hour alone late at night, when I can re-read your last letter in the library before going to bed. And talking of bed let's hope only the enclosed kind of letter is read by censors (are you quite sure you are right about officers' mail arriving uncensored?) because, although I can write shamelessly once I've locked the door I must admit to a blush or two when I get the kind of reply sparked off by the one I wrote last week! Good-bye for a little while, Paul darling, your ever loving, ever yearning Claire.*"

The postscript pleased him and he sat thinking awhile on her strange and, to him, unexpected skill as a writer of love-letters. They came, perhaps, once a fortnight, spaced by two or three gossipy bulletins such as the one he had just received and each time he received one he marvelled at the range and freedom of her self-expression, reflecting how much their relationship had matured in the last few years, particularly since their quarrel over that idiot at the camp and her crazy suspicions regarding Hazel Palfrey. He remembered the Claire Derwent he had met and flirted with when he first arrived in the Valley, a pert and rather vain nineteen-year-old, without a thought in her head beyond hunting and dancing and catching a husband who would spoil her on account of her red mouth and corn-coloured hair. How much of the present Claire had existed when they

794

met and how much was the fruit of the fulfilment she had found in children and her leading social position in the Valley? He took out her last, intimate letter and read it for the twentieth time, astonished to find that it produced the same excitement it had stirred in him when he first received it before going up the line on the night his friend Guy Manners had been blown to bits at Vesuvius Cutting. It was fortunate that he had had her letter to take his mind off death during the twenty-four hours that followed, for out here the memory of friends' voices and faces was short and Guy was almost forgotten in a matter of days. He now re-read the letter as if it proclaimed some extraordinary dazzling feat on his part, something that was still able to inspire him with almost unlimited confidence in himself and this was understandable, for his pride had never completely recovered from the wound inflicted by Grace's rejection of him. "*Oh my darling,*" she wrote, in that clear, rounded fist of hers that recalled the pages of the estate diary, "*I feel so desolate when I am alone at night in here and when, after torturing myself with longing, I go upstairs to invite an even more intense yearning by seeing your things about the room. Then I tell myself I ought not to be miserable, not really, when I remember the wonderful years we've had, and the years that I know with absolute certainty we shall have again! And the odd thing is this reassurance does seem to work, perhaps because I have such sharp and sweet memories of your love in this room right back to the day you brought me here. So, when I've locked the door, I am yours again, as completely as if you were sitting on the side of the bed tugging off those long boots (which I keep oiled because Chivers thinks of them as just boots) watching me undress and sometimes being tiresome about letting my hair down, so that it wastes a half-hour in the morning getting it presentable again! Dear God, Paul how I enjoy being a wife to you and basking in your admiration at times like that. I swear to myself that I shall more than make up for every minute we're missing! I like to think we have enjoyed each other far more than most married couples but I think I can still surprise you a little! I mean to try anyhow! I won't ever hold anything back when you take me in your arms again. What I mean is, I'll do and say everything that comes into my head no matter how abandoned it is! I shall say how I revel in your male gentleness and even more in your male roughness and occasional impatience, which you might be surprised to learn I find rather flattering after sharing a bed with you for — wait, I'm counting! — twenty-one days short of ten years! Good night my darling; I feel so much better for writing this and if you don't mind having such frightfully immodest letters from a*
795

woman old enough to know better I'll write another every time I feel desperate!"

It seemed to him a wonderful thing that he should have been capable of inspiring a letter like that and it crossed his mind, musing on it once again, that he might have Grace Lovell to thank for it. Looking back he realised now how raw and ingenuous he had been as a lover when he and Grace had honeymooned in Paris at the beginning of the Edwardian era, a time when only a street-walker dared admit to a knowledge of the art of love, when complete ignorance of all physical aspects of marriage was a bride's (and often a groom's) title to respectability. It had been Grace and no one else who had taught him what little he knew of women. Because of her Claire had been spared the painful, clumsy initiation reserved for the majority of young wives. Yet, she could surely take some credit to herself for the success of their marriage, for all she had needed from the outset was his frank admiration of her body and she had brought to their relationship a prevailing sense of humour that was strange in a daughter of a glum old stick like Edward Derwent.

It was because his thoughts turned to Grace more than once that day that the encounter on the road up to Messines thirty-six hours later made such a profound impression upon him. Pot-bellied old General Plumer, probably the only high-ranking officer in the Salient who enjoyed the respect of his troops, blew his famous mines early that morning and their effect was as devastating as his chief-of-staff, Harington, had promised. The roar that accompanied the detonation of the nineteen undiscovered galleries under Messines sounded like the crack of doom and news filtered back that the attack had been a triumph, the first wave of troops walking over with virtually no opposition, for the German trenches opposite were a shambles. Paul realised this when he saw some of the gibbering survivors that afternoon, and although he pitied them he felt more optimistic about the war than he had felt for years. If it was ever to end, he told himself, then this was surely the way to wage it and the mere trickle of British wounded, compared to the flood that had accompanied every other push, was corroboration.

He went up the line that night with a convoy of corrugated iron for revetting the captured trenches. The outward journey was less eventful than any he had made since his arrival in the sector, and it was a quiet, windless dawn when he started back and became snarled up in a traffic jam two miles short of the dump. An ambulance, heading in

796

the opposite direction, had swerved off the road and become bogged down on the edge of a flooded shell-hole and he sat watching as a party of pioneers attached a cable to the ditched vehicle in an attempt to drag it back on the road. Then, as he half dozed, he seemed to have had a particularly vivid dream for there was something familiar about the slim, uniformed W.A.A.C., obviously the ambulance driver, who stood nonchalantly by the running board of the pioneers' lorry smoking a cigarette.

She looked, he thought, more like a boy than a woman in her laced-up boots and loose-fitting trench coat. She did not appear much concerned over the fate of her vehicle but rested her weight on the spare tyre of the lorry, inhaling deeply and letting the smoke trickle from her nose. Then he shook himself awake with a shout of amazement; the W.A.A.C. was Grace whom he had last seen after her hectic involvement in the House of Commons riot six years ago and although he knew this with complete certainty he was so amazed by her presence there that, for almost a minute, he stood half in half out of his lorry before shaking himself, jumping down and squelching across the slimed pavé to greet her in a voice hoarse and cracked with emotion. "*Grace!* It *is* you! It's you, by God!", and for some reason that he found difficult to himself to explain, he felt a tremendous surge of exhilaration as he seized both her hands and pumped them up and down so energetically that the cigarette fell from her lips and some of the pioneers, hearing him shout, looked up from their work to stare at them.

She did not seem to be so surprised as he but her eyes lit up and she smiled, slowly, almost sleepily, so that he noticed she was not only dog tired but also that she must have lost two stones since their last meeting. Her dark hair, crammed under the ungainly cap, had been cut short and there were flecks of grey over the temples. He had always thought of her as rather stocky and well-made, particularly about the shoulders but now she seemed so slim and fragile that, despite the few grey hairs and the circles under her eyes, she looked younger and infinitely more vulnerable than he recalled. He groped for his cigarettes and offered her one, noting that her hand shook a little as she put it to her lips. She said, in the low, controlled voice that was the only thing about her unchanged, "I heard you were out, Paul. Uncle Franz wrote and told me about a month ago but it's a bore that you've caught me at such a disadvantage! I'm not usually this inefficient, it was a bloody staff car hogging the centre of the road. It

797

would have been all the same if I'd been loaded with abdominals, blast them! However, what can you expect from red-tabs? Everyone is expected to make way for them, even the poor devils they've fed into the Mincing Machine!"

He was struck by the bitterness of her voice and also by the terrible exhaustion it expressed, as though the effort of greeting him made substantial demands on her vitality.

"Franz never told me you were out here!" Paul said, indignantly, "I thought you were nursing in London."

"I was," she told him, "but when I discovered women handle authority even more despotically than men I got a transfer! It was either that or braining the matron with a bed-pan! How long have you been out?"

Only three months, he told her, so apologetically that she laughed and said, "Well, don't sound so bloody humble about it! After all, you're rising forty now and I daresay you could have dodged the column easily enough!" Then she looked at him rather pensively, adding, "You wouldn't tho', would you? You were always a glutton for punishment!"

"Damn it, so were you!" he laughed. "At least I enjoyed creature comforts when they were available! Look here, let me get some of my chaps to work on that crate of yours, those bloody pioneers will be fiddling about until Jerry drops something heavy on us!" and he shouted to his sergeant and walked over to supervise the salvage operations while she continued to watch, standing with her legs squarely apart, still dribbling smoke through her nose.

The ambulance was hauled clear at last, not before time for a range-finder crumped down in a field about three hundred yards to the west. Drivers in both halted columns began to hoot and shout ribald advice, and in the resultant flurry he almost lost her, for she scrambled into the driving seat and addressed herself to the controls while Paul's sergeant swung the starting handle, beaming with relief when the engine coughed and ticked over. Paul ran round to the off-side just as the column began to move.

"Where can I get in touch with you? Let's have dinner some where?"

She called over her shoulder, "Base hospital, I'm free tonight, six until midnight! Ask for Driver Lovell!"

She reversed expertly across the road and then edged away leaving him to scramble back into his lorry and move off in the opposite

798

direction. He was heady with excitement, reflecting, as they nosed down the road to the dump, "By God, but she's a remarkable woman! I don't think I ever realised how remarkable!" And then he pondered the startling changes in her looks and manner, neither of which, he felt, could be wholly explained by her occupation and drab uniform, for notwithstanding her almost insane embroilment in The Cause, he had always thought of her as all woman and now she was four-fifths male and as tough and embittered as the hardiest trench veteran. She was also, he thought soberly, near the end of her tether, used up, physically and spiritually but sticking it out in the way most of the men were sticking it, fortified to some extent by the mystic comradeship of the Western Front.

V

She succeeded in surprising him again that night after he had picked her up at the hospital transport depot and driven her into Béthune in the Douglas motor-cycle combination he had scrounged. She had changed her uniform and used a little lipstick and powder and the grey hair above her ears must have been camouflaged in some way for the tendrils that strayed below the rim of her cap were now as dark and curling as he remembered. She seemed also to have performed the miracle of developing a small bust during the day and was at least half a woman again but she did not seem to mind when he referred jokingly to this startling recapture, saying, carelessly, "Well, it isn't every night one is taken out to dinner by an ex-husband! Other men will be there and I wouldn't like them to think you were that hard up for a girl!"

He found her surprisingly relaxed and easy to talk with, as though they were not an estranged husband and wife, who had been parted for twelve years, but a couple of old friends who occasionally spent an evening together. While they were waiting to give their order she said, looking round at tables occupied exclusively by officers and nurses from Advanced Base Hospital, "It's almost a club, isn't it? Entrance fee a hole in you somewhere, or the permanent shakes!"

"You used to be just as hard on politicians," he reminded her, laughing. "Have you shifted your sights to the General Staff?"

"Oh no," she said, "I'm not murderous about anyone any more; I was, when I first came out and drove wounded back after the Loos fiasco but not now. It's got 'way beyond anyone's control! The politicians lost their grip years ago and even at H.Q. the old ex-cavalry Has-beens are the prisoners of their own inadequacies. You might say

799

I've succeeded in reversing the Bourbon outlook – I've forgotten everything and am learning all the time."

Paul realised that he was enjoying her society for the first time since their relationship had fallen foul of Roddy Rudd's motor-car, just before she ran away. "I can understand what you've forgotten," he said, recalling the free-for-all in Westminster Yard in Coronation week, "but what exactly have you learned?"

"Compassion," she said simply, "and enormous admiration for the guts and patience of the underprivileged. Many other things of course but those in particular." She spoke now, he thought, more as a Socialist than as a suffragette, and he asked her what she thought about the revolution in Russia. Did it mean there was a possibility of world revolution before all the licensed killing was done?

"That's difficult to prophesy," she said, "it depends on the breaking strain of us, the French, and even poor old Fritz over there. Big changes are already occurring in the European social structures but if we can adapt ourselves to this we can probably evolve some kind of compromise when it's over – providing the peace is reasonably merciful whichever side impose it!"

She talked easily of all kinds of things arising out of political, social, industrial and even strategic problems and he was impressed not only by her width of vision and lucidity, but also by her tolerance that seemed even to enfold men who had flung her into gaol and forcibly fed her not once but many times. He was shocked by his own political ignorance and by the relative fatuity of the theorists, professionals like poor old Grenfell struggling with his conscience at home.

"You've changed tremendously, Grace," he told her, "I don't think I'd ever have the impudence to quarrel with you again," and she laughed, her old, musical laugh and replied, "You aren't obliged to, you've got a new wife to dominate!"

"I never came anywhere near dominating you," he protested, "and I can't ever recall trying!"

"No," she said, seriously, "I only meant that as a joke. The one real regret I've had about it is that I hurt you so badly at the time but even that regret is qualified."

"How do you mean, 'qualified'?"

"Well," she said, "I imagine you got a much better wife out of it all and certainly more lasting happiness. One only has to look at you to discover that! You are very happy with Claire, aren't you? All my informants tell me so."

When she moved from politics and world affairs to human relationships her certainty abandoned her, exposing a slightly naïve facet of her compact personality, and through this chink in her assurance he realised that she had deliberately understated her feelings of guilt about him and was trying to convince herself that subsequent events exonerated her. It moved him a little that she should find this necessary after so many years and after witnessing so much real suffering at uncomfortably close range. He said, quickly, "What happened was best for both of us, Grace, I don't bear any malice and never have, at least, not since I remarried. Yes, I am happy with Claire, happier than I deserve in the circumstances but if it's any comfort to you I can remind you of two things. One—it was you who virtually threw her at me and two—well, I don't imagine I could have succeeded anything like so well in a second marriage if you hadn't taught me how to treat a woman in and out of bed!"

"Did I do that?" she said, genuinely astonished but he could see that she was flattered all the same.

"You certainly did!" and acting on a sudden impulse he did a strange thing, tugging out his wallet, extracting the most thumbed of Claire's letters and pushing it across the table. "You'll probably think I'm only being amiable by admitting that," he went on, hurriedly, "so there's proof of it! Go ahead, read that last page!"

"But it's a letter from her?"

"Yes but read it, or skim it if you like. I want you to!"

"Are you sure?"

"Quite sure. I owe you that!"

She took the folded sheets from the envelope and smoothed them out on the table, turning over the first three pages and glancing at the final page with unconcealed curiosity. The girl came with coffee and cognac but she did not look up although she was careful to shade the letter with her hand. Watching her he saw colour flood her cheeks and only then realised how parchment pale they were, not with the attractively smooth waxiness of the old days but a dry tautness that puckered the skin under the eyes and somehow deprived the face of width. Seeing her flush like that he felt a sudden tenderness for her. She seemed so small, lonely and desperate, so hopelessly inadequate to the fearful demands made upon her strength. She said, returning the letter, "Don't ever be such an idiot as to tell Claire you showed me this, Paul! Ordinarily it would have been unforgivable but I can understand what made you do it and it was very generous on your

801

part! She's lucky and you're lucky! I do remember telling you that what she quotes here is the basis of every successful marriage and it was obviously one of the less fanciful theories I had and still have! You've found something rare and precious, so hang on to it all your life! But I don't have to tell you that, do I?"

"No," he said, "I value it and so does Claire although I could never be absolutely sure of that until I came out here. We never put it to the test, I suppose,"

"Oh," she said, smiling as the colour in her cheeks faded, "that's rubbish! She's woman enough to have valued it from the beginning for I do remember that much about her! 'Ripe' was the adjective I used, I believe, and you plucked her at the right time judging by that letter! I suppose you carry a photograph?"

He showed her snapshots taken with Simon's box camera, pictures of Claire alone and members of the family individually and as a group. He noticed that she studied the one of Simon intently but unemotionally.

"Is he troublesome, like his mother?" she wanted to know and Paul said no, not troublesome but far more introspective than the twins and even more sensitive to reproof than the six-year-old Mary.

"He'll be thirteen now. Have you any plans for him?"

"No," Paul told her, "except that he's bright enough to go on to 'Varsity if he wants to. He has your passion for facts and your wonderful memory. He's very good at history and writes a good essay, I'm told." Then, seeing that she was interested, "Look here, Grace, Claire isn't the least bit inclined to jealousy. When you get leave why don't you run down and see him? Or, if that would embarrass you, why don't you have him to stay? He knows all the essentials about what happened."

"Not quite all," she said, "and neither, for that matter, do you. Anyway, I don't take my leaves at home, I use them to practise my other occupation."

"What on earth is that?"

She looked at him steadily. "Saluting men who are about to die," she said. "Youngsters mostly, some of them young enough to shock you but all young enough to need a little mothering."

He was not shocked or even embarrassed. Somehow it was precisely what he would have expected of her essentially generous nature. "I don't write them Claire's kind of letter afterwards," she went on, smiling, "but if I'm honest I get as much out of giving as they do taking and sometimes more! It keeps me sane, anyway."

"Damn it," he burst out, "you've been out here far too long! Why the hell don't you apply for a rest? They can't keep you the way they can us."

"I'll rest when it's all over," she said, "or maybe before, if I'm unlucky. In the meantime I get satisfaction from the thought that at last I'm of real use to someone," and as though she did not wish to prolong the discussion she stood up and crammed on her ugly cap. "Come on," she said, "if I don't show up one of the kids will be hauled out of bed to drive my ambulance," and marched out, leaving him to pay the bill.

When he regained the street she was sitting in the sidecar and the engine was warming up. He said, stuffing the change into his pocket, "How are you off for money, Grace? If you wanted any I hope you'd have the sense to ask for it."

"Now what," she said, "can a woman buy out here? There's nothing worth having in the few shops that are open and no shortage of escorts with money to burn! Even at Advanced Base we're out-numbered twenty to one. Get moving, Paul, but in case I forget when you drop me off thank you for everything."

"Will you meet me again, same time same place next week?"

"Certainly I will, that's the best meal I've had in months and the best wine too! They probably know you tip well."

"Then next Thursday," he said, revving up and they bumped off over the pavé in the direction of the hospital.

She rushed away as soon as they drove into the compound although it still wanted twenty minutes to midnight. He saw her flit like a shadow between two Nissen huts and disappear with a casual lift of the hand.

He got a message to her six days later and arranged to call at dusk and take her into Béthune again. He was surprised to realise how keenly he looked forward to meeting her and on the way to the hospital amused himself going over all the things he had forgotten to ask her. When he inquired for her at the transport section, however, a little Cockney driver, her voice muffled by adenoids, told him that Driver Lovell, " 'Er Ladyship" as she called her, was on duty having volunteered for an extra run to the Field Dressing Station because she, the informant, had a heavy cold. "I woulden've let 'er go," the Cockney girl said, "but I was asleep, see? We was busy las' night and I slep' on. She did her trip earlier today an' scrubbed out an' all but she's like that! Proper sport 'Er Ladyship is!"

"When is she likely to get back?" Paul inquired.

"Oh, any minnit now," the girl replied, "she's bin gone since dinner-time. I come out to scrub the crate for 'er. Least I c'n do, ain't it?"

Half-an-hour passed but the ambulance did not show up and Paul occupied the time amusingly enough pumping the Cockney driver about Grace. He soon realised that she was the acknowledged leader of the section, not only on account of her long service overseas (she was the only original member of the section still serving) but because she made everyone's problems her own, writing letters to parents, interceding with the M.O. on defaulters' behalf and generally mothering the group, especially new arrivals. "Mindjew," the girl said, with a wink, "she's a rare one for the boys! Never withaht one and we younguns don't stand a look-in! Goes all the way too or so they say, 'though she's old enough to be mother to some of 'em who come sniffin' round! But what I say is, who cares? I mean, it ain't as if she's got anyone waitin' back in Blighty, is it? And you don't get no 'elpin' 'and from the 'oly sort, do yer? Catch one o' the Sacred Virgins standin' in for someone else's run to Casualty Clearing!"

The Sacred Virgins, he learned, were W.A.A.C.s who, according to the Cockney, had reputations for "leading men up the garden path an' slamming the summer-'ouse door in their dials!" Paul was still chuckling at this when a despatch-rider roared into the compound reporting a shambles a mile or so up the Messines road. A lone-flying Gotha, he said, had taken a crack at a convoy and there had been a few casualties. The road was temporarily blocked and two ambulances were required at once.

The Cockney girl had a vehicle ticking over in a matter of minutes and there was a good deal of scurrying to and fro. Paul, who was off duty until midnight, abandoned his Douglas and jumped up beside the girl shouting to the convoy leader that he was a transport officer and would help clear the road. Twenty minutes later, just as dusk was falling, they came to the scene of the incident. Two Leyland lorries, full of captured material from the Ridge, had been blown off the road, their crews killed outright by an aerial bomb that had cratered the pavé midway between them. Close behind the wreck of the second lorry an ambulance lay on its side and orderlies were trying to extricate a screaming patient from inside. Two other patients, dead or unconscious, lay on stretchers close by. The ambulance driving cabin was empty. Suddenly the Cockney girl became frantic. "Where's 'Er

Ladyship?" she kept asking hurrying men, who brushed her aside as they lifted the stretchers into the first ambulance, and then he found her, about twenty yards back along the road, a small, huddled form under a muddy blanket, guarded by her orderly nursing a broken collar bone.

Paul lifted the blanket and looked down at the calm, waxen face for a moment. It was dirty but not disfigured in any way and the orderly, another Cockney, told him he had already examined the body but could find no wound to account for death.

"Muster bin blast, sir," he told Paul, despondently, "seen it happen offen enough. Do fer anyone with a bad ticker, an' I always reckoned she weren't strong enough fer the job. Game tho', by Christ! Bin on the run four months with her an' never see a woman with 'er nerve!"

He was sorry, Paul noted, but not overwhelmed and why should he have been? If he had been helping her to shuttle wounded to and fro for four months he must have seen scores of men die on this stretch of road. Paul replaced the blanket and the Cockney driver, who came running as soon as she was told, burst into tears, rocking to and fro like a child with a grazed knee. Then, quite abruptly, she pulled herself together and got Grace and the orderly into the second ambulance as an R.A.M.C. sergeant arrived to take charge. Paul, feeling numb, went back to help the pioneers' trouble squad fill in the crater and make the road usable. While he was directing the work the sergeant rejoined him.

"That driver, sir," he said casually, "a W.A.A.C. over there says you knew her?"

"Yes, I knew her," Paul said, "she was a very old friend of mine. I was to have taken her out to dinner in Béthune tonight. We would have been there now if she hadn't volunteered for someone else's run."

"That's the way it goes," the sergeant said, philosophically, "it don't never do to volunteer, sir!" and Paul said, bitterly, "A stray bloody Gotha! What the hell is a Gotha doing over here in daylight, for God's sake? I'll never stop hating those bastards!"

The sergeant looked at him quizzically for a moment, as though trying to assess his grief and then said, gently, "It's not *them* so much, sir. Save your hate for the bloody fools up yonder who sandwiched the Red Cross between lorries carrying captured machine-guns and ammo!" and he moved off, shouting to the pioneers to get a bloody move on if they didn't want to cause a pile-up a mile long.

They buried her in a temporary war cemetery near the advanced base hospital and Paul got permission to attend. It was a brief, simple ceremony but they gave her all the honours, including the "Last Post". Apart from the M.O. and the pioneer grave diggers he was the only man present. The rest were girls of the transport section and two or three nurses.

He stood watching them shovel the clay into the grave and tried to come to terms with the crazy improbability of the scene; Grace Lovell, once his wife and mistress of Shallowford, neatly tucked away out of sight under a French plain after being killed by the blast of a German aeroplane bomb. It was closer to fantasy than reality, the kind of twist that tangled the skein of a bad dream, like foliage growing out of a carpet or a coach lurching along on elliptical wheels driven by a two-headed dog; it was madly and hopelessly illogical and past thinking about.

Before they were done it began to rain, the thin, slanting rain that seemed always to be falling on this plain. He thought, "God in Heaven, who could have believed it would end this way when I first saw her standing in the nursery the night I arrived in the Valley?" and then, as the notes of the bugle opened a sluice on his emotions, he had difficulty in holding himself rigid for he recalled her reply to his advice to apply for a rest—"I'll rest when it's all over, or maybe before, if I'm unlucky!" Well, she had been unlucky. She had been unlucky the whole of her life, with a father who goaded her mother into drowning herself, a wretched and rootless adolescence, a failed marriage, years of prison and persecution for a principle, and finally a foreign bomb out of the sky. And yet, as he made his way back to his lorry, he remembered to be glad they had met again and, to a great extent, buried the past, and also that he was here to salute her as a war comrade rather than a woman whom he had held in his arms.

The rain began to fall faster, driving in from the north-west and the group around the grave dispersed. Only the pioneer corporal remained to bank the earth round the wooden cross, inscribed, *"Driver G. Lovell, W.A.A.C. Transport Section. Killed in action, 14.4.17"*.

CHAPTER SIX

I

HENRY PITTS, known in "B" Company as "Smiler", had never quarrelled with mud. It had always puzzled him why people got excited about it when it transferred itself to their boots and clothes, or why so many should go out of their way to avoid contact with it. His mother, Martha, was such a person, and so was his wife, Gloria. As soon as he presented himself at the kitchen door on a wet day they would rush out like a couple of furies, screaming, "Dornee bring that mud in, boy!" or "Keep that bliddy mud where it b'longs!" It astonished him, this almost universal hatred of mud which was, after all, only earth in a glutinous form and as the years passed he developed what amounted to mild affection for it, partly because it seemed to him a warm, friendly element, lacking the malevolence of rain, hail, snow and the east wind but also because it was his silent ally against the assault of women's tongues.

Out here, in the autumn of 1917, mud enfolded him on every side and Henry's comrades had come to regard it as an enemy second only to German trench mortars. When, in the winter of 1916–17, a hard frost set in, and it was possible to walk the length of a communication trench without soiling one's boots, the men rejoiced in the weather, as though it was an advantage to have to stamp one's feet for half-an-hour to restore circulation, or wear so many garments that even a waddle round a traverse was an effort. He took issue with them on this, pointing out that, under these conditions, shells were far more lethal than when they pitched into soft, friendly mud but they dismissed him as a lunatic, a man who had been out so long that he had grown to tolerate mud and the curious thing was they were half right about this for when he was alone on watch Henry would sometimes mould handfuls of the thick, yellow stuff into elephants, or snub-nosed howitzers, or cottages, or, if it was not solid enough for use as plasticine, trace patterns on its shining surfaces with a cartridge tip.

It might have been his alliance with mud, or his natural amiability, or his slow, plodding, thoughtful way of making war that enabled him to survive the Passchendaele battle that summer and autumn and not merely survive it but emerge from it as an infantryman whom the Germans could neither kill, wound nor discourage. Men were swallowed up in their thousands during the successive stages of the offensive, falling in groups under murderously accurate machine-gun fire, disappearing in the brimming craters that pocked the landscape, going sick by the hundred or, in some instances, choosing suicide to a prolongation of their misery but Henry survived without so much as catching a cold in the head. When it was over, and the shattered remains of the army was pulled back after penetrating a mile or two at a cost of about 300,000 casualties, he had not only preserved his bland imperturbability intact but had also won the Military Medal, just like Smut Potter, downalong.

His acquisition of glory was due less to his invulnerability that had become a legend in the unit than a desire to prove a point involving mud, or mud as related to the new-fangled weapon now appearing on the Front and known, for some unexplained reason, as The Tank.

Henry had a profound distrust of all mechanical contrivances on wheels dating from his first glimpse of Roddy Rudd's motor on its initial trip down the Valley and when he saw his first tank he was derisive, sharing the prejudice of his commander-in-chief, Sir Douglas Haig, and expecting even less of tanks than the most prejudiced cavalryman waiting to advance against an entrenched enemy over ground marked on pre-war maps as "*Marsh, sometimes passable in summer*".

"They contrapshuns!" he declared, "why, dam' me, I could bellycrawl across faster'n a bliddy great snail like that! Theym not only useless theym a bliddy menace to everyone walking in front of 'em! Even the cripples yerabout could cross ahead of 'em, you zee if I baint right when us goes over!"

He was about as right as he could be. On the first day of the assault the tanks got bogged down far short of their first objectives and Henry, passing one stranded in no-man's-land, shouted, "Why dornee get out an' push, maister?" to an infuriated sergeant who found himself the target for half the artillery behind Château Wood. The attacks continued, more or less abortively, throughout July, August and September and it was during a despairing attempt to push down the Menin Road in the final phase of the offensive that Henry had the satisfaction of passing the famous tank graveyard, where a dozen or more of the helpless monsters lay like a swarm of dying beetles trapped in a pool of syrup. It was this day that he proved his theory, won his medal and was promoted sergeant.

About half-a-mile east of the tank graveyard the battalion was pinned down by a single, expertly sited machine-gun. The survivors of the first wave had been there all morning and despite urgent appeals to the artillery to silence it the gun was still traversing and keeping everybody immobile in a line of waterlogged shell-holes. It was only a matter of time, Henry's sergeant said, before the German guns located and exterminated them but the machine-gun had already accounted for a score of men who had tried to get within bombing-range and the only thing to do was to stay under cover until one of the tanks could deal with it or cause it to withdraw. This was heresy to Henry, who said, emphatically, "No bliddy tank'll get this far, Sarge, and I'll bet 'ee a tin o' Goldflake on that! Us'll have to come at it on the flank or not at all, and it baint very healthy here, be it? You wait on the tank and I'll zee what us c'n do in the meantime."

He took a haversack of bombs and set out on a wide detour, moving from hole to hole across the tormented landscape and at length arriving within extreme throwing distance of the gun that was still firing in an arc of about a hundred and eighty degrees; then, suddenly, it stopped firing.

Two years on the Western Front had taught Henry Pitts how to gauge the exact point where risk coincides with what the training manuals called "the inherent military probability" but what Henry would have called "plain, bliddy gappy". His "gappy" told him that the machine-gun, having been firing at intervals for over an hour, must be running short of belts and as he saw no signs of reinforcements arriving with replenishments a long silence implied that the gunners, if not helpless, were at least conserving every bullet to stop a concerted rush. He sat there weighing his chances very carefully; then he half-rose and gently lobbed a bomb over the lip of his crater. On the heels of its explosion he heard a short, hoarse cry that did not sound like the bellow of a victim but more like a despairing shout of "Kamerad" and this, in fact, was what he had expected. He waited another moment before extricating himself from the embrace of the mud and plodding across the lips of several keyholed craters in the direction of the gun. No sound came from the emplacement and neither burst nor bullet was aimed at him from the summit of the ridge. For a few seconds he appeared as the only man alive in all that vast, glutinous landscape, a sole survivor of a race swallowed in miles and miles of soft, putrefying mud. At last, as he negotiated a spread of half-immersed corpses, to look down into the shell-hole, he knew triumph. There was the machine-gun team, their hands raised and there, huddled close by, were about a dozen other mud-caked figures too dazed and despairing to surrender, who looked up at him apathetically, hardly recognisable as human beings in their sodden, shapeless clothes and abject postures. The Devil's immunity must have been working overtime that day. It even succeeded in diverting the artillery and machine-gunners higher up the ridge for not a burst was directed at the group when Henry, a bomb in either hand, shepherded his fifteen prisoners out of the emplacement and back towards the halted British line of advance by the overland route. They got there almost intact. The last of the Germans, a whimpering boy who looked about sixteen, got hung up for a moment on wire and yelped like a terrier when a stray bullet struck his hand. The sergeant looked at Henry with awe, too astonished to congratulate him but later, when they were back at the starting-point and digging in against the inevitable counter-attack, he listened with great respect to Henry's simple explanation of his coup and how it demonstrated the superiority of legs over tanks. "Now take what happened outalong, Sarge," he said, pausing in his revetting to scrape a pound of mud from his puttees. "There I was 'avin' to maake up me own mind whether or not they was out of ammo and ready to give up. And so I did, an' you zeed the result. But suppose—just suppose—I'd been one o' they bliddy contrapshuns, all racket an' no bliddy brains? Could I have sat quiet an' worked it out for meself? And suppose I had? Ah, now, there's the real rub! Could I ha' clawed me way along them ridges without bringing down a box barrage as would ha' blown us all to tatters? Would 'ee tell me that, Sarge?"

The sergeant, himself a Devonian, shook his head and admitted that Henry was probably right but he did not yield the argument unconditionally, saying, thoughtfully, "'Tiz all a matter o' the ground, Smiler. On terra-firma tanks could make a clean breakthrough, providing there's enough of them mind you, but in a bloody mudbath like this they can't get started, can 'em? Youm right but it baint a fair test, boy! No, it baint a fair test!", and he went away down the trench to despatch Henry's fifteen prisoners to Battalion H.Q. for interrogation. He sent a note along with them, explaining how and by whom they had been acquired, but Henry did not hear about this until much later when, with the exhausted remnant of his unit, he was informed of official recognition whilst delousing his shirt over a candle-flame in a cellar behind Ypres.

II

The sergeant's claim that tanks had not had a fair trial at Passchendaele was advanced by an embittered tank officer in Gough's Fifth Army that same month. Among the most insistent that tanks should not be judged on their third Ypres performance was Captain Palfrey, now the commander of a squadron of Mark IV tanks, two male and two female, affectionately christened Alfie, Bertha, Charlie and Daisy.

It was given to very few during the twenty-four months intervening between Loos and Passchendaele to see their dreams come true but Ikey was of that minority for the vision he had had whilst artillery-spotting during the 1915 battle had materialised in the later stages of the Somme offensive when, as one of the first tankmen to pilot a Mark I machine into battle, he had cursed the idiotic use of the weapon by High Command. Tanks were dribbled into the line in ones and twos and although their initial impact upon the enemy was sensational, and those reaching the German line swept everything before them, the determination of the strategists to precede every big attack with a barrage that churned up the ground and advertised their objectives, effectually prevented exploitation of the arm. The tankmen were withdrawn as failures when the offensive petered out but instead of despairing they returned to their maps, probing and probing for a sector where they could prove their claim that tanks were the only answer to the Western Front stalemate.

By this time Ikey had been in and out of the line for three years but he was a bad example of the theory that a man's usefulness declined in direct relation to his length of service in the field. He had ridden out the shock of Hazel's strange death, had not become an alcoholic or been seriously wounded and after two years' active service his nervous system was more or less intact although some of his closest associates were beginning to think that he had deluded himself into thinking he was no longer engaged in a war against the Central Powers but against the cavalry-generals in their châteaux fifty miles behind the lines. Before the war Ikey's attitude to senior officers had been one of ironic and affectionate contempt. His mimicry of those above field rank had been a star-turn wherever subalterns assembled out of earshot of their superiors. With a little make-up he could even look like one as he delivered imaginary lectures by members of the staff, interspersing every sentence with the obligatory "Haw-Haw"! and ad libbing long and rambling reminiscences of campaigns fought in Upper Burma and the Sudan.

Long before the end of the Somme offensive, however, he had decided that senior officers were now beyond a joke, especially the over-sixties and their gilded protégés who infested Supreme Headquarters. They had enlarged themselves, he declared, from mere buffoons into homicidal maniacs and should be locked out of harm's way until the war was over, when they could be trotted out and driven through the streets of London, preceded by a banner with the legend: "Victory in Spite of US". In the meantime he placed his reliance in the improved Mark IV tank and when news came that at long last the tankmen were to be allowed a chance to show what they could do in a sector of their own choosing he was so elated that he told his crews they now had a chance of ending the war single-handed.

They were denied this distinction. The chosen sector was opposite Cambrai and at the insistence of the tankmen the attack was preceded by the briefest of bombardments. At first it looked as if Ikey's reckless prophecy would be fulfilled. In a matter of hours the tanks, with cheering infantry in close support, had advanced a distance of four miles, tearing just such a gap in the German lines as Douglas Haig (and before him Sir John French) had been promising since the spring of 1915. The tank experts had reckoned, however, without the price of Passchendaele. There were no fresh divisions left to exploit this astounding advance and when the Germans counter-attacked there was nothing for it but to withdraw and yield up two-thirds of the territory won. At the close of the battle all that remained on H.Q. maps to demonstrate the usefulness of tanks on the Western Front was a blunted salient a mile or two wide that ultimately became as big an embarrassment to troops in the line as the famous "prestige" salient at Ypres.

Yet Ikey enjoyed his private victory. Inside the inferno of the leading tank he sweated and stewed as they rumbled forward over first, second and third lines of defence, barriers that would have cost the lives of a hundred thousand men on Somme and Passchendaele estimates. He came through it all unwounded and sent in a detailed report on the engagement but with the advance of winter, activities in the new Flesquiéres salient came to a standstill and he was sent back to Étaples for a three months' technical course and here, to his mild astonishment, he learned that he had been promoted major.

812

His elevation, following closely upon the strain of the autumn battles, completed the profound psychological change in Ikey that had begun with news that his wife's reason had succumbed to the shock of what most people would have called her awakening. Paul had told him the truth in a long, tactfully-worded letter but even Paul was largely unaware of the forces and stresses that had persuaded Hazel to appoint herself beacon-lighter to the doomed men of the Valley and, as Ikey saw it, every other Valley in Europe. Ikey, who understood her processes of thought better than anyone, not excluding Meg Potter, saw Hazel's act of madness as a protest, an instinctive protest against the more cynical and infinitely more lethal madness of civilisation and although, all things considered, he joined Maureen in regarding her death as an unlooked-for mercy, the events that had led up to it confirmed him in his steadfast belief that Hazel had been more sane than most people were nowadays; among this majority he numbered the patriots on both sides of the lines and, more particularly, the politicians and generals directing the Allied war effort.

For a long time now, ever since his first term at High Wood and up to, say, the beginning of the Somme offensive, Ikey had been armoured against fate by his ironic sense of humour and, even more effectively, by his social neutrality for it was this that set him apart from even the most detached of his fellows. He had never wholly rejected his childhood in a Thames-side slum but neither had he wholly accepted his status as the adopted son of a country squire and an officer in the forces of the Crown. He continued to maintain a foot in each camp for while his natural adaptability enabled him to survive the narrow atmosphere of the mess and polo ground, Hazel Potter had safely anchored him to his original habitat. He enjoyed, as it were, a unique lookout post in a private no-man's-land. He found the position amusing and sometimes absorbing from an intellectual standpoint and it had special advantages in his dealings with the men who came under his command. He could communicate without patronage and they were not slow to recognise as much, so that among the other ranks he was always the most popular officer in every unit in which he served. He was also, because of his lifelong habit of taking a situation apart and studying the pieces individually before putting them together again, an accomplished professional and his seniors soon came to rely on him to a degree that encouraged their built-in contempt for technicalities that was a feature of the pre-war army. Ikey was not slow to exploit this trust and when he found himself in France, where professional ability often meant economy in lives, there was considerable competition for his services. His transfer from the artillery to the Tank Corps had cost him the goodwill of his superiors but because he was convinced that tanks, and tanks alone, could break the deadlock in the West, he had persisted and had ultimately been successful. He never regretted the transfer. The officers of the Tank Corps were mostly ex-civilians, un-hampered by the prejudices of gunners who had soldiered in India, and here Ikey found his creativeness given free rein. He also dis-covered that at last he could communicate without having to keep tongue in cheek.

As a major, a professional, and a man who had been out more than two years he could have adopted a superior attitude towards his fellow-officers without incurring their resentment but he now reserved the professional touch for comic turns in the mess. Yet, deep in his heart, Ikey no longer searched for humour in the present situation. As the months went by, as more and more conscripts were fed into the Mincing Machine, he grew bitter and desperate, not so much against the war itself but against the manner in which it was being waged. There were times when, like Siegfried Sassoon, he was tempted to voice his protest openly in the newspapers or through one or other of the left-wing organisations at home but the habit of discipline was strong in him and he reasoned that the only result of a one-man revolt would be his transfer to a mental ward. This, in fact, had already happened in one or two cases when Authority, unwilling to brand a man with a good war-record coward or traitor, found it convenient to downgrade him as shell-shocked and put him out of harm's way for the duration.

He was actually discussing one of these cases with fellow-officers in a bar in Étaples towards the end of his course, when his cast of thought was broken and remoulded by a chance meeting with a wounded French officer, employed about the camp as an interpreter.

He had noticed the Frenchman standing apart from the group, a man so hideously disfigured that it was difficult not to look at him with embarrassing directness. He was a tall, slim officer, lacking a right arm, and from his temples to the right side of his chin was what appeared at first glance to be a wide smear of plum jam but was, in fact, a terrible scar partially disguised by skin-grafting. When Ikey's companions left to go on duty the Frenchman came forward and said, in faultless English, "You won't remember me, Major Palfrey?" and when Ikey admitted this but invited him to have a drink in any case, went on, "I recall you very well! We met in India when I was French attaché, at Cawnpore, in 1912. We had a long discussion one night, on Napoleon's Russian Campaign. I believe I convinced you that it was not the blunder claimed in the history books!"

Ikey recalled him then and clearly, a handsome, intelligent, friendly individual called Bouvet, an expert on the new French "75", still regarded as the best field-gun in existence. Bouvet said, "It is natural you should not recall my face. I was left for dead in the first Ardennes battle and was in hospital until February this year."

Ikey murmured an expression of formal sympathy and they chatted on their Indian service but he soon realised that the man was impatient to be done with small-talk and express his opinion on Allied prospects and the general conduct of the war. No sooner had he broached the topic, however, than the Frenchman said, "Not in here, my friend! We will talk elsewhere I think!", and led the way to his billet, a small cottage hemmed in by three-storey warehouses. They went in and Bouvet lit the lamp, revealing a room containing very little furniture but a great many books, papers and files.

"You must not think you British have the prerogative of stupidity," he said. "I could not help hearing your conversation in the bistro but it is even worse with us. There can be no hope of victory until we have a unified command and younger men at the top."

"Well, that's on its way," Ikey said. "We already have a Joint Planning Commission and a central reserve and I imagine, as time goes on, it will take over from men like Haig."

"As time goes on," Bouvet sneered, "that is very British of you, my friend!" and then, pulling his mouth into a hard line that tautened the ravaged flesh of his cheek, "But we have no time! The Germans will attack in strength as soon as they can transfer their freed divisions from the Russian front and the result of that attack will be the finish!"

Ikey was familiar with this theory, an access of German strength in the spring after an armistice with Russia, but in spite of himself, he began to defend a more optimistic view, pointing out that the superiority of defence over offence had been proved over and over again in the last three years and that the war would probably end in a stalemate. The Frenchman listened politely but when he had finished he said, quietly, "The enemy have their quota of idiots, my friend, but unfortunately their system of command is such that Junkers are ciphers, like Hindenburg, real power resting with the climbers, like Ludendorff. Ludendorff is no fool! Do you imagine he has not profited by the lessons of Verdun, the Somme and Passchendaele? I tell you, he will break through and dictate peace by midsummer! Everything points to that, including our mutinies!"

It was the first direct reference Ikey had heard from a Frenchman of mutinies that had resulted from the total failure of the Nivelle offensive and he was curious to learn more.

"You know about the mutinies?" he asked. "They were more than a few isolated incidents?"

"I know enough about them to get me court-martialled if I so much as mentioned them to an Englishman!" Bouvet said, "yet I think it is my duty to mention them to you, if only to convince you that you have no one but yourselves to rely on once the German offensive is launched! The French south of the Somme cannot help you. They will hold the line, perhaps, but it is accepted that they will do no more than that until the Americans arrive in force. By then it will be too late."

Bouvet then disclosed all he knew of the French mutinies and Ikey was shocked by his account. He learned that whole divisions of French infantry had walked away from the front, heading for Paris, and that the situation had only been saved by the prompt dismissal of General Nivelle, his successor's decision not to sacrifice another drop of French blood in an offensive, and by mass arrests and an unspecified number of executions. It was one of the methods employed to restore order that appalled Ikey. A small number of men, so Bouvet told him, had been shot but others, ostensibly pardoned, had been sent to a quiet sector of the line and there exterminated by their own artillery, supposedly firing at enemy defences. Bouvet could not say how many had died this way but he thought it was over a thousand and Ikey left his billet that night with his education on modern war complete. He no longer despised the Allied High Command buffoons but thought of them as a group of men from whom nothing could be expected but an eternity of blood-letting. It was this conversation, more than anything of his personal experiences in the last three years, that blasted him from his seat on the fence. The war had to be fought out, he supposed, but afterwards, immediately afterwards there must be a reckoning. The entire social structure of the old world would have to be changed, either by revolution on the Russian pattern, or by some less drastic process but changed anyway if human dignity was to survive. From then on he was committed and took little care to conceal as much notwithstanding the bright new crown over his shoulder.

The day she received Paul's letter saying that he had been promised nine days' leave in October Claire turned her back on patients, children, staff and all other time-robbers, saddled old Snowdrop and crossed the dunes to the gully to satisfy herself that Eph Morgan had kept his word about making the shanty habitable by the end of the month.

All good Shallowfordians had their inner tabernacle on or about the estate and Claire's preference was for the steep, narrow goyle that gave on to the beach within a couple of hundred yards of the rock-pool where her mother had taught her to swim and where Paul had proposed. She did not go there often but when she did she preferred to go alone.

In the mouth of the gully was a single dwelling, a tumbledown shanty once occupied by a local character known in the Valley as Crabpot Willie. Crabpot had been a very old man when Claire was a child but she recalled him as a shaggy-whiskered old rascal, who lived by catching and selling shellfish, who walked rather like a crab and who was said, on slender authority, to have rounded the Horn on a windjammer. Here he had lived until his death in the early 'nineties after which his cabin had fallen into decay for nobody cared to live this far from the village or so near high-water mark where spring tides would sometimes lap Willie's doorstep.

Claire first revisited the area whilst prospecting for a shorter cut to the beach for hospital bathing parties and recalling that the old man had been a favourite of her mother's she turned aside to inspect his former home. She was surprised to find that the main roof timbers and pine floor were more or less intact, and that the shingle roof had been partially saved by overhanging firs marking the edge of the wood on the shoulder of the landslip. It was a secluded, pleasant spot in the summer. Sand had blown in from the beach, half-filling the little cleft and was held there by marram grass and sea holly. Higher up, beyond the pine-needles, grew campion, bugloss, trefoil and wood anemone in a grove of dwarf oaks and the place was sheltered from easterly and south-westerly winds. Claire's first thought was to convert the shanty into a beach chalet for the convalescents but then she knew that she would resent sharing it with anyone save Paul and another plan began to form in her mind, resulting in her approach to Eph Morgan (then building Nissen huts under Government contract in the paddock) and an appeal to make it habitable as her retreat. Eph carried out an inspection and said the shanty could be weather-proofed easily enough but warned her that the only way she could get the necessary materials was by compounding a felony and signing a form to the effect that the work was a hospital extension. She signed without a qualm and he went to work on the promise of cash payment, hauling materials along the beach at low tide and later helping her transport furniture, bedding and kitchen utensils across the dunes.

When the job was finished, and the shanty looked snug and inviting, she locked the door and kept the key on her personal ring, against the time that she should have news of Paul's homecoming, for the shanty was to be a place where they could enjoy a few hours' blessed privacy away from the racket of wards and nursery and safe from those who might use his precious leave to importune for one thing or another. There was also, she admitted to herself, a selfish element in the scheme. She had long since made up her mind that she needed him far more desperately than did anyone else in the Valley and was prepared to maintain her claim at the expense of tenants, employees and even the children.

In early October he wired asking if she would care to meet the leave train at Charing Cross and spend a day or two in town doing the popular shows but she wrote at once declining the offer, saying that she would meet him at Sorrel Halt in the trap. She knew that he would prefer this and her plans were now well advanced.

On the morning of the day he was due to arrive she drove the trap over the dunes for a last-minute inspection and unloaded enough stores at the shanty to withstand a short siege. The cabin looked spic and span under its new coat of tar and creosote, crouching under the cluster of firs like a weatherbeaten toadstool. Inside it smelled fresh and clean and Claire spent an hour there, lighting a fire and banking it high with green wood, airing the bed with stone hot-water bottles, offloading eggs, bacon, flour, and some bottles of wine laid down for Simon's twenty-first birthday and adding a touch of colour with some bronze and yellow chrysanthemums.

She sat for a moment watching the fire burn up feeling more like a young bride than a woman approaching middle age with a growing family and over a hundred convalescent soldiers on her conscience, but the latter could not have troubled her much for, as she laid her best silk nightdress across the pillow, she thought, gaily, "I daresay he'll remind me it's autumn and hustle me back to the house in search of

818

comfort after nine months at the Front but I'm damned if I don't do my best to maroon him here for twenty-four hours!" Then she locked the door and led the pony up the incline to the dunes, noting with satisfaction that the weather, although crisp, looked settled over Nun's Bay, the source of all the gales at this time of year.

She was astonished to note how fit and young he looked when he swung his valise from the train and came striding down the platform towards her. For so long, it seemed, she had been shut up with sick, shambling men, short of a limb, jumpy and indecisive in their movements. She knew, of course, that he had been spared the worst of it and had at least slept under a roof since the spring offensive but she had not expected him to come home to her looking braced, healthier and obviously more tranquil in mind than when he had been grappling with multiple problems during the first half of the war. She experienced a moment of embarrassment when he embraced her, recalling all those things she had poured into her letters during the last few months but the moment passed after they climbed into the trap and he took the reins with an air of having been met after one of his rare trips to London.

He told her a little of what had been happening over there, of the failure of the latest Ypres battle on account of the mud and how lucky he had been then to be in the relatively quiet sector far to the south and she began to feel slightly deflated, as though her role now was no more than that of dutiful audience to the returning warrior. Then, just as they were dipping down from the crest near the place where he had stopped to reassure himself after the suffragette scrimmage, he surprised her by pulling off the road, dropping the reins and kissing her with such zest that she exclaimed, laughing, "I expected something like that on the platform but all I got was a peck and a war bulletin!"

"You can forget the damned war from now on," he said, seriously, "I only used it as a smokescreen while I got my bearings! If it was dark I'd let the pony nibble on that gorse for a spell and whisk you off into the heather before we got buried alive by well-meaning old busybodies like Mrs. Handcock and the local Home Fronters! I was glad when you said you preferred not to meet me in London but we ought to have had the sense to find a place temporarily removed from everyone!"

He could hardly have given her a more welcome opening. She said, eagerly, "Listen, Paul, do you remember that tumbledown old shack in the gully near the rock-pool where you proposed? I had an idea a month or so ago and I talked Eph Morgan into restoring it and when it was done I fixed it up. We can go there now. I took food over this morning and lit a fire. We can stay there for a day or so if we like because I took Maureen into my confidence and she said she'll think of something to spare our blushes! You don't *have* to go, of course, we could ride over tomorrow but . . . well, it's the only way I could think of to make sure the tenants don't descend on us in a body!"

She broke off, embarrassed to discover that she was blushing furiously under his amused stare and said, lifting up the reins, "Well, there it is! Suit yourself! I don't mind either way!"

"By God I will!" he said, snatching the reins and flicking them across the pony's back. "How the devil do you get there from here? There's no road, is there?" and as she directed him to cross Codsall Bridge and cut across the stubble fields to the dunes, "And you don't have to apologise, either! I half thought that you . . . all right, let it pass!"

"What were you going to say?"

He looked at her with a grin. "Only that I had a rather depressing thought at the back of my head — that those letters you wrote were prompted by loneliness more than anything else and that when we came face to face you'd feel shamefaced about putting your name to them!"

"And what makes you think I'm not?"

"Like hell you are, you little liar!" he said, chuckling, "you've been plotting for months and why not? By God, Claire, I don't regret getting into the war when I might have stayed here but I don't think I realised how vital you were to my peace of mind, or how desperately I would miss you! I used to think it had to do with your identification with this place and so it had, in the beginning, but not any longer! It's you Claire Derwent and not the Valley! I could live anywhere if I had to, so long as I could be sure of waking up nights and finding you within reach!", and he threw his arm round her as they bumped off the Four Winds track and headed across the stubble for the coast. She said, choosing her words carefully: "I've always pretended to be the Spirit-of-the-Valley, Paul, for I knew that was the kind of wife you wanted and played up to it! Even in the very beginning I admired your nerve taking on a job this size, and being a rather sensual little beast there never was a time when I didn't enjoy you as a man. Deep, spiritual need, however — real love, that's something one has to learn

820

and I didn't begin learning until we had that stupid quarrel over poor Hazel and its sequel. Since then, and since your being away put responsibility on me, I understand your purpose better than anyone — except maybe John Rudd. I know somehow you'll come back for good, if only because you were meant to make this out-of-the-way corner live and flower. That's why, although I'm desolate without you, I don't worry myself sick like all the other women."

He nodded, understanding and valuing every word she uttered. Then, as they reached the grove of dwarf oaks, he climbed down and led the pony along the ruts made by her hauls earlier in the year. When they reached the bottom it was dusk and the orange sun was playing a losing game with the silhouettes of the firs behind the cabin. He said, with the deepest satisfaction, "This was an inspiration, Claire, and we'll keep this place for ourselves! We won't even have the children here," and turned aside to unharness the pony and bed her down in the lean-to stable while she went inside to stir up the fire and prepare a meal. She had, he noticed, overlooked nothing. There was even a truss of hay and a bucket of oats for the animal.

IV

Of the eight days he remained in the Valley they spent four in seclusion and the rest up at the house. The ninth he devoted to Simon who had gone to High Wood the previous month.

For Claire the time they spent alone was the highwater mark of her marriage, a lamp that was to shine down the years to the end of her life, lighting up periods of doubt and frustration, a fixed point to which she could always look for reassurance when her hair ceased to crackle under the comb and she began to thicken and lose some of her suppleness. Their hunger for one another denied them the leisurely love-making of pre-war days but instead followed a kind of graph, with a dozen rapturously high peaks and any number of swift dips into laughter. But midway between these two extremes were long, placid intervals when she would bring him up-to-date on Valley affairs and gossip so that when it was time for him to go a clear, balanced picture of Valley trends and Valley economics was etched upon his memory. The picture was to console him in the calamitous period ahead but he remembered more vividly the gaiety of their conversations and the blessed silence of the gully, disturbed only by the whisper of the firs and the measured suck of the tide, advancing and retreating up and down the deserted beach. The children brought him joy too, each in their several ways, Simon's adolescent earnestness, the twins' boisterous enthusiasm for all things military, the independence of little Whiz and six-year-old Mary's solemnity when she sat on his knee, begging him to make the other available to her protégé, Rumble Patrick, whom he noticed she mothered like a little spaniel bitch foster-rearing a fox-cub.

But for Claire there was no such overall domestic pattern as this; for her the interval was at once more intense and far more personal, a time when she had reason to bless her forethought in providing a retreat where she was under no obligation to share him and where no exchanges between them were too unlikely and extravagant for a man and woman denied one another for so long.

After the initial transport, when they let the meal she had prepared go cold upon the table, she made up her mind to prolong the ecstasy of reunion by the exercise of some restraint but her resolutions came to nothing. As soon as he touched her her yearning became a frenzy so that she would not wait for him to take the initiative, as in the past, but would translate all her written promises into action demanding of him as much as he could give and exalting in his greed for her. Yet always, as in the earliest days of their marriage, there was a residual of humour, for when they were still again she would say, teasing him, "You don't act like a man home from a place where they work you hard! I believe you must have landed the cushiest job in France with nothing better to do but loiter about storing up energy on a honeymoon diet of oysters and champagne!" And he would respond with some such rejoinder as, "It was generated by your shameless letters — refined cruelty to a much-married man away from home and living in the open on a diet of bully beef!" Or, if she teased him about his techniques, saying he must have acquired them from the mademoiselles, he would heave her across his knee and spank her broad bottom for disobeying his orders to keep the war out of their conversation. As a honeymoon it was far more enriching than its predecessor ten years before and it was this she had in mind when she denigrated honeymoons as a whole, declaring that it was too much to expect young couples to adjust themselves so soon after the fuss of a tribal ceremony with the din of wedding bells in their ears. "Why can't honeymoons be postponed for as long as this?" she demanded, and he had laughed, saying, "Because, you idiot, they are designed for the prompt procreation of children! Suppose we'd waited ten years? We should have been a tetchy old couple of nearly sixty while the twins and Mary were still at school!"

"Well," she said, with a conceit that made him chuckle, "if you haven't procreated a second clutch in the last forty-eight hours I must be past bearing! If the estate falls into disarray because I'm busy nursing all next summer you'll have no one but yourself to blame, Squire!"

This was the way they talked and this was the rhythm of the days and nights they spent together, wild, ungovernable moments, spaced with intervals of laughter, speculation and reminiscence, but there were some inexpressibly tender moments too, as when they were undressing before the fire late one night after stealing back to the cabin like a pair of clandestine lovers.

She was in the act of slipping on her nightgown when he took it from her, bidding her to stand before the green and violet sputter of blazing apple logs, and when she did as he asked he sat absorbing the strength and symmetry of her body, as a painter might ponder the complexities of transferring physical perfection to canvas. She had already loosed her hair, and its lights danced the measure of the flames. She stood quite still, receiving and relishing his homage as he appraised every part of her, her long, slender feet and dimpled knees, the glowing health of her skin, the smooth sweep of her hips where they ended in a still-neat waist — every aspect of her that he had worshipped over the years. There was not a part of her, he thought, that was less than perfect in his eyes; the sturdy columns of her thighs balanced by wide buttocks and a long, straight back, her full, firm breasts, her strong neck and powerful shoulders offsetting the curious smallness and neatness of her head and, above all, those features of her that were so eager to demonstrate subjection to him, her generous, pouting mouth, her lips, and eyes that seemed to him at this moment never to have held in their depths anything but promise. He said, soberly, "You're not just Rubens' model, Claire, you're Velazquez's and every other perfectionist who ever tried to express a feminine ideal! You're quite beautiful and far nearer physical perfection than you were in your early twenties! I swear to you that isn't flattery and it isn't because I've been starved of you either! A man could go on looking at you for ever and find something new and exciting every second! How could any man in his senses help desiring you, even if he did no more than keep you to look at at moments like this?"

She emerged from the sensual reverie praise of this kind induced and forked a shaft of mischief at him, the instinctive provocation of a woman secure in the tenure of her lover.

"No one else ever has looked at me like this. If they ever do I'll get the verdict endorsed! After all, one as flattering as that deserves corroboration!", and then the mischief died and moved by an impulse his commendation stirred in her she pressed his face to her breasts, saying, "I'm only beautiful as long as you remember me like this, Paul! As long as the memory of our time alone here is vivid and close to you! For as long as that nothing can change for us dearest, not even if everything and everybody around us changes!"

He was to remember that cry of hers at a moment when the world around him was not merely changing but disintegrating in an everlasting series of thunder flashes and the reek of cordite filled his lungs.

V

Although it was not for want of trying on Paul's part he had never succeeded in establishing a relationship with Simon that he had achieved with the other children, or, for that matter, with some of his numerous godchildren in the Valley. The boy hedged himself about with a special kind of privacy that rebuffed most people and only Ikey, and, to some extent Claire, could overcome. He was on friendly terms with most of the tenantry, and some of the craftsmen and hired labourers, so that it had sometimes irritated Paul to admit to himself that Simon would talk more freely to Sam Potter, the woodsman, or the hare-lipped dairymaid at the Home Farm than he would talk to his father. In Paul's presence Simon was respectful and noncommittal.

One of the by-products of Paul's 1917 leave was a partial bridging of this gap, for Paul was lucky to catch Simon with some of his defences down, moping through his first term at a sadly disorganised High Wood, staffed by an asthmatic temporary headmaster, invalided trench veterans and Grade III civilians.

Paul was depressed by the boy's dispirited manner when summoned to the Headmaster's study to meet his father and at once his heart went out to him, for he was reminded very sharply of Grace as Paul had last seen her in Béthune. He knew Claire had told Simon of her death and wondered if the boy was grieving, notwithstanding the fact that he could have no memory of her. There was no transport available so at the Head's suggestion the two of them set out across the moor to an isolated inn near Five Barrows, an ancient Celtic monument four miles from the school.

At first Paul thought it was going to be a miserably embarrassing expedition, for Simon answered his questions regarding school life with mumbled monosyllables. As they were threading their way through a beech grove, however, heading for the open moor, Paul succeeded in breaking the ice by chance when he said, "I've really come to tell you what a brave woman your mother was, son!", and the boy stopped, looking up at him with a trembling lip and saying, in a cracked voice that Paul recognised as half-broken, "Mrs. Handcock said you were there when she was killed, sir, but I didn't believe it. I didn't see how you could be but that was what she said. I – I'd like to know if that was true, sir."

Paul found to his embarrassment that his own voice was unsteady. They stood together on the edge of the wood, overlooking a tumbling moorland stream and then, by common consent, sat down side by side on a broken piece of fencing. Paul began, "I didn't know how much you'd been told but – " and then, impatiently, "Look here, you don't have to call me 'sir'! Ikey always called me 'Gov'nor'. You can call me Gov'nor if you like."

The boy grinned and Paul realised what perfect teeth he had and how, just like Grace, he was able to dissipate any impression of surliness or distrust by a smile. He put his hand on Simon's shoulder and when the boy did not withdraw, as he half-expected he might, said, "Well, it so happens that old chatterbox had it right for once! I *was* there when your mother was killed. She was driving badly wounded men from Advanced Dressing Station to hospital, and I came on the scene a few minutes after it happened but before that we'd met by chance and had dinner together and we talked about you. She was coming to see you when she came on leave." The lie, he thought, could be classified as snow-white, for somehow it seemed important he should draw them together in this roundabout way. Simon said, "Do you mind telling me about her . . . Gov'nor?"

"Not in the least. I always had a great respect for her courage but after meeting her again in France, and talking to some of the girls she was working with, I came away with a tremendous admiration for her! She was as much a heroine as any chap with the V.C. and don't ever forget it! That was her second trip under fire that day and she volunteered for it."

He told as much of the circumstances as he thought the boy could

825

absorb without feeding him material for morbid reflections but Simon surprised him none the less, for after Paul had told him Grace had been given a military funeral, the boy said, "Why did she leave us in the first place? Did you quarrel over me?"

"Good God, no! Why should we do that? You were only a few months old at the time." He sat thinking hard, wondering how to explain such an unlikely set of circumstances to a thirteen-year-old child and finally compromised, saying, "It's difficult to put into words, old chap, but I suppose the truth is your mother was never in love with me, not in the way your stepmother is. It had to do with our aims in life. You see, she wasn't a 'country' person, so we ought never to have married. If we hadn't we should have stayed good friends, the way we ended up in France. Then she got a bee in her bonnet about votes for women and in the end this became more important to her than—well—me or the estate."

"Were you against votes for women?"

"No, I wasn't, and neither was our M.P., Jimmy Grenfell, who also admired her but the odd thing is I've come to believe your mother left because, in a funny sort of way, she thought it was unfair to me to stay." He looked sideways at the boy. "Do you find that hopeless to understand?"

"No," said Simon, "I believe I can see what you mean, Gov'nor."

"Then try and tell me," Paul said, gratefully, and Simon went on, "She must have thought you ought to be married to someone keen on the Valley."

"That's exactly it!" said Paul, excited by the boy's perception, "she told me I ought to have married a farmer's daughter in the first place but what I'd really like to get home to you is that just because we got divorced she wasn't a mother to be ashamed of but rather the opposite. She didn't run off with anyone else, she just had to give herself to politics and she was prepared to go to prison for her beliefs which is a damned sight more than most politicians are!"

"Some of those Labour chaps have," Simon said, unexpectedly, and Paul wondered how, in a conservative school like High Wood Simon could have known this and commented on it without labelling Socialist M.P.s "dirty conchies".

"Yes, that's so," he replied. "Some people feel about the war that way and most of the fighting men respect them for it."

"They do?" He saw that he had astonished the boy at last and went on, "Yes, they do, because people at home haven't any real idea what

826

it's like, so they can't help talking nonsense about it like the newspapers and politicians. Did Ikey tell you about his friend Keith Horsey, the parson's son? He was a C.O. but he's out there in the thick of it stretcher-bearing."

"Yes," said Simon, thoughtfully, "I know about Horsey. Fellows here are ashamed he was a Highwodian you know, so I wrote to Ikey and told him and he wrote back saying they must be chumps because Horsey was braver than anyone if the truth was known!"

"Did you pass that on?" asked Paul, curiously.

"No," Simon said, "because I'd get hell for sticking up for a C.O. You don't go around looking for trouble as a first-termer!"

Paul laughed and felt a rush of affection for the boy, thinking how badly he had misjudged him in the past.

"I see your point," he said, "it must be damned difficult to hold an unpatriotic point of view in a place like this!"

"What do *you* think about the war, Gov'nor?"

This was almost as difficult as explaining why Grace had exchanged home and husband for Holloway, for Paul feared to express himself too freely on the subject in case Simon quoted him in an unguarded moment.

"I *don't* think about it any more than I can help, son," he said, realising he was evading the question, "I just get on with it, like most of the chaps out there," but the boy was not to be fobbed off with this and again reminded Paul of Grace when one of her principles was challenged.

"But you must know whether you think it right or wrong."

"Well then, it's wrong," Paul said, reluctantly, "it's the biggest crime against humanity that's ever happened but I daresay some good will come out of it, at least, that's what most of us out there like to think, the Germans as well as the English."

"If everybody fighting thinks that why isn't it stopped?" Simon persisted, with his mother's maddening logic.

"Because, for the moment, neither side is ready to give in. The men in the trenches would be very happy to call it a day but the war isn't directed by them. They just do what they're told and all the orders come from older men, most of them warming their backsides beside a comfortable fire. That's why it has to be fought to a finish."

"It seems a stupid way to carry on," the boy said and Paul agreed that it was indeed but that when the men came back they intended to

827

make certain nothing like it would happen again so perhaps it would benefit their children and grandchildren.

After that they spent a rewarding day, talking easily of all kinds of things but when they parted in the quad as the bell rang for tea he realised Simon had absorbed every word he had been told about Grace for he said, shaking hands and pocketing Paul's tip, "If they give my mother a medal could I have it? To keep?"

Paul had difficulty concealing the extent to which the request moved him but promised he certainly could keep the medal if there was one and the boy went off then, cheerfully enough Paul thought, envying the ability of the young to discard emotional problems in the struggle to adapt themselves to their immediate surroundings. The tedious journey home, however, was not wholly depressing, for at least he could congratulate himself on having got nearer to Simon than ever before and as he crossed the moor in the ramshackle motor-cab he had engaged at Paxtonbury he thought how small a part environment played in promoting character and how manifestly clear it was that Simon's personality was the legacy of the sallow, exhausted woman he had last seen lying under a groundsheet on the road to Messines Ridge. "They can talk as much as they like about the influences of social backgrounds," he told himself, "but what's in the blood stays there! Look at Ikey and that crazy marriage of his? And look at the way Eveleigh is making a fool of himself over that damned shop-girl! Come to that look at Simon—his stream of political thought already veering left at thirteen!" The rain slashed against the canvas hood of the cab and the darkness deprived him of his favourite view of the Valley.

CHAPTER SEVEN

I

JANUARY, 1918; snow blanketed the entire Valley, from the farthest fold of Blackberry Moor to the bleak, crusted dunes, from the blur of Shallowford Woods down through eight-foot drifts to the frozen Sorrel where the ice was said to be six inches thick. The frost had held fast since Boxing Day and even those with menfolk in the ice-bound ditches of Flanders were too cold, too tired and too discouraged to spare them much sympathy. For this was the fourth winter of the war that would never end and external pressures had shrivelled souls to the size and toughness of dried peas, sometimes putting an impossible price on neighbourliness.

Claire, depressed by this collective withdrawal, fought it wherever she could, for it seemed to her a loss more painful and damaging than the drain on Valley manpower. From time to time she went out of her way to marshal the survivors, reviving their flagging spirits with reminders of the approach of spring and the promise of a record yield from meadows now gripped fast by the frost and scoured by an east wind that searched through the heaviest garments a person could wear and still waddle up and down the lifeless lanes. The Valley, she would remind herself, was not only more populous but more productive than it had ever been. There were never less than two thousand men in the hutted camp at Nun's Bay, and often a hundred convalescents at Shallowford House. All seven farms had a record number of acres under the plough and were supporting twice as much livestock as in pre-war years and although so many familiar faces had disappeared, some of them for ever, their places had been taken by others not all of whom came into the category of foreigners, like the soldiers in camp or the German prisoners in the depot north of the woods. Men and girls had drifted in from the neighbouring estate of Heronslea which had lost impetus since Lord Gilroy had been killed on the Italian Front leaving no heir and two Whinmouth conscientious objectors were now employed by her brother Hugh at High Coombe, Hugh having neither the patriotic scruples of Eveleigh nor his preference for buxom land-girls. Yet the shifts and changes in the tempo of life were so various and manifold that Claire had the greatest difficulty in keeping track of them all when she sat in the library late at night writing to Paul, or keeping the estate diary up-to-date. She applied herself to these tasks religiously, for the one was her sole emotional outlet and the other seemed to her a bridge to post-war continuity. The list of Valley soldiers and Valley casualties had now entered upon a second page. Dick Marlowe, the sexton's younger son, had gone down somewhere off the west coast of Africa bringing home a cargo of maize from Capetown, and news crossed the Teazel of the death in action of Dave Buller, Gilroy's keeper, who had carried the scars of Smut Potter's gunstock to his grave in a shell-hole on the slopes of Vimy Ridge. Then, as January passed, and the hard frost held on into February, news came of Parson Horsey's loss. His son Keith had been blown to pieces when a Minnenwerfer scored a direct hit on a stretcher party passing down a communication trench in front of St. Quentin, and this time Claire had to do more than record the casualty, feeling under an obligation to call on the little rector.

She always hated these duty visits to the bereaved for whatever could one say to a broken old widower, whose hopes for years had been centred on an only son who had taken a double-first at Oxford and whose brains were now at the bottom of a French ditch? Expressions of sympathy had been all very well in 1914 and even in 1915 but they were fatuous after years of slaughter and the actual presence in the Valley of so many maimed men. She made the effort, however, borrowing Maureen's battered Ford, for she was now close on five months' pregnant just as she had predicted, although it no longer seemed a subject to joke about. A baby on the way was just one more responsibility at a time when she needed the maximum freedom of movement.

She found the rector at work in his glacial, book-filled study and although he looked tired and ill he seemed to her to have derived some kind of fortitude from his faith which was more than could be said of most of his flock in identical circumstances. He seemed also to have acquired a kind of pride in his son's share in the war, for he said, after showing her Keith's last letter praising the courage of some of the wounded he had tended, "I was against him going to begin with, you know, but I realise now that he was right and I was wrong! I've since wondered if the early martyrs wouldn't have made their point just as forcibly by electing to serve in the arena, perhaps attending to wounded gladiators and animals. I always knew Keith would justify

me but I never imagined it would occur in this roundabout way!"
Claire, somewhat puzzled, asked him to explain and he went on,
earnestly, "Oh come, Mrs. Craddock, you and your husband have
never had any illusions about me being a failure here, just as I was in
my last parish and the one before that! I was never unaware of it but
I could at least say to myself, 'I fathered a first-class scholar, whose
personal impact may be as feeble as mine but whose brains will win
him a real place in the world! And they would have done that, you
know. Now, I suppose, I must find consolation in the thought that his
presence out there must have been instrumental in bringing a hundred
or so back from the dead and I could hardly think that if Keith had
been just one more man with a gun." He smiled, politely and nervously, just as he did every Sunday on ascending the pulpit to begin
sermons that were barely tolerated by his war-time congregations, and
then he pointed at a large framed photograph of Parson Bull, his
predecessor, still hanging over the fireplace. Bull had had himself
photographed in hunting rig and contemplating the former rector's
Hogarthian build, and insolent, bulging eye, it occurred to Claire that
one could spend a lifetime looking for two more dissimilar priests.
Horsey said, "I keep it there to remind me there are various ways of
preaching the gospel, Mrs. Craddock. Bull's way was a century or
more out-of-date but it worked far more effectively than mine. You
have to admit that!"

"No," said Claire, beginning to assess the parson's true stature for
the first time, "I don't admit it! Bull's way wouldn't work any longer
and I think the people about here are going to need your methods in
the very near future. My husband never has thought of you as a
failure, for at least you achieved something he always wanted by
reconciling the Anglicans and the Nonconformists in the Valley. All
Bull ever did was to hold them apart by brute strength!" Horsey
accepted the compliment with a slight inclination of the head and
thanked her for calling. At the door she said, suddenly, "Look here,
Rector, why don't you come up to the house and hold a non-
denominational service for the convalescents? I daresay most of them
are beyond any parson's reach but you might catch the odd lost sheep.
Anyway, even the scoffers would like a change. The camp padre
doesn't impress them very much."

"Then I'm sure I should impress them less, Mrs. Craddock. After
all, can you wonder they've lost their faith? I don't think we parsons
have come very well out of this war. Keith wrote saying every German

has the words '*Gott Mit Uns*' emblazoned on his belt. Besides, what would I talk to them about?"

She had a sudden inspiration. "Your son!" and he looked at her sharply, saying, "Wouldn't that be parading a personal grief, Mrs. Craddock?"

"No, I don't think it would. Many of them wouldn't be alive now if they hadn't been brought in by stretcher-bearers."

He seemed vaguely impressed by this and stood holding the door, his eyes on the yellow slush that had accumulated on the step.

"Well, I'll think it over," he said at length. "Anyway, it was kind of you to ask and kinder still to call." She went down the path to the car and heaved herself in, relieved to be done with the visit. "Poor little beggar," she thought as Marlowe, the sexton, who had lost two sons swung the engine, "he's putting a brave face on it but I think this has about finished him." But the Reverend Horsey was far from finished. Within the week he not only surprised Claire but several hundred others, including himself.

When the sound of the car had died away Parson Horsey went back into his study and sat down at his desk, poking about among the mass of papers until he found a closely-written sheaf of manuscript left by Keith after his last leave, in December. Horsey studied each page carefully, sitting there until the light faded. Then, lighting the lamp, he put the manuscripts away and began to re-read his son's letters, more than a score of them, written from France. When the house-keeper came in with his cocoa he was writing to Claire and his letter, delivered by hand the following morning, puzzled her. He said he would accept her offer to conduct a non-denominational service in the big ward next Sunday, subject to two conditions; attendance was to be optional and she must on no account circulate news of Keith's death among the patients. She sent a message to Nun's Bay camp informing the resident padre that the local rector would conduct the service on the following Sunday but was already half-regretting having invited Horsey to preach. The men, as she well knew, had shed what religious beliefs they held in France, and their approach to parsons was at best negative and sometimes hostile. "We on'y saw a few o' the R.C.s up the line," one of the men told her. "Them others, they'd slip across during a quiet spell, dish out a few Woodbines an' nip orf ruddy quick! It's nice to 'ave one 'andy when you're buried they say but me, I don' go much on 'em! Sooner put me money on

832

Jumbo I would," and he showed her a small ivory elephant attached to his identity discs. Because Horsey was coming at her own invitation, however, she felt responsible for his reception and knowing that most of the more mobile patients would make themselves scarce before the service began she filled a couple of benches in the ward with household staff and a few of the V.A.D.s who had been allocated to her before Christmas. She was not really Commandant now, although she kept the title by courtesy. Her pregnancy had curtailed her nursing activities and a professional matron was due to arrive any day to cope with an influx of more seriously wounded men.

Horsey arrived about ten-thirty and the tepid service began, attended by no more than half-a-dozen of the active convalescents and, perforce, by those confined to bed. After the second hymn Horsey walked briskly behind the table they used as an altar and stood midway between the two nearest beds, blinking and fumbling with some notes he held in his hand. One of the men at the far end of the ward began to cough and deliberately prolonged the spasm but the rector waited quietly and when there was silence began, in an unexpectedly firm voice, "I daresay most of you chaps are familiar with stretcher-bearers! I'm not going to bore you with a sermon and I haven't even thought of a text. All I want is to read you a piece of writing sent me by a young man who spent a year in France and has since died. He calls this piece '*Truce, 1917*' and it tells of an incident that happened on the edge of a place called Pilckem Wood, near Ypres."

There were several men present who had unpleasant memories of Pilckem Wood and one of them, who had lain under it a day and a night with a broken thigh, involuntarily advertised as much by exclaiming, "Christ!", and left it at that. His exclamation had an unlooked-for effect on some of the others, who scowled and hissed "Shhh!" whereas the man who had shown Claire his elephant charm, sat up and said, very sternly, "Stow it, mate!" Claire, sitting on the end of the form under the window, glanced at Horsey and noticed that he seemed unruffled by the stir. He cleared his throat and at once began to read.

It was a straightforward piece of prose telling a simple, factual story of a fifty-minute cessation of hostilities towards the end of the Passchendaele battle, when men of both sides came out into the open to collect the wounded. There was nothing very remarkable about this, Claire decided. Paul had told her that it often happened but it

833

occurred to her that the writing was remarkable for its restraint. It made no attempt whatever to imitate the purple passages of a magazine story and, what was even more unusual, it contained no irony so that it was neither a conventional "call-to-arms" nor an indictment of war but simply an account of what actually occurred during the lull, as seen from the point of view of someone grubbing about in the shell-holes in search of men with a chance of recovery. The dying, it said, were given morphine and the dead were left lying where they had fallen in the morass. Time was an essential factor in the operation. Every man in the open knew that the firing would begin again at any moment and soon enough it did when infantrymen on both sides fired shots over the stretcher-parties' heads, warning them to return to their own lines.

When the rector had finished there was a silence such as Claire had never heard in the ward. At first she thought it was due to embarrassment but then, looking at the man she thought of as "Jumbo", she realised that this was not so, for he was looking at Parson Horsey with a respect that she had never seen him bestow on any visitor, commissioned, civilian or clerical. It was as though, at any moment, he would embarrass them all by applauding but to Claire's relief he continued to stare straight at the little man standing between the two beds. Horsey used the pause to grope under his surplice and his hand re-emerged holding a small packet of letters tied with tape. He shuffled them carefully, selecting one with the air of a man who considers himself unobserved and then, clearing his throat once more, he said, "The chap who wrote that was killed at the beginning of this month. The night before he was killed, however, he wrote two letters and one of them was passed on to me by his wife. I hope you will forgive me if I read this letter to end this little service. It isn't very long but I think it helps to clarify the motives of many of the conscientious objectors. You see, this chap was classified as a C.O. who felt strongly enough about his beliefs to go to face gaol for them. At the last minute, however, a friend home from France persuaded him to enlist as a stretcher-bearer. Now I don't know what you think of conscientious objectors; not much I imagine and therefore I would be less than honest if I failed to tell you this man once came to me and asked my advice and I told him he ought not to compromise in any way. I told him that partly because he was a brilliant scholar, the kind of man who might have something useful to contribute to the world after the war, but on reading this final letter of his I see very clearly

834

that I was wrong. Perhaps you will agree, perhaps not, I don't know. I'm not nearly as sure of anything as I was a year or so ago."

He laid the packet of letters on the makeshift altar and took the one he had selected from its field service envelope. While he was doing this Claire looked round the hut expecting some kind of reaction to an introduction that she found utterly uncharacteristic of the Horsey she had watched begin so many half-apologetic sermons in the parish church on pre-war Sundays. There was no reaction and Horsey began reading:

"This is the first anniversary of my arrival in France and it seems a good time to jot down a thought or two that I should have put on paper months ago but somehow never seemed to find time, either before or since the Ypres fighting. First, please don't bother to send the books you promised. I shouldn't have a chance to read them and in any case it seems a shame to subject a book to the kind of treatment it gets out here. It was thinking of books, however, that led me to think of the places they belong —libraries, schools and universities where, on looking back, it seems to me I spent so much time and largely wasted time at that because, in making out what you might call my first annual report, I see that a man would have to be a fool not to learn more in one week out here than he could cram into a lifetime in a university that is, regarding essentials! Do you remember that old poem, the one in which Abou Ben Adam tells the recording angel to write him down as a chap who loved his fellow-men? Old Ben Adam could survive out here and might even enlarge himself but I doubt if poor old Shelley and Keats would last a week without going crazy!

"Well now, from annual reports to balance sheets. I've done some balancing up since we came out of the Passchendaele show and it's a pretty rum set of figures. On the debit side—carried forward from last year and the year before that—is death, blood, mud, lice, fear and boredom and on the other side?—call them hidden credits, sheer wonder at what a terrific pounding the average chap can take without breaking; the strength of the bond between men who survive the same near-miss three days in a row and, above all, the comforting thought that Hell can't be so bad after all for this is Hell right enough but men can still laugh in it—laugh and sing and are doing both right now in this half a cellar, the one group over a game of pontoon, the other accompanied by a concertina. End of annual report and presentation of balance sheet—with time to say, in the light of the last half-inch of candle, that I'm glad I'm here, even though I don't retract a word of anything I ever said about the stupidity and brutality of war for

if I hadn't come here I should have gone on cuddling my resentment behind prison bars and thinking myself no end of a martyr whereas here every poor devil is a martyr and there aren't enough stakes to go round! Some will survive, perhaps enough to draw up a fresh set of rules for the nations that used to call themselves civilised. Candle's going out. Good night. God bless."

Horsey repeated his shuffling act with the flimsy sheets and then, retrieving the letters on the table, returned the one he had read to its sheaf. Nobody spoke and nobody moved. Not a cough or a shuffle broke the silence, until Claire heard a dry, indeterminable sound on her left and turning saw Mrs. Handcock's handkerchief go to her nose as she blew and then blushed because everybody turned to look at her as though, by looking, they diverted attention from any emotional display on their part. Mrs. Handcock, Claire recalled, would be one of those present who remembered Keith Horsey as a shambling adolescent drifting about the Valley with his long nose stuck in a book, a boy who had later married (or been married by) pretty Rachel Eveleigh of Four Winds, in defiance of her presently whoring father, but Keith's anonymity did not diminish the impact of Parson Horsey's sermon. Looking at him, and again at his congregation, Claire realised that here was a man who would never fear or falter again. She knew this, and the men knew it, but neither she nor they could have expressed in words precisely what he had told them that was new and therefore absent in any other sermon they had ever heard, or any sermon Horsey had preached in the past. She was aware of something else too — the enormous margin of error present in the snap judgments one sometimes made of other human beings.

II

Corporal "Jumbo" Bellchamber, one of the few enlisted men present when Parson Horsey preached on conscientious objectors, came face to face with the rector a month later at a double wedding in the parish church. On that occasion Jumbo was a groom, together with his inseparable companion, Lance-Corporal Georges Brissot. The occasion was the only cheerful one in the Valley that season, a time when General Ludendorff and his highly-trained infiltration squads demonstrated that there was, after all, one way of breaking the deadlock in the West.

The Bellchamber-Brissot alliance was one of those improbable

836

partnerships that sometimes emerge from service in the field. For a long time now they had never operated apart and it was therefore entirely fitting that they should take, as brides, two other inseparables, Cissie and Violet Potter, who had privately agreed that it was time they looked to the future and made a grab while there were still eligible men alive in the Valley.

They might have done worse. Jumbo, although wan and short of breath after three years in France ending with double pneumonia and pleurisy, was still more or less whole, whereas his big, swarthy, mild-mannered friend had a cork foot but, to offset this disadvantage, practical experience in farming dating from pre-war days in the province of Quebec. Brissot's injury had left him with an ungainly, bobbing limp, that gave people the impression he was forever on the point of tumbling head over heels but otherwise he was quite a catch, being strong, genial and capable of running a small farm. It was after Jumbo had discovered that the two Potter girls were in a position (once respectably wed) to obtain the lease of the Dell from the Squiress that a casual association developed into courtship and sundry slaps, chuckles and squeals were replaced with long, sighing glances and heavy breathing on the few occasions when Cissie and Vi could retreat to their familiar refuge in the laurels at the top of the drive.

Although Jumbo was barely half the size of his companion he was senior partner in the alliance, his ascendancy over the French Canadian dating from very early in the war, when the two had met by chance in the yard of an abandoned French farmhouse, near Château Thierry. Georges was a civilian then, who had been visiting French cousins when Von Kluck's hordes swept across north-eastern France and the visitor had been overlooked when his relatives decamped ahead of the British rearguard. Jumbo was a stray too, having been sent with a message to a British corps on the right, where he lost himself in a maze of unsignposted roads. He took refuge in the barn of the farm where Georges was stranded and they did not meet until a patrol of four Uhlans rode into the farmyard in search of forage. From an attic window the French Canadian watched all four German cavalry-men fall to the rifle of a single British straggler who had installed himself in a loft.

Georges was dumbfounded by the speed at which it happened. Down they went—one, two, three, four, just like wooden ducks at a shooting booth, the saddles emptying so quickly that Georges was persuaded the entire British Army had returned to rescue him. When he realised that his saviour was a single, bow-legged little soldier he was so impressed that he never recovered from the shock. From then on he was Jumbo's man and after helping him recover the Uhlan's horses on which they caught up with Smith-Dorrien's footsore columns, he joined the Cockney's unit as interpreter, later enlisting and sharing his friend's varying fortunes through Neuve Chapelle, Loos and the Somme. They emerged from these disasters unscathed but the weather at Passchendaele was too much for Jumbo, despite a remarkable toughness, resilience and unfailing optimism. Then a carelessly-handled dud shell gave Georges the privilege of prolonging the alliance indefinitely, so that they found themselves wintering at Shallowford, where Jumbo's high spirits made him a great favourite with the Potter girls, who had always preferred the noisy, boisterous lovers.

The double proposal was put to the girls the day that Jumbo received his discharge, Georges having been invalided out a month or so before. Until then Georges had never thought of marriage or settling in England for good but he accepted all his friend's decisions and reposed complete and utter trust in his judgments, despite the fact that Jumbo's speech was still largely incomprehensible to him. Georges spoke and understood English well but the Cockney idiom defeated him. He could never learn, for instance, that a "butcher's" meant a "look" or that when Jumbo announced he was ready to climb stairs and retire to bed he did not say so in as many words but said he was "hitting the apples-an'-pears fer a kip". Thus his announcement that marriage to the Potter girls would be an investment in the future bewildered him. Jumbo said, after studying his discharge papers, "This is it, cock! We're both aht on our ear and we gotter get weavin' bloody quick, mate! I did think o' going fer moonishuns where they say you c'n earn a fortune but seein' as ol' Jerry 'as nearly shot 'is bolt, I don't reckon we'd 'ave time ter dig ourselves in before we start scrambling fer jobs with all the other bleeders in Civvy Street! Do yer fancy a nice bit o' country, like this here?"

Georges, understanding nothing but the final sentence, said that he found the locality very much to his taste, for it reminded him somewhat of wooded areas on the shores of the St. Lawrence. Jumbo took this for unqualified assent, saying, "Right! Then, Bob's your uncle! Them two bints 'ave got a farm, an' since they're only working 'ere while they look for a couple o' mugs to run it we'd better get stuck in before some other greedy baskit catches on! Since there ain't a pin to

838

choose between 'em ser far as looks goes we'll toss for 'em an' after that you leave me to do the torkin'!"

They tossed, Jumbo winning Cissie and Georges Violet. When a local busybody pointed out that, although well over thirty and unwed, the girls had already raised a small family between them Jumbo was indignant, not with the brides-to-be but with the informant. "What of it?" he demanded, unconsciously reiterating the claim of Edward of York, "I'm a bachelor and I reckon I've got 'arf a dozen running around somewhere! Besides, they're bringing us house, farm an' furniture as a bleedin' dowry, ain't they? Gor blimey, whose askin' for jam on it?"

It was Parson Horsey's impressive performance in the ward that inclined Jumbo in favour of a church wedding and the ceremony was probably the best attended in the history of the church. Everyone was there, including Claire, all her family, and a motley guard of honour representing half-a-dozen regiments from the convalescents. Later the happy foursome repaired to the Dell to fortify themselves with a quart or two of Meg's hedgerow wine before beginning the task of spring-cleaning the decrepit farmhouse.

Claire wrote an amusing account of the ceremony to Paul that same night but it was a long time before the Squire of Shallowford was aware that the Dell, always the odd man out among his farms, had entered upon a new era under Anglo-French management. He never, in fact, received her letter, for the Potter girls were married on Saturday, the sixteenth of March and five days later the entire British line opposite St. Quentin had collapsed, Ludendorff's stormtroops gaining as much ground in twelve hours as combined French and British offensives of the war had won in three and a half years.

There was another matter that would have interested him in the letter Claire posted the day after the Dell wedding; this concerned her personal handling of yet another Four Winds' crisis, events having reached a point where intervention on her part seemed essential.

Everybody in the Valley knew that Farmer Eveleigh kept a mistress but the scandal had died down after Marian Eveleigh had pulled herself together, turned her back on the spirits and spent all her working days at the big house where she was regarded as the most reliable local hand on the staff. One day in early March, however, Claire had found her weeping and distraught and persistent questioning uncovered the cause. Eveleigh, Marian said, had now taken his land-girl mistress into the house, offering his wife a choice between the room formerly occupied by the boys and the cottage lodging vacated by the land-girl. The affront to a woman who had borne Eveleigh six children and lost looks and figure in the process, so outraged Claire that without even consulting John Rudd, she checked the terms of the Four Winds' lease, borrowed Maureen's Ford and drove to the farm at such speed that Old Honeyman, herding sheep along the river road, had to scramble up the bank to avoid her onrush. She went in by the back door without stopping to knock and finding no one in the kitchen stormed upstairs shouting Eveleigh's name. He came out of the bedroom, his face covered with lather and razor in hand, standing gaping at her and looking, she thought, very seedy in his long-sleeved woollen vest and dangling braces. It was some time since she had seen him for he had kept clear of the big house since Paul's last visit and Claire, who admired his pluck and capacity for work without being able to like him, was surprised at the change in his appearance. He looked like an ageing man who was over-eating, drinking too much and possibly over-worrying. She went straight to the point, making no apology for her presence on his landing at eight-thirty in the morning.

"You and I are going to have words, Eveleigh!" she snapped, and when his hand went to his chin added, "Never mind shaving, come down just as you are!"

He followed her downstairs to the big, stone-floored kitchen, looking bewildered and alarmed.

"Has anything happened up at the house, Mrs. Craddock? Is aught amiss wi' Marian?"

"You may well ask that!" Claire snapped at him. "I've just learned from her what's been happening here and I came at once. It's got to stop, do you hear?"

His expression hardened and she realised that his initial anxiety had stemmed from a guess that his wife had had some kind of accident. As soon as he understood that his own behaviour was in question he began to bluster but not, Claire thought, with much conviction.

"I don' see what the 'ell it's got to do with you," he mumbled, "I'm not behind wi' me rent, am I?"

"I don't know," Claire said, impatiently, "I didn't stop to consult Rudd but I do know that if the Squire was here he wouldn't stand for what's going on at Four Winds!"

"But he knew about Jill," protested Eveleigh, "it's no dam' secret in the Valley!"

"He doesn't know that the girl has been installed in one of his farms and your wife turned out!"

"If she said that she's a liar!" said Eveleigh, flushing and wiping lather from his blue chin. "We haven't been man and wife for nigh on two years but I never turned her out! You c'n ask Jill or any one about here!"

"I'm not going to ask that girl anything," Claire said, "except to pack her stuff and move out before I leave! I can't stop you making a damned fool of yourself, or making your wife miserable, but I won't stand for a chit like that being mistress of a Shallowford farm! I'll give her ten minutes and no longer; I'm busy!"

He looked at her open-mouthed and it struck her then that the change in him since the war had invaded his home and deprived him of his boys was almost as great as that wrought in Will Codsall by his spell in the trenches. She remembered that Paul had always spoken of Four Winds as the most prosperous but the unluckiest farm in the Valley, and had sometimes half-jested about it being hag-ridden by Arabella's ghost. She could understand what he meant now, less on account of this hesitant, truculent man, standing with his back to the door and trying, almost pitifully, to strike a balance between the respect he owed her as his landlord's wife and his rights as an individual than on account of the cheerlessness of the kitchen which had no feeling of home. In pre-war days this had been a cheerful room with its brasses gleaming, its hearth swept, its oak furniture highly polished. Now it smelled of dry rot and looked drab and tarnished, as though nobody used it except as a place to eat and loaf about. One or two grubby garments lay on the settle, and dirty dishes, coated with grease, were piled on the centre board of the great oak dresser. The fire was smoking and the curtains were stained and wrinkled. She said, with deliberate contempt, "Jill seems to me a pretty poor exchange for a wife like Marian who gave you good service and loyalty! If this kitchen is anything to go by you made a damned bad bargain, Eveleigh!"

At the mention of the girl he scowled, drawing his heavy brows together. "Leave Jill out' o' this, Mrs. Craddock," he growled, "you got no call to insult her and none to order her out neither! I'm master o' this place so long as I pay up quarter-days, and you show me another farm in the Valley that has my yield, year in year out!"

"I'm not discussing your yield," Claire said, half-wishing she had brought John along to bully the fool, "but I stand by what I said. Out she goes or you'll live to regret it!"

The door behind him opened so suddenly that it struck him and he lurched forward a pace to reveal Jill Chilcott. Claire remembered her now as a sullen, generously-built girl, who had once served behind the counter at a Paxtonbury draper's. She was dark and coarse-featured but possessed a heavy sensuality that would appeal to a man of Eveleigh's taciturn temperament. She was also every bit as sluttish as the kitchen suggested, her uncombed hair hanging in great hanks either side of a petulant face. She had obviously just risen from bed and had not bothered to dress. All she had on was a dirty whalebone corset that nipped her waist and forced her breasts so high that she looked as grotesque as one of the dummies in the window of the draper's where she had worked before the war. Her skin was very white but an unhealthy white, as though she ate too much starch and avoided exercise.

Eveleigh said, roughly, "For Chris' sake get something on, girl! This is Mrs. Craddock from the Big House," and he threw her a flannel dressing gown that had been hanging on the back of the settle. She caught the gown but did not put it on, staring at Claire with far less embarrassment than her lover. Her wide, moist mouth was clamped in a little girl's sulk and she looked, Claire thought, rather too sure of herself in the circumstances.

"I bin listening," she announced, "I heard everythin' she said, an' you don't need to take no notice of 'er! None at all, see? Fact is, she's got no right 'ere an' you can order 'er out if you please!" She turned back to Claire who was now shaking with rage. "You wouldn't have no court order, would you? You know, one o' them notice-to-quit papers, signed be a Magistrate?"

The girl's insolence was so insufferable that Claire regained the initiative, ignoring her and concentrating on Eveleigh, who was now losing his truculence and was very embarrassed by the scene.

"I took the trouble to study your lease before I came," she said, "and I could have you out of here in three months! The Squire let you take over the Codsall lease on a triennial basis but it was never transferred to you. I'm sure Sydney, Martin's heir, would be very glad to let it revert to the Codsalls. He's already bought a farm in Nun's Bay and if he knew the circumstances of your tenure he'd probably apply to me for a re-transfer at once! Now get this slut out of here and reinstate your wife. If you do I'll ask Rudd to make out a new seven-year lease in your name but if you don't I'll write to Sydney Codsall this very day!"

It was a shot in the dark, or at least in the twilight, for Claire's study of the Four Winds' lease had been cursory but its effect upon Eveleigh was deadly and she saw this at once. Resentment and obstinacy ebbed from him and for a moment he almost cringed. She saw too that her threat had cut the ground from under the girl, who obviously knew Eveleigh as Paul and Rudd knew him, a man dedicated to these acres, someone whose entire life was bound up in stock and pasture between Sorrel and Teazel. She knew then that she had him, that nothing would be allowed to threaten his hold of the farm and that, in his heart and belly, he valued the least of his Friesian cows above the woman who had found a means of making a bad joke of his years of toil since Codsall's death.

The girl was a fighter, however, and made a final, desperate appeal, catching Eveleigh by the forearm and hanging there in what struck Claire as a kind of parody of an imploring wife in a Temperance magic-lantern show.

"Don' lissen Norman, she can't touch yer! She *can't*, I tell yer! She's bin put up to this by the old cow, Norman . . . !" but that was as far as she got for suddenly Eveleigh ceased to look either surly or hesitant but shook himself, like a man coming out of a daze and thrust her aside so violently that she was sent spinning across the room.

"Don't you call my missis names you bliddy whore!" he shouted, "I told you before 'bout that and I'll not tell you again! Do like Mrs. Craddock says! Pack yer things and go back to the cottage! Go on, damn you!" and swinging open the door he spun her round, planted a stockinged foot in her behind and projected her right across the hall to the foot of the stairs.

She fell on her hands and knees and remained crouching there but the terrible indignity of rejection must have sparked off her pride for, after a moment, she rose slowly and not ungracefully and said, in little above a whisper, "You won't get rid o' me as easily as this, Norman! I'll make you pay one way an' another, you see if I don't!", and as Eveleigh took a couple of strides in her direction she ran up the stairs and he came back into the kitchen, closing the door and crossing to the fireplace where he stood with head bowed and hands resting on the mantel as though the effort had exhausted him. It was so quiet that Claire could hear a hen clucking in the yard. She said: "You didn't have to do that, Eveleigh. She didn't move in without your invitation."

"Sometimes I could ha' killed her," he said, "*lots* o' times I could

843

ha' killed her and I daresay I would in the end if you hadn't come!"

He shivered and glanced round the room, so fearfully that Claire's flesh crept. It was as though she was listening to an echo of a scene enacted in the room during Arabella's time and described to her by Paul, years after the tragedy and this fancy was underlined by his next words. He said, bitterly: "This is an unlucky house, Mrs. Craddock. Sometimes I get the notion they'm still yer, the pair of 'em! I never thought o' that until my boy Gilbert got blown to tatters an' then my woman turned queer and didn't seem to take no pleasure in me but I've thought of it a lot since and maybe that's why I took up wi' that little bitch! She took me mind off me troubles I reckon," and he spat in the fire, shaking himself like a big dog scrambling from water.

Suddenly she felt a terrible compassion for him, a far deeper and more urgent pity than she felt for his wife, or his dead son Gilbert, or his daughter Rachel now mourning Keith and involved in pity for him was a little for the girl upstairs, who had tasted power for the first time in her wretched life only to be thrown out in the end like a pan of washing-up water. But he had suffered and was suffering far more than any of them, a man whose lifetime of hard, disciplined toil had led him to this—his wife a neurotic, his children dead or scattered and his self-respect in ruins. She said, gently, "Take a drink, Eveleigh. Is there whisky or brandy in the cupboard?"

Without shifting his position in front of the fireplace, he said, quietly, "There's gin and bitters. That was her tipple!" and Claire crossed to the dresser finding there a bottle of gin and a jug of apple juice. She fetched glasses, washed them, and poured him a stiff measure and a smaller one for herself, carrying it across to him and bending to give the sullen fire a poke.

"I'll get Mr. Rudd to make out a proper lease," she said. "You don't have to worry any more but you'll be far happier with Marian back to look after you. It's done her a lot of good working up there with the convalescents. She's almost over losing Gilbert now and I hear that Harold, your other boy, is doing splendidly in Palestine. He's commissioned, isn't he?" and when he nodded, "We're all going through a bad time but it'll end, sooner or later. Would you like me to send Marian over to clean this place as soon as the girl moves out?"

She did not know whether her words brought him any comfort. He heaved himself away from the mantel, swallowed his gin and sat

844

heavily in the inglenook, his big, brown hands clasped between his knees.

"I daresay it's hard for a lady like you to understand," he said at length, "but she helped get me through that time I heard about Gil and all that bliddy table-rapping Marian took to. That, and all the work an' worry and conniving, with everyone on at me to squeeze quarts into pint pots, an' dam' near every man and girl in the Valley going off to war or munitions! She was outside it all somehow. Never seemed to touch her, one way or the other. All she wanted was a strong man two-three times a night. It's hard to explain but . . ." Suddenly he got up and walked over to the window, as though confession was embarrassing him more than he could bear. Claire said, "You don't have to apologise to me. I understand better than you think. And I'm not really a lady you know, just a farmer's daughter, who was lucky to get a good man and stay in love with him. That's why I'm here, I suppose. The Squire isn't just a landlord. He thinks of people like you as his friends not his tenants, and he feels about this place just the way you do. You can say anything you like to me. It won't go further than this room!"

He looked at her gratefully and she saw that he was master of himself again and was glad for it excused the impulsive way she had challenged his privacy. He said, slowly, "What I was going to say was, her being a young woman made me think a bit of myself, I reckon, took me back to the old days, when I first come here to work for Old Maister an' Arabella. I'm turned fifty now and it comes hard on a man that age to see most o' what he's worked for shredding away, a bit here, a bit there. The boys went off, then two o' the girls but me an' Marian never fell out over aught 'till Rachel took up with that parson's son, poor little sod an' then Gil joined an' got hisself killed. I was wrong both times and I'll own to that now but I didden know it at the time. You don't, do you? You just say an' do first thing as comes into your head and then the damage is done! I'd have come through it all right if Marian had turned to me fer comfort instead o' they bliddy spirits and suchlike! Then Jill see how things were between us an' tried her luck so to speak. She come to me in the barn one day after I'd had no sense nor comfort out o' Marian for three months or more. I was about desperate I suppose, an' one thing soon led to another. So long as she was there, ready to parade all she got any time I was minded I could muddle along wi' the work but youm right o' course, there's no future to it!" He stopped suddenly and looked at her under

845

his heavy brows. "Do you think Marian'd cry quits an' come back, same as we used to be?"

"Yes," Claire said, "I'm sure she'd be glad to do just that."

"Right!" he said, "then I'll pay that bliddy volcano off an' have done with her and we'll pick up where we left off!"

Claire heard the girl bumping a case down the stairs and Eveleigh went out to her. There was a low rumble of voices, then a pause and finally the front door banged. He came back rather jauntily with a reluctant grin on his face and the tread of a man who has just settled a matter of business to his own satisfaction.

"I give her fifty pounds," he said, "that stopped her snivelling! A pair o' trousers an' a bit to spend on herself is all she needs to keep her contented. We won't hear no more of Jill," and then, resignedly, "it'll mean tellin' the Squire, won't it? If you're thinking of getting the lease straightened out, I mean?"

"Only the essentials," Claire told him, "although I daresay it would cheer him up to learn we had our own kind of troubles over here."

"Well, you tell him all you've a mind to, Mrs. Craddock and send Marian over soon as you like." He looked round the disordered kitchen with impatience. "This place needs a doin' over, don't it? I reckon Marian'll make the dust fly! Funny thing about most women—present company excepted o' course—either they can't have enough of a man one way, or they can't do enough for him another! Now Marian, backalong, she was different. She kept the place fresh but didden seem to mind how many kids come along!" He smiled to himself and Claire thought his ability to do that again was the most encouraging thing to emerge from the interview.

III

On the night of March 20th, 1918, Paul took a convoy of lorries carrying ammunition up to a battery about two miles behind the Green Defence Zone, in front of St. Quentin. The night was dry, muggy and unusually quiet. Not a single shell whined overhead and only very occasionally did a flare of one sort or another light up the blackness for a few moments. It was difficult to believe that somewhere up ahead were hundreds of thousands of men slopping about in trenches that were only just beginning to dry out after the thaw.

After arranging for the shells to be off-loaded, the major command ing the battery invited Paul into his spacious dug-out for a drink.

846

He was hardly more than a boy, with a boy's exuberance and lack of ceremony, and speculated gaily on the date of the long-awaited German offensive, saying that Jerry would probably wait for things to dry out a little more before trying his luck in the quagmire over which the British had tried to advance in the autumn, and when Paul asked if he thought the initial attack would be successful, he said, off-handedly, "Oh, they expect Old Fritz to gain some ground but our defences are fluid enough to cope with it. We shall just bring up reserves and counter-attack and in the end everything will be as-you-were I imagine. Well, here's to a safe trip back and I wish to God I was going with you! Things are devilish dull here lately and I'm overdue for leave."

Things remained dull until Paul's lorries were about half-way back to the dump. Then, about 3 a.m., all hell broke loose, first in the areas nearer base, then in the artillery zone behind him and finally right where the convoy was travelling, a mixture of high-velocity and gas shells straddling the road with terrifying accuracy. It was suicide to push on so Paul ordered the men out of the vehicles and let them disperse in the fields and they were pinned here for more than half-an-hour as the shifting barrage grew more and more intense and the landscape erupted under a continuous rain of shells. Paul was not long in doubt that this was it, the big push they had been promised as soon as Jerry had transferred a sufficient number of troops from the Russian front but what appalled him was the terrible intensity and accuracy of the barrage, as though thousands of guns of all calibres were concentrating on a relatively small area, switching back and forth with a horrid rhythm that prevented anyone making a dash for it. With the first lightening in the eastern sky came fog and Paul spared a thought for the poor devils trapped in the undermanned front line, saturated with gas, crouching in crumbling trenches and awaiting the first waves of the German infantry to appear through the mist that now lay heavily over the countryside.

About six o'clock, when the barrage seemed to be reconcentrating on the forward areas, he started the convoy moving again but before they had gone far a howitzer shell landed smack on the head of the column and the road was impassable. The pattern of the drumfire now resolved itself into a steady pounding of extreme back and front areas and only occasional shells, mostly gas, fell in the intermediate zone so that there was no alternative but to return to the battery site and await the arrival of trouble-spot engineers to clear the road. The men in the leading lorries had been killed outright so, unencumbered with wounded, they were able to turn and head back the way they had come, driving directly into the sheet of flame on the horizon.

Moving fast they covered the distance in just over twenty minutes but there was no sanctuary at the battery, nor was there much shelter in the gunners' dug-outs. A direct hit, possibly two or three, had registered on the site and the place was a shambles. Every gun but one had been destroyed and the only living member of the crews seemed to be a bombardier nursing an injured hand. He was able to tell him that, apart from a team over on the right, he was the sole survivor.

"We'd only fired a few rounds," he said, "they had us taped to an inch! I was over by the dump which didn't go up, thank Christ. I bin out two years but never seen anything like this, not even on the Somme. It's a different *kind* of straffing, sir, a proper your-turn-next carpet pattern. Jerry 'as all the bloody luck, don't 'ee? Look at the fog out there!"

Paul's sergeant put a field-dressing on the man and sent him over to the remains of the officers' dug-out. It was useless to send him back to the dressing station for the fog belt in the west was masking a leaping sheet of orange indicating that the barrage had switched yet again and was now firing at extreme range.

The gun on the right was still in action but its detonations sounded like apologetic coughs against the roar of the overall barrage. The ground quivered and heaved and the din penetrated the deepest recesses of the brain, slamming the door on every impulse not directly concerned with self-preservation. Paul staggered across to the battery H.Q. post and on his way recognised the remains of the boyish major who had entertained him three hours before, identifying him from among several blood-stained bundles by his military moustache and the crown on the lapel of his tunic. There was nothing he could do but get his surviving fourteen men under what cover was still available and there they remained until, through the tormented fog-belt, came the first of the beaten infantry.

They arrived in twos and threes, stumbling, blear-eyed men, some without rifles and about half of them walking wounded trying forlornly to find their way to a dressing station. Only one, a hard-bitten sergeant of a Midland regiment, was coherent and told Paul of chaos and carnage up the line where break-throughs had occurred right and left of the sectors his company had been holding.

"Couldn't do a damned thing to stop 'em!" the man said, with a curse. "The saturation strafe they sent over at first light wiped out two-thirds of us. All the trenches up there are shallow and under-manned and then down comes this bloody fog to cap all! We held 'em off for a time with two machine-guns but they by-passed us and went round the flanks. It's a real bloody cave-in if you ask me and it'll take days to harden up, even if we've got plenty o' reserves back there!" He glanced bitterly at the fog which lay low on the ground all about them. "By God!" he muttered, "if we'd had fog like this at Third Wipers we could have gone all the way to Berlin!"

Then a wounded captain arrived and with him an astonishingly composed Engineer, a tall, angular Scotsman with iron-grey hair who had been up in the support line all night installing a pump. Paul never forgot him, a polite, methodical man of well over forty who took com-mand of the half-demoralised mob of wounded and stragglers now milling about the littered gun-site. The Scotsman said they would have to organise a road-block and rallying point until reserves came up and a counter-attack could be mounted and his quiet confidence spread to Paul and some of the unwounded N.C.O.s, who at once set to work, driving the three remaining lorries broadside on across the road, digging in each side and hauling timber and wire from the shattered gunpits and dug-outs to make some kind of entanglement to protect front and flanks. Men and more men trickled in until there were about two or three hundred to man the strongpoint, and as soon as the barrage lifted Paul sent off two despatch-riders to the rear with scribbled messages reporting their strength and position. The Scots-man told him that they were on the furthest edge of the Green Zone that had been designed for defence in depth but that the German attack had been launched before the new trenches were much more than surface scratches. There were plenty of tools available, and the men dug furiously after they realised they were out of range of all but long-range artillery and that the very speed of the German advance would mean a long interval must elapse before field batteries could be moved forward to give their infantry support. The bombardment had slackened appreciably and what there was of it seemed to be concen-trated on areas further back, probably in the hope of checking the flow of reserves in the Green Zone. They had dug and wired a semi-circular strongpoint by nine o'clock and sited their three light machine-guns and two Lewis-guns by the time the first parties of German infantry appeared through the thinning fog at a range of perhaps four hundred yards. By then the gun on the right, that had been firing over open sites, was silent, having run out of ammunition and the Scotsman, walking upright along the curving trench, did not give the order to fire until the scattered groups on the edge of the mist were within close range. They went to ground at once and during the lull that followed some of Paul's men brought up rations and a small jar of rum salvaged from the battery command post. Paul tried to contact the rear by telephone but the wire must have been cut to pieces by the bombardment, so the Scotsman despatched several of the walking wounded with orders to fan out both sides of the road and take their chance getting through with first-hand reports on the situation.

About midday the Germans attacked again, this time in greater strength and with at least two heavy machine-guns, but they were again beaten off and the Midland sergeant, who seemed to Paul the kind of man badly needed at Supreme Headquarters forty miles back, said that in his view the enemy was employing completely revolutionary tactics in this offensive, pushing on wherever the resistance was weak and leaving the strongpoints to be mopped up by reserve divisions armed with mortars and supported by light artillery.

They were there in the improvised defence-hedgehog until dusk but had nothing worse than light machine-gun fire and sniping to contend with. The Germans out ahead had a flame-thrower but were never able to get close enough to use it. About six, to everyone's relief, a despatch-rider arrived on a Douglas motor-cycle, with orders to retreat to a map reference three miles in the rear and they pulled out, taking the less badly wounded along with them and probed their way over the shattered plain for hours, occasionally being fired on by other groups of stragglers from sectors south and north of the St. Quentin trenches. In one of these blind encounters the Scots captain was shot through the head; Paul never knew his name.

In the early hours of the morning they came unexpectedly upon a new line of strongpoints where reserves, rushed up earlier in the day, were furiously digging in. Paul and the survivors of his group were sorted out and directed to a scratch M.T. centre, established in front of Rouy le Grand. It was, they told him, thirteen miles from the previous front line. At Third Ypres, Paul reflected, it had taken the British four months and something like half-a-million casualties to capture a couple of miles of liquid mud.

He remembered that first day clearly enough. The intensity of the switched barrages, the bloody shambles of the battery site, the cool, angular Engineer who had organised the defence, and even irrelevant details, like the dead gunner's pathetic moustache and the bombardier's shattered hand, but he could never recall the day-to-day life of the next few weeks, remembering the period only as a grey, misted-over interval, shot through with stress, fear and constant movement that resulted in a terrible physical exhaustion. More often than not throughout April and early May he seemed to be asleep on his feet or driving a Leyland lorry over the remains of roads and tracks, weaving between an eternal patchwork of shell-holes and breathing stale air through his respirator. His senses were numbed by shock, noise and lack of sleep so that there was no rhythm to his existence, as during his previous fifteen months in the field. His unit, merged into other decimated units, was flung here and there, north, south and back again, wherever it was needed to bring up rations and wire and ammunition and sometimes the lorries seemed to be moving to no purpose for days on end. All the men whose names he remembered disappeared into the chaos of the shifting front but others replaced them, half-trained boys of eighteen and wary, workshy men of nearly fifty, who waddled about much like Old Honeyman tending sheep in the big paddock at home. No mail came through, or if it did he was never there to receive it and everywhere the front seemed to be crumbling and the war as good as lost. As soon as the St. Quentin break-through was plugged outside Albert he went north into the dismal basin of the Lys, again fighting as an infantryman during the break-through at Bailleul. Then, when the northern offensive was held, he was sent south again to lovely, unspoiled country round Vailly, north of the River Vesle, where the exhausted survivors of St. Quentin and the Lys were just in time for the May offensive on Chemin des Dames, and Ludendorff's stormtroops smashed through on a broad front, penetrating to the Marne.

It was here, just before the supreme German effort, that he had a few days' respite, drifting up and down quiet country roads through villages still inhabited by civilians and during this blessed period he sometimes let his mind drift back to the Valley, to the view of the meandering Sorrel seen from the south-west corner of Hermitage Wood but before he had made contact with home, or even caught up on his arrears of sleep, the third hammer blow fell on the exhausted divisions manning the Vauxaillon-Craonne Line and suddenly he was a rifleman again, holding out in forlorn little centres of resistance and washed back by the indefatigable grey tide from the east, escaping death sometimes by inches and going back and back with the wreck of British and French units blasted from their positions by mathematically plotted barrages, like the one that had shattered the old front line opposite St. Quentin. On the morning of the 29th of May the tide finally engulfed him, blotting out past and present for a period of fifty-nine days.

It came without pain, without even realisation. Just a soundless explosion like the red-gold wink of distant shell fire at night and then an eternity of dreams, some troubled, like the recurring dream of his fever in hospital sixteen years before, some tranquil, like the memory of long summer afternoons in the Valley, with Claire coming down the goyle to Crabpot Willie's shack wearing an old-fashioned sun bonnet and waving as she approached yet never seeming to reach his side.

They had just made one more lurch south-westwards towards Soissons, no longer really an army after days of marching, countermarching, of losing touch with their flanks, and being pounded by artillery and whipped by machine-gun fire that seemed sometimes to come from the rear. They retired, still struggling, a rabble of British, French poilus, and French civilians caught up in the backward heaves of the shattered divisions and it was Paul's quixotic concern for a wounded poilu that brought him down.

He had never shared the British contempt for their allies, seeing the French not as ragamuffins, whose trenches were filthy and uninhabitable, nor yet, romantically, as the inheritors of the Austerlitz tradition but as a nation of peasants and small craftsmen, like the people of the Valley who had been cruelly used by their militarists and politicians. Their countryside, parts of which reminded him vividly of the Valley, had been fouled by the passage of armies and their dwellings reduced to rubble by the cannon of both sides. And all this time their blood had been poured out like dish-water in the Ardennes, in Champagne, and in witless offensives like that of General Nivelle, the previous summer. Yet somehow they fought on, doggedly and savagely, little swarthy men, for the most part, with blue-black whiskers and dark, burning eyes and lately, or so it had seemed to Paul, they fought without hope.

Some such thought must have crossed his mind when he saw the poilu making a feeble attempt to apply a field-dressing as he lay on the blind side of a grassy hummock. They were retiring over fields not yet reduced to the grey morasses of the north, a rolling countryside where hawthorn blossomed and wild flowers grew. Two Northumbrian privates were humping the company's surviving Lewis-gun and clumsy ammunition buckets, so Paul was comparatively unencumbered. The Frenchman rolled his eyes upward as Paul knelt beside him. His shoulder had been laid open by shrapnel that was still scything down from a battery behind the hill and as Paul raised him, grunting under his weight, another splinter whanged through the poilu's helmet, scattering his brains and ricocheting into Paul's temple. They fell together, locked in a grotesque embrace and the Northumbrians, leaving their stray M.T. officer for dead, ran down the slope to find cover in a farmhouse, promising each other that they would go back for his papers and identity discs as soon as it was dark.

They never did of course, for dusk found them caught up in the mass exodus from Soissons and it was a German stretcher-party that found Paul still breathing at dawn the next day and conveyed him, with some of their own stretcher cases, to the Soissons infirmary.

He owed his life to the presence there of a Leipzig brain specialist called Quirnheim. Bored with abdominals and fractured limbs the man took a mild interest in the case, extracting the splinter but telling his orderly that the English lieutenant would almost certainly die during the next twenty-four hours. When, on his rounds the following day, Paul was seen to be alive the specialist's interest in the patient revived. He took a closer look, skilfully removed another half-ounce splinter from a shallow wound forward of the left ear and told the grinning orderlies that the Englishman evidently possessed an even thicker skull than his commander-in-chief, Sir Douglas Haig, and thus stood a chance of recovery. Quirnheim had no opportunity of following the case through for the tide of war swept back through Soissons and all the seriously wounded were left behind when the Germans abandoned the railhead to counter-attacking French and Americans. He lay in a ward alongside twenty to thirty other critical cases and in late July the Americans moved in, so that there was nobody who could identify him, his discs having been mislaid, his uniform burned and his few personal belongings looted.

The war rolled away to the north-east and days passed before a few muttered words, overheard by an American nurse, identified him as an

Englishman, after which he was moved to a private ward and given individual attention. His ultimate emergence from the coma astonished and delighted the American surgeon, who, in the period ahead, was prone to take as much credit for Paul's recovery as his countrymen took for the overthrow of the German Empire. It was not until he was being invalided via Paris to England that a British doctor told him he probably owed his life to two factors, one French and one German. The shell-splinters, it seemed, had spent most of their force on the poilu's head but without Quirnheim's skill in replacing a section of bone with a silver plate the largest of them would have caused death. The information made Paul thoughtful. In later life he always felt diffident about the Croix de Guerre the French Government ultimately awarded him for his puny share in the Chemin des Dames battle; neither could he bring much enthusiasm to the post-war Hang-the-Kaiser campaign.

V

Claire's fifth child, another girl born early in the morning of July 1st, gave her as little trouble as her sisters, Mary and Whiz. Maureen said, when she returned to the Big House after her morning rounds, that Claire was an example of the law of compensation, "carrying with difficulty but bringing forth with despatch". It was not until the baby was safely delivered, and Maureen, paying her return visit, was enjoying a quiet cigarette before beginning her evening rounds, that the doctor began to understand Claire's obstinate and utterly irrational optimism concerning Paul. It was not, she decided, simply a pregnant woman's talisman, for although both she and John considered Paul dead, along with all the others except those three indestructibles, Ikey, Smut and Henry Pitts, Claire's faith had never faltered. Maureen said, admiring her patient's composure, "You're an unlikely cuss, Claire! You really have made up your mind that he'll soon be lounging in here on those long legs of his, haven't you?" and Claire said, "Yes, I have. He'll be along soon enough and not all that much the worse for it—but this isn't just a lifebuoy, Maureen, of the kind all women grab at when they get a 'Missing' telegram—there's a link between people who have spent years building up a deep, personal relationship like mine and Paul's, and yours and John's. Separation and distance can't sever it and if death did then one would know. I'm not sure of much any longer but I'm confident of that! Now let me have another look at my baby."

She struggled into a sitting position as Maureen lifted the child out of the cot and placed her in her arms. " 'Now baint her a pretty li'l maid'?" Claire demanded, " *baint* her, now'?" and Maureen, whose familiarity with babies had warped her judgment on these matters, agreed that she was indeed, with features of almost classic regularity, great tufts of hair a shade more blonde than her mother's and perfectly formed hands and feet. "I'm so proud of her I could ask Parson Horsey to ring a peal of bells!" Claire said and Maureen added glumly that they could reserve that for news of Paul and an end to this idiotic slaughter, for although relieved for Claire, for whom she had always had a deep affection, she was miserably depressed by the hopelessness of life, what with poor old John laid up with the Spanish influenza scourge, half the Valley down with the same epidemic, and twice as much work as she could handle at her time of life. She came home, tired out, at eight o'clock and poured herself a stiff double whisky, carrying it up to sit with John for a spell. She tried to inject him with some of Claire's irrational cheerfulness, telling him what a handsome daughter the Squiress had just produced but John Rodd was gloomier than ever these days. He had never believed "missing" was more than an indirect way of saying "dead" and she knew that his friendship with Paul Craddock had always meant a great deal to him, as much and perhaps more than their marriage, or their seven-year-old boy, now boarding with Mary Willoughby at Deepdene in the hope that he would elude the 'flu virus.

"Well, I daresay it'll sustain her a bit," he grumbled, "but you know and I know that it's damned nonsense!"

"This morning I wasn't convinced it was," she admitted. "Claire talked about a thread between two people who grew fond of one another over the years and somehow it seemed to make sense, as though one spins a kind of strand from the heart and a final break registers itself physically."

"By God we shall have you table-rapping before long!" he exclaimed and then, "No! It's better to face facts and make one's dispositions accordingly!" For a moment he was racked with a violent fit of coughing and Maureen noticed, with renewed concern, how old and tired he looked.

"What *kind* of dispositions?" she asked, after he had taken a sip of his blackcurrant syrup.

"Oh, don't ask me now," he said, irritably, "let's wait until the war's over! I don't see how she can run a place this size as a widow even though she won't be short of cash. Besides, all the heart will go out of her the moment she gets confirmation of his death and she'll sell up. Before we know where we are we'll have a damned profiteer moving in and when that happens I'm off, I can tell you! I shall put my feet up and spend the time left to me fishing and reading!"

She said, doubtfully, "Suppose she never gets confirmation?" and he growled, as he pulled the bedclothes up to his chin, "So much the worse for everybody, especially her! She'll turn into one of those damned neurotic women like Victoria, sniffing about the place and complaining that someone has moved his toothbrush out of line! I know Claire Derwent, my dear. Without that lanky great dreamer she'd be lost and the children wouldn't mean a damn thing to her," and although Maureen did not relish the thought she believed him for she too knew Claire and it had always intrigued her how far Claire's children had lagged behind in her affections. She recalled how eagerly she had turned her back on the family when Paul had been last on leave and how jealously she had kept him closeted in that love-nest of theirs, down in the goyle. "I suppose the truth is she's got an excessive amount of animal vitality," she mused aloud, "and he's the only man with the key to release it. I've noticed it often and, to tell the truth, it sometimes amused me. The poor gel almost has an orgasm every time he slips his arm around her waist!" She sat beside him for a few moments before saying, "It isn't just Paul, John! Everywhere I call nowadays the sparkle and zest has gone, and most of the hope too. How can any of us start fresh again, at our age?"

"We can't," he said, "but that isn't important. The new arrivals, like that youngster born today will and I daresay they'll make something better of it! A third of Europe's population died in the Black Death and ten years later this country alone was exporting enough wool to mine gold for a thousand families like the Gilroys and the Lovells. You, me, Paul, Claire, Will Codsall and the rest, we're just the latter-day Black Death generation, the unlucky bunch caught at the bottom of the dip. I daresay the replacements will learn from it and if they don't they deserve all they get! Turn the light down, old girl, I'm going to try and sleep before this blasted cough gets a hold!" but Maureen's Celtic curiosity had been awakened, not only by what he had said but by the memory of Claire's steadfast faith in the face of near certainty regarding Paul's fate. She said, "Wait John — I'll give you a tablet and some hot milk to quieten the cough and make you sleep — but you've said that much, tell me a little more. Where does Paul Craddock's archaic dream fit into this switchback pattern? Is there any justification for his stick-in-the-muddery, in an age dominated by machines when the best brains in Europe seem to have lost their way? What I mean is, what made him succeed here? Was it simply obstinacy, vanity?"

He thought a while before answering. It was a question that had occurred to him often over the years for, in its answer he imagined, lay the core of his deep attachment to the man.

"It isn't either," he said, at length, "but something a good deal more uncommon. Fundamental too. Nothing like it has been seen around here in a very long time!"

"What makes you say that?"

"I've spent most of my life among people with their noses in dirt," he went on, thoughtfully, "and he was the only one who neither looked on land as property or as a way of life that carried an insurance against hunger. To him it was the flesh and bones of humanity, the only true essential and whatever success he had here was the result of that plus a natural talent for administration inherited from money-grubbing ancestors on some other side of his family! And that isn't the whole of it either! There was something else that held him in — two things, and kept him from overreaching himself and getting the backing of men he couldn't afford to lose."

"Men like you, John?"

"Not just me, all the farmers and the craftsmen about here."

"Well?"

"He never once put money before human dignity. All the time I knew him he only made one serious mistake."

"Grace Lovell?"

"No, by God! That wasn't a mistake! He learned from Grace in all kinds of ways. The mistake was that a person with as much to give as Paul Craddock should go and get killed in a battle that was a damned shoddy affair compared with the one he was fighting. That wasn't simply his tragedy either, it was a tragedy for everyone in the Valley!"

She saw that he was hot and flushed and at once felt contrite. "All right, John, I'm sorry I had to get you worked up at a time like this. I'll get your tablet and drink now," and she hurried downstairs, shocked and confused by his bitterness and by his acceptance of Paul's death as a fact.

And yet, as she pottered about in the kitchen waiting for the milk to warm, she was conscious of a sudden and inexplicable lift in spirits, so

857

that she said to herself aloud, "I wonder? I wonder if there could be anything in that thread-theory of Claire's?" She turned off the gas-ring and threw open the window, looking up at the stars in the clear, summer night and as she leaned there anticipation warmed her as it might a child counting the hours to Christmas Eve. "Would *I* know?" she thought, "if John had got himself blown to bits in China or Timbuctoo? Would *I* feel a sudden smart, like a half-healed scab coming off? Maybe I would, for who the devil am I to throw everything out the window that hasn't been laboratory tested? I learn something new about my job every day!" She poured the milk, dissolved the tablet and went up the narrow stairs a good deal more cheerfully than she had descended them ten minutes before.

CHAPTER EIGHT

I

THE influenza epidemic ran its course from Whin to Sorrel and across the Valley to the county border, striking down about one in four and killing some of the very young and the elderly. Arthur Pitts of Hermitage died that autumn and so did Marlowe, the sexton, whose two boys had been killed, one in France and one at sea. Sam and Joannie Potter lost their youngest, a baby of eighteen months, and Cissie Potter, now Cissie Bellchamber, lost the child sired by Jem, the Bideford Goliath. Before that, however, there was a brief season of hope, when the country rang with news of the collapse of the famous Hindenburg Line and it really did begin to look as if the end might be round the corner. Then, just as the harvest was being gathered in, the Valley folk noticed a stricken look on the face of the Squiress and could only suppose that she had received confirmation of Squire's death and, for some reason, was loath to broadcast the news. They were not long in discovering the truth. The latest telegram to reach the Valley concerned not the Squire but his protégé, the boy whom they remembered him treating as a son from the days of his first coming among them, and although most of them were fond of Ikey they were none the less slightly relieved, for there was still hope that Squire would turn up, just as old Smut had returned from the dead a year or so ago.

Claire tore open the telegram with fumbling, sweating fingers. It told her that Major Palfrey, M.C., of the Tank Corps, had died of wounds in a base hospital early in August and the heavy blow made her reel for somehow she had had almost as much faith in Ikey's survival as she had in Paul's. A day or so later a letter arrived from Ikey's Commanding Officer. Ikey, he said, had named her next-of-kin and it might comfort her a little to know that he had received his wounds actually in the Hindenburg Line, a few days after playing an important part in the decisive victory over the Hun. It did not comfort her at all. Apart from her own grief she realised how deeply Paul would mourn the boy and how much a part of the family he had become since that far-off day when he had unexpectedly sided with her in the matter of

859

young Simon's renunciation of fox-hunting. She might have derived a little comfort, however, could she have known that Ikey Palfrey was one of the very few serving soldiers on the Western Front who had at least seen his theories of the war completely vindicated before his death and also, in the few moments of consciousness vouchsafed to him after his transfer from Field Dressing Station to hospital, had been able to direct a nurse to mail a letter that had been several days in the writing.

On August 1st his had been one of the reserve squadrons of a massed tank attack on what looked like an impregnable section of the line, protected by formidable wire-belts and, as far as the attackers were aware, manned by resolute troops armed with the new anti-tank guns and well supported by artillery. Yet it cracked like a stick when the tanks waddled over it and Ikey's squadron, brought up for a heave against the support line, was equally successful for the ground was dry and the heart had gone out of many of the defenders. The advance went on all that week until the tanks were probing Proyart and Le Fisque, and the entire German defence line seemed to be crumbling.

A day or so later, feeling rather like the junior partner of a huge, floundering enterprise saved from bankruptcy by policies devised and initiated by him, Ikey went off to explore part of the famous line and descended into a deep, concrete-faced dugout, drawn there by curiosity and the lure of souvenirs. That evening he could view the war as something virtually over and done with and felt himself on the threshold of a new era in which the long roll of dead would have to be justified by the living and a new social structure more flexible than its predecessor. The sense of achievement made him pleasantly relaxed and reflective. It also made him criminally careless.

He directed his electric torch into the bunk recesses of the vast shelter, seeing a litter of abandoned blankets and items of kit and then, hanging on a bulkhead near the door, he saw the pickelhaube, the famous dress-helmet of the German Army symbolic of the very early days of the war, its patent leather and metal-tipped spike gleaming in the rays of his torch. Pickelhaubes were greatly prized as souvenirs and as he looked at it he suddenly thought of old Horace Handcock, the Valley patriot, who had been breathing fire and slaughter at the Germans ever since the dreadnought race of 1908 and the thought of old Horace made him smile for it occurred to him that Horace, crowned by this helmet, would caricature a fat German feldwebel. He had the same self-important gait, the same prominent

860

blue eyes and thick, brick-red neck and Ikey made up his mind on the spot to present Horace with the pickelhaube as soon as he got home.

He stood up and unhooked the helmet from the nail on which it hung and there was a blinding flash, a roaring in his ears and then an advancing wall of blankness that lifted him and blasted him clear across the dugout. The pickelhaube was a very obvious booby-trap and as a man who, off and on, had served on the Western Front since November, 1914, he should have known better. Much, much better.

II

Another and equally freakish stroke of bad luck came close to depriving the Valley of one of its most celebrated soldiers in the last few hours of the war.

Smut Potter, who had sniped at Germans in the flooded trenches east of Armentiéres as long ago as autumn, 1914, had then spent almost a year masquerading as a French idiot in German-occupied Péronne and had since survived Passchendaele and battles in open country that followed the break-throughs, was shot and crippled by a machine-gun bullet on the morning of November 11th, only three hours before the cease-fire.

There was a kind of justice surrounding the circumstances in which Smut got his Blighty and got it far too late to show a profit except in the way of a small disability pension. In the four years he had been in action he had killed, or had a hand in killing, over a hundred Germans some of whom were notched on his rifle stock although he stopped keeping score after they had trained him to use the Mills bomb. He had collected a wound or two here and there but never one serious enough to keep him out of the line for more than a month or so and this he had in no way resented. He liked Army life, balancing the bad items against the good, the loss of sleep, danger and discomfort against the acquisition of an enormous variety of goods all of which he redistributed to his friends and favourite officers. He had lost his stripes three times for drunkenness but had always regained them in the next push and like most front-line soldiers, fought without rancour, looking on the war as a kind of gigantic poaching expedition and the men in the trenches opposite as homicidal but impersonal game-keepers.

There had been rumours of an armistice for a week or more as he

861

entered upon his fifth winter of active service but Smut did not take them very seriously. From what he had seen of Fritz lately there was still a good deal of fight left in him and, as it turned out, he was right about that. On the final day of the war his battalion was advancing on a village east of Valenciennes, where a wounded German officer told them the enemy rearguard had gone back before dawn. So they went in, some hundreds of them and were milling about the Square when two well-sited machine-guns opened up and Smut went down with a bullet in the hip. He would have been hit again, probably fatally, had not his poacher's sixth sense somersaulted him into a doorway where he was protected by the bodies of less experienced men while the last-ditch Germans, including the wounded officer, were rooted out and despatched with bayonet and bomb. The orderly who dressed Smut's wound commiserated with him, pointing out that hostilities were due to cease that very day but Smut, lying on a stretcher await- ing transportation down the line, was philosophical, deciding that he had had more luck than any one man deserved and that luck did not use a calendar. While the wounded were awaiting ambulances to take them back to the advanced Field Hospital an airman on the stretcher beside him died. With a good deal of wriggling, and a certain amount of agony, Smut managed to acquire the airman's fur-lined boots, reasoning that they would almost certainly be looted by the R.A.M.C. orderly who removed the body and that boots such as these would come in handy on the soggy fields above the Dell.

During his long spell in hospital at St. Omer Smut's thoughts returned to Madame Viriot, the baker's widow who had sheltered him during his spell behind the enemy lines. In retrospect she seemed a homely, friendly and industrious body. He remembered then that she had talked about setting up a bakery in the Valley after the war and ordered him to get in touch with her at Lille as soon as the opportunity presented itself. He was not much of a hand at writing so he dictated a letter to a V.A.D. and, in due course, Madame arrived in person, quite beside herself with delight at being so miraculously restored to her stray Tommy. As soon as Smut could hobble about on crutches they were married by the Mayor of St. Omer, an occasion for much merry- making by the patients and hospital staff. Then, to Madame Potter's chagrin, the authorities began to make a ridiculous fuss about her accompanying her husband back to England before numerous formalities had been completed. The business proved so protracted that in the end she was left behind to cope with it, while Smut was shipped across the Channel to await discharge. He limped home to the Valley, a civilian once more, in the spring of 1919, and when he told his friends that he had married a Frenchwoman, and that she would soon be starting a bakery in Coombe Bay they thought it was just another of Smut's leg-pulls. They soon discovered that it was not for Madame arrived a fortnight later, with a mountain of baggage and commercial instincts that proved disastrous to George Endicott, whose bakery had run down during the war and was now offered for sale. Madame got it for two hundred pounds and within weeks of moving in was putting inches on the waistlines of Coombe Bay housewives. She did not expect Smut to contribute to the running of the little business, except for driving the old delivery van that she herself had assembled from a number of derelict vehicles rusting on the dump behind Nun's Bay camp. She was inclined to think that Smut had done his bit by ridding France of a hundred or so of the hated Boche and was entitled to rest on his not inconsiderable laurels that included the Military Medal. Smut took his good fortune for granted at the time but came to appreciate it when he ran across war comrades who were having the greatest difficulty in getting jobs and settling back into civilian life.

"I got to admit," he would tell his cronies in The Raven, "that I struck it cushy the day I met my ole woman! Them Frogs are diff'rent in all kinds o' ways but 'specially so when it comes to marryin' an' settlin' down. Now take Marie! She's boss from first light 'till lights out but from then on it's me who takes over and a Frenchwoman wouldn't 'ave it no other way! In public you minds your P's and Q's with 'em but soon as the shutters is up it's three paces be'ind fer the wimmin, just like the Wogs! Seems to work, too, seems to keep 'em happy and hard at it, although I offen wonder how we'd 'ave managed if Marie hadn't bin well past puppin'!"

He was to find out; before 1919 was done Madame Potter was proudly announcing to all her customers that the Ostend fortune-teller had been wrong after all. She was, by her reckoning, forty-two and had enjoyed, just as prophesied, three husbands but now (the Virgin be praised) she was *enceinte*, which Smut sheepishly translated as "in the family way".

"He will be a boy!" Madame declared with a whirl of gesture, "and he will grow up to kill hundreds of the Boche like his father!"

III

Henry Pitts, the Valley immortal, faced the end as he had faced the beginning, with mild surprise, with a touch of awe, with patience, amiability and the slow rubbery smile so seldom absent from his genial face.

Most of the men fighting on the Western Front were bewildered by the abrupt cessation of gunfire at 11 a.m., on the morning of November 11th, but they soon adapted themselves to it. It was otherwise with Henry Pitts; the occasion made a deep and lasting impression on him.

Sergeant Pitts, D.C.M., was sitting on the firestep of a hastily dug trench in a turnip field, north-east of Mons, when the guns stopped firing. He too had heard rumours of an armistice but like his neighbour Smut he refused to take them seriously for by now he was completely absorbed in the war and it was not often that he thought of the Valley, or his wife Gloria, or even of his beloved saddlebacks in their sties under Hermitage Wood.

At eleven o'clock, when it sounded as though every gunner and every rifleman in the Western Front was competing for the honour of having fired the final shot of the war, Henry's mind was more humbly engaged. He was trying to open a tin of bully beef with a very blunt bayonet and concentration had temporarily erased the rubbery smile from his face. Watching him, one on either side, were his two special pals, Corporal Watts and L/Corporal Eley, the one a former Blackburn cotton operative, the other a Cockney, who was entered on the battalion strength as bookmaker's clerk. They missed Henry's smile. It was like the sun going out and its absence augured badly for the peace for each of them had come to regard it as a Company barometer, indicating fair weather or foul in terms of light, heavy or medium straffing. The magic hour, and its accompanying explosion of fire-arms, seemingly left Henry unmoved for he could usually only think of one thing at a time but it stirred the imagination of his two companions. About five minutes past eleven L/Corporal Eley began to jump up and down like a child seeking permission to visit the lavatory. It was only when the racket had died away, and a rocket or two was soaring from the German lines, that Eley's fidgetings distracted Henry to the extent of causing him to rise, cock an ear in the manner of a man who suspects himself the victim of a practical joke, and say, "Be it true then? Do 'ee reckon there's aught in it, after all?", and without waiting for an answer he unslung his rifle saying, "Reckon I'll get up over an' take a look!"

At once they began to remonstrate with him. To a cautious man like Watts, one of the very few survivors of Kitchener's 1915 drive for recruits, it seemed madness to make a target of oneself on the strength of information supplied by officers a few months out of school and he laid a restraining hand on Henry's shoulder. "Nay lad!" he pleaded, "don't be so bloody daaft! Give 'em an' hour or so to cool off!" but by now Henry's rubbery smile was back again and he said, impatiently, "Oh, giddon with 'ee, Bert! Hark to the silence! Tiz all over, baint it?", and clawed his way over the parapet rising to his full height and standing there, the only living thing above ground in all that vast, dreary landscape.

He remained there for almost a minute and they gazed up at him unbelievingly, expecting, any second, to accord him the honours due to the last man killed in the war. Nothing happened, so presently Henry squelched purposefully out into no-man's-land, walking with his familiar splay-footed gait that anyone born in the Valley would have recognised a mile away. What astonished him most was the absence of shell-holes in his path until he remembered that Fritz had been leap-frogging back so rapidly that the area had never been subjected to heavy bombardment or cluttered with belts of wire. He was half-way between the lines when he saw a large, grey blob emerge from the earth and begin to plod directly towards him and in the first wake of the blob came other, smaller blobs, looking like a trail of disconsolate snails evacuating a cabbage patch. He stopped then and waited, aware that his mouth was dry and his stomach mutinous, as though he had swallowed a quart of canteen beer in a great hurry. The leading blob was now only some thirty yards distant and Henry identified it as a German sergeant approximating his own build, a big-boned, broad-shouldered man, very plump about the jowls so that his coal-scuttle helmet adorned his head like a small extinguisher on a fat Christmas candle.

The German did not seem as unsure of himself as Henry but advanced steadily and close behind him came half-a-dozen other Germans, still in file and led by a very thin officer, who seemed to walk very slowly, as though he found the clay too heavy for his boots. Then Henry noticed that the sergeant was smiling and pointing with his left hand to his right palm which held something that glittered and then raising his other hand to his mouth.

865

"Well Christ A'mighty!" Henry said to himself, "I reckon he wants to trade fags for them bliddy cap-badges he's holding!" and he hurried forward, fumbling in his tunic pocket for his Woodbines.

Then the Germans came forward at a run and suddenly he was surrounded by infantrymen of a Saxon regiment and his Woodbines disappeared in a flash as the Germans pressed upon him a variety of badges and emblems, including a matchbox holder emblazoned with a double-eagle and the legend *"Gott Mit Uns"* that Henry recognised as having begun life as a belt buckle. The German officer now came up with them and Henry saw that he was a very sick young man and was breathing hard, as though he had run a mile. In contrast to the plump sergeant the officer's helmet was too big for him, making his face look cavernous and pinched. He could hardly have been more than twenty and he looked, Henry thought, as if he was consumptive. The sergeant said something in German and the officer translated, flashing a pale smile at the Englishman. He spoke in rather lisping accents that reminded Henry of the occasional nob like Roddy Rudd and Bruce Lovell, who had strayed into the Valley from time to time.

"The sergeant asks if you will shake the hand," he said and Henry, impressed but embarrassed, said that he would gladly shake hands and did so. He had always respected the German front-line troops and, like most of the infantry, dismissed most of the atrocity stories as newspaper twaddle. Then the sergeant said something else and the officer, after a spluttering cough, again translated, telling Henry that the sergeant said he looked as though he was a farmer. Henry was so delighted at this that he seized the Saxon's hand again and shouted, "Youm right first time, Jerry! Now for Chrisaake 'ow did 'ee work that one out?" and after some difficulty, arising perhaps from the officer's unfamiliarity with the Valley dialect, the officer said Henry's hands had given him away whereupon Henry turned enthusiastically to L/Corporal Eley, who had come up at a run to harvest more cap-badges in exchange for the half-opened tin of bully, exclaiming, "Damme, Bert, theym smart as paint, baint 'em? Smart as paint they be, the whole bliddy lot o' them!", and Eley said he had never doubted it and searched his pockets for more Woodbines.

They stood there for perhaps ten minutes before officers came out from the British lines and ordered them back, announcing that an edict from Divisional H.Q. had strictly forbidden fraternisation. Henry was unfamiliar with the word "fraternisation" and said so but when it was explained to him by a lieutenant of "B" Company he was indignant. "Why damme," he said to Corporal Watts, in an uncharacteristically heated voice, "the bliddy thing's over an' done with, baint it? That Fritz was a farmer like me, an' that poor toad of a lieutenant, the one who could speak our lingo, was half-dead a'ready! Whyfore shoudden us pass the time o' day with 'em?"

He continued to brood on the fraternisation ban. It seemed to distress him far more than all the straffing and discomfort he had undergone in the past and his natural respect for officers, particularly frontline officers, began to fade, together with his enthusiasm for the war. He remained aloof from the unofficial celebrations (including a spectacular firework display of coloured flares from both sides of the line) and his mind continued to dwell on the bovine, broad-shouldered Saxon, who had instantly recognised him as a fellow farmer. Somehow it never occurred to him that the men he had been fighting all this time were identical, men who, in better times, plodded about tending pigs, herding cows, ploughing up land and banking swedes for winter cattle feed. He had thought of them, if at all, as a race of efficient robots whose trade—if they had one—was war, who had never lived anywhere but in holes in the ground and whose tools included mustard gas and shrapnel. The encounter in no-man's-land undermined his entire philosophy of war and now, looking back, it seemed to him a very stupid, profitless business and he wanted nothing so much as to be done with it and go home. His dourness puzzled his platoon commander and also his intimates, men like Watts and Eley. Throughout all the bad times they had been able to look to him for reassurance, waiting for his slow, rubbery smile to indicate that the barrage had shifted further back, or north and south along the line but now his essential cheerfulness had deserted him and in its place was impatient pessimism.

They never really got to the bottom of it, although, from time to time, he tried to explain what had wrought such a change in his outlook and when, in late November, they followed the Germans across the winter landscape and entered Cologne he could be seen almost any day distributing pieces of chocolate and tins of plum and apple to clusters of pale, listless children at the street corners, thus openly defying the fraternisation order that he would describe as "a bliddy lot o' red tape that dorn maake no zense no'ow!"

In late January he was weeded out on account of his age group and sent home for demobilisation and about a month later, when there was a light flurry of snow over the Valley, he detrained at Sorrel Halt and came tramping over the moor to the river road. It felt strange to be swinging along without the usual Christmas tree of equipment hanging about him and until he got used to the feeling he did not know what to do with his left hand that had always gripped the sling of the rifle hooked to his shoulder. Then the sky cleared a little and a fitful winter sun gleamed over the Teazel watershed, pin-pointing a million beads of moisture on the broad blades of the river rushes and he stopped to contemplate the scene, comparing it with the porridge aspect of the Salient. "By Jesus," he said to himself, "I'm bliddy glad to be back! I'd clean forgotten how diff'rent it was!" and he marched on, unconsciously adjusting his route march stride to the slow, splayfooted tread of a countryman crossing the ridges of a ploughed field.

IV

Paul had been home three months then, having been discharged from a convalescent centre in Wales a day or so after the armistice.

His comparatively rapid recovery surprised everybody, including Claire, who had rushed all the way to Rhyl to visit him the moment she received a letter confirming the wonderful telegram telling her that he was alive and lying wounded at Soissons. Alone in the Valley she was not overwhelmed by this news for she had never, not for a moment, thought of him as dead. She was relieved, however, when she found him unmaimed and more or less himself, although he complained of severe headaches that his doctors warned would persist for some months but would grow more and more infrequent as time passed. Although delighted to see her he was somewhat abstracted, as though he could not yet accept the fact that he was not only alive but whole. He remembered very little of the last few months and nothing at all between the moment of stooping to lift the wounded poilu and that of hearing the voice of an American nurse in the ward some ten weeks later. Between headaches he felt fairly fit but he tired very easily and sometimes slept dreamlessly, ten hours at a stretch.

Claire's two brief visits did a good deal to encourage a steady self-adjustment. He relished the soft, warm plumpness of her hand in his and was touched by her timid hospital smile, saying, "Don't fret, old girl, I'll be all right when I get out of here," and although the doctor warned her that he ought to remain under direct medical care at least until spring she had an uneasy certainty that she was more aware of what was good for him than someone who had never ridden down into the Valley and through the autumn woods about the mere, and that what he needed far more urgently than drugs was the balm of familiar surroundings.

When she returned home for the second time she brought these thoughts into the open during a discussion with Maureen and it was Maureen's letter to the M.O. that swung the balance in favour of an early discharge. Less than a month after her second visit news came that he would be arriving on the afternoon train into Paxtonbury and so he did, descending slowly from the carriage and looking about anxiously until he saw the family clustered outside the refreshment room, a rather nervous Claire with seven-year-old Mary holding her hand, five-year-old Whiz holding Mary's hand, and the twins dancing a jig among a stream of passengers. Mary reached him first and he was touched by the abandon with which she embraced him. He remarked also how pretty and cuddly she looked, with her dark clusters of sausage curls and soft brown eyes, "brown an' mild as a heifer's" as Mrs. Handcock once described them. Then he was almost bowled over by the two-pronged assault of the twins, who came at him like a couple of bullet-headed fugitives from a barrage, squealing with the excitement, and he thought, fleetingly, "I've always considered all four of them babies and here they are half-grown children, and each so individual that it hardly seems possible they are all mine and Claire's!" Claire stood back, letting the children enjoy their moment and looking, he thought, as though she was going to disgrace them all by bursting into tears. Then, pulling herself together, she shepherded them into Maureen's battered Ford and they bumped off across the moor and down between the banks of crisp, half-dead bracken to the river. All the time the twins chattered gaily while Mary nestled against his shoulder and he thought, as they swung left and along under the paddock wall, "It's a miracle! An absolute bloody miracle to be here again, seeing it and smelling it, with Claire as calm and pretty as ever sitting at the wheel, the twins prattling on about horses and conkers and school, and Mary and Whiz preening themselves but saying little except to tell him that poor Rumble Patrick, Ikey's boy, had been prevented from joining the welcome home party by "the 'flu that everybody caught!" And then he remembered that he had yet another child, a girl Claire had named Jill, whom he had never seen and his mind leapt back more than a year to the hour of this child's conception in old Crabpot Willie's shanty during their second honeymoon, when the war had looked as if it was going on for ever.

869

He felt an immense rush of tenderness and thankfulness for all of them and for everything about him; for the gleaming Sorrel and its sorry-looking autumn rushes, the sprays of late meadowsweet in the hedge, the twenty shades of brown in the avenue chestnuts and the breath-taking peace of a scene unencumbered by rusting wire, unpocked by gaping shell-holes and with every building roofed with thatch and pantiles that still held something of the summer's warmth.

They made no great fuss of him at the house, having been warned against a demonstration in advance so that soon enough everyone had gone to bed or returned to their own pursuits and he and Claire were alone again in front of the study fire.

It seemed to him a smaller, cosier room than he remembered, with firelight reflecting on the coloured bindings of the books and the comforting smell of leather and old, ineradicable dust that lay between the dark oak shelves. She sat with the hem of her skirt on her knees and her long, elegant legs stretched to the blaze. Seeing her like that, after so long a deprivation, he would have thought that she would have hurried him into beginning one of their study-fireside tumbles but for the moment he could only contemplate her, letting relief and gratitude warm him like the logs in the grate. She had lost a good deal of weight he would have said, was thinner about the face, and in her eyes was a maturity that was new to him. And yet, if anything, it heightened her allure and he said, involuntarily, "I'd almost forgotten how beautiful you were, Claire, how much of a woman!" and when she smiled absently but made no reply, "I suppose it will take me time to get adjusted. So far it's a little disturbing, no more than returning to a place one hasn't visited since childhood but remembers as a source of joy and laughter."

She said, "It won't take you long, Paul! It won't take you forty-eight hours if you can relax and let the Valley seep into your bones!" She looked at him speculatively then, wondering whether she should take the initiative to search out the boisterous male in him that had so often responded to isolation here late at night but he was looking into the fire with a quizzical expression and she knew that she must be patient and walk carefully. His silence disconcerted her somewhat, for such silences were uncommon between them and one would have thought they had so much to discuss.

"What did you think of the baby? You were up there a long time but when you came down you didn't say?"

He recollected himself but she saw that he did so with an effort.

"Jill? She's quite beautiful!" and then, with a welcome flicker of his old-time raillery, "She'll have the edge on Claire Derwent at seventeen plus! She's got perfect features."

"Do you like 'Jill'? Do you want to change it for any other name?"

"Since you ask me, yes. I'd like to call her Claire."

She felt tremendously encouraged without knowing why. "For any special reason?"

"She's the most like you for one thing and for another . . ."

"Well?"

She knew precisely what he had in mind but she wanted very much to hear him say it. He looked across at her and grinned and her heart gave a leap. It was going to be all right. It was going to be the same, in spite of her intermittent misgivings ever since she had looked down on a stranger when they showed her into the ward at the hospital. He said, "You know damned well why? Do I really have to tell you?"

"Yes, you do!"

"All right. She's far more of a love-child than any of them. She had to be when you look back on how you came by her. That's a fact isn't it?"

"Yes, that's a fact," she said. "They say a woman always knows precisely when she comes by a child but I'm hanged if I could give you chapter and verse regarding the other two girls. Who could with a man like you about the place?"

"Right then," he said, settling back and feeling the room and her presence grow on him like a skin, "it's 'Claire' from now on! What made you think of 'Jill' anyway?"

"I daresay because she came tumbling after," she said and he laughed. It was the first time she had heard him laugh for longer than she cared to remember.

They were finding their way again and the certainty of this excited her so much that she had to make an effort to sit still and appear to share his mood.

"She's going to be a handful, I can tell you that already. I daresay it's because I worried so much all the time I was carrying her but you can't expect everything. She'll probably grow up into a thoroughly spoiled little brat, with everyone billing and cooing round her and all the young men within miles making silly excuses to call on us."

"Well, damned good luck to her," said Paul, emphatically. "After what we've had to put up with I'm all for the next generation grabbing all they can get!" And then, suddenly, he thought of poor old

871

Ikey and Hazel and of their child now asleep upstairs in the room he shared with the twins. He said, bitterly, "It's a bloody shame Ikey couldn't have made it! To cop it like that, three months before the end!" and he scrambled up and looked down on her anxiously. "Look here, Claire, if I have occasional fits of depression don't run away with the idea that you or the children are involved. I shall be remembering chaps like Ikey and Tom Williams and Will Codsall and all the other poor devils who went west!"

She looked at him doubtfully for a moment, as though debating with herself whether or not to pursue the subject. Finally she said, "Was it *worth* it, Paul? Was it really worth it, do you think? I mean, couldn't it have been avoided with a little commonsense and more tolerance all round?"

He did not have to reflect long on an answer. He had already given the question a great deal of thought. "It will have been well worth it if everybody has grown up sufficiently to throw bombast and national prejudice on the ash heap! Anyway, for what it's worth, that's the general opinion among the troops and they ought to know! As to whether it could have been avoided that's a different question. I suppose not, really. It could have been put off for a few years but no more, I think, not when you had gilded idiots like the Kaiser and the Tsar, and so many of our own windbags directing things! Sooner or later somebody would have pooped off the first shot so I suppose one has to regard it as inevitable in terms of the pre-war way of running things. It'll be different now, though, if only because it has to be! Nobody would ever stand for it again in any case and that goes for Fritz as well as us, and certainly the poor devils of French, who bore the brunt of it, for all our share in winning."

The fire rustled and a half-burned log slipped, ejecting a spark with a sharp crack that made him wince. She saw the instinctive movement and suddenly she was beside him, holding him tightly and covering his face with kisses.

"Let's put a ban on mentioning it," she said, "let's rake the fire out and go to bed. You must be tired out and I ought to have sent you to bed hours ago!" and she seized his hands but perhaps, in doing so, defeated her intentions for the movement brought them face to face on the hearthrug and he kissed her on the mouth, not hungrily but with a flourish that was at least a positive reassertion. "I'm not as tired as all that," he said and then it was she who laughed.

On June 1st, 1919, the day of his fortieth birthday, he went out into the yard and asked old Chivers if Snowdrop, twenty-one by his calculation, was still capable of an hour or two of walking exercise and Chivers asserted that he certainly was and was even good for a trot on level ground, so Paul watched the old man saddle the mild-eyed grey and then hoisted himself up and climbed the orchard path through a forest of bluebells to the gap near the stile that gave on to the high-banked lane connecting Hermitage with the western edge of the woods.

There seemed to him promise of a long, baking summer, with everything far forward after a warm and windless spring. He skirted the fringe of Hermitage Wood and picked up the narrow, circular bridle path that led to the little plateau that was his favourite vantage point. As he jogged along he looked up into a cloudless sky, enjoying the sun on his face and thinking that the weather was doing its best to make up for early autumns and long winters that had depressed the troops more than the shelling in France but then, he reflected, Flanders always had had a reputation for all-the-year-round drizzle and no matter where you dug out there you were bound to strike water a couple of feet below the surface. Then, as he had learned to do in the last six months, he was able to put France and the war out of his mind. Profit, he reminded himself, lay in the future and it was no use regretting an era when every child returning home from Mary Willoughby's little school would automatically tug his cap, or drop a dutiful little curtsy whenever he or John Rudd rode by. Not all that had disappeared was bad and surely patronage of that kind was something country life could do without in the years ahead. There were, of course, uglier trends, like the steady infiltration of men of Sydney Codsall's type into the coastal area east of Nun's Bay, war profiteers who seemed determined to disfigure the entire countryside with gimcrack bungalows, most of them in cahoots with faceless allies on local and county councils. "Development" they called it, pretending their object was that of providing homes for old people and ex-service men but having watched Sydney Codsall grow from a toothy child into a scheming young shyster Paul had no confidence in this theory. Sydney now owned almost a third of Coombe Bay, including the old inn, The Raven, which he had already "developed" into a Tudor sham but Paul made up his mind that he would see murder done before Sydney's tide pushed inland beyond the old brickyard, reflecting that he was nicely placed to hold it at bay for he was a war profiteer himself and a far more successful one than Sydney Codsall or any of his partners, not excluding Codsall's father-in-law, reported to have made a fortune in sugar.

The comforting reflection slammed a door in his resentment so that he found he could indulge himself in the luxury of a chuckle. All the time he had been wrestling with estate problems, all the months he had spent in France and in hospital, money had been piling up in his bank, the harvest of other acres he owned within a penny tram-ride of Tower Bridge. Its total had staggered him when Franz had come down with his ledgers and balance sheets in the spring and for a week or more Paul had gone about with a Bunyan's pack of guilt on his shoulders. It was not a very pleasant thought to realise one might have enriched oneself at the expense of the blood and bones of men like Ikey Palfrey and Big Jem of the Dell and his first impulse had been to get rid of it in a single dramatic gesture, as the politician Stanley Baldwin had done when he returned a third of his war profits to its source. Then he had a better idea and nothing Franz could say could make him drop it. He made over his holdings in the firm of Zorndorff and Craddock to the National Fund for War Disabled and afterwards transferred two-thirds of his accumulated capital, something like a hundred and twenty thousand pounds, to a special Trust Fund earmarked exclusively for estate development. Not Sydney Codsall's development but real development, the restocking and re-equipping of every farm in the Valley, the rebuilding of every cottage over fifty years old and the purchase of stocks of fertiliser and tractors for all who would use them and plough teams for diehards like Henry Pitts who would not. Not one penny of this money, Paul told Claire and a sceptical John Rudd, would ever be rechannelled to his personal account, or be included in legacies to his children or grandchildren. Capital and incidental interest would be used to re-hearten and reclaim land and modernise each of the seven farms. In the meantime (and this was what sent Uncle Franz away tapping his forehead) the Craddocks, one and all, would live on rents frozen at pre-war level plus the yield of pre-war investments and whatever the Home Farm produced under the management of Honeyman's nephew.

He had expected opposition from Claire, if only in defence of her children but she made no protest. She understood, far better than he realised, the compulsions under which he acted and being Edward

Derwent's daughter she had always accepted land as the only true wealth, notwithstanding all the fortunes made by speculators and Paxtonbury tradesmen in the last four years.

It was signed and settled now, less than six months after his discharge and today was the first morning in over a month that he had deserted the office. The doctors at Rhyl had not lied to him. His headaches were now spaced by weeks instead of days and the worst discomfort he suffered from wounds in two wars was the occasional nag of rheumatism in the small crater left by a Boer bullet at the turn of the century.

The magic of the morning began to work on him as his shoulder brushed the lower branches of the elms overlooking Hermitage and at last he reined in on the spur of turf at the extreme edge of the escarpment. It was all under his eye, more than ten miles of it, with the silver sliver of the river curving south-east like a bent rapier aimed at the heart of the Bluff. To the left and behind stood the big timber of Shallowford Woods, trees he had nearly lost in 1916 but which had miraculously survived while every wood in north-eastern France had been shredded to bare poles. To the south he could just see a grey-blue strip of water where the Channel lapped the edge of the dunes; to the west was Four Winds, squatting snugly among green wheat and well-trimmed hedges, and beyond, three miles or more, the gentle slope to the Teazel watershed rising more steeply as it curved north to melt into the moor. This was the outlook, south-east, south and south-west but there was as much to savour within yards of where old Snowdrop stood like a pipe-clayed veteran, comfortably at ease. A towering elm marked the precise corner of the wood, its green buds clothing the bole as far as the lowest branches. Ferns had come creeping out of the wood to seed themselves on the extreme limit of the shade and among them was a riot of colour, jostling for space. Foxgloves stood there, some of them six feet high and already shaking out pink mittens a month earlier than usual; campion ran along the southern margin of the wood like a belt of crimson fire and lower down the bank grew clusters of dandelion, daisy, periwinkle, stitchwort, bugloss and buttercup. There was only a pretence of silence up here. If you listened and thought about listening, there was subdued uproar, an orchestra of buzzing and whizzing and whispering and a rich, heady scent, the overall smell of everything that grows in England in the months of May and June.

He sat there with slack reins until Snowdrop began to shuffle and

875

arch his neck and then he went on slowly down the escarpment to the point where the footpath joined the approach lane of Hermitage Farm. Clouds of flies followed him, seeking Snowdrop's eyes and the heat haze lay on the Valley like a blue, trembling veil. Prudence Pitts, Henry's girl, saw him approach and shouted, "Me Dad be upalong wi' the pigs, Mr. Craddock!" but he only smiled and lifted his hand. Of all the people in the Valley, save only Claire and possibly John Rudd and his wife, he preferred Henry's company but today he wanted to make the circuit alone, without having to wrench his mind from contemplation of the Valley as a domain rather than a community.

He reached the river road and let the grey nose the shallows, waiting while he drank his fill. A kingfisher flashed by and he remembered seeing one on this same reach the very first evening he passed here in the company of old John Rudd. Deliberately he counted both years and phases; that first hectic season when everything was new and strange and the whole Valley burning a sackcloth-brown under what Mrs. Handcock called "a praper ol' scorcher"; the false dawn of his first marriage and all the grief and confusion that came of it; the long, rewarding period with Claire that endured until another and more catastrophic "scorcher" was over, and finally the interminable war years, with everything falling to pieces and hardly any of his former allies surviving to pull them together again. Well, it had been a long haul, getting on for a fifth of a century of ups and downs, but he was still here, sitting the same horse in the same river bottom; there was time enough, at forty, for the fulfilment of lingering dreams.

Book Five

CHAPTER ONE

I

On the afternoon of September 1st, 1929, the eve of the twins' 21st birthday, Paul saddled the sedate skewbald (who had replaced Snowdrop as his estate transport) and rode up to French Wood, the young plantation now growing up on the extreme south-western corner of the Hermitage plateau. He told himself he was going there with the object of calling on Henry Pitts and making one more attempt to convert him to tractor ploughing, but this was no more than an excuse to escape from the frenzied upheaval accompanying preparations for the all-night dance The Pair had organised, with the active connivance of their mother and sisters.

The house was already full of young people, most of them strangers to Paul, who bustled round and about him carrying armfuls of decorations, chairs, trestle tables and weird-looking band instruments and maintained a ceaseless hammering that made work in the office an impossibility. He said to Claire, standing on a stepladder with her mouth full of tacks, "I'm going over to Hermitage, I won't be long!" but she only nodded absentmindedly. Clearly she had no thoughts for him today and neither, it seemed, had anyone else, for even Mary, the quiet one, had been sucked into the whirlpool of the first big-scale social event at Shallowford since Simon's twenty-first, more than four years before.

Paul rode up the orchard to the sunken lane, noting that the apple crop promised well and that Young Honeyman and Henry Pitts had almost done with harvesting. He never rode to the new wood without a feeling that he was going to church, for French Wood, which had been his own way of commemorating the Valley dead, was a kind of church, much more of one than the precincts of all the other war memorials in the district—plain granite crosses and pseudo-heroic statues of glaring infantrymen, without the vitality or validity of his private memorial to the eighteen local men who had died between August 1914 and November 1918.

He remembered as he rode across the plateau how the eccentric notion had come to him the week of his fortieth birthday in June,

1919, when he had sat Snowdrop on the crest overlooking the Valley and thought of all the cheery souls who had turned their faces to the sun at this spot and now lay in tidy graves in Picardy and Gallipoli. He thought too of the maimed, of poor devils like Reg Willis the wheel-wright's son, who had lost the sight of both eyes and Davy Tozer, the smith's son, who had come home minus a leg. There had been talk of memorial stones and statues in all the papers just then, for the Armistice was only seven months behind them but now, as he entered the little wood growing up around him, he was very glad he had planted a tree for each man instead of carving their names on a lump of granite in the churchyard. A living tree was surely more pleasant to behold than most of the conventional war memorials up and down the country and here, in "French Wood" as the Valley folk insisted on calling it, every man had individual representation, so long as a comrade lived to come here and remember them once in a while.

The plantation was fenced with a stout wooden paling to keep out the wild deer and against all the predictions of the local wiseacres it was prospering, as though the wood spirits favoured the idea. Paul had chosen each young tree with care—a mountain ash for Ikey; oaks for the older men like Tremlett, the huntsman and Tom Williams, the fisherman; an elm for Jem Pollock already as thick as the Dell giant's thigh and a small cluster of silver birches for the younger set, men like Tod Glover who had once flown low over this spot showing off his wind-riding skill like a buzzard. In the centre of the wood was a flowering cherry for Grace, killed hauling wounded back from Vimy and as he crossed the turf Paul was not much surprised to find his eldest son Simon sitting there, with a cherrywood pipe in his mouth contemplating the metal plaque which read: "*Grace Craddock, ambulance driver, killed April 1917,*" and underneath the only Scriptural quotation inscribed on a plaque—"*Greater love hath no man . . .*" Simon said, without looking round, "You should have done your bit of Bible thumping under old Tom Williams' tree, Gov'nor! He was a Methodist and would have thought it fitting." Then, with laughter in his eyes, "She never had much truck with organised religion, did she?"

"No," Paul said, aware that the boy was teasing him but not resenting it in any way, "she didn't! As a matter of fact she didn't have much truck with anything except Women's Rights and Compassion."

The boy looked at him in a way that Paul had learned to associate
880

with his questing, mildly cynical nature, akin to his mother's but more tolerant and far less likely to give offence.

"It was a sentimental idea, this wood of the dead," he said, "but taken all round it does you credit, Gov'nor."

"Thank you," said Paul with a grin, for he suddenly remembered after all these years when and where he had invited Simon to call him "Gov'nor" — sitting on a fence near his school, during a hurried visit on Paul's leave from the Front in the autumn of 1917. He thought of reminding the boy and then decided not. Simon affected to despise the past and to regard everything that had happened up to the Labour Government's first term of office, in 1924, as a pitiable failure of all human achievement. He said, instead, "What made you come here, today of all days?"

"For the same reason as you; to get away from the racket! Anyway, I had some thinking to do. I've had a letter from Ned Stokes. He wants to know if I'd care to take over the literary editorship of *The Forum*. It's a new magazine his uncle is backing. Might have a future now that Labour is back again."

Paul was resigned to Simon's false starts and news that he was contemplating a journalistic career, after turning his back on teaching and forestry, had no power to irritate him. He said, tolerantly, "You're old enough to dispense with my advice, Si. I daresay you'd find it amusing for a time but those magazines don't last long as a rule, do they?"

"No," Si said seriously, "but what does?"

"Land," said Paul, not unexpectedly, and Simon smiled and shook his head as though he had long ago accepted the fact that, when it came to the estate, his father was slightly off his head and everybody in the Valley acknowledged as much.

"I suppose your mob will want to nationalise us," Paul said and without waiting for an answer, "Well, I daresay it'll come to that in the end but until it does I'm staying put! It will take more than your precious Ramsay Mac' to shift me."

Simon took his pipe from his mouth and ran his hand through his dark hair. It was a gesture that always reminded Paul vividly of his first wife, one of the many quirks she had passed on to the child she had abandoned for the Women's Suffrage Campaign, when he was no more than a few months old. He said, resignedly, "You might just as well go over to the Tories, Gov'nor. You're a Tory in everything but name you know."

"Don't be so damned patronising!" Paul told him. "Jimmy

Grenfell and I were the two people who showed the Tories the door round here before you were born!"

"Oh, I know about the 1906 landslide and all that," Simon said, "but for all your sound and fury you Radicals are as deeply rooted in the past as eighteenth-century landlords. Even the Tories subscribe to something new if there's a quick profit in it but you and Jimmy Grenfell don't. Surely you can see we've taken your place as Progressives?"

"I can't see anything of the kind," Paul said, but genially, for secretly he never cared to quarrel with Simon's championship of the underdog, not even when it was larded with left-wing jargon borrowed from dull-looking books translated from the Russian. "The fact is we were content to nibble whereas you lot will overeat yourselves and give the electorate chronic indigestion. As soon as you begin to burp all your reforms will emerge as hot air and the Tories will be more firmly entrenched than ever! You see if I'm not right! However, I don't propose to spend a pleasant afternoon discussing politics with you, I'm going over to Hermitage to see Henry Pitts. Do you want to come along?"

"No thanks," Simon said. "I'd better go back and give The Pair a hand. Do you know how many those idiots have invited to stay with us overnight? Seventy-four! Where the devil are they going to sleep?"

"I don't suppose they will until the sun gets up and then they can doss down in the barns for all I care," Paul said. "Your mother and I are going to the shanty after the midnight toasts. You'll be in charge from then on!"

"An honour," said Si, grinning, "but one I could easily duck! The twins' set are morons but come to that so are the twins themselves. Have you talked to them since they came back from town yesterday?"

"Good God, no!" Paul said, "they never talk to me! Mary is the only one of you who regards me as anything more than an amiable old stick-in-the-mud with a fortune in loose change!" and he sauntered out of the enclosure and swung himself in the saddle, setting the skewbald at the steep path down to the river road and turning right towards the Hermitage farm track. Simon moved clear of the trees and watched him until he passed out of sight behind the Hermitage elms. "Well, Gov," he said to himself, "Steve and Andy will be 'talking' tomorrow or the day after and I daresay they'll succeed in knocking you more than I ever have! I've always been odd-man-out here and had time to get used to it!" He lit his pipe again and stood puffing thoughtfully and then, as he turned away, he passed the young beech planted for

Keith Horsey, the parson's son, whom he remembered as an old boy of High Wood and sometime school friend of his boyhood hero, Ikey. He stopped to read the words on the plaque: "*To Keith Horsey, R.A.M.C. Killed February 1917.*" He recalled that Horsey had once been the Valley's conscientious objector and also that Number Ten Downing Street was now occupied by another. He thought, "You should have held on a bit. Who knows? A chap with a good degree might have had a place in the Cabinet and then every damned flag-flapper in the Valley would have licked your boots!"

He lunged off, hands in pockets, pipe in mouth. He knew his duty as the heir of Shallowford at the forthcoming celebrations but he did not look forward to hours of junketing in the company of hearty young men who drove high-powered sports cars with overlong bonnets and leggy girls who pretended they were hot stuff and shouted "Stop!" as soon as they felt a hand above their knee. At twenty-five, and with his future still undecided, he considered himself too adult for this sort of nonsense; too old and too disillusioned with the entire bloody decade.

II

Claire had been so busy preparing for the dance that she had neglected to enter the momentous date in the estate diary. Keeping the diary up-to-date was still largely her prerogative, although Paul sometimes wrote brief entries in it and she knew that he always read every word she wrote between the heavy leather Bible covers of what had once been old Sir George Lovell's pornographic photograph album. It was a task she always found congenial inasmuch as it made her aware of continuity and now that her youngest child was eleven, and she herself forty-five, continuity was important to her. About four-thirty, when the decorations were complete and the buffet tables laid and covered with tablecloths, she made a last-minute check of the guest rooms, and the Nissen hut fortuitously left behind by the R.A.M.C. ten years before and then went into the library and shut the door against intruders.

She had always liked this room and liked being alone in it. Its smell of stale dust and old leather reminded her of the early days of her marriage and it always seemed to her that when she was here at night, with Paul reading or dozing in the big armchair on the other side of the hearth they recaptured the intimacy that eluded them in a house full of strident young things and servants who lacked the permanence of

883

dear old bodies like Mrs. Handcock, long since retired to a cottage, or Thirza Tremlett, who had been nursemaid until John Rudd's boy had been born and she had moved down to the Lodge.

She fetched the diary and carried it back to the library table but as she set it down she caught a swift and not altogether pleasing glimpse of her reflection in the mirror over the sideboard. In the old days she had worried about putting on weight despite Paul's constant assurance that he liked rounded women but now she wondered if current fashions had not encouraged her to proceed too boldly in the reverse direction for her breasts seemed to have disappeared altogether and her behind, viewed sideways, looked nearly as flat as a board. Her hair had been bobbed as long ago as 1926 and the shearing of her long, golden tresses, for thirty years her pet vanity, had been an occasion almost as catastrophic as the declaration of war. Paul had stormed and she had wept, and the fact that the entire family had taken up her cause had not helped to convince either of them that her smooth, oval face was suited to the fashion. Since then she had compromised, unknowingly anticipating the long-bob of the immediate future, and now her hair reached her shoulders and curled under, masking what she called her "rats-tails" on the nape of her neck. Her skin was still very clear and her eyes retained their blue depths but as she turned her back on the mirror she could not help regretting that the craze for boyish figures was taking such a long time to die, or consoling herself that the one aspect of current fashions to her advantage was that of short skirts, for her legs were still shapely and her ankles slim, whereas some poor wretches were condemned to expose calves as thick as banister rails and knees as knobbly as applewood faggots.

She opened the book and wrote: "*Today the Twins celebrated their 21st birthday with an all-night ball . . .*" and then stopped, thinking how Stephen and Andrew would hoot with laughter if they ever saw to-night's event described as a "ball", as though there would be sets of lancers and the mazurka, and all the gentlemen would wear gloves and the girls wait hopefully for their programmes to be filled. The thought took her back, however, to the first celebration she had ever attended in this house—the Coronation soirée in October, 1902, when she had driven here with her father, stepmother, brother Hugh and sister Rose, one and all convinced that new Squire would round off the occasion by announcing that he intended marrying Claire Derwent of High Coombe in the New Year. They had all taken a terrible tumble that night and she could smile at it now but it had taken her close on five

884

years to ride out and perhaps she would be nursing a grievance yet if Paul's first wife had not been such a goose as to run off to London to smash windows and get herself locked up in Holloway prison.

It was a day for musing. She wrote: "... *about two hundred guests attended and toasts were proposed by the Squire at midnight,*" but then she did what she usually did when making a special entry of this kind and began browsing her way back through the pages, noting entries relating to early triumphs of her second daughter Karen (universally known as "Whiz") in the County show-ring, Simon's decorous 21st birthday celebrations, in January, 1925, John Rudd's retirement in the following year, and on to the outbreak of foot and mouth disease at Four Winds in the summer of the General Strike, the crash of a Handley Page aircraft on the dunes, Jimmy Grenfell's narrow electoral victories in 1924 and again last May and all kinds of relevant and irrelevant happenings since Paul's miraculous return from the dead in the last weeks of the war. It was all here in her own or his handwriting and browsing over his entries she found a theme that was absent from her own recordings, a pattern of subdued anxiety running from page to page, an undertone to the orchestra of Valley events. There were terse entries like one in May, 1924, that read, "*Codsall is developing east of Nun's Bay, blast him ...*" and enigmatic ones such as "*Quarry project through County Council; will block it one way or another.*" It was the first time she had noticed that he was using the diary as a safety valve or, indeed, that Sydney Codsall's activities around the periphery of the estate were so important to him and it worried her a little, the more so because she could not remember him having confided in her beyond making a glum comment or two on local jerry building and the sins of war profiteers. She went into the office and rummaged among the estate maps. John Rudd had always praised Paul's administrative capacity and although he was proverbially untidy everywhere else he was never slipshod in here, the plainly furnished room that was the hub of the estate and had been since he had converted old Sir George's dark-room into an office. Everything was docketed and filed; every map, every lease and catalogue indexed with neatly printed cards. It was, she reflected, a side of him she hardly knew, even after twenty-two years of marriage, and today it intrigued her. She found a map dated 1929 and unrolled it, holding the ends down with ledgers and a glance at it confirmed her suspicion regarding his fear of encirclement, for whilst Shallowford land was shaded light pink and the sea pale

885

blue, there were three areas shaded black and when she looked at the key she was not surprised to see them identified as "*Threatened Development*". The extent of the areas surprised her. She knew that ever since the war had ended Sydney Codsall's Whinmouth Development Company (Bricks and Tiles), Ltd. had been building bungalows on what had once been Blair's Farm, in Nun's Bay, a coastal island of freehold dividing the southern boundaries of the Shallowford and Heronslea Estates but she was largely unaware of Sydney's steady infiltration into Coombe Bay, two miles or more to the east, where, from time immemorial, most of the property had been owned by the Squire of Shallowford. There was a tracing pinned to the map which showed details of this infiltration. The old Manson brickyard was shaded in and so was The Raven, once owned by a local brewery and run by Minnie Flowers and her husband but now a Tudor sham renamed "The Lovell Arms". Now that she thought about it the deliberate reintroduction of the word "Lovell" into the district smacked of an insult aimed at Paul and she wondered if there existed some quarrel between Paul and the toothy child he had tried to befriend when Sydney's father went raving mad all those years ago and killed Arabella Codsall with a hay-knife. There was a patch of black away up in the northeasterly corner of the map in the area where, during the war, there had been a prisoner-of-war camp. She had always thought of this parcel as land owned and administered by the Forestry Commission but it was clear that this too had now passed into the hands of the Whinmouth Development Company, for it was ringed in pencil and across it Paul had written "Quarry Site?"

She was still bent over the map, the twins' celebrations forgotten, when she heard his step beyond the office door and at once felt guilty, as though she had been prying like Bluebeard's wife. He came in with a tired smile, however, that at once reassured her so that her protective instinct drove her anxieties into the open and she said, "I've been reading the diary and I came in here to check up. Why didn't you tell me you've been brooding about Sydney Codsall's antics?" He looked hard at her then, trying to make up his mind whether she was genuinely interested and she understood his caution. He had never quite forgotten his first wife's contempt for his obsession with Shallowford and it had always seemed to her that this was the one wound of the many he had received at the hands of Grace Lovell that had been beyond her power to heal.

"It's a fair question," he said at length, "but right now we have to change for the big do tonight. I'll explain when the tumult has died down."

"No, Paul," she said obstinately, "there's no hurry to change. Tell me now or I shall worry about it when I should have my mind on my job tonight."

"Very well," he said, "although there can't be much you haven't heard. That little bastard won't be happy until he's boxed us in. His shantytown already extends as far as the dunes. He has about a third of the property in Coombe Bay under his hand and he's just bought the quarry behind the woods."

"It looks frightening on paper," Claire said, "but hasn't he gone as far as he can? With farm prices at their present level you don't want any more land, do you?"

"No," he said, "I don't want more land. As a matter of fact I wouldn't mind unloading some, providing it went to a farmer and not to rascals who haven't the slightest interest in it beyond the quick profits they make exploiting it and fouling the countryside into the bargain!"

It was common knowledge that the shantytown on the old Blair farmland was the Squire's *bête noire* and privately she considered his attitude unreasonable. The bungalows there were almost all occupied by elderly retired couples from Whinmouth and Paxtonbury and, much as she shared his love of the Valley, she was not prepared to claim a monopoly of the coastline. She said, carefully, "He's already built on every square inch of the Blair holding. There isn't room over there to put a shed up and all the land east is included in the county coastal preservation strip. Rudd told me that years ago, no one can build on it."

"No one can build houses!"

"What else could be built?"

"A road," he said, "a glorified promenade right across the dunes as far as Coombe Bay and once that was approved we should soon have a little Blackpool on our doorstep!"

"This is possible? A motor road, between Nun's Bay and Coombe Bay?"

"Sydney and his Council stooges have been agitating for it for years. Why else do you suppose he's bought up so many Coombe Bay freeholds?"

She understood and shared his concern because her resentment had deeper roots than his. A road along the coast would cut and probably choke the series of goyles that led down to the beach and one of the first to go would surely be Crabpot Willie's goyle, where lay the shanty that had a significance for her that she could never have explained to anyone, not even him.

"They've been trying, you say. What stopped them succeeding?"

He grinned and rolled up the plan. "I've got my stooges as well," he said. "Fortunately it's a pretty expensive project and nobody likes to pay more county rates than they can help."

"What about the land he's got behind the woods? Can he build another shantytown there?"

"It wouldn't pay him to," Paul said, suddenly quite cheerful again, "even if the coastal development matures, as I daresay it will in the end. His holdings in Coombe Bay and north of the woods will always be blocked by High Coombe, so he'll have to confine his activities in that area to quarrying. I daresay he'd give his eye-teeth to get hold of some of your brother's pasture and have direct access to the sea from that side."

"What is he *really* after?" she asked. "I mean, apart from money."

"Me!"

"But why? You were almost a father to him when he was a boy. Ikey saved him from his crazy father, didn't he?"

"Yes he did," Paul said. "He fetched him down from the bedroom by ladder but Ikey would have saved everybody a lot of trouble if he'd left him there! Sydney hates me—I can't tell why exactly—it's probably because he knew I disliked his mother and because I showed him the door that time he came here during the war with his plan to cut me in on a side profit he was making out of pitprops. However, don't run away with the idea that I hate him back. I don't you know, just what he stands for, what all Sydney Codsalls stand for. There are one or two operating in every area of the country. They stand up in public spouting about development and progress but what they really mean is exploitation and rural rape! They are the new *condottiere*, marching through England as the medieval mercenaries marched across France, taking everything out and putting nothing back! Some of them are old men who helped to push us into the war and drank blood for four years but there are plenty of others younger than me, men who made damned sure they stayed home and staked their claim while the going was good! Somebody has to stand up to the bastards or the country won't be worth living in in a generation from now."

She had heard it all before, when some of the ex-servicemen called on him for advice or a loan, but never so exactly stated. She said, "If you feel as strongly as that about Sydney Codsall why don't you run for the County Council yourself, Paul?"

"Not me!" he said fervently. "I'll fight them where I find them, in my own fields and woods, thank you! Councils? They're for two varieties, well-meaning windbags and backscratchers, like Sydney's mob! I know better than to fight them in the open. How long would it take them to tack a war-profiteer's label on me?"

"That's nonsense! There isn't a soul about here that doesn't know you've ploughed everything back into the estate. Suppose you had behaved like half the other landlords and unloaded the farms on the tenants as soon as taxes went up and prices kept going down? You've nothing to be ashamed of and a good deal to be proud of, Paul."

He said nothing to this but dropped his glance to the diary, thumbing idly through the stiff, scrawl-covered pages. She did not have to be told where he had been all afternoon. Whenever he was in this mood she knew he had been to French Wood, as though a visit there established contact with men who had shared his intense love of the Valley and were able to renew his faith in the future. She was aware also that his return to the wood had some link with the day itself, the coming-of-age of the two handsome young extroverts she had borne him, and as she thought this she remembered something else that would have made her chuckle had she thought of it earlier. They had been conceived here, in this very room and not in a bed either, bless you, but on that old bearskin rug in front of the fire, one gusty night after they had come home cider-merry from one of old Arthur Pitt's Hallowe'en parties! She knew, after twenty-two years, how to coax him out of this things-aren't-what-they-were mood and surely tonight was an occasion he should enjoy as much if not more than the twins and a lot of boisterous strangers. She said: "Right! We'll all battle along with you, Paul, but was there a special reason why you kept this to yourself so long? Kept it from me, I mean?"

"Yes," he said, "I suppose there was. You've always been so damned expert at keeping pace with change, Claire. Look at yourself! You don't appear more than a year or two older than some of those cropped-eared, flat-chested girls the twins bring into the place but my clock stopped after the war and I sometimes think of myself as constitutionally incapable of keeping abreast of the times. It worries me sometimes and that's the truth! I hate change but one day I'll catch myself resisting changes for the better. Simon as good as told me that today."

"Well," she said, smiling at his earnestness, "you weren't always so desperately traditionist. Can you see any direct link between that moth-eaten old rug we ought to have thrown out long ago and those lumping great boys, whose health you'll be proposing tonight?"

"No," he said, looking very puzzled. "I'm jiggered if I can! Is there one?"

"There certainly is!" she said and reminded him, laughing at his slightly startled expression and the way he stared down at the rug as though he half expected it to turn back into a bear. He said, his features relaxing slowly, "I might have known you would remember a thing like that! Will they be serving cider tonight, do you think?"

"We're not staying here tonight."

"That's so," he said. "We're off to the shanty, aren't we? Well, you don't have to remind me of what happened there a long time ago. Come to think of it, it's a wonder we haven't a baker's dozen coming-of-age parties ahead of us!" and he kissed her on the mouth in a manner that implied Sydney Codsall and all his works would be out of mind for at least twenty-four hours.

III

It was not often that John Rudd came to the big house these days. At seventy-seven, and with a heart condition that had given him one or two frights over the last few years, he found the long drive too steep and the effort of climbing in and out of his wife's fussy little cars more exhausting than the ascent on foot. He was here tonight, however, and enjoying himself in an unexpected way, for this was the first big event at Shallowford in the past forty years when nothing was expected of him but to sit still, sip well-watered toddy and look amiable.

Maureen was off helping Claire and the staff with the buffet and Paul was consorting with some of his more active cronies—Henry Pitts, Smut Potter and the like, so that John, comfortably seated in what Claire was pleased to call the Minstrel Gallery (actually a kind of landing built on when the room was enlarged after the war) could look down on the swirling mob and make cynically good-humoured comparisons with other special occasions that had occurred here since the days of "that old goat George Lovell and his rackety sons, Hubert

890

and Ralph". The new dances puzzled him somewhat, prancing embraces of the kind that were always popular among young people but were confined, as far as he could recall, to the bushes and would never have been allowed on a dance floor, not even George Lovell's dance floor. The tunes puzzled him even more, the old stamping music having been replaced by a variety of near-dirges, almost all concerned with moons waxing or waning over definitive portions of the United States, with here and there a snatch or two reminiscent of the songs coons used to sing at concerts. Even the band instruments in use were nothing like he recalled, not even in the early days of the Craddock régime. The basic melody, it seemed, no longer emanated from the piano or the violins but from a kind of trombone called, he understood, "a sax", the notes of which were augmented and often drowned by the rattle of kettledrum and clash of cymbals. The youngsters seemed to enjoy it all and take the cacophony for granted but then, in the decade that was just about to end, youngsters took everything for granted—noise, speed, half-nakedness and what was perhaps the most surprising, the virtual elimination of class-distinctions. If he needed proof of this he had only to lean forward an inch or so and look over the balustrade to see Stephen Craddock, the stockier of the twins, whirling round with Prudence Pitts, the red-headed daughter of Henry and Gloria of Hermitage, a girl who was almost exactly Stephen's age. Now that, he thought, would have been enough to bring the ceiling down thirty years ago whereas, in the more free and easy Edwardian decade, the glimpse of the girl's underclothes as she was swung round in a final flourish would have almost certainly led to her being ordered home by her blushing mama and clouted on the way out by the father.

They were at it again, with hardly a pause for breath, one of the swoonier tunes now—pretty enough in an unremarkable way but tinged, as were nearly all their songs, with melancholy and defeatism. He tried to catch the words of the lyric bawled into a mechanical amplifier by the hired girl vocalist (another undreamed-of innovation) but could make no sense of it, for she seemed to be pleading for kisses from somebody called "Babette" and Babette, unless he was far in his dotage, had always been a woman's name and a rather tarty one at that. His observations and the reflections they provoked switched from the general to the particular. He spotted and contemplated each of Paul's brood in order of precedence, beginning with Simon, the Lovell girl's boy, and ending with the Craddock postscript, the beautiful eleven-year-old, who had been given special permission to stay up until 1 a.m. for the occasion. They were a handsome bunch but also, as he knew from their parents and from Maureen's fireside gossip, a highly unpredictable spread of children. Simon, already twenty-five, was said to be as mulish as his mother and likely to go her way if Paul failed to pull him up short whereas the twins, Stephen and Andrew, were as happy-go-lucky a pair as one would be likely to encounter anywhere but had not, so far as he was aware, done a day's work in their lives, if one excepted the repeated stripping and reassembling of motor-bikes and their redesigning of old Hocking's motor-launch into a speed boat that had capsized at high speed in the bay a month ago and came close to drowning them. There was Simon, serious but tricky, and The Pair, feather-witted but likeable, and then came the three girls, with more permutations—Mary, the eldest and her father's favourite, Whiz, the long-faced sixteen-year-old who rode superbly, won bushels of awards and reminded everybody of her Aunt Rose away in Gloucestershire, and finally the family Aphrodite, Claire, whose classic profile, natural poise and astounding precocity marked her down as a future Emma Hamilton or Du Barry. Well, thank God, he only had one child to worry about since poor old Roddy had drowned under the guns of *Von Spee* and his Paul seemed normal enough, with plenty of his mother's sense of humour but none of her pseudo-Irish feyness, praise be to God! He sipped his whisky, pondering the not inconsiderable compensations of old age as he saw Paul come through from the hall, mount the rostrum and motion the perspiring drummer to give a long roll on the drums as a preface to the midnight toasts.

They swarmed into the already overcrowded room from all parts of the house and garden, some of the latecomers looking a little dishevelled and removing wisps of grass from their dinner jackets and dresses. In the old days, John thought, only the Potter girls slipped out into the shrubbery between dances but now almost everybody made these stealthy exits and re-entrances. There was a general laugh when Stephen made a breathless reappearance with the daughter of the Paxtonbury Archdeacon in tow, and then Paul gestured for silence and made a pleasant little speech, not too long and not too flippant but spiced with a little salty humour about his sons' shortcomings which was offset by the geniality Paul Craddock could always summon for a gathering such as this. There was not a man or a woman over forty present, John thought, who would not bear witness to the staying-power of the young greenhorn whom he had met off the London train more than twenty-seven years ago, and who had since rooted himself in the Valley as no Lovell had ever done.

John stood up to drink the twins' health but it was not of them he thought as he downed his final whisky that night. His congratulations —if he offered any—were reserved for the tall, slightly stooping man of fifty, raising his glass and looking down on the slightly tipsy company, and on the blonde woman who stood smiling at his side and whose attention, he suspected, was also directed at Paul rather than her sons, for no one who knew Claire Derwent (as he still thought of her) doubted that any one of her children came better than a poor second to the man she had come home to nurse and marry at the time of the German wreck in Tamer Potter's Cove. "Dear God it seems a dozen lifetimes away!" muttered John aloud, as the music began to bray again and the couples swung off into the one recognisable dance of the evening, the Gay Gordons, and Maureen Rudd, appearing suddenly at his side, said, "What's that you're saying, John?" But John was not prepared to admit to sentimentality, not even with only his wife as an audience, and replied, "Nothing, old girl, only that it's time I toddled off. Stay on if you like, I'm for my bed!"

"I'll tell Paul and Claire and get our coats," Maureen said and disappeared again while John took a final glance at the kaleidoscopic scene below, thinking, "Who'll be next? Mary, the quiet one? She's eighteen and has three years to go but maybe she'll marry and won't have a big house celebration. I doubt if I'll be around to see it anyway but good luck to them all, damned good luck, if only for his sake!"

Soon after two a.m., when most of the older guests had left, the blare of a hunting horn expertly blown by Robbie Eveleigh, youngest of the Eveleigh boys (he had taken Tremlett's place as huntsman when the Sorrel Vale Farmers' Hunt was revived in the early 'twenties) summoned the younger generation of the Valley to join the traditional Tally-Ho crocodile, without which no Westcountry celebration could be said to be complete. Simon, as M.C., thanked God that Paul and Claire had departed for the shanty, for already several of The Pair's inner circle were a little the worse for wear and the passage of the Tally-Ho crocodile through the house seemed to him a direct threat to furniture and fabric. There was no help for it, however, and the best he could do was to insist on a single crocodile weaving in one direction instead of two working towards one another with the object of head-on collisions. They set off to the scream of three horns, Robbie's and two others blown by Stevie and Andrew, and the uproar of their ascent of the stairs and progress along the main corridor from the old nursery to the west wing, shook the house in its foundations. The orchestra did not take part but added to the general din by playing hunting music at full blast, so that elderly folk abed as far away as Coombe Bay stirred in their sleep as the waves of sound that launched Squire's twins into their twenty-second year crossed the stubble fields and lapped the inshore sandbanks of the bay. Paul and Claire, climbing into bed in the shanty heard the distant uproar and exchanged wry smiles; Marian Eveleigh heard it in the big bedroom at Four Winds, tut-tutting lest it should wake Norman who had been sleeping badly since his heart attack in the spring and had been persuaded to take a sleeping-draught against the noisy homecoming of his children; old Martha Pitts heard it over at Hermitage and wondered if Henry was home and whether Gloria, her daughter-in-law, had managed to keep him sober. Francis Willoughby at Deepdene, who had politely declined an invitation heard it, for it set his Welsh collie barking and the yaps were answered by the deep-throated bay of Jumbo Bellchamber's mastiff lower down the Bluff slopes at the Potters' old farm. Nobody minded much, however, least of all Simon who was bored by his six-hour stint as Master of Ceremonies. Alone among the family (young Claire had flagrantly disobeyed her mother's instructions and stayed up for the fun) he did not hitch himself on to the braying procession but wandered out on the terrace and down the broad, flagstoned path to the sunken rose garden, inhaling the night air with pleasure after the fug of the ballroom and watching the harvest moon ride over the avenue chestnuts down by the ford.

He had descended the steps that led to the lily pond before he saw a shadow and the glow of a cigarette over by the sundial. The lights from the terrace did not reach this far and the area round the column was cut off from moonlight by a tall copper-beech marking the southern limit of Grace Lovell's single contribution to Shallowford. He saw, however, that a woman stood there and that she was not a guest, for she had a coat thrown loosely over her shoulders and beneath it wore a high-necked sweater and tweed skirt. There was also something about her posture that suggested here was someone else impatient with noise and buffoonery, so he called:

"Hello there? It's only me, Simon Craddock. Can I find someone for you?"

894

The figure straightened itself and tossed the cigarette in a wide arc across the pond.

"No, thank you. I'm only waiting for my sister, Esther. Robbie, my brother, is staying on to help clear up so I brought the trap over for her; I'll give her another ten minutes."

He realised then that he was talking to Rachel Eveleigh, one of the two elder of the Four Winds' girls and remembered in time that she wasn't Rachel Eveleigh now but Rachel Horsey, having married Keith Horsey, the parson's son, whose memorial plaque he had read that same afternoon. He remembered her clearly as a pretty, fresh-faced girl, with light brown hair, who used to help her mother make cream in the Four Winds' buttery but had forgotten until now that Keith Horsey, the C.O., had had a wife, much less a local one. Her presence here as an outsider puzzled him, especially as her brother Robbie, the huntsman, and at least one of her sisters, were among the more boisterous of the younger set in the house. He said, diffidently, "How is it you weren't invited? I helped make out the list. You must have been overlooked. I'm most terribly sorry," and suddenly she laughed so that he felt embarrassed for there was nothing diffident about her laughter. Then she must have realised she had disconcerted him for she said, earnestly, "I'm sorry! I wasn't laughing at you, Mr. Craddock, just at the idea that anyone should be expected to remember me when making out invitation lists for a Shallowford beano! I've been away from here since before my husband was killed. You may remember him better than me, he went to your school, I believe."

"I remember you both," Simon said, still a little ruffled. "As a matter of fact I was thinking of Keith only this afternoon."

"You were?" She sounded not merely surprised but defensive. "Why should anyone around here ever think of Keith?"

"For the same reason as they think occasionally of all the other poor chaps who went west. Oh, I'm not referring to that mob"—he jerked his head towards the house—"they're incapable of thinking about anything of the smallest importance but local ex-service chaps must think of people like Keith Horsey a good deal. My father does for one!"

She moved aside so that the moonlight fell on his face and he had a curious certainty that she was weighing him up and trying to make up her mind whether to continue the conversation or break it off abruptly by walking away.

"You're different, aren't you?" she said, finally. "They never told me about you but—wait a minute, something gells—I remember! You were madly anti-blood sports, weren't you?"

This time he could laugh for her directness, once you got used to it, was refreshing.

"I still am," he said, "it's a kink they never managed to straighten out but now they just pull my leg about it."

"Ikey told us," she said. "I remember there was a family row over it at the time." As she said this she recalled also that the Squire's eldest son, his child by the suffragette, had always worshipped Ikey Palfrey, and the memory of this bridged the gap between them so that her prickliness changed to a kind of relief. She said, before he could reply, "Would you have a cigarette about you? That was my last and I'm an addict."

He took out his case, a twenty-first birthday gift from his sister Mary and they lit up, moving by common consent across to the low wall that surrounded the lily pond; they were reconciled by each other's company to the uproar still issuing from the house. He said, rather glumly, "Ah now, Ikey was one up on both of us! He would have *thought* the same as we do of that kind of horse play but it wouldn't have prevented him from joining in and outdoing the wildest of them! Then he would have gone to bed stone sober and laughed himself to sleep!"

"How do you know so much about him? You were still a child when he was killed."

"I was fourteen-and-a-half and I should remember. The day they told me he was dead was the last time I shed tears. That was when Claire sent his last letter on."

"A letter to you?"

"He wrote me many letters, fifty-three actually."

"Describing what it was like out there?"

"About pretty well everything. I once thought of publishing them but then I thought better of it. It was the only legacy Ikey left to any-one, so why the hell should I share it with boneheads like The Pair, and the other idiots up there?"

"You don't share things at all, do you? Don't get me wrong, I'm not implying that you're mean but that you hate sharing yourself and anything important to you, anything you believe in or regard as fundamental?"

Her prodding among the private storehouse of his thoughts made him feel sufficiently resentful to stand up in protest but when she

896

reached out quickly, and caught him by the hand, he suddenly felt more cheerful and expectant than for a very long time. He hardly knew why this should be so; he could not even see the girl's face clearly where she sat with her face turned away from the moonlight and he reminded himself that she was not a girl but a woman in her early thirties, widowed more than ten years ago. And yet there was assurance in her voice and touch and as her hand tugged at him he sat down again saying, "What the hell is wrong with us? What's eating the bloody heart out of us? Why is it we can't *be* young and *act* young, like all the others up there?"

"Well, I'm not young any more," she said equably, "but in your case I imagine it's part heredity and part on account of those letters Ikey Palfrey wrote you."

"Do you remember my mother?"

"No, not really, but everybody in the Valley knew of her. I was about seven when she was headline news about here. She has significance for me because you might say that in a way she broke the ice for Keith."

"How did she do that?"

"They were the only two rebels the Valley produced in a generation so it's fitting they should both leave their bones on the same battlefield, particularly as most of those who threw the brickbats are home and dry!"

She had given him the clue he had been fumbling for ever since her harsh laugh at his apology about the invitations. She had been embittered not so much by Keith's early death as by the patriotic persecution that had hounded him within range of the guns. His curiosity concerning her increased, perhaps nudged by the "Oxford" accent she used, something utterly foreign to anyone growing up in the kitchen of Four Winds but sounding like the half-way voice of someone who had worked hard to shed the Valley burr.

"Keith was killed twelve years ago," he said, "what have you done with yourself all that time?"

"All kinds of things except marry again."

"You don't sound like a Valley girl any more."

She laughed, pleasantly this time. "Should I? I left here for the North in 1914."

"It always shows up in the vowels."

She was silent for a moment. The racket in the house had died down and dancing had evidently been resumed for the sound of a

897

waltz drifted across to them, a thin, warbling tune, pleasant to hear after the frenzied scream of the hunting-horns.

"What's that they're playing?" she asked suddenly.

"It's one of the talking-picture tunes called 'I met her in Monterey'."

"Ah," she said, "one of their 'if-only' tunes! You might think they were all in their 'fifties if you judged them on their dance music."

"You haven't told me what happened to you."

She said with what seemed to him something of an effort, "The real waste of the war wasn't the blood you know, it was the brains! That's the currency your generation will have to pay in. Keith had brains, not just exam-passing brains but the ability to select and interpret what he learned. After he was killed it seemed to me I should at least make some effort to compensate for the waste. I took a degree in Economics at Leeds University."

It did not surprise him overmuch. There was something about her that suggested not only stamina but initiative.

"You went back to school?"

"Night school up to Matric standard; then I got a county grant. They go out of their way to cater for the morally earnest in the North, you know."

"And then?"

"I ran headlong into the sex-barriers your mother spent her life storming. They are still there, you know, bristling with patronage, complacency and fly-buttons! I tried accountancy, then teaching, then actuarial work and flopped in all three! They say the professions are open to women now but it isn't true of course, not unless a woman is prepared to wear a tight skirt and leave all the decisions to the men, even the one about what time she likes to go to bed."

He ignored all her jibes. "What do you do now?"

"I supervise a chain of working men's clubs and do part-time secretarial work for a Member of Parliament. The clubs interest me. The M.P. doesn't, I'm afraid."

"A Socialist M.P.?"

"A very temporary one; he'll be looking for a job himself before he's acquired a taste for House of Commons sherry."

There were so many things he wanted to ask her—how secure was the recent Labour victory at the polls, how sincere was her avowed contempt for men of whatever political persuasion, and above all what remedies, if any, she prescribed for the anaemia of Western civilisa-

898

tion but at that moment the music stopped and he heard Stephen bawling for him from the terrace.

"I'll have to go," he said. "Won't you at least come up and have a drink of some sort?"

"No thanks," she said. "I'll bring our trap round to the front if you tell my sister I'm waiting. I promised Mother I'd get her back at a reasonable hour and I suppose three o'clock is reasonable by Esther's standards."

He offered his hand and she took it absentmindedly.

"Couldn't we meet again before I go back to town?" he suggested. "I'm thinking of going on the staff of a new magazine but nothing's settled yet."

"What kind of magazine?"

"A long-hair; it's to be called *The Forum*. Have you heard about it?"

"Yes," she said, "I've heard about it," and then, with another crackle of candour, "You could do a lot better than that, Simon!"

"Then let's meet and discuss it. Tomorrow evening? I can pick you up and we could have a bite to eat at The Mitre, in Paxtonbury."

"Very well." She sounded unenthusiastic but he was still young enough and vain enough not to care. He went off along the flagged wall calling to Stephen but as he went he wished he could have seen her in the light, especially when she was talking about Beanpole Horsey.

IV

The twins "did their talking" that same week, before all traces of the celebrations had been removed and it was as well for them perhaps that Simon was still at home to act as a buffer, and also that they had had the foresight to summon reserve artillery in the person of Uncle Franz Zorndorff who had been talked into paying one of his rare visits to the Westcountry.

The old man, whom Paul declared was going to live for ever, appeared the Monday after the party, spruce and chipper as ever, although, by Paul's reckoning, he was now only a year short of ninety. He bowled up the drive soon after lunch in his huge, black Daimler, driven by a chauffeur wearing chocolate livery and Paul thought, as he watched the flunkey double round and give Franz an unnecessary arm as far as the porch, "The old rascal loves ostentation everywhere but in his counting-house. In there he's too damned careful to spend sixpence on a new blotter!" But he was pleased to see his father's old partner nonetheless and made a mental note to seek his advice about farm prices and land values. The wily old Croat might spend his entire life between his luxury flat in the West End and his disreputable Thames-side scrapyard, but his advice on any subject remotely connected with money was worth having and usually worth following. He called from the garden door as Claire ran out on to the porch, "Now what the devil brings you down here? Is the plague raging in town?"

The aged dandy waved his silver-topped cane and submitted gracefully to Claire's embrace, and then Simon and Mary ran out, and after them the twins whooping with glee, so that Paul began to suspect there was more in this than met the eye and went back into the study to rake among memories of recent hints on Claire's part connected in some way with the twins' harebrained schemes for making money—for "getting aboard the jolly old bandwaggon" as they would have put it. Their bandwaggons, Paul reflected, were gaudier than Simon's but just as flimsily constructed and somehow far more calculated to irritate him. Simon's false starts had about them a few rags of dignity whereas the twins' were balloons full of blather that soared and were forgotten in a matter of days. The presence of Franz, however, made him more than usually curious to know what was brewing and he would have gone through into the hall had not Stephen appeared suddenly in the doorway and said, "Uncle Franz is swilling tea, Gov! He says to leave him with Mother for a jiffy. Andy and I want to jaw first, is that okay with you?"

"You don't have to tell me something's afoot," Paul said and grinned in spite of himself for it was impossible to resist the impact of The Pair. "Come on in, both of you, and out with it! Your brother told me you had another rod in pickle for me."

"Won't cost you a sou, Gov, and that's a fact," said Stephen, sidling in and shutting the door after his twin. "Isn't it a fact, Andy?"

"Fact," said Andy, who habitually used far fewer words than his brother.

"Well, what is it? Not another madcap scheme like that marine engineering lark, I hope."

"Nothing like it," said Stephen, sitting and throwing his long legs over the arm of the chair, "this is a corker and Uncle Franz is right behind us, isn't that so, Andy?"

"Money in it," Andy said, "real money! No outlay either."

"At least not from your standpoint, Gov," Stevie added promptly.

"Well that's a change anyway," Paul said watching their exchange of glances with sardonic amusement. "I suppose it's too much to hope that you've decided to take my advice and pick up where you both left off at Agricultural College?"

"Look, Gov, farming's a dead duck. Honestly it is!"

"Dead and buried," confirmed Andy. "Ask any of your tenants, they'll soon get you up-to-date!"

He knew it was useless to argue with them. They had been over the ground so often since both had left school without matriculating; they had been over it, through it and round it, with and without benefit of supplementary arguments and suggestions contributed by Claire, John Rudd and the Principal of the County Agricultural College they had attended for a couple of terms. "Well," he said, resignedly, "get to the point, I'm listening."

"Uncle Franz has asked us to take over his Birmingham Branch," said Andy, rather too bluntly it would seem for his brother's liking for Stevie swung round in protest but was checked by a gesture on the part of Andy, confirming Paul's theory that although Stephen was the more dominant of the two Andy was the brains of the alliance. He said, trying to keep his voice level, "What the devil do you mean? *What* Birmingham branch? And branch of what, for God's sake?"

Stevie, already out of his depth, was content to leave the matter with his twin but Andy went on, deliberately, "Uncle Franz has a yard up there. It's been open a year but it's being run by a crook and isn't paying off! It could tho', particularly with another slump around the corner. Uncle Franz thinks we'd make a go of it."

"A 'yard'?" Paul queried, repressing an impulse to shout. "You mean—a *scrapyard*?"

"What else? Franz is the king of scrap, isn't he?"

"Yes," Paul said, "he is, and when I was a year or two older than you he did his best to make me the Crown Prince! I declined the honour and looking back on my life I count myself very fortunate!"

"But that's just it," Andy said, leaning forward and speaking with great emphasis, "looking back on *your* life, Gov! We're concerned with *our* lives and neither of us have the slightest inclination to vegetate down here!"

Out of the corner of his eye Paul saw Stephen wince but Andy, unrepentant, went on before either of them could comment. "I don't mean that you've vegetated, Gov! Nobody around here could accuse you of that, but what you've done you wanted to do and were good at whereas Stevie and I, we're neither of us particularly bright and have to grab at what chances present themselves! I reckon we could tackle this lark and might even make a go of it! Anyway, we've talked it over and we'd like to try."

It was a longish speech for Andy and left him a little breathless and red in the face. Paul said, as his mind still boggled at the project, "You say you've talked it over? Do you mean with your mother, as well as with Uncle Franz and Simon?"

"No," admitted Stephen, "we thought of doing so but didn't. It didn't seem fair to involve her in case you blew your top!"

Strange that, Paul reflected, calming somewhat. Strange and a little touching that they should have reservations in that respect. It did them credit he supposed, but it also showed how accurately they had measured Claire's loyalty. Then, as he got his second wind, he had leisure to ponder the irony of the situation. From scrap to scrap in one generation! How Franz must relish the proposal after all he had heard from Paul on the subject of scrapyards over the last twenty-seven years! He said, curtly, "Very well, you've had your say. Run along and let me talk this over with that old rascal."

"Don't you want to hear details?" Stevie asked and Paul said no but if he had to listen to them he preferred hearing them from Franz.

They got up gratefully enough but as they reached the door he relented slightly and said, "Well, at least you didn't taunt me for using scrap money to keep the Valley alive since the war!"

"We thought of it, Gov, but decided it was below the belt!" Stevie said and they both vanished under cover of his grunt of laughter.

Paul went over to the window and looked down the curving line of the avenue of chestnuts. He still felt winded and was glad of a moment to compose himself before Franz appeared. From the angle of the window he could see the glint of afternoon sun on the ford and the shadow-play on the long swell of the Codsall stubble fields where they climbed to the watershed on the edge of the moor. He remembered the first time he had stood here and looked westward to the boundary, the day before the Lovell sale, in the long, dry summer of 1902, just before he had made up his mind to buy the place and years before those two young idiots had been thought of; well, it was pretty well full circle now, with all three of his sons opting out of the estate and the demands it made on a man. They would find their way, he supposed, but it would be their way not his or Claire's and there was, after all, some justice in their argument. He had a right to want at least one of them to follow on here but he had no right to insist on it and he knew before he heard Franz's step what the outcome would be. If he had a successor here it would have to be a grandson and even that, he felt, was unlikely.

The old man advertised himself with a cough, then shuffled in and stood with his back to the door. Paul thought he had seldom seen Franz so unsure of himself and it cheered him. It was not often he had the old man at a disadvantage.

"Well, Franz," he said. "I suppose they told you I took it on the chin, although I must say it makes nonsense of everything I had in mind for them. Was it their idea or yours?"

"Mine, Paul," Franz said, "and common decency demands I make some effort to hammer the motive into your thick skull." He lowered himself gently into Claire's armchair and lit one of his long Dutch cheroots. He looked, Paul thought, like a centenarian gnome got up for a wedding—trim Van Dyke beard and sidewhiskers, razor-sharp creases in his striped trousers, puffed grey stock fixed with a diamond pin, gnarled fingers crowded with gold rings. He said, puffing a thin stream of bluish smoke, "I *have* a motive and it's a disinterested one, I assure you."

"You imply you agree with Andy when he says British agriculture is dead and buried?"

"No," Franz said, "but it soon would be if their sort had a hand in it! The fact is, Paul, my boy, you haven't made allowances for the gap between their generation and yours. It's a great deal wider than the usual gulf between father and son."

"The thing that defeats me," Paul said suddenly, "is that those boys are good farming stock on their mother's side. Simon I could understand—any child of Grace would have to behave eccentrically but Claire's boys—old Derwent's grandchildren . . . !"

"It isn't eccentric to want to clear a fresh circle for yourself at twenty-one, Paul! After all, you did and were damned obstinate about it if I remember rightly! In any case, those boys are as far away from us as we were from men born during the French Revolution. You can blame the war for that but don't blame them."

"But what the hell could they do in a Birmingham scrapyard? They'll only lose you money and you'll ship them back to me the moment they do. I know you that well, Franz!"

"My boy," said Franz, with the air of taut patience that always irritated Paul when they disagreed, as they did over almost everything they discussed. "Why will you persist in looking on the scrap-metal

903

industry as the prerogative of a man in a leather apron, driving a donkey-cart? Did you ever see me touch a piece of salvage? What will they do up there? They'll do what I tell them to do, make friends and contacts, hob-nob with steelmasters, used-car dealers, machinists, boiler-makers, wholesale meat-purveyors and wiremen! They'll join clubs, buy drinks, dress well, drive fast cars, back steeplechasers and flirt with women, I hope; anything calculated to broaden their outlook and nail down new sources. I've done precisely that for the past fifty years and you can't tell me that it hasn't paid dividends!"

"It sounds the kind of occupation well suited to them," Paul said, "but I hope you realise they can't add a column of figures three times without getting three different totals, and that their scrawl is usually illegible."

"We maintain clerks and book-keepers," said Franz, acidly. "It wasn't to learn how to run my business that I made the effort to come here, Paul."

"Neither was it to win my approval to my sons leaving me in the lurch," said Paul cheerfully, "for you've always been too damned arrogant to seek a blessing from anyone!"

Franz smiled, accepting the thrust as a compliment. "I won't quarrel with you there, my boy, but the fact is I was wrong about you and admit it! The only real success is living one's life the way one wants to live it and, taken all round, you've been successful. Damn it, how many men have survived two wars and two marriages and stayed sane and solvent?"

"It wasn't just luck, Franz, it was often more a matter of holding on."

"Whatever it was timing had something to do with it, which brings me to the only real point I want to make."

"Well?"

"You had a twelve-year apprenticeship before the rot set in. You settled in here smug and cosy when the pound stood for something abroad, when everybody knew their place and you and all your bucolic friends could take tea on the lawn without the tablecloth blowing away and wasps crawling up your corduroys! You ought to remember that when you expect those boys to use your set of values! I'm nearly twice your age and I don't expect them to use mine! They have to make a new mould and they can't do it here growing prize artichokes and playing cricket on the green! Make 'em and they'll go sour on you, sour and rotten, I promise you! I've seen too many rich men's sons warped by Papa's conceits not to know what I'm talking about.

904

I've given you good advice in the past—it was me who put you on to this place at the start of it all—and I'm giving you more now! Let 'em go, and Simon as well if he wants to, and do it with good grace! Let 'em find out for themselves what it's really like out there in among the grime and brickstacks. Either they'll adjust and do you credit or they'll come home with their tails between their legs, in which case you might found your neo-yeoman family after all!"

By the time Franz had finished and thrown his cheroot butt into the grate as a kind of full-stop Paul was chuckling, not so much because, in his heart, he agreed with the old man, but because his explosive vitality had the effect of cutting everything down to size and making Paul's initial distaste for the project seem as prejudiced as Henry Pitts' stonewall opposition to selling his plough horses and accepting the gift of a tractor. He said, pacifically, "All right, Franz, you don't have to break a blood-vessel on their behalf! They're all three of age, anyway, and I couldn't stop them doing what they wanted. Good luck to them and to you and you're the one who is going to need it most! However, since you seem to be in such a pontifical mood, and since I rarely see you where we're not interrupted by the telephone, will you give *me* some advice? There are pretty clear signs of another slump setting in. Is it likely to be easier or more difficult to ride out than the last one, from my viewpoint I mean?"

"Now why the devil should you ask me that?" Franz said, playing at being ruffled. "What do I know of livestock and land values this far from civilisation?"

"About a hundred times more than the best-informed local Agricultural Adviser who ever quoted an out-of-date white paper to me," Paul told him, remembering that all the success the old man had achieved since landing in England as a political refugee had not made him immune to flattery.

"You're genuinely asking my advice? About selling or buying land?"

"About selling it; I've come out of things better than most farmers since the war but it's time I retrenched if I want to keep money in hand against emergencies. One of my tenants has been pestering me to sell for some time."

"You trust him?"

"Good God, yes, he's my brother-in-law. It's Claire's brother, Hugh."

"Then sell! Sell tomorrow! And retrench too if you have time!"

"It's as bad as that?"

"We're heading directly into the worst economic blizzard of our lifetime."

"Oh come, Franz, you aren't that scared of another Socialist Government?"

"The Socialists have nothing to do with it this time. The Tories ought to be damned glad they're not holding the baby. As a matter of fact some that I know are!"

Paul was more interested than alarmed. He knew that the sensitive fingers of this dry old stick never left the economic pulse and recalled how, on the night of August 1st, 1914, he had been hauled out of bed to answer Franz's laconic telephone call urging him to insure against a long war; only Kitchener and Uncle Franz had been right about that! He said, "If it isn't all this talk about the investors going abroad and taking their money out of reach of our tame Bolshies what's causing the anxiety?"

"The American Stock-market. You don't still cherish the fiction we're still the financial hub of the world, do you? We're in for a bad time, the whole lot of us!"

"Well," said Paul resignedly, "the first to feel it will be the farmers."

"Oh don't try that one on me," Franz said testily. "I've never seen a poor one yet and at least they can always eat! By this time next year that'll be a privilege among the unemployed."

"Then why are you branching out in Birmingham? Wouldn't you do well to retrench?"

The old man smiled and stood up, brushing the ash from his faultlessly cut jacket.

"I always maintained, Paul, that you were not a man of business and certainly not of the scrap business! In a month those boys of yours will make rings round you. The scrap market is the vulture in the flock. That's why I can smell carrion long before anyone else's nostrils twitch. Sell to your brother-in-law and count yourself fortunate. I would advise you to pretend to sell reluctantly and keep the price up but I know your Nonconformist conscience would torment you if you didn't tell the buyer everything I've said to you today! Besides, you have a duty to your wife's family, I suppose, you owe her something for putting up with you all these years! What time do you dine in this wilderness?"

"We don't," Paul told him, "we have high tea at six-thirty and don't expect any frills."

906

The Croat took out a large gold watch and studied it. "Time for a nap," he said, affably. "Half-an-hour with you, my friend, is as good as a day's grind."

He went out with his curious shuffling step and Paul, still grinning, escorted him as far as the landing, pointing the way to the guest room. As he descended the stairs his grin broadened. Simon, Andrew, Stephen and, behind them, Claire, were all gazing up at him from the threshold of the hall. They looked like a group of anxious children whose ball has just sailed over an alien fence and were calculating the risks of retrieving it.

CHAPTER TWO

I

PAUL remembered, looking back on that time, that Franz had used the word "blizzard" and had seemed to mean it but the depression that resulted in three million unemployed in Britain, and had most of its cities and great areas of the countryside sick and gasping by 1931, did not visit the Valley as a blizzard, or anything like a blizzard. Instead it crept in from the north and east like a malign, leisurely blight, touching first one family then another, plucking at a farm here, a man there, leaving any number of small, scabrous wounds that were slow to heal and seemed at first unrelated to one another or to hurts such as those caused, say, by the war. Yet, in some instances, the wounds were just as lethal. At Periwinkle, for example, which decayed structurally, and in the relationship between the Big House and Higher Coombe, where the period of stress left a scar that never did heal while there was breath in the body of Paul Craddock and his wife, formerly Claire Derwent.

Echoes of the Wall Street crash reached the Valley by courtesy of Fleet Street. During the autumn Stevie and Andrew left for what Paul thought of as its storm-centre, the industrial Midlands, but when they reappeared on Christmas Eve that same year they did not look like the survivors of the economic disaster. They roared up in a red M.G. sports car, with long silk scarves round their necks and golf clubs protruding from an overloaded boot. They rampaged about the Valley for a spell shouting at everyone they encountered, coming home at four in the morning and spending freely in the Paxtonbury pubs. Then they disappeared again without anyone having the least idea what they did in Birmingham or how they acquired sports car, golf clubs or the skill to use them.

It was a hard winter. Snow fell early and Valley noises were muted for a period of weeks; then, with the arrival of a cheerless, seeping spring, came news that foxes were active west of Hermitage Wood and that luckless Elinor Codsall had lost thirty-seven point-of-lay birds in a single night.

Paul went over to pay her hunt compensation, knowing that she was having a struggle with the price of eggs at an all-time low and her son Mark laid up with a broken leg caused by a motor-cycle skid during the cold snap. He was accustomed, by now, to Elinor's pessimism but was puzzled by the way she took her loss of hens to heart, as though the dog-fox who got into the run had singled her out for special persecution.

"'Er made straight for me, zame as all bad luck do!" she said and when Paul tried to laugh her out of her grievance she said, challengingly, "Well, baint it zo? Baint it alwus zo? My man was the first to get called up an' be blown to tatters! Then us struggles on 'till that red-headed bitch Gloria Pitts comes yer raisin' creation about me an' that German! Then us loses the pigs in the first voot an' mouth outbrak an' when us is making headway again Mark has to break his bliddy leg. Now, to top all, nigh on forty point-o'-lay crossbreds, the best I ever reared, makes one meal for bliddy Reynard!"

There was no comforting her and she continued to grumble through the summer when Mark was back at work but likely to be slightly lame for the rest of his life for the accident left him with one leg an inch shorter than the other.

The Codsalls perked up for a time after Paul found them a hired hand called Rutter but after a few months at Periwinkle the new man had an invitation from his brother-in-law in Tasmania and announced that farming here was a mug's game and he was getting out while the going was good. After that Paul noticed that land Will Codsall had patiently reclaimed from the moor began to go back, so that before the year was out Periwinkle was reduced to its original holding, a mere sixty acres and although Elinor was only paying a pre-war rent she fell behind in that and Paul, only too aware of the narrow profit margin of more prosperous farms, could not be persuaded by John Rudd to find a billet for Mark Codsall somewhere else and cut his losses by letting Elinor live on in the old Hardcastle farmhouse while her land was divided between Four Winds and Hermitage.

It was the final piece of advice John was to give him. In the event the Periwinkle problem was solved by a near miracle but before Paul could justify his extreme reluctance to do as the agent suggested John was dead.

If a man can be said to have died thoroughly at peace with his world this was achieved by John Rudd. He died in the cramped bedroom of the lodge that he had occupied ever since the Lovells had left and in the presence of the only three people in his life who mattered to him, his wife Maureen, the slim, fair-haired boy, whom she had astonished everyone by producing soon after her late marriage, and Paul Craddock, whom John always claimed to have restored to him a purpose in life.

He caught a severe chill in early autumn and coughing aggravated his heart condition. On the third day after he had taken to his bed it was arranged that he should be admitted to Whinmouth Hospital and Maureen sent for Paul asking him to come before the ambulance was due. Paul was shocked at John's appearance. He lay propped up by pillows looking more than his age and his gruff voice was reduced to a dry whisper. Yet he seemed philosophic about his chances of survival. "Tried to tell Maureen to leave me be," he said, "but she fussed, so I couldn't be bothered arguing. Prefer to die here if I've got to go. Been my life best part of fifty years."

Paul reminded him that Maureen's purpose in transferring him to hospital was his need of an oxygen tent but he made no attempt to indulge in conventional sick-bed denials. He knew Rudd better than that and recognised an old, tired and moderately satisfied man when he saw one. John went on, after some coughing, "Should like to have left you on a crest instead of deep in a damned trough. Think you'll struggle out of it?"

"We've always bobbed up before, John," Paul told him, "and there's no sense in you worrying about it at your time of life."

The agent's old-fashioned moustache twitched. "You're a damned sight tougher than you look, Paul," he said grudgingly. "A Boer bullet in your knee, lump of Hun shrapnel in your head, your ribs bashed in that time of the wreck, and this white elephant on your back! But you wouldn't have it otherwise, would you?"

"I could have done without the bullet and the shrapnel," Paul said, "but I'm not nearly as bothered as you seem to be by current land values and farm prices. These things come and go like women's fashions."

"Talking of fashions . . ." whispered John and stopped as his son came in with a draught of medicine, put it down on the bedside table and said, in a sickroom voice, "Mother has just heard on the 'phone the ambulance will be a bit late, Father. It seems they're clearing up after a road smash on the main road, a bad one."

"Good," John croaked, "hope it keeps 'em busy all night!" and as the boy tiptoed out and he reached out to pick up his medicine, "I wish to God he and his mother would be as realistic as you, Paul. She's tough enough with her patients but she clucks all day long over me! Like a schoolmaster spoiling his own children!" and he chuckled at his own modest joke.

Paul said, for something to say, "You were making some comment on fashions."

"Ah yes," John muttered, his medicine glass clutched in a hand that shook so much that Paul reached across to steady it, "it made me think of bosoms!"

"Whose bosom in particular?"

"Eveᵢybody's! Time was when every woman about the Valley tortured herself to look like an hour-glass. Now every damned one of them, your wife included, delights in making herself look like a tube!"

It struck Paul as so grotesque that bluff old John Rudd should beguile the time awaiting his ambulance by jesting about bosoms that he laughed outright and the patient, catching the infection of laughter, joined in so that for a moment they were both comparatively young again, riding together through Shallowford on their way home from a day's hunting before the war. Then, with tragic suddenness, John's laugh changed to a rasping cough and the draught of medicine shot over the coverlet as he bent forward spluttering and groping with outflung arms. Maureen rushed into the room and after her the boy but it was over before they could hoist him back into his former position.

It was sobering, Paul thought, to witness the extremity of their distress, for although death was a new experience to the boy his mother must have seen a thousand die in almost identical circumstances. She looked across at Paul with her face ravaged and Paul, taking control, motioned to the boy to leave which he did at once, trying in vain to stem an unmanly flow of tears. Paul said, "He loathed the prospect of dying outside the Valley, Maureen! He told me so the minute I came in here. Surely you must have known what his chances were!"

She made a gesture of hopelessness and turned her back on the disordered bed, crossing to the window and opening it a notch so that a swishing wind threading the chestnuts banished the stuffiness of the little room. Paul took advantage of the moment to lay the body straight and arrange the sheet, after which, thinking to give her son something to occupy his mind, he called down and gave instructions to cancel the ambulance and notify the hospital. He turned back to Maureen, still standing by the window. "Can I get you a drink, Maureen?" and when she shook her head, "He had a good life once the Lovells went out of it and especially good after you came to share it."

"He told you that?"

"He implied it often enough. It was a tremendous piece of luck for him to find you about half-way through."

"For me too, Paul," she said, and he saw that she had herself in hand again.

There seemed nothing more to say, or not at this stage, and when Maureen indicated she would like to stay a while and compose herself before she went back to the boy, he left without saying anything more to his godson who was talking hoarsely into the telephone. He went out into the drive and found the night warmish but gusty, with only a sliver of moon over the Bluff and a hurrying breathlessness in the south-westerly wind that promised more rain, possibly an autumn gale. He went through the open iron gates to the ford which was high and noisy and stood there a moment gulping down mouthfuls of the moist air, quickly coming to terms with the sharp break in a line of continuity that led right back to the blazing afternoon nearly thirty years ago, when he had first trotted along this road with John. That was all that John had cared about—continuity, pattern, ordered progress and it was that, he supposed, that had linked them from the beginning, building a relationship that had resulted in each of them having complete confidence in the other and in Shallowford as an institution. Yet he remembered John telling him before the war that he no longer needed an agent, that he was perfectly capable of running this place alone. It wasn't true of course, no single man's care and capital could nourish the Valley, no matter how single-minded and dedicated that man might be. It needed a dozen or more and they were getting fewer as time went on. Some were not being replaced as surely as Arthur Pitts at Hermitage had been and Edward Derwent, his father-in-law at Higher Coombe but he had been lucky so far. Of the seven farms only Periwinkle and Four Winds were in rough water, the one because it had always been too small and inadequately staffed, the other because Eveleigh's eldest son had been killed in the war and none of the others seemed interested in carrying on. He stood there in the wet wind making a sort of accounting to the dead man in the lodge. Prices were atrocious, more and more skilled men were drifting into the towns, hedging and ditching was in arrears because of labour shortage, reliefs and government subsidies were unrealistic, and older men like Henry Pitts and the failing Eveleigh were slow to take to new methods and develop new markets like those for sugar-beet, cereal wheat and peas for local canning. If it were not for Paul's policy of keeping rents at a minimum figure, and feeding fresh capital into the estate by way of pedigree livestock, farm machines hired out at nominal rates and free gifts of chemical manure to those who would use it, the estate would have contracted long ago and land would have been sold off to keep what remained in good heart. As it was only Hugh Derwent's Higher Coombe had broken away and even that was still in the family and might return some time seeing that Hugh was a bachelor and likely to remain one. John had seemed worried in his last moments regarding his ability to hold on to the place and now Paul wondered if he had convinced him of his determination and wished that he had emphasised it more. "Well," he muttered to himself, as he turned for home, "he ought to know me after all this time! I'll see it through one way or another until one of the boys comes to his senses, or one of the girls marries a sensible chap and has children to pass it to!" and feeling renewed rather than depressed he repassed the lodge and lifted his hand in salute to the man who lay behind the little latticed window. It was very difficult to think of old John as dead.

II

John Rudd was buried on one of those left-over days from late summer when the broad, steep street leading down to the church glowed in pale sunlight that suggested rather than provided warmth for the mourners. After the committal, when he was heading for the lych-gate to rejoin Claire (no women had attended at the graveside although many had been present in the church), Paul found himself noting any number of odd, inconsequential things that John might have remarked upon had he been in a tranquil mood—a squadron of rooks circling the church elms, the drunkard's flight of a bumble bee who had evidently lost his calendar, the curious, crab-like progress of old Aaron Stokes, the reed-gatherer, who must, by Paul's reckoning, have attended two hundred funerals during his eighty-odd years in the village but his reflections were cut short by confrontation with young Mark Codsall, yet another godchild, at the fork in the church path and Mark's apologetic—"Could I have a word with 'ee, Squire? Worn taake but a moment; tiz about Mother!"

He turned aside, wondering if this meant fresh trouble but Mark seemed no more than bashful and said, as they drew aside from the

913

stream of mourners, "She's thinkin' on gettin' married again, Squire! Tiz true! I baint jokin'! But it'll mean her leaving Periwinkle an' she abben the nerve to tell 'ee! Anyway, tiz all happened zo zudden I'm praper mazed meself, that I be!"

Paul said, "I'm absolutely delighted to hear it, Mark, and so, I'm sure, would your father have been. She needs to make a new life for herself and that's been her main trouble but I hadn't the faintest notion she . . ." and he stopped, noticing that Mark was now flushed with embarrassment.

"Nor had I, nor our Floss, nor any of us," Mark added, "but on'y me's in favour of it! Them others, they don't understand, havin' gone off an' lived away so long, but I remember the bloke well enough. Reckon I ought to—he saved my life when I was a tacker."

"Who did?" asked Paul, more mystified than ever and the young man blurted out that the German prisoner who had been loaned to the farm twelve years before had reappeared on the doorstep a fortnight ago and informed his mother that he was not only a widower but a prosperous one, having inherited an extensive market-garden from an uncle in some unpronounceable German province like "Shinivwig".

"Schleswig? Schleswig-Holstein?" suggested Paul and Mark said yes, that was it, and Elinor had asked him in for a meal and afterwards they had driven off to Paxtonbury in his hired Essex saloon and that his mother had "shown up that night in a praper old tizzy, laughin' an' cryin',", and that since then the German, who was called Willi Meyer, had called every day and had finally taken Mark aside and asked him his views on the prospect of having a German stepfather.

"Good God!" said Paul laughing and then, recalling where he was, straightened his face. "What did you say to that?"

"I told un 'twas no biziness o' mine," Mark said, "seein' 'er was old enough to marry whom 'er plaised! Point is, I got no hankering to stay on there meself. I bin courtin' Liz Pascoe and Liz has zet her heart on one o' they new houses in Nun's Bay and woulden give us a thank-you for our ratty old plaace. Besides," he looked a little ashamed, "I baint zet on varmin' like Mother and Dad were, I'd as zoon try something wi' steady money, zo long as it had to do wi' driving and mebbe a chance to ride once in a while."

Paul knew very well what Mark was hinting at. Chivers, the Shallowford groom, had died a year ago and had never been replaced and Mark Codsall was a judicious compromise between the post-war motor-mad youngsters and older men who still liked a day's hunting.

He said, on impulse, "How would it suit you to move into Chivers' old quarters at Shallowford and be our chauffeur, groom and odd-job man in the garden? The stable flat has mod cons, tell Liz, and it's a damned sight more comfortable than any of those jerry-built bungalows at Nun's Bay. You won't make a fortune but I daresay you'd earn more than you've been getting lately."

"It'd suit me fine," Mark said, his eyes shining, "Liz an' me could get married zoon as mother but . . . well . . . dornee *mind* about her marryin' a Jerry, Squire?"

"Not in the least," said Paul, "a Jerry saved my life soon after that prisoner-of-war tackled your snakebite. Would she be embarrassed if I rode over and wished her luck?"

"Well, I daresay 'er'd blush an' carry on a bit," Mark admitted, grinning, "but if I was you I'd call unexpected an' catch 'em at it! He's always around dinner-times but you worn have no trouble with 'ee, 'ee's a nice enough chap, even if he does click his heels and bob about all the time. He's got our lingo off too! Damned if he don't sound like he'd swallowed a bliddy dictionary sometimes!"

Paul rode over to Periwinkle about noon the next day and it cheered him to see the astonishing change in the Elinor Codsall, who flitted out to the gate in a way that reminded him of the Elinor Willoughby wooed by Will Codsall over at Deepdene all those years ago. Her greying hair was neatly dressed and her apron (a piece of sacking when he had last called) was clean, frilled and gaily patterned. She was so shy and excited that she whisked him into the presence of the tall, sombre Willi Meyer, a man about her own age and then disappeared into the scullery like a rabbit into a hedge burrow. Fortunately, at this point, Mark stumped into the kitchen and dispensed tankards of home-brewed cider, so that Paul and the German soon found common ground in battlefield reminiscences which led, naturally enough, to an expression of Meyer's doubts about the local reaction to a marriage between a German and the widow of a man killed by Germans fourteen years before, explaining earnestly that Elinor herself seemed entirely free of prejudice and regarded the entire conflict as an act of folly on the part of their respective rulers. As for him, he did not blame the luckless Kaiser (as most English people did) so much as the Junkers, who had always been a thorn in the side of the South Germans. He himself, he hastened to add, had nothing but admiration for the British, who had treated him with far more lenience than he had been led to expect after his capture near St.

915

Quentin. All the time he talked he stood stiffly to attention, making his points with a series of stiff half-bows from the waist and every time he bowed Mark Codsall choked into his cider. Paul could not help comparing Meyer's elaborate courtesy with the bucolic manners of poor old Will, his predecessor, and it crossed his mind, whilst listening patiently to the German's preamble, that it was not every woman who could achieve such a range in husbands. This led him to reflect upon what this punctilious Saxon could find to admire in the tubby, middle-aged widow, still hiding out in the scullery, or, for the matter, how Elinor herself could have taken his proposal seriously. The German answered one of these questions almost at once, declaring that he had forgotten neither Elinor's kindness when he was a prisoner nor her skill in raising poultry and it seemed to Paul that his determination to take her back to Schleswig with him was prompted largely by her promise of extreme usefulness when he got her there. In Germany, as in England, he pointed out, poultry was the prerogative of the farmer's wife. He had no children and after eight years as a widower looked upon marriage as an insurance against lonely old age. What did the Graf think? Was it not a very sensible arrangement for both parties?

Paul explained, as well as he could, that he had no jurisdiction whatever over Elinor, that she was his tenant and had been for nearly thirty years but that his interest in her was limited to that of an old friend. If she was anxious to become Frau Meyer he could give assurance that nobody in the Valley, much less himself, would think any the less of her and that a majority, he felt, would wish them luck. The people round here, he told the German, now resented the French more than the Germans, particularly since it had been made public that the French Government charged rent for the use of track and rolling stock employed to repatriate British wounded, whereas in recent years, especially since the publication of Remarque's *All Quiet*, anti-German hysteria had spent itself.

"Ach, so!" said Meyer, thoughtfully, "that is good to hear from the lips of an English Graf! It has never been otherwise in my country. Tommy fed our children in the Ruhr and in defiance of orders, yes?"

He seemed to regard this as a suitable point to terminate the interview, clicking his heels and conjuring a blushing Elinor from the scullery with a despotic clap of his hands. Elinor's prompt response to the summons released another spring of conjecture in Paul's mind, for he reflected how, when Will Codsall was nominal master here, it was common knowledge in the Valley that Elinor wore the trousers. Elinor said Willi was anxious to get married before his return early in the New Year and this meant that everybody concerned would have to hustle. Mark could take what he liked of the furniture and the remainder would be put up to auction for she was taking nothing but her linen.

"John Rudd's notion was to split Periwinkle acres between Hermitage and Four Winds," Paul told her, wondering if Elinor would resent seeing half her acreage pass to the Pitts' family, for she had never forgiven Gloria for her unique expression of patriotism during the war.

"Tiz your land, Squire," Elinor said carelessly, "and tiz for you to parcel it out but I'd be plaised if you could see your way to givin' me away when the time comes! Would 'ee now? Would Mrs. Craddock think it zeemly?"

"I'm sure she would," Paul said, "but wouldn't your brother Francis like to do it?"

"Giddon no," said Elinor, impatiently. "Francis baint had collar an' tie on zince Father died and he give up attending chapel! Us'd zooner it was you, woulden us, Willi?"

"Please?" said Willi, never having mastered the Devon dialect, whereupon Paul translated and the German said it would be an honour, none of his family having had a Graf present at their weddings.

"For God's sake what *is* a 'Graf'?" demanded the indulgent Mark but Paul said he would explain later and they parted on a cordial note, Elinor accompanying Paul to the post where he had tethered his skewbald.

"What do 'ee really think, Squire?" she asked as he put his foot in the stirrup, "do 'ee think I'm mazed to go marryin' a forriner at my time o' life? I dorn mind if you says zo tho' my mind's zet on it, whether or no!"

"I think it's a splendid arrangement," Paul said, laughing, "so long as you're sure you'll be happy in a strange land, away from all the folk you've grown up with. He's a thoroughly decent chap but I suppose you've considered the obvious difficulties, language and so on?"

"Arr," she said thoughtfully, "I have that and I daresay I'll be terrible homesick come springtime an' autumn but a woman's plaace is where her man has his work. If old Will had up an' trotted off to Australia that time his folks tried to come between us I would ha' followed to whistle an' neither Arabella nor my folks could have stopped

917

me! Zeems away off, that ole fuss dorn it, like another lifetime? To tell 'ee the real truth, Squire, Willi Meyer showin' up like he did saved me from actin' about as stupid as Will's father! Things was closin' in like they do sometimes an' you can't fight free of 'em like you can when youm young an' spry!"

"You're as young and spry as the best of us," Paul told her and then, looking down at her earnest face, his curiosity broke the bounds of propriety and he said, "Was there ever anything between you and Willi Meyer when he was working here during the war? I don't give a damn one way or the other, but *was* there?" and was not the least surprised when a sly grin lit up her face and she said, cheerfully, "Arr, nought but slap an' tickle in the barn a time or two, Squire, but dornee ever let Gloria Pitts know, will 'ee now?"

"What kind of a fool do you take me for?" Paul said, chuckling, and before he swung himself into the saddle he turned and kissed her weather-roughened cheek, not waiting to witness her surprise but riding down over the weed-grown western slope to the track that led to the river road. "By George!" he said to himself, as he broke into a trot, "what the devil do any of us know about the people we live among? I don't think I ever thought of that story Henry told me about the fight in the Periwinkle kitchen without choking with indignation but it seems Gloria had it right after all! Maybe everyone was a little mad those days, even Claire with that ass at the camp, the one who came close to prompting me to tan the hide off her!" He went on down to the river, riding into a flurry of rain and feeling a good deal more cheerful than he had for a long time.

III

There were three Valley weddings that winter but only those of Elinor Codsall and her unlikely German, and Mark Codsall and his Liz Pascoe, were on home ground. The third, a ceremony entirely without trimmings, took place in a Manchester Registry Office on the same day as Elinor's wedding.

Valley gossips were wrong when they told each other Squire Craddock had refused to attend the wedding of his eldest son, Simon, to Rachel, the widowed daughter of his tenant, Norman Eveleigh, and they were equally wrong surmising that neither Squire nor Squiress had been aware of the match until it was accomplished. Their failure to attend was due to the clash of dates and no other reason. Paul had

918

been given a bare twenty-four hours' notice of the wedding by telephone but would have hurried north, grumpily enough no doubt, had he not felt that Elinor Codsall had prior claim on him.

Simon telephoned his father and stepmother with reluctance. Only the prospect of an eve-of-wedding quarrel with his fiancée got him into the 'phone booth for her insistence seemed to him maddeningly illogical having regard to her refusal to notify her own parents. She could not make him understand that their cases differed or that she had never found grace to forgive her father for his bitter opposition to her marriage to Keith Horsey during the war. She and Norman Eveleigh had never exchanged a word since that day and she still held him partly responsible for Keith's death, which was even more illogical. It was not Eveleigh's bellicose patriotism that had made Keith Horsey a conscientious objector, nor his sour nagging that had encouraged Keith to enlist as a stretcher-bearer instead of sweating it out in gaol. The rift remained however, and when Simon tried to strike a bargain with her, offering to delay the wedding a week and invite all four parents, she refused point blank but still held to her view that Paul should be notified and given the chance to attend.

"It's a damned lopsided arrangement," Simon grumbled, "but I'll do it if you insist. I've got nothing against the Gov'nor or your father and I don't see much sense in asking either of them to make a five-hundred-mile round trip in mid-winter to attend a five-minute civil ceremony! However, if we ask one we should ask the other. What on earth has our difference in age to do with it!"

Rachel, who, since his proposal, had not drawn attention to the fact that she was eight years his senior flashed out at this.

"It hasn't really any bearing at all except, possibly, that you were a child of ten when my father made everybody at home wretched about my marrying Keith! Can't you get it into your thick Craddock-Lovell skull that I still find his attitude unforgivable?"

"There's your mother," he argued, "you've nothing against her, have you?"

"Marian's very loyal," she told him, "and she'd stick by Father no matter what but that's as it should be, particularly since all the bite has gone out of him! Do as I say! Go into that kiosk and tell your father when and where, for if you don't I'm hanged if I won't change my mind after all!"

He capitulated at that. He knew her by now, a woman of strange inflexibility in whom infinite prejudice was mixed with infinite compassion in about equal proportions. He had seen her in draughty church institutes and parish halls, raging against social injustices to an apathetic audience of a dozen people, and he had watched her help an incompetent midwife deliver a child in a bug-infested tenement where whole families lived in single rooms on diets of fish, chips, and bread and margarine when they were lucky. He had admired her, worshipped her, and sometimes feared her, knowing that dedication to a cause to the degree that Rachel Horsey was dedicated could make sentimental mush of his own dilettante socialism. He went into the booth and dialled trunks, watching her through the streaked panes as she stood with her coat collar turned up against the wind and her brooding eyes fixed on some point beyond the spot where the railway bridge laid a shadow across glistening setts. He felt desperately sorry for her, standing there in the cold and drizzle, sorry and half-choked with a range of emotions in which awe and a deep yearning to share her life were the two extremes. The operator told him he was through and he heard Paul's voice on the line.

"Hullo? Craddock here! Who is it?"

"Simon."

"*Simon!*" The voice sounded agreeably surprised. "Are you coming home?"

"Soon Gov'nor, but I've got news. It'll rock you but it's nothing unpleasant."

"Are you all right?" The voice was urgent now.

"Sure I'm all right. I rang to say I was getting married to Rachel Horsey."

"Married?" The voice sounded incredulous. "For God's sake— *When?*"

"The day after tomorrow."

"Day after *tomorrow*! Great God! Wait a minute, I'll fetch Claire . . ."

"No don't, Gov! No, I don't mind her knowing—of course I don't —but, well . . . I haven't any more change and Rachel is standing in the rain. Can you come up? It's only a Register Office 'do' but Rachel seems to think you and Claire should be invited. Otherwise I'd have written and left it at that! Are you still there?"

Paul's voice broke the silence and sounded a little less cordial Simon thought. "Yes, I'm still here. Listen, I've got to give Elinor Codsall away the same day. Can't you postpone it?"

"No Gov, I'm afraid not. We had to fit it in with all kinds of things up here, including a bye-election. *Who* did you say you've got to give away?"

"Elinor Codsall of Periwinkle. The widow! She's marrying a Jerry she met during the war! I've promised and she's relying on me. I honestly don't see how I could let her down flat at the last moment."

"Of course you couldn't!" Simon tried to keep the relief out of his voice. "You go ahead and wish her the best from both of us."

"It's damned sickening tho'. Claire will be very disappointed. You say Rachel Eveleigh is there?"

"Right here but she isn't Rachel Eveleigh, Gov. She's a widow too!"

"Of course, I'd forgotten." He had forgotten, not only the fact that she had been a bride at one of those rushed war-time weddings but also that she must be years older than Simon, he could not say how many until he consulted Claire or the diary.

"Do her parents know?"

"Not yet," said Simon, "she's writing her mother."

"I see!" He understood the girl's prejudice far better than his son. He had thought of that strange contretemps at Four Winds several times since Simon had written saying he was engaged in some kind of social work in association with the girl. Yet it had never occurred to him for a moment that one of Norman Eveleigh's daughters would end up as his daughter-in-law and bewilderment prevented him from getting a clear mental picture of the girl. There were so many Eveleighs. There had always been so many Eveleighs, ever since that awful night he had hammered on Norman's door in the teeth of a south-westerly gale and told him his employer was hanging from a beam of the barn. Then he remembered something relevant. That was the night Simon had been born, and one of the children who had peeped over the banisters and been shooed back to bed must have been the Rachel, now "waiting in the rain". He said, emphatically, "Listen, Simon, if the operator cuts in tell her to reverse the charges. Get Rachel into the box, you idiot, boy!"

There was a pause and he heard Claire calling from the library, "Who is it, Paul?"

"Simon! He's 'phoning from Manchester," and she came into the hall as Paul heard a crisp, unrecognisable voice on the line. "Mr. Craddock? You remember me?"

"Good Lord, of course I remember you, Rachel! Listen, before we're cut off. Would you like me to go over and tell Marian? I'm sure she'd appreciate it."

There was a brief pause, during which Claire joggled his elbow and he shook her off, impatiently. "Did you hear, Rachel?"

"Yes," she said quietly, "I'd like that, Mr. Craddock, and tell her I'll write. I'm sorry you can't come but we both understand—and, Mr. Craddock . . ."

"Yes?"

"I'll look after him well. You don't have to worry."

"I hope he'll look after you, Rachel but—thank you, I . . . I'm happy about it, even if it is a bit sudden, and I'm sure Mrs. Craddock will be. Can we ring you anywhere later?"

"Yes, you can. We're going to town just for the weekend to a conference actually," and she gave him a number that he jotted down on the pad.

"There are the pips," she said, "don't reverse! Simon's getting wet now! Good-bye, Mr. Craddock."

"Good-bye, my dear. And good luck, both of you."

The wire clicked and began to purr. Slowly he replaced the receiver and turned to meet Claire's bewildered gaze.

"Who on earth was it? You said 'Simon', didn't you?"

"Yes," he said, "it was Simon who called but that was Rachel Horsey, née Eveleigh."

"Eveleigh's second daughter? The one who married the parson's son and never came back?"

He nodded. "What do you remember about her?"

"Only that she was a pretty girl with a generous share of Norman Eveleigh's pigheadedness. Why?"

"She'll need it, she's marrying Simon the day after tomorrow," and as she gasped and her hand shot to her mouth as it always did when she was surprised, "Come out of this damned draught and I'll tell you what little I know. Fix me a drink too. It's a wonder I'm not a dipsomaniac with my crazy family."

Simon's letter duly arrived, a breezy statement of fact, "Like an extract from one of his damned statistical reviews on malnutrition," Paul muttered, but he made no such comment about a letter Marian Eveleigh handed to him a day or so later, after he had ridden over and told her the news. Marian was flushed and excited, although half-inclined to apologise for her daughter having married into the Squire's family but it seemed to Paul that Norman, her husband, had some difficulty in taking it in. He kept shaking his head and fidgeting with his hands and his only remark when his wife repeated the news into his one sound ear was, "Arr, Rachel's alwus gone her orn way! Nothin' new about that, be there?"

When Marian walked him to the yard he said, "How is he these days, Marian? He doesn't seem too great," and she said, defiantly, that he could still do a good day's work but that the deafness that had followed his partial stroke a year or so ago sometimes gave people the idea that he was wool-gathering. The Lady Doctor, she went on, using the term the Valley had applied to Maureen Rudd since 1906, had urged him to give up work altogether but she knew this would be fatal to him. "He'd only moon about and die of boredom," she said, "so let un carry on, long as he can. As to our Rachel, she's a hard one and no mistake! She's never forgotten that war-time bust-up. Maybe this'll make a difference. I wouldn't like to think they kept it up until he was taaken."

She seemed, Paul thought, resigned to him dying although he could hardly be more than seventy and looked strong enough physically. She was equally resigned to tending him and sticking by him, having found it easy to erase the memory of a war-time peccadillo with the land-girl who had once moved into her bedroom and been ejected by Claire. He said, briefly, "Well, I don't know what you think about it, Marian, but I hope you'll believe me when I tell you I think Rachel is what Simon needs. She's had plenty of trouble of her own and I dare-say she'll mother him and persuade him to settle down somewhere."

"None of 'em will ever do that be our standards, Squire," she replied, "and I don't reckon it's their fault altogether. Nothing's ever been quite the same since, has it?"

"No," said Paul, cheerfully, for he heard this kind of remark every day from one or other of the older generation, "but there's a good deal I'm not sorry to see gone. Taken all round people are kinder and at least we're unlikely to see another war again, so we must have learned something from it."

"Lord God, I do hope you're right," said Marian fervently. "Would you like to see the letter she writes me if 'er does?"

"Yes indeed," Paul said, privately hoping it would be more explicit than Simon's telephone conversation.

It wasn't, or not much. Marian sent it over a day or so later and it looked fat enough to be informative until he realised that the envelope contained a sealed letter addressed to him as well as a brief letter to Mrs. Eveleigh. He thought, as he took it out, "Now why the devil didn't she write direct? She hasn't forgotten where we live has she?"

923

but he ceased to wonder when he saw, written slantways across the inside envelope, "*For Mr. Paul Craddock: Personal*" and his jaw dropped at the first paragraph, which read: "Dear Squire Craddock, — I'm sorry, I can't think of you as a plain 'Mr.' although, to be frank, I wouldn't like you to think I subscribe to patronage of any kind!" His curiosity overcame his surprise as he read on—"I haven't told Simon I'm writing for obvious reasons and therefore enclose this with Mother's letter. I wouldn't have thought of writing if I hadn't got to know Simon well enough to understand *you* far more than I did in the old days, when I was a child growing up in the Valley. Ordinarily I set my face against landlords of all kinds but you are an exception apart from the fact that (whether we like it or not) we're now related. Any prejudice I might have had in your respect has gone long ago and not only because—as I say—I've learned about you through Simon, but also because you've never shown my family, particularly my mother, anything but consideration and therefore you don't qualify as a landlord in my book!"

His unpredictable sense of humour was already at work and he found himself grinning broadly. "By God," he muttered aloud, "young Simon's met his match here and no mistake!" and because her uncompromising style reminded him so vividly of Grace riding her sex-equality hobby-horse he readdressed himself to the letter with enthusiasm.

"Well," she went on, blandly, "that will do for a preamble; now to the grist. Honestly, Mr. Craddock, you've made a real mess of Simon and sometimes I feel it's almost too late to unravel him! I'm going to try, though, for Keith persevered with me and I was even more hopeless material. I remember the fearful row we had about the time we married when I curtsied to his father! You see, Simon has terrific potential—a receptive mind, good reasoning powers, good health, a first-class memory and so on, but what are these worth without *drive* and *purpose* and *direction*? When I met him he was ambling along like a sick mule, feeling so sorry for himself that whatever capacity he had to do something practical for anyone else was a spluttering fuse that led nowhere and would have ended blowing himself up with a faint pop! I imagine you were always handicapped by the fact that his mother dodged the job of bringing him up and that made you lean over backwards to make allowances for him. That damned public school you sent him to didn't help either but that's another story. The point is, he's my responsibility now and I want you to know that I'm

924

serious to the point of priggery about any responsibilities I take on! That's why I always take my time accepting a new one as I did by marrying Si. After all, he's twenty-six and I'm thirty-four, so there was plenty to worry about had he been adult, which he certainly wasn't when I met him the night of his brothers' twenty-first party."

He knew it was important to digest this letter line by line so he went back and started again. He knew, also, that she was not merely forthright to the point of arrogance but that her judgment was sound and that every shot she fired scored a bull's-eye. He had leaned over backwards to make allowances; Simon had all those qualities she named and he did lack purpose and direction; he was not fully adult and never had been, as though some hidden streak of Lovell indolence blunted his natural talents to a degree that made him seem rootless and ineffectual and yet, somewhere inside him, was a persistent flicker of Grace's fire. That a child of Norman and Marian Eveleigh, whose education could not have exceeded a rudimentary grounding at Mary Willoughby's little school, should have perceived this astonished him. Could she have learned so much in her brief marriage to Keith Horsey? Or had it been dinned into her during the long struggle to make ends meet and keep her head above water, without whining to a father she despised? He realised that this was something he would never know. Clearly she was not a person to proclaim her own triumphs. He read on: "I'm going to make something of Si, Mr. Craddock—*really* make something of him! What emerges may not be the kind of person you admire but at least that person will amount to something. I think it's right that I should tell you this because, in a way, I need your help. *I want you to promise you'll never send him money.* He has a little (about three pounds a week) from his mother's estate and that's more than enough to tide us over until he can stand on his own feet. If he thinks he can always come back to you I'm beaten from the start. Some of the people we work among raise families on less than this and if there is one thing I can't stand it's a theorist who preaches Socialism when his own belt is let out to the last notch! Believe me, Mr. Craddock, we get plenty of those in the Movement and I wish to God they would stop pretending and go over to the Opposition! I haven't made up my mind yet exactly what Simon will go for but meantime he's teaching in the W.E.A. (Workers' Education Association) and soon I'm hoping he'll take an external in Economics. After that, if things work out as I hope, he'll get electoral experience in a hopeless seat and finally, with more luck, stand for somewhere

925

with a chance of winning. All this, of course, is dependent upon him and also on my hunch about him. Meantime, if Mrs. Craddock fusses (and I wouldn't blame her a bit if she did, for she obviously knows him better than you!), do try and convince her I'll make him as good a wife as he'll let me. He's a very lovable boy and although I'm sure I don't sound it I'm a naturally affectionate person. Yours very sincerely, Rachel Craddock."

It took his breath away for a moment and then the chuckle that had been trying to escape for the last ten minutes emerged as a bellow and he stood by the window with the letter still in his hand and enjoyed the joke as he had not enjoyed one in a long time.

Slowly the more sober aspects of the situation filtered through to him and he thought, with some satisfaction, "Dammit, it might be the best day's work he ever did in his life marrying that girl! She's got all his mother's idealism pickled in several generations of Eveleigh commonsense. Shall I show this letter to Claire or shall I let well alone? It's something I shall have to think about damned carefully!" and he folded the pages, put them back in the envelope and locked it in a drawer of his desk, along with his Will and insurance policies.

He was preoccupied for several days, so much so that Claire mistook his withdrawal for worry about the failure of the new Government to halt the decline in agriculture. As was her custom she challenged him when they were going to bed one night.

"There's no sense in worrying yourself silly, Paul," she said, for perhaps the hundredth time in the last decade. "Farming will bob up just as it always does. That's the one sure thing about the land. It's indestructible and indispensable."

"Who the devil is worrying?" he demanded, off guard. "Did I say I was particularly worried?"

"I can always tell, it's the Tudor look again!"

The "Tudor look" was a family joke. Ikey, the family jester, had once produced a miniature, supposedly by Hillyard, of a long-faced Elizabethan worrier, and pointed out the close resemblance of the portrait to Paul in one of his baffled moods.

"Ah," he said, beginning to brush his teeth vigorously, "you're 'way off course this time, old girl! I wasn't worrying, just pondering. About the newly-weds!" He put down his toothbrush and glanced at her humorously. "Come to think of it you haven't had much to say on the subject. The last time one of the family married a tenant's daughter you sulked for weeks!"

She was long since proof against this kind of gibe and laughed over her shoulder as she climbed into bed. "That's a libel," she said, "and you know it! I began sulking about Ikey marrying Hazel Potter but there were other reasons for maintaining it and I don't have to remind you of those, do I?"

"No," he said, "you don't! It was a guilty conscience about that young squirt up at the camp . . . what was his name again?"

"You haven't forgotten his name, you fraud but why worry about newly-weds of their age? Were you thinking of mailing them one of those Marie Stopes books there's so much talk about?"

He said, slowly, "I had a letter from her, Claire, and I've been wondering whether or not to pass it to you. I've decided I will. I think you'll enjoy it as much as I did!"

She had been drowsy for the last hour but she was wide awake now. "Give it to me at once! Go on, give it to me!" and when he protested that it was locked in his office she said, "I don't give a damn where it is! Go and get it this instant, you traitor!"

He fetched it and sat on the edge of the bed watching her read it and any misgivings he might have had disappeared when he saw her stifle a giggle, then a series of giggles. "Oh dear," she said, laying it down, "poor Simon! All those capitals and underlinings! The Movement! Opposition! The W.E.A.! There wouldn't be any point in sending him Marie Stopes would there? He's gone and married one, the silly boy!"

"Now how can you justify that?" he demanded. "I'm all for Simon having a sober wife as a sheet-anchor but don't tell me any fun and games will go along with it!"

"Rubbish!" she said, "she gives herself away in the tailpiece. Don't take that crusading preamble of hers at face value, it's no more than a smokescreen!"

"Are you trying to tell me she isn't in earnest about her determination to make something of the boy?"

"Oh, I daresay she thinks she is," Claire said, "but she's covering up nevertheless and any woman could tell you as much. See here—she's healthy, Valley-bred and thirty-four. She's been without a man twelve years and if she's an Eveleigh she's no prude! Along comes Simon, young, good-looking but, what's more important, pliable! Why bless you, she needs him more than he needs her but because of the age gap she has to justify herself! So what does she do? Sets about convincing herself the marriage is near-platonic but you can take it

927

from me that now she's got him she won't address herself exclusively to the task of healing sick society!"

She always amused him when she came out with one of these down-to-earth pronouncements and he chuckled as he switched off the light and climbed into bed, saying, "The trouble with you is you've got a one-track mind and always have had!" whereupon, not altogether to his surprise she said, "Thank God we're old enough to let the world get on with it and concentrate on essentials," and enfolded him in a way that left him in no doubt at all about what she regarded as essential.

CHAPTER THREE

I

THAT was the season of Rumble Patrick's disgrace, the time when the long-suffering Headmaster of High Wood decided that a less conventional establishment was required to battle with the young man's restless sense of humour. Whilst it could not be said that Rumble Patrick made family history by being expelled from school it is certain that his career there ended prematurely, following a letter from the Headmaster suggesting that withdrawal would save everyone concerned a great deal of unpleasantness.

So Rumble came home at seventeen, puzzled but not deflated by the world's rejection of his efforts to cheer it up and Paul was not surprised by the turn of events. Indeed, the surprising factor was that High Wood had tolerated Rumble so long.

And yet was it all that surprising? From earliest childhood Rumble Patrick Palfrey had been able (and that simultaneously) to bewitch and exasperate his peers and nobody knew this better than Claire, who had been slightly awed by the child ever since the day she had brought him to Shallowford after Hazel Palfrey had been run down and killed by the Army staff car. There was something demoniac about Rumble who was, as Mary once declared, half-cherub, half-poltergeist. It was as though, shortly before his birth, he had been given the rare privilege of assembling his own psychological make-up from material available from both sides of his family and had rejected all but the risible and the bizarre. He had, for example, a broad streak of urchin impudence, the legacy of Ikey's Thames-side forbears and fused with this was the cheerful contempt for authority that had been a characteristic of the Potter clan for generations. This was by no means all. Woven into his character were the strands of Ikey's objectiveness, Mother Meg's pride, Old Tamer's cussedness and Uncle Smut's initiative, all subject, it would seem, to a belief that every day was April Fool's Day. It added up to a most engaging personality but one that offered certain problems to those charged with fitting him for a career in a competitive world.

Paul had sent him to High Wood out of habit. Neither Ikey nor

Simon had taken kindly to the credo of the late Doctor Arnold of Rugby, and whereas The Pair had distinguished themselves at games, both had failed the Junior Cambridge examination three times in a row, having taken six years to grind from Second Form to Lower Fifth. With the arrival of Rumble Patrick in 1926, however, High Wood faced an altogether sterner challenge. By the time Rumble was fourteen his explosive energy had settled into a deadly rhythm that expressed itself in volleys of elaborate practical jokes, many of which would, no doubt, become hallowed by tradition but at the time of launching did nothing for the peace of mind of the staff.

It would be unprofitable to list the efforts of Rumble Patrick Palfrey to enliven the school's day-to-day life. They began, conventionally enough, with run-of-the-mill pranks—the sudden elevation of the chalk on a length of thread suspended across the blackboard, the insertion of a dead rat under the teacher's rostrum, the ghostly creakings of an isolated upright piano moved on to the edge of a warped floorboard shortly before Speech Day ritual began, the organic rumblings in blocked hot water pipes to illustrate a geography lesson about earthquakes and so on, but it was soon evident that Rumble was warming up for the big league, in Middle School. At fifteen he abandoned this kind of nonsense to the professional time-wasters, devoting himself to the planning and execution of more ambitious diversions and the inspiration of some of them must have derived from long-dead ancestors, jesters and tumblers in medieval Hungary perhaps, passed onto him by his emigrant grandmother. He was not only as good a mimic as his father had been but a better actor and was able, by the exercise of some strange Jekyll and Hyde alchemy, to assume all manner of personalities with the minimum of disguise. His voice had a wide range, his soft, cherubic features astonishing mobility and he was, above all, a persuasive salesman of comic ideas. There was never any malice in his jokes but his intense curiosity to witness what would occur if a certain number of actions were put into effect sometimes produced alarming results, as when he opened the sluice-gates of High Wood's millpond and flooded a road to the depth of two feet or when, in less desperate mood, he persuaded the village signwriter to paint and erect a large board advertising an isolated section of school property for sale by public auction. Sometimes he would operate as leader of a band of jokers but more often he would work alone, as when he disguised himself as a grizzled labourer and rode about the country all one Sunday on a Douglas motor-cycle owned by the school cricket coach. He took his inevitable punishments cheerfully enough, counting them mild in exchange for the entertainment they represented, and for all his crazy unpredictability and nuisance value he somehow contrived to remain popular with the staff, even the Headmaster, who sat down to write his ultimatum to Paul with reluctance, reasoning perhaps, that life at High Wood after Rumble Patrick's departure would be restful but dull. The letter was sent the day after Rumble, disguised as a deputy stationmaster, sent the school eleven on a cross-country trip into Cornwall when they should have been playing away to Somerset Stragglers. In writing to Paul the Head admitted that "the boy could, if trained and tamed, prove a credit to himself and family" but honesty compelled him to qualify this by adding "he might find it difficult to adjust in a society where the patterns of general behaviour were already established", which Paul took as a hint to despatch Rumble Patrick to an outpost of the Empire where his originality would have free play among the primitives.

The day Rumble and his school trunk returned to Shallowford Paul left word that the boy was to report at once to the library. He did not consult Claire on the matter, knowing that she had long since succumbed to Rumble's spell. In any case he always hated these occasions which embarrassed him and left him with a feeling of inadequacy as a father. When Rumble arrived, however, he saw at once that the boy was determined to make things as easy as possible, for he entered with Ikey's engaging grin and said, without preamble and without hypocrisy, "I'm sorry I let you down, Gov'nor, but you don't have to involve yourself any more, you know. After all, I'm not a kid any more."

Paul looked at him as he stood by the tall window and found himself comparing the boy to Ikey in his scrapyard days. He had Ikey's sense of detachment and Ikey's small, neat head but his frame was all Potter, sturdy, thick-set, suggestive of speed as well as power. He thought, sadly, "I wonder what the devil poor old Ikey would have made of him? Or Old Tamer, his grandfather?" and his spirits lifted somewhat when he recalled that on both sides of his family Rumble had heroes of a kind and stamina that ought to be good survival currency in a world drained of security by the demands of the last sixteen years. He said, with more curiosity than reproach:

"Why is it you prefer to live in hot water, Rumble, when most chaps your age are content to take a dip in it now and again?" and the boy answered, with unexpected promptness, "The world is so lopsided,

931

Gov'nor. Everyone is tearing themselves to pieces looking for answers and all they come up with are more and more questions!" and he looked across at Paul shrewdly, as though it occurred to him he would have to elaborate a little if he was to make his point but Paul understood, having not only known and reared Ikey, but also observed Hazel when she was running wild in the woods. He meant, of course, that most people were so reluctant to laugh at themselves and that Rumble's pranks were no more than an attempt to redress the balance.

"Everybody's finding life pretty tough these days, Rumble, and they aren't all endowed with your kind of bounce. The point is, what the devil am I to do with you now? You can't earn a living pulling people's legs! Your father was a rare handful but at least he compromised and made a success of the Army. Suppose I passed you on to a crammer's? Would you promise to stop acting the goat for once? It's high time you did, you know!"

The boy, serious for once, said, "Simon and The Pair have gone off and only the girls are left. It must be a bit frustrating for you, Gov'nor—to have no one to carry on, I mean."

"You think you could make a career of farming?"

"I wouldn't want to step in ahead of them, it wouldn't be fair, would it?"

"Then what?"

"I'd like to get out and about for a couple of years. Not like Simon —politics are a fearful bore—and not like Steve and Andy either, for I'd make a fearful hash of a commercial career. I mean *really* out and about; overseas."

So here it was again; none of them had a particle of affection for the Valley. All they wanted was to escape as from a noose that threatened to throttle their initiative. They saw him, one and all, as an anachronism, clinging to a way of life that had begun to wither as long ago as the summer of 1914. The conviction that this was so made him feel defeated and old beyond his years.

"Have you anywhere particular in mind?"

"Yes," said Rumble, unexpectedly, "I'd go to Australia first. There was a chap I was friendly with at school, a fellow called McPherson, whose pater had a sheep farm inland from Brisbane. He was always keen for me to visit and I've heard from him lately and the offer is still open. It's a big place, Queensland."

Paul glanced down at the Headmaster's letter and remembered the hint, ". . . a place where the patterns of behaviour were not fully established . . ." Claire wouldn't like it, or Mary, who, of all his children, had been the closest to Rumble. Yet the idea had obvious advantages. Australia was probably populated with unconventional people and any one of the numerous Diggers he had met in France during the war would be more than capable of knocking common-sense into the boy with the flat of his hand. Maybe a year or two rough-ing it among strangers was what he needed and yet, with Simon and The Pair already gone, he was reluctant to help empty the Valley of young men. He said, resignedly, "Check on that invitation, it might have gone cold; in the meantime I'll think things over but while I'm doing it for God's sake try and keep out of trouble, Rumble!"

Suddenly the boy was himself again, mischief sparkling in his eyes, so that Paul, recalling Ikey's impudence, hardly knew whether to laugh or clout him across the head as he rushed into the hall calling to Mary. Paul heard his daughter's joyous shout from the top of the stairs and then, as she relayed the news of Rumble's home-coming to her sisters, a rush of feet across the landing. He went out of the garden door and down the drive to see Maureen, who had always shown a great interest in Rumble Patrick, but she only gave the advice he expected.

"Damned good idea!" she said. "Head him that way and don't let Claire or the girls talk you out of it!" and when he protested that all the young to whom one might look for succession were leaving the Valley, she added, "*He'll* come back! That one will always come back! Too much of his mother in him to stay away long!" and went briskly about her business, leaving him to reflect glumly that she herself had not been much help since John had died and her own boy had gone off to study medicine in Dublin.

These days he was beginning to feel more and more isolated, more and more turned in upon himself. The decade that had closed with the death of old John, his chief confidant, had not only deprived him of all three of his sons but several of his intimates, men like Arthur Pitts, of Hermitage, and his dour father-in-law Edward Derwent, who, on his son buying the freehold of Higher Coombe, had deliberately placed himself beyond the sphere of interference by moving into a quayside cottage overlooking Whinmouth harbour. Mary, the dreamer of the family, kept to herself when she wasn't mooning after Rumble Patrick and even Claire seemed to have withdrawn from him a little as her two younger daughters claimed more of her attention, Whiz with her eternal round of gymkhanas and hunter trials, the youngest with

933

the business of growing into the most sought-after adolescent within riding distance. Sometimes, as today, he was very sorry for himself, wishing the whole boiling of them would give him leisure to concentrate on his own concerns whilst making themselves available to help form a decision once in a while. He went down the river road a mile or so and for once found a little comfort in the distant prospect of Henry Pitts hup-hupping his three-horse plough team across the red down-slope of Undercliff, the farm's southernmost field. He stood leaning on a rail watching Henry's broad back from a safe distance, reflecting how often and how fruitlessly he had tried to talk him into selling his horses and buying a tractor like Francis Willoughby, Eveleigh's foreman, and Brissot, the cork-footed co-tenant of the once sterile Potter holding. "Well," he told himself, as Henry dragged his team round and came back towards him, "there's one thing that won't change—Henry's methods of husbandry and his hatred of 'bliddy contrivances'!" and although he had no wish to talk to Henry today the sight encouraged him to make his way to French Wood, a direction he often took when he was in the dumps.

He approached it from the south, climbing the escarpment above the big bend in the Sorrel and pushing his way through the tall thistles and docks that crowned the little plateau in front of the plantation but here, on the very edge of trees, he stopped short, seeing the hunched form of a girl sitting with her back to him on a log near Grace's flowering cherry. It was his daughter Mary and he did not need to see her face to realise that she was in tears.

She had not heard his approach so he stopped and drew back below the crest, his mind assembling the pieces of the puzzle with a speed and certainty that surprised him. Less than an hour ago he had heard her greet Rumble from the stairs and the note of pleasurable excitement in her voice told him that she must have been unaware until that moment of Rumble's return; now she was here alone, more than a mile from the house, and even a man to whom feminine changes of mood remained a mystery after two marriages did not need to be told why. Rumble must have blurted out his harebrained plan and, equally obviously, the prospect of Rumble removing himself half-way across the world had devastated her. Here then, was something new, Mary and Rumble Patrick, linked in a way that he had never suspected and he wondered if Claire had an inkling and if she had whether she was amused, displeased or indifferent. The revelation, complicating an already teasing problem, irritated him and he thought, impatiently,

934

"Damn it, surely I must be imagining things! He's not eighteen yet and she's less than two years older!" and he stole back to take another look but found, to his relief, that she had disappeared and the distant crackle of dry bracken below the crest told him that she must have ridden up here on one of the ponies. He made up his mind then to watch her closely at supper and if she gave herself away to consult Claire at once but then, as though it had dropped through the trees and struck his head like a pebble, he had another and even more extravagant idea. What if it turned out that his eldest daughter and the son of Ikey Palfrey and Hazel Potter were to succeed him, the Valley passing not to his sons, as he had always assumed, but to his grandsons? He sat down on the stump to think and it astonished him that he could contemplate the irony of such a twist without resentment, could even find in it a kind of inevitability as he followed a loose end of the skein all the way back to the scrapyard beside the Thames. "I daresay it's no more than wishful thinking on my part!" he grumbled to himself. "But then, do I really wish it? Would I prefer events to have taken a more natural course and the Valley to pass to Simon, or one of the twins?" He found himself unable to answer the question but he could not put it out of mind; the memory of his daughter's hunched figure was too poignant to support the theory that he was deducing too much from too little. He sat musing a long time and then, crossing the grove, he picked up the pony's tracks in the dust that lay thickly on the path around the northern bulge of Hermitage Wood. As he left the trees and walked into bright sunlight a hen pheasant whirred up less than a yard ahead and flew squawking across the dip. "I daresay you're wiser than I am, old girl!" he said aloud. "Kark-kark—Kark-kark! That's about all any of us can say when it comes to explaining other people's motives, especially when they are your own flesh and blood!"

II

It would have astonished him even more to have learned that he made his discovery, or half-discovery, only an hour or so before Mary herself gauged the strength of the bond that linked her to Rumble Patrick. Alone among the Craddock children she remembered his actual arrival at Shallowford, a small, plump, easily-delighted child of four, speaking an even broader Devon brogue than Mrs. Handcock and Martha Pitts, and because she was the eldest girl, and no one in

935

their senses vested responsibility in The Pair, her mother had taken her aside that same evening and told her frankly that Rumble's mother had been killed and that his father, Ikey, was away at the war and that she was to do all in her power to make Rumble feel at home in the Big House. It was not, she soon discovered, a particularly onerous charge. Rumble Patrick made himself at home anywhere and in a week or two seemed to have forgotten everything about his mother and the enclosed life he shared with her at Mill Cottage, becoming almost at once one of the Craddocks, sleeping in Mary's room until he was six, riding her ponies, sharing her toys and Claire's good-night kisses. Mary soon noticed that her mother showed him special tenderness and would have found it difficult to believe that Rumble's appearance in the world, and the war-time marriage that followed it, had sparked off the only important quarrel between her father and mother in the history of their marriage. When the child had been thoroughly absorbed, however, Mary did not relinquish her post as playmate extraordinary. Her maternal instinct, naturally strong (she was the only one of the Craddock girls who played with dolls), had been matured by Rumble's presence and as her sisters grew up to develop their own interests and needed her less and less, she became Rumble's sole companion in his eternal wanderings about the woods and valleys, where he constantly surprised her with his knowledge of fieldcraft, wild flowers and the habits of the thousand and one creatures who lived out their lives within a mile of the Sorrel springs on the moor. He never treated her as a girl, as did Simon and The Pair, but expected her to climb the same trees, wade the same streams, and disdain tears when brambles clawed at her bare legs and nettles left their smart on her wrists. Because he never seemed to want to ride but preferred to penetrate into places inaccessible to ponies, Mary soon ceased trying to compete with Whiz, the equestrienne of the family and thus lost favour with her Aunt Rose, who sometimes invited them all to stay at her sprawling Gloucestershire home that was a kind of horse-barracks. But there were compensations. By the time she was ten, and Rumble was eight-and-a-half, each of them knew the Valley better than Paul, or John Rudd, and among the tenants only Smut Potter, who drove the bakery van for his French wife's business in Coombe Bay, could challenge them on the termini of the rabbit-runs in Shallowford Woods or the exact location of the principal otter holts along the weaving courses of the Sorrel and Teazel. They liked Smut, who would often stop his van and pass a pleasant half-hour with them during his rounds, telling them where to find nests and sometimes recounting his poaching exploits of pre-war days, and they had their favourites among the tenants, farmworkers and Valley craftsmen. They liked old Martha Pitts up at Hermitage, who would sometimes bake them savoury pasties, telling them she had done as much for Rumble Patrick's mother when she had lived wild in the woods before her marriage. They liked and respected Grandmother Meg, whom they encountered in out-of-the-way places where she was gathering herbs or selling her rush mats and baskets and Meg, unsmilingly and with a deliberation that fascinated Mary, would sometimes tell their fortunes and prophesy that Mary would marry a gypsy and have blue-eyed children, a pledge that Mary secretly doubted for she could not imagine marrying anyone but Rumble, whose eyes were the colour of his mother's name. They were fond of Henry Pitts, with his great, rubbery smile and were well-received by the Timberlakes at the saw-mill, and also by the cork-footed Frenchman, Brissot, who did most of the work in the Dell while his partner, Jumbo, stood around cracking jokes in his thin, Cockney voice. Mary found it difficult to believe that both Mrs. Brissot and Jumbo's wife were Rumble's aunts. Each of them seemed so old and each treated him with the same respect they showed the Squire's children but it was so, for Paul made no mystery of Rumble's background and once took them up to French Wood, pointing out the two trees he had planted in memory of Rumble's parents, saying that Ikey, his father, had been a very brave soldier and his mother, Hazel, had known even more of what went on in the coverts and goyles of the estate than Smut Potter, a statement that helped Mary to understand Rumble's instinctive knowledge of wood-craft and fieldcraft. They had their dislikes too, usually avoiding High Coombe and thinking of Mary's uncle, Hugh Derwent, as an aloof, tetchy man plodding about his business without a smile, and although they got along well enough with Marian Eveleigh, at Four Winds, it was never a farm they frequented much for they were half-convinced that old Norman Eveleigh was a little soft in the head, partly because he looked at them as though they were not there but also because one side of his mouth dribbled a little, as though he had left his handkerchief at the farm. Rumble told Mary this was nothing to wonder at; Norman Eveleigh had evidently been touched by the Four Winds' curse and sooner or later every master of this particular farm went mad.

So they wandered about, looking for and finding small, everyday

937

adventures, but the idyll came to a sudden end in 1922, when Rumble Patrick was sent away to prep school and Mary put up her hair and had to pay some heed to her clothes. Then Mary went as a weekly boarder to the Convent of the Holy Family, in Paxtonbury, and there were only the holidays when they tried but failed to pick up where they had left off. Something went missing and neither of them could discover what it was; then Whiz grew old enough to invite her pony-mad friends back to the house, and some of the twins' friends from Paxtonbury and Whinmouth began to notice Mary's dark, shy charm and employ all kinds of strategems to get her alone and kiss her behind the barns or in dark corners of the house. At first she was indignant at such tomfoolery, thinking them very soppy but later both her mother and Whiz urged her to be "more sociable" and she did try very hard, and even fancied for a week or two that she was in love with a red-headed boy called Gussie whom Stephen brought home to stay for a fortnight one summer. Yet the secret bond between them was never completely severed; it only stretched as the years went by, and the house was full of strangers who kept passing between them with their crazy dance steps and ukeleles and horseplay, so it was not until the week Rumble disgraced himself at school and came home with wild, frightening talk of going to Australia to learn sheep-farming, that the memory of their childhood alliance became vivid to her. Before that, *just* before that, something happened that made her particularly sensitive to Rumble's callous declaration of independence.

A night or two before Rumble's return there had been a Junior Hunt Ball at Whinmouth and, as was usual on these occasions, Mary was told off to chaperon her younger sisters, Whiz and Claire, respectively seventeen and fourteen, after they had been driven to the dance in the family Austin by Mark Codsall. The role of chaperone was largely fictitious these days, especially in the Craddock household, but Mary got her routine instructions—"Keep an eye on them and make sure you're all ready to leave by midnight." Claire Craddock was very broadminded in the matter of her daughters' upbringing, not only because she trusted Mary implicitly and remembered her own youth had been singularly free of restrictions but also because, far more than Paul, she had come to terms with the new freedoms. It seemed to her both natural and healthy that young people should want to grow up fast and enjoy themselves out of range of adults, and whenever Paul challenged the wisdom of her tolerance she could be relied upon to dismiss his growls as evidence of a hangover from an era dead and buried in the 1914–18 earthquake.

"No one quarrels with your preference for horse-transport and horn-lanterns, dear," she told him on this occasion, "but you really must try and see the world through their eyes! All I'm concerned with is getting them there safely and getting them back at a reasonable hour. I've enough faith in my daughters to know that they'll conduct themselves sensibly in company and this is a perfectly respectable company, composed of people we know. It might interest you to learn that it actually goes on until two a.m. but I've told Mary to have them back here by one!"

"I should damn well think so!" he replied but he did not make an issue of it. He would never have admitted as much but he had respect for her judgment in these matters and was obliged to admit that she had made a more successful job of raising the girls than he had of tailoring the boys.

Whiz was particularly excited, being currently involved in a double flirtation with two young thrusters from the Paxtonbury Farmers' Hunt and looked forward to the certainty of being sure of partners for every dance and perhaps the cause of a quarrel. Fourteen-year-old Claire (who everybody mistook for sixteen) was eager to show off her new apple-green organdie, her first real dance frock bought on the occasion of her fourteenth birthday, in June. Mark got them there too early and the first hour or so was dull but the dance warmed up when all the young men came in from The Mitre and Mary soon lost track of Whiz, suspecting that she was spending more time in the parked cars than on the dance floor, whereas it intrigued her to see young Claire blush for the first time in her serene existence, when the Master's son, a willowy young man with a reputation for being Paxtonbury's most expert ballroom dancer, partnered her to win the fox-trot competition. She was watching her sister come down from the platform and marvelling, as she often did on these occasions, at Claire's breathtaking poise and composure, when Bob Halberton lounged across and asked her for the next dance. She was glad to see him, even though he did seem to have consumed rather more than a safe quota of beer, for up to then her dancing had been limited to pot-luck stumbles in the Paul Jones. She had known Bob all her life. His father was a doctor, practising in Whinmouth and he was a genial, heavy-featured boy, who was often out with the Sorrel Vale Hunt on Saturdays. He was engaged, he told her, in studying law and was

939

finding it a terrible bore, so much so that he was thinking of throwing it up and trying for a short-service commission in the Air Force.

"That's the life!" he told her, clutching her tightly as they shuffled round the crowded floor. "I've already joined a Flying Club at Reading, where I'm bogged down in an office so I get a flip most weekends. Who the devil wants to be chained to a stool grubbing among conveyances and affiliation orders? If it wasn't for the fact that the old man has sworn to cut me off I'd sign on without even asking him and to hell with the consequences!"

She had always rather liked Bob Halberton, who had the gaiety of the twins plus, she suspected, a good deal more intelligence and she thought of him as kind-hearted and masculine. She also liked him for not being sure of himself, or as good-looking as most of Whiz's friends and the amateur sheikhs the twins brought home but she had never suspected that he was interested in her so that when he said, on the long drum roll, "Look here, Mary, it's stuffy in here. Let's go out for some air!" she was flattered but reminded him of her responsibilities as chaperone. He said, laughing, "Oh, to the devil with that! They ought to be looking after you!" and then, as though she was feinting, "Is there someone else? I always took you for the unsophisticated one!"

The gibe (for she accepted it as one) hurt a little and she replied, with a crackle of defiance, "I'll get my wrap!" and on the way to the cloakroom told Whiz that "she was going out with Bob Halberton for a cooler". Whiz laughed and looked surprised. "*You*. And Bob Halberton? My word, Mar, you're coming on but watch out, they say he's hot stuff!"

"He won't be 'hot stuff' with me," Mary retorted, suddenly feeling annoyed with herself and everyone in the room, excluding Bob Halberton, to whom she felt she owed her escape from the company of wallflowers but as they made for his car, an Austin Seven painted to look like a racing car, she decided that he was not safe to drive and told him so and to her relief he said, "I daresay you're right!" and motioned her into the back, climbing in after her and losing no time in clasping her in a bearlike embrace.

She did not mind being kissed by him, accepting the sad fact that almost every man who kissed you at a dance, or a celebration of any sort, was certain to smell of liquor but she had never been kissed so enthusiastically as Bob kissed her and wondered if it had anything to do with him being in need of solace. People usually were when they sought her out and his grumblings about office life were still fresh in her mind. She drew back at last and said, "Could I have a cigarette, Bob?"

He laughed rather unpleasantly at this, recognising it as a time-honoured manœuvre in the art of self-defence but he gave her one, saying, "I didn't know you smoked?"

"Well, I've started!" she said, so sharply that he laughed again, saying, "Don't think I don't understand! All your life you've been stuck with the job of Little Mother. Well, it's time you started having fun, so why not let rip!" and he kissed her again, this time letting his hand slip over her shoulder and rest on her breast. She remembered then what Whiz had said about him being "hot stuff" but in her new role as a rebel she did not see how she could protest without seeming a prude, so she puffed stolidly at the cigarette as he stealthily extended his hold but realised, rather forlornly, that she was deriving no pleasure at all from his mauling and wondered how all her contemporaries could welcome this kind of thing as they apparently did whenever they were alone in the dark with boys. He said, as though to relax her, "You're very sweet, Mary! I've always thought of you as the flower of the flock!" but instead of pleasing her the comment touched her pride and she replied, "If you're referring to my brothers and sisters I should like to know what's wrong with them!"

He took up her challenge more ruthlessly than she expected. "Well, let's face it, Mary; your brother Simon is a bolshie, the twins are a pair of nitwits, and although both your sisters are damned pretty they know it, even that kid Claire! I'm not a fool, it must be sheer hell living with younger sisters who do everything so well that everyone looks over your head at them!"

His appalling honesty made her shudder but because she recognised a strong element of truth in what he said she kept her temper in check, thinking, "At least he has the guts to say what everyone else thinks! That's more than anyone will, even Mother!" and she said miserably, "I suppose that implies I'm the flop of the family? Well, I am! I'm not at ease with people like young Claire and I can't win prizes at every field event like Whiz. I'm not gay and dressy and gregarious like the twins, or even bolshie and clever like Simon! Would you mind telling me exactly why you asked me to come out here? Was it out of pity?"

It was his turn to recoil. He sat back, taking her by the shoulders and turning her face to him under the unflattering glow of the parking-ground lamp and for a moment seemed at a loss what to say. Then her instinctive sympathy for him gave him the wrong clue, as she said, hastily, "I'm sorry, Bob! That was a beastly thing to say! Let's go back inside," and she reached to open the door.

"Don't be such a damned fool, Mary!" he growled, throwing his arm round her. "Have fun yourself for once!" and he began to kiss her with such determination that she was crushed against the hard leather cushions of the tiny car. Then he was almost on top of her, his hand slipping the shoulder strap of her dress over her arm in a clumsy attempt to fondle her small bosom. There was hardly enough space to resist but she did her best, pressing herself against the door and drawing up her knees so that her short dress wrinkled high on her thighs but even this he took as a gesture of encouragement, extricating his other hand and groping between her knees. Then fear and distaste gave way to fury and she dragged her nails down the side of his face and taking advantage of his wincing recoil rolled to the floor, grabbed for the handle and fell out on to the tarmac. She heard him shout, "Mary, I'm sorry . . . *wait!*" but she picked herself up and ran, not back to the hall but round the building into the shadow and across the little square to the quay where she stopped, steadying herself against the harbour guard-rail. She felt sick with misery and shame but still consumed with a terrible anger, not for Bob, whom she reasoned would be very sorry for himself when he sobered up, but with the world as a whole and her allotted place in it, the plainest, gawkiest and shyest of a family of six, a girl who had no more finesse when faced with a routine dance-hall hazard than to scratch a man's face raw and then rush off into the dark like an outraged virgin pursued by a satyr. Whiz was two years her junior but Whiz would have extricated herself from such a situation with dignity and hauteur and surely even Claire, at fourteen, would have had enough sense not to climb into the back of a car with a half-tipsy boy, imagining that all he wanted from her was a dry peck or two and a sympathetic audience. Bob Halberton was clearly right when he implied that she was the family flop, the pre-destined maiden aunt, who would sit at home knitting woollies for a chain of nieces and nephews until her life grew dim and purposeless. Why was she so different from all the others? Why did she find a tussle in the back of a car degrading and humiliating, when most girls her age would have shrugged it off as no more than tiresome and others, a majority, perhaps, would have found it flattering, especially

942

if they had spent two hours watching others enjoy themselves. She could find no answer to these questions that did not point to personal inadequacy and suddenly, to her renewed shame, tears began to flow and her whole world clouded over as she went back over Bob Halberton's coarse and shattering summary of the Craddocks of Shallowford—a bolshie, a couple of empty-headed idiots, two vain extroverts and a reject! Did everyone outside the Valley—and perhaps those inside it— view the family in this light? It was a chilling thought for, until that moment, she had always tended to think of the Craddocks as the acknowledged leaders of the community. Perhaps this was a fallacy? Perhaps people in places like Whinmouth and Paxtonbury had always regarded her father as a man who was playing Squire with money earned in a scrapyard, and her mother as a lucky farmer's daughter, shrewd enough to have grabbed him on the rebound after a disastrous marriage to real gentry?

Bob found her there dabbing her eyes and trying, in the wan light of the harbour lamps, to repair her make-up. He seemed contrite and deflated, showing three curving lines of nail-furrows on each cheek and said, as soon as he saw her, "I'm sorry, Mary! I didn't realise what an ass I was making of myself . . . I've always liked you a lot, honestly, and after all you did give a chap the impression . . ." and he tailed off, shuffling from one foot to the other and dabbing his scratches with a handkerchief. There was, she decided, small comfort to be derived from his abjectness, for even now he was careful to use the verb "like" rather than risk a second misunderstanding. Then her fatal pity took a hand again and she said, quietly, "You can't go back in the hall with your face in that state, you'd better go home and forget what happened. It was my fault really, I shouldn't have come out. At eighteen, it's time I learned what's expected of a girl who does," and she walked back across the square with Bob trotting alongside like a terrier who has been whipped and is hoping to find a way of wriggling back into grace. He found none; she said, decisively, "Good night, Bob," and went straight into the hall, where everyone was bobbing round the floor to the rhythm of the latest bit of nonsense:

> "There ain't no sense,
> Sitting on the fence,
> All by yourself in the moonlight . . ."

and although Mary found the theme appropriate to her mood its irony had no power to cheer as she sat waiting for Mark Codsall to call and take them home. When he did appear, on the stroke of midnight, she summoned her sisters with such impatience that Whiz complained, "You needn't be in such a panic just because your Bob has taken himself off!" and Mary felt she could have boxed her ears on the spot. To Whiz's subsequent demand for an account of what happened, she snapped, "Nothing! Nothing but silliness!" and that was her sole contribution to the lively recapitulation of the evening's triumphs that beguiled her sisters all the way home.

And then, after a day and a night of brooding, Rumble was restored to her and she tore downstairs in response to his shout only to learn, to her bewilderment, that he had been politely expelled and had made up his mind, presumably with her father's blessing, to remove himself to Australia! What was more galling than this monstrous decision was the eagerness with which Rumble embraced it. All through the autumn, while letters and cables were passing to and fro between him and his future hosts, and his great black cabin trunk was being filled, he ranged about the house practising a ridiculous Australian accent and spicing his conversation with outlandish words like "pommie", "outback" and "fair dinkum". It was as though, like Simon and the twins before him, he could hardly wait to scrape Valley mud from his shoes and whilst she had understood the restlessness of her brothers, Rumble's rejection of the old life—a time that had once seemed eternal—mystified and depressed her.

It was not until his last afternoon that she had an inkling of what lay behind this renunciation of their past. It was almost Christmas then and a cheerless Christmas it promised to be, for there was little point in decorating the house for a family reunion that might last two or three days and would not, in any case, include the twins, who were in the Tyrol, and Rumble, who was due to sail on December 22nd. The weather, however, did its best to help the Valley show off its autumn clothes and when she accepted his invitation for a final ramble she found that October still lingered among the oaks and chestnuts of the southern rim of the woods, and that when they went down the long, tangled slope to the mere the water was slate-blue in pale sunshine and the evergreens on the islet were fortified against winter by a gloss that still held the ripeness of June. She noticed, a little maliciously, that he had lost some of his bounce and that his fresh, squarish face now had an almost stoical expression. He said nothing, however, until they moved along level with the ruinous old pagoda where he stopped, took her arm and said with rare earnestness, "Will you

944

promise something, Mar? Will you come here sometimes, to this spot, and—well, remember me once in a while?"

The finality as well as the strangeness of the request dried her mouth and her voice was as strange to him as his sudden seriousness was to her.

"Yes, of course—of course I will, Rumble, but, oh God, you make it sound as if I won't ever see you again! You make it so horribly final! Why do you *have* to go? You needn't! Even now you could cry off and we'd all understand! I think Daddy would be relieved really and I'm sure Mummy would!"

He seemed to consider a moment so that hope fluttered in her but then he said, slowly, "I couldn't you know—cry off, I mean. I've let him down just like the others but at least I know it and can do something about it and I think he understands that or will do, some day!"

"But I don't understand! What has Daddy got to do with you going all that way off? He hasn't thrown you out, he wasn't even upset about you getting sacked from High Wood. Where does he enter into it?"

He looked at her solemnly for a moment and then, relaxing, gently pushed her down on a stump where the path crossed one of old Aaron Stokes' tracks to the reed beds.

"It's because of him I got into this, Mar," he said, "but I'll never forgive you if you pass that on, even to your mother or to Simon! Don't you realise what a sickener it was for him? The twins going off like that, and Simon never having the remotest wish to carry on? It was part of his dream that at least one of them would finish what he started. I imagine that's why he had a family in the first place!"

"Well, even if that were true," she said, and privately thought he was taking far too much for granted, "you could go to Agricultural College and take on the Home Farm in time."

"It wouldn't be the same," he said, shaking his head. "I'm not his son you see, just the byblow of a kid he fished out of the slums and the scattiest of the Potters. We respect one another and he's been more than a father to me. It would be a poor sort of return if I paid him back by horning in ahead of his children! Surely you can understand that, Mar?"

"No I can't!" she said, stubbornly. "For you've just said neither Simon, Steve nor Andy want to stay here and farm. The Valley has never meant a thing to either one of them!"

"They may come round to it, one or other of them, sooner or later,"

945

he said, "but they certainly wouldn't if I got my oar in first and staked a claim! Simon is too unselfish and the twins would just use me as an excuse. You must see that, Mar."

She did see it and gave him credit for his sagacity. Until then her sense of deprivation had been so personal that it had never occurred to her he might be making a deliberate or half-deliberate sacrifice, and the realisation enlarged him enormously. She said, with awe in her voice, "Then you aren't really so . . . so *keen* to go, Rumble?"

"*Keen!*" He sounded outraged. "Leaving *here*? Why, turning my back on this place is the hardest thing I've ever done or ever will do! And there's more to it than that too! Leaving you makes it that much harder. The Valley is my home and you're the one person that makes it so, and it's never been any other way with me, although I don't think I understood that until a week or two ago, until . . . well . . . until I'd burned my boats!"

There was sweetness as well as pain in his declaration, a sweetness that seemed to rend her and gush into her breast so that she reached out and took both his hands and held them tremulously. In the pincer grip of fear and relief she was unable to utter a word of protest or pleasure and they sat there on the many-ringed stump, linked less by physical contact as by the intensity of their emotions, by a tangle of ties reaching back to their earliest childhood compounding all the days they had spent together soaking up sunshine and drinking wind and rain. It was a magic moment, less transitory for her than for him, for now, out of understanding, came reassurance of a kind and a conviction that, if a person as splendidly resourceful and enterprising as Rumble could travel to the ends of the earth, he might well find his way back again, so that this might not be the end of everything but a beginning. She said, in a steady voice, "I love you, Rumble! I want you to know that I love you and could never love anyone else, could never want anyone else to touch me, you understand?" and as she said this she thought fleetingly of Bob Halberton's prying hands on the night of the dance and was conscious of a release from shame, as though Rumble's touch had exorcised an unwholesome memory and restored tranquillity to her being.

He looked at her in a way that he had never done in the past. There was joy in his glance but apprehension also, as though he welcomed her pledge but doubted her strength to make it good against the demands of time and distance. Then he raised his hand and touched her lightly on the cheek and in the shy gesture was all she needed to

946

know, at all events for the present, until she had leisure to contemplate this moment of time in privacy. He kissed her mouth so gently that she was half afraid to return the kiss but did so with hardly less restraint and it was a bestowal that must have liberated him from the silence of wonder, for he said, stroking her hair, "I've thought of this, Mar. Many times! I've imagined it but that's as far as it went. It's late enough in the day for us but it has happened, and I suppose that's the important thing!" And then, nerving himself, "But it doesn't bind you, Mar! You must understand that! It mustn't spoil things for you after I've gone!"

"But I want it to bind me, Rumble," she said, fervently. "I wouldn't want to remember it any other way and I don't care for how long, you understand? I don't care any more!"

They sat through the last moments of the short winter's afternoon, saying little of any consequence, too shy now to do more than utter short, broken sentences about letters, pledges, promises and a raggle taggle of trivialities, but for Mary all the stresses of the last few weeks had been eased, like the slackening of a cable hitching her to a drag-load of despondency and deprivation. She wondered, as they went hand in hand up the escarpment to the slope above the house, whether anyone would notice and comment on the change in her when they assembled for high tea but decided that she did not care a rap if they did.

Nobody exclaimed. They were all too concerned with the ritual of his departure and in any case it would be days before the great change in her advertised itself in an added brightness of the eye, a lightness of step or a tendency to hum a tune instead of taking up a challenge thrown down by Whiz or young Claire. By that time he was gone and they had received his first card posted at Lisbon. Claire read it aloud and Paul, catching Mary's eye and seeking confirmation of his thoughts in French Wood back in the summer, was reassured by what he saw, or thought he saw, thinking, "Well, she seems to have reconciled herself to his going after all! I daresay I was imagining something that wasn't there," and he dismissed the subject, forgetting it in a welter of new troubles. It was some time before he realised that he had been right after all.

III

The seasons had their cycles and the years their rhythms, a small graph within a larger one that was then caught up in the rhythm of the

947

world outside. There were good years and bad, years recalled with laughter and others with memories that the people of the Valley stowed away like lumber to take out only in times of prosperity and good cheer. The war years fell into this grouping but even these had faces that reflected an odd note of laughter or excitement, like the arrival of the first aeroplane in the Valley, or the ripple that ran down the Sorrel when news came that Smut Potter had returned from the dead. Some of the slump years had this same, mitigating sparkle. The year 1926, when prices were down and foot and mouth rampant and the general gloom was relieved to some extent by the astounding news that Francis Willoughby had won a national cattle award and was taking one of his bulls all the way to the Argentine. Paul watched these rhythms closely and sometimes wrote of them in the estate diary, jotting down forecasts between solid wedges of Claire's trivia, and his extreme sensitivity regarding all things pertaining to the Valley regulated his alternating moods of optimism and pessimism, particularly round about January, the bleakest time of year. He would say, "This year will be good in most respects . . ." or, "This year's damp is already in my bones . . . !" pretending that his barometer was the wound in his knee, or the small crater in his temple where the last piece of shrapnel had been extracted in 1918, but this was only a family joke, like his "Tudor look". His gift of local prophecy, if indeed he possessed one, was geared to a far more complicated machine assembled from the cogs and wheels plucked from the years, from signs and portents passed to him by gypsy Meg, or by weather sages like Arthur Pitts and old John Rudd, but even Paul himself never mastered the art of starting or stopping this machine at will. It seemed to generate itself and run on through a given number of revolutions and when at length it stopped of its own accord he knew they were all set for one of their unmemorable spells, when things were neither good nor bad and the seasons came and went unnoticed.

The machine began to roll in the first week of January, 1931, and its whirring was so urgent that he was worrying hard before the year was forty-eight hours old, the nag setting him reading through the pages of the diary as far back as 1904 when the new year had opened with the Codsall tragedy and the tempo built to the whirlwind of Grenfell's first victory and Grace's flight. Perhaps it was the vivid memory of this time, and its link with the first event of 1931, that put him on his guard, for just as the bumpy run of 1904 began at Four Winds, so the 1931 run of bad luck began with an event that left Four

948

Winds masterless and laid open the flank to the west. It was a vulnerable flank, particularly since Elinor Codsall had given up and Periwinkle had gone derelict, for although in the east Higher Coombe had been pinched out by the sale of freehold Paul never considered this as a sign of impending dissolution. Hugh Derwent was his own brother-in-law and also a first-class farmer. It did not matter if his land had been erased from the estate map for Hugh had told Claire more than once that he was unlikely to marry now and he had no kith or kin other than the Craddock children, and his childless sister, Rose. To the west, however, it was another matter. Not only was Four Winds the largest and most prosperous farm of the original six, it was also the closest to Nun's Bay shantytown and the proposed route of the coastal road to Coombe Bay. Failure, or withdrawal in this direction might mean all manner of things and could not be shrugged off like the break-up of Periwinkle in the north-west. Four Winds was a bastion in the economy of the estate; it needed a strong man in possession.

It was with these thoughts that Paul, learning of Norman Eveleigh's second stroke on January 3rd, threw a saddle over the skewbald and took the shortest route to the gate in the park wall. It was the route, he reminded himself, that he and Ikey had taken the night he answered a previous summons to Four Winds when Norman Eveleigh, tousled but cool-headed at three in the morning, had recommended himself as a likely successor to the man hanging in the barn. Now, according to Marian, Eveleigh was done for, lying in the kitchen where he had been carried by two of his men after collapsing in the yard an hour or so before whilst clearing a blocked drain. He did not recognise anyone, not even his wife, but lay on a makeshift bed staring up at them with uncomprehending eyes. The thick fingers of his left hand twitched and his left leg kicked but these were the only movements he made when Doctor Maureen peeled off his long, woollen pants and probed the flesh. Marian stood beside the log fire and old Ben, Eveleigh's aged pigman, remained in the doorway, twisting the ends of his white moustaches in embarrassment at witnessing the sudden helplessness of a man he had feared and respected for more than thirty years.

"Will us get un upstairs?" Marian asked, after Maureen had finished her examination. "Us coulden manage it at first but I daresay us could now, tho' he's a turrible weight."

"He'll do here for the time being," Maureen said and then, without lowering her voice, "I'm afraid this is it, Marian!" and when Eveleigh's wife shot her a look of reproach, added, "He can't hear and he can't

949

see much either. Maybe the difference between light and dark with his left eye but no more."

Marian's face crumpled and she began to sniff so that Maureen at once summoned Debbie, Eveleigh's unmarried daughter, telling her to look after her mother. Paul said nothing but remained after Debbie, Marian and Ben had left the room. The hulk on the makeshift couch was enough to depress anyone who had known Norman Eveleigh in his prime, a tireless machine that could harvest round the clock, and milk faster than anyone in the Valley, a man to whom hard and regular toil was the breath of life, so much so that he had somehow carried on after his first stroke years ago and still managed a better day's work than some of the younger hands who had come to the Valley since the war.

"I'd sooner see him dead!" he said suddenly. "He'd have wished it, I can tell you that!"

"Most people wish it," Maureen said, repacking her bag, "but we have to take what comes our way. We were right about keeping him hard at work as long as possible. Any other finish would have been cruel." Then, straightening herself, "He was a damned hard man, Paul. Hard on himself and hard on everyone around him."

"He was a good farmer," Paul said, "and taken all round a good family man. I never regretted putting him in here after Codsall. It was one of the few times I followed a hunch and wouldn't let John turn me aside."

"How old would he be?"

"Sixty-seven," Paul said and she smiled, recalling that Paul and her John had vied with one another on knowing the exact age of everyone in the Valley. It was one of the small vanities they shared.

"Well," she said, "I suppose you might say he worked himself into the ground but the older ones do, don't they? There aren't many of the originals left now, are there?"

"There are none," he told her gravely, "but the farms of four of the six I began with have passed from father to son. That's not a bad average and I'll warrant it can't be said of any other estate round here." He lifted Eveleigh's hand, holding it for a moment and setting it down on the blanket when Eveleigh's stare did not waver. "How long is he likely to last?"

"Hard to say," Maureen replied, "but not long. We could get him into Paxtonbury Hospital if Marian prefers that. It'll save her trouble for he'll have to be nursed day and night. What do you think?"

950

She had grown accustomed to deferring to him on matters like this. The Valley people trusted her by now but not in the way they trusted him.

"He ought to die here," said Paul.

"But he won't be conscious of where he dies and he'll certainly survive longer in hospital if we can get him there."

"There isn't any point in him surviving, Maureen, and no matter how stricken he is he'll know if you shift him!"

"How? He can't see or hear?"

"He can smell!" Paul said, "and I don't want him to go with the stench of a hospital in his nostrils! He's one of us, Maureen, and he'd prefer to die on his own land."

She did not argue with him; John had taught her that he knew all these people better than anyone alive and she was confident that he could handle Marian Eveleigh, a woman who had always accepted him as God's deputy.

"Very well, Paul, tell them to fix him up down here. It'll kill him to be dragged up that stairway. I'll look back tonight." She went out and climbed into her ramshackle car, touched by his sadness and finding in it confirmation of an accelerated rate of change and the merciless shift of pattern in their lives lately. Who would he get in Eveleigh's place, she wondered? There was no son or son-in-law to follow on, for Gilbert, the only real farmer of the brood, had been blown to pieces practising with a short-fuse hand-grenade in 1916, and the eldest daughter, Debbie, was one of those Valley girls who preferred to go to their graves mourning a man killed in the war—who was it now?—one of the Marlowe boys, or Dave Williams, the fisherman? Well, that was Paul's problem, she had plenty of her own with a mild 'flu epidemic on her hands and she slammed the car in gear and drove off towards Codsall bridge, noting that the river was high and that another day's rain would flood the lower road as it usually did at this time of year.

Paul remained at Four Winds most of the morning, helping Marian and Debbie convert the kitchen into a sickroom but he was more concerned with the problem of succession. He said, when Norman had been made as comfortable as possible, "Do you suppose your youngest boy, Robbie, would be interested?" and Marian said Robbie wouldn't, he was far happier as a hunt servant whereas Harold, the second boy, was doing too well in the North to exchange his factory job for farming.

"You can't blame him for that," Paul grunted but he could see they

951

were worried about their future and said, hoping to reassure them, "Don't think I'll ever send you packing, we'll think of something. In the meantime you had better let Rachel know and see if you can get her home to take her turn at nursing. Someone will have to sit with him night and day and there are only two of you."

He went out and rode slowly down the track to the river road, unable to shake off his gloom. Eveleigh's death had not been entirely unexpected but it was a pity that it had to happen now with skilled labour so scarce, all the younger men drifting into the cities, and the Valley feeling the pinch of war-time losses more sharply than at any time since the Armistice. What a splendid thing it would have been if young Gilbert had been there to step into his father's place or, failing that, his own son Simon bring Eveleigh's daughter home and work out an apprenticeship at Four Winds under Marian's experienced eye? He thought, savagely, "Damn the younger ones! Where's the sense in them turning their backs on the land and joining the bloody dole queues in the city?" and then it occurred to him that this was unfair because the natural successors were not children who had grown up in the last decade but those who lay in graveyards all over France and the Near East. Who could blame their younger brothers and sisters for seeking a more rewarding life than that of the hulk sprawled in the kitchen at Four Winds, used up at the age of sixty-seven? One needed to have had a glimpse of what the Valley could offer in pre-war days before one could be reconciled to the sweat and grind of the job. Maybe, after all, he had it wrong and his sons, and young sparks like Rumble Patrick, had it right; maybe The Pair had talked sense when they described farming in England as a dead duck.

In the event Eveleigh lasted no more than a month and they buried him a pebble-toss from old Willoughby, Tamer Potter and Arthur Pitts. All the family were briefly united for the funeral and Paul had a word or two with Harold, the second boy, now in his early thirties and serving as Welfare Officer (whatever that was) at a jam-making factory in Manchester. He looked, Paul thought, an odd man out among Valley mourners, in his neat black overcoat, trilby hat and striped pants. Paul asked him how he was doing and he said, wryly, "Oh, so-so, Mr. Craddock! There's a hell of a lot of unemployment up there but I'm on the permanent staff, thank God! I cashed in on the welcome-home-the-heroes boom in 1919 and flashed my 'accustomed-to-handling-men' qualifications under their noses! I had damn all else to offer, except a good line in killing Turks!" Paul also had a chance to meet and reappraise Rachel, his daughter-in-law, but found to his dismay that both Simon and his wife bored him with their clichés and endless chatter about the dictatorship of the proletariat and the various manifestations of the class-struggle. "Don't they ever come down off the bloody platform and become human beings?" he complained to Claire, after Simon and Rachel had rushed north again to take part in yet another bye-election but Claire only chuckled and said, "They'll get over it, poor dears. They are talking about adopting a child so all we have to do is to wait until the proletariat has to be fed at four in the morning!" and privately he thanked God for her commonsense and was ashamed of his own intolerance. Then, as March came round, he was sucked into the political maelstrom himself, for Jimmy Grenfell, Liberal Member for the Paxtonbury Division since half-way through King Edward's reign, announced that he would not stand again when the present Parliament dissolved and intended to devote what remained of his life to writing a history of the Chartist Movement, a task that seemed to him more rewarding than shoring up a Labour Minority led by the Duchess-kissing Ramsay MacDonald, now a prisoner of the Tory Opposition. Paul, who hated abrupt changes of any kind, was shocked by his decision.

"Who the devil can we find to take your place, Jimmy?" he grumbled. "I've looked to you as our spokesman up there ever since I came here."

"Why don't you stand yourself, Paul?" Jimmy said but only in jest, for he knew that his backer would as soon go and live in Hong Kong as spend most of his time in London.

"We'll lose the seat if a Socialist makes a three-cornered fight of it," Paul warned him but Grenfell said, dryly, "We'll lose it anyway. The Tories are putting up a local man, a real local, not a phoney like they have in the past."

"Who?"

"You know him; a young speculator called Codsall, the son of one of your former tenants, I believe."

"*Sydney* Codsall? That young bastard? You must be joking!"

"I'm not joking, they've had their eye on him ever since he got on the County Council a year or so back."

"Then we have to find someone with an even chance of beating that young scoundrel," Paul declared and his emphasis puzzled Grenfell for it had seemed to him that Paul had been losing interest in politics of late. "He's the man behind everything shoddy round here and he doesn't know a damned thing about representing an agricultural constituency! He's a small-town shyster on the make and I've known him since he was a child. Even then he was a slippery little swine!"

"They say he's made a pile," Grenfell said. "Is that true?"

"I daresay, he's dabbled in jerry-built property and runs a quarry over beyond High Coombe. He had hopes of 'developing' Coombe Bay, God help us, but I've scotched that by blocking his direct access to the sea."

"Maybe that's what set him on his way to Westminster," said Grenfell, grinning. "You'd be surprised what they get up to there nowadays. It's one of my reasons for getting out."

"You're absolutely resolved on it, Jimmy?"

"Yes I am," said Grenfell and gave Paul a narrow glance. "You've taken a beating since the slump set in and your boys went off. Could you take another wallop?"

"You've decided there's no longer an alternative to Tories and Socialism?"

"No," said Grenfell, "nothing so dramatic. That last time I was in dock—just before the last General Election—I asked them to give it to me straight. They did! Cancer! I'd like to have a crack at something creative before I go."

It should not have been much more of a shock than Eveleigh's stroke. For a long time now Claire had been worried about Jimmy Grenfell's health and his spells in hospital, but Paul, regarding him as a frail man but knowing him for a fighter had never shared her concern, certainly not to the degree it merited. Grenfell gave him a moment to ride the punch and said, placidly, "I told Claire months ago and advised her to keep it from you. I didn't really believe she would but I see I misjudged her. Come now, it's not all that of a shock. You knew I'd never make old bones and I'm pretty well satisfied with the run I've had for my money."

"How long did they give you?" Paul asked, feeling like a child in the presence of Jimmy's size and toughness.

"Oh, they blathered about another operation," Grenfell said, "but who the devil wants to die the death of a thousand cuts in a clinic noisy with lamentation? I'm like your old friend Eveleigh, I prefer to die on my feet. However, I might as well choose the locality and I'm damned if I want to spend my last few months listening to professional liars like Stan Baldwin and Ramsay. They're all pitiful when you measure 'em against real men, chaps like Asquith, Grey, Haldane and even poor old Bonar Law. Post-war change isn't limited to the Valley, Paul. You'd have to face it no matter where you went."

"What are your plans, Jimmy? Will you wait for another election?"

"Oh yes, it'll be this autumn in my view and I need daily access to the Public Record Office and the library of the House while I finish my research. This book means a lot to me, Paul. I've been at it, off and on, for ten years. After that, I'll find somewhere down here and watch the sunset."

"You'll watch it from Shallowford," Paul said, "and don't let's have any polite excuses! Claire would wish it, Maureen will be on tap, and the place has been half-empty since the boys left."

Grenfell's face lit up with pleasure. "You mean that? It isn't a sympathetic reflex?" and when Paul grunted impatiently, "Then I'd like that, Paul. It has shape, for in a way it all began in your library— that time I called uninvited, remember? And I'm not such a fool as to imagine I should have ever won the seat if I hadn't had you behind me. I've never had more than a slim majority and it was made up of people who trusted me because they liked and trusted you. Will you write to me after you've talked to Claire? It's her decision, you know."

He talked to Claire that same night, anticipating her approval and getting it. She had always understood the strength of the bond between the two men and, like most of the women in the Valley, had long since succumbed to Jimmy Grenfell's shy charm and integrity. She said, "He can have Simon's old room. It faces south and is big enough to use as a study. He can do his writing there and come and go as he pleases by the garden stair. When will he move in?"

Paul said he thought after Parliament had dissolved for the summer recess but that between then and now they had to get busy looking for a challenger to Sydney Codsall's pretensions. She said, with a yawn, "I wouldn't try too hard, Paul. If Jimmy says he'll get in he will. We only scraped home last time because of Jimmy's personal following."

"But we can't just hand that little bastard the seat on a plate! I'd sooner stand myself than let that happen!"

"You won't do anything so silly!" she said emphatically and when, like a thwarted boy he challenged her, she got up and crossed to the rug, looking down at him with a mixture of sympathy and impatience.

"You ask why? For any number of reasons! In the first place an M.P. has to spend at least half his time in London; in the second you don't really give a damn what happens outside this Valley and never have, but most of all because, as an M.P., you'd lose the thing about

955

you that's more important to me and everyone else about here, that makes you different and easy to love!"

"Now what the hell would that be?" he demanded, laughing at her but she did not smile.

"Your faith in people and your instinctive trust in them! You wouldn't keep that once you started bandying words with that glib bunch! No, Paul, you can put that out of mind, and Jimmy, Henry Pitts or anyone else with your true interests at heart will tell you the same if they're honest!" and she went off to bed, leaving him to ponder her advice by the dying fire. She was right, of course, and in any case, when it came to the touch, he doubted if his pride was equal to a defeat at the hands of a man like Sydney Codsall. It occurred to him, however, that she might be out-of-date in her estimate of human beings and Valley folk in particular. He still liked and trusted the hard core, men like Henry, Francis Willoughby, Sam and Smut Potter, and women like Marian Eveleigh and Martha Pitts, and even some of the latecomers like the French Canadian, Brissot, and his sky-larking partner, Jumbo Bellchamber, but he was not nearly so sure of the youngsters, of his own sons, of second-generation Potters and the Valley flappers who plastered their faces with make-up and seemed to spend most of their time waiting for the 'bus to Paxtonbury and Whinmouth. Sydney himself was of this generation, too young to have suffered in the war but old enough to join in the scramble for the wreckage of a civilisation that had once offered security and serenity to anyone who did not complain of an aching back or expect much in the way of bonuses.

"Well, I daresay she knows what she's talking about," he thought, heaving himself up and shelving a final decision until he could assess the prospects of drumming up a candidate with a sporting chance. "Maybe most people see Sydney as I've always seen him and won't take him too seriously."

Some did, however, as he was obliged to admit before this year of setbacks had lurched into a crisis that rang alarm bells as far west as the Sorrel Valley.

CHAPTER FOUR

I

PERHAPS the first of the Valley uncommitted to take a markedly serious view of Sydney Codsall was Hugh Derwent, freeholder of High Coombe.

No one had ever seemed to get the true measure of Hugh. At the age of fifty he was unmarried, seldom moved more than twenty miles east or west of the Bluff and was, in a sense, the Valley sphinx, a man who kept very much to himself and had no real friend, apart from Francis Willoughby, his next-door neighbour at Deepdene. Often enough his dogged neutrality puzzled Francis, who nevertheless ambled to Hugh's defence when his name came up for periodical speculation in the bar of The Raven or the Paxtonbury cattle-market, those two changing-houses of Valley gossip.

Paul had confessed to Claire often enough that he had never been able to guess what her brother Hugh was thinking and Claire said this was not really surprising for Hugh had never had a thought at all but got by very well on instinct. He was a prudent if unenterprising farmer, without his father's prickly pride, his sister Rose's amiability, or his sister Claire's natural sparkle and quick temper. In a sense, but without setting out to deceive or conciliate, Hugh Derwent was all things to all men. Some said he was "near", which, in the Valley idiom, meant careful with loose change. Others said he was not mean, silent and withdrawn by nature but was exceptionally shy and shyness made him difficult to know. The children thought of him as even crustier than old Edward Derwent and kept clear of his neat fields but Francis Willoughby held Hugh was not so much crusty as lonely, and missed the bustle that had prevailed at High Coombe when Rose's riding school had been based there and the place was always full of laughing girls and young men mooning after Claire before her elevation to Squiress. His purchase of the freehold from his brother-in-law, towards the end of 1929 surprised nobody, for it had long been known that all the Derwents were land-hungry. On becoming a freeholder, however, and taking over from his father, Hugh had withdrawn even more from his neighbours and although he gave them all the tradi-

957

tional Valley salute—a circular flourish of the right hand and a sound midway between a grunt and a cough—he rarely gave them anything else but went about his business with ponderous tread and level gaze. Paul, who had always been curious about him, occasionally plied Claire for information about his youth. Had he ever been any different? Had he ever shown an inclination to specialise, as had Francis Willoughby with his beef cattle? Had he ever fallen in love? To the last question Claire, taxing her memory, said there had been a phase in Hugh's life when he was about nineteen when he had begun to brush his clothes, wear a necktie instead of a choker, and plaster his hair with grease and that these actions were outward manifestations of his obsession with Queenie Pitts, a cousin of Henry's, who had spent summer holidays at Hermitage. But Queenie had married a sergeant of the Royal Marines, after which Hugh had reverted to his old morose habits and had seemed, she recalled, more relieved than heart-sore. What was Queenie Pitts like, he asked, and she said she was a plump, jolly girl, with Henry's smile, lots of freckles and a propensity to say "Ooo-ahhh!" in her earnestness to agree with everybody and keep the atmosphere congenial.

"She sounds as if she might have done him a lot of good," Paul said and Claire agreed, adding that the Derwents were a warm-blooded lot and that Hugh's moroseness was probably caused by his never having enjoyed a woman, for she was ready to swear he was still a virgin.

Virgin or not Hugh Derwent set Valley tongues wagging in the summer of 1931.

Francis Willoughby was the first to get an inkling of what was happening. He was crossing his top field adjoining Derwent's land one day when he noticed a smart new car parked in High Coombe's approach lane but did not remark on it until, on the third occasion it was there, he saw Hugh and Sydney Codsall emerge from the yard, stand talking for a moment and shake hands before parting. After Sydney had backed out he went along the hedge and called, genially, "What's young Bighead after, Hugh?" using the name Sydney's detractors had coined for a son of old Martin, who had taken to wearing town clothes. To his surprise Hugh Derwent flushed, mumbled something non-committal and at once withdrew, obviously disinclined to discuss the visit but a surprise of a more dramatic nature was in store for Francis that week. A day or so later an earth-moving machine arrived in charge of a squad of Whinmouth navvies and began to bite

958

into Derwent's northern boundary hedge, clawing its way across two clover fields and swallowing soil and hedgerows like a starving mastodon let loose on the countryside. This was too much, even for an incurious man like Francis. He crossed over to High Coombe, sought out its master and said, with the resentment of a traditionist witnessing a landscape change, "What the hell be 'em about, Hugh? Be 'em laying a culvert or zummat?"

Hugh looked, he recounted later, very shifty but said, "They'm coming through, Francis! Tiz all zigned and zettled!" and when pressed for more detailed information, admitted that he had sold a freeway connecting Codsall's quarry and the main road north of Shallowford, to the cliff-top fields east of the Bluff. Francis was amazed and said so but Hugh, with a flash of Derwent temper, replied, "What business is it of anyone else? Tiz my land now and I paid for it!" after which he stumped off and Francis, greatly troubled, pondered developments a day or two before seeking out Claire and telling her what was happening on the eastern edge of the Valley. He was prepared for indignation but not the dismay she displayed the moment he explained what was occurring.

"You're sure of this? Codsall's men are actually working there now?" and when he confirmed that this was the case and it looked as though the new road would pass within fifty yards of the farmhouse, she said, quietly, "Thank you, Francis! Don't tell anyone else and be sure you keep it from Squire! I'm going over there right away."

She was bumping down High Coombe approach track within the hour and found her brother drinking his morning cocoa at the kitchen table. He seemed displeased but not surprised when she burst into the room and sent his daily woman Flossie Waring packing, with a curt "Leave us, Floss!"

"What the devil is going on here, Hugh?" she demanded. "Have you leased Codsall a right-of-way, or have you been such a fool as to let him talk you into selling a strip?"

He said, with defiance that did not fool her, "He's bought it! Paid a crazy price for it! It's like I told Francis, tiz all zigned and zettled, and nobody's business but mine!"

"*What* is signed and settled?"

"The sale! What else? I've done wi' farming, drat it! I got more sense than any of 'em, I reckon."

Claire was so appalled that she could only echo his words, the full meaning of which took some time to register. "*Done* with farming?

959

What on earth do you mean 'done with farming'? How can you be done with farming? You're still here, aren't you?"

"Yes," he said, "but I won't be, come Quarter Day! I'll be long ways off and married too, mostlike."

At any other time the mere possibility of her brother Hugh marrying, or even contemplating marriage, would have put every other thought out of her head but under the shock of his admission she let the incidental news pass as irrelevant and said, breathlessly, "Look here, Hugh, who do you think you're fooling? Paul sold you the freehold because he knew you and Father always hankered after it! It was me who persuaded him and you can't sell it, not even if you wanted to!"

He put down his mug and stood up. She had never realised how much weight had been added to his lumbering frame since the war. Today he looked gross and out of condition, and his eyes, which had always held a puzzled, slightly worried expression, were as cold and blue as a March sky. She said, with sudden concern, "What *is* it, Hugh? You aren't sick, are you? If you are . . ."

"Never felt better!" he said shortly, "nor more pleased wi' meself! And tidden a particle o' use asking me to change my mind because it's like I said, all zigned and zettled!"

"I keep asking you *what* is signed and settled!" she almost screamed, and his rather pursey mouth twitched, almost as though he found her extreme exasperation amusing.

"You'd better get it straight and go back so as your man can swallow it in one piece," he said. "It'll be less sour than nibbling, piece at a time! Codsall been badgering me for more than a year to sell him Eight Acre and Top Warren. Offered me near as much for two meadows as I paid for the whole parcel. Well, I held him off until I run across Queenie—Queenie Pitts that was. She's been a widow twelve year or more, did you know that?"

"Never mind Queenie Pitts! Did you sell Sydney Eight Acre and Top Warren? Did you?"

"Aye, I did," he said, watching her carefully, "and more!"

"How much more?"

"The whole of it."

"High Coombe? The *house*? *This* house?"

"He woulden have it no other way, so we settled on Saturday."

Suddenly her knees began to buckle and she half turned from him to sit on the end of the long oak bench running the length of the big

960

refectory table. There wasn't a thing about this kitchen that lacked association with her childhood, especially those years before the day they brought her mother into the yard and she saw her through the inglenook window, a bundle under a covering of coats. Sitting here, her head in a whirl and her body shaking, it was as though the most terrible moment of her life had returned to gloat and reduce her once again to a little ghost with two swinging plaits and pointed dancing shoes, worn for the first time that day in anticipation of Mary Willoughby's Christmas party. She said, in a whisper, "Is it final, Hugh? There's no crying off?" and he answered gruffly that there was not, for he had made up his mind to change the entire pattern of his life and Codsall's price was "the daftest ever paid for a Valley farm and likely to be 'till the crack of doom!" The mention of money seemed to relax him and iron away some of his truculence, for he stood over her grinning and said, "Here, lass, what's there to fuss about? I only sold what was mine since Father took himself off. Dammit, your husband would have sold at that price if he'd known about it!"

His reference to Paul restored to her the power of protest. She shouted, "That's a damned lie, Hugh! Paul wouldn't have, no matter what Sydney was offering!" but his grin broadened so that suddenly he was no longer a paunched, balding man of fifty but a teasing brother, enjoying the time-honoured High Coombe game of "making Claire's eyes spark". He said, genially, "Now see here, Claire, what's wrong with me sitting in a dish o' cream for a change? You been squatting in one ever since you nabbed young Squire and Rose weren't long following suit! Why damme, girl, you've got pretty nigh the whole Valley under your hand, an' Rose spends more on her hunters in one year than I earn in two! I'm gone fifty; I don't want to stay an' wear out, like old Norman Eveleigh yonder. Besides, like I said, I ran into Queenie, and she's that bonny you'd never believe and her not a year younger'n you!"

It was his seeming inability to understand the nature of his betrayal that baffled her for when she turned away he grabbed her arm and she saw that he was holding up a snapshot for her inspection, almost as though he felt confident that she had only to glance at it to approve his act. She saw that it was a picture of a blowzy, smirking woman in a bathing costume, and although just recognisable as Queenie Pitts, it had little relation to the bucolic girl she remembered in her teens. It was inconceivable, she thought, that a cautious, unimaginative man like Hugh should be eager to exchange land he had farmed all his life

961

for a late-flowering courtship with a fat, rather coarse-looking woman, but perhaps he did not see her as she was but as she had seemed to him the better part of thirty years ago. It was this that prompted her to make a final attempt to shame him if he was capable of being shamed. Behind him, hanging where it had hung throughout much of her childhood, was a large, oval-framed portrait of their mother, a picture sadly dated and taken God knows how many years ago in a Whinmouth studio, of a handsome, smiling woman, under a broad picture hat and wearing a blouse with leg-o'-mutton sleeves that looked like a pair of waterwings. She pushed past him and unhooked the picture, tucking it under her arm and making for the door but the action increased his truculence and he moved to stop her, shouting, "Now lissen here, Claire, tidden a particle o' use your man storming over here, and making a scene . . ." but when she evaded him he followed her out into the yard, trotting alongside as she climbed in the car, started the engine and began to reverse rapidly up the lane. Tears blurred her vision so that she struck the bank more than once but she outdistanced him easily enough and swung into the Dell road, leaving him behind in a cloud of exhaust. She thought, "I've got to be the one to tell Paul! I won't be answerable for what he might do if it is passed to him as Valley gossip!" and she calmed a little, pushing the car up the one-in-four gradient on the shoulder of the Bluff.

She found him in the Home Farm strawyard talking to young Honeyman and drew him aside, pouring out her tale and waiting for him to erupt. He did not; instead he heard her out, interposing one or two terse, factual questions about the farm's conveyance, the proposed route of the new road and other aspects of the sale, questions that she was unable to answer. His voice was steady but she noticed that his face paled a little under its summer tan and that his cheek twitched when she repeated what Hugh had said about herself and Rose. Then, quite suddenly, she realised that he was not angry at all but was regarding her with sympathy, and his arm went round her as he led her to the far side of the rick, out of earshot of Honeyman and his men. He said, briefly, "You're taking this on yourself, aren't you? Well don't! It was my decision to sell to your father and how the hell were you to know he'd pass it to Hugh almost at once? For that matter, how could you or anyone else anticipate a thing like this? The real wrong Hugh has done is not giving me a chance to buy it back again; I don't care what that young bastard Codsall gave him, I would have covered it, even if I had had to mortgage the entire bloody Valley!

However, it's done, and I don't suppose it can be reversed at this stage—that depends on the conditions your father handed over to Hugh. I'll drive over and see him right away and I'd prefer you not to come. Will you walk across the fields, or shall I ask Honeyman to run you home in the trap?"

"I'll walk," she said gratefully, "and . . . thank you, Paul!" and she brushed his cheek. She wanted to say much more. She wanted to tell him he had never seemed so big or so dignified as at that moment, when it must have seemed that everything he had striven for over the years had been mocked and belittled but he turned and left her and a moment later was driving down the river road towards Whinmouth.

Edward Derwent was not at home when Paul knocked at the door of his quayside cottage but Liz told him that he had had a letter from the local solicitor that morning and it had seemed to upset him. He had gone out with his breakfast half eaten and that was unusual for he "did zo take to his bacon an' eggs". Paul said, "Where's the nearest 'phone-box, Liz?" and she pointed to one outside the harbour-master's office no more than a step away, so he said good-bye and crossed the quay to telephone Snow and Pritchard, the firm the Derwents used on the few occasions they needed a lawyer. They told him that Mr. Derwent had indeed called that morning but had gone again, they understood to visit his son. The information troubled Paul. He knew Edward Derwent for an impulsive man if his dander was up so, he jumped in the car and put his foot down all the way to the moor highway that linked up with the dust road running across the head-waters of the two rivers. It was the longest way round but the way the old man would have taken if he made the journey by trap, and he remembered that Edward Derwent neither hired cars nor drove them. He reached the junction of roads in half-an-hour and it was not until he was descending the hill that the sourness of Claire's news rose in his throat, tainting his palate like bile. He had a swift and agonising vision of what the estate map would look like when Codsall had finished with High Coombe, had cut his road and blocked the whole eastern boundary of the estate with bungalows, quarry shacks and God knew what else. Shallowford would be punched into an ungainly figure eight, with "development" reaching as far as the edge of the Dell and then all the way to the coast. Coombe Bay would change overnight, becoming, no doubt, a snappy little resort, with a prim promenade, shelters and "attractions" of one sort and another, and whom would they attract? Not men with a craft at their fingertips, like

963

old Tom Williams and Abe Tozer the smith but carloads of week-enders, strewing paper bags and cigarette packets all over the gutters and townees to man shops displaying mass-produced goods behind chromium-plated windows! Well, no one alive could stop it altogether, he supposed, but where was the sense in accelerating the process and this, it would seem, was what Sydney and his kind had in mind, and for no better purpose than to line their own pockets. God damn the lot of them, he thought, and especially that bloody traitor Hugh Derwent, and he swung the car off the road into a passing bay to allow the passage of a two-horse farm waggon approaching at a walk.

It was not until the vehicle had drawn almost level that he noticed the waggoner was Hugh Derwent himself, hunched on the box with the reins slack in his hand. He shot out his hand to open the offside door and leap out and then he stopped half-way out, checked partly by his brother-in-law's dejected air but more so by a livid cut spotted with congealed blood on his cheekbone. He opened his mouth to say something but Hugh did not even glance at the car. In a moment the waggon had gone creaking on its way leaving a debris of twigs and leaves where it had brushed the nearside hedge. In another moment it had passed out of sight round the bend in the narrow track.

Edward Derwent was standing in the centre of the yard when he drove up, waiting beside the pump almost as though he expected him and Paul noticed that he looked very trim in his serviceable tweeds and the deerstalker he had affected since his retirement. "More like a retired colonel than a farmer," Paul thought, with a grin, and without knowing why suddenly felt a great deal more cheerful although, from where they stood, he could hear the chink of spades on flint as Cod-sall's workmen dug their way across Eight Acre. Paul said, "I saw Hugh near the crossroads and he looked pretty sorry for himself! You're not going to tell me you thrashed him?"

"I caught him one or two before he ran for it," the old man said but with no answering smile. "It's damned lucky for him I brought this instead of a double-barrel!" and he lifted a heavy walking-stick tipped with a brass ferrule. "I was coming over if you hadn't shown up. Not that there's much to say, you can't do a thing to stop it, lad."

"I didn't imagine I could," Paul told him. "I just hoped, I suppose. Claire was very upset. What happened exactly?"

"I threw him off," the old man said, "the same as I would a poacher. Oh, he owns the place legally, at least until Codsall moves in on

Quarter Day, but I told him if I found him about the place between then and now I'd shoot him, even if I had to hang for it! Aye, and I would too, that's no boast!" Paul said, quietly, "Is there a drink in the house? We could both do with one, Edward!" and led the way inside, noting that the kitchen showed signs of a hasty evacuation, with dresser drawers open and furniture pushed to one side. Old Derwent went into the scullery and came back with a bottle of gin in one hand and an orange in the other and Paul watched as he poured two measures, sliced the orange with his penknife and squeezed a half into each glass. "That's so like him," he thought. "The old boy has probably never heard of bottled fruit-juice of the kind they'll soon be selling from kiosks in Coombe-Bay-on-Sea!" and they sipped in silence. Paul said, at length, "Someone will have to tend the stock, Edward. Shall I tell your man Gregory to carry on?"

"No," Edward said. "I'll have a word with Gregory before I go to bed. I shall stay until the last minute. I ought never to have left here; never!" and his eyes ranged the room, stopping at the patch of discoloured wallpaper between window and fireplace.

"Claire took it," Paul told him, "it was a gesture, I suppose, but I'll ask her to bring it back when she comes over."

"You never knew Claire's mother, did you?"

"No, she was killed a few years before I got here. She was very popular and very beautiful, I believe."

The old man walked across to the slate hearth and stood with one arm on the mantel looking into the empty grate. Paul had always thought of him as a prematurely aged man; this afternoon he looked ninety, although Paul knew he was no more than seventy odd.

"She was the pride of the Valley," Edward said. "To see her in full-cry was to see wind crossing standing corn, boy! Claire favours her in looks, and Rose in style, but neither one could hold a candle to Molly in her prime! Damned if I ever could understand what she saw in me. Thought about that many a time and never found an answer."

"I could give him one," Paul thought, "but it would only embarrass him. The readiness of a man ready to kill his only son for selling off land to a jobbing builder probably had something to do with it; that, plus his guts and integrity. With five men like him I could hold the Valley against all comers but there aren't five, only three now—him, me and Henry Pitts. The reinforcements haven't shown up so, from here on, it's digging in and that's an end to it!" Something still puzzled
965

him, however, and he said, "Didn't Hugh fight back? He could have held you off with one hand and laughed in your face, Edward!"

"He hasn't a ha'porth of real guts," the old man said. "I don't know how Molly and me came to spawn a boy like Hugh. Seems all our spunk went into the girls!" And then, cocking an eye, "He'll not show his face in the Valley again until I'm six foot under! You'd better warn Claire of that."

"She'll lose no sleep over it," Paul said but the old man shook his head. "A family ought to stick together to the end. I always tried to teach 'em that after their mother went but I must have taken a wrong turn somewhere."

"You didn't," Paul said, "but I daresay Hugh did when that girl of his showed him her backside. There's a lot of us who would like a chance to catch time by the tail and I suppose he sees the chance of doing it, or thinking he can," and as he said this he felt an alien current of sympathy for Hugh Derwent, remembering his own desperate loneliness after Grace had gone and before Claire took her place. He said, in an effort to cheer Edward, "I suppose we've got a lot to be thankful for. I could never bear a brother of Claire permanent ill-will and I'll tell you something else too. Whatever I've managed to do here in the last quarter century I couldn't have done without Claire, so you still have a generous share in it, Edward."

The old man pushed himself off the mantel, turned and retraced his steps to the table and as he reached for his glass his moustache twitched. In a man of Edward Derwent's temperament this was the equivalent of Henry Pitts' braying laugh. He said, "I'll tell you one thing young-feller-me-lad! When you first settled in here I wouldn't have wagered a flagon of cider on your chances! I was wrong about Hugh and wrong about you, so you can write me off as a dam' bad judge o' character! Nobody could have done more for this place and the way you've gone about it has been right—right all the way down the line, so don't let that Martin Codsall's boy or my boy, or any other Clever Dick tell you that isn't so, now or ever! I'll drink to you, lad, to get the taste of my own kin out of my mouth!" and he drained the glass and began moving round methodically shutting drawers and straightening furniture.

"Will you want your things sent over tonight?" Paul asked and Edward said he would. Claire could telephone the harbour-master and ask him to tell Liz to pack them up and get ready to move back.

"Will she want to do that just for a few weeks?"

"She'll do as I bliddy well tell her!" the old man retorted. "I've yet to get a back-answer from my second wife, although I got plenty from the first!" He stopped what he was doing and looked at Paul. "Tell me, lad," he said, "have you ever had any tussles with my girl? I always reckoned she'd take some managing. Did you ever have call to belt her?"

"Only once," Paul said, smiling, "and it was a long time ago. Maybe that once was enough."

The old man looked at him with admiration. "I always did tell Willoughby and old Arthur Pitts that there was a deal more to you than you could tell by looking," he said, "so at least I was right about one thing!"

Paul left him on that and went out into the yard. The hot sun sucked humid steam from a neatly-piled stack of manure and already the farm seemed half-deserted. A dog was sound asleep over by the pump and a blue-check pigeon was the only moving thing between byre and house. From over the hedge came the persistent chink of spade and the rumble of a wheelbarrow rolling along a plank track. He looked over the wall beside the building where Rose had had her stables and saw a seam of earth glowing red, like the wound on Hugh Derwent's cheek. A few workmen pottered to and fro and beyond was a man in town clothes setting up a surveyor's tripod. He went back to the car and eased it along the lane until he could turn and then drove home, thinking not of the eastern defences, which had crumbled, but those in the west, of the deserted Periwinkle and the masterless Four Winds. "It's time," he told himself, "we had a little luck but I daresay it will all run Sydney's way until the election. After that who knows? Who knows anything at all?"

II

By the time Quarter Day came round he had other things to think about and so, for that matter, had most people. The alarm bells of national bankruptcy were ringing in Fleet Street and urgency ruffled the bland voices of radio announcers so that even in the Valley, where people were very slow to panic, folk became aware of the crisis and the possibility of a general election, "To Give the Government a Mandate For Economy". That, thought Paul, was how it was always projected, in stunning capitals, with the emphasis on what was expected from the governed rather than what could be expected from the governors.

967

Henry Pitts must have noticed as much for one morning, meeting Paul on the river road, he shouted, " 'Ave 'ee 'eard the latest, Maister? We'm goin' broke, on account of all that bliddy cash you an' me 'ave been sploshing about zince us was demobbed, backalong!"

That was about it, thought Paul. The men in charge muddled along, bickering one with the other and trying this and that expedient until the machine slithered to a halt. Then, like the feckless head of an improvident household, they announced that there would have to be a cut in housekeeping, sacrifices all round and no more pocket money for anyone. His cynical attitude towards politics, fostered by a decade of agricultural depression, had been deepened by the arrival of Jimmy Grenfell, with the benefit of thirty years' close-range experience of professional politicians. Sentence of death had put a cutting edge on Grenfell's sense of humour and he beguiled some of his sleepless hours in front of the library fire after Claire had gone to bed sketching for Paul a gallery of lively portraits of the shady, the earnest and the pompous with whom he had hobnobbed since he first entered "The Club", as he called it, about the time the Tsar's fleet fired on British fishing smacks in the belief that they were Japanese warships. Listening to him Paul began to doubt the practicability of democracy but when he admitted his doubts Jimmy only said, with a shrug, "There are really only two choices, Democracy and Muddle, or Dictatorship and Tyranny. I admit I've sometimes wondered which is preferable but I've always come down in favour of muddle, if only because it can always be temporarily tidied without a blood bath. I daresay we shall stagger on for another decade or so, but as for finding the right answers, as we believed ourselves capable of doing in 1906, that's just a pipe-dream! The Holy Grail was lost long ago and it's not likely to turn up in Westminster."

Paul went along, accompanied by Henry Pitts and Smut Potter, to Sydney Codsall's adoption meeting in the Paxtonbury Drill Hall and found it a less humiliating experience than he had anticipated, largely on account of his companions' lively commentary. The prospect of Sydney Codsall as a Member of Parliament struck Henry as so uproariously funny that all the shushing on the part of rosetted stewards could not prevent him from expressing opinions that would have led to him being thrown out in days when Paxtonbury folk took their politics seriously.

"Giddon, tiz a bliddy miracle!" he kept muttering. "Marty Codsall's boy, zitting up there like a tailor's dummy, askin' us to zend un

968

to Parlyment! Why damme, I never zeed ole Marty in a collar an' tie in his life and all the politics he ever knowed was how much water to add to 'is milk!"

When Henry was only warned to keep quiet, and not expelled from the meeting, Smut joined in, saying that they ought to have had his mother, Arabella, up there on the platform. " 'Er voice could carry furthest of anyone in the Valley," he added, half-way through Sydney's personal promise to build the League of Nations into an effective instrument for peace. "You could have heard Arabella from the far zide o' Cathedral Close and I can't catch no more'n the odd word o' the boy's, can you, Henry?"

"No," said Henry, "but I'm sure o' one thing, I baint missin' much!" and Smut's barking laugh made so many people turn that Paul hustled them out and they adjourned to the public bar of The Mitre where Henry, suddenly more serious, said, "Lookit, Maister, is us goin' to let un get away with it? Tiz the daftest thing ever happened yerabouts, a toad like 'ee standin' for farmers! Baint there nothin' us can do about it?"

"Not much," Paul told him, "for we still haven't got a candidate. He won't be unopposed, however, a Labour chap is putting up, a University lad sent down to get experience."

Smut said, with a picturesque oath, "A bolshie is wastin' his time yerabouts. If you stood us'd 'ave a sportin' chance anyway. Dammit, we voted solid Liberal here nigh on thirty years, so why have us let this happen? Politics never bothered me much, apart from the larks us got up to in the old days, but to see Marty Codsall's boy standing gives me the gripes, I can tell 'ee!" to which Henry added, "Why *dornee* 'ave a go, Squire? 'Twould liven things up any road."

It was not the first pressures that had been applied to him as the weeks passed and still no acceptable successor to Grenfell presented himself. Liberal farmers from the villages north of Paxtonbury made approaches and some of the Old Guard, who had helped to send Jimmy back to Westminster several times in succession, seemed to resent his steadfast refusal to involve himself. He continued to stand aloof until mid-September, when the date of the election was announced and the Socialist party split down the middle with the Premier, Ramsay MacDonald, and others making common cause with the Opposition. Grenfell said, on hearing this news over Claire's new, four-valve radio set, "Well, there's an end to the Liberal Party. We've been slowly bleeding to death ever since Lloyd George knifed us, in

December, 1916. Now we shall have to choose Right or Left, with no hedging of bets! Thank God Asquith didn't live to see it!"

It was Grenfell's comments on this occasion that reminded Paul of his own broadly-based faith in Democracy, a credo that, in his view, offered few fireworks but rather a steady promise of improvement for those dedicated to the ideal of personal liberty practised within a framework of disciplined free enterprise. It was very difficult for him to stand aside altogether and see a man who despised farmers as clod-hoppers seek to represent the Valley in national councils, yet nomination day would have come and gone without him taking positive action had not Claire done a sudden right-about-face and ranged herself on the side of Henry, Smut and all the others urging him to take up the challenge.

They were sitting before the library fire one night listening to the midnight news-bulletin when she said, without preamble, "*Do* it, Paul! I was wrong! You won't win but do it anyway, as a gesture!"

He was amused but also slightly alarmed at her insistence. It was not losing he feared but losing ignominiously. He said, "You weren't wrong, you know; all the arguments you used against my standing were valid. Why this sudden change of heart?"

"I think Hugh has something to do with it, Hugh and the man who bought him. I went over there today to help Father and Liz pack up."

"Well?"

"It was pitiful, not just the old couple having to leave but the place itself, so empty and lifeless, with the stock sold off and not even a hen scratching about in the nettles. It was a kind of death."

"I don't see the connection between the write-off of High Coombe and me standing for Parliament."

"There is a connection," she insisted, "but I'm not clever enough to state it. It has to do with standing up for our way of life, a banner that has to be picked up and waved by someone, if only for a few moments!"

He pondered this and with it the issues, most of them unconnected with the everyday life of the few hundred people living between the main line and the sea—far wider issues, involving tariffs, overseas payments, war debts, the League of Nations, the guilt of Germany, the truculence of France, on which he would be asked to pronounce and in which he was not, and never had been, deeply interested. If he stood at all it would be as a candidate in the old-fashioned sense, a local man seeking to represent local causes which was a role not even Jimmy

Grenfell had been able to play for much of his time in Westminster. And yet, she was right again, even if she did stand in flat contradiction to herself. "A banner to be picked up and waved, if only for a few moments . . ."

"All right," he said, finally, "if you're behind me I'll have a go and to hell with it! Do we go up and tell Jimmy now? He's probably awake and readng."

"No," she said, "it can keep for tonight!" and then she did something that she had not done for a long time, kicking off her shoes, coiling herself on his knee and saying, "I know I'm a good deal heavier but you'll have to put up with that! After all, it's an occasion!"

It was a brief, breathless campaign, waged, for the most part, in thin rain that seemed now to have been falling for months, ruining the harvest and converting the Sorrel streams into brown floods that burst their banks and spread far across the flats, greatly hindering movement from one point to another. Looking back on that autumn election Paul found his memories of it fragmentary and insubstantial, a succession of dashes to and from draughty village halls and littered committee rooms, of open-air meetings in a dripping raincoat, and intervals of talk and endless cups of tea in steamy kitchens. He remembered the smells after he had forgotten the occasions, a salad of drying laundry, wet macintoshes, stale dust rising from the cracks of Institute platforms, and the sharp, schoolroom smell of freshly-printed leaflets and election addresses. His speeches were short and factual, concerned almost exclusively with the heavy slack of farm economy since the all-too-brief boom of ten years ago. He warned listless town audiences of the steady drift from the land, urging the necessity of a sound agricultural policy if the country was not to become completely dependent on imported food. It was, he supposed, a very parochial campaign, with little appeal to voters living in the suburbs of the cathedral city, or elderly couples who had retired on fixed incomes to bungalows in places like Nun's Bay but it won over a sizeable number of the farmers who had been Tories all their lives and it detached from Labour's interests some of the unemployed who, in better times, had been rooted in local crafts like coach-building, shoeing, fishing, thatching and brick-making. He had a very zealous committee headed by Henry Pitts, Sam and Smut Potter, Marian Eveleigh, Parson Horsey and a few of the faithful living north of Paxtonbury. He also had a number of unexpected allies whom he used as supplementary speakers, men like the humorist, Jumbo Bell-chamber, and Rose's aged husband, Major Barclay-Jones, who came down from Gloucestershire and cantered about the Valley like a vintage Paul Revere, scorning the use of committee cars. Mary, his eldest daughter, was with him heart and soul, endlessly addressing envelopes and answering the telephone, or waiting for him with a Thermos flask of coffee in the brief intervals between one meeting and another, and Claire's enthusiasm touched him even more for she had always professed to regard politics as a bore, as though to emphasise the contrast between herself and Grace. The constant rushing to and fro, and the vast expenditure of nervous energy listening to constituents' grumbles and remembering so many names and faces, made him feel his age but with only a few days to go he began, almost subconsciously, to rate his chances far better than at the outset of the campaign. He met, and made friends with, the young Socialist candidate, a rather forlorn figure who reminded him a little of his son Simon, and he found it possible to admire the earnestness of a lad whose deprived youth in a north-eastern shipbuilding town had made him an apostle of militant socialism. The Socialist candidate was called Hardcastle and his appearance in the Valley was a forlorn hope on the part of Labour but he fought cleanly and doggedly, and Paul went so far as to put him in touch with Simon and Rachel, currently campaigning in a Welsh mining area. He did not come face to face with Sydney Codsall during the campaign. It was not until all the ballot boxes had been collected in Paxtonbury Town Hall that he saw him, outwardly smug but showing nervousness when the counting began, and wondered what attitude he would take if Sydney was disposed to be patronising. He was spared a decision; Sydney and his agent kept their distance while he stood waiting with young Hardcastle, watching the votes pile up on the long trestle tables, three creeping stacks, his own and Sydney's maintaining a level advance and Hardcastle's almost a non-starter. He was familiar with the tense atmosphere of a count, having attended any number in the past and was surprised at his own indifference. He had picked up the banner and waved it, and that was all that mattered. When Claire and Mary joined him, and Claire (far more concerned with the result than he was himself) sought his hand for comfort, he said, with a grin, "You needn't worry, old girl! It isn't going to be a walkover!" and shuttled her on to Hardcastle, who looked as if he needed mothering.

The result was far closer than anyone had anticipated having regard to the landslide in favour of the National Government all over the country. They told him the totals but he was almost too astonished to take them in and at one p.m., with everyone congratulating both leading candidates, the Returning Officer went out on to the balcony where a crowd awaited the result in the eternal drizzle. Only at the very last moment did Paul feel a void in the pit of his stomach and a parched feeling in the back of his throat that reminded him of nights behind Vimy, when he had been on the point of moving up to support areas with a convoy of shells or wire. Then, as he pulled himself together, he heard the fruity voice of the Returning Officer challenging the steady hiss of the rain:

". . . Codsall, Sydney Algernon; thirteen thousand, one hundred and forty-nine . . . Craddock, Paul; thirteen thousand . . ." but the next words were drowned in the roar that ascended from a crowd raised to a pitch of enthusiasm by the obvious closeness of the contest.

". . . Craddock, Paul; thirteen thousand, one hundred and one!" Sydney had won but by so small a margin that it was nothing to crow about and certainly not so when his massive organisation was taken into account. To Paul it was better than a victory, for it meant justification without the horrid necessity of turning his back on the Valley and his relief was so great that he felt almost sorry for his opponent faced with the prospect of making good his electoral promises and discovering, as Grenfell had prophesied, that attendance at Westminster called for a great deal more stamina than the old-pals atmosphere of County and Urban politics in the provinces. Perhaps Sydney already realised this; his formal speech of thanks was delivered in a high, piping voice and interrupted by a volley of catcalls, organised, Paul suspected, by stalwarts like Henry and Smut. He left them at it and went back into the hall where Claire, pink with excitement, said, "You don't look like a defeated candidate!" and plucked his sleeve nervously when he said, with unabashed heartiness, "I don't feel like one either, old girl! Don't you ever push me that near the cliff again!" He shook off a swarm of supporters, saying, "For God's sake let's get on home and pick up where we left off! Codsall can keep the seat warm until we can find someone who means business!"

Claire remained in what old Mrs. Handcock always described as "a bit of a tizzy" for the rest of the day but when the house was quiet, unnaturally so after the turmoil of the last three weeks, he poured her a double brandy and stood watching her sip it. He said, thankfully, "My God, it's like coming home from the war! Like being turned

973

loose again from hospital or the trenches! Why did we ever take such a risk?"

"We neither of us realised it was a risk. Frankly I thought you'd poll about a third of his total. It only goes to show."

"To show what?"

She turned her back on him to set down her glass, at the same time throwing a glance at him over her shoulder that somehow reminded him of the saucy, provocative girl who had once helped him decorate this room for King Edward's Coronation soirée. "It's like Father always says! There's a lot more to you than meets the eye!"

"Well," he said, crossing to her, slipping his hands behind her and genially pinching her bottom, "you should know! I suppose you would call this another of your famous 'occasions'?"

"Look here," she protested, "all our married life you've been hard at work convincing yourself that I was a wanton! I daresay it flatters you but it isn't true!"

"Oh yes it is," he said, "and you've got six children to prove it! Do you want another drink?"

"No," she said, "and neither do you it seems!" and disengaged herself to throw a log on the fire and switch off the light.

"You're a lusty fifty-two, Paul," she told him, "so maybe I'm lucky you didn't win and get yourself a London flat and an admiring secretary!" but as she said this her mood shifted again and holding his face between her hands she said, "We've been wonderfully lucky in spite of everything and we ought never to forget that when we run into the occasional bad patch! I was beginning to and so, I think, were you," but his relief was too deep to share her sudden earnestness and all he replied was, "Stop preaching, woman, it doesn't become you!" and began to treat her as though they had just returned, laughing and half-tipsy, from one of old Arthur Pitts' Hallowe'en parties in days when fashions in clothes made this kind of frolic a far less casual enterprise than it was today.

III

The long run of bad luck ended almost at once. Within days of the landslide election, when supporters were still pointing out that he, alone of Westcountry candidates, had increased the Liberal vote notwithstanding a massive Coalition victory, Claire came into the office and said young Eveleigh wanted to talk to him. Paul looked up, expecting to see Robbie, the baby of the family, now huntsman to the

974

Sorrel Vale pack but it was Robbie's elder brother, Harold, whom he had not seen since Norman Eveleigh's funeral. Harold, the war hero who had been commissioned in the field and decorated for gallantry, looked apologetic and declined a drink, saying, "Perhaps later, Mr. Craddock, I'd prefer to talk first. The fact is, I'm in the fashion—on the dole and have come to you with half an idea."

News that Harold was unemployed surprised him for he had got the impression from Marian, as well as Harold himself, that the temporary gentleman of the long family had done very well for himself and had continued to earn good money throughout the Depression.

"I thought you were dug in," he said and Harold replied, bitterly, "So did I, but it seems I didn't dig deeply enough! The boss had a son down from 'Varsity and didn't know where to place him. Then he remembered me and reckoned the war was so long ago that we were due for the next, so out I went on my ear! They didn't put it that way, of course—just the usual cock about hard times and unavoidable economies! Odd how these chaps can make a virtue of necessity. This crisis has been a Godsend to some of them I can tell you!"

Paul said, sympathetically, "We all get a kick in the pants now and again and ex-service chaps more than their ration. What was the idea you had?"

"Mother wondered if you would consider me as tenant at Four Winds."

Paul made no attempt to conceal his astonishment. Like all the Eveleighs Harold had grown up on a farm but he had enlisted at eighteen, and after the war had gone straight into industry. To come home with the notion of running Four Winds implied that he was either supremely self-confident or desperate; it was important to discover which for Four Winds was no place for a desperate man, using it as a temporary haven and Marian would surely be aware of that.

"You say it was your mother's idea?"

"No, it was mine; Mother doesn't think I could make it and she only let me apply because she's sorry for Connie and the kids."

"You've got kids?"

"A boy and a girl, seven and five."

"You've been able to save a bit?"

"A bit, but not much, the pay wasn't all that good." He hesitated, then went on, "I pretended it was better than it was when I came home! I always was a bit of a show-off, remember? The pips went to

975

my head, I suppose. I daresay you heard about the time the old man had to clear my mess debts?"

"No, I didn't and you don't have to tell me."

"I'd prefer to!"

"Well?"

"I never really settled after demob. Everything seemed stale and flat. It was a come-down to have to take one's place in the queue and be grateful for the odd glass of beer after whisky! I soon got out of my depth and the old man paid up but only on condition I resigned my commission. That was back in 1922."

It was, Paul reflected, a familiar story—a boy boosted by his own courage and initiative and being spoiled by older men, whose experiences on the Western Front bred in them a terrible pity for the very young. Then peace and reaction, with any number of sprees in the Mess, and maybe a love-affair or two with girls overseas, who would encourage him to show off and spend freely. Finally Father's ultimatum and the bump back to earth, the assumption of parental responsibilities and the need to hold down a job in a competitive world. It must have happened a million times since 1918. He looked sharply at the young man and thought he could detect fear behind the eyes. Harold Eveleigh must have faced death many times but it needed a different kind of courage to tackle the challenges of the last year or so. And yet, pitying him and understanding his situation so well, Paul resisted the impulse to welcome him with open arms. Four Winds needed a dedicated man unless it was to go the way of High Coombe and tear yet another gap in Valley defences. He said, aware that he was temporising, "You're over thirty now, Harold, and I don't suppose you've milked a cow or ploughed a furrow since you were seventeen. So far as I'm aware you've never even wanted to! That's what's important and that's why your mother was reluctant to encourage you. It won't be news to you that agriculture is down and out, or that it's damned low on the priority list of politicians."

Harold said nothing but Paul could see he was digesting every world. "It isn't that I wouldn't like to see an Eveleigh back at Four Winds," he went on, "but there's more to it than sentiment. I've poured a small fortune into the estate since the war but I can't go on doing it. Unless things mend very soon I shall be obliged to contract or throw in my hand."

Harold Eveleigh shifted his weight from one foot to the other, trying, without much success, to conceal his growing desperation. "I see your point, Mr. Craddock. You need someone with experience, the kind of farmer my brother Gilbert would have been if he hadn't had the bad luck to meet a bloody fool of a bomb-instructor."

"No," Paul said, "not necessarily but I need someone with Gilbert's instinctive love of the place. I daresay your mother could supply the experience but let me put it this way; what I *don't* want is a man using Four Winds as a bolt-hole, someone who will move on when something less mucky turns up! I daresay that sounds priggish but I don't care if it does. This place means everything to me and I'll fight for it the way you fought Johnny Turk, with every bloody weapon I can lay my hands on!"

He gave him a moment or so to ponder, crossing to the sideboard and pouring two drinks. When he turned the young man was hunched by the window, hands deep in pockets, chin lowered as he looked beyond the leafless chestnuts to the point where Four Winds' boundary met the skyline midway between the rivers.

"Here's to Gilbert and all the others anyway," Paul said, nudging his elbow and Harold said, slowly, "I daresay I should have been as good a farmer as Gil if I'd stayed behind like Francis Willoughby, over at Deepdene. Come to that, we can't swear to how Gil would have reacted if he had survived and had to pitch in with the rest of us and make the best of it. Sometimes I think they were the lucky ones, Mr. Craddock; chaps like Ikey Palfrey, Big Jem and all the others who went West! At least they died still believing in one another!"

"I still believe in the Valley and Four Winds is a vital part of it," Paul said but he was touched nonetheless. There had been times when identical thoughts had occurred to him, particularly during the last few months.

Eveleigh went on, "What can I say that won't sound like a bleat? I can't tell you I'm longing to trudge behind a plough, or that I think raising a crop of mangolds is Mankind's noblest endeavour, but ten years in industry has at least taught me there are far dirtier ways of earning a living! If I had my time over again I'd settle for mangold-raising as the least of two evils. I've got farming in my blood, I imagine, the same as Gil and all of us and I've got a flair with some animals. Apart from that I've got a duty to Connie and the kids, and two other things in my favour are that I'm fit and still old-fashioned enough to keep my word if I give it. If you like to take a chance on those qualifications I'll do my best and at least I'd accept guidance. I was pigheaded once but not any longer!"

977

Paul found himself drawn to the man, liking both his honesty and his awkward humility. It must, he thought, cost a son of Norman Eveleigh a great effort to admit so many shortcomings. He said, on impulse, "Would you bring your wife over to see me, Harold?" and Harold said, "She's here now, I left her in the kitchen having a cup of tea with Miss Mary but she knows even less than I do about running a farm. She gets on with Mother, however. She's a Lancashire lass and worked in a chocolate factory up to the time we married. Shall I fetch her?"

He sounded eager and Paul wrote this down as a point in his favour. He remembered Arabella, and how essential it was for a farmer's wife to accept the limits of the life if her husband was to succeed. A Lancashire girl, who had worked in a chocolate factory and who got along with Marian Eveleigh, sounded promising material. "By all means," he said, "and bring Mary with her in case she's shy."

Harold shot off like a boy at the end of an unpleasant interview and was back almost at once with a pretty brunette in tow, a tall girl with a very clear skin, soft brown eyes and a child's mouth. Mary, always at her best with shy people, came to the rescue saying, "Shake hands with him, Mrs. Eveleigh! He always scowls like that when he's introduced to anyone!" and Harold laughed, adding, "She's not such a mouse! She thinks we're a soft lot in the South but says the climate makes up for us!"

"She can make Lancashire cream cheese," Mary said, "and I think she'll like it here," but Harold said quickly, "She might not get the chance, Miss Craddock! Your father is chewing it over and I'm hanged if I blame him! We're both rank amateurs and it isn't as if Mother was still young."

"She's young enough to teach you a thing or two," Paul said, "so I'll get the new lease drawn up this afternoon. You and Marian can be joint tenants for three years and we'll see how things shape. Will that satisfy you?"

He saw young Eveleigh and his wife exchange a quick glance and read their relief. The girl Connie said, in a strong Lancashire accent, "We'll make a go of it, Mr. Craddock, I'll see to that!" and suddenly Paul knew that they would, that Harold and this pretty young wife of his were much-needed reinforcements and that Four Winds would soon regain its place as the natural bastion in the West. After they had gone Mary confirmed this impression. "I took to her at once," she said, "she's down-to-earth and doesn't say things she doesn't mean!"

"That's a Lancashire characteristic," he told her, "we had hundreds of them about here during the war. The thing that decided me was the fact that they're prepared to take advice from Marian!" and then he smiled and when Mary asked the reason, added, "I was thinking of the buzz in Four Winds' kitchen that led up to this—Harold and his wife trying every trick in the pack to talk Marian into acting as their spokesman, knowing that she would be a damned sight more likely to win me over than he would!"

"Well, it so happens you're wrong, Daddy. Marian wanted to come but that girl wouldn't let her. She told me she didn't want his mother talking-up for Harold. If you had turned them down they were leaving in the morning to look for work in London!"

He was struck by this and it reinforced him in the rightness of his decision. They had their troubles, these youngsters, but were probably maturing under them and somehow the entire interview now presented itself as a hopeful signpost into the future. Then, following this chain of thought, he remembered Rumble Patrick's last letter in which he talked of quitting Queensland for Alberta.

"You hear from Rumble a good deal more frequently than we do," he said. "Does this Canadian venture mean he's tired of sheep-farming and must needs fly off at another tangent?"

He saw the colour rush to her cheeks and instantly regretted the question. Her head came up sharply and she said, defensively, "He's having to feel his way, like anyone else far from home! You don't have to worry about Rumble. He'll surprise you one of these days!" and she left the room with an abruptness that left him in no doubt at all but that she preferred to keep Rumble and Rumble's letters to herself. He thought, with a smile, "Well, she's damned touchy about him! I wonder if Claire knows as much as I think I know, and whether we ought to pool the evidence?" but postponed a decision as something that could wait and went into the office to find the old Four Winds' lease, drawn up the day after the inquest on Martin Codsall and his wife. Searching for it he came across the estate diary and opened it to see what Claire had written about the election. The entry startled him. Under October 19th, 1931, she had written: "*General Election: a three-cornered fight here with Paul Craddock standing as successor to James Grenfell, Liberal M.P. for Paxtonbury since 1904. He was defeated, but only just. General opinion is he could have won if he had tried.*" That was all, a reasonable if prejudiced statement of fact, for he had to admit that he was more elated over the Eveleigh succession than

979

he was deflated by defeat at the polls and this must surely mean that he would carry his parochialism to the grave. He turned a page and wrote, "*Harold Eveleigh, second son of the late Norman Eveleigh, tenant of Four Winds for twenty-five years and foreman prior to succeeding Martin Codsall, today applied for and was granted the lease which he will hold jointly with his mother, Marian Eveleigh. He is aged 32, married and has two children.*" It seemed incredible that the man who had just asked for the lease had been the smaller of the two night-shirted boys peering down at him the night he thundered on the Eveleigh front door to pass the news that Martin Codsall had killed Arabella and hanged himself.

CHAPTER FIVE

I

TRAVELLER, the oldest and craftiest fox inhabiting the country of the two rivers, could usually be found in Folly Wood, north of Heronslea, when said to be at home but it was not by remaining for long in one covert that he had survived any number of cracking days on the part of the Sorrel Vale Hunt. Robbie Eveleigh, huntsman to the local pack, had ceased to regard Traveller as a legitimate quarry and had his hounds succeeded in running the old rake to earth (which was un-likely, for Traveller had come to doubt the security of earths before he was half-grown) he would have probably called them off and cast around for a fresh scent; Traveller, he might have reasoned, had pro-vided everybody in the district with so much sport for so many years that he had earned the right to die of old age.

Traveller was readily identifiable by less experienced men than Robbie. All the Heronslea keepers knew him, recognising his drooping left ear and abbreviated brush when they caught a swift glimpse of him on routine patrols beside the pseudo-Gothic tower raised by the mad Gilroy nearly a century ago. They also recognised his curious lopsided gait, caused by an old injury in a gin-trap when he was in his prime and now that he was very old his coat was so shot with grey as to pass for brindled. Yet age and infirmities had done little to restrict Traveller's movements about the country or impair in any way his prodigious memory for nooks, crannies, short-cuts or places where a decoy scent could be found, or a stream forded on dry pads. And with-in this web of knowledge was another, with threads feeding back to an instinct that taught him how to differentiate between danger areas and safe areas, dependent upon the people occupying them. He knew the Valley and Valley folk far better than Paul Craddock and Smut Potter, better than Smut's gypsy mother, or Marian Eveleigh, neither of whom had ventured far beyond the Whin or the county border. Indeed, the only two-legged creature who had known it as well had been Hazel Potter and she had died before Traveller was born.

He had not acquired this detailed knowledge without working hard for it and neither had it been dinned into him by being chased over it in peril of his life several times a season. He had built it up bit by bit during countless forays, east and south-east as far as the backyards of Coombe Bay cottages and the marram grass tunnels of the dunes, sometimes going there in search of food and sometimes to look for a mate, for there were always young vixens to be found in Shallowford Woods and a favourite of Traveller, who had already borne him several litters, still hunted the landslip terrace under the Bluff. His survival was therefore no miracle of hardihood or ingenuity but simply the result of keeping abreast of every change that took place in the country of the two rivers. As regards this, the constant revision of the map imprinted on his mind, he was a pedant among foxes, like an old man who has sworn on oath to achieve the age of a hundred and is prepared to regulate his life accordingly. At certain seasons of the year he would make one of his great, circular sweeps of the Valley, noting every minute change as it presented itself—a sagging gate here, a new plank footbridge there, a different pattern of lights at one farm, a variation in an occupier's step at the next. Methodically and pains-takingly the new scents and sounds were absorbed and filed away for future use. Not one was overlooked or forgotten.

In the late spring of 1932 Traveller padded free of the trailing briars of Folly Wood and set out on one of his routine reconnaissances, moving swiftly over the mile or so of bracken as far as the barrows on Blackberry Moor, for there was no profit in lingering near home where nothing had changed for a long time. His goal lay further east, where things were constantly changing, and he did not slacken his urgent pace until he reached the old hunting ground above Periwinkle Farm. Here he lingered a few moments, his pace slowed more by nostalgia than curiosity. The farmhouse was empty. He knew that well enough, having passed this way often since Elinor Codsall had gone, taking her succulent hens with her. Periwinkle had been a winter larder to Traveller in his heyday for all Elinor's vigilance had never succeeded in denying him occasional access to a hen or a duck. Tonight he did not have to descend into the hollow to make certain that the yard was still derelict, or the rotting hen-houses empty of anything larger than a shrew. He climbed to the top of the hill, looking across the dip at Hermitage Wood, then turned north heading for Hermitage itself but tensed himself nevertheless for the Pitts family was unpredictable and many a buckshot had come his way in these fields and the rutted lane that bisected them. Old Arthur had never fired at him (he had not seen the old man about for some time) and Henry, the ponderous, splay-footed master was content to bellow "Be off, you bliddy varmint!" if Traveller broke cover in his line of vision, but the younger Pitts, David, did not hunt and regarded all foxes as vermin to be extermi-nated by any means, fair or foul. Tonight, however, none of the men-folk were astir although there was a car parked at the head of the lane and as he slipped by he heard a woman's soft laugh and a voice say, "Dornee now! Tiz late, boy . . ." but he paid little heed to sounds or taint. Whenever he descended Hermitage lane between late spring or early autumn there was a car of some sort in the passing bay and Prudence Pitts was sitting in it, with one man or another. Traveller knew it was her, identifying her by the sickly scent that clung to her, a scent that suggested dog violets but was not violets or any other flower of the woods but a bastard alloy of some kind and usually competing with whiffs of human scent and petrol exhaust. He went on down to the yard, noting a fresh rat-hole that would give access to the cattlecake store and the mice who lived there but he did not explore, preferring to reconnoitre on an empty belly. There was a square of orange light above the rain tub so he scrambled up and looked into the kitchen. There was not much to be seen. Henry, and his son David and the old crone were there, all three crouched round the oblong box with a trumpet on the top, their attention devoted to the caterwauling issuing from it, a medley of sounds dominated by one not unlike the bray of a hunting-horn. He jumped down, skirted the yard where there was a chained and very unobservant collie and went past the sties, wrinkling his lip at the sour stench of pigs. Then he climbed the long, sloping field to the sunken lane that circled the escarpment and headed north-east for Shallowford Woods where, in his day, he must have given hounds the slip on a hundred occasions.

It was a mild, pleasant night and he was enjoying himself in his own quiet way. The woods were full of safe, springtime scents, so that his nose told him precisely what ride he was crossing at any one time. Down here by the mere anemones and irises grew and the sap in the split reeds gave off a scent that recalled long summer days in the holts under the bank, where he often met otters. Otters fished for a living and had no quarrel with him but he knew they were hunted like him-self and sometimes envied their ability to take to the water. He passed the pagoda and circled Sam Potter's cottage, recalling the big man's joyous whoop whenever he saw him bound out of a bracken in the area further north, where Sam spent most of his time felling timber.

Traveller liked Sam, who had no malice but he did not care for his younger boy, Ted, who was prodigiously fast on his feet and could leap across broken ground at the speed of a whippet. Once or twice, in this part of the woods, he had come close to running Traveller down but there was no risk tonight, for Ted was always early to bed like his father. Only Joannie Potter and her long-faced daughter, Pauline, sat up late and as Traveller paused outside the tightly wired hen enclosure Pauline came out of the back door calling the cats to their supper. She was, he recalled, crazy about cats, who were strangely pampered at this house and not left to fend for themselves as at all the other farms in the Valley. Coddling them had made them soft so that he did not fear them as he feared the half-wild cats at Deepdene or the Dell. He jumped the stream, threaded the rhododendron maze and climbed the hill where the Shallowford badgers lived. One or two of them were pottering about and bristled at his approach. They were excessively fastidious animals and only a dire emergency would drive him to use their holts as a refuge but he had refuged there from time to time until hounds were called off to another part of the woods. Every animal in the woods was leagued against Man and the badgers were no exception.

He padded through a forest of bluebells to the head of the slope and then, at a leap, dropped down into Derwent territory, or what had been Derwent but was now a wilderness, recalling in its sordid disarray, the old camp on Blackberry Moor before it was overgrown by creeping colour. Unlike the camp, however, there were few pickings to be had here now. He did not understand what had been happening in this part of his preserve but had remained curious ever since the downslope of the hill above the farm had been ripped open by great, clanking machines, like those that rushed down the shining rails near Sorrel Halt and now, he noted, there were other changes, none of which fitted into the broad pattern of agricultural pursuits as he had observed them over the years. Some of the great engines stood about, protected by tarpaulins that lifted in the breeze and momentarily deceived him into thinking men were on hand although the wind carried no taint of men. Then he saw them for what they were, coverings of the kind used on haystacks and he snarled at them and crossed the red weals in Eight Acre to inspect a long row of squarish pits, cross-covered with beams and surfaced underneath with a hard, gritty substance that was neither earth, grass, rubble nor the familiar tar of made-up roads. The pits puzzled and disturbed him and he wondered

984

if they were a row of gigantic traps of a new and hazardous design; then it occurred to him that they were not unlike dwellings, although it seemed improbable that a man like Derwent would have so many people cluttering his land. His reasoning powers were considerable but they were limited by his experience and he had no previous experience of building sites, Nun's Bay having been completed shortly before he was born. The changes here were immense since his last visit and instinct warned him against change of such catastrophic proportions so that he could not help but link the disarray at High Coombe with the dissolution at Periwinkle on the far side of the woods. Viewed separately they were singular; taken together they were alarming.

He padded down the long slope towards the sea and whilst crossing the approach lane of Deepdene he wondered what had become of the old woman who had so many children for whom she would sometimes ring a bell, the clang of which carried over the river on certain winds. Then he heard the heavy crunch of hobnail boots on gravel and at once took cover in a bed of docks as Dick Potter, Farmer Willoughby's cowman, checked his stride, sniffing the air before moving on with a grunt. Dick, as Traveller well knew, had affiliations with the cottage back in the woods and it struck him that the Potters, one and all, were a tribe to be watched. Each of them, it seemed, possessed some special skill; Sam, the woodsman, could throw a hatchet and kill a rabbit on the run and his son Ted, could outpace a whippet over a given distance; now here was Dick, Ted's brother, who could smell a fox on a windless night and Traveller was grateful that the moon had yet to rise. He waited until the sound of footsteps had died before taking the steep, winding path to the Dell. Here there was nothing to fear. The two farmers and their fat wives were an amiable lot and Traveller had a special interest in one of the men because he had a curious, lopsided walk, not unlike Traveller's own. There had been a time when the Dell was sown with traps but that was before Traveller's time. Today neither Farmer Bellchamber, Farmer Brissot, nor anyone else about here bothered to keep down the conies which abounded in Low Coombe. Traveller killed one in passing and then wished he had not for the rabbit's shriek set the dogs barking and one of the women came out into the yard and shouted to them to be quiet. The dogs he knew were chained so he lingered in the area for a spell, remembering times he had given hounds the slip in the fields of kale about here; then he trotted off and turned left-handed, emerging from the wood at the head of the Bluff where he was just in time to see the moon rise and tip twenty cartloads of silver into the bay. He paused, looking down, half inclined to descend the rock-ledges to the landslip terrace and visit the vixen who lived there but he thought better of it. He was already tired and it was a long way home and his need of vixens was less urgent than in the past.

It was in an enclosed garden above the forge that he was made aware of other changes since he had passed this way. The village seemed to be extending up the hill and, whereas evening loiterers had usually gathered under the one roof of The Raven, tonight a group of them, all men, were standing in the soft glow of the forge that spread beyond the open door. He went closer and looked directly down on them, their taint reaching him like an advancing wall, their cigarettes glowing like a scatter of watch fires. Some he recognised and some he did not, according to their occupations and habitat. Abe Tozer, the aged smith, was there, leaning on a long-shafted hammer, his white whiskers reaching the top of his leather apron and close by two or three of Abe's cronies—Morgan, the pot-bellied builder, Noah Williams, the sailor who never went to sea, and Thorn, the new sexton whom Traveller had often watched at work on the churchyard. With them was a sprinkling of younger men, like the hideously disfigured Gappy Saunders, and the blind man, Willis, who walked with a white stick. The rumble of their voices came up to the fox as he rested and again the pattern of change was revealed to him for not so long ago this street would have been empty under the stars at this time of night.

He circled the forge, crossed the street and climbed the hill to the dunes where the smell of the sea vanquished every other scent until he caught the reek of gorse growing among the marram grass. Then he turned inland along the river bank as far as Timberlake's sawmill, a place where he had often refuged from hounds and watched them overrun his scent among the newly-sawn logs before he doubled back to the nearest covert. The house behind the sawpit was silent and shuttered, as though its occupants had turned their backs on the Valley like Elinor Codsall and Farmer Derwent, and for the third time that evening Traveller sensed change and a shifting pattern, so that suddenly, from being merely curious he felt uneasy, despite the reassuring scents of resin, dry sawdust and woodsmoke and leaving the yard hurried on his way, crossing the river at the ford and taking a short cut across the stubble to Four Winds. Here, to his relief, nothing had changed at all. The yards were still tidy and spotlessly clean, the fences in repair, barns and byres bolted. There were no rat-holes in the weather-boarding and lights burned behind neatly-curtained windows; all the same he went on through to the watershed without pause. The fat Boxer kept by the new landlord was a pet and was therefore almost certainly asleep beside the fire in the kitchen but all his life Traveller had feared the Four Winds cats of which there seemed to be a baker's dozen, all as aggressive as stoats. By the time the moon was high he was safe across the Teazel and heading through Heronslea coverts and within minutes of reaching his culvert beside the tower he was curled muzzle to brush, or what little remained of his brush, but before he slept the changes he had marked during his circuit had been filed away in his memory. Hunting had finished until autumn but when it began again every scrap of information acquired that night would multiply his chances of outwitting hounds and the tyrant who fed them as a reward for betraying every other beast of the field.

II

The changes Traveller had marked during his fact-finding foray seemed abrupt to him for, alone in the valley, he and Squire Craddock were half-rebel, half-conservative. To most people in the Valley post-war changes were accepted as the wear and tear of years—incidents like the death of old Arthur Pitts, or the decision of Mary Willoughby to close her little school and spend the remainder of her days sharing a bungalow with an elderly cousin, in Dawlish. Everyone had noted, of course, the inroads of Codsall's shock troops at High Coombe, and some of them smiled and shrugged when they heard the story of the irascible old farmer's assault on his son Hugh at the time of the sell-out, but for the most part they did not share the resentment of father, sister and brother-in-law. A man was entitled to do as he liked with land bought and paid for and the bungalows Codsall's partner Tapscott built in Top Warren were soon sold, the row of shops in Coombe Bay High Street soon let. The proposal to build a permanent camping site for tents and caravans, with its own row of shops in Eight Acre, caused a somewhat wider ripple of comment but once the site was cleared and the foundations that had so mystified Traveller marked out, few were outraged by what was happening along the eastern border of the estate. Farms were being sold off everywhere nowadays and it was accepted that there was no future in agriculture. Young men like Dick Potter, and Will Codsall's younger son Mick, who clung to the industry were the exceptions. Maybe they were too idle to leave the Valley and learn a trade in Paxtonbury, maybe they were too stupid.

Most of the young ones had left by the end of 1932, some to look for work in the cities, others to marry and one or two, despairing of finding regular jobs, to join the Services or go abroad like Rumble Patrick Palfrey. The Valley was not at all surprised to learn that he had sailed away to Australia; anything might be expected of a child born in a cave above the Shallowford badger sets but as the Depression deepened, and the national tally of unemployed topped the three million mark, some of Rumble's contemporaries had second thoughts about his hereditary daftness and themselves wrote away for details of Government-sponsored emigrant schemes. Young Sally Pascoe, for instance, the younger daughter of Walt Pascoe and "Pansy-Potter-that-was", left in 1931, writing within six months to say that she had found herself a husband in Ontario. Brother Albert (the hidden persuader of Pansy's second marriage) soon followed her and after him went Esther Eveleigh and her husband George, only son of the blind wheelwright, Willis. Yet somehow the broad outlines of the Valley did not change much, at least not along its northern and western boundaries. Periwinkle remained derelict; nobody would be fool enough to move into Elinor Codsall's farm, where the acres Will had reclaimed from the moor were already waist-high with dock and thistle and the farmhouse, never much shakes as a dwelling, was partially roofless and soggy with damp. In the south-east the Willoughby holding continued to prosper, Francis Willoughby having proved that it paid to specialise and his success with beef had attracted two local youngsters to sign on with him at the new agricultural rates. Deepdene was a very democratic farm these days, Francis and his two hired hands (one a Potter and the other a Timberlake), living a carefree life with a daily woman to cook and clean for them. Master and men made regular jaunts to Paxtonbury where, it was rumoured, Francis learned to lose his woman shyness in the roystering company of young Dick Potter, his foreman. Whether this was true or not Francis must have mellowed since his trip to the Argentine for when teased by Claire on the subject of his bachelor status he had shocked her by quoting the famous Churdles Ash quip – that the act of taking a wife at his age was akin to leaping into a river to quench thirst! Claire thought this evidence that Francis' success had done much to enlarge the son of Preacher Willoughby, the old prophet who had once stalked the Valley warning the unrepentant against an eternity of hell fire.

988

Lower down the long slope, where the unlikely partnership of the lame French Canadian Brissot and the Cockney Jumbo Bellchamber had now entered its second decade, there was hope that the Dell would continue to hold its own, for Brissot was a good farmer and his talkative friend a better salesman. The two Potter girls had sobered beyond local recognition and had even been known to express disapproval concerning the shameless behaviour of girls like Prudence Pitts who, to some extent, had inherited the Potter reputation of tasting every dish in the Valley before making a final decision. Prudence's mother, the once tawny, now greying Gloria, was outraged when the comment reached her as it did within hours. Like everyone else among the older generation she had vivid memories of the Potter girls' reputations up to the moment they had married at the end of the war and it seemed to her grossly hypocritical on their part to quarrel with her daughter's efforts to make the most of the shrinking supply of men in the Valley. She carried her complaint to Henry, demanding that he confront the slanderers but Henry only laughed and said, "Dornee talk so bliddy daaft, woman! Us dorn mind what the Potters zay an' never did! Besides, tiz true baint it? I baint zeed 'er with the zame chap three times in a row!" Gloria complained that he was deficient in family loyalty but she said it without emphasis. During the early years of her marriage she had regarded herself as the dominant partner but the shearing episode, in the disordered kitchen of Elinor Codsall in 1917, had taught her otherwise. Since then she had made one or two half-hearted attempts to regain the ascendancy but all they had earned her was the traditional penance of a valley shrew, a profound reluctance to sit upon anything unupholstered for a day or so. Apart from an occasional flare-up between man and wife, and a brief sulk on the part of Prudence when she was between boy friends, life pursued an uneventful course at Hermitage. Henry's son David, now twenty-six, had his father's and grandfather's reverence for large whites and saddlebacks and in the main he upheld Henry's refusal to abandon traditional tools for one or other of "they bliddy machines". Paul declared that Hermitage was the most old-fashioned farm in the county, a holding that had never heard the stutter of a tractor, or the clatter of the muck-spreader but deep in his heart he counted Henry Pitts his most reliable tenant. Their relationship, always cordial, had now ripened into friendship and they would sometimes ride the rounds together, talking of old friends and old adventures that led all the way back to the rescue of shipwrecked sailors in Tamer Potter's cove. Paul was not alone in his affection for Henry. Everyone in the valley welcomed his broad, rubbery smile and his high-pitched " 'Ow *be* 'ee then?" His aged mother, Martha, still treated him like a child but she respected his judgment as she had never minded that of her amiable husband, Arthur.

Over at Four Winds Harold Eveleigh had made good his pledge to regard farming as a way of life rather than a temporary alternative to the dole queue. The farm had almost regained its pre-war rhythm for Harold's wife, the pretty Lancashire girl, was quick to learn from Marian and from Deborah, her sister-in-law, whereas Harold brought to his new occupation the serious application that had promoted him from private to captain in three years of active service in the East and afterwards in Ireland. It heartened Paul to see Four Winds surface again and shake off its gloomy reputation, and when Harold's son Norman was born he broke his resolution to cease adding to the long roll of his Valley godchildren. Mary, his daughter, and Harold's wife Connie, became close friends and Whiz, his second daughter, taught Connie to ride. Paul never had cause to regret his snap decision; from the time Harold took over his western flank was secure.

The fox's uneasiness when he paused outside the silent, shuttered sawmill was justified, for that very day Dandy Timberlake had died, indirectly as the result of the lung wound he had received in the Dardanelles seventeen years before. He and Pansy Potter had made a good marriage and Walt Pascoe's children found him a tolerant and conscientious stepfather. Walter's eldest son, Tim, stayed on at the mill as sawyer, assisted by Dandy's own child, who bore the name of Pascoe notwithstanding the fact that everyone in the valley was aware that he was the product of a walk home in a storm on the night of the Coronation fête, in 1911. The boys were both single and after Dandy's death their mother lived on at Mill Cottage, where Hazel had settled after bearing Ikey's child in the woods. In spite of having had a largish family and two husbands Pansy held middle-age at bay more successfully than either of her sisters. At forty-nine she was still a very handsome woman, with enormous reserves of Potter vitality, and although she regretted Dandy in the way she had regretted Walt, she made no secret of her intention to marry a third time as soon as opportunity presented itself.

"I made two of 'em comfortable and I baint ready for the rocking-chair yet!" she told Claire, the day after the funeral. "Poor old Dandy was only half the man 'er was before 'er was shot about be they ole

990

Turks but the poor ole toad did his best, bless 'un! Las' thing 'er zed to me bevore he give up was, 'Panse midear, dornee wear no widdow's weeds for me! You show a leg an' get yourself a bit o' winter comfort zoon as may be! Youm too lusty o' woman to run to waste and youm not fifty yet so get out an' about midear, and dornee mind what the gossips zay!' "

Pansy took him strictly at his word. That summer, by means of Dandy's insurance money, she transformed herself and then took a job as barmaid in The Raven where, at first glance, even her oldest associates had some difficulty in recognising her. Her hair, that had been a dead-leaf brown flecked with grey at the time of Dandy's death, now shone like sun-kissed brass and her mouth was as red and welcoming as a coal fire on a cold night. She disdained the slimming diets urged upon her by her daughters but settled for the policy of making the utmost of what she had, lacing herself into a pair of pre-war stays that induced a pink and permanent flush on her cheeks without recourse to rouge. Pansy's new self, indeed, was a study in pink. She wore coral-pink earrings and tight pink blouses that revealed a bewitching cleavage. Round her waist she wore a patent leather belt of piratical design, relieved by a pink rose the petals of which were proof against fading for they had been made by Pansy herself from part of a window-blind, a trick learned in one of the many women's magazines she read. Her black shiny skirt was so tightly stretched across her hips that it would never have remained there when she leaned over to draw beer had she not equipped it with press-studs as large as the bosses on a suit of mail. Her shapely legs were encased in flesh-pink stockings and the heels of her patent leather shoes obliged the new landlord to renew the bar linoleum every six months. He did not complain, however, for the new barmaid proved a transfusion to an establishment that had been going downhill since it was rebuilt to look like a Tudor tithe barn. Bar profits took a sudden upward leap and there was soon civil war between the regular patrons of private and public saloons, both of whom clamoured for Pansy's ministrations. She was an enormous success from any point of view and, next to her figure, the male clientele admired her endearing trick of pretending to be shocked at the remarks tossed at her when she was teetering across the floor with a tray of drinks balanced on the tips of vermilion finger nails. Men began to drift back again from Abe Tozer's forge in ones and twos so that old Abe and Eph Morgan, who were both lifelong teetotallers, soon had it to themselves again and resumed their interminable games of draughts on the anvil. Among the reclaimed was Alf Willis, the wheelwright, who had been blinded by gas on the Somme and had recently become a widower. Alf (christened 'Reginald') was thankful that he had learned a trade before losing his sight and was still able to pursue it as well as draw a disability pension. His wife had been a rather anaemic woman and the strain of living with him during the difficult period of his readjustment had exhausted her, so that now he was looked after by his thirteen-year-old daughter Bessie and occupied one of the new bungalows at the top of the village. Willis could not see Pansy's late-flowering charms but he had not lost his sense of touch and because he was sightless, and everyone pitied him, she went out of her way to be especially kind to him, allocating him a reserved seat in a corner where she had to brush against him every time she served the tables under the window. Her sidelong passage past Alfie became a regular source of Raven ribaldry as the weeks went by for every time she lisped " 'Scuse me, Alfie!" and pressed herself against him, his broad face glowed with unabashed pleasure and Alfie's cronies would pretend to offer cash for his seat. Encouraged by this, or by Pansy's thoughtful offer to relieve his daughter Bessie of the nightly walk to The Raven to fetch Father home, Alfie soon proposed and Pansy promptly accepted, so that Smut, whose experience of his sister went back a very long way, declared, " 'Er had it in mind from the day she took the job, the crafty bitch!" but at once qualified this implied criticism by adding, "She'll play the game by 'un tho'! Panse usually does, pervidin' o' course, that Alfie's minded to keep 'er served!" Presumably Alfie was for, to the delight of The Raven's regulars, Pansy presented her astonished husband with a ten-pound boy thirty-seven weeks to the day he led her to the altar. It was her sixth child and she celebrated her fiftieth birthday two months before delivery. Although inclined to be a trifle vain of her record (three husbands and progeny by each) she worried over the possibility of being replaced at the pub but her employer hastened to reassure man and wife that Pansy was irreplaceable and promised to keep open her job if she liked to come in and serve five evenings a week. Her wages and tips, added to Alfie Willis's earnings and pension, were more than enough to offset the cost of a regular baby-sitter so she soon made a triumphant reappearance, still in pink and showing, if anything, rather more cleavage. Dandy would have been delighted and so, perhaps, would Walt, whose happiest hours had been spent in the court where Pansy now reigned.

That was the period Claire called "The Marriage Year", the twelve months between the spring of 1932 and the early summer of 1933, and Pansy's marriage to Alfie Willis was only the final peal of wedding bells in the Valley. Mark Codsall led off by marrying Liz Pascoe, Pansy's eldest daughter and taking the cottage her mother vacated on moving into the pub. Then, to the vast relief of Gloria Pitts, Prudence accepted Young Honeyman, manager of the Home Farm, and the least hopeful of her many suitors. Gloria Pitts suspected that it was panic rather than Honeyman's relatively good prospects that inclined her daughter to choose Honeyman instead of one of her flashier beaux, young men with oiled hair who had raced her about the countryside in their second-hand cars and lingered so long in the passing bay of the lane. She was, in fact, on the point of demanding of her daughter specific information regarding matters that had come to her notice when Prudence announced the engagement. She went on to say—as if it was the most natural thing in the world—that they had "decided not to wait and would be married almost at once" and that "this was Nelson's idea because he was scared I might change my mind!" Young Honeyman's name "Nelson", derived from his father's obsession with the Navy League in pre-war days and only a threat on his wife's part to shame him at the christening, had prevented the boy being named Horatio-Grenville-Hood, Nelson being a compromise. Gloria kept her suspicions to herself and Henry, who liked Honeyman, swore that he would give his daughter a "rare ole zend-off, like us had in the old days yerabouts". He kept his promise. Over a hundred guests attended the wedding and Squire himself proposed the principal toast, for Prudence was one of his tribe of godchildren. Everyone declared that Prudence was the most radiant Valley bride of recent years and the junketings at the Hermitage that day were reminiscent of a less sophisticated era. There was an open-air breakfast and a procession down the track to the festooned honeymoon car, the couple riding the first stage on a farm-waggon drawn by drag-ropes. After that there was rice, old shoes, nosegays and silver horseshoes all the way to Sorrel Halt, where Nelson and Prudence entrained for "an unknown destination" that proved, disappointingly, to be Ilfracombe. Young Honeyman could hardly believe his luck when he found himself alone in the compartment with the most popular girl in the Valley but Prudence, carefully combing confetti from her red-gold hair, looked more relieved than ecstatic when he shyly showed her the marriage licence. It had been, she reflected, a very close call. Notwithstanding the falseness of the alarm that had precipitated the engagement,

Henry would have had her marry Ronnie Stokes if she had not had the sense to keep her suspicions to herself and the odd thing was, now that she had Nelson, she actually preferred him to Ronnie. He was rather stolid she supposed, and his courting tactics were years behind the times, but he was healthy, high in the Squire's good graces, and had no eyes for anyone but her; as to the techniques, she could supply those as part of her dowry.

Within two months of Prudence Pitts' marriage Whiz, Paul's second daughter, announced that she was engaged to a Flight-Lieutenant Ian McClean, recently attached to the new R.A.F. base, a mile or so east of Paxtonbury. She told her parents that they would probably be married before Ian left to complete a tour of duty in the Near East. Whiz had had almost as many local admirers as Prudence but the name of "Ian" was new to Paul, although not to Claire who, although appearing to pursue a policy of extreme tolerance, nonetheless maintained a watchful eye on the least tractable of her three daughters. Up to the moment Whiz announced her news Paul had always pretended to be piqued by his daughters' disinclination to "look about with an idea of settling down" and had seemed, indeed, to take it as an affront that nobody had asked either one of them for her hand. Now, to Claire's amusement, he began to bluster, demanding to know if "this Ian McShane was present to make a formal request". Whiz laughed outright at this. "Good heavens, of course he isn't!" she said, "what year do you think this is? 1066? And anyway, you might as well get his name right. It's 'McClean!'—a small 'c' and then a big one!"

"I'm obliged to you for pointing that out," Paul grumbled, disconcerted when he sensed that Claire shared her daughter's view in that he was behaving like a Victorian papa, "but how the devil am I expected to approve of a prospective son-in-law I've never even met?"

"You have met him," Whiz said coolly, "he was one of a tennis party here at Whitsun but even if you hadn't it wouldn't make much difference, would it? After all, I'll be twenty in April."

Claire stepped in quickly now. She had no illusions regarding the lack of communications between Paul and all his children, with the exception of Simon, whom he had come to understand of late, and Mary, whom he adored. Between him and Whiz there had always existed a zone of neutrality that extended, to some extent, to their youngest child, whom he accused her of spoiling on account of her striking good looks.

994

"Listen you two," she said, briskly, "what's the point of quarrelling over the poor boy? Ask him to lunch tomorrow and let him speak up for himself! I'm sure your father will like him, Whiz, he seemed a polite, level-headed sort of chap to me," and with that Whiz drifted off to bed, reappearing at noon the following day with a uniformed Scot in tow, a cautious, thick-set young man, with sandy hair, good if rather distant manners, and a profound disinclination to engage in small talk. Paul spent an uncomfortable half-hour with him alone but neither of them mentioned Whiz and as the day wore on Paul realised that his daughter had been quite right—there was little expected from him one way or the other. Everyone of her generation was obviously equipped to make their own decisions, even at the age of nineteen. He noted with approval, however, that Ian McClean was neither fool nor weakling but a man who kept his emotions, if he had any, double-locked and chained and instinct told him that this kind of man might get the best out of a girl who had been inclined to put on side after so many successes in the show ring. Ian, it seemed, had a little money of his own, an income of about three hundred a year plus his pay and was due to fly off to the Suez Canal zone in September, returning the following spring. After that, he said, he would move about here, there and everywhere, sometimes in this country but more often in far off places like Hong Kong, Singapore, the Arabian Gulf and India. Whiz, once married, could accompany him to most of these places but not all, for there were certain areas closed to the wives of junior officers. When, at last, the subject of the actual wedding nosed itself into the general conversation and Ian bucked at delay, Paul had a gleam of insight, reading into the young Scot's insistence on a short engagement determination to stake his claim before Whiz went out of circulation, and he felt a certain sympathy for the man. Although by no means as beautiful as young Claire, Whiz (Ian gravely referred to her by her given name, Karen) was pretty enough to prove a bad risk and, like her twin brothers, she had the knack of attracting about her a small court of admirers, some of whom Paul reminded himself, were far less eligible than this taciturn Celt. In the end he found himself wholeheartedly approving the match and it made him chuckle to see the subtle change that the prospect of marriage wrought in Whiz, for she became almost affectionate towards him as her moods ranged from one of brittle excitement to a kind of dithering uncertainty, not as regards Ian but the trivia inseparable from weddings. Claire, however, seemed to have an instinctive knowledge of how to cope, both with her daughter and with the mounting tensions in the house as the day approached. She was quite prepared, he noted, to organise the most spectacular wedding ever witnessed in the Valley but by mid-August Whiz had backed down, settling for a comparatively quiet affair, with a mere sixty guests, most of them family or local equestriennes. Mary and young Claire were bridesmaids (Paul thought he had never seen anyone look quite so enchanting as Mary in her sprigged organdie and long, Victorian mittens) and in the absence of any close friend at Ian's temporary base, Stephen, the more talkative of the twins, stood as best man. To Paul's relief he was not called upon to entertain the groom's family. McClean's father had died with most of the Cameronians at Loos, and his mother a year or so later, in India. Aside from a few R.A.F. acquaintances from the camp the groom was represented by a formidable aunt from Perth, whose speech was as broad in its way as old Mrs. Handcock's, and who seemed to regard everyone living south of the Cheviots as something midway between a tyrant oppressor and a confidence trickster. Paul made the mistake of trying to draw her out on Scottish history but was soon sent packing with a flea in his ear, Aunt Elspeth being unaware that the last blood-letting between English and Scot had occurred at Culloden Moor, nearly two centuries ago. Picking up his dignity he wandered among the guests, feeling rather like a lucky amateur exhibitor at a professional flower show whose entry, the bride, had unexpectedly won first prize. He was consoled, however, by the presence of the wanderers among his brood, finding a sympathiser in Simon who dismissed all religious ceremonies as "social opiates", a view that did not seem to be shared by his wife Rachel, who was clearly enjoying the occasion and looked, Paul thought, attractive in her simple blue dress, wide straw hat and elbow-length gloves. Simon told him a little of their life in the mining valleys and shipyard towns and it all sounded desperately dull and unrewarding but he noticed that the boy seemed to be maturing under the stresses of his nonstop guerrilla war against what he called The Establishment. He was, for instance, more restrained in his judgments and more disposed to make allowances for the terrible complexities of building a social system that guaranteed fair shares for all; he was also prepared to find room in his brave new world for a revitalised agriculture and for this small blob of jam Paul was duly grateful.

The Pair were as irrepressible as ever. They came skidding up the drive in a huge car of American make, scrambled out and at once proceeded to fill the house with noise and strangers, of the kind that attached themselves to the twins wherever they went. They must have introduced him to a baker's dozen of their friends but he forgot their names instantly and could only think of them as carbon copies of his own boys and of each other. The young men, he noticed, used a laconic argot of their own that was almost a foreign language and drank a great deal without becoming the worse for it; their womenfolk—who reminded him of a bevy of medieval pages in a Flemish picture—had nicely waved peroxided hair, doll-like faces and were not above letting themselves be pawed in public, although they received these attentions absentmindedly, as though they were thinking of more important matters like their next hairdressing appointment. He found himself wondering how many of them were virgins, or whether their silly talk was no more than the backlash of Victorian and Edwardian cant. It was Henry Pitts, another wanderer in this post-war wilderness, who put these thoughts into words when he said, watching the young people milling about at the reception, "Us is vallin' behind, Maister, and there baint two ways o' lookin' at it! There's a bliddy great hairy fence betwext them an' us, an' whereas the wimmin zeem to be able to jump it when they've a mind to, I'm jiggered if I c'n nerve myself to take off! I can't never be zertain zure what's on t'other zide!" There really was such a fence, Paul thought, and the only gap in it accessible to him was Mary, who seemed to have a password enabling her to move to and fro between the generations but preferred, on the whole, to stay in the safe old world that she could not have recalled, having been no more than three when the gates slammed on it in 1914.

One big surprise did emerge from the wedding, the totally unpredictable recapture of Stephen by his old flame, Monica Dearden, the Archdeacon's daughter from Paxtonbury, whom Paul had almost forgotten. Claire met her in the Cathedral Close a week or two before the wedding and sent her an invitation, saying that it was at Stephen's request, which was not true although he had asked after her in one of his infrequent letters. Paul could never imagine either of the twins married. They seemed so self-sufficient, so satisfied with their hectic round of golf, jaunts to the Continent and business luncheons with potential suppliers of scrap iron in the North and Midlands. He was wrong, however. Before the end of Claire's "wedding year" both were brought into the fold, Stephen by the elegant Monica, who seemed to combine the unlikely roles of blue-stocking and playgirl, Andy by a little Welsh nurse whom he met during a spell in hospital after a road crash in one of his dashes down to South Wales in search of scrap.

997

Paul liked both his new daughters-in-law, although he was slightly intimidated by Monica Dearden and bored by the Archdeacon's wife. Stevie and Monica were married and off on their honeymoon to Venice before he had the slightest inkling that Claire had, in fact, manipulated the match and regarded it as a personal triumph. He learned of this the day of the wedding in Paxtonbury Cathedral, when Stevie and his bride had gone, and he and Claire were driving back over the moor after seeing the couple off.

"Well, I think I managed that very neatly indeed!" she crowed, "and moreover my part in it will establish just the right relationship between mother-in-law and daughter-in-law!"

"I suppose you're boasting of your share in helping that dull, well-meaning old duck to cope with all those beaming clergymen?" he asked and she laughed and said, "Oh dear, Paul, you really are dim about some things! Haven't you realised I arranged that wedding singlehanded?"

He stopped the car on the first stage of the descent, pulling off the road not fifty yards from the point where, more than twenty years before, she had helped him to adjust himself to all that had happened as a result of the suffragette riot in Westminster Yard.

"What the devil are you talking about, Claire. *How* did you arrange it? Stevie has been blowing hot and cold about that girl for years and it seems to me all that happened is that he got a fresh look at her when she turned up at Whiz's wedding, looking extremely fetching!"

"Well, to begin with it was *me* who invited her with that end in view," she said, "and after that it was *me* who told Monica where he was based and advised her to manufacture an excuse to bump into him!"

"Good God, you did that?" he exclaimed, genuinely amazed. "But why? What made it so important to you to see Stevie married?"

"I don't see why a mother shouldn't work as hard to get her sons safely married as to find someone suitable for her daughters! As a matter of fact sons usually stand in greater need of the push, especially ours! In this case, however, I had a special incentive. I was determined to split the partnership and now Andy will have to get married too, you see if I'm not right!"

"Have you anyone special in mind?" he asked but his sarcasm was tinged with admiration.

"No," she admitted, seriously, "but he'll find someone and soon for he won't enjoy himself nearly so much without Stevie as an audience! Don't you realise that most of their trouble stems from the fact that they have been playing 'Betcher!' ever since they were toddlers?"

He knew it of course but her talent for practical intrigue startled him. He said, "What exactly did you do? Apart from the invitation and the tip-off?"

"Oh, I had a long and rather blushing talk with Monica when she came home after 'meeting' him in Birmingham. We met by appointment at The Mitre and, as the saying goes, she emptied her heart, poor dear! Well, it wasn't in vain, I told her to leave it all to me and that I'd have Stevie roped and delivered in less than a week!"

"Knowing The Pair that was a damned reckless offer but I'll wager the cards fell your way. They usually do in the matrimonial field."

"No," she said, unblushingly, "as a matter of fact they didn't, or not at first. Those two maniacs of ours got involved in the crash the next day. You remember—the first we heard about it was Stevie ringing up after being discharged from hospital."

He chuckled, recalling the way she had exploited his own helplessness shortly before he proposed but his only comment was, "Well, go on, finish it."

"In a way I *was* lucky. Andy was crocked but Stevie escaped with scratches, tho' I daresay I should have thought up something if it had been the other way round."

"You bet your life you would! What precisely *did* you do, you scheming hussy?"

"I just mentioned, ever so casually, that there was talk of Monica Dearden marrying Alderman Gratwick's son—you know, the ironmonger one—and then I told Monica to get young Gratwick to take her to the Territorial Ball. I knew Steve would rise to that bait and sure enough he did! He was in Paxtonbury Town Hall before the orchestra had tuned up and now—well, now they're on their way in a gondola!"

"Well, I'll be damned!" he said. "Did it occur to you that if the marriage goes on the rocks you'll be directly responsible?"

"No, it didn't and doesn't! He's kept that poor girl on tenterhooks for years and with all the opportunities he must have had that must mean something! Monica played up much better than I expected, however, and in view of her ecclesiastical background that was rather surprising."

"Just what do you mean by that?"

He saw that she was not only enjoying her triumph but also the prospect of shocking him. "Well," she said, "knowing The Pair, and the fact that, behind their display of fireworks, they are basically decent human beings with tender consciences, I encouraged her to let Stevie go almost the entire length of the garden path providing she didn't let him into the summer-house! It seemed to work. She brought him to the boil in less than a month!"

She had often amused him with her half-baked schemes, and her transparently counterfeit logic, but never quite so much as on this occasion. He said, when he had done laughing, "You're an absolute travesty of a wife and mother! I don't know where you get it from—certainly not from your father—and I can't bring myself to believe from your mother either. Now, I suppose, you'll go to work on Andy?"

"No," she said, "I don't have to. You see, Andy will go wife-hunting himself now that he's thrown on his own resources. Stevie was always the real leader."

"And how about Mary?" he asked cautiously but there was no mischief in her eye as she replied, very levelly, "Mary? Oh, she's your problem, not mine! That's one for you to tackle without any help from me!"

He had no need to be reminded of that and thought briefly of Rumble Patrick, now in Alberta doing God alone knew what, but still, he was sure, holding Mary's heart to ransom. She had been very quiet of late, an island of serenity in a sea of to-ing and fro-ing, willing to smile at the antics of her brothers and sisters but not to contribute much to family high jinks. How far did one's parental responsibilities extend? His eldest, Simon, was now twenty-eight, and his youngest, Claire's favourite, was fifteen and quite the daintiest creature he had ever seen. Of the six of them three were now "safely" married and two of the others likely to be in no time at all but of the six not one had inherited his obsession with the Valley, or was prepared to get behind it and help to push into the future. Simon, inheriting Grace's wider outlook, was already immersed in the troubles of the world at large and perhaps, like his mother before him, secretly despised the limits Paul had always set upon himself. The Pair made no secret at all of their impatience with his parochialism and had reverted to type, deriving more satisfaction from a discarded boiler than a good harvest. As to the girls, Mary loved beauty and seemed content to seek it at home but suppose Rumble Patrick turned up "whispering of lands where blaze the unimaginable flowers"? Then, he supposed, she would turn her back on the Valley without another thought and he would never see her again, except for an occasional visit from somewhere thousands of miles away. As for the remaining two, Whiz and young Claire, he expected nothing at all from them. Whiz was married anyway and the Valley had never been more to her than a place to cross at breakneck speed on a mettlesome horse. Claire, the baby, whom his wife and almost everyone else spoiled outrageously, would find nothing more absorbing in a Sorrel pool than her own reflections, so that, taken all round, they were a disappointing bunch. Claire said, with a smile, "I don't need a penny for them! I suppose you were wondering whether they've been much of an investment after all?" and he replied, without rancour, "Something like that but a man is a fool who expects a dividend from flesh and blood. I look for my return in the by-products!"

"Such as?"

"I've still managed to hang on to most of my capital, haven't I?" and he made a wide sweep with his hand; she realised that he was not referring to money.

III

Claire made good her boast. Within three months of Stevie's marriage to Monica Dearden, and their settling in what Paul thought of as a rather vulgar Edwardian house in a suburb of Birmingham, Andy appeared and presented his intended with the flourish a magician uses when he whips the curtains aside to reveal the missing lady still in one piece. Claire did not say "I told you so!" but her glance implied it when Andy came bounding into the hall one crisp, February morning, having driven through the night from the Welsh valleys where, he crowed, he had gone to rescue his Margaret and whisk her over the border like a marauding moss-trooper in search of a bride.

His choice presented Paul with no puzzles. Contemplating Margaret he reflected that perhaps, after all, at least one of his sons had inherited something from him, for at Andy's age Margaret Highton's ripeness would have made instant appeal to him. The girl's qualifications for an extrovert's bride were all on show—a happy-go-lucky temperament, a trim little figure, Celtic sensuality and an obvious capacity for enjoying the bonuses of life, good food, pretty clothes, lots of laughter and a regular roll in the hay. She was small and neat, with exceptionally pretty legs and a fashionable pageboy bob framing a fresh, gently rounded face. Her brown hair reflected firelight in the way sunshine teases the polished husk of a chestnut and she had large, brown eyes, a *retroussé* nose and a wide red mouth that turned up at the corners and would probably stay that way if kissed often enough. Paul took to her at once and Claire, watching him, understood why; Margaret had promise and to Paul a woman without it was not worth a moment's attention. Claire, for her part, was fascinated by the girl's Welsh lilt that suggested sad Celtic songs sung round the camp-fires of forgotten kings with long, unpronounceable names full of "u"s and double "d"s. She thought, the moment she saw her, "Well, I'd say Andy was luckier than Stevie! She's got something, apart from pretty-prettiness and I daresay they'll have a string of handsome children and enjoy watching them grow up!" and she left Paul to show Margaret around while she listened to Andy's unlikely account of his courtship that began in the casualty ward of a cottage hospital in Glamorgan, and ended a few days ago with Andy storming the dispensary at three in the morning, being ejected by an indignant night sister, and returning at breakfast time to persuade Margaret that, until the British paid its nurses better wages, they didn't deserve to have any! Claire said, laughing, "Did she take much persuading, Andy?" and he said not after she had seen the ring that he had purchased from one of his seedier contacts in Cardiff, getting a seventeen-and-a-half per cent reduction on condition he gave "Solly" (who dealt in scrap metals as well as expensive jewellery) twenty-five shillings a ton "over the odds" for the rusting remains of a coaling barge!

"I hope you didn't tell her as much as you're telling me!" Claire laughed, "for the idea of a man bargaining for my engagement ring would have made me think twice at Margaret's age!" but as she said this she felt a wave of affection for him that embraced not only Andy, and his sexy little Welsh girl, but the whole of Andy's generation who seemed so miraculously liberated from the conventions of the preceding generations. The very notion of buying an engagement ring from a scrap dealer, rushing into a girl's place of work, and carrying her off like a freebooting soldier at the sack of a city, would have been preposterous in her day and she remembered the scandal that had led to her virtual exile from the Valley throughout the years of Paul's first marriage. She could never agree with Paul and other traditionalists that all post-war changes were regrettable. A few were but the majority were long overdue and one was surely the disappearance of hypocrisy among the young, giving them the freedom to act on impulse and indulge their natural appetites without artlessness. Andy had simply looked at this plump little partridge and, after prodding her here and there, had decided that he liked what he saw and here they were, as good as in bed together, and enjoying every moment of it! "Damned good luck to them!" she thought. "I wish Paul and I had been able to use that kind of short-cut! It would have saved us both a good deal of misery!" and she bustled off to order a special dinner but found time during the afternoon to enter Andy's engagement into the diary immediately under recent entries devoted to Whiz and Stevie.

The April wedding was a very simple affair, more intimate and relaxing than either of its forerunners. Margaret's father, a retired miner, made no excuses for his inability to do more than provide a modest reception in the institute adjoining the local chapel and Paul found both him and his wife refreshing contrasts to Ian McClean's formidable aunt, and the patrician dignity of the Archdeacon and his wife. Claire, watching them talking and laughing together, was amused and relieved, for although she freely admitted to being a bit of a snob she would have hated to witness her husband or children putting on side. These were his kind of people, she reflected, whose company he had sought ever since she had known him and they brought out the best in him, whereas the twins seemed equipped to move freely on all levels of society. She noticed, however, that Stevie's wife, Monica, tilted her nose an inch or so as she took her seat at the trestle table and toyed with lettuce salad, and thought, briefly, "It's odd they should have been so close all their lives but split on their choice of wives! I still think Monica was absolutely right for Stevie and there's no doubt at all that the little Welsh girl is ideal for Andy, but will this prove the fork in the road that The Pair have travelled all these years?" Then she found herself looking directly into the eyes of Simon, saw that he was smiling and realised that they were sharing the same thought. He came over and said, in his diffident voice, "It's all right, Claire, you don't have to worry! If Monica tries to snub her Stevie will sit on her, hard!"

"There's not even privacy in thought when you're around, Simon," she said. "Sometimes I think you must be Ikey, reincarnated."

"Well, at least I was trained by Ikey," he said. "Thank your lucky stars he never taught Gov the noble art of thought-reading!"

She laughed, feeling, as always, relaxed in Simon's company. He was mellowing a good deal, she thought, since leaving home and marrying that earnest but tiresomely intense wife of his and she wondered if Paul was right when he said Simon was growing a shell. She held to her point, saying, "How can you be so certain? Stevie might even agree with her!"

"No," he said seriously, "the twins are vulgarians but just ones! They'll make money, pots of it I daresay, but they'll never let money make fools of them. How could they? You and Gov had them until they were seven and you know what the Jesuits say!"

It struck her that he was paying her a rather gracious compliment, that he was saying, in effect, no one who had grown up at Shallowford would find it easy to lose the classlessness that had been such a feature of the Valley since Paul had reigned there but she was never less than honest with Simon and said, "I can't take a ha'porth of credit for that, Simon! I was a terrible snob when I married your father."

"Oh, I daresay," he said, cheerfully, "but you were humble enough to learn from him and loved him enough to want to. As a matter of fact, Claire, that's something I've always admired about you two, you borrowed tolerance from one another, whenever you needed it! I suppose that's what made the marriage so successful."

"Stop it," she said, "you'll have me blushing in a minute!"

"So what? If you can't fly a happy marriage like an ensign on a wedding day when can you? You don't have to apologise for it, it's rare enough these days."

"Yours seems to be working out well enough."

"Yes, but 'well enough' doesn't win prizes, does it? You have to remember Rachel took a beating over Keith. She'll never quite get it out of her system."

She would have liked to have asked him to be more explicit but at that moment the bridal pair took their seat at the top table and Stevie, as toastmaster, called for order. She continued to ponder his rather enigmatic conversation and it bothered her so much that she missed half the fun of the send-off, when all Margaret's neighbours converged on the pavement shouting expressions of goodwill that sounded like Celtic battle-cries. It was during the inevitable anti-climax, when they were returning to the hotel to say their good-byes and disperse, that she was able to draw him aside again and say, "I've been thinking . . . it was Paul's second go, you know, and that gave me a flying start . . ." and she stopped, remembering too late that she was addressing the son of Grace Lovell. He noticed her confusion and rescued her with a smile and a squeeze of the elbow.

"There was a big difference, Claire. Rachel was in love with poor old Beanpole Horsey but you and Paul . . . it was in the cards from the start! I was the product of a misdeal!"

"And a very lucky one for me," she said quickly and kissed him, remembering how she had once felt impelled to kiss Ikey Palfrey for roughly the same reasons. It was strange, she thought, as she watched Simon and Rachel drive off in their battered Morris, with the tatters of the last election posters still adhering to the doors—strange and a little spooky how vividly that boy recalled Ikey Palfrey, whose understudy he had always been.

And yet, taken all round, she felt elated, reflecting that if the success of her marriage was so obvious to him, the son of the woman she had replaced, it must be doubly so to everyone and perhaps this was something to crow about after all. Her elation bubbled over when they were packing for the drive home and she said, suddenly, "Look here, Paul, why do we have to go home? It's spring, and not all Wales is as down and out as this place! Why don't we take a few days off?"

He never liked staying away from the Valley for more than a day or two but she saw by his smile that she had anticipated him and suddenly remembered why. Last year had been their Silver Wedding anniversary but there had been no celebration for it had clashed with Prudence Pitts' wedding, then the whirl of Whiz's engagement and marriage and, within weeks, Stevie's marriage to Monica Dearden. He had always promised her some kind of celebration and now it was far too late to arrange one they could share with all their old friends in the Valley.

"I had it in mind to suggest we slipped off and did some overdue honeymooning ourselves," he said. "Maybe it's all this nuptial syrup we've been dosed with lately! Suppose we 'go back', just for the weekend?"

She knew what he meant by "go back". Never, in the twenty-six years of their marriage, had they revisited Anglesey, where they had spent their first fortnight together in 1907, and now, Heaven help them both, it was 1933, and the same season of the year. She said, eagerly, "I'd love that, Paul! And Mary and young Claire have never seen the mountains. Why not drop a line to Honeyman . . ." but he interrupted her, saying, impatiently, "Don't be so damned silly, woman! Do you want to hawk proofs of fruitfulness all over the island? Mary and Claire can tour the mountains under their own steam if they want to and if not they can go home by train!" and he went downstairs to telephone the Home Farm and tell Honeyman that he would not be back until early the following week. In the meantime Claire had collected the two girls to tell them of the change of plan and was annoyed to find herself blushing when she said, in response to her youngest daughter's "Why can't we come along?" "I don't think your father wants that, my dear . . . it's . . . well . . . it's his idea of a Silver Wedding trip, and you know what a sentimentalist he is!" and she was vastly obliged to Mary when she helped her out by saying, "I think it's wonderful for you both! Come on, Claire, we'll check the trains and if there's one tonight we'll take it, no matter what. I only hope North Wales is a bit less dingy than South, Mother!"

"Believe me, it is!" Claire told her. "From what I recall of it it's not unlike home!" and she hurried away to redistribute the contents of the cases.

They set off that same evening, driving almost due north, putting up for the night at a little hotel among the low hills of Radnorshire and moving on after an early breakfast along the southern valleys of Snowdonia. She took her turn at driving the big Austin so that he could look around a bit and sometimes they travelled for miles without exchanging a word but both, in their own way, were enjoying the experience of being cut off from the Valley, with the family turmoil of the last hectic months behind them. As they crossed Menai Bridge, meeting a stream of returning Easter traffic, he said, "I don't recall seeing anything but a horse and trap up here in those days. One might think it was a century ago judging by externals!" and she said, with a smile, "How about internals? Do you feel your age? No hedging, tell the truth without bragging!"

"Mentally I do," he admitted, "but not physically. That's the result of making the effort to ride and walk as much as I could. The youngsters will have to pay for this tearing around in cars when they come up to the fifty mark. No, I don't feel more than forty. How about you?"

"Forty-one," she said, "and a year or so younger after dark!" and he gave one of his sudden schoolboy laughs and pinched her knee as they turned inland towards the north-west corner of the island, where they had stayed the second and more rewarding week of their honeymoon in a farmhouse, after making an excuse to vacate a hotel full of Methodist clergymen assembled for a conference. Over here there were changes to be noted but they were not remarkable, a limited amount of new buildings on what had been open country, a few caravans in fields on either side of the unsurfaced road leading to the bay where, twenty-six years before, they had bathed and picnicked all day, without seeing anyone but children with shrimping nets. The old Roman road beyond Tynygongl had not changed at all and wild flowers, rarely seen in the Sorrel area, still grew in profusion among the outcrops of rock about the Druids' Circle. Everyone about here spoke Welsh and used English with difficulty, and, to their delight, the old farmhouse was still there, overlooking the bay, a snug, Tudor homestead, squatting so close to the soil it looked as permanent as the rocks that broke the shallow soil and made ploughing here a tedious business. They knocked on the door with some trepidation and the old woman who answered them, and gave them a polite Welsh greeting, was the same who, as a woman in her early forties, had bustled about her unexpected guests seven years before the war. She did not recognise them, of course, but when Paul explained who they were she broke into a torrent of Welsh, rushed to the dresser and produced a photograph album containing a yellowing snapshot taken with Paul's box camera on the porch, a picture of himself and Claire taken at his direction and with, he recalled, a great deal of fussing on the landlady's part. They all peered at the blurred images and Claire said, "My goodness! Look at my waist in those days! And I'd quite forgotten you had a moustache, Paul!"

The woman, Mrs. Hughes, told them that her husband had died several years before and Paul said, "You had a son. He was called . . . wait a minute . . . David, and couldn't speak a word of English! Does he still carry on farming?"

"No, David was took," the farmer's wife replied, unsentimentally, "he was took an' never come home, you see!" and she pointed to a photograph standing on the oak sideboard showing David in khaki presenting bayoneted rifle in the inevitable pose of Kitchener's volunteers, when they rushed into studios within hours of being kitted out. "There's not so many of the younger ones left around here," she went on. "Those who come back look you had different ideas, and crossed over to the mainland. There's no money to be earned farming and Evan's land iss sold off, mostly. My daughter Dilys's man, Owen, he works what iss left, but there are no children whateffer! There's a pity it iss but things is that changed, don't you know?"

Paul consoled her by saying his part of the world had changed too and from similar causes and it consoled him to think that post-war problems were universal among the farming communities. The old woman asked if they had a family and when Claire told her two boys

1007

and three girls she exclaimed with delight and patted her, as though she had been a prize-winning cow, so that Paul had to turn away to hide his grin and leave them together, lifting the cases out of the car without asking if the farm still accommodated visitors.

It was soon arranged, however, and he was directed to the same low-ceilinged bedroom with its enormous, locally-made oak bedstead and view of the sea through the mullioned window. He thought, as he began to unpack, "I suppose, taken all round, we've been a damned sight luckier than most! Hardly more than one in three of the chaps who were young then would be alive now, or, if they were, sound in wind and limb," and then Claire came in and said, practising Simon's thought-reading trick, "I felt desperately sorry for the old dame, Paul. It's almost as though we were flaunting our survival! That boy of hers married before he went off and got killed but she hasn't any grandchildren and no prospect of any."

"She's still got the farm or what's left of it," he said, "and that's more than some of them have. Do you really want to stay?"

"Yes," she said, "but more for her sake than ours. It's all rather chastening, don't you think?"

"It always is," he replied, "and I imagine that's what they mean when they say one shouldn't look back." Then, seeing her raise her arms to take off her little straw hat and noting, notwithstanding her continual complaints regarding her waistline, that her figure was very trim for a woman a few months short of fifty, he was glad they had returned and catching her round the waist, said, "I don't give a damn if I do feel smug about us! We've earned the right to preen ourselves a bit, Claire!" and he spun her round and kissed her mouth with an urgency that was communicated to him not only by an awareness of where they stood but also by the thought that there was a limit to the span when a man could kiss his wife as though he was still courting her.

It was this thought, and the deliberate nostalgia they were invoking, that injected a special kind of gaiety and youthful abandon into the brief period they remained in hiding at Tynygongl. Paul, for his part, found himself recalling some of the spring tides of the years. As he lay in bed watching her undress, for instance, he remembered with amusement his impatience with the fiendish complexities of her 1911 Coronation finery, in the hotel room overlooking Green Park and again, when she teased him by prolonging her going-to-bed ritual involving creams and lotions, he saw her as the laughing girl who had thrown her cap at him in the long, dry summer of 1902. He did not communicate these memories to her, preferring to enjoy them in private but deduced from her lightheartedness that she had equally stimulating memories of her own, for she came to him each night with an enthusiasm reminiscent of the time they had spent together in Crabpot Willie's cabin during his final leave from France, encouraging him to use her not gently and diffidently, as he had done when they first lay in this room together, but as though she too had heard a clock ticking in the bowels of the old house.

It was within these terms of reference, or something like them, that she communed with herself while he slept. Had their marriage never had much more than a strong, physical basis, and if so would the colours fade altogether when time finally caught up with them and remembered ecstasy was all they had? It was a sombre thought but the terminus still seemed immeasurably far off, for they derived more satisfaction from one another than when they were under thirty and far more than when they had first come here, she as nervous and gawky as a Valley milkmaid, he curbed by the failure of his first marriage. How quickly and finally those initial handicaps had been overcome! And how smoothly had they arrived at a stage where intimacy was achieved on her part with the uninhibited enthusiasm of a Potter wench, and on his with the casual expectancy of an uncomplicated creature like Henry Pitts? Well, if that was all there was to it, a bed and the procreation of healthy children, she couldn't help it and, what was more to the point, she didn't care! Not a hoot! Not one of his hearty smacks on the bottom signifying his impatience to have her naked in his arms caressing every part of her body. It was not quite what she had expected of marriage in that beginning but it had worked and that was all that mattered.

She turned over, tucking his arm under her breasts and returned the wink of phosphorescent light in the bay.

CHAPTER SIX

I

THE year of weddings ended with a funeral. Paul and Claire arrived back in the Valley on May Day, the first anniversary of the wedding of Prudence Pitts, to learn that Jimmy Grenfell had persuaded Mary to shift him to a Paxtonbury Nursing Home, declaring that there were limits to the hospitality one man could claim from another, and that it was bad taste to die in an old friend's bed. He must have known that Paul would never have agreed to him going, and would, indeed, have done all in his power to dissuade him from submitting to another operation, so he took advantage of his hosts' absence and convinced Mary that her parents would have fallen in with his plan. Paul hurried over to see him the day before his operation and found him very weak but as cheerful and resigned as ever. The history of the Chartist Movement was proofed, he said, and all that remained now was for Paul to send the MSS. to the publishers and countersign a document he would find in the drawer of the desk on which it lay.

"What is it, Jimmy?" he demanded. "I must know what I'm signing before I promise anything."

"Only some mumbo-jumbo drawn up by the agent," Grenfell told him, "allocating the royalties, if any, to you."

"Dammit, man," Paul protested, "I don't want to profit by your death! Haven't you any relatives you want to pass it to?" but Jimmy said all his relations were staunch Tories who would be embarrassed by a book on a revolutionary movement. "In any case," he added, "the money isn't a straight bequest, it's an endowment. I'm told the book is expected to do well, both here and in America, and I had an idea that I could flatter you and, at the same time, make a post-mortem gesture! It ought, over the years, to produce enough to give one boy, or girl for that matter, a decent education and send them on to university. It's laid down in the deed that if any such person is found, and named by you, that they read modern history and philosophy. You'll administrate, of course, so I leave it to you to see the clause is followed."

"That alters things," Paul said, "and I think it's a splendid idea! What kind of geographical limits had you in mind?"

"Only that whoever takes advantage of this is the child of one of your tenants, or, if there are no local takers, the child of one of our old stalwarts in the constituency, someone who stood with us through the heat of the day."

"Well," Paul said, "let's hope you can tackle the paper work yourself, Jimmy," but Grenfell said, "You don't believe that, Paul! I'm a gonner and you know it; I only agreed to this operation because I knew it would mean curtains. There's really no point in hanging on any longer and becoming a damned nuisance to everyone. I've already had a couple of years more than I expected and I owe that to you, to Claire, and that charming daughter of yours. I'm afraid this is goodbye, Paul."

Paul said nothing. He was aware, more than anyone, of the pain Jimmy had endured over the last few years and could no more regret his release than he had regretted old John Rudd's more merciful death not so long ago. Both men, he reflected, had been bonny fighters and it was pitiful to see them grow entirely dependent on others. He said, finally, "It's been fun, Jimmy, and an adventure in its way, ever since you bowled up the drive in that yellow trap, wearing that damned silly billycock hat and looking more like a squire than I ever did! I've learned a hell of a lot from you; it was you who kept me in touch with what was going on outside and stopped me from becoming dangerously parochial."

"Taken all round you had the right idea from the beginning, Paul," Grenfell said. "I didn't always think so but I do now."

"Well, I believe we're getting on top of things, Jimmy," and as he said this it struck him that, in his final moments, old John Rudd had also been concerned with the future of the Valley, as though each of these men had donated part of themselves to a task that had absorbed his own interests throughout the greater part of a lifetime. He left then, with the certainty that he would never see Jimmy Grenfell again and neither did he. Within twenty-four hours they rang through to say the patient had died under the anaesthetic.

Parson Horsey called as soon as the news got around and said Grenfell had asked him if he could be buried in the Valley and Paul was more impressed by this than by Grenfell's eccentric legacy.

"He wasn't a local man, he belonged up North," he told Horsey. "Jimmy didn't set foot in the Valley until he got himself adopted as

Liberal candidate at the beginning of the century. What did you promise him?"

"I told him we would certainly find room for him when his time came," Horsey said. "He's one of the few politicians I ever met who based his election addresses on the Sermon on the Mount. There aren't so many of his kind left, Mr. Craddock. Will Wednesday suit you? His grave will be the first in the new annexe, beyond the wall."

Paul remembered then that Horsey had recently acquired a triangular plot east of Churchyard Lane, directly behind the church and its overcrowded graveyard. It brought home to him that the rate of wastage in the Valley was accelerating and, for the first time perhaps, he realised that the Craddocks, when their turn came round, would not lie in the same acre as old Tamer Potter, Edwin Willoughby, John Rudd, and Norman Eveleigh, of Four Winds.

He completed arrangements with the parson and went into the office to record Grenfell's death in the diary but when he turned the book to its first blank page he saw that Claire had anticipated him and had written, under Monday's date, *"Today James Grenfell, M.P. (with a single brief break) for Paxtonbury from 1904 until 1929, and who spent his last years in Shallowford writing his 'The History of the English Chartists', died at the age of sixty-five years. He was a good man, genuinely regretted by everyone in the Valley, and particularly so by the Squire, whose close friend he was during the whole of that time."* The entry touched him. Claire had never been one for national politics and what she had written underlined the respect and affection she felt for Grenfell as a man, rather than as a politician. There was nothing he could add to the entry so he went upstairs to the room Jimmy had occupied since retiring to Shallowford. To his surprise he found Mary sitting at the desk, so absorbed in the proofs of Jimmy's book that she did not hear him come in. He knew his eldest daughter was an enthusiastic devotee of lyrical poetry (she was the only female member of the family, he would say, whose mind strayed outside a woman's magazine) but he had never before seen her reading a political book.

She said, noting his smile, "All right, so it's a new field! But it's one of the most absorbing books I've ever read. Have you read it?"

"In manuscript. What makes it specially interesting to you?"

"The way people lived, the working people and the fight they had. You don't hear about that kind of thing in school history lessons, at least I never did—just kings, battles and treaties."

"You must have had a very old-fashioned history teacher!"

"No, seriously," she went on, folding her hands and clasping her wrists, a gesture he always thought of as Mary's equivalent of putting her hands in pockets, "what staggers me is that it wasn't all that time ago, less than a century. Your father, and Grandpa Derwent, must have been alive, and realising that makes everything so much—well—relevant, even things about here if you see what I mean?"

He did not but he was anxious to; he had never held a conversation like this with any member of his family except Simon and Simon always retreated into bluebooks and party pamphlets.

"How do you mean, 'even things around here'?"

She said, cautiously, "Well, you know how we've always teased you about having a bee in your bonnet as regards the Valley . . . ?"

"You don't have to apologise. As regards that my skin is several inches thick! How does the Valley come into it?"

"This book, which I began dipping into simply because I liked Uncle Jimmy made it so clear that there have always been two kinds of people in charge, those out for all they could get and those—well, those like you!"

It was, he felt, one of the most roundabout but acceptable compliments he had ever received, certainly out of the mouth of one of his children and it confirmed his prejudice in favour of this willowy, inarticulate, sensitive girl, whom he had always preferred (and been ashamed of preferring) above her brothers and sisters. He straddled Jimmy's chair and said, gravely, "I see. It looks as if it has finally got through to you. It's about time I must say! Does this mean the rest of the family still regard me as half-dotty?"

"Oh no," she said, earnestly, "not dotty, just . . . well . . . just the tiniest bit eccentric about the Good Earth, and The-Man-With-Mud-On-His-Boots! And in any case, you mustn't include Mummy in the family write-off. Your word has always been gospel to her."

"For quite different reasons, I'm afraid. Well, you'd better finish it and if you want to talk about it after you can, any time. Incidentally, 'The Good Earth' is an article of faith with me and always has been ever since the day I came here."

"Why did you come here, Daddy?"

"Why?" He had to think hard. It was a question he had not asked himself for more than twenty years now. He said, at length, "Because of a dream, I suppose, a dream I had when I was in hospital after the Boer War but it's far too complicated to recount and right now I have to arrange Uncle Jimmy's funeral."

"*Will* you explain? Some other time?"

"Yes, if you like but it will only convince you the bees must have been in my bonnet when I was born. It's too late in the day to expect them to swarm!"

"I'll hold you to that," she said and turned back to the proofs while he went out, quite forgetting what had brought him there but musing on the conversation for the rest of the day as he sat telephoning and writing to everybody who might want to attend Jimmy's funeral.

It happened that, about this time, there was a very active bee in Claire Craddock's bonnet but it was a recent lodger and she had yet to come to terms with it. Within a month of Jimmy Grenfell's death, however, it led her to pay one of her rare calls on Doctor Maureen.

She saw Maureen almost every day, for the Lady Doctor (as everyone still called her) lived on alone at the lodge that she used as a surgery, but it was a long time since Claire had had occasion to seek her professional advice. Unlike a majority of Maureen's patients Claire was deeply ashamed of ill-health and had, in fact, never sought a doctor in her life except during confinements. She went now much against her will, convinced that she was approaching, if not entering, the dreaded Change.

She had returned from the Welsh holiday in splendid health but ever since had lacked an appetite and had been subject to mild spells of dizziness when she got up in the morning. Nothing to worry about, she told herself, but enough to set her thinking. Her horror of The Change (she always saw it in capital letters) dated back to her childhood when she had overheard a doctor tell her father that this had been a contributory factor to her mother's death, inasmuch as it had probably warped her judgment at the fatal jump. Yet this half-recalled episode from a time of trouble was not the main cause of her anxiety. She was aware of others, with sources far closer the surface, and they were all rooted in a fixation about the milestone of fifty.

On her fiftieth birthday she took a good long look at herself in the dressing-table mirror and the scrutiny failed to reassure her, notwithstanding recent memories of the second honeymoon. She saw facial muscles that were undeniably sagging a little, wisps of hair over the ears that had outgrown their last rinse in a fortnight, eyes that, in her view, had lost a good deal of their sparkle, lips that seemed slightly less full and—this was certainly no fancy—an inclination to put on

1014

weight notwithstanding years of dieting. She weighed herself on the bathroom scales and at once regretted it, for the needle proclaimed an impossible increase of two pounds in just over a week. She said, stepping down, "It's wrong! The damned scales need seeing to!" but Paul and the children noticed that she did not open her birthday presents with much enthusiasm and when they teased her about it she had to make a genuine effort to pretend not to mind. A few days later, telling herself that she needed a tonic, or change of diet, she walked across the paddock to catch Maureen between morning surgery and her forenoon rounds, knowing that with no time to spare Maureen would probably confine herself to questions and a prescription. Maureen called from upstairs, "Hullo there! Don't tell me you're for surgery! I've just got rid of the last malingerer!"

"Come on down," Claire said shortly, "I'd like a word with you!" and Maureen said, "*Professionally?* You must be joking!" Then, judging Claire's tetchy mood from a distance, "Go along in then, I won't be a moment," and Claire went in, looking round distastefully at the cheerless little room with its dog-eared calendar, row of hard chairs and worn oilcloth. There were no magazines; Maureen did not encourage her patients to linger.

"You do look a bit off colour," Maureen said as she bustled in. "I noticed it as a matter of fact but knowing you I wasn't going to be the first to mention it!"

"You noticed it?"

"Oh, it's nothing, I can tell you that from here! I daresay you've been over-dieting. Overtiring yourself too—all those family upheavals on lettuce leaves and charcoal biscuits! Don't say I didn't warn you!"

"I think it's more than that," Claire said, ignoring her banter. "I think it's The Change and if it is you can give me a tonic and some advice!" but in Maureen's presence her confidence returned. They had been friends now for over a quarter of a century and if there was one thing Claire knew it was that she could count on directness and no "Now-now-there-there" talk from Maureen Rudd. She spoke of her occasional dizziness, her increase in weight despite dieting, loss of appetite and, above all, recurring spells of depression. Maureen was as blunt as she had expected. "Well, I daresay you're right, girl, but there's very little I can do about it! There are tablets, of course, but I never had much faith in 'em. It's more of a mental than physical readjustment and its effect on a woman is often regulated by willpower and plain commonsense. You've got more than most women around here and should get through it easily enough, providing, of course, that you don't mind me having a word with Paul on the subject. His attitude is important, or will be in your case. He mustn't mind you flying off the handle every now and again!" She looked at Claire with amused affection. "Cheer up! Most of the women round here who reach the point of no return are delighted. I can tell you that for nothing!"

"I don't suppose you'll believe me," Claire said, "but Paul and I have never tried not to have children, not once!" and Maureen, with an appreciative chuckle, replied, "I certainly do believe you! What kind of a family doctor do you think I am?" and then, because Claire's mood made her seem a great deal younger than fifty, she put her arm round her, saying, "Getting old inside a family circle is nothing to be frightened of! It's getting old alone that's the real spectre!" and Claire suddenly felt ashamed of her neglect and made her promise to come up to supper, remembering that she must be very lonely in the evenings now that John was gone, and her son rarely returned to the Valley after qualifying and taking a practice in Scotland.

She remained cheerful for a spell but then the steady increase in her weight, and a tendency to tire very quickly, began to disturb her again. The tablets made her sleepy by day and restless at night, and she found that she was morose on wakening, so that it was with less hesitation that she paid her second call on Maureen and submitted to a check-up despite a protest that all she really needed was sanction to throw "the damned tablets in the dustbin". Maureen said, sharply for her, "If there's one type of patient who makes me swear it's the sort who come here with their own prescriptions and expect me to sign 'em! Get your clothes off, girl, and let's take a good look at you! There's not a thing wrong with you that isn't in your mind and I must say you surprise me! Next thing you'll be joining the procession of middle-aged women who come in here insisting they have cancer of the breast!"

Maureen's cavalier handling of her patients was notorious so she submitted with good grace as Maureen made her check, grunting a little, Claire noticed, when she stooped, so that the patient got one back, saying, "You sound as if you could do with a diet yourself! You must turn the scale to something around twelve stone!"

"Twelve-three to be exact," Maureen said, straightening, "but I'm not pregnant and you most certainly are, my girl!"

The certainty that Maureen must be joking irritated Claire, who thought this was carrying a joke too far. She sat up, swung off the cold leather couch and said, "For heaven's sake, Maureen, I'm not one of your silly hypochondriacs who has to be bullied into . . ." but then she stopped, for something in Maureen's expression, as she stood with arms akimbo and back to the window, made her pause. Maureen said with a shrug, "You can protest as much as you like but it's a fact, so don't let's have any more snivelling about grey hairs, and youth calling from the far side of the hill! You're three months pregnant and there's an end to it! I don't know whether I should congratulate you or ask Parson Horsey to ring the church bells!"

Then she waited. Half-minute elapsed before Claire could make any kind of reply, for her tongue was stilled by the confusion of mind resulting from such a preposterous explanation. Pregnant, at fifty-plus! Pregnant, after a gap of how many years since the birth of her youngest child?—1918—and now it was 1933, and young Claire would be sixteen next birthday! She said, in a voice so strained and uncertain that it seemed not to belong to her, "There can't be any mistake? It's a certainty, you say?" but she did not seriously challenge the fact, reasoning that Maureen would be very unlikely to fall into such an error after seeing her through all her previous pregnancies, including an unsuccessful one as long ago as December 1907. She said, hoarsely, "What is it, Maureen, a . . . kind of . . . freak-miracle?" and Maureen, who seemed to be extracting a certain amount of sardonic amusement from the situation, retorted, "Good God, woman, of course it isn't! I told you you were exceptionally healthy and it isn't all that uncommon when a woman has already had a string of children. Nature's last fling, I imagine, and it will be the last if that's any consolation!" but Claire continued to sit balanced on the edge of the couch, gasping and blinking, as though she had just been dragged from cold water. Maureen said, curiously, "Once you've got over the shock will you be pleased? Will Paul, do you think?"

"How would I know that? It's all I can do to . . . to absorb it! I feel as if—well, as if I'd been caught out in something shameful," and then, correcting herself, "no, not shameful exactly, but something horribly embarrassing, a practical joke in very bad taste that didn't amuse anybody!"

Maureen, who thought she knew her patient as well as anybody, was not only baffled but a little worried. She said, "Look here, Claire, I've always thought of you and that hulking husband of yours as two people marvellously adjusted to one another, a couple who had the sense to give their instincts a chance, instead of relying on one or other

1017

of these damn silly books on sex and psychology that people are churning out nowadays! I haven't been wrong, have I?"

"No," Claire said, slowly, "you haven't been wrong, Maureen. I've always found joy and fulfilment in the physical side of our marriage and I think he has too, but—how can I explain? We don't have to . . . to proclaim it from the housetops do we?"

"You were proud enough of the others," Maureen said, not liking this turn of talk at all, "so why worry about a few sly giggles at your age?"

"Age is the operative word," Claire said, beginning to dress at a speed that suggested she could not be out of the surgery quickly enough. "The 'others' are all grown up, and going their own way, so to the devil with starting all over again, and having Paul's attention directed elsewhere! I've earned the right to have him to myself, haven't I?"

She went out with a rush, not even pausing to say good-bye and Maureen, who was rarely astonished, looked after her with mouth wide open. "Great God!" she said aloud, as she watched Claire cross the stepping stones to the ford instead of turning for home, "I do believe the woman's madly jealous of her own womb! Her appetite for that man has never had anything to do with children at all—they were just by-products!" and suddenly she felt angry with herself for her total failure to plumb the emotional depths of a patient she had always thought of as an open book and a well-thumbed book at that. She thought, "Well, I don't know how Paul will react but he's going to hear about this from me and I hope I can find him before she does!"

She was lucky, meeting Paul in the drive before Claire returned from her breathless walk along the river road and, to Maureen's relief, he let his sense of humour take over, once he had ridden out the shock. But although glad enough to hear him laugh she deliberately sobered him, saying, "Right, but see that you straighten your face before she comes to you with the news, and I don't have to tell you to pretend it's first-hand when you get it! You're going to need more tact over the next six months than I've ever seen you display!"

"Oh, stuff and nonsense!" he said. "I daresay it's staggered her but once she's got used to the idea she'll be delighted. She isn't likely to have a bad time, is she?"

"Physically, no, she's always produced children with less difficulty than most women but what I'm trying to prepare you for is something quite different. I'm beginning to get an inkling of what's bothering her

1018

and I must be half-way into my dotage not to have spotted it before. How can I put it without seeming fanciful? Listen—in the old days she had youth, and the vanity that goes along with youth. The children were close enough together to amuse one another, the house full of women to attend to them and you were out and about your business most of the day. It's very different now. The children are grown up or scattered and the staff, such as they are, won't do a stroke more than they have to! On top of that you're now of an age when you'll be more likely to spend more time at home but, above all, remember that when Claire looks in the glass she sees a middle-aged woman whose figure isn't going to be improved by another child! If you think I'm exaggerating ask yourself how she behaved towards the children when they were toddlers."

"She was a damned good mother to them."

"I'm not questioning that but what was her overall approach to them? Was it mother-hennish?"

"No it wasn't! Now that I come to think of it it was always pretty casual."

"Right, well I'm asking you to think about that and for your sake as much as hers."

He said, wrinkling his brow, "You know it is odd, Maureen, I don't think I've ever remarked on it before but there was something undemonstrative about her approach to the kids, all except young Claire that is."

"Don't be taken in by that," Maureen said, "I've noticed her approach to Claire myself and it's no more than an inclination to bask in the reflected glory of the child's looks and poise! No, Paul, we might as well face it. She fell head over heels in love with you the minute you rode into High Coombe yard when you were youngsters and all the years between have done nothing but pile coals on the fire! That's why you're in this pickle, isn't it?"

"You really think of it as 'a pickle', Maureen?"

"Well, let's put it another way, it's a six months' walk through a mine field and all I'm saying, as your doctor and friend, is watch where you put your feet, lad!"

It was as well that he had this warning for Claire's humour during that summer and autumn baffled him to such an extent that it was difficult to believe he was sharing bed and board with the same woman. It was not that she was quarrelsome or intractable—in some ways he would have described her as subdued and withdrawn—but that he, and everyone else about Shallowford, found her wildly unpredictable. Sometimes she would show a spurt of temper over a trivial omission on the part of one or other of them but at other times she seemed to have lost contact with the family. In between these two extremes she was unsure of herself to a degree that recalled the very earliest days of her marriage, when she found herself in authority over such well-established limpets as old Mrs. Handcock and the unsmiling Thirza Tremlett. Towards early autumn, when her pregnancy had ceased to cause much comment in the Valley, she took to wandering off alone in the old yellow trap (Paul had forbidden Mark Codsall to let her saddle a horse) and the curious would watch her drive out along the river road to the moor, or across the pasture track to the head of the goyle that led down to Crabpot Willie's cabin and the beach. Paul was nervous of these solitary excursions but, after a word with Maureen, he made no protest and had to admit that they had a calming effect on her nerves, for she was often more herself when she returned to preside over family high tea at six. Then, as the evenings drew in, she took to retiring early and would be asleep when he came upstairs but she rarely slept until dawn and sometimes she would be up by the time he awoke, pottering about the house before the earliest riser was astir. Not always, however. There were occasions when he caught a swift and disturbing glimpse of the pressures a fancied insecurity was exerting on her mind, as when he awoke one night to find her out of bed and crouched on the floor beside him, her head touching his pillow. He reached out to turn on the bedside light, thinking that she must be unwell and had blundered round to his side in an effort not to disturb him but she dragged his hand from the bulb and then began kissing him with a desperation that stirred his pity. He said, gently, "What *is* it, dear? Tell me what's worrying you so badly? I'll help if I can, we'll all help . . ." but he learned very little even then, for once she had climbed back to bed he realised that it was not words of comfort she wanted so much as reassurance that her swollen body was not repugnant to him. He gathered this from her impatient dismissal of his half-hearted protests and his silent possession of her, without either the tenderness or the humour that had attended their love-making in the past. After that he followed Maureen's advice to drop the half-invalid approach and a subdued Christmas came and went, the family assembling and dispersing without anyone making more than an indirect reference to her condition. She seemed to approve of this collective disregard of the embarrassingly obvious yet she remained withdrawn, so that Paul found himself noting the passage of days with the attentiveness of a castaway or a prisoner.

When at last it happened—on the 30th of January, 1934—he was away from home, just as he had been in 1910 when Thirza Tremlett met him at the gate with news of Mary's arrival. Henry Pitts' wife, Gloria, had died whilst on a visit to her sister in Cornwall, the victim of her own obstinacy and a virulent influenza epidemic, for Henry said she had been severely troubled with her chest throughout the winter but had insisted, against his advice, on making the trip to the remote village where she had been born in order to attend her aged mother's funeral early in the New Year. She caught a severe chill at the graveside, developed pneumonia and had been too ill to recognise him when he responded to an urgent summons to the bedside. To his surprise and indignation he learned that Gloria had expressed a death-bed wish to be buried in the family grave near her original home and it required the united pressure of all Gloria's Cornish relatives to overcome his objections to such an act of disloyalty. Paul, who thought it his duty to attend Gloria's funeral, found Henry's grief somewhat mitigated by his wife's eccentric preference to lie in foreign soil, and on their way back from the funeral tea (it was, Henry grudgingly admitted, a very sumptuous one) he voiced his complaints with what seemed to Paul an exaggerated bitterness.

"Tidden right!" he kept saying, "an' tidden zeemin' that 'er should lie down yer, half-way across the bliddy country! Never 'eard o' such a thing, not in all me born days! A Pitts, buried all the way down yer, among a horde o' flamin' Cornishmen! Tiz 'er own wish I know but 'er won't rest easy! There's been a Pitts in the Valley for I don't know how long and 'er's the first to be buried out of it! 'Er was alwus obstinit mind but I never dreamed 'er was so mazed about Cornishmen!"

Henry's rumbling complaints took some of the sting out of the occasion as they recrossed Bodmin Moor in driving January sleet and Paul, a tolerant listener, was tempted to confide some of his own troubles to his old friend, if only to distract him from his grievance but he thought better of it and held his peace until they drove into the frontier town of Launceston, where he left Henry to console himself with a tankard of beer and telephoned Shallowford to say he expected to be home in two or three hours.

Mary answered so quickly that she might have had the receiver to her ear. She said, quietly but incisively, "Come straight away, Daddy! The baby's arrived! It's a boy and everything's fine but we need you!"

Paul said, with a gasp, "Your mother is all right? You aren't keeping anything back?"

"No, honestly. Maureen says it was a very straightforward affair but . . ."

"To hell with what Maureen says! Maureen told me there was no possibility of the baby arriving until partway through February! When was he born?"

"It started soon after you left."

"Why the devil didn't somebody get in touch?"

"We couldn't. I wasn't sure of the address and there wouldn't have been a 'phone, would there?"

"No, you're quite right. Give her my love and tell her I'll be with her in about three hours. And Mary . . ."

"Well?"

"How has she taken it?"

Mary said, carefully, "It's a bit odd, Dad. You know how she's been but I thought—well, when the baby actually arrived I thought she'd change."

"And she hasn't?"

"No, she doesn't seem interested. Just hurry along, she'll be all right when you show up!"

He replaced the receiver and stood looking across the hotel lobby at the sleet slashing down on the little square and leaping up from the cobbles. He felt tired and dispirited, finding no pleasure in the news although, secretly, he had been hoping for another boy. He thought, impatiently, "Claire's right! We're both too old for this kind of nonsense and it's time we both had a little peace and quiet!" and then homesickness came down on him, as it always did when he was more than an hour's ride from the Valley, and he called to Henry to hurry along and went out into the rain to the car.

It was like playing an old, old scene over again, with words and actions clearly remembered but all the spring and gaiety gone from the step. She was in the same room and the same bed and the only difference, as he was quick to notice, was that the baby's cot was not by the window as it had been on every previous occasion. She looked, he thought, extraordinarily fresh and young but there was still hostility in the eyes, or perhaps it was not hostility but simply an unconscious expression of the same baffling impatience with life he himself was experiencing. He said, with an effort, "I'm sorry I wasn't here,

Claire, I could kick myself for not trying to find a public 'phone in that Godforsaken country. I ought not to have gone, I suppose, but Henry is our oldest friend left around here and he wanted me at a time like this. Mary said it was quick, like the others. Is that true?"

"Yes, it was very quick," she said. "I suppose you're pleased it's a boy?"

"Yes, I am but all I really wanted was to get it over and done with."

He wanted badly to use this opportunity to talk frankly to her, to make some attempt to climb the fence that had grown up between them during the drift of the last few months, but she would not give him the necessary encouragement so he remained standing by the window, feeling more shy and gawky than when he came here to visit her after the birth of the twins. What they had lost, he decided, was the sense of humour that had always been able to bridge these embarrassing moments. When she asked if he had any name in mind he said, groping wildly for laughter, "I don't know . . . something to single him out from all the others ten laps ahead; how about 'Tailpiece'?" The small joke was a failure. After a wretched pause she said, settling herself, "Yes . . . well you had better go and look at him. After all, he's all yours, Paul!"

He would have protested and perhaps, stung by injustice, hit back in some way but he remembered in time that she was at a disadvantage and that if this tension between them persisted it must be met and faced as soon as she came downstairs. He went along the corridor to the old nursery where, to his astonishment, he found Thirza Tremlett sitting beside the cot making the obligatory noises she had made over the cots of all the children up to the time she left the Big House and became nanny to John Rudd's boy. She was wearing her faded nanny's "uniform" and for some reason her presence cheered him a little.

"Now what the devil prompted you to rejoin the column?" he asked, remembering that Thirza had married after leaving Maureen's service and had not been seen in the Valley for some time past. Thirza told him that she had heard through old Mrs. Handcock that Mrs. Craddock was "expecting again" and had applied for reinstatement after she and her husband had "gone their seprit ways". He recalled then that Thirza had ultimately married a Whinmouth sailor who had, it was rumoured, been courting her since the bustle was in vogue. He said, looking down on the fat little bundle who was gesticulating with a small, business-like fist, "And what do you think of this surprise packet, Thirza?" She replied that she supposed he would do but pointed out that, with a gap of fifteen years between him and his youngest sister, "he was zertain zure to be spoiled" and he might depend upon her to do her best to see that he wasn't.

" 'Ave 'er got a given naame yet, Squire?" she asked and Paul said no, it was something he would have to think about, and because Thirza was more of an old friend than an employee, added, "Mrs. Craddock doesn't seem particularly pleased with him, Thirza? Have you any idea why?" She did not seem in any way embarrassed by this mark of confidence, considering, no doubt, that it was her prerogative to pronounce upon such matters. "Well," she said, unsmilingly, "I baint surprised to learn that! Mebbe Mrs. Craddock thinks tiz high time 'er was done wi' such tiresomeness!" and the look she gave him as he withdrew was loaded with reproach.

He drifted off to seek Mary, wondering whether "tiresomeness" on the part of Thirza's sailor-husband had played its part in the failure of the marriage but he was far too grateful to see a fragment of the old pattern restored to resent the implied rebuke. Mary was not to be found so he went up across the long orchard, conjuring with names and recalling the fun he and Claire had naming the other children, sometimes amusing themselves for nearly a week before settling on Andrew, Stephen and Mary. "Karen", the name Whiz never used, had been Claire's choice, he remembered, and she had hit on an equally fanciful name for young Claire which he had rejected on his return from France, in 1918. As he went down the lane towards the western tongue of the woods confidence began to return to him, a bonus, perhaps, of crossing a landscape where every tree and every contour was as familiar to him as his own features. "I daresay it's something to do with the metabolism of the body" he told himself, still pondering the baffling changes in Claire, "and as time goes on it will sort itself out, like everything always does in and about the Valley." After all, there had been times when he had despaired of finding his own way, and plenty of occasions when whole families, like the Eveleighs at Four Winds, had been written off but something always turned up to adjust the balance in the way spring converted this belt of trees from a witches' backdrop to a maze of green tunnels. He turned away from the woods and went down the long, sloping field to the house, just as a watery sun came out and the sky over the Sorrel cleared for a few moments. It looked quiet and workaday down there, with wavering columns of bluish smoke rising from the twisted chimneys and a line of limp washing on the cord that crossed the kitchen garden. Peace returned to him and with it the memory of the fat little bundle in the cot knuckling his fist and looking up at him through eyes slitted against the light. "John!" he exclaimed suddenly. "It will be good to have a John around the place again and if there is a more English name for a farmer I've yet to hear it!" He went on down the slope feeling almost cheerful again.

II

"Almost" was as far as he got that season. As spring came round Claire edged back into the family circle but far too guardedly for Paul's liking, so that imperceptibly their roles were now reversed, with his own edginess causing his daughters and the men about Home Farm to tread warily, whereas it was Claire who held the watching brief that had been his throughout autumn and winter. He was aware of the sources from which his surliness stemmed, not merely his semi-estrangement from Claire but a long, rumbling quarrel with circumstances that held any number of new problems in reserve, depriving him of the mental ease he had enjoyed in pre-war days when the world was sane and the wary peace he had enjoyed in the years leading up to the slump, when his children were growing up around him and he was still young enough to respond to a challenge. Yet, even now, there existed no open quarrel between him and Claire. She had abandoned her solitary expeditions in the trap and was, in fact, less inclined than he was to fly off the handle when something displeased her, but what exasperated him most was her neutral attitude to the baby and her tendency, at least in his view, to give free rein to young Claire who was now, as Mrs. Handcock would have said, "of an age", which meant she was too old to be smacked and too young to respond to reason. It was no consolation to reflect that Claire had never been over zealous in her duties as a mother, that she had left all the fussing to people like Thirza, Mrs. Handcock and old Chivers, the groom, for he remembered also that the children, one and all, had always been able to make her laugh and arouse her interest, so that her relationship with them had been that of an elder sister rather than a mother and he had never quarrelled with this. As to the new baby, she breast-fed him, as she had all her children but that was all. She took no pains to conceal that he was little more than a tiresome addition to household chores and Paul sometimes wondered if the baby's plainness had anything to do with her attitude. At this stage in their lives all her children had a pink and white prettiness whereas John, a sturdy child and one that gave little enough trouble, was surprisingly sallow and even Thirza had to admit that his wrinkles had something in common with those of old Aaron Stokes, the doyen of the Valley, still to be seen outside his cottage on fine mornings making bird-tables to supplement his pension.

When the baby was about six months old Paul stopped by the lodge one morning seeking further advice from Maureen but was not surprised by her impatience with his complaints.

"Women are often withdrawn after childbirth," she reassured him, "so in the name of God don't be cultivating another fancied grievance!"

"Now why the hell should I go looking for trouble?" he demanded but she said, with a laugh, "Oh, I'm not saying it's deliberate on your part but she tried your patience pretty sorely all winter so this is your subconscious getting its own back!"

Neither he nor old John Rudd had ever had much patience with Maureen's pseudo-Freudian explanations for human oddities of one sort or another, so he protested that she was now talking nonsense, "Damn it, you admitted yourself that she was jealous of the poor little beggar before he arrived. Now that I've come round to your point of view you back down on it and feed me a lot of psychological claptrap! It would have made John hoot with laughter and you know it!"

She said, regarding him with affectionate amusement, "Oh, you and my John were two of a kind. Everything you came up against had to be black, white or khaki and stated in two-syllable words! Well, thank God, we've learned something about human beings since those days and the plain fact is life isn't that simple! A thing like this could have gone either way. A majority of women producing a healthy child at fifty would have whipped up their husbands' temper for quite another reason!"

"How?"

"They would have screamed with triumph, turned their backs on their man for good and gone to goo-gooing over the new arrival and if it had taken Claire that way we should have had you in here with an even bigger chip on your shoulder! Very well, you've asked for it. I'm going to give it you straight whether you like it or not! How often have you made love to the girl since the package was delivered?"

"Now you're just a nosy old woman dredging for prurient details but if you don't wheedle them out of me I daresay you'll get them from her so I'll tell you! We haven't been man and wife since John

1026

arrived, and as things are right now we look like heading for honourable retirement!"

"Then you're both bigger fools than I took you for!" Maureen replied. "There's not the slightest chance of her conceiving again and setting up a new record in the Valley!"

"I don't think it's that, Maureen."

"Then what is it? Are you both sulking, at your age?"

He said, trying to state his case as honestly as he could, "We never have been lovers from habit and what's more I can't remember a time when an occasion wasn't mutually prompted and mutually enjoyed but the impetus has gone somehow. Maybe it's burned itself out and the very lack of it is poisoning our relationship."

"But that just isn't true," she said with an earnestness that half-convinced him in spite of himself. "This is no more than a phase and both of you are prolonging it artificially. Listen here, Paul, I know an old stick-in-the-mud like you finds it difficult to take psychological factors into consideration but they do exist and very much so in a woman as sensual as Claire and a man as vigorous as you! The years ahead of you could be your happiest yet for I never saw a better-matched or a healthier pair, but you are letting your prejudices react against one another and if you don't do something about it you might have a real issue on your hands before you've realised it!"

"What do you suggest? That I don't wait for the propitious moment and demand my rights, as they say?"

"No, I don't," she said emphatically, "for that might easily result in your making an ass of yourself and coming back here waving your pride at me like a head on a pike! I know it's asking a lot of you to be subtle—neither you nor my John ever really understood the damned word—but subtlety is your cue now. Stop bellyaching and start courting and I promise you the propitious moment will appear without any prompting on your part, you great numbskull!"

"Well," he said slowly, "you're beginning to make sense but even if you're right I don't see how a thing like this can be resolved by a tumble or two on the bed," and she sighed, so deeply that he had to smile.

"You can be so *thick* sometimes!" she said. "Who am I, a woman who married an elderly man when I was over thirty, to be giving you and Claire lessons in this kind of thing? I'll spell it out for you. Claire Derwent, as I've told you before is crazy about you, not as Squire of Shallowford but as a man—M.A.N.— and the only man she has ever enjoyed or ever wanted to and when I say enjoy I mean it! I remember telling John more than once that she goes limp at the knees every time you enter a room and women like her don't change, not even when they produce 'proofs of affection' as they used to say, at the age of fifty! Well, here she is, back in the race again you might say, but how are you giving expression to the relief she must be feeling? By holding back out of mistaken consideration and by working off your bad temper looking for qualities in her that aren't there and never were, not even when she was a day-old bride! You remember what I told you in the beginning of all this? That the children are no more than by-products to her, this last one especially, but if she ever suspects that baby is causing a permanent rift between you you'll really have something to blow about! You haven't put this in words to her, I hope?"

"No, I haven't said anything but Mary and Thirza must have noticed her attitude to the kid."

"Let them both mind their own damned business! One's made a mess of her own marriage and the other is still waiting on Mr. Right! This concerns no one but you and Claire, and my advice is to stop expecting her to sit opposite you with a shawl on her shoulders and rock the cradle! Dammit, when I think of most of the middle-aged couples you don't deserve your luck, either of you! There won't *be* an old age for you or her unless you open the door to it!" She paused for breath and concluded, "Have I made any impression on you at all?"

"Yes," he said, "I think maybe you have but I'm not one of your wide-eyed witch-doctor patients, who swallow everything you prescribe without question. I like to be told the ingredients and make up my own mind. Would you give me a hint how to start courting at fifty-four? You ought to know something about it, John was about that age when he married you. What was his line?"

"He pretended to anticipate my every wish. It was only later I discovered that his technique was simplicity itself. He would pay out three yards of slack and pull in two-and-a-half when I wasn't looking and I loved him for it! You start with an advantage no man deserves. Claire's already broken and the jerks won't even surprise her!"

"Well," he said, "you won't find that in any of your Psychology-for-the-Million textbooks but I suppose it's the kind of advice I was looking for and I'll take it. There's a big supper-dance at the Paxton-bury Town Hall on Thursday, the annual 'do' of the County Dairy-men's Association. The girls wanted to make it a family excursion but I turned them down. I've suddenly changed my mind."

"Quite proper!" she said. "Why the hell should the kids have all the fun? Has she got a new frock to go in?"

"No, but she's got her eye on one!" and he walked out almost jauntily so that she called after him, "Don't waste my surgery time coming back here with a progress report! I live on your doorstep, remember?" and slammed the door feeling justifiable pride in her achievement but regretting that old John wasn't on hand to hear an account and share the joke. Time and again he had prevailed upon her to break confidence with the patients he liked as well as those he did not.

The dance was in full swing when they arrived about nine o'clock and the two girls at once disappeared to find their friends, leaving Paul and Claire to begin the evening with the Military Two-Step, this kind of item predominating an event organised by and for the middle-aged rather than youngsters. By Paxtonbury standards it was an impressive gathering and reckoned the event of the season, if Paxtonbury could be said to enjoy a season. Most of the local landowners were present, including the Somerset Gilroys, near relatives of the Heronslea family, who had recently let their property and gone to live in France. Humphrey Gilroy asked Claire to dance and Paul found himself partnering Gilroy's wife, a statuesque woman who seemed to tolerate him solely on account of his relationship with Rose Barclay-Jones, organiser of the well-known two-day event in Gloucestershire and described by Mrs. Gilroy as "a dashing gel", which struck Paul as a curious description of his gaunt, fifty-nine-year-old sister-in-law. After they had shed the Gilroys, danced a waltz, and watched Mary win a spot-prize (young Claire seemed to have adjourned to the car-park but Paul, in tolerant mood, did not remark on it) they sat out eating cold turkey and Claire, who had seemed nervously elated ever since he had insisted on buying her a green velvet dance frock she had admired in a Cathedral Close window said, "I suppose you know all about the Dairy Queen Contest? They have the preliminary canter tonight and we've never had a finalist all the years it's been going."

"Yes," he told her, he knew all about the Dairy Queen Contest. Old John Rudd had always referred to it as "The Heifer Parade", declaring that its popularity lay less in its avowed purpose of advertising Britain's farm products than in the opportunity it offered farmer-judges from all over the provinces to enjoy a close-up of young women in bathing costumes. "I'd forgotten it was on the programme," he admitted and she said, doubtfully, "Honestly? You aren't holding out on us?" and then laughed so that he at once linked her expectant air with the mysterious flutter in the family when he had announced that they would be attending the dance after all.

"Look here," he demanded, "what *is* all this? What gave you, young Claire and even Mary the jitters when I suddenly changed my mind about coming tonight?"

"Oh, never mind," she said, smiling, "just sit back and wait! Frankly I thought you were double-bluffing us but it seems I was wrong!" and before he could dig deeper the drums rolled, the floor cleared, and the Paxtonbury Town Clerk stepped on stage to proclaim in a town-crier's voice that there would now be an interval while Mr. Humphrey Gilroy, C.B.E., and three other judges representing four Westcountry counties, would select Devon's entry for the national final of the British Dairy Queen of 1934.

It was then, as the curtains swung aside to reveal a dozen contestants grouped in a half-circle on the dais, that Paul experienced one of the sharpest jolts of his life. Fourth from the right, looking like a young Aphrodite in her scarlet swimsuit and ermine-trimmed cloak, was his youngest daughter, and Claire, watching her nervously, saw his body go taut as he exclaimed, "Good God! It's young Claire! Whose idea was this? And why the devil wasn't I consulted?"

She said, rather desperately, "Shhh, Paul, not here—please! I'll explain everything but don't make a scene, she'd never forgive you!" and she let him simmer as the audience cooed, the band struck up a Danubian waltz and the girls began to circle the dais, their high heels clattering as they passed to and fro in front of the judges in the orchestra pit.

She was, he had to admit, the most staggeringly attractive female he had ever seen but it was not the classic regularity of her features, or the singular maturity of figure in one so young that gave her such obvious advantages over the others. Her distinction was centred on her poise, a kind of relaxed sophistication that armoured her against the nervous embarrassment of the older girls. She was, he reflected grimly, a smooth professional among a crop of buxom amateurs; then his attention switched from the stage to his own predicament.

He knew that if he made no effort to hold himself in he would make a scene of their conspiracy of silence, if not here then the moment they returned home. Alternatively, if he once admitted to feeling slighted and belittled by their exclusion, such progress as he had made with

Claire in the last day or so would be cancelled out. In the resultant flare up (for she would certainly side with her daughters) the chance to recapture the elusive rhythm of their lives would be lost, perhaps for good. He saw then, and clearly, that he must either capitulate or compromise but there was really no room to manœuvre. He knew his youngest daughter sufficiently well to appreciate how much this occasion meant to her, particularly if—as was barely credible considering her age—she went forward to the national final. He was so absorbed in making private decisions that he paid little heed to the judges and it was the familiar ring of his own name issuing from the mouth of the Town Clerk that jolted him into an awareness that the stage was now empty of bathing beauties, and a decision was on hand. He thought, as sweat struck cold under his armpits, "Damn it, why should I let a prejudice destroy the peace and quiet of my own home? This is a time to borrow old John Rudd's trick of paying out slack and not haul in again until my feet are on surer ground than they have been during the last twelve months!" and then the tension broke in the seats behind and he felt Claire's hand grasp his wrist as a fanfare of uncertain trumpets summoned his youngest daughter back on stage and he watched her advance towards the Lady Mayoress who had materialised from the wings carrying a garish-looking crown on a red, velvet cushion. "Good God!" he exclaimed, "she's won!" but because he saw in his wife's face a radiance that had not been there for a very long time, he found it easy to counterfeit a nonchalance he did not feel and even to add, "There was never a doubt about it, was there?"

He got his reward on the spot. Her relief seemed to burst like a bubble and for the first time in almost a year she looked at him in a way that he recognised and remembered.

"You rotten fraud!" she whispered, enlarging her grip on his hand, "you had me scared for a moment!" and then, to his acute embarrassment, she and Mary began to applaud as frenziedly as anyone in the hall.

III

"In for a penny, in for a pound," Maureen told him when she heard the news and again he took her advice so that the Craddocks descended upon London in a body in September to swell the gathering of provincials from all over England and Wales who were involved in the Dairy Queen finals, held in a Park Lane hotel.

The competitors, viewed as a contingent, taxed the ingenuities of all but the most ingenious of the Press corps, who found most of the girls blushingly inarticulate when faced with the stock questions. All but Claire that is, of whom the journalists made a mascot, not only because she was the youngest finalist by almost two years but because she seemed to know exactly where she was going and why. This was something that Fleet Street not only understood but applauded.

Mary, who was present at most of her interviews, looked on with awe as Claire fenced, joked and flirted with hardbitten men more than twice her age and seemed, by exercising an inborn skill, to know precisely what they required in the way of copy, so that Claire's profile, Claire's expectations, and even Claire's pronouncements on such diverse topics as clothes, love, cows and cheese were featured in all the journals and periodicals. She even made a fleeting appearance on Gaumont British News, assisting at the opening of a hospital wing.

One way and another it was a sensational week and the first occasion for Paul when London, as a city, touched him with her magic for the weather was fine and warm, their quarters comfortable and the general excitement contrived to keep at bay that depressing anonymity he had always felt when caught up in this whirl of traffic and stampede of grey-faced millions who somehow reminded him of prisoners-of-war milling about the compounds behind Compiègne.

Perhaps the sense of family unity had something to do with it, for on the second day the twins and their wives roared up in their big, shiny cars, Monica and the laughing Welsh girl, Margaret, both dripping with furs and inclined, he noticed, to convert their *"a"*s into *"e"*s and discard the *"g"* in words like "ripping" and "topping", which they used a great deal. Like Claire, and a few of the Pressmen, the twins were already assured of victory and Paul feared for them all when finalists intermingled for the first time at a tea dance and he realised that the competition here was far more formidable than at Paxtonbury. She could, he thought, outclass some of the chubbier girls from the remote counties, places like Cardigan and Cumberland (although, if he were in search of a living advertisement for cream and butter these were the very girls he would choose) but it was obvious that city sophistication had lapped over the farmlands within shouting distance of the big cities and Miss Suffolk, for instance, looked far more like a film star than a dairymaid. He enjoyed talking to Garstin Schroeder, the improbably-named Organising Secretary of the British Dairymen's Association, finding him extremely well-informed on the subject of farming prospects generally, and he found common ground talking to some of the fathers of competitors, whose dolorous experiences on the land during the nineteen-twenties were identical with his own. As a rule, however, he stood aside and let the women enjoy themselves, grateful for Mary's watchful chaperonage of Claire, even more grateful for his wife's sparkle which dated from the very moment he gave his reluctant blessing of the enterprise in the Paxtonbury Town Hall. He did not have to follow Maureen's advice literally; so far, he told himself, he had paid out a great deal of slack and gathered none in but it was a relief to hear her laugh again, to see her preen herself in her smart new clothes and watch her soar off on a series of shopping sprees with her elegant daughters-in-law, Monica and Margaret, neither of whom, he reflected, seemed eager to pause in their eternal gallivanting long enough to produce a grandchild for his delight. It was reflection on his lack of grandchildren, in fact, that modified his pleasure in the reunion. The Pair had now been married more than two years and Simon, who showed up on the final day, for four years, but neither one had yielded a dividend, male or female. Whiz, they told him, was expecting a child but Whiz and her dour Scots husband were far away in Singapore and if things went on like this it might be years before he could hoist a toddler on to the crupper of his saddle and ride down across the Codsall stubble fields, as he had ridden with all his own children at one time or another. He mentioned this to Claire one night after they had returned from a noisy drinking session in the hotel lounge but she did not seem to share his regrets.

"Oh, there's time enough," she said carelessly, "they're all young and healthy and girls nowadays want a bit of fun before they settle down the way we did in our day. I can't say as I blame them, either. Everything has been so topsy-turvy since the war that one can't see more than a few weeks ahead."

One could not indeed, as Simon was not slow to point out when they had a quiet chat during the parade rehearsal on the morning of the grand final. The boy, he thought, was a great contrast to his splendid brothers, in his off-the-peg suit and weather-beaten trilby. He had some kind of job, he said, editing a left-wing paper in Manchester, and Rachel, his wife, who did not accompany him, brought in extra money as a lecturer for the Workers' Education Association. Between them they had contested three by-elections and had emerged at the bottom of the poll at each of them but repeated failure to penetrate beyond the fringe of politics seemed neither to depress nor surprise him.

"I'm living the kind of life I want to live, the only kind I could live, Gov'nor," he said, when Paul suggested he should swim with the tide until a real opportunity presented itself. "The fact is the whole damned lot of us are living on borrowed time but so few people seem to realise it. Take what's happening in Germany. All pretence of freedom has disappeared over there and anyone who opposes that little bastard Hitler has his throat cut, or is slammed into one of his concentration camps. Nobody seems to bother. All that really concerns most people is how to make a fast buck, how to find the money for the new Morris Eight, or the down payment on 'Mon Repos' and 'Shangri-La'. They'll wake up eventually, however. They'll have to or go under overnight!"

It was the first time Paul had considered Adolf Hitler as a potential menace and he could not help feeling that Simon's obsession with the underdog had led him to exaggerate. He said, "I'll go along with you, son, when you say things aren't all they should be, and that the Government is the laziest, shiftiest bunch we've had for a very long time, but surely nobody takes tinpot ranters like Hitler and Mussolini seriously? From where I stand it's ninety-five per cent blather!"

"The Kaiser blathered," Simon said, and not for the first time of late Paul had the impression that, in his quiet way, his son had the same political prescience as old Franz Zorndorff, who boasted that he could smell burning powder half-way across the world.

"What are the chances of a general turnover at the next election?" he asked, remembering that since Jimmy Grenfell's death he had lost contact with the political scene, apart from a perusal of leading articles and Simon said, "None! We'll dodder on and on, doped by our football, films, greyhounds and the distractions that even dairymen go for nowadays. Then, one bright morning, we shall wake up and find the Fascists not merely on our doorstep but in bed with us, and chaps like Mosley and his Blackshirts hanging a 'To Let' notice on the Houses of Parliament. That is, of course, providing Hitler doesn't take a crack at Russia; if he does he'll get all the backing he needs in the West."

Paul wondered, as Simon said this, precisely how far to the left his son had travelled in the years since the Slump and asked, bluntly, "Do you still look at Russia with starry eyes, Simon? Is it really any better than Fascism?"

"No, I don't go along with it," Simon replied unexpectedly, "it's not the answer and never can be—people handing down decisions from the top. We have the real answer here if the mass of people would use the machinery got together by the pioneers, like the Tolpuddle Martyrs and old Tom Paine!" He smiled, and added, "You see? Basically I'm just as old-fashioned as you, Gov'nor! At least, Rachel says I am."

"You and she seem to get along well enough," Paul said, more as a feeler than a statement, and Simon replied, "As people? Yes, we do; I respect her and she tolerates me, but she's a Marxist and the trouble with poor old Karl was he never learned how to laugh."

Somewhere near at hand trumpets brayed and ushers appeared to shepherd everyone to their seats. Paul regretted the interruption, knowing that in the scurry that followed the verdict he would have no chance to continue the discussion and it was so rarely these days that he had a chance to talk to the only one of his children whose intelligence he respected. Soon, however, he forgot Simon, being drawn, willy-nilly, into the vortex as the twenty finalists were whittled down to twelve, then seven, and then four, with Claire still in the running and his wife, daughter and daughters-in-law gibbering with excitement, and triumph still hidden behind the red and gold curtains where the survivors had retired to await the ultimate choice. The Pair, Paul noticed, although jubilant, were far more realistic than their womenfolk, Andy declaring that young Claire would forfeit the title on account of her age, Stevie trying to console his mother by saying, "Look here, she's got this far, and holds the Devon title for a year! That's something to be going on with, isn't it?"

"It's not enough," Claire said, emphatically, "she's got to win! She's just got to win!" and when Paul said, "Why, Claire? What's so terribly important about it? And why is it so vital to you?" the cold glance she turned on him reminded him uncomfortably of her recent moods. "It isn't important to me but it's terribly important to her! Why? Because it's all she's got, don't you see?" and to Paul's astonishment Monica came out in full support of this astonishing verdict, saying, "I go along with that! I was a Claire, not as pretty maybe but with nothing to offer but a face and curves in the right places! I never had any real confidence in myself in a last year's dress; no brains, no special skills, nothing but myself."

"And the pity of it is that it's expendable," Claire added. "One loses a little of it every day after one's twentieth birthday. Now a thing like this—public recognition I mean—is something one can look back on all one's life without having to console oneself with a photograph album!"

As she said this, almost as though addressing herself, the cancer of the last year was suddenly revealed to him for he remembered how vain she had always been of her body, and her ability to keep pace with changing fashions, all the way from leg-o'-mutton sleeves and picture hats to the bandeaux and short skirts of the "twenties", and the more feminine styles of today. It occurred to him then that she must always have thought of their partnership as something that owed very little to the shared adventures of three decades but hung upon factors like the weight of flesh about her thighs, the size and sag of her breasts and the clarity of her skin. Comprehending this for the first time in nearly a year he had an inarticulate desire to comfort her but at that moment the curtains swung aside and the Master of Ceremonies emerged with a slip of paper in his hand and announced, "The final decision of the judges, ladies and gentlemen . . . Miss Cheshire, fourth place, Miss Shropshire third place . . ." He saw Claire, then Mary and the others, rise in their seats and heard the Twins yelp with triumph. "Miss Kent, runner up . . . Miss Devonshire, Dairy Queen of England and Wales for the year 1934–1935 . . ."

The orchestra crashed out and the applause stormed over their heads. He saw the other finalists file in, noting their glumness and pathetic attempts to smile as Claire was led to the central dais, moving with infinite grace, utterly composed as the silly little crown was placed on her head by last year's winner, and beside him his wife looked so pale that he thought for a moment she was going to faint and caught her arm as trumpets blared and everyone rose to their feet, clapping. He said, with relief, "Well, there you are! She'll have something to look back on after all!" but the thought struck him that, at the age of sixteen, the salting away of memories was a macabre compulsion.

By the following day they had dispersed, the twins and their wives roaring away up the Great North Road, Simon, about some mysterious business in the East End and then to Euston for Manchester, Paul and Mary by taxi to Waterloo, with Claire left behind to stay with her daughter until Tuesday. At the last minute Schroeder, the Organising Secretary, came to them with a sudden change of plan. Arrangements had been made, he said, for the winner to fulfil her first public engagement at an Agricultural Fair, due to open in The Hague later that week but prior to that she had to be "groomed", whatever that meant. Paul was anxious to get home. The harvest was late and in any case he and Mary had arranged to take part in a County Gymkhana but he would have waived Valley commitments if he had been persuaded that wife or daughter needed him. As it was, in the upheaval that followed the triumph, he was almost overlooked and when Claire said that she would like to stay on a day or two to help choose dresses, and that he would be bored by a two-day shopping expedition in the West End, he took the broad hint and said, "You don't mind if I go back with Mary? I'm a droop when it comes to this kind of thing!" she regarded him with her head on one side and replied, "You're dying to get out of here and I must say you've been far more patient than I expected! Go along home with Mary and meet me on the three o'clock from Waterloo, on Tuesday. I can't really leave her alone until she flies off and I have a feeling she'd sooner have me around than Mary!"

"I'm quite sure she would," Paul said, "and I believe you're getting an even bigger kick out of it than she is!"

"Yes, I am," Claire admitted, "for it's something I should have loved to have happened to me at her age, although I couldn't have carried it off with her aplomb!"

"I'm damned certain you could," he said, "but I don't think your father would have stood for it for one moment!"

"Neither would you! I can just see your face if I wiggled up and down in front of all those latterday George Lovells in a tight bathing costume! Did you think of that old rascal when the judging was going on?"

"Why yes, I did as a matter of fact," he admitted, surprised and pleased at this evidence of a return to their old-time jocular plane, "but I would have said it was the last thought to occupy your mind."

She said, frankly but without looking at him, "It's been a difficult time for you, Paul, and don't imagine I don't realise as much! But we're over the hump now, I can tell you that! This has been a real tonic to me! Would you be interested in learning how, exactly?"

"Yes, I would. Very interested indeed!"

"Well, I suppose, up to the moment of young Claire winning the preliminary I was just plain envious—envious and resentful of their youth and high spirits, of the freedoms they enjoy that we never had and of their good looks and expectation of life! I was even jealous of Mary's tranquillity but now, well—now I've got the whole thing into better focus, just a matter of counting blessings I imagine! After all, we're still solvent and in good health and Claire owes this triumph to

1037

the legacy of our health. But the really important thing is I'm still important to you! I'm convinced of that at any rate!"

"Did you ever doubt it?"

"Yes, both before and after John was born. Don't ask me why but I did!"

"I wonder what happened to all that famous Derwent commonsense?"

"It evaporated the minute I knew I was pregnant. Maureen tried to explain it but she didn't really get through to me."

"Or to me either," he admitted.

"It's partly a physical change, I suppose. I told her before I left that I'd try and put it on paper some time so that she could write an article for one of her medical journals."

"Don't you do anything so damned silly," he said, "it's one thing having a daughter displaying all her equipment in public, but quite another having one's wife strip herself naked for the British Medical Journal! I'll say good-bye to Claire and wish her luck," and he turned to go with a sense of enormous relief but as he reached the door he said, as an afterthought, "From now on it's going to be us, Claire! They can bloody well fend for themselves, one and all! One thing Maureen said did get through to me—that the time we've got left could be the happiest years of our life. Did she say that to you?"

"Yes and I didn't believe her but I do now. That's all that counts, isn't it?"

"It's what counts with me," he replied emphatically and crossed the corridor to the room shared by the two girls.

Mary was in the lobby arranging about luggage but his youngest daughter was there and he was at once struck by her remoteness of expression which was something new to him, although she had always been a very self-contained person, far more so than any of his other children. She was so still and rapt as she sat by the window that she did not turn her head as he entered and he felt the curious embarrassment that had always plagued their relationship. He said, with assumed heartiness, "Well, Kiddo, you saw them all off and your mother's bursting with pride! She's staying until you take off at Croydon and I've come to wish you luck, I'm going home with Mary."

The child looked at him as though he had said something she only half understood and again he caught the half-puzzled, half-anxious expression in her eyes, eyes a shade bluer than her mother's and half veiled by long, golden lashes. He thought, "Well, here's an odd turn-

1038

up! She isn't as confident as all that now that she's launched!" and somehow felt closer to her than ever before, the shift prompting a protectiveness she had never seemed to demand of him.

"Are you scared after all, Claire? If you are it's nothing to be ashamed of, and if you want to talk about it I'll listen."

"No," she said, in hardly more than a whisper, "I'm not scared, Daddy. I'm terribly excited but—" and suddenly, against all probability, she seemed on the verge of tears so that he went across and put his arm on her shoulder, saying, "You can still back out if you want to! Nobody can make you go through with it. After all, it's only a kind of advertisement, and apart from expenses you aren't being paid for the job."

"Oh, I wouldn't want that," she said, "I'd want to go through with it, no matter what happens."

"But what could happen, Kiddo? Apart from pleasant things?"

"I don't know," she said, uncertainly, "nothing, I suppose, but it's queer—I had a feeling it was all—well—*bound* to happen, just the way it has! Just now, before you came in, it seemed—well rather *creepy* somehow. Does that sound stupid?"

"No, not a bit stupid. The fact is you've had a devil of a lot of excitement and no matter how much you pretend to be adult you're still only a kid. It's perfectly understandable you should feel nervous. If it was me, I'd be scared stiff."

She made the only joke he ever recalled her making, saying, with a smile, "You'd look like hell under a crown, Daddy!" and because it was the first time there had ever been real communication between them he threw his arm round her, saying, "Neither you, nor Whiz, nor your brothers, ever had the slightest respect for me! However, if you'd like me to stay and see you off I can easily 'phone through and get Henry Pitts to do my judging at the Gymkhana. Would you like me to do that, Claire?"

"No," she said, "because I know you hate London and I think you've been pretty sporting over the whole business. You haven't even warned me not to talk to strange men in foreign cities! Go on back to your precious Valley and let me find one of my own, like Whiz and The Pair! All I'd like you to be sure of is that—well—that I don't *really* take everything for granted! It's just that I'm not very good at saying 'thank you'," and she took both his hands, stood on tiptoe and kissed him very deliberately on both cheeks. The unexpectedness of words and gesture overwhelmed him so much that all he could say

1039

was, "Do you need any money?" She shook her head, held him for a moment and then resumed her seat by the window. He may have fancied it but it seemed to him that she turned her head away deliberately and he went out hurriedly, never having suspected her of doing anything so human as to shed a tear at the prospect of leaving home and family.

IV

It was a rather sombre journey back to the Valley. He found it difficult to rid himself of a feeling of guilt, of having abandoned her at a time when, for the first time in her life, she seemed to need him but when he tried to describe what had passed between them, first to Claire and then to Mary, it sounded trivial and insubstantial so that he was not surprised when they told him that maybe young Claire had bitten off just a tiny bit more than she could chew and that a little humility, the product of nervousness, would do her far more good than harm. When he urged that he should stay after all, or even accompany her to Holland, they laughed at him for reverting to one of his "duty-moods", another hoary source of merriment among the family, yet the feeling of unease persisted, clouding his pleasure at his sight of the Valley under warm September sunshine, with its fields dotted with golden stooks and its streams unseasonably high after a wet August.

All that day and all the next he had difficulty in picking up his routine, his mind constantly returning to the picture of young Claire sitting at the hotel window looking out on nothing or perhaps on something only she could see, and he thought too of her sudden spurt of affection, wondering what instinctive fears might have prompted it. The feeling was strong enough to drive him to the telephone on the second night, the last of her stay in London, only to learn from an impersonal receptionist that "Mrs. and Miss Craddock had gone to a theatre and were not expected back until after midnight." He declined an invitation to leave a message and went to bed with his favourite copy of Jorrocks and when Jorrocks failed to entertain him he lay awake a long time listening to the screech of owls in the paddock, thinking it was the one night-sound of Shallowford he preferred not to hear on the rare occasions sleep evaded him.

If Shallowford House could have been said to possess a radio fan the title would have gone to Mary, the only member of the family

1040

whose musical tastes extended beyond Strauss waltzes and jazz. Mary's room, the first on the nursery corridor facing west, was the most feminine in the house. She had chosen her own carpet and curtains and converted two deep alcoves into arched bookshelves. Her furniture was small and neat, an assortment of birthday and Christmas presents over the years and she had accompanied Paul to local auction sales to buy little pieces of Coalport and Rockingham china, mostly vases and baskets which she kept filled with wild flowers from February until late autumn. These little posies, dotted about the room, were her calendars. In late winter there were usually snowdrops and celandines on the mantelshelf and the lower shelves of the alcoves. In March and April there were primroses and dog-violets, with arrangements of pigmy daffodils and narcissi as spring advanced and after that came the blue and yellow iris that everyone else in the Valley called "flags". Later still the room was gay with foxgloves and bluebells (cut short to spare the bulbs), honeysuckle, meadowsweet, campion, bugloss and shyer flowers gathered in remote corners of the woods revealed to her by old Meg Potter, with whom Mary was on intimate terms. She spent a great deal of her free time in this room writing in her diary, trying to compose rustic sonnets on the style of Wilfred Blunt (her favourite poet) and writing long, rambling letters to Rumble Patrick, with whom she had now maintained a regular correspondence for more than three years. Rumble's photograph stood in a silver frame on a papier-mâché bedside table, not the round-faced Rumble Patrick who had decamped to Australia as long ago as December, 1930, and had since wandered half-way round the world, but a lean, cheerful-looking young man, in what she took to be a Canadian trapper's outfit of fur cap, fringed jacket and top boots. The photo was signed "*As always, Rumble*" which satisfied her but did not seem to impress anyone else.

On the afternoon Paul drove to Paxtonbury to meet the 3 p.m. out of Waterloo she declined his invitation to come along, saying that she had to write Rumble an account of the Dairy Queen final so that it was about half-past five, just after Paul had left, that she sat down at her little rosewood desk and began to marshal her facts, making no effort to restrain the pride she felt in the family triumph and pinning caption slips on each of the snipped-out photographs of Claire, on which she wrote such comments as "*This doesn't do our Claire justice, it was one of those awful flashlights and she looks startled!*" or "*The girl next to Claire is Miss Cheshire who was a very pretty brunette but a cat!*" About ten minutes to six she reached out and turned her wireless on, continuing writing against a background of Jack Payne's light orchestral music, a Palm Court broadcast dribbling out tinkling tunes like "Little Man you've had a busy day", or dreamier ones like "A Night in Napoli" and "Little Old Church in the Valley". Mary paid no heed to them but unconsciously cocked an ear when the announcer began to read the news. Then she stopped writing, in the middle of the word "gorgeous", used to describe the white satin ball-dress the Dairymen's Association had presented to Claire to wear at her maiden public appearance. Her hand clutched the pen so tightly that its nib spluttered and for a moment the little room, flooded with early evening sunshine, rocked and receded as the announcer said, in a voice nicely pitched for tragic announcements, ". . . there are believed to be no survivors in this afternoon's air disaster, involving the British Dairymen's contingent on their way to exhibit British products at The Hague. Among those aboard the aircraft, which is believed to have crashed about twelve miles north-west of the Hook of Holland, was the recently-chosen British Dairy Queen, Miss Claire Craddock, aged only sixteen. Rescue craft went out on receipt of the first distress signals and, together with other aircraft, are still searching the area. A report has come in that one body, believed to be that of a crew member, has been recovered but apart from a small amount of wreckage no traces of the fuselage have been found. The total complement of the aircraft was sixteen. Further bulletins will be issued at nine o'clock and midnight . . ."

Mary waited, her hand on the knob, until the announcer went on to talk about something else. Then she switched off and stood up, steadying herself by the little brass rail that surmounted the desk and it was necessary to grip hard for the walls continued to expand and contract and all the time the sun poured into the window like a blinding light, causing her to raise a hand still holding the pen and press the palm to her eyes. The movement left a smear of ink on her cheek.

Claire dead! Drowned and probably mangled, somewhere off the coast of Holland! Claire, the spoiled beauty of the family, whose photographs lay strewn across the desk covering the pages of Rumble's letter. Claire! Who had somehow stood for success and glitter and adventure in the world outside the Valley, the beautiful little child whom she had accompanied to so many dances, gymkhanas and fêtes, noting how everyone turned their heads when they passed, the girl who had caused men of all ages to stand aside and pay silent homage to her radiance and grace, as though she was some classical statue transformed into flesh and blood and loaned for each occasion. It was incredible and yet, as Mary fought for her breath, she knew that it was true and that even at this stage to hope would be futile. There had been clinical finality in the announcement but away and beyond this there was also a terrible inevitability about it, as though young Claire had come at the end of the road the very moment the little crown had been settled on her head and that somehow, if only they had taken the trouble to find out, it could all have been found in Meg Potter's pack of cards.

And then, as tears began to flow, she forced herself to think of the effect of this appalling news on the others, on her mother, now more than half-way home and isolated from news in a speeding train, and of her father, half-way to Paxtonbury, likewise ignorant of what had happened and liable, she thought with a shudder, to read it in a news-paper whilst awaiting the arrival of the express.

She crossed over to the window groping for handholds on bed-head and table and her blundering hand brushed and tipped over a small vase of flowers spilling water and a shower of yellow blossoms across the table-top. At last she found the window seat, summoning every ounce of resolution to think, to hit on some way of softening the blow if God was merciful and Paul and Claire arrived home unaware of the disaster. For she would have to break it to them. Somehow they would have to be cushioned against the savagery of a flat, impersonal wireless announcement, or the professionally sympathetic voice of a policeman telling the story over the telephone. From far away down-stairs she heard the telephone ringing insistently and levering herself up went out into the corridor to the stairhead. Thirza, crossing the hall, turned aside to lift the receiver but Mary called, with an urgency that made Thirza's head jerk upwards, "*Don't!* It's for me!" and ran downstairs as Thirza, shrugging, marched through the swing door into the kitchen quarters.

A voice said, quietly but distinctly, "Shallowford House? Is Mr. Craddock available?" and Mary said, choking back her tears, "Who is it? Who wants him? This is Mary Craddock, his daughter!" and when the voice said, "Ah yes, is your father anywhere about, Miss Crad-dock?" she recognised it as that of Sergeant Beeworthy, the police-man stationed at Whinmouth and responsible for the Coombe Bay area. She said, with a tremendous effort, "Is it . . . is it about the air-crash? About my sister Claire?"

"Yes, Miss Craddock, I'm afraid it is. You know about it?"

"I just heard it, on the six o'clock news."

"I see." The voice expressed relief and there was a pause before it went on: "Have you told your father? Is he there?" and Mary said no, he had gone to Paxtonbury to meet her mother on a train due in about six o'clock. "Listen, Sergeant," she went on, as the power of coherent thought returned to her, "I . . . I'd much sooner you left this to me! Unless he buys a paper at the station he won't know, he'll simply pick up Mother and come straight back here without stopping! I'd much sooner you left it to me and didn't try to contact him! Will you do that? *Will* you?"

"Certainly, Miss Craddock," and Beeworthy sounded grateful. "I think that would be best in the circumstances. I just had word from London and it would have been my job to make sure that he knew."

"There's no further news?"

"Nothing good, I'm afraid. They've located the wreck, it seems, but there's very little hope. There were no survivors. It was some kind of engine-failure they say. I'm . . . I'm terribly sorry for all of you, I knew her well of course."

"Everybody did. Thank you, Sergeant. I'll tell Father you rang."

"There's one thing more, Miss Craddock."

"Well?"

"In the circumstances the Press will soon be on to you. I expect they'll jam your line."

"What can I do . . . just for the time being?"

"You could leave the receiver off the hook but then nobody else could get you. I think it might be wiser to ring the Coombe Bay operator and ask her to put all incoming calls through to me. I could filter them for you, for a couple of hours or so, and I daresay I could head the Press off. I could say you were all in London."

"That would be very kind, Sergeant."

"Right, then ring the operator right away. Perhaps Mr. Craddock or you would ring me later. I might have more news."

She rang off, passed the message to the operator without comment and looked at her watch. It was six-twenty. Paul would be meeting the train in a few minutes and it would take him less than an hour to drive back. By eight o'clock they would be coming through the door and she would know by looking at them whether or not they had heard. She went upstairs to the bathroom. Any weeping that had to be done had better be done now.

She waited until they had had some tea, listening over the banisters to the rise and fall of their voices and hearing Claire's laugh. Then she went down to the library and Paul, jumping up, said, "I thought you must have popped out somewhere, Mary . . ." but stopped, looking hard at her as she stood with her back pressed to the door, groping for the words but finding none.

"What is it, dear? You're upset? You've been crying!" and Claire put down her empty cup and turned towards her so that, fleetingly, Mary was grateful she had been betrayed by her eyes despite incessant bathing, for this surely meant that they would not be swung from a mood of relief at being home and together again, with all the excitement behind them, to one of utter despair. They had warning; some kind of warning.

She said, biting her lip, "Something's happened. Something . . . bad! Don't let anyone in, I've got to tell you first!" and then stopped, her tongue filling her mouth.

All her life she had admired him at times of crisis. He had always seemed to her a big, dependable man, whose inclination to fuss was reserved for the smaller, unimportant irritants, a broken harness strap, a sudden quarrel resulting in unnecessary noise but in the wider sphere she had never once seen him rattled and it came to her now, faced with this hideous task, that this might be the secret of his reputation in the Valley. He came over to her and took her by the hand, leading her to a chair near the tall window, saying, "Is it about Rumble, Mary?" She shook her head and swallowed and they waited until her tongue became manageable.

"Claire, *our* Claire."

Her mother's head came up sharply. "She's ill? Someone's telephoned from London?"

She wished now that she had tackled Paul alone. It would have been much easier to have told him and let him pass it on, for her mother's favouritism of Claire had never been a secret in the house, just another family joke, and surely a shock like this would be too great for her to absorb without collapse. The thought gave Mary a little strength. She said, choosing her words with the utmost care, "There's been an accident. A bad accident!"

"Where?"

It was Paul who spoke and he sounded tired rather than frightened.

"Flying to Holland—it was on the wireless—then the police rang. No one was saved!" and she bowed her head and was silent.

There was no sudden outcry, no movement of any kind. The library clock ticked on. The mellow light filtered by the avenue chestnuts flooded the room as each of them fought with the whole of their strength to ward off horror from each other and then Claire, twisting her handkerchief into a hard knot, stood up and she said, quietly:

"There's *no* hope? None at all?"

Mary shook her head and there was silence again. Claire crossed to the sideboard cupboard taking out a brandy glass and a decanter. She poured four fingers and carried it back across the room.

"Take a drink, Paul!"

"You— ?"

"It doesn't help me but it will you." He took and swallowed it like a child taking medicine and it was in the act of putting the decanter away that Claire, out of the corner of her eye, saw Mary sitting with her head bowed, her hands limp on her lap. The abject pose communicated the girl's misery to her as nothing else could have done. She moved to the window and touched her head lightly, the gesture releasing a spring of tenderness that had never flowed for a daughter who seemed to belong less to her than did Paul's son by Grace Lovell. "I'll never forget you made yourself tell us, Mary! *Never*, you understand?" Then she went out leaving them alone, understanding that, at a juncture such as this, she was the odd one out.

She paused in the hall undecided which way to go and what to do first, yet astonished by her own steadiness. Then she made her decision and climbed the stairs to Claire's room, one room along from Mary's. It was still strewn with the debris of Claire's departure and she wondered for a moment why nobody had tidied up after they had gone. Then she remembered that Claire had always been the litterbug of the family and that long ago instructions had been issued to Thirza and the others not to encourage her slatternly habits by following her round and picking up discarded garments.

Tears began to flow as she set about the job of clearing up and as the first of them fell she knew the source of her strange, numb calm. It was not, as she had thought on quitting the study, the almost instinctive lurch towards the routine obligations of telephoning and writing, or a summoning of willpower to withstand the flow of condolences or the clamour of the Press. This rally would occur in an hour or so but for the moment she found a reserve of strength in a deep conviction that what had occurred was not a terrible accident but a cycle of circumstances, all of which were inevitable and quite beyond anyone's power to alter or mitigate. She had always known that something like this would deprive her of Claire, suddenly and completely, and it was because of this that she had spoiled the child so shamelessly. She was very far from being a superstitious woman in the accepted sense of the word and yet, as regards Claire, a child conceived against a background of death and deprivation in the deepest trough of the war, she had always been half-aware of a kind of bargain made with death that involved not only the child but her father whom everyone in the Valley, herself excepted, believed dead at that time. All the time the child had lain in her womb death had squatted over the Valley and his favourite roosting-spot had been the chimney-pots of this house. Yet, in the end, he had been vanquished, or perhaps not vanquished but bought off, and now, after a respite of more than sixteen years, he had returned to claim the talisman. She did not know why or how such a train of reasoning could cushion her against the terrible shock of Claire's death but it did, so that a kind of emotional petrification checked her tears and she braced herself against the demands that Paul and Mary and all the others would be certain to make on her in the weeks ahead, weeks of mourning that were denied even the focal point of a committal.

When the room was tidy she opened the window, took a last look round and went downstairs to the telephone, lifting the receiver and asking for the number of the Whinmouth police station. Her hand and her voice was steady as the bell tinkled, and when Thirza emerged from the kitchen to answer it, she turned aside and said, crisply, "Go and fetch the Lady Doctor, Thirza. Tell her Mr. Craddock wants her urgently and hurry!"

She turned her back on the woman's puzzled expression and re-addressed herself to the telephone but there was no more news, only confirmation of the disaster. She replaced the receiver and wondered whether to await Maureen in the hall but then she had another thought, retracing her steps upstairs, and going along to the nursery. The baby was awake, threshing away with his fat little fists, and as she stared down at him she found herself smiling. She thought, "I wonder why he always struck me as a plain child? He isn't plain, just— comical!" She picked him up, carried him downstairs and out on to the terrace, holding him tightly and occasionally brushing his head with her lips. They were still standing so when Maureen and Thirza came hurrying up the drive.

CHAPTER SEVEN

I

No other bodies were recovered so it was as Claire had suspected, a mourning without a corpse, with a memorial service in Coombe Bay Church that Paul authorised only after strong pressure from The Pair and their wives, who were, it seemed, very conventional in some respects and thought it essential Claire should have her public tribute.

The weather broke the day following and autumn rain seeped down on the stubble and a countryside that had rallied during the sunny spell following a wet summer; by the end of the week it might have been late November. The Sorrel was in flood and all its culverts choked with sodden leaves.

It was strange that the elimination of Claire, who had never been noisy and energetic like her brothers, or even gregarious like her sister Whiz, should invest the house with such gloom and emptiness, but this was so and it was Mary, without an absorbing occupation, who noticed it more than the others. Sometimes, when it pressed too heavily upon her, she put on macintosh and gumboots and slogged up across the orchard to the lane and round the rim of the woods to the mere, or, turning left instead of right, climbed to French Wood and dropped down past Hermitage Farm to the stream that fed the Sorrel here, then up the long slope to the ruin of Periwinkle. She had always liked Elinor Codsall and it increased her depression to see the rain dripping through the thatch and thistles marching down the slope that Will, whom she dimly recalled, had reclaimed from the moor before he went off and got himself "blowed to tatters", as Martha Pitts used to say.

She was here one October afternoon, about a fortnight after Claire's death, when she heard, or thought she heard, the sound of footsteps in what had been Elinor's kitchen. She stood on the bank and listened, half-deciding that she must have been wrong but then she noticed a wisp of smoke rising from the chimney and guessed who must be inside, almost certainly old Meg Potter. Meg sometimes used the ruin for boiling herbs she gathered this side of the Valley and thus saved herself the trouble of hauling them all the way to Low Coombe where she still lived if she could be said to live anywhere. It would be comforting, Mary thought, to take a brew of tea with Meg and tell her her troubles. Maybe she would tell her fortune again, as she often did when they met by chance in isolated places. Meg did not tell anybody's fortune but she was always ready to tell Mary's and would never accept silver for her services. "You'll never maake money, tho' you'll live a long time in peace," she would tell her gravely, "and I dorn't need me palm crossed to tell that to man nor maid!"

She jumped down from the bank and crossed the muddy farmyard, meaning to stand beside the rain-tub and peep in the window, in case it wasn't Meg but one or other of the wayfarers, who sometimes slept a night in there *en route* for Paxtonbury's tramps' lodging-house. Then she stopped, convinced that she was the victim of a hallucination brought on by delayed shock, for inside, engaged in measuring the room with a long, notched yardstick, was Rumble Patrick!

At least, she thought it was Rumble Patrick, although the young man absorbed in the task of estimating the floor-space of the littered room was much taller, more broad-shouldered and somehow more rawboned than the Rumble who had kissed her beside the mere all those years ago, and to whom she must have written at least two hundred and fifty letters during the last three and a half years. He was much browner too and more weather-beaten about the face and his dark hair, that had been thick and unruly, was now close-cropped, so that his reddened ears, always inclined to protrude, seemed set at an angle of about forty-five degrees. His clothes were outlandish, serviceable breeches and a kind of lumber-jacket with a fur-lined hood, and strong, laced-up boots, like those her mother was seen to be wearing in photographs taken before the war, only these had metal-tipped high heels that looked oddly effeminate on the long legs of a broad-shouldered young man.

She remained by the window oblivious of the dripping thatch as warmth stole into her, animating every nerve in her body and bringing the blood rushing to cheeks already whipped by the wind. She tried to call out but her tongue was as unresponsive as it had been when she had brought the news of Claire's death to her father and mother and it was all she could do to lift her hand to the pane and drum with her fingers on the cracked glass. He turned then, as sharply as a hare surprised in long grass but when he saw her he did not seem surprised but grinned broadly and beckoned, so that she ran along the slippery cobbles and under the cascade of drips at the porch and the next moment she was in his arms, laughing and crying and still struggling with a sluggish tongue.

He said, holding her and running his big, rough hands over her damp hair, "I suppose that rascal Smut Potter gave me away? He was the only one who saw me jump the train, at Sorrel Halt. I meant to tip him to keep his mouth shut but I had to run back along the line for my rucksack and forgot!"

She told him at last that she had not had the least idea he was home and that he was a pig to have given her such a shock, and that he couldn't have come from Sorrel Halt that day because the first train that stopped there was the four-thirty and it was only three-forty-five now but he said, still grinning, "Who said it stopped? It slowed down and I couldn't see the sense of going on to Paxtonbury and hiring a taxi so I jumped for it! We're going to need all I've saved to put this joint in order! What's the matter with Gov'nor, to let one of his places run down to this extent? Another year and even I couldn't have fixed it!"

He spoke, she noticed, with a slight but unmistakable Colonial drawl, using words like "fixed" and "joint" without self-consciousness so that for a moment the implication of what he said did not strike her; when it did she could have cried out with relief and joy. Being Mary, however, she only admonished herself for leaping to the most exciting of conclusions and said, instead, "You mean you intend to *farm* Periwinkle. To do it up yourself and . . . and *settle* in it?"

"You bet," he said, casually, "unless there's anything better going and I'm pretty sure from your letters there isn't! The others are all occupied, aren't they? Even if they are operating on a horse-and-buggy economy!"

Yes, she told him, almost gobbling with excitement, all the other farms in the Valley were tenanted and High Coombe had been sold off and was now a building estate and caravan camp. Her father had long since written-off Periwinkle and what remained free of weeds had been split between Hermitage and Four Winds, after Elinor Codsall had married her German prisoner-of-war. He looked thoughtful at this and she noticed that when he concentrated his expression reminded her sharply of his grandmother, Meg Potter; he had Meg's deep-set eyes and bushy brows and the same obstinate chin.

"That's bad," he said, "for I don't suppose either Pitts or Harold Codsall will take kindly to surrendering land. They could be compensated, I suppose. I've earmarked two thousand dollars for contingencies."

"Good heavens!" she said. "Daddy wouldn't let you pay money for that! He'd come to some kind of arrangement with Henry and Harold," but he said, sharply, "If they can be persuaded to let it revert I'll pay for it! I'm aiming to be a freeholder, not a tenant farmer. Come to think of it, it's probably a good idea the Gov let the place run to seed. He might even be glad to get it off his hands. Would he, do you think? After we're married, of course?"

The sheer casualness of the afterthought made her gasp and she said, drawing back a little, "*Married?* Good Lord, Rumble, you haven't even proposed to me yet! I was always hoping you would in your letters but for every paragraph in them that made me hope there were five hundred about sheep-dip!"

He said, with his slow grin, "Ah, you'd be surprised how many trial proposals I used to light my pipe winter evenings! Fact is, I'm too down-to-earth to put that kind of guff on paper but then, where's the point, seeing I never looked twice at any other Sheila?"

"Sheila?" she said, with a sharp stab of jealousy, "who is Sheila?" and he threw back his head and laughed, telling her that "Sheila" was nobody in particular, just Australian slang for "girl-friend".

"Well," she said, much relieved, "you haven't even told me how and why you're here. I suppose you decided to come as soon as you got my letter telling you the awful news about poor little Claire?"

"No," he said, "I didn't wait for a letter. I went East the day after I read about it in the papers. She was only about eleven when I left, poor kid, but she would have had my vote at a beauty contest even then. How has your mother taken it, Mary?"

"Oddly enough a good deal better than Father," she told him. "He's frightfully low but you being here will cheer him up. He was always asking about you and I had to read him all the farming bits from your letters. I think he approves of you very much, Rumble."

"Well, I hope so," he said, "seeing that he's likely to be stuck with me for a son-in-law!" and suddenly he reached out and grabbed her again with a kind of proprietary flourish that made her giggle but his embrace was no laughing matter; his grip promised to crack her ribs.

"Oh, Rumble," she cried, as he swung her off her feet and carried her triumphantly into the yard, "you'll never know what a difference it made, looking in that filthy window and just seeing you there! I can't get Claire out of my mind and the others can't, either. It seems almost wrong to feel happy after what happened to her but I do, I do, terribly happy, and . . . safe somehow! Can you understand that? No, I don't suppose you can, not having been here when it happened, and not having seen any of us in years!"

He said, cheerfully, "Whether I can understand it or not it sounds very flattering!" and when he seemed disposed to march clear across the yard and into the lane with her, she said, "For heaven's sake put me *down*, Rumble! Suppose Henry Pitts or anyone came down moor road?"

"Oh, they wouldn't begrudge me a celebration," he said, "not even in England, where they still go for the gooseberry-bush guff!" but he set her down, kissed her mouth with the air of a man sealing a bargain and set off down the eastern slope at such a pace that she had to trot to keep up with him. When they reached the wicket gate in the park wall, however, he suddenly became shy and said, "Hadn't you better run on ahead and warm them up a little? After all, this isn't the Outback or the Rockies, where anyone passing by is expected to stay a fortnight!" but she seized him by the hand saying that Paul and Claire would be delighted to see him and that he was just what was needed up there, so they crossed the Big Paddock, skirted the Home Farm and came on the drive near the final curve, Mary running across the gravel forecourt shouting, "Mummy! Daddy! Look who's here!" and thinking that even decorous Claire would have whooped for joy to see Rumble back in the Valley at last and at a time when they could all do with a little good news.

II

He had his father's flair for lighting up shadows, for coaxing laughter from such reluctant subjects as the poker-faced Thirza and the solemn Mark Codsall. From the moment he flung down his rucksack in the hall, and was dragged by Mary into the library, stillness left the house and voices were raised again. He was, Paul thought, like the sun and the wind, radiating vitality just as Ikey had done whenever he chose and it was quite astonishing to see the effect he had upon Mary, who hardly ever took her eyes from him, although she had an irritating habit of interrupting and throwing him off on a fresh tack just when he was explaining something interesting, like the latest kind of reaper operating in the wheatlands of the North-West. The two men soon got down to business and, as Mary had predicted, Paul was very willing to have Periwinkle reoccupied, promising to see what he could do to recover the hundred-odd acres leased to Hermitage and Four Winds. Harold Eveleigh, he said, would probably be glad of a shrinkage, for Four Winds was about as much as he could handle with only one man and one boy but Henry's son, David, might protest at yielding up the Undercliff pasture, for he had put a good deal of work into it since it was ceded. Supposing this could be achieved, however, Periwinkle would still be a farm of well under two hundred acres and not, he would have thought, an economical unit these days. Would not Rumble be better advised to cross the river and take one of Gilroy's run-down properties? He understood that the Heronslea estate was in very bad shape, with some of the smaller farmers being welded into larger units, and two or three ruinous and tenantless at the moment.

"I wouldn't care to go outside the Valley," Rumble said. "I've done all the travelling I intend to do. From now on, if you catch me north of the railway line, or east of the Coombe, you can take a shot at me with a twelve-bore!" and he obviously meant it, for he at once plunged into a detailed description of what he intended doing with Will Codsall's old place, and how he could make it as prosperous a farm as Four Winds in Norman Eveleigh's heyday. "Two-thirds of it are southern slopes," he said, "and dear old Elinor, bless her, had her nose so deep in the hen-roosts that I don't think she ever realised it, or Will Codsall before her! Once I've reclaimed the moor strip there's not much I couldn't raise there and I've learned what can and can't be done in a climate like ours! Cereals can be produced here cheaper than in Canada, providing mechanisation is one hundred per cent and the biscuit factories prefer English wheat to any other kind."

"Then why has three million acres passed out of cultivation since the war?" Paul asked, and Rumble said it was largely on account of the English farmer's resistance to new methods and reluctance to combine for the purposes of buying and marketing. Paul, who had been trying to build a co-operative system ever since 1911, had to admit that Rumble was right and asked if Periwinkle would specialise or follow a policy of mixed farming, like that practised by most of the Valley farmers for generations.

"That depends entirely on available markets and the growth of Government subsidies," Rumble said. "The canning industry is bound to go on expanding and when it does it might pay to try fruit on the western side. In the meantime I shan't bother with beef or pigs, and if I follow Elinor in the matter of hens you won't catch mine outside of a deep-litter! Free range is old-hat, and damned wasteful on farms as small as they are in this country. What do you want for Periwinkle as it stands, Gov? I shall have to make a start right away if I'm to be ready for spring sowing, and there's not so much as a fence in repair over there!"

Paul said, smiling, "What shall we say? Ninety acres at sixpence an acre . . . ?" but Rumble's jaw shot out and he said, briskly, "I'm not joking, Gov'nor! If I can't buy it I won't have it!"

"Then have it as a wedding present," Paul said, "providing I got the message in Mary's eyes!" and he thought how times had changed, for here was everybody blandly assuming that Rumble and Mary would marry almost at once and so far no one had mentioned the matter either to him or to Claire, save by implication.

"No, I'll not have that," Rumble said obstinately. "I wouldn't feel I owned it and I always wanted to own a piece of the Valley, ever since I was a kid."

"Did you now?" said Paul, much surprised, and reflecting how odd it was that such a thought had never entered the head of either one of his own sons. "Well, I see your point, and I daresay I'd have felt the same at your age, but the farmhouse itself is derelict and it's my responsibility to get that put right before I make the place over. I'll ask Eph Morgan to look at it. He'll give me good advice."

"I've already looked at it," Rumble said, "and I don't want anyone else messing about over there! I can make that place shipshape in three months, providing I can hire one pair of unskilled hands. Where I've been we don't waste money on builders, plumbers and electricians, we do things ourselves. All I want out of you is your price. And your daughter!"

"Ah, I was wondering when you were coming round to that," Paul said, "but supposing you can make Periwinkle habitable, when do you intend getting married?"

"The day the last shingle goes on the roof," Rumble told him, "for I'm damned if I'm going to re-thatch! It looks pretty enough but a man's never done with it. Can you buy Canadian shingles around here?"

"I'm sure *you* can," Paul said, responding to the boy's tremendous zest, and remembering precisely how he himself had felt when he first vowed to put new life into the Valley, "but if you won't let me set you up there I'll buy you a tractor for a wedding present and Claire will chip in with some furniture. By God, but it does me good to see somebody with a bit of real enthusiasm for land! I'd begun to think we'd seen the last of it in your generation and quite made up my mind that you would stay in the Dominions. Weren't you tempted to? Honestly?"

"No, never, although it was fun while it lasted and the best place to learn because class cuts no ice at all over there! A man's judged on the skill in his hands and the ideas in his head."

"Then apart from Mary what made you return?"

Rumble said, wrinkling his brow and looking, for a moment, extraordinarily like his Grandfather Tamer assessing the cash value of a piece of flotsam, "It's home, I guess. I could have sent for Mary and I daresay she would have come but there wasn't a day out there when I didn't sniff the air and find something missing! Spring-time and Fall were the worst. You could never smell rain, or come to terms with the colours. All manner of things tug at a man but one can't put a name to 'em until one's back. In the train, on the way down, I got a clue—everything's real green—that is, neither parched up, as it most always was in Queensland, or green-sombre, like the pine forests back of the Rockies. And the sky is different too, maybe because it doesn't stay the same for two minutes together!"

"Well," Paul said, laughing, "Mary often told us you weren't any great shakes at writing a love-letter, Rumble, but you seem to me to have the instincts of a poet, of the Walt Whitman variety! Did you ever read him?"

"Never," Rumble admitted, "but Mary's been threatening me with poetry ever since I got back! Maybe I should be grateful to all the guys she quotes. They seem to have kept her in cold storage while I was away."

"I don't think it was the poets altogether," Paul told him, remembering the glimpse he had of his daughter in French Wood the day Rumble made up his mind to go overseas. "I think it was Valley magic. After all, your roots here are a lot deeper than mine!" and he got up as Mary came bouncing in, shouting that Henry Pitts and his son David had called, that she had shown them into the office, and that a message had come from Harold Eveleigh saying he would be over as soon as he could see about the redivision of land and when Paul, astonished, said he had not even broached the matter to either of them, Mary said gaily, "No, but I did and I think you ought to see to it at once, Daddy!"

He went along the corridor hiding his smile. It was extraordinary, he thought, how the certainty that she was coveted put sparkle into the girl. Maybe there was more of Claire in her than either of them had suspected.

Mary's was far more of a Valley wedding in the old-fashioned sense than that of any of his other children, all of whom had married what Mrs. Handcock or Old Tamer would have dismissed as "forriners", notwithstanding the fact that Whiz's groom, Ian, and both the twins' wives, were a mixture of Saxon and Celt. Here, however, both bride and groom had been born within hailing distance of the Sorrel, and nobody (except possibly Claire) recalled that the latter had first seen the light of day in a cave over the badger slope in Shallowford Woods.

So many responded to the general invitation that Paul was reminded of the wedding of John Rudd and Maureen O'Keefe, getting on for thirty years ago, the last occasion he could recall when children presented horseshoes to the happy pair on their way down the drive.

He prayed for a fine day and his prayers were answered, April borrowing a few hours from June and the sun throwing down a cloth-of-gold cloak that spread from the summit of the Bluff to the crown of the Teazel watershed. It was the first family reunion since the day of the Dairy Queen final but, as though by common consent, nobody mentioned this and the occasion was further heightened for Claire by a sight of her first grandchild, the three months' old daughter of Whiz, home on leave from Malaya. There were prospects of more to come, she noted, when the twins' wives appeared, putting all the women to shame with their smart London clothes but unable to disguise the fact that both were pregnant. Simon and Rachel turned up, both, she thought, looking rather tired and old, and Smut Potter, by virtue of the fact that he was uncle of the groom, hired himself a topper and striped pants from Whitby's, in Paxtonbury, and so astounded his brother Sam that he exclaimed to Henry Pitts, "Would 'ee think, to look at 'un, that he ever did time for poachin'? Damme, you could almost mistake him for old Gilroy himself!" All the Valley originals attended the church and reception; Marian Eveleigh, Eph Morgan, now in his eighties, and Martha Pitts also in hers, Maureen and her son Paul, Abe Tozer, the smith (who now shoed no more than two horses a week), together with a score of second-generation couples, mostly Pascoes, Timberlakes or Codsalls. Old Edward Derwent was bedridden but he sent Liz along and Rose came down from Gloucestershire. To Paul, looking out of the library window while the guests were assembling after the ceremony, it was proof that many of his fears regarding the Valley's vitality were groundless but perhaps this was less because so many familiar faces were to be seen than the reassurance that had been his watching Rumble rebuild Periwinkle almost single-handed, and also the light in his daughter's eyes, when she came downstairs to share a ten-minute vigil with him after Claire and all the others had left for the church.

"There's no hurry, sir," the car-hire man had told him on the telephone, when he was dressed, fidgety and waiting for Claire to come down, "it's customary for the bride to be five minutes late at the church. There's only the one car, I believe?"

"Yes," Paul told him, "just the bridal car, my wife and the others are finding their own transport but you will be here sharp at eleven, won't you?" Then, having survived the last-minute panic surrounding the departure of the family in what looked like a motorcade, he retired to the library for a double brandy and was enjoying it when the door opened and Mary came in, looking as serene and composed as young Claire would have looked in similar circumstances but, to his mind, the most ravishing bride of the century. The brandy had steadied his nerves and he said, gratefully, "This is something very special for me, Mary. All the other weddings—well, perhaps I shouldn't say it—but they were just occasions! You and Rumble represent the continuity I always wanted and worked for and my only regret is that Ikey didn't live to see it! I think he would have derived as much satisfaction from it as I do. You don't remember him, I suppose?"

"No, and I've only the vaguest memory of Rumble's mother, but you loved the pair of them, didn't you?"

"Yes I did," he admitted, "as much as my own children, although they were probably the most unlikely pair who ever produced a child, even in a community like ours which has been throwing up eccentrics for generations! You don't look as if you need a drink but you can have a small one if you like."

"No," she said, arranging herself on the humpty as deftly as a swan on a nest, "I'll wait, I think. I always thought I'd be sick with panic but I'm not and when you come to think of it why should I be? How old was Rumble when Mother brought him home that day?"

"Four; you're not telling me you remember his arrival here, are you?"

"That's the funny thing," she said, "I do, and quite distinctly! It was only an hour after his mother was killed, wasn't it? Mother told

1057

us he'd just been orphaned and we had to make it up to him but I think I was the only one impressed!"

He thought he knew what she was thinking—of the seeming inevitability of this marriage, something that had seeded itself and emerged from a shared childhood but he could remember the original link in the chain that connected her Rumble Patrick Palfrey to the Valley—an impulsive act of his street-urchin father in the scrapyard during the long, hot summer of 1902, a tiny, insignificant incident that had prompted him to adopt Ikey, first as a stable-boy, later as a kind of son; he did not remember ever having told her how casually it had all begun.

There was no time now; the car advertised its arrival by a screech of tyres on the gravel and she stood up, unhurriedly rearranging the folds of her gown.

"Well," he said, offering his arm, "here goes the last of the Craddock girls!" and she replied, rising to the occasion, "Well you needn't sound so beastly relieved about it! I may have been the retiring one of the family but I had my chances!"

"I'm damned glad you didn't take 'em!" he said, and they passed out on to the terrace and into the forecourt where the car stood flaunting its broad, white ribbons.

III

Edward Derwent died that spring and neither Paul, Claire, nor anyone else who was on intimate terms with the old man could regret his death. He had been bedridden for the better part of a year and had confessed, often enough, that confinement to a bedroom was purgatory. Liz told Paul he was a tetchy invalid and Paul could believe it. He had always been a very active man, even in his declining years, and when Paul called on him for the last time he admitted that he had made the biggest mistake of his life retiring at seventy and "handing over to that damned son o' mine!"

"I should have carried on and died on my own acres, same as Norman Eveleigh!" he said, "for that way High Coombe would ha' stayed inside the boundaries and I shouldn't have to lie here knowing there was a rash o' red-brick spreading across Eight Acre and Cliff Warren! However, tiz too late to think o' that now!"

"I don't ever think of it," Paul had comforted him, "and neither does Claire! At the time it happened it stuck in my gullet but at least it was a means of keeping the coastline open. If Sydney hadn't got direct access to Coombe Bay through your land he would have hammered away at the County Council until he got a road over the dunes from the west. As it is we got off fairly cheaply. Young Harold Eveleigh's return to Four Winds shored up the landslide to some extent."

"Ah!" Derwent said, with real regret in his voice, "I should ha' had more sons and I would have had if I hadn't lost my first wife, backalong."

"You've done all right by your daughters, Edward," Paul reminded him, "and you can't expect your bread buttered both sides. I daresay, if you had had a spread of sons, they would have been killed in the war!" and the old man must have pondered this for presently he said, "Arr, I daresay you're right at that, boy! It never struck me that way before and the girls did me credit, just as you say, tho' I should have liked our Rose to have married a bit earlier and had children!"

It occurred to Paul, looking down at the broad, red face, spiked with grey bristles, that Edward Derwent had always been a man who concerned himself exclusively with fundamentals. Land, stock, and children to follow him, were the only things that he had ever considered worthy of serious contemplation. Everything else could go hang. He wondered if this was one of the reasons why he had always got along with his gruff old father-in-law and said, hoping to comfort him a little, "Well, Edward, you did me a damned good turn producing Claire. It's been a good marriage, right from the start."

"Aye, you don't have to tell me that, son," the old man replied, "although I daresay she's been a bit of a handful now and again. You can lay that to my door for I spoiled her after her mother went and sometimes it looked to me as if you did the same. The times were against us, mind you! A man's position in the house baint what it was, I can tell you! Why, even Liz'll answer back when she's a mind to!" and as though making a final effort to assert the doctrine of male superiority he raised his voice and bellowed for his wife, who at once made nonsense of his complaints by popping into the room like a cuckoo on the hour-strike, saying, "What *is* it, dear? Do 'ee want for anything?" and Paul had to turn to the window to hide a smile.

Rose came down when the old man's condition grew worse and she and Claire were with him when he died. He was buried in the churchyard extension, within swearing distance—as Smut Potter irreverently observed, of his one-time neighbour Tamer, with whom he had once maintained a long-standing feud about water-rights and the depredations of the Potter clan on his well-kept acres. "I sometimes wonder," Smut told Paul at the funeral, "what might have happened downalong if the Almighty, in His infinite wisdom, hadn't planted Preacher Willoughby between the two of 'em. I reckon you would have come looking for an estate and found a bliddy battlefield!"

Paul offered Liz a home at Shallowford but she declined. Edward, she said, had left her sufficient to buttress her old age and she had made many friends in Whinmouth and preferred to live out her years in the quayside cottage. "Us likes to watch the people go by," she said unexpectedly, "and I would miss my whist so! Tiz kind o' Claire to want me, tell her, but I'll stop where I be, thanking you!"

A more cheerful entry found its way into the estate record a week or so later, when preparations for celebrating the Silver Jubilee of George V and Queen Mary were in progress. Paul was leaving the Rectory one morning in early May, having been discussing with Horsey the street-luncheon and the distribution of commemorative mugs to the schoolchildren, when he saw a blue Morris Cowley zigzag down the village street, its horn blaring and its course so erratic that pedestrians instinctively withdrew into shop doorways until it came to an uncertain halt a few yards short of the church. Paul saw the driver waving but the sun was in his eyes and it was not until he crossed the street that he realised, to his amazement, the driver was Henry Pitts. Beside him, snuggled down like a sleek little dormouse, sat a pretty, very diminutive woman of about thirty-five, whom he recognised as one of the newcomers to the area who had recently bought one of Sydney Codsall's bungalows at the top of the village. Henry, who was in an ebullient mood, insisted they all adjourn to The Raven close by. Like everyone else in the Valley he deliberately avoided calling the pub by its new name, "The Lovell Arms". Paul was so astounded to see Henry driving a car that he followed them without a word and it was not until they were sipping their drinks that he found his tongue and asked Henry to introduce him to the lady and incidentally explain his inexplicable surrender to the twentieth century.

"Well, Maister," Henry said, breezily, "I had to come to it, zame as everybody else yerabouts, but 'twas a pistol held to me head and Ellie's finger on the trigger, baint that zo, midear?" and he slid his arm round the little woman's waist and drew her towards him with a familiarity that left Paul in no doubt at all but that Henry was planning to fill the gap left in his life by the death of his wife, Gloria. "Do 'ee know Ellie? Do 'ee know the Squire, midear?" and when Paul said he had not the pleasure, and Ellie giggled her denial, he continued expansively, " 'Er's new yerabouts, you zee, and a widder, baint 'ee, midear? Us on'y made up our minds this morning, zo tiz fitting you should be the first to know. Truth is, I told Ellie you'd stand for me when us gets down to bizness. Will 'ee, now?"

"Certainly I will and I'm delighted to hear it," said Paul, reaching down to shake hands with Ellie, who seemed to stand no higher than Henry's massive chest, "but I don't see the connection between finding a wife and buying a motor-car, Henry. Damn it, you've always set your silly face against everything that's appeared on the market since Edward the Seventh was crowned!"

Ellie seemed to regard this remark as a brilliant witticism on Paul's part, laughing so heartily that she spilled half her gin-and-orange down her chest and Henry bought her another and made a great show of removing the droplets from the front of her frock. When his ministrations were complete he said gravely that the car was not his but had belonged to Ellie's late husband, a commercial traveller for a well-known brand of pickles, who had died of thrombosis whilst opening up new territory in Hampshire, six months ago. " 'Twas very suddenlike, wasn't it, midear?" he said gaily. "Dropped stone dade, he did, in the act o' taking his boots off! And him all alone, poor toad, in one o' they dismal little places commercials stay in when they'm peddling!"

If it had not been for the fact that Henry was acknowledged to have the largest and softest heart in the Valley Paul might have found elements of near-relish in this recital, particularly as, all the time Henry talked of her husband's fatal collapse, little Ellie beamed at him and then added, by way of extenuation, "Oswald was twenty years older than me, Mr. Craddock, so it weren't that much of a shock, if you follow me!"

"I see," said Paul, reflecting that, although only half her size, Henry's intended had the same philosophic approach to life and death as her predecessor, and at once bought another round, asking, "What finally overcame that daft prejudice of yours towards all things mechanical, Henry?" and Henry explained that Ellie had the car but could not drive and that he, at fifty-eight, declined to walk the four miles between Hermitage and Coombe Bay every night to do a bit of courting, so he had hired a man from the Whinmouth Motor Company, taken a course of driving lessons and could now "push her along middling-like!"

"Middling-like is about right," Paul commented but comforted himself with the reflection that a man who had survived three years on the Western Front without a wound would almost certainly die in his bed, especially as his grandfather had come close to breaking the Valley record for longevity.

"Perhaps Ellie can talk you into getting a tractor after you're married," he suggested, "for it's something I've never been able to do! Here's to both of you, and jolly good luck! Will it be a church wedding or a quiet affair at the Registry Office?"

"Oh, not church, Mr. Craddock," said Ellie, in a shocked tone, very much at odds with the congeniality she had shown over the eclipse of the traveller in pickles, "I mean, it wouldn't *look* right, would it? Not with the pair of us hardly out of mourning!"

"No, perhaps not," conceded Paul and suddenly decided that he liked her for her honesty and remarkable inconsistency, both of which promised to contribute something towards the happiness of his oldest friend in the Valley.

"Well, tiz a rare bit o' luck us running into you today," Henry said, "for us was racking our brains about how to break it to young David and Mother! Seeing you reminded me o' the part you played getting Elinor Codsall clear away, with that bliddy Squarehead she married! Do 'ee think you could bring yourself to sound the boy on how he'd feel about me bringing Ellie back to Hermitage? I dorn mind tellin' 'ee, Squire, tiz something I don't relish doin'."

"Damn it, that's surely a job for you, isn't it?" Paul protested but Ellie said, earnestly, "Oh, we've already given 'em the *hint*, Mr. Craddock! What Henry means is—well—could you bring yourself to pop over today and sort of walk in on us, after we'd put it to 'em? Henry told me his Ma thinks a rare lot of you, and if we can bring her round to it I don't reckon we shall have trouble with Henry's boy. You see, I always get along with men!" and she winked so impudently that it was Henry's turn to soil his waistcoat with liquor.

It began to look like a conspiracy and must have been hatched, Paul decided, the moment they saw him in the street. He said, with a sigh, "Your father warned me thirty years ago what I was taking on with this place, Henry! I'll come but only providing you take the plunge now. For all that I don't see how my presence will help much."

"Giddon, doan you believe it," said Henry, finishing his pint at a gulp, "Mother alwus did think the sun shined from your backside, Squire! Hop in, Ellie, and us'll get it over an' done with, midear!"

and he led the way out to the little car and after killing the engine five times managed to start and drive down to the river road, where he soon built up to thirty-five miles per hour. It was a breathless but triumphant journey. Along every yard of the route Henry kept his finger on the horn and when he had occasion to change gear the car proceeded in violent leaps and bounds, so that Paul was relieved to be put out at the top of Hermitage Lane and watch them drive on to the farm, "to warm things up a bit" as Henry put it.

He gave them fifteen minutes' grace and then ambled into the yard advertising his approach by calling to the dogs, so that Henry emerged on the porch and exclaimed, for the benefit of his aged mother and son, David, "Why damme if it baint Squire himself! Come along in! Youm just in time for the shock of a lifetime, Squire! I was just tellin' Mother I was thinkin' o' bringing Ellie to care for her in her old age, wadden I, Davey boy?" whereupon he solemnly reintroduced Paul to Ellie and then treacherously withdrew, on the feeble pretext of showing Ellie his saddlebacks.

It was obvious that the news had not come as a thunderbolt to the old lady and her grandson and equally clear that they were not wholly in favour of the arrangement, for Martha Pitts, invariably cheerful and welcoming, now had her nutcracker jaws well clamped and Young David was glowering at the stone flags, his enormous red hands hanging loose, like a pair of hams in a butcher's window. Paul realised that the initiative was his and took it, as much out of his sympathy for them as Henry.

"You might have done a good deal worse, Martha!" he said, bluntly. "She's a cheerful little body and I think she'll make Henry a good wife. These things are never easy for the people concerned but when a man has been married as long as Henry he's far easier to live with if he cuts his losses and starts all over again."

"She baint varmin' stock!" Martha grumbled, "and you c'n zee that be lookin' at her!"

"And suppose I had it in mind to marry an' zettle in yer?" demanded David, and they both awaited his verdict, not exactly resentfully but with a certain shared glumness.

"She may not be farming stock but she's obviously used to a hard day's work," Paul said. "Morover, she's genuinely fond of Henry and certainly isn't after what money he's got. In fact, it seems to me she's doing precisely what he's doing—finding a means to insure against a lonely old age!"

"He's got us!" said Martha, defensively.

"Both of you are different generations and that's important to a man his age. And talking of ages, he's not old enough to retire and hand over to you, David. If he did he'd soon run to seed if I know Henry. *Were* you thinking of getting married yourself?"

"Well, no, I got no one particular in mind," the young man admitted, "but I got a right to if I do want!"

It occurred to Paul now that here was a situation that often cropped up in local farming families, where life revolved around a single, indivisible unit of land but it was a problem he had never been called to solve. Sometimes the older generation lived on and the sons soldiered as junior partners until they wanted to marry, but so far none of the Shallowford farms had supported three working generations under a single roof. He said, on impulse, "Suppose I agreed to build a house nearer the river if and when you think of marrying, Davey? Hermitage is large enough to support two families and I daresay Martha would get along with Ellie well enough, once she set her mind to it. If she didn't could she move in with you?" and he was relieved to see the old lady's face relax, for it was known that she had always worshipped Henry's son and that the boy's presence here had made it easy for her to get along with the sharp-tempered Gloria in the past.

"What do 'ee say to that, midear?" she asked, glancing at her grandson with the furtiveness of the very old and insecure, and Davey' wrinkling his brow, said, "Well, I daresay 'twould be the best way out, Gran! I'd always be glad to 'ave 'ee, you knows that well enough!"

"Very well, you've got my word for it," Paul said. "There's an ideal site on that flat piece below Undercliff where the brook runs under the road. I'll get my son-in-law Rumble to survey it tomorrow, for he seems to have made a first-class job of tidying up Periwinkle. You're good neighbours, I hope?"

"Arr," said David, with a flicker of enthusiasm, "he's a dabster an' no mistake! Can do well-nigh anything with his own two hands an' most of it a bliddy sight better'n a tradesman! Coulden wish for a better chap upalong, I couldn't!"

"Then it's settled," Paul said, "and the pair of you do what you can to make Ellie feel she's wanted in the meantime!" and he withdrew to find Henry and Ellie hanging about the yard, having eavesdropped on most of the conversation at the scullery window. They were obviously relieved and Henry said, " 'Ow much will it cost to build that bungalow downalong, Squire?" and Paul said, shortly, "A good deal less than it would to have a bad atmosphere up here, Henry! This has always been a happy farm and I want to keep it that way!"

"Arr," Henry replied, thoughtfully, "youm right about that, Maister! Gloria had her moods, mind you, but Martha could always manage her, 'cept that one time, when she left it to me and a pair o' scissors!"

"What was that?" piped Ellie but he replied, with one of his slow, rubbery smiles, "Mind your own bliddy bizness, Ellie! Tiz between me an' Squire and I won't tell 'ee 'till I 'ave a mind to!" and he emphasised Valley dominance of male over female by the proprietary slap on the behind that made them seem man and wife already.

Paul declined an offer of Henry's to run him back to the house, walking over the shoulder of Undercliff pasture to the slope below French Wood and congratulating himself on a good morning's work, albeit one that would set him back by several hundred pounds. High Coombe was gone but Four Winds had been saved and Periwinkle was burgeoning under the hands of Rumble and Mary. Now Hermitage, always one of his favourites, had been insured against dissolution, so that, taken as a whole, the future was more promising than it had been for a long time. He stopped at the crest and looked down across the Valley. Next week, he remembered, there would be Silver Jubilee celebrations, and although it seemed probable they would lack the spontaneity (and certainly the imperial aggressiveness) of 1902 and 1911, official jollifications were at least evidence of continuity and that alone, in a rapidly changing world, brought him a measure of satisfaction. He felt the urge to hurry on home and write in the estate diary about proposed changes this side of the Valley and relief must have shown in his face when he appeared at lunch, for Claire greeted him with a cheerful, "What's cooking? You look smug?" and he replied, "I feel smug, and I've every right to! No one in this house ever has fully appreciated my stupendous talents as an arbitrator!"

IV

It was, one might have said, his Indian summer of smugness. With the Slump behind him and the family, apart from the baby, off his hands, even his feud with Sydney Codsall became almost extinct after the bricks of the bungalows on the eastern border had mellowed and the County Council (with whom Sydney seemed to have lost his grip) compelled him to shift the caravan-park nearer the main road where it was screened, to some degree, by the tongue of the woods.

The Silver Jubilee celebrations were tepid judged by earlier and more robust jamborees, as though the British were honouring the royal family from habit. Public luncheons were eaten, races run, mugs distributed, loyal addresses delivered but purely local festivities had lost their appeal in an age when radios were switched on all day and there was a two-hourly 'bus service between Coombe Bay and Paxtonbury, and all the youngsters roared about the countryside on motorcycles. People went further afield these days and looked for more sophistication in their leisure. There were two cinemas in Paxtonbury and one in Whinmouth, and their bills were displayed regularly in the window of Smut Potter's baker's shop, giving him and his French wife free access to Hollywood entertainment every day of the week had they cared to avail themselves of this tremendous privilege.

And yet the Valley remained a unit, buttressed in the east by dedicated, middle-aged men, like the cork-footed Brissot of Lower Coombe and Francis Willoughby of Deepdene, and in the west by the bastions of Four Winds, Hermitage and the resurrected Periwinkle. There was still no more than a wandering path along the dunes and over the goyles and liaison between the estate and the National Trust kept the great woods in being and the slopes of Blackberry Moor free of bricks and mortar.

On Midsummer's Day, 1935, when all the Jubilee litter had been gathered up and burned, a casual perusal of the estate diary sent Paul off on one of his great circular sweeps, his first in a long time. He had been entering up after breakfast when something prompted him to turn back the pages, a whole fistful of pages, to the same season of the year a quarter-century ago, when he had made the rounds to acquaint tenants of King Teddy's death, in 1910. The recollection of this set him musing on the great patterns of change that had overlapped one another in the last two-and-a-half decades. It struck him that the very act of conveying such news across country on horseback was something linking him to Tudor and Stuart eras, for today, supposing the ailing George V died, everyone in the Valley would be aware of the fact within minutes. There was hardly a cottage that did not possess its radio and London papers arrived in Coombe Bay at breakfast-time on the morning 'bus. The bright sun threw golden darts across the little room so that the prospect of paperwork depressed him and he pushed his tray aside, letting his mind rove back to the day, clearly recalled, when he had ridden old Snowdrop over the Sorrel and back across the edge of the moor to the mere and the farms in the east. It seemed more than twenty-five years ago. Four of his seven children had been unborn and young Ikey Palfrey had only just left school. Old Tamer and Willoughby were already dead but Arthur Pitts, John Rudd, Norman Eveleigh and most of the old brigade were thriving and so were the second generation, Will Codsall, Big Jem, and a score of others commemorated in French Wood. The sight of a motor-car in those days had set everyone running and no one in the Valley had ever seen an aeroplane, or heard of Hollywood. There had been but one telephone in the district, a thing that looked like an ear-trumpet in Coombe Bay Post Office and the main road running behind the woods had been white with dust all summertime. He said aloud, as he re-read his 1910 entry, "God, it's another world!" and then, hearing Claire clearing the breakfast things, shouted, "I'm going out for a spell! I'll be home to lunch!" and went along the terrace to the yard calling Mark Codsall to saddle the skewbald.

He took the same route, across Big Paddock to Home Farm, where he stopped for a brief chat with his goddaughter, formerly Prudence Pitts, now mistress of the place, and as he sat his horse talking to her he reflected how quickly these flighty girls let themselves go once they had settled for a man. Prudence had once been the belle of the Valley and the giddiest flirt for miles around; today she looked as though she had been married almost as long as her landlord. He gave her good-day and rode on, his mind occupied working out her age which he judged to be twenty-seven. She was not, he thought, wearing so well, despite her lavish use of cosmetics and fortnightly visits to the Paxton-bury hairdresser. Her figure had already begun to sag and rumour had reached him that she nagged her husband but the farm itself seemed in good order, with its outbuildings freshly whitewashed and its yard free of nettles. He emerged on to the river road and crossed the bridge, once a plank affair but now of metal plates bedded in concrete piers and rode on down the Four Winds' approach lane to the biggest but no longer the most prosperous farm on the estate. Harold Eveleigh and his eldest boy were there, tinkering with a tractor parked along-side the barn where Martin Codsall had hanged himself more than thirty years ago. He called, "Lovely morning, Harold! Anything you can't fix yourself?" and Eveleigh straightened himself and grinned.

"If I can't, Bob can," he said and the boy beside him grunted, "Carburettor trouble! This fuel is second-rate and she clogs. Dad will start her on it, no matter how many times I tell him to switch over and start on pure gas!" He tinkered awhile and then, with a stuttering roar, the engine suddenly burst into life and the boy leaped up and tuned it to a smooth *bub-bub-bub*.

"Got to keep him handy all the time," Harold said. "I wish to God he didn't have to go to school! I could do with Bob around all the week. I was going in for a mug of tea. Will you join me, Mr. Craddock?"

"Thanks no," Paul told him, "but give my regards to your wife. I'm just doing the rounds and I've promised to be home for lunch. Everything okay over here?"

"Ticking over," Harold said. "Milk yield is up but we're down on pigs. Poor old Ben is past it, I'm afraid. Time we pensioned him off!" and he nodded in the direction of an incredibly old man doddering across the yard carrying two buckets of swill, completely absorbed in the task of keeping his balance on the sun-slippery flags.

"He must be nearly ninety!" Paul said, recognising the labourer to whom he had once delivered the drunken Martin Codsall after taking him home from the bay one winter's afternoon, shortly before the Four Winds' tragedy, and he called, "Hi there, Ben!" but the old man disappeared round the corner of the barn without looking up.

"Stone deaf!" Harold said, "but a better worker than most of them for all that! I've tried to persuade him to pack it in but either he can't hear or deliberately misunderstands. He was here in Codsall's time, wasn't he?"

"Yes," Paul said, "and I daresay he's another who would prefer to die in his boots. If you retired him he'd fade out in a fortnight. It's routine that keeps that kind going."

"By God, it won't keep me going at his age!" Harold said. "I shall be damned glad to put my feet up and let the boys carry on."

"Do they want to?"

"Bob does, he's got a mechanical flair. Must be from his mother's side, it certainly isn't from mine."

"Well, there's hope for you yet," Paul said. "You heard Henry Pitts has acquired a tractor since he remarried?"

"I never believed it until I saw him cruising across Undercliff the other day but if he drives it the way he drives his Morris we shan't have him around for long!"

"Don't bank on it," Paul said, moving on. "Henry came through Third Ypres. It'll take a damned sight more than a tractor spill to kill him!"

He rode down to the river, feeling, as he would have said, "comfortable" about Four Winds. Harold Eveleigh would never be the kind of farmer his father was, or his brother Gilbert would have been, but he had more than enough staying power to see him through, and domestic peace anchored him to the place in a way that was rarer today than it had been a generation ago. He forded the river where it was no more than fetlock deep and pushed on up the swell of Undercliff and under the lee of French Wood to Hermitage, passing on his way the cleared site for Davey Pitts' new bungalow. Davey, it seemed, had been evasive when he had told him a month ago that he had no plans to marry, or perhaps his father's second marriage had jogged his elbow. He had appeared at Shallowford within three days of the confrontation and taken Paul up on his offer to provide alternative accommodation for himself and the old lady. Later it had leaked out that he had become engaged to one of the Timberlake girls living in Whinmouth, so that the danger of relationships going sour at Hermitage had been sidestepped.

The old lady was sunning herself in the porch when Paul rode up and he was just in time to see Ellie emerge with her tea and biscuits. Old Martha, he noticed, received her ministrations as a right and he thought, "The sooner the old girl goes and leaves Henry and his new wife to themselves the better!" and apparently Ellie thought so too, for she made a grimace of resignation with her mouth as if to say, "It isn't for long, thank God! But I'm not giving her a stick to beat me with!"

He passed the time of day with them both and learned that Henry had taken his new tractor down in the hollow near the moor road fork. On the rim of the western boundary he saw him, trailing blue exhaust along the bowl of a field they called Barley Mow and it was obvious, even from this distance, that he was using his tractor as a plaything and not as an implement, for the trailer he was towing was empty and Paul watched as Henry, hunched like a chariot driver, charged a narrow gateway and roared up the incline towards the north-westerly tip of the wood. It was, he felt, a cheering sight, and evidence that none were proof against the lure of gadgets. Not a hundred yards from where Henry joyously tackled the gradient was the road junction where, in the early years of the century, he had stood on the bank and gaped at his first horseless carriage, the fidgety little contrivance driven into the Valley by Roddy Rudd. From that moment, it seemed, his mind had hardened against machines and his prejudices had been increased rather than diminished by his experiences in the glutinous mud of Passchendaele, yet here he was, wedded to the machine age by a widow and an eight-horse-power car. In a way, Paul thought, it was a comic miracle.

He left Henry to his play and rode across the shallow valley to the Periwinkle boundary where the skewbald, full of spring grass, and with the hunting season well behind her, threw up her heels and took the ascent at a gallop, Paul entering into the spirit of the frolic and hallooing Mary as she emerged from the wash-house with her mouth full of pegs—rubber pegs, he noticed. Rumble Patrick must have talked her into throwing her wooden pegs on to the ash-heap.

Every time he had come this way in the last few months there had been changes and all of them good. The new shingled roof of the farmhouse, the creosoted split-rail fences and the general air of sleekness that the ugly duckling of the Valley had acquired under Rumble Patrick's dynamic direction, made his heart swell with pride, not only because the marriage was so clearly a happy one but because he felt he could take credit to himself for having produced a daughter with enough sense to sit waiting for the right husband when other girls would have compromised. And yet, although the wedding was only three months distant in time, he found it difficult to regard the new occupants of Periwinkle as newlyweds. To him they seemed always to have been man and wife elect and what had happened last April was no more than ratification of contract. As he reined in at the gate Rumble appeared from the kitchen wearing nothing but a pair of khaki shorts and, improbably, an apron. The boy's back and shoulders were burned a golden brown and Paul thought, "Now dammit, why can't I tan like that? If I take my shirt off I go brick-red, endure two days' agony, peel and then go fish-belly white again!"

"What's the idea of the badge of servitude?" he asked. "No other man in the Valley would be seen dead in an apron!" and Mary, spitting her pegs into a basket, called, "Don't come between man and wife! Rumble does the cooking on washdays and he's a better hand at it than most of the women around here! Are you going to stay and sample one of his hashes?"

"Not likely," he said, dismounting and leading the skewbald into the lean-to stable, "but I'd like to see what kind of a job you've made of it inside? You're about finished now, aren't you?"

Yes they were, she told him, and he smiled at the queenly way she marched ahead of him into the house leaving Rumble to offsaddle the mare and resume his weekly chore. He had seen the renovations in various stages but was unprepared for the pleasant impact of Elinor's old kitchen, always a tumbledown old place, with its crumbling beams and bulging cob. Today the place seemed not only solid and commodious but one of the most cheerful rooms he had ever entered, its great stone fireplace softened by large earthenware jars filled with lupins, delphiniums and gladioli, the slate floor laid with brightly patterned rugs and primrose curtains over the windows. There was a new stove in the enlarged scullery, a covered-way for boots, coals and logs, and what had once been a deeply recessed bacon cupboard had been converted into a backstair leading to the landing where the beams had been treated with a preservative that gave off a pleasing, resinous smell. She obviously took immense pride in showing him all they had done and pouted when he said the place looked more like a pocket Manor House than a run-down farm.

"I don't see why all farmers should have to share a sty with their pigs," she said, "and most of them around here do! Rumble can solve any problem once he puts his mind to it but it was me who took charge up here," and she led the way into the low-ceilinged bedroom, where the walls were painted the colour of old parchment, every piece of cottage furniture gleamed and the double bed was covered with a lavender-blue bedspread. There were night tables either side of the bed and on them were gleaming silver candlesticks, complete with the original snuffers. It all looked so trim, fresh and elegant that he thought, "They aren't really farmers at all, they're more like a couple of kids playing house!" He said:

"I was only teasing. You've got a better home-making instinct than any of us, Mary, and this would have made old Elinor Codsall's eyes start from her head. As for poor old Will, he would have rolled himself in a blanket and slept on the floor!" Then, looking at her pink nightie and Rumble's striped pyjamas folded on the pillows like props in a magazine advertisement, "You're obviously well-matched and I don't have to ask if you're happy."

"No," she said, without a trace of the shyness that had characterised her up to the very moment of Rumble Patrick's reappearance in the Valley, "No, you don't, Daddy! He's wonderful but sometimes I find it very hard to believe he's only twenty-two. He seems so much more mature than any of the younger set round here and yet — well — it doesn't make him in the least stodgy, if you know what I mean."

"I know exactly what you mean," he said, "for his father Ikey

1071

had the same quality. It was something I always envied him!" and he gave her a swift hug to express his extreme satisfaction and they went downstairs to the scullery where Rumble was stirring a savoury-smelling stew in a large, black saucepan which he lifted aside and said, as he slipped his arm round her waist, "Did he think it was a bit fussy up there? Above stairs it was her doing, not mine, Gov'nor!"

Paul said, seriously, "You've made a wonderful start here and it frightens me to think I thought of bulldozing the place after Elinor left, and letting it revert to rough pasture. What have you got in the way of stock?"

"Nothing to boast about as yet," Rumble said, "but I'm buying some Friesians from Eveleigh. The new generator's installed and the milking machine arrives on Friday. I shan't bother with pigs while the price is so low but I'm going ahead with the cereal wheat as I planned. That way I can manage with one extra hand. After we've re-claimed fifteen acres of moor we'll see about getting another on piece-work basis. Would you and Claire like to come over to a meal on Saturday night? It's rather special, the official switch-on!" and he pointed to the empty light-socket over the stove.

"We should be delighted," he said and Rumble told Mary to watch the stew while he showed Paul the electric plant housed in what had been Will Codsall's cowshed and then, as Rumble led the way out of the house, his face assumed a slightly wary expression as he said, "Did she drop the dutiful hint about a little stranger, Gov?" and went on, before Paul could exclaim, "Oh, I talked the usual guff about waiting until there was money in the bank but . . . well . . . you know these things have a way of making up their own minds! Maybe there's some sense in her view—that kids are the better for having young parents!"

"Well, you certainly haven't wasted much time, Rumble," he said, smiling, "but taken all round I think she's right and you're wrong!" He glanced down the slope to where the river gleamed between the willow clump on the wide bend above Codsall bridge. "It's a nice spot to be born in and grow up, so damned good luck to the three of you!"

He rode off along the crest towards the bulge of Hermitage Wood feeling more elated than ever. He already had three grandchildren, all girls, but Mary's, he felt sure, would be a boy and perhaps take his place here in the 'fifties and 'sixties. Somehow he had always known that his successor would derive from Mary and also that, somewhere along the line, Ikey would have a stake in it, and it was to Ikey that his thoughts returned as he cut across the northern boundary of Hermitage to enter the woods by a little-used bridle path running round the shoulder of the badgers' slope. It was about here, so Maureen told him, that Hazel Potter had been delivered of Rumble Patrick in a cave, on a summer evening the year before hell broke loose and changes rushed down on them so rapidly that it seemed the pattern of life would be shattered for all time. It had not, thank God. Somehow they had been able to save the main fabric, sort out the pieces, and begin all over again and this, surely, was what Oliver Cromwell (himself a well-meaning vandal) would have called "a crowning mercy".

The woods were at their midsummer best, the bracken shoots mushrooming as high as the skewbald's ears, the flowering rhododendrons immediately below looking like a fleet of purple galleons anchored in an olive-green bay with their crews asleep or ashore. Beyond the stream, in the hollow east of the mere, Sam Potter's cottage reminded him of the cottage Tom had seen from Hearthover Fell, in his favourite childhood book, *The Water Babies*, and as he advanced down the steep slope he caught a glimpse of the ponderous figure of Joannie Potter, wearing red, just like the old lady who had befriended the fugitive sweep. The mere itself, on his right, was very still but as he reached its northernmost tip he could see the tiny V-ripples of voles swimming along the bank towards Smut Potter's old hideout, and, over by the islet, a moorhen and her chicks making the circuit and again suggesting a fleet, only this time one of rowboats led by a small, brown ketch. The orchestra began as the path flattened out, a low, muted hum of innumerable rustlings and warblings and dronings, pitched in the identical key that he heard when he first rode here in the drought of 1902, and he thought, "This will almost certainly be the last place to change! Even Sydney's bulldozers would be defeated by this tangle, thank God!" and he called to Joannie Potter, twice as heavy as when Sam first brought her here at his instance and she answered in her high-pitched, broad-vowelled voice, "Zam's downalong! Word came Mother Meg wanted un. Do 'ee want un special, Squire?" and Paul said no, he was just taking the air, and asked after Pauline, his first Valley godchild, now married to a railwayman in Paxtonbury.

" 'Er s vine," Joannie said, "and expectin' another. That'll mak' zix grandchildren, what wi' Georgie's last one! Who'd ha' thought it now?'

"Who indeed," said Paul, with a smile, for he had always had a

1073

warm corner in his heart for Sam and Joannie, the very first of the second generation round here to raise a family and name one of their children for him, although her sex called for a little cheating and one extra syllable.

"What's Sam doing downalong?" he asked and Joannie told him that word had come from the Dell that Meg had had "one of her spells" a week since and Smut had had to take the van and fetch her back from the moor, leaving her horse to find its own way home.

" 'Er's over eighty now and 'er reely shoulden keep traapsing about, the way she does," Joannie complained.

"You'll not stop Meg moving around," said Paul, "not unless you tie her down!" and he rode on beside the mere, passing the spot where, on the left, he had first romped in the grass with Claire, and on the right was the islet holding his happiest memory of Grace. At the sloping field he turned left, hugging the edge of the woods past the favourite haunt of the Shallowford butterflies for about here, years before he came to the Valley, someone had begun planting an ornamental shrubbery and a few of the imported shrubs had lingered on, notably a buddleia that seemed to hold a special delight for butterflies of all kinds. They were here now, wavering irresolutely over the flowers, a host of Red Admirals, Peacocks, Meadow Browns, Tortoiseshells and Cabbage Whites, two or three hundred of them going about their business whatever it was, and pausing to watch them Paul remembered the neighbours of the old German professor who had been driven from the Valley in 1914, for his hobby had been lepidoptery and he had had cases of butterflies in his study.

He gave Deepdene a miss and rode instead down the winding path to the Dell to inquire after Mother Meg but she was not there and neither was Sam, the French Canadian Brissot telling him that, against her daughters' advice, Meg had set out on one of her basket-selling trips early that morning.

The Dell looked far tidier than it had ever looked under the hands of Old Tamer, his wife, or even Big Jem. There was not a nettle or dock to be seen and green wheat stood shoulder high in what had once been a tangle of briars on the southern slope of the wood.

"You seem to be keeping hard at it about here," he said to Brissot, a man he respected, although he could never understand why he had carried the Cockney Bellchamber on his back all these years. "Do you ever feel homesick for Quebec?" and the Frenchman said politely that he had never regretted settling in England because the winters were so mild, particularly down here, and even as a child he had hated snow. Violet, Jumbo Bellchamber's wife, came out with her washing while they stood talking and smiled a welcome. Like Joannie Potter she had put on a great deal of weight and it was difficult to picture her as a slim, fleet-footed girl, who had once set Valley tongues clacking and driven the young sparks wild. "They all seem to have settled for a quiet life at last," he told himself, "though I would never have bet a shilling on it happening!" and he took the track that led over the western shoulder of the Bluff and was soon clattering down Coombe Bay High Street.

Not much of the original village was left and what little there was seemed populated with strangers, loafing about the church green in holiday garb. Almost everyone about here, he reflected, catered for summer visitors and in a month or two, when the school holidays began, this street would teem with Cockneys and Midlanders in shorts and coloured shirts, with children scrambling about in the harbour with shrimping nets and toy boats. He was in such a relaxed mood, however, that the thought of Coombe Bay as a holiday resort did not bother him this morning. It was probably good for trade and who the devil was he to deny city families a fortnight by the sea, or begrudge people like Smut Potter and that French wife of his selling their confections? As he drew level with the Vicarage he saw Parson Horsey, a bent, shrunken old man now, with a halo of silvery hair circling his brown, polished skull. The old man was still very active, however, for here he was hoeing his flower-beds and stooping every now and again to pluck a weed and toss it in a seed-box close by.

"I had to get out in the sun this morning," Horsey confessed, after Paul had hailed him and Paul said, "Me too!" and reined in, asking after Abe Tozer, the smith, who had taken to his bed a week or so before.

"He'll not last the summer," Horsey said, "but he hasn't any regrets. After all, he was swinging a hammer up to last week and his wife tells me he's well over eighty. I suppose the forge will close when he dies. There's more call here for a good garage than a smithy. Your good lady is well, I trust?" and Paul said she was and told him the news from Periwinkle. Horsey said, with a smile, "Well, it doesn't surprise me, Squire. That girl of yours is a lovable lass and as for that lad of Hazel Potter's, one should never be surprised at how a Potter turns out! I've just seen Pansy taking her third husband for an airing. He's a powerful swimmer, you know, and she marches him down to the beach every morning of the week about this time between May and October. There's some very good stuff in that woman somewhere. They say she's made that poor chap a very happy man. It isn't everyone who would take him on."

It was a judgment, Paul thought, that old Parson Bull would never have passed and not for the first time he congratulated himself in installing this little gnome of a man as rector all those years ago after Parson Bull, last of the sporting parsons, had ridden himself into the ground chasing foxes.

"Do you ever hear from Rachel these days?" he asked and Horsey said he did, now and again, and that the last time she wrote she said she had just been adopted as Socialist candidate for a Glasgow constituency and seemed to have a chance of being elected if Baldwin went to the country in the autumn. He waited to see if Paul would respond with news of a letter from Simon but when he did not, added, "Your boy is her agent. I expect you'll be hearing!"

"I doubt it," said Paul. "They're generally too absorbed in politics to waste propaganda time writing to an old Diehard like me! What do you really make of them? Honestly now?"

Horsey said, with a smile, "I think maybe they have the right idea—broadly speaking that is! Things are badly shared, no one can deny that, so perhaps it's right that the younger generation should chivvy those in authority. Frankly I find their outlook a bit cold-blooded and I daresay you do as well, but if they can goad the Establishment into knocking down a few slums, raising the general standard of living, and stopping another war, then all power to their elbow! Our lot were a bit too complacent, don't you think?"

"You weren't," Paul said, remembering Claire's tale of the sermon he had preached to wounded soldiers, "but probably I was and still am! I've always known my limitations and they don't extend beyond the Teazel and the Bluff, yonder!"

He said good-bye and walked the skewbald down to the harbour where he saw the blind Alf Willis, supple and well-muscled for a handicapped man of over forty, emerge from the water and watched Pansy hand him his towel and help him on with his sweater. It was just another facet of the morning's ride that pleased him and he turned the horse into the sandhills, meaning to follow the coastline as far as Crabpot Willie's goyle before riding the last mile home in time for lunch.

It was much cooler here by the sea and the flies, which had bothered the skewbald in the woods, dropped away so that he put her into a steady trot. In five minutes he had reached the gully and turned inland, heading through the scattered pines above the shanty but halfway up the incline he reined in, his eye catching a sparkle of metal on the summit of the opposite hillock. There was a trap over there, stationary in a cleared patch about a hundred yards west of the goyle, and when he looked more closely he could see someone sitting motionless on the box, slumped against the iron backrest. He rose in his stirrups and called "Hi, there!" but the figure did not move and the pony, after raising its head, went on cropping the sparse grass. He thought, "That's odd, it looks like Old Meg's trap," and crossed the goyle at its shallow head, circling round to the clearing and coming alongside the shabby little equipage. It was Meg's trap and Meg was in it. The reins had slipped from her hands and she sat with her eyes wide open, looking out over the tops of the lower pines to the bay. He did not need to dismount to discover that she was dead.

The sight of her sitting here, staring out across the Channel, was impressive and a little awesome. She looked rooted and statuesque, her knees spread and her hands resting lightly in her lap. She might have been part of the background, something that belonged there, like one of the fully-grown pines or the outcrop of sandstone against which the trap-wheel had come to rest in the pony's search for grass. He dismounted, hitched the mare's reins to the rear step and, after feeling her pulse, knelt on the footboard and eased her into the trap-well, which was half-full of rush mats and besom brooms. She was very heavy and the effort required all his strength but he managed it and that gently, for he had a great affection for this hulk of a woman, who had always gone her own way with dignity, earning her own bread and keeping herself, and often her indolent family, with coppers coaxed from the twin trades of hawking and fortune-telling. It was strange, he thought, that she should die the morning he had news for her of another grandchild, one among so many, yet he did not find her death shocking or startling. It must have come upon her very stealthily, while she was returning home across the dunes and perhaps, hearing its rustle, she had reined in to take a last look at the sun baking the sandbanks a mile or so out to sea. It was, after all, a pleasant way to die and one he might envy her some day, death in the open and the fresh air, after a long lifetime of breathing fresh air; a good deal better than John Rudd's death in a stuffy little room and a far more natural one than poor Claire's. He thought of Old Tamer's death in the breakers off the Cove, hardly a mile east of this spot, and wondered if man and wife would now meet again after all this time and if so what they would have to say to one another. It seemed unlikely. If Heaven and Hell were Old Testament realities, then Tamer would still be working out his time in Purgatory, whereas Old Meg, who had never stolen so much as a clothes-peg, would surely get her reward if rewards were going.

He lifted the reins and clicked his tongue at the pony, turning the trap in a half-circle and setting off across the fields in the direction of the ford.

v

Uncle Franz Zorndorff paid his last visit to Shallowford that September, his last visit anywhere as it happened, for a few months later he died at the age of ninety-three. His final meeting with Paul was almost accidental.

He had written in May saying that he was going to Austria for a holiday and Paul was very surprised, not so much that a man of his advanced years should feel a sudden urge to travel, but because Franz's wish to see his homeland again after so many years indicated an unsuspected streak of sentiment in the old man. By Paul's calculations Franz had fled the Continent seventy years ago, when the Emperor Franz Joseph had ruled over his hotch-potch of a dozen quarrelsome races of which Franz's people, the Croats, were then a persecuted minority. Paul had never heard the Croat speak of Austria-Hungary with affection. It was the home, he would say, of *Schlamperei* —which he translated as a policy of deliberate drift, a tolerance for romantic nonsense, and to a man with a lifelong dedication to money-making *Schlamperei* was an unforgivable sin. It was therefore with some astonishment that Paul had read into the old man's letter a kind of confession, for Franz had written, "... I've had a very long run, my boy, and can't expect more than another year or so. Before I go I should dearly love to see what they have made of it over there, since the old Empire broke up and everybody chose their own road to perdition. You might find it difficult to believe but I have always had a filial affection for the Old Man" (he meant, presumably, Franz Joseph, who had ruled from 1848 until 1916) "and before I die I have a ridiculous desire to ride in a carriage along the Prater, and take a final sniff of the air of Transylvania. I daresay the journey will kill me but if it does then I shall have no complaints. Whilst the City of

1078

London is undeniably the only place on earth where a man can put on weight whilst making a fortune, it is not, I think, a place where one would wish to leave one's bones! Last week I made a shorter sentimental journey to your father's grave, in Nunhead Cemetery. It was, perhaps, the sight of those grey acres that suggested this grandiose display of sentiment!"

Franz did not leave his old bones in Transylvania. Judging by the series of luridly-coloured picture postcards received by the twins, by Claire and others, his return to Vienna, after a lapse of almost three-quarters of a century, invigorated him and in mid-September that year Paul was again surprised to hear Franz's precise voice on the telephone and to learn that he had that day landed in Plymouth.

"What the devil are you doing in Plymouth, you restless old rascal?" Paul demanded, and Franz said that he had made the outward journey by trans-Continental express but had returned home by sea from Trieste and would be passing through Paxtonbury in an hour or so. If Paul cared to meet him there he was welcome; there was a later train on to town and they could spend an afternoon together.

"I'll meet you, of course I'll meet you," he said, beginning to wonder if the old chap was senile, "but why on earth don't you stop off and stay with us for a week or two? There isn't all that hurry to get back to London at your age, is there?"

"As a matter of fact there is," Franz replied, unexpectedly. "To my way of thinking even minutes count but don't expect me to explain that from a public telephone-box! My train gets in at one-fifteen and if you intend meeting me be there, because I shan't get out unless you are, do you understand?"

"I'll be there," Paul said, resignedly, and replaced the receiver with a suspicion that Uncle Franz's apparent hurry might have something to do with the twins who had been left in charge of the patron's various enterprises during his absence. He mentioned as much to Claire but all Claire said was, "You're a born worrier, Paul! Why on earth should you suppose anything like that? Those boys are perfectly capable of looking after his interests. They've been more or less running his business for years!"

"Nobody runs Uncle Franz's business!" Paul said, "and I shall get to the bottom of this! It wouldn't surprise me in the least if those two hadn't been monkeying on the Stock Exchange while he was away!" and he drove off across the moor, his disquiet causing him to arrive

1079

far too early and spend an impatient three-quarters of an hour stamping up and down the platform, awaiting the boat train.

He saw Franz leaning from the window before the train came to a halt and was relieved by his obvious chirpiness. The old fellow was as spruce as ever, his face sunburned the colour of an old walnut and his Van Dyck beard curled Continental fashion, so that he looked like the most elderly character in Rembrandt's "Night Watch", one of Paul's favourite pictures.

He went along to the compartment and supervised the unloading of Franz's cases, more than enough to load a barrow, and with the note of tolerant impatience he reserved for the Croat, said, "You don't have to bother with all this clutter. I'm taking you along home whether you like it or not. Put all this stuff in the left-luggage office and we'll have lunch at The Mitre and get back to Shallowford for tea. Claire's expecting you."

"Then I shall have to disappoint her," Franz said, flatly. "I'm catching the late-afternoon train and only my duty to you disposed me to break my journey to this desert staging-post. If I survive I may well join you for Christmas but in the meantime there's salvaging to be done, I assure you."

"So those boys of mine let you down after all?" Paul said and the old Croat's Father Christmas eyebrows shot up an inch as he looked at Paul with humorous concern.

"Good heavens, no!" he said. "Whatever gave you that idea? I've been in constant touch with them and they've been splendid, quite splendid! I can't imagine how you produced a pair of smart operators like Steve and Andy. Are you quite sure Claire didn't cuckold you one day while you were out ploughing?"

"Then what the devil is your hurry?" Paul demanded. "At ninety-three you can't be all that essential to the business!" and Franz said, with a twinkle, "I don't suppose I am but I like to pretend to myself that it is so! After all, it's all I've got to hold me to life and I daresay, at my age, you'll feel precisely the same about your damned fields and dripping woods! The fact is, I've learned a good deal in the last few months, and perhaps it's lucky for all of us that I made that trip. I had my suspicions, mind you, but I have to admit that I was scared once I saw it at close quarters."

"Suspicions about what? You've only been on holiday in Vienna, haven't you?"

"To get there I crossed Germany," Franz said, "and I was suffi-

1080

ciently misguided to stop overnight in Munich. A month or so later I stayed a few days in Nuremberg, and even in Austria I was able to confer with certain associates. The truth is, my dear fellow, the balloon is almost ready to ascend!"

"Damn it, *what* balloon?" said Paul, impatiently, and Franz replied, settling himself in the car and adjusting the impeccable creases in his trousers, "Ah, I thought that would confound you! It's what follows from having your nose in the dirt all your life! I suppose you have heard of Hitler, have you not?"

"Well, of course I have," Paul said, "who hasn't? He makes more noise than the Kaiser used to but what of it?"

"What of it?" said Franz crisply. "The Kaiser turned everything upside down, didn't he? And made you a small fortune into the bargain."

"Are you trying to tell me you think there's danger of war?"

"Indeed I am," Franz said, "but a very different kind of war from anything in the past. There won't be anything gentlemanly about this one!"

"There wasn't anything gentlemanly about the last!" Paul retorted, "ask anyone who was at Ypres or on the Somme!"

"Oh, I'm not talking about the actual waging of it, the mere fisticuffs part!" Franz said, with a blandness that Paul found irritating. "I'm talking about the political aspects, the impact on Western civilisation as a whole! That maniac means business and unless we people wake up in time that disgusting swastika of his will fly in all manner of unlikely places; Buckingham Palace maybe! Oh, you can chortle, but I don't think you would if you've seen what I've seen this summer, or talked to people whose near relatives are actually populating his extermination centres!"

As usual Paul found himself impressed, in spite of private reservations that the old man was exaggerating. Franz was a Jew, of course, and he supposed that made a difference, for even Henry Pitts had expressed indignation of *pogroms* in Germany since the Nazi party had taken control, and yet, the prospect of actually being called upon to fight Germany again, had never cost Paul, or anyone else in the Valley, a moment's loss of sleep. He said, more soberly, "Very well, Uncle Franz, what did you actually see? One of those idiotic rallies, with everyone goosestepping, wearing fancy shirts and shouting 'Heil Hitler'?"

"Yes," said Franz, without the customary spice of his professional cynicism, "I saw that but I also saw elderly women and seven-year-olds scrubbing the streets and being kept at it by arrogant young thugs with dog whips! I saw whole Jewish shopping centres wrecked and looted and, in Vienna, I was infected by the panic of men I have known gamble twenty thousand pounds on a hunch and then spend the evening drinking schnapps and listening to folk music without so much as telephoning their broker! I have lived a very long time, my boy, and seen a very great deal. I have not lost my touch or my sense of smell and can still sniff powder a long way off. And even though I find it difficult to read small print without spectacles I can still recognise a vulture when I see one."

He seemed abstracted during the meal they had at The Mitre in the Cathedral Close and reluctant to return to the subject but over their coffee, after Paul had given him the family news, he said, suddenly, "There was a reason for my returning by sea! I couldn't bring myself to cross Germany again, not even to fly over it, you understand?"

"I can't help feeling you're exaggerating a little," Paul said, "for I can't imagine anyone, even the Germans, starting another war. Incidents and an occasional bickering, no doubt, with plenty of sabre-rattling and a financial crisis or two, but when it comes to the actual point anyone would think twice; three times! Anyone, that is, who was actually there and Hitler served on the Western Front."

"Precisely the same might be said of 1914," Franz said. "I defer to you when it comes to recalling actual conditions on the battlefield but someone like me, a man whose ear has been to the ground for nearly a century, doesn't have to read history books to know that in August 1914, no one, not even the Junkers, actually willed the war! It simply happened. All but the lunatic fringe were terrified of the actuality by the time the guns started firing themselves."

"Aren't there enough of us to contain him?" Paul argued. "What about Russia and France?"

"You can write off France! I've done business there lately and count myself fortunate I collected fifty per cent of my bad debts. As to Russia, there are plenty of wiseacres who think he'll turn East and if he did they would encourage him, finance him I don't doubt, but they would be doing themselves a very poor service. It's no more than a question of who is first. That man is after world domination."

It was difficult not to be convinced by the old man, particularly when one looked back on his accurate prophecies of 1906, 1914 and 1929. He had forecast, among lesser catastrophes, the German Naval race, the World War and the Wall Street crash, when those in a position to know, people like James Grenfell for instance, had been hopelessly wrong. Paul said, "Isn't there a way to head it off?"

"Yes," Franz said, "but I very much doubt if you English are realistic or ruthless enough to use the means at your disposal! You could blow Mussolini's transports out of the water when he gobbles up Abyssinia in a week or two. That might convince German financiers and chauvinists that they were playing with fire. The Abyssinians are barbarians, of course, but we might as well confine barbarism to Africa if we can." His eyes, usually as bright as a ferret's, seemed to cloud and he looked across at a portly Dickensian waiter and a couple of clergymen toying with their fish course. "You know, Paul," he said, "it's your world that's at stake, not mine! We people, the usurers of this world, learn to come to terms with these things but you never could. Win or lose you'll sacrifice all you managed to salvage from the last dog-fight—provincial peace and social patterns, a code of decent behaviour and places like this, that are the focal points of your out-dated civilisation. You'll be lucky if you don't lose your precious Valley."

"How do you suggest I insure against it?" Paul asked grimly, for it began to dawn on him that Zorndorff's telephone call and his decision to break his journey, were no more than thinly-disguised manœuvres to exercise the protectiveness shown towards the son of his old partner, a habit that had coloured their relationship for more than thirty years.

"I can tell you that, my boy," Franz said, cheering up at once, "you can act independently of that idiot Baldwin and any windbag who succeeds him, and set course between the present and Dooms-day."

"Well?"

"Buy!" Franz said, earnestly. "Lay up the treasure of the fat years against the dearth of the lean! Buy all the pedigree stock you can afford and all the latest machinery. Build a reservoir at a safe distance from the house for reserve fuel, for fuel will be one of the first things to run short. Make yourself as tight and self-contained as Noah, who received his warning from a somewhat more infallible source, but above all, ignore anything you read in the newspapers about pacts and arms agreements and Germany being too poor to wage a war of aggression! Even over there plenty of people old enough to know better are depending on that and more still are falling into the error

1083

that they are still in the driver's seat. I daresay they were until a year or so ago but time doesn't stand still for people like Adolf Hitler. It's get on or get out, the same as it is in any competitive business, and nobody seems to have recognised him as that very rare phenomenon indeed!"

"Come again!"

Franz said, with his familiar, sneering smile, "They do not recognise an Austrian who is uniquely free of the taint of *schlamperei*! I am such a one, and Hitler is another. Dangerous fellows both! Like an Englishman unhindered by tolerance, someone who would even cheat at cricket if there was a sizeable stake on the match! Well, it is time for my train, I think," and he stood up, taking out his wallet and putting a five-pound note on top of the two-pound bill.

"I'll pay for this, Uncle Franz," Paul said but the old man waved his hand.

"Certainly not," he said. "I doubt if I shall ever have the pleasure of lunching with you again," and, to the hovering waiter, "The meal was excellent! My compliments to the chef and share the change!" He swept out, past the two clergymen and the gratified waiter, and Paul reflected that for all his shrewdness he was still as vain as a mongrel who has confounded the judges by winning a first at Cruft's.

He drove home very slowly, pondering the old man's Jeremiad and wondering if, in the next year or so, he should plough his reserve (only just replenished after the drain of the slump) into building the fuel-tank and investing in stock and machinery at the County Show. "Maybe I will," he told himself, "the old rascal was right about everything else but I'm not that much impressed, in spite of it all! At the age of fifty-six there's really no reason why I should be." But then, as he looked up and saw the slender silhouette of French Wood on the sky-line, he remembered that he had sons and sons-in-law, the eldest thirty-one, the youngest still a baby, and he hurried on, saying, "Christ! Not again! Not after what we endured for four years at the hands of boneheads like Haig!" Then, as the park wall began, and he caught the gleam of sun on the shallow river, he compromised, "I'll buy, just as he advised," he told himself, "but as an investment in sanity not in suicide!"

He swung into the drive and blew his horn to give Claire warning of his approach.

CHAPTER EIGHT

I

FRANZ did not return to the West for Christmas. In mid-December Stephen wrote to say that the old man had gone into a nursing home and in late January, the week Valley radio sets broadcast news that King George lay dying, Zorndorff died in his sleep.

Paul thought it his duty to travel to London in thick, January murk to attend the cremation at Woking and when he returned to the old man's home in Sloane Street one of a small army of the solicitors Zorndorff had employed drew him on one side and gave him a letter Franz had dictated, with orders that it be handed to Paul Craddock after his death.

"He made a number of codicils to his will during the last few months," the man said, rather resentfully. "All in all it made matters very complicated! Up to that time his dealings with us had been very straightforward."

"I daresay you were well paid for it," Paul said, shortly, and the solicitor, regretting his unguarded remark, buttoned his lip and said, "Oh, I certainly wouldn't like you to think we objected in any way, Mr. Craddock. It was just that—well—we felt some of his last-minute changes were rather impulsive!"

"Since you've told me this much you can tell me what they were," Paul grunted, for he was always a little edgy in London, particularly when required to go there in winter.

"I . . . er . . . I think perhaps your sons are better qualified to explain that, sir," the man said. "After all, we handled his latest will but we were not his exclusive advisers. The Five-Year dispersal of the estate was executed by another firm. He only came to us when the partner of his regular solicitors died."

Paul relented somewhat, reflecting that Uncle Franz must have been a particularly troublesome client to men whose minds ran along prescribed grooves and when he was alone with Stevie and Andrew he reported his conversation with the lawyer, asking them how much they expected to benefit from the will. The boys were practically strangers to him now. It was getting on for seven years since they had launched themselves into this bizarre world of scrap metal, golf tournaments, mysterious trips up and down the country in bigger and better cars, and hole-in-corner conferences with shady characters who lived, Paul suspected, on their wits, and only just inside the law. Neither Stephen nor Andrew had maintained any real links with the Valley or, as far as he could judge, with any aspect of country life that was not synthetic. They wore Savile Row suits and smoked big cigars but there was still something vaguely flashy about both them and their equally well dressed wives, so that he thought with relief of Rumble Patrick and Mary, in their snug farmhouse overlooking the Sorrel.

"There's not all that much duty to pay," Andy explained, with a grin. "Uncle Franz saw to that when he split everything up a year or so after we horned in on the racket! It was lucky for us he lived out the span. Stevie and I were made partners, you know, but most of his capital was ploughed back in the Birmingham and Liverpool branches and since then we've opened yards in half-a-dozen other places. You might say that what the Old Boy really left us was goodwill, bricks and mortar. Plenty of it but not much cash. About five thou apiece I'd say, wouldn't you, Stevie?"

"Plus legacies in trust for the kids," Stevie said. "They won't have to bother, I can tell you that, Gov, so if you ever think of making a will you can cut us out and no hard feelings."

It was impossible not to respond towards the sheer impudence of The Pair, Paul thought, and he could readily understand how the old buccaneer had taken them to his heart.

"I'm not at the will-making stage yet," he told them, "but I should be interested to know how the old fellow disposed of his cash. He had hordes of Austrian relatives, most of whom sponged on him for years, but somehow I don't think the hangers-on will benefit. The lawyer I spoke to seemed to imply he had had all manner of second thoughts after his trip abroad."

"Yes he did," Andy said, "and he was damned cagey about them but from what I can gather he left a hell of a dollop to the Zionist Movement. He was very needled about what was happening to the Jews over there but, aside from that, I hope he didn't overlook you, Gov! You mightn't believe it, but he had a lot of time for you, even though, privately, he thought you were a bit . . . well . . . a bit set in your ways, if you follow me."

"I follow you," Paul said, "and it's about the politest way either of you have ever put it! He left me a letter to be read after his death and

1086

I've got it here. I purposely didn't open it until I could share it with you," and he thumbed open the stiff, parchment envelope, extracting a single, folded sheet, with an antedated cheque attached to it by a paper-clip. The cheque was for ten thousand pounds.

"Good God!" Paul exclaimed, "this is absolute nonsense! I parted with what interests I retained in the firm during the slump!"

The letter was brief and very much to the point. "My dear Paul," it ran. "I enclose this because, knowing lawyers, I realise that it might be a year before you get your hands on it. You can draw on this almost at once and, as I warned you, there isn't that much time! I don't suppose you followed my advice and stocked up but this may prompt you to begin. You ought to be a rich man in your own right but I know very well that you are not. You still might be, in spite of yourself, if you ever approach my age! It's my guess that in the years ahead land and property will skyrocket as never before and for all manner of reasons, among them over-population and slum-clearance by bombing squadrons. However, I found on getting back here, that I was in a very small minority. Few people take that little rascal any more seriously than you did. That's why I made some last-minute alterations in my will and left the bulk of my pile to those who are going to need a refuge few of them deserve! Despite your holier-than-thou judgment of me, my boy, I never really had much use for money *as* money. It was making it, beating them all at it, that was the breath of life to me, even in your father's time! One small thing; I had someone do a little digging in Somerset House after our last meeting and uncovered a little that explains your life-long obsession with mud, red necks, thatch, well-water and hairy forearms! Your mother's maiden name was 'Endicott' and she came from a Somerset Village, either Curry Rivel or Chard, I was unable to determine which, although I daresay you could find out by checking parish records. She was born in 1848 but I couldn't get a copy of the birth certificate as there were hordes of Endicotts thereabouts. All I wanted to prove to myself was that you did, after all, revert to type! Good luck always, dear ploughboy—affectionately, Franz Zorndorff."

He read the letter aloud and the twins listened respectfully. Andy said, finally, "Well what do you know? He was an amazing old bird, wasn't he? But I can't help feeling that last trip of his threw him off balance a bit. After all, who the hell cares about a bloody little whipper-snapper who used to hang wallpaper and bites carpets whenever he gets stoked up? Someone will bump him off sooner or later!"

"As a matter of fact the cheque isn't all that much of a surprise to me," Stevie admitted. "The last time I talked to the Old Boy he launched into a diatribe about the submarine fleet Hitler is building and how we should all be starved out in war. Damned funny the bats that start whizzing around in your belfry when you get to that age! There was that final instruction we found on his desk, the day the ambulance called for him."

"What was that?" Paul asked sharply, not sure that he cared for their flippancy.

"He asked us to scatter his ashes in the boneyard," Andy said. "Can you beat that? Down among the scrap! Ashes to ashes you might say."

"That's a revolting idea!" Paul protested, "and if it was left to me I should ignore it"

"Well, it was a special request," Andy said, "we've got it in black and white."

"Have you told the solicitors?"

"No," they said together, obviously awaiting a lead.

"Well don't!" Paul said. "He was a wonderful friend to me, and although we seldom saw eye to eye, I had more respect for him than you seem to have! I'll take care of his ashes and I'll do what he advised about stocking up."

"You mean you really fell for that stuff about war?" Steve asked and Paul said, no, he didn't, but he wasn't going to be caught off balance by another slump and it amounted to the same thing! Then they all took a drink, and felt better for it and the twins drove him to Waterloo in time for the five o'clock train. It was not until he had shaken them off that he could laugh at them, and as the train gathered speed, and the yellow-brick labyrinth was left behind, he re-read Franz's letter, finding that the old man's quixotic search for his mother's antecedents touched him more than the legacy. He thought, "I'll drive over to Curry Rivel and Chard in the spring and take a look at those parish records. It's odd that I never thought of contacting Somerset House myself but had to leave it to him!" Then his mind conjured with expansion on the basis of the money. One could do a very great deal with ten thousand and it seemed disloyal to spend it in any other way, or simply to invest it against a repetition of 1929–31. Two thousand would cover all the stock and machinery he could house at Home Farm and perhaps another thousand would provide a fuel-storage tank and pumping equipment, housed in the hollow on the western edge of Big Paddock. What could he do with the remaining seven? Some of it, he supposed, could be used to foster the co-operative that he had been nibbling at for years, a couple of heavy lorries, a combined harvester for the use of every farm on the estate, perhaps improved outbuildings, Dutch barns and modern byres at places like Deepdene, Low Coombe and Four Winds. That French Canadian, Brissot, and Young Eveleigh could do with some help—he didn't know about Francis Willoughby and Henry Pitts, who had always preferred to solve their own problems but they were tenants and he was entitled to improve his own property if he wished. Peri-winkle was the exception. It was being bought by Rumble Patrick over a period and already a third of the money had been paid over. Then, as the train glided into Salisbury, he had an idea, and as it took shape it appealed to his sense of humour. He explored it for flaws and could find none and by the time he had finished dinner, and the train was rattling into Paxtonbury, he was resolved on it and made up his mind that he would confide in no one but Claire.

He left the train and made his way in driving sleet to his car, set-ting the windscreen wipers threshing and settling himself for the sixteen-mile trip over the moor. It was fortunate, he reflected, that he knew every bend in the road for there were patches of fog wherever the trees fell away and his eyes were not as keen as they had been when he drove up to the artillery positions behind Vimy nearly twenty years ago. He was relieved when the gradient told him he was over the crest and dropping down to the river where the elms behind the park wall kept the mist high and comparatively thin. "Tomorrow," he told himself, shivering, "providing Claire doesn't head me off, I'll ride to Hermitage with the news. Rain or no rain it's always a damned sight warmer with a horse between one's thighs!"

Claire did not head him off. All she did was laugh and say that she supposed he was interpreting the spirit of Uncle Franz's implied con-ditions. She did suggest, however, that Simon and Whiz should bene-fit to some extent, pooh-poohing his argument that he was pledged to Rachel never to give Simon money, even supposing he was willing to accept any.

"Nonsense," she scoffed, "Rachel has had time to outlive those high-minded notions! You offer her a little and see! As for Whiz and Ian, they don't really need any, but I won't have any of them saying we're showing favouritism. I know you always have done as regards

Mary and that I did towards little Claire, but never as regards money. That's the one sure way to split a family."

"You're right about that," he said. "Suppose we send them £500 apiece?"

"You'll have to do better than that," she said. "Rumble won't accept a penny if he thinks it's a gift. You'll have to make it appear a direct legacy from Uncle Franz to Mary. Get one of the twins to forge a letter of confirmation and produce it in a day or so."

"I had something like that in mind myself," he said, "but not enough guile to put it into words!" and he kissed her, absurdly grateful to be home again and reflecting that, when they were alone here, with all the older children grown and dispersed, and two-year-old John and the staff asleep upstairs, there was a tranquillity and time-lessness about the old house that made him feel half his age.

He rode over to Periwinkle the next day, a mild, damp morning, with the mist lying in the bottoms and everything drooping and glistening in the hedges. Mary, busily baking her bread, looked pon-derous but very fit and when he asked her if any precise date had been quoted she told him Maureen had "pencilled in" St. Valentine's Day.

"Don't let her take you in," he said, "she generally contrives to get things wrong. I was away from home when four out of my seven were born!" and he called through the covered-way to Rumble who could be heard swinging an axe in the strawyard.

"Come in for a minute, I've got news for you!"

Mary said, laughing, "He won't like it, whatever it is. The one thing he really enjoys is chopping. Someone in Canada taught him to split sixpences edgeways and whenever he's out of sorts all I have to do is to hand him the axe and lead him to the chopping block! In ten minutes we've not only got more than enough for the evening's burning but he's worked off all his bad temper on stumps."

"I don't believe that boy ever shows bad temper," Paul said, as they went back into the pleasant kitchen, where a great log fire burned and everything twinkled, and Mary told him he was happy enough most of the time but had been worrying over the struggle to maintain monthly payments on the farm, and also the fact that he couldn't expand as fast as he had planned without hiring another hand. "He says farmers will never get a square deal in this country until they find a way to cut out the middleman," she added.

"He sounds just like his grandfather," said Paul. "Every time I called on the Dell in the old days Tamer blathered about bankruptcy. When you're as old as me you'll realise this is no more than a built-in pessimism that the British farmer claims as a birthright! It comes from thousands of years' sparring with our weather!"

Rumble came in, his face streaked with sweat and said, nodding at Mary, "She looks like a penguin, doesn't she?" and Mary countered with, "Kick off those filthy boots! I don't want half the yard in here!" so that again Paul thought how easy was their relationship and how greatly it differed from the more guarded exchanges between Simon and Rachel, or between the twins and their sophisticated wives. He said,

"I've got a windfall for you; Uncle Franz Zorndorff left money to split between the family and Mary will get her share in a week or two."

He saw them exchange glances and it seemed to him that Rumble's eye sparkled.

"That's encouraging! How much?"

"Round about fifteen hundred," Paul lied happily and Rumble's cheeks turned a deeper shade of pink as his arm slipped over Mary's shoulders and they stood with their backs to the fire looking, Paul thought, like a couple of children on Christmas morning.

"That was damned decent of the old boy!" Rumble said. "I don't recall seeing him more than twice. Why didn't the twins get the lot? After all, they worked for him."

"The twins have done very well," Paul told him. "They get the Empire and we get the leavings! He left us ten thousand on condition I spent half on the estate. I've earmarked five and the rest, less lawyer's fees, passes to Mary, Whiz and Simon. That was what he had in mind when I last talked to him and that's how it will be split!"

He wondered if Rumble suspected that this was largely a fiction and also how he would maintain it if Simon and Rachel declined to accept their share of the money. Rumble said, deliberately, "That's terrific, Gov, but don't give us Mary's share, keep it towards the balance of the freehold and I'll make it up to her later. It will mean this place is really ours that much sooner!" He glanced at Mary; "Do you go along with that, Mar?"

"Of course!" she said, "it's by far the best way of using it. We don't want for anything right now and in a couple of years we shall be in the clear. Do what Rumble says, Daddy!"

They had, he reflected, outwitted him after all, and he thought how Claire would laugh when he got home and reported as much.

"There's at least one thing you can say about my brood," he told himself, "not one of them is greedy for money and that's something to crow about these days!"

"You're sure you wouldn't rather have it as a float?" he persisted. "I'm in no hurry to be paid off and I never cared for the arrangement in the first place. I realise you want to be independent and admire you for it, but you might just as well have stayed tenants until you got some capital together!"

"That's the way I want it," Rumble said, looking very obstinate, "for I don't care to be a tenant, not even with you as my landlord! If I farm land I've got to own it! Maybe it's something they dinned into me in the Dominions."

"Very well," Paul said, "that's the way it will be. It will mean Periwinkle is two-thirds yours already and that's not bad going for twelve months." He looked at Mary again. "Are you determined to have the baby here? You wouldn't rather your mother made arrangements to go in St. Theresa's, at Paxtonbury?"

"He'll be born right here!" she confirmed. "Mother had all her children at home and Rumble was born in the Valley. It wouldn't be the same if he was born elsewhere, even tho' Paxtonbury is just over the hill, and now I must see to my bread!" and she went out leaving Rumble to walk him to the gate.

"I've had the telephone installed," Rumble said, expressing an anxiety Paul had never felt for Claire, "and Doctor Maureen looks in every day." Then, with a diffidence that struck Paul as uncharacteristic, "Do you happen to know Grandfather Potter's real name? I always meant to ask Mother Meg and never did!" and Paul, racking his brains, said this was a teaser, for he had never heard anyone in the Valley call the old man anything but "Tamer".

"Do you want to name your boy after him?" he asked and Rumble said, almost apologetically, "Yes, I should like to but don't ask me why, something to do with your famous 'continuity' I imagine. Do you think Uncle Sam or Uncle Smut would know?"

"If they don't we can easily look in the parish records," Paul told him. "I'll ride down there right away and ring through. What's your number?" and he jotted it down in the memoranda block he was never without when he rode about the Valley.

An hour later he was chuckling and when Parson Horsey asked him the joke he said, returning the register, "I look like being saddled with a grandson called Jeremiah and I must say it's an apt name for anyone destined to farm hereabouts! Do you christen many babies with Biblical names these days?"

"Not one in fifty," Horsey said, "all the boys are named something fancy, like 'Trevor' or 'Bevis', and all the girls are named after film stars!"

"Well, thank God we can shorten it to something manageable," said Paul and rang through from Coombe Bay public 'phone booth to pass the information to Rumble.

He was there again in under a fortnight and for once Maureen had calculated the date accurately. The baby, christened Jerry ("Jeremiah is asking too much of family loyalty!" Rumble declared) was born on February 14th. Mary was exhausted but delighted, and Claire said the baby had "an Italianate look", having inherited Paul's narrow features and his parents' dark complexion. "There's certainly not much Derwent about him," she said ruefully, when she came downstairs, and Rumble had promised to add the name "Edward" to keep the record straight. Then, Valley-fashion, they all wet the baby's head and Thirza was loaned as nurse for a fortnight, less because Mary needed her than for fear of giving offence, for Thirza regarded this function as an hereditary right and would have sulked for a week if she had been denied it.

"Well," said Claire, as they drove down the track to the river road, "I suppose you're satisfied now! You look almost as smug as Rumble I must say!"

"It's a matter of satisfaction to both of us," he said, "for it means that at least one of our children is anchored here. If young John stays put, and doesn't take it into his head to go rooting in scrap-yards, or taking the world's troubles on his shoulders like Simon, then we're in business for another two generations!"

She glanced at him affectionately, wondering at the astounding durability of the roots he had thrown down since the day he had first ridden into High Coombe yard in his stained Yeomanry uniform, and she had handed him sherry and pikelets and held his hand a little longer than necessary. In some ways it seemed a thousand years ago and in others only a month, and as she thought this she experienced the familiar, comforting desire to be possessed by him as though it was twenty years ago. "Maybe it's an instinctive awareness of the cycle caused by another birth," she thought and wondered, even whilst laughing at herself, how she could get him to go to bed earlier than usual that night without making it obvious and pandering his vanity, for even at fifty-six he was still inclined to parade his virility.

II

In the old days the ripples of the world beyond Paxtonbury seldom reached the lower reaches of the Sorrel. A few did, much trumpeted events, like the death of a monarch and the coronation of another but it was not often that Valley folk involved themselves, even objectively, in international topics. Before 1914 the latest titbit of scandal from the Dell could always be sure of winning more word-coverage in The Raven than, say, an Agadir crisis, or the latest Armenian massacre. The first international event that really captured the imagination in the Valley had been the war but even then not because Valley men were claimed and killed but on account of the invasion of the Valley by so many foreigners passing through the moor training camp and the convalescent home. After the war the Valley did its best to revive the policy of deliberate isolation, counting London, and the affairs of the Continent, well lost after so much cackling, scurrying and heartbreak. They were aware, of course, that all kinds of things did happen east of Sorrel Halt and west of the Whin, but no one, not even Horace Handcock (whose patriotism had managed to survive the General Strike and the Invergordon Mutiny) made more than a passing reference to events such as Lindbergh's flight of the Atlantic, the Saar dispute, or the airship disaster at Beauvais. Farm prices interested them, and so did sporadic outbreaks of foot and mouth disease, but events like the trials of Metro-Vickers men in Moscow, and the perennial squabbles of French poli-ticians went unread. The Valley was like a tiny community in the hinterland of a remote island; everyone living in it was intelligently aware of what went on in the local capital but only vaguely conscious of events further afield, especially those enacted in places separated from them by stretches of salt water. Few people in the Valley took a newspaper other than the *County Weekly* and not all that number listened, with much attention, to the news bulletins although there was a radio of sorts in most of the farms and cottages.

All this began to change rather abruptly between the autumn of 1935 and the summer of 1936 and Paul, whose finger and thumb never really left the Valley pulse, was the first to notice this and be-come aware of the end of a deliberate dissociation with the world outside. The realisation came to him quite suddenly one frosty

1094

morning in October, 1935, when he was hailed by Henry Pitts from the lower stretch of Undercliff.

Henry, riding his tractor like a Roman charioteer, saw him testing the ice in one of the oxbows of the river and called, cheerily, "I zee that ole varmint be zettin' about 'em niggermen, Maister!" and somehow Paul at once knew that he was referring to Mussolini's attack upon Abyssinia.

He went across to him and they talked for a spell on world events and it was soon after that, in the public bar of The Raven, that he heard people like Smut Potter and the blind veteran, Willis, engaged in argument over the probable fate of the sad-eyed Negus, currently a fugitive on his way to Britain.

Paul's personal interest in world affairs had waned since Jimmy Grenfell's death. Jimmy had always kept him in touch with the broad outlines of what was happening outside but now that both Jimmy and Uncle Franz were dead he found himself less and less addicted to reading leading articles in *The Times* and the *Mail*, preferring late-night symphony concerts to the nine o'clock or midnight news-bulletins on the air. It was the voice of Adolf Hitler, that he heard by accident one night, that first made him conscious of his withdrawal and he said to Claire, absorbed in her favourite Priestley, "Good God! Can you imagine a man who sounds like that running a country populated by chaps with as much sense as Old Scholtzer? It's fantastic! He sounds like a maniac in a fit!"

"What was that, dear?" Claire asked, mildly, dragged from the interminable odyssey of *The Good Companions*, and he said, smiling, "I'm sorry, I was only thinking aloud!" but all the next day his mind returned to the phenomenon and although he spoke no word of German the speech had seemed to him to contain elements that a man could associate with the howl of the long-dead sheepdog of Preacher Willoughby, a dog that had caught rabies and had been shot by Smut Potter.

Then he noticed that others were equally concerned or, if not concerned, at least interested in the antics of the German Fuehrer and, to a somewhat lesser extent, in those of the Italian Duce and his eternal postures and extravagant claims to the Mediterranean, Corsica and Nice. Both of them became, in a sense, comedians, always good for a wry joke or a gibe, in a way that men like Stanley Baldwin and Ramsay MacDonald were not, for these men were at least recognisable whereas Hitler and Mussolini were not and seemed different

1095

even from such flamboyant characters as the ageing Kaiser, now reported to be chopping trees in Holland.

Then the Spanish Civil War began and circumstances combined to compel Paul to take a more than casual interest in world affairs, for one morning, when he was at work in his office, Claire came in carrying baby John and said, "We've got a visitor, Paul. It's Rachel!" and when he said, with pleased surprise, "Simon too?" Claire said Rachel was alone and wanted to see him at once. "She's in the kitchen," she told him, "she was wet through, the silly girl! She walked up from the 'bus stop in Coombe Bay!"

"Why the devil didn't she ring and ask one of us to fetch her?" he demanded and then, because Claire looked worried, "Is she all right? Is Simon all right?" and he got up to go into the hall but she stopped him, saying "I think she wants to talk to you alone. I'll take John down to Maureen for his inoculation and join you at lunch. She's agreed to stay on a day or so," and Rachel appeared, looking, he thought, not merely bedraggled after a two-mile walk in pelting rain but extremely unsure of herself.

Claire took her hat, coat and gloves, told her to stand against the fire and went out, carrying the protesting two-year-old with her. Paul said, "I've forgotten, Rachel. Do you drink or don't you?" and Rachel said she would be glad of a whisky if there was one going and her clothes began to steam in the heat of the library fire.

"I ought to have had more sense, I suppose," she said, "but the fact is I just didn't think of telephoning. I've got too much on my mind and that's why I'm here!"

"Is Simon ill?"

"No, he's very well, or was the last time I saw him."

"You . . . you've not parted?"

"No, at least, not in the conventional way. We've had a big row tho', the first in six years, and it doesn't make it any easier to reflect that basically he was right and I was wrong! But even if I climbed down it wouldn't stop him now. You might but I couldn't and that isn't surprising when you think of it. It was me who headed him that way in the beginning."

He said, handing her a large whisky and soda, "Sit down and take it easy. Where is Simon right now?"

"In Falmouth, unless he's already sailed."

"Sailed where?"

"For Spain, as a volunteer."

"Good God!" Paul exclaimed, deeply shocked. "What the devil made him do a damned silly thing like that?"

She said, regarding him carefully over the rim of the glass, "How much are you interested down here? I mean, it's common currency with us but I realise it mightn't be for you. He got it into his head that every able-bodied man who gives a damn about the future ought to stop talking and do something and, as I said, he's probably right! But after all, he's well over thirty and was almost certain to win a seat in Glasgow next election. I think he could do more good right here, fighting this non-intervention farce but maybe that's only my way of kidding myself. What really frightens me is the idea of him being killed or captured. It's a no-holds-barred war you know!"

"He must be off his head!" Paul said. "What can he hope to do out there? One man, caught up in a war between two bunches of foreigners? What possible purpose does he think he'll achieve?"

"Solidarity of the Left I imagine," Rachel said. "That's what got him as far as Falmouth. There's an International Brigade forming, people like us, who think this is a dress-rehearsal for the Fascist take-over in Europe."

"*You* think that, or only Simon does?"

"Oh, I think it, and surely it's evident, even to our home-grown Fascists, but that doesn't reconcile me to losing him. You remember what I wrote to you at the time we married? I said I'd do everything I could to make him a good wife and I seem to have succeeded too well. He's quite dedicated now, far more than I am or ever could be! I found that out when we argued about his going. I suppose you'd call me a Frankenstein, of the rose-pink variety. In the last year or so I've paled but he's gone several shades deeper red!"

"How on earth do you think I can help?"

"I don't know really, I came here because I was . . . well . . . desperate I suppose. I thought you might hurry down to Falmouth before the boat sails for Bordeaux—that's where they're said to be congregating—and try and talk him out of it one way or another."

"If you can't how can I? He thinks of me as an anachronism and always has!"

"He's got a very great affection for you nonetheless."

Paul was surprised to hear it; mild respect, perhaps, in a slightly contemptuous way, but hardly affection. "What makes you think that?"

"We were talking about it a night or two ago. What he admires

1097

about you is your consistency. That, and your genuine concern for the few people you think you can influence along broadly progressive lines."

"The trouble with you and Simon and everyone else of your persuasion," he complained, "is that you slot every idea and abstract into a labelled bin and forget that politics consist of people with toothache, mother-in-law troubles and rate-summonses! I daresay I seem very old-fashioned to you but at least I've never overlooked that! And touching his mother I might as well tell you she's still very much alive in Simon and always has been. She seems to have passed on this . . . this mania for banner-waving, like a congenital defect, like cross-eyes or a weak chest!"

He sounded so exasperated that she laughed and then he laughed too, adding, "Listen to me! Preaching at you! I'll go to Falmouth right away if you can tell me where to locate him but only on condition you stop here and let Claire mother you for a week or two. Will you do that?"

"Yes," she said earnestly, "and I'll never cease to be grateful if you can talk sense into him."

"I can't promise to do that," he said, "but I'll try. Of my seven children only Mary ever regarded me as anything more than an amiable fuddy-duddy. Maybe I should have been a bit more Victorian in my methods of bringing them up."

"You did all right, Squire," she said, "ask my mother or anyone else about here!" and she walked across to the tall window and looked out across the dripping paddock at the distant outbuildings of Home Farm. "It's odd," she said, with an air of apology, "a bit of me is beginning to think you might have been far closer to the truth than any of us—accidentally one might say, like a man who made up his mind to pursue a path even if it did appear to lead in the opposite direction! After all, the world's round isn't it? You might be the odd one who goes the whole way while all we short-cutters get lost in the woods!"

It seemed to him the most oblique endorsement of his policy that anyone ever stated to his face.

The directions she gave him were vague. Simon was supposed to be boarding a coaster in Falmouth and crossing to Brest where, if everything went according to plan, he would meet volunteers from countries as widely separated as Mexico and Bulgaria and travel

1098

overland to Bordeaux. Here a Republican coaster was scheduled to pick them up and take them on to San Sebastian. It was typical, Paul thought, of the sheer muddle-headedness of the Left, an itinerary based on hope, faith and slogans, rather than steamship tickets and a thick-soled pair of walking shoes. He found the coaster easily enough, a grubby little cockleshell called *Hans Voos*, out of Amsterdam, but the only man aboard her appeared to speak no English save the single word "Okay", which he repeated, with varying degrees of emphasis, whenever Paul asked a question. He booked bed and breakfast at an hotel near the harbour, fortified himself with a couple of stiff whiskies and went looking for Simon but it was not until the following day that he located him through a wharf-loafer, who said the Dutch vessel was due to sail the following morning and that some young Englishmen had been recruited as crew. Paul never learned how the vessel arrived there from Amsterdam with a crew of one, or what the ship was supposed to be transporting apart from British idealism.

Simon was in high spirits, looking and talking like a young missionary who, after innumerable setbacks, had just been given sailing instructions to New Guinea and promised the likelihood of being eaten by cannibals. He did not seem surprised to see his father, admitting that he had thought it probable Rachel would approach him in the hope of bringing about a last-minute cancellation of plans.

"I can tell you now, Gov'nor," he said, "that there won't be any change, although I appreciate you coming all this way for her sake. She ought to have known better than to involve you for, damn it, J'm thirty-two not seventeen! I know precisely what I'm doing and what's at stake."

"It's my belief that you don't!" growled Paul, "and frankly I think you're in for some nasty shocks once you embroil yourself in that free-for-all! Don't think I'm not on your side—in the general sense that is. I hope to God these chaps give Franco and his mercenaries a damned good thrashing and bundle them back to Africa but I think it's their concern, not ours, nor Russia's, Italy's or anyone else's! I've seen two wars and unless Britain was directly involved they could fight another in my stableyard before I'd join in!"

"But hang it, Gov'nor, this is a dress-rehearsal and how it goes will resolve the future for every one of us!" Simon argued although good-humouredly. "We don't expect chaps your age to join in but how the devil can I preach solidarity against Fascism if I'm not prepared to peel off my own coat and take a crack at them? I tried to make Rachel see that, and she ought to see it, but all she could say was that I would do more good staying home and helping to organise public opinion against Non-intervention."

"And I'm by no means persuaded she isn't right at that," Paul said, wishing Jimmy Grenfell was alive to back him up. "I'll grant you we've been drifting pretty hopelessly since the war, and that things are getting in a hopeless muddle one way and another, but if that's so isn't it the duty of chaps your age to become legislators rather than Robin Hoods? She says you would win your next fight at the hustings."

"Suppose I did?" Simon said, bitterly, "where would I go from there? I've been stumping the country for six years and Capital is more firmly entrenched in Westminster than it was when you and old Jimmy Grenfell held the platform, in pre-world war days! We were getting somewhere then, if history books are to be believed, but we've been backsliding ever since and if you don't believe me look what's happening in Germany and Italy right now! Anyone with enough guts to oppose racialism and rule-by-rubber-truncheon is shot out of hand or sent to rot behind barbed wire! Have you really thought about the logical outcome of Fascism, as practised by bastards like Hitler and Mussolini?"

"I've thought about it a great deal," Paul said, "and all I'm saying is that insurance against that kind of thing happening here won't be bought by your death in a Spanish ditch!"

"Well, we must agree to differ I suppose," Simon said, cheerfully. "You'll wake up sooner or later and I hope to God it isn't too late!" Then, with a boyish grin, "Would you like to meet the troops? Deckhands all, tho' I doubt if any one of them has ever sailed further than the Isle of Wight on Bank Holiday," and without waiting for his father to accept this dubious honour he led the way to a ramshackle pub where Paul was introduced as "the Gov'nor" to a group of piratical-looking young men drinking beer out of tankards and seemingly as full of missionary zeal as his son. There was a slim, pallid youth, whose clothes looked as if they had been borrowed from a younger brother's wardrobe, a squat, broad-shouldered Scot, who spoke with a thick Glasgow accent and was addressed as "Tam" by the others, but the recruit who impressed Paul the most was a handsome young chap with a public-school accent, who said his name was Barnaby and had, Paul learned, interrupted his studies at Cambridge to sign on as a deckhand on the *Hans Voos*, which was the only legal way of leaving the country for the rendezvous in Bordeaux. The obvious sincerity of the group touched him in spite of himself and deep in his heart he envied their faith in their own convictions, their high spirits and derring-do. He thought, "They're only a later edition of the young idiots who thronged into the Yeomanry after Black Week, 1899, and went off to fight Kruger, and I daresay they'll soon be as disenchanted with International Socialism as we were with Imperialism." Then, glancing at Simon (deep in a dialectical discussion with the Glaswegian and talking, as far as Paul could hear, straight from the textbook) "I wish Grace could see him now! He's so very like her in her suffragette days, with the same passionate belief in theory and the same compulsion to put theory to the touch! Well, I only hope he's luckier than she was and neither rots in gaol or finishes six feet down on a Continental plain!"

Simon said, "Will you stay and see us off, Gov?" and Paul said no, he wouldn't, because he had a strong suspicion that they wouldn't get further than the harbour entrance before a Government official came aboard with a court order and returned them to the shore. "I'll bail the lot of you out if I have to," he promised, "but only on condition you all go home and tackle whatever you're trying to do in a country where you can be understood from a platform!"

They seemed to think this was meant as a joke and certainly accepted it as one, thumping his shoulders and forcing him to drink another tankard of beer, as though he had been a parent conferring with daredevil prefects on Speech Day. Then he and Simon went outside and back along the quay to his hotel. "It's coming in thick again," Paul said, "and it's a four hours' drive, so I'll say good-bye and good luck and try and think of something cheerful to tell Rachel when I get home."

"Tell her to keep my candidature warm," Simon said. "I'll be back inside six months and you'll find out what it's like to have an M.P. in the family. You haven't said anything about Mother and the kids. Are they all well and happy?"

"Mary is," he said, dolefully, "but I wouldn't know about the others. Whiz seems settled enough with that airman of hers but they spend most of their time abroad. As for The Pair, they're still making money I suppose, spending most of it on their wives and the rest on the sort of rubbish everyone prefers to something worth having these days!"

"Well, cheer up, Gov!" he said. "You look good for another thirty years as an eighteenth-century squire and by that time things will almost certainly have sorted themselves out a bit, even if all the surviving squires are in museums!" but suddenly his smile faded and he looked serious as he said, "Listen Gov, I'll write . . . I'll write anything important direct to you, understand? I'm more glad that I can say I had this chance of seeing you and all I want you to understand is that I'm doing what I think to be right—what I think *has* to be done by some of us, some time, so why not now? Put like that I suppose it sounds like an attitude but even if it is it's my attitude and deeply felt! The minute I get an address I'll write and . . ." he stopped suddenly and came as near to blushing as anyone with his sallow complexion could.

"Well?"

"I daresay this sounds hopelessly sentimental but . . . would you have a photograph of my mother at home somewhere?"

The question startled him so much that, for a moment, he was too occupied controlling his emotions to reply. He had come down here prepared to be persuasive, angry, contemptuous even, but he had not expected to be ravaged. The boy might be thirty-two but when making that request he looked no older than on the day they sat side by side on a log near his school in 1917 and he told him of Grace's death in France. Simon was sensitive enough to give him a moment or two to recover and looked out across the harbour so that finally Paul managed to say, "I've got several. Studio portraits and early snapshots. I'll pick the best of them and send them if you like."

"Thanks!" Simon said and they shook hands, and after that Paul could not be gone quickly enough. He glanced in the mirror as he drove back along the littered quay and there was Simon, his raincoat fluttering in the stiff wind, his mop of dark hair, the same texture as his mother's, streaming out like a black pennant. Paul thought, "God help us all, will I ever see the boy again? I very much doubt it, for it seems to me he's been heading for this all his life, before he was born even! In some ways I'm damned unlucky with my children!" and he drove into the rain, pressing up the central road of the peninsula at twice the speed he generally travelled. The open country on each side shared his deep depression and he remembered the last time he had driven across Bodmin Moor, nearly three years ago, when little John was being born and he was half-way through that uncomfortable interlude with Claire. Well, that had turned out well enough, so perhaps this would in the long run. He badly needed a drink but decided not to stop and waste driving time for, as usual, he felt lost and lonely out of range of the Valley and almost envied Simon the companionable squalor of the forecastle of the *Hans Voos*. "At least he has someone to share his convictions," he thought, "and that's more than I have, or have had since old John Rudd died! Claire and Mary are all very well but they're women and can't really understand, whereas Rumble Patrick, who comes closest to my way of thinking, is another generation and can't range back far enough." The struggle, it seemed to him, was too long and too demanding. One ought, by now, to have entered upon an era of serenity, with little or no risk of switchbacks ahead, but the long hauls and the steep dips that succeeded them were becoming more frequent every year and used up far too much of a man's nervous energy. What was even more depressing was a conviction that, week by week almost, the struggle was enlarging itself, so that a man now had to worry about factors entirely outside his control, like this damned war in Spain, and the creeping tide of barbarism in Europe. He thought about the span of years before the world ran off its rails in 1914—"The Edwardian Afternoon" people were already calling it, as though it had been a marathon garden-party but had it? There had been the pleasure of working and planning within settled terms of reference but even then one needed the resilience of youth to absorb the shocks and disappointments of life. Grace had tinged his days with sadness and the element of strife within her seemed to have clung to Simon ever since. Then, when he had survived that breaker, the war had rushed down on them, and after that the stresses of the 'twenties culminating in the slump. One accepted personal tragedies, like the death of young Claire, and with them the ransoms of time, like the elimination of old friends and old partners, but lately—just when they seemed to be adjusting themselves to the post-war pattern—fresh shock waves came out of nowhere and a man was flat on his back again if he didn't keep looking over his shoulder! People like Henry Pitts and Smut Potter seemed to ride them without much trouble, and Claire had acquired the knack of bracing herself to meet every new crosscurrent but he couldn't, or not indefinitely; unlike them he was burdened with a sense of involvement that was at once a curse and an inspiration.

His sense of isolation joined forces with the wind-driven sleet that rushed at him across the open moor and he pressed on over the border like a tired fugitive on the run.

Simon wrote within the month, giving a Madrid address but no personal news beyond the fact that he was well. For progress of the war Paul had to turn to the newspapers and one needed a good deal of ingenuity to thread the maze of prejudice implicit in the reports. Even the names of the antagonists were interchangeable. To Right-Wing journalists Franco's Moors were "Nationalists" and the elected government "Reds"; to others, who shared Simon's dress-rehearsal theory Franco's side were "The Fascists", or "Insurgents", and their opponents "The People's Army". Paul hardly knew what to make of it and was still trying to puzzle it out when, in common with everyone else in the Valley who read newspapers or listened to radio bulletins, he was caught up in a different kind of civil war, one of words raging around the bachelor King whom everyone had assumed would replace his father in the days when there was still a real, personal relationship between Monarch and subjects. Here was an issue, he thought, that did not require Fleet Street guidance and Paul came down heavily in favour of the morganatic marriage to Mrs. Simpson (whoever she was) and was mortified to find himself in the minority when the topic was discussed in the Valley. Only Henry Pitts and Smut Potter proclaimed their allegiance to "The King's Party", whereas people like Marian Eveleigh, Thirza Tremlett, and even the former Potter girls (whom he would have thought could have been relied upon to take a tolerant view) ranged themselves alongside Baldwin and the pharisaical Archbishop of Canterbury, Violet Bellchamber declaring, "Us dorn want the likes of '*Er* for Queen, do us? 'Er's been divorced twice and if he can't do no better'n that then he should bide single and vind his bit o' comfort where he can, zame as King Teddy did!"

At first Paul found this attitude amusing, especially when it was adopted by women who seemed to have forgotten their own carefree youth but as the crisis mounted, and the cleavage of opinion became sharper, their intolerance exasperated him and Claire, sensitive to his moods, called him to task when he admitted losing his temper with Harold Codsall's wife on the subject.

"You're getting everything out of proportion these days," she told him bluntly, "and if you don't watch yourself you'll develop into a real old griper in your old age! What on earth does it matter to you whether he marries Mrs. Simpson or not? You never had much time for royalty in what you're now pleased to call the Good Old Days just because they're behind you!"

"I had a lot of time for him!" he countered, "and it makes me vomit to hear people discard loyalties like sweaty socks! Damn it, there was a time when that chap was the most popular man in the world, and unlike most of his kind he bloody well earned it, trapesing all over the world advertising the damned country! I remember him in France too! He wasn't like all the other Brass Hats, warming their fat backsides at a fire at Supreme Headquarters. He did everything he could to get up to the front and the chaps loved him for it! Now, because he happens to fall for a mature, intelligent woman, everybody suddenly becomes a bloody Sunday School superintendent! I tell you, it turns my guts sour!", and he flung himself out of the house and took it out on the skewbald in a breakneck gallop across the dunes where, as luck would have it, he ran into Maureen driving her ancient Morris up from the red-tiled bungalows in Nun's Bay. Maureen had news that took his mind off the troubles of the King and Mrs. Simpson. She braked and hooted the moment she saw him and shouted:

"Hi! Hold on there! I've just heard a rumour that will set tongues wagging! Sydney Codsall is flat broke and resigning his seat. Have you heard anything to confirm it?"

It was not quite true but it had elements of truth, as everybody between Whin and Sorrel soon learned. Sydney's business associate, Tapscott, the builder, had gone bankrupt for what seemed to Valley folk the astronomical sum of £28,000, but it soon leaked out that Sydney, although partially involved, had saved his bacon by withdrawing capital before the crash. It was true that he was resigning the Parliamentary seat, won in 1931 but this, it seemed, was due to domestic rather than financial difficulties for his wife was suing for divorce on evidence gathered by a private detective, so that the Valley soon found itself featured in the Sunday newspapers for the first time since the wreck of the German ship off the Cove, in 1906. It made, as Vi Potter declared, "tolerable gude readin' ", particularly in one of the Sunday papers that featured a picture of Sydney's alleged mistress and horsefaced wife side by side, under the banner headline, "*M.P. flees Love-Nest by Fire Escape*" and below, "*Nude Woman hits Photographer with Table Lamp*".

In the resultant scramble for details the King and Mrs. Simpson departed for France almost unnoticed and Paul, never a malicious man, nonetheless commented to Claire that weekend, "Well, he's been sailing close to the wind twenty years and was due to capsize! I wonder if Tapscott would be interested in an offer for what's left of High Coombe? It would be a feather in our cap to get it back, don't you think?"

She could not be sure whether or not he was joking so she temporised. "What would you do with half a farm if you got it? They've already built all over Eight Acre and Cliff Warren. I don't suppose there's more than a hundred acres left of the original."

"Periwinkle was smaller than that to begin with," he said, rubbing his hands and looking so pleased with himself that she felt ashamed for him. "There's no harm in getting Snow & Pritchard to put out a feeler!" and he left the table whistling between his teeth so that she thought, a little ruefully, "He's hardening up! There's no doubt about that, and I'm not at all sure that I like it!"

Tapscott was only too eager to sell and before the New Year was a fortnight old the rump of the old Derwent Farm had been repurchased, a parcel consisting of the original farmhouse, some ruinous outbuildings and about ninety-five acres between the tail-end of Tapscott's bungalows and the north-eastern tip of Shallowford Woods. Paul got it, he told Claire, for a song—less than half the price paid to Hugh Derwent by Sydney five years before, and not much more than Paul had been paid by Hugh two years before that. She drove out there with him one windless March day and they poked about the farm and grass-grown yards, finding that the old building was still in reasonable repair, Sydney's agents having used it as an administration centre for the caravan camp inland from Eight Acre. For all that the air of neglect depressed Claire so much that she said, pointing at the cracked and peeling paint on what had once been Rose's stables, "I wish I hadn't come. It's revived all my anger against Hugh! I suppose we shall have to pull it down and include what's left in Willoughby's farm."

"Not a bit of it!" he assured her. "I've got an idea but it'll need time to work on. Anyway, I'm glad some damned speculator didn't jump in ahead of us, for this is like recapturing occupied territory. High Coombe was always my private Alsace-Lorraine!"

He went to work at once, making an appointment with Francis Willoughby that same evening and when Francis, guessing why he had called, asked "It'll be about what's left of High Coombe, won't it?" he said that unless Francis was desperate for more pasture he had a plan that required a sacrifice on the part of Deepdene and he would appreciate Francis speaking his mind, notwithstanding the landlord-tenant relationship between them.

They made an appointment and Francis was awaiting him at the extreme southern end of his land when he rode up from the Dell about ten o'clock the following morning. He looked, Paul thought, about as unlike his father, Preacher Willoughby, as was possible. The preacher had been tall and spare, with a saint's halo of soft white hair, whereas Francis, broad-shouldered and grizzled, looked precisely what he was, a middle-aged man who had never had a thought unconnected with cattle-rearing. He was short and square, his thick calves encased in spotless leggings and a hard hat wedged firmly on his round head, as though to advertise that inside there was no room for frivolities of any kind. He was respectful, however, greeting Paul with the grave politeness that still lingered among the older tenants.

"I come downalong to saave 'ee the journey up to the house," he said. "My two varmints are upalong in the rickyard and they stop work if I bide talking to anyone!"

"It's about one of your varmints I've called," Paul said, dismounting. "How would you feel about young Dick Potter branching out on his own? I'm sure a chap with your reputation wouldn't have trouble replacing him."

Francis looked blank and then thoughtful. Not given to making snap judgments he took his time answering.

"Dick's got the maakings of a good farmer," he said at length, "which is surprising, considering the blood that runs in him but then, you can't judge by that, or not entirely. That Potter son-in-law of yours over at Periwinkle is a lively spark and may do well once he's outgrown his fancy notions! Where would you be thinking of zettling my cowman? On what's left of old Edward Derwent's plaace?"

"Why not? There's over a hundred acres if I threw in the sloping meadow that backs on the Big House. It's small I know but he'd be on his own, except for a boy if he could get one and I believe he's a good man with dairy cattle?"

"Arr!" said Francis, guardedly, "he is that! Better than he be wi' the beef. If he hadn't been I wouldn't have kept him all this time!"

It occurred to Paul that this eastern side of the estate bred an altogether different kind of man than the west or south. Within living memory Edward Derwent, Tamer Potter, Willoughby Senior and now Willoughby Junior had all grown to maturity on the exposed side of the Bluff. Perhaps the eastwinds, sweeping across the Downs, had tempered them in a way that it had not tempered amiable families like the Pitts, the Honeymans and the younger Eveleighs.

"Dick Potter, by my reckoning, is twenty-six. If he stays on with you another year or so he won't want to shift and he'll be a hired man all his life. I've already had a word with Sam, his father, and he's desperately keen we give the lad a chance, Francis. I'd appreciate it if you'd part with him and forgo any hopes you had of enclosing High Coombe within your own borders. However, I'm not going to do more than put it to you. If you're opposed to the idea then we'll forget it and say nothing to him. You've been a first-class tenant ever since your father died and I wouldn't want to upset you. Take a day or so to think it over."

"Nay," Francis said, slowly, "I don't need time to think on that. Tiz right to give the lad the chance, for I've not forgotten you gave me mine backalong. I can make do on the land I've got, I've managed well enough so far!" His last sentence was a challenge and Paul, recognising as much, said, "You certainly have and there isn't a man in the Valley who isn't proud of you. Should I put it to Dick or would you like to sound him?"

"I'll do it," Francis said and heaved himself off his five-barred gate, "but I wouldn't bank on him accepting. There's a lazy streak in the Potters but us'll zee what us'll zee!"

Paul never learned what took place between Francis and Dick Potter, son of his woodsman, but the upshot of it was that Dick set about repairing the Derwent farmhouse and outbuildings and somehow contrived to find time to do some spring sowing on the neglected acres inland from the cliff fields. Paul and Claire went over in late April to see how he was getting along and found him with Smut Potter's lad, the impish, seventeen-year-old son of the ponderous Fleming, who had clasped Smut to her corseted bosom in 1917 and had never let him go. Dick favoured his father, Sam, a tall, rangy young man, with the Potter trademarks of brown, impudent eyes, stiff unruly hair and bouncing, spring-heeled gait. Paul handed the new tenant of High Coombe his lease and learned that Dick proposed to specialise in dairy products.

"Not Friesians, Guernseys," he told Paul. "There's a big local demand for clotted cream in Coombe Bay and Whinmouth and it's growing all the time. 'Bonbon' is going to work for me, so he says, but I doan reckon he'll stay; he's always cracking on about Australia!"

Paul remembered then that Smut's boy was known in the Valley as "Bonbon", a name derived from his mother's impatient response to all enquiries when she first came here, soon after the Armistice. He recalled also that the two cousins had always been close friends, notwithstanding the eight-year gap in their ages. It was comforting, he thought, to have two Potters at work in the Coombe again and asked if he could see what sort of job they were making of the inside of the farm. Repairs were obviously rough and ready and Claire must have noticed as much, for she said, "This is well enough for men who don't mind pigging it, Dick, but you'll have to get a real builder in if you ever think of marrying!" and Dick said, grinning, "Bless you, Mrs. Craddock, I got no time to think o' marrying now, and no one in mind either! I shall have all my work cut out gettin' this place in shape!"

"I've heard you young chaps talk like that before," Claire said, "but you all come round to it sooner or later!" and she looked round the big kitchen, adding rather wistfully, "This is a place for children, Rose and I were happy here and if my brother Hugh had married at your age he would have been poorer but a good deal happier I think."

She was thoughtful on the way home and it occurred to Paul that she resented seeing the old farm change hands but he was wrong, for when he asked if this was so she said, with a chuckle, "No, I wasn't brooding on that! I was just thinking it's lucky Father didn't live to see it; if people really do turn in their graves the poor old chap must be positively threshing about to witness a Potter on his land! He feuded with them for years, remember? It was only old Preacher Willoughby who kept them from tearing each other's throats!"

"You can say what you like of the Potters," he replied, "but you have to grant them staying power! They were hanging on by their fingertips when I came here thirty-five years ago and look at them now! One grandson farming at Periwinkle and married to our daughter, two other grandsons reclaiming High Coombe and two of the originals still rooted in the Dell! Damn it, they practically dominate the Valley and I daresay it would have astonished old Tamer, bless his old heart!"

The Coronation junketings that year were so tame, Paul thought, as to be hardly worth organising. Everybody went through the usual motions — public luncheons, a service in the parish church, some tepid sports in the water-meadows, and the ritual distribution of mugs to schoolchildren, but the heart had gone out of the cult of royalty-worship and it seemed to him that people found it laborious to light fire-crackers and get drunk in honour of the new King. Victoria had been an awesome figure, a kind of arch-priestess deputising for the Almighty and even prompting Him on occasion, whereas her son, the portly Edward, had been a man licensed to gamble and womanise and hobnob with bookmakers without losing his dignity. Then came Squire George, Vicky's solemn grandson, and everyone respected his rectitude, even though he never enjoyed the prestige of his father, and after that everyone in the Valley had been prepared to welcome the cheerful young man who had outraged them by running off with a handsome divorcee, but for George VI, perhaps because of his shyness and slight stammer, there was little more than tolerance tinged with sympathy and somehow this did not add up to reverence or even enthusiasm. In any case, by this time the front of the stage was cluttered with clowns, the noisiest and most grotesque troop anyone in the Valley could remember, not excluding the Kaiser, who had always been seen with an eagle perched on his helmet. The clamour from across the water grew louder and louder as more and more grotesques, with sinister-sounding names and extravagant characters, claimed attention. There was Dr. Goebbels, with his big head and clumping foot, Goering with his chestful of medals, Himmler, who was said to cause those who displeased him to disappear in puffs of smoke, The Duce (whom the Valley folk knew as "Musso") with a chin that jutted like a ledge of the Bluff but, dominating all, the ringmaster himself, with his lank forelock, Charlie Chaplin moustache, hysterical oratory and extraordinary reputation for gnawing carpets when thwarted. Altogether an extravagant and totally ridiculous bunch thought the Valley, and their opinion of Squire Craddock's good sense dropped a point or two when the word went round that he thought the nation was threatened by them and was reported to have spent thousands of pounds on farm machinery and pedigree stock at the County Show, and also (could caution go further?) in digging a huge, concrete-lined pit in the dip between the big house paddock and Home Farm rickyard, rumoured by some to be an air-raid shelter and by others a fuel-storage tank against the day when storm-troopers would come goosestepping up from Coombe Bay.

It was a combination of factors that encouraged Paul to prepare for the worst. He had never forgotten Franz Zorndorff's infallibility in these matters, nor the fact that even Franz's nerve had been shaken by his visit to the Continent just before his death. Then there were Simon's letters, full of a kind of desperate bitterness against the democracies for continuing the farce of non-intervention in Spain, when it was obvious to a child that the war was being won for Franco by Germany and Italy. There was also his deep distrust of waffling politicians like Chamberlain, who behaved like startled chickens in the face of any demand for a show-down but perhaps his most unnerving conclusions were those reached after reading books like Koestler's *Spanish Testament*, and other first-hand accounts of life in Spain, Italy and Germany, sedulously fed him by his daughter-in-law Rachel, with whom he had formed a regular postal-link since Simon had sailed away on the coaster, *Hans Voos*. Until then, notwithstanding the war to end wars, Paul's politics had been largely parochial and his overall policy had been to conserve most of his energy for use in a purely local sphere but now, as the months went by, he found his sympathies inclining more and more towards the militant Left and he began to wonder if, after all, there might not be something to be said for Simon's theories. When men he respected, like the dapper Anthony Eden, resigned from the Government in protest against a policy of weakness towards Mussolini, he found himself chafing under the smart of humiliation but he had come to realise that his anxieties were not shared among the Valley people, not even by men whom he would have expected to favour a stronger line at Westminster. Henry Pitts, for instance, openly laughed at his fears and made him feel a little like old Horace Handcock, the ultrapatriotic gardener, when he admitted the true purpose of the new fuel-storage tank.

"Giddon Maister," Henry had said, "whatever be thinking of? You dorn honestly reckon Old Fritz wants another basinful, do 'ee? Why, damme, I mind the poor toads I swapped fags with between trenches, the day us stopped pooping off at 'em, and I dorn care 'ow much that bliddy Hitler rampages, I'd lay a pound note to a farden 'ee worn't get they into the firing-line again! They got more bliddy zense, I c'n tell 'ee! And as for they Eyeties—Gordamme, you baint zayin' youm scared o' they, be 'ee?"

Smut Potter, it seemed, held similar views but in his case they were fostered by the policy of playing down his French wife's anxieties

IIII

regarding a resurgence of the hated Boche, who had already robbed her of a husband. Marie Potter was one of the few people in the Valley who shared Paul's disposition to fear the worst, as he discovered when he called at the Coombe Bay bakery on the morning soon after Hitler's invasion of Austria. She was building a pyramid of cakes in her window and emerged thinking his shout from the bakery was that of the representative of a wholesale sugar firm with whom she did business. When he saw, in the adjoining store, mountains of bagged sugar and remarked on it she only said, with a frown, "It will disappear one morning and then, *poof*! No cakes! No business! No cash to carry to the bank! Today they are glad enough to sell it in bulk. Tomorrow they will sell it by the half-kilo, M'sieur!"

He talked to her then of current affairs and was surprised to find that, unlike himself, who was no more than uneasy, she was convinced that Germany would invade France within a matter of months.

"There is no doubt in my mind," she said, "the Boche will come seeking *revanche*, and my people will be the first to suffer; as always!"

"You've got the Maginot Line, Madame," he reminded her but she said "*Poof*" again, as if the new fortifications were made of sugaricing. He said, with a shrug, "Well then, if they do come I daresay we'll give them another thrashing. After all, we managed it well enough the last time."

"At a cost!" she said, buttoning her heavily moustached lip. She had great respect for him, not because he was her landlord but because he had the Croix de Guerre, and she did not berate him for lack of realism, as she did every other Englishman who came here talking politics.

In the early spring of 1938 news came that Simon was a prisoner-of-war, captured at a place called Teruel and Paul, learning of this through Rachel, who got it from a source she would not disclose over the telephone, asked what they could do to help the boy. She said there was only one thing they could do, contact the local Member of Parliament and ask him to make representations to Franco's people at Government level, for she understood some kind of machinery had been established for exchanging non-nationals captured by one side or the other. Paul saw the new M.P. without much hope but was cheered by the kindness and cordiality of his reception. Major Harries, M.C., who had recently taken Sydney's place as Member for Paxtonbury, was a retired gunner and it might have been Ikey's association with the Artillery that helped for they had served together as sub-alterns in India, and later on the Western Front. Paul said, when he was introduced, "It's only fair to tell you, Major, that I've been opposing your party all my life but I daresay you're aware of that already."

"You're one of my constituents whether you like it or not," said the ex-gunner, cheerfully, "so don't let's hear any more of that! I'll do what I can and be glad to! I've been watching that bloody business closely and frankly, irrespective of any political views your son holds, I think he's right when he says the Italians and Germans are flexing their muscles for something a little more ambitious! I'm in a minority up there, of course, just as anyone is who heeds Churchill's warnings!"

Paul found himself warming towards the man and over lunch at The Mitre repeated Zorndorff's warnings and spoke of his own modest insurances against war. The Major approved wholeheartedly: "I was in Germany six months ago," he said, "and I was scared stiff by what I witnessed. It goes against the grain to be forced, on pain of being rough-housed, to have to salute that little bastard, but that's what happened to me while I was watching a procession in Bremen. I'll do everything I can to get your boy turned loose and if I'm success-ful I'd like the privilege of hearing a first-hand account of his recent experiences."

Major Harries was as good as his word or better. He rang Paul within the week saying that contact had been established with the British Consul in Burgos, and that negotiations had already begun. "Don't expect rapid results," he warned, "you know how long it takes a Spaniard to make a decision but we have ways and means of putting some heat on so maybe the boy will be home for Christmas. He's unwounded, I'm told, so that's something to be thankful for!"

Paul thanked him and 'phoned Rachel, inviting her down to await further developments, but before she arrived he had another 'phone call from the Member to say that a batch of about a dozen British prisoners were being sent home via Gibraltar, and that Simon might well be among them.

Rachel arrived the next day, looking close to breaking point Paul thought and Claire packed her off to stay with Mary at Periwinkle. There had always been a close link between Rachel and Rumble Patrick after Rachel had personally delivered the boy in Hazel's cave one summer evening, in 1913. She was still staying there when Simon arrived, weighing about nine stones and suffering from the after-effects of three months in a verminous Spanish gaol in daily expectation of being marched out and shot with batches of Basques and Catalans. He was stunned, Paul thought, by the miracle of his delivery and it was during their almost wordless drive across the top of the moor from Paxtonbury that Paul said, "You owe your release to a Tory, Simon. He went to a great deal of trouble and wondered if you could find time to see him and give him an account of what happened over there."

Simon said, with a tired smile, "Major Harries? I've already seen him. He met us and gave us lunch at Tilbury yesterday!" and when Paul exclaimed Simon added, stifling a yawn, "Soon it won't be a question of Tories, Socialists and Liberals, Gov'nor, just for and against—those who oppose the clock being put back a thousand years, and those with nothing else in mind! There won't be any neutrals. Everyone here will have to step one side of the line and that's what I intend to stress when I lecture."

"Before you dive back into the mill-race you'll damn well get some rest and put on a bit of weight!" Paul said, gruffly. "Rachel means to see to that and I intend to back her up!"

"Oh, sure, sure," Simon said, "I'll get fit first. That's obligatory if I'm to do any good, but I'm not 'cured' as you might say, just confirmed! I daresay it sounds vainglorious but I wouldn't have missed it and I don't regret a bloody day of it! At least I've satisfied myself I was on the right tack. How about you?"

"We'll discuss that when you've had a good meal and ten hours' sleep," Paul said, "Doctor Maureen is waiting to give you a good going-over. However, just for the record, I'm your side of the line and so are a minority of thinking people, although not many hereabouts."

Simon looked across the Sorrel to the watershed as they topped the rise and began the winding descent to the river road. It was a mild spring day and the Valley looked patiently expectant, not yet in its uniform of spring-green but half-dressed, one might have said, in hourly anticipation of its coming-out date.

"I thought about this place a good deal while I was in Spain," he admitted. "You mightn't believe me but it exerts its magic on me as powerfully as on you, although maybe I'm too inhibited to make a fetish of it. It must have been a very wonderful place to live in in the old, carefree days when you came rampaging down from London."

"They weren't all that carefree. We had our problems, just as your generation has. The main difference was most people were content with three square meals a day, a good night's rest and to leave it at that!"

"Ah! 'Bread alone'!" Simon commented. "Well, it's all the poor devils in Spain ask but there are plenty ready to deny them even that!"

"No!" Paul countered, almost savagely, "not 'bread alone' Simon! A man who wants to be more than a cabbage needs a dream to spread on his bread! Otherwise one might as well take one's place alongside the cows and wait to be milked night and morning!" And then, seeing Simon look at him quizzically, "I'm sorry, I made up my mind on my way over to meet you that I'd talk platitudes at least for a day or so," and Simon, grinning, said, "Well, that comes under the heading of a platitude Gov'nor but I'll not quarrel with it and I don't suppose my mother would have done", and as they turned on to the river road Paul saw him fumble in his inside pocket and pull out a cheap folder containing the two soiled photographs of Grace he had sent to Spain a month or two after their parting in Falmouth. Impulsively he stopped the car and said, "Let me look at those, Simon!" and Simon handed him the folder and sat silently while he scrutinised the pictures, one a faded snapshot of Grace in the rose garden she had created, the other a formal studio-portrait, taken on their Paris honeymoon, in 1903. He said, handing them back, "Environment doesn't count for a damned thing! You're as alike as peas in a pod, physically and temperamentally! What's in the blood stays there!" and he let the clutch in and pulled back on to the road. They drove the rest of the way home in silence.

CHAPTER NINE

I

SIMON and Rachel remained in the Valley until early summer but Paul was relieved they were gone before the Munich crisis set everybody (including constitutional optimists like Claire, Henry Pitts and Smut Potter) by the ears. They came to him one by one, freely admitting their misjudgments but when it was all over, and Chamberlain had returned waving his piece of paper, they joined the tumultuous acclamation of the man who had "saved the peace". Their complacency angered him, although he went out of his way not to show it. Instead he spent long hours in his office, planning, conserving, getting his stock records up-to-date and cautiously adding to his purchases of seed, chemical manures and machinery. His fear now was not so much that there would be a war but that there would not, that he was laying up stock against a day when the Valley lost its identity in an almost bloodless absorption of Western Europe. For that, it would seem, was the alternative that most people preferred, including those he would have classed as rebels in the old society.

He began thinking along these nightmarish lines after a discussion with Smut Potter round about Christmas-time. Smut, carelessly going his rounds, called to him one day as he was crossing Codsall bridge and said, "Well, Squire, dree months ago I would have bet my favourite twelve-bore to a pound o' tay us would have been keepin' Christmas in they bliddy trenches but it's blown over after all!" and although it was no more than a casual greeting, of the kind that Smut offered to almost everyone he met between Coombe Bay and Periwinkle, Paul was sour enough to challenge him, saying sharply, "It's a damned pity we aren't while we've still got a few twelve-bores to put to our shoulders!" and Smut at once lowered his van window, apparently to hear the news that had put so much grit into Paul's voice.

"You abben heard nothin' new, 'ave 'ee?" he asked. "That bliddy Hitler baint jumped the gun, has he?" and Paul, mollified by the anxiety in his voice, replied, "No, I've heard nothing new, but I daresay we shall soon enough!"

Smut looked relieved then and also a little sheepish. "Gordamme, you put the fear o' God into me, Squire!" he admitted and then, in a puzzled voice, "Don't you reckon us is over it? I had the bliddy jitters backalong but it zeems quiet enough now according to the papers and radio."

Paul was tempted to stay and preach, to use Smut as a captive audience for his forebodings but he changed his mind, saying, ill-humouredly, "Well that's very reassuring! I'll sleep a lot better for hearing that, Smut!" and went his way hands in pockets so that Smut looked after him with concern, wondering what factors were at work to make Squire so crusty these days, and whether his own wife, Marie, had infected him with her non-stop Jeremiads about *les salles Boches* but he was not left wondering for long. Winter passed and spring followed and with spring came the pounce on Prague, and after that Mussolini's grab at Albania, and in the confused weeks that followed they began to drift back to him, bringing with them what he most needed, a feeling of unity of purpose and comradeship, that made him feel less like a prophet of doom stalking the Valley and muttering of wrath to come.

Henry Pitts was the first of the prodigals, declaring that " 'Twas time us stopped the rot", and Harold Codsall was the next, sending his boy over with the trailer to buy chemical manure against the arrival of a stock he had ordered in Paxtonbury. Then Smut, holding forth in the bar of The Raven one night, declared that "only Squire and his boy" had been right about what would follow Munich and word of this reached Paul the next day by Parson Horsey who confessed, sadly, that sooner or later someone would have to do something about Hitler and that whatever it was would be inconsistent with the charters of the Peace Pledge and the League of Nations. But none of these affirmations brought him as much comfort as Claire's, who said one night, as they sat by the fire, "Did I tell you I had a word on the 'phone with two of your daughters-in-law while you were out?"

"No," he said, without displaying much interest, "you didn't; anything new?"

"Yes there was," she said, knitting her brows, "and perhaps you can make sense of it for I can't and neither, it seemed, could Monica or Margaret, both of whom appear convinced that their respective husbands—our sons that is—have gone raving mad! They've joined the Air Force!"

He dropped the book he was reading and stood up with such a jerk that his Boer scar gave a twinge.

"They've *what*?"

"Well, not joined exactly but put themselves on some kind of Reserve. You remember one of their crazes was gliding or flying? Well, now they go up every Sunday and they're both going on some kind of course for a fortnight. It's all to do with the scare—you know, flying balloons or something."

"The Balloon Barrage?"

"Yes, that was it, that's what Margaret said."

"Well I'm damned," he said, subsiding, "they are about the last two I would have thought to join that kind of outfit at a time like this!" and suddenly he laughed. "I'm not laughing at them but at what old Franz would have said. I hope he's where he can't see them wasting their time fiddling about with barrage balloons when the price of scrap is at an all-time high."

"What exactly *are* barrage balloons?" she asked, mildly, and he told her, adding that the very fact amateurs like The Pair had been enrolled meant that somebody somewhere was taking a more serious view than he had supposed.

"You sound very cheerful about it," she said, and he replied that he was, in spite of all it might mean, for even a war was better than watching Europe taken over piecemeal and half the world enslaved without so much as a whimper on the part of the victims.

"You never used to think like that, Paul. You were always utterly opposed to war, even when everyone about here was war-crazy in 1914."

"It was quite different then," he said, "and it amazes me that everybody doesn't *see* it's different! I still think the last war was an act of madness on everybody's part—certainly continuing it after 1916 was—but there's simply no other way of containing that bunch of psychopaths. They haven't a damn thing in common with the Kaiser's bunch. Losing to Germany in '14 or '15 would have been bad but if we'd agreed to a patched-up peace after a year or so, it would have all been forgotten by now!" He leaned forward, earnestly, and she was impressed by the note of pleading in his voice. "Tell me, Claire, tell me honestly, do *you* think I'm a nervous old maid laying in all these stocks and building that fuel-storage tank? If you do then for God's sake say so and give me a chance to convince you!"

She said, quietly, "No, I think you know what you're doing, Paul. I think you always know what you're doing if it concerns the Valley."

"You've been in a minority of two then," he said, but with relief in

1118

his voice. "Only Smut's wife, old Marie, encouraged me at the time. You didn't! Why didn't you?"

"Why didn't I what?"

"Back me up, tell me I was right. I would have appreciated it."

She said, levelly, "You show me any woman about here with sons who is ready to admit, even to herself, to the prospect of seeing them face what you faced last time, or the possibility of suffering what wives and mothers like me and Marian Eveleigh and Elinor Codsall suffered all the time you were out there. No Paul, you don't bring it into the open, you go on pretending it's a bad dream that will fade out as soon as it's light! That's what I've been doing ever since Simon went off to fight in Spain."

He pondered her confession, finding it not only human but logical. One was so apt to think of war as a man's business whereas, of course, it was not and involved everybody one way or another, not because the methods of waging war had changed with the introduction of bombers but because feather-distributing women of Gloria Pitts' type were rare. The majority, the Claires, the Marians and the Elinors of this world, seldom came forward to claim their fair share of misery when their menfolk were lying out in mud under a barrage, or were home again, flaunting their medals and heroism. Usually, as in Claire's case, they kept their thoughts and misgivings to themselves, and tried to look interested when they had to listen to stories of blood and privation. This was the first time in twenty years he had ever given a thought to all she must have suffered during the period he had been in France. Was it any different in any other home in the Valley? He said, gently, "You should have told me that before, Claire, but I'm glad it popped out!" and suddenly she was on the rug beside him with her arms round his knees, as though interposing herself between him and the pointing finger of Kitchener in 1914. "You won't go again, Paul! You wouldn't? I couldn't face that time again, no matter what!" and he said, stroking her hair, "Good heavens, no, I shan't go! How could I, at my age? Besides, if it does come there will be more than enough to do right here, I can tell you." She nodded, eagerly, and he thought it strange that his reassurance, which did not include immunity for Simon, Stevie, Andy or her two sons-in-law, Ian and Rumble, should bring her such immediate comfort. Then he remembered what Maureen had said, what he himself had always suspected. She didn't give a damn about her children now they were grown and dispersed. All her adult life her eggs had been in one basket.

1119

There had always been a rhythm to their relationship, a swing and a drift that seemed not to be governed by external pressures, or by their own impulses but rather the chances that struck high and low notes in the harmony of the marriage. A trivial misunderstanding might promote a period of coolness, a casual mental adjustment, such as that resulting from this talk of war, bring them close together again so that for weeks together they would respond to one another far more like lovers than man and woman who had shared a bed for thirty years.

In that final summer of the old world, or rather the world that had tried so unavailingly to resolve itself into the older pattern, they were closer than they had ever been since the long interval between the children growing up and the birth of John, now a chubby, mischievous child of five. They would sometimes take him down to the shanty where Claire would teach him to swim in the rock-pool where she herself had learned and Paul would squat on a rock at the mouth of the goyle and watch them, marvelling a little at her patience and also at the curious sinuosity of her body in the water. The thrust of her American crawl never ceased to surprise him and these days she was unencumbered by the heavy, serge bathing dress she had worn the day he proposed to her within shouting distance of this favourite spot of theirs. Her figure, he thought, had withstood the years and successive pregnancies astonishingly well. It was thickening about the waist but not appreciably so for a woman over fifty. Her long legs were still, in his view at least, the shapeliest in the Valley, her breasts were full but high and her behind, always ample, had for him the pleasing flow of a ripe pear, so that when he saw her stand poised at the deepest end of the pool, flash down into the clear water and forge the entire length of the trough under water he would gloat over her as some sensual memory stirred in him and sometimes he would select a specially bright coin from his hoard of memories and, as it were, hold it momentarily as between finger and thumb.

He did not always accompany her there. He had work to do, although it was now confined, in the main, to checking his defences, like a conscientious garrison-commander anticipating a siege but uncertain when the first enemy hull would show over the horizon. There were times, indeed, when he doubted if there would be a siege, and then he would chide himself for a man who had let fancy dominate him but always, via newspapers, radio or the telephone links he had established with Simon, Rachel and the twins, would come sinister hints and rumours that hardened his sense of purpose and then she would have to spend her afternoons at the pool alone with John, or in the company of the Lee Gibsons, an elderly American couple who had rented the tall Victorian villa once occupied by Celia Lovell and used as a penitentiary for the erring Bruce Lovell.

Cyrus and Myra Lee Gibson were of the select company of expatriates who, from time to time, strayed into the Valley and never found their way out again. The first of them, in Paul's experience, had been the old German professor, and since then Brissot, the French Canadian, and Marie Potter, Smut's wife, had been added to their number. Mrs. Lee Gibson had allegedly come to the West to trace ancestors but her husband, a successful portrait artist (who, as a young man had hob-nobbed with the Paris Impressionists) had stayed on to paint landscapes, confessing himself fascinated by the quality of light in and around the Valley which, in high summer, was the nearest British equivalent to his native Arizona and in early autumn reminiscent of the filtered sunlight of Provence. Paul did not take these compliments seriously, recognising Cyrus as a dabbler in everything but portraiture but both he and Claire had become attached to the old couple. They had no family of their own and made favourites of young John and Mary's son, Jerry, who was often dumped on his grandmother for the afternoon.

During a spell of hot May weather Claire was down here every day and one blazing afternoon, when she had ordered the children out of the pool and was standing with her back to the goyle drying her hair, Lee Gibson hailed from beside the shanty, calling "Hold it! Don't move, gal!" and she thought he was taking a snapshot but when she went up the beach saw that he was touching up a series of charcoal sketches, all of herself in various postures in and about that rock-ledge.

"Can't you find a better model than a grandmother playing Nannie to a couple of toddlers," she joked but he said, adding a touch here and there, "I think we've hit on something! Myra thinks so too. If you're interested we could build on it. Come up to the cabin and see for yourself. Myra will watch over the children," and he led her into the shanty which Paul let him use as a studio whenever he worked west of the Bluff.

She was astonished at what she saw propped against the empty grate—a full-length portrait, two-thirds completed, of herself, seated on a spur of rock casually engaged in drying herself with a blue towel. He had caught her in a moment of abstraction, half-facing the Channel seen in the right background, with her shoulder-length hair tousled and bunched by the upward thrust of her right hand, and the sun playing strongly on her half-exposed breast and loosely braced thigh. The picture had a quality that was rare, a kind of breadth and freedom so often absent from a posed portrait, and it pleased her enormously not only because it was an excellent likeness but because some good fairy had enabled him to bring out her vitality and with it a strong echo of her youth. She said, throwing modesty aside, "Cyrus, it's wonderful! It makes me look—well—not more than forty! And although nobody could say it wasn't me you've been gallant enough to slant it so that I look ten stone instead of getting on for twelve!" and she was so flattered and excited that she kissed him, saying, "Does Paul know? Have you shown it to him yet?"

"Certainly not! For one thing it isn't finished and you'll have to pose in here for the final touches; for another I'm not at all sure he'd approve of an uncommissioned semi-nude of his wife. He's old-fashioned enough to hound me out of the Valley for taking such a liberty!"

"He'll love it!" she declared, and then, "Look here, his birthday is next week. Could you finish it by then?"

"With your co-operation I could," he said and she could see that he was pleased by her enthusiasm. "I'll cover it now. If the children see it they'll go running to him and I take it you want to surprise him?"

"Yes, I do and I will!" she said, helping him to drape it with a sheet and told him of a day long ago, when they were lean and young and vain, and Paul had proposed having her painted in oils by a London artist but somehow the project had been shelved and forgotten. "We've left it rather late," she said ruefully, "for I think I was worth painting in those days!"

"You're worth it now in my eyes and his," he reassured her, "in mine because your figure is more interesting than it was then—and if you doubt it take a look at Renoir's 'Anna'—and in his because you haven't changed at all, my dear! I happened to see him looking down at you when you were streaking across that pool a day or so ago and, quite frankly, it struck me that his mouth was watering! So there you have it!"

It was a thought to cheer her all the way home and prompt her to do something she did infrequently these days which was to change for high tea, wondering if he would notice. To her relief he did, for although he made no comment she heard him telling Mary on the 'phone that "Mother had got herself up" as a dress-rehearsal, no doubt, for the family reunion on the occasion of his birthday next week when, for the first time in years, they would reassemble at Shallowford and drink champagne sent on in advance by the twins.

On the last day of May, the day prior to his sixtieth birthday, they began to drift in from the North, the Midlands and Camberley, where Whiz and her husband were currently based, and it was after the last of them had arrived, and they had retired bemused by talk and bustle, that she warned him not to expect his birthday present from her until the children had gone. When, unsuspecting, he enquired if it was coming by post she blushed and her moment of confusion intrigued him, so that he said:

"What are you driving at? Do you mean you would prefer the children not to see it?"

"Not exactly," she stammered, "I don't mind them seeing it once it's—well—once it's *established* but it would embarrass me very much if they realised it was a birthday gift. You'll understand when you see it." He sat on the edge of the bed scratching his head and looking so completely baffled that she laughed, saying, "I'll tell you what! It's past midnight so have it now! But you must give me your word of honour you won't go whooping downstairs with it, won't even refer to it in front of them!"

His curiosity was now so engaged that he would have promised anything, so she went along the passage to the room that had been Jimmy Grenfell's and came back carrying a package measuring about four feet by three carefully tied in brown paper and sacking. He cut the string with her nail scissors and his expression, when the canvas was revealed, was worth all the self-doubts she had suffered since entering into the conspiracy with Cyrus. He propped it against the dressing-table and stood back studying it from every angle. Then he moved it so as to catch the bedside light and walked cautiously round it, as though he was playing Peeping Tom on a bathing beach. Finally he said, sombrely, "It's a bloody miracle! He's seen you not only as you *are* but as you always *were*! I've never looked at a picture so alive and exciting! It's got everything I ever saw in you, from the day you took me swimming there over thirty years ago! It's the most wonderful birthday present you've ever given me, that anyone's ever given me!" and he threw his arms round her and kissed her in a way that convinced her the instinct that had prompted the gift had been as accurate as were most of her instincts concerning him.

1123

"Where are we going to hang it?" he demanded.

"Not downstairs certainly," she said. "Everyone who comes into the house will make that awful music-hall joke about dressing mutton to look like lamb! It's—well Paul—it's a very *private* present, and I certainly don't want it on exhibition! It was just an idea I had the moment I saw it half-done and it seems to have worked, so that's all I care. Hang it in your dressing-room."

He studied it again, so carefully that she said, laughing, "For heaven's sake, Paul, you've got the original right here! If you look at it much longer with that leery expression I shall begin to think it's idealised and you're reminiscing!"

"It isn't in the least idealised," he said, seriously, "it's a melting-pot of everything about you that has made me look at other women objectively rather than subjectively all the years we've been married! And I'll tell you something else too, if it flatters you!"

"It'll flatter me," she promised.

"I've led a pretty active life and therefore I've always had plenty to do and mostly have enjoyed doing it but every time you walk into a room I find myself wishing everybody else would walk out of it! Every time I touch you I get the impression of physical renewal and that must be a very rare tonic for a man my age! I can't reasonably expect it to last into my seventies, so I'm damned if I don't hang this picture over the bed where I hope it'll keep me from flagging as time runs on!"

"When you flag in that respect I'll 'phone Jonas Whiddon, the undertaker," she said, chuckling, "for you'll be ready for him! Now get me out of this party dress so that I can breathe freely again!" and she stood while he unhooked her, reflecting that the strictures she had endured to look as slim and young as possible that evening had been largely unnecessary, for she did not really care a curse what the assembled children thought of her figure and, as far as he was concerned, the picture seemed to have provided him with ample excuse to turn the calendar to the wall.

They were awakened early next morning by a stir below the window and Claire, who could slough off morning drowsiness in a matter of seconds, jumped out of bed and took a peep through the curtains, retiring promptly when confronted with Henry Pitts' melon-slice smile. She said, scrambling into her dressing gown, "Wake up, Paul! Henry and some of his cronies are outside!" and she shook him so that he sat up, rubbing his eyes and grumbling that it was still too early to get up.

1124

"It's twenty minutes to seven," she told him, seizing a comb and struggling with her hair, "and maybe you can tell me why half the Valley is milling about outside our front door! I came within an inch of making a Lady Godiva bow to them!"

"They couldn't have noticed or they would have cheered," he said and went yawning to the window where, seeing Henry's upturned face, he called down, "What's up, Henry? Trouble somewhere?"

"No trouble, Maister," Henry called back, "but the top o' the marning to 'ee, an' the missis too!" Then, turning to Smut Potter close by he called, "Tell Mark to bring 'un out, Smut! Let the gentleman zee the rabbit!" and there was a prolonged stir behind the big rhododendron clump and Claire, joining Paul at the window, recognised Harold Eveleigh, Rumble Patrick, Farmer Brissot, Jumbo Bellchamber, and, standing a little apart, Francis Willoughby and Dick Potter. As they stared down Mark Codsall emerged from behind the shrubbery leading an unsaddled grey some seventeen hands high and of a build that reminded Claire instantly of old Snowdrop, the well-mannered gelding Paul had ridden about the Valley from the day of his arrival until the early 'twenties. Paul must have noticed the resemblance too for he exclaimed, "My God! It's Snowdrop's ghost! Where do you suppose they got him and why . . . ?" and then the significance of the assembly dawned on him as he saw her laughing and Henry shouted, "Come on down, just as you be, Squire! Us baint leavin' without drinking your health an' me, Smut an' Mark have been up an' about zince daylight!"

Paul withdrew, lost for words, blundering round to the wrong side of the bed in search of his slippers. She found them, pushed him down on the bed and slipped them on his feet as though he had been a boy late for school, saying, "I'll stay and get dressed but you go right on down! I can't feed that lot at short notice!" and she hustled him out and slammed the door so that he stood bewildered for a moment before going down through the kitchen and into the stable-yard, where the big grey now stood, surrounded by more than a dozen of them with its rope halter held by Mark Codsall, Shallowford's groom-handyman.

Some of them, he thought, looked vaguely embarrassed but this number included neither Henry Pitts nor Smut, who stood close together, clearly enjoying the occasion. Henry said, "Tiz the nearest us could come to old Snowdrop, Maister! Didden zeem right somehow, you ridin' about the Valley on that bottlenosed skewbald o' yours, so when Smut zeed this one at Bampton Fair us clubbed together and sent Smut to buy 'un! He got ten pound off what they were asking but us knowed he would, the bliddy old thief!"

"He's rising eight," Smut said, "but well-mannered. I knows that because I rode 'un all the way home, just to make sure the nagsman at Bampton weren't lying when he said 'er was traffic-broken! On'y thing he shied at was a bliddy motor-bike doing nigh on seventy mile an hour! He's been out two seasons with the Eggesford Hunt, so I reckon us have catched a bargain one way and another! He'll go, mind you, and I daresay he can jump too but seein' you baint so young as you were us zettled for a soft-mouth and easy temperament!"

"You *all* had a hand in it?" Paul said at length. "Everyone here?"

"Giddon no," Henry said, "us baint all here! There was nigh on fifty subscribed and I got a list here if you can read my writing!" and he presented a soiled sheet of foolscap, containing a long list of names, each of them familiar and representing not only the tenants but all the local craftsmen, men like old Aaron Stokes and Abe Tozer's son. Goss, the new sexton, had contributed and so had Willis, the blind wheelwright, and there were a couple of names from outside the Valley, Ben Godbeer, the Paxtonbury seedsman, and ex-Police Sergeant Price, long since retired, from Whinmouth.

He was too moved to make adequate response but they seemed to understand his confusion and silently made way for him as he walked round the gelding, noting a broad back and heavy quarters proclaiming it a stayer who would carry him over heavy ground all day and still be good for a turn of speed towards dusk. It was, he thought, one of the best all-rounders he had ever seen and he did not need to be told it had good manners. Even Snowdrop would have stood chafed at standing unsaddled in the midst of such a crowd, all of them strangers.

He said, quietly, "He's magnificent, and I can't thank you all enough. It's ... it's quite the kindest thing anyone ever did for me ..." and he trailed off, feeling that anything he said in the way of acknowledging their loyalty and generosity would sound trite. Henry came to his rescue with—"Put 'un away in the loose-box, Mark boy! Let's drink Squire's health and get about our biziness!" and they all trooped into the kitchen where Claire was drawing tankards of ale and The Pair and Simon were on hand to serve them, each of his sons displaying a jocularity suitable to the occasion. Then they drank his health, mercifully without speeches and presently, after wishing him Many Happy Returns, they drifted away so that he was left alone with Simon who said, with a smile, "I wouldn't have missed that, Gov! It

1126

was quite something in this day and age!" and Paul, automatically collecting tankards and piling them into the sink, agreed that it was but could find no words to convey to the most perceptive of his children the warmth of the glow in his heart but went quietly upstairs to shave, glad of an excuse to take his time over dressing. "Some of the older ones used to say there were compensations in passing the sixty-mark," he reflected, "but I never believed them until this moment," and he paused in the act of scraping his chin with the open razor he had bought in Cape Town on his twenty-first birthday and glanced out of the little window across the fields, already shimmering in the morning heat-haze. "I've got this place by the tail at last," he thought, "and it's taken me close on forty years to do it! They would never have done a thing like that for the Lovells and I'm damned glad all the children were here to see it!" He wiped the lather from his face and looked hard at himself in the glass, noting the mop of iron-grey hair and brown, lined face that now had a permanent "Tudor look". He wondered if the marks of the struggle were as obvious to others as they were to him and then, lowering his glance, noted with satisfaction that he had no paunch, that his body looked more youthful than his face. He pulled on boots and breeches and drifted into the bedroom, hearing the babel from below as his family assembled for breakfast but feeling no immediate inclination to join them. He threw wide the window sniffing the air like a pointer, playing his old game of identifying its components—dew-soaked grass, clover, the scent of roses from Grace's sunken garden and the overall tang of the sea. Well, there it was, looking precisely as it had looked when he first came here limping from the effects of a Boer bullet and as it had looked on all his other birthdays. Many of them he had forgotten but he could remember the notches of successive decades—the day he was thirty for instance, when he and Claire had taken the eight-months-old twins to Coombe Bay in the waggonette and the day he was forty, when he had ridden alone up to the spur of Hermitage Wood and picked the spot for the memorial plantation. On his fiftieth birthday, just before the twins' coming-of-age, he had gone the rounds with old John Rudd, bless his heart, and now that he was sixty they roused him from bed to present him with a hunter that reminded them of Snowdrop, thus underlining the fact that they too, in their way, clamoured for continuity. He looked from the rumpled bed to Claire's portrait, still leaning against the dressing-table, and the memory of last night's frolic made him smile. He didn't feel sixty and he didn't act sixty but then, why should be, with a fine woman like her in his arms and the Valley calling to him outside? And as he thought of Claire and the Valley in relation to one another he reminded himself that they were indivisible, that the vitality they fed him sprang from the same source. The knowledge that it was there, would always be there, put a spring in his step as he went along to the head of the stairs listening to the clatter-chatter from the dining-room. A verse occurred to him and he fumbled for it as he went down to the hall—something of Hardy's that he had read recently and had memorised because it seemed to him to epitomise the life he and Claire had shared in this house and would, he supposed, continue to share throughout their remaining years:

> "When down to dust we glide
> Men will not say askance,
> As now; 'How all the countryside
> Rings with their mad romance!'
> But as they graveward glance
> Remark; 'In them we lose
> A worthy pair, who helped advance
> Sound parish views.' "

Dullish and perhaps a little pie-faced, he thought, smiling at his vanity, but an apt epitaph for both of them. "Sound parish views!" No more and no less. It was about all he had ever striven after.

III

It seemed to him, as he watched them all at supper that night, that the tensions of the world were reproduced round his own dining-table. On the left sat Simon and Rachel and on the right the conventional Whiz and her rather stuffy husband, Ian. Simon would be thinking, perhaps, of pitiful processions of fugitives and refugees trudging ahead of the victorious Fascists in Spain, whereas Whiz and Ian, if they thought of Spain at all, would dismiss it as none of their business. In between were his other children, The Pair, who almost certainly regarded the prospect of a collision with Hitler as a tremendous lark, and Rumble and Mary, who, like himself, would see their contribution to any struggle for survival in efforts to coax the last blade of wheat from Valley soil. Nobody discussed politics, Simon having been briefed by Claire to keep his views to himself lest they should promote strife between him and his brother-in-law, Ian. The atmosphere re-

1128

mained cordial but the tension was there all right, as he could see when they listened to the nine o'clock news-bulletin. When they broke up and went their several ways the next morning he had a brief word with Simon, whose opinions he valued, but he took care to do it out of earshot of the others. It was Simon, in fact, who promoted the conversation while he stood waiting for Rachel to bring their single hand-grip down.

"It will be a long time before we're all here together again, Gov'nor," he said, watching The Pair stow their wives' luggage in the boot of the big Wolseley. "Fact is, I doubt if it'll ever happen, for the whole damned lot of us are standing on a fused bomb. I gather, however, that you are one of the few who admits as much."

"Yes Si, I admit it and have done for some time but I don't think Ian and Whiz do, and I don't think The Pair regard it as anything more than an excuse to play with balloons at weekends. Could you give an approximate date to it?"

"No," Simon told him, "and neither could anyone else but it shouldn't be long now. That mad bastard Hitler has to keep moving in the same direction and Franco's triumph will encourage him to prod us that much harder! I never thought of myself as a man who would look forward to flashpoint but delaying it isn't going to help."

"What will you do when it does come? Have you made any plans?"

"I shall join the foot-sloggers I suppose," Simon said, "the R.A.F. is too jazzy for me, I'm afraid."

"Could you get a commission?"

"I wouldn't have one as a gift. In any case, my International Brigade associations would put paid to that. They might be compelled to fight Fascists but, taken all round, they prefer them to Bolshies!"

Paul said, without challenging the dubious logic of this, "If it does happen would you like Rachel to come here for the duration? She grew up on a farm and could make herself very useful, both to me and Rumble Patrick."

"Yes," he said, brightening a little, "I'd like that very much," and as Rachel appeared with Monica and Margaret he gave Paul a swift grin and added, "So long, Gov! You're a spry sixty and I doubt if any of us will make it without a bath chair!" It was meant as a joke, Paul thought, but to a man like himself, who had seen thousands of shattered men occupying invalid carriages in two wars, it was singularly unfunny. He watched them drive off, all six of them piled into Stevie's car and the girls squealing as Stevie, ever a madcap driver, careered

1129

round the sharp bend of the drive and skidded a couple of feet on the canting gravel. Then Whiz and Ian said their grave good-byes and after that Mary and Rumble wandered off hand in hand across the orchard, moving slowly, like a couple of village lovers.

"Well," said Claire, and he could not miss the note of thankfulness in her voice, "That's that until Christmas, I suppose!" and he replied, slipping his arm around her, "Let's hope so at all events. Glad as I am to have them all under one roof occasionally, a little goes a long way!" but he said this because he knew she needed his corroboration. Secretly he felt a little sad, even frightened, for it occurred to him that although nothing was likely to occur until the harvest was gathered all over Europe, a lot could happen between the end of August and the first snow. Harvest-thanksgiving, he recalled, was the traditional season of war, always providing mountebanks like Adolf Hitler followed traditions.

Even then he was caught on the hop; not quite as ludicrously as in August 1914 but ludicrously enough, after all his months of planning and worrying. Either he had resigned himself to another Munich, or Simon and Rachel had laid too much stress upon Hitler's hatred of Communism. Or perhaps, like Henry, he found it very difficult to believe that a generation of Germans who had shared the mud of Passchendaele would actually start another war. He had relaxed during July and early August but when Hitler began to threaten Poland he called a meeting of the Valley co-operative and laid his plans before them in detail, a pooling of resources on a scale not even practised in 1917, and every farm in the area, tied and freehold, operating as a unit under a standing committee composed of Brissot, Honeyman, Harold Codsall, David Pitts, Willoughby and himself. He had invited Felton, the county agricultural adviser, to attend the meeting and Felton was impressed, 'phoning later to say that he would appreciate Paul's co-operation in fostering similar co-operatives north and east of Paxton-bury. By then, however, the harvest was upon them and because the weather was patchy everyone, including himself, was too busy to pay overmuch attention to the screaming threats from Berlin, or the cock-sure rantings from Rome. In any case, the cacophony had now contnued so long—ever since the autumn of 1935, when Mussolini had attacked Abyssinia—and everybody had become so bored with it, that it acted on them like the beat of surf on the shore throughout an overlong winter. It was not until the evening of the 23rd August, that the telephone bell rang and he heard Simon say, "Well Gov, this is it, I imagine!" and when Paul admitted that he had been out helping Rumble Patrick until dusk, that Claire was away fetching young John from the annual Sunday School treat, and that he had not heard a news-bulletin for twenty-four hours, Simon said, with a bitterness the telephone could not disguise, "Germany and Russia have signed a non-aggression pact! You'd better listen to the next news and then ring me. Make it tonight, I'll be off tomorrow."

"For God's sake—off where? There's no war yet, is there?"

"Camp. Local Terriers. We were going anyway but this will almost certainly mean mobilisation."

"I'll ring," Paul promised and hung up, hurrying back to the library and switching on just in time to hear the news delivered as though it had been part of a sports commentary. He heard it out and went back to the 'phone, finding that his steps dragged a little and suddenly feeling the tug of tired muscles after twelve hours in the fields.

"When would Rachel like to come?" he asked as soon as Simon answered, "Will she wait until something actually happens?"

"She's packing now," Simon said and then, after a slight pause, "I'd better say good-bye, Gov. God knows where I shall end up or if I'll be able to ring. There's some talk of actually landing chaps on the Continent as a kind of peace force, if you've ever heard anything so bloody silly! Keep an eye on Rachel, as well as the home fires burning!"

"Good luck wherever you go—if anywhere," Paul said hoarsely and quickly replaced the receiver. He was not given to premonitions but he had one now. In the half-hour or so before he heard the scrape of Claire's car on the gravel he was as sure as he had ever been of anything that he would never hear Simon's voice again. All the others', possibly, but not the voice of Grace's son.

CHAPTER TEN

I

ABOUT half-past five, on the last morning of May, 1940, Paul émerged from Crabpot Willie's cabin in time to see his relief, Henry Pitts, top the rise and descend the shallow tail of the goyle on his pony. He looked, Paul thought, exactly like a burgher commando rider moving down into a donga. The pony was far too small for him and his legs swung barely a foot from the ground. Over his shoulder, supported by a length of whipcord, was a 12-bore and the Boer touch was heightened by the shapeless trilby hat he wore, a hat that had weathered the Valley sun, wind and sleet ever since it had been issued as part of Henry's demobilisation togs in the long dry summer of 1919.

It was strange, Paul reflected, that all the important pattern changes of the Valley were signposted by what the locals called "a praper ole scorcher". The sun had burned the grass a dark brown in 1902, the season Paul settled in, and the Valley had withered under its non-stop glare in 1914. The first year of the peace had been just as hot and airless but between then and now, a matter of twenty-one years, he could not recall a dry spell lasting more than a fortnight or so. Perhaps they had come and gone without him noticing but now, with the rhythm of the seasons broken more finally than ever before, one took note of the weather. Somehow the brassiness of the sky, and the windlessness of the dunes above the beach, had within them elements of mockery to men condemned to play soldiers when they should have been making the very most of such sunshine.

He called, "You're ahead of time, Henry, I didn't expect you until six!" and Henry, sliding down without disturbing the creases of his habitual grin, replied, "I was woke be they bliddy aircraft passing over. Taaken all round 'twas too early to get up but too late to drop off again, zo I slipped out without wakin' Ellie an' brewed meself a cup o' tay!"

"I was just about to put the kettle on," Paul said, "but seeing you're here I'll leave it to you. I'm off along the beach to the Fort, then over to Bluff to check with Francis. It's been very quiet, nothing but the aircraft. Blenheims I think they were, off bombing somewhere I imagine!"

"They all gives Ellie the jitters!" Henry said, "and tidden a particle o' use me zayin' they'm ours. She knows bliddy well I can't tell the diff'rence. Who be inside, Maister?"

"Only Robbie Eveleigh. He was relieved by Noah Williams just after three o'clock when I came on but you can send them both home at seven. Nothing's likely to happen now!"

He looked down the gully to the sea, as flat and motionless as he had ever seen it, with its eastern edges turning whitish pink as the sun hoisted itself clear of the Bluff. Birds were chirping in the thicket beyond the pines and a solitary gull dipped over the criss-cross of iron stanchions, sown along the outer edge of the sandbanks, a token of discouragement to ehrmacht landing-parties.

"Tiz a funny thing," Henry said, passing his hand over his un-unshaven jowls, "you remember us always said in France that ole Jerry could pick his own weather. If 'er maade up 'is mind to pay us a call he could get ashore without gettin' 'is veet wet, an' what's more the glass zays it's zet fair, zame as it's been for a month or more a'ready!"

"And a damned good job too," Paul reminded him. "If we had had our usual summer Dunkirk would have been a fiasco and I doubt whether we should have fished the half of them off."

"Arr," Henry condoned, "that's true, but then, if us had had the kind o' weather you an' me had to put up with over there, I dorn reckon his bliddy ole panzers would o' crossed our old stamping ground so fast! Not nearly so fast!" he added, emphatically and then seriously, "I suppose you baint heard nowt o' your boys?"

"No word so far," Paul told him, "but as far as I know only Simon was over there. The Pair had switched to Air-Sea Rescue and Ian, Whiz's husband, was still out East last time I heard. Will you be free to take on tonight, same as usual?"

"Ah, I'll do that. Tiz worked well enough zo far baint it?"

"It'll work a damnèd sight better when the telephone people give us the outside line they've promised," Paul said. "Imagine having to rely on word-of-mouth alerts in this day and age! I can't see Jerry doing it if he was in our shoes!" and he went round the cabin to the lean-to shed where his birthday grey was saddled and tethered, Henry following and tethering his pony in its place at the hay net. The animals accepted the routine as though it had begun a year ago instead

1133

of a matter of days, dating from the formation of the coastal patrol of Churchill's L.D.V.s, or Lame-Duck-Vagabonds as Henry designated the Local Defence Volunteers. Valley men were responsible for guarding the coast from a mile west of the landslip, where their right-hand man was in contact with the Whinmouth group, to a mile east of the Bluff, where Francis Willoughby's patrols were in touch with the next section. They were thinly stretched, a mere dozen or so, operating over more than four miles of coastline. As Smut Potter said the first night they took station, "It baint much more than a bluff, be it? If Jerry was minded to come ashore in the dark he'd be eatin' his bliddy breakfast at The Mitre, in Paxtonbury, bevore us knowed he was around!" Yet the group took themselves seriously. At least they were better armed than the majority of the lookouts around the coasts, having, between them, eight shot-guns and three .22 rifles, as well as Paul's Smith & Wesson revolver. They might, as Henry said, blow a few hats off before they ran for it.

Paul turned east directly into the sun, shading his eyes as he walked the grey along the tideline towards Coombe Bay and perhaps because the morning was so sparkling and he had enjoyed two hours' sleep in the cabin after Noah Williams had reported, he felt reasonably encouraged, despite the incredible tale of disasters that had been theirs since the invasion of Norway, in April. To a man who had spent more than eighteen months on the Western Front it was hard to believe France had been overrun in a month, that Poland, Holland and Belgium had thrown in the sponge, that Paris was already occupied by jubilant, jackbooted Nazis, that British ships had fired on the French fleet, and that all that remained of the British Expeditionary Force was about a quarter-million shaken men lacking guns, transport and every kind of material. Already, however, they were calling Dunkirk a triumph, instead of the disaster it undoubtedly was. Already people like Smut Potter and Henry Pitts, who should know better, had slipped into the easy optimism that had swept down the Valley in the first weeks of the 1914–18 war, when everyone scrambled into uniform for fear it would be over by Christmas. Nobody, or nobody he had encountered since the news of the breakthrough, considered defeat by Hitler a possibility, although surely the speed and terrible finality of recent events made even temporary survival unlikely. They might, he supposed, fight some kind of delaying action, that would harden as it was edged northward, but after that, when the men who had frightened Uncle Franz in Munich and Nuremberg, had overrun the entire island, the war could only continue from Canada and how could such a war, even if it resulted in ultimate victory, save the Valley from the bombs of the Luftwaffe and tanks that had carved their way from the Rhine to the Biscay coast in less than a month?

That was the overall picture. What of the personal tragedy, as it affected him and Claire? Of his four sons and two sons-in-law four were already involved, The Pair (tiring of playing balloons, as he knew they would once they realised their role was static) were now sea-based; Ian was flying Gladiators in Egypt, and Simon—it would be poor old Simon—was probably already dead, or a prisoner marching into endless captivity! So far the Valley had not fared too badly. Only one man, a reservist from Coombe Bay, had been certified dead, after a submarine had found its way into Scapa Flow and sunk the *Royal Oak*, but others would soon qualify for another page at the back of the estate record book. Young Eveleigh, Harold's boy, of Four Winds, had his name down for the R.E.s, and Smut's lad, "Bon-Bon", who had helped farm the shrunken High Coombe holding, was waiting to be called into the R.A.F. Paul Rudd, Maureen's only son, had written from Scotland to say he was joining the R.A.M.C., and Albert Pascoe, whose real name was Timberlake, had left a week ago to join the Devons. "God knows!" Paul told himself, as he kicked the grey into a trot, "I've enough to make me despondent but for the life of me I don't *feel* despondent! Is it because the entire bloody shambles has passed beyond the bounds of sanity, or has the "miracle of Dunkirk" had the same effect on me as on all the others, notwithstanding the dictates of ordinary commonsense?"

The question interested him deeply and he continued to ponder it as he headed for the harbour slipway and the bizarre structure beyond that was now known as "The Fort". It was not really a fort but a café, idiotically disguised as a pillbox, of the kind that had caused the deaths of so many men in the morasses about Pilckhem Ridge, Passchendaele. Someone had had the notion of painting it battleship-grey and knocking a loophole or two in the seaward side, but to any-one with poor eyesight and second-rate binoculars it still looked like a café and a gimcrack one at that. As he rode along the last stretch of beach Paul found himself pondering the curious contradictions of the British race, indolent to the point of national suicide in the face of so many stark warnings, and then, given a lead from Westminster, in such a hurry to make up for lost time that they became eager victims of ten thousand bureaucrats. Two months ago, apart from the tiresome (and, to Paul, useless blackout), no one could have supposed the country committed to a war. Today the entire countryside was in an uproar, with signposts torn down, the names removed from such tiny stations as Sorrel Halt, tank-traps showing their teeth all the way to Paxtonbury, sandbars covered by a *chevaux de frise* of tubular ironwork, and finally, this absurd little sea-front café disguised as a pillbox! And in a way everyone seemed to be enjoying themselves hugely, as though it was a vast relief to face the prospect of meeting heavy tanks and dive-bombers with a few rabbit-guns and petrol bombs made out of ginger-beer bottles. It was commendable, perhaps, this illogical upsurge of defiance, but it was also pitiful. A people who had survived the Somme and Third Ypres should be waging total war with a better prospect of winning it.

The beach looked deserted so he clattered up the slipway along to the fort where he dismounted and tethered the grey to the guard-rail of the sea-wall. Then, hearing the rattle of stones below, he looked over the drop into the sunburned face of Rumble Patrick, perhaps the best beloved of all the males in the Valley, and the current freeholder of Periwinkle. Rumble, as usual, wore nothing but singlet and shorts and still, thought Paul, looked more like a boy than the master of a farm and the father of two children.

"Lovely morning, Gov!" he called, cheerily. "Saw you a mile off but you didn't spot us, did you now?"

"No, I didn't," admitted Paul. "Where were you? Playing in a sandpit?"

"Getting warm!" Rumble called back and then, with a knowing grin, "Okay! Come out Uncle Smut and show the Gov the welcome we've prepared for Jerry!" and Smut Potter suddenly materialised from a rash of pebbles, all about the size of a clenched fist, so that Paul, looking closer, saw that a cunningly constructed tank-trap now protected the approach to the wall under the pillbox, a trench about ten feet deep and two yards wide, screened by a huge boat-tarpaulin strong enough to bear the weight of camouflage shingle.

"That's not bad!" he said, admiringly, "but suppose Jerry resists the invitation and prefers to tackle the slipway?"

"We've got a better one down there," Rumble said. "Smut organised local slave-labour yesterday and my guess is that anything leaving a tank-landing craft would either try the slipway or head

1136

straight up the beach to bring point-blank fire on the Fort. He'd want to get over the sea-wall in the shortest possible time, wouldn't he?"

"I daresay, and in any case it's better than sitting waiting and playing cards in the café, as Smut was last time I looked in. Are you two the only ones on patrol over here?"

"We were six strong last night," Smut said. "Brissot and Jumbo Bellchamber turned up, as well as Mark Codsall and Willis."

"Willis?" Paul queried. "What the hell is the good of a blind chap on this sort of job?"

"Just what I thought, Squire," Smut said, apologetically, "but the fact is I didn't have the heart to turn him away. Panse brought un down, zoon as it was dimpsy, and he said he could sit inside and relay messages when us got the phone laid on. He could too, I reckon, and you can't help admiring his pluck!"

No, Paul thought, you couldn't; a man of over fifty, blinded by mustard gas on the Lys in 1918 but still anxious to prove to himself that he wasn't utterly useless in an emergency.

"Tell him this is his post from now on," he said. "I'm going to blitz the G.P.O. people the moment I've had breakfast. We should have the 'phone link-up between here, the Bluff lookout, and shanty H.Q. within twenty-four hours."

Smut waved his hand and disappeared under the shingle again, Rumble swinging himself up the short rope-ladder that connected rampart and tank-trap to sit dusting the sand from his long, dark hair while Paul untethered the grey and swung himself into the saddle. So often Rumble had reminded him painfully of his father, Ikey Palfrey, but never more so than this morning, with his overlong hair, smooth brown skin and easy good humour that was encouraged, no doubt, by being early abroad on such a pleasant morning.

"Mary all right?" Paul asked and Rumble said she was although he had the impression she considered the L.D.V. lark a male excuse to indulge in children's games and evade serious work.

"Claire has much the same viewpoint if that's any comfort," Paul told him, "but to my mind it's somebody's job to keep a close lookout early evenings and early mornings. If a German aircraft skims over it wouldn't do for the pilot to report that there was nothing awake but gulls. If I were you I'd slip back for your breakfast now. He isn't likely to try it in broad daylight and until we've got a gun here there's no sense in maintaining day and night patrols. Love to Mary!" and he trotted on, turning left off the sea-front at the junction of High Street and climbing the steep street to the church.

No one else was astir as yet and he remembered the first time he had ridden along this road in the early morning, the second day he had arrived here, now almost exactly thirty-eight years ago, when he was a lame young man of twenty-three madly in love with a girl he had met by chance in the Shallowford nursery the previous evening. He smiled grimly, recalling the flutter in his breast as he rode past her house on the hill and wondered, not for the first time, if he would have bought the estate at all had it not been for Grace. Probably, although John Rudd always declared she had been the deciding factor, and as he thought of old John and Grace he remembered other old faces and dismounted at the lych-gate of the churchyard, again tethering the horse and making his way between grass-grown graves to the west door, then hard left to the section of the yard where lay most of the men and women of his first decade in the Valley.

They were none of them really dead to him, and never would be so long as there was breath in his body. He glanced across at the granite obelisk marking the grave of Old Tamer that might so easily have been his own. Close by lay Preacher Willoughby who should, by rights, have been buried in the Nonconformist patch but somehow had not been, and remembering the rosy, saintlike face of the former master of Deepdene he thought of Elinor, his daughter, and wondered how she would fare now, an Englishwoman married to a German and living somewhere in the Württemberg area. Behind Willoughby's grave was the Codsall family plot, man and wife quiet at last, and beyond them, the grave of Arthur Pitts and that of Edward Derwent, his father-in-law, who had always been gruff and uncommunicative but had proved a trump once his ruffled pride was soothed by his pretty daughter's elevation to Squiress. He grinned, recalling Edward's honest, shamefaced acceptance of him as a prospective son-in-law, the day of old John Rudd's wedding in the fall of 1906. Dear Heaven! It all seemed so long ago and so improbable, like pondering the dynasties of Plantagenets and Tudors. Could any one of the people lying around him have dreamed up this summer, with a raving mad-man bestriding Europe and Britain the only country between him and a very promising bid for world domination? Perhaps that was just possible. Some of them had known the Kaiser's ambition but surely there was no real comparison, for not even Horace Handcock, the Valley fire-eater who had so hated Germans had envisaged concentra-

1138

tion camps and the deliberate destruction of open cities, like Rotterdam and Warsaw.

He stood for a moment over John Rudd's grave, wondering what kind of advice John would have given him this morning. "Hold on" perhaps; no more and no less for what else was there to do anyway? He circled the church and went past the Rectory, his riding boots striking hard on the asphalt path so that a dormer window opened and the snow-white head of Parson Horsey appeared, like the head of a gnome emerging from a crooked little house in a fairy-tale book illustration.

"You're up and about betimes!" the old man called. "Coast-watching, I imagine?"

"Doing the rounds," Paul told him, "I can't sit waiting for it at home."

"You never could," Horsey threw at him, with a chuckle, "and I envy you! The only good thing about this war is that one doesn't have the obligatory tussle with one's conscience over participating. I don't think my Keith would have been content to be a stretcher-bearer in this flare-up!"

"I don't think so either!" said Paul, and then, "What's the latest on the evacuee situation?"

"Another batch of thirty due on Saturday to replace some of those who have gone back, pining for fish and chips!" said the rector. "I imagine this lot will stay, however. It wouldn't surprise me a bit if that dreadful little man didn't start bombing London any day now. I hear there's talk of sending shiploads of children to the States and Canada. Would you consider sending your John and Mary's babies if you get the chance?"

Paul had already made his decision on this and had his answer pat. "No! Saving your presence, Rector, I'm damned if I would! This is where they were born and this is where they belong. They can take their chance with the rest of us and if they come through they'll grow up with more self-respect than if they sat it out three thousand miles away! That may sound vainglorious but it's how both Claire and Mary look at it. Besides, there's the U-boats!"

"I see your point," said Horsey and waving his hand withdrew, leaving Paul to remount and take the cliff path to the head of the Bluff, then down the gentle eastern slope of what had been Edward Derwent's cliff meadow as far as the coastguard hut where Francis Willoughby had his lookout post.

Francis was there, sunning himself, with an old briar gripped between his teeth and close by was "Bon-Bon", Smut's only child by his French wife, brewing tea on an open fire. The boy seemed glad of Paul's arrival as a break in the monotony of the long watch.

"Have you two been up here all night?" Paul asked and Francis said they had, taking turn and turn about because no reliefs were available.

"Can't you find a couple in the village?" Paul demanded and Francis said perhaps but he was "not minded to go begging for help from townsfolk".

"You'll have to find somebody when Bon-Bon's deferred service expires," he said. "When do you have to report, Bon-Bon?"

"Saturday," the boy said, "at Cardington. Basic training and then I'm down as an air-gunner."

"I'll rustle up a couple of tradespeople," Paul told Francis, "it's ridiculous you sitting here all night and then trying to run your farm in the daytime. You didn't see anything unusual I suppose?"

"Only a rabbit!" said Bon-Bon with a grin and held up a largish buck by its ears. "I know you said not to waste ammo, Squire, but this one sat up an' begged for it!"

"You're your father all over again!" Paul said, and turned north-west, crossing the fields over which Tamer had once hurried with news of the wreck and striking the head of the Dell path short of the well Jem Pollock had dug when, as Lord of Low Coombe, he exercised dominion over two captive wives. From here he could have descended to the river road but it was still very early, not quite six-thirty, so he skirted Dell Wood, and the corner of the sloping meadow that had been added to the reconstructed Derwent holding, and rode along the southern crest of Shallowford Woods until he passed the buddleia bush with its hovering cloud of butterflies. Everything looked much the same, he decided, as though Hitler's storming advance across Europe should have changed the very landscape, and he entered the woods near Hazel Potter's squirrel oak and coaxed the big grey down the steep, tree-studded slope to the mere.

The bird chorus was deafening and behind it, like the wash of a distant sea, he could hear the summer insect murmur, always audible about here whenever the temperature rose above the sixties. As he rode he looked about him sharply, noting the great banks of foxgloves that grew in the clearings and the last of the bluebell drifts under the trees. Suppose they were not playing soldiers? Suppose, on a morning like this, next week or the week after, German parachutists should crash into this cover and Panzers storm ashore to batter the Coombe Bay cob and thatch into rubble? He forced himself to review the possibility. Where would they run and what would become of them? How and where could the enemy be stopped or even checked? There was no kind of precedent for such a calamity. Men of the Valley had gone out to fight in wars over the last thousand years but no fields and woods nearer than Normandy had been their battleground, if one excepted the local brawls, like the Wars of the Roses, the Great Rebellion, and Monmouth's sorry venture in the west. There was, he supposed, some kind of parallel here. Getting on for three hundred years ago Jeffreys and Colonel Kirke had ridden into Paxtonbury, with their summary justice and hangman's ropes, but today a far worse threat hovered over every man, woman and child living hereabouts. The Bloody Assizes had been a very short-lived tyranny, whereas Hitler and his Nazis promised to establish themselves for all time and boasted of a Reich that would last a thousand years! Nobody, not even the most optimistic in the Valley, had any illusions as to the kind of future that faced them if the Nazis did establish a permanent bridgehead. There would, no doubt, be murder and rape and pillage, on a scale that had not been practised in civilised countries since the Thirty Years War. And as he thought this and dropped down the last terrace to the mereside track, the heat went out of the sun and he shivered, finding the entire situation too terrible to contemplate. One would fight, he supposed, fight with shot-gun, Service revolver and pitchfork, with Molotov cocktails and brickbats, but what would it avail in the end? Up in Westminster Churchill was breathing fire and slaughter and undoubtedly people had taken heart from his words, but who among them had heard Winston's ironic aside after making his famous fight-on-the-beaches oration? Paul had, having passed the time of day with the local M.P. when he went into Paxtonbury to buy ammunition a week since. The Member had been close to Churchill when he sat down and claimed to have heard him say, in that curious, slurred growl of his, "I don't know what we'll fight with — bloody axes and pick-handles, I imagine!"

About half-way along the track, almost opposite the ruinous Folly and the island, he met Sam Potter, spare, grizzled and well into his sixties but still swinging along with the stride of a man half his age. Sam, he learned, had made an early call on Harold Codsall, also in search of 12-bore ammunition and the sight of him injected Paul with confidence. Sam, he thought, would defend his cottage to the last gasp and it would take more than a squad of stormtroopers to eject him. He said, "Any news of the family, Sam?" and Sam told him that his daughter's husband, an anti-aircraft gunner, had been among those rescued at Dunkirk the previous week and was due on leave any day. He seemed in need of reassurance himself for he hesitated when Paul was on the point of moving off, saying, half-apologetically, "What do 'ee maake of it, Squire? Tiz a bliddy ole mix-up, baint it? Do 'ee reckon they'll try their luck at comin' yer?"

"They might," Paul said, "but if they do I daresay they'll get more than they bargained for. The Army will need time to reorganise but we've still got a Navy and an Air Force!"

"Arr!" Sam said, brightening, "a man forgets that, but for once in my life, Squire, I'd welcome grey skies and a choppy sea outalong. If the Channel turned nasty I reckon us'd maake mincemeat o' the bastards. 'Ave 'ee got enough chaps to cover the landslip-Bluff stretch night times?"

"Francis Willoughby will need a partner when young Bon-Bon goes this weekend. Would you take on, until we can get properly organised and the police let us have some rifles?"

"Arr, I'll do that an' glad to," Sam said, with a sigh. "I'll walk over an' fix it up with un after Joannie has put up a bit o' breakfast." Then, looking up at him earnestly, "Tiz a real bliddy upset at our time o' life, baint it?"

"Yes," Paul said, "it certainly is, Sam, but I don't doubt we'll come through it, the same as we did all our other troubles and you and I have seen plenty in the last forty years. My regards to Joannie!" and he rode on, reflecting that, of all the Valley men, his link with Sam Potter was the strongest, for the instalment of Sam, as woodsman-game-keeper, had been his first independent act as Squire of Shallowford.

He emerged from the woods and rode down the sunken lane to the stile at the top of the orchard. Looking at his watch he saw that it was ten minutes to seven and suddenly he felt both tired and hungry, ready for one of Claire's generous breakfasts and maybe an hour's nap in the study armchair. "I'm getting too old for this kind of larkabout," he told himself, "and so are most of us around here. Surely to God it's time we had leisure to enjoy this kind of weather, without gadding up and down the Valley half the night!" And then, bracing himself, he succumbed to the spur of vanity, putting his grey at the two-rail fence beside the stile, clearing it easily and recalling, as he swung erect in the saddle, a phrase about "young men skylarking over fences on their way home after a blank day in the hunting field". It had not been such a blank night. He had seen the tribal spirit of the Valley at work again, with almost every able-bodied man from Blackberry Moor to the far side of the Bluff caught up in a collective task that reached back and back to the days when Celts and Normans had put themselves in a position of defence against French sea-raiders and Napoleon's flat-bottomed barges. He unsaddled the grey and put him up in the stable, going in through the kitchen and putting the big iron kettle to boil for tea that he would take up to Claire. As he did so, however, he heard the telephone bell shrill and his heart missed a beat, although he told himself sternly that it was probably only the Whinmouth police, checking up on his local organisation. He went into the hall and lifted the receiver, and then his heart began to hammer and his eyes misted a little, for the voice at the end of the line was Simon's and within it was a crackle of cheerfulness that was uncharacteristic of the boy. He said, breathlessly, "*Simon!* It's really *you!* You're . . . you're home and dry, lad?"

"Not so dry!" Simon said, "but home okay! I'm ringing from near Folkestone. I got in during the night. Pretty well the last of 'em I'd say!"

"God, but I'm glad to hear from you!" Paul said, fumbling for a cigarette to steady himself. "What happened? How did you make it?"

"Too long a yarn to spin from a public call-box but the bare bones aren't so remarkable. I just walked into the bloody sea and swam for it!"

"You're joking!"

"No I'm not!" He heard Simon smother a chuckle. "I could see 'em mopping up along the beaches, north of Calais, so as it was every man for himself I stripped off and struck out. I was damned lucky, mind, I not only found an empty oil-drum a mile or so out but I was sighted by a destroyer late in the afternoon. That's why I've been so long getting in; they only docked last night!"

"You're . . . you're quite fit?"

"Fit as a fiddle! They gave me lashings of Navy rum on board and I don't think I've sobered up yet. We're getting nine days survival leave. Tell Rachel I'll be down some time during the next forty-eight hours. Look, I can't stop, Gov, there's a queue outside . . . see you soon!" and the line went dead.

He stood holding the receiver to his ear, thinking not so much of

1143

Simon, whom he had half-decided was dead, but of some or the other times he had stood here being fed with information from the world outside the Valley; a night in 1914, when Uncle Franz had rung; the day Simon had 'phoned to tell him he was marrying Rachel Eveleigh; all manner of minor milestones through the years, concerning the comings and goings of The Pair, of Whiz, Mary and young Claire. He thought, "He's luckier than his mother! He survived that Spanish nightmare and he's survived this! He obviously takes some killing, like me and Smut and old Henry Pitts. *Swam* for it, by God!", and he gave a short, barking laugh, catching sight of himself in the cheval mirror hanging on the cloakroom door. The reflection arrested him. Earlier that morning he had compared Henry to a Boer commando but now he himself looked like an ageing bandit, with tousled grey locks and a Smith & Wesson strapped to his side. He cocked his head on one side, wondering if others would agree with him that he did not look sixty-one, no more than, say, fifty-four or -five, and still good for a rough and tumble if one was waiting him down on the beach. Then he heard the kettle-lid rattling and went back into the kitchen to make the tea, pouring it into the morning ritual mugs, taking one in each hand, and going slowly up the broad, shallow stairs.

He opened the bedroom door with his knee and was surprised, and not a little amused, to find Claire was still heavily asleep. Then he remembered she had got up with him at two o'clock to make his coffee before he rode off to the shanty and had probably had some trouble getting off to sleep again after he had gone. He gently set down the mugs and pulled the curtain aside so that dazzling sunshine filled the room and she stirred and heaved herself over without waking. He went across and looked down at her, conscious of a warm current of relief and pleasure that was only partially due to the cheering news of Simon's escape. She was still, he thought, lovely to look at, particularly when she was relaxed as now. Her hair showed evidence of its fortnightly rinse and there was a suggestion of grey about the temples but one had to look for it, it didn't proclaim itself, as it did in most of the Valley women midway through their fifties. Her skin was still very clear and her cheeks, now slightly pendulous, were as fresh and rosy as on the day he had first ridden into High Coombe farmyard on his initial tour of the estate. Her mouth, showing faint traces of lipstick, was just as inviting and slightly parted lips revealed square, white teeth, the product, as she often told him, of her great weakness for cheese, which made calcium. Suddenly she blinked her eyes and when she saw him sat up very suddenly, her pink nightdress slipping over one shoulder and her expression very bemused.

"What is it? What's the time?"

"Time you were up and about," he said, handing her a mug. It's lucky you woke up when you did. Another moment and I should have been in beside you and half the morning wasted. I've just heard from Simon."

"*Simon!* He's . . . here? He's all right?"

"Near Folkestone and coming on leave. Not even wounded. Sounded as though he subscribes to the general belief that Dunkirk was an even more shattering victory than Waterloo!"

"Oh God, I'm glad, Paul! Glad for you but gladder still for me!" and she set down the mug and hugged herself with a little girl's glee.

He said, sitting on the edge of the bed, "I knew you would be. He always was rather special for you, wasn't he? Perhaps because you always leaned over backwards in attempts to disprove the wicked stepmother theory! Well, I daresay he owes his survival to you. He tells me he swam for it. No! I mean it! He actually struck out across Channel and was picked up by a destroyer a mile or so out! It was you who taught him to swim, Claire."

"Yes, I did," she said, with enormous satisfaction, "and he was always the best swimmer of the lot of them. The Pair wouldn't have got beyond the breakwater. Have you told Rachel yet?"

"No, I only heard as I was making the tea ten minutes ago."

"Then I'll drive over right away!" she said, scrambling out of bed, but he protested. "No you won't, woman! You'll get me some breakfast first and while it's cooking you can scout around for Mark Codsall. He came off duty more than seven hours ago and he can take her the news!"

He yawned and suddenly she looked contrite. "You must be tired out! Why don't you pull off your clothes and slip into bed for an hour or so? Tell you what—I'll bring your breakfast up on a tray!"

He could not remember when he had last breakfasted in bed and the idea was appealing. Then he remembered all the things he had to do and stopped in the act of unbuckling his webbing belt. "Hell no, I can't do that . . . !" but she had gauged his approval and said, sharply, "You can and you will! Here, give me those things!" and began peeling off his jacket so that he surrendered and quickly undressed, sliding into a bed that was still warm and smelled very pleasantly of her perfume. He lay back watching her struggle into her clothes,

1145

smiling to himself as she inched a frivolous and inadequate foundation-garment over her heavy hips and marvelling at the impression of slimness it lent her when it was in position. Then, after a tug or two at her hair, she was gone and he was drifting into a doze when the dressing-room door opened very cautiously and the bullet head of his six-year-old son John appeared round the crack. He said, sleepily, "All right, either come in or go out, John!" and John came in, his eyes immediately fastening on the discarded holster.

"Can I look at it, Dad?"

"No you can't, it's loaded!"

"Have you shot any Nazis?"

"No, there were none within range unfortunately!"

John looked mildly disappointed and mooched across to the tall window where Paul saw that he was arrayed in the cowboy outfit the doting Thirza Tremlett had made for him at his urgent demand. It consisted of a loud check shirt, fringed corduroys and a gun-belt slung with two beaded and brass-studded holsters, each sporting a cap pistol.

"Uncle Rumble says the sea will be a-wash with their corpses if they try for Coombe Bay!" John said solemnly. "Was he pulling my leg, do you think?"

"No," said Paul, judiciously, "he wasn't! Every one who tries to get ashore will certainly be picked off from the dunes. Everyone's waiting with a gun and the Navy is all set to drive them right into our line of fire. If you want your breakfast your mother's getting it now!"

"Okay!" said the boy and left abruptly, without noticing the reluctant grin that made his father conscious of the night's bristles on his chin. "Okay!" And dressed as an American cowboy at a time like this! It was a little incongruous to see a six-year-old adopting a role of make-believe violence when there was so much real violence threatening over the Channel and in the skies overhead. He was nodding off when Claire bustled in with his tray and although, just then, he would have preferred to sleep, he made the effort and sat up while she lifted the cover from a plate of bacon and eggs. Then the smell revived his appetite and he began to eat ravenously as she watched with approval.

"Was it all quiet on the Coombe Bay front?"

Quiet enough, he told her, describing Henry's arrival, Rumble Patrick's tank-trap and his own casual visit to the churchyard before riding home through the woods. His detour interested her. She said, looking down on him with a smile, "I'd like to see the German who could run you off this land, Paul! He'd have to be a six-headed monster armed with a death-ray!"

"A company of second-line troops could do it with last-war rifles," he said. "We've only got a few sporting guns and an odd revolver or two!"

"You don't have to worry," she said, with a finality that made him half-ashamed of his fears, "they won't even try! And we'll win all right, the same as we always do after the initial flutter in the hen-house. You'll finish your days here and so will I. And so will Mary's children and young John and probably their children! And by that time there won't be anything to worry about except jerry-builders for by then you men will have grown up and learned to attend to the serious business!"

He was exasperated in spite of the assurance she brought him and said, petulantly, "It isn't that kind of war, Claire! Not this time. It's very real war, with all-or-nothing stakes. You ought to get that into your head and keep it there!"

"Oh, it's in my head," she said, off-handedly, "but I can't get so worked up about it as you. I can't really believe that anybody as idiotic as Hitler will be tolerated anywhere for long. Too much Derwent commonsense, maybe. Breakfast to your liking, sir?"

"First-rate. You can make a habit of this after the war!"

"You'd be lucky!" and suddenly she laughed, reached out and rumpled his already rumpled hair. "I'll see to John's breakfast and get the message over to Rachel!" and she turned to go but he steadied the tray with his right hand and shot out his left, catching her by the wrist.

"Steady on!" she warned him, "you'll have the lot over the bed-clothes!" but when he lifted her plump hand to his mouth and kissed it she smiled, saying, "An early ride in Shallowford Woods always takes you this way! Did you pass alongside the mere?"

"Yes," he admitted, "past the exact spot where you once tried to seduce me, you huzzy. And me a gangling, city-bred boy with money in the bank!"

"I wish I'd succeeded!" she said. "We would have had nearly five extra years to look back on!"

"And five more children!"

"Without a shadow of doubt. Help yourself to more tea if you want it. I'll give you a call about ten."

She went out and he disposed of the tray, stretching and luxuriating in the warmth of the bed and the glow of strong, morning sunlight. Suddenly and improbably the war seemed to recede and with it went all thought of Hitler, a stricken Continent, L.D.V. patrols and Rumble Patrick's tank-traps. All that remained, all that mattered on this earth or beyond it was Claire and Shallowford, Claire's children and Claire's children's children, together with all the old originals and their descendants, living their humdrum lives between the railway line and the sea, between the Teazel in the west and the Bluff in the east. Nothing else was worth a moment's anxiety, and, resolving this, he slept.

She returned about ten but she did not disturb him. He was sleeping very peacefully and she thought, briefly, "To hell with his orders. He'll be out again half the night and he isn't as young as he likes to pretend!" And then, for the first time in a long while, she took a dispassionate look at him, not so much to assess the toll of the years that drove her to study her own reflection often enough, but in search of the man himself. What was it, she asked herself, that had held her to him all these years, had made his business hers, his trickle of hopes and fears, anxieties and exultations the threads of her existence and led, one and all, back to this sprawling house on the southern slope of a valley by-passed by the century? She looked closely and seriously at the long, narrow face, hedged with bluish stubble, the thick grey hair tumbled on her pillow, the long, relaxed form under the white coverlet. His loins undoubtedly. They had always brought her fulfilment but outside the bed, in day-to-day life, there was a quality about him that was astonishingly rare in this age — an enduring faith and ceaseless endeavour that was utterly divorced from the besetting preoccupation of his generation, concerned, in the main, with greed of one sort or another. He might, she reflected, have been a very rich man and he was not, had never wanted to be, for all the money he had ever had had been poured into these acres and dribbled away without a sigh on his part, and he was not even rich in kind, for most of it had gone to those whose lives, in a sense, he had held in trust over the years. And yet, she decided, it was not his generosity that made him the acknowledged leader here but his terrible earnestness, his sense of purpose and dedication that only today was finding wider expression from one end of the country to the other. Realising this, and identifying his steadfastness with the national mood in the face of final

1148

disaster, she decided something else about him that was both old and new. He had been right all the time, every moment of his working life, since he had first ridden into the Valley when she was a girl of nineteen. He had, as it were, selected a target that most men of his means and single-mindedness would have regarded as far too modest, but whereas the big-game hunters had missed he had scored a succession of bull's-eyes and was still scoring. It gave her a queer sense of pride to realise that, over most of the time, she had been loading for him. He had prescience but also a kind of innocence. The one had enabled him to evaluate soil and comradeship in excess of everything else that touched his life and the other had matured him as a human being and brother to whom everyone about here turned, in good times and bad, for advice, steadfastness and friendship. In a way he was the antithesis of the spirit of the century, of the dismal trends of laissez-faire, usury and triviality that had led, after all, to another global calamity and yet he had never lost a certain modesty that some mistook for naïvety, forgetting that, under his seeming mildness was a core of proofed steel. Perhaps she was the only person in the world who was fully aware of this, having seen it tempered over the years but there were still plenty who thought of him as an anachronism, a reactionary, a benevolent autocrat or a genial soft touch but she knew otherwise. He was all these things on the surface but primarily he was a man of faith and a romantic, whose fibres were far tougher and more weatherproof than the fibres of professional adventurers and men in counting-houses, if only because, by now, they probed so deeply into Valley soil. There was enormous strength here, and abundant tenderness. There was virility, at sixty-one, that still retained the power to make her wilt and there was also self-assurance equal to all the stresses of peace and war, change and catastrophe. A woman who troubled herself to understand and appreciate this would always be safe with him; safe, satisfied and grateful for the hand she had been dealt.

She went to the window, remembering how she had stood on this same spot through the long afternoons watching him recover from his tremendous exertions after the wreck in the Cove. Thirty-three years with the same man, and she could still feel about him as she had felt the day he rode over that hill where the south-easterly tongue of the woods melted into the tip of the sloping meadow running down the near side of the Coombe. It was something to be thankful for. She went out, softly closing the door, leaving him to whatever dreams he had. They must have been rewarding. He was smiling slightly as he slept.

He appeared, dressed and shaved, just before noon after she had carried her coffee into the library and entered the bare facts of Simon's survival into the estate diary. He grumbled a little at being left so long, pointing out that the leisurely days were behind them, but she shrugged off his complaint, reminding him that he would be out again half the night and was due to celebrate his sixty-first birthday in the morning. That stopped him dead, as she knew it would, for she was sure that he had forgotten. He said, scratching his head, "Sixty-one, by God! What an orchestra to play a man into his dotage! Why, they couldn't even ring a peal of bells in the village without having everyone assume that the balloon had gone up!" And then he laughed, recounting how, that same morning, he had put the grey at the orchard rail and cleared it with eighteen inches in hand.

"The grey is only nine!" she said, and closing the diary crossed to the long cupboard under the lowest bookshelf, returning with a carefully wrapped parcel about four feet in length. "Since you seem determined to go on playing young men's games until you have a seizure you may as well have your newest toy now!" she said.

"I'm more likely to have one playing games with you!" he told her, a joke aimed at concealing his boyish curiosity of the kind he invariably displayed on these occasions. He cut the string very deliberately and threw back the wrappings. On the table lay a brand new ·22 deer rifle, together with a worn bandolier weighted with ammunition.

He recognised the bandolier at once as the sole remaining item of kit he had brought home from the Cape, in 1902, and she smiled as he stood staring down at the gift, as genuinely surprised and overwhelmed as he had been a year ago, when she had given him the bathing-pool portrait that now hung over the bed. He looked, she thought, more like sixteen than sixty as he said, sombrely, "It's magnificent! It's the best vermin gun on the market. It can kill at half-a-mile, did you know that?"

"Smut advised me to handle it carefully," she said. "I had to ask him to get it but don't enquire too closely where. It's my belief he bent the law a little!"

"I'll warrant he did!" and he picked it up, balanced it and let his hand glide over the gleaming stock. Then, after breaking it to make sure it was unloaded, he brought it slowly to his shoulder and clicked the trigger. "Well," he said, at length, "let 'em come! Let 'em all come! I'll knock a few gaps in their bloody ranks before they chase me out of the Valley!" and suddenly she realised that what had seemed at first an extravagant notion was, in fact, an inspiration on her part.

"Last year a provocative oil-painting of a grandmother in half a swimsuit, this year a gun to shoot Stormtroopers! I suppose it's me who encourages you never to grow up!" she said but her sigh was thoroughly counterfeit and when he threw his arms round her and kissed her mouth she strained herself towards him, giving expression to the nostalgic yearning she had felt for him in the bedroom an hour or so earlier. He said, seriously, "I shall enjoy going on patrol tonight. I can lend my shot-gun to Eveleigh's boy until the rifles arrive. Is there any fresh coffee going?"

"I'll get some," she said and went out, guessing that, boy-like, he wanted a few minutes alone to relish his gift. She was quite right. The moment her back was turned he threw open the garden door and moved out on to the terrace, slipping a round into the breech and looking about for a likely mark. He found one at the angle of the rose garden, a very amateur scarecrow that Mark Codsall had rigged up to guard the freshly-turned vegetable rows in Little Paddock. It was hardly more than a cross of peasticks, hung about with an old sports jacket and a hard hunting hat, thrown aside by one of the children. He brought the gun to his shoulder and fired, almost without sighting. The hat went spinning and the peastick frame lurched to an angle of sixty degrees. "Well," he told himself, with the utmost satisfaction, "I haven't forgotten how to shoot and that must mean there's nothing wrong with my eyesight!" and then, as though the mood of self-satisfaction demanded enlargement, "And there was nothing wrong with the post-war generation after all! Most of them turned up trumps in the end — young Bon-Bon falling over himself to get into the R.A.F., The Pair turning their backs on money-making for the duration, Rumble Patrick down there on the beach building his tank-traps, and dear old Simon, bless his suffragette heart, taking a cool look at those bloody Nazis and deciding to swim for it!" He heard Claire call "Coffee!" from the library and threw the rifle over his forearm, walking slowly back along the baking terrace and raising his nose an inch to sniff the heavy scent of parched grass. He had walked these flags in many moods over the last four decades but never, he told himself, with a more compelling sense of uplift and dedication.

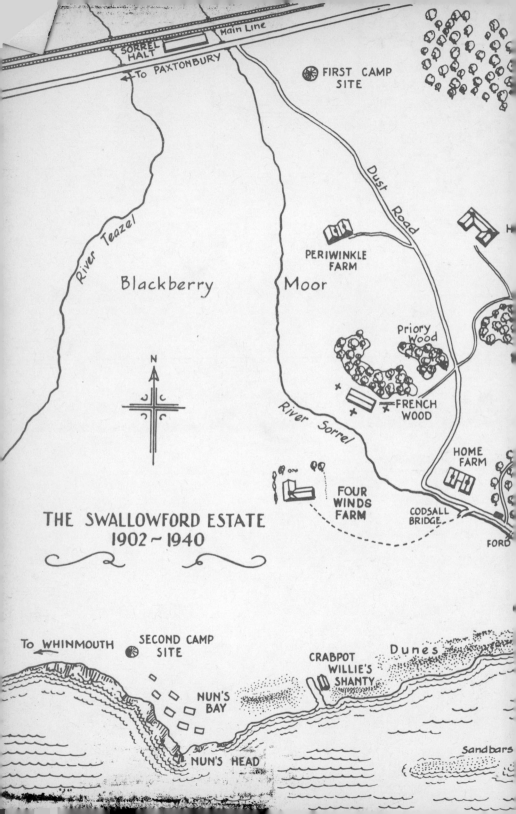

SORREL HALT

Main Line

To PAXTONBURY

FIRST CAMP SITE

Dust Road

River Teazel

Blackberry   Moor

PERIWINKLE FARM

N

Priory Wood

FRENCH WOOD

River Sorrel

HOME FARM

THE SWALLOWFORD ESTATE
1902~1940

FOUR WINDS FARM

CODSALL BRIDGE

FORD

To WHINMOUTH

SECOND CAMP SITE

Dunes

CRABPOT WILLIE'S SHANTY

NUN'S BAY

NUN'S HEAD

Sandbars